extraordinary acclaim

for

INFINITE

JEST

"Diving into the riches of *Infinite Jest* is an exhilarating, breath-taking experience. The book teems with so much life and death, so much hilarity and pain, so much gusto in the face of despair that one cheers for the future of our literature. Rarely does one read such audaciously inventive prose. . . . A triumphant, high-energy linguistic rush."

— NEWSDAY

"Truly remarkable. . . . What weird fun *Infinite Jest* is to read."

— NEWSWEEK

"Uproarious. . . . It shows off Wallace as one of the big talents of his generation, a writer of virtuosic talents who can seemingly do anything."

— NEW YORK TIMES

"Spectacularly good. . . . It's as though Paul Bunyan had joined the NFL or Wittgenstein had gone on 'Jeopardy'! *Infinite Jest* is that colossally disruptive. . . . Next year's book awards have been decided."

— NEW YORK

"God, I love this book. If you buy it on the strength of this review and don't grow to adore it, make a fetish out of it, keep it strapped to your body at all times . . . I personally promise to buy it back at full price."

— TIME OUT NEW YORK

"An acidic, free-styling 1,088-page encyclopedia of hurt. . . . *Infinite Jest* wrangles an enormous cast of engagingly wacked-out characters into a frequently hilarious but ultimately tragic epic."

— SPIN

"A big, brilliant book. . . . Wallace is a mesmerizing storyteller."

— NEW YORK OBSERVER

"A work of genius . . . *Infinite Jest* is a grandly ambitious, wickedly comic epic on par with such great, sprawling novels of the 20th century as *Ulysses, The Recognitions,* and *Gravity's Rainbow.* . . . With a sophisticated lexicon and mesmerizing syntax reminiscent of William Gaddis and William T. Vollmann, *Infinite Jest* is our most thorough dissection of America's addiction to just about everything, including treatment itself. . . . A wild, surprisingly readable tour de force, a high-energy satire of '90s America in the savagely funny tradition of Swift and Sterne."

— SEATTLE TIMES

"One of the most talked about books of the season. . . . *Infinite Jest* is a sprawling piece of intellectual wizardry and social satire, a work whose largeness alone would make it newsworthy, even if its size were not matched by a display of formidable ambition and skill. . . . At once serious, diagnostic, frightening, comic, and lyrical."

— HARPER'S BAZAAR

"A blockbuster comedy. . . . No other writer now working communicates so dazzlingly what life will feel like the day after tomorrow."

— ELLE

"Brilliant. . . . There's no doubt that Wallace's talent is immense and his imagination limitless. . . . A consistently innovative, sensitive, and intelligent writer."

— SAN FRANCISCO CHRONICLE

"Brashly funny and genuinely moving. . . . This one is worth the long haul. . . . *Infinite Jest* will confirm the hopes of those who called Wallace a genius."

— CHICAGO TRIBUNE

"Challenging and provocative."

— ORLANDO SENTINEL

"Wallace is the funniest writer of his generation."

— VOICE LITERARY
SUPPLEMENT

"*Infinite Jest* is a stunning novel, a comic masterpiece. . . . Submit to the addiction and receive *Infinite Jest*'s pleasures unadulterated, unabridged, and magnificent."

— BOOK PAGE

"Wallace offers huge entertainment. . . . Only Gaddis and Pynchon have this range. So brilliant you need sunglasses to read it, but it has a heart as well as a brain. *Infinite Jest* is both a vast, comic epic and a profound study of the postmodern condition . . . a *Naked Lunch* for the nineties."

— REVIEW OF CONTEMPORARY
FICTION

"Ambitious and frequently brilliant . . . a raucous Falstaffian, deadly serious vision of a cartwheeling culture in the self-pleasuring throes of self-destruction. . . . Almost certainly the biggest and boldest novel we'll see this year . . . and probably one of the best."

— KIRKUS REVIEWS

INFINITE JEST

ALSO BY DAVID FOSTER WALLACE

THE BROOM OF THE SYSTEM

GIRL WITH CURIOUS HAIR

A SUPPOSEDLY FUN THING I'LL NEVER DO AGAIN

BRIEF INTERVIEWS WITH HIDEOUS MEN

EVERYTHING AND MORE

OBLIVION

CONSIDER THE LOBSTER

INFINITE

JEST

A Novel

DAVID FOSTER WALLACE

Foreword by Dave Eggers

BACK BAY BOOKS
Little, Brown and Company
New York   Boston   London

Back Bay Books / Little, Brown and Company
Hachette Book Group
237 Park Avenue, New York, NY 10017
www.hachettebookgroup.com

Originally published in hardcover by Little, Brown and Company, February 1996
First Back Bay paperback edition, February 1997
Back Bay 10th anniversary paperback edition, November 2006

Back Bay Books is an imprint of Little, Brown and Company. The Back Bay Books name and logo are trademarks of Hachette Book Group, Inc.

The publisher is not responsible for websites (or their content) that are not owned by the publisher.

The characters and events in this book are fictitious. Any apparent similarity to real persons is not intended by the author and is either a coincidence or the product of your own troubled imagination.
Where the names of real places, corporations, institutions, and public figures are projected onto made-up stuff, they are intended to denote only made-up stuff, not anything presently real.
Besides Closed Meetings for alcoholics only, Alcoholics Anonymous in Boston, Massachusetts, also has Open Meetings, where pretty much anybody who's interested can come and listen, take notes, pester people with questions, etc. A lot of people at these Open Meetings spoke with me and were extremely patient and garrulous and generous and helpful. The best way I can think of to show my appreciation to these men and women is to decline to thank them by name.

Portions have appeared in somewhat different form in the following: *Harvard Review, The Iowa Review, Grand Street, Conjunctions, Harper's, The Review of Contemporary Fiction, The Pushcart Prize XIII, The New Yorker.*

ISBN 978-0-316-92004-9 (hc)
ISBN 978-0-316-06652-5 (pb)
LCCN 2006934927

10
RRD-IN

Printed in the United States of America

For F. P. Foster: R.I.P.

FOREWORD

In recent years, there have been a few literary dustups — how insane is it that such a thing exists in a world at war? — about readability in contemporary fiction. In essence, there are some people who feel that fiction should be easy to read, that it's a popular medium that should communicate on a somewhat conversational wavelength. On the other hand, there are those who feel that fiction can be challenging, generally and thematically, and even on a sentence-by-sentence basis — that it's okay if a person needs to work a bit while reading, for the rewards can be that much greater when one's mind has been exercised and thus (presumably) expanded.

Much in the way that would-be civilized debates are polarized by extreme thinkers on either side, this debate has been made to seem like an either/or proposition, that the world has room for only one kind of fiction, and that the other kind should be banned and its proponents hunted down and, why not, dismembered.

But while the polarizers have been going at it, there has existed a silent legion of readers, perhaps the majority of readers of literary fiction, who don't mind a little of both. They believe, though not too vocally, that so-called difficult books can exist next to, can even rub bindings suggestively with, more welcoming fiction. These readers might actually read *both* kinds of fiction themselves, *sometimes in the same week*. There might even be — though it's impossible to prove — readers who find it possible to enjoy Thomas Pynchon one day and Elmore Leonard the next. Or even: readers who can have fun with Jonathan Franzen in the morning while wrestling with William Gaddis at night.

David Foster Wallace has long straddled the worlds of difficult and not-as-difficult, with most readers agreeing that his essays are easier to read than his fiction, and his journalism most accessible of all. But while much of his work is challenging, his tone, in whatever form he's exploring, is rigorously unpretentious. A Wallace reader gets the impression of being in a room with a very talkative and brilliant uncle or cousin who, just when he's about to push it too far, to try our patience with too much detail, has the good sense to throw in a good lowbrow joke. Wallace, like many other writers who could be otherwise considered too smart for their own good — Bellow comes to mind — is, like Bellow, always aware of the reader, of the idea that books are essentially meant to entertain, and so almost unerringly balances his prose to suit. This had been Wallace's hallmark for years before this book, of course. He was already known as a very smart and challenging and funny and preternaturally gifted writer when *Infinite Jest* was released in 1996, and thereafter his reputation included all the adjectives mentioned just now, and also this one: Holy shit.

No, that isn't an adjective in the strictest sense. But you get the idea. The book is 1,079 pages long and there is not one lazy sentence. The book is drum-tight and relentlessly smart, and though it does not wear its heart on its sleeve, it's deeply felt and incredibly moving. That it was written in three years by a writer under thirty-five is very painful to think about. So let's not think about that. The point is that it's for all these reasons — acclaimed, daunting, not-lazy, drum-tight, very funny (we didn't mention that yet but yes) — that you picked up this book. Now the question is this: Will you actually read it?

In commissioning this foreword, the publisher wanted a very brief and breezy essay that might convince a new reader of *Infinite Jest* that the book is approachable, effortless even — a barrel of monkeys' worth of fun to read. Well. It's easy to agree with the former, more difficult to advocate the latter. The book is approachable, yes, because it doesn't include complex scientific or historical content, nor does it require any particular expertise or erudition. As verbose as it is, and as long as it is, it never wants to punish you for some knowledge you lack, nor does it want to send you to the dictionary every few pages. And yet, while it uses a familiar enough vocabulary, make no mistake that *Infinite Jest* is something *other*. That is, it bears little resemblance to anything before it, and comparisons to anything since are desperate and hollow. It appeared in 1996, *sui generis,* very different from virtually anything before it. It defied categorization and thwarted efforts to take it apart and explain it.

It's possible, with most contemporary novels, for astute readers, if they are wont, to break it down into its parts, to take it apart as one would a car or Ikea shelving unit. That is, let's say a reader is a sort of mechanic. And let's say this particular reader-mechanic has worked on lots of books, and after a few hundred contemporary novels, the mechanic feels like he can take apart just about any book and put it back together again. That is, the mechanic recognizes the components of modern fiction and can say, for example, *I've seen this part before, so I know why it's there and what it does. And this one, too — I recognize it. This part connects to this and performs this function. This one usually goes here, and does that. All of this is familiar enough.* That's no knock on the contemporary fiction that is recognizable and breakdownable. This includes about 98 percent of the fiction we know and love.

But this is not possible with *Infinite Jest*. This book is like a spaceship with no recognizable components, no rivets or bolts, no entry points, no way to take it apart. It is very shiny, and it has no discernible flaws. If you could somehow smash it into smaller pieces, there would certainly be no way to put it back together again. It simply *is*. Page by page, line by line, it is probably the strangest, most distinctive, and most involved work of fiction by an American in the last twenty years. At no time while reading *Infinite Jest* are you are unaware that this is a work of complete obsession, of a stretching of the mind of a young writer to the point of, we assume, near madness.

Which isn't to say it's madness in the way that Burroughs or even Fred Exley used a type of madness with which to create. Exley, like many writers of his generation and the few before it, drank to excess, and Burroughs ingested every controlled substance he could buy or borrow. But Wallace is a different sort of madman, one in full control of his tools, one who instead of teetering on the edge of this precipice or that, under the influence of drugs or alcohol, seems to be heading ever-inward, into the depths of memory and the relentless conjuring of a certain time and place in a way that evokes — it seems so wrong to type this name but then again, so right! — Marcel Proust. There is the same sort of obsessiveness, the same incredible precision and focus, and the same sense that the writer wanted (and arguably succeeds at) nailing the consciousness of an age.

Let's talk about age, the more pedestrian meaning of the word. It's to be expected that the average age of the new *Infinite Jest* reader would be about twenty-five. There are certainly many collegians among you, probably, and there may be an equal number of thirty-year-olds or fifty-year-olds who have for whatever reason reached a point in their lives where they have determined themselves finally ready to tackle the book, which this or that friend has urged upon them. The point is that the average age is appropriate enough. I was twenty-five myself when I first read it. I had known it was coming for about a year, because the publisher, Little, Brown, had been very clever about building anticipation for it, with monthly postcards, bearing teasing phrases and hints, sent to every media outlet in the country. When the book was finally released, I started in on it almost immediately.

And thus I spent a month of my young life. I did little else. And I can't say it was always a barrel of monkeys. It was occasionally trying. It demands your full attention. It can't be read at a crowded café, or with a child on one's lap. It was frustrating that the footnotes were at the end of the book, rather than on the bottom of the page, as they had been in Wallace's essays and journalism. There were times, reading a very exhaustive account of a tennis match, say, when I thought, well, okay. I like tennis as much as the next guy, but enough already.

And yet the time spent in this book, in this world of language, is absolutely rewarded. When you exit these pages after that month of reading, you are a better person. It's insane, but also hard to deny. Your brain is stronger because it's been given a monthlong workout, and more importantly, your heart is sturdier, for there has scarcely been written a more moving account of desperation, depression, addiction, generational stasis and yearning, or the obsession with human expectations, with artistic and athletic and intellectual possibility. The themes here are big, and the emotions (guarded as they are) are very real, and the cumulative effect of the book is, you could say, seismic. It would be very unlikely that you would find a reader who, after finishing the book, would shrug and say, "Eh."

Here's a question once posed to me, by a large, baseball cap–wearing English major at a medium-size western college: Is it our duty to read *Infinite Jest*? This is a good question, and one that many people, particularly literary-minded people, ask themselves. The answer is: Maybe. Sort of. Probably, in some way. If we think it's our duty to read this book, it's because we're interested in genius. We're interested in epic writerly ambition. We're fascinated with what can be made by a person with enough time and focus and caffeine and, in Wallace's case, chewing tobacco. If we are drawn to *Infinite Jest,* we're also drawn to the Magnetic Fields' *69 Songs,* for which Stephin Merritt wrote that many songs, all of them about love, in about two years. And we're drawn to the ten thousand paintings of folk artist Howard Finster. Or the work of Sufjan Stevens, who is on a mission to create an album about each state in the union. He's currently at State No. 2, but if he reaches his goal, it will approach what Wallace did with the book in your hands. The point is that if we are interested in human possibility, and we are able to cheer each other on to leaps in science and athletics and art and thought, we must admire the work that our peers have managed to create. We have an obligation, to ourselves, chiefly, to see what a brain, and particularly a brain like our own — that is, using the same effluvium we, too, swim through — is capable of. It's why we watch *Shoah,* or visit the unending scroll on which Jack Kerouac wrote (in a fever of days) *On the Road,* or William T. Vollmann's 3,300-page *Rising Up and Rising Down,* or Michael Apted's *7-Up, 28-Up, 42-Up* series of films, or . . . well, the list goes on.

And now, unfortunately, we're back to the impression that this book is daunting. Which it isn't, really. It's long, but there are pleasures everywhere. There is humor everywhere. There is also a very quiet but very sturdy and constant tragic undercurrent that concerns a people who are completely lost, who are lost within their families and lost within their nation, and lost within their time, and who only want some sort of direction or purpose or sense of community or love. Which is, after all and conveniently enough for the end of this introduction, what an author is seeking when he sets out to write a book — any book, but particularly a book like this, a book that gives so much, that required such sacrifice and dedication. Who would do such a thing if not for want of connection and thus of love?

Last thing: In attempting to persuade you to buy this book, or check it out of your library, it's useful to tell you that the author is a normal person. Dave Wallace — and he is commonly known as such — keeps big sloppy dogs and has never dressed them in taffeta or made them wear raincoats. He has complained often about sweating too much when he gives public readings, so much so that he wears a bandanna to keep the perspiration from soaking the pages below him. He was once a nationally ranked tennis player, and he cares about good government. He is from the Midwest — east-central Illinois, to be specific, which is an intensely normal part of the country (not far, in fact, from a city, no joke, named Normal). So he is normal, and regular, and ordinary, and this is his extraordinary, and irregular, and not-normal achievement, a thing that will outlast him and you and me, but will help future people understand us — how we felt, how we lived, what we gave to each other and why.

— Dave Eggers
  September 2006

INFINITE JEST

O

YEAR OF GLAD

I am seated in an office, surrounded by heads and bodies. My posture is consciously congruent to the shape of my hard chair. This is a cold room in University Administration, wood-walled, Remington-hung, double-windowed against the November heat, insulated from Administrative sounds by the reception area outside, at which Uncle Charles, Mr. deLint and I were lately received.

I am in here.

Three faces have resolved into place above summer-weight sportcoats and half-Windsors across a polished pine conference table shiny with the spidered light of an Arizona noon. These are three Deans — of Admissions, Academic Affairs, Athletic Affairs. I do not know which face belongs to whom.

I believe I appear neutral, maybe even pleasant, though I've been coached to err on the side of neutrality and not attempt what would feel to me like a pleasant expression or smile.

I have committed to crossing my legs I hope carefully, ankle on knee, hands together in the lap of my slacks. My fingers are mated into a mirrored series of what manifests, to me, as the letter X. The interview room's other personnel include: the University's Director of Composition, its varsity tennis coach, and Academy prorector Mr. A. deLint. C.T. is beside me; the others sit, stand and stand, respectively, at the periphery of my focus. The tennis coach jingles pocket-change. There is something vaguely digestive about the room's odor. The high-traction sole of my complimentary Nike sneaker runs parallel to the wobbling loafer of my mother's half-brother, here in his capacity as Headmaster, sitting in the chair to what I hope is my immediate right, also facing Deans.

The Dean at left, a lean yellowish man whose fixed smile nevertheless has the impermanent quality of something stamped into uncooperative material, is a personality-type I've come lately to appreciate, the type who delays need of any response from me by relating my side of the story for me, to me. Passed a packet of computer-sheets by the shaggy lion of a Dean at center, he is speaking more or less to these pages, smiling down.

'You are Harold Incandenza, eighteen, date of secondary-school graduation approximately one month from now, attending the Enfield Tennis Academy, Enfield, Massachusetts, a boarding school, where you reside.' His reading glasses are rectangular, court-shaped, the sidelines at top and bottom. 'You are, according to Coach White and Dean [unintelligible], a regionally, nationally, and continentally ranked junior tennis player, a potential O.N.A.N.C.A.A. athlete of substantial promise, recruited by Coach White via correspondence with Dr. Tavis here commencing . . . February of this year.' The top page is removed and brought around neatly to the bottom of the sheaf, at intervals. 'You have been in residence at the Enfield Tennis Academy since age seven.'

I am debating whether to risk scratching the right side of my jaw, where there is a wen.

'Coach White informs our offices that he holds the Enfield Tennis Academy's program and achievements in high regard, that the University of Arizona tennis squad has profited from the prior matriculation of several former E.T.A. alumni, one of whom was one Mr. Aubrey F. deLint, who appears also to be with you here today. Coach White and his staff have given us —'

The yellow administrator's usage is on the whole undistinguished, though I have to admit he's made himself understood. The Director of Composition seems to have more than the normal number of eyebrows. The Dean at right is looking at my face a bit strangely.

Uncle Charles is saying that though he can anticipate that the Deans might be predisposed to weigh what he avers as coming from his possible appearance as a kind of cheerleader for E.T.A., he can assure the assembled Deans that all this is true, and that the Academy has presently in residence no fewer than a third of the continent's top thirty juniors, in age brackets all across the board, and that I here, who go by 'Hal,' usually, am 'right up there among the very cream.' Right and center Deans smile professionally; the heads of deLint and the coach incline as the Dean at left clears his throat:

'— belief that you could well make, even as a freshman, a real contribution to this University's varsity tennis program. We are pleased,' he either says or reads, removing a page, 'that a competition of some major sort here has brought you down and given us the chance to sit down and chat together about your application and potential recruitment and matriculation and scholarship.'

'I've been asked to add that Hal here is seeded third, Boys' 18-and-Under Singles, in the prestigious WhataBurger Southwest Junior Invitational out at the Randolph Tennis Center —' says what I infer is Athletic Affairs, his cocked head showing a freckled scalp.

'Out at Randolph Park, near the outstanding El Con Marriott,' C.T. inserts, 'a venue the whole contingent's been vocal about finding absolutely top-hole thus far, which —'

'Just so, Chuck, and that according to Chuck here Hal has already justified his seed, he's reached the semifinals as of this morning's apparently impressive win, and that he'll be playing out at the Center again tomorrow,

4

against the winner of a quarterfinal game tonight, and so will be playing tomorrow at I believe scheduled for 0830 —'

'Try to get under way before the godawful heat out there. Though of course a dry heat.'

'— and has apparently already qualified for this winter's Continental Indoors, up in Edmonton, Kirk tells me —' cocking further to look up and left at the varsity coach, whose smile's teeth are radiant against a violent sunburn — 'Which is something indeed.' He smiles, looking at me. 'Did we get all that right Hal.'

C.T. has crossed his arms casually; their triceps' flesh is webbed with mottle in the air-conditioned sunlight. 'You sure did. Bill.' He smiles. The two halves of his mustache never quite match. 'And let me say if I may that Hal's excited, excited to be invited for the third year running to the Invitational again, to be back here in a community he has real affection for, to visit with your alumni and coaching staff, to have already justified his high seed in this week's not unstiff competition, to as they say still be in it without the fat woman in the Viking hat having sung, so to speak, but of course most of all to have a chance to meet you gentlemen and have a look at the facilities here. Everything here is absolutely top-slot, from what he's seen.'

There is a silence. DeLint shifts his back against the room's panelling and recenters his weight. My uncle beams and straightens a straight watchband. 62.5% of the room's faces are directed my way, pleasantly expectant. My chest bumps like a dryer with shoes in it. I compose what I project will be seen as a smile. I turn this way and that, slightly, sort of directing the expression to everyone in the room.

There is a new silence. The yellow Dean's eyebrows go circumflex. The two other Deans look to the Director of Composition. The tennis coach has moved to stand at the broad window, feeling at the back of his crewcut. Uncle Charles strokes the forearm above his watch. Sharp curved palm-shadows move slightly over the pine table's shine, the one head's shadow a black moon.

'Is Hal all right, Chuck?' Athletic Affairs asks. 'Hal just seemed to . . . well, grimace. Is he in pain? Are you in pain, son?'

'Hal's right as rain,' smiles my uncle, soothing the air with a casual hand. 'Just a bit of a let's call it maybe a facial tic, slightly, at all the adrenaline of being here on your impressive campus, justifying his seed so far without dropping a set, receiving that official written offer of not only waivers but a living allowance from Coach White here, on Pac 10 letterhead, being ready in all probability to sign a National Letter of Intent right here and now this very day, he's indicated to me.' C.T. looks to me, his look horribly mild. I do the safe thing, relaxing every muscle in my face, emptying out all expression. I stare carefully into the Kekuléan knot of the middle Dean's necktie.

My silent response to the expectant silence begins to affect the air of the room, the bits of dust and sportcoat-lint stirred around by the AC's vents dancing jaggedly in the slanted plane of windowlight, the air over the table like the sparkling space just above a fresh-poured seltzer. The coach, in a slight accent neither British nor Australian, is telling C.T. that the whole application-interface process, while usually just a pleasant formality, is probably best accentuated by letting the applicant speak up for himself. Right and center Deans have inclined together in soft conference, forming a kind of tepee of skin and hair. I presume it's probably *facilitate* that the tennis coach mistook for *accentuate*, though *accelerate*, while clunkier than *facilitate*, is from a phonetic perspective more sensible, as a mistake. The Dean with the flat yellow face has leaned forward, his lips drawn back from his teeth in what I see as concern. His hands come together on the conference table's surface. His own fingers look like they mate as my own four-X series dissolves and I hold tight to the sides of my chair.

We need candidly to chat re potential problems with my application, they and I, he is beginning to say. He makes a reference to candor and its value.

'The issues my office faces with the application materials on file from you, Hal, involve some test scores.' He glances down at a colorful sheet of standardized scores in the trench his arms have made. 'The Admissions staff is looking at standardized test scores from you that are, as I'm sure you know and can explain, are, shall we say . . . subnormal.' I'm to explain.

It's clear that this really pretty sincere yellow Dean at left is Admissions. And surely the little aviarian figure at right is Athletics, then, because the facial creases of the shaggy middle Dean are now pursed in a kind of distanced affront, an I'm-eating-something-that-makes-me-really-appreciate-the-presence-of-whatever-I'm-drinking-along-with-it look that spells professionally Academic reservations. An uncomplicated loyalty to standards, then, at center. My uncle looks to Athletics as if puzzled. He shifts slightly in his chair.

The incongruity between Admissions's hand- and face-color is almost wild. '— verbal scores that are just quite a bit closer to zero than we're comfortable with, as against a secondary-school transcript from the institution where both your mother and her brother are administrators —' reading directly out of the sheaf inside his arms' ellipse — 'that this past year, yes, has fallen off a bit, but by the word I mean "fallen off" to outstanding from three previous years of frankly incredible.'

'Off the charts.'

'Most institutions do not even *have* grades of A with multiple pluses after it,' says the Director of Composition, his expression impossible to interpret.

'This kind of . . . how shall I put it . . . incongruity,' Admissions says, his expression frank and concerned, 'I've got to tell you sends up a red flag of potential concern during the admissions process.'

'We thus invite you to explain the appearance of incongruity if not outright shenanigans.' Students has a tiny piping voice that's absurd coming out of a face this big.

'Surely by *incredible* you meant very very very impressive, as opposed to literally quote "incredible," surely,' says C.T., seeming to watch the coach at the window massaging the back of his neck. The huge window gives out on nothing more than dazzling sunlight and cracked earth with heat-shimmers over it.

'Then there is before us the matter of not the required two but *nine* separate application essays, some of which of nearly monograph-length, each without exception being —' different sheet — 'the adjective various evaluators used was quote "stellar" —'

Dir. of Comp.: 'I made in my assessment deliberate use of *lapidary* and *effete.*'

'— but in areas and with titles, I'm sure you recall quite well, Hal: "Neoclassical Assumptions in Contemporary Prescriptive Grammar," "The Implications of Post-Fourier Transformations for a Holographically Mimetic Cinema," "The Emergence of Heroic Stasis in Broadcast Entertainment" —'

' "Montague Grammar and the Semantics of Physical Modality"?'

' "A Man Who Began to Suspect He Was Made of Glass"?'

' "Tertiary Symbolism in Justinian Erotica"?'

Now showing broad expanses of recessed gum. 'Suffice to say that there's some frank and candid concern about the recipient of these unfortunate test scores, though perhaps explainable test scores, being these essays' sole individual author.'

'I'm not sure Hal's sure just what's being implied here,' my uncle says. The Dean at center is fingering his lapels as he interprets distasteful computed data.

'What the University is saying here is that from a strictly academic point of view there are admission problems that Hal needs to try to help us iron out. A matriculant's first role at the University is and must be as a student. We couldn't admit a student we have reason to suspect can't cut the mustard, no matter how much of an asset he might be on the field.'

'Dean Sawyer means the court, of course, Chuck,' Athletic Affairs says, head severely cocked so he's including the White person behind him in the address somehow. 'Not to mention O.N.A.N.C.A.A. regulations and investigators always snuffling around for some sort of whiff of the smell of impropriety.'

The varsity tennis coach looks at his own watch.

'Assuming these board scores are accurate reflectors of true capacity in this case,' Academic Affairs says, his high voice serious and sotto, still looking at the file before him as if it were a plate of something bad, 'I'll tell you right now my opinion is it wouldn't be fair. It wouldn't be fair to the other applicants. Wouldn't be fair to the University community.' He looks at me. 'And it'd be especially unfair to Hal himself. Admitting a boy we see as simply an athletic asset would amount to just using that boy. We're under myriad scrutiny to make sure we're not using anybody. Your board results, son, indicate that we could be accused of using you.'

Uncle Charles is asking Coach White to ask the Dean of Athletic Affairs whether the weather over scores would be as heavy if I were, say, a revenue-raising football prodigy. The familiar panic at feeling misperceived is rising, and my chest bumps and thuds. I expend energy on remaining utterly silent in my chair, empty, my eyes two great pale zeros. People have promised to get me through this.

Uncle C.T., though, has the pinched look of the cornered. His voice takes on an odd timbre when he's cornered, as if he were shouting as he receded. 'Hal's grades at E.T.A., which is I should stress an *Acad*emy, not simply a camp or factory, accredited by both the Commonwealth of Massachusetts and the North American Sports Academy Association, it's focused on the total needs of the player and student, founded by a towering intellectual figure whom I hardly need name, here, and based by him on the rigorous Oxbridge Quadrivium-Trivium curricular model, a school fully staffed and equipped, by a fully certified staff, should show that my nephew here can cut just about any Pac 10 mustard that needs cutting, and that —'

DeLint is moving toward the tennis coach, who is shaking his head.

'— would be able to see a distinct flavor of minor-sport prejudice about this whole thing,' C.T. says, crossing and recrossing his legs as I listen, composed and staring.

The room's carbonated silence is now hostile. 'I think it's time to let the actual applicant himself speak out on his own behalf,' Academic Affairs says very quietly. 'This seems somehow impossible with you here, sir.'

Athletics smiles tiredly under a hand that massages the bridge of his nose. 'Maybe you'd excuse us for a moment and wait outside, Chuck.'

'Coach White could accompany Mr. Tavis and his associate out to reception,' the yellow Dean says, smiling into my unfocused eyes.

'— led to believe this had all been ironed out in advance, from the —' C.T. is saying as he and deLint are shown to the door. The tennis coach extends a hypertrophied arm. Athletics says 'We're all friends and colleagues here.'

This is not working out. It strikes me that EXIT signs would look to a native speaker of Latin like red-lit signs that say HE LEAVES. I would yield to the urge to bolt for the door ahead of them if I could know that bolting for the door is what the men in this room would see. DeLint is murmuring something to the tennis coach. Sounds of keyboards, phone consoles as the door is briefly opened, then firmly shut. I am alone among administrative heads.

'— offense intended to anyone,' Athletic Affairs is saying, his sportcoat

8

tan and his necktie insigniated in tiny print — 'beyond just physical abilities out there in play, which believe me we respect, *want*, believe me.'

'— question about it we wouldn't be so anxious to chat with you directly, see?'

'— that we've known in processing several prior applications through Coach White's office that the Enfield School is operated, however impressively, by close relations of first your brother, who I can still remember the way White's predecessor Maury Klamkin wooed that kid, so that grades' objectivity can be all too easily called into question —'

'By whomsoever's calling — N.A.A.U.P., ill-willed Pac 10 programs, O.N.A.N.C.A.A. —'

The essays are old ones, yes, but they are mine; *de moi*. But they are, yes, old, not quite on the application's instructed subject of Most Meaningful Educational Experience Ever. If I'd done you one from the last year, it would look to you like some sort of infant's random stabs on a keyboard, and to you, who use *whomsoever* as a subject. And in this new smaller company, the Director of Composition seems abruptly to have actuated, emerged as both the Alpha of the pack here and way more effeminate than he'd seemed at first, standing hip-shot with a hand on his waist, walking with a roll to his shoulders, jingling change as he pulls up his pants as he slides into the chair still warm from C.T.'s bottom, crossing his legs in a way that inclines him well into my personal space, so that I can see multiple eyebrow-tics and capillary webs in the oysters below his eyes and smell fabric-softener and the remains of a breath-mint turned sour.

'. . . a bright, solid, but very shy boy, we know about your being very shy, Kirk White's told us what your athletically built if rather stand-offish younger instructor told him,' the Director says softly, cupping what I feel to be a hand over my sportcoat's biceps (surely not), 'who simply needs to swallow hard and trust and tell his side of the story to these gentlemen who bear no maliciousness none at all but are doing our jobs and trying to look out for everyone's interests at the same time.'

I can picture deLint and White sitting with their elbows on their knees in the defecatory posture of all athletes at rest, deLint staring at his huge thumbs, while C.T. in the reception area paces in a tight ellipse, speaking into his portable phone. I have been coached for this like a Don before a RICO hearing. A neutral and affectless silence. The sort of all-defensive game Schtitt used to have me play: the best defense: let everything bounce off you; do nothing. I'd tell you all you want and more, if the sounds I made could be what you hear.

Athletics with his head out from under his wing: '— to avoid admission procedures that could be seen as primarily athletics-oriented. It could be a mess, son.'

'Bill means the appearance, not necessarily the real true facts of the matter, which you alone can fill in,' says the Director of Composition.

'— the appearance of the high athletic ranking, the subnormal scores, the over-academic essays, the incredible grades vortexing out of what could be seen as a nepotistic situation.'

The yellow Dean has leaned so far forward that his tie is going to have a horizontal dent from the table-edge, his face sallow and kindly and no-shit-whatever:

'Look here, Mr. Incandenza, Hal, please just explain to me why we couldn't be accused of using you, son. Why nobody could come and say to us, why, look here, University of Arizona, here you are using a boy for just his body, a boy so shy and withdrawn he won't speak up for himself, a jock with doctored marks and a store-bought application.'

The Brewster's-Angle light of the tabletop appears as a rose flush behind my closed lids. I cannot make myself understood. 'I am not just a jock,' I say slowly. Distinctly. 'My transcript for the last year might have been dickied a bit, maybe, but that was to get me over a rough spot. The grades prior to that are *de moi*.' My eyes are closed; the room is silent. 'I cannot make myself understood, now.' I am speaking slowly and distinctly. 'Call it something I ate.'

It's funny what you don't recall. Our first home, in the suburb of Weston, which I barely remember — my eldest brother Orin says he can remember being in the home's backyard with our mother in the early spring, helping the Moms till some sort of garden out of the cold yard. March or early April. The garden's area was a rough rectangle laid out with Popsicle sticks and twine. Orin was removing rocks and hard clods from the Moms's path as she worked the rented Rototiller, a wheelbarrow-shaped, gas-driven thing that roared and snorted and bucked and he remembers seemed to propel the Moms rather than vice versa, the Moms very tall and having to stoop painfully to hold on, her feet leaving drunken prints in the tilled earth. He remembers that in the middle of the tilling I came tear-assing out the door and into the backyard wearing some sort of fuzzy red Pooh-wear, crying, holding out something he said was really unpleasant-looking in my upturned palm. He says I was around five and crying and was vividly red in the cold spring air. I was saying something over and over; he couldn't make it out until our mother saw me and shut down the tiller, ears ringing, and came over to see what I was holding out. This turned out to have been a large patch of mold — Orin posits from some dark corner of the Weston home's basement, which was warm from the furnace and flooded every spring. The patch itself he describes as horrific: darkly green, glossy, vaguely hirsute, speckled with parasitic fungal points of yellow, orange, red. Worse, they could see that the patch looked oddly incomplete, gnawed-on; and some of the nauseous stuff was smeared around my open mouth. 'I ate this,' was what I was saying. I held the patch out to the Moms, who had her contacts out for the dirty work, and at first, bending way down, saw only her crying child, hand out, proffering; and in that most maternal of reflexes she, who feared and loathed more than anything spoilage and filth, reached to take whatever her baby held out — as in how many used heavy Kleenex, spit-back candies, wads of chewed-out gum in how many theaters, airports, backseats, tournament lounges? O. stood there, he says, hefting a cold clod, playing with the Velcro on his puffy coat, watching as the Moms, bent way down to me, hand reaching, her lowering face with its presbyopic squint, suddenly stopped, froze, beginning to I.D. what it was I held out, countenancing evidence of oral contact with same. He remembers her face as past describing. Her outstretched hand, still Rototrembling, hung in the air before mine.

'I ate this,' I said.

'Pardon me?'

O. says he can only remember (sic) saying something caustic as he limboed a crick out of his back. He says he must have felt a terrible impending anxiety. The Moms refused ever even to go into the damp basement. I had stopped crying, he remembers, and simply stood there, the size and shape of a hydrant, in red PJ's with attached feet, holding out the mold, seriously, like the report of some kind of audit.

O. says his memory diverges at this point, probably as a result of anxiety. In his first memory, the Moms's path around the yard is a broad circle of hysteria:

'God!' she calls out.

'Help! My son ate this!' she yells in Orin's second and more fleshed-out recollection, yelling it over and over, holding the speckled patch aloft in a pincer of fingers, running around and around the garden's rectangle while O. gaped at his first real sight of adult hysteria. Suburban neighbors' heads appeared in windows and over the fences, looking. O. remembers me tripping over the garden's laid-out twine, getting up dirty, crying, trying to follow.

'God! Help! My son ate this! Help!' she kept yelling, running a tight pattern just inside the square of string; and my brother Orin remembers noting how even in hysterical trauma her flight-lines were plumb, her footprints Native-American-straight, her turns, inside the ideogram of string, crisp and martial, crying 'My son ate this! Help!' and lapping me twice before the memory recedes.

'My application's not bought,' I am telling them, calling into the darkness of the red cave that opens out before closed eyes. 'I am not just a boy who plays tennis. I have an intricate history. Experiences and feelings. I'm complex.

'I *read*,' I say. 'I study and read. I bet I've read everything you've read. Don't think I haven't. I consume libraries. I wear out spines and ROM-drives. I do things like get in a taxi and say, "The library, and step on it." My instincts concerning syntax and mechanics are better than your own, I can tell, with due respect.

'But it transcends the mechanics. I'm not a machine. I feel and believe. I have opinions. Some of them are interesting. I could, if you'd let me, talk and talk. Let's talk about anything. I believe the influence of Kierkegaard on Camus is underestimated. I believe Dennis Gabor may very well have been the Antichrist. I believe Hobbes is just Rousseau in a dark mirror. I believe, with Hegel, that transcendence is absorption. I could interface you guys right under the table,' I say. 'I'm not just a creātus, manufactured, conditioned, bred for a function.'

I open my eyes. 'Please don't think I don't care.'

I look out. Directed my way is horror. I rise from the chair. I see jowls sagging, eyebrows high on trembling foreheads, cheeks bright-white. The chair recedes below me.

'Sweet mother of Christ,' the Director says.

'I'm fine,' I tell them, standing. From the yellow Dean's expression, there's a brutal wind blowing from my direction. Academics' face has gone instantly old. Eight eyes have become blank discs that stare at whatever they see.

'Good God,' whispers Athletics.

'Please don't worry,' I say. 'I can explain.' I soothe the air with a casual hand.

Both my arms are pinioned from behind by the Director of Comp., who wrestles me roughly down, on me with all his weight. I taste floor.

'What's *wrong*?'

I say '*Nothing* is wrong.'

'It's all *right*! I'm *here*!' the Director is calling into my ear.

'Get help!' cries a Dean.

My forehead is pressed into parquet I never knew could be so cold. I am arrested. I try to be perceived as limp and pliable. My face is mashed flat; Comp.'s weight makes it hard to breathe.

'Try to listen,' I say very slowly, muffled by the floor.

'What in God's name are those . . . ,' one Dean cries shrilly, '. . . those *sounds*?'

There are clicks of a phone console's buttons, shoes' heels moving, pivoting, a sheaf of flimsy pages falling.

'*God!*'

'*Help!*'

The door's base opens at the left periphery: a wedge of halogen hall-light, white sneakers and a scuffed Nunn Bush. 'Let him *up*!' That's deLint.

'There is nothing wrong,' I say slowly to the floor. 'I'm in here.'

I'm raised by the crutches of my underarms, shaken toward what he must see as calm by a purple-faced Director: 'Get a *grip*, son!'

DeLint at the big man's arm: '*Stop* it!'

'I am not what you see and hear.'

Distant sirens. A crude half nelson. Forms at the door. A young Hispanic woman holds her palm against her mouth, looking.

'I'm not,' I say.

You have to love old-fashioned men's rooms: the citrus scent of deodorant disks in the long porcelain trough; the stalls with wooden doors in frames of cool marble; these thin sinks in rows, basins supported by rickety alphabets of exposed plumbing; mirrors over metal shelves; behind all the voices the slight sound of a ceaseless trickle, inflated by echo against wet porcelain and a cold tile floor whose mosaic pattern looks almost Islamic at this close range.

The disorder I've caused revolves all around. I've been half-dragged, still pinioned, through a loose mob of Administrative people by the Comp. Director — who appears to have thought variously that I am having a seizure (prying open my mouth to check for a throat clear of tongue), that I am somehow choking (a textbook Heimlich that left me whooping), that I am psychotically out of control (various postures and grips designed to transfer that control to him) — while about us roil deLint, trying to restrain the Director's restraint of me, the varsity tennis coach restraining deLint, my mother's half-brother speaking in rapid combinations of polysyllables to the trio of Deans, who variously gasp, wring hands, loosen neckties, waggle digits in C.T.'s face, and make *pases* with sheaves of now-pretty-clearly-superfluous application forms.

I am rolled over supine on the geometric tile. I am concentrating docilely on the question why U.S. restrooms always appear to us as infirmaries for public distress, the place to regain control. My head is cradled in a knelt Director's lap, which is soft, my face being swabbed with dusty-brown institutional paper towels he received from some hand out of the crowd overhead, staring with all the blankness I can summon into his jowls' small pocks, worst at the blurred jaw-line, of scarring from long-ago acne. Uncle Charles, a truly unparalleled slinger of shit, is laying down an enfilade of same, trying to mollify men who seem way more in need of a good brow-mopping than I.

'He's fine,' he keeps saying. 'Look at him, calm as can be, lying there.'

'You didn't see what *happened* in there,' a hunched Dean responds through a face webbed with fingers.

'Excited, is all he gets, sometimes, an excitable kid, impressed with —'
'But the *sounds* he made.'
'Undescribable.'
'Like an animal.'
'*Sub*animalistic noises and sounds.'
'Nor let's not forget the *gestures*.'
'Have you ever gotten *help* for this boy Dr. Tavis?'
'Like some sort of animal with something in its mouth.'
'This boy is damaged.'
'Like a stick of butter being hit with a mallet.'
'A writhing animal with a knife in its eye.'
'What were you possibly *about*, trying to enroll this —'
'And his *arms*.'
'You didn't see it, Tavis. His arms were —'
'Flailing. This sort of awful reaching drumming wriggle. *Waggling*,' the group looking briefly at someone outside my sight trying to demonstrate something.
'Like a time-lapse, a flutter of some sort of awful . . . growth.'
'Sounded most of all like a drowning goat. A goat, drowning in something viscous.'
'This strangled series of bleats and —'
'Yes they *waggled*.'
'So suddenly a bit of excited waggling's a crime, now?'
'You, sir, are in trouble. You are *in trouble*.'
'His face. As if he was strangling. Burning. I believe I've seen a vision of hell.'
'He has some trouble communicating, he's communicatively challenged, no one's denying that.'
'The boy needs *care*.'
'Instead of caring for the boy you send him here to *enroll, compete?*'
'Hal?'
'You have not in your most dreadful fantasies dreamt of the amount of *trouble* you have bought yourself, Dr. so-called Headmaster, *educator*.'
'. . . were given to understand this was all just a formality. You took him aback, is all. Shy —'
'And you, White. You sought to *recruit* him!'
'— and terribly impressed and excited, in there, without us, his support system, whom you asked to leave, which if you'd —'
'I'd only seen him play. On court he's gorgeous. Possibly a genius. We had no idea. The brother's in the bloody NFL for God's sake. Here's a top player, we thought, with Southwest roots. His stats were off the chart. We watched him through the whole WhataBurger last fall. Not a waggle or a noise. We were watching ballet out there, a mate remarked, after.'

'Damn right you were watching ballet out there, White. This boy is a balletic athlete, a player.'

'Some kind of athletic savant then. Balletic compensation for deep problems which *you* sir choose to disguise by muzzling the boy in there.' An expensive pair of Brazilian espadrilles goes by on the left and enters a stall, and the espadrilles come around and face me. The urinal trickles behind the voices' small echoes.

'— haps we'll just be on our way,' C.T. is saying.

'The integrity of my sleep has been forever compromised, sir.'

'— think you could pass off a damaged applicant, fabricate credentials and shunt him through a kangaroo-interview and inject him into all the rigors of college life?'

'Hal here *functions,* you ass. Given a supportive situation. He's fine when he's by himself. Yes he has some trouble with excitability in conversation. Did you once hear him try to deny that?'

'We witnessed something only marginally *mammalian* in there, sir.'

'Like hell. Have a look. How's the excitable little guy doing down there, Aubrey, does it look to you?'

'You, sir, are quite possibly ill. This affair is not concluded.'

'What *ambulance?* Don't you guys *listen?* I'm telling you there's —'

'Hal? Hal?'

'Dope him up, seek to act as his mouthpiece, muzzling, and now he lies there catatonic, staring.'

The crackle of deLint's knees. 'Hal?'

'— inflate this publicly in any distorted way. The Academy has distinguished alumni, litigators at counsel. Hal here is provably competent. Credentials out the bazoo, Bill. The boy reads like a vacuum. *Digests* things.'

I simply lie there, listening, smelling the paper towel, watching an espadrille pivot.

'There's more to life than sitting there interfacing, it might be a newsflash to you.'

And who could not love that special and leonine roar of a public toilet?

Not for nothing did Orin say that people outdoors down here just scuttle in vectors from air conditioning to air conditioning. The sun is a hammer. I can feel one side of my face start to cook. The blue sky is glossy and fat with heat, a few thin cirri sheared to blown strands like hair at the rims. The traffic is nothing like Boston. The stretcher is the special type, with restraining straps at the extremities. The same Aubrey deLint I'd dismissed for years as a 2-D martinet knelt gurneyside to squeeze my restrained hand and say 'Just hang in there, Buckaroo,' before moving back into the administrative fray at the ambulance's doors. It is a special ambulance, dispatched from I'd rather not dwell on where, with not only paramedics but some kind of psychiatric M.D. on board. The medics lift gently and are handy with straps. The M.D., his back up against the ambulance's side, has both hands up in dispassionate mediation between the Deans and C.T., who keeps stabbing skyward with his cellular's antenna as if it were a sabre, outraged that I'm being needlessly ambulanced off to some Emergency Room against my will and interests. The issue whether the damaged even have interested wills is shallowly hashed out as some sort of ultra-mach fighter too high overhead to hear slices the sky from south to north. The M.D. has both hands up and is patting the air to signify dispassion. He has a big blue jaw. At the only other emergency room I have ever been in, almost exactly one year back, the psychiatric stretcher was wheeled in and then parked beside the waiting-room chairs. These chairs were molded orange plastic; three of them down the row were occupied by different people all of whom were holding empty prescription bottles and perspiring freely. This would have been bad enough, but in the end chair, right up next to the strap-secured head of my stretcher, was a T-shirted woman with barnwood skin and a trucker's cap and a bad starboard list who began to tell me, lying there restrained and immobile, about how she had seemingly overnight suffered a sudden and anomalous gigantism in her right breast, which she referred to as a titty; she had an almost parodic Québecois accent and described the 'titty's' presenting history and possible diagnoses for almost twenty minutes before I was rolled away. The jet's movement and trail seem incisionish, as if white meat behind the blue were exposed and widening in the wake of the blade. I once saw the word *KNIFE* finger-written on the steamed mirror of a nonpublic bathroom. I have become an infantophile. I am forced to roll my closed eyes either up or to the side to keep the red cave from bursting into flames from the sunlight. The street's passing traffic is constant and seems to go 'Hush, hush, hush.' The sun, if your fluttering eye catches it even slightly, gives you the blue and red floaters a flashbulb gives you. 'Why *not*? Why *not*? Why not *not*, then, if the best reasoning you can contrive is why not?' C.T.'s voice, receding with outrage. Only the gallant stabs of his antenna are now visible, just inside my sight's right frame. I will be conveyed to an Emergency Room of some kind, where I will be detained as long as I do not respond to questions, and then, when I do respond to questions, I will be sedated; so it will be inversion of standard travel, the ambulance and ER: I'll make the journey first, then depart. I think very briefly of the late Cosgrove Watt. I think of the hypophalangial Grief-Therapist. I think of the Moms, alphabetizing cans of soup in the cabinet over the microwave. Of Himself's umbrella hung by its handle from the edge of the mail table just inside the Headmaster's House's foyer. The bad ankle hasn't ached once this whole year. I think of John N. R. Wayne, who would have won this year's WhataBurger, standing watch in a mask as Donald Gately and I dig up my father's head. There's very little doubt that Wayne would have won. And Venus Williams owns a ranch outside Green Valley; she may well attend the 18's Boys' and Girls' finals. I will be out in plenty of time for tomorrow's semi; I trust Uncle Charles. Tonight's winner is almost sure to be Dymphna, sixteen but with a birthday two weeks under the 15 April deadline; and Dymphna will still be tired tomorrow at 0830, while I, sedated, will have slept like a graven image. I have never before faced Dymphna in tournament play, nor played with the sonic balls the blind require, but I watched him barely dispatch Petropolis Kahn in the Round of 16, and I know he is mine.

It will start in the E.R., at the intake desk if C.T.'s late in following the ambulance, or in the green-tiled room after the room with the invasive-digital machines; or, given this special M.D.-supplied ambulance, maybe on the ride itself: some blue-jawed M.D. scrubbed to an antiseptic glow with his name sewn in cursive on his white coat's breast pocket and a quality desk-set pen, wanting gurneyside Q&A, etiology and diagnosis by Socratic method, ordered and point-by-point. There are, by the *O.E.D. VI*'s count, nineteen nonarchaic synonyms for *unresponsive,* of which nine are Latinate and four Saxonic. I will play either Stice or Polep in Sunday's final. Maybe in front of Venus Williams. It will be someone blue-collar and unlicensed, though, inevitably — a nurse's aide with quick-bit nails, a hospital security guy, a tired Cuban orderly who addresses me as *jou* — who will, looking down in the middle of some kind of bustled task, catch what he sees as my eye and ask So yo then man what's *your* story?

O

YEAR OF THE DEPEND ADULT UNDERGARMENT

Where was the woman who said she'd come. She said she would come. Erdedy thought she'd have come by now. He sat and thought. He was in the living room. When he started waiting one window was full of yellow light and cast a shadow of light across the floor and he was still sitting waiting as that shadow began to fade and was intersected by a brightening shadow from a different wall's window. There was an insect on one of the steel shelves that held his audio equipment. The insect kept going in and out of one of the holes on the girders that the shelves fit into. The insect was dark and had a shiny case. He kept looking over at it. Once or twice he started to get up to go over closer to look at it, but he was afraid that if he came closer and saw it closer he would kill it, and he was afraid to kill it. He did not use the phone to call the woman who'd promised to come because if he tied up the line and if it happened to be the time when maybe she was trying to call him he was afraid she would hear the busy signal and think him disinterested and get angry and maybe take what she'd promised him somewhere else.

She had promised to get him a fifth of a kilogram of marijuana, 200 grams of unusually good marijuana, for $1250 U.S. He had tried to stop smoking marijuana maybe 70 or 80 times before. Before this woman knew him. She did not know he had tried to stop. He always lasted a week, or two weeks, or maybe two days, and then he'd think and decide to have some in his home one more last time. One last final time he'd search out someone new, someone he hadn't already told that he had to stop smoking dope and please under no circumstances should they procure him any dope. It had to be a third party, because he'd told every dealer he knew to cut him off. And the third party had to be someone all-new, because each time he got some he knew this time had to be the last time, and so told them, asked them, as a favor, never to get him any more, ever. And he never asked a person again once he'd told them this, because he was proud, and also kind, and wouldn't put anyone in that kind of contradictory position. Also he considered himself creepy when it came to dope, and he was afraid that others would see that he was creepy about it as well. He sat and thought and waited in an uneven X of light through two different windows. Once or twice he looked at the phone. The insect had disappeared back into the hole in the steel girder a shelf fit into.

She'd promised to come at one certain time, and it was past that time. Finally he gave in and called her number, using just audio, and it rang several times, and he was afraid of how much time he was taking tying up the line and he got her audio answering device, the message had a snatch of ironic pop music and her voice and a male voice together saying we'll call you back, and the 'we' made them sound like a couple, the man was a handsome black man who was in law school, she designed sets, and he didn't leave a message because he didn't want her to know how much now he felt like he needed it. He had been very casual about the whole thing. She said she knew a guy just over the river in Allston who sold high-resin dope in moderate bulk, and he'd yawned and said well, maybe, well, hey, why not, sure, special occasion, I haven't bought any in I don't know how long. She said he lived in a trailer and had a harelip and kept snakes and had no phone, and was basically just not what you'd call a pleasant or attractive person at all, but the guy in Allston frequently sold dope to theater people in Cambridge, and had a devoted following. He said he was trying to even remember when was the last time he'd bought any, it had been so long. He said he guessed he'd have her get a decent amount, he said he'd had some friends call him in the recent past and ask if he could get them some. He had

18

this thing where he'd frequently say he was getting dope mostly for friends. Then if the woman didn't have it when she said she'd have it for him and he became anxious about it he could tell the woman that it was his friends who were becoming anxious, and he was sorry to bother the woman about something so casual but his friends were anxious and bothering him about it and he just wanted to know what he could maybe tell them. He was caught in the middle, is how he would represent it. He could say his friends had given him their money and were now anxious and exerting pressure, calling and bothering him. This tactic was not possible with this woman who'd said she'd come with it because he hadn't yet given her the $1250. She would not let him. She was well off. Her family was well off, she'd said to explain how her condominium was as nice as it was when she worked designing sets for a Cambridge theater company that seemed to do only German plays, dark smeary sets. She didn't care much about the money, she said she'd cover the cost herself when she got out to the Allston Spur to see whether the guy was at home in the trailer as she was certain he would be this particular afternoon, and he could just reimburse her when she brought it to him. This arrangement, very casual, made him anxious, so he'd been even more casual and said sure, fine, whatever. Thinking back, he was sure he'd said *whatever*, which in retrospect worried him because it might have sounded as if he didn't care at all, not at all, so little that it wouldn't matter if she forgot to get it or call, and once he'd made the decision to have marijuana in his home one more time it mattered a lot. It mattered a lot. He'd been too casual with the woman, he should have made her take $1250 from him up front, claiming politeness, claiming he didn't want to inconvenience her financially over something so trivial and casual. Money created a sense of obligation, and he should have wanted the woman to feel obliged to do what she'd said, once what she'd said she'd do had set him off inside. Once he'd been set off inside, it mattered so much that he was somehow afraid to show how much it mattered. Once he had asked her to get it, he was committed to several courses of action. The insect on the shelf was back. It didn't seem to do anything. It just came out of the hole in the girder onto the edge of the steel shelf and sat there. After a while it would disappear back into the hole in the girder, and he was pretty sure it didn't do anything in there either. He felt similar to the insect inside the girder his shelf was connected to, but was not sure just how he was similar. Once he'd decided to own marijuana one more last time, he was committed to several courses of action. He had to modem in to the agency and say that there was an emergency and that he was posting an e-note on a colleague's TP asking her to cover his calls for the rest of the week because he'd be out of contact for several days due to this emergency. He had to put an audio message on his answering device saying that starting that afternoon he was going to be unreachable for several days. He had to clean his bedroom, because once he had dope he would not leave his bedroom except to go to the refrigerator and the bathroom, and even then the trips would be very quick. He had to throw out all his beer and liquor, because if he drank alcohol and smoked dope at the same time he would get dizzy and ill, and if he had alcohol in the house he could not be relied on not to drink it once he started smoking dope. He'd had to do some shopping. He'd had to lay in supplies. Now just one of the insect's antennae was protruding from the hole in the girder. It protruded, but it did not move. He had had to buy soda, Oreos, bread, sandwich meat, mayonnaise, tomatoes, M&M's, Almost Home cookies, ice cream, a Pepperidge Farm frozen chocolate cake, and four cans of canned chocolate frosting to be eaten with a large spoon. He'd had to log an order to rent film cartridges from the Inter-Lace entertainment outlet. He'd had to buy antacids for the discomfort that eating all he would eat would cause him late at night. He'd had to buy a new bong, because each time he finished what simply had to be his last bulk-quantity of marijuana he decided that that was it, he was through, he didn't even like it anymore, this was it, no more hiding, no more imposing on his colleagues and putting different messages on his answering device and moving his car away from his condominium and closing his windows and curtains and blinds and living in quick vectors between his bedroom's InterLace teleputer's films and his refrigerator and his toilet, and he would take the bong he'd used and throw it away wrapped in several plastic shopping bags. His refrigerator made its own ice in little cloudy crescent blocks and he loved it, when he had dope in his home he always drank a great deal of cold soda and ice water. His tongue almost swelled at just the thought. He looked at the phone and the clock. He looked at the windows but not at the foliage and blacktop driveway beyond the windows. He had already vacuumed his venetian blinds and curtains, everything was ready to be shut down. Once the woman who said she'd come had come, he would shut the whole system down. It occurred to him that he would disappear into a hole in a girder inside him that supported something else inside him. He was unsure what the thing inside him was and was unprepared to commit himself to the course of action that would be required to explore the question. It was now almost three hours past the time when the woman had said she would come. A counselor, Randi, with an *i*, with a mustache like a Mountie, had told him in the outpatient treatment program he'd gone through two years ago that he seemed insufficiently committed to the course of action that would be required to remove substances from his lifestyle. He'd had to buy a new bong at Bogart's in Porter Square, Cambridge because whenever he finished the last of the substances on hand he always threw out all his bongs and pipes, screens and tubes and rolling papers and roach clips, lighters and Visine and Pepto-Bismol and cookies and frosting, to eliminate all future temptation. He always felt a sense of optimism and firm resolve after he'd discarded the materials. He'd bought the new bong and laid in fresh supplies this morning, getting back home with everything well before the woman had said she would come. He thought of the new bong and new little packet of round brass screens in the Bogart's bag on his kitchen table in the sunlit kitchen and could not remember what color this new bong was. The last one had been orange, the one before that a dusky rose color that had turned muddy at the bottom from resin in just four days. He could not remember the color of this new last and final bong. He considered getting up to check the color of the bong he'd be using but decided that obsessive checking and convulsive movements could compromise the atmosphere of casual calm he needed to maintain while he waited, protruding but not moving, for the woman he'd met at a design session for his agency's small campaign for her small theater company's new Wedekind festival, while he waited for this woman, with whom he'd had intercourse twice, to honor her casual promise. He tried to decide whether the woman was pretty. Another thing he laid in when he'd committed himself to one last marijuana vacation was petroleum jelly. When he smoked marijuana he tended to masturbate a great deal, whether or not there were opportunities for intercourse, opting when he smoked for masturbation over intercourse, and the petroleum jelly kept him from returning to normal function all tender and sore. He was also hesitant to get up and check the color of his bong because he would have to pass right by the telephone console to get to the kitchen, and he didn't want to be tempted to call the woman who'd said she would come again because he felt creepy about bothering her about something he'd represented as so casual, and was afraid that several audio hang-ups on her answering device would look even creepier, and also he felt anxious about maybe tying up the line at just the moment when she called, as she certainly would. He decided to get Call Waiting added to his audio phone service for a nominal extra charge, then remembered that since this was positively the last time he would or even could indulge what Randi, with an *i*, had called an addiction every bit as rapacious as pure alcoholism, there would be no real need for Call Waiting, since a situation like the present one could never arise again. This line of thinking almost caused him to become angry. To ensure the composure with which he sat waiting in light in his chair he focused his senses on his surroundings. No part of the insect he'd seen was now visible. The clicks of his portable clock were really composed of three smaller clicks, signifying he supposed preparation, movement, and readjustment. He began to grow disgusted with himself for waiting so anxiously for the promised arrival of something that had stopped being fun anyway. He didn't even know why he liked it anymore. It made his mouth dry and his eyes dry and red and his face sag, and he hated it when his face sagged, it was as if all the integrity of all the muscles in his face was eroded by marijuana, and he got terribly self-conscious about the fact that his face was sagging, and had long ago forbidden himself to smoke dope around anyone else. He didn't even know what its draw was anymore. He couldn't even be around anyone else if he'd smoked marijuana that same day, it made him so self-conscious. And the dope often gave him a painful case of pleurisy if he smoked it for more than two straight days of heavy continuous smoking in front of the Inter-Lace viewer in his bedroom. It made his thoughts jut out crazily in jagged directions and made him stare raptly like an unbright child at entertainment cartridges — when he laid in film cartridges for a vacation with marijuana, he favored cartridges in which a lot of things blew up and crashed into each other, which he was sure an unpleasant-fact specialist like Randi would point out had implications that were not good. He pulled his necktie down smooth while he gathered his intellect, will, self-knowledge, and conviction and determined that when this latest woman came as she surely would this would simply be his very last marijuana debauch. He'd simply smoke so much so fast that it would be so unpleasant and the memory of it so repulsive that once he'd consumed it and gotten it out of his home and his life as quickly as possible he would never want to do it again. He would make it his business to create a really bad set of debauched associations with the stuff in his memory. The dope scared him. It made him afraid. It wasn't that he was afraid of the dope, it was that smoking it made him afraid of everything else. It had long since stopped being a release or relief or fun. This last time, he would smoke the whole 200 grams — 120 grams cleaned, destemmed — in four days, over an ounce a day, all in tight heavy economical one-hitters off a quality virgin bong, an incredible, insane amount per day, he'd make it a mission, treating it like a penance and behavior-modification regimen all at once, he'd smoke his way through thirty high-grade grams a day, starting the moment he woke up and used ice water to detach his tongue from the roof of his mouth and took an antacid — averaging out to 200 or 300 heavy bong-hits per day, an insane and deliberately unpleasant amount, and he'd make it a mission to smoke it continuously, even though if the marijuana was as good as the woman claimed he'd do five hits and then not want to take the trouble to load and one-hit any more for at least an hour. But he would force himself to do it anyway. He would smoke it all even if he didn't want it. Even if it started to make him dizzy and ill. He would use discipline and persistence and will and make the whole experience so unpleasant, so debased and debauched and unpleasant, that his behavior would be henceforward modified, he'd never even want to do it again because the memory of the insane four days to come would be so firmly, terribly emblazoned in his memory. He'd cure himself by excess. He predicted that the woman, when she came, might want to smoke some of the 200 grams with him, hang out, hole up, listen to some of his impressive collection of Tito Puente recordings, and probably have intercourse. He had never once had actual intercourse on marijuana. Frankly, the idea repelled him. Two dry mouths bumping at each other, trying to kiss, his self-conscious thoughts twisting around on themselves like a snake on a stick while he bucked and snorted dryly above her, his swollen eyes red and his face sagging so that its slack folds maybe touched, limply, the folds of her own loose sagging face is it sloshed back and forth on his pillow, its mouth working dryly. The thought was repellent. He decided he'd have her toss him what she'd promised to bring, and then would from a distance toss back to her the $1250 U.S. in large bills and tell her not to let the door hit her on the butt on the way out. He'd say *ass* instead of *butt*. He'd be so rude and unpleasant to her that the memory of his lack of basic decency and of her tight offended face would be a further disincentive ever, in the future, to risk calling her and repeating the course of action he had now committed himself to.

He had never been so anxious for the arrival of a woman he did not want to see. He remembered clearly the last woman he'd involved in his trying just one more vacation with dope and drawn blinds. The last woman had been something called an appropriation artist, which seemed to mean that she copied and embellished other art and then sold it through a prestigious Marlborough Street gallery. She had an artistic manifesto that involved radical feminist themes. He'd let her give him one of her smaller paintings, which covered half the wall over his bed and was of a famous film actress whose name he always had a hard time recalling and a less famous film actor, the two of them entwined in a scene from a well-known old film, a romantic scene, an embrace, copied from a film history textbook and much enlarged and made stilted, and with obscenities scrawled all over it in bright red letters. The last woman had been sexy but not pretty, as the woman he now didn't want to see but was waiting anxiously for was pretty in a faded withered Cambridge way that made her seem pretty but not sexy. The appropriation artist had been led to believe that he was a former speed addict, intravenous addiction to methamphetamine hydrochloride[1] is what he remembered telling that one, he had even described the awful taste of hydrochloride in the addict's mouth immediately after injection, he had researched the subject carefully. She had been further led to believe that marijuana kept him from using the drug with which he really had a problem, and so that if he seemed anxious to get some once she'd offered to get him some it was only because he was heroically holding out against much darker deeper more addictive urges and he needed her to help him. He couldn't quite remember when or how she'd been given all these impressions. He had not sat down and outright bold-faced lied to her, it had been more of an impression he'd conveyed and nurtured and allowed to gather its own life and force. The insect was now entirely visible. It was on the shelf that held his digital equalizer. The insect might never actually have retreated all the way back into the hole in the shelf's girder. What looked like its reemergence might just have been a change in his attention or the two windows' light or the visual context of his surroundings. The girder protruded from the wall and was a triangle of dull steel with holes for shelves to fit into. The metal shelves that held his audio equipment were painted a dark industrial green and were originally made for holding canned goods. They were designed to be extra kitchen shelves. The insect sat inside its dark shiny case with an immobility that seemed like the gathering of a force, it sat like the hull of a vehicle from which the engine had been for the moment removed. It was dark and had a shiny case and antennae that protruded but did not move. He had to use the bathroom. His last piece of contact from the appropriation artist, with whom he had had intercourse, and who during intercourse had sprayed some sort of perfume up into the air from a mister she held in her left hand as she lay beneath him making a wide variety of sounds and spraying perfume up into the air, so that he felt the cold mist of it settling on his back and shoulders and was chilled and repelled, his last piece of contact after he'd gone into hiding with the marijuana she'd gotten for him had been a card she'd mailed that was a pastiche photo of a doormat of coarse green plastic grass with WELCOME on it and next to it a flattering publicity photo of the appropriation artist from her Back Bay gallery, and between them an unequal sign, which was an equal sign with a diagonal slash across it, and also an obscenity he had assumed was directed at him magisculed in red grease pencil along the bottom, with multiple exclamation points. She had been offended because he had seen her every day for ten days, then when she'd finally obtained 50 grams of genetically enhanced hydroponic marijuana for him he had said that she'd saved his life and he was grateful and the friends for whom he'd promised to get some were grateful and she had to go right now because he had an appointment and had to take off, but that he would doubtless be calling her later that day, and they had shared a moist kiss, and she had said she could feel his heart pounding right through his suit coat, and she had driven away in her rusty unmuffled car, and he had gone and moved his own car to an underground garage several blocks away, and had run back and drawn the clean blinds and curtains, and changed the audio message on his answering device to one that described an emergency departure from town, and had drawn and locked his bedroom blinds, and had taken the new rose-colored bong out of its Bogart's bag, and was not seen for three days, and ignored over two dozen audio messages and protocols and e-notes expressing concern over his message's emergency, and had never contacted her again. He had hoped she would assume he had succumbed again to methamphetamine hydrochloride and was sparing her the agony of his descent back into the hell of chemical dependence. What it really was was that he had again decided those 50 grams of resin-soaked dope, which had been so potent that on the second day it had given him an anxiety attack so paralyzing that he had gone to the bathroom in a Tufts University commemorative ceramic stein to avoid leaving his bedroom, represented his very last debauch ever with dope, and that he had to cut himself off from all possible future sources of temptation and supply, and this surely included the appropriation artist, who had come with the stuff at precisely the time she'd promised, he recalled. From the street outside came the sound of a dumpster being emptied into an E.W.D. land barge. His shame at what she might on the other hand perceive as his slimy phallocentric conduct toward her made it easier for him to avoid her, as well. Though not shame, really. More like being uncomfortable at the thought of it. He had had to launder his bedding twice to get the smell of the perfume out. He went into the bathroom to use the bathroom, making it a point to look neither at the insect visible on the shelf to his left nor at the telephone console on its lacquer workstation to the right. He was committed to touching neither. Where was the woman who had said she'd come. The new bong in the Bogart's bag was orange, meaning he might have misremembered the bong before it as orange. It was a rich autumnal orange that lightened to more of a citrus orange when its plastic cylinder was held up to the late-afternoon light of the window over the kitchen sink. The metal of its stem and bowl was rough stainless steel, the kind with a grain, unpretty and all business. The bong was half a meter tall and had a weighted base covered in soft false suede. Its orange plastic was thick and the carb on the side opposite the stem had been raggedly cut so that rough shards of plastic protruded from the little hole and might well hurt his thumb when he smoked, which he decided to consider just part of the penance he would undertake after the woman had come and gone. He left the door to the bathroom open so that he would be sure to hear the telephone when it sounded or the buzzer to the front doors of his condominium complex when it sounded. In the bathroom his throat suddenly closed and he wept hard for two or three seconds before the weeping stopped abruptly and he could not get it to start again. It was now over four hours since the time the woman had casually committed to come. Was he in the bathroom or in his chair near the window and near his telephone console and the insect and the window that had admitted a straight rectangular bar of light when he began to wait. The light through this window was coming at an angle more and more oblique. Its shadow had become a parallelogram. The light through the southwest window was straight and reddening. He had thought he needed to use the bathroom but was unable to. He tried putting a whole stack of film cartridges into the dock of the disc-drive and then turning on the huge teleputer in his bedroom. He could see the piece of appropriation art in the mirror above the TP. He lowered the volume all the way and pointed the remote device at the TP like some sort of weapon. He sat on the edge of his bed with his elbows on his knees and scanned the stack of cartridges. Each cartridge in the dock dropped on command and began to engage the drive with an insectile click and whir, and he scanned it. But he was unable to distract himself with the TP because he was unable to stay with any one entertainment cartridge for more than a few seconds. The moment he recognized what exactly was on one cartridge he had a strong anxious feeling that there was something more entertaining on another cartridge and that he was potentially missing it. He realized that he would have plenty of time to enjoy all the cartridges, and realized intellectually that the feeling of deprived panic over missing something made no sense. The viewer hung on the wall, half again as large as the piece of feminist art. He scanned cartridges for some time. The telephone console sounded during this interval of anxious scanning. He was up and moving back out toward it before the first ring was completed, flooded with either excitement or relief, the TP's remote device still in his hand, but it was only a friend and colleague calling, and when he heard the voice that was not the woman who had promised to bring what he'd committed the next several days to banishing from his life forever he was almost sick with disappointment, with a great deal of mistaken adrenaline now shining and ringing in his system, and he got off the line with the colleague to clear the line and keep it available for the woman so fast that he was sure his colleague perceived him as either angry with him or just plain rude. He was further upset at the thought that his answering the telephone this late in the day did not jibe with the emergency message about being unreachable that would be on his answering device if the colleague called back after the woman had come and gone and he'd shut the whole system of his life down, and he was standing over the telephone console trying to decide whether the risk of the colleague or someone else from the agency calling back was sufficient to justify changing the audio message on the answering device to describe an emergency departure this evening instead of this afternoon, but he decided he felt that since the woman had definitely committed to coming, his leaving the message unchanged would be a gesture of fidelity to her commitment, and might somehow in some oblique way strengthen that commitment. The E.W.D. land barge was emptying dumpsters all up and down the street. He returned to his chair near the window. The disk drive and TP viewer were still on in his bedroom and he could see through the angle of the bedroom's doorway the lights from the high-definition screen blink and shift from one primary color to another in the dim room, and for a while he killed time casually by trying to imagine what entertaining scenes on the unwatched viewer the changing colors and intensities might signify. The chair faced the room instead of the window. Reading while waiting for marijuana was out of the question. He considered masturbating but did not. He didn't reject the idea so much as not react to it and watch as it floated away. He thought very broadly of desires and ideas being watched but not acted upon, he thought of impulses being starved of expression and drying out and floating dryly away, and felt on some level that this had something to do with him and his circumstances and what, if this grueling final debauch he'd committed himself to didn't somehow resolve the problem, would surely have to be called his problem, but he could not even begin to try to see how the image of desiccated impulses floating dryly related to either him or the insect, which had retreated back into its hole in the angled girder, because at this precise time his telephone and his intercom to the front door's buzzer both sounded at the same time, both loud and tortured and so abrupt they sounded yanked through a very small hole into the great balloon of colored silence he sat in, waiting, and he moved first toward the telephone console, then over toward his intercom module, then convulsively back toward the sounding phone, and then tried somehow to move toward both at once, finally, so that he stood splay-legged, arms wildly out as if something's been flung, splayed, entombed between the two sounds, without a thought in his head.

O

1 APRIL — YEAR OF THE TUCKS MEDICATED PAD

'All I know is my dad said to come here.'

'Come right in. You'll see a chair to your immediate left.'

'So I'm here.'

'That's just fine. Seven-Up? Maybe some lemon soda?'

'I guess not, thanks. I'm just here, is all, and I'm kind of wondering why my dad sent me down, you know. Your door there doesn't have anything on it, and I was just at the dentist last week, and so I'm wondering why I'm here, exactly, is all. That's why I'm not sitting down yet.'

'You're how old, Hal, fourteen?'

'I'll be eleven in June. Are you a dentist? Is this like a dental consult?'

'You're here to converse.'

'Converse?'

'Yes. Pardon me while I key in this age-correction. Your father had listed you as fourteen, for some reason.'

'Converse as in with you?'

'You're here to converse with me, Hal, yes. I'm almost going to have to implore you to have a lemon soda. Your mouth is making those dry sticky inadequate-saliva sounds.'

'Dr. Zegarelli says that's one reason for all the caries, is that I have low salivary output.'

'Those dry sticky salivaless sounds which can be death to a good conversation.'

'But I rode my bike all the way up here against the wind just to converse with you? Is the conversation supposed to start with me asking why?'

'I'll begin by asking if you know the meaning of *implore*, Hal.'

'Probably I'll go ahead and take a Seven-Up, then, if you're going to implore.'

'I'll ask you again whether you know *implore*, young sir.'

'Young sir?'

'You're wearing that bow tie, after all. Isn't that rather an invitation to a *young sir?*'

'*Implore*'s a regular verb, transitive: to call upon, or for, in supplication; to pray to, or for, earnestly; to beseech; to entreat. Weak synonym: urge. Strong synonym: beg. Etymology unmixed: from Latin *implorare, im* meaning in, *plorare* meaning in this context to cry aloud. *O.E.D.* Condensed Volume Six page 1387 column twelve and a little bit of thirteen.'

'Good lord she didn't exaggerate did she?'

'I tend to get beat up, sometimes, at the Academy, for stuff like that. Does this bear on why I'm here? That I'm a continentally ranked junior tennis player who can also recite great chunks of the dictionary, verbatim, at will, and tends to get beat up, and wears a bow tie? Are you like a specialist for gifted kids? Does this mean they think I'm gifted?'

SPFFFT. 'Here you are. Drink up.'

'Thanks. SHULGSHULGSPAHHH . . . Whew. Ah.'

'You *were* thirsty.'

'So then if I sit down you'll fill me in?'

'. . . professional conversationalist knows his mucous membranes, after all.'

'I might have to burp a little bit in a second, from the soda. I'm alerting you ahead of time.'

'Hal, you are here because I am a professional conversationalist, and your father has made an appointment with me, for you, to converse.'

'MYURP. Excuse me.'

Tap tap tap tap.

'SHULGSPAHHH.'

Tap tap tap tap.

'You're a professional conversationalist?'

'I am, yes, as I believe I just stated, a professional conversationalist.'

'Don't start looking at your watch, as if I'm taking up valuable time of yours. If Himself made the appointment and paid for it the time's supposed to be mine, right? Not yours. And then but what's that supposed to mean, "professional conversationalist"? A conversationalist is just one who converses much. You actually charge a fee to converse much?'

'A conversationalist is also one who, I'm sure you'll recall, "excels in conversation." '

'That's *Webster's Seventh*. That's not the *O.E.D.*'

Tap tap.

'I'm an *O.E.D.* man, Doctor. If that's what you are. Are you a doctor? Do you have a doctorate? Most people like to put their diplomas up, I notice, if they have credentials. And *Webster's Seventh* isn't even up-to-date. *Webster's Eighth* amends to "one who converses with much enthusiasm." '

'Another Seven-Up?'

'Is Himself still having this hallucination I never speak? Is that why he put the Moms up to having me bike up here? Himself is my dad. We call him Himself. As in quote "the man Himself." As it were. We call my mother the Moms. My brother coined the term. I understand this isn't unusual. I understand most more or less normal families address each other internally by means of pet names and terms and monikers. Don't even think about asking me what my little internal moniker is.'

Tap tap tap.

'But Himself hallucinates, sometimes, lately, you ought to be apprised, was the thrust. I'm wondering why the Moms let him send me pedalling up here uphill against the wind when I've got a challenge match at 3:00 to converse with an enthusiast with a blank door and no diplomas anywhere in view.'

'I, in my small way, would like to think it had as much to do with me as with you. That my reputation preceded me.'

'Isn't that usually a pejorative clause?'

'I am wonderful fun to talk to. I'm a consummate professional. People leave my parlor in states. You are here. It's conversation-time. Shall we discuss Byzantine erotica?'

'How did you know I was interested in Byzantine erotica?'

'You seem persistently to confuse me with someone who merely hangs out a shingle with the word *Conversationalist* on it, and this operation with a fly-by-night one strung together with chewing gum and twine. You think I have no support staff? Researchers at my beck? You think we don't delve full-bore into the psyches of those for whom we've made appointments to converse? You don't think this fully accredited limited partnership would have an interest in obtaining data on what informs and stimulates our con-versees?'

'I know only one person who'd ever use *full-bore* in casual conversation.'

'There is nothing casual about a professional conversationalist and staff. We delve. We obtain, and then some. Young sir.'

'Okay, Alexandrian or Constantinian?'

'You think we haven't thoroughly researched your own connection with the whole current intra-Provincial crisis in southern Québec?'

'What intra-Provincial crisis in southern Québec? I thought you wanted to talk racy mosaics.'

'This is an upscale district of a vital North American metropolis, Hal. Standards here are upscale, and high. A professional conversationalist flat-out full-bore *delves*. Do you for one moment think that a professional plier of the trade of conversation would fail to probe beak-deep into your family's sordid liaison with the pan-Canadian Resistance's notorious M. DuPlessis and his malevolent but allegedly irresistible amanuensis-cum-operative, Luria P——?'

'Listen, are you okay?'

'*Do you?*'

'I'm *ten* for Pete's sake. I think maybe your appointment calendar's squares got juggled. I'm the potentially gifted ten-year-old tennis and lexical prodigy whose mom's a continental mover and shaker in the prescriptive-grammar academic world and whose dad's a towering figure in optical and avant-garde film circles and single-handedly founded the Enfield Tennis Academy but drinks Wild Turkey at like 5:00 A.M. and pitches over sideways during dawn drills, on the courts, some days, and some days presents with delusions about people's mouths moving but nothing coming out. I'm not even up to *J* yet, in the condensed *O.E.D.*, much less Québec or malevolent Lurias.'

'. . . of the fact that photos of the aforementioned . . . liaison being leaked to *Der Spiegel* resulted in the bizarre deaths of both an Ottawan paparazzo and a Bavarian international-affairs editor, of an alpenstock through the abdomen and an ill-swallowed cocktail onion, respectively?'

'I just finished *jew's-ear*. I'm just starting on *jew's-harp* and the general theory of oral lyres. I've never even *skied*.'

'That you could dare to imagine we'd fail conversationally to countenance certain weekly shall we say maternal . . . assignations with a certain unnamed bisexual bassoonist in the Albertan Secret Guard's tactical-bands unit?'

'Gee, is that the exit over there I see?'

'. . . that your blithe inattention to your own dear grammatical mother's cavortings with not one not two but over *thirty* Near Eastern medical attachés . . . ?'

'Would it be rude to tell you your mustache is askew?'

'. . . that her introduction of esoteric mnemonic steroids, stereo-chemically not dissimilar to your father's own daily hypodermic "mega-vitamin" supplement derived from a certain organic testosterone-regeneration compound distilled by the Jivaro shamen of the South-Central L.A. basin, into your innocent-looking bowl of morning Ralston. . . .'

'As a matter of fact I'll go ahead and tell you your whole face is kind of running, sort of, if you want to check. Your nose is pointing at your lap.'

'That your quote-unquote "complimentary" Dunlop widebody tennis racquets' super-secret-formulaic composition materials of high-modulus-graphite-reinforced polycarbonate polybutylene resin are organochemically identical I say again *identical* to the gyroscopic balance sensor and *mise-en-scène* appropriation card and priapistic-entertainment cartridge implanted in your very own towering father's anaplastic cerebrum after his cruel series of detoxifications and convolution-smoothings and gastrectomy and prostatectomy and pancreatectomy and phalluctomy . . .'

Tap tap. 'SHULGSPAHH.'

'. . . could possibly escape the combined investigative attention of. . . ?'

'And it strikes me I've definitely seen that argyle sweater-vest before. That's Himself's special Interdependence-Day-celebratory-dinner argyle sweater-vest, that he makes a point of never having cleaned. I know those stains. I was there for that clot of veal marsala right there. Is this whole appointment a date-connected thing? Is this April Fools, Dad, or do I need to call the Moms and C.T.?'

'. . . who requires only daily evidence that you *speak?* That you recognize the occasional vista beyond your own generous Mondragonoid nose's fleshy tip?'

'You rented a whole office and face for this, but leave your old unmistakable sweater-vest on? And how'd you even get down here before me, with the Mercury up on blocks after you . . . did you fool C.T. into giving you the keys to a functional car?'

'Who used to pray daily for the day his own dear late father would sit, cough, open that bloody issue of the *Tucson Citizen,* and not turn that newspaper into the room's fifth wall? And who after all this light and noise has apparently spawned the same silence?'

'. . .'

'Who's lived his whole ruddy bloody cruddy life in five-walled rooms?'

'Dad, I've got a duly scheduled challenge match with Schacht in like twelve minutes, wind at my downhill back or no. I've got this oral-lyrologist who's going to be outside Brighton Best Savings wearing a predesignated necktie at straight-up five. I have to mow his lawn for a month for this interview. I can't just sit here watching you think I'm mute while your fake nose points at the floor. And are you hearing me talking, Dad? It speaks. It accepts soda and defines *implore* and converses with you.'

'Praying for just one conversation, amateur or no, that does not end in terror? That does not end like all the others: you staring, me swallowing?'

'. . .'

'Son?'

'. . .'

'Son?'

◯

9 MAY — YEAR OF THE DEPEND ADULT UNDERGARMENT

Another way fathers impact sons is that sons, once their voices have changed in puberty, invariably answer the telephone with the same locutions and intonations as their fathers. This holds true regardless of whether the fathers are still alive.

Because he left his dormitory room before 0600 for dawn drills and often didn't get back there until after supper, packing his book bag and knapsack and gear bag for the whole day, together with selecting his best-strung racquets — it all took Hal some time. Plus he usually collected and packed and selected in the dark, and with stealth, because his brother Mario was usually still asleep in the other bed. Mario didn't drill and couldn't play, and needed all the sleep he could get.

Hal held his complimentary gear bag and was putting different pairs of sweats to his face, trying to find the cleanest pair by smell, when the telephone console sounded. Mario thrashed and sat up in bed, a small hunched shape with a big head against the gray light of the window. Hal got to the console on the second ring and had the transparent phone's antenna out by the third.

His way of answering the phone sounded like 'Mmmyellow.'

'I want to tell you,' the voice on the phone said. 'My head is filled with things to say.'

Hal held three pairs of E.T.A. sweatpants in the hand that didn't hold the phone. He saw his older brother succumb to gravity and fall back limp against the pillows. Mario often sat up and fell back still asleep.

'I don't mind,' Hal said softly. 'I could wait forever.'

'That's what you think,' the voice said. The connection was cut. It had been Orin.

'Hey Hal?'

The light in the room was a creepy gray, a kind of nonlight. Hal could hear Brandt laughing at something Kenkle had said, off down the hall, and the clank of their janitorial buckets. The person on the phone had been O.

'Hey Hal?' Mario was awake. It took four pillows to support Mario's oversized skull. His voice came from the tangled bedding. 'Is it still dark out, or is it me?'

'Go back to sleep. It isn't even six.' Hal put the good leg into the sweatpants first.

'Who was it?'

Shoving three coverless Dunlop widebodies into the gear bag and zipping the bag partway up so the handles had room to stick out. Carrying all three bags back over to the console to deactivate the ringer on the phone. He said, 'No one you know, I don't think.'

O

YEAR OF THE DEPEND ADULT UNDERGARMENT

Though only one-half ethnic Arab and a Canadian by birth and residence, the medical attaché is nevertheless once again under Saudi diplomatic immunity, this time as special ear-nose-throat consultant to the personal physician of Prince Q——, the Saudi Minister of Home Entertainment, here on northeastern U.S.A. soil with his legation to cut another mammoth deal with InterLace TelEntertainment. The medical attaché turns thirty-seven tomorrow, Thursday, 2 April in the North American lunar Y.D.A.U. The legation finds the promotional subsidy of the North American calendar hilariously vulgar. To say nothing of the arresting image of the idolatrous West's most famous and self-congratulating idol, the colossal Libertine Statue, wearing some type of enormous adult-design diaper, a hilariously apposite image popular in the news photos of so many international journals.

The attaché's medical practice being normally divided between Montreal and the Rub' al Khali, it is his first trip back to U.S.A. soil since completing his residency eight years ago. His duties here involve migrating with the Prince and his retinue between InterLace's two hubs of manufacture and dissemination in Phoenix, Arizona U.S.A. and Boston, Massachusetts U.S.A., respectively, offering expert E.N.T. assistance to the personal physician of Prince Q——. The medical attaché's particular expertise is the maxillofacial consequences of imbalances in intestinal flora. Prince Q—— (as would anyone who refuses to eat pretty much anything but Töblerone) suffers chronically from *Candida albicans*, with attendant susceptibilities to monilial sinusitis and thrush, the yeasty sores and sinal impactions of which require almost daily drainage in the cold and damp of early-spring Boston, U.S.A. A veritable artist, possessed of a deftness nonpareil with cotton swab and evacuation-hypo, the medical attaché is known among the shrinking upper classes of petro-Arab nations as the DeBakey of maxillofacial yeast, his staggering fee-scale as wholly *ad valorem*.

Saudi consulting fees, in particular, are somewhere just past obscene, but the medical attaché's duties on this trip are personally draining and sort of nauseous, and when he arrives back at the sumptuous apartments he had his wife sublet in districts far from the legation's normal Back Bay and Scottsdale digs, at the day's end, he needs unwinding in the very worst way. A more than averagely devout follower of the North American sufism promulgated in his childhood by Pir Valayat, the medical attaché partakes of neither kif nor distilled spirits, and must unwind without chemical aid. When he arrives home after evening prayers, he wants to look upon a spicy and 100% *shari'a-halal* dinner piping hot and arranged and steaming pleasantly on its attachable tray, he wants his bib ironed and laid out by the tray at the ready, and he wants the living room's teleputer booted and warmed up and the evening's entertainment cartridges already selected and arranged and lined up in dock ready for remote insertion into the viewer's drive. He reclines before the viewer in his special electronic recliner, and his black-veiled, ethnically Arab wife wordlessly attends him, loosening any constrictive clothing, adjusting the room's lighting, fitting the complexly molded dinner tray over his head so that his shoulders support the tray and allow it to project into space just below his chin, that he may enjoy his hot dinner without having to remove his eyes from whatever entertainment is up and playing. He has a narrow imperial-style beard which his wife also attends and keeps free of detritus from the tray just below. The medical attaché sits and watches and eats and watches, unwinding by visible degrees, until the angles of his body in the chair and his head on his neck indicate that he has passed into sleep, at which point his special electronic recliner can be made automatically to recline to full horizontal, and luxuriant silk-analog bedding emerges flowingly from long slots in the appliance's sides; and, unless his wife is inconsiderate and clumsy with the recliner's remote hand-held controls, the medical attaché is permitted to ease effortlessly from unwound spectation into a fully relaxed night's sleep, still right there in the recumbent recliner, the TP set to run a recursive loop of low-volume surf and light rain on broad green leaves.

Except, that is, for Wednesday nights, which in Boston are permitted to be his wife's Arab Women's Advanced League tennis night with the other legation wives and companions at the plush Mount Auburn Club in West Watertown, on which nights she is not around wordlessly to attend him, since Wednesday is the U.S.A. weekday on which fresh Töblerone hits Boston, Massachusetts U.S.A.'s Newbury Street's import-confectioners' shelves, and the Saudi Minister of Home Entertainment's inability to control his appetites for Wednesday Töblerone often requires the medical attaché to remain in personal attendance all evening on the bulk-rented fourteenth floor of the Back Bay Hilton, juggling tongue-depressors and cotton swabs, nystatin and ibuprofen and stiptics and antibiotic thrush salves, rehabilitating the mucous membranes of the dyspeptic and distressed and often (but not always) penitent and appreciative Saudi Prince Q———.
So on 1 April, Y.D.A.U., when the medical attaché is (it is alleged) insuffi-

ciently deft with a Q-Tip on an ulcerated sinal necrosis and is subjected at just 1800h. to a fit of febrile thrushive pique from the florally imbalanced Minister of Home Entertainment, and is by high-volume fiat replaced at the royal bedside by the Prince's personal physician, who's summoned by beeper from the Hilton's sauna, and when the damp personal physician pats the medical attaché on the shoulder and tells him to pay the pique no mind, that it's just the yeast talking, but to just head on home and unwind and for once make a well-deserved early Wednesday evening of it, and but so when the attaché does get home, at like 1840h., his spacious Boston apartments are empty, the living room lights undimmed, dinner unheated and the attachable tray still in the dishwasher and — worst — of course no entertainment cartridges have been obtained from the Boylston St. InterLace outlet where the medical attaché's wife, like all the veiled wives and companions of the Prince's legatees, has a complimentary goodwill account. And even if he weren't far too exhausted and tightly wound to venture back into the damp urban night to pick up entertainment cartridges, the medical attaché realizes that his wife has, as always on Wednesdays, taken the car with the diplomatic-immunity license plates, without which your thinking alien wouldn't even dream of trying to park publicly at night in Boston, Massachusetts U.S.A.

The medical attaché's unwinding-options are thus severely constricted. The living room's lavish TP receives also the spontaneous disseminations of the InterLace Subscription Pulse-Matrix, but the procedures for ordering specific spontaneous pulses from the service are so technologically and cryptographically complex that the attaché has always left the whole business to his wife. On this Wednesday night, trying buttons and abbreviations almost at random, the attaché is able to summon up only live U.S.A. professional sports — which he has always found brutish and repellent — Texaco Oil Company–sponsored opera — which the attaché has seen today more than enough of the human uvula thank you very much — a redisseminated episode of the popular afternoon InterLace children's program 'Mr. Bouncety-Bounce' — which the attaché thinks for a moment might be a documentary on bipolar mood disorders until he catches on and thumbs the selection-panel hastily — and a redisseminated session of the scantily clad variable-impact early-A.M. 'Fit Forever' home-aerobics series of the InterLace aerobics-guru Ms. Tawni Kondo, the scantily clad and splay-limbed immodesty of which threatens the devout medical attaché with the possibility of impure thoughts.

The only entertainment cartridges anywhere in the apartment, a foul-tempered search reveals, are those which have arrived in Wednesday's U.S.A. postal delivery, left on the sideboard in the living room along with personal and professional faxes and mail the medical attaché declines to read until it's been pre-scanned by his wife for relevant interest to himself.

The sideboard is against the wall opposite the room's electronic recliner under a triptych of high-quality Byzantine erotica. The padded cartridge-mailers with their distinctive rectangular bulge are mixed haphazardly in with the less entertaining mail. Searching for something to unwind with, the medical attaché tears the different padded mailers open along their designated perforations. There is an O.N.A.N.M.A. Specialty Service film on actinomycete-class antibiotics and irritable bowel syndrome. There is 1 April Y.D.A.U.'s CBC/PATHÉ North American News Summary 40-minute cartridge, available daily by a wife's auto-subscription and either transmitted to TP by unrecordable InterLace pulse or express-posted on a single-play ROM self-erasing disk. There is the Arabic-language video edition of April's *Self* magazine for the attaché's wife, *Nass*'s cover's model chastely swathed and veiled. There is a plain brown and irritatingly untitled cartridge-case in a featureless white three-day standard U.S.A. First Class padded cartridge-mailer. The padded mailer is postmarked suburban Phoenix area in Arizona U.S.A., and the return-address box has only the term '*HAPPY ANNIVER-SARY!*,' with a small drawn crude face, smiling, in ballpoint ink, instead of a return address or incorporated logo. Though by birth and residence a native of Québec, where the language of discourse is not English, the medical attaché knows quite well that the English word *anniversary* does not mean the same as *birthday*. And the medical attaché and his veiled wife were united in the eyes of God and Prophet not in April but in October, four years prior, in the Rub'al Khali. Adding to the padded mailer's confusion is the fact that anything from Prince Q———'s legation in Phoenix, Arizona U.S.A. would carry a diplomatic seal instead of routine O.N.A.N. postage. The medical attaché, in sum, feels tightly wound and badly underappreciated and is prepared in advance to be irritated by the item inside, which is merely a standard black entertainment cartridge, but is wholly unlabelled and not in any sort of colorful or informative or inviting cartridge-case, and has only another of these vapid U.S.A.-type circular smiling heads embossed upon it where the registration- and duration-codes are supposed to be embossed. The medical attaché is puzzled by the cryptic mailer and face and case and unlabelled entertainment, and preliminarily irritated by the amount of time he's had to spend upright at the sideboard attending to mail, which is not his task. The sole reason he does not throw the unlabelled cartridge in the wastecan or put it aside for his wife to preview for relevance is because there are such woefully slim entertainment-pickings on his wife's irritating Americanized tennis-league evening away from her place at home. The attaché will pop the cartridge in and scan just enough of its contents to determine whether it is irritating or of an irrelevant nature and not entertaining or engaging in any way. He will heat the prepared *halal* lamb and spicy *halal* garnish in the microwave oven until piping-hot, arrange it attractively on his tray, preview the first few moments of the puzzling and/or irritating or possibly mysteriously blank entertainment cartridge first, then unwind with the news summary, then perhaps have a quick unlibidinous look at *Nass*'s spring line of sexless black devout-women's-wear, then will insert the recursive surf-and-rain cartridge and make a well-deserved early Wednesday evening of it, hoping only that his wife will not return from her tennis league in her perspiration-dampened black ankle-length tennis ensemble and remove his dinner tray from his sleeping neck in a clumsy or undeft fashion that will awaken him, potentially.

When he settles in with the tray and cartridge, the TP's viewer's digital display reads 1927h.

YEAR OF THE TRIAL-SIZE DOVE BAR

Wardine say her momma aint treat her right. Reginald he come round to my blacktop at my building where me and Delores Epps jump double dutch and he say, Clenette, Wardine be down at my crib cry say her momma aint treat her right, and I go on with Reginald to his building where he live at, and Wardine be sit deep far back in a closet in Reginald crib, and she be cry. Reginald gone lift Wardine out the closet and me with him crying and I be rub on the wet all over Wardine face and Reginald be so careful when he take off all her shirts she got on, tell Wardine to let me see. Wardine back all beat up and cut up. Big stripes of cut all up and down Wardine back, pink stripes and around the stripes the skin like the skin on folks lips be like. Sick down in my insides to look at it. Wardine be cry. Reginald say Wardine say her momma aint treat her right. Say her momma beat Wardine with a hanger. Say Wardine momma man Roy Tony be want to lie down with Wardine. Be give Wardine candy and 5s. Be stand in her way in Wardine face and he aint let her pass without he all the time touching her. Reginald say Wardine say Roy Tony at night when Wardine momma at work he come in to the mattresses where Wardine and William and Shantell and Roy the baby sleep at, and he stand there in the dark, high, and say quiet things at her, and breathe. Wardine momma say Wardine tempt Roy Tony into Sin. Wardine say she say Wardine try to take away Roy Tony into Evil and Sin with her young tight self. She beat Wardine back with hangers out the closet. My momma say Wardine momma not right in her head. My momma scared of Roy Tony. Wardine be cry. Reginald he down and beg for Wardine tell Reginald momma how Wardine momma treat Wardine. Reginald say he Love his Wardine. Say he Love but aint never before this time could understand why Wardine wont lie down with him like girls do their man. Say Wardine aint never let Reginald take off her shirts until tonight she come to Reginald crib in his building and be cry, she let Reginald take off her shirts to see how Wardine momma beat Wardine because Roy Tony. Reginald Love his Wardine. Wardine be like to die of scared. She say no to Reginald beg. She say, if she go to Reginald momma, then Reginald momma go to Wardine momma, then Wardine momma think Wardine be lie down with Reginald. Wardine say her momma say Wardine let a man lie down before she sixteen and she beat Wardine to death. Reginald say he aint no way going to let that happen to Wardine.

Roy Tony kill Dolores Epps brother Columbus Epps at the Brighton Projects four years gone. Roy Tony on Parole. Wardine say he show Wardine he got some thing on his ankle send radio signals to Parole that he still here in Brighton. Roy Tony cant be leave Brighton. Roy Tony brother be Wardine father. He gone. Reginald try to hush Wardine but he can not stop Wardine cry. Wardine look like crazy she so scared. She say she kill herself if me or Reginald tell our mommas. She say, Clenette, you my half Sister, I am beg that you do not tell you momma on my momma and Roy Tony. Reginald tell Wardine to hush herself and lie down quiet. He put Shedd Spread out the kitchen on Wardine cuts on her back. He run his finger with grease so careful down pink lines of her getting beat with a hanger. Wardine say she do not feel nothing in her back ever since spring. She lie stomach on Reginald floor and say she aint got no feeling in her skin of her back. When Reginald gone to get the water she asks me the truth, how bad is her back look when Reginald look at it. Is she still pretty, she cry.

I aint tell my momma on Wardine and Reginald and Wardine momma and Roy Tony. My momma scared of Roy Tony. My momma be the lady Roy Tony kill Columbus Epps over, four years gone, in the Brighton Projects, for Love.

But I know Reginald tell. Reginald say he gone die before Wardine momma beat Wardine again. He say he take his self up to Roy Tony and say him to not mess with Wardine or breathe by her mattress at night. He say he take his self on down to the playground at the Brighton Projects where Roy Tony do business and he go to Roy Tony man to man and he make Roy Tony make it all right.

But I think Roy Tony gone kill Reginald if Reginald go. I think Roy Tony gone kill Reginald, and then Wardine momma beat Wardine to death with a hanger. And then nobody know except me. And I am gone have a child.

In the eighth American-educational grade, Bruce Green fell dreadfully in love with a classmate who had the unlikely name of Mildred Bonk. The name was unlikely because if ever an eighth-grader looked like a Daphne Christianson or a Kimberly St.-Simone or something like that, it was Mildred Bonk. She was the kind of fatally pretty and nubile wraithlike figure who glides through the sweaty junior-high corridors of every nocturnal emitter's dreamscape. Hair that Green had heard described by an over-wrought teacher as 'flaxen'; a body which the fickle angel of puberty — the same angel who didn't even seem to know Bruce Green's zip code — had visited, kissed, and already left, back in sixth; legs which not even orange Keds with purple-glitter-encrusted laces could make unserious. Shy, irides-cent, coltish, pelvically anfractuous, amply busted, given to diffident move-ments of hand brushing flaxen hair from front of dear creamy forehead, movements which drove Bruce Green up a private tree. A vision in a sun-dress and silly shoes. Mildred L. Bonk.

And then but by tenth grade, in one of those queer when-did-that-happen metamorphoses, Mildred Bonk had become an imposing member of the frightening Winchester High School set that smoked full-strength Marl-boros in the alley between Senior and Junior halls and that left school alto-gether at lunchtime, driving away in loud low-slung cars to drink beer and smoke dope, driving around with sound-systems of illegal wattage, using Visine and Clorets, etc. She was one of them. She chewed gum (or worse) in the cafeteria, her dear diffident face now a bored mask of Attitude, her flaxen locks now teased and gelled into what looked for all the world like the consequence of a finger stuck into an electric socket. Bruce Green saved up for a low-slung old car and practiced Attitude on the aunt who'd taken him in. He developed a will.

And, by the year of what would have been graduation, Bruce Green was way more bored, imposing, and frightening than even Mildred Bonk, and he and Mildred Bonk and tiny incontinent Harriet Bonk-Green lived just off the Allston Spur in a shiny housetrailer with another frightening couple and with Tommy Doocey, the infamous harelipped pot-and-sundries dealer who kept several large snakes in unclean uncovered aquaria, which smelled, which Tommy Doocey didn't notice because his upper lip completely cov-ered his nostrils and all he could smell was lip. Mildred Bonk got high in the afternoon and watched serial-cartridges, and Bruce Green had a steady job at Leisure Time Ice, and for a while life was more or less one big party.

YEAR OF THE DEPEND ADULT UNDERGARMENT

'Hal?'

'. . .'

'Hey Hal?'

'Yes Mario?'

'Are you asleep?'

'Booboo, we've been over this. I can't be asleep if we're talking.'

'That's what I thought.'

'Happy to reassure you.'

'Boy were you on today. Boy did you ever make that guy look sick. When he hit that one down the line and you got it and fell down and hit that drop-volley Pemulis said the guy looked like he was going to be sick all over the net, he said.'

'Boo, I kicked a kid's ass is all. End of story. I don't think it's good to rehash it when I've kicked somebody's ass. It's like a dignity thing. I think we should just let it sort of lie in state, quietly. Speaking of which.'

'Hey Hal?'

'. . .'

'Hey Hal?'

'It's late, Mario. It's sleepy-time. Close your eyes and think fuzzy thoughts.'

'That's what the Moms always says, too.'

'Always worked for me, Boo.'

'You think I think fuzzy thoughts all the time. You let me room with you because you feel sorry for me.'

'Booboo I'm not even going to dignify that. I'll regard it as like a warning sign. You always get petulant when you don't get enough sleep. And here we are seeing petulance already on the western horizon, right here.'

'. . .'

'. . .'

'When I asked if you were asleep I was going to ask if you felt like you believed in God, today, out there, when you were so on, making that guy look sick.'

'This again?'

'. . .'

'*Really* don't think midnight in a totally dark room with me so tired my hair hurts and drills in six short hours is the time and place to get into this, Mario.'

'. . .'

'You ask me this once a week.'

'You never say, is why.'

'So tonight to shush you how about if I say I have administrative bones to pick with God, Boo. I'll say God seems to have a kind of laid-back management style I'm not crazy about. I'm pretty much anti-death. God looks by all accounts to be pro-death. I'm not seeing how we can get together on this issue, he and I, Boo.'

'You're talking about since Himself passed away.'

'. . .'

'See? You never say.'

'I do too say. I just did.'

'. . .'

'I just didn't happen to say what you wanted to hear, Booboo, is all.'

'. . .'

'There's a difference.'

'I don't get how you couldn't feel like you believed, today, out there. It was so *right there*. You moved like you totally believed.'

'. . .'

'How do you feel inside, not?'

'Mario, you and I are mysterious to each other. We countenance each other from either side of some unbridgeable difference on this issue. Let's lie very quietly and ponder this.'

'Hal?'

'. . .'

'Hey Hal?'

'I'm going to propose that I tell you a joke, Boo, on the condition that afterward you shush and let me sleep.'

'Is it a good one?'

'Mario, what do you get when you cross an insomniac, an unwilling agnostic, and a dyslexic.'

'I give.'

'You get somebody who stays up all night torturing himself mentally over the question of whether or not there's a dog.'

'That's a good one!'

'Shush.'

'. . .'

'. . .'

'Hey Hal? What's an insomniac?'

'Somebody who rooms with you, kid, that's for sure.'

'Hey Hal?'

'. . .'

'How come the Moms never cried when Himself passed away? I cried, and you, even C.T. cried. I saw him personally cry.'

'. . .'

'You listened to *Tosca* over and over and cried and said you were sad. We all were.'

'. . .'

'Hey Hal, did the Moms seem like she got happier after Himself passed away, to you?'

'. . .'

'It seems like she got happier. She seems even taller. She stopped travelling everywhere all the time for this and that thing. The corporate-grammar thing. The library-protest thing.'

'Now she never goes anywhere, Boo. Now she's got the Headmaster's House and her office and the tunnel in between, and never leaves the grounds. She's a worse workaholic than she ever was. And more obsessive-compulsive. When's the last time you saw a dust-mote in that house?'

'Hey Hal?'

'Now she's just an *agoraphobic* workaholic and obsessive-compulsive. This strikes you as happification?'

'Her eyes are better. They don't seem as sunk in. They look better. She laughs at C.T. way more than she laughed at Himself. She laughs from lower down inside. She laughs more. Her jokes she tells are better ones than yours, even, now, a lot of the time.'

'. . .'

'How come she never got sad?'

'She did get sad, Booboo. She just got sad in her way instead of yours and mine. She got sad, I'm pretty sure.'

'Hal?'

'You remember how the staff lowered the flag to half-mast out front by the portcullis here after it happened? Do you remember that? And it goes to half-mast every year at Convocation? Remember the flag, Boo?'

'Hey Hal?'

'Don't cry, Booboo. Remember the flag only halfway up the pole? Booboo, there are two ways to lower a flag to half-mast. Are you listening? Because no shit I really have to sleep here in a second. So listen — one way to lower the flag to half-mast is just to lower the flag. There's another way though. You can also just raise the pole. You can raise the pole to like twice its original height. You get me? You understand what I mean, Mario?'

'Hal?'

'She's plenty sad, I bet.'

At 2010h. on 1 April Y.D.A.U., the medical attaché is still watching the unlabelled entertainment cartridge.

OCTOBER — YEAR OF THE DEPEND ADULT UNDERGARMENT

For Orin Incandenza, #71, morning is the soul's night. The day's worst time, psychically. He cranks the condo's AC way down at night and still most mornings wakes up soaked, fetally curled, entombed in that kind of psychic darkness where you're dreading whatever you think of.

Hal Incandenza's brother Orin wakes up alone at 0730h. amid a damp scent of Ambush and on the other side's dented pillow a note with phone # and vital data in a loopy schoolgirlish hand. There's also Ambush on the note. His side of the bed is soaked.

Orin makes honey-toast, standing barefoot at the kitchen counter, wearing briefs and an old Academy sweatshirt with the arms cut off, squeezing honey from the head of a plastic bear. The floor's so cold it hurts his feet, but the double-pane window over the sink is hot to the touch: the beastly metro Phoenix October A.M. heat just outside.

Home with the team, no matter how high the AC or how thin the sheet, Orin wakes with his own impression sweated darkly into the bed beneath him, slowly drying all day to a white salty outline just slightly off from the week's other faint dried outlines, so his fetal-shaped fossilized image is fanned out across his side of the bed like a deck of cards, just overlapping, like an acid trail or timed exposure.

The heat just past the glass doors tightens his scalp. He takes breakfast out to a white iron table by the condo complex's central pool and tries to eat it there, in the heat, the coffee not steaming or cooling. He sits there in dumb animal pain. He has a mustache of sweat. A bright beach ball floats and bumps against one side of the pool. The sun like a sneaky keyhole view of hell. No one else out here. The complex is a ring with the pool and deck and Jacuzzi in the center. Heat shimmers off the deck like fumes from fuel. There's that mirage thing where the extreme heat makes the dry deck look wet with fuel. Orin can hear cartridge-viewers going from behind closed windows, that aerobics show every morning, and also someone playing an organ, and the older woman who won't ever smile back at him in the apartment next to his doing operatic scales, muffled by drapes and sun-curtains and double panes. The Jacuzzi chugs and foams.

The note from last night's Subject is on violet bond once folded and with a circle of darker violet dead-center where the subject's perfume-spritzer had hit it. The only interesting thing about the script, but also depressing, is that every single circle — o's, d's, p's, the #s 6 and 8 — is darkened in, while the i's are dotted not with circles but with tiny little Valentine hearts, which are not darkened in. Orin reads the note while he eats toast that's mainly an excuse for the honey. He uses his smaller right arm to eat and drink. His oversized left arm and big left leg remain at rest at all times in the morning.

A breeze sends the beach ball skating all the way across the blue pool to the other side, and Orin watches its noiseless glide. The white iron tables have no umbrellas, and you can tell where the sun is without looking; you can feel right where it is on your body and project from there. The ball moves tentatively back out toward the middle of the pool and then stays there, not even bobbing. The same small breezes make the rotted palms along the condominium complex's stone walls rustle and click, and a couple of fronds detach and spiral down, hitting the deck with a slap. All the plants out here are malevolent, heavy and sharp. The parts of the palms above the fronds are tufted in sick stuff like coconut-hair. Roaches and other things live in the trees. Rats, maybe. Loathsome high-altitude critters of all kinds. All the plants either spiny or meaty. Cacti in queer tortured shapes. The tops of the palms like Rod Stewart's hair, from days gone by.

Orin returned with the team from the Chicago game two nights ago, red-eye. He knows that he and the place-kicker are the only two starters who are not still in terrible pain, physically, from the beating.

The day before they left — so like five days ago — Orin was out by himself in the Jacuzzi by the pool late in the day, caring for the leg, sitting in the radiant heat and bloody late-day light with the leg in the Jacuzzi, absently squeezing the tennis ball he still absently squeezes out of habit. Watching the Jacuzzi funnel and bubble and foam around the leg. And out of nowhere a bird had all of a sudden fallen into the Jacuzzi. With a flat matter-of-fact *plop*. Out of nowhere. Out of the wide empty sky. Nothing overhung the Jacuzzi but sky. The bird seemed to have just had a coronary or something in flight and died and fallen out of the empty sky and landed dead in the Jacuzzi, right by the leg. He brought his sunglasses down onto the bridge of his nose with a finger and looked at it. It was an undistinguished kind of bird. Not a predator. Like a wren, maybe. It seems like no way could it have been a good sign. The dead bird bobbed and barrel-rolled in the foam, sucked under one second and reappearing the next, creating an illusion of continued flight. Orin had inherited none of the Moms's phobias about disorder, hygiene. (Not crazy about bugs though — roaches.) But he'd just sat there squeezing the ball, looking at the bird, without a conscious thought in his head. By the next morning, waking up, curled and entombed, it seemed like it had to have been a bad sign, though.

Orin now always gets the shower so hot it's to where he can just barely stand it. The condo's whole bathroom is done in this kind of minty yellow tile he didn't choose, maybe chosen by the free safety who lived here before the Cardinals sent New Orleans the free safety, two reserve guards and cash for Orin Incandenza, punter.

And no matter how many times he has the Terminex people out, there are still the enormous roaches that come out of the bathroom drains. Sewer roaches, according to Terminex. *Blattaria implacablus* or something. Really huge roaches. Armored-vehicle-type bugs. Totally black, with Kevlar-type cases, the works. And fearless, raised in the Hobbesian sewers down there. Boston's and New Orleans's little brown roaches were bad enough, but you could at least come in and turn on a light and they'd run for their lives. These Southwest sewer roaches you turn on the light and they just look up at you from the tile like: 'You got a problem?' Orin stomped on one of them, only once, that had come hellishly up out of the drain in the shower when he was in there, showering, going out naked and putting shoes on and coming in and trying to conventionally squash it, and the result was explosive. There's still material from that one time in the tile-grouting. It seems unremovable. Roach-innards. Sickening. Throwing the shoes away was preferable to looking at the sole to clean it. Now he keeps big glass tumblers in the bathroom and when he turns on the light and sees a roach he puts a glass down over it, trapping it. After a couple days the glass is all steamed up and the roach has asphyxiated messlessly and Orin discards both the roach and the tumbler in separate sealed Ziplocs in the dumpster complex by the golf course up the street.

The yellow tile floor of the bathroom is sometimes a little obstacle course of glasses with huge roaches dying inside, stoically, just sitting there, the glasses gradually steaming up with roach-dioxide. The whole thing makes Orin sick. Now he figures the hotter the shower's water, the less chance any small armored vehicle is going to feel like coming out of the drain while he's in there.

Sometimes they're in the bowl of the toilet first thing in the A.M., dog-paddling, trying to get to the side and climb up. He's also not crazy about spiders, though more like unconsciously; he's never come anyplace close to the conscious horror Himself had somehow developed about the Southwest's black widows and their chaotic webs — the widows are all over the place, both here and Tucson, spottable on all but the coldest nights, their dusty webs without any kind of pattern, clotting just about any right-angled place that's dim or out of the way. Terminex's toxins are more effective on the widows. Orin has them out monthly; he's on like a subscription plan over at Terminex.

Orin's special conscious horror, besides heights and the early morning, is roaches. There'd been parts of metro Boston near the Bay he'd refused to go to, as a child. Roaches give him the howling fantods. The parishes around N.O. had been having a spate or outbreak of a certain Latin-origin breed of sinister tropical *flying* roaches, that were small and timid but could fucking *fly,* and that kept being found swarming on New Orleans infants, at night, in their cribs, especially infants in like tenements or squalor, and that reportedly fed on the mucus in the babies' eyes, some special sort of optical-mucus — the stuff of fucking nightmares, mobile flying roaches that wanted to get at your eyes, as an infant — and were reportedly blinding them; parents'd come in in the ghastly A.M.-tenement light and find their infants blind, like a dozen blinded infants that last summer; and it was during this spate or nightmarish outbreak, plus July flooding that sent over a dozen nightmarish dead bodies from a hilltop graveyard sliding all gray-blue down the incline Orin and two teammates had their townhouse on, in suburban Chalmette, shedding limbs and innards all the way down the hillside's mud and one even one morning coming to rest against the post of their roadside mailbox, when Orin came out for the morning paper, that Orin had had his agent put out the trade feelers. And so to the glass canyons and merciless light of metro Phoenix, in a kind of desiccated circle, near the Tucson of his own father's desiccated youth.

It's the mornings after the spider-and-heights dreams that are the most painful, that it takes sometimes three coffees and two showers and sometimes a run to loosen the grip on his soul's throat; and these post-dream mornings are even worse if he wakes unalone, if the previous night's Subject is still there, wanting to twitter, or to cuddle and, like, spoon, asking what exactly is the story with the foggy inverted tumblers on the bathroom floor, commenting on his night-sweats, clattering around in the kitchen, making kippers or bacon or something even more hideous and unhoneyed he's supposed to eat with post-coital male gusto, the ones who have this thing about they call it Feeding My Man, wanting a man who can barely keep down A.M. honey-toast to eat with male gusto, elbows out and shovelling, making little noises. Even when alone, able to uncurl alone and sit slowly up and wring out the sheet and go to the bathroom, these darkest mornings start days that Orin can't even bring himself for hours to think about how he'll get through the day. These worst mornings with cold floors and hot windows and merciless light — the soul's certainty that the day will have to be not traversed but sort of climbed, vertically, and then that going to sleep again at the end of it will be like falling, again, off something tall and sheer.

So now his own eye-mucus is secure, in the Desert Southwest; but the bad dreams have gotten worse since the trade to this blasted area Himself himself had fled, long ago, as an unhappy youngster.

As a nod to Orin's own unhappy youth, all the dreams seem to open briefly with some sort of competitive-tennis situation. Last night's had started with a wide-angle shot of Orin on a Har-Tru court, waiting to receive serve from someone vague, some Academy person — Ross Reat maybe, or good old M. Bain, or gray-toothed Walt Flechette, now a teaching pro in the Carolinas — when the dream's screen tightens on him and abruptly dissolves to the blank dark rose color of eyes closed against bright light, and there's the ghastly feeling of being submerged and not knowing which way to head for the surface and air, and after some interval the dream's Orin struggles up from this kind of visual suffocation to find his mother's head, Mrs. Avril M. T. Incandenza's, the Moms's disconnected head attached face-to-face to his own fine head, strapped tight to his face somehow by a wrap-around system of VS HiPro top-shelf lamb-gut string from his Academy racquet's own face. So that no matter how frantically Orin tries to move his head or shake it side to side or twist up his face or roll his eyes he's still staring at, into, and somehow through his mother's face. As if the Moms's head was some sort of overtight helmet Orin can't wrestle his way out of.[2] In the dream, it's understandably vital to Orin that he disengage his head from the phylacteryish bind of his mother's disembodied head, and he cannot. Last night's Subject's note indicates that at some point last night Orin had clutched her head with both hands and tried to sort of stiff-arm her, though not in an ungentle or complaining way (the note, not the stiff-arm). The apparent amputation of the Moms's head from the rest of the Moms appears in the dream to be clean and surgically neat: there is no evidence of a stump or any kind of nubbin of neck, even, and it is as if the base of the round pretty head had been sealed, and also sort of rounded off, so that her head is a large living ball, a globe with a face, attached to his own head's face.

The Subject after Bain's sister but before the one just before this one, with the Ambush scent and the hearts over i's, the previous Subject had been a sallowly pretty Arizona State developmental psychology grad student with two kids and outrageous alimony and penchants for sharp jewelry, refrigerated chocolate, InterLace educational cartridges, and professional athletes who thrashed in their sleep. Not real bright — she thought the figure he'd trace without thinking on her bare flank after sex was the numeral 8, to give you an idea. Their last morning together, right before he'd mailed her child an expensive toy and then had his phone number changed, he'd awakened from a night of horror-show dreams — woke up with an abrupt fetal spasm, unrefreshed and benighted of soul, his eyes wobbling and his wet silhouette on the bottom sheet like a coroner's chalk outline — he woke to find the Subject up and sitting up against the reading pillow, wearing his sleeveless Academy sweatshirt and sipping hazelnut espresso and watching, on the cartridge-viewing system that occupied half the bedroom's south wall, something horrific called 'INTERLACE EDUCATIONAL CARTRIDGES IN CONJUNCTION WITH CBC EDUCATIONAL PROGRAMMING MATRIX PRESENTS *SCHIZOPHRENIA: MIND OR BODY?*' and had had to lie there, moist and paralyzed, curled fetal on his own sweat-shadow, and watch on the viewer a pale young guy about Hal's age, with copper stubble and a red cowlick and flat blank affectless black doll's eyes, stare into space stage-left while a brisk Albertan voiceover explained that Fenton here was a dyed-in-the-wool paranoid schizophrenic who believed that radioactive fluids were invading his skull and that hugely complex high-tech-type machines had been specially designed and programmed to pursue him without cease until they caught him and made brutal sport of him and buried him alive. It was an old late-millennial CBC public-interest Canadian news documentary, digitally sharpened and redisseminated under the Inter-Lace imprimatur — InterLace could get kind of seedy and low-rent during early-morning off-hours, in terms of Spontaneous Disseminations.

And so but since the old CBC documentary's thesis was turning out pretty clearly to be *SCHIZOPHRENIA: BODY*, the voiceover evinced great clipped good cheer as it explained that well, yes, poor old Fenton here was more or less hopeless as an extra-institutional functioning unit, but that, on the up-side, science could at least give his existence some sort of meaning by studying him very carefully to help learn how schizophrenia manifested itself in the human body's brain . . . that, in other words, with the aid of cutting-edge Positron-Emission Topography or 'P.E.T.' technology (since supplanted wholly by Invasive Digitals, Orin hears the developmental psychology graduate student mutter to herself, watching rapt over her cup, unaware that Orin's paralytically awake), they could scan and study how different parts of poor old Fenton's dysfunctional brain emitted positrons in a whole different topography than your average hale and hearty nondelusional God-fearing Albertan's brain, advancing science by injecting test-subject Fenton here with a special blood-brain-barrier-penetrating radioactive dye and then sticking him in the rotating body-sized receptacle of a P.E.T. Scanner — on the viewer, it's an enormous gray-metal machine that looks like something co-designed by James Cameron and Fritz Lang, and now have a look at this Fenton fellow's eyes as he starts to get the gist of what the voiceover's saying — and in a terse old Public-TV cut they now showed subject Fenton in five-point canvas restraints whipping his copper-haired head from side to side as guys in mint-green surgical masks and caps inject him with radioactive fluids through a turkey-baster-sized syringe, then good old Fenton's eyes bugging out in total foreseen horror as he's rolled toward the huge gray P.E.T. device and slid like an unrisen loaf into the thing's open maw until only his decay-colored sneakers are in view, and the body-sized receptacle rotates the test-subject counterclockwise, with brutal speed, so that the old sneakers point up and then left and then down and then right and then up, faster and faster, the machine's blurps and tweets not even coming close to covering Fenton's entombed howls as his worst delusional fears came true in digital stereo and you could hear the last surviving bits of his functional dye-permeated mind being screamed out of him for all time as the viewer digitally superimposed an image of Fenton's ember-red and neutron-blue brain in the lower-right corner, where InterLace's Time/Temp functions usually appear, and the brisk voiceover gave capsule histories of first paranoid schizophrenia and then P.E.T. With Orin lying there slit-eyed, wet and neuralgic with A.M. dread, wishing the Subject would put her own clothes and sharp jewelry on and take the rest of her Töblerone out of the freezer and go, so he could go to the bathroom and get yesterday's asphyxiated roaches into an E.W.D. dumpster before the dumpsters all filled for the day, and decide what kind of expensive present to mail the Subject's kid.

And then the matter of the dead bird, out of nowhere.

And then news of pressure from the AZ Cardinal administration to cooperate with some sort of insipid-type personality-profile series of interviews with some profiler from *Moment* magazine, with personal backgroundish questions to be answered in some blandly sincere team-PR way, the unexamined stress of which drives him to start calling Hallie again, reopen that whole Pandora's box of worms.

Orin also shaves in the shower, face red with heat, wreathed in steam, by feel, shaving upward, with south-to-north strokes, as he was taught.

O

YEAR OF THE DEPEND ADULT UNDERGARMENT

Here's Hal Incandenza, age seventeen, with his little brass one-hitter, getting covertly high in the Enfield Tennis Academy's underground Pump Room and exhaling palely into an industrial exhaust fan. It's the sad little interval after afternoon matches and conditioning but before the Academy's communal supper. Hal is by himself down here and nobody knows where he is or what he's doing.

Hal likes to get high in secret, but a bigger secret is that he's as attached to the secrecy as he is to getting high.

A one-hitter, sort of like a long FDR-type cigarette holder whose end is packed with a pinch of good dope, gets hot and is hard on the mouth — the brass ones especially — but one-hitters have the advantage of efficiency: every particle of ignited pot gets inhaled; there's none of the incidental secondhand-type smoke from a party bowl's big load, and Hal can take every iota way down deep and hold his breath forever, so that even his exhalations are no more than slightly pale and sick-sweet-smelling.

Total utilization of available resources = lack of publicly detectable waste.

The Academy's tennis courts' Lung's Pump Room is underground and accessible only by tunnel. E.T.A. is abundantly, embranchingly tunnelled. This is by design.

Plus one-hitters are small, which is good, because let's face it, anything you use to smoke high-resin dope with is going to stink. A bong is big, and its stink is going to be like commensurately big, plus you have the foul bong-water to deal with. Pipes are smaller and at least portable, but they always come with only a multi-hit party bowl that disperses nonutilized smoke over a wide area. A one-hitter can be wastelessly employed, then allowed to cool, wrapped in two baggies and then further wrapped and sealed in a Ziploc and then enclosed in two sport-socks in a gear bag along with the lighter and eyedrops and mint-pellets and the little film-case of dope itself, and it's highly portable and odor-free and basically totally covert.

As far as Hal knows, colleagues Michael Pemulis, Jim Struck, Bridget C.

Boone, Jim Troeltsch, Ted Schacht, Trevor Axford, and possibly Kyle D. Coyle and Tall Paul Shaw, and remotely possibly Frannie Unwin, all know Hal gets regularly covertly high. It's also not impossible that Bernadette Longley knows, actually; and of course the unpleasant K. Freer always has suspicions of all kinds. And Hal's brother Mario knows a thing or two. But that's it, in terms of public knowledge. And but even though Pemulis and Struck and Boone and Troeltsch and Axford and occasionally (in a sort of medicinal or touristic way) Stice and Schacht all are known to get high also, Hal has actually gotten actively high only with Pemulis, on the rare occasions he's gotten high with anybody else, as in in person, which he avoids. He'd forgot: Ortho ('The Darkness') Stice, of Partridge KS, knows; and Hal's oldest brother, Orin, mysteriously, even long-distance, seems to know more than he's coming right out and saying, unless Hal's reading more into some of the phone-comments than are there.

Hal's mother, Mrs. Avril Incandenza, and her adoptive brother Dr. Charles Tavis, the current E.T.A. Headmaster, both know Hal drinks alcohol sometimes, like on weekend nights with Troeltsch or maybe Axford down the hill at clubs on Commonwealth Ave.; The Unexamined Life has its notorious Blind Bouncer night every Friday where they card you on the Honor System. Mrs. Avril Incandenza isn't crazy about the idea of Hal drinking, mostly because of the way his father had drunk, when alive, and reportedly his father's own father before him, in AZ and CA; but Hal's academic precocity, and especially his late competitive success on the junior circuit, make it clear that he's able to handle whatever modest amounts she's pretty sure he consumes — there's no way someone can seriously abuse a substance and perform at top scholarly and athletic levels, the E.T.A. psych-counselor Dr. Rusk assures her, especially the high-level-athletic part — and Avril feels it's important that a concerned but un-smothering single parent know when to let go somewhat and let the two high-functioning of her three sons make their own possible mistakes and learn from their own valid experience, no matter how much the secret worry about mistakes tears her gizzard out, the mother's. And Charles supports whatever personal decisions she makes in conscience about her children. And God knows she'd rather have Hal having a few glasses of beer every so often than absorbing God alone knows what sort of esoteric designer compounds with reptilian Michael Pemulis and trail-of-slime-leaving James Struck, both of whom give Avril a howling case of the maternal fantods. And ultimately, she's told Drs. Rusk and Tavis, she'd rather have Hal abide in the security of the knowledge that his mother trusts him, that she's trusting and supportive and doesn't judge or gizzard-tear or wring her fine hands over his having for instance a glass of Canadian ale with friends every now and again, and so works tremendously hard to hide her maternal dread of his possibly ever drinking like James himself or James's father, all so that

Hal might enjoy the security of feeling that he can be up-front with her about issues like drinking and not feel he has to hide anything from her under any circumstances.

Dr. Tavis and Dolores Rusk have privately discussed the fact that not least among the phobic stressors Avril suffers so uncomplainingly with is a black phobic dread of hiding or secrecy in all possible forms with respect to her sons.

Avril and C. T. know nothing about Hal's penchants for high-resin Bob Hope and underground absorption, which fact Hal obviously likes a lot, on some level, though he's never given much thought to why. To why he likes it so much.

E.T.A.'s hilltop grounds are traversable by tunnel. Avril I., for example, who never leaves the grounds anymore, rarely travels above ground, willing to hunch to take the off-tunnels between Headmaster's House and her office next to Charles Tavis's in the Community and Administration Bldg., a pink-bricked white-pillared neo-Georgian thing that Hal's brother Mario says looks like a cube that has swallowed a ball too big for its stomach.[3] Two sets of elevators and one of stairs run between the lobby, reception area, and administrative offices on Comm.-Ad.'s first floor and the weight room, sauna, and locker/shower areas on the sublevel below it. One large tunnel of elephant-colored cement leads from just off the boys' showers to the mammoth laundry room below the West Courts, and two smaller tunnels radiate from the sauna area south and east to the subbasements of the smaller, spherocubular, proto-Georgian buildings (housing classrooms and subdormitories B and D); these two basements and smaller tunnels often serve as student storage space and hallways between various prorectors'[4] private rooms. Then two even smaller tunnels, navigable by any adult willing to assume a kind of knuckle-dragging simian posture, in turn connect each of the subbasements to the former optical and film-development facilities of Leith and Ogilvie and the late Dr. James O. Incandenza (now deceased) below and just west of the Headmaster's House (from which facilities there's also a fair-diametered tunnel that goes straight to the lowest level of the Community and Administration Bldg., but its functions have gradually changed over four years, and it's now too full of exposed wiring and hot-water pipes and heating ducts to be really passable) and to the offices of the Physical Plant, almost directly beneath the center row of E.T.A. outdoor tennis courts, which offices and custodial lounge are in turn connected to E.T.A.'s Lung-Storage and -Pump Rooms via a pargeted tunnel hastily constructed by the TesTar All-Weather Inflatable Structures Corp., which together with the folks over at ATHSCME Industrial Air Displacement Devices erects and services the inflatable dendriurethane dome, known as the Lung, that covers the middle row of courts for the winter indoor season. The crude little rough-sided tunnel between Plant and Pump is traversable only via all-fours-type crawling and is essentially unknown to staff and Administration, popular only with the Academy's smaller kids' Tunnel Club, as well as with certain adolescents with strong secret incentive to crawl on all fours.

The Lung-Storage Room is basically impassable from March through November because it's full of intricately folded dendriurethane Lung-material and dismantled sections of flexible ducting and fan-blades, etc. The Pump Room is right next to it, though you have to crawl back out into the tunnel to get to it. On the engineering diagrams the Pump Room's maybe about twenty meters directly beneath the centermost courts in the middle row of courts, and looks like a kind of spider hanging upside-down — an unfenestrated oval chamber with six man-sized curved ducts radiating up and out to exit points on the grounds above. And the Pump Room has six radial openings, one for each upcurving duct: three two-meter vents with huge turbine-bladed exhaust fans bolted into their grilles and three more 2M's with reversed ATHSCME intake fans that allow air from the ground above to be sucked down and around the room and up into the three exhaust vents. The Pump Room is essentially like a pulmonary organ, or the epicenter of a massive six-vectored wind tunnel, and when activated roars like a banshee that's slammed its hand in a door, though the P.R.'s in full legit operation only when the Lung is up, usually November–March. The intake fans pull ground-level winter air down into and around the room and through the three exhaust fans and up the outtake ducts into networks of pneumatic tubing in the Lung's sides and dome: it's the pressure of the moving air that keeps the fragile Lung inflated.

When the courts' Lung is down and stored, Hal will descend and walk and then hunch his way in to make sure nobody's in the Physical Plant quarters, then he'll hunch and crawl to the P.R., gear bag in his teeth, and activate just one of the big exhaust fans and get secretly high and exhale palely through its blades into the vent, so that any possible odor is blown through an outtake duct and expelled through a grille'd hole on the west side of the West Courts, a threaded hole, with a flange, where brisk white-suited ATHSCME guys will attach some of the Lung's arterial pneumatic tubing at some point soon when Schtitt et al. on Staff decide the real weather has moved past enduring for outdoor tennis.

During winter months, when any expelled odor would get ducted up into the Lung and hang there conspicuous, Hal mostly goes into a remote sub-dormitory lavatory and climbs onto a toilet in a stall and exhales into the grille of one of the little exhaust fans in the ceiling; but this routine lacks a certain intricate subterranean covert drama. It's another reason why Hal dreads Interdependence Day and the approach of the WhataBurger classic and Thanksgiving and unendurable weather, and the erection of the Lung.

Recreational drugs are more or less traditional at any U.S. secondary school, maybe because of the unprecedented tensions: post-latency and puberty and angst and impending adulthood, etc. To help manage the intrapsychic storms, etc. Since the place's inception, there's always been a certain percentage of the high-caliber adolescent players at E.T.A. who manage their internal weathers chemically. Much of this is good clean temporary fun; but a traditionally smaller and harder-core set tends to rely on personal chemistry to manage E.T.A.'s special demands — dexedrine or low-volt methedrine[5] before matches and benzodiazapenes[6] to come back down after matches, with Mudslides or Blue Flames at some understanding Comm. Ave. nightspot[7] or beers and bongs in some discreet Academy corner at night to short-circuit the up-and-down cycle, mushrooms or X or something from the Mild Designer class[8] — or maybe occasionally a little Black Star,[9] whenever there's a match- and demand-free weekend, to basically short out the whole motherboard and blow out all the circuits and slowly recover and be almost neurologically reborn and start the gradual cycle all over again . . . this circular routine, if your basic wiring's OK to begin with, can work surprisingly well throughout adolescence and sometimes into one's like early twenties, before it starts to creep up on you.

But so some E.T.A.s — not just Hal Incandenza by any means — are involved with recreational substances, is the point. Like who isn't, at some life-stage, in the U.S.A. and Interdependent regions, in these troubled times, for the most part. Though a decent percentage of E.T.A. students aren't at all. I.e. involved. Some persons can give themselves away to an ambitious pursuit and have that be all the giving-themselves-away-to-something they need to do. Though sometimes this changes as the players get older and the pursuit more stress-fraught. American experience seems to suggest that people are virtually unlimited in their need to give themselves away, on various levels. Some just prefer to do it in secret.

An enrolled student-athlete's use of alcohol or illicit chemicals is cause for immediate expulsion, according to E.T.A.'s admissions catalogue. But the E.T.A. staff tends to have a lot more important stuff on its plate than policing kids who've already given themselves away to an ambitious competitive pursuit. The administrative attitude under first James Incandenza and then Charles Tavis is, like, why would anybody who wanted to compromise his faculties chemically even come here, to E.T.A., where the whole point is to stress and stretch your faculties along multiple vectors.[10] And since it's the alumni prorectors who have the most direct supervisory contact with the kids, and since most of the prorectors themselves are depressed or traumatized about not making it into the Show and having to come back to E.T.A. and live in decent but subterranean rooms off the tunnels and work as assistant coaches and teach laughable elective classes — which is what the eight E.T.A. prorectors do, when they're not off playing Satellite tournaments or trying to make it through the qualifying rounds of some serious-money event — and so they're morose and low on morale, and feel bad about themselves, often, as a rule, and so also not all that surprisingly tend to get high now and then themselves, though in a less covert or exuberant fashion than the hard-core students' chemical cadre, but so given all this it's not hard to see why internal drug-enforcement at E.T.A. tends to be flaccid.

The other nice thing about the Pump Room is the way it's connected by tunnel to the prorectors' rows of housing units, which means men's rooms, which means Hal can crawl, hunch, and tiptoe into an unoccupied men's room and brush his teeth with his portable Oral-B and wash his face and apply eyedrops and Old Spice and a plug of wintergreen Kodiak and then saunter back to the sauna area and ascend to ground level looking and smelling right as rain, because when he gets high he develops a powerful obsession with having nobody — not even the neurochemical cadre — know he's high. This obsession is almost irresistible in its force. The amount of organization and toiletry-lugging he has to do to get secretly high in front of a subterranean outtake vent in the pre-supper gap would make a lesser man quail. Hal has no idea why this is, or whence, this obsession with the secrecy of it. He broods on it abstractly sometimes, when high: this No-One-Must-Know thing. It's not fear per se, fear of discovery. Beyond that it all gets too abstract and twined up to lead to anything, Hal's brooding. Like most North Americans of his generation, Hal tends to know way less about why he feels certain ways about the objects and pursuits he's devoted to than he does about the objects and pursuits themselves. It's hard to say for sure whether this is even exceptionally bad, this tendency.

At 0015h., 2 April, the medical attaché's wife is just leaving the Mount Auburn Total Fitness Center, having played five six-game pro-sets in her little Mideast-diplomatic-wife-tennis-circle's weekly round-robin, then hung around the special Silver-Key-Members' Lounge with the other ladies, unwrapping her face and hair and playing Narjees[11] and all smoking kif and making extremely delicate and oblique fun of their husbands' sexual idiosyncrasies, laughing softly with their hands over their mouths. The medical attaché, at their apartment, is still viewing the unlabelled cartridge, which he has rewound to the beginning several times and then configured for a recursive loop. He sits there, attached to a congealed supper, watching, at 0020h., having now wet both his pants and the special recliner.

Eighteen in May, Mario Incandenza's designated function around Enfield Tennis Academy is filmic: sometimes during A.M. drills or P.M. matches he'll be assigned by Coach Schtitt et al. to set up an old camcorder or whatever video stuff's to hand on a tripod and record a certain area of court, video-taping different kids' strokes, footwork, certain tics and hitches in serves or running volleys, so the staff can show the tapes to the kids instructionally, letting the kids see on the screen exactly what a coach or prorector's talking about. The reason being it's a lot easier to fix something if you can see it.

AUTUMN — YEAR OF DAIRY PRODUCTS FROM THE AMERICAN HEARTLAND

Drug addicts driven to crime to finance their drug addiction are not often inclined toward violent crime. Violence requires all different kinds of energy, and most drug addicts like to expend their energy not on their professional crime but on what their professional crime lets them afford. Drug addicts are often burglars, therefore. One reason why the home of someone whose home has been burglarized feels violated and unclean is that there have probably been drug addicts in there. Don Gately was a twenty-seven-year-old oral narcotics addict (favoring Demerol and Talwin[12]), and a more or less professional burglar; and he was, himself, unclean and violated. But he was a gifted burglar, when he burgled — though the size of a young dinosaur, with a massive and almost perfectly square head he used to amuse his friends when drunk by letting them open and close elevator doors on, he was, at his professional zenith, smart, sneaky, quiet, quick, possessed of good taste and reliable transportation — with a kind of ferocious jolliness in his attitude toward his livelihood.

As an active drug addict, Gately was distinguished by his ferocious and jolly élan. He kept his big square chin up and his smile wide, but he bowed neither toward nor away from any man. He took zero in the way of shit and was a cheery but implacable exponent of the Don't-Get-Mad-Get-Even school. Like for instance once, after he'd done a really unpleasant three-month bit in Revere Holding on nothing more than a remorseless North Shore Assistant District Attorney's circumstantial suspicion, finally getting out after 92 days when his P.D. got the charges dismissed on a right-to-speedy brief, Gately and a trusted associate[13] paid a semiprofessional visit to the private home of this Assistant D.A. whose zeal and warrant had cost Gately a nasty impromptu detox on the floor of his little holding-cell. Also a believer in the Revenge-Is-Tastier-Chilled dictum, Gately had waited patiently until the 'Eye On People' section of the *Globe* mentioned the A.D.A. and his wife's presence at some celebrity charity sailing thing out in Marblehead. Gately and the associate went that night to the A.D.A.'s private home in the upscale Wonderland Valley section of Revere, killed the power to the home with a straight shunt in the meter's inflow, then clipped just the ground wire on the home's pricey HBT alarm, so that the alarm'd sound after ten or so minutes and create the impression that the perps had somehow bungled the alarm and been scared off in the middle of the act. Later that night, when Revere's and Marblehead's Finest summoned them home, the A.D.A. and his wife found themselves minus a coin collection and two antique shotguns and nothing more. Quite a few other valuables were stacked on the floor of the living room off the foyer like the perps hadn't had time to get them out of the house. Everything else in the burglarized home looked undisturbed. The A.D.A. was a jaded pro: he walked around touching the brim of his hat[14] and reconstructed probable events: the perps looked like they'd bungled disabling the alarm all the way and had got scared off by the thing's siren when the alarm's pricey HBT alternate ground kicked in at 300 v. The A.D.A. soothed his wife's sense of violation and uncleanliness. He calmly insisted on sleeping there in their home that very night; no hotel: it was like crucial to get right back on the emotional horse, in cases like this, he insisted. And then the next day the A.D.A. worked out the insurance and reported the shotguns to a buddy at A.T.F.[15] and his wife calmed down and life went on.

About a month later, an envelope arrived in the A.D.A.'s home's exquisite wrought-iron mailbox. In the envelope were a standard American Dental Association glossy brochure on the importance of daily oral hygiene — available at like any dentist's office anywhere — and two high-pixel Polaroid snapshots, one of big Don Gately and one of his associate, each in a Halloween mask denoting a clown's great good professional cheer, each with his pants down and bent over and each with the enhanced-focus handle of one of the couple's toothbrushes protruding from his bottom.

Don Gately had sense enough never to work the North Shore again after that. But he ended up in hideous trouble anyway, A.D.A.-wise. It was either bad luck or kismet or so forth. It was because of a cold, a plain old human rhinovirus. And not even Don Gately's cold, is what made him finally stop and question his kismet.

The thing started out looking like tit on a tray, burglary-wise. A beautiful neo-Georgian home in a wildly upscale part of Brookline was set nicely back from an unlit pseudo-rural road, had a chintzy SentryCo alarm system that fed, idiotically enough, on a whole separate 330 v AC 90 Hz cable with its own meter, didn't seem to be on anything like a regular P.M.-patrol route, and had, at its rear, flimsily tasteful French doors surrounded by dense and thorn-free deciduous shrubbery and blocked off from the garage's halogen floods by a private E.W.D.-issue upscale dumpster. It was in short a real cock-tease of a home, burglary-wise, for a drug addict. And Don Gately straight-shunted the alarm's meter and, with an associate,[16] broke and entered and crept around on huge cat feet.

Except unfortunately the owner of the house turned out to be still home, even though both of his cars and the rest of his family were gone. The little guy was asleep sick in bed upstairs in acetate pajamas with a hot water bottle on his chest and half a glass of OJ and a bottle of NyQuil[17] and a foreign book and copies of *International Affairs* and *Interdependent Affairs* and a pair of thick specs and an industrial-size box of Kleenex on the bedside table and an empty vaporizer barely humming at the foot of the bed, and the guy was to say the least nonplussed to wake up and see high-filter flashlights crisscrossing over the unlit bedroom walls and bureau and teak chiffonnier as Gately and associate scanned for a wall-safe, which surprisingly like 90% of people with wall-safes conceal in their master bedroom behind some sort of land- or seascape painting. People turned out so identical in certain root domestic particulars it made Gately feel strange sometimes, like he was in possession of certain overlarge private facts to which no man should be entitled. Gately had a way stickier conscience about the possession of some of these large particular facts than he did about making off with other people's personal merchandise. But then all of a sudden in mid-silent-search for a safe here's this upscale homeowner turning out to be home with a nasty head-cold while his family's out on a two-car foliage-tour in what's left of the Berkshires, writhing groggily and Ny-Quilized around on the bed and making honking adenoidal sounds and asking what in bloody *hell* is the meaning of this, except he's saying it in Québecois French, which means to these thuggish U.S. drug addicts in Halloween-clowns' masks exactly nothing, he's sitting up in bed, a little and older-type homeowner with a football-shaped head and gray van Dyke and eyes you can tell are used to corrective lenses as he switches on the bright bedside lamp. Gately could easily have screwed out of there and never looked back; but here indeed, in the lamplight, is a seascape over next to the chiffonnier, and the associate has a quick peek and reports that the safe behind it is to laugh at, it can be opened with harsh language, almost; and oral narcotics addicts tend to operate on an extremely rigid physical schedule of need and satisfaction, and Gately is at this moment firmly in the need part of the schedule; and so D. W. Gately disastrously decides to go ahead and allow a nonviolent burglary to become in effect a robbery — which the operative legal difference involves either violence or the coercive threat of same — and Gately draws himself up to his full menacing height and shines his flashlight in the little homeowner's rheumy eyes and addresses him the way menacing criminals speak in popular entertainment — *d*'s for *th*'s, various apocopes, and so on — and takes hold of the guy's ear and conducts him down to a kitchen chair and binds his arms and legs to the chair with electrical cords neatly clipped from refrigerator and can-opener and M. Café-brand Automatic Café-au-Lait-Maker, binds him just short of gangrenously tight, because he's hoping the Berkshire foliage is prime and the guy's going to be soloing in this chair for a good stretch of time, and Gately starts looking through the kitchen's drawers for the silverware — not the good-silver-for-company silverware; that was in a calfskin case underneath some neatly folded old spare Christmas wrapping in a stunning hardwood-with-ivory-inlay chest of drawers in the living room, where over 90% of upscale people's good silver is always hidden, and has already been promoted and is piled[18] just off the foyer — but just the regular old everyday flatware silverware, because the vast bulk of homeowners keep their dish towels two drawers below their everyday-silverware drawer, and God's made no better call-for-help-stifling gag in the world than a good old oily-smelling fake-linen dish towel; and the bound guy in the cords on the chair suddenly snaps to the implications of what Gately's looking for and is struggling and saying: Do not gag me, I have a terrible cold, my nose she is a brick of the snot, I have not the power to breathe through the nose, for the love of God please do not gag my mouth; and as a gesture of goodwill the homeowner tells Gately, who's rummaging, the combination of the bedroom's seascape safe, except in French numbers, which together with the honking adenoidal inflection the guy's grippe gives his speech doesn't even sound like human speech to Gately, and but also the guy tells Gately there are some antique pre-British-takeover Québecois gold coins in a calfskin purse taped to the back of an undistinguished Impressionist landscape in the living room. But everything the Canadian homeowner says means no more to poor old Don Gately, whistling a jolly tune and trying to look menacing in his clown's mask, than the cries of, say, North Shore gulls or inland grackles; and sure enough the towels are two drawers under the spoons, and here comes Gately across the kitchen looking like a sort of Bozo from hell, and the Québecer guy's mouth goes oval with horror, and into that mouth goes a balled-up, faintly greasy-smelling kitchen towel, and across the guy's cheeks and over the dome of protruding linen goes some fine-quality fibrous strapping tape from the drawer under the decommissioned phone — why does everybody keep the serious mailing supplies in the drawer nearest the kitchen phone? — and Don Gately and associate finish their swift and with-the-best-of-intentions nonviolent business of stripping the Brookline home as bare as a post-feral-hamster meadow, and they relock the front door and hit the unlit road in Gately's reliable and double-mufflered 4×4. And the bound, wheezing, acetate-clad Canadian — the right-hand man to probably the most infamous anti-O.N.A.N. organizer north of the Great Concavity, the lieutenant and trouble-shooting trusted adviser who selflessly volunteered to move with his family to the savagely American area of metro Boston to act as liaison between and general leash-holder for the half-dozen or so malevolent and mutually antagonistic groups of Québecer Separatists and Albertan ultra-rightists united only in their fanatical conviction that the U.S.A.'s Experialistic 'gift' or 'return' of the so-calledly 'Recon-

figured' Great Convexity to its northern neighbor and O.N.A.N. ally constituted an intolerable blow to Canadian sovereignty, honor, and
hygiene — this homeowner, unquestionably a V.I.P., although admittedly
rather a covert V.I.P., or probably more accurately a 'P.I.T.,'[19] in French,
this meek-looking Canadian-terrorism-coordinator — bound to his chair,
thoroughly gagged, sitting there, alone, under cold fluorescent kitchen
lights,[20] the rhinovirally afflicted man, gagged with skill and quality
materials — the guy, having worked so hard to partially clear one clotted
nasal passage that he tore intercostal ligaments in his ribs, soon found even
that pinprick of air blocked off by mucus's implacable lava-like flow once
again, and so has to tear more ligaments trying to breach the other nostril,
and so on; and after an hour of struggle and flames in his chest and blood
on his lips and the white kitchen towel from trying frantically to tongue the
towel out past the tape, which is quality tape, and after hopes skyrocketing
when the doorbell rings and then hopes blackly dashed when the person at
the door, a young woman with a clipboard and chewing gum who's offering promotional coupons good for Happy Holidays discounts on member-
ships of six months or more at a string of Boston non-UV tanning salons,
shrugs in her parka and makes a mark on the clipboard and blithely retreats
down the long driveway to the pseudo-rural road, an hour of this or more,
finally the Québecois P.I.T., after unspeakable agony — slow suffocation,
mucoidal or no, being no day at the Montreal Tulip-Fest — at the height of
which agony, hearing his head's pulse as receding thunder and watching his
vision's circle shrink as a red aperture around his sight rotates steadily in
from the edges, at the height of which he could think only, despite the pain
and panic, of what a truly dumb and silly way this was, after all this time,
to die, a thought which the towel and tape denied expression via the rueful
grin with which the best men meet the dumbest ends — this Guillaume
DuPlessis passed bluely from this life, and sat there, in the kitchen chair,
250 clicks due east of some really spectacular autumn foliage, for almost
two nights and days, his posture getting more and more military as rigor
mortis set in, with his bare feet looking like purple loaves of bread, from the
lividity; and when Brookline's Finest were finally summoned and got him
unbound from the coldly lit chair, they had to carry him out as if he were
still seated, so militarily comme-il-faut had his limbs and spine hardened.
And poor old Don Gately, whose professional habit of killing power with
straight shunts to a meter's inflow was pretty much a signature M.O., and
who had, of course, a special place in the heart of a remorseless Revere
A.D.A. with judicial clout throughout Boston's three counties and beyond,
an of course particularly remorseless A.D.A., as of late, whose wife now
needed Valium even just to floss, and was patiently awaiting his chance, the
A.D.A. was, coldly biding his time, being a patient Get-Even and Cold-Dish
man just like Don Gately, who was, through no will to energy-consuming

violence on his part, in the sort of a hell of a deep-shit mess that can turn a man's life right around.

Year of the Depend Adult Undergarment: InterLace Telentertainment, 932/1864 R.I.S.C. power-TPs w/ or w/o console, Pink$_2$, post-Primestar D.S.S. dissemination, menus and icons, pixel-free Internet Fax, tri- and quad-modems w/ adjustable baud, Dissemination-Grids, screens so high-def you might as well be there, cost-effective videophonic conferencing, internal Froxx CD-ROM, electronic *couture*, all-in-one consoles, Yushityu nanoprocessors, laser chromotography, Virtual-capable media-cards, fiber-optic pulse, digital encoding, killer apps; carpal neuralgia, phosphenic migraine, gluteal hyperadiposity, lumbar stressae.

3 NOVEMBER — YEAR OF THE DEPEND ADULT UNDERGARMENT

Rm. 204, Subdormitory B: Jim Troeltsch, age seventeen, hometown Narberth PA, current Enfield Tennis Academy rank in Boys' 18's #8, which puts him at #2 Singles on the 18's B-team, has been taken ill. Again. It came on as he was suiting up warmly for the B-squad's 0745h. drills. A cartridge of a round-of-16 match from September's U.S. Open had been on the small room viewer with the sound all the way down as usual and Troeltsch'd been straightening the straps on his jock, idly calling the match's action into his fist, when it came on. The illness. It came out of nowhere. His breathing all of a sudden started hurting the back of his throat. Then that overfull heat in various cranial meatus. Then he sneezed and the stuff he sneezed out was thick and doughy. It came on ultra-fast and out of the pre-drill blue. He's back in bed now, supine, watching the match's fourth set but not calling the action. The viewer's right under Pemulis's poster of the paranoid king[21] that you can't escape looking at if you want to look at the viewer. Clotted Kleenex litter the floor around his bed's wastebasket. The bedside table is littered with both OTC and prescription expectorants and pertussives and analgesics and Vitamin-C megaspansules and one bottle of Benadryl and one of Seldane,[22] only the Seldane bottle actually contains several Tenuate 75-mg. capsules Troeltsch has incrementally promoted from Pemulis's part of the room and has, rather ingeniously he thinks, stashed in bold plain sight in a bedside pill bottle where the Peemster would never think to check. Troeltsch is the sort that can feel his own forehead and detect fever. It's definitely a rhinovirus, the sudden severe kind. He speculated on if yesterday when Graham Rader pretended to sneeze on J. Troeltsch's lunch-tray at the milk-dispenser at lunch if Rader might have really sneezed and only pretended to pretend, transferring virulent rhinoviri to Troeltsch's delicate mucosa. He feverishly mentally calls down various cosmic retributions on Rader. Neither of Troeltsch's roommates is here. Ted Schacht is getting the knee's first of several whirlpools for the day. Pemulis has geared up and left for 0745 drills. Troeltsch offered Pemulis rights to his breakfast to fill up his vaporizer for him and call the first-shift nurse for 'yet more' Seldane nuclear-grade antihistamine and a dextromethorphan nebulizer and a written excuse from A.M. drills. He lies there sweating freely, watching digitally recorded professional tennis, too worried about his throat to feel loquacious enough to call the action. Seldane is not supposed to make you drowsy but he feels weak and unpleasantly drowsy. He can barely make a fist. He's sweaty. Nausea/vomiting like not an impossibility by any means. He cannot believe how fast it came on, the illness. The vaporizer seethes and burps, and all four of the room's windows weep against the outside cold. There are the sad tiny distant-champagne-cork sounds of scores of balls being hit down at the East Courts. Troeltsch drifts at a level just above sleep. Enormous ATHSCME displacement fans far up north at the wall and border's distant roar and the outdoor voices and *pock* of cold balls create a kind of sound-carpet below the digestive sounds of the vaporizer and the squeak of Troeltsch's bedsprings as he thrashes and twitches in a moist half-sleep. He has heavy German eyebrows and big-knuckled hands. It's one of those unpleasant opioid feverish half-sleep states, more a fugue-state than a sleep-state, less a floating than like being cast adrift on rough seas, tossed mightily in and out of this half-sleep where your mind's still working and you can ask yourself whether you're asleep even as you dream. And any dreams you do have seem ragged at the edges, gnawed on, incomplete.

It's literally 'daydreaming,' sick, the kind of incomplete fugue you awaken from with a sort of psychic clunk, struggling up to sit upright, convinced there's someone unauthorized in the dorm room with you. Falling back sick on his circle-stained pillow, staring straight up into the prolix folds of the Turkish blanketish thing Pemulis and Schacht had Krazy-Glued to the ceiling's corners, which billows, hanging, so its folds form a terrain, like with valleys and shadows.

I am coming to see that the sensation of the worst nightmares, a sensation that can be felt asleep or awake, is identical to those worst dreams' form itself: the sudden intra-dream realization that the nightmares' very essence and center has been with you all along, even awake: it's just been . . . *overlooked;* and then that horrific interval between realizing what you've overlooked and turning your head to look back at what's been right there all along, the *whole time*. . . . Your first nightmare away from home and folks, your first night at the Academy, it was there all along: The dream is that you awaken from a deep sleep, wake up suddenly damp and panicked and are overwhelmed with the sudden feeling that there is a distillation of total evil in this dark strange subdorm room with you, that evil's essence and center is right here, in this room, right now. And is for you alone. None of the other little boys in the room are awake; the bunk above yours sags dead, motionless; no one moves; no one else in the room feels the presence of something radically evil; none thrash or sit damply up; no one else cries out: whatever it is is not evil *for them*. The flashlight your mother name-tagged with masking tape and packed for you special pans around the institutional room: the drop-ceiling, the gray striped mattress and bulged grid of bunksprings above you, the two other bunkbeds another matte gray that won't return light, the piles of books and compact disks and tapes and tennis gear; your disk of white light trembling like the moon on water as it plays over the identical bureaus, the recessions of closet and room's front door, door's frame's bolections; the cone of light pans over fixtures, the lumpy jumbles of sleeping boys' shadows on the snuff-white walls, the two rag throw-rugs' ovals on the hardwood floor, black lines of baseboards' reglets, the cracks in the venetian blinds that ooze the violet nonlight of a night with snow and just a hook of moon; the flashlight with your name in maternal cursive plays over every cm. of the walls, the rheostats, CD, Inter-Lace poster of Tawni Kondo, phone console, desks' TPs, the face in the floor, posters of pros, the onionskin yellow of the desklamps' shades, the ceiling-panels' patterns of pinholes, the grid of upper bunk's springs, recession of closet and door, boys wrapped in blankets, slight crack like a creek's course in the eastward ceiling discernible now, maple reglet border at seam of ceiling and walls north and south *no floor has a face* your flashlight showed but didn't no never did *see* its eyes' pupils set sideways and tapered like a cat's its eyebrows' \/ and horrid toothy smile leering right at your light all the time you've been scanning oh mother a face in the *floor* mother oh and your flashlight's beam stabs jaggedly back for the overlooked face misses it overcorrects then centers on what you'd felt but had seen without seeing, just now, as you'd so carefully panned the light and looked, a face in the *floor* there all the time but unfelt by all others and unseen by you until you knew just as you felt it didn't belong and was evil: *Evil.*

And then its mouth opens at your light.

And then you wake like that, quivering like a struck drum, lying there awake and quivering, summoning courage and spit, roll to the right just as in the dream for the nametagged flashlight on the floor by the bed just in case, lie there on your shank and side, shining the light all over, just as in the dream. Lie there panning, looking, all ribs and elbows and dilated eyes. The awake floor is littered with gear and dirty clothes, blond hardwood with sealed seams, two throw-rugs, the bare waxed wood shiny in the windows' snowlight, the floor neutral, faceless, you cannot see any face in the floor, awake, lying there, faceless, blank, dilated, playing beam over floor again and again, not sure all night forever unsure you're not missing something that's right there: you lie there, awake and almost twelve, believing with all your might.

O

AS OF YEAR OF THE DEPEND ADULT UNDERGARMENT

The Enfield Tennis Academy has been in accredited operation for three pre-Subsidized years and then eight Subsidized years, first under the direction of Dr. James Incandenza and then under the administration of his half-brother-in-law Charles Tavis, Ed.D. James Orin Incandenza — the only child of a former top U.S. jr. tennis player and then promising young pre-Method actor who, during the interval of J. O. Incandenza's early formative years, had become a disrespected and largely unemployable actor, driven back to his native Tucson AZ and dividing his remaining energies between stints as a tennis pro at ranch-type resorts and then short-run productions at something called the Desert Beat Theater Project, the father, a dipsomaniacal tragedian progressively crippled by obsessions with death by spider-bite and by stage fright and with a bitterness of ambiguous origin but consuming intensity toward the Method school of professional acting and its more promising exponents, a father who somewhere around the nadir of his professional fortunes apparently decided to go down to his Raid-sprayed basement workshop and build a promising junior athlete the way other fathers might restore vintage autos or build ships inside bottles, or like refinish chairs, etc. — James Incandenza proved a withdrawn but compliant student of the game and soon a gifted jr. player — tall, bespectacled, domineering at net — who used tennis scholarships to finance, on his own, private secondary and then higher education at places just about as far away from the U.S. Southwest as one could get without drowning. The United States government's prestigious O.N.R.[23] financed his doctorate in optical physics, fulfilling something of a childhood dream. His strategic value, during the Federal interval G. Ford–early G. Bush, as more or less the top applied-geometrical-optics man in the O.N.R. and S.A.C., designing neutron-scattering reflectors for thermo-strategic weapons systems, then in the Atomic Energy Commission — where his development of gamma-refractive indices for lithium-anodized lenses and panels is commonly regarded as one of the big half-dozen discoveries that made possible cold annular fusion and approximate energy-independence for the U.S. and its various allies and protectorates — his optical acumen translated, after an early retirement from the public sector, into a patented fortune in rearview mirrors, light-sensitive eyewear, holographic birthday and Xmas greeting cartridges, videophonic Tableaux, homolosine-cartography software, nonfluorescent public-lighting systems and film-equipment; then, in the optative retirement from hard science that building and opening a U.S.T.A.-accredited and pedagogically experimental tennis academy apparently represented for him, into 'après-garde' experimental- and conceptual-film work too far either ahead of or behind its time, possibly, to be much appreciated at the time of his death in the Year of the Trial-Size Dove Bar — although a lot of it (the experimental- and conceptual-film work) was admittedly just plain pretentious and unengaging and bad, and probably not helped at all by the man's very gradual spiral into the crippling dipsomania of his late father.[24]

The tall, ungainly, socially challenged and hard-drinking Dr. Incandenza's May–December[25] marriage to one of the few bona fide bombshell-type females in North American academia, the extremely tall and high-strung but also extremely pretty and gainly and teetotalling and classy Dr. Avril Mondragon, the only female academic ever to hold the Macdonald Chair in Prescriptive Usage at the Royal Victoria College of McGill University, whom Incandenza'd met at a U. Toronto conference on Reflective vs. Reflexive Systems, was rendered even more romantic by the bureaucratic tribulations involved in obtaining an Exit- and then an Entrance-Visa, to say nothing of a Green Card, for even a U.S.-spoused Professor Mondragon whose involvement, however demonstrably nonviolent, with certain members of the Québecois-Separatist Left while in graduate school had placed her name on the R.C.M.P.'s notorious *Personnes à Qui On Doit Surveiller Attentivement'* List. The birth of the Incandenzas' first child, Orin, had been at least partly a legal maneuver.

It is known that, during the last five years of his life, Dr. James O. Incandenza liquidated his assets and patent-licenses, ceded control over most of the Enfield Tennis Academy's operations to his wife's half-brother — a former engineer most recently employed in Amateur Sports Administration at Throppinghamshire Provincial College, New Brunswick, Canada — and devoted his unimpaired hours almost exclusively to the production of documentaries, technically recondite art films, and mordantly obscure and obsessive dramatic cartridges, leaving behind a substantial (given the late age at which he bloomed, creatively) number of completed films and cartridges, some of which have earned a small academic following for their technical feck and for a pathos that was somehow both surreally abstract and CNS-rendingly melodramatic at the same time.

Professor James O. Incandenza, Jr.'s untimely suicide at fifty-four was held a great loss in at least three worlds. President J. Gentle (F.C.), acting on behalf of the U.S.D.D.'s O.N.R. and O.N.A.N.'s post-annular A.E.C., conferred a posthumous citation and conveyed his condolences by classified ARPA-NET Electronic Mail. Incandenza's burial in Québec's L'Islet County was twice delayed by annular hyperfloration cycles. Cornell University Press announced plans for a festschrift. Certain leading young quote 'après-garde' and 'anticonfluential' filmmakers employed, in their output for the Year of the Trial-Size Dove Bar, certain oblique visual gestures — most involving the chiaroscuro lamping and custom-lens effects for which Incandenza's distinctive deep focus was known — that paid the sort of deep-insider's elegaic tribute no audience could be expected to notice. An interview with Incandenza was posthumously included in a book on the genesis of annulation. And those of E.T.A.'s junior players whose hypertrophied arms could fit inside them wore black bands on court for almost a year.

DENVER CO, 1 NOVEMBER
YEAR OF THE DEPEND ADULT UNDERGARMENT

'I hate this!' Orin yells out to whoever glides near. He doesn't loop or spiral like the showboats; he sort of tacks, the gliding equivalent of snowplowing, unspectacular and aiming to get it over ASAP and intact. The fake red wings' nylon clatters in an updraft; ill-glued feathers keep peeling off and rising. The updraft is the oxides from Mile-High's thousands of open mouths. Far and away the loudest stadium anyplace. He feels like a dick. The beak makes it hard to breathe and see. Two reserve ends do some kind of combined barrel-roll thing. The worst is the moment right before they make the jump off the stadium's rim. Hands in the top rows reaching and clutching. People laughing. The InterLace cameras panning and tightening; Orin knows too well the light on the side that means Zoom. Once they're out over the field the voices melt and merge into oxides and updraft. The left guard is soaring up instead of down. A couple beaks and a claw fall off somebody and go pinwheeling down toward the green. Orin tacks grimly back and forth. He's among those who steadfastly refuse to whistle or squawk. Bonus or no. The stadium loudspeaker's a steely gargle. You can never hear it clearly even on the ground.

The sad old ex-QB who now just holds on place-kicks falls in beside Orin's slow back-and-forth about 100 meters over the 40. He's one of the token females, his beak blunter and wings' red nongarish.

'Hate and loathe this with a clusterfucking *passion,* Clayt!'

The holder tries to make a resigned wing-gesture and is almost blown into Orin's pinfeathers. 'Almost down! Enjoy the ride! Yo — cleavage-check in 22G, just by the —' and then lost in the roar as the first player touches down and sheds the red-feathered promotional apparatus. You have to scream to even be heard. At some point it starts sounding like the crowd's roaring at its own roar, a doubling-back quality like something'll blow. One of the Broncos in the rear end of a costume takes a header at midfield so it looks like the thing's ass went flying off. Orin has told no Cardinal, not even the team's counselor and visualization-therapist, about his morbid fear of heights and high-altitude descent.

'I punt! I'm paid to punt long, high, well, and always! Making me do personal interviews on my personal side's bad enough! But this crosses every line! Why do we stand for this! I'm an athlete! I'm not a freak-show performer! Nobody mentioned flying at the trade-table. In New Orleans it was just robes and halos and once a season a zither. But just once a season. This is fucking awful!'

'Could be worse!'

Spiralling down toward the line of X's and the bill-capped guys that help strip the wings off, runty potbellied volunteer front-office-connected guys who always smirk in a way you couldn't quite level the accusation.

'I'm paid to punt!'

'It's worse in Philly! . . . had fucking water-drops in Seattle for three seaso—'

'Please Lord, spare the Leg,' Orin whispers each time just before touchdown.

'. . . of how you could be an Oiler! You could be a *Brown*.'

The organopsychedelic muscimole, an isoxazole-alkaloid derived from *Amanita muscaria,* a.k.a. the fly agaric mushroom — by no means, Michael Pemulis emphasizes, to be confused with *phalloides* or *verna* or certain other kill-you-dead species of North America's *Amanita* genus, as the little kids sit there Indian-style on the Viewing Room floor, glassy-eyed and trying not to yawn — goes by the structural moniker 5-aminomethyl-3-isoxazolol, requires about like maybe ten to twenty oral mg. per ingestion, making it two to three times as potent as psilocybin, and frequently results in the following alterations in consciousness (not reading or referring to notes in any way): a kind of semi-sleep-like trance with visions, elation, sensations of physical lightness and increased strength, heightened sensual perceptions, synesthesia, and favorable distortions in body-image. This is supposed to be a pre-dinner 'Big Buddy' powwow, where the littler kids receive general big-brotherly-type support and counsel from an upperclassman. Pemulis sometimes treats his group's powwows like a kind of colloquium, sharing personal findings and interests. The viewer's on Read from the room's laptop, and the screen's got block-capitaled METHOXYLATED BASES FOR PHENYLKYLAMINE MANIPULATION on it, and underneath some stuff that might as well be Greek to the Little Buds. Two of the kids squeeze tennis balls; two rock and bob Hasidically to stay alert; one has a hat with a pair of fake antennae made of tight-coiled spring. More or less revered by the aboriginal tribes of what's now southern Québec and the Great Concavity, Pemulis tells them, the fly agaric 'shroom was both loved and hated for its powerful but not always unless carefully titrated pleasant psycho-spiritual effects. A boy probes at his own navel with great interest. Another pretends to fall over.

Some of the more marginal players start in as early as maybe twelve, I'm sorry to say, particularly 'drines before matches and then enkephaline[26] after, which can generate a whole vicious circle of individual neurochemistry; but I myself, having taken certain vows early on concerning fathers and differences, didn't even get downwind of my first bit of Bob Hope[27] until fifteen, more like nearly sixteen, when Bridget Boone, in whose room a lot of the 16 and Unders used to congregate before lights-out, invited me to consider a couple of late-night bongs, as a kind of psychodysleptic Sominex, to help me sleep, perhaps, finally, all the way through a really unpleasant dream that had been recurring nightly and waking me up *in medias* for weeks and was beginning to grind me down and to cause some slight deterioration in performance and rank. Low-grade synthetic Bob or not, the bongs worked like a charm.

In this dream, which every now and then still recurs, I am standing publicly at the baseline of a gargantuan tennis court. I'm in a competitive match, clearly: there are spectators, officials. The court is about the size of a football field, though, maybe, it seems. It's hard to tell. But mainly the court's complex. The lines that bound and define play are on this court as complex and convoluted as a sculpture of string. There are lines going every which way, and they run oblique or meet and form relationships and boxes and rivers and tributaries and systems inside systems: lines, corners, alleys, and angles deliquesce into a blur at the horizon of the distant net. I stand there tentatively. The whole thing is almost too involved to try to take in all at once. It's simply huge. And it's public. A silent crowd resolves itself at what may be the court's periphery, dressed in summer's citrus colors, motionless and highly attentive. A battalion of linesmen stand blandly alert in their blazers and safari hats, hands folded over their slacks' flies. High overhead, near what might be a net-post, the umpire, blue-blazered, wired for amplification in his tall high-chair, whispers Play. The crowd is a tableau, motionless and attentive. I twirl my stick in my hand and bounce a fresh yellow ball and try to figure out where in all that mess of lines I'm supposed to direct service. I can make out in the stands stage-left the white sun-umbrella of the Moms; her height raises the white umbrella above her neighbors; she sits in her small circle of shadow, hair white and legs crossed and a delicate fist upraised and tight in total unconditional support.

The umpire whispers Please Play.

We sort of play. But it's all hypothetical, somehow. Even the 'we' is theory: I never get quite to see the distant opponent, for all the apparatus of the game.

O

YEAR OF THE DEPEND ADULT UNDERGARMENT

Doctors tend to enter the arenas of their profession's practice with a brisk good cheer that they have to then stop and try to mute a bit when the arena they're entering is a hospital's fifth floor, a psych ward, where brisk good cheer would amount to a kind of gloating. This is why doctors on psych wards so often wear a vaguely fake frown of puzzled concentration, if and when you see them in fifth-floor halls. And this is why a hospital M.D. — who's usually hale and pink-cheeked and poreless, and who almost always smells unusually clean and good — approaches any psych patient under his care with a professional manner somewhere between bland and deep, a distant but sincere concern that's divided evenly between the patient's subjective discomfort and the hard facts of the case.

The doctor who poked his fine head just inside her hot room's open door and knocked maybe a little too gently on the metal jamb found Kate Gompert lying on her side on the slim hard bed in blue jeans and a sleeveless blouse with her knees drawn up to her abdomen and her fingers laced around her knees. Something almost too overt about the pathos of the posture: this exact position was illustrated in some melancholic Watteau-era print on the frontispiece to Yevtuschenko's *Field Guide to Clinical States*. Kate Gompert wore dark-blue boating sneakers without socks or laces. Half her face obscured by the either green or yellow case on the plastic pillow, her hair so long-unwashed it had separated into discrete shiny strands, and black bangs lay like a cell's glossy bars across the visible half of the forehead. The psych ward smelled faintly of disinfectant and the Community

Lounge's cigarette smoke, the sour odor of medical waste awaiting collection with also that perpetual slight ammoniac tang of urine, and there was the double bing of the elevator and the always faraway sound of the intercom paging some M.D., and some high-volume cursing from a manic in the pink Quiet Room at the other end of the psych-ward hall from the Community Lounge. Kate Gompert's room also smelled of singed dust from the heat-vent, also of the over-sweet perfume worn by the young mental health staffer who sat in a chair at the foot of the girl's bed, chewing blue gum and viewing a soundless ROM cartridge on a ward-issue laptop. Kate Gompert was on Specials, which meant Suicide-Watch, which meant that the girl had at some point betrayed both Ideation and Intent, which meant she had to be watched right up close by a staffer twenty-four hours a day until the supervising M.D. called off the Specials. Staffers rotated Specials-duty every hour, ostensibly so that whoever was on duty was always fresh and keenly observant, but really because simply sitting there at the foot of a bed looking at somebody who was in so much psychic pain she wanted to commit suicide was incredibly depressing and boring and unpleasant, so they spread the odious duty out as thin as they possibly could, the staffers. They were not technically supposed to read, do paperwork, view CD-ROMs, do personal grooming, or in any way divert their attention from the patient on Specials, on-duty. The patient Ms. Gompert seemed both to be fighting for breath and to be breathing rapidly enough to induce hypocapnia; the doctor could not be expected not also to notice that she had fairly large breasts that rose and fell rapidly inside the circle of arms with which she hugged her knees. The girl's eyes, which were dull, had registered his appearance in the doorway, but they didn't seem to track as he came toward the bed. The staffer was also employing an emery board. The doctor told the staffer that he was going to need a few moments alone with Ms. Gompert. It is a sort of requirement that a doctor whenever possible be reading or at least looking down at something on his clipboard when addressing a subordinate, so the doctor was looking studiously at the patient's Intake and the sheaf of charts and records Med-Netted over from trauma and psych wards in some other city hospitals. Gompert, Katherine A., 21, Newton MA. Data-clerical in a Wellesley Hills real estate office. Fourth hospitalization in three years, all clinical depression, unipolar. One series of electro-convulsive treatments out at Newton-Wellesley Hospital two years back. On Prozac for a short time, then Zoloft, most recently Parnate with a lithium kicker. Two previous suicide attempts, the second just this past summer. Bi-Valium discontinued two years, Xanax discontinued one year — an admitted history of abusing prescribed meds. Depressions unipolar, fairly classic, characterized by acute dysphoria, anxiety w/panic, diurnal listlessness/agitation patterns, Ideation w/w/o Intent. First attempt a CO-episode, garage's automobile had stalled before lethal hemotoxicity achieved. Then last year's attempt — no scarring now visible, her wrists' vascular nodes obscured by the insides of the knees she held. She continued to stare at the doorway where he'd first appeared. This latest attempt a straightforward meds O.D. Admitted via the E.R. three nights past. Two days on ventilation after a Pump & Purge. Hypertensive crisis on the second day from metabolic retox — she must have taken a hell of a lot of meds — the I.C.U. charge nurse had beeped the chaplain, so the retox must have been bad. Almost died twice this time, Katherine Ann Gompert. Third day spent on 2-West for observation, Librium reluctantly administered for a B.P. that was all over the map. Now here on 5, his present arena. B.P. stable as of the last four readings. Next vitals at 1300h.

The attempt had been serious, a real attempt. This girl had not been futzing around. A bona fide clinical admit right out of Yevtuschenko or Dretske. Over half the admits to psych wards are things like cheerleaders who swallow two bottles of Mydol over a high-school breakup or gray lonely asexual depressing people rendered inconsolable by the death of a pet. The cathartic trauma of actually going in somewhere officially Psych-, some understanding nods, some bare indication somebody gives half a damn — they rally, back out they go. Three determined attempts and a course of shock spelled no such case here. The doctor's interior state was somewhere between trepidation and excitement, which manifested outwardly as a sort of blandly deep puzzled concern.

The doctor said Hi and that he wanted to ascertain for sure that she was Katherine Gompert, as they hadn't met before up till now.

'That's me,' in a bit of a bitter singsong. Her voice was oddly lit-up for one who lay fetal, dead-eyed, w/o facial affect.

The doctor said could she tell him a little bit about why she's here with them right now? Can she remember back to what happened?

She took an even deeper breath. She was attempting to communicate boredom or irritation. 'I took a hundred-ten Parnate, about thirty Lithonate capsules, some old Zoloft. I took everything I had in the world.'

'You really must have wanted to hurt yourself, then, it seems.'

'They said downstairs the Parnate made me black out. It did a blood pressure thing. My mother heard noises upstairs and found me she said down on my side chewing the rug in my room. My room's shag-carpeted. She said I was on the floor flushed red and all wet like when I was a newborn; she said she thought at first she hallucinated me as a newborn again. On my side all red and wet.'

'A hypertensive crisis will do that. It means your blood pressure was high enough to have killed you. Sertraline in combination with an MAOI[28] will kill you, in enough quantities. And with the toxicity of that much lithium besides, I'd say you're pretty lucky to be here right now.'

'My mother sometimes thinks she's hallucinating.'

'Sertraline, by the way, is the Zoloft you kept instead of discarding as instructed when changing medications.'

'She says I chewed a big hole out of the carpet. But who can say.'

The doctor chose his second-finest pen from the array in his white coat's breast pocket and made some sort of note on Kate Gompert's new chart for this particular psych ward. Crowded in among his pocket's pens was the rubber head of a diagnostic plexor. He asked Kate if she could tell him why she had wanted to hurt herself. Had she been angry at herself. At someone else. Had she ceased to feel as though her life had meaning to it. Had she heard anything like voices suggesting that she hurt herself.

There was no audible response. The girl's breathing had slowed to just rapid. The doctor took an early clinical gamble and asked Kate whether it might not be easier if she rolled over and sat up so that they could speak with each other more normally, face to face.

'I am sitting up.'

The doctor's pen was poised. His slow nod was studious, blandly puzzled-seeming. 'You mean to say you feel right now as if your body is already in a sitting-up position?'

She rolled an eye up at him for a long moment, sighed meaningfully, and rolled and rose. Katherine Ann Gompert probably felt that here was yet another psych-ward M.D. with zero sense of humor. This was probably because she did not understand the strict methodological limits that dictated how literal he, a doctor, had to be with the admits on the psych ward. Nor that jokes and sarcasm were here usually too pregnant and fertile with clinical significance not to be taken seriously: sarcasm and jokes were often the bottle in which clinical depressives sent out their most plangent screams for someone to care and help them. The doctor — who by the way wasn't an M.D. yet but a resident, here on a twelve-week psych rotation — indulged this clinical reverie while the patient made an elaborate show of getting the thin pillow out from under her and leaning it up the tall way against the bare wall behind the bed and slumping back against it, her arms crossed over her breasts. The doctor decided that her open display of irritation with him could signify either a positive thing or nothing at all.

Kate Gompert stared at a point over the man's left shoulder. 'I wasn't trying to hurt myself. I was trying to kill myself. There's a difference.'

The doctor asked whether she could try to explain what she felt the difference was between those two things.

The delay that preceded her reply was only marginally longer than the pause in a regular civilian conversation. The doctor had no ideas about what this observation might indicate.

'Do you guys see different kinds of suicides?'

The resident made no attempt to ask Kate Gompert what she meant. She used one finger to remove some material from the corner of her mouth.

'I think there must be probably different types of suicides. I'm not one of the self-hating ones. The type of like "I'm shit and the world'd be better off without poor me" type that says that but also imagines what everybody'll say at their funeral. I've met types like that on wards. Poor-me-I-hate-me-punish-me-come-to-my-funeral. Then they show you a 20 × 25 glossy of their dead cat. It's all self-pity bullshit. It's bullshit. I didn't have any special grudges. I didn't fail an exam or get dumped by anybody. All these types. Hurt themselves.' Still that intriguing, unsettling combination of blank facial masking and conventionally animated vocal tone. The doctor's small nods were designed to appear not as responses but as invitations to continue, what Dretske called Momentumizers.

'I didn't want to especially hurt myself. Or like punish. I don't hate myself. I just wanted out. I didn't want to play anymore is all.'

'Play,' nodding in confirmation, making small quick notes.

'I wanted to just stop being conscious. I'm a whole different type. I wanted to stop feeling this way. If I could have just put myself in a really long coma I would have done that. Or given myself shock I would have done that. Instead.'

The doctor was writing with great industry.

'The last thing more I'd want is hurt. I just didn't want to feel this way anymore. I don't . . . I didn't believe this feeling would ever go away. I don't. I still don't. I'd rather feel nothing than this.'

The doctor's eyes appeared keenly interested in an abstract way. They looked severely magnified behind his attractive but thick glasses, the frames of which were steel. Patients on other floors during other rotations had sometimes complained that they sometimes felt like something in a jar he was studying intently through all that thick glass. He was saying 'This feeling of wanting to stop feeling by dying, then, is —'

The way she suddenly shook her head was vehement, exasperated. 'The feeling is *why* I want to. The feeling is the *reason* I want to die. I'm here because I want to die. That's why I'm in a room without windows and with cages over the lightbulbs and no lock on the toilet door. Why they took my shoelaces and my belt. But I notice they don't take away the feeling do they.'

'Is the feeling you're explaining something you've experienced in your other depressions, then, Katherine?'

The patient didn't respond right away. She slid her foot out of her shoes and touched one bare foot with the toes of the other foot. Her eyes tracked this activity. The conversation seemed to have helped her focus. Like most clinically depressed patients, she appeared to function better in focused activity than in stasis. Their normal paralyzed stasis allowed these patients' own minds to chew them apart. But it was always a titanic struggle to get them to do anything to help them focus. Most residents found the fifth floor a depressing place to do a rotation.

'What I'm trying to ask, I think, is whether this feeling you're communicating is the feeling you associate with your depression.'

Her gaze moved off. 'That's what you guys want to call it, I guess.'

The doctor clicked his pen slowly a few times and explained that he's more interested here in what *she* would choose to call the feeling, since it was her feeling.

The resumed study of the movement of her feet. 'When people call it that I always get pissed off because I always think *depression* sounds like you just get like really sad, you get quiet and melancholy and just like sit quietly by the window sighing or just lying around. A state of not caring about anything. A kind of blue kind of peaceful state.' She seemed to the doctor decidedly more animated now, even as she seemed unable to meet his eyes. Her respiration had sped back up. The doctor recalled classic hyperventilatory episodes being characterized by carpopedal spasms, and reminded himself to monitor the patient's hands and feet carefully during the interview for any signs of tetanic contraction, in which case the prescribed therapy would be I.V. calcium in a saline percentage he would need quickly to look up.

'Well *this*' — she gestured at herself — 'isn't a state. This is a *feeling*. I feel it all over. In my arms and legs.'

'That would include your carp— your hands and feet?'

'All *over*. My head, throat, butt. In my stomach. It's all over everywhere. I don't know what I could call it. It's like I can't get enough outside it to call it anything. It's like horror more than sadness. It's more like horror. It's like something horrible is about to happen, the most horrible thing you can imagine — no, worse than you can imagine because there's the feeling that there's something you have to do right away to stop it but you don't know what it is you have to do, and then it's happening, too, the whole horrible time, it's about to happen and also it's happening, all at the same time.'

'So you'd say anxiety is a big part of your depressions.'

It was now not clear whether she was responding to the doctor or not. 'Everything gets horrible. Everything you see gets ugly. *Lurid* is the word. Doctor Garton said *lurid*, one time. That's the right word for it. And everything sounds harsh, spiny and harsh-sounding, like every sound you hear all of a sudden has teeth. And smelling like I smell bad even after I just got out of the shower. It's like what's the point of washing if everything smells like I need another shower.'

The doctor looked intrigued rather than concerned for a moment as he wrote all this down. He preferred handwritten notes to a laptop because he felt M.D.s who typed into their laps during clinical interviews gave a cold impression.

Kate Gompert's face writhed for a moment while the doctor was writing. 'I fear this feeling more than I fear anything, man. More than pain, or my mom dying, or environmental toxicity. Anything.'

'Fear is a major part of anxiety,' the doctor confirmed.

Katherine Gompert seemed to come out of her dark reverie for a moment. She stared full-frontal at the doctor for several seconds, and the doctor, who'd had all discomfort at being stared at by patients trained right out of him when he'd rotated through the paralysis/-plegia wards upstairs, was able to look directly back at her with a kind of bland compassion, the expression of someone who was compassionate but was not, of course, feeling what she was feeling, and who honored her subjective feelings by not even trying to pretend that he was. Sharing them. The young woman's expression, in turn, revealed that she had decided to take what amounted for her to her own gamble, this early in a therapeutic relationship. The abstract resolve on her face now duplicated what had been on the doctor's face when he'd taken the gamble of asking her to sit up straight.

'Listen,' she said. 'Have you ever felt sick? I mean nauseous, like you knew you were going to throw up?'

The doctor made a gesture like Well sure.

'But that's just in your stomach,' Kate Gompert said. 'It's a horrible feeling but it's just in your stomach. That's why the term is "sick to your stomach." ' She was back to looking intently at her lower carpopedals. 'What I told Dr. Garton is OK but imagine if you felt that way all over, inside. All through you. Like every cell and every atom or brain-cell or whatever was so nauseous it wanted to throw up, but it couldn't, and you felt that way all the time, and you're sure, you're positive the feeling will never go away, you're going to spend the rest of your natural life feeling like this.'

The doctor wrote down something much too brief to correspond directly to what she'd said. He was nodding both while he wrote and when he looked up. 'And yet this nauseated feeling has come and gone for you in the past, it's passed eventually during prior depressions, Katherine, has it not?'

'But when you're in the feeling you forget. The feeling feels like it's always been there and will always be there, and you forget. It's like this whole filter drops down over the whole way you think about everything, a couple weeks after —'

They sat and looked at each other. The doctor felt some combination of intense clinical excitement and anxiety about perhaps saying the wrong thing at such a crucial juncture and fouling up. His last name was needle-pointed in yellow braid on the left breast of the white coat he was required to wear. 'I'm sorry? A couple weeks after — ?'

He waited for seven breaths.

'I want shock,' she said finally. 'Isn't part of this whole concerned kindness deal that you're supposed to ask me how I think you can be of help? Cause I've been through this before. You haven't asked what I want. Isn't it? Well how about either give me ECT[29] again, or give me my belt back. Because I can't stand feeling like this another second, and the seconds keep coming on and on.'

'Well,' the doctor said slowly, nodding to indicate he had heard the feelings the young woman was expressing, 'Well, I'm happy to discuss treatment options with you, Katherine. But I have to say right now I'm curious about what you started it sounded like to me to maybe start to indicate what might have occurred, something, two weeks ago to make you feel these feelings now. Would you be comfortable talking to me about it?'

'Either ECT or you could just sedate me for a month. You could do that. All I'd need is I think a month at the outside. Like a controlled coma. You could do that, if you guys want to help.'

The doctor gazed at her with a patience she was meant to see.

And she gave him back a frightening smile, a smile empty of all affect, as if someone had contracted her circumorals with a thigmotactic electrode. The teeth of the smile evidenced a clinical depressive's classic inattention to oral hygiene.

She said 'I was thinking I was about to say you'll think I'm crazy if I tell you. But then I remembered where I am.' She made a small sound that was supposed to be laughter; it did sound jagged, dentate.

'I was going to say I've thought sometimes before like the feeling maybe had to do with Hope.'

'Hope.'

Her arms had been crossed over her breasts the whole time, and though the room was overheated the patient rubbed each palm continually over her upper arms, behavior one associates with chill. The position and movement shielded her inner arms from view. The doctor's eyebrows had gone synclinal from puzzlement without his awareness.

'Bob.'

'Bob.' The doctor was anxious that his failure to have any idea what the girl was referring to would betray itself and accentuate her feelings of loneliness and psychic pain. Classic unipolars were usually tormented by the conviction that no one else could hear or understand them when they tried to communicate. Hence jokes, sarcasm, the psychopathology of unconscious arm-rubbing.

Kate Gompert's head was rolling like a blind person's. 'Jesus what am I *doing* here. Bob Hope. Dope. Sinse. Stick. Grass. Smoke.' She made a quick duBois-gesture with thumb and finger held to rounded lips. 'The dealers down where I buy it some of them make you call it Bob Hope when you call, in case anybody's accessed the line. You're supposed to ask is Bob in town. And if they have some they say "Hope springs eternal," usually. It's like a code. One kid makes you ask him to please commit a crime. The dealers that stay around any length of time tend to be on the paranoid side. As if it would fool anybody who knew enough to bother to access the band on the call.' She seemed decidedly more animated. 'And one particular guy with snakes in a tank in a trailer in Allston, he —'

'So drugs, then, you're saying you feel may be a factor,' the doctor inter-rupted.

The depressed young woman's face emptied once more. She engaged briefly in something the staffers on Specials called the Thousand-Meter Stare.

'Not "*drugs,*"' she said slowly. The doctor smelled shame in the room, sour and uremic. Her face had become distantly pained now.

The girl said: 'Stopping.'

The doctor felt comfortable saying once again that he was not sure he understood what she was trying to share with him.

She now went through a series of expressions that made it clinically im-possible for the doctor to determine whether or not she was entirely sincere. She looked either pained or trying somehow to suppress hilarity. She said 'I don't know if you'll believe me. I'm worried you'll think I'm crazy. I have this thing with pot.'

'Meaning marijuana.'

The doctor was oddly sure that Kate Gompert pretended to sniff instead of engaging in a real sniff. 'Marijuana. Most people think of marijuana as just some minor substance, I know, just like this natural plant that happens to make you feel good the way poison oak makes you itch, and if you say you're in trouble with Hope — people'll just laugh. Because there's much worse drugs out there. Believe me I know.'

'I'm not laughing at you, Katherine,' the doctor said, and meant it.

'But I love it *so much.* Sometimes it's like the center of my life. It does something to me, I know, that's not good, and I got told point-blank not to smoke, on the Parnate, because Dr. Garton said no one knew what certain combinations do yet and it'd be roulette. But after a while I always think to myself it's been a while and things will be different somehow this time if I do, even on the Parnate, so I do again, I start again. I'll start out doing just like a couple of hits off a duBois after work, to get me through dinner, because dinner with my mother and me is — well, but and pretty soon after a while I'm in my room with the fan pointed out the window all night, doing one-hitters and exhaling at the fan, to kill the smell, and I make her say I'm not there if anybody calls, and I lie about what I'm doing in there all night even if she doesn't ask, sometimes she asks and sometimes she doesn't. And then after a while I'm smoking joints at work, at breaks, going in the bath-room and standing on the toilet and blowing it out the window, there's this tiny window up high with the glass frosted and all filthy and cobwebby, and I hate having my face up next to it, but if I clean it off I'm afraid Mrs. Diggs or somebody will be able to tell somebody's been doing something up around the window, standing there in high heels on the rim of the toilet, brushing my teeth all the time and using up Collyrium[30] by the bottleful and switching the console to audio and always needing more water before I answer the console because my mouth's too dry to talk, especially on the Parnate, the Parnate makes my mouth dry anyways. And pretty soon I'm totally paranoid they know I'm stoned, at work, sitting there in the office, high, reeking and I'm the only one that can't tell I reek, I'm like so obsessed with Do They Know, Can They Tell, and then after a while I'm having my mother call in sick for me so I can stay home after she goes in to work and have the whole place to myself with nobody to worry about Do They Know, and smoke out the fan, and spray Lysol all over and stir Ginger's litter box around so the whole place reeks of Ginger, and smoke and draw and watch terrible daytime stuff on the TP because I don't want my mother to see any cartridge-orders on days I'm supposed to be in bed sick, I start to get obsessed with Does She Know. I'm getting more and more miserable and fed up with myself for smoking so much, this is after a couple weeks of it, is all, and I start getting high and thinking about nothing except how I have to quit smoking all this Bob so I can get back to work and start saying I'm here when people call, so I can start living some kind of damn *life* instead of just sitting around in pajamas pretending I'm sick like a third-grader and smoking and watching TP again, and so after I've smoked the last of whatever I've got I always say No More, This Is It, and I throw out my papers and my one-hitter, I've probably thrown about fifty one-hitters in dumpsters, including some nice wood and brass ones, including a couple from Brazil, the land-barge guys must go through our sector's dumpster once a day looking to get another good one-hitter. And anyways I quit. I do stop. I get sick of it, I don't like what it does to me. And I go back to work and work my fanny off, to make up for the last couple weeks and get a leg up on like building momentum for a whole new start, you know?'

The young woman's face and eyes were going through a number of ranges of affective configurations, with all of them seeming inexplicably at gut-level somehow blank and maybe not entirely sincere.

'And so,' she said, 'but then I quit. And a couple of weeks after I've smoked a lot and finally stopped and quit and gone back to really living, after a couple of weeks this *feeling* always starts creeping in, just creeping in a little at the edges at first, like first thing in the morning when I get up, or waiting for the T to go home, after work, for supper. And I try to deny it, the feeling, ignore it, because I fear it more than anything.'

'The feeling you're describing, that starts creeping in.'

Kate Gompert finally took a real breath. 'And then but no matter what I do it gets worse and worse, it's there more and more, this filter drops down, and the feeling makes the fear of the feeling way worse, and after a couple weeks it's there all the time, the feeling, and I'm totally inside it, I'm in it and everything has to pass through it to get in, and I don't want to smoke any Bob, and I don't want to work, or go out, or read, or watch TP, or go out, or stay in, or either do anything or not do anything, I don't want *anything* except for the feeling to go *away*. But it doesn't. Part of the feeling is being like willing to do anything to make it go away. Understand that. *Anything.* Do you understand? It's not wanting to hurt myself it's wanting to *not hurt.*'

The doctor hadn't even pretended to try to take notes on all this. He couldn't keep himself from trying to determine whether the ambient blank insincerity the patient seemed to project during what appeared, clinically, to be a significant gamble and move toward trust and self-revealing was in fact projected by the patient or was somehow counter-transferred or -projected onto the patient from the doctor's own psyche out of some sort of anxiety over the critical therapeutic possibilities her revelation of concern over drug-use might represent. The time this thinking required looked like sober and thoughtful consideration of what Kate Gompert said. She was again gazing at her feet's interactions with the empty boating sneakers, her face moving between expressions associated with grief and suffering. None of the clinical literature the doctor had read for his psych rotation suggested any relation between unipolar episodes and withdrawal from cannabinoids.

'So this has happened in the past, prior to your other hospitalizations, then, Katherine.'

Her face, foreshortened by its downward angle, was working in the spread, writhing configurations of weeping, but no tears emerged. 'I just want you to shock me. Just get me out of this. I'll do anything you want.'

'Have you explored this possible connection between your cannabis use and your depressions with your regular therapist, Katherine?'

She did not respond directly as such. Her associations began to loosen, in the doctor's opinion, as her face continued to work dryly.

'I had shock before and it got me out of this. Straps. Nurses with their sneakers in little green bags. Anti-saliva injections. Rubber thing for your tongue. General. Just some headaches. I didn't mind it at *all.* I know everybody thinks it's horrible. That old cartridge, Nichols and the big Indian. Distortion. They give you a general here, right? They put you under. It's not that bad. I'll go willingly.'

The doctor was summarizing her choice of treatment-option, as was her right, on her chart. He had extremely good penmanship for a doctor. He put her *get me out of this* in quotation marks. He was adding his own post-assessment question, *Then what?*, when Kate Gompert began weeping for real.

And just before 0145h. on 2 April Y.D.A.U., his wife arrived back home and uncovered her hair and came in and saw the Near Eastern medical attaché and his face and tray and eyes and the soiled condition of his special recliner, and rushed to his side crying his name aloud, touching his head, trying to get a response, failing to get any response to her, he still staring straight ahead; and eventually and naturally she — noting that the expression on his rictus of a face nevertheless appeared very positive, ecstatic, even, you could say — she eventually and naturally turning her head and following his line of sight to the cartridge-viewer.

Gerhardt Schtitt, Head Coach and Athletic Director at the Enfield Tennis Academy, Enfield MA, was wooed fiercely by E.T.A. Headmaster Dr. James Incandenza, just about begged to come on board the moment the Academy's hilltop was shaved flat and the place was up and running. Incandenza had decided he was going to bring Schtitt on board or bust — this even though Schtitt had then just lately been asked to resign from the staff of a Nick Bollettieri camp in Sarasota because of a really unfortunate incident involving a riding crop.

By now, though, pretty much everybody now at E.T.A. feels as though stories about Schtitt's whole corporal-punitive thing must have been pumped up out of all sane proportion, because even though Schtitt still does favor those high and shiny black boots, and yes the epaulets, still, and now a weatherman's telescoping pointer that's a clear stand-in for the now-forbidden old riding crop, he has, Schtitt, at near what must be seventy, mellowed to the sort of elder-statesman point where he's become mostly a dispenser of abstractions rather than discipline, a philosopher instead of a king. His felt presence is here mostly verbal; the weatherman's pointer has not made corrective contact with even one athletic bottom in Schtitt's whole nine years at E.T.A.

Still, although he now has all these *Lebensgefährtins*[31] and prorectors to administer most of the necessary little character-building cruelties, Schtitt does like his occasional bit of fun, still.

So but when Schtitt dons the leather helmet and goggles and revs up the old F.R.G.-era BMW cycle and trails the sweating E.T.A. squads up the Comm. Ave. hills into East Newton on their P.M. conditioning runs, making judicious use of his pea-shooter to discourage straggling sluggards, it's usually eighteen-year-old Mario Incandenza who gets to ride along in the side-car, carefully braced and strapped, the wind blowing his thin hair straight back off his oversized head, beaming and waving his claw at people he knows. It's possibly odd that the leptosomatic Mario I., so damaged he can't even grip a stick, much less flail at a moving ball with one, is the one kid at E.T.A. whose company Schtitt seeks out, is in fact pretty much the one person with whom Schtitt speaks candidly, lets his pedagogical hair down. He's not close to his prorectors, particularly, Schtitt, and treats Aubrey deLint and Mary Esther Thode with a formality that's almost parodic. But often of a warm evening sometimes Mario and Coach Schtitt will find themselves out alone under the East Courts' canvas pavilion or the towering copper beech west of Comm.-Ad., or at one of the initial-scarred redwood picnic tables off the path out behind the Headmaster's House where Mario's mother and uncle live, Schtitt savoring a post-prandial pipe, Mario enjoying the smells of the calliopsis alongside the grounds' quincunx paths, the sweetish pines and the briers' yeasty musk coming up from the hillside's slopes. And he actually likes the sulphury odor of Schtitt's obscure Austrian blend. Schtitt talks, Mario listens, generally. Mario is basically a born listener. One of the positives to being visibly damaged is that people can sometimes forget you're there, even when they're interfacing with you. You almost get to eavesdrop. It's almost like they're like: If nobody's really in there, there's nothing to be shy about. That's why bullshit often tends to drop away around damaged listeners, deep beliefs revealed, diary-type private reveries indulged out loud; and, listening, the beaming and bradykinetic boy gets to forge an interpersonal connection he knows only he can truly feel, here.

Schtitt has the sort of creepy wiriness of old men who still exercise vigorously. He has surprised blue eyes and a vivid white crewcut of the sort that looks virile and good on men who have lost a lot of hair anyway. And skin so clean-sheet-white it almost glows; an evident immunity to the sun's UV; in pine-shaded twilight he is almost glowingly white, as if cut from the stuff of moons. He has a way of focusing his whole self's concentration very narrowly, adjusting his legs' spread for the varicoceles and curling one arm over the other and sort of drawing himself in around the pipe he attends to. Mario can sit motionless for really long periods. When Schtitt exhales pipe-smoke in different geometric shapes they both seem to study intently, when Schtitt exhales he makes little sounds variant in plosivity between P and B.

'Am realizing whole myth of efficiency and no waste that is making this continent of countries we are in.' He exhales. 'You know myths?'

'Is that like a story?'

'Ach. A made-up story. For some children. An efficiency of Euclid only: flat. For flat children. Straight ahead! Plow ahead! Go! This is myth.'

'There aren't any flat children, really.'

'This myth of the competition and bestness we fight for you players here: this myth: they assume here always the efficient way is to plow in straight, go! The story that the shortest way between two places is the straight line, yes?'

'Yes?'

Schtitt can use the stem of the pipe to point, for emphasis: 'But what then when something is in the *way* when you go between places, no? Plow ahead: go: collide: *kabong*.'

'Willikers!'

'Where is their straight shortest then, yes? Where is the efficiently quickly straight of Euclid then, yes? And how many two places are there without there is something in the way between them, if you go?'

It can be entertaining to watch the evening pines' mosquitoes light and feed deeply on luminous Schtitt, who is oblivious. The smoke doesn't keep them away.

'When I am boyish, training to compete for best, our training facilities on a sign, very largely painted, stated WE ARE WHAT WE WALK BETWEEN.'

'Gosh.'

It's a tradition, one stemming maybe from Wimbledon's All-England locker rooms' tympana, that every big-time tennis academy has its own special traditional motto on the wall in the locker rooms, some special aphoristic nugget that's supposed to describe and inform what the academy's philosophy's all about. After Mario's father Dr. Incandenza passed away, the new Headmaster, Dr. Charles Tavis, a Canadian citizen, either Mrs. Incandenza's half-brother or adoptive brother, depending on the version, C.T. had taken down Incandenza's founding motto — *TE OCCIDERE POSSUNT SED TE EDERE NON POSSUNT NEFAS EST*[32] — and had replaced it with the rather more upbeat THE MAN WHO KNOWS HIS LIMITATIONS HAS NONE.

Mario is an enormous fan of Gerhardt Schtitt, whom most of the other E.T.A. kids regard as probably bats, and as w/o doubt mind-looseningly discursive, and show the old pundit even token respect mostly because Schtitt still personally oversees the daily drill-assignments and can, if aggrieved, have Thode and deLint make them extremely uncomfortable more or less at will, out there in A.M. practice.

One of the reasons the late James Incandenza had been so terribly high on bringing Schtitt to E.T.A. was that Schtitt, like the founder himself (who'd come back to tennis, and later film, from a background in hard-core-math-based optical science), was that Schtitt approached competitive tennis more like a pure mathematician than a technician. Most jr.-tennis coaches are basically technicians, hands-on practical straight-ahead problem-solving statistical-data wonks, with maybe added knacks for short-haul psychology and motivational speaking. The point about not crunching serious stats is that Schtitt had clued Incandenza in, all the way back at a B.S. 1989[33] U.S.T.A. convention on photoelectric line-judging, that he, Schtitt, knew real tennis was really about not the blend of statistical order and expansive potential that the game's technicians revered, but in fact the opposite — *not*-order, *limit,* the places where things broke down, fragmented into beauty. That real tennis was no more reducible to delimited factors or probability curves than chess or boxing, the two games of which it's a hybrid. In short, Schtitt and the tall A.E.C.-optics man (i.e. Incandenza), whose fierce flat serve-and-haul-ass-to-the-net approach to the game had carried him through M.I.T. on a full ride w/ stipend, and whose consulting report on high-speed photoelectric tracking the U.S.T.A. mucky-mucks found dense past all comprehending, found themselves totally simpatico on tennis's exemption from stats-tracking regression. Were he now still among the living, Dr. Incandenza would now describe tennis in the paradoxical terms of what's now called 'Extra-Linear Dynamics.'[34] And Schtitt, whose knowledge of formal math is probably about equivalent to that of a Taiwanese kindergartner, nevertheless seemed to know what Hopman and van der Meer and Bollettieri seemed not to know: that locating beauty and art and magic and improvement and keys to excellence and victory in the prolix flux of match play is not a fractal matter of reducing chaos to pattern. Seemed intuitively to sense that it was a matter not of reduction at all, but — perversely — of expansion, the aleatory flutter of uncontrolled, metastatic growth — each well-shot ball admitting of n possible responses, n^2 possible responses to those responses, and on into what Incandenza would articulate to anyone who shared both his backgrounds as a Cantorian[35] continuum of infinities of possible move and response, Cantorian and beautiful because *in*foliating, *contained,* this diagnate infinity of infinities of choice and execution, mathematically uncontrolled but humanly *contained,* bounded by the talent and imagination of self and opponent, bent in on itself by the containing boundaries of skill and imagination that brought one player finally down, that kept both from winning, that made it, finally, a game, these boundaries of self.

'You mean like the baselines are boundaries?' Mario tries to ask.

'*Lieber[1] Gott[1] neih,*with a plosive disgusted sound. Schtitt likes best of all smoke-shapes to try to blow rings, and is kind of lousy at it, blowing mostly wobbly lavender hot dogs, which Mario finds delightful.

The thing with Schtitt: like most Europeans of his generation, anchored from infancy to certain permanent values which — yes, OK, granted — may, admittedly, have a whiff of proto-fascist potential about them, but which do, nevertheless (the values), anchor nicely the soul and course of a life — Old World patriarchal stuff like honor and discipline and fidelity to some larger unit — Gerhardt Schtitt does not so much dislike the modern O.N.A.N.ite U.S. of A. as find it hilarious and frightening at the same time. Probably mostly just *alien*. This should not be rendered in exposition like this, but Mario Incandenza has a severely limited range of verbatim recall. Schtitt was educated in pre-Unification *Gymnasium* under the rather Kanto-Hegelian idea that jr. athletics was basically just training for citizenship, that jr. athletics was about learning to sacrifice the hot narrow imperatives of the Self — the needs, the desires, the fears, the multiform cravings of the individual appetitive will — to the larger imperatives of a team (OK, the State) and a set of delimiting rules (OK, the Law). It sounds almost frighteningly simple-minded, though not to Mario, across the redwood table, listening. By learning, in *palestra,* the virtues that pay off directly in competitive games, the well-disciplined boy begins assembling the more abstract, gratification-delaying skills necessary for being a 'team player' in a larger arena: the even more subtly diffracted moral chaos of full-service citizenship in a State. Except Schtitt says *Ach,* but who can imagine this training serving its purpose in an experialist and waste-exporting nation that's forgotten privation and hardship and the discipline which hardship teaches by requiring? A U.S. of modern A. where the State is not a team or a code, but a sort of sloppy intersection of desires and fears, where the only public consensus a boy must surrender to is the acknowledged primacy of straight-line pursuing this flat and short-sighted idea of personal happiness:

'The happy pleasure of the person alone, yes?'

'Except why do you let deLint tie Pemulis and Shaw's shoes to the lines, if the lines aren't boundaries?'

'Without there is something bigger. Nothing to contain and give the meaning. Lonely. *Verstiegenheit.*'[36]

'Bless you.'

'Any something. The *what:* this is more unimportant than that there is *something.*'

Schtitt one time was telling Mario, as they respectively walked and tottered down Comm. Ave. eastward into Allston to see about getting a gourmet ice cream someplace along there, that when he was Mario's age — or maybe more like Hal's age, whatever — he (Schtitt) had once fallen in love with a tree, a willow that from a certain humid twilit perspective had looked like a mysterious woman aswirl with gauze, this certain tree in the public *Platz* of some West German town whose name sounded to Mario like the sound of somebody strangling. Schtitt reported being seriously smitten with the tree:

'I went daily to there, to be with the tree.'

They respectively walked and tottered, ice-cream-bound, Mario moving like the one of them who was truly old, mind off his stride because he was trying to think hard about what Schtitt believed. Mario's thinking-hard expression resembles what for another person would be the sort of comically distorted face made to amuse an infant. He was trying to think how to articulate some reasonable form of a question like: But then how does this surrender-the-personal-individual-wants-to-the-larger-State-or-beloved-tree-or-*something* stuff work in a deliberately *individual* sport like competitive junior tennis, where it's just you v. one other guy?

And then also, again, still, what are those boundaries, if they're not baselines, that contain and direct its infinite expansion inward, that make tennis like chess on the run, beautiful and infinitely dense?

Schtitt's thrust, and his one great irresistible attraction in the eyes of Mario's late father: The true opponent, the enfolding boundary, is the player himself. Always and only the self out there, on court, to be met, fought, brought to the table to hammer out terms. The competing boy on the net's other side: he is not the foe: he is more the partner in the dance. He is the what is the word *excuse* or *occasion* for meeting the self. As you are his occasion. Tennis's beauty's infinite roots are self-competitive. You compete with your own limits to transcend the self in imagination and execution. Disappear inside the game: break through limits: transcend: improve: win. Which is why tennis is an essentially tragic enterprise, to improve and grow as a serious junior, with ambitions. You seek to vanquish and transcend the limited self whose limits make the game possible in the first place. It is tragic and sad and chaotic and lovely. All life is the same, as citizens of the human State: the animating limits are within, to be killed and mourned, over and over again.

Mario thinks of a steel pole raised to double its designed height and clips his shoulder on the green steel edge of a dumpster, pirouetting halfway to the cement before Schtitt darts in to catch him, and it almost looks like they're doing a dance-floor dip as Schtitt says this game the players are all at E.T.A. to learn, this infinite system of decisions and angles and lines Mario's brothers worked so brutishly hard to master: junior athletics is but one facet of the real gem: life's endless war against the self you cannot live without.

Schtitt then falls into the sort of silence of someone who's enjoying mentally rewinding and replaying what he just came up with. Mario thinks hard again. He's trying to think of how to articulate something like: But then is battling and vanquishing the self the same as destroying yourself? Is that like saying life is pro-death? Three passing Allstonian street-kids mock and make fun of Mario's appearance behind the pair's backs. Some of Mario's thinking-faces are almost orgasmic: fluttery and slack. And then but so what's the difference between tennis and suicide, life and death, the game and its own end?

It's always Schtitt who ends up experimenting with some exotic ice-cream flavor, when they arrive. Mario always chickens out and opts for good old basic chocolate when the moment of decision at the counter comes. Thinking along the lines of like Better the flavor you know for sure you already love.

'And so. No different, maybe,' Schtitt concedes, sitting up straight on a waffle-seated aluminum chair with Mario beneath an askew umbrella that makes the flimsy little table it's rooted to shake and clank in the sidewalk's breeze. 'Maybe no different, so,' biting hard into his tricolored cone. He feels at the side of his white jaw, where there's some sort of red welt, it looks like. 'Not different' — looking out into the Ave.'s raised median at the Green Line train rattling past downhill — 'except the chance to play.' He brightens in preparation to laugh in his startling German roar, saying 'No? Yes? The chance to play, yes?' And Mario loses a dollop of chocolate down his chin, because he has this involuntary thing where he laughs whenever anyone else does, and Schtitt is finding what he has just said very amusing indeed.

YEAR OF THE DEPEND ADULT UNDERGARMENT

There is no jolly irony in Tiny Ewell's name. He is tiny, an elf-sized U.S. male. His feet barely reach the floor of the taxi. He is seated, being driven east into the grim three-decker districts of East Watertown, west of Boston proper. A rehabilitative staffer wearing custodial whites under a bombardier's jacket sits beside Tiny Ewell, big arms crossed and staring placid as a cow at the intricately creased back of the cabbie's neck. The window Tiny is next to has a sticker that thanks him in advance for not smoking. Tiny Ewell wears no winter gear over a jacket and tie that don't quite go together and stares out his window with unplacid intensity at the same district he grew up in. He normally takes involved routes to avoid Watertown. His jacket a 26S, his slacks a 26/24, his shirt one of the shirts his wife had so considerately packed for him to bring into the hospital detox and hang on hangers that won't leave the rod. As with all Tiny Ewell's business shirts, only the front and cuffs are ironed. He wears size 6 Florsheim wingtips that gleam nicely except for one big incongruous scuff-mark of white from where he'd kicked at his front door when he'd returned home just before dawn from an extremely important get-together with potential clients to find that his wife had had the locks changed and filed a restraining order and would communicate with him only by notes passed through the mail-slot below the white door's black brass (the brass had been painted black) knocker. When Tiny leans down and wipes at the scuff-mark with a slim thumb it only pales and smears. It is Tiny's first time out of Happy Slippers since his second day at the detox. They took away his Florsheims after 24 abstinent hours had passed and he started to perhaps D.T. a little. He'd kept noticing mice scurrying around his room, mice as in rodents, vermin, and when he lodged a complaint and demanded the room be fumigated at once and then began running around hunched and pounding with the heel of a hand-held Florsheim at the mice as they continued to ooze through the room's electrical outlets and scurry repulsively about, eventually a gentle-faced nurse flanked by large men in custodial whites negotiated a trade of shoes for Librium, predicting that the mild sedative would fumigate what really needed to be fumigated. They gave him slippers of green foam-rubber with smiley-faces embossed on the tops. The detox's in-patients are encouraged to call these

Happy Slippers. The staff refer to the footwear in private as 'pisscatchers.' It is Tiny Ewell's first day out of rubber slippers and ass-exposing detox pajamas and striped cotton robe in two weeks. The early-November day is foggy and colorless. The sky and the street are the same color. The trees look skeletal. There is bright wet wadded litter all along the seams of street and curb. The houses are skinny three-deckers, mashed together, wharf-gray w/ salt-white trim, madonnas in the yards, bowlegged dogs hurling themselves against the fencing. Some schoolboys in knee-pads and skallycaps are playing street hockey on a passing school's cement playground. Except none of the boys seems to be moving. The trees' bony fingers make spell-casting gestures in the wind as they pass. East Watertown is the obvious straight-line easement between St. Mel's detox and the halfway house's Enfield, and Ewell's insurance is paying for the cab. With his small round shape and bit of white goatee and a violent flush that could pass for health of some jolly sort, Tiny Ewell looks like a radically downscaled Burl Ives, the late Burl Ives as an impossible bearded child. Tiny looks out the window at the rose window of the church next to the school playground where the boys are playing/not playing. The rose window is not illuminated from either side.

The man who for the last three days has been Tiny Ewell's roommate at St. Mel's Hospital's detoxification unit sits in a blue plastic straight-back chair in front of his and Ewell's room's window's air conditioner, watching it. The air conditioner hums and gushes, and the man gazes with rapt intensity into its screen of horizontal vents. The air conditioner's cord is thick and white and leads into a three-prong outlet with black heel-marks on the wall all around it. The November room is around 12° C. The man turns the air conditioner's dial from setting #4 to setting #5. The curtains above it shake and billow around the window. The man's face falls into and out of amused expressions as he watches the air conditioner. He sits in the blue chair with a trembling Styrofoam cup of coffee and a paper plate of brownies into which he taps ashes from the cigarettes whose smoke the air conditioner blows straight back over his head. The cigarette smoke is starting to pile up against the wall behind him, and to ooze and run chilled down the wall and form a sort of cloud-bank near the floor. The man's raptly amused profile appears in the mirror on the wall beside the dresser the two in-patients share. The man, like Tiny Ewell, has the rouged-corpse look that attends detox from late-stage alcoholism. The man is in addition a burnt-yellow beneath his flush, from chronic hepatitis. The mirror he appears in is treated with shatterproof Lucite polymers. The man leans carefully forward with the plate of brownies in his lap and changes the setting on the air conditioner from 5 to 3 and then to 7, then 8, scanning the screen of gushing vents. He finally turns the selector's dial all the way around to 9. The air conditioner roars and blows his long hair straight back, and his beard blows back over his shoulder, ashes fly and swirl around from his plate of brownies, plus crumbs, and his rodney's tip glows cherry and gives sparks. He is deeply engaged by whatever he sees on 9. He gives Tiny Ewell the screaming meemies, Ewell has complained. He wears pisscatchers, a striped cotton St. Mel's robe, and a pair of glasses missing one lens. He has been watching the air conditioner all day. His face produces the little smiles and grimaces of a person who's being thoroughly entertained.

When the big black rehabilitative staffer placed Tiny Ewell in the taxi and then squeezed in and told the cabbie they wanted Unit #6 in the Enfield Marine VA Hospital Complex just off Commonwealth Ave. in Enfield, the cabbie, whose photo was on the Mass. Livery License taped to the glove compartment, the cabbie, looking back and down at little Tiny Ewell's neat white beard and ruddy complexion and sharp threads, had scratched under his skallycap and asked if he was sick or something.

Tiny Ewell had said, 'So it would seem.'

By mid-afternoon on 2 April Y.D.A.U.: the Near Eastern medical attaché; his devout wife; the Saudi Prince Q——'s personal physician's personal assistant, who'd been sent over to see why the medical attaché hadn't appeared at the Back Bay Hilton in the A.M. and then hadn't answered his beeper's page; the personal physician himself, who'd come to see why his personal assistant hadn't come back; two Embassy security guards w/ sidearms, who'd been dispatched by a candidiatic, heartily pissed-off Prince Q——; and two neatly groomed Seventh Day Adventist pamphleteers who'd seen human heads through the living room window and found the front door unlocked and come in with all good spiritual intentions — all were watching the recursive loop the medical attaché had rigged on the TP's viewer the night before, sitting and standing there very still and attentive, looking not one bit distressed or in any way displeased, even though the room smelled very bad indeed.

O

30 APRIL — YEAR OF THE DEPEND ADULT UNDERGARMENT

He sat alone above the desert, redly backlit and framed in shale, watching very yellow payloaders crawl over the beaten dirt of some U.S.A. construction site several km. to the southeast. The outcropping's height allowed him, Marathe, to look out over most of U.S.A. area code 6026. His shadow did not yet reach the downtown regions of the city Tucson; not yet quite. Of sounds in the arid hush were only a faint and occasional hot wind, the blurred sound of the wings of sometimes an insect, some tentative trickling of loosened grit and small stones moving farther down the upslope behind.

And as well the sunset over the foothills and mountains behind him: such a difference from the watery and somehow sad spring sunsets of south-western Québec's Papineau regions, where his wife had need of care. This (the sunset) more resembled an explosion. It took place above and behind him, and he turned some of the time to regard it: it (the sunset) was swollen and perfectly round, and large, radiating knives of light when he squinted. It hung and trembled slightly like a viscous drop about to fall. It hung just above the peaks of the Tortolita foothills behind him (Marathe), and slowly was sinking.

Marathe sat alone and blanket-lapped in his customized *fauteuil de roll-ent*[37] on a kind of outcropping or shelf about halfway up, waiting, amusing himself with his shadow. As the lowering light from behind came at an angle more and more acute, Goethe's well-known '*Bröckengespenst*' phenome-non[38] enlarged and distended his seated shadow far out overland, so that the spokes of his chair's rear wheels cast over two whole counties below gigantic asterisk-shadows, whose fine black radial lines he could cause to move by playing slightly with the wheels' rubber rims; and his head's shadow brought to much of the suburb West Tucson a premature dusk.

He appeared to remain concentrated on his huge shadow-play as gravel and then also breath sounded from the steep hillside back above him, grit and dirty stones cascading onto the outcropping and gushing past his chair and off the front lip, and then the unmistakable yelp of an individual's impact with a cactus somewhere up behind. But Marathe, he had all the time without turning watched the other man's clumsy sliding descent's own mammoth shadow, cast as far east as the Rincon range just past the city Tucson, and could see the shadow rush in west toward his own as Un-specified Services' M. Hugh Steeply descended, falling twice and cursing in U.S.A. English, until the shadow collapsed nearly into Marathe's monstrous own. Another yelp took place as the Unspecified Services field-operative's fall and slide the last several meters carried him upon his bottom down onto the outcropping and then nearly all the way out and off it, Marathe having to release the machine pistol under his blanket to grab Steeply's bare arm and halt this sliding. Steeply's skirt was pulled obscenely up and his hosiery full of runs and stubs of thorns. The operative sat at Marathe's feet, glowing redly in the backlight, legs hanging over the shelf's edge, breathing with difficulty.

Marathe smiled and released the operative's arm. 'Stealth becomes you,' he said.

'Go shit in your chapeau,' Steeply wheezed, bring up his legs to survey the hosiery's damage.

They spoke for the most part U.S.A. English when they met like this, covertly, in the field. M. Fortier[39] had wished Marathe to require that they interface always in Québecois French, as for a small symbolic concession to the A.F.R. on the part of the Office of Unspecified Services, which the Québecois Sepératiste Left referred to always as B.S.S., the 'Bureau des Services sans Spécificité.'

Marathe watched a column of shadow spread again out east over the desert's floor as Steeply got a hand under himself and rose, a huge and well-fed figure tottering on heels. The two men sent together a strange Bröckengespenst-shadow out toward the city Tucson, a shadow round and radial at the base and jagged at the top, from Steeply's wig becoming uncombed in his descent. Steeply's gigantic prosthetic breasts pointed in wildly different directions now, one nearly at the empty sky. The matte curtain of sunset's true dusk-shadow was moving itself very slowly in across the Rincons and Sonora desert east of the city Tucson, still many km. from obscuring their own large shadow.

But once Marathe had committed not just to pretend to betray his Assassins des Fauteuils Rollents in order to secure advanced medical care for the medical needs of his wife, but to in truth do this — betray, perfidiously: now pretending only to M. Fortier and his A.F.R. superiors that he was merely pretending to feed some betraying information to B.S.S.[40] — once this decision, Marathe was without all power, served now at the pleasures of the power of Steeply and the B.S.S. of Hugh Steeply: and now they spoke mostly the U.S.A. English of Steeply's preference.

In fact, Steeply's Québecois was better than Marathe's English, but c'était la guerre, as one says.

Marathe sniffed slightly. 'Thus, so, we now are both here.' He wore a windbreaker and did not perspire.

Steeply's eyes were luridly made up. The rear area of his dress was dirty. Some of his makeup had started to run. He was forming a type of salute to shade his eyes and looking upward behind them at what remained of the explosive and trembling sun. 'How in God's name did you get up here?'

Marathe slowly shrugged. As usual, he appeared to Steeply as if he were half-asleep. He ignored the question and said only, shrugging, 'My time is finite.'

Steeply had also with him a woman's handbag or purse. 'And the wife?' he said, gazing upward as yet. 'How's the wife doing?'

'Holding her own weight, thank you,' Marathe said. His tone of his voice betrayed nothing. 'And so thus what is it your Offices believe they wish to know?'

Steeply tottered on a leg as he removed one shoe and poured from it grit.

'Nothing terribly surprising. A bit of razzle-dazzle up northeast in your so-called Ops-area, certainly you heard.'

Marathe sniffed. A large odor of inexpensive and high-alcohol perfume came not from Steeply's person but from his handbag, which failed to complement his shoes. Marathe said, 'Dazzle?'

'As in a civilian-type individual receives a certain item. Don't tell me this is news to you guys. Not on InterLace pulse, this item. Arrives via normal physical mail. We're sure you heard, Rémy. A cartridge-copy of a certain let's call it between ourselves "the Entertainment." As in in the mail, without warning or motive. Out of the blue.'

'From somewhere blue?'

The B.S.S. operative had perspired also through his rouge, and his mascara had melted to become whorish. 'A person with no political value to anybody except that the Saudi Ministry of Entertainment made one the hell of a shrill stink.'

'The medical attaché, the specialist of digesting, you refer to.' Marathe shrugged again in that maddening Francophone way that can mean several things. 'Your offices wish to ask was the Entertainment's cartridge disseminated through our mechanisms?'

'Don't let's waste your finite time, ami old friend,' Steeply said. 'The mischief happens to occur in metropolitan Boston. Postal codes route the package through the desert Southwest, and we know your dissemination-scheme's routing mechanism is proposed for somewhere between Phoenix and the border down here.' Steeply had worked hard at feminizing his expressions and gesturing. 'It would be a bit starry-eyed of O.U.S. not to think of your distinguished cell, no?'

Beneath Marathe's windbreaker was a sportshirt whose breast pocket was filled with many pens. He said: 'Us, we don't have the information on even casualties. From this blue dazzle you speak of.'

Steeply was trying to extract something stubborn from inside his other shoe. 'Upwards of twenty, Rémy. Out of commission altogether. The attaché and his wife, the wife a Saudi citizen. Four more raggers, all with embassy cards. Couple neighbors or something. The rest mostly police before word got to a level they could stop police from going in before they killed the power.'

'Local police forces. Gendarmes.'

'The local constabulary.'

'The minions of the law of the land.'

'The local constabulary were shall we say *unprepared* for an Entertainment like this.' Steeply even removed and replaced his pumps in the upright-on-one-leg-bringing-other-foot-up-behind-his-bottom way of a feminine U.S.A. woman. But he appeared huge and bloated as a woman, not merely unattractive but inducing something like sexual despair. He said, 'The attaché had diplomatic status, Rémy. Mideast. Saudi. Said to be close to minor members of the royal family.'

Marathe sniffed hard, as if congested of the nose. 'A puzzling,' he said.

'But also a compatriot of yours. Canadian citizenship. Born in Ottawa, to Arab émigrés. Visa lists a residence in Montreal.'

'And Services Without Specificity wishes maybe to ask were there below-the-surface connections that make the individual not such a civilian, unconnected. To ask of us would the A.F.R. wish to make of him the example.'

Steeply was removing dirt from his bottom, swatting himself on the bottom. He stood more or less directly over Marathe. Marathe sniffed. 'We have neither digestive medicals nor diplomatic entourages on any lists for action. You have personally seen A.F.R.'s initial lists. Nor in particular Montreal civilians. We have, as one will say, larger seafood to cook.'

Steeply was looking out over the desert and city, also, as he swatted at himself. He seemed to have noticed the *gespenst*-phenomenon of his own shadow. Marathe for some reason pretended again to sniff the nose. The wind was moderate and constant and of about the temperature of a U.S.A. clothes-dryer set on Low. It made the shrill whistling sounds. Also sounds of the blowing grit. Weeds-of-tumbling like enormous hairballs rolled often across the Interstate Highway of I-10 far below. Their specular perspective, the reddening light on vast tan stone and the oncoming curtain of dusk, the further elongation of their monstrous agnate shadows: all was almost mesmerizing. Neither man seemed able to look at anything but the vista below. Marathe could simultaneously speak in English and think in French. The desert was the tawny color of the hide of the lion. Their speaking without looking at one another, facing both the same direction — this gave their conversing an air of careless intimacy, as of old friends at the cartridge-viewer together, or a long-married couple. Marathe thought this as he opened and closed his upheld hand, making over the city Tucson a huge and black blossom open itself and close itself.

And Steeply raised his bare arms and held them out and crossed them, maybe as if signalling for distant aid; this made X's and pedentive V's over much in the city Tucson. 'Still, Rémy, but born in the hated-by-you Ottawa, this civilian attaché, and connected to a major buyer of trans-grid entertainment. And follow-up out of the Boston offices reports possible indications of the victim's prior possible involvement with the widow of the *auteur* we both know was responsible for the Entertainment in the first place. The *samizdat*.'

'Prior?'

Steeply produced from his handbag Belgian cigarettes of a many-mm. and habitually female type. 'Film director's wife'd taught out at Brandeis where the victim'd done his residency. The husband was on board over at A.E.C., and different agencies' background checks indicated the wife was fucking just about everything with a pulse.' With the slight pause of which Steeply could excel: 'Particularly a Canadian pulse.'

'Involvement of sexuality is what you are meaning, then, not politics.'

Steeply said, 'This wife herself a Québecer, Rémy, from L'Islet county — Chief Tine says three years spent on Ottawa's "*Personnes Qui On Doit*" list. There's such a thing as political sex.'

'I have said to you all we know. Civilians as individual warnings to O.N.A.N. are not our desire. This is known by you.' Marathe's eyes looked nearly closed. 'And your tits, they have become cock-eyed, I will tell you. Services Without Specificity, they have given you ridiculous tits, and now they point differently.'

Steeply looked down at himself. One of the false breasts (surely false: surely they would not go as far as the hormonal, Marathe thought) nearly touched the chins of Steeply when his looking down produced his double chins. 'I was asked to secure personal verification, is all,' he said. 'My general sense at the Office is the brass consider the whole incident a stumper. There're theories and countertheories. There are even antitheories positing error, mistaken identity, sick hoax.' His shrugging, with his hands on the prosthesis, appeared not at all Gallic. 'Still: twenty-three human beings lost for all time: that'd be some hoax, no?'

Marathe sniffed. 'Asked to verify by our mutual M. Tine? How you call him: "Rod, a God"?'

(Rodney Tine, Sr., Chief of Unspecified Services, acknowledged architect of O.N.A.N. and continental Reconfiguration, who held the ear of the White House of U.S.A., and whose stenographer had long doubled as the stenographer-cum-*jeune-fille-de-Vendredi* of M. DuPlessis, former asst. coordinator of the pan-Canadian Resistance, and whose passionate, ill-disguised attachment (Tine's) to this double-amaneunsis — one Mlle. Luria Perec, of Lamartine, county L'Islet, Québec — gave rise to these questions of the high-level loyalties of Tine, whether he 'doubled'[41] for Québec out of the love for Luria or 'tripled' the loyalties, pretending only to divulge secrets while secretly maintaining his U.S.A. fealty against the pull of an irresistible love, it was said.)

'*The*, Rémy.' It was clear that Steeply could not fix his breasts' directions without pulling down severely his décolletage, which he was shy to do. He produced from his handbag sunglasses and put on the sunglasses. They were embellished with rhinestones and looked absurd. 'Rod *the* God.'

Marathe forced himself to say nothing of their appearance. Steeply tried with several matches to light a cigarette in the wind. The encroachment of true dusk began to erase his wig's chaotic shadow. Electric lights began to twinkle in the Rincon foothills east of the city. Steeply tried somewhat to cup his body around the match, for shelter for the flame.

It's a herd of feral hamsters, a major herd, thundering across the yellow plains of the southern reaches of the Great Concavity in what used to be Vermont, raising dust that forms a uremic-hued cloud with somatic shapes interpretable from as far away as Boston and Montreal. The herd is descended from two domestic hamsters set free by a Watertown NY boy at the beginning of the Experialist migration in the subsidized Year of the Whopper. The boy now attends college in Champaign IL and has forgotten that his hamsters were named Ward and June.

The noise of the herd is tornadic, locomotival. The expression on the hamsters' whiskered faces is businesslike and implacable — it's that implacable-herd expression. They thunder eastward across pedalferrous terrain that today is fallow, denuded. To the east, dimmed by the fulvous cloud the hamsters send up, is the vivid verdant ragged outline of the annularly overfertilized forests of what used to be central Maine.

All these territories are now property of Canada.

With respect to a herd of this size, please exercise the sort of common sense that come to think of it would keep your thinking man out of the southwest Concavity anyway. Feral hamsters are not pets. They mean business. Wide berth advised. Carry nothing even remotely vegetablish if in the path of a feral herd. If in the path of such a herd, move quickly and calmly in a direction perpendicular to their own. If American, north not advisable. Move south, calmly and in all haste, toward some border metropolis — Rome NNY or Glens Falls NNY or Beverly MA, say, or those bordered points between them at which the giant protective ATHSCME fans atop the hugely convex protective walls of anodized Lucite hold off the drooling and piss-colored bank of teratogenic Concavity clouds and move the bank well back, north, away, jaggedly, over your protected head.

The heavy-tongued English of Steeply was even more difficult to understand with a cigarette in the mouth. He said, 'And you'll of course report this little interface of you and me right back to Fortier.'

Marathe shrugged. ''n sûr.'

Steeply got it lit. He was a large and soft man, some type of brutal-U.S.-contact-sport athlete now become fat. He appeared to Marathe to look less like a woman than a twisted parody of womanhood. Electrolysis had caused patches of tiny red pimples along his jowls and upper lip. He also held his elbow out, the arm holding the match for lighting, which is how no woman lights a cigarette, who is used to breasts and keeps the lighting elbow in. Also Steeply teetered ungracefully on his pumps' heels on the stone's uneven surface. He never for a moment turned his back completely at Marathe as he stood on the lip of the outcropping. And Marathe had his chair's wheels' clamps now locked down tight and a firm grip on the machine pistol's pebbled grip. Steeply's purse was small and glossy black, and the sunglasses he wore had womanly frames with small false jewels at the temples. Marathe believed that something in Steeply enjoyed his grotesque appearance and craved the humiliation of the field-disguises his B.S.S. superiors requested of him.

Steeply now looked at him, in probability, behind the dark glasses. 'And also that I just right now asked you if you'd report it, and that you said *bien sûr?*'

Marathe's laugh had this misfortune to sound false and overhearty, whether or not sincere. He made a mustache of his finger, pretending for some reason to stifle a need to sneeze. 'You verify this because of why?'

Steeply scratched under the hem of his blonde wig with (stupidly, dangerously) the thumb of his hand that held the cigarette. 'Well you are already tripling, Rémy, aren't you? Or would it be quadrupling. We know Fortier and the A.F.R. know you're here with me now.'

'But do my brothers on wheels know that you are knowing this, that they have sent me to pretend I double?'

Marathe's sidearm, a Sterling UL35 9 mm machine pistol with a Mag Na Port silencer, did not have a safety. Its fat and texture-of-pebbles grip was hot from Marathe's palm, and in turn caused Marathe's palm to perspire beneath the blanket. From Steeply there merely was silence.

Marathe said: '. . . have I merely *pretended* to pretend to pretend to betray.'[42]

And the desert U.S.A.'s light had become now sad, more than half the round sun gone behind the Tortolitas. Only now the chair's wheels and Steeply's thick legs cast shadows below the dusk-line, and these shadows were becoming squat and retreating back up toward the two men.

Steeply did a brief pretend-Charleston, playing with his legs' shadows. 'Nothing personal. You know that. It's the obsessive caution. Who was it — who once said we get paid to drive ourselves crazy, the caution thing? You guys and Tine — your DuPlessis always suspected he tried to hold back on the information he passed sexually to Luria.'

Marathe shrugged hard. 'And abruptly M. DuPlessis has now passed away from life. Under circumstances of almost ridiculous suspicion.' Again with the false-sounding laugh. 'An inept burglary and grippe indeed.'

Both men were silent. Steeply's left arm had on it a nasty mesquite scratch, Marathe could observe.

Marathe finally glanced at his watch, its dial illuminated in his body's shadow. Both men's shadows were now climbing the steep incline, returning up to them. 'Me, I think that we go about our affairs in a more simple manner than your B.S.S. office. If M. Tine's betrayal were incomplete, we of Québec would be aware.'

'Because of Luria.'

Marathe pretended to fuss with his blanket, rearranging it. 'But yes. The caution. Luria would be aware.'

Steeply stepped gingerly up to the edge and tossed out his cigarette's stub. The wind caught the stub and it soared slightly upward from his hand, moving east. Both men were silent until the butt fell and hit the dark mountainside off below them, a tiny bloom of orange. Their silence then became contemplative. Something tight in the air between them loosened. Marathe no longer felt the sun on his skull. Dusk settled about them. Steeply had found his triceps' scratch and twisted the flesh of his arm to examine it, his rouged lips rounded with concern.

YEAR OF THE DEPEND ADULT UNDERGARMENT

Tuesday, 3 November, Enfield Tennis Academy: A.M. drills, shower, eat, class, lab, class, class, eat, prescriptive-grammar exam, lab/class, conditioning run, P.M. drills, play challenge match, play challenge match, upper-body circuits in weight room, sauna, shower, slump to locker-room floor w/ other players.

'. . . to even realize what they're sitting there feeling is unhappiness? Or to even feel it in the first place?'

1640h.: the Comm.-Ad. Bldg.'s males' locker room is full of clean upperclassmen in towels after P.M. matches, the players' hair wet-combed and shining with Barbicide. Pemulis uses the comb's big-toothed end to get that wide-furrowed look that kids from Allston favor. Hal's own hair tends to look wet-combed even when it's dry.

'So,' Jim Troeltsch says, looking around. 'So what do you think?'

Pemulis lowers himself to the floor by the sinks, leaning up against the cabinet where they keep all the disinfectants. He has this way of looking warily to either side of him before he says anything. 'Was there like a central point to all that, Troeltsch?'

'The exam was talking about the syntax of Tolstoy's sentence, not about real unhappy families,' Hal says quietly.

John Wayne, as do most Canadians, lifts one leg slightly to fart, like the fart was some kind of task, standing at his locker, waiting for his feet to get dry enough to put on socks.

There is a silence. Showerheads dribble on tile. Steam hangs. Distant ghastly sounds from T. Schacht over in one of the stalls off the showers. Everyone stares into the middle distance, stunned with fatigue. Michael Pemulis, who can stand about ten seconds of communal silence tops, clear his throat deeply and sends a loogie up and back into the sink behind him. The plate mirrors caught part of its quivering flight, Hal sees. Hal closes his eyes.

'Tired,' someone exhales.

Ortho Stice and John ('N.R.') Wayne seem less fatigued than detached; they have the really top player's way of shutting the whole neural net down for brief periods, staring at the space they took up, hooded in silence, removed, for a moment, from the connectedness of all events.

'Right then,' Troeltsch says. 'Pop quiz. Pop test-question. Most crucial difference, for Leith tomorrow, between your historical broadcast TV set and a cartridge-capable TP.'

Disney R. Leith teaches E.T.A.'s History of Entertainment I and II as well as certain high-level esoteric Optics things you needed Permission of Inst. to get into.

'The Cathodeluminescent Panel. No cathode gun. No phosphenic screen. Two to the screen's diagonal width in cm. lines of resolution, total.'

'You mean a high-def. viewer in general, or a specifically TP-component viewer?'

'No analogs,' Struck says.

'No snow, no faint weird like ghostly double next to UHF images, no vertical roll when planes fly over.'

'Analogs v. digitals.'

'You referring to broadcast as in network versus a TP, or network-plus-cable versus a TP?'

'Did cable TV use analogs? What, like pre-fiber phones?'

'It's the digitals. Leith has that word he uses for the shift from analogs to digitals. That word he uses about eleven times an hour.'

'What did pre-fiber phones use, exactly?'

'The old tin-can-and-string principle.'

' "Seminal." He keeps saying it. "Seminal, seminal." '

'The biggest advance in home communications since the phone he says.'

'In home entertainment since the TV itself.'

'Leith might say the Write-Capable CD, for entertainment.'

'He's hard to pin down if you get him on entertainment qua entertainment.'

'The Diz'll say use your own judgment,' Pemulis says. 'Axford took it last year. He wants an argument made. He'll skewer you if you treat it like there's an obvious answer.'

'Plus there's the InterLace de-digitizer instead of an antenna, with a TP,' Jim Struck says, squeezing at something behind his ear. Graham ('Yardguard') Rader is checking his underarm for more hair. Freer and Shaw might be asleep.

Stice has pulled his towel down slightly and is fingering the deep red abdominal stripe a jock's waistband leaves. 'Boys, I ever become president, the first thing to go's elastic.'

Troeltsch pretends to shuffle cards. 'Next item. Next like flash-card. Define *acutance*. Anybody?'

'A measure of resolution directly proportional to the resolved ratio of a given pulse's digital code,' Hal says.

'The Incster has the last word once again,' says Struck. Which invites a chorus:

'The Halster.'

'Halorama.'

'Halation.'

'Halation,' Rader says. 'A halo-shaped exposure-pattern around light sources seen on chemical film at low speed.'

'That most angelic of distortions.'

Struck says 'We'll be like *vying* for the seats all around Inc tomorrow.' Hal shuts his eyes: he can see the page of text right there, all highlighted, all yellowed up.

'He can scan the page, rotate it, fold the corner down and clean under his nails with it, all mentally.'

'Leave him alone,' Pemulis says.

Freer opens his eyes. 'Do a dictionary-page for us, man, Inc.'

Stice says 'Leave him be.'

It's all only half-nasty. Hal is placid about getting his balls smacked around; they all are. He does his share of chops-busting. Some of the littler kids who take their showers after the upperclassmen are hanging around listening. Hal sits on the floor, quiescent, chin on his chest, just thinking it's nice finally to breathe and get enough air.

The temperature had fallen with the sun. Marathe listened to the cooler evening wind roll across the incline and desert floor. Marathe could sense or feel many million floral pores begin slowly to open, hopeful of dew. The American Steeply produced small exhalations between his teeth as he examined his scratch of the arm. Only one or two remaining tips of the digitate spikes of the radial blades of the sun found crevices between the Tortolitas' peaks and probed at the roof of the sky. There were the slight and dry locationless rustlings of small living things that wish to come out at night, emerging. The sky was violet.

Everyone in the locker room's got a towel around his waist like a kilt. Everyone except Stice has a white E.T.A. towel; Stice uses his own sort of trademark towels, black ones. After a silence Stice shoots some air out through his nose. Jim Struck picks liberally at his face and neck. There are one or two sighs. Peter Beak and Evan Ingersoll and Kent Blott, twelve, eleven, ten, are up sitting on the blond-wood benches that run in front of the lockers' rows, sitting there in towels, elbows on knees, not taking part. So is Zoltan Csikzentmihalyi, who's sixteen but speaks very little English. Idris Arslanian, new this year, ethnically vague, fourteen, all feet and teeth, is a shadowy lurking presence just outside the locker-room door, poking the non-Caucasoid snout in occasionally and then withdrawing, terribly shy.

Each E.T.A. player in 18-and-Unders has like four to six 14-and-Unders kids he's supposed to keep his more experienced wing over, look out for. The more the E.T.A. administration trusts you, the younger and more generally clueless the little kids in your charge. Charles Tavis instituted the practice and calls it the Big Buddy System in the literature he sends new kids' parents. So the parents can feel their kid's not getting lost in the institutional shuffle. Beak, Blott, and Arslanian are all in Hal's Big Buddy group for Y.D.A.U. He also in effect has Ingersoll, having traded Todd ('Postal-Weight') Possalthwaite to Axford off the books for Ingersoll, because Trevor Axford found he so despised the Ingersoll kid for some unanalyzable reason that he was struggling against a horrible compulsion to put Ingersoll's little fingers into the gap by the hinges of an open door and then very slowly close the door, and came to Hal almost in tears, Axford had. Though technically Ingersoll is still Axford's and Possalthwaite Hal's. Possalthwaite, the great lobber, has a weird young-old face and little wet lips that lapse into a sucking reflex under stress. In theory, a Big Buddy's somewhere between an R.A. and a prorector. He's there to answer questions, ease bumpy transitions, show ropes, act as liaison with Tony Nwangi and Tex Watson and the other prorectors specializing in little kids. Be somebody they can come to off the record. A shoulder to climb up on a footstool and cry on. If a 16-and-Under gets made a Big Buddy it's kind of an honor; it means they think you're going places. When there's no tournament or travel, etc., Big Buddies get together with their quar-to-sextet in small-group private twice a week, in the interval between P.M. challenge matches and dinner, usually after saunas and showers and a few minutes of sitting slumped around the locker room sucking air. Sometimes Hal sits with his Little Buddies at dinner and eats with them. Not often, however. The savvier Big Buddies don't get too overly close with their L.B. ephebes, don't let them forget about the unbridgeable gaps of experience and ability and general status that separate ephebes from upperclassmen who've hung in and stuck it out at E.T.A. for years and years. Gives them more to look up to. The savvy Big Buddy doesn't rush in or tread heavy; he holds his own ground and lets the suppliants realize when they need his help and come to him. You have to know when to tread in and take an active hand and when to hang back and let the littler kids learn from the personal experience they'll have to learn from, inevitably, if they want to be able to hang. Every year, the biggest source of attrition, besides graduating 18s, is 13–15s who've had enough and just can't hang. This happens; the administration accepts it; not everyone's cut out for what's required of you here. Though C.T. makes his administrative assistant Lateral Alice Moore drive the prorectors bats trying to ferret out data on littler kids' psychic states, so he can forecast probable burnouts and attritive defections, so he'll know how many slots he and Admissions'll have to offer Incomings for the next term. Big Buddies are in a tricky position, requested to keep the prorectors generally informed about who among their charges seems shaky in terms of resolve, capacity for suffering and stress, physical punishment, homesickness, deep fatigue, but at the same time wanting to remain a trust-worthy confidential shoulder and wing for their Little Buddies' most private and delicate issues.

Though he, too, has to struggle with a strange urge to be cruel to Inger-soll, who reminds him of someone he dislikes but can't quite place, Hal on the whole rather likes being a Big B. He likes being there to come to, and likes delivering little unpretentious minilectures on tennis theory and E.T.A. pedagogy and tradition, and getting to be kind in a way that costs him nothing. Sometimes he finds out he believes something that he doesn't even know he believed until it exits his mouth in front of five anxious little hair-less plump trusting clueless faces. The twice-weekly (more like once-weekly, as things usually pan out) group interfaces with his quintet are unpleasant only after a particularly bad P.M. session on the courts, when he's tired and on edge and would far rather go off by himself and do secret stuff in under-ground ventilated private.

Jim Troeltsch feels at his glands. John Wayne is of the sock-and-a-shoe, sock-and-a-shoe school.

'Tired,' Ortho Stice again sighs. He pronounces it 'tard.' To a man, now, the upperclassmen are down slumped on the locker room's blue crush car-pet, their legs straight out in front of them, toes pointing out at that distinc-tive morgue-angle, their backs up against the blue steel of the lockers, careful to avoid the six sharp little louvered antimildew vents at each locker's base. All of them look a bit silly naked because of their tennis tans: legs and arms the deep sienna of a quality catcher's mitt, from the summer, the tan just now this late starting to fade, but feet and ankles of toadbelly-white, the white of the grave, with chests and shoulders and upper arms more like off-white — the players can sit shirtless in the stands at tourna-ments when they're not playing and get at least a bit of thoracic sun. The faces are the worst, maybe, most red and shiny, some still deep-peeling from three straight weeks of outdoor tournaments in August-September. Besides Hal, who's atavistically dark-complected anyway, the ones here with the least bad piebald coloring are the players who can tolerate spraying them-selves down with Lemon Pledge before outdoor play. It turns out Lemon Pledge, when it's applied in pre-play stasis and allowed to dry to a thin crust, is a phenomenal sunscreen, UV-rating like 40+, and the only stuff anywhere that can survive a three-set sweat. No one knows what jr. player at what academy found this out about Pledge, years back, or how: rather bizarre discovery-circumstances are envisioned. The smell of sweat-wet Pledge out on the court makes some of the more delicately constituted kids sick, though. Others feel sunscreen of any kind to be unconscionably pussified, like white visors or on-court sunglasses. So most of the E.T.A. upperclassmen have these vivid shoe-and-shirt tans that give them the classic look of bodies hastily assembled from different bodies' parts, especially when you throw in the heavily muscled legs and usually shallow chests and the two arms of different sizes.

'Tard tard tard,' Stice says.

Group empathy is expressed via sighs, further slumping, small spastic gestures of exhaustion, the soft clanks of skulls' backs against the lockers' thin steel.

'My bones are ringing the way sometimes people say their ears are ringing, I'm so tired.'

'I'm waiting til the last possible second to even breathe. I'm not expanding the cage till driven by necessity of air.'

'So tired it's out of *tired*'s word-range,' Pemulis says. '*Tired* just doesn't do it.'

'Exhausted, shot, depleted,' says Jim Struck, grinding at his closed eye with the heel of his hand. 'Cashed. Totalled.'

'Look.' Pemulis pointing at Struck. 'It's trying to think.'

'A moving thing to see.'

'Beat. Worn the heck out.'

'Worn the *fuck*-all out is more like.'

'Wrung dry. Whacked. Tuckered out. More dead than alive.'

'None even come close, the words.'

'Word-inflation,' Stice says, rubbing at his crewcut so his forehead wrinkles and clears. 'Bigger and better. Good greater greatest totally great. Hyperbolic and hyperbolicker. Like grade-inflation.'

'Should be so lucky,' says Struck, who's been on academic probation since fifteen.

Stice is from a part of southwest Kansas that might as well be Oklahoma. He makes the companies that give him clothes and gear give him all black clothes and gear, and his E.T.A. cognomen is 'The Darkness.'

Hal raises his eyebrows at Stice and smiles. 'Hyperbolicker?'

'My daddy as a boy, he'd have said "tuckered out"'ll do just fine.'

'Whereas here we are sitting here needing whole new words and terms.'

'Phrases and clauses and models and structures,' Troeltsch says, referring again to a prescriptive exam everyone but Hal wishes now to forget. 'We need an inflation-generative grammar.'

Keith Freer makes a motion as if taking his unit out of his towel and holding it out at Troeltsch: 'Generate this.'

'Need a whole new syntax for fatigue on days like this,' Struck says. 'E.T.A.'s best minds on the problem. Whole thesauruses digested, analyzed.' Makes a sarcastic motion. 'Hal?'

One semion that still works fine is holding your fist up and cranking at it with the other hand so the finger you're giving somebody goes up like a drawbridge. Though of course Hal's mocking himself at the same time. Everybody agrees it speaks volumes. Idris Arslanian's shoes and incisors appear briefly in the doorway's steam, then withdraw. Everyone's reflection is sort of cubist in the walls' shiny tiling. The name handed down paternally from an Umbrian five generations past and now much diluted by N.E. Yankee, a great-grandmother with Pima-tribe Indian S.W. blood, and Canadian cross-breeding, Hal is the only extant Incandenza who looks in any way ethnic. His late father had been as a young man darkly tall, high flat Pima-tribe cheekbones and very black hair Brylcreemed back so tight there'd been a kind of enforced widow's peak. Himself had looked ethnic, but he isn't extant. Hal is sleek, sort of radiantly dark, almost otterish, only slightly tall, eyes blue but darkly so, and unburnable even w/o sunscreen, his untanned feet the color of weak tea, his nose ever unpeeling but slightly shiny. His sleekness isn't oily so much as moist, milky; Hal worries secretly that he looks half-feminine. His parents' pregnancies must have been all-out chromosomatic war: Hal's eldest brother Orin had got the Moms's Anglo-Nordo-Canadian phenotype, the deep-socketed and lighter-blue eyes, the faultless posture and incredible flexibility (Orin was the only male anybody at E.T.A.'d ever heard of who could do a fully splayed cheerleader-type split), the rounder and more protrusive zygomatics.

Hal's next-oldest brother Mario doesn't seem to resemble much of anyone they know.

On most of the nontravel days that he doesn't Big Buddy with his charges, Hal will wait till most everybody's busy in the sauna and shower and stow his sticks in his locker and stroll casually down the cement steps into E.T.A.'s system of tunnels and chambers. He has some way he can casually drift off and have quite a while go by before anyone even notices his absence. He'll often stroll casually back into the locker room just as people are slumped on the floor in towels discussing fatigue, carrying his gear bag and substantially altered in mood, and go in when most of the littler kids are in there peeling Pledge-husks off their limbs and taking their turn showering, and shower, using one of the kids' shampoo out of a bottle shaped like a cartoon character, then hike the head back and apply Visine in a Schacht-free stall, gargle and brush and floss and dress, usually not even needing to comb his hair. He carries Visine AC, mint-flavored floss, and a traveller's toothbrush in a pocket of his Dunlop gear bag. Ted Schacht, big into oral hygiene, regards Hal's bag's floss and brush as an example to them all.

'So tired it's like I'm almost high.'

'But not pleasantly high,' Troeltsch says.

'It'd be a pleasanter tiredness-high if I didn't have to wait till fucking 1900 to start all this studyin',' Stice says.

'You'd think Schtitt could at least not turn up the juice the week before midterms.'

'You'd think that the coaches and the teachers could try and get together on their scheduling.'

'It'd be like a pleasant fatigue if I could just go up after dinner and hunker on down with the mind in neutral and watch something uncomplex.'

'Not have to worry about prescriptive forms or acutance.'

'Kick back.'

'Watch something with chase scenes and lots of stuff blowing up all over the place.'

'Relax, do bongs, kick back, look at lingerie catalogues, eat granola with a great big wooden spoon,' Struck says wistfully.

'Get laid.'

'Just get one night off to like R and R.'

'Slip on the old environmental suit and listen to some atonal jazz.'

'Have sex. Get laid.'

'Bump uglies. Do the nasty. Haul ashes.'

'Find me one of them Northeast Oklahoma drive-in burger-stand waitresses with the great big huge titties.'

'Those enormous pink-white French-painting tits that sort of like *tumble* out.'

'One of those wooden spoons so big you can barely get your mouth around it.'

'Just one night to relax and indulge.'

Pemulis belts out two quick verses of Johnny Mathis's 'Chances Are,' left over from the shower, then subsides to examine something on his left thigh. Shaw has a spit-bubble going, growing to such exceptional size for just spit that half the room watches until it finally goes at the same moment Pemulis breaks off.

Evan Ingersoll says 'We get off Saturday for Interdependence Day Eve, though, the board said.'

Several upperclass heads are cocked up at Ingersoll. Pemulis makes a bulge in his cheek with his tongue and moves it around.

'Flubbaflubba': Stice makes his jowls fly around.

'We get off classes is all. Drills and challenges go merrily on, deLint says,' Freer points out.

'But no drills Sunday, before the Gala.'

'But still matches.'

Every jr. player presently in this room is ranked in the top 64 continentally, except Pemulis, Yardley and Blott.

There'd be clear evidence that T. Schacht's still in one of the toilet stalls off the showers even if Hal couldn't see the tip of one of Schacht's enormous purple shower thongs under the door of the stall right by where the shower-area entryway cuts into his line of sight. Something humble, placid even, about inert feet under stall doors. The defecatory posture is an accepting posture, it occurs to him. Head down, elbows on knees, the fingers laced together between the knees. Some hunched timeless millennial type of waiting, almost religious. Luther's shoes on the floor beneath the chamber pot, placid, possibly made of wood, Luther's 16th-century shoes, awaiting epiphany. The mute quiescent suffering of generations of salesmen in the stalls of train-station johns, heads down, fingers laced, shined shoes inert, awaiting the acid gush. Women's slippers, centurions' dusty sandals, dockworkers' hobnailed boots, Popes' slippers. All waiting, pointing straight ahead, slightly tapping. Huge shaggy-browed men in skins hunched just past the firelight's circle with wadded leaves in one hand, waiting. Schacht suffered from Crohn's Disease,[43] a bequest from his ulcerative-colitic dad, and had to take carminative medication with every meal, and took a lot of guff about his digestive troubles, and had developed of all things arthritic gout, too, somehow, because of the Crohn's Disease, which had settled in his right knee and caused him terrible pain on the court.

Freer's and Tall Paul Shaw's racquets fall off the bench with a clatter, and Beak and Blott move fast to pick them up and stack them back on the bench, Beak one-handed because the other hand is keeping his towel fastened.

'Because so that was let's see,' Struck says.

Pemulis loves to sing around tile.

Struck's hitting his palm with a finger for either emphasis or ordinal counting. 'Close to let's call it an hour run for the A-squads, an hour-fifteen drills, two matches back to back.'

'I only played one,' Troeltsch injects. 'Had a measurable fever in the A.M., deLint said to throttle down today.'

'Folks that went three sets only played one match, Spodek and Kent for an instance,' Stice says.

'Funny how Troeltsch how his health always seems to rally when A.M. drills get out,' Freer says.

'— like conservatively two hours for the matches. Conservatively. Then half an hour on the machines under fucking Loach's beady browns, sitting there with the clipboard. That's let's call it five hours of vigorous nonstop straight-out motion.'

'Sustained and strenuous exertion.'

'Schtitt's determined this year we ain't singing no silly songs at Port Washington.'

John Wayne hasn't said one word this whole time. The contents of his locker are neat and organized. He always buttons his shirt all the way up to the top button as if he were going to put on a tie, which he doesn't even own. Ingersoll's also getting dressed out of his underclassman's small square locker.

Stice says 'Except they seem to forget we're still in our puberty.'

Ingersoll is a kid seemingly wholly devoid of eyebrows, as far as Hal can see.

'Speak for yourself, Darkness.'

'I'm saying how stressing the pubertyizing skeleton like this, it's real short-sighted.' Stice's voice rises. ' 'm I supposed to do when I'm twenty and in the Show playing nonstop and I'm skeletally stressed and injury-proned?'

'Dark's right.'

A curled bit of cloudy old Pledge-husk and a green thread from a strip of GauzeTex wrap are complexly entwined in the blue fibers of the carpet near Hal's left ankle, which ankle is faintly swollen and has a blue tinge. He keeps flexing the ankle whenever it occurs to him to. Struck and Troeltsch spar briefly with open hands, feinting and bobbing their heads, both still seated on the floor. Hal, Stice, Troeltsch, Struck, Rader, and Beak are all rhythmically squeezing tennis balls with their racquet-hands, as per Academy mandate. Struck's shoulders and neck have furious purple inflammations; Hal had also noticed a boil on the inside of Schacht's thigh, when Ted'd sat down. Hal's face's reflection just fits inside one of the wall-tiles opposite, and then if he moves his head slowly the face distends and comes back together with an optical twang in the next tile. That post-shower community feeling is dissipating. Even Evan Ingersoll looks quickly at his watch and clears his throat. Wayne and Shaw have dressed and left; Freer, a major Pledge-devotee, is at his hair in the mirror, Pemulis also rising now to get away from Freer's feet and legs. Freer's eyes have a protrusive wideness to them that the Axhandle says makes Freer always look like he's getting shocked or throttled.

And time in the P.M. locker room seems of limitless depth; they've all been just here before, just like this, and will be again tomorrow. The light saddening outside, a grief felt in the bones, a sharpness to the edge of the lengthening shadows.

'I'm thinking it's Tavis,' Freer says to them all in the mirror. 'Where there's excess work and suffering can fucking Tavis be far behind.'

'No, it's Schtitt,' Hal says.

'Schtitt was short a few wickets out of the old croquet set long before he got hold of us, men,' Pemulis says.

'Peemster and Hal.'

'Halation and Pemurama.'

Freer purses his little lips and expels air like he's blowing out a match, blowing some tiny grooming-remnant off the big mirror's glass. 'Schtitt just does what he's told like a good Nazi.'

'What the *hail* is that supposed to mean?' asks a Stice who's well known for asking How High Sir when Schtitt says Jump, now feeling at the carpet around him for something to throw at Freer. Ingersoll tosses Stice a woppsed-up towel, trying to be helpful, but Stice's eyes are on Freer's in the glass, and the towel hits him on the head and sits there, on his head. The room's emotions seem to be inverting themselves every couple seconds. There's half-cruel laughter at Stice as Hal struggles to his feet, rising in careful stages, putting most of his weight on the good ankle. Hal's towel falls off as he does his combination. Struck says something that's lost in the roar of a high-pressure toilet.

The feminized American stood at a slight angle to Marathe upon the outcropping. He stared out at the dusk-shadow they were now inside, and as well the increasingly complicated twinkle of the U.S.A. city Tucson, seeming slackly transfixed, Steeply, in the way vistas too large for the eye to contain transfix persons in a kind of torpid spectation.

Marathe seemed on the edge of sleep.

Even the voice of Steeply had a different timbre inside the shadow. 'They say it's a great and maybe even timeless love, Rod Tine's for your Luria person.'

Marathe grunted, shifting slightly in the chair.

Steeply said 'The sort that gets sung about, the kind people die for and then get immortalized in song. You got your ballads, your operas. Tristan and Isolde. Lancelot and what's-her-name. Agamemnon and Helen, Dante and Beatrice.'

Marathe's drowsy smile continued upward to become a wince. 'Narcissus and Echo. Kierkegaard and Regina. Kafka and that poor girl afraid to go to the postbox for the mail.'

'Interesting choice of example here, the mailbox.' Steeply pretended to chuckle.

Marathe came alert. 'Take off your wig and be shitting inside it, Hugh Steeply B.S.S. And the ignorance of you appalls me. Agamemnon had no relation with this queen. Menelaus was husband, him of Sparta. And you mean *Paris*. Helen and Paris. He of Troy.'

Steeply seemed amused in the idiotic way: 'Paris and Helen, the face that launched vessels. The horse: the gift which was not a gift. The anonymous gift brought to the door. The sack of Troy from inside.'

Marathe rose slightly on his stumps in the chair, showing some emotions at this Steeply. 'I am seated here appalled at the naïveté of history of your nation. Paris and Helen were the *excuse* of the war. All the Greek states in addition to the Sparta of Menelaus attacked Troy because Troy controlled the Dardanelles and charged the ruinous tolls for passage through, which the Greeks, who would like very dearly the easy sea passage for trade with the Oriental East, resented with fury. It was for commerce, this war. The one-quotes "love" one-does-not-quote of Paris for Helen merely was the excuse.'

Steeply, genius of interviewing, sometimes affected more than usual idiocy with Marathe, which he knew baited Marathe. 'Everything reduces itself to politics for you guys. Wasn't that whole war just a song? Did that war even really take place, that anybody knows of?'

'The point is that what launches vessels of war is the state and community and its interests,' Marathe said without heat, tiredly. 'You only wish to enjoy to pretend for yourself that the love of one woman could do this, launch so many vessels of alliance.'

Steeply was stroking the perimeters of the mesquite-scratch, which made his shrug appear awkward. 'I don't think I'd be so sure. Those around Rod the God say the man would die twice for her. Say he wouldn't have to even think about it. Not just that he'd let the whole of O.N.A.N. come down, if it came to that. But'd die.'

Marathe sniffed. 'Twice.'

'Without even having to pause and think,' Steeply said, stroking at his lip's electrolysistic rash in a ruminative fashion. 'It's the reason most of us think he's still there, why he's still got President Gentle's ear. Divided loyalties are one thing. But if he does it for *love* — well then you've got a kind of tragic element that transcends the political, wouldn't you say?' Steeply smiled broadly down at Marathe.

Marathe's own betrayal of A.F.R.: for medical care for the conditions of his wife; for (Steeply might imagine to think) love of a person, a woman. '*Tragic* saying as if Rodney Tine of Nonspecificity were not responsible for choosing it, as the insane are not responsible,' said Marathe quietly.

Steeply now was smiling even more broadly. 'It has a kind of tragic quality, timeless, musical, that how could Gentle resist?'

Marathe's tone now became derisive despite his legendary sangfroid in matters of technical interviews: 'These sentiments from a person who allows them to place him in the field as an enormous girl with tits at the cock-eyed angle, now discoursing on tragic love.'

Steeply, impassive and slackly ruminative, picked at the lipstick of the corner of his mouth with a littlest finger, removing some grain of grit, gazing out from their shelf of stone. 'But sure. The fanatically patriotic Wheelchair Assassins of southern Québec scorn this type of interpersonal sentiment between people.' Looking now down at Marathe. 'No? Even though it's just this that has brought you Tine, yours for Luria to command, should it ever come to that?'

Marathe had settled back on his bottom in the chair. 'Your U.S.A. word for fanatic, "fanatic," do they teach you it comes from the Latin for "temple"? It is meaning, literally, "worshipper at the temple." '

'Oh Jesus now here we go again,' Steeply said.

'As, if you will give the permission, does this *love* you speak of, M. Tine's grand love. It means only the *attachment*. Tine is attached, fanatically. Our attachments are our temple, what we worship, no? What we give ourselves to, what we invest with faith.'

Steeply made motions of weary familiarity. 'Herrrrrre we go.'

Marathe ignored this. 'Are we not all of us fanatics? I say only what you of the U.S.A. only pretend you do not know. Attachments are of great seriousness. Choose your attachments carefully. Choose your temple of fanaticism with great care. What you wish to sing of as tragic love is an attachment not carefully chosen. Die for one person? This is a craziness. Persons change, leave, die, become ill. They leave, lie, go mad, have sickness, betray you, die. Your nation outlives you. A cause outlives you.'

'How are your wife and kids doing, up there, by the way?'

'You U.S.A.'s do not seem to believe you may each choose what to die for. Love of a woman, the sexual, it bends back in on the self, makes you narrow, maybe crazy. Choose with care. Love of your nation, your country and people, it enlarges the heart. Something bigger than the self.'

Steeply laid a hand between his misdirected breasts: 'Ohh ... Canada. . . .'

Marathe leaned again forward on his stumps. 'Make amusement all you wish. But choose with care. You are what you love. No? You are, completely and only, what you would die for without, as you say, the *thinking twice*. You, M. Hugh Steeply: you would die without thinking for what?'

The A.F.R.'s extensive file on Steeply included mention of his recent divorce. Marathe already had informed Steeply of the existence of this file. He wondered how badly Steeply doubted what he reported, Marathe, or whether he assumed its truth simply. Though the persona of him changed, Steeply's car for all field assignments was this green sedan subsidized by a painful ad for aspirin upon its side — the file knew this stupidity — Marathe was sure the sedan with its aspirin advertisement was somewhere below them, unseen. The fanatically beloved car of M. Hugh Steeply. Steeply was watching or gazing at the darkness of the desert floor. He did not respond. His expression of boredom could be real or tactical, either of these.

Marathe said, 'This, is it not the choice of the most supreme importance? Who teaches your U.S.A. children how to choose their temple? What to love enough not to think two times?'

'This from a man who —'

Marathe was willing that his voice not rise. 'For this choice determines all else. No? All other of our you say *free* choices follow from this: what is our temple. What is the temple, thus, for U.S.A.'s? What is it, when you fear that you must protect them from themselves, if wicked Québecers conspire to bring the Entertainment into their warm homes?'

Steeply's face had assumed the openly twisted sneering expression which he knew well Québecers found repellent on Americans. 'But you assume it's always choice, conscious, decision. This isn't just a little naïve, Rémy? You sit down with your little accountant's ledger and soberly decide what to love? Always?'

'The alternatives are —'

'What if sometimes there *is* no choice about what to love? What if the temple comes to Mohammed? What if you just *love?* without deciding? You just *do:* you see her and in that instant are lost to sober account-keeping and cannot choose but to love?'

Marathe's sniff held disdain. 'Then in such a case your temple is self and sentiment. Then in such an instance you are a fanatic of desire, a slave to your individual subjective narrow self's sentiments; a citizen of nothing. You become a citizen of nothing. You are by yourself and alone, kneeling to yourself.'

A silence ensued this.

Marathe shifted in his chair. 'In a case such as this you become the slave who believes he is free. The most pathetic of bondage. Not tragic. No songs. You believe you would die twice for another but in truth would die only for your alone self, its sentiment.'

Another silence ensued. Steeply, who had made his early career with Unspecified Services conducting technical interviews,[44] used silent pauses as integral parts of his techniques of interface. Here it defused Marathe. Marathe felt the ironies of his position. One strap of Steeply's prostheses' brassiere had slipped into view below his shoulder, where it cut deeply into his flesh of the upper arm. The air smelled faintly of creosote, but much less strongly smelling than the ties of train tracks, which Marathe had smelled at close range. Steeply's back was broad and soft. Marathe eventually said:

'You in such a case have nothing. You stand on nothing. Nothing of ground or rock beneath your feet. You fall; you blow here and there. How does one say: "tragically, unvoluntarily, lost." '

Another silence ensued. Steeply farted mildly. Marathe shrugged. The B.S.S. Field Operative Steeply may not have been truly sneering. The city Tucson's lume appeared a bleached and ghostly white in the unhumid air. Crepuscular animals rustled and perhaps scuttled. Dense and unbeautiful spider webs of the poisonous U.S.A. species of spider Black Widow were beneath the shelf and the incline's other outcroppings. And when the wind hit certain angles in the mountainside it moaned. Marathe thought of his victory over the train that had taken his legs.[45] He attempted in English to sing:

' "*Oh Say, Land of the Free.*" '

And they both could feel this queer dry night-desert chill descend with the moon's gibbous rise — a powdery wind down below making dust to shift and cactus needles whistle, the sky's stars adjusting to the color of low flame — but were themselves not yet chilled, even Steeply's sleeveless dress: he and Marathe stood and sat in the form-fitting astral spacesuit of warmth their own radiant heat produced. This is what happens in dry night climes, Marathe was learning. His dying wife had never once left southwestern Québec. Les Assassins des Fauteuils Roulents' remote embryonic disseminatory Ops base down here in Southwest U.S.A. seemed to him like the surface of the moon: four corrugated Quonsets and kiln-baked earth and air that swam and shimmered like the area behind jet engines. Empty and dirty-windowed rooms, doorknobs hot to touch and hell-stench inside the empty rooms.

Steeply was continuing saying nothing while he tamped down another of his long Belgian cigarettes. Marathe continued to hum the U.S.A. song, all over the map in terms of key.

3 NOVEMBER Y.D.A.U.

'Because none of them really meant any of it,' Hal tells Kent Blott. 'The end-of-the-day hatred of all the work is just part of the work. You think Schtitt and deLint don't know we're going to sit in there together after showers and bitch? It's all planned out. The bitchers and moaners in there are just doing what's expected.'

'But I look at these guys that've been here six, seven years, eight years, still suffering, hurt, beat up, so tired, just like I feel tired and suffer, I feel this what, dread, this dread, I see seven or eight years of unhappiness every day and day after day of tiredness and stress and suffering stretching ahead, and for what, for a chance at a like a pro career that I'm starting to get this dready feeling a career in the Show means even *more* suffering, if I'm skeletally stressed from all the grueling here by the time I get there.'

Blott's on his back on the shag carpet — all five of them are — stretched out splay-limbed with their heads up supported on double-width velourish throw-pillows on the floor of V.R.6, one of the three little Viewing Rooms on the second floor of the Comm.-Ad. Bldg., two flights up from the locker rooms and three from the main tunnel's mouth. The room's new cartridge-viewer is huge and almost painfully high-definition; it hangs flat on the north wall like a large painting; it runs off a refrigerated chip; the room's got no TP or phone-console; it's very specialized, just a player and viewer, and tapes; the cartridge-player sits on the second shelf of a small bookcase beneath the viewer; the other shelves and several other cases are full of match-cartridges, motivational and visualization cartridges — InterLace, Tatsuoka, Yushityu, SyberVision. The 300-track wire from the cartridge-player up to the lower-right corner of the wall-hung viewer is so thin it looks like a crack in the wall's white paint. Viewing Rooms are windowless and the air from the vent is stale. Though when the viewer's on it looks like the room has a window.

Hal's put on an undemanding visualization-type cartridge, as he usually does for a Big Buddy group-interface when they're all tired. He's killed the volume, so you can't hear the reinforcing mantra, but the picture is bright and bell-clear. It's like the picture almost leaps out at you. A graying and somewhat ravaged-looking Stan Smith in anachronistic white is at a court's baseline hitting textbook forehands, over and over again, the same stroke, his back sort of osteoporotically hunched but his form immaculate, his footwork textbook and effortless — the frictionless pivot and back-set of weight, the anachronistic Wilson wood stick back and pointing straight to the fence behind him, the fluid transfer of weight to the front foot as the ball comes in, the contact at waist-level and just out front, the front leg's muscles bunching up as the back leg's settle, eyes glued to the yellow ball in the center of his strings' stencilled **W** — E.T.A. kids are conditioned to watch not just the ball but the ball's rotating seams, to read the spin coming in — the front knee dipping slightly down under bulging quads as the weight flows more forward, the back foot up almost *en-pointe* on the gleaming sneaker's unscuffed toe, the no-nonsense flourishless follow-through so the stick ends up just in front of his gaunt face — Smith's cheeks have hollowed as he's aged, his face has collapsed at the sides, his eyes seem to bulge from the cheekbones that protrude as he inhales after impact, he looks desiccated, aged in hot light, performing the same motions over and over, for decades, his other hand floating up gently to grasp the stick's throat out in front of the face so he's flowed back into the Ready Stance all over again. No wasted motion, egoless strokes, no flourishes or tics or excesses of wrist. Over and over, each forehand melting into the next, a loop, it's hypnotizing, it's supposed to be. The soundtrack says 'Don't Think Just See Don't Know Just Flow' over and over, if you turn it up. You're supposed to pretend it's you on the bell-clear screen with the fluid and egoless strokes. You're supposed to disappear into the loop and then carry that disappearance out with you, to play. The kids're lying there limp and splayed, supine, jaws slack, eyes wide and dim, a relaxed exhausted warmth — the flooring beneath the shag is gently heated. Peter Beak is asleep with his eyes open, a queer talent E.T.A. seems to instill in the younger ones. Orin had been able to sleep with his eyes open at the dinner table, too, at home.

Hal's fingers, long and light brown and still slightly sticky from tincture of benzoin,[46] are laced behind his upraised head on the pillow, cupping his own skull, watching Stan Smith, eyes heavy too. 'You feel as though you'll be going through the exact same sort of suffering at seventeen you suffer now, here, Kent?'

Kent Blott has colored shoelaces on his sneakers with 'Mr.-Bouncety-Bounce-Program'-brand bow-biters, which Hal finds extraordinarily artless and young.

Peter Beak snores softly, a small spit-bubble protruding and receding.

'But Blott surely you've considered this: Why are they all still here, then, if it's so awful every day?'

'Not every day,' Blott says. 'But pretty often it's awful.'

'They're here because they want the Show when they get out,' Ingersoll sniffs and says. The Show meaning the A.T.P. Tour, travel and cash prizes and endorsements and appearance fees, match-highlights in video mags, action photos in glossy print-mags.

'But they know and we know one very top junior in twenty even gets all the way to the Show. Much less survives there long. The rest slog around on the satellite tours or regional tours or get soft as club pros. Or become lawyers or academics like everyone else,' Hal says softly.

'Then they stay and suffer to get a scholarship. A college ride. A white cardigan with a letter. Girl coeds keen on lettermen.'

'Kent, except for Wayne and Pemulis not one guy in there needs any kind of scholarship. Pemulis'll get a full ride anywhere he wants, just on test-scores. Stice's aunts'll send him anywhere even if he doesn't want to play. And Wayne's headed for the Show, he'll never do more than a year in the O.N.A.N.C.A.A.'s.' Blott's father, a cutting-edge E.N.T. oncologist, flew all over the world removing tumors from wealthy mucous membranes; Blott has a trust fund. 'None of that's the point and you guys know it.'

'They love the game, you're going to say.'

Stan Smith has switched to backhands.

'They sure must love something, Ingersoll, but how about for a second I say that's not Kent's point either. Kent's point's the misery in that room just now. K.B., I've taken part in essentially that same bitter bitchy kind of session hundreds of times with those same guys after bad P.M.s. In the showers, in the sauna, at dinner.'

'Very much bitching also in the lavatories,' Arslanian says.

Hal unsticks his hair from his fingers. Arslanian always has a queer faint hot-doggish smell about him. 'The point is it's ritualistic. The bitching and moaning. Even assuming they feel the way they say when they get together, the point is notice we were all sitting there all feeling the same way *together*.'

'The point is togetherness?'

'Shouldn't there be violas for this part, Hal, if this is the point?'

'Ingersoll, I — '

Beak's cold-weather adenoids wake him periodically, and he gurgles and his eyes roll up briefly before they level out and he settles back, seeming to stare.

Hal creatively visualizes that Smith's velvety backhand is him slo-mo slapping Evan Ingersoll into the opposite wall. Ingersoll's parents founded the Rhode Island version of the service where you order groceries by TP and teenagers in fleets of station wagons bring them out to you, instead of supermarkets. 'What the point is is that we'd all just spent three hours playing challenges against each other in scrotum-tightening cold, assailing each other, trying to take away each other's spots on the squads. Trying to defend them against each other's assaults. The system's got inequality as an axiom. We know where we stand entirely in relation to one another. John Wayne's over me, and I'm over Struck and Shaw, who two years back were both over me but under Troeltsch and Schacht, and now are over Troeltsch who as of today is over Freer who's substantially over Schacht, who can't beat anyone in the room except Pemulis since his knee and Crohn's Disease got so much worse, and is barely hanging on in terms of ranking, and is showing incredible balls just hanging on. Freer beat me 4 and 2 in the quarters of the U.S. Clays two summers ago, and now he's on the B-squad and five slots below me, six slots if Troeltsch can still beat him when they play again after that illness-default.'

'I am over Blott. I am over Ingersoll,' Idris Arslanian nods.

'Well Blott's just ten, Idris. And you're under Chu, who's on an odd year and is under Possalthwaite. And Blott's under Beak and Ingersoll simply by virtue of age-division.'

'I know just where I stand at all times,' muses Ingersoll.

SyberVision edits its visualization sequences with a melt-filter so Stan Smith's follow-through loops seamlessly into his backswing for the exact same next stroke; the transitions are gauzy and dreamlike. Hal struggles to hike himself up onto his elbows:

'We're all on each other's food chain. All of us. It's an individual sport. Welcome to the meaning of *individual*. We're each deeply alone here. It's what we all have in common, this aloneness.'

'*E Unibus Pluram*,' Ingersoll muses.

Hal looks from face to face. Ingersoll's face is completely devoid of eyebrows and is round and dustily freckled, not unlike a Mrs. Clarke pancake. 'So how can we also be together? How can we be friends? How can Ingersoll root for Arslanian in Idris's singles at the Port Washington thing when if Idris loses Ingersoll gets to challenge for his spot again?'

'I do not require his root, for I am ready.' Arslanian bares canines.

'Well that's the whole point. How can we be friends? Even if we all live and eat and shower and play together, how can we keep from being 136 deeply alone people all jammed together?'

'You're talking about community. This is a community-spiel.'

'I think alienation,' Arslanian says, rolling the profile over to signify he's talking to Ingersoll. 'Existential individuality, frequently referred to in the West. Solipsism.' His upper lip goes up and down over his teeth.

Hal says, 'In a nutshell, what we're talking about here is loneliness.'

Blott looks about ready to cry. Beak's palsied eyes and little limb-spasms signify a troubling dream. Blott rubs his nose furiously with the heel of his hand.

'I miss my dog,' Ingersoll concedes.

'Ah.' Hal rolls onto one elbow to hike a finger into the air. 'Ah. But then so notice the instant group-cohesion that formed itself around all the pissing and moaning down there why don't you. Blott. You, Kent. This was your question. The what looks like sadism, the skeletal stress, the fatigue. The suffering *unites* us. They want to let us sit around and bitch. Together. After a bad P.M. set we all, however briefly, get to feel we have a common enemy. This is their gift to us. Their medicine. Nothing brings you together like a common enemy.'

'Mr. deLint.'

'Dr. Tavis. Schtitt.'

'DeLint. Watson. Nwangi. Thode. All Schtitt's henchmen and henchwomen.'

'I hate them!' Blott cries out.

'And you've been here this long and you still think this hatred's an accident?'

'Purchase a clue Kent Blott!' Arslanian says.

'The large and economy-size clue, Blott,' Ingersoll chimes.

Beak sits up and says 'God no not with *pliers!*' and collapses back again, again with the spit-bubble.

Hal is pretending incredulity. 'You guys haven't noticed yet the way Schtitt's whole staff gets progressively more foul-tempered and sadistic as an important competitive week comes up?'

Ingersoll up on one elbow at Blott. 'The Port Washington meet. I.D. Day. The Tucson WhataBurger the week after. They want us in absolute top shape, Blott.'

Hal lies back and lets Smith's *ballet de se* loosen his facial muscles again, staring. 'Shit, Ingersoll, we're all in top shape already. That's not it. That's the least of it. We're off the charts, shape-wise.'

Ingersoll: 'The average North American kid can't even do one pull-up, according to Nwangi.'

Arslanian points down at his own chest. 'Twenty-eight pull-ups.'

'The point,' Hal says softly, 'is that it's not about the physical anymore, men. The physical stuff's just pro forma. It's the heads they're working on here, boys. Day and year in and out. A whole program. It'll help your attitude to look for evidence of design. They always give us something to hate, really hate together, as big stuff looms. The dreaded May drills during finals before the summer tour. The post-Christmas crackdown before Australia. The November freezathon, the snot-fest, the delay in upping the Lung and getting us under cover. A common enemy. *I* may despise K. B. Freer, or' (can't quite resist) 'Evan Ingersoll, or Jennie Bash. But *we* despise Schtitt's men, the double matches on top of runs, the insensitivity to exams, the repetition, the stress. The loneliness. But we get together and bitch, all of a sudden we're giving something group expression. A community voice. Community, Evan. Oh they're cunning. They give themselves up to our dislike, calculate our breaking points and aim for just over them, then send us into the locker room with an unstructured forty-five before Big Buddy sessions. Accident? Random happenstance? You guys ever see evidence of the tiniest lack of coolly calculated structure around here?'

'The structure's what I hate the most of all,' Ingersoll says.

'They know what's going on,' Blott says, bouncing a little on his tailbone. 'They *want* us to get together and complain.'

'*Oh* they're cunning,' Ingersoll says.

Hal curls himself a bit on one elbow to put in a small plug of Kodiak. He can't tell whether Ingersoll's being insolent. He lies there very slack, visualizing Smith pounding overheads down onto Ingersoll's skull. Hal some weeks back had acquiesced to Lyle's diagnosis that Hal finds Ingersoll — this smart soft caustic kid, with a big soft eyebrowless face and unwrinkled thumb-joints, with the runty, cuddled look of a Mama's boy from way back, a quick intelligence he squanders on an insatiable need to advance some impression of himself — that the kid so repels Hal because Hal sees in the kid certain parts of himself he can't or won't accept. None of this ever occurs to Hal when Ingersoll's in the room. He wishes him ill.

Blott and Arslanian are looking at him. 'Are you OK?'

'He is tired,' Arslanian says.

Ingersoll drums idly on his own ribcage.

Hal usually gets secretly high so regularly these days this year that if by dinnertime he hasn't gotten high yet that day his mouth begins to fill with spit — some rebound effect from B. Hope's desiccating action — and his eyes start to water as if he's just yawned. The smokeless tobacco started almost as an excuse to spit, sometimes. Hal's struck by the fact that he really for the most part believes what he's said about loneliness and the structured need for a *we* here; and this, together with the Ingersoll-repulsion and spit-flood, makes him uncomfortable again, brooding uncomfortably for a moment on why he gets off on the secrecy of getting high in secret more than on the getting high itself, possibly. He always gets the feeling there's some clue to it on the tip of his tongue, some mute and inaccessible part of the cortex, and then he always feels vaguely sick, scanning for it. The other thing that happens if he doesn't do one-hitters sometime before dinner is he feels slightly sick to his stomach, and it's hard to eat enough at dinner, and then later when he does go off and get off he gets ravenous, and goes out to Father & Son Market for candy, or else floods his eyes with Murine and heads down to the Headmaster's House for another late dinner with C.T. and the Moms, and eats like such a feral animal that the Moms says it does something instinctively maternal in her heart good to see him pack it away, but then he wakes before dawn with awful indigestion.

'So the suffering gets less lonely,' Blott prompts him.

Two curves down the hall in V.R.5, where the viewer's on the south wall and doesn't get turned on, the Canadian John Wayne's got LaMont Chu and 'Sleepy T.P.' Peterson and Kieran McKenna and Brian van Vleck.

'He's talking about developing the concept of tennis mastery,' Chu tells the other three. They're on the floor Indian-style, Wayne standing with his back against the door, rotating his head to stretch the neck. 'His point is that progress towards genuine Show-caliber mastery is slow, frustrating. Humbling. A question of less talent than temperament.'

'Is this right Mr. Wayne?'

Chu says '. . . that because you proceed toward mastery through a series of plateaus, so there's like radical improvement up to a certain plateau and then what looks like a stall, on the plateau, with the only way to get off one of the plateaus and climb up to the next one up ahead is with a whole lot of frustrating mindless repetitive practice and patience and hanging in there.'

'Plateaux,' Wayne says, looking at the ceiling and pushing the back of his head isometrically against the door. 'With an X. *Plateaux*.'

The inactive viewer's screen is the color of way out over the Atlantic looking straight down on a cold day. Chu's cross-legged posture is textbook. 'What John's saying is the types who don't hang in there and slog on the patient road toward mastery are basically three. Types. You've got what he calls your Despairing type, who's fine as long as he's in the quick-improvement stage before a plateau, but then he hits a plateau and sees himself seem to stall, not getting better as fast or even seeming to get a little worse, and this type gives in to frustration and despair, because he hasn't got the humbleness and patience to hang in there and slog, and he can't stand the time he has to put in on plateaux, and what happens?'

'Geronimo!' the other kids yell, not quite in sync.

'He bails, right,' Chu says. He refers to index cards. Wayne's head makes the door rattle slightly. Chu says, 'Then you've got your Obsessive type, J.W. says, so eager to plateau-hop he doesn't even know the word *patient,* much less *humble* or *slog,* when he gets stalled at a plateau he tries to like *will* and *force* himself off it, by sheer force of work and drill and will and practice, drilling and obsessively honing and working more and more, as in frantically, and he overdoes it and gets hurt, and pretty soon he's all chronically messed up with injuries, and he hobbles around on the court still obsessively overworking, until finally he's hardly even able to walk or swing, and his ranking plummets, until finally one P.M. there's a little knock on his door and it's deLint, here for a little chat about your progress here at E.T.A.'

'Banzai! El Bailo! *See* ya!'

'Then what John considers maybe the worst type, because it can cunningly masquerade as patience and humble frustration. You've got the Complacent type, who improves radically until he hits a plateau, and is content with the radical improvement he's made to get to the plateau, and doesn't mind staying at the plateau because it's comfortable and familiar, and he doesn't worry about getting off it, and pretty soon you find he's designed a whole game around compensating for the weaknesses and chinks in the armor the given plateau represents in his game, still — his whole game is based on this plateau now. And little by little, guys he used to beat start beating him, locating the chinks of the plateau, and his rank starts to slide, but he'll say he doesn't care, he says he's in it for the love of the game, and he always smiles but there gets to be something sort of tight and hangdog about his smile, and he always smiles and is real nice to everybody and real good to have around but he keeps staying where he is while other guys hop plateaux, and he gets beat more and more, but he's content. Until one day there's a quiet knock at the door.'

'It's DeLint!'

'A quiet chat!'

'Geronzai!'

Van Vleck looks up at Wayne, who's now turned away with his hands against the door frame, shoving, one leg back, stretching the right calf. 'This is your advice, Mr. Wayne sir? This isn't Chu palming himself off as you again?'

They all want to know how Wayne does it, #2 continentally in 18's at just seventeen, and very likely #1 after the WhataBurger and already getting calls from ProServ agents Tavis has Lateral Alice Moore screen. Wayne's the most sought-after Big Buddy at E.T.A. You have to apply for Wayne as Buddy by random drawing.

LaMont Chu and T. P. Peterson are sending van Vleck optical daggers as Wayne turns around to stretch a hip-flexor and says he's said pretty much all he has to say.

'Todder, I admire your savvy, I admire a kid's certain worldly skepticism, no matter how misplaced it is here. So even though it fucks me on the odds, so there's now like practically no way I can come out square,' M. Pemulis says in V.R.2, subdorm C, sitting on the very edge of the divan with a few feet of beige shag between him and his four kids, all cross-legged on cushions; he says, 'I'll reward your worldly skepticism this once by letting you try it with only two, so like I've got just two cards here, and I hold them up,

116

one in each hand. . . .' He stops abruptly, knocks his temple with the heel of a hand that holds a Jack. 'Whoa, what am I thinking. We all gotta put in our fiveski here first.'

Otis P. Lord clears his throat: 'The ante.'

'Or it's called the pot,' says Todd Possalthwaite, laying a five on the little pile.

'Jaysus I'm thinking, sweet Jaysus what am I getting into with these kids that speak the lingo like veteran Jersey-shore croupiers. I got to be missing a widget or something. 't the fuck, though, you know what I'm saying? So Todd man you choose just one of the cards, we got the clubby Jack and the spade Queen here, and you choose . . . and so down they go both of them face-down, and I like swirl them around on the floor a little, not shuffle but swirl so they're in plain view the whole time, and you folllllllowwwwwwww the card you chose, around and around, which like with three cards maybe I've got some chance you lose track but with two? With just *two?*'

Ted Schacht in V.R.3 at his giant plasticene oral demonstrator, the huge dental mock-up, white planks of teeth and obscene pink gums, twine-size floss anchored around both wrists:

'The vital thing here gentlemen being not the force or how often you rotate to particulate-free floss but the *motion*, see, a soft sawing motion, gently up and down both ancipitals of the enamel' — demonstrating down the side of a bicuspid big as the kids' heads, the plasticene gum-stuff yielding with sick sucking sounds, Schacht's five kids all either glazed-looking or glued to their watch's second-hand — 'and then here's the key, *here's* the thing so few people understand: *down* below the ostensible gumline into the basal recessions at either side of the gingival mound that obtrudes between the teeth, down *below*, where your most pernicious particulates hide and breed.'

Troeltsch holds court in his, Pemulis and Schacht's room in Subdorm C, supinely upright against both of his and one of Schacht's pillows, the vaporizer chugging, one of his kids holding Kleenex at the ready.

'Boys, what it is is I'll tell you it's repetition. First last always. It's hearing the same motivational stuff over and over till sheer repetitive weight makes it sink down into the gut. It's making the same pivots and lunges and strokes over and over and over again, at you boys's age it's reps for their own sake, putting results on the back burner, why they never give anybody the boot for insufficient progress under fourteen, it's repetitive movements and motions for their own sake, over and over until the accretive weight of the reps sinks the movements themselves down under your like consciousness into the more nether regions, through repetition they sink and soak into the hardware, the C.P.S. The machine-language. The autonomical part that makes you breathe and sweat. It's no accident they say you Eat, Sleep, Breathe tennis here. These are autonomical. Accretive means accumulating, through sheer mindless repeated motions. The machine-language of the muscles. Until you can do it without thinking about it, play. At like four-teen, give and take, they figure here. Just do it. Forget about is there a point, of course there's no point. The point of repetition is there is no point. Wait until it soaks into the hardware and then see the way this frees up your head. A whole shitload of head-space you don't need for the mechanics anymore, after they've sunk in. Now the mechanics are wired in. Hardwired in. This frees the head in the remarkablest ways. Just wait. You start thinking a whole different way now, playing. The court might as well be inside you. The ball stops being a ball. The ball starts being something that you just know *ought* to be in the air, spinning. This is when they start getting on you about concentration. Right now of course you have to concentrate, there's no choice, it's not wired down into the language yet, you have to think about it every time you do it. But wait till fourteen or fifteen. Then they see you as being at one of the like crucial plateaus. Fifteen, tops. Then the con-centration and character shit starts. Then they really come after you. This is the crucial plateau where character starts to matter. Focus, self-consciousness, the chattering head, the cackling voices, the choking-issue, fear versus whatever isn't fear, self-image, doubts, reluctances, little tight-lipped cold-footed men inside your mind, cackling about fear and doubt, chinks in the mental armor. Now these start to matter. Thirteen at the ear-liest. Staff looks at a range of thirteen to fifteen. Also the age of manhood-rituals in various cultures. Think about it. Until then, repetition. Until then you might as well be machines, here, is their view. You're just going through the motions. Think about the phrase: Going Through The Motions. Wiring them into the motherboard. You guys don't know how good you've got it right now.'

James Albrecht Lockley Struck Jr. of Orinda CA prefers one long Q&A-type interface, with V.R.8's viewer playing ambient stuff against relaxation-vistas of surf, shimmering ponds, fields of nodding wheat.

'Time for about maybe two more, me droogies.'

'Say it's close and the guy starts kertwanging you. Balls are way in and he's calling them out. You can't believe the flagrancy of it.'

'Implicit this is a no-linesman situation, Traub, you're saying.'

Creepily-blue-eyed Audern Tallat-Kelpsa chimes in: 'This is early rounds. The kind they give you only two balls. Honor systems. All of a sudden there he is kertwanging on you. It happens.'

'I know it happens.'

Traub says, 'Whether he's outright kertwanging or just head-fucking you. Do you start kertwanging back? Tit for tat? What do you do?'

'Do we assume there's a crowd.'

'Early round. Remote court. No witnesses. You're on your own out there. Do you kertwang back.'

'You do not kertwang back. You play the calls, not a word, keep smiling. If you still win, you'll have grown inside as a person.'

'If you lose?'

'If you lose, you do something private and unpleasant to his water-jug right before his next round.'

A couple of the kids have notebooks and studious nods. Struck is a prized tactician, very formal in B.B. group-sessions, something scholarly and detached about him his charges often revere.

'We can discuss private water-jug unpleasantness on Friday,' Struck says, looking at his watch.

A hand raised by the violently cross-eyed Carl Whale, age thirteen. Acknowledgment from Struck.

'Say you have to fart.'

'You're serious, Mobes, aren't you.'

'Jim sir, say you're playing out there, and suddenly you have to fart. It feels like one of those real hot nasty pressurized ones.'

'I get the picture.'

Now some empathic murmurs, exchanged looks. Josh Gopnik is nodding very intensely. Struck stands very straight to the right of the viewer, hands behind his back like an Oxford don.

'I mean the kind that's real urgent.' Whale looks briefly around him. 'But that it's not impossible it's actually a need to go to the bathroom, instead, masquerading as a fart.'

Now five heads are nodding, pained, urgent: clearly a vexing sub-14 issue. Struck examines a cuticle.

'Meaning defecate is what you mean, then, Mobes. Go to the bathroom.'

Gopnik looks up. 'Carl's saying the kind where you don't know what to do. What if you think you have to fart but it's really that you have to shit?'

'As in it's a competitive situation, it's not a situation where you can go bearing down and forcing and see what happens.'

'So out of caution you don't,' Gopnik says.

'— fart,' Philip Traub says.

'But then you've denied yourself an urgent fart, and you're running around trying to compete with a terrible hot nasty uncomfortable fart riding around the court inside you.'

Two levels down, Ortho Stice and his brood: the little libraryish circle of soft chairs and lamps in the warm foyer off the front door to subdorm C:

'And what he says he says it's about more than tennis, mein kinder. *Mein kinder*, well it sort of means my family. He eyeballs me right square in the eye and says it's about how to reach down into parts of yourself you didn't know were there and get down in there and live inside these parts. And the only way to get to them: sacrifice. Suffer. Deny. What are you willing to give. You'll hear him ask it if you're privileged to ever get an interface. The call could come at anytime: the man wants a mano-to-mano interface. You'll hear him say it over and over. What have you got to give. What are you willing to part with. I see you're looking a little pale there, Wagenknecht. Is this scary you bet your little pink personal asses it's scary. It's the big time. He'll tell you straight the fuck out. It's about discipline and sacrifice and honor to something way bigger than your personal ass. He'll mention America. He'll talk patriotism and don't think he won't. He'll talk about it's patriotic play that's the high road to the thing. He's not American but I tell you straight out right here he makes me proud to be American. Mein kinder. He'll say it's how to learn to be a good American during a time, boys, when America isn't good its own self.'

There's a long pause. The front door is newer than the wood around it.

'I'd chew fiberglass for that old man.'

The only reason the Buddies in V.R.8 can hear the little burst of applause from the foyer is because Struck won't hesitate to pause and consider silently as long as he has to. To the kids the pauses spell dignity and integrity and the still-water depth of a guy with nine years in at three different academies, and who has to shave daily. He exhales a slow breath through rounded lips, looking off up at the ceiling's guilloche border.

'Mobes, if it's me: I let it ride.'

'You let it out come what may?'

'A la contraire. I let it ride around inside all day if I have to. I make an iron rule: nothing escapes my bottom during play. Not a toot or a whistle. If I play hunched over I play hunched over. I take the discomfort in the name of dignified caution, and when it's especially bad I look up at sky between points and I say to the sky Thank You Sir may I have another. Thank You Sir may I have another.'

Gopnik and Tallat-Kelpsa are writing this down.

Struck says, 'That's if I want to hang for the long haul.'

'*One* side of the gingival mound, then up over the apex and down over the *other* side of the gingival mound, using you should cultivate a certain amount of touch with the string.'

'Now the big question of character is do we let a fluke of a probably one-in-a-hundred lapse in concentration make us throw up our faggy hands and go dragging characterlessly back to our dens to lick the whimpering wounds, or do we narrow our eyes and put out the chin and say Pemulis we say we say Pemulis, Double or Nothing, when the odds remain so almost crazily stacked in our favor today.'

'So they do it on purpose?' Beak is asking. 'Try to make us hate them?'

Limits and rituals. It's almost time for communal dinner. Sometimes Mrs. Clarke in the kitchen lets Mario ring a triangle with a steel ladle while she rolls back the dining-room doors. They make the servers wear hairnets and little Ob/Gynish gloves. Hal could take out the plug and nip down into the tunnels, maybe not even all the way down into the Pump Room. Be only twenty minutes late. He's thinking in an abstract absent way about limits and rituals, listening to Blott give Beak his aperçu. Like as in is there a clear line, a quantifiable difference between need and just strong desire. He has to sit up to spit in the wastebasket. There is a twinge in a tooth on his mouth's left side.

MARIO INCANDENZA'S FIRST AND ONLY EVEN REMOTELY ROMANTIC EXPERIENCE, THUS FAR

In mid-October Y.D.A.U., Hal had invited Mario for a post-prandial stroll, and they were strolling the E.T.A. grounds between the West Courts and the hillside's tree-line, Hal with his gear bag. Mario could sense that Hal wanted to be able to go off by himself briefly, so he contrived (Mario did) to be very interested in some sort of leaf-and-twig ensemble off the path, and let Hal sort of melt away down the path. The whole area running along the tree-line and the thickets of like shrubbery and stickery bushes and heaven knew what all was covered with fallen leaves that were dry but had not yet quite all the way lost their color. The leaves were underfoot. Mario kind of tottered from tree to tree, pausing at each tree to rest. It was @ 1900h., not yet true twilight, but the only thing left of the sunset was a snout just over Newton, and the places under long shadows were cold, and a certain kind of melancholy sadness was insinuating itself into the grounds' light. The staggered lamps by the paths hadn't come on yet, however.

A lovely scent of illegally burned leaves wafting up from East Newton mixed with the foody smells from the ventilator turbines out of the back of the dining hall. Two gulls were in one place in the air over the dumpsters over by the rear parking lot. Leaves crackled underfoot. The sound of Mario walking in dry leaves was like: crackle crackle crackle stop; crackle crackle crackle stop.

An Empire Waste Displacement displacement vehicle whistled past overhead, rising in the start of its arc, its one blue alert-light atwinkle.

He was around where the tree-line bulged herniatically out toward the end of the West Courts' fencing. From deeper inside the thickets on the lip of the hillside came a tremendous crackling and thrashing of underbrush and trailing willow-branches, and who should heave into unexpected view but the U.S.S. Millicent Kent, a sixteen-year-old out of Montclair NJ, #1 Singles on the Girls 16's-A squad and two hundred kilos if she was a kilo. Southpaw, one-hander off the backhand side, a serve Donnie Stott likes to clock with radar, and chart. Mario's filmed the U.S.S. Millicent Kent for staff-analysis on several occasions. They exchange hearty Hi's. One of only a couple female E.T.A.s with visible veins in her forearms, object of a fiercely-wagered-on bench-press challenge against Schacht, Freer, and Petropolis Kahn that M. Pemulis had organized last spring, in which she'd topped Kahn and Freer refused to show and Schacht finally beat her but doffed his cap. Out for a staff-ordered weight-management post-dinner stroll, squeezing Penn 5's in both hands, in E.T.A. sweat pants and with an enormous violet bow either Scotch-taped or glued to the blunt rounded top of her hair. She told Mario she'd just seen the strangest thing farther back deeper in the thickets off the lip. Her hair was tall and rounded off in the shape of a kind of pill, not unlike a papal hat or a British constable's tall hat. Mario said the bow looked terrific, and what a surprise to come face to face like this out here in the chill dusk. Bridget Boone had said the U.S.S. Millicent Kent's coiffure looked like a missile protruding from its silo in preparation for launch. The last of the sun's snout was setting just over the tip of the U.S.S. Millicent's hair, which was almost osseously hard-looking, composed of dense woven nests of reticulate fibers like a dry loofa sponge, which she said over the summer a home-perm had misfired and left her hair a system of reticulate nests, and was only now loosening up enough even to attach a bow to. Mario said that well the bow set her off to a T, was all he had to say on the matter. (He hadn't literally said 'chill dusk.') The U.S.S.M.K. said she'd been amusing herself beating her way through one of the brambly thickets Mrs. Incandenza had — when she'd still spent time outdoors at all — planted to discourage part-time employees from short-cutting up the hillside to E.T.A., and had come upon a Husky VI-brand telescoping tripod, new and dully silvery-looking and set up on its three legs, right in the middle of the thicket. For no visible reason and with no footprints or visible evidence of path-beating anywhere around except the U.S.S. Millicent's own. The U.S.S. Millicent Kent stowed a tennis ball in each hip pocket and took Mario's claw and said here to walk this way and she'd show him real quick, and get his like feedback on the issue, and plus have a witness when they got back and she told people about it. Mario said the Husky VI came with its own pan head and cable release. With the girl supporting him with one hand and beating an easement through the brush with the other they proceeded deeper into the thicket on the lip. The outdoor light was now the same hue as U.S.S.M.K.'s hairbow. She said she swore to God it was around here someplace. Mario said his late dad had used a somewhat less snazzy IV-model Husky back in his early days of making art-films, when he also used a homemade dolly and sandbags and halogen spots instead of kliegs. Several different species and types of birds were twittering.

The U.S.S. Millicent Kent told Mario that off the record she'd always felt he had the longest lushest prettiest lashes of any boy on two continents, three if you counted Australia. Mario thanked her kindly, calling her Ma'am and trying to fake a Southern accent.

The U.S.S. Millicent Kent said she wasn't sure what were her old footprints from finding the thicket with the tripod and what were their more recent footprints from trying to find the old footprints, and that she was worried because it was starting to get dark and they might not be able to find it and then Mario wouldn't believe she'd seen something as batshit-sounding as a gleaming silvery tripod all set up for no reason in the middle of nowheresville.

Mario said he was pretty sure that Australia was a continent. Walking, he came up to around the bottom of U.S.S. Millicent's ribcage.

Mario heard crackling and thrashing from some other thicket nearby but was certain it wasn't Hal, since Hal very rarely made a lot of motion-noise either outside or in-.

The U.S.S. Millicent Kent told Mario that though she was an admittedly great player, w/ an overwhelming haul-ass-up-to-the-net-and-loom-over-it-like-a-titan game in the Betty Stove/Venus Williams power-game tradition, and headed for an almost limitless future in the Show, she'd confide in him in private out here that she'd never really loved competitive tennis, that her real love and passion was modern interpretive dance, at which she admittedly had less unconsciously native gifts and talents to bring to bear, but which she loved, and had spent just about all her off-court time as a little girl practicing in a leotard in front of a double-width mirror in her room at home in suburban Montclair NJ, but that tennis was what she had limitless talent at and got emotional strokes and tuition-waiver boarding-school offers in, and that she'd been desperate to get into a boarding school. Mario asked if she could recall if the Husky-VI tripod had been the TL one with waffle-gridded rubber tips on the legs and a 360° pan head or the SL one with unwaffled tips and only a 180° pan head that swiveled in an arc instead of a full circle. The U.S.S. Millicent revealed that she'd accepted a scholarship to E.T.A. at age nine for the sole reason of getting away from her father. She referred to her father as her Old Man, which you can just tell she capitalizes. Her mother had left home when the U.S.S. Millicent was only five, running off very abruptly with a man sent by what had then been called Con-Edison to do a free home-energy-efficiency assessment. It had been six years since she'd laid an eyeball on her Old Man, but to the best of her recall he was almost three meters tall and morbidly obese, which had been why every mirror and bathtub in the house had been double-width. One older sister who'd been deeply involved in synchronized swimming had got pregnant and married in high school soon after her mother's departure.

All this time there's been more crackling and crashing off up the hillside. Mario has trouble on any kind of declined grade. Some sort of bird's sitting in the top branch of a little tree and looking at them without saying anything. Mario thinks suddenly of a joke he remembers hearing Michael Pemulis tell:

'If two people get married in West Virginia and then pull up stakes and move to Massachusetts and then if they decide they want to get a divorce, what's the biggest problem getting a divorce?'

The U.S.S.M.K. says her other older sister had at just fifteen joined the Ice Capades of all things, and was in the back-up-like chorus where the biggest artistic challenge was not bumping into people and either falling or making them fall.

'Getting a divorce from your sister, because in West Virginia Pemulis said a lot of people who get married are brother and sister.'

'Hold my hand.'

'He was only joking, though.'

By now the light was about the same color as the ash and clinkers in the bottom of a Weber Grill. The U.S.S. Millicent Kent was leading them in a set of slightly diminishing circles. Then, she said, at age eight she came home early from after-school drills at the U.S.T.A. Jr. Facility in Passaic NJ looking forward to slipping into the old leotard and getting in some modern interpretive dancing up in her room, only to come home suddenly and find her father wearing her leotard. Which needless to say didn't fit very well. And with the small front portion of his huge bare feet squeezed into a pair of strapless pumps Mrs. Kent had left behind in her haste. In the dining room he'd moved all the furniture over to the side of, in front of the really wide mirror, in a grotesquely tiny and bulging violet leotard, capering. Mario says violet's really the U.S.S. Millicent's color. She says that was the exact creepy word for it: *capering*. Pirouetting and rondelling. Simpering, as well. The crotch of her leotard looked like a slingshot, it was so deformed. He hadn't heard her come in. U.S.S. Millicent asked Mario if he'd ever seen a girl's yin-yang before. Obscene mottled hirsute flesh had pooched and spilled out over every centimeter of the leotard's perimeter, she recalled. She'd had a voluptuous figure even at eight, she told Mario, but the Old Man was in a whole different-sized ballpark altogether. Mario kept saying Golly Ned, all he could think of to say. His flesh jiggled and bounced as he capered. It was repellent, she said. There was no sign of a Husky VI or any other model of tripod in any of the thickets and boscages. Her literal term for it was 'yin-yang.' But her Old Man wasn't just a cross-dressing transvestite, she said; it turned out they always had to be a *relative*'s female clothes. She said she always used to wonder why her sisters' one-pieces and figure-skating skirts always looked so askewly baggy and elastic-shot, since the sisters didn't exactly wear tiny little malnourished sizes themselves. The Old Man didn't hear her come in and he capered and jetéed for several more minutes until she happened to catch his simpering eye in the mirror, she said. That's when she knew she had to get away, she said. And Mario's own old man's Admissions lady had called out of the blue that very evening, she said. Like it had been fate. Serendipity. Kismet.

'Yin-yang,' Mario offered, nodding. The U.S.S. Millicent's hand was large and hot and at the level of sogginess of a bathmat that's been used several times in a row in quick succession.

Her second-oldest sister, many years later, had informed the U.S.S.M.K. that the first time anybody'd had any inklings about the Old Man was an episode when the older sister was very small and Mrs. K. had sewed her a special costume complete with gold-lamé bow & arrow for playing Cupid in the school Valentine's Day pageant, and the sister's school had got out early one day after an asbestos scare and she'd come unexpectedly home and found the Old Man in the basement rumpus room in tiny wings and hideously distended diaper striking a pose from a rather well-known Titian oil in the Met's High Renaissance Wing, and had struggled with denial and own-perceptions-doubting for quite some time thereafter, until a hysterical episode during rehearsals for an Ice Capades Valentine's Day number brought all the feelings surging up and broke the denial, and the Ice Capades' Employee Assistance Office counselling staff helped her start to work it all through.

At which point U.S.S. Millicent stopped them in an unprickly thicket of what later turned out to be poison sumac and turned with a strange glint in the one eye that wasn't in pine-shadow and crushed Mario's large head to the area just below her breasts and said she needed to confess that Mario's eyelashes and vest with extendable police lock he used for staying upright in one place had for quite some time now driven her right around the bend with sensual feeling. What Mario perceived as a sudden radical drop in the prevailing temperature was in fact the U.S.S. Millicent Kent's sexual stimulation sucking tremendous quantities of ambient energy out of the air surrounding them. Mario's face was so squashed against the U.S.S. Millicent's thorax that he had to contort his mouth way out to the left to breathe. U.S.S.M.K.'s hairbow became detached and fluttered down through Mario's sightline like a giant crazed violet moth. U.S.S.M.K. was trying to undo Mario's corduroys but was frustrated by the complex system of snaps and fasteners at the bottom of his police lock's Velcro vest, which overlapped his trouser's own fasteners, and Mario tried to reconfigure his mouth somehow to both breathe and warn the U.S.S.M.K. that he was incredibly ticklish in the area of the bellybutton and directly below. He could now start to hear his brother Hal somewhere to the above and east, calling Mario's name at a moderate volume. The U.S.S. Millicent Kent was saying there was no way Mario could be any more nervous than she was about what was happening between them. It's true that the sounds of Mario sucking air out of a severely leftward-contorted mouth could have been interpretable as the heavy breathing of sexual stimulation. It was when the U.S.S. Millicent wrapped one arm around his shoulder for leverage and forced her other hand up under the hem of the tight vest and then down inside the trousers and briefs, rooting for a penis, that Mario became so ticklish that he began to double up, clearing his face of U.S.S. Millicent's front and laughing out loud in such a distinctive high-pitched way that Hal had no trouble beelining right upon them, compromised though his navigational systems were after fifteen or so secret minutes alone in the fragrant pines.

Mario later said it was just like when there was a word on the tip of your tongue that try as you might you can't remember until the exact second you stop trying, and in it pops, right into your head: it was when the three of them were walking together back up the hillside toward the tree-line's lip, not trying to do anything but get back to Comm.-Ad. by the most direct route in the dark, that they stumbled upon the cinematic tripod, a dully glinting TL waffle-tipped Husky, in the middle of what wasn't such a very tall or thick thicket at all.

30 APRIL — YEAR OF THE DEPEND ADULT UNDERGARMENT

Steeply said 'Choosing Boston as your Ops center, after all, which to us signifies: the place of the supposed Entertainment's origin.'

Marathe made a gesture of being willing to take time and play along, if Steeply wished it. 'But also the city Boston U.S.A. has logic. Your closest city to the Convexity. Closest therefore to Québec. Within as you say the distance of spit.' His wheelchair squeaked very slightly whenever he moved. An automobile horn somewhere between the city and themselves blew a sustained blast. It grew always colder down on the desert floor; they could feel this. He felt gratitude for his windbreaker.

Steeply flicked some ashes from his cigarette with a coarse thumb-gesture that was not yet feminine. 'But we're not any more sure that they actually do have copies. Also, does this quote "anti"-Entertainment the film's director supposedly made to counter the lethality: does it really also exist; this really could be some sort of game for you and the F.L.Q.,[47] to hold out the promise of the anti-Entertainment as a chip for concessions. As some kind of remedy or antidote.'

'Of this anti-film that antidotes the seduction of the Entertainment we have no evidence except craziness of rumors.'

Steeply used a technical interviewer's device of pretending to occupy himself with small physical chores of preening and hygiene, delaying, to have Marathe elaborate himself more fully. The lights of the city Tucson with their movements and twinkling made a globe of light such as on ceilings at les salles de danser in Val d'Or, Québec. Marathe's wife was dying slowly of ventricular restenosis.[48] He thought: *die twice.*

Marathe said: 'And also why do they never send you into the field as

yourself, Steeply? This is to say in appearance. The last time you were —
what is it I hope to say — a Negro, for almost one year, no?'

U.S.A. persons' shrugs are always as if trying to lift a heavy thing. 'Haitian,' Steeply said. 'I was Haitian. Some negroid tendencies in the persona,
maybe.' Marathe listened to Steeply be silent. A U.S.A. coyote sounds more
like a high-strung dog. The automobile's horn continued, sounding to the
men forlorn and somehow nautical out below in the dark. The feminine
manner to examine the fingernails was to raise the whole hand's back into
view instead of malely curling the nails in over the upturned palm; Marathe
recalled knowing this from a very young age. Steeply would pick at the
corners of his lip, then for an interval change to examining the fingernails.
His silences seemed always comfortable and contained. He was a competent
operative. More cold air came, odd eddied breezes up in over the shelf from
the desert's floor, puffs of sudden air as if from the turning of a volume's
pages. His bare arms had the plucked-chicken look of chilled and bare skin
in his grotesque sleeveless dress. Marathe had not been aware of when during the falling of night Steeply had removed the absurd sunglasses, but decided the exact moment of this did not matter for reporting every word and
gesture back to M. Fortier. Again the coyote, and also another farther off,
perhaps to answer. The sounds were like that of a domestic dog being given
low voltage. Les Assassins' M. Fortier and M. Broullîme and some others of
his comrades-on-wheels believed Rémy Marathe to be eidetic, near-perfect
in recall and detail. Marathe, who could remember several incidents of crucial observations he had failed to later recall, knew this was not true.

30 APRIL — YEAR OF THE DEPEND ADULT UNDERGARMENT

Several times also Marathe called U.S.A. to Steeply 'Your walled nation'
or 'Your murated nation.'

O

An oiled guru sits in yogic full lotus in Spandex and tank top. He's maybe
forty. He's in full lotus on top of the towel dispenser just above the
shoulder-pull station in the weight room of the Enfield Tennis Academy,
Enfield MA. Saucers of muscle protrude from him and run together so that
he looks almost crustacean. His head gleams, his hair jet-black and extravagantly feathered. His smile could sell things. Nobody knows where he

comes from or why's he's allowed to stay, but he's always in there, sitting yogic about a meter off the rubberized floor of the weight room. His tank top says TRANSCEND in silkscreen; on the back it's got *DEUS PRO-VIDEBIT* in Day-Glo orange. It's always the same tank top. Sometimes the color of the Spandex leggings changes.

This guru lives off the sweat of others. Literally. The fluids and salts and fatty acids. He's like a beloved nut. He's an E.T.A. institution. You do like maybe some sets of benches, some leg-curls, inclined abs, crunches, work up a good hot shellac of sweat; then, if you let him lick your arms and forehead, he'll pass on to you some little nugget of fitness-guru wisdom. His big one for a long time was: 'And the Lord said: Let not the weight thou wouldst pull to thyself exceed thine own weight.' His advice on conditioning and injury-prevention tends to be pretty solid, is the consensus. His tongue is little and rough but feels good, like a kitty's. It isn't like a faggy or sexual thing. Some of the girls let him, too. He's harmless as they come. He supposedly went way back with Dr. Incandenza, the Academy's founder, in the past.

Some of the newer kids think he's a creep and want him out of there. What kind of guru wears Spandex and lives off others' perspiration? they complain. God only knows what he does in there when the weight room's closed at night, they say.

Sometimes the newer kids who won't even let him near them come in and set the resistance on the shoulder-pull at a weight greater than their own weight. The guru on the towel dispenser just sits there and smiles and doesn't say anything. They hunker, then, and grimace, and try to pull the bar down, but, like, lo: the overweighted shoulder-pull becomes a chin-up. Up they go, their own bodies, toward the bar they're trying to pull down. Everyone should get at least one good look at the eyes of a man who finds himself rising toward what he wants to pull down to himself. And I like how the guru on the towel dispenser doesn't laugh at them, or even shake his head sagely on its big brown neck. He just smiles, hiding his tongue. He's like a baby. Everything he sees hits him and sinks without bubbles. He just sits there. I want to be like that. Able to just sit all quiet and pull life toward me, one forehead at a time. His name is supposedly Lyle.

It was yrstruly and C and Poor Tony that crewed that day and everything like that. The AM were wicked bright and us a bit sick however we scored our wake ups boosting some items at a sidewalk sale in the Harvard Squar where it were warm upping and the snow coming off onnings and then later Poor Tony ran across an old Patty citizen type of his old aquaintance from like the Cape and Poor Tony got over and pretended like he would give a blow job On The House and we got the citizen to get in his ride with us and crewed on him good and we got enough $ off the Patty type to get straight-ened out for true all day and crewed on him hard and C wanted we should elemonade the Patty's map for keeps and everything like that and take his ride to this understanding slope strip shop he knows in Chinatown but Poor Tony turns white as a shit and said by no means and put up an arguement and everything like that and we just left the type there in his vehicle off Mem Dr we broke the jaw for insentive not to eat no cheese and C insisted and was not 2Bdenied and took off one ear which there was a mess and every-thing like that and then C throws the ear away after in a dumster so yrstrulys' like so what was the exact pernt to that like. The dumster was with the dumsters out by Steves' donuts in the Enfield Squar. We go back to the Brighton Projects to cop and Roy Tony was always there on his bench in the Playground in late AM but now all the Project Nigers was awake and out in the Playground and it was tense but it was day time and everything like that and we cop half a bundle from Roy Tony and we go down to the library at Copley where we stash our personnel works when we crewed and went into the mensroom where there was severel works on the floor allready that early and got straight in the stall and C and yrstruly had a beef about who shot three and who got two and we made Poor Tony give us up his third bag and then but we had to cop for that nite and tomorrow AM still which was XMas and had to cop in advance, its' a never ending strugle its' a full time job to stay straight and there is no vacation for XMas at anytime. Its' a fucking bitch of a life dont' let any body get over on you diffrent. And back we go to the Harvard Squar however on arrival Poor Tony wanted he should hang for lunch time with his red leather fags in the Bow&Arrow and pretty much I can tolerate fags when alone but together yrstruly I cant' fucking stand fags and yrstruly and C said fuck this shit and we screwed out and go up to the Central Squar where it was cool offing and the onnings re freezing and everything like that and snowing and boosted NyQuil at the CVS Drug where we go to the mop aile and employ a mophandle in tilting the mirror over the NyQuil aile and boosted NyQuil in Cs' coat and got messed up on NyQuil and scored a bookbag off a foran slope studn type kid on the Redline platform but it only had books and disks and the diskcase was fucking plastic and into a dumster with it it goes but also at this time we come up and run into Kely Vinoy that was working her corner by the dum-ster by Cheap-O records in the Squar by the email place and shes' dopesick having a conversession with Eckwus and an other man and Eckwus said he said Stokely Darkstar just got freetested again at the Fenway and confirmed a big Boot 8.8 hes' got the Virus for sure and Purpleboy said he said Dark-star said how if he was going down he didnt' give a shit and wasnt' going to give a shit if he gave some others the Virus thru trancemission and the Word was out&about dont' share Stokely Darkstars' works dont' use works off Stokely Darkstar no matter how sick you are even if your' dyng for it get other works. Like C said any thing would count in your mind when your' sick and had copped and was minus works and Darkstar had works. We all every crew with heads left have personnel works for only ourselves that we use except blownout old hose like Kely and Purpleboy there Man takes there $ and there works and Hes' the only one can give them there shots and keep Kely just this side of dopesick 24-7 for insentive for her to make him more $ and everything like that, theres' nothing wurse than a Pimp and Boston Pimps are the wurst there' 10X wurse than NYC Pimps that are supperst to be so hartless in NYC where yrstruly petaled ass in the Columbus Squar for a time of my youth like Stokely Darkstar before departing for green pastures, and we had a conversession but were' coming down and it was getting dark and snowing for a White XMas and if we didnt' crew before like 2200 Roy Tonys' Nigers would be too drunk to keep them from beefing with us and thered' be a beef and everything like that if we go to cop after 2200 and who needs a grief so back we Redline to the Harvard Squar and all the foran studns are in the bars and we locate Poor Tony smoking hash with fags back of Au Bon Pain and say lets roll a foran studn stuck here for XMas in the bars and cop before 2200 and so we all go on the ice from the frozen melted snow to the Bow&Arrow in the Squar with Poor Tony and Lolasister and Susan T. Cheese who I fucking cant' stand and got in there and made Susan T. Cheese buy beers and we wait and no studns are leaving alone to roll but a older type individual who any body could see is no studn but is legless on shots alone at the bar fucking shatered slumped over is getting ready to depart for green pastures and Poor Tony tells Lolasister to screw she crews with Poor Tony some times but not if its' wet work and with Cs' involvement its' always wet work, and yrstruly I inform Susan T. Cheese she new better than not to screw as well and the older individual de parts shatered and holding onto walls in a hiclass and promising coat for the possibility of $ and pernts his old nose this way and that and everything like that thru the Bow&Arrow window C wipes the steam off, and has a conversession with a Santaclaus ringing a big bell for the kettle and were' like Jesus its' a never ending strugle to wait and cop but after awhile finally after stifing the Santaclaus we watch he picks a direction finally at last up Mass Ave toward the Central Squar on foot, and Poor Tony beats it around the block to get up in front of him around the block on the ice in his fucking heels and feather snake around his neck and gets him some how Poor Tony always knows how over to the dumsters' alley by Bay Bank off Sherman St, and yrstruly and C crew on the individual and roll him and C messes up his older map to a large degree and we leave him in no condition to eat cheese in a snow drift of materil under the dumster, and C again wants to siphon out a vehicle on Mass Av and set him on fire but he has 400 $ on his person and then some and a coat with a fury collar and a watch we realy scored and C even gosofar to take the non studns' shoes which they dont' fit, and in the dumster they go.

And but so but back we go to the Brighton Projects but its' post 2200 its'

130

too late Roy Tony hasnt' got his pissboys out hes' not open for comerce and yet it is like a Niger Convenssion in the Playground of the Brighton Projects with there glass pipes and there Crown Royal in purple bags and everything like that in the Playground of the Projects and if they smell were' holding this kindof $ amounts they will crew on us in numbers there' animals at nite with there purple velvet bags and p-dope and Redi Rok crack, one large Niger in a Patriots hat has a hart incident and downhegoes on the black top by the swing set right in front of us and none of his *brothers* unquot gosofar to do any thing he lays there there' animals at nite and we screw out with rickytick speed from the Brighton Projects, and we converse. And Poor Tony wants to just go over the line to the Enfield Squar and try and just cop p-dope from Delphina down by the Empire hangers or else what else hang with the fags at Steves' donuts and hear who else is holding weight in Enfield or Allston and everything like that, but Delphinas' p is from bunk the Word is out&about that its' all Manitol and kwai9 you might as well fucking cop XLax or Schweppes and C dopeslaps Poor Tony and C wants to Redline down to Chinatown but Poor Tony turns white as a shit and says Chinatowns' too dear in $ and everything like that, even for like bundles, Dr. Wo is 200 $ but atleast its' always good and but we have 400 $ and then some and C pernts out we can fucking well afford Wos' well known exellent skeet for once at XMas and Poor Tony stamps a hiheel and says but how weve' got enough $ to stay straight and get Lolasister straight for XMas and all lay up and not have to never ending strugle at XMas and two or more days after that if we dont' blow it on XMas Eve in Chinatown instead of waiting which is a good pernt but when has any body known C to ever wait he gets dopesick faster than us and everything like that and is all piss and vinegar for Wo and starting with the Shivers and with the noses' mucis all ready and everything like that and C is not 2Bdenied and we say we are screwing down to Chinatown and if Poor Tony dont' want to come he can take a like a giant breath and hold it in the Squar until we get back and well' cop for him, and Poor Tony says he might be a dicksucking fag but hes' not a starry eyed' moroon.

And so offwego and everything like that with 400 $ on the Orangeline, and thru a fucked up circumstances yrstruly and C almost end up raping a older type nurse in a white nurses' uniform and coat on the train but we dont' and but Poor Tony seems white and detracted on the train playng with his feather snake and says he says he seems in his mind maybe to recall an involvment in some type deal where Dr. Wo might of got slightly got over on and burnt and that maybe down in Chinatown we could air on the side of low profiles and try to cop some where else except from the Wos'. Except Dr. Wo is who we know. C is Wos' former aquaintance from crewing with slopes on the North shore for Whity Sorkin in the days of his youth. C is not 2Bdenied. And so at the Orangeline Tstop we grab a fat cab to about two blocks from Hung Toys and screw out of the cab at a light and the thing with fat cabbies is they cant' run after you and Poor Tony is pisser to watch tearassing it down the street in hiheels with a feather stoal. Poor Tony runs right by the front of Hung Toys, this is by pryor agreement to wait for us low profile down the street and yrstruly and C go in Hung Toys where they dont' open till 2300 and sell *tea* unquot like 100 Proof tea till all hours and everything like that and never get Inspected because Dr. Wo has arrangements with Chinatowns' Finest. XMas is noncelebrated in Chinatown. Dr. Wo a good thing about Wo is hes' always there in Hung Toys at known times. Here theres' all old slope racial type ladies sitting in booths eating noddles and drinking quot tea out of white cups the size of a shotglass and everything like that. With small slope kids tearassing it all over and older men in like jew caps and skinny beerds out of just the middle of there chin but Dr. Wo is only middle aged and wears iron glasses and a tie and looks more like a banker for a slope but he is 100 % business and icecold all the way down for slope type comerce plus hes' connected bigtime and not to be fucked or got over on if some body has a head left and yrstruly I cant' believe Poor Tony would ever take part of tryng to crew on Wo who he knows thru C in even the smallest comerce and if he did C says he sure never heard about it nor saw any of the skeet or anything like that, and why. Cs' the one that knows Wo. We arranged Poor Tony to wait for us out side and try to be low profile. Its' sub 0 snow and hes' in a leather spring coat and stoal and brown wig thats' not as good as a hat and hell' freeze his low profile balls off and C was tryng to smile and he told Dr. Wo we needed three bundles and Dr. Wo was smiling in his slope manner said the boosting life must surely be exellent and C laughed and said *most* exellent Cs' tight with slopes he does the talking and everything like that, and he says were' going to lay up low profile for the XMas vacation and not crew because I had a rape type situation from an older nurse last nite on the T and almost got pinched by the Ts' Finest and Dr. Wo nods in a special subservant manner he uses for non slopes who hes' realy polite with but hes' a dictater to his slopes when we see him with his subservant slopes but with us were' allike most polite and everything like conversession and its' nice but expensive but it feels nice at the time but Wo finishes his so called *tea* and Wo goes back behind the curtains in the back of Hung Toys thats' a giant brightred curtain with purple mountains or hills and clouds that are flyng snakes with leather wings that is one curtain yrstruly would want to boost for personnel hanging use that no body that isnt' a slope and isnt' in with Wo cant' never go behind it but you can see when he opens it and goes behind the curtain it looks like merly more old slope ladies sitting on packing cases with slope writing eating more noddles in bowls they hold about like a millmeter from their yellow maps and everything like that. Slopes rarly stop shovling in the old noddles. Stokely Darkstar calls them maggoteaters and subservant slopes keep going in and out of the curtain while Wos' back there a longer than avrege time and Cs' got the Shivers and starting to jones and dope-fiends are full of super station and he says to yrstruly he says the fuck he says maybe what if Poor Tony realy did take part with burning Wo and what if a slope sees Poor Tony out side and is one of these slopes going in and out of the curtain maybe telling Wo, like ratting out Poor Tony as our aquaintance, and my mucis is starting and were' jonesing super statiously over PT and wheres' Wo behind the curtain and everything like that, tryng to smile and conversession ultralow, drinking quot tea thats' like schnapps only wurse and green. And we jones and Dr. Wo comes back finally at last out smiling subservantly with all the wonderful skeet three bundles in a newspaper who could fucking read it but the pictures are of slope VIPs' in suits and Wo sits down, and Wo never sits down at the booth with the skeet it isnt' done in his comerce, and Wos' hands are folded over our skeet in the thing and Wo smiling says he asks C if weve' seen goodold Poor Tony or Susan T. Cheese around we crew with Poor Tony in boosting life did we not he said. C he says PT is a fucking dicksucking fag queer and a proven cheeseater and wed' fucked up his map and Cheese and Lolasisters' map in a beef and didnt' crew with fags since aprox the autum period. C is pouring mucis and tryng to smile cusually, Dr. Wo laughed in a harty fashion and said exellent and Wo leaned over our skeet sayng if we should happenbychance to see Poor Tony or them to please give Poor Tony his quite best regards and wish him prosparity and a thousand *blisses*. And everything like that. And we promote the newspaper of skeet and Wo promotes our $ and very politely outwego and I admit it yrstruly wanted we should burn Poor Tony and rickytick the fuck out of Chinatown but we go over down more by the China Pearl Place and Poor Tony is sortof hunched behind a lightpoal with his gray teeth chatting in his dress and thin coat tryng to be low profile in his red coat and heels around a million+ slopes that all are subservants of Wo. And later after screwing out we didnt' tell him of what Wo said about sitting down and asking about him and Cheeses' *blisses* and we screw to the Orangeline to our hot air blowergrate we use at nite at the library behind the Copley Squar and we get our personnel works out from behind the brickworks behind the bush by the hot blowergrate where we stash our works and were' eggerly into the first bundle and were' cooking up and notice Poor Tony doesnt' the least bitch when yrstruly and C tie off first in line seeing as were' the ones that copped it and Poor Tonys' gotto wait as usal, except I notice he doesnt' bitch even a little, normally Poor Tony keeps up this usal wine yrstruly learned how to not notice, but when he doesnt' wine now that were' jonesing and the skeets' right there I notice hes' cusually looking like every place but at the skeet which is unusal and C jonesing and with the Shivers cooking up tryng to keep his lighter lit in the hot airs' wind and snow of nite, and I admit it yrstruly I get a wicked cold inside feeling even with all this hot air from the blowergrate blowing up from under us and making our hair blow around and Tonys' feather snake pernt upword I yrstruly get a cold feeling of super station once more, you get wicked super stations in this fucked up kindof shit life because its' a never ending chase and you get too tired to go by much more than never ending habit and super station and everything like that so but I dont' say any thing but yrstruly I have a cold super station about Poor Tony not wining while he makes like he has to cusually piss and takes a piss and the piss steams up around the lower ares of the bush with his back turned away and isnt' looking around with interst or anything like that you never turn your back on the skeet when its' partly your skeet which is wicked unusal which C is so eggerly dopesick he doesnt' notice any thing past keeping the lighter lit. And so I admit it I yrstruly did yrstruly purplously let C tie off and boot up first while I still cooked up, I did cook up unusally slow, fucking with the getting the snowmelt hot in the spoon and everything like that yrstruly I let the lighter go out and took more time with the cotton and C had the Shivers wurst of us and cooks up the fastest and would of got it anyway. Later with Cs' map elemonaded Poor Tony later conceited admitting Susan T. Cheese helped a Worcester fag get over on Wo for a fronted bundle in autum is why. And all three bundles Wo give us in slope news was Hotshots. Laced. It started the instantly C undid the belt and booted up we knew allready, yrstruly I and PT thearized it was Drano with the blue like glittershit and everything like that taken out by subservant slopes it had that Drano like effect on C and everything like that it was laced what ever it was C started with the screaming in a loud hipitch fashion instantly after he unties and boots and downhegoes flopping with his heels pouning on the metal of the blower-grate and hes' at his throat with his hands tearing at him self in the most fucked up fashions and Poor Tony is hiheeling rickytick over over C zipping up sayng he screams sweety C but and stuffing the feather snake from his necks' head in Cs' mouth to shut him up from hipitch screaming in case Bostons' Finest can hear involvment and blood and bloody materil is coming out Cs' mouth and Cs' nose and its' allover the feathers its' a sure sign of Drano, blood is and Cs' eyes get beesly and bulge and hes' cryng blood into the feathers in his mouth and tryng to hold onto my glove but Cs' arms are going allover and one eye it like allofa sudden pops outof his map, like with a Pop you make with fingers in your mouth with all this blood and materil and a blue string at the back of the eye and the eye falls over the side of Cs' map and hangs there looking at the fag Poor Tony. And C turned lightblue and bit thru the snakes' head and died for keeps and shit his pants instanly with shit so bad the hot air blowergrate is blowing small bits of fart and blood and missty shit up into our maps and Poor Tony backs offof over C and puts his hands over his madeup map and looks at C thru his fingers. And yrstruly I take the belt off it goes without saying, and dont' even rethink or dream about tryng maybe a diffrent bag out of a diffrent bundle from C for how could Wo know what bundle wed' cook up outof first so all three bundles must be Hot so I dont' even dream even tho yrstrulys' Shiverng and mucis sick allready and now in payback Wo has our only $ to get straight with for XMas. It might sound fucking low but the reason we had to leave the decesed body C in one of the librarys' dumsters is the reason is because the Copley Squars' Finest know it is our personnel hot air blowergrate and if we leave C there its' a sure pinch for us as known aquaintance and a period of Kicking The Bird in holding in a cell but the dumster was empty of materil and Cs' head made a fucked up sound when it hit the empty bottom and Poor Tony cried and wined and said he said he had no inkling that beast Wo was that vindicative and poorold decesed C and how this was it hes' going to get clean from heronout and get a straightjob dancing in a Patty type Club in the Fenway and everything like that on and on piss and wine. I didnt' say any thing. I had to rethink on the T to the Squar if yrstruly I should elemonade Poor Tonys' map for keeps for payback on how he purplously lets C shoot up first and wouldof' let yrstruly shoot first even knowing, or make that cheese move and go back down the Orangeline to Wo and try and get enough bags to get true straight eating cheese to Wo about the wherehouse that Poor Tony and Susan T. Cheese and Lolasister with Eckwus crashed at now. Or like *what*. Yrstruly I almost was cryng. It was when Poor Tony took off his hiheels and wanted yrstruly I should boost him like over the edge of Cs' bodies' dumster to get back what was left of his feather stoal out of Cs' mouth that yrstruly I thought I decided what to do. But the connected slope Wo wasnt' even there in front of the Hung Toys curtain in the early XMas AM, and then Poor Tony departed for green pastures and ate cheese, and it took yrstruly two days of Kicking The Bird in the hall out side my Mumsters' apartment that for payback she locked the door before I yrstruly can get in a Detox to atleast cop some methedoan and get three squars to stay down in yrstruly to start to thearize on what to try and do after I could standup straight and walk upright again once more.

3 NOVEMBER Y.D.A.U.

Hal could hear the phone console ringing as he dropped his gear bag and took the room key from around his neck. The phone itself had been Orin's and its plastic case was transparent and you could see the phone's guts.
'Mmyellow.'
'Why do I always get the feeling I'm interrupting you in the middle of

some like vigorous self-abuse session?' It was Orin's voice. 'It's always multiple rings. Then you're always a little breathless when you do.'

'Do what.'

'A certain sweaty urgency to your voice. Are you one of the 99% of adolescent males, Hallie?'

Hal never liked talking on the phone after he'd gotten high in secret down in the Pump Room. Even if there was water or liquid handy to keep the cotton at bay. He didn't know why this was so. It just made him uneasy.

'You're sounding hale and fit, O.'

'You can tell me, you know. No shame in it. Let me tell you, boy, I did myself raw for years on end on that hill.'

Hal estimated over 60% of what he told Orin on the phone since Orin had abruptly started calling again this spring was a lie. He had no idea why he liked lying to Orin on the phone so much. He looked at the clock. 'Where are you?'

'Home. Snug and toasty. It's 90+ out.'

'That would be Fahrenheit I'm assuming.'

'This city is made of all glass and light. The windows are like high-beams coming at you. The air has that spilled-fuel shimmer to it.'

'So to what do we owe.'

'Sometimes I wear sunglasses even in the house. Sometimes at the stadium I hold my hand up and look at it and I swear I can see right through it. Like that thing with the flashlight and your hand.'

'Hands seem to be sort of a theme to this call, thus far.'

'On the way in from the lot off the street here I saw a pedestrian in a pith helmet stagger and like claw at the air and pitch forward onto his face. Another Phoenician felled by the heat I think to myself.'

It occurred to Hal that although he lied about meaningless details to Orin on the phone it had never occurred to him to consider whether Orin was ever doing the same thing. This induced a spell of involuted marijuana-type thinking that led quickly, again, to Hal's questioning whether or not he was really all that intelligent. 'SATs are six weeks away and Pemulis is less and less helpful on the math, if you want to know what I'm doing all day.'

'The man's face made a sizzling noise when it hit the pavement. Like bacon-caliber sizzling. He's still lying there, I see out the window. He's not moving anymore. Everyone's avoiding him, going around him. He looks too hot to touch. A little Hispanic kid made off with his hat. Have y'all had snow yet? Describe snow for me again, Hallie, I'm begging you.'

'So you go around with this image of me sitting around during the day masturbating, is what you're saying.'

'I've actually been thinking of maneuvering for the whole Kleenex concession at E.T.A., as a venture.'

'That of course would mean actually contacting C.T. and the Moms.'

'Me and this forward-looking reserve QB have been making inquiries.

Putting out feelers. Volume discounts, preferred-vendor status. Maybe a sideline in unscented lubricants. Any thoughts?'

'O.?'

'I'm sitting here actually missing New Orleans, kid. It'd be just coming up on Advent I think. The Quarter always gets really quaint and demure during Advent. It almost never rains down there during Advent for some reason. People remark on it, the phenomena.'

'You sound somehow a little off to me, O.'

'I'm heat-crazed. I might be dehydrated. What's that word? Everything's looked all beige and powdery all day. Trash bags have been swelling up and spontaneously combusting out in the dumpsters. These sudden rains of coffee grounds and orange peels. The Displacement guys in the barges have to wear asbestos gloves. Also I met somebody. Hallie, a possibly very special somebody.'

'Uh oh. Dinnertime. Triangle's a-clangin' over in West.'

'Hey Hallie though? Hang on. Kidding aside for a second. What all do you know about Separatism?'

Hal stopped for a moment. 'You mean in Canada?'

'Is there any other kind?'

Ennet House Drug and Alcohol Recovery House[49] was founded in the Year of the Whopper by a nail-tough old chronic drug addict and alcoholic who had spent the bulk of his adult life under the supervision of the Massachusetts Department of Corrections before discovering the fellowship of Alcoholics Anonymous at M.D.C.-Walpole and undergoing a sudden experience of total self-surrender and spiritual awakening in the shower during his fourth month of continuous AA sobriety. This recovered addict/ alcoholic — who in his new humility so valued AA's tradition of anonymity that he refused even to use his first name, and was known in Boston AA simply as the Guy Who Didn't Even Use His First Name — opened Ennet House within a year of his parole, determined to pass on to other chronic drug addicts and alcoholics what had been so freely given to him in the E-Tier shower.

Ennet House leases a former physicians' dormitory in the Enfield Marine Public Health Hospital Complex, managed by the United States Veterans Administration. Ennet House is equipped to provide 22 male and female clients a nine-month period of closely supervised residency and treatment.

Ennet House was not only founded but originally renovated, furnished, and decorated by the nameless local AA ex-con, who — since sobriety doesn't exactly mean instant sainthood — used to lead select teams of early-recovery dope fiends on after-hours boosting expeditions at area furniture and housewares establishments.

This legendary anonymous founder was an extremely tough old Boston AA galoot who believed passionately that everyone, no matter how broad the trail of slime they dragged in behind them, deserved the same chance at sobriety through utterly total surrender he'd been granted. It's a kind of extremely tough love found almost exclusively in tough old Boston galoots.[50] He sometimes, the founder, in the House's early days, required incoming residents to attempt to eat rocks — as in like rocks from the ground — to demonstrate their willingness to go to any lengths for the gift of sobriety. The Massachusetts Department of Public Health's Division of Substance Abuse Services eventually requested that this practice be discontinued.

Ennet was not any part of the nameless Ennet House founder's name, by the way.

The rock thing — which has become a grim bit of mythopoeia now trotted out to illustrate how cushy the present Ennet residents have it — was probably not as whacko as it seemed to Division of S.A.S., since many of the things veteran AA's ask newcomers to do and believe seem not much less whacko than trying to chew feldspar. E.g. be so strung out you can feel your pulse in your eyeballs, have the shakes so badly you make a spatter-painting on the wall every time somebody hands you a cup of coffee, have the life-forms out of the corner of your eye be your only distraction from the chainsaw-racing chatter in your head, sitting there, and have some old lady with cat-hair on her nylons come at you to hug you and tell you to make a list of all the things you're grateful for today: you'll wish you had some feldspar handy, too.

In the Year of the Yushityu 2007 Mimetic-Resolution-Cartridge-View-Motherboard-Easy-To-Install Upgrade For Infernatron/InterLace TP Systems For Home, Office Or Mobile,[51] the nameless founder's death of a cerebral hemorrhage at age sixty-eight went unremarked outside the Boston AA community.

FROM INTERNAL INTERLACE-SYSTEM E-MAIL MEMO
CAH-NNE22-3575634-22, CLAIMS ADJUSTMENT
HEADQUARTERS, STATE FARM INSURANCE COMPANIES, INC.,
BLOOMINGTON IL 26 JUNE
YEAR OF DAIRY PRODUCTS FROM THE AMERICAN
HEARTLAND

FROM: murrayf @clmshqnne22.626INTCOM
TO: powellg/sanchezm/parryk @ clmhqnne.626INTCOM
MESSAGE: guys, get a load. my def. of a bad day. metro boston region 22 this spring, comp claim. witnesses deposed by boston wrkmans comp. establish claimant Impaired and the emerg. room

rept. lists a blood-alcohol of .3+, so be pleased to know we're clear on the 357-5 liability end. but basic facts below confirmed by witnesses and CYD accident rept. here's just the first page, get a load:

murrayf @clmshqnne22.626INTCOM 626YDPAH0112317/p. 1

Dwayne R. Glynn
176N. Faneuil Blvd.
Stoneham, Mass. 021808754/4
June 21, YODPFTAH

Workmans Accident Claims Office
State Farm Insurance
1 State Farm Plaza
Normal, Ill. 617062262/6

Dear Sir:

I am writing in response to your request for additional information. In block #3 of the accident reporting form, I put "trying to do the job alone", as the cause of my accident. You said in your letter that I should explain more fully and I trust that the following details will be sufficient.

I am a bricklayer by trade. On the day of the accident, March 27, I was working alone on the roof of a new six story building. When I completed my work, I discovered that I had about 900 kg. of brick left over. Rather than laboriously carry the bricks down by hand, I decided to lower them in a barrel by using a pulley which fortunately was attached to the side of the building at the sixth floor. Securing the rope at ground level, I went up to the roof, swung the barrel out and loaded the brick into it. Then I went back to the ground and untied the rope, holding it tightly to insure a slow descent of the 900 kg of bricks. You will note in block #11 of the accident reporting form that I weigh 75 kg.

Due to my surprise at being jerked off the ground so suddenly, I lost my presence of mind and forgot to let go of the rope. Needless to say, I proceeded at a rapid rate up the side of the building. In the vicinity of the third floor I met the barrel coming down. This explains the fractured skull and the broken collar bone.

Slowed only slightly, I continued my rapid ascent not stopping until the fingers of my right hand were two knuckles deep into the pulleys. Fortunately, by this time, I had regained my presence of mind, and was able to hold tightly to the rope in spite of considerable pain. At approximately the same time, however, the barrel of bricks hit the ground and the bottom fell out of the barrel from the force of hitting the ground.

Devoid of the weight of the bricks, the barrel now weighed approximately 30 kg. I refer you again to my weight of 75 kg in block #11. As you could imagine, still holding the rope, I began a rather rapid descent from the pulley down the side of the building. In the vicinity of the third floor, I met the barrel coming up. This accounts for the two fractured ankles and the laceration of my legs and lower body.

The encounter with the barrel slowed me enough to lessen my impact with the brick-strewn ground below. I am sorry to report, however, that as I lay there on the bricks in considerable pain, unable to stand or move and watching the empty barrel six stories above me, I again lost my presence of mind and unfortunately let go of the rope, causing the barrel to begin a

endtransINTCOM626

HAL INCANDENZA'S FIRST EXTANT WRITTEN COMMENT ON ANYTHING EVEN REMOTELY FILMIC, SUBMITTED IN MR. OGILVIE'S SEVENTH-GRADE 'INTRODUCTION TO ENTERTAINMENT STUDIES' (2 TERMS, REQUIRED), ENFIELD TENNIS ACADEMY, 21 FEBRUARY IN THE YEAR OF THE PERDUE WONDERCHICKEN, @ FOUR YEARS AFTER THE DEMISE OF BROADCAST TELEVISION, ONE YEAR AFTER DR. JAMES O. INCANDENZA PASSED FROM THIS LIFE, A SUBMISSION RECEIVING JUST A B/B+, DESPITE OVERALL POSITIVE FEEDBACK, MOSTLY BECAUSE ITS CONCLUDING ¶ WAS NEITHER SET UP BY THE ESSAY'S BODY NOR SUPPORTED, OGILVIE POINTED OUT, BY ANYTHING MORE THAN SUBJECTIVE INTUITION AND RHETORICAL FLOURISH.

Chief Steve McGarrett of 'Hawaii Five-0' and Captain Frank Furillo of 'Hill Street Blues' are useful for seeing how our North American idea of the hero changed from the B.S. 1970s era of 'Hawaii Five-0' to the B.S. 1980s era of 'Hill Street Blues.'

Chief Steve McGarrett is a classically modern hero of action. He acts out. It is what he does. The camera is always on him. He is hardly ever off-screen. He has just one case per week. The audience knows what the case is and also knows, by the end of Act One, who is guilty. Because the audience knows the truth before Steve McGarrett does, there is no mystery, there is only Steve McGarrett. The drama of 'Hawaii Five-0' is watching the hero in action, watching Steve McGarrett stalk and strut, homing in on the truth. Homing in is the essence of what the classic hero of modern action does.

Steve McGarrett is not weighed down by administrative State-Police-Chief chores, or by females, or friends, or emotions, or any sorts of conflicting demands on his attention. His field of action is bare of diverting clutter. Thus Chief Steve McGarrett single-mindedly acts to refashion a truth the audience already knows into an object of law, justice, modern heroism.

In contrast, Captain Frank Furillo is what used to be designated a 'post'-modern hero. Viz., a hero whose virtues are suited to a more complex and corporate American era. I.e., a hero of reaction. Captain Frank Furillo does not investigate cases or single-mindedly home in. He commands a precinct. He is a bureaucrat, and his heroism is bureaucratic, with a genius for navigating cluttered fields. In each broadcast episode of 'Hill Street Blues,' Captain Frank Furillo is beset by petty distractions on all sides from the very beginning of Act One. Not one but eleven complex cases, each with suspects and snitches and investigating officers and angry community leaders and victims' families all clamoring for redress. Hundreds of tasks to delegate, egos to massage, promises to make, promises from last week to keep. Two or three cops' domestic troubles. Payroll vouchers. Duty logs. Corruption to be tempted by and agonized over. A Police Chief who's a political parody, a hyperactive son, an ex-wife who haunts the frosted-glass cubicle that serves as Frank Furillo's office (whereas Steve McGarrett's B.S. 1970s office more closely resembled the libraries of landed gentry, hushed behind two heavy doors and wainscotted in thick, tropical oak), plus a coldly attractive Public Defendress who wants to talk about did this suspect get Mirandized in Spanish and can Frank stop coming too soon he came too soon again last night maybe he should get into some kind of stress counselling. Plus all the weekly moral dilemmas and double binds his even-handed bureaucratic heroism gets Captain Frank Furillo into.

Captain Frank Furillo of 'Hill Street Blues' is a 'post'-modern hero, a virtuoso of triage and compromise and administration. Frank Furillo retains his sanity, composure, and superior grooming in the face of a barrage of distracting, unheroic demands that would have left Chief Steve McGarrett slumped, unkempt, and chewing his knuckle in administrative confusion.

In further contrast to Chief Steve McGarrett, Captain Frank Furillo is rarely filmed tight or full-front. He is usually one part of a frenetic, moving pan by the program's camera. In contrast, 'Hawaii Five-o' 's camera crew never even used a dolly, favoring a steady tripodic close-up on McGarrett's face that today seems more reminiscent of romantic portraiture than filmed drama.

What kind of hero comes after McGarrett's Irishized modern cowboy, the lone man of action riding lonely herd in paradise? Furillo's is a whole different kind of loneliness. The 'post'-modern hero was a heroic *part of* the herd, responsible for all of what he is part of, responsible to everyone, his lonely face as placid under pressure as a cow's face. The jut-jawed hero of action ('Hawaii Five-0') becomes the mild-eyed hero of reaction ('Hill Street Blues,' a decade later).

And, as we have observed thus far in our class, we, as a North American audience, have favored the more Stoic, corporate hero of reactive probity ever since, some might be led to argue 'trapped' in the reactive moral ambiguity of 'post-' and 'post-post'-modern culture.

But what comes next? What North American hero can hope to succeed the placid Frank? We await, I predict, the hero of *non*-action, the catatonic hero, the one beyond calm, divorced from all stimulus, carried here and there across sets by burly extras whose blood sings with retrograde amines.

ENORMOUS, ELECTROLYSIS-RASHED 'JOURNALIST' 'HELEN' STEEPLY'S ONLY PUTATIVE PUBLISHED ARTICLE BEFORE BEGINNING HER SOFT PROFILE ON PHOENIX CARDINALS PUNTER ORIN J. INCANDENZA, AND HER ONLY PUTATIVE PUBLISHED ARTICLE TO HAVE ANYTHING OVERTLY TO DO WITH GOOD OLD METROPOLITAN BOSTON, 10 AUGUST IN THE YEAR OF THE DEPEND ADULT UNDERGARMENT, FOUR YEARS AFTER OPTICAL THEORIST, ENTREPRENEUR, TENNIS ACADEMICIAN, AND AVANT-GARDE FILMMAKER JAMES O. INCANDENZA TOOK HIS OWN LIFE BY PUTTING HIS HEAD IN A MICROWAVE OVEN

Moment Magazine has learned that the tragic fate of the second North American citizen to receive a Jarvik IX Exterior Artificial Heart has, sadly, been kept from the North American people. The woman, a 46-year-old Boston accountant with irreversible restenosis of the heart, responded so well to the replacement of her defective heart with a Jarvik IX Exterior Artificial Heart that within weeks she was able to resume the active lifestyle she had so enjoyed before stricken, pursuing her active schedule with the extraordinary prosthesis portably installed in a stylish Etienne

Aigner purse. The heart's ventricular tubes ran up to shunts in the woman's arms and ferried life-giving blood back and forth between her living, active body and the extraordinary heart in her purse.

Her tragic, untimely, and, some might say, cruelly ironic fate, however, has been the subject of the all too frequent silence needless tragedies are buried beneath when they cast the callous misunderstanding of public officials in the negative light of public knowledge. It took the sort of searching and fearless journalistic doggedness readers have come to respect in *Moment* to unearth the tragically negative facts of her fate.

The 46-year-old recipient of the Jarvik IX Exterior Artificial Heart was actively window shopping in Cambridge, Massachusetts' fashionable Harvard Square when a transvestite purse snatcher, a drug addict with a criminal record all too well known to public officials, bizarrely outfitted in a strapless cocktail dress, spike heels, tattered feather boa, and auburn wig, brutally tore the life sustaining purse from the woman's unwitting grasp.

The active, alert woman gave chase to the purse snatching 'woman' for as long as she could, plaintively shouting to passers by the words 'Stop her! She stole my heart!' on the fashionable sidewalk crowded with shoppers, reportedly shouting repeatedly, 'She stole my heart, stop her!' In response to her plaintive calls, tragically, misunderstanding shoppers and passers by merely shook their heads at one another, smiling knowingly at what they ignorantly presumed to be yet another alternative lifestyle's relationship gone sour. A duo of Cambridge, Massachusetts, patrolmen, whose names are being withheld from *Moment*'s dogged queries, were publicly heard to passively quip, 'Happens all the time,' as the victimized woman staggered frantically past in the wake of the fleet transvestite, shouting for help for her stolen heart.

That the prosthetic crime victim gave spirited chase for over four blocks before collapsing onto her empty chest is testimony to the impressive capacity of the Jarvik IX replacement procedure, was the anonymous comment of a public medical official reached for comment by *Moment*.

The drug crazed purse snatcher, informed officials passively speculated, may have found even his hardened conscience moved by the life saving prosthesis the ill gotten woman's Aigner purse revealed, which runs on the same rechargeable power cell as an electric man's razor, and may well have continued to beat and bleed for a period of time in the rudely disconnected purse. The purse snatcher's response to this conscience appears to have been cruelly striking the Jarvik IX Exterior Artificial Heart repeatedly with a stone or small hammer-like tool, where its remains were found some hours later behind the historic Boston Public Library in fashionable Copley Square.

Is medical science's awe inspiring march forward, however, always doomed to include such tragic incidents of ignorance and callous loss, one might ask. Such seems to be the stance of North American officials. If indeed so, the victims' fate is frequently kept from the light of public knowledge.

And the facts of the case's outcome? The 46-year-old deceased woman's formerly active, alert brain was removed and dissected six weeks later by a Brigham and Women's City of Boston Hospital medical student reportedly so moved by her terse toe tag's account of the victim's heartless fate that he confessed to *Moment* a temporary inability to physically wield the power saw of his assigned task.

ALPHABETICAL TALLY OF SÉPARATISTEUR / ANTI-O.N.A.N.
GROUPS WHOSE OPPOSITION
TO INTERDEPENDENCE / RECONFIGURATION IS
DESIGNATED BY R.C.M.P. AND U.S.O.U.S. AS
TERRORIST / EXTORTIONIST IN CHARACTER

(Q=Québecois, E=Environmental, S=Separatist, V=Violent,
VV=Extremely Violent)

— *Les Assassins des Fauteuils Rollents* (Q, S, VV)
— *Le Bloc Québecois* (Q, S, E)
— Calgarian Pro-Canadian Phalanx (E, V)
— *Les Fils de Montcalm* (Q, E)
— *Les Fils de Papineau* (Q, S, V)
— *Le Front de la Libération de la Québec* (Q, S, VV)
— *Le Parti Québecois* (Q, S, E)

WHY — THOUGH IN THE EARLY DAYS OF INTERLACE'S
INTERNETTED TELEPUTERS THAT OPERATED OFF LARGELY
THE SAME FIBER-DIGITAL GRID AS THE PHONE COMPANIES,
THE ADVENT OF VIDEO-TELEPHONING (A.K.A. 'VIDEOPHONY')
ENJOYED AN INTERVAL OF HUGE CONSUMER POPULARITY —
CALLERS THRILLED AT THE IDEA OF PHONE-INTERFACING
BOTH AURALLY AND FACIALLY (THE LITTLE FIRST-
GENERATION PHONE-VIDEO CAMERAS BEING TOO CRUDE
AND NARROW-APERTURED FOR ANYTHING MUCH MORE
THAN FACIAL CLOSE-UPS) ON FIRST-GENERATION TELEPUTERS
THAT AT THAT TIME WERE LITTLE MORE THAN HIGH-TECH
TV SETS, THOUGH OF COURSE THEY HAD THAT LITTLE
'INTELLIGENT-AGENT' HOMUNCULAR ICON THAT WOULD

APPEAR AT THE LOWER-RIGHT OF A BROADCAST/CABLE PROGRAM AND TELL YOU THE TIME AND TEMPERATURE OUTSIDE OR REMIND YOU TO TAKE YOUR BLOOD-PRESSURE MEDICATION OR ALERT YOU TO A PARTICULARLY COMPELLING ENTERTAINMENT-OPTION NOW COMING UP ON CHANNEL LIKE 491 OR SOMETHING, OR OF COURSE NOW ALERTING YOU TO AN INCOMING VIDEO-PHONE CALL AND THEN TAP-DANCING WITH A LITTLE ICONIC STRAW BOATER AND CANE JUST UNDER A MENU OF POSSIBLE OPTIONS FOR RESPONSE, AND CALLERS DID LOVE THEIR LITTLE HOMUNCULAR ICONS — BUT WHY, WITHIN LIKE 16 MONTHS OR 5 SALES QUARTERS, THE TUMESCENT DEMAND CURVE FOR 'VIDEOPHONY' SUDDENLY COLLAPSED LIKE A KICKED TENT, SO THAT, BY THE YEAR OF THE DEPEND ADULT UNDERGARMENT, FEWER THAN 10% OF ALL PRIVATE TELEPHONE COMMUNICATIONS UTILIZED ANY VIDEO-IMAGE-FIBER DATA-TRANSFERS OR COINCIDENT PRODUCTS AND SERVICES, THE AVERAGE U.S. PHONE-USER DECIDING THAT S/HE ACTUALLY *PREFERRED* THE RETROGRADE OLD LOW-TECH BELL-ERA VOICE-ONLY TELEPHONIC INTERFACE AFTER ALL, A PREFERENTIAL ABOUT-FACE THAT COST A GOOD MANY PRECIPITANT VIDEO-TELEPHONY-RELATED ENTREPRENEURS THEIR SHIRTS, PLUS DESTABILIZING TWO HIGHLY RESPECTED MUTUAL FUNDS THAT HAD GROUND-FLOORED HEAVILY IN VIDEO-PHONE TECHNOLOGY, AND VERY NEARLY WIPING OUT THE MARYLAND STATE EMPLOYEES' RETIREMENT SYSTEM'S FREDDIE-MAC FUND, A FUND WHOSE ADMINISTRATOR'S MISTRESS'S BROTHER HAD BEEN AN ALMOST MANICALLY PRECIPITANT VIDEO-PHONE-TECHNOLOGY ENTREPRENEUR ... AND BUT SO WHY THE ABRUPT CONSUMER RETREAT BACK TO GOOD OLD VOICE-ONLY TELEPHONING?

The answer, in a kind of trivalent nutshell, is: (1) emotional stress, (2) physical vanity, (3) a certain queer kind of self-obliterating logic in the microeconomics of consumer high-tech.

(1) It turned out that there was something terribly stressful about visual telephone interfaces that hadn't been stressful at all about voice-only interfaces. Videophone consumers seemed suddenly to realize that they'd been subject to an insidious but wholly marvelous delusion about conventional voice-only telephony. They'd never noticed it before, the delusion — it's like it was so emotionally complex that it could be countenanced only in the context of its loss. Good old traditional audio-only phone conversations

allowed you to presume that the person on the other end was paying complete attention to you while also permitting you not to have to pay anything even close to complete attention to her. A traditional aural-only conversation — utilizing a hand-held phone whose earpiece contained only 6 little pinholes but whose mouthpiece (rather significantly, it later seemed) contained (6^2) or 36 little pinholes — let you enter a kind of highway-hypnotic semi-attentive fugue: while conversing, you could look around the room, doodle, fine-groom, peel tiny bits of dead skin away from your cuticles, compose phone-pad haiku, stir things on the stove; you could even carry on a whole separate additional sign-language-and-exaggerated-facial-expression type of conversation with people right there in the room with you, all while seeming to be right there attending closely to the voice on the phone. And yet — and this was the retrospectively marvelous part — even as you were dividing your attention between the phone call and all sorts of other idle little fuguelike activities, you were somehow never haunted by the suspicion that the person on the other end's attention might be similarly divided. During a traditional call, e.g., as you let's say performed a close tactile blemish-scan of your chin, you were in no way oppressed by the thought that your phonemate was perhaps also devoting a good percentage of her attention to a close tactile blemish-scan. It was an illusion and the illusion was aural and aurally supported: the phone-line's other end's voice was dense, tightly compressed, and vectored right into your ear, enabling you to imagine that the voice's owner's attention was similarly compressed and focused . . . even though your own attention was *not,* was the thing. This bilateral illusion of unilateral attention was almost infantilely gratifying from an emotional standpoint: you got to believe you were receiving somebody's complete attention without having to return it. Regarded with the objectivity of hindsight, the illusion appears arational, almost literally fantastic: it would be like being able both to lie and to trust other people at the same time.

Video telephony rendered the fantasy insupportable. Callers now found they had to compose the same sort of earnest, slightly overintense listener's expression they had to compose for in-person exchanges. Those callers who out of unconscious habit succumbed to fuguelike doodling or pants-crease-adjustment now came off looking rude, absentminded, or childishly self-absorbed. Callers who even more unconsciously blemish-scanned or nostril-explored looked up to find horrified expressions on the video-faces at the other end. All of which resulted in videophonic stress.

Even worse, of course, was the traumatic expulsion-from-Eden feeling of looking up from tracing your thumb's outline on the Reminder Pad or adjusting the old Unit's angle of repose in your shorts and actually seeing your videophonic interfacee idly strip a shoelace of its gumlet as she talked to you, and suddenly realizing your whole infantile fantasy of commanding

146

your partner's attention while you yourself got to fugue-doodle and make little genital-adjustments was deluded and insupportable and that you were actually commanding not one bit more attention than you were paying, here. The whole attention business was monstrously stressful, video callers found.

(2) And the videophonic stress was even worse if you were at all vain. I.e. if you worried at all about how you looked. As in to other people. Which all kidding aside who doesn't. Good old aural telephone calls could be fielded without makeup, toupee, surgical prostheses, etc. Even without clothes, if that sort of thing rattled your saber. But for the image-conscious, there was of course no such answer-as-you-are informality about visual-video telephone calls, which consumers began to see were less like having the good old phone ring than having the doorbell ring and having to throw on clothes and attach prostheses and do hair-checks in the foyer mirror before answering the door.

But the real coffin-nail for videophony involved the way callers' faces looked on their TP screen, during calls. Not their callers' faces, but their own, when they saw them on video. It was a three-button affair, after all, to use the TP's cartridge-card's Video-Record option to record both pulses in a two-way visual call and play the call back and see how your face had actually looked to the other person during the call. This sort of appearance-check was no more resistible than a mirror. But the experience proved almost universally horrifying. People were horrified at how their own faces appeared on a TP screen. It wasn't just 'Anchorman's Bloat,' that well-known impression of extra weight that video inflicts on the face. It was worse. Even with high-end TPs' high-def viewer-screens, consumers perceived something essentially blurred and moist-looking about their phone-faces, a shiny pallid *indefiniteness* that struck them as not just unflattering but somehow evasive, furtive, untrustworthy, *unlikable*. In an early and ominous InterLace/G.T.E. focus-group survey that was all but ignored in a storm of entrepreneurial sci-fi-tech enthusiasm, almost 60% of respondents who received visual access to their own faces during videophonic calls specifically used the terms *untrustworthy, unlikable,* or *hard to like* in describing their own visage's appearance, with a phenomenally ominous 71% of senior-citizen respondents specifically comparing their video-faces to that of Richard Nixon during the Nixon-Kennedy debates of B.S. 1960.

The proposed solution to what the telecommunications industry's psychological consultants termed *Video-Physiognomic Dysphoria* (or *VPD*) was, of course, the advent of High-Definition Masking; and in fact it was those entrepreneurs who gravitated toward the production of high-definition videophonic imaging and then outright masks who got in and out of the short-lived videophonic era with their shirts plus solid additional nets.

Mask-wise, the initial option of High-Definition Photographic Imaging — i.e. taking the most flattering elements of a variety of flattering multi-angle photos of a given phone-consumer and — thanks to existing image-configuration equipment already pioneered by the cosmetics and law-enforcement industries — combining them into a wildly attractive high-def broadcastable composite of a face wearing an earnest, slightly overintense expression of complete attention — was quickly supplanted by the more inexpensive and byte-economical option of (using the exact same cosmetic-and-FBI software) actually casting the enhanced facial image in a form-fitting polybutylene-resin mask, and consumers soon found that the high up-front cost of a permanent wearable mask was more than worth it, considering the stress- and *VPD*-reduction benefits, and the convenient Velcro straps for the back of the mask and caller's head cost peanuts; and for a couple fiscal quarters phone/cable companies were able to rally *VPD*-afflicted consumers' confidence by working out a horizontally integrated deal where free composite-and-masking services came with a videophone hookup. The high-def masks, when not in use, simply hung on a small hook on the side of a TP's phone-console, admittedly looking maybe a bit surreal and discomfiting when detached and hanging there empty and wrinkled, and sometimes there were potentially awkward mistaken-identity snafus involving multi-user family or company phones and the hurried selection and attachment of the wrong mask taken from some long row of empty hanging masks — but all in all the masks seemed initially like a viable industry response to the vanity,-stress,-and-Nixonian-facial-image problem.

(2 and maybe also 3) But combine the natural entrepreneurial instinct to satisfy *all* sufficiently high consumer demand, on the one hand, with what appears to be an almost equally natural distortion in the way persons tend to see themselves, and it becomes possible to account historically for the speed with which the whole high-def-videophonic-mask thing spiralled totally out of control. Not only is it weirdly hard to evaluate what you yourself look like, like whether you're good-looking or not — e.g. try looking in the mirror and determining where you stand in the attractiveness-hierarchy with anything like the objective ease you can determine whether just about anyone else you know is good-looking or not — but it turned out that consumers' instinctively skewed self-perception, plus vanity-related stress, meant that they began preferring and then outright demanding videophone masks that were really quite a lot better-looking than they themselves were in person. High-def mask-entrepreneurs ready and willing to supply not just verisimilitude but aesthetic enhancement — stronger chins, smaller eye-bags, air-brushed scars and wrinkles — soon pushed the original mimetic-mask-entrepreneurs right out of the market. In a gradually unsubtlizing progression, within a couple more sales-quarters most consumers were now using masks so undeniably better-looking on videophones than their real faces were in person, transmitting to one another such horrendously skewed

and enhanced masked images of themselves, that enormous psychosocial stress began to result, large numbers of phone-users suddenly reluctant to leave home and interface personally with people who, they feared, were now habituated to seeing their far-better-looking masked selves on the phone and would on seeing them in person suffer (so went the callers' phobia) the same illusion-shattering aesthetic disappointment that, e.g., certain women who always wear makeup give people the first time they ever see them without makeup.

The social anxieties surrounding the phenomenon psych-consultants termed *Optimistically Misrepresentational Masking* (or *OMM*) intensified steadily as the tiny crude first-generation videophone cameras' technology improved to where the aperture wasn't as narrow, and now the higher-end tiny cameras could countenance and transmit more or less full-body images. Certain psychologically unscrupulous entrepreneurs began marketing full-body polybutylene and -urethane 2-D cutouts — sort of like the headless muscleman and bathing-beauty cutouts you could stand behind and position your chin on the cardboard neck-stump of for cheap photos at the beach, only these full-body videophone-masks were vastly more high-tech and convincing-looking. Once you added variable 2-D wardrobe, hair- and eye-color options, various aesthetic enlargements and reductions, etc., costs started to press the envelope of mass-market affordability, even though there was at the same time horrific social pressure to be able to afford the very best possible masked 2-D body-image, to keep from feeling comparatively hideous-looking on the phone. How long, then, could one expect it to have been before the relentless entrepreneurial drive toward an ever-better mousetrap conceived of the *Transmittable Tableau* (a.k.a. *TT*), which in retrospect was probably the really sharp business-end of the videophonic coffin-nail. With *TTs*, facial and bodily masking could now be dispensed with altogether and replaced with the video-transmitted image of what was essentially a heavily doctored still-photograph, one of an incredibly fit and attractive and well-turned-out human being, someone who actually resembled you the caller only in such limited respects as like race and limb-number, the photo's face focused attentively in the direction of the videophonic camera from amid the sumptuous but not ostentatious appointments of the sort of room that best reflected the image of yourself you wanted to transmit, etc.

The Tableaux were simply high-quality transmission-ready photographs, scaled down to diorama-like proportions and fitted with a plastic holder over the videophone camera, not unlike a lens-cap. Extremely good-looking but not terrifically successful entertainment-celebrities — the same sort who in decades past would have swelled the cast-lists of infomercials — found themselves in demand as models for various high-end videophone Tableaux.

Because they involved simple transmission-ready photography instead of computer imaging and enhancement, the Tableaux could be mass-produced and commensurately priced, and for a brief time they helped ease the tension between the high cost of enhanced body-masking and the monstrous aesthetic pressures videophony exerted on callers, not to mention also providing employment for set-designers, photographers, airbrushers, and infomercial-level celebrities hard-pressed by the declining fortunes of broadcast television advertising.

(3) But there's some sort of revealing lesson here in the beyond-short-term viability-curve of advances in consumer technology. The career of videophony conforms neatly to this curve's classically annular shape: First there's some sort of terrific, sci-fi-like advance in consumer tech — like from aural to video phoning — which advance always, however, has certain unforeseen disadvantages for the consumer; and then but the market-niches created by those disadvantages — like people's stressfully vain repulsion at their own videophonic appearance — are ingeniously filled via sheer entrepreneurial verve; and yet the very advantages of these ingenious disadvantage-compensations seem all too often to undercut the original high-tech advance, resulting in consumer-recidivism and curve-closure and massive shirt-loss for precipitant investors. In the present case, the stress-and-vanity-compensations' own evolution saw video-callers rejecting first their own faces and then even their own heavily masked and enhanced physical likenesses and finally covering the video-cameras altogether and transmitting attractively stylized static Tableaux to one another's TPs. And, behind these lens-cap dioramas and transmitted Tableaux, callers of course found that they were once again stresslessly invisible, unvainly makeup- and toupeeless and baggy-eyed behind their celebrity-dioramas, once again free — since once again unseen — to doodle, blemish-scan, manicure, crease-check — while on their screen, the attractive, intensely attentive face of the well-appointed celebrity on the other end's Tableau reassured them that they were the objects of a concentrated attention they themselves didn't have to exert.

And of course but these advantages were nothing other than the once-lost and now-appreciated advantages of good old Bell-era blind aural-only telephoning, with its 6 and (6^2) pinholes. The only difference was that now these expensive silly unreal stylized Tableaux were being transmitted between TPs on high-priced video-fiber lines. How much time, after this realization sank in and spread among consumers (mostly via phone, interestingly), would any micro-econometrist expect to need to pass before high-tech visual videophony was mostly abandoned, then, a return to good old telephoning not only dictated by common consumer sense but actually after a while culturally approved as a kind of chic integrity, not Ludditism but a kind of retrograde transcendence of sci-fi-ish high-tech for its own sake, a transcendence of the vanity and the slavery to high-tech fashion that people view as so unattractive in one another. In other words a return to aural-only telephony became, at the closed curve's end, a kind of status-symbol of anti-vanity, such that only callers utterly lacking in self-awareness continued to use videophony and Tableaux, to say nothing of masks, and these tacky facsimile-using people became ironic cultural symbols of tacky vain slavery to corporate PR and high-tech novelty, became the Subsidized Era's tacky equivalents of people with leisure suits, black velvet paintings, sweater-vests for their poodles, electric zirconium jewelry, NoCoat LinguaScrapers, and c. Most communications consumers put their Tableaux-dioramas at the back of a knick-knack shelf and covered their cameras with standard black lens-caps and now used their phone consoles' little mask-hooks to hang these new little plasticene address-and-phone diaries specially made with a little receptacle at the top of the binding for convenient hanging from former mask-hooks. Even then, of course, the bulk of U.S. consumers remained verifiably reluctant to leave home and teleputer and to interface personally, though this phenomenon's endurance can't be attributed to the videophony-fad per se, and anyway the new panagoraphobia served to open huge new entrepreneurial teleputerized markets for home-shopping and -delivery, and didn't cause much industry concern.

Four times per annum, in these chemically troubled times, the Organization of North American Nations Tennis Association's Juniors Division sends a young toxicologist with cornsilk hair and a smooth wide button of a nose and a blue O.N.A.N.T.A. blazer to collect urine samples from any student at any accredited tennis academy ranked higher than #64 continentally in his or her age-division. Competitive junior tennis is meant to be good clean fun. It's October in the Year of the Depend Adult Undergarment. An impressive percentage of the kids at E.T.A. are in their divisions' top 64. On urine-sample day, the juniors form two long lines that trail out of the locker rooms and up the stairs and then run agnate and coed across the E.T.A. Comm.-Ad. Bldg. lobby with its royal-blue shag and hardwood pan-elling and great glass cases of trophies and plaques. It takes about an hour to get from the middle of the line to your sex's locker room's stall-area, where either the blond young toxicologist or on the girls' side a nurse whose severe widow's peak tops her square face with a sort of bisected forehead dispenses a plastic cup with a pale-green lid and a strip of white medical tape with a name and a monthly ranking and 10-15-Y.D.A.U. and *Enf.T.A.* neatly printed in a six-pt. font.

Probably about a fourth of the ranking players over, say, fifteen at the Enfield Tennis Academy cannot pass a standard North American GC/MS[52] urine scan. These, seventeen-year-old Michael Pemulis's nighttime customers, now become also, four times yearly, his daytime customers. Clean urine is ten adjusted dollars a cc.

'Get your urine here!' Pemulis and Trevor Axford become quarterly urine vendors; they wear those papery oval caps ballpark-vendors wear; they spend three months collecting and stashing the urine of sub-ten-year-old players, warm pale innocent childish urine that's produced in needly little streams and the only G/M scan it couldn't pass would be like an Ovaltine scan or something; then every third month Pemulis and Axford work the agnate unsupervised line that snakes across the blue lobby shag, selling little Visine bottles of urine out of an antique vendor's tub for ballpark wieners, snagged for a song from a Fenway Park wienerman fallen on hard off-season times, a big old box of dull dimpled tin with a strap in Sox colors that goes around the back of the neck and keeps the vendor's hands free to make change.

'Urine!'

'Clinically sterile urine!'

'Piping hot!'

'Urine you'd be proud to take home and introduce to the folks!'

Trevor Axford handles cash-flow. Pemulis dispenses little conical-tipped Visine bottles of juvenile urine, bottles easily rendered discreet in underarm, sock or panty.

'Urine trouble? Urine luck!'

Quarterly sales breakdowns indicate slightly more male customers than female customers, for urine. Tomorrow morning, E.T.A. custodial workers — Kenkle and Brandt, or Dave ('Fall Down Very') Harde, the well-loved old janitor laid off from Boston College for contracting narcolepsy, or thick-ankled Irish women from the semi-tenements down the hill across Comm. Ave., or else sullen and shifty-eyed residents from Ennet House, the halfway facility at the bottom of the hill's other side in the old VA Hospital complex, hard-looking and generally sullen types who come and do nine months of menial-type work for the 32 hours a week their treatment-contract requires — will empty scores of little empty plastic Visine bottles from subdorm wastebaskets into the dumpster-nest behind the E.T.A. Employee parking lot, from which dumpsters Pemulis will then get Mario Incandenza and some of the naïver of the original ephebic urine-donators themselves to remove, sterilize, and rebox the bottles under the guise of a rousing game of Who-Can-Find,-Boil,-And-Box-The-Most-Empty-Visine-Bottles-In-A-Three-Hour-Period-Without-Any-Kind-Of-Authority-Figure-Knowing-What-You're-Up-To, a game which Mario had found thumpingly weird when Pemulis introduced him to it three years ago, but which Mario's really come to look forward to, since he's found he has a real sort of mystical intuitive knack for finding Visine bottles in the sedimentary layers of packed dumpsters, and always seems to win hands-down, and if you're poor old Mario Incandenza you take your competitive strokes where you can find them. T. Axford then stashes and recycles the bottles, and packaging overhead is nil. He and Pemulis keep the wiener-tub stashed under a discarded Yarmouth sail in the back of the used tow truck they'd chipped in on with Hal and Jim Struck and another guy who's since graduated E.T.A. and now plays for Pepperdine, and paid to have reconditioned and the rusty chain and hook that hung from the tow truck's back-tilted derrick replaced with a gleamingly new chain and thick hook — which get used really only twice a year, spring and late fall, for brief intervals of short-distance hauling during the all-weather Lung's dismantling and erection, plus occasionally pulling a paralyzed rear-wheel-drive student or employee vehicle either back onto or all the way up the E.T.A. hillside's long 70° driveway during bad snowstorms — and the whole thing derusted and painted in E.T.A.'s proud red and gray school colors, with the complex O.N.A.N. heraldic ensign — a snarling full-front eagle with a broom and can of disinfectant in one claw and a Maple Leaf in the other and wearing a sombrero and appearing to have about half-eaten a swatch of star-studded cloth — rather ironically silk-screened onto the driver's-side door and the good old pre-Tavis E.T.A. traditional motto TE OCCIDERE POSSUNT . . . unironically emblazoned on the passenger door, and which they all share use of, though Pemulis and Axford get slight priority, because the truck's registration and basic-liability insurance get paid for out of quarterly urine-revenues.

Hal's older brother Mario — who by Dean of Students' fiat gets to bunk in a double with Hal in subdorm A on the third floor of Comm.-Ad. even though he's too physically challenged even to play low-level recreational tennis, but who's keenly interested in video- and film-cartridge production, and pulls his weight as part of the E.T.A. community recording assigned sections of matches and drills and processional stroke-filming sessions for later playback and analysis by Schtitt and his staff — is filming the congregated line and social interactions and vending operation of the urine-day lobby, using his strap-attached head-mounted camera and thoracic police-lock and foot-treadle, apparently getting footage for one of the short strange Himself-influenced conceptual cartridges the administration lets him occupy his time making and futzing around with down in the late founder's editing and f/x facilities off the main sub-Comm.-Ad. tunnel; and Pemulis and Axford do not object to the filming, nor do they even do that hand-to-temple face-obscuring thing when he aims the head-mounted Bolex their way, since they know nobody will end up seeing the footage except Mario himself, and that at their request he'll modulate and scramble the vendors' and customers' faces into undulating systems of flesh-colored squares, by means of his late father's reconfigururing matte-panel in the editing room, since facial scrambling will heighten whatever weird conceptual effect Mario's usually after anyway, though also because Mario's notoriously fond of undulating flesh-colored squares and will jump at any opportunity to edit them in over people's faces.

They do brisk business.

Michael Pemulis, wiry, pointy-featured, phenomenally talented at net but about two steps too slow to get up there effectively against high-level pace — so in compensation also a great offensive-lob man — is a scholar-ship student from right nearby in Allston MA — a grim section of tract housing and vacant lots, low-rise Greek and Irish housing projects, gravel and haphazard sewage and indifferent municipal upkeep, a lot of depressed petrochemical light industry all along the Spur, an outlying district zoned for sprawl; an old joke in Enfield-Brighton goes ' "Kiss me where it smells" she said so I took her to Allston' — where he discovered a knack playing Boys Club tennis in cut-off shorts and no shirt and a store-strung stick on scuzzy courts with blacktop that discolored your yellow balls and nets made of spare Feeny Park fencing that sent net-cord shots spronging all the way out into traffic. An Inner City Development Program tennis prodigy at ten, recruited up the hill at eleven, with parents who wanted to know how much E.T.A.'d pay up front for rights to all future possible income. Cavalier about practice but a bundle of strangled nerves in tournaments, the rap on Pemulis is that he's way lower-ranked than he could be with a little hard work, since he's not only E.T.A.'s finest Eschatonic[53] marksman off the lob but Schtitt says is the one youth here now who knows truly what is it to *pünch* the volley. Pemulis, whose pre-E.T.A. home life was apparently hackle-raising, also sells small-time drugs of distinguished potency at reasonable retail prices to a large pie-slice of the total junior-tournament-circuit market. Mario Incandenza is one of those people who wouldn't see the point of trying recreational chemicals even if he knew how to go about it. He just wouldn't get it. His smile, below the Bolex camera strapped to his large but sort of withered-looking head, is constant and broad as he films the line's serpentine movement against glass shelves full of prizes.

M. M. Pemulis, whose middle name is Mathew (*sic*), has the highest Stanford-Bïnet of any kid on academic probation ever at the Academy. Hal Incandenza's most valiant efforts barely get Pemulis through Mrs. I's triad of required Grammars[54] and Soma R.-L.-O. Chawaf's heady Literature of Discipline, because Pemulis, who claims he sees every third word upside-down, actually just has a born tech-science wienie's congenital impatience with the referential murkiness and inelegance of verbal systems. His early tennis promise quick-peaking and it's turned out a bit dilettantish, Pemulis's real enduring gift is for math and hard science, and his scholarship is the coveted James O. Incandenza Geometrical Optics Scholarship, of which there is only one, and which each term Pemulis manages to avoid losing by just one dento-dermal layer of overall G.P.A., and which gives him sanctioned access to all the late director's lenses and equipment, some of which turn out to be useful to unrelated enterprises. Mario's the only other person sharing the optic-and-editing labs off the main tunnel, and the two have the kind of transpersonal bond that shared interests and mutual advantage can inspire: if Mario's not helping Pemulis fabricate the products of independent-optical-study work M.P. isn't really much into doing — you should see the boy with a convex lens, Avril likes to say within Mario's hearing; he's like a fish in brine — then Pemulis is giving Mario, who's a film-nut but no great tech-mind, serious help with cinemo-optical praxis, the physics of focal-length and reflective compounds — you should see Pemulis with an emulsion curve, yawning blasély under his bill-reversed yachting hat and scratching an armpit, juggling differentials like a boy born to wear a pocket-protector and high-water corduroys and electrician's tape on his hornrims' temples, asking Mario if he knows what you call three Canadians copulating on a snowmobile. Mario and his brother Hal both consider Pemulis a good friend, though friendship at E.T.A. is nonnegotiable currency.

Hal Incandenza for a long time identified himself as a lexical prodigy who — though Avril had taken pains to let all three of her children know that her nonjudgmental love and pride depended in no way on achievement or performance or potential talent — had made his mother proud, plus a really good tennis player. Hal Incandenza is now being encouraged to identify himself as a late-blooming prodigy and possible genius at tennis who is on the verge of making every authority-figure in his world and beyond very proud indeed. He's never looked better on court or on monthly O.N.A.N.T.A. paper. He is erumpent. He has made what Schtitt termed a 'leap of exponents' at a post-pubescent age when radical, plateaux-hopping, near-J.-Wayne-and-Show-caliber improvement is extraordinarily rare in tennis. He gets his sterile urine gratis, though he could well afford to pay: Pemulis depends on him for verbal-academic support, and dislikes owing favors, even to friends.

Hal is, at seventeen, as of 10/Y.D.A.U., judged *ex cathedra* the fourth-best tennis player under age eighteen in the United States of America, and the sixth-best on the continent, by those athletic-organizing bodies duly charged with the task of ranking. Hal's head, closely monitored by deLint and Staff, is judged still level and focused and unswollen/-bludgeoned by the sudden éclat and rise in general expectations. When asked how he's doing with it all, Hal says Fine and thanks you for asking.

If Hal fulfills this newly emergent level of promise and makes it all the way up to the Show, Mario will be the only one of the Incandenza children not wildly successful as a professional athlete. No one who knows Mario could imagine that this fact would ever even occur to him.

Orin, Mario, and Hal's late father was revered as a genius in his original profession without anybody ever realizing what he really turned out to be a genius at, even he himself, at least not while he was alive, which is perhaps bona-fidely tragic but also, as far as Mario's concerned, ultimately all right, if that's the way things unfolded.

Certain people find people like Mario Incandenza irritating or even think they're outright bats, dead inside in some essential way.

Michael Pemulis's basic posture with people is that Mrs. Pemulis raised no dewy-eyed fools. He wears painter's caps on-court and sometimes a yachting cap turned around 180°, and, since he's not ranked high enough to get any free-corporate-clothing offers, plays in T-shirts with things like *ALLSTON HS WOLF SPIDERS* and *CHOOSY MOTHERS* and *THE FIENDS IN HUMAN SHAPE Y.D.A.U. TOUR* or like an ancient *CAN YOU BELIEVE IT THE SUPREME COURT JUST DESECRATED OUR FLAG* on them. His face is the sort of spiky-featured brow-dominated Feenian face you see all over Irish Allston and Brighton, its chin and nose sharp and skin the natal brown color of the shell of a quality nut.

Michael Pemulis is nobody's fool, and he fears the dealer's Brutus, the potential eater of cheese, the rat, the wiretap, the pubescent-looking Finest sent to make him look foolish. So when somebody calls his room's phone, even on video, and wants to buy some sort of substance, they have to right off the bat utter the words 'Please commit a crime,' and Michael Pemulis will reply 'Gracious me and mine, a crime you say?' and the customer has to insist, right over the phone, and say he'll pay Michael Pemulis money to commit a crime, or like that he'll harm Michael Pemulis in some way if he refuses to commit a crime, and Michael Pemulis will in a clear and I.D.able voice make an appointment to see the caller in person to 'plead for my honor and personal safety,' so that if anybody eats cheese later or the phone's frequency is covertly accessed, somehow, Pemulis will have been entrapped.[55]

Secreting a small Visine bottle of urine in an armpit in line also brings it up to plausible temperature. At the entrance to the male stall-area, the ephebic-looking O.N.A.N.T.A. toxicologist rarely even looks up from his clipboard, but the square-faced nurse can be a problem over on the female side, because every so often she'll want the stall door open during production. With Jim Struck handling published-source plagiarism and compressed iteration and Xerography, Pemulis also offers, at reasonable cost, a small *vade mecum*ish pamphlet detailing several methods for dealing with this contingency.

O

WINTER B.S. 1960 — TUCSON AZ

Jim not that way Jim. That's no way to treat a garage door, bending stiffly down at the waist and yanking at the handle so the door jerks up and out jerky and hard and you crack your shins and my ruined knees, son. Let's see you bend at the healthy knees. Let's see you hook a soft hand lightly over the handle feeling its subtle grain and pull just as exactly gently as will make it come to you. Experiment, Jim. See just how much force you need to start the door easy, let it roll up out open on its hidden greasy rollers and pulleys in the ceiling's set of spiderwebbed beams. Think of all garage doors as the well-oiled open-out door of a broiler with hot meat in, heat roiling out, hot. Needless and dangerous ever to yank, pull, shove, thrust. Your mother is a shover and a thruster, son. She treats bodies outside herself without respect or due care. She's never learned that treating things in the gentlest most relaxed way is also treating them and your own body in the most efficient way. It's Marlon Brando's fault, Jim. Your mother back in California before you were born, before she became a devoted mother and long-suffering wife and breadwinner, son, your mother had a bit part in a Marlon Brando movie. Her big moment. Had to stand there in saddle shoes and bobby sox and ponytail and put her hands over her ears as really loud motorbikes roared by. A major thespian moment, believe you me. She was in love from afar with this fellow Marlon Brando, son. Who? Who. Jim, Marlon Brando was the archetypal new-type actor who ruined it looks like two whole gen-erations' relations with their own bodies and the everyday objects and bodies around them. No? Well it was because of Brando you were opening that garage door like that, Jimbo. The disrespect gets learned and passed on. Passed down. You'll know Brando when you watch him, and you'll have learned to fear him. *Brando,* Jim, Jesus, B-r-a-n-d-o. Brando the new arche-typal tough-guy rebel and slob type, leaning back on his chair's rear legs, coming crooked through doorways, slouching against everything in sight, trying to *dominate* objects, showing no artful respect or care, yanking things toward him like a moody child and using them up and tossing them crudely aside so they miss the wastebasket and just lie there, ill-used. With the over-clumsy impetuous movements and postures of a moody infant. Your mother is of that new generation that moves against life's grain, across its warp and baffles. She may have loved Marlon Brando, Jim, but she didn't understand him, is what's ruined her for everyday arts like broilers and garage doors and even low-level public-park knock-around tennis. Ever see your mother with a broiler door? It's carnage, Jim, it's to cringe to see it, and the poor dumb thing thinks it's tribute to this slouching slob-type she loved as he roared by. Jim, she never intuited the gentle and cunning economy behind this man's quote harsh sloppy unstudied approach to objects. The way he'd oh so clearly practiced a chair's back-leg tilt over and over. The way he studied objects with a welder's eye for those strongest centered seams which when pressured by the swinishest slouch still support. She never ... never sees that Marlon Brando felt himself as body so keenly he'd *no need* for manner. She never sees that in his quote careless way he actually really touched whatever he touched as if it were part of him. Of his own body. The world he only seemed to manhandle was for him sentient, feeling. And no one ... and she never understood that. Sour sodding grapes indeed. You can't envy someone who can be that way. Respect, maybe. Maybe *wistful* respect, at the very outside. She never saw that Brando was playing the equivalent of high-level quality tennis across sound stages all over both coasts, Jim, is what he was really doing. Jim, he moved like a careless fingerling, one big muscle, muscularly naïve, but always, notice, a fingerling at the center of a clear current. That kind of animal grace. The bastard wasted *no* motion, is what made it art, this brutish no-care. His was a tennis player's dictum: touch things with consideration and they will be yours; you will own them; they will move or stay still or move for you; they will lie back and part their legs and yield up their innermost seams to you. Teach you all their tricks. He knew what the Beats know and what the great tennis player knows, son: learn to do nothing, with your whole head and body, and everything will be done by what's around you. I know you don't understand. Yet. I know that goggle-eyed stare. I know what it means all too well, son. It's no matter. You will. Jim, I know what I know.

I'm predicting it right here, young sir Jim. You are going to be a great tennis player. I was near-great. You will be truly great. You will be the real thing. I know I haven't taught you to play yet, I know this is your first time, Jim, Jesus, relax, I know. It doesn't affect my predictive sense. You will overshadow and obliterate me. Today you are starting, and within a very few years I know all too well you will be able to beat me out there, and on the day you first beat me I may well weep. It'll be out of a sort of selfless pride, an obliterated father's terrible joy. I feel it, Jim, even here, standing on hot gravel and looking: in your eyes I see the appreciation of angle, a prescience re spin, the way you already adjust your overlarge and apparently clumsy child's body in the chair so it's at the line of best force against dish, spoon, lens-grinding appliance, a big book's stiff bend. You do it unconsciously. You have no idea. But I watch, very closely. Don't ever think I don't, son.

You will be poetry in motion, Jim, size and posture and all. Don't let the posture-problem fool you about your true potential out there. Take it from me, for a change. The trick will be transcending that overlarge head, son. Learning to move just the way you already sit still. Living in your body.

This is the communal garage, son. And this is our door in the garage. I know you know. I know you've looked at it before, many times. Now . . . now *see* it, Jim. See it as body. The dull-colored handle, the clockwise latch, the bits of bug trapped when the paint was wet and now still protruding. The cracks from this merciless sunlight out here. Original color anyone's guess, boyo. The concave inlaid squares, how many, bevelled at how many levels at the borders, that pass for decoration. Count the squares, maybe . . . let's see you treat this door like a lady, son. Twisting the latch clockwise with one hand that's right and. . . . I guess you'll have to pull harder, Jim. Maybe even harder than that. Let me . . . *that's* the way she wants doing, Jim. Have a look. Jim, this is where we keep this 1956 Mercury Montclair you know so well. This Montclair weighs 3,900 pounds, give or take. It has eight cylinders and a canted windshield and aerodynamic fins, Jim, and has a maximum flat-out road-speed of 95 m.p.h. per. I described the shade of the paint job of this Montclair to the dealer when I first saw it as bit-lip red. Jim, it's a machine. It will do what it's made for and do it perfectly, but only when stimulated by someone who's made it his business to know its tricks and seams, as a body. The stimulator of this car must know the car, Jim, feel it, be inside much more than just the . . . the compartment. It's an object, Jim, a body, but don't let it fool you, sitting here, mute. It will *respond*. If given its due. With artful care. It's a body and will respond with a well-oiled purr once I get some decent oil in her and all Mercuryish at up to 95 big ones per for just that driver who treats its body like his own, who *feels* the big steel body he's inside, who quietly and unnoticed feels the nubbly plastic of the grip of the shift up next to the wheel when he shifts just as he feels the skin and flesh, the muscle and sinew and bone wrapped in gray spiderwebs of nerves in the blood-fed hand just as he feels the plastic and metal and flange and teeth, the pistons and rubber and rods of the amber-fueled Montclair, when he shifts. The bodily red of a well-bit lip, parping along at a silky 80-plus per. Jim, a toast to our knowledge of bodies. To high-level tennis on the road of life. Ah. Oh.

Son, you're ten, and this is hard news for somebody ten, even if you're almost five-eleven, a possible pituitary freak. Son, you're a body, son. That quick little scientific-prodigy's mind she's so proud of and won't quit twittering about: son, it's just neural spasms, those thoughts in your mind are just the sound of your head revving, and head is still just body, Jim. Commit this to memory. Head is body. Jim, brace yourself against my shoulders here for this hard news, at ten: you're a machine a body an object, Jim, no less than this rutilant Montclair, this coil of hose here or that rake there for the front yard's gravel or sweet Jesus this nasty fat spider flexing in its web over there up next to the rake-handle, see it? See it? *Latrodectus mactans*, Jim. Widow. Grab this racquet and move gracefully and feelingly over there and kill that widow for me, young sir Jim. Go on. Make it say 'K.' Take no names. There's a lad. Here's to a spiderless section of communal garage. Ah.

Bodies bodies everywhere. A tennis ball is the ultimate body, kid. We're coming to the crux of what I have to try to impart to you before we get out there and start actuating this fearsome potential of yours. Jim, a tennis ball is the ultimate body. Perfectly round. Even distribution of mass. But empty inside, utterly, a vacuum. Susceptible to whim, spin, to force — used well or poorly. It will reflect your own character. Characterless itself. Pure potential. Have a look at a ball. Get a ball from the cheap green plastic laundry basket of old used balls I keep there by the propane torches and use to practice the occasional serve, Jimbo. Attaboy. Now look at the ball. Heft it. Feel the weight. Here, I'll . . . tear the ball . . . open. Whew. See? Nothing in there but evacuated air that smells like a kind of rubber hell. Empty. Pure potential. Notice I tore it open along the seam. It's a body. You'll learn to treat it with consideration, son, some might say a kind of love, and it will open for you, do your bidding, be at your beck and soft lover's call. The thing truly great players with hale bodies who overshadow all others have is a way with the ball that's called, and keep in mind the garage door and broiler, *touch*. Touch the ball. Now that's . . . that's the touch of a player right there. And as with the ball so with that big thin slumped overtall body, sir Jimbo. I'm predicting it right now. I see the way you'll apply the lessons of today to yourself as a physical body. No more carrying your head at the level of your chest under round slumped shoulders. No more tripping up. No more overshot reaches, shattered plates, tilted lampshades, slumped shoulders and caved-in chest, the simplest objects twisting and resistant in your big thin hands, boy. Imagine what it feels like to be this ball, Jim. Total physicality. No revving head. Complete presence. Absolute potential, sitting there potentially absolute in your big pale slender girlish hand so young its thumb's unwrinkled at the joint. My thumb's wrinkled at the joint, Jim, some might say gnarled. Have a look at this thumb right here. But I still treat it as my own. I give it its due. You want a drink of this, son? I think you're ready for a drink of this. No? Nein? Today, Lesson One out there, you become, for better or worse, Jim, a man. A player. A body in commerce with bodies. A helmsman at your own vessel's tiller. A machine in the ghost, to quote a phrase. Ah. A ten-year-old freakishly tall bow-tied and thick-spectacled citizen of the. . . . I drink this, sometimes, when I'm not actively working, to help me accept the same painful things it's now time for me to tell you, son. Jim. Are you ready? I'm telling you this now because you have to know what I'm about to tell you if you're going to be the more than near-great top-level tennis player I know you're going to be eventually very soon. Brace yourself. Son, get ready. It's glo . . . gloriously painful. Have just maybe a taste, here. This flask is silver. Treat it with due care. Feel its shape. The near-soft feel of the warm silver and the calfskin sheath that covers only half its flat rounded silver length. An object that rewards a considered touch. Feel the slippery heat? That's the oil from my fingers. My oil, Jim, from my body. Not my hand, son, feel the flask. Heft it. Get to know it. It's an object. A vessel. It's a two-pint flask full of amber liquid. Actually more like half full, it seems. So it seems. This flask has been treated with due care. It's never been dropped or jostled or crammed. It's never had an errant drop, not drop *one*, spilled out of it. I treat it as if it can feel. I give it its due, as a body. Unscrew the cap. Hold the calfskin sheath in your right hand and use your good left hand to feel the cap's shape and ease it around on the threads. Son ... son, you'll have to put that what is that that *Columbia Guide to Refractive Indices Second Edition* down, son. Looks heavy anyway. A tendon-strainer. Fuck up your pronator teres and surrounding tendons before you even start. You're going to have to put down the book, for once, young Sir Jimbo, you never try to handle two objects at the same time without just aeons of diligent practice and care, a Brando-like dis ... and well *no* you don't just drop the book, son, you don't just just don't *drop* the big old *Guide to Indices* on the dusty garage floor so it raises a square bloom of dust and gets our nice white athletic socks all gray before we even hit the court, boy, *Jesus* I just took five minutes explaining how the key to being even a potential player is to treat the things with just exactly the ... here lemme have this ... that books aren't just *dropped* with a crash like bottles in the trashcan they're *placed,* guided, with senses on Full, feeling the edges, the pressure on the little floor of both hands' fingers as you bend at the knees with the book, the slight gassy shove as the air on the dusty floor ... as the floor's air gets displaced in a soft square that raises no dust. Like soooo. Not like *so*. Got me? Got it? Well now don't be that way. Son, don't be that way, now. Don't get all oversensitive on me, son, when all I'm trying to do is help you. Son, Jim, I *hate* this when you do this. Your chin just disappears into that bow-tie when your big old overhung lower lip quivers like that. You look chinless, son, and big-lipped. And that cape of mucus that's coming down on your upper lip, the way it shines, don't, just don't, it's revolting, son, you don't want to revolt people, you have to learn to control this sort of oversensitivity to hard truths, this sort of thing, take and exert some goddamn *control* is the whole point of what I'm taking this whole entire morning off rehearsal with not one but two vitally urgent auditions looming down my neck so I can show you, planning to let you move the seat back and touch the shift and maybe even ... maybe even drive the Montclair, God knows your feet'll reach, right Jimbo? Jim, hey, why not drive the Montclair? Why not you drive us over, starting today, pull up by the courts where today you'll — here, look, see how I unscrew it? the cap? with the soft very outermost tips of my gnarled fingers which I wish they were steadier but I'm exerting control to control my anger at that chin and lip and the cape of snot and the way your eyes slant and goggle like some sort of mongoloid child's when you're threatening to cry but just the very tips of the fingers, here, the most sensitive parts, the parts bathed in warm oil, the

161

whorled pads, I feel them singing with nerves and blood I let them extend
. . . further than the warm silver hip-flask's cap's very top down its broadening cone where to where the threads around the upraised little circular
mouth lie hidden while with the other warm singing hand I gently grip the
leather holster so I can feel the way the whole flask feels as I guide . . . guide
the cap around on its silver threads, hear that? stop that and listen, hear
that? the sound of threads moving through well-machined grooves, with
great care, a smooth barbershop spiral, my whole hand right through the
pads of my fingertips less . . . less unscrewing, here, than guiding, persuad-
ing, reminding the silver cap's body what it's built to do, machined to do,
the silver cap knows, Jim, I know, you know, we've been through this before, leave the book *alone,* boy, it's not going anywhere, so the silver cap
leaves the flask's mouth's warm grooved lips with just a snick, hear that?
that faintest snick? not a rasp or a grinding sound or harsh, not a harsh
brutal Brando-esque rasp of attempted domination but a snick a . . . nuance,
there, ah, oh, like the once you've heard it never mistakable *ponk* of a true-
hit ball, Jim, well pick it *up* then if you're afraid of a little dust, Jim, pick the
book *up* if it's going to make you all goggle-eyed and chinless honestly Jesus
why do I try I try and try just wanted to introduce you to the broiler's garage
and let you drive, maybe, feeling the Montclair's body, taking my time to let
you pull up to the courts with the Montclair's shift in a neutral glide and the
eight cylinders thrumming and snicking like a healthy heart and the wheels
all perfectly flush with the curb and bring out my good old trusty laundry
. . . laundry basket of balls and racquets and towels and flask and my *son,*
my flesh of my flesh, white slumped flesh of my flesh who wanted to embark
on what I predict right now will be a tennis career that'll put his busted-up
used-up old Dad back square in his little place, who wanted to maybe for
once be a real boy and learn how to play and have fun and frolic and play
around in the unrelieved sunshine this city's so fuck-all famous for, to enjoy
it while he can because did your mother tell you we're moving? That we're
moving back to California finally this spring? We're moving, son, I'm hark-
ing one last attempted time to that celluloid siren's call, I'm giving it the one
last total shot a man's obligation to his last waning talent deserves, Jim,
we're headed for the big time again at last for the first time since she announced she was having you, Jim, hitting the road, celluloid-bound, so say
adios to that school and that fluttery little moth of a physics teacher and
those slumped chinless slide-rule-wielding friends of no now wait I didn't
mean it I meant I wanted to tell you *now,* ahead of time, your mother and I,
to give you plenty of notice so you could *adjust* this time because oh you
made it so unmisinterpretably *clear* how this last move to this trailer park
upset you so, didn't you, to a mobile home with chemical toilet and bolts to
hold it in place and widow-webs everyplace you look and grit settling on
everything like dust out here instead of the Club's staff quarters I got us

162

removed from or the house it was clearly my fault we couldn't afford any-more. It was my fault. I mean who else's fault would it be? Am I right? That we moved your big soft body with allegedly not enough notice and that east-side school you cried over and that Negro research resource librarian there with the hair out to here that . . . that lady with the upturned nose on tiptoe all the time I have to tell you she seemed so consummate east-side Tucsonian all self-consciously not of this earth's grit urging us to quote nurture your optical knack with physics with her nose upturned so you could see up in there and on her toes like something skilled overhead had sunk a hook between her big splayed fingerling's nostrils and were reeling skyward up toward the aether little by little I'll bet those heelless pumps are off the floor altogether by now son what do you say son what do you think . . . no, go on, cry, don't inhibit yourself, I won't say a word, except it's getting to me less all the time when you do it, I'll just warn you, I think you're overwork-ing the tears and the . . . it's getting less effec . . . effective with me each time you use it though we know we both know don't we just between you and me we know it'll always work on your mother, won't it, never fail, she'll every time take and bend your big head down to her shoulder so it looks obscene, if you could see it, pat-patting on your back like she's burping some sort of slumping oversized obscene bow-tied infant with a book strain-ing his pronator teres, crying, will you do this when you're grown? Will there be episodes like this when you're a man at your own tiller? A citizen of a world that won't go pat-pat-there-there? Will your face crumple and bulge like this when you're six-and-a-half grotesque feet tall, six-six-plus like your grandfather may he rot in hell's rubber vacuum when he finally kicks on the tenth tee and with your flat face and no chin just like him on that poor dumb patient woman's fragile wet snotty long-suffering shoulder did I tell you what he did? Did I tell you what he did? I was your age Jim here take the flask no give it here, oh. Oh. I was thirteen, and I'd started to play well, seriously, I was twelve or thirteen and playing for years already and he'd never been to watch, he'd never come once to where I was playing, to watch, or even changed his big flat expression even once when I brought home a trophy I won trophies or a notice in the paper TUCSON NATIVE QUALI-FIES FOR NATIONAL JR CH'SHIPS he never acknowledged I even existed as I was, not as I do you, Jim, not as I take care to bend over backwards way, *way* out of my way to let you know I *see* you recognize you am aware of you as a body care about what might go on behind that big flat face bent over a homemade prism. He plays golf. Your grandfather. Your grand-pappy. Golf. A golf man. Is my tone communicating the contempt? Billiards on a big table, Jim. A bodiless game of spasmodic flailing and flying sod. A quote unquote sport. Anal rage and checkered berets. This is almost empty. This is just about it, son. What say we rain-check this. What say I put the last of this out of its amber misery and we go in and tell her you're not feeling up to snuff enough again and we're rain-checking your first introduction to the Game till this weekend and we'll head over this weekend and do two straight days both days and give you a really extensive intensive intro to a by all appearances limitless future. Intensive gentleness and bodily care equals great tennis, Jim. We'll go both days and let you plunge right in and get wet all over. It's only five dollars. The court fee. For one lousy hour. Each day. Five dollars each day. Don't give it a thought. Ten total dollars for an intensive weekend when we live in a glorified trailer and have to share a garage with two DeSotos and what looks like a Model A on blocks and my Montclair can't afford the kind of oil she deserves. Don't look like that. What's money or my rehearsals for the celluloid auditions we're moving 700 miles for, auditions that may well comprise your old man's last shot at a life with any meaning at all, compared to my *son*? Right? Am I right? Come here, kid. C'mere c'mere c'mere c'mere. That's a boy. That's my J.O.I. of a guy of a joy of boy. That's my kid, in his body. He never came once, Jim. Not once. To watch. Mother never missed a competitive match, of course. Mother came to so many it ceased to mean anything that she came. She became part of the environment. Mothers are like that, as I'm sure you're aware all too well, am I right? Right? Never came once, kiddo. Never lumbered over all slumped and soft and cast his big grotesque long-even-at-midday shadow at any court I performed on. Till one day he came, once. Suddenly, once, without precedent or warning, he . . . came. Ah. Oh. I heard him coming long before he hove into view. He cast a long shadow, Jim. It was some minor local event. It was some early-round local thing of very little consequence in the larger scheme. I was playing some local dandy, the kind with fine equipment and creased white clothing and country-club lessons that still can't truly play, even, regardless of all the support. You'll find you often have to endure this type of opponent in the first couple rounds. This gleaming hapless lox of a kid was some client of my father's son . . . son of one of his clients. So he came for the client, to put on some sham show of fatherly concern. He wore a hat and coat and tie at 95° plus. The client. Can't recall the name. There was something canine about his face, I remember, that his kid across the net had inherited. My father wasn't even sweating. I grew up with the man in this town and never once saw him sweat, Jim. I remember he wore a boater and the sort of gregariously plaid uniform professional men had to wear on the weekends then. They sat in the indecisive shade of a scraggly palm, the sort of palm that's just crawling with black widows, in the fronds, that come down without warning, that hide lying in wait in the heat of midday. They sat on the blanket my mother always brought — my mother, who's dead, and the client. My father stood apart, sometimes in the waving shade, sometimes not, smoking a long filter. Long filters had come into fashion. He never sat on the ground. Not in the American Southwest he didn't. There was a man with a healthy respect for

spiders. And *never* on the ground under a palm. He knew he was too grotesquely tall and ungainly to stand up in a hurry or roll screaming out of the
way in a hurry in case of falling spiders. They've been known to be willing
to drop right out of the trees they hide in, in the daytime, you know. Drop
right on you if you're sitting on the ground in the shade. He was no fool, the
bastard. A golfer. They all watched. I was right there on the first court. This
park no longer exists, Jim. Cars are now parked on what used to be these
rough green asphalt courts, shimmering in the heat. They were right there,
watching, their heads going back and forth in that windshield-wiper way of
people watching quality tennis. And was I nervous, young sir J.O.I.? With
the one and only Himself there in all his wooden glory there, watching, half
in and out of the light, expressionless? I was not. I was in my body. My body
and I were one. My wood Wilson from my stack of wood Wilsons in their
trapezoid presses was a sentient expression of my arm, and I felt it singing,
and my hand, and they were alive, my well-armed hand was the secretary of
my mind, lithe and responsive and *senza errori,* because I knew myself as a
body and was fully inside my little child's body out there, Jim, I was in my
big right arm and scarless legs, safely ensconced, running here and there, my
head pounding like a heart, sweat purled on every limb, running like a veldt-
creature, leaping, frolicking, striking with maximum economy and minimum effort, my eyes on the ball and the corners both, I was two, three, a
couple shots ahead of both me and the hapless canine client's kid, handing
the dandy his pampered ass. It was carnage. It was a scene out of nature in
its rawest state, Jim. You should have been there. The kid kept bending over
to get his breath. The smoothly economical frolicking I was doing con-
trasted starkly compared to the heavily jerky way he was being forced to
stomp around and lunge. His white knit shirt and name-brand shorts were
soaked through so you could see the straps of his jock biting into the soft ass
I was handing him. He wore a flitty little white visor such as fifty-two-year-
old women at country clubs and posh Southwestern resorts wear. I was, in a
word, deft, considered, prescient. I made him stomp and stagger and lunge. I
wanted to humiliate him. The client's long sharp face was sagging. My father had no face, it was sharply shadowed and then illuminated in the wag-
ging fronds' shadow he half stood in but was wreathed in smoke from the
long filters he fancied, long plastic filtered holders, yellowed at the stem, in
imitation of the President, as courtiers once spluttered with the King . . .
veiled in shade and then lit smoke. The client didn't know enough to keep
quiet. He thought he was at a ball game or something. The client's voice
carried. Our first court was right near the tree they sat under. The client's
legs were out in front of them and protruded from the sharp star of frond-
shade. His slacks were lattice-shadowed from the pattern of the fence his
son and I played just behind. He was drinking the lemonade my mother had
brought for me. She made it fresh. He said I was good. My father's client

did. In that emphasized way that made his voice carry. You know, son? Good godfrey Incandenza old trout but that lad of yours is *good*. Unquote. I heard him say it as I ran and whacked and frolicked. And I heard the tall son of a bitch's reply, after a long pause during which the world's whole air hung there as if lifted and left to swing. Standing at the baseline, or walking back to the baseline, to either serve or receive, one of the two, I heard the client. His voice carried. And then later I heard my father's reply, may he rot in a green and empty hell. I heard what . . . what he said in reply, sonbo. But not until after I'd fallen. I insist on this point, Jim. Not until after I'd started to fall. Jim, I'd been in the middle of trying to run down a ball way out of mortal reach, a rare blind lucky dribbler of a drop-shot from the over-groomed lox across the net. A point I could have more than afforded to concede. But that's not the way I . . . that's not the way a real player plays. With respect and due effort and care for every point. You want to be great, near-great, you give every ball everything. And then some. You concede nothing. Even against loxes. You play right up to your limit and then pass your limit and look back at your former limit and wave a hankie at it, embarking. You enter a trance. You feel the seams and edges of everything. The court becomes a . . . an extremely unique place to be. It will do everything for you. It will let nothing escape your body. Objects move as they're made to, at the lightest easiest touch. You slip into the clear current of back and forth, making delicate X's and L's across the harsh rough bright green asphalt surface, your sweat the same temperature as your skin, playing with such ease and total mindless effortless effort and and and entranced concentration you don't even stop to consider whether to run down every ball. You're barely aware you're doing it. Your body's doing it for you and the court and Game's doing it for your body. You're barely involved. It's magic, boy. Nothing touches it, when it's right. I predict it. Facts and figures and curved glass and those elbow-straining books of yours' lightless pages are going to seem flat by comparison. Static. Dead and white and flat. They don't begin to. . . . It's like a dance, Jim. The point is I was too bodily respectful to slip up and fall on my own, out there. And the other point is I started to fall forward even *before* I started to hear him reply, standing there: Yes, But He'll *Never Be Great*. What he said in no way made me fall forward. The unlovely opponent had dribbled one just barely over the too-low public-park net, a freak accident, a mishit drop-shot, and another man on another court in another early-round laugher would have let it dribble, conceded the affordable, not tried to wave a hankie from the vessel of his limit. Not race on all eight healthy scarless cylinders desperately forward toward the net to try to catch the goddamn thing on the first bounce. Jim, but any man can slip. I don't know what I slipped on, son. There were spiders well-known to infest the palms' fronds all along the courts' fences. They come down at night on threads, bulbous, flexing. I'm thinking it could have been a bulbous goo-filled widow I stepped and slipped on, Jim, a spider, a mad rogue spider come down on its thread into the shade, flabby and crawling, or that leapt suicidally right from an overhanging frond onto the court, probably making a slight flabby hideous sound when it landed, crawling around on its claws, blinking grotesquely in the hot light it hated, that I stepped on rushing forward and killed and slipped on the mess the big loathsome spider made. See these scars? All knotted and ragged, like something had torn at my own body's knees the way a slouching Brando would just rip a letter open with his teeth and let the envelope fall on the floor all wet and rent and torn? All the palms along the fence were sick, they had palm-rot, it was the A.D. year 1933, of the Great Bisbee Palm-Rot epidemic, all through the state, and they were losing their fronds and the fronds were blighted and the color of really old olives in those old slim jars at the very back of the refrigerator and exuded a sick sort of pus-like slippery discharge and sometimes abruptly fell from trees curving back and forth through the air like celluloid pirates' paper swords. God I hate fronds, Jim. I'm thinking it could have been either a daytime *latrodectus* or some pus from a frond. The wind blew cruddy pus from the webbed fronds onto the court, maybe, up near the net. Either way. Something poisonous or infected, at any rate, unexpected and slick. All it takes is a second, you're thinking, Jim: the body betrays you and down you go, on your knees, sliding on sandpaper court. Not so, son. I used to have another flask like this, smaller, a rather more cunning silver flask, in the glove compartment of my Montclair. Your devoted mother did something to it. The subject has never been mentioned between us. Not so. It was a *foreign* body, or a substance, not my body, and if anybody did any betraying that day I'm telling you sonny kid boy it was something *I* did, Jimmer, I may well have betrayed that fine young lithe tan unslumped body, I may very well have gotten rigid, overconscious, careless of it, listening for what my father, who I respected, I *respected* that man, Jim, is what's sick, I knew he was there, I was conscious of his flat face and filter's long shadow, I knew him, Jim. Things were different when I was growing up, Jim. I hate . . . Jesus I hate saying something like this, this things-were-different-when-I-was-a-lad-type cliché shit, the sort of cliché fathers back then spouted, assuming he said anything at all. But it was. Different. Our kids, my generation's kids, they . . . now you, this post-Brando crowd, you new kids can't like us or dislike us or respect us or not as human beings, Jim. Your parents. No, wait, you don't have to pretend you disagree, don't, you don't have to say it, Jim. Because I know it. I could have predicted it, watching Brando and Dean and the rest, and I know it, so don't splutter. I blame no one your age, boyo. You see parents as kind or unkind or happy or miserable or drunk or sober or great or near-great or failed the way you see a table square or a Montclair lip-red. Kids today . . . you kids today somehow don't know how to *feel*, much less love, to say nothing of respect. We're just bodies to you. We're just bodies and shoulders and scarred knees and big bellies and empty wallets and flasks to you. I'm not saying something cliché like you take us for granted so much as I'm saying you cannot ... imagine our absence. We're so present it's ceased to mean. We're environmental. Furniture of the world. Jim, I could imagine that man's absence. Jim, I'm telling you you cannot imagine my absence. It's my fault, Jim, home so much, limping around, ruined knees, overweight, under the Influence, burping, nonslim, sweat-soaked in that broiler of a trailer, burping, farting, frustrated, miserable, knocking lamps over, overshooting my reach. Afraid to give my last talent the one shot it demanded. Talent is its own expectation, Jim: you either live up to it or it waves a hankie, receding forever. Use it or lose it, he'd say over the newspaper. I'm ... I'm just afraid of having a tombstone that says HERE LIES A PROMISING OLD MAN. It's ... potential may be worse than none, Jim. Than no talent to fritter in the first place, lying around guzzling because I haven't the balls to ... God I'm I'm so *sorry*. Jim. You don't deserve to see me like this. I'm so scared, Jim. I'm so scared of dying without ever being really *seen*. Can you understand? Are you enough of a big thin prematurely stooped young bespectacled man, even with your whole life still ahead of you, to understand? Can you see I was giving it all I had? That I was *in* there, out there in the heat, listening, webbed with nerves? A self that touches all edges, I remember she said. I felt it in a way I fear you and your generation never could, son. It was less like falling than being shot out of something, is the way I recall it. It did not did *not* happen in slow motion. One minute I was at a dead and beautiful forward run for the ball, the next minute there were hands at my back and nothing underfoot like a push down a stairway. A rude whip-lashing shove square in the back and my promising body with all its webs of nerves pulsing and firing was in full airborne flight and came down on my knees this flask is empty right down on my knees with all my weight and inertia on that scabrous hot sandpaper surface forced into what was an exact parody of an imitation of contemplative prayer, sliding forward. The flesh and then tissue and bone left twin tracks of brown red gray white like tire tracks of bodily gore extending from the service line to the net. I slid on my flaming knees, rushed past the dribbling ball and toward the net that ended my slide. Our slide. My racquet had gone pinwheeling off Jim and my racquetless arms out before me sliding Jim in the attitude of a mortified monk in total prayer. It was given me to hear my father pronounce my bodily existence as not even potentially great at the moment I ruined my knees forever, Jim, so that even years later at USC I never got to wave my hankie at anything beyond the near- and almost-great and would-have-been-great-*if,* and later could never even hope to audition for those swim-trunk and Brylcreem beach movies that snake Avalon is making his mint on. I do not insist that the judgment and punishing fall are ... were connected, Jim. Any man can slip out there. All it takes is a second of misplaced respect. Son, it was more than a father's voice, carrying. My mother cried out. It was a religious moment. I learned what it means to be a body, Jim, just meat wrapped in a sort of flimsy nylon stocking, son, as I fell kneeling and slid toward the stretched net, myself seen by me, frame by frame, torn open. I may have to burp, belch, son, son, telling you what I learned, son, my . . . my love, too late, as I left my knees' meat behind me, slid, ended in a posture of supplication on my knees' disclosed bones with my fingers racquetless hooked through the mesh of the net, across which, the net, the sopped dandy had dropped his pricey gut-strung Davis racquet and was running toward me with his visor askew and his hands to his cheeks. My father and the client he was there to perform for dragged me upright to the palm's infected shade where she knelt on the plaid beach-blanket with her knuckles between her teeth, Jim, and I felt the religion of the physical that day, at not much more than your age, Jim, shoes filling with blood, held under the arms by two bodies big as yours and dragged off a public court with two extra lines. It's a pivotal, it's a seminal, religious day when you get to both hear and feel your destiny at the same moment, Jim. I got to notice what I'm sure you've noticed long ago, I know, I know you've seen me brought home on occasions, dragged in the door, under what's called the Influence, son, helped in by cabbies at night, I've seen your long shadow grotesquely backlit at the top of the house's stairs I helped pay for, boy: how the drunk and the maimed both are dragged forward out of the arena like a boneless Christ, one man under each arm, feet dragging, eyes on the aether.

4 NOVEMBER
YEAR OF THE DEPEND ADULT UNDERGARMENT

From Cambridge's Latinate Inman Square, Michael Pemulis, nobody's fool at all, rides one necessary bus to Central Square and then an unnecessary bus to Davis Square and a train back to Central. This is to throw off the slightest possible chance of pursuit. At Central he catches the Red Line to Park St. Station, where he's parked the tow truck in an underground lot he can more than afford. The day is autumnal and mild, the east breeze smelling of urban commerce and the vague suede smell of new-fallen leaves. The sky is pilot-light blue; sunlight reflects complexly off the smoked-glass sides of tall centers of commerce all around Park St. downtown. Pemulis wears button-fly chinos and an E.T.A. shirt beneath a snazzy blue Brioni sportcoat, plus the bright-white yachting cap that Mario Incandenza calls his Mr. Howell hat. The hat looks rakish even when turned around, and it has a detachable lining. Inside the lining can be kept portable quantities of just about anything. Having indulged in 150 mg. of very mild 'drines, post-transaction. Wearing also gray-and-blue saddle oxfords w/o socks, it's such a mild autumn day. The streets literally *bustle*. Vendors with carts instead of tubs sell hot pretzels and tonics and those underboiled franks Pemulis likes to have them put the works on. You can see the State House and Common and Courthouse and Public Gardens, and beyond all that the cool smooth facades of Back Bay brownstones. The echoes in the underground Park Pl. garage — PARK — are pleasantly complex. Traffic westward on Common-wealth Avenue is light (meaning things can move) all the way through Ken-more Square and past Boston U. and up the long slow hill into Allston and Enfield. When Tavis and Schtitt and the players and ground crew and Testar and ATHSCME teams inflate the all-weather Lung for the winter over Courts 16–32, the domed Lung's nacelle is visible against the horizon all the way down by the Brighton Ave.–Comm. Ave. split in lower Allston.

The incredibly potent DMZ is apparently classed as a para-methoxylated amphetamine but really it looks to Pemulis from his slow and tortured sur-vey of the MED.COM's monographs more like more similar to the anticholinergic-deliriant class, way more powerful than mescaline or MDA or DMA or TMA or MDMA or DOM or STP or the I.V.-ingestible DMT (or Ololiuqui or datura's scopolamine, or Fluothane, or Bufotenine (a.k.a. 'Jackie-O.'), or Ebene or psilocybin or Cylert[56]; DMZ resembling chem-ically some miscegenation of a lysergic with a muscimoloid, but significantly different from LSD-25 in that its effects are less visual and spatially-cerebral and more like *temporally*-cerebral and almost ontological, with some sort of manipulated-phenylkylamine-like speediness whereby the ingester perceives his relation to the ordinary flow of time as radically (and euphorically, is where the muscimole-affective resemblance shows its head) altered.[57] The incredibly potent DMZ is synthesized from a derivative of fitviavi, an ob-scure mold that grows only on other molds, by the same ambivalently lucky chemist at Sandoz Pharm. who'd first stumbled on LSD, as a relatively ephebic and clueless organic chemist, while futzing around with ergotic fungi on rye. DMZ's discovery was the tail-end of the B.S. 1960s, just about the same time Dr. Alan Watts was considering T. Leary's invitation to be-come 'Writer in Resonance' at Leary's utopian LSD-25 colony in Millbrook NY on what is now Canadian soil. A substance even just the accidental-synthesis of which sent the Sandoz chemist into early retirement and serious unblinking wall-watching, the incredibly potent DMZ has a popular-lay-chemical-underground reputation as the single grimmest thing ever con-ceived in a tube. It is also now the hardest recreational compound to acquire in North America after raw Vietnamese opium, which forget it.

DMZ is sometimes also referred to in some metro Boston chemical circles as *Madame Psychosis*, after a popular very-early-morning cult radio per-sonality on M.I.T.'s student-run radio station WYYY-109, 'Largest Whole

Prime on the FM Band,' which Mario Incandenza and E.T.A. stats-wienie and Eschaton game-master Otis P. Lord listen to almost religiously.

The day-shift Ennet House kid at the booth who raises the portcullis to let him onto the grounds had a couple times in October approached Pemulis about a potential transaction. Pemulis has a rigid policy about not transacting with E.T.A. employees who come up the hill from the halfway house, since he knows some of them are at the place on Court Order, and knows for a fact they pull unscheduled Urines all over the place down there, and types like the Ennet House types are just the sorts of people Pemulis's talents let him get away from in terms of like social milieu and mixing and transacting; and his basic attitude with these low-rent employees is one of unfoolish discretion and like why tempt fate.

The East Courts are empty and ball-strewn when Pemulis pulls in; most of them are still at lunch. Pemulis, Troeltsch, and Schacht's triple-room is in subdorm B in the back north part of the second floor of West House and so superjacent to the Dining Hall, from which through the floor Pemulis can hear voices and silverware and can smell exactly what they're having. The first thing he does is boot up the phone console and try Inc and Mario's room over in Comm.-Ad., where Hal is sitting in windowlight with the Riverside *Hamlet* he told Mario he'd read and help with a conceptual film-type project based on part of, his uncushioned captain's chair partly under an old print of a detail from the minor and soft-core Alexandrian mosaic *Consummation of the Levirates,* eating an AminoPal® energy-bar and waiting very casually, the phone with its antenna already out lying ready on the arm of the chair and two folio-size *Baron's* SAT-prep guides and a spine-shot copy of the B.S. 1937 *Tilden on Spin* and his keys on their neck-chain lying on the Lindistarne carpet by his shoe, waiting in a very casual posture. Hal deliberately waits till the audio console's third ring, like a girl at home on Saturday night.

'Mmyellow.'

'The turd emergeth.' Pemulis's clear and digitally condensed voice on the line. 'Repeat. The turd emergeth.'

'Please commit a crime,' is Hal Incandenza's immediate reply.

'Gracious me,' Pemulis says into the phone tucked under his jaw, carefully de-Velcroing the lining of his Mr. Howell hat.

TENNIS AND THE FERAL PRODIGY, NARRATED BY HAL INCANDENZA, AN 11.5-MINUTE DIGITAL ENTERTAINMENT CARTRIDGE DIRECTED, RECORDED, EDITED, AND — ACCORDING TO THE ENTRY FORM — WRITTEN BY MARIO INCANDENZA, IN RECEIPT OF NEW-NEW-ENGLAND REGIONAL HONORABLE MENTION IN INTERLACE TELENTERTAINMENT'S ANNUAL 'NEW EYES, NEW VOICES' YOUNG FILMMAKERS' CONTEST, APRIL IN THE YEAR OF THE YUSHITYU 2007 MIMETIC-RESOLUTION-CARTRIDGE-VIEW-MOTHERBOARD-EASY-TO-INSTALL UPGRADE FOR INFERNATRON/INTERLACE TP SYSTEMS FOR HOME, OFFICE OR MOBILE (*SIC*), ALMOST EXACTLY THREE YEARS AFTER DR. JAMES O. INCANDENZA PASSED FROM THIS LIFE

Here is how to put on a big red tent of a shirt that has *ETA* across the chest in gray.

Please ease carefully into your supporter and adjust the elastic straps so the straps do not bite into your butt and make bulged ridges in your butt that everyone can see once you've sweated through your shorts.

Here is how to wrap your torn ankle so tightly in its flesh-tone Ace bandages your left leg feels like a log.

Here is how to win, later.

This is a yellow iron-mesh Ball-Hopper full of dirty green dead old balls. Take them to the East Courts while the dawn is still chalky and no one's around except the mourning doves that infest the pines at sunrise, and the air is so sopped you can see your summer breath. Hit serves to no one. Make a mess of balls along the base of the opposite fence as the sun hauls itself up over the Harbor and a thin sweat breaks and the serves start to boom. Stop thinking and let it flow and go boom, boom. The shiver of the ball against the opposite fence. Hit about a thousand serves to no one while Himself sits and advises with his flask. Older men's legs are white and hairless from decades in pants. Here is the set of keys a stride's length before you in the court as you serve dead balls to no one. After each serve you must almost fall forward into the court and in one smooth motion bend and scoop up the keys with your left hand. This is how to train yourself to follow through into the court after the serve. You still, years after the man's death, cannot keep your keys anywhere but on the floor.

This is how to hold the stick.

Learn to call the racquet a stick. Everyone does, here. It's a tradition: The Stick. Something so much an extension of you deserves a sobriquet.

Please look. You'll be shown exactly once how to hold it. This is how to hold it. Just like this. Forget all the near-Eastern-slice-backhand-grip bafflegab. Just say Hello is all. Just shake hands with the calfskin grip of the stick. This is how to hold it. The stick is your friend. You will become very close.

Grasp your friend firmly at all times. A firm grip is essential for both control and power. Here is how to carry a tennis ball around in your stick-hand, squeezing it over and over for long stretches of time — in class, on the phone, in lab, in front of the TP, a wet ball for the shower, ideally squeezing it at all times except during meals. See the Academy dining hall, where tennis balls sit beside every plate. Squeeze the tennis ball rhythmically month after year until you feel it no more than your heart squeezing blood and your right forearm is three times the size of your left and your arm looks from across a court like a gorilla's arm or a stevedore's arm pasted on the body of a child.

Here is how to do extra individual drills before the Academy's A.M. drills, before breakfast, so that after the thousandth ball hit just out of reach by Himself, with his mammoth wingspan and ghastly calves, urging you with nothing but smiles on to great and greater demonstrations of effort, so that after you've gotten your third and final wind and must vomit, there is little inside to vomit and the spasms pass quickly and an east breeze blows cooler past you and you feel clean and can breathe.

Here is how to don red and gray E.T.A. sweats and squad-jog a weekly 40 km. up and down urban Commonwealth Avenue even though you would rather set your hair on fire than jog in a pack. Jogging is painful and pointless, but you are not in charge. Your brother gets to ride shotgun while a senile German blows BBs at your legs both of them laughing and screaming *Schnell*. Enfield is due east of the Marathon's Hills of Heartbreak, which are just up Commonwealth past the Reservoir in Newton. Urban jogging in a sweaty pack is tedious. Have Himself hunch down to put a long pale arm around your shoulders and tell you that his own father had told him that talent is sort of a dark gift, that talent is its own expectation: it is there from the start and either lived up to or lost.

Have a father whose own father lost what was there. Have a father who lived up to his own promise and then found thing after thing to meet and surpass the expectations of his promise in, and didn't seem just a whole hell of a lot happier or tighter wrapped than his own failed father, leaving you yourself in a kind of feral and flux-ridden state with respect to talent.

Here is how to avoid thinking about any of this by practicing and playing until everything runs on autopilot and talent's unconscious exercise becomes a way to escape yourself, a long waking dream of pure play.

The irony is that this makes you very good, and you start to become regarded as having a prodigious talent to live up to.

Here is how to handle being a feral prodigy. Here is how to handle being seeded at tournaments, signifying that seeding committees composed of old big-armed men publicly expect you to reach a certain round. Reaching at least the round you're supposed to is known at tournaments as 'justifying your seed.' By repeating this term over and over, perhaps in the same rhythm at which you squeeze a ball, you can reduce it to an empty series of phonemes, just formants and fricatives, trochaically stressed, signifying zip.

Here is how to beat unseeded, wide-eyed opponents from Iowa or Rhode Island in the early rounds of tournaments without expending much energy but also without seeming contemptuous.

This is how to play with personal integrity in a tournament's early rounds, when there is no umpire. Any ball that lands on your side and is too close to call: call it fair. Here is how to be invulnerable to gamesmanship. To keep your attention's aperture tight. Here is how to teach yourself, when an opponent maybe cheats on the line-calls, to remind yourself that what goes around comes around. That a poor sport's punishment is always self-inflicted.

Try to learn to let what is unfair teach you.

· Here is how to spray yourself down exactly once with Lemon Pledge, the ultimate sunscreen, then discover that when you go out and sweat into it it smells like close-order skunk.

Here is how to take nonnarcotic muscle relaxants for the back spasms that come from thousands of serves to no one.

Here is how to weep in bed trying to remember when your torn blue ankle didn't hurt every minute.

This is the whirlpool, a friend.

Here is how to set up the electric ball machine at dawn on the days Himself is away living up to what will be his final talent.

Here is how to tie a bow tie. Here is how to sit through small openings of your father's first art films, surrounded by surly foreign cigarette smoke and conversations so pretentious you literally cannot believe them, you're sure you have misheard them. Pretend you're engaged by the jagged angles and multiple exposures without pretending you have the slightest idea what's going on. Assume your brother's expression.

Here is how to sweat.

· Here is how to hand a trophy to Lateral Alice Moore to put in the E.T.A. lobby's glass case under its system of spotlights and small signs.

What is unfair can be a stern but invaluable teacher.

Here is how to pack carbohydrates into your tissues for a four-singles two-doubles match day in a Florida June.

Please learn to sleep with perpetual sunburn.

Expect some rough dreams. They come with the territory. Try to accept them. Let them teach you.

Keep a flashlight by your bed. It helps with the dreams.

Please make no extramural friends. Discourage advances from outside the circuit. Turn down dates.

If you do exactly the rehabilitative exercises They assign you, no matter how silly and tedious, the ankle will mend more quickly.

This type of stretch helps prevent the groin-pull.

Treat your knees and elbow with all reasonable care: you will have them with you for a long time.

Here is how to turn down an extramural date so you won't be asked again. Say something like I'm terribly sorry I can't come out to see $8\frac{1}{2}$ revived on a wall-size Cambridge Celluloid Festival viewer on Friday, Kimberly, or Daphne, but you see if I jump rope for two hours then jog backwards through Newton till I puke They'll let me watch match-cartridges and then my mother will read aloud to me from the O.E.D. until 2200 lights-out, and c.; so you can be sure that henceforth Daphne/Kimberly/Jennifer will take her adolescent-mating-dance-type-ritual-socialization business somewhere else. Be on guard. The road widens, and many of the detours are seductive. Be constantly focused and on alert: feral talent is its own set of expectations and can abandon you at any one of the detours of so-called normal American life at any time, so be *on guard*.

Here is how to *schnell*.

Here is how to go through your normal adolescent growth spurt and have every limb in your body ache like a migraine because selected groups of muscles have been worked until thick and intensile and they resist as the sudden growth of bone tries to stretch them, and they ache all the time. There is medication for this condition.

If you are an adolescent, here is the trick to being neither quite a nerd nor quite a jock: be no one.

It is easier than you think.

Here is how to read the monthly E.T.A. and U.S.T.A. and O.N.A.N.T.A. rankings the way Himself read scholars' reviews of his multiple-exposure melodramas. Learn to care and not to care. They mean the rankings to help you determine where you are, not who you are. Memorize your monthly rankings, and forget them. Here is how: never tell anyone where you are.

This is also how not to fear sleep or dreams. Never tell anyone where you are. Please learn the pragmatics of expressing fear: sometimes words that seem to express really *invoke*.

This can be tricky.

Here is how to get free sticks and strings and clothes and gear from Dunlop, Inc. as long as you let them spraypaint the distinctive Dunlop logo on your sticks' strings and sew logos on your shoulder and the left pocket of your shorts and use a Dunlop gear-bag, and you become a walking lunging sweating advertisement for Dunlop, Inc.; this is all as long as you keep justifying your seed and preserving your rank; the Dunlop, Inc. New New England Regional Athletic Rep will address you as 'Our gray swan'; he wears designer slacks and choking cologne and about twice a year wants to help you dress and has to be slapped like a gnat.

Be a Student of the Game. Like most clichés of sport, this is profound. You can be shaped, or you can be broken. There is not much in between. Try to learn. Be coachable. Try to learn from everybody, especially those who fail. This is hard. Peers who fizzle or blow up or fall down, run away, disappear from the monthly rankings, drop off the circuit. E.T.A. peers waiting for deLint to knock quietly at their door and ask to chat. Opponents. It's all educational. How promising you are as a Student of the Game is a function of what you can pay attention to without running away. Nets and fences can be mirrors. And between the nets and fences, opponents are also mirrors. This is why the whole thing is scary. This is why all opponents are scary and weaker opponents are especially scary.

See yourself in your opponents. They will bring you to understand the Game. To accept the fact that the Game is about managed fear. That its object is to send from yourself what you hope will not return.

This is your body. They want you to know. You will have it with you always.

On this issue there is no counsel; you must make your best guess. For myself, I do not expect ever really to know.

But in the interval, if it is an interval: here is Motrin for your joints, Noxzema for your burn, Lemon Pledge if you prefer nausea to burn, Contracol for your back, benzoin for your hands, Epsom salts and anti-inflammatories for your ankle, and extracurriculars for your folks, who just wanted to make sure you didn't miss anything they got.

SELECTED TRANSCRIPTS OF THE RESIDENT-INTERFACE-DROP-IN-HOURS OF MS. PATRICIA MONTESIAN, M.A., C.S.A.C.,[58] EXECUTIVE DIRECTOR, ENNET HOUSE DRUG AND ALCOHOL RECOVERY HOUSE (*SIC*), ENFIELD MA, 1300–1500H., WEDNESDAY, 4 NOVEMBER — YEAR OF THE DEPEND ADULT UNDERGARMENT

'But there's this *way* he drums his fingers on the table. Not even like really drumming. More like in-way between drumming and like this *scratching, picking,* the way you see somebody picking at dead skin. And without any kind of rhythm, see, constant and never-stopping but with no kind of rhythm you could grab onto and follow and stand. Totally like *whacked, insane.* Like the kind of sounds you can imagine a girl hears in her head right before she kills her whole family because somebody took the last bit of peanut butter or something. You know what I'm saying? The sound of a fucking mind coming apart. You know what I'm saying? So yeah, yes, OK, the short answer is when he wouldn't quit with the drumming at supper I sort of poked him with my fork. Sort of. I could see how maybe somebody could have thought I sort of stabbed him. I offered to get the fork out, though. Let me just say I'm ready to make amends at like anytime. For my part in it. I'm *owning* my part in it is what I'm saying. Can I ask am I going to get Restricted for this? Cause I have this Overnight tomorrow that Gene he approved already in the Overnight Log. If you want to look. But I'm not trying to get out of owning my part of the, like, occurrence. If my Higher Power who I choose to call God works through you saying I've got some kind of a punishment due, I won't try to get out of a punishment. If I've got one due. I just wanted to ask. Did I mention I'm grateful to be here?'

'I'm not *denying* anything. I'm simply asking you to define "alcoholic." How can you ask me to attribute to myself a given term if you refuse to define the term's meaning? I've been a reasonably successful personal-injury attorney for sixteen years, and except for that one ridiculous so-called seizure at the Bar Association dinner this spring and that clot of a judge banning me from his courtroom — and let me just say that I can support my contention that the man masturbates under his robe behind the bench with *detailed* corroboration from both colleagues and Circuit Court laundry personnel — with the exception of less than a handful of incidents I've held my liquor and my head as high as many a taller advocate. Believe you me. How old are you, young lady? I am not *in denial* so to speak about anything empirical and objective. Am I having pancreas problems? Yes. Do I have trouble recalling certain intervals in the Kemp and Limbaugh administrations? No contest. Is there a spot of domestic turbulence surrounding my intake? Why yes there is. Did I experience yes some formication in detox? I did. I have no problem forthrightly admitting things I can grasp. Formicate, with an *m*, yes. But what is this you demand I admit? Is it *denial* to delay signature until the vocabulary of the contract is clear to all parties so bound? Yes, yes, you don't follow what I mean here, good! And you're reluctant to proceed without clarification. I rest. I cannot deny what I don't understand. This is my position.'

'So I'm sitting there waiting for my meatloaf to cool and suddenly there's a simply *sphincter*-loosening shriek and here's Nell in the air with a steak-fork, positively *aloft, leaping* across the table, in *flight*, horizontal, I mean Pat the girl's body is literally *parallel* to the surface of the table, *hurling* herself at me, with this upraised fork, shrieking something about the sound of *peanut* butter. I mean my God. Gately and Diehl had to pull the fork out of my hand and the tabletop both. To give you an idea. Of the *savagery*. Don't even ask me about the pain. Let's don't even get into that, I assure you. They *offered* me Percocet[59] at the emergency room, is all I'll say about the levels of pain involved. I told them I was in recovery and powerless over narcotics of any sort. Please don't even ask me how moved they were at my courage if you don't want me to get weepy. This whole experience has me right on the edge of a complete hysterical *fit*. So but yes, guilty, I may very well have been tapping on the table. Excuse me for occupying space. And then she ever so *magnaminously* says she'll apologize if I will. Well come again I said? Come *again?* I mean my God. I'm sitting there attached to the table by tines. I know bashing, Pat, and this was unabashed bashing at its most fascist. I respectfully ask that she be kicked out of here on her enormous rear-end. Let her go back to whatever fork-wielding district she came from, with her Hefty bag full of gauche clothes. Honestly. I know part of this process is learning to live in a community. The give and take, to let go of personality issues, turn them over. Et cetera. But is it not also supposed to be and here I quote the handbook a *safe* and *nurturing* environment? I have seldom felt less nurtured than I did impaled on that table I have to say. The pathetic harassments of Minty and McDade are bad enough. I can get bashed back at the Fenway. I did not come here to get bashed on some pretense of table-tapping. I'm dangerously close to saying either that . . . that *specimen* goes or I do.'

'I'm awful sorry to bother. I can come back. I was wondering if maybe there was any special Program prayer for when you want to hang yourself.'

'I want understanding I have no denial I am drug addict. Me, I know that I am addicted since the period of before Miami. I am no trouble to stand up in the meetings and say I am Alfonso, I am drug addict, powerless. I am knowing powerlessness since the period of Castro. But I cannot stop even since I know. This I have fear. I fear I do not stop when I admit I am Alfonso, powerless. How does to admit I am powerless make me stop what the thing is I am powerless to stop? My head it is crazy from this fearing of no power. I am now hope for *power*, Mrs. Pat. I want to advice. Is hope of power the bad way for Alfonso as drug addict?'

'Sorry to barge, there, P.M. Division called again about the thing with the vermin. The word was *ultimatum* that they said.'

'Sorry if I'm bothering you about something that isn't a straightforward treatment interface thing. I'm up there trying to do my Chore. I've got the men's upstairs bathroom. There's something . . . Pat there's something in the toilet up there. That won't flush. The thing. It won't go away. It keeps reappearing. Flush after flush. I'm only here for instructions. Possibly also protective equipment. I couldn't even describe the thing in the toilet. All I can say is if it was produced by anything human then I have to say I'm really worried. Don't even ask me to describe it. If you want to go up and have a look, I'm a 100% confident it's still there. It's made it real clear it's not going anywhere.'

'Alls I know is I put a Hunt's Pudding Cup in the resident fridge like I'm supposed to at 1300 and da-da-da and at 1430 I come down all primed for pudding that I paid for myself and it's not there and McDade comes on all concerned and offers to help me look for it and da-da, except if you look I look and here's the son of a whore got this big thing of pudding on his chin.'

'Yeah but except so how can I answer just yes or no to do I want to stop the coke? Do I think I want to absolutely I think I want to. I don't have a septum no more. My septum's been like fucking dissolved by coke. See? You see anything like a septum when I lift up like that? I've absolutely with my whole heart thought I wanted to stop and so forth. Ever since with the septum. So but so since I've been wanting to stop this whole time, why couldn't I stop? See what I'm saying? Isn't it all about wanting to and so on? And so forth? How can living here and going to meetings and all do anything except make me want to stop? But I think I already want to stop. How come I'd even be here if I didn't want to stop? Isn't being here proof I want to stop? But then so how come I can't stop, if I want to stop, is the thing.'

'This kid had a harelip. Where it goes like, you know, *thith*. But his went way up. Further up. He sold bad speed but good pot. He said he'd cover our part of the rent if we kept his snakes supplied with mice. We were smoking up all our cash so what's to do. They ate mice. We had to go into pet stores and pretend to be real heavily into mice. Snakes. He kept snakes. Doocy. They smelled bad. He never cleaned the tanks. His lip covered his nose. The harelip. My guess he couldn't smell what they smelled like. Or something would have got done. He had a thing for Mildred. My girlfriend. I don't know. She probably has a problem too. I don't know. He had a thing for her. He'd keep saying shit like, with all these *t-h*'s, he'd go Tho you want to fuck me, Mildred, or what? We don't hath t'eat each other or nothin. He'd say shit like this with me right there, dropping mice into these tanks, holding my breath. The mice had to be alive. All in this godawful voice like somebody's holding their nose and can't say *s*. He didn't wash his hair for two years. We had like an in-joke on how long he wouldn't wash his hair and we'd make X's on the calendar every week. We had a lot of these in-type jokes, to help us stand it. We were wasted I'd say 90% of the time. Nine-O.

But he never did the whole time we were there. Wash. When she said we had to leave or she was taking off and taking Harriet was when she said when I was at work he started telling her how to have sex with a chicken. He said he had sex with the chickens. It was a trailer out past the dumpster-dock in the Spur, and he kept a couple chickens under it. No wonder they ran like hell when anybody came. He'd been like sexually abusing fowls. He kept talking to her about it, with all *t-h*'s, like You hath to like *thcrew* them on, but when you come they jutht thort of *fly* off of you. She said she drew the line. We left and went to Pine Street shelter and she stayed for a while till this guy with a hat said he had a ranch in New Jersey and off she goes, and with Harriet. Harriet's our daughter. She's going to be three. She says it *free*, though. I doubt now the kid'll ever say a single *t-h* her whole life. And I don't even know where in New Jersey. Does New Jersey even have ranches? I'd been in school with her since grade school. Mildred. We were like childhood sweethearts. And then this guy who got her old cot at the shelter I got lice from. He moves into her cot and then I start to get lice. I was still trying to deliver ice to machines at gas stations. Who wouldn't have to get high just to stand it?'

'So this purports to be a disease, alcoholism? A disease like a cold? Or like cancer? I have to tell you, I have never heard of anyone being told to pray for relief from cancer. Outside maybe certain very rural parts of the American South, that is. So what is this? You're *ordering* me to pray? Because I allegedly have a disease? I dismantle my life and career and enter nine months of low-income treatment for a *disease,* and I'm prescribed prayer? Does the word *retrograde* signify? Am I in a sociohistorical era I don't know about? What exactly is the story here?'

'Fine, fine. Fine. Just completely fine. No problem at all. Happy to be here. Feeling better. Sleeping better. Love the chow. In a word, couldn't be finer. The grinding? The tooth-grinding? A tic. A jaw-strengthener. Expression of all-around fineness. Likewise the thing with the eyelid.'

'But I did *too* try. I been trying all *month*. I been on four interviews. They didn't none of them start till 11, and I'm like what's the point get up early sit around here I don't have to be down there till 11? I filled out applications *ever*day. Where'm I suppose to go? You can't kick me out just for the moth— they don't call me back if I'm *trying*. Snot my *fault*. Go on and ask Clenette. Ask that Thrale girl and them if I ain't been trying. You *can't*. This is just so *fucked up*.

'I *said* where'm I suppose to *go* to?'

'I'm on a month's Full-House Restriction for using freaking mouthwash? Newsflash: news bulletin: mouthwash is for spitting out! It's like 2% proof!'

'It's about somebody *else*'s farting, why I'm here.'

'I'll gladly identify myself if you'll first simply explain what it is I'm identifying myself *as*. This is my position. You're requiring me to attest to facts I do not possess. The term for this is "duress." '

'So my offense is what, misdemeanor gargling?'

'I'll come back when you're free.'

'It's back. For a second there I hoped. I had hope. Then there it was again.'

'First just let me say one thing.'

O

LATE OCTOBER
YEAR OF THE DEPEND ADULT UNDERGARMENT

'Open me anothowone of those boy and I'll tell you the highlight of that season of my season tickets was I got to see that incwedible son of a bitch set his fiwst wecord in the flesh. It was y'bwother's Cub Scout twoop outing you wouldn't join because I wemember this you w'afwaid you'd lose the online time in fwont of the TP. Wemember? Well I'll always wemember this one day, boy. It was against Sywacuse, what, eight seasons back. The little son of a bitch had a long of seventy-thwee that day and a avewage of sixty-fwigging-nine. *Seventy-thwee* for Chwist's sake. Open me anothowone, boy, use the exowcise. I wecall the sky was cloudy. When he punted you spent a weal long time studying the sky. They weally hung. He had a long hang-time of eight-point-thwee seconds that day. That's sewious hanging, boy. Me I nevewit five in my day. Chwist. The whole twoop said they never heawd anything like the sound of the son of a bitch's seventy-thwee. Won Wichardson, you wemember Wonnie, the twoop-leadawhateva, petwoleum jelly salesman outta Bwookline, Wonnie's a wetired pilot from the Sewvice, from a bomma-squadwon, Wonnie we's down at t'pub that night Wonnie says he says that seventy-thwee sounded just like fucking *bombs* sounded, that kind of cwacking WHUMP, when they hit, to the boys in the squadwon in the planes when they let them go.'

The radio show right before Madame Psychosis's midnight show on M.I.T.'s semi-underground WYYY is 'Those Were the Legends That Formerly Were,' one of those cruel tech-collegiate formats where any U.S. student who wants to can dart over from the super-collider lab or the Fourier Transforms study group for fifteen minutes and read on-air some parodic thing where he'd pretend to be his own dad apotheosizing some sort of thick-necked historic athletic figure the dad'd admired and had by implication compared with woeful distaste to the pencil-necked big-headed asthmatic little kid staring up through Coke-bottle lenses from his digital keyboard. The show's only rule is that you have to read your thing in the voice of some really silly cartoon character. There are other, rather more exotic patricidal formats for Asian, Latin, Arab, and European students on select weekend evenings. The consensus is Asian cartoon characters have the silliest voices.

Albeit literally sophomoric, 'Those Were the Legends . . .' is a useful drama-therapy-type catharsis-op — M.I.T. students tend to carry their own special psychic scars: nerd, geek, dweeb, wonk, fag, wienie, four-eyes, spazola, limp-dick, needle-dick, dickless, dick-nose, pencil-neck; getting your violin or laptop TP or entomologist's kill-jar broken over your large head by thick-necked kids on the playground — and the show pulls down solid FM ratings, though a lot of that's due to reverse-inertia, a Newton's-II-like backward shove from the rabidly popular Madame Psychosis Hour, M–F 0000h.–0100h., which it precedes.

Y.D.A.U.'s WYYY late-shift student engineer, unfond of any elevator that follows a serpentine or vascular path, eschews the M.I.T. Student Union's elevator. He has an arrival routine where he skips the front entrances and comes in through the south side's acoustic meatus and gets a Millennial Fizzy® out of the vending machine in the sephenoid sinus, then descends creaky back wooden stairs from the Massa Intermedia's Reading Room down to about the Infundibular Recess, past the *Tech Talk Daily* CD-ROM student paper's production floor and the sick chemical smell of the Read-Only cartridge-press's developer, down past the epiglottal Hillel Club's dark and star-doored HQ, past the heavier door to the tiled lattice of hallways to the squash and racquetball courts and one volleyball court and the airy corpus callosum of 24 high-ceiling tennis courts endowed by an M.I.T. alum and now so little used they don't even know now where the nets are, down three more levels to the ghostly-clean and lithium-lit studios of FM 109–WYYY FM, broadcasting for the M.I.T. community and selected points beyond. The studio's walls are pink and laryngeally fissured. His asthma's better down here, the air thin and keen, the tracheal air-filters just below the flooring and the ventilators' air the freshest in the Union.

The engineer, a work-study graduate student with bad lungs and occluded pores, settles alone at his panel in the engineer's booth, adjusts a couple needles' bob, and sound-checks the only paid personality on the nightly docket, the darkly revered Madame Psychosis, whose cameo shadow is just visible outside the booth's thick glass, her screen half-obscuring the on-air studio's bank of phones, checking cueing and transition for the Thursday edition. She is hidden from all view by a jointed triptych screen of cream chiffon that glows red and green in the lights of the phone bank and the cueing panel's dials and frames her silhouette. Her silhouette is cleanly limned against the screen, sitting cross-legged in its insectile microphonic headset, smoking. The engineer always has to tighten his own headset's cranial band down from the 'Those Were' engineer's mammoth parietal breadth. He activates the intercom and offers to check Madame Psychosis's levels. He requests sound. Anything at all. He hasn't opened his can of pop. There is a long silence during which Madame Psychosis's silhouette doesn't look up from something she looks like she's collating at her little desk.

After a while she makes some little sounds, little plosives to check for roaring sounds in exhalations, a perennial problem in low-budget FM.

She makes a long *s*-sound.

The student engineer takes a hit from his portable inhaler.

She says 'He liked that sort of dreamy, dreaming music that had the rhythm of long things swinging.'

The engineer's movements at the panel's dials resemble someone adjusting the heater and sound system while driving.

'The Dow that can be told is not the eternal Dow,' she says.

The engineer, age twenty-three, has extremely bad skin.

'Attractive paraplegic female seeks same; object:'

The windowless laryngeal studio is terribly bright. Nothing casts a shadow. Recessed-lit fluorescence with a dual-spectrum lithiumized corona, developed two buildings over and awaiting O.N.A.N. patent. The chilly shadowless light of surgical theaters, convenience stores at 0400. The pink wrinkled walls sometimes look more gynecological than anything else.

'Like most marriages, theirs was the evolved product of concordance and compromise.'

The engineer shivers in the bright chill and lights a gasper of his own and tells Madame Psychosis through the intercom that the whole range of levels is fine. Madame Psychosis is the only WYYY personality who brings in her own headset and jacks, plus a triptych screen. Over the screen's left section are four clocks set for different Zones, plus a numberless disk someone hung for a joke, to designate the annularized Great Concavity's No-Time. The E.S.T. clock's trackable hand carves off the last few seconds from the five minutes of dead air Madame Psychosis's contract stipulates gets to precede her show. You can see her silhouette putting out the cigarette very methodically. She cues tonight's synthesized bumper and theme music; the engineer flicks a lever and pumps the music up the coaxial medulla and through the amps and boosters packed into the crawlspaces above the high false ceiling of the corpus callosum's idle tennis courts and up and out the aerial that protrudes from the gray and bulbous surface of the Union's roof. Institutional design has come a ways from I. M. Pei. M.I.T.'s near-new Student Union, off the corner of Ames and Memorial Dr.,[60] East Cambridge, is one enormous cerebral cortex of reinforced concrete and polymer compounds. Madame Psychosis is smoking again, listening, head cocked. Her tall screen will leak smoke for her show's whole hour. The student engineer is counting down from five on an outstretched hand he can't see how she sees. And as pinkie meets palm, she says what she's said for three years of midnights, an opening bit that Mario Incandenza, the least cynical person in the history of Enfield MA, across the river, listening faithfully, finds, for all its black cynicism, terribly compelling:

Her silhouette leans and says 'And Lo, for the Earth was empty of form, and void.

'And Darkness was all over the Face of the Deep.

'And We said:

'Look at that fucker *Dance*.'

A toneless male voice is then cued in to say It's Sixty Minutes More Or Less With Madame Psychosis On YYY-109, Largest Whole Prime On The FM Band. The different sounds are encoded and pumped by the student engineer up through the building's corpus and out the roof's aerial. This aerial, low-watt, has been rigged by the station's EM-wienies to tilt and spin, not unlike a centrifugal theme-park-type ride, spraying the signal in all directions. Since the B.S. 1966 Hundt Act, the low-watt fringes of the FM band are the only part of the Wireless Spectrum still licensed for public broadcast. The deep-water green of FM tuners all over the campus's labs and dorms and barnacled clots of grad apartments align themselves slowly toward the spatter's center, moving toward the dial's right, a little creepily, like plants toward light they can't even see. Ratings are minor-league by the pre-InterLace broadcast standards of yore, but they are rock-solid consistent. Audience demand for Madame Psychosis has been, from the very start, inelastic. The aerial, inclined at about the angle of a 3-km. cannon, spins in a blurred ellipse — its rotary base is elliptical because that's the only shape the EM-wienies could rig a mold for. Obstructed on all sides by the tall buildings of East Cambridge and Commercial Drive and serious Downtown, though, only a couple thin pie-slices of signal escape M.I.T. proper, e.g. through the P.E.-Dept. gap of barely used lacrosse and soccer fields between the Philology and Low-Temp Physics complexes on Mem. Dr. and then across the florid-purple nighttime breadth of the historic Charles River, then through the heavy flow of traffic on Storrow Dr. on the Chuck's other side, so that by the time the signal laps at upper Brighton and Enfield you need almost surveillance-grade antennation to filter it in out of the EM-miasma of cellular and interconsole phone transmissions and TPs' EM-auras that crowd the FM fringes from every side. Unless, that is, your tuner is lucky enough to be located at the apex of a tall and more or less denuded hill, in Enfield, in which case you find yourself right in YYY's centrifugal line of fire.

Madame Psychosis eschews chatty openings and contextual filler. Her hour is compact and no-nonsense.

After the music fades, her shadow holds collated sheets up and riffles them slightly so the sound of paper is broadcast. 'Obesity,' she says. 'Obesity with hypogonadism. Also morbid obesity. Nodular leprosy with leonine facies.' The engineer can see her silhouette lift a cup as she pauses, which reminds him of the Millennial Fizzy in his bookbag.

She says 'The acromegalic and hyperkeratosistic. The enuretic, this year of all years. The spasmodically torticollic.'

The student engineer, a pre-doctoral transuranial metallurgist working off massive G.S.L. debt, locks the levels and fills out the left side of his time sheet and ascends with his bookbag through a treillage of interneural stairways with semitic ideograms and developer-smell and past snack bar and billiard hall and modem-banks and extensive Student Counseling offices around the rostral lamina, all the little-used many-staired neuroform way up to the artery-red fire door of the Union's rooftop, leaving Madame Psychosis, as is S.O.P., alone with her show and screen in the shadowless chill. She's mostly alone in there when she's on-air. Every so often there's a guest, but the guest will usually get introduced and then not say anything. The monologues seem both free-associative and intricately structured, not unlike nightmares. There's no telling what'll be up on a given night. If there's one even remotely consistent theme it's maybe film and film-cartridges. Early and (mostly Italian) neorealist and (mostly German) expressionist celluloid film. Never New Wave. Thumbs-up on Peterson/Broughton and Dali/Buñuel and -down on Deren/Hammid. Passionate about Antonioni's slower stuff and some Russian guy named Tarkovsky. Sometimes Ozu and Bresson. Odd affection for the hoary dramaturgy of one Sir Herbert Tree. Bizarre Kaelesque admiration for goremeisters Peckinpah, De Palma, Tarantino. Positively poisonous on the subject of Fellini's 8½. Exceptionally conversant w/r/t avant-garde celluloid and avant- and après-garde digital cartridges, anticonfluential cinema,[61] Brutalism, Found Drama, etc. Also highly literate on U.S. sports, football in particular, which fact the student engineer finds dissonant. Madame takes one phone call per show, at random. Mostly she solos. The show kind of flies itself. She could do it in her sleep, behind the screen. Sometimes she seems very sad. The engineer likes to monitor the broadcast from a height, the Union's rooftop, summer sun and winter wind. The more correct term for an asthmatic's inhaler is 'nebulizer.' The engineer's graduate research specialty is the carbonated translithium particles created and destroyed billions of times a second in the core of a cold-fusion ring. Most of the lithioids can't be smashed or studied and exist mostly to explain gaps and incongruities in annulation equations. Once last year,

Madame Psychosis had the student engineer write out the home-lab process for turning uranium oxide powder into good old fissionable U-235. Then she read it on the air between a Baraka poem and a critique of the Steeler defense's double-slot secondary. It's something a bright high-schooler could cook and took less than three minutes to read on-air and didn't involve one classified procedure or one piece of hardware not gettable from any decent chemical-supply outlet in Boston, but there was no small unpleasantness about it from the M.I.T. administration, which it's well-known M.I.T. is in bed with Defense. The hot-fuel recipe was the one bit of verbal intercourse the engineer's had with Madame Psychosis that didn't involve straight levels and cues.

The Union's soft latex-polymer roof is cerebrally domed and a cloudy pia-mater pink except in spots where it's eroded down to pasty gray, and everywhere textured, the bulging rooftop, with sulci and bulbous convolutions. From the air it looks wrinkled; from the roof's fire door it's an almost nauseous system of serpentine trenches, like water-slides in hell. The Union itself, the late A.Y. ('V.F.') Rickey's *summum opus,* is a great hollow brain-frame, an endowed memorial to the North American seat of Very High Tech, and is not as ghastly as out-of-towners suppose it must be, though the vitreally inflated balloon-eyes, deorbited and hung by twined blue cords from the second floor's optic chiasmae to flank the wheelchair-accessible front ramp, take a bit of getting used to, and some like the engineer never do get comfortable with them and use the less garish auditory side-doors; and the abundant sulcus-fissures and gyrus-bulges of the slick latex roof make rain-drainage complex and footing chancy at best, so there's not a whole lot of recreational strolling up here, although a kind of safety-balcony of skull-colored polybutylene resin, which curves around the midbrain from the inferior frontal sulcus to the parietooccipital sulcus — a halo-ish ring at the level of like eaves, demanded by the Cambridge Fire Dept. over the heated pro-mimetic protests of topological Rickeyites over in the Architecture Dept. (which the M.I.T. administration, trying to placate Rickeyites and C.F.D. Fire Marshal both, had had the pre-molded resin injected with dyes to render it the distinctively icky brown-shot off-white of living skull, so that the balcony resembles at once corporeal bone and numinous aura) — which balcony means that even the worst latex slip-and-slide off the steeply curved cerebrum's edge would mean a fall of only a few meters to the broad butylene platform, from which a venous-blue emergency ladder can be detached and lowered to extend down past the superior temporal gyrus and Pons and abducent to hook up with the polyurethane basilar-stem artery and allow a safe shimmy down to the good old oblongata just outside the rubberized meatus at ground zero.

Topside in the bitter river wind, wearing a khaki parka with a fake fur fringe, the student engineer makes his way and settles into the first intra-parietal sulcus that catches his fancy, makes a kind of nest in the soft trench — the convoluted latex is filled with those little non-FHC Styrofoam peanuts everything industrially soft is filled with, and the pia-mater surface gives rather like one of those old beanbag-chairs of more innocent times — settles in and back with his Millennial Fizzy and inhaler and cigarette and pocket-size Heathkit digital FM-band receiver under a high-CO night sky that makes the stars' points look extra sharp. The Boston P.M. is 10°C. The postcentral sulcus he sits in is just outside the circumference of the YYY aerial's high-speed spin, so five m. overhead its tip's aircraft-light describes a blurred oval, vascularly hued. His FM receiver's power cells, tested daily against the Low-Temp Lab's mercuric resistors, are fresh, the wooferless tuner's sound tinny and crisp, so that Madame sounds like a faithful but radically miniaturized copy of her studio self.

'Those with saddle-noses. Those with atrophic limbs. And yes chemists and pure-math majors also those with atrophic necks. Scleredema adultorum. Them that seep, the serodermatotic. Come one come all, this circular says. The hydrocephalic. The tabescent and chachetic and anorexic. The Brag's-Diseased, in their heavy red rinds of flesh. The dermally wine-stained or carbuncular or steatocryptotic or God forbid all three. Marin-Amat Syndrome, you say? Come on down. The psoriatic. The exzematically shunned. And the scrofulodermic. Bell-shaped steatopygiacs, in your special slacks. Afflictees of Pityriasis Rosea. It says here Come all ye hateful. Blessed are the poor in body, for they.'

The pulsing aircraft-alert light of the aerial is magenta, a sharp and much closer star, now, with his fingers laced behind his head, reclined and gazing upward, listening, the centrifugal whirl's speed making its tip's light trail color across the eyes. The light's oval a bloody halo over the very barest of all possible heads. Madame Psychosis has done U.H.I.D. stuff before, once or twice. He is listening to her read four levels below the Oblangated Recess that becomes the heating shaft's nubbin of spine, ad-lib-style reading from one of the PR-circulars of the Union of the Hideously and Improbably Deformed, an agnostic-style 12-step support-group deal for what it calls the 'aesthetically challenged.'[62] She sometimes reads circulars and catalogues and PR-type things, though not regularly. Some things take several succes-sive shows to get through. Ratings stay solid; listeners hang in. The engineer's pretty sure he'd hang in even if he weren't paid to. He does like to settle into a sulcus and smoke slowly and exhale up past the blurred red ellipse of the aerial, monitoring. Madame's themes are at once unpredictable and some-how rhythmic, more like probability-waves for subhadronics than anything else.[63] The student engineer has never once seen Madame Psychosis enter or leave WYYY; she probably takes the elevator. It's 22 October in the O.N.A.N.ite year of the Depend Adult Undergarment.

Like most marriages, Avril and the late James Incandenza's was an evolved product of concordance and compromise, and the scholastic curriculum at E.T.A. is the product of negotiated compromises between Avril's academic hard-assery and James's and Schtitt's keen sense of athletic pragmatics. It is because of Avril — who quit M.I.T. entirely and went down to half-time at Brandeis and even turned down an extremely plummy-type stipended fellowship at Radcliffe's Bunting Institute that first year to design and assume the helm of E.T.A.'s curriculum — that the Enfield Tennis Academy is the only athletic-focus-type school in North America that still adheres to the trivium and quadrivium of the hard-ass classical L.A.S. tradition,[64] and thus one of the very few extant sports academies that makes a real stab at being a genuine pre-college school and not just an Iron Curtainish jock-factory. But Schtitt never let Incandenza forget what the place was supposed to be about, and so Avril's flinty *mens-sana* pedagogy wasn't diluted so much as *ad-valorem*ized, pragmatically focused toward the *corpore-potis*-type goals kids were coming up the hill to give their childhoods for. Some E.T.A. twists Avril'd allowed into the classic L.A.S. path are e.g. that the seven subjects of the T and Q are mixed and not divided into Quadrivial Upperclass v. Trivial Ephebic; that E.T.A. geometry classes pretty much ignore the study of closed figures (excepting rectangles) to concentrate (also except for Thorp's Trigonometry of Cubes, which is elective and mostly aesthetic) for two increasingly brutal semesters on the involution and expansion of bare angles; that the quadrivial requirement of astronomy has at E.T.A. become a two-term elementary optics survey, since vision issues are obviously more germane to the Game, and since all the hardware required for everything from aphotic to apochromatic lenswork were and are right there in the lab off the Comm.-Ad. tunnel. Music's been pretty much bagged. Plus the triviumoid fetish for classical oratory has by now at E.T.A. been converted to a wide range of history and studio courses in various types of entertainment, mostly recorded film — again, way too much of Incandenza's lavish equipment lying around not to exploit, plus the legally willed and endowed-for-perpetuity presence on the academic payroll of Mrs. Pricket, Mr. Ogilvie, Mr. Disney R. Leith, and Ms. Soma Richardson-Levy-O'Byrne-Chawaf, the late founder/director's loyal sound engineer, Best Boy, production assistant, and third-favorite actress, respectively.

Plus also the six-term Entertainment Requirement because students hoping to prepare for careers as professional athletes are by intension training also to be entertainers, albeit of a deep and special sort, was Incandenza's line, one of the few philosophical points he had to pretty much ram down the throats of both Avril and Schtitt, who was pushing hard for some mix of theology and the very grim ethics of Kant.

Mario Incandenza has sat in on a back-row stool for every session of an E.T.A. Entertainment Dept. offering ever since he was finally three years ago December asked to disenroll from the Winter Hill Special School in Cambridgeport for cheerfully declining even to try to learn to really read, explaining he'd way rather listen and watch. And he is a fanatical listener/observer. He treats the lavish Tatsuoka fringe-FM-band tuner in the living room of the Headmaster's House like kids of three generations past, listening the way other kids watch TP, opting for mono and sitting right up close to one of the speakers with his head cocked dog-like, listening, staring into that special pocket of near-middle distance reserved for the serious listener. He really does have to sit right up close to listen to 'Sixty Minutes +/− . . .' when he's over at the HmH[65] with C.T. and sometimes Hal at his mother's late suppers, because Avril has some auditory thing about broadcast sound and gets the howling fantods from any voice that does not exit a living corporeal head, and though Avril's made it clear that Mario's free at any time to activate and align the Tatsuoka's ghostly-green tuner to whatever he wishes, he keeps the volume so low that he has to be lowered onto a low coffee table and lean in and almost put his ear up against the woofer's tremble and concentrate closely to hear YYY's signal over the conversation in the dining room, which tends to get sort of manically high-pitched toward the end of supper. Avril never actually asks Mario to keep it down; he does it out of unspoken consideration for her thing about sound. Another of her unspoken but stressful things involves issues of enclosure, and the HmH has no interior doors between rooms, and not even much in the way of walls, and the living and dining rooms are separated only by a vast multileveled tangle of house-plants in pots and on little stools of different heights and arrayed under hanging UV lamps of an intensity that tends to give the diners strange little patterns of tan that differ according to where someone usually sits at the table. Hal sometimes complains privately to Mario that he gets more than enough UV during the day thank you very much. The plants are incredibly lush and hale and sometimes threaten to block off the whole easement from dining to living room, and the rope-handled Brazilian machete C.T. had mounted on the wall by the tremulous china-case has stopped really being a joke. The Moms calls the houseplants her Green Babies, and she has a rather spectacular thumb, plant-wise, for a Canadian.

'The leukodermatic. The xanthodantic. The maxillofacially swollen. Those with distorted orbits of all kinds. Get out from under the sun's cove-lighting is what this says. Come in from the spectral rain.' Madame Psychosis's broadcast accent is not Boston. There are r's, for one thing, and there is no cultured Cambridge stutter. It's the accent of someone who's spent time either losing a southern lilt or cultivating one. It's not flat and twangy like Stice's, and it's not a drawl like the people at Gainesville's academy. Her voice itself is sparely modulated and strangely empty, as if she were speaking from inside a small box. It's not bored or laconic or ironic or tongue-in-cheek. 'The basilisk-breathed and pyorrheic.' It's reflective but not judgmental, somehow. Her voice seems low-depth familiar to Mario the way certain childhood smells will strike you as familiar and oddly

sad. 'All ye peronic or teratoidal. The phrenologically malformed. The sup-
puratively lesioned. The endocrinologically malodorous of whatever ilk.
Run don't walk on down. The acervulus-nosed. The radically -ectomied.
The morbidly diaphoretic with a hankie in every pocket. The chronically
granulomatous. The ones it says here the ones the cruel call Two-Baggers —
one bag for your head, one bag for the observer's head in case your bag falls
off. The hated and dateless and shunned, who keep to the shadows. Those
who undress only in front of their pets. The quote aesthetically challenged.
Leave your lazarettes and oubliettes, I'm reading this right here, your closets
and cellars and TP Tableaux, find Nurturing and Support and the Inner
Resources to face your own unblinking sight, is what this goes on to say, a
bit overheatedly maybe. Is it our place to say. It says here Hugs Not Ughs. It
says Come don the veil of the type and token. Come learn to love what's
hidden inside. To hold and cherish. The almost unbelievably thick-ankled.
The kyphotic and lordotic. The irremediably cellulitic. It says Progress Not
Perfection. It says Never Perfection. The fatally pulchritudinous: Welcome.
The Actaeonizing, side by side with the Medusoid. The papuled, the macu-
lar, the albinic. Medusas and *odalisques* both: Come find common ground.
All meeting rooms windowless. That's in ital: all meeting rooms windowless.' Plus the music she's cued for this inflectionless reading is weirdly compelling. You can never predict what it will be, but over time some kind of
pattern emerges, a trend or rhythm. Tonight's background fits, somehow, as
she reads. There's not any real forwardness to it. You don't sense it's straining to get anywhere. The thing it makes you see as she reads is something
heavy swinging slowly at the end of a long rope. It's minor-key enough to be
eerie against the empty lilt of the voice and the clinks of tines and china as
Mario's relations eat turkey salad and steamed crosiers and drink lager and
milk and vin blanc from Hull over behind the plants bathed in purple light.
Mario can see the back of the Moms's head high above the table, and then
over to the left Hal's bigger right arm, and then Hal's profile when he lowers
it to eat. There's a ball by his plate. The E.T.A. players seem to need to eat
six or seven times a day. Hal and Mario had walked over for 2100 supper at
HmH after Hal had read something for Mr. Leith's class and then disappeared for about half an hour while Mario stood supported by his police
lock and waited for him. Mario rubs his nose with the heel of his hand.
Madame Psychosis has an unironic but generally gloomy outlook on the
universe in general. One of the reasons Mario's obsessed with her show is
that he's somehow sure Madame Psychosis cannot herself sense the compelling beauty and light she projects over the air, somehow. He has visions of
interfacing with her and telling her she'd feel a lot better if she listened to her
own show, he bets. Madame Psychosis is one of only two people Mario
would love to talk to but would be scared to try. The word *periodic* pops
into his head.

'Hey Hal?' he calls across the plants.

Like for months in the spring semester of Y.D.P.A.H. she referred to her own program as 'Madame's Downer-Lit Hour' and read depressing book after depressing book — *Good Morning, Midnight* and *Maggie: A Girl of the Streets* and *Giovanni's Room* and *Under the Volcano,* plus a truly ghastly Bret Ellis period during Lent — in a monotone, really slowly, night after night. Mario sits on the low little van der Rohe–knockoff coffee table with bowed legs (the table) with his head cocked right up next the speaker and his claws in his lap. His toes tend to point inward when he sits. The background music is both predictable and, within that predictability, surprising: it's periodic. It suggests expansion without really expanding. It leads up to the exact kind of inevitability it denies. It is heavily digital, but with something of a choral bouquet. But unhuman. Mario thinks of the word *haunting,* like in 'a haunting echo of thus-and-such.' Madame Psychosis's cued music — which the student engineer never chooses or even sees her bring in — is always terribly obscure[66] but often just as queerly powerful and compelling as her voice and show itself, the M.I.T. community feels. It tends to give you the feeling there's an in-joke that you and she alone are in on. Very few devoted WYYY listeners sleep well M-F. Mario has horizontal breathing-trouble sometimes, but other than that he sleeps like a babe. Avril Incandenza still sticks with the old L'Islet-region practice of taking just tea and nibbles at U.S. suppertime and waiting to eat seriously until right before bed. Cultured Canadians tend to think vertical digestion makes the mind unkeen. Some of Orin and Mario and Hal's earliest memories are of nodding off at the dining-room table and being gently carried by a very tall man to bed. This was in a different house. Madame Psychosis's cued musics stir very early memories of Mario's father. Avril is more than willing to take some good-natured guff about her inability to eat before like 2230h. Prandial music holds little charm or associations for Hal, who like most of the kids on double daily drills makes fists around his utensils and eats like a wild dog.

'Nor are excluded the utterly noseless, nor the hideously wall- and cross-eyed, nor either the ergotic of St. Anthony, the leprous, the varicelliformally eruptive or even the sarcoma'd of Kaposi.'

Hal and Mario probably eat/listen late over at the HmH twice a week. Avril likes to see them outside the awkward formality of her position at E.T.A. C.T.'s the same at home and office. Both Avril and Tavis's bedrooms are on the second floor, as a matter of fact right next to each other. The only other room up there is Avril's personal study, with a big color Xerox of M. Hamilton as Oz's West Witch on the door and custom fiber-wiring for a tri-modem TP console. A stairway runs from her study down the backside of HmH, north, down to a tributary-tunnel leading to the main tunnel to Comm.-Ad., so Avril can commute over to E.T.A. below ground. The HmH tunnel connects with the main at a point between the Pump Room and Comm.-Ad., meaning Avril never like hunches idly past the Pump Room, which fact Hal obviously endorses. Late suppers at HmH for Hal are limited by deLint to twice a week tops because they get him excused from dawn drills, which also means late-night mischief possibilities. Sometimes they bring Canada's John ('No Relation') Wayne over with them, whom Mrs. I. likes and speaks to animatedly even though he rarely says anything the whole time he's there and also eats like a wild dog, sometimes neglecting utensils altogether. Avril also likes it when Axford comes; Axford has a hard time eating, and she likes to exhort him to eat. Very rarely anymore does Hal bring Pemulis or Jim Struck, to whom Avril is so faultlessly, brittlely polite that the dining room's tension raises hair.

Whenever Avril parts ficus leaves to check, Mario's still hunched pigeon-toed and cocked in the same RCA-Victorish posture, with the little horizontal forehead-crease that means he's either listening or thinking hard.

'The multiple amputee. The prosthetically malmatched. The snaggle-toothed, wattled, weak-chinned, and walrus-cheeked. The palate-clefted. The really large-pored. The excessively but not necessarily lycanthropically hirsute. The pin-headed. The convulsively Tourettic. The Parkinsonianly tremulous. The stunted and gnarled. The teratoid of overall visage. The twisted and hunched and humped and halitotic. The in any way asymmetrical. The rodential- and saurian- and equine-looking.'

'Hey Hal?'

'The tri-nostriled. The invaginate of mouth and eye. Those with those dark loose bags under their eyes that hang halfway down their faces. Those with Cushing's Disease. Those who look like they have Down Syndrome even though they don't have Down Syndrome. You decide. You be the judge. It says You are welcome regardless of severity. Severity is in the eye of the sufferer, it says. Pain is pain. Crow's feet. Birthmark. Rhinoplasty that didn't take. Mole. Overbite. A bad-hair *year*.'

The WYYY student engineer in his sulcus contemplates the moon, which looks sort of like a full moon that somebody's bashed in a little bit with a hammer. Madame Psychosis asks rhetorically whether the circular's left anyone out. The engineer finishes his Fizzy and makes ready to descend again for the hour's close, his skin turned toward the terrible cerebral chill off the Charles, which is windy and blue. Sometimes Madame Psychosis takes one random call to start '60 +/−.' Tonight the one caller she ends by taking has a cultured stutter and invites M.P. and the YYY community to consider the fact that the moon, which of course as any sot knows revolves around the earth, does not itself revolve. Is this true? He says it is. That it just stays there, hidden and disclosed by our round shadow's rhythms, but never revolving. That it never turns its face away.

The little Heathkit can't receive signals inside the Cerebrum's subdural stairwells, during descent, but the student engineer can anticipate she'll make no direct reply. Her sign-off is more dead air. She almost reminds the engineer of certain types in high school whom everyone adored because you sensed it made no difference to them whether you adored them. It had sure made a difference to the engineer, though, who hadn't been invited to even one graduation party, with his inhaler and skin.

The dessert Avril serves when Hal's over is Mrs. Clarke's infamous high-protein-gelatin squares, available in bright red or bright green, sort of like Jell-O on steroids. Mario's wild for them. C.T. clears the table and loads the dishwasher, since he didn't cook, and Hal gets into his coat at like 0101h. Mario's still listening to the WYYY nightly sign-off, which takes a while because they not only list the station's kilowattage specs but go through proofs for the formulae by which the specs are derived. C.T. always drops at least one plate out in the kitchen and then bellows. Avril always brings some hell-Jell-O squares in to Mario and adopts a mock-dry tone and tells Hal it's been reasonably nice to see him outside les bâtiments sanctifiés. The whole thing to Hal sometimes gets ritualistic and almost hallucinatory, the post-prandial farewell routine. Hal stands under the big framed poster of *Metropolis* and whumps his gloves together casually and tells Mario there's no reason for him to leave too; Hal's going to blast down the hill for a bit. Avril and Mario always smile and Avril asks casually what his plans are.

Hal always whumps his gloves together and smiles up at her and says 'Make trouble.'

And Avril always puts on a sort of mock-stern expression and says 'Do not, under any circumstances, have fun,' which Mario still always finds clutch-your-stomach funny, every time, week after week.

Ennet House Drug and Alcohol Recovery House is the sixth of seven exterior Units on the grounds of an Enfield Marine Public Health Hospital complex that, from the height of an ATHSCME 2100 industrial displacement fan or Enfield Tennis Academy's hilltop, resembles seven moons orbiting a dead planet. The hospital building itself, a VA facility of iron-colored brick and steep slate roofs, is closed and cordoned, bright pine boards nailed across every possible access and aperture, with really stern government signs about trespassing. Enfield Marine was built during either WWII or Korea, when there were ample casualties and much convalescence. About the only people who use the Enfield Marine complex in a VA-related way now seem to be wild-eyed old Vietnam veterans in fatigue jackets de-sleeved to make vests, or else drastically old Korea vets who are now senile or terminally alcoholic or both.

The hospital building itself stripped of equipment and copper wire, defunct, Enfield Marine stays solvent by maintaining several smaller buildings on the complex's grounds — buildings the size of like prosperous homes, which used to house VA doctors and support staff — and leasing them to different state-related health agencies and services. Each building has a Unit-number that increases with the Unit's distance from the defunct hospital and with its proximity, along a rutted cement roadlet that extends back from the hospital's parking lot, to a steep ravine that overlooks a particularly unpleasant part of Brighton MA's Commonwealth Avenue and its Green Line train tracks.

Unit #1, right by the lot in the hospital's afternoon shadow, is leased by some agency that seems to employ only guys who wear turtlenecks; the place counsels wild-eyed Vietnam vets for certain very-delayed stress disorders, and dispenses various pacifying medications. Unit #2, right next door, is a methadone clinic overseen by the same MA Division of Substance Abuse Services that licenses Ennet House. Customers for the services of Units #1 and #2 arrive around sunup and form long lines. The customers for Unit #1 tend to congregate in like-minded groups of three or four and gesture a lot and look wild-eyed and generally pissed-off in some broad geopolitical way. The customers for the methadone clinic tend to arrive looking even angrier, as a rule, and their early-morning eyes tend to bulge and flutter like the eyes of the choked, but they do not congregate, rather stand or lean along #2's long walkway's railing, arms crossed, alone, brooding, solo acts, stand-offish — 50 or 60 people all managing to form a line on a narrow walkway waiting for the same small building to unlock its narrow front door and yet still managing to appear alone and stand-offish is a strange sight, and if Don Gately had ever once seen a ballet he would, as an Ennet House resident, from his sunup smoking station on the fire escape outside the Five-Man bedroom upstairs, have seen the movements and postures necessary to maintain this isolation-in-union as balletic.

The other big difference between Units #1 and #2 is that the customers of #2 leave the building deeply changed, their eyes not only back in their heads but peaceful, if a bit glazed, but anyway in general just way better put-together than when they arrived, while #1's wild-eyed patrons tend to exit #1 looking even more stressed and historically aggrieved than when they went in.

When Don Gately was in the very early part of his Ennet House residency he almost got discharged for teaming up with a bad-news methedrine addict from New Bedford and sneaking out after curfew across the E.M.P.H.H. complex in the middle of the night to attach a big sign on the narrow front door of Unit #2's methadone clinic. The sign said CLOSED UNTIL FURTHER NOTICE BY ORDER COMMONWEALTH OF MASSACHUSETTS. The first staffer at the methadone clinic doesn't get there to open up until 0800h., and yet it's been mentioned how #2's customers always begin to show up with twisting hands and bulging eyes at like dawn, to wait; and Gately and the speed freak from New Bedford had never seen anything like the psychic crises and near-riot among these semi-ex-junkies — pallid blade-slender chain-smoking homosexuals and bearded bruiser-types in leather berets, women with mohawks and multiple sticks of gum in, upscale trust-fund-fritterers with shiny cars and computerized jewelry who'd arrived, as they'd been doing like hyper-conditioned rats for years, many of them, arrived at sunup with their eyes protruding and with Kleenexes at their noses and scratching their arms and standing on first one foot and then the other, doing basically everything but truly congregating, wild for chemical relief, ready to stand in the cold exhaling steam for hours for that relief, who'd arrived with the sun and now seemed to be informed that the Commonwealth of MA was suddenly going to withdraw the prospect of that relief, until (and this is what really seemed to drive them right over the edge, out there in the lot) until Further Notice. *Apeshit* has rarely enjoyed so literal a denotation. At the sound of the first windowpane breaking and the sight of a blown-out old whore trying to hit a leather-vested biker with an old pre-metric GRASS GROWS BY INCHES BUT IT DIES BY FEET sign from #2's clinic's pathetic front lawn, the methedrine addict began laughing so hard that she dropped the binoculars from the Ennet House upstairs fire escape where they were watching, at like 0630h., and the binoculars fell and hit the roof of one of the Ennet House counselors' cars right below in the little roadlet, with a ringing clunk, just as he was pulling in, the counselor, his name was Calvin Thrust and he was four years sober and a former NYC porn actor who'd gone through the House himself and now took absolutely zero in terms of shit from any of the residents, and his pride and joy was his customized 'Vette, and the binoculars made rather a nasty dent, and plus they were the House Manager's amateur-ornithology binoculars and had been borrowed out of the back office without explicit permission, and the long fall and impact didn't do them a bit of good, to say the least, and Gately and the methedrine addict got pinched and put on Full House Restriction and very nearly kicked out. The addict from New Bedford picked up the aminating needle a couple weeks after that anyway and was discovered by a night staffer simultaneously playing air-guitar and polishing the lids of all the donated canned goods in the House pantry way after lights out, stark naked and sheened with meth-sweat, and after the formality of a Urine she was given the old administrative boot — over a quarter of incoming Ennet House residents get discharged for a dirty Urine within their first thirty days, and it's the same at all other Boston halfway houses — and the girl ended up back in New Bedford, and then within like three hours of hitting the streets got picked up by New Bedford's Finest on an old default warrant and sent to Framingham Women's for a 1-to-2 bit, and got found one morning in her bunk with a kitchen-rigged shiv protruding from her privates and another in her neck and a thoroughly eliminated personal map, and Gately's individual counselor Gene M. brought Gately the news and invited him to see the methedrine addict's demise as a clear case of There But For the Grace of God Goeth D. W. Gately.

Unit #3, across the roadlet from #2, is unoccupied but getting reconditioned for lease; it's not boarded up, and the Enfield Marine maintenance guys go in there a couple days a week with tools and power cords and make a godawful racket. Pat Montesian hasn't yet been able to find out what sort of group misfortune #3 will be devoted to servicing.

Unit #4, more or less equidistant from both the hospital parking lot and the steep ravine, is a repository for Alzheimer's patients with VA pensions. #4's residents wear jammies 24/7, the diapers underneath giving them a lumpy and toddlerish aspect. The patients are frequently visible at #4's windows, in jammies, splayed and open-mouthed, sometimes shrieking, sometimes just mutely open-mouthed, splayed against the windows. They give everybody at Ennet House the howling fantods. One ancient retired Air Force nurse does nothing but scream 'Help!' for hours at a time from a second-story window. Since the Ennet House residents are drilled in a Boston-AA recovery program that places great emphasis on 'Asking For Help,' the retired shrieking Air Force nurse is the object of a certain grim amusement, sometimes. Not six weeks ago, a huge stolen HELP WANTED sign was found attached to #4's siding right below the retired shrieking nurse's window, and #4's director was less than amused, and demanded that Pat Montesian determine and punish the Ennet House residents responsible, and Pat had delegated the investigation to Don Gately, and though Gately had a pretty good idea who the perps were he didn't have the heart to really press and kick ass over something so much like what he'd done himself, when new and cynical, and so the whole thing pretty much blew over.

Unit #5, kittycorner across the little street from Ennet House, is for catatonics and various vegetablish, fetal-positioned mental patients subcontracted to a Commonwealth outreach agency by overcrowded LTIs. Unit #5 is referred to, for reasons Gately's never been able to pinpoint, as The Shed.[67] It is, understandably, a pretty quiet place. But in nice weather, when its more portable inmates are carried out and placed in the front lawn to take the air, standing there propped-up and staring, they present a tableau it took Gately some time to get used to. A couple newer residents got discharged late in Gately's treatment for tossing firecrackers into the crowd of catatonics on the lawn to see if they could get them to jump around or display affect. On warm nights, one long-limbed bespectacled lady who seems more autistic than catatonic tends to wander out of The Shed wrapped in a bedsheet and lay her hands on the thin shiny bark of a silver maple in #5's lawn, stands there touching the tree until she's missed at bedcheck and retrieved; and since Gately graduated treatment and took the offer of a live-in Staffer's job at

Ennet House he sometimes wakes up in his Staff cellar bedroom down by the pay phone and tonic machine and looks out the sooty ground-level window by his bed and watches the catatonic touching the tree in her sheet and glasses, illuminated by Comm. Ave.'s neon or the weird sodium light that spills down from the snooty tennis prep school overhead on its hill, he'll watch her standing there and feel an odd chilled empathy he tries not to associate with watching his mother pass out on some piece of living-room chintz.

Unit #6, right up against the ravine on the end of the rutted road's east side, is Ennet House Drug and Alcohol Recovery House, three stories of whitewashed New England brick with the brick showing in patches through the whitewash, a mansard roof that sheds green shingles, a scabrous fire escape at each upper window and a back door no resident is allowed to use and a front office around on the south side with huge protruding bay windows that yield a view of ravine-weeds and the unpleasant stretch of Commonwealth Ave. The front office is the director's office, and its bay windows, the House's single attractive feature, are kept spotless by whatever residents get Front Office Windows for their weekly Chore. The mansard's lower slope encloses attics on both the male and female sides of the House. The attics are accessed from trapdoors in the ceiling of the second floor and are filled to the beams with trash bags and trunks, the unclaimed possessions of residents who've up and vanished sometime during their term. The shrubbery all around Ennet House's first story looks explosive, ballooning in certain unpruned parts, and there are candy-wrappers and Styrofoam cups trapped throughout the shrubs' green levels, and gaudy homemade curtains billow from the second story's female side's bedroom windows, which are open what seems like all year round.

Unit #7 is on the west side of the street's end, sunk in hill-shadow and teetering right on the edge of the eroding ravine that leads down to the Avenue. #7 is in bad shape, boarded up and unmaintained and deeply slumped at the red roof's middle as if shrugging its shoulders at some pointless indignity. For an Ennet House resident, entering Unit #7 (which can easily be entered through the detachable pine board over an old kitchen window) is cause for immediate administrative discharge, since Unit #7 is infamous for being the place where Ennet House residents who want to secretly relapse with Substances sneak in and absorb Substances and apply Visine and Clorets and then try to get back across the street in time for 2330 curfew without getting pinched.

Behind Unit #7 begins far and away the biggest hill in Enfield MA. The hillside is fenced, off-limits, densely wooded and without sanctioned path. Because a legit route involves walking north all the way up the rutted road through the parking lot, past the hospital, down the steep curved driveway to Warren Street and all the way back south down Warren to Commonwealth, almost half of all Ennet House residents negotiate #7's back fence and climb the hillside each morning, short-cutting their way to minimum-wage temp jobs at like the Provident Nursing Home or Shuco-Mist Medical Pressure Systems, etc., over the hill up Comm., or custodial and kitchen jobs at the rich tennis school for blond gleaming tennis kids on what used to be the hilltop. Don Gately's been told that the school's maze of tennis courts lies now on what used to be the hill's hilltop before the Academy's burly cigar-chomping tennis-court contractors shaved the curved top off and rolled the new top flat, the whole long loud process sending all sorts of damaging avalanche-type debris rolling down and all over Enfield Marine's Unit #7, something over which you can sure bet the Enfield Marine VA administration litigated, years back; and but Gately doesn't know that E.T.A.'s balding of the hill is why #7 can still stand empty and unrepaired: Enfield Tennis Academy still has to pay full rent, every month, on what it almost buried.

6 NOVEMBER
YEAR OF THE DEPEND ADULT UNDERGARMENT

1610h. E.T.A. Weight Room. Freestyle circuits. The clank and click of various resistance-systems. Lyle on the towel dispenser conferring with an extremely moist Graham Rader. Schacht doing sit-ups, the board almost vertical, his face purple and forehead pulsing. Troeltsch by the squat rack blowing his nose into a towel. Coyle doing military presses with a bare bar. Carol Spodek curling, intent on the mirror. Rader nodding as Lyle bends and leans in. Hal up on the spotter-shelf in back of the incline-bench in the shadow of the monster copper beech through the west window doing single-leg toe-raises, for the ankle. Ingersoll at the shoulder-pull, steadily upping the weight against Lyle's advice. Keith ('The Viking') Freer[68] and the steroidic fifteen-year-old Eliot Kornspan spotting each other on massive barbell-curls next to the water cooler's bench, taking turns bellowing encouragement. Hal keeps pausing to lean down and spit into an old NASA glass on the floor by the little shelf. E.T.A. Trainer Barry Loach walking around with a clipboard he doesn't write anything down on, but watching people intently and nodding a lot. Axford with one shoe off in the corner, doing something to his bare foot. Michael Pemulis seated cross-legged on the cooler's bench just off Kornspan's left hip, doing facial isometrics, trying to eavesdrop on Lyle and Rader, wincing whenever Kornspan and Freer roar at each other.

'Three more! Get it up there!'
'Hoooowaaaaa.'
'Get that shit up there man!'

'Gwwwhoooooow*aaaaa!*'

'It raped your sister! It killed your fucking mother man!'

'Huhl huhl huhl huhl *gwwwww.*'

'*Do it!*'

Pemulis makes his face very long for a while and then very short and broad, then all sort of hollow and distended like one of Bacon's popes.

'Well suppose' — Pemulis can just make out Lyle — 'Suppose I were to give you a key ring with ten keys. With, no, with a hundred keys, and I were to tell you that one of these keys will unlock it, this door we're imagining opening in onto all you want to be, as a player. How many of the keys would you be willing to try?'

Troeltsch calls over to Pemulis, 'Do the deLint-jerking-off face again!' Pemulis for a second lets his mouth gape slackly and his eyes roll way up and flutters his lids, moving his fist.

'Well I'd try every darn one,' Rader tells Lyle.

'Huhl. Huhl. Gwww*wwwww.*'

'Motherfucker! Fucker!'

Pemulis's wince looks like a type of facial isometric.

'Do Bridget having a tantrum! Do Schacht in a stall!'

Pemulis makes a shush-finger.

Lyle never whispers, but it's just about the same. 'Then you *are* willing to make mistakes, you see. You are saying you will accept 99% error. The paralyzed perfectionist you say you are would stand there before that door. Jingling the keys. Afraid to try the first key.'

Pemulis pulls his lower lip down as far as it will go and contracts his cheek muscles. Cords stand out on Freer's neck as he screams at Kornspan. There's a little hanging mist of spittle and sweat. Kornspan looks like he's about to have a stroke. There are 90 kg. on the bar, which itself is 20 kg.

'One more you *fuck.* Fucking *take* it.'

'Fuck me. *Fuck me* you *fuck.* Gwwwwww.'

'*Take the pain.*'

Freer has one finger under the bar, barely helping. Kornspan's red face is leaping around on his skull.

Carol Spodek's smaller bar goes silently up and down.

Troeltsch comes over and sits down and saws at the back of his neck with the towel, looking up at Kornspan. 'I don't think all the curls I've ever done all together add up to 110,' he said.

Kornspan's making sounds that don't sound like they're coming from his throat.

'Yes! *Yiiissss!*' roars Freer. The bar crashes to the rubber floor, making Pemulis wince. Every vein on Kornspan stands out and pulses. His stomach looks pregnant. He puts his hands on his thighs and leans forward, a string of something hanging from his mouth.

'Way to fucking take it ba*by*,' Freer says, going over to the box on the dispenser to get rosin for his hands, watching himself walk toward the mirror.

Pemulis starts very slowly to lean over toward Kornspan, looking around confidentially. He gets so his face is right up near the side of Kornspan's mesomorphic head and whispers. 'Hey. Eliot. Hey.'

Kornspan, bent over, chest heaving, rolls his head a little his way.

Pemulis whispers: 'Pussy.'

If, by the virtue of charity or the circumstance of desperation, you ever chance to spend a little time around a Substance-recovery halfway facility like Enfield MA's state-funded Ennet House, you will acquire many exotic new facts. You will find out that once MA's Department of Social Services has taken a mother's children away for any period of time, they can always take them away again, D.S.S., like at will, empowered by nothing more than a certain signature-stamped form. I.e. once deemed Unfit — no matter why or when, or what's transpired in the meantime — there's nothing a mother can do.

Or for instance that people addicted to a Substance who abruptly stop ingesting the Substance often suffer wicked papular acne, often for months afterward, as the accumulations of Substance slowly leave the body. The Staff will inform you that this is because the skin is actually the body's biggest excretory organ. Or that chronic alcoholics' hearts are — for reasons no M.D. has been able to explain — swollen to nearly twice the size of civilians' human hearts, and they never again return to normal size. That there's a certain type of person who carries a picture of their therapist in their wallet. That (both a relief and kind of an odd let-down) black penises tend to be the same general size as white penises, on the whole. That not all U.S. males are circumcised.

That you can cop a sort of thin jittery amphetaminic buzz if you rapidly consume three Millennial Fizzies and a whole package of Oreo cookies on an empty stomach. (Keeping it down is required, however, for the buzz, which senior residents often neglect to tell newer residents.)

That the chilling Hispanic term for whatever interior disorder drives the addict back again and again to the enslaving Substance is *tecato gusano*, which apparently connotes some kind of interior psychic worm that cannot be sated or killed.

That black and Hispanic people can be as big or bigger racists than white people, and then can get even more hostile and unpleasant when this realization seems to surprise you.

That it is possible, in sleep, for some roommates to secure a cigarette from their bedside pack, light it, smoke it down to the quick, and then extinguish it in their bedside ashtray — without once waking up, and without setting anything on fire. You will be informed that this skill is usually acquired in penal institutions, which will lower your inclination to complain about the practice. Or that even Flents industrial-strength expandable-foam earplugs do not solve the problem of a snoring roommate if the roommate in question is so huge and so adenoidal that the snores in question also produce subsonic vibrations that arpeggio up and down your body and make your bunk jiggle like a motel bed you've put a quarter in.

That females are capable of being just as vulgar about sexual and eliminatory functions as males. That over 60% of all persons arrested for drug- and alcohol-related offenses report being sexually abused as children, with two-thirds of the remaining 40% reporting that they cannot remember their childhoods in sufficient detail to report one way or the other on abuse. That you can weave hypnotic Madame Psychosis–like harmonies around the minor-D scream of a cheap vacuum cleaner, humming to yourself as you vacuum, if that's your Chore. That some people really do look like rodents. That some drug-addicted prostitutes have a harder time giving up prostitution than they have giving up drugs, with their explanation involving the two habits' very different directions of currency-flow. That there are just as many idioms for the female sex-organ as there are for the male sex-organ.

That a little-mentioned paradox of Substance addiction is: that once you are sufficiently enslaved by a Substance to need to quit the Substance in order to save your life, the enslaving Substance has become so deeply important to you that you will all but lose your mind when it is taken away from you. Or that sometime after your Substance of choice has just been taken away from you in order to save your life, as you hunker down for required A.M. and P.M. prayers, you will find yourself beginning to pray to be allowed literally to lose your mind, to be able to wrap your mind in an old newspaper or something and leave it in an alley to shift for itself, without you.

That in metro Boston the idiom of choice for the male sex-organ is: *Unit*, which is why Ennet House residents are wryly amused by E.M.P.H. Hospital's designations of its campus's buildings.

That certain persons simply will not like you no matter what you do. Then that most nonaddicted adult civilians have already absorbed and accepted this fact, often rather early on.

That no matter how smart you thought you were, you are actually way less smart than that.

That AA and NA and CA's 'God' does not apparently require that you believe in Him/Her/It before He/She/It will help you.[69] That, *pace* macho bullshit, public male weeping is not only plenty masculine but can actually feel *good* (reportedly). That *sharing* means talking, and *taking somebody's inventory* means criticizing that person, plus many additional pieces of

Recoveryspeak. That an important part of halfway-house Human Immuno-Virus prevention is not leaving your razor or toothbrush in communal bathrooms. That apparently a seasoned prostitute can (reportedly) apply a condom to a customer's Unit so deftly he doesn't even know it's on until he's history, so to speak.

That a double-layered steel portable strongbox w/ tri-tumblered lock for your razor and toothbrush can be had for under $35.00 U.S./$38.50 O.N.A.N. via Home-Net Hardware, and that Pat M. or the House Manager will let you use the back office's old TP to order one if you put up a sustained enough squawk.

That over 50% of persons with a Substance addiction suffer from some other recognized form of psychiatric disorder, too. That some male prostitutes become so accustomed to enemas that they cannot have valid bowel movements without them. That a majority of Ennet House residents have at least one tattoo. That the significance of this datum is unanalyzable. That the metro Boston street term for not having any money is: *sporting lint*. That what elsewhere's known as Informing or Squealing or Narcing or Ratting or Ratting Out is on the streets of metro Boston known as 'Eating Cheese,' presumably spun off from the associative nexus of *rat*.

That nose-, tongue-, lip-, and eyelid-rings rarely require actual penetrative piercing. This is because of the wide variety of clip-on rings available. That nipple-rings do require piercing, and that clitoris- and glans-rings are not things anyone thinks you really want to know the facts about. That sleeping can be a form of emotional escape and can with sustained effort be abused. That female chicanos are not called chicanas. That it costs $225 U.S. to get a MA driver's license with your picture but not your name. That purposeful sleep-deprivation can also be an abusable escape. That gambling can be an abusable escape, too, and work, shopping, and shoplifting, and sex, and abstention, and masturbation, and food, and exercise, and meditation/prayer, and sitting so close to Ennet House's old D.E.C. TP cartridge-viewer that the screen fills your whole vision and the screen's static charge tickles your nose like a linty mitten.[70]

That you do not have to like a person in order to learn from him/her/it. That loneliness is not a function of solitude. That it is possible to get so angry you really do see everything red. What a 'Texas Catheter' is. That some people really do steal — will steal things that are *yours*. That a lot of U.S. adults truly cannot read, not even a ROM hypertext phonics thing with HELP functions for every word. That cliquey alliance and exclusion and gossip can be forms of escape. That logical validity is not a guarantee of truth. That evil people never believe they are evil, but rather that *everyone else* is evil. That it is possible to learn valuable things from a stupid person. That it takes effort to pay attention to any one stimulus for more than a few seconds. That you can all of a sudden out of nowhere want to get high with your Substance so bad that you think you will surely die if you don't, and but can just sit there with your hands writhing in your lap and face wet with craving, can want to get high but instead just sit there, wanting to but not, if that makes sense, and if you can gut it out and not hit the Substance during the craving the craving will eventually *pass,* it will go away — at least for a while. That it is statistically easier for low-IQ people to kick an addiction than it is for high-IQ people. That the metro Boston street term for panhandling is: *stemming,* and that it is regarded by some as a craft or art; and that professional stem-artists actually have like little professional colloquia sometimes, little conventions, in parks or public-transport hubs, at night, where they get together and network and exchange feedback on trends and techniques and public relations, etc. That it is possible to abuse OTC cold- and allergy remedies in an addictive manner. That Nyquil is over 50 proof. That boring activities become, perversely, much less boring if you concentrate intently on them. That if enough people in a silent room are drinking coffee it is possible to make out the sound of steam coming off the coffee. That sometimes human beings have to just sit in one place and, like, *hurt.* That you will become way less concerned with what other people think of you when you realize how seldom they do. That there is such a thing as raw, unalloyed, agendaless kindness. That it is possible to fall asleep during an anxiety attack.

That concentrating intently on anything is very hard work.

That addiction is either a disease or a mental illness or a spiritual condition (as in 'poor of spirit') or an O.C.D.-like disorder or an affective or character disorder, and that over 75% of the veteran Boston AAs who want to convince you that it is a disease will make you sit down and watch them write *DISEASE* on a piece of paper and then divide and hyphenate the word so that it becomes *DIS-EASE,* then will stare at you as if expecting you to undergo some kind of blinding epiphanic realization, when really (as G. Day points tirelessly out to his counselors) changing *DISEASE* to *DIS-EASE* reduces a definition and explanation down to a simple description of a feeling, and rather a whiny insipid one at that.

That most Substance-addicted people are also addicted to thinking, meaning they have a compulsive and unhealthy relationship with their own thinking. That the cute Boston AA term for addictive-type thinking is: *Analysis-Paralysis.* That cats will in fact get violent diarrhea if you feed them milk, contrary to the popular image of cats and milk. That it is simply more pleasant to be happy than to be pissed off. That 99% of compulsive thinkers' thinking is about themselves; that 99% of this self-directed thinking consists of imagining and then getting ready for things that are going to happen to them; and then, weirdly, that if they stop to think about it, that 100% of the things they spend 99% of their time and energy imagining and trying to prepare for all the contingencies and consequences of are *never good*. Then that this connects interestingly with the early-sobriety urge to pray for the literal loss of one's mind. In short that 99% of the head's thinking activity consists of trying to scare the everliving shit out of itself. That it is possible to make rather tasty poached eggs in a microwave oven. That the metro-street term for really quite wonderful is: *pisser*. That everybody's sneeze sounds different. That some people's moms never taught them to cover up or turn away when they sneeze. That no one who has been to prison is ever the same again. That you do not have to have sex with a person to get crabs from them. That a clean room feels better to be in than a dirty room. That the people to be most frightened of are the people who are the most frightened. That it takes great personal courage to let yourself appear weak. That you don't have to hit somebody even if you really really want to. That no single, individual moment is in and of itself unendurable.

That nobody who's ever gotten sufficiently addictively enslaved by a Substance to need to quit the Substance and has successfully quit it for a while and been straight and but then has for whatever reason gone back and picked up the Substance again has *ever* reported being glad that they did it, used the Substance again and gotten re-enslaved; not ever. That *bit* is a metro Boston street term for a jail sentence, as in 'Don G. was up in Billerica on a six-month bit.' That it's impossible to kill fleas by hand. That it's possible to smoke so many cigarettes that you get little white ulcerations on your tongue. That the effects of too many cups of coffee are in no way pleasant or intoxicating.

That pretty much everybody masturbates.

Rather a lot, it turns out.

That the cliché 'I don't know who I am' unfortunately turns out to be more than a cliché. That it costs $330 U.S. to get a passport in a phony name. That other people can often see things about you that you yourself cannot see, even if those people are stupid. That you can obtain a major credit card with a phony name for $1500 U.S., but that no one will give you a straight answer about whether this price includes a verifiable credit history and line of credit for when the cashier slides the phony card through the register's little verification-modem with all sorts of burly security guards standing around. That having a lot of money does not immunize people from suffering or fear. That trying to dance sober is a whole different kettle of fish. That the term *vig* is street argot for the bookmaker's commission on an illegal bet, usually 10%, that's either subtracted from your winnings or added to your debt. That certain sincerely devout and spiritually advanced people believe that the God of their understanding helps them find parking places and gives them advice on Mass. Lottery numbers.

That cockroaches can, up to a certain point, be lived with.

That 'acceptance' is usually more a matter of fatigue than anything else.

That different people have radically different ideas of basic personal hygiene.

That, perversely, it is often more fun to want something than to have it.

That if you do something nice for somebody in secret, anonymously, without letting the person you did it for know it was you or anybody else know what it was you did or in any way or form trying to get credit for it, it's almost its own form of intoxicating buzz.

That anonymous generosity, too, can be abused.

That having sex with someone you do not care for feels lonelier than not having sex in the first place, afterward.

That it is permissible to *want*.

That everybody is identical in their secret unspoken belief that way deep down they are different from everyone else. That this isn't necessarily perverse.

That there might not be angels, but there are people who might as well be angels.

That God — unless you're Charlton Heston, or unhinged, or both — speaks and acts entirely through the vehicle of human beings, if there is a God.

That God might regard the issue of whether you believe there's a God or not as fairly low on his/her/its list of things s/he/it's interested in re you.

That the smell of Athlete's Foot is sick-sweet v. the smell of podiatric Dry Rot is sick-sour.

That a person — one with the Disease/-Ease — will do things under the influence of Substances that he simply would not ever do sober, and that some consequences of these things cannot ever be erased or amended.[71] Felonies are an example of this.

As are tattoos. Almost always gotten on impulse, tattoos are vividly, chillingly permanent. The shopworn 'Act in Haste, Repent at Leisure' would seem to have been almost custom-designed for the case of tattoos. For a while, the new resident Tiny Ewell got first keenly interested and then weirdly obsessed with people's tattoos, and he started going around to all the residents and outside people who hung around Ennet House to help keep straight, asking to check out their tattoos and wanting to hear about the circumstances surrounding each tattoo. These little spasms of obsession — like first with the exact definition of *alcoholic,* and then with Morris H.'s special tollhouse cookies until the pancreatitis-flare, then with the exact kinds of corners everybody made their bed up with — these were part of the way Tiny E. temporarily lost his mind when his enslaving Substance was taken away. The tattoo thing started out with Tiny's white-collar amazement at just how many of the folks around Ennet House seemed to have tattoos. And the tattoos seemed like potent symbols of not only whatever they were pictures of but also of the chilling irrevocability of intoxicated impulses.

Because the whole thing about tattoos is that they're permanent, of course, irrevocable once gotten — which of course the irrevocability of a tattoo is what jacks up the adrenaline of the intoxicated decision to sit down in the chair and actually get it (the tattoo) — but the chilling thing about the intoxication is that it seems to make you consider only the adrenaline of the moment itself, not (in any depth) the irrevocability that produces the adrenaline. It's like the intoxication keeps your tattoo-type-class person from being able to project his imagination past the adrenaline of the impulse and even consider the permanent consequences that are producing the buzz of excitement.

Tiny Ewell'll put this same abstract but not very profound idea in a whole number of varied ways, over and over, obsessively almost, and still fail to get any of the tattooed residents interested, although Bruce Green will listen politely, and the clinically depressed Kate Gompert usually won't have the juice to get up and walk away when Tiny starts in, which makes Ewell seek her out vis-à-vis tattoos, though she hasn't got a tattoo.

But they don't have any problem with showing Tiny their tatts, the residents with tatts don't, unless they're female and the thing is in some sort of area where there's a Boundary Issue.

As Tiny Ewell comes to see it, people with tattoos fall under two broad headings. First there are the younger scrofulous boneheaded black-T-shirt-and-spiked-bracelet types who do not have the sense to regret the impulsive permanency of their tatts, and will show them off to you with the same fake-quiet pride with which someone more of Ewell's own social stratum would show off their collection of Dynastic crockery or fine Sauvignon. Then there are the more numerous (and older) second types, who'll show you their tattoos with the sort of stoic regret (albeit tinged with a bit of self-conscious pride about the stoicism) that a Purple-Hearted veteran displays toward his old wounds' scars. Resident Wade McDade has complex nests of blue and red serpents running down the insides of both his arms, and is required to wear long-sleeved shirts every day to his menial job at Store 24, even though the store's heat always loses its mind in the early A.M. and it's always wicked motherfucking hot in there, because the store's Pakistani manager believes his customers will not wish to purchase Marlboro Lights and Mass. Gigabucks lottery tickets from someone with vascular-colored snakes writhing all over his arms.[72] McDade also has a flaming skull on his left shoulderblade. Doony Glynn has the faint remains of a black dotted line tattooed all the way around his neck at about Adam's-apple height, with instruction-manual-like directions for the removal of his head and maintenance of the disengaged head tattooed on his scalp, from the days of his Skinhead youth, which now the tattooed directions take patience and a comb and three of April Cortelyu's barrettes for Tiny even to see.

Actually, a couple weeks into the obsession Ewell broadens his dermo-taxonomy to include a third category, Bikers, of whom there are presently none in Ennet House but plenty around the area's AA meetings, in beards and leather vests and apparently having to meet some kind of weight-requirement of at least 200 kilos. *Bikers* is the metro Boston street term for them, though they seem to refer to themselves usually as Scooter-Puppies, a term which (Ewell finds out the hard way) non-Bikers are not invited to use. These guys are veritable one-man tattoo festivals, but when they show them to you they're disconcerting because they'll bare their tatts with the complete absence of affect of somebody just showing you like a limb or a thumb, not quite sure why you want to see or even what it is you're looking at.

A like *N.B.* that Ewell ends up inserting under the heading *Biker* is that every professional tattooist everybody who can remember getting their tattoos remembers getting them from was, from the sound of everybody's general descriptions, a Biker.

W/r/t the Stoic-Regret group within Ennet House, it emerges that the male tattoos with women's names on them tend, in their irrevocability, to be especially disastrous and regretful, given the extremely provisional nature of most addicts' relationships. Bruce Green will have *MILDRED BONK* on his jilted right triceps forever. Likewise the *DORIS* in red-dripping Gothic script just below the left breast of Emil Minty, who yes apparently did love once. Minty also has a palsied and amateur swastika with the caption *FUCK NIGERS* on a left biceps he is heartily encouraged to keep covered, as a resident. Chandler Foss has an undulating banner with a redly inscribed *MARY* on one forearm, said banner now mangled and necrotic because Foss, dumped and badly coked out one night, tried to nullify the romantic connotations of the tatt by inscribing *BLESSED VIRGIN* above the *MARY* with a razor blade and a red Bic, with predictably ghastly results. Real tattoo artists (Ewell gets this on authority after a White Flag Group meeting from a Biker whose triceps' tattoo of a huge disembodied female breast being painfully squeezed by a disembodied hand which is *itself* tattooed with a disembodied breast and hand communicates real tattoo-credibility, as far as Tiny's concerned) real tatt-artists are always highly trained professionals.

What's sad about the gorgeous violet arrow-pierced heart with *PAMELA* incised in a circle around it on Randy Lenz's right hip is that Lenz has no memory either of the tattoo-impulse and -procedure or of anybody named Pamela. Charlotte Treat has a small green dragon on her calf and another tattoo on a breast she's set a Boundary about letting Tiny see. Hester Thrale has an amazingly detailed blue and green tattoo of the planet Earth on her stomach, its poles abutting pubis and breasts, an equatorial view of which cost Tiny Ewell two weeks of doing Hester's weekly Chore. Overall searing-regret honors probably go to Jennifer Belbin, who has four uncoverable black teardrops descending from the corner of one eye, from one night of mescaline and adrenalized grief, so that from more than two meters away she always looks like she has flies on her, Randy Lenz points out. The new

black girl Didi N. has on the plane of her upper abdomen a tattered screaming skull (off the same stencil as McDade's, but w/o the flames) that's creepy
because it's just a tattered white outline: Black people's tattoos are rare, and
for reasons Ewell regards as fairly obvious they tend to be just white outlines.

Ennet House alumnus and volunteer counselor Calvin Thrust is quietly
rumored to have on the shaft of his formerly professional porn-cartridge-
performer's Unit a tattoo that displays the magiscule initials *CT* when the
Unit is flaccid and the full name *CALVIN THRUST* when hyperemic. Tiny
Ewell has soberly elected to let this go unsubstantiated. Alumna and v.c.
Danielle Steenbok once got the bright idea of having eyeliner-colored tattoos put around both eyes so she'd never again have to apply eyeliner, not
banking on the inevitable fade that over time's turned the tattoos a kind of
nauseous dark-green she now has to constantly apply eyeliner to cover up.
Current female live-in Staffer Johnette Foltz has undergone two of the six
painful procedures required to have the snarling orange-and-blue tiger removed from her left forearm and so now has a snarling tiger minus a head
and one front leg, with the ablated parts looking like someone determined
has been at her forearm with steel wool. Ewell decides this is what gives
profundity to the tattoo-impulse's profound irrevocability: Having a tatt
removed means just exchanging one kind of disfigurement for another.
There are Tingly and Diehl's identical palmate-cannabis-leaf-on-inner-wrist
tattoos, though Tingly and Diehl are from opposite shores and never
crossed paths before entering the House.

Nell Gunther refuses to discuss tattoos with Tiny Ewell in any way or
form.

For a while, Tiny Ewell considers live-in Staffer Don Gately's homemade
jailhouse tattoos too primitive to even bother asking about.

He'd made a true pest of himself, though, Ewell did, when at the height
of the obsession this one synthetic-narc-addicted kid came in who refused to
be called anything but his street name, Skull, and lasted only like four days,
but who'd been a walking exhibition of high-regret ink — both arms tattooed with spiderwebs at the elbows, on his fishy-white chest a naked lady
with the same kind of overlush measurements Ewell remembered from the
pinball machines of his Watertown childhood. On Skull's back a half-m.-
long skeleton in a black robe and cowl playing the violin in the wind on a
crag with *THE DEAD* in maroon on a vertical gonfalonish banner unfurling below; on one biceps either an icepick or a mucronate dagger, and
down both forearms a kind of St. Vitus's dance of leather-winged dragons
with the words — on both forearms — *HOW DO YOU LIK YOUR
BLUEYED BOY NOW MR DETH!?*, the typos of which, Tiny felt, only
served to heighten Skull's whole general tatt-gestalt's intended effect, which
Tiny presumed was primarily to repel.

208

In fact Tiny E.'s whole displacement of obsession from bunks' hospital corners to people's tattoos was probably courtesy of this kid Skull, who on his second night in the newer male residents' Five-Man Room had shed his electrified muscle-shirt and was showing off his tattoos in a boneheaded regretless first-category fashion to Ken Erdedy while R. Lenz did headstands against the closet door in his jockstrap and Ewell and Geoffrey D. had their wallets' credit cards spread out on Ewell's drum-tight bunk and were trying to settle a kind of admittedly childish argument about who had the more prestigious credit cards — Skull flexing his pectorals to make the over-developed woman on his chest writhe, reading his forearms to Erdedy, etc. — and Geoffrey Day had looked up from his AmEx (Gold, to Ewell's Platinum) and shaken his moist pale head at Ewell and asked rhetorically what had ever happened to good old traditional U.S. tattoos like *MOM* or an anchor, which for some reason touched off a small obsessive explosion in Ewell's detox-frazzled psyche.

Probably the most poignant items in Ewell's survey are the much-faded tattoos of old Boston AA guys who've been sober in the Fellowship for decades, the crocodilic elder statesmen of the White Flag and Allston Groups and the St. Columbkill Sunday Night Group and Ewell's chosen Home Group, Wednesday night's Better Late Than Never Group (Non-smoking) at St. Elizabeth's Hospital just two blocks down from the House. There is something queerly poignant about a deeply faded tattoo, a poignancy something along the lines of coming upon the tiny and poignantly unfashionable clothes of a child long-since grown up in an attic trunk some-where (the clothes, not the grown child, Ewell confirmed for G. Day). See, e.g., White Flag's cantankerous old Francis ('Ferocious Francis') Gehaney's right forearm's tatt of a martini glass with a naked lady sitting in the glass with her legs kicking up over the broad flaring rim, with an old-style Rita Hayworth–era bangs-intensive hairstyle. Faded to a kind of underwater blue, its incidental black lines gone soot-green and the red of the lips/nails/ *SUBIKBAY'62USN4-07* not lightened to pink but more like decayed to the dusty red of fire through much smoke. All these old sober Boston blue-collar men's irrevocable tattoos fading almost observably under the low-budget fluorescence of church basements and hospital auditoria — Ewell watched and charted and cross-referenced them, moved. Any number of good old U.S.N. anchors, and in Irish Boston sooty green shamrocks, and several little frozen tableaux of little khaki figures in G.I. helmets plunging bayonets into the stomachs of hideous urine-yellow bucktoothed Oriental carica-tures, and screaming eagles with their claws faded blunt, and *SEMPER FI*, all autolyzed to the point where the tattoos look like they're just under the surface of a murky-type pond.

A tall silent hard-looking old black-haired BLTN-Group veteran has the terse and hateful single word *PUSSY* in what's faded to pond-scum green down one liver-spotted forearm; but yet the fellow transcends even stoic regret by dressing and carrying himself as if the word simply wasn't there, or was so irrevocably there there was no point even thinking about it: there's a deep and tremendously compelling dignity about the old man's demeanor w/r/t the *PUSSY* on his arm, and Ewell actually considers approaching this fellow re the issue of sponsorship, if and when he feels it's appropriate to get an AA sponsor, if he decides it's germane in his case.

Near the conclusion of this two-month obsession, Tiny Ewell approaches Don Gately on the subject of whether the jailhouse tattoo should maybe comprise a whole separate phylum of tattoo. Ewell's personal feeling is that jailhouse tattoos aren't poignant so much as grotesque, that they seem like they weren't a matter of impulsive decoration or self-presentation so much as simple self-mutilation arising out of boredom and general disregard for one's own body and the aesthetics of decoration. Don Gately's developed the habit of staring coolly at Ewell until the little attorney shuts up, though this is partly to disguise the fact that Gately usually can't follow what Ewell's saying and is unsure whether this is because he's not smart or educated enough to understand Ewell or because Ewell is simply out of his fucking mind.

Don Gately tells Ewell how your basic-type jailhouse tatt is homemade with sewing needles from the jailhouse canteen and some blue ink from the cartridge of a fountain pen promoted from the breast pocket of an unalert Public Defender, is why the jailhouse genre is always the same night-sky blue. The needle is dipped in the ink and jabbed as deep into the tattooee as it can be jabbed without making him recoil and fucking up your aim. Just a plain ultraminimal blue square like Gately's got on his right wrist takes half a day and hundreds of individual jabs. How come the lines are never quite straight and the color's never quite all the way solid is it's impossible to get all the individualized punctures down to the same uniform deepness in the, like, twitching flesh. This is why jailhouse tatts always look like they were done by sadistic children on rainy afternoons. Gately has a blue square on his right wrist and a sloppy cross on the inside of his mammoth left forearm. He'd done the square himself, and a cellmate had done the cross in return for Gately doing a cross on the cellmate. Oral narcotics render the process both less painful and less tedious. The sewing needle is sterilized in grain alcohol, which Gately explains that the alcohol is got by taking mess-hall fruit and mashing it up and adding water and secreting the whole mess in a Ziploc just inside the flush-hole thing of the cell's toilet, to, like, foment. The sterilizing results of this can be consumed, as well. Bonded liquor and cocaine are the only things hard to get inside of M.D.C. penal institutions, because the expense of them gets everybody all excited and it's only a matter of time before somebody goes and eats cheese. The inexpensive C-IV oral narcotic Talwin can be traded for cigarettes, however, which can in turn be got at the canteen or won at cribbage and dominoes (M.D.C. regs prohibit straight-out cards) or got in mass quantities off smaller inmates in return for protection from the romantic advances of larger inmates. Gately is right-handed and his arms are roughly the size of Tiny Ewell's legs. His wrist's jailhouse square is canted and has sloppy extra blobs at three of the corners. Your average jailhouse tatt can't be removed even with laser surgery because it's incised so deep in. Gately is polite about Tiny Ewell's inquiries but not expansive, i.e. Tiny has to ask very specific questions about whatever he wishes to know and then gets a short specific answer from Gately to just that question. Then Gately stares at him, a habit Ewell tends to complain about at some length up in the Five-Man Room. His interest in tattoos seems to be regarded by Gately not as invasive but as the temporary obsession of a still-quivering Substanceless psyche that in a couple weeks will have forgot all about tattoos, an attitude Ewell finds condescending in the extremus. Gately's attitude toward his own primitive tattoos is a second-category attitude, with most of the stoicism and acceptance of his tatt-regret sincere, if only because these irrevocable emblems of jail are minor Rung Bells compared to some of the fucked-up and *really* irrevocable impulsive mistakes Gately'd made as an active drug addict and burglar, not to mention their consequences, the mistakes', which Gately's trying to accept he'll be paying off for a real long time.

Michael Pemulis has this habit of looking first to one side and then over to the other before he says anything. It's impossible to tell whether this is unaffected or whether Pemulis is emulating some film-noir-type character. It's worse when he's put away a couple 'drines. He and Trevor Axford and Hal Incandenza are in Pemulis's room, with Pemulis's roommates Schacht and Troeltsch down at lunch, so they're alone, Pemulis and Axford and Hal, stroking their chins, looking down at Michael Pemulis's yachting cap on his bed. Lying inside the overturned hat are a bunch of fair-sized but bland-looking tablets of the allegedly incredibly potent DMZ.

Pemulis looks all around behind them in the empty room. 'This, Incster, Axhandle, is the incredibly potent DMZ. The Great White Shark of organo-synthesized hallucinogens. 'The gargantuan feral infant of —'

Hal says 'We get the picture.'

'The Yale U. of the Ivy League of Acid,' says Axford.

'Your ultimate psychosensual distorter,' Pemulis sums up.

'Think you mean psycho*sensory,* unless I don't know the whole story here.'

Axford gives Hal a narrow look. Interrupting Pemulis means having to watch him do the head-thing all over again each time.

'Hard to find, gentlemen. As in very hard to find. Last lots came off the line in the early 70s. These tablets here are artifacts. Certain amount of decay in potency probably inevitable. Used in certain shady CIA-era military experiments.'

Axford nods down at the hat. 'Mind-control?'

'More like getting the enemy to think their guns are hydrangea, the enemy's a blood-relative, that sort of thing. Who knows. The accounts I've been reading have been incoherent, gistless. Experiments conducted. Things got out of hand. Let's just say things got out of control. Potency judged too incredible to proceed. Subjects locked away in institutions and written off as casualties of peace. Formula shredded. Research team scattered, reassigned. Vague but I've got to tell you pretty sobering rumors.'

'These are from the early 70s?' Axhandle says.

'See the little trademark on each one, with the guy in bell-bottoms and long sideburns?'

'Is that what that is?'

'Unprecedentedly potent, this stuff. The Swiss inventor they say was originally recommending LSD-25 as what to take to come *down* off the stuff.' Pemulis takes one of the tablets and puts it in his palm and pokes at it with a callused finger. 'What we're looking at. We're looking here at either a serious sudden injection of cash —'

Axford makes a shocked noise. 'You'd actually try to peddle the incredibly potent DMZ around this sorry place?'

Pemulis's snort sounds like the letter K. 'Get a large economy-size clue, Axhandle. Nobody here'd have any clue what they'd even be dealing with. Not to mention be willing to pay what they're worth. Why, there are pharmaceutical museums, left-wing think tanks, New York designer-drug consortiums I'm sure'd be dying to dissect these. Decoct like. Toss into the spectrometer and see what's what.'

'That we could get bids from, you're saying,' Axford says. Hal squeezes a ball, silently looking at the hat.

Pemulis turns the tablet over. 'Or certain very progressive and hip-type nursing homes I know guys that know of. Or down at Back Bay at that yogurt place with that picture of those historical guys Inc was saying at breakfast was up on the wall.'

'Ram Das. William Burroughs.'

'Or just down in Harvard Square at Au Bon Pain where all those 70s-era guys in old wool ponchos play chess against those little clocks they keep hitting.'

Axford's pretending to punch Hal's arm in excitement.

Pemulis says 'Or of course I'm thinking I could just go the sheer-entertainment route and toss them in the Gatorade barrels at the meet with Port Washington Tuesday, or down at the WhataBurger — watch everybody run around clutching their heads or whatever. I'd be *way* into watching Wayne play with distorted senses.'

Hal puts one foot up on Pemulis's little frustum-shaped bedside stool and leans farther in. 'Would it be prying to ask how you finally managed to get hold of these?'

'It wouldn't be prying at all,' Pemulis says, removing from the yachting cap's lining every piece of contraband he's got and spreading it out on the bed, sort of the way older people will array all their valuables in quiet moments. He has a small quantity of personal-consumption Lamb's Breath cannabis (bought back from Hal out of a 20-g. he'd sold Hal) in a dusty baggie, a little Saran-Wrapped cardboard rectangle with four black stars spaced evenly across it, the odd 'drine, and it looks like a baker's dozen of the incredibly potent DMZ, Sweet Tart–sized tablets of no particular color with a tiny mod hipster in each center wishing the viewer peace. 'We don't even know how many hits this is,' he muses quietly. There's sun on the wall with the hanging viewer and poster of the paranoid king and an enormous hand-drawn Sierpinski gasket. In one of the three big mullioned west windows — the Academy is nothing if not well-fenestrated — there's an oval flaw that's casting a bubble of ale-colored autumn sunlight from the window's left side to elongate onto Pemulis's tightly made bed,[73] and he moves everything his hat's got into the brighter bubble, going down on one knee to study a tablet between his forceps (Pemulis owns stuff like philatelic forceps, a loupe, a pharmaceutical scale, a postal scale, a personal-size Bunsen burner) with the calm precision of a jeweler. 'The literature's mute on the titration. Do you take one tablet?' He looks up on one side and then back around on the other at the boys' faces leaning in above. 'Is like half a tab a regulation hit?'

'Two or even three tablets, maybe?' Hal says, knowing he sounds greedy but unable to help himself.

'The accessible data's vague,' Pemulis says, his profile contorted around the loupe in his socket. 'The literature on muscimole-lysergic blends is spotty and vague and hard to read except to say how massively powerful the supposed yields are.'

Hal looks at the top of Pemulis's head. 'Did you hit a medical library?'

'I got on MED.COM off Lateral Alice's WATS line and went back and forth and up and down through MED.COM. Plenty on lysergics, plenty on methoxy-class hybrids. Vague and almost gossip-columny shit on fitviavi-compounds. To get anything you got to cross-key Ergotics with the phrase *muscimole* or *muscimolated*. Only a couple things ring the bell when you key in *DMZ*. Then they're all potent this, sinister that. Nothing with any specifics. And jumbly polysyllables out the ass. Whole thing gave me a migraine.'

'Yes but did you actually hop in the truck and actually *go* to a real med-library?' Hal's his mother Avril's child when it comes to databases, software Spell-Checks, etc. Axford now really does punch him once in the shoulder, albeit the right one. Pemulis is scratching absently at the little hair-hurricane at the center of his hair. It's close to 1430h., and the flawed bubble of light on the bed is getting to be the slightly sad color of early winter P.M. There are still no sounds from the West Courts outside, but there's high song of much volume through the wall's water-pipes — a lot of the guys who are drilled past caring in the A.M. don't get it up to shower until after lunch, then sit through P.M. classes with wet hair and different clothes than their A.M. classes.

Pemulis rises to stand between them and looks around the empty three-bedded room again, with neat stacks of three players' clothes and bright gear on shelves and three wicker laundry hampers bulging slightly. There is the rich scent of athletic laundry, but other than that the room looks almost professionally clean. Pemulis and Schacht's room makes Hal and Mario's room look like an insane asylum, Hal thinks. Axford drew one of only two single upperclass rooms in last spring's lottery, the other having gone to the Vaught twins, who get counted as one entry in Room Draw.

Pemulis still has his cheek screwed up to keep the loupe in as he looks around. 'One monograph had this toss-off about DMZ where the guy invites you to envision acid that has itself dropped acid.'

'Holy *crow*.'

'One article out of fucking *Moment* of all sources talks about how this one Army convict at Leavenworth got allegedly injected with some massive unspecified dose of early DMZ as part of some Army experiment in Christ only knows what and about how this convict's family sued over how the guy reportedly lost his mind.' He directs the loupe dramatically at first Hal and then Axford. 'I mean literally *lost* his mind, like the massive dose picked his mind up and carried it off somewhere and put it down someplace and forgot where.'

'I think we get the picture, Mike.'

'Allegedly *Moment* says how the guy's found later in his Army cell, in some impossible lotus position, singing show tunes in a scary deadly-accurate Ethel-Merman-impression voice.'

Axford says maybe Pemulis stumbled on a possible explanation for poor old Lyle and his lotus position down in the weight room, gesturing with the bad right hand in the direction of Comm.-Ad.

Again Pemulis with the thing with the head. The slackening of a cheek lets the loupe fall out and bounce off the drum-tight bed, and Pemulis gets it to rebound into his palm without even looking. 'I think we can err on the side of not dickying the Gatorade barrels, anyway. This soldier's story's moral was proceed with caution, big time. The guy's mind's still allegedly AWOL. An old soldier, now, still belting out Broadway medleys in some secretive institution someplace. Blood-relatives try to sue on the guy's behalf, Army apparently came up with enough arguments to give the jury reasonable doubt about if the guy can even be said to legally exist enough to bring suit, anymore, since the dose misplaced his mind.'

Axford feels absently at his elbow. 'So you're saying let's proceed with care why don't we.'

Hal kneels to prod one of the tablets up against the dusty baggie's side. His finger looks dark in the elongated bubble of light. 'I'm thinking these look like two tablets are possibly a hit. A kind of Motrinish look to them.'

'Visual guesswork isn't going to do it. This is not Bob Hope, Inc.'

'We could even designate it "Ethel," for on the phone,' Axford suggests.

Pemulis watches Hal arranging the tablets into the same general cardioid-shape as E.T.A. itself. 'What I'm saying. This is not a fools-rush-in-type substance, Inc. This show-tune soldier like left the *planet*.'

'Well, so long as he waves every so often.'

'The sense I got is the only thing he waves at is his food.'

'But that was from a massive early dose,' Axford says.

Hal's arrangement of the tablets on the red-and-gray counterpane is almost Zen in its precision. 'These are from the 70s?'

After intricate third-party negotiations, Michael Pemulis finally landed 650 mg. of the vaunted and elusive compound DMZ or 'Madame Psychosis' from a small-arms-draped duo of reputed former Canadian insurgents who now undertook small and probably kind of pathetic outdated insurgency-projects from behind the front-operation of a cut-rate mirror, blown-glass, practical joke 'n gag, trendy postcard, and low-demand old film-cartridge emporium called Antitoi Entertainment, just up Prospect St. from Inman Square in Cambridge's decayed Portugo/Brazilian district. Because Pemulis always conducts business solo and speaks no French, the whole transaction with the Nuck in charge had to be negotiated in dumbshow, and since this lumberjackish Antitoi Nuckwad tended to look from side to side before he communicated even more than Pemulis looked all around himself, with his dim-looking partner standing there cradling a broom and also scanning for eavesdroppers in the closed shop the whole time, the whole negotiated deal had resembled a kind of group psychomotor seizure, with different bits of whipping and waggling heads reflected in dislocated sections and at jagged angles in more mirrors and pebbled blown-glass vases than Pemulis had ever seen crammed into anywhere. A very low-rent TP indeed had a hardcore-porn cartridge going at five times the normal speed so it looked like crazed rodents and may have turned Pemulis's sexual glands off for all time, he feels. God alone knew where these clowns had acquired thirteen incredibly potent 50-mg. artifacts of the B.S. 1970s. But the good news is they were Canadians, and like fucking Nucksters about almost anything they had no idea what what they were in possession of was worth, as it slowly emerged. Pemulis, w/ aid of 150 mg. of time-release Tenuate Dospan, almost danced a little post-transaction jig on his way up the steps of the otiose Cambridge bus, feeling the way W. Penn in his Quaker Oats hat in like the 16th century must have felt trading a few trinkets to babe-in-the-woods Natives for New Jersey, he imagines, doffing the nautical cap to two nuns in the aisle.

Over the course of the next academic day — the incredibly potent stash now wrapped tight in Saran and stashed deep in the toe of an old sneaker that sits atop the aluminum strut between two panels in subdorm B's drop ceiling, Pemulis's time-tested entrepôt — over the course of the next day or so the matter's hashed out and it's decided that while there's no real reason to involve Boone or Stice or Struck or Troeltsch, it's really Pemulis and Axford and Hal's right — duty, almost, to the spirits of inquiry and good trade practice — to sample the potentially incredibly potent DMZ in predeterminedly safe amounts before unleashing it on Boone or Troeltsch or any unwitting civilians. Axford having been allowed in on the front end, the question of Hal's defraying the opportunity-cost of his part in the experiment is tactfully broached and turns out to be no problem. Pemulis's mark-up isn't anything beyond accepted norms, and there's always room in Hal's budget for spirited inquiry. Hal's one condition is that somebody tech-literate actually take the truck down to B.U. or M.I.T.'s medical library and physically verify that the compound is both organic and nonaddictive, which Pemulis says a physical hands-on library assault is already down in his day-planner in pen, anyway. After P.M. drills on Thursday, as Hal Incandenza and Pemulis with camera-mounted Mario Incandenza in tow stand with their hands in the chainlink mesh of one of the Show Courts' fencing and watch Teddy Schacht play a private exhibition against a Syrian Satellite-pro who's at E.T.A. for two paid weeks of corrective instruction on a service-motion that's eroding his rotator cuff — the guy wears thick glasses with a black athletic band around his head and plays with an upright square-jawed liquid precision and is dispatching Ted Schacht handily, which Schacht is taking with his customary sanguine good temper, giving his stolid all, learning what he can, one of very few genuinely stocky players at E.T.A. and one of the even fewer ranked junior players around without an apparent ego, wholly noninsecure since he blew out his knee on a *contre-pied* in the pre-Thanksgiving exhibition three years back, which is odd, now still in and at it for just the fun — and more or less doomed, therefore, to a purgatorial existence in 128-256 Alphabetville — as Pemulis and Hal stand there sweaty in full red-and-gray E.T.A. sweats on a raw 11/5 P.M., the sweat in their hair starting to accrete and freeze, Mario's head bowed under the weight of the head-mount rig and his hideously arachnodactylic fingers whitening as the fence takes his forward weight, Hal's posture subtly but warmly inclined ever so slightly toward his tiny older brother, who resembles him the way creatures of the same Order but not the same Family might resemble one another — as they stand watching and hashing matters out, Hal and Pemulis, there's the thud and sprong of an E.W.D. transnational catapult off way below to their left and then the high keen sound of a waste-displacement projectile the clouds are too low to let them see the flight of — though a weirdly yellow sheep-shaped cloud is visible somewhere up off past Acton, connecting the horizon's seam to some kind of coming storm-front held off by the ATHSCME fans along the Lowell-Methuen stretch of border, northwest. Pemulis finally nixes the notion of performing the spirited controlled experiment here in Enfield, where Axford has to be at the A squad's dawn drills every morning at 0500, and also Hal, unless he's slept over at HmH the night before, with HmH just not being a good DMZ-dropping venue at all. Pemulis, scanning up and down the length of the fence and winking at Mario, posits that a solid 36 hours of demand-free time will be advisable for any interaction with the incredibly potent you-know-whatski. That also lets out the inter-academy thing with Port Washington tomorrow, for which Charles Tavis has chartered two buses, because so many E.T.A. players are getting to go and do battle in this one — Port Washington Academy is gargantuan, the Xerox Inc. of North American tennis academies, with over 300 students and 64 courts, half of which they'll have already put under warm inflatable TesTar cover as of like Halloween, P.W.'s staff being less into the value of elemental suffering than Schtitt & Co. — so many that Tavis will almost surely go ahead and bus them all back up from Long Island just as soon as the post-competition dance is over, rather than shell out for all those motel rooms without corporate support. This E.T.A.–P.W. meet and buffet and dance are a private, inter-academy tradition, an epic rivalry almost a decade old. Plus Pemulis says he'll need a couple weeks of quality med-library-stacks-tossing time to do the more exacting titration and side-effects re-search Hal agrees the soldier's sobering story seems to dictate. So, they conclude, the window of opportunity looks to be 11/20–21 — the weekend right after the big End-of-Fiscal-Year fundraising exhibition with the E.T.A. A & B squads in singles against (this year) Québec's notoriously hapless Jr. Davis and Jr. Wightman Cup squads,[74] invited down under very quiet low-profile political conditions via the good expatriate offices of Avril Incan-denza to get vivisected by Wayne and Hal et al for the philanthropic amusement of E.T.A. patrons and alums, then to dance the P.M. away at a catered supper and Alumni Ball — the weekend right before Thanksgiving week and the WhataBurger Invitational in sunny AZ, because this year in addition to Friday 11/20 they also get Saturday 11/21 off, as in from both class and practice, because C.T. and Schtitt have arranged a special one-match doubles exhibition for the Saturday A.M. following the big meet, one between two female coaches of the Québecois Wightmans and E.T.A.'s infamous Vaught twins, Caryn and Sharyn Vaught, seventeen, O.N.A.N.'s top-ranked junior women's doubles team, unbeaten in three years, an unbeatable duo, uncanny in their cooperation on the court, moving as One at all times, playing not just as if but in fact because they shared a brain, or at least the psychomotor lobes of one, the twins Siamese, fused at the left and right temple, banned from Singles by O.N.A.N. regs, the broadshadow-casting Vaughts, flinty-eyed tire-executive's daughters out of Akron, using her/their four legs to cover chilling amounts of court, plus to sweep the Charleston competition at every post-exhibition formal ball for the last five years running. Tavis'll be on Wayne to play some sort of exhibitory thing, too, though asking Wayne to publicly smear a second Québecer in two days might be a bit much. And but everyone who's anyone'll be down at the Lung, watching the Vaughts vivisect some adult-ranked Nucks, plus maybe Wayne,[75] then the E.T.A.s will get Saturday to rest and recharge before starting both the pre-WhataBurger training week and the bell-lap of prep for 12/12's Boards, meaning late Friday night–Sunday A.M. will give Pemulis, Hal, and Axford (and maybe Struck if Pemulis needs to let Struck in, for help with library-tossing) enough time to psychospiritually rally from whatever meninges-withering hangover the incredibly potent DMZ might involve ... and Axford in the sauna predicted it would be a witherer indeed, since even just LSD alone he observed left you the next day not just sick or down but utterly empty, a shell, void inside, like your soul was a wrung-out sponge. Hal wasn't sure he concurred. An alcohol hangover was definitely no frolic in the psychic glade, all thirsty and sick and your eyes bulging and receding with your pulse, but after a night of involved hallucinogens Hal said the dawn seemed to confer on his psyche a kind of pale sweet aura, a luminescence.[76] Halation, Axford observed.

Pemulis appears to have left out of his calculations the fact that he'll get that Saturday P.M. off classes only if he makes the travelling list for the Tucson-WhataBurger the following week, and that unlike Hal and Axford he's not a lock: Pemulis's U.S.T.A. rank, excepting his halcyon thirteenth year in the Year of the Perdue Wonderchicken, has never gotten higher than 128, and the WhataBurger draws kids from all over O.N.A.N. and even Europe; the draw will have to be weak indeed for him to get even one of the 64 Qualifying-Round invitations. Axford's on the fringes of the top 50, but he got to go last year at seventeen, so he's almost got to get to go. And Hal is looking at getting a Third or maybe Fourth Seed in 18's Singles; he's definitely going, barring some sort of cataclysmic ankle-relapse against either Port Wash. or Québec. Axford postulates that Pemulis isn't miscalculating so much as simply showing a slitty-eyed confidence, which as far as his match-play outlook is concerned would be unusual and rather a fine thing — prorector Aubrey deLint says (publicly) that seeing M. Pemulis in practice v. seeing M. Pemulis in a real match that means anything is like getting to know some girl through e-mail as like e-mail-keyboard-type penpals and really falling for her and then finally meeting her in person and finding out she's got like just one enormous tit in the exact middle of her chest or something like that.[77]

Mario will get to come along if Avril can convince C.T. to bring him along to get WhataBurger footage for this year's E.T.A. promotional Xmas-giveaway-to-private-and-incorporated-patrons cartridge.

Schacht and the glossy Syrian are laughing together about something up at the net-post, where they've walked to gather gear and various spare rotator-cuff- and knee-appliances after the Syrian kind of cornily jumped the net and pumped Schacht's hand, breath and sweat-steam rising up off and moving off through the fence's mesh toward the manicured western hills as Mario's laugh rings out at some broad mock-supplicant's gesture Schacht's just now made.

O

7 NOVEMBER
YEAR OF THE DEPEND ADULT UNDERGARMENT

You can be at certain parties and not really be there. You can hear how certain parties have their own implied ends embedded in the choreography of the party itself. One of the saddest times Joelle van Dyne ever feels anywhere is that invisible pivot where a party ends — even a bad party — that moment of unspoken accord when everyone starts collecting his lighter and date, jacket or greatcoat, his one last beer hanging from the plastic rind's five rings, says certain perfunctory things to the hostess in a way that acknowledges their perfunctoriness without seeming insincere, and leaves, usually shutting the door. When everybody's voices recede down the hall. When the hostess turns back in from the closed door and sees the litter and the expanding white V of utter silence in the party's wake.

Joelle, at the end of her rope and preparing to hang from it, listening, is supported by a polished hardwood floor above both river and Bay's edge, perched uncomfortably in striated light in one of Molly Notkin's chairs molded in the likeness of great filmmakers from the celluloid canon, seated between empty Cukor and frightening Murnau in Méliès's fiberglass lap, his trousers' crease uncomfortable and his cummerbund M.I.T.-crested. The lurid chairs' directors are larger than life: Joelle's feet dangle well off the floor, her squished hamstrings beginning to burn under a damp thick cotton Brazilian skirt which is vivid, curled pale purples and fresh red against a

Latin black that seems to glow above pale knees and white rayon kneesocks and feet in clogs that are hanging half off, legs swinging like a child's, always feeling like a child in Molly's chairs, conspicuously perched in the eye of a bad party's somewhat forced-feeling storm of wit and good cheer, sitting by herself under what used to be her window, the daughter of a low-pH chemist and homemaker from western Kentucky, a lot of fun to be with, normally, if you can get over the disconcerting veil.

Among pernicious myths is the one where people always get very upbeat and generous and other-directed right before they eliminate their own map for keeps. The truth is that the hours before a suicide are usually an interval of enormous conceit and self-involvement.

There are decorative bars, slender and of black iron that pigeon droppings have made piebald, over the west windows to this third-floor cooperative apartment on the East Cambridge fringes of the Back Bay, where near-Professor Notkin is holding a party to celebrate passing her Orals in Film & Film-Cartridge Theory, the doctoral program where Joelle — before her retreat into broadcast sound — had met her.

Molly Notkin often confides on the phone to Joelle van Dyne about the one tormented love of Notkin's life thus far, an erotically circumscribed G. W. Pabst scholar at New York University tortured by the neurotic conviction that there are only a finite number of erections possible in the world at any one time and that his tumescence means e.g. the detumescence of some perhaps more deserving or tortured Third World sorghum farmer or something, so that whenever he tumefies he'll suffer the same order of guilt that your less eccentrically tortured Ph.D.-type person will suffer at the idea of, say, wearing baby-seal fur. Molly still takes the high-speed rail down to visit him every couple weeks, to be there for him in case by some selfish mischance he happens to harden, prompting in him black waves of self-disgust and an extreme neediness for understanding and nonjudgmental love. She and poor Molly Notkin are just the same, Joelle reflects, seated alone, watching doctoral candidates taste wine — sisters, sororal twins. With her fear of direct light, Notkin. And the disguises and whiskers are simply veiled veils. How many sub-rosa twins are there, out there, really? What if heredity, instead of linear, is branching? What if it's not arousal that's so finitely circumscribed? What if in fact there were ever only like two really distinct individual people walking around back there in history's mist? That all difference descends from this difference? The whole and the partial. The damaged and the intact. The deformed and the paralyzingly beautiful. The insane and the attendant. The hidden and the blindingly open. The performer and the audience. No Zen-type One, always rather Two, one upside-down in a convex lens.

Joelle is thinking about what she has in her purse. She sits alone in her linen veil and pretty skirt, obliquely looked at, listening to bits of conversation she reels in out of the overall voices' noise but seeing no one really else, the absolute end of her life and beauty running in a kind of stuttered old hand-held 16mm before her eyes, projected against the white screen on her side, for once, from Uncle Bud and twirling to Orin and Jim and YYY, all the way up to today's wet walk here from the Red Line's Downtown stop, walking the whole way from East Charles St., employing a self-conscious and kind of formal stride, but undeniably pretty, the overall walk toward her last hour was, on this last day before the great O.N.A.N.ite Interdependence revel. East Charles to the Back Bay today is a route full of rained-on sienna-glazed streets and upscale businesses with awnings and wooden signs hung with cute Colonial script, and people looking at her like you look at the blind, naked gazes, not knowing she could see everything at all times. She likes the wet walk for this, everything milky and halated through her veil's damp linen, the brick sidewalks of Charles St. unchipped and impersonally crowded, her legs on autopilot, she a perceptual engine, holding the collar of her overcoat closed at her poncho's neckline in a way that lets her hold the veil secure against her face with a finger on her chin, thinking always about what she has in her purse, stopping in at a discount tobacconist and buying a quality cigar in a glass tube and then a block later placing the cigar inside carefully in among the overflowing waste atop a corner receptacle of pine-green mesh, but keeps the tube, puts the glass tube in her purse, can hear the rain's *thup* on tight umbrellas and hear it hiss in the street, and can see droplets broken and regathering on her polyresin coat, cars sheening by with the special lonely sound of cars in rain, wipers making black rainbows on taxis' shining windshields. In every alley are green I.W.D. dumpsters and the smaller red I.W.D. dumpsters to take the overflow from the green dumpsters. And the sound of her wood-sole clogs against the receding staccato of brittle women's high heels on brick westward as Charles St. now approaches Boston Common and becomes less quaint and upscale: sodden litter — flat the way only wet litter can be flat — appears on the sidewalk and in the curb's seam, and now murky-colored people with sacks and grocery carts appraising that litter, squatting to lift and sift through litter; and the rustle and jut of limbs from dumpsters being sifted by people who all day do nothing but sift through I.W.D. dumpsters; and other people's blue shoeless limbs extending in coronal rays from refrigerator boxes in each block's three alleys, and the little cataract of rainwater off the edge of each dumpster's red annex's downsloping side and hitting refrigerator boxes' tops with a rhythmless thappathappappathap; somebody going *Pssssst* from an alley's lip, and ghastly-white or blotched faces declaiming to thin air from recessed doorways curtained by rain, and for an other-directed second Joelle wishes she'd hung on to the cigar, to give away, and moving westward into the territory of the Endless Stem near the end of Charles she starts to dispense change she is asked for from doorways and inverted up-tilted boxes; and she gets asked about the deal with the veil with a lack of delicacy she rather prefers. A sooty wheelchaired man with a dead white face below a NOTRE RAI PAYS cap silently extends a hand for coins — a puffed red cut across that businesslike palm is half-healed and almost visibly closing. It looks like a dent in dough. Joelle gives him a folded U.S. twenty and likes that he says nothing.

She buys a .473-liter Pepsi Cola in a blunt plastic bottle at a Store 24 whose Jordanian clerk just looks at her blankly when she asks if they carry Big Red Soda Water, and settles for the Pepsi and comes out and pours the pop out down a storm-drain and watches it pool there foaming brownly and stay put because the drain's grate is clogged solid with leaves and sodden litter. She walks on toward the Common with the empty bottle and glass tube in her purse. There was no need to buy Chore Boy pads at the Store 24.

Joelle van Dyne is excruciatingly alive and encaged, and in the director's lap can call up everything from all times. What will be that most self-involved of acts, self-cancelling, to lock oneself in Molly Notkin's bedroom or bath and get so high that she's going to fall down and stop breathing and turn blue and die, clutching her heart. No more back and forth. Boston Common is like a lush hole Boston's built itself around, a two-k. square of shiny trees and dripping limbs and green benches over wet grass. Pigeons all over, the same sooty cream as the willows' rinds. Three young black men perched like tough crows along a bench's back approve her body and call her *bitch* with harmless affection and ask where's the wedding at. No more deciding to stop at 2300h. and then barely getting through the hour's show and hurtling back home at 0130h. and smoking the Chore Boy's resins and not stopping after all. No more throwing the Material away and then half an hour later rooting through the trash, no more all-fours scrutiny of the carpet in hopes of a piece of lint that looks enough like the Material to try to smoke. No more singeing the selvage of veils. The Common's south edge is Boylston Street with its 24/7 commerce, upscale, cashmere scarves and cellular holsters, doormen with gold braid, jewelers with three names, women with valence-curtain bangs, stores disgorging shoppers with their wide white monogrammed twine-handle bags. The rain's wet veil blurs things like Jim had designed his neonatal lens to blur things in imitation of a neonatal retina, everything recognizable and yet without outline. A blur that's more deforming than fuzzy. No more clutching her heart on a nightly basis. What looks like the cage's exit is actually the bars of the cage. The afternoon's meshes. The entrance says *EXIT*. There isn't an exit. The ultimate annular fusion: that of exhibit and its cage. Jim's own *Cage III: Free Show*. It is the cage that has entered *her,* somehow. The ingenuity of the whole thing is beyond her. The Fun has long since dropped off the Too Much. She's lost the ability to lie to herself about being able to quit, or even about enjoying it, still. It no longer delimits and fills the hole. It no longer delimits the hole. There's a certain smell to a rain-wet veil. Something about that caller and the moon, saying the moon never looked away. Revolving and yet not. She had hurtled on back home on the night's final T and gone home and at least finally not turned her face away from the situation, the predicament that she didn't love it anymore she hated it and wanted to stop and also couldn't stop or imagine stopping or living without it. She had in a way done as they'd made Jim do near the end and admitted powerlessness over this cage, this unfree show, weeping, literally clutching her heart, smoking first the Chore Boy-scrap she'd used to trap the vapors and form a smokable resin, then bits of the carpet and the acetate panties she'd filtered the solution through hours earlier, weeping and veilless and yarn-haired, like some grotesque clown, in all four mirrors of her little room's walls.

CHRONOLOGY OF ORGANIZATION OF NORTH AMERICAN NATIONS' REVENUE-ENHANCING SUBSIDIZED TIME™, BY YEAR

(1) Year of the Whopper
(2) Year of the Tucks Medicated Pad
(3) Year of the Trial-Size Dove Bar
(4) Year of the Perdue Wonderchicken
(5) Year of the Whisper-Quiet Maytag Dishmaster
(6) Year of the Yushityu 2007 Mimetic-Resolution-Cartridge-View-Motherboard-Easy-To-Install-Upgrade For Infernatron/InterLace TP Systems For Home, Office, Or Mobile (*sic*)
(7) Year of Dairy Products from the American Heartland
(8) Year of the Depend Adult Undergarment
(9) Year of Glad[78]

Jim's eldest, Orin — punter extraordinaire, dodger of flung acid extraordinaire — had once shown Joelle van Dyne his childhood collection of husks of the Lemon Pledge that the school's players used to keep the sun off. Different-sized legs and portions of legs, well-muscled arms, a battery of five-holed masks hung on nails from an upright fiberboard sheet. Not all the husks had names below them.

Boylston St. east means she passes again the black-bronze equestrian statue of Boston's Colonel Shaw and the MA 54th, illuminated now by a patch of emergent sunlight, Shaw's metal head and raised sword illicitly draped in a large Québecois fleur-de-lis flag with all four irises' stems altered to red blades, so it's absurdly now a red white and blue flag; three Boston cops on ladders with poles and shears; the Canadian militants come in the night, on the eve of Interdependence, thinking anyone cares whether they hang things from historic icons, hang anti-O.N.A.N. flags, as if anyone not paid to remove them cares one way or the other. The encaged and suicidal have a really hard time imagining anyone caring passionately about anything. And here too are E. Boylston's dealers, sirens of the other, second cage, standing as always outside F.A.O. Schwartz, young little black boys, boys so black they're blue, horrifically skinny and young, little more than living shadows in knit caps and knee-length sweatshirts and very white hightops, shifting and blowing into their cupped hands, alluding to the availability of a certain Material, just barely alluding is all, with their postures and bored blank important gaze. Certain salesmen have only to stand there. Certain types of sales: the customer comes to you; and Lo. The cops at the flag across the street don't give them a look. Joelle hurries past the line of dealers, she tries to, her clogs loose and clocking, tarrying for just a moment at the end, just past the gauntlet's end, still within two extended hands' reach of the last bored dealer; for here on the street outside Schwartz is placed an odd adverting display, not a live salesman of any sort but rather a humanoid figure of something that's better than cardboard, untouched by the vendors who don't seem even to look, a display on an angled rear-mount stand like a photo-frame's stand, 2-D, the figure a man in a wheelchair, in a coat and tie, his lap blanketed and no legs below, his well-fed face artistically reddened with some terrible joy, his smile's arc of the extreme curvature that exists between mirth and fury, his ecstasy terrible to see, his head hairless and plastic and cast back, his eyes on the blue harlequin-patches of the post-storm sky, looking straight up, or having a seizure, or ecstatic, his arms also up and out in a gesture of submission or triumph or thanks, his oddly thick right hand the receptacle for the black spine of the case of some new film cartridge being advertised for distribution, the cartridge stuck like a tongue out of a slot in his (lineless) palm; except there is only this display, this ecstatic figure and a cartridge no feral vendor's removed, no mention of title, no blurbs or quoted references to critics' thumbs, the case's spine itself bare black slightly pebbled generic plastic, conspicuously unlabelled. Two Oriental women's shopping bags catch and make her raincoat billow slightly as Joelle stands there briefly, feeling the lines' dealers looking at her, assessing; and then someone calls something to one of the cops halfway up the statue, using his first name, which echoes slightly and breaks the spell; the little black boys look away. None of the passersby seem to notice the display she stands before, reflecting. It's some kind of anti-ad. To direct attention at what is not said. Lead up to an inevitability you deny. Not new. But an expensive and affecting display. The film-cartridge itself would be a blank, too, or the case empty, worthless because it really can be removed all the way from the slot in the figure's hand. Joelle removes it and looks at it and puts it back. She's had her last fling with film cartridges. Jim had used her several times. Jim at the end had filmed her at prodigious and multilensed length, and refused to share what he'd made of it, and died w/o a note.[79] Her mental name for the man had been 'Infinite Jim.' The display cartridge shoves home with a click. One of the such young dealers calls her Mama and asks where's the funeral at.

For a while, after the acid, after first Orin left and then Jim came and made her sit through that filmed apology-scene and then vanished and then came back but only to — only four years seven months six days past — to leave, for a while, after taking the veil, for a while she liked to get really high and clean. Joelle did. Scrub sinks until they were mint-white. Dust the ceilings without using any kind of ladder. Vacuum like a fiend and put in a fresh vacuum-bag after each room. Imitate the wife and mother they both declined to shoot. Use Incandenza's toothbrush on tiles' grout.

In places along Boylston cars are triple-parked. People's wipers are on that setting that Joelle, who does not drive, imagines to read OCCASIONAL on the controls. Her own personal Daddy's old car had wipers' controls on the turn-signal stalk by the wheel. Available yellow cabs pass, hissing in the streets. Over half the passing cabs out here in the rain are advertising themselves as available, purple numbers lit below *TAXI*. As she remembers things Jim was, besides a great filmic mind and her true heart's friend, the world's best hailer of Boston cabs, known to have less hailed than conjured cabs in spots where Boston cabs by all that's right just aren't, a hailer of Boston cabs in places like Veedersburg, Indiana and Powell, Wyoming, something in the authority of the lifted arm's height, the oncoming taxi undergoing a sort of parallax as it bore down over tumbleweed streets, appearing under Incandenza's upraised palm as if awaiting benediction. He was a tall and physically slow-moving man with a great love of taxis. And they loved him back. Never again a cab in four-plus years, after that. And so Joelle van Dyne, a.k.a. Madame P., surrendered, suicidal, eschews tumbrel or hack, her solid clogs sounding formal on the smooth cement down Boylston's sidewalk past fine stores' revolving doors southeast toward serious brownstone-terrain, open coat swirling over poncho and hanging rain breaking into stutters and drips.

After she had smoked homemade freebase cocaine this A.M. for the last time and then fired up the Chore Boys and good panties she'd used as a last filter and choked on burnt acetate when she shredded and smoked them, and had wept and imprecated at the mirrors and thrown away her paraphernalia again for the final time, when an hour later she'd walked not formally to her T-stop under a parliament of gathering storm-clouds and faint sticky bits of autumn thunder to ride to Upper Brighton and find Lady Delphina, get real weight from Lady Delphina, so hard to just cut it off in mid-binge, on a Saturday, unless you just passed out, to tell L.D. when she'd said goodbye and it was the last time it had been really the penultimate time but that *this* was the last time, this was goodbye for real, and get serious weight from Lady Delphina, pay her twice the 8-gram rate as a generous farewell, as she walked without much real formality to her T-stop and stood on the platform, each time mistaking little mutters of thunder for the approach of the train, wanting more of it so badly she could feel her brain heaving around in its skull, then a pleasant and gentle-faced older black man in raincoat and hat with a little flat black feather in the band and the sort of black-frame styleless spectacles pleasant older black men wear, with the weary but dignified mild comportment of the older black, waiting alone with her on the chill dim Davis Square subway platform, this man had folded his *Herald* neatly lengthwise and had it under the same arm he tipped his hat with and said to excuse him if this was an intrusion, he said, but he'd had occasion to see one or two of these linen veils before, around, like what she wore, and was interested and rendered curious. He pronounced all four syllables of *interested,* which Joelle, from Kentucky, enjoyed. If he might be so bold, he said, tipping his hat. Joelle had engaged with him completely, which was extremely rare, even off the air. She rather welcomed the chance to think about anything else at all, with the train surely never pulling in. She reflected that the anecdote had gotten about, but not the incident's legacy, she said, as if that part were hidden. The Union of the Hideously and Improbably Deformed was unofficially founded in London in B.S. 1940 in London U.K. by the cross-eyed, palate-clefted, and wildly carbuncular wife of a junior member of the House of Commons, a lady whom Sir Winston Churchill, P.M.U.K., having had several glasses of port plus a toddy at a reception for an American Lend-Lease administrator, had addressed in a fashion wholly inappropriate to social intercourse between civilized gentlemen and ladies. Unwittingly all but authoring the Union designed to afford the scopophobic empathic fellowship and the genesis of sturdy inner resources through shame-free and unconstrained concealment, W. Churchill — when the lady, no person's doormat, informed him with prim asperity that he appeared to be woefully inebriated — made the anecdotally famous reply that while, yes, yea verily, he was indeed inebriated, he would the following A.M. be once again sober, while she, dear lady, would tomorrow still be hideously and improbably deformed. Churchill, doubtless under weighty emotional pressures during this period in history, had then proceeded to extinguish his cigar in the lady's sherry and to place a finger-bowl napkin delicately over the ruined features of her flaming visage. The laminated non-photo U.H.I.D. membership card Joelle showed the interested old black gentleman related all this data and more in a point-size so tiny the card looked somehow both blank and defaced.

PUTATIVE CURRICULUM VITAE OF HELEN P. STEEPLY, 36, 1.93 M., 104 KG., A.B., M.J.A.

1 Year, *Time* (graduate intern, 'Newsmakers' Section);

16 Months, *Decade Magazine* ('Hottest and Nottest,' a trends-and-style-analysis column) until *Decade* folded;

5 Years, *Southwest Annual* (human-interest, geriatric-medical, personality and tourism articles);

5 Months, *Newsweek* (11 small features on trends and entertainment until her Executive Editor, with whom she was in love, left *Newsweek* and took her with him);

1 Year, *Ladies Day* (personality and medical-cosmetic features — some research first-hand — until one week in which the Executive Editor reconciled with his wife and H.P.S. got mugged and purse-snatched on W. 62nd and vowed never again to live in Manhattan);

15 Months–Present, *Moment* magazine, Southwest Bureau, Erythema AZ (medical, soft sports, personality, and home-entertainment-trends reporting, masthead byline, contributing-editor status).

Thereafter proceeding first to the Upper Brighton and now to the cooperative Back Bay–edge brownstone she had lived in once with Orin and performed in with his father and then passed on to Molly Notkin, today's party's guest of honor and hostess in one, as of yesterday enjoying A.B.D. pre-doctoral status in Film & Film-Cartridge Theory at M.I.T., having cleared the notorious hurdle of Oral Examinations on that day by offering her examination committee a dramatically rendered and if she did say so herself devastating oral critique of post-millennial Marxist Film-Cartridge Theory from the point of view of Marx himself, Marx as pretend-film-cartridge theorist and scholar. Still dressed as K.M. a day later, in celebration — the glued beard matted and pubic-black, Homburg ordered direct from Wiesbaden, soot from a terribly obscure British souvenir-filth shop — she has no idea that Joelle's been in a cage since Y.T.S.D.B., has no idea what she and Jim Incandenza were even about for twenty-one months, whether they were lovers or what, whether Orin left because they were lovers or what,[80] or that Joelle even now lives hand-to-lung on a grossly generous trust willed her by a man she unveiled for but never slept with, the prodigious punter's father, infinite jester, director of a final *opus* so *magnum* he'd claimed to have had it locked away. Joelle's never seen the completed assembly of what she'd appeared in, or seen anyone who's seen it, and doubts that any sum of scenes as pathologic as he'd stuck that long quartzy auto-wobbling lens on the camera and filmed her for could have been as entertaining as he'd said the thing he'd always wanted to make had broken his heart by ending up.

Climbing to the third-floor, stairs pale from wear, still trembling from the A.M.'s interruptus, Joelle finds herself having a hard time, climbing, as if the force of gravity goes up as she does. The party-sounds start around the second landing. Here is Molly Notkin dressed as a crumbling Marx again greeting Joelle at her door with the sort of delighted mock-surprise U.S. hostesses use for greetings. Notkin secures Joelle's veil for her during removal of the beaded coat and poncho, then lifts the veil slightly in a practiced two-finger gesture to deliver a double-cheek kiss that is sour with cigarettes and wine — Joelle never smokes when veiled — asking how Joelle got here and then without waiting for an answer offering her that odd kind of British-Columbian apple juice they'd found they both liked so, and that Joelle at home's abandoned and gone back to the Big Red Soda Water of childhood, which Notkin doesn't know, and still cluelessly considers extra-sweet Canadian juice to be pretty much both her and Joelle's biggest vices. Molly Notkin's the kind of soul you want desperately to be polite to but have to hide it with because she'd be mortified if she suspected you were ever just being polite to her about anything.

Joelle makes a get-out-of-here gesture. 'The really really good kind?'

'The kind that looks *muddy* it's so fresh.'

'Where'd you get it this late this far east?'

'The kind you just about have to *strain* it's so fresh.'

The living room is full and hot, campy mambo playing, walls still the same off-white but all the trim now a confectioner's rich brown. Or plus there's wine, Joelle sees, a whole assortment on the old sideboard it took three men with cigars in gray jumpsuits to get up the stairs when they got it, an assortment of bottles of different shapes and dim colors and different levels of what's inside. Molly Notkin has one dirty-nailed hand on Joelle's arm and one on the head of a chair of Maya Deren brooding avant-gardedly in vivid spun-glass polymers, and is telling Joelle about her Orals in a party's near-shout that will leave her hoarse well before this big one's sad end.

A good muddy juice fills Joelle's mouth with spit that's as good as the juice, and her linen veil is drying and beginning once again comfortingly to flutter with her breath, and, perched alone and glanced at covertly by persons who don't know they know her voice, she feels the desire to raise the veil before a mirror, to refine some of her purse's untouched Material, raise the veil and set free the encaged rapacious thing inside to breathe the only uncloth'd gas it can stomach; she feels ghastly and sad; she looks like death, her mascara's all over the place; no one can tell. The plastic Pepsi bottle and glass cigar tube and lighter and packet of glycine bags are a shape in the corner of the rain-darkened cloth purse that rests on the floor just below her dangling clogs. Molly Notkin is standing with Rutherford Keck and Crosby Baum and a radically bad-postured man before the school-supplied Infernatron viewer. Baum's wide back and pompadour obscure whatever's on the screen. Academics' voices sound nasal, with a cultivated stutter at sentences' start. A good many of James O. Incandenza's films were silent. He was a self-acknowledged visual filmmaker. His damaged grinning boy Joelle never got to know because Orin had disliked him often carried the case with the lenses, grinning like somebody squinting into bright light. That insufferable child actor Smothergill used to contort his face at the boy and he'd just laugh, which sent Smothergill into tantrums that Miriam Prickett would resolve in the bathroom somehow. An old Latin-revival CD issues at acceptable volume from the speakers screwed into planters and hung with thin chains from each corner of the cream ceiling. Another large loose group is dancing in the cleared space between the cluster of directorial chairs and the bedroom door, most favoring Y.D.A.U.'s Minimal Mambo, this autumn's East Coast anticraze, the dancers appearing to be just this side of standing still, the subtlest possible hints of fingers snapping under right-angled elbows. Orin Incandenza, she has not forgotten, had a poor mottled swollen elbow above a forearm the size of a leg of lamb. He had switched neatly from arm to leg. Joelle was Orin Incandenza's only lover for twenty-six months and his father's optical beloved for twenty-one. A foreign academic with an almost Franciscan bald spot has the swirling limp of someone with a prosthesis — hired by M.I.T. after her time. The better dancers' movements are so tiny they are evocative and compel watching, their near-static mass curdled and bent somehow subtly around one beautiful young woman, quite beautiful, her back undulating minimally in a thin tight blue-and-white-striped sailorish top as she alludes to a cha-cha with maracas empty of anything to rattle, watching herself almost dance in the full-length mirror of quality plate that after Orin left Joelle had forbidden Jim to hang and had slid beneath her bed face-down; now it's the west wall's framed mirror, hung between two empty ornate gilt frames Notkin thinks she's been retroironic by having the frames themselves framed, in rather less or-nate frames, in wry allusion to the early-Experialist fashion of making art out of the accessories of artistic presentation, the framed frames hanging not quite evenly on either side of the mirror he'd cut for the scenes of that last ghastly thing he'd made her stand before, reciting in the openly empty tones she'd gone on to use on-air; the girl stands transfixed in alternating horizontal blue and white, then vertically sliced by bar-cut sunlight, diced, drunk, so wrecked on good vintage her lips hang slack and the reflected cheeks' muscles have lost all integrity and the cheeks jiggle like the outstanding paps in her little sailor's top. Apocalyptic rouge and a nose-ring that's either electrified or is catching bits of light from the window. She is watching herself with unselfconscious fascination in the only serviceable mirror here outside the bathroom. This absence of shame at the self-obsession. Is she Canadian? Mirror-cult? Not possibly a U.H.I.D.: the bearing's all wrong. But now, whispered to by a near-motionless man in an equestrian helmet, she turns abruptly falling away from her own reflection to explain, not to the man so much as no one in particular, the whole dancing mass: I was just looking at my *tits* she says looking down at herself aren't they *beautiful,* and it's moving, there's something so heartbreakingly sincere in what she says Joelle wants to go to her, tell her it is and will be completely all right, she's pronounced *beautiful* like the earlier *interested* in four syllables, splitting the diphthong, betraying her class and origin with the heartbreaking openness Joelle's always viewed as either terribly stupid or terribly brave, the girl raising her striped arms in triumph or artless thanks for being constructed this way, these 'tits,' built by whom and for whom never occurring, artlessly ecstatic, she is not drunk Joelle now sees but has taken Ecstasy, Joelle can see, from the febrile flush and eyes jacked so wide you can make out brain-meat behind the balls' poles, a.k.a. X or MDMA, a beta-something, an early synthetic, emotional acid, the Love Drug so-called, big among the artistic young under say Bush and successors, since fallen into relative disuse because its pulverizing hangover has been linked to the impulsive use of automatic weapons in public venues, a hangover that makes a freebase hangover look like a day at the emotional beach, the difference between suicide and homicide consisting perhaps only in where you think you discern the cage's door: Would she kill somebody else to get out of the cage? Was the allegedly fatally entertaining and scopophiliac thing Jim alleges he made out of her unveiled face here at the start of Y.T.S.D.B. a cage or really a door? Had he even cut the tape into something coherent? There was nothing coherent in the mother-death-cosmology and apologies she'd repeated over and over, inclined over that auto-wobbled lens propped up in the plaid-sided pram. He never let her see it, not even the dailies. He killed himself less than ninety days later. Fewer than ninety days? How much must a person want out, to put his head in a microwave oven? A dim woman all the kids had known of in Boaz had put her cat in a microwave to dry it after a tick-bath and set the oven just on Defrost and the cat ended up all over the woman's kitchen's walls. How would you rig the thing so it would activate with the door open? Is there just some sort of refrigerator-light button you could hold down and secure with tape? Would the tape melt? She cannot remember thinking of it once in four years. Did she kill him, somehow, just inclining veilless over that lens? The woman in love with her own breasts is being congratulated with the subtlest possible allusions to clapping hands from barely animate dancers with their glass tulips held between their teeth, and Vogelsong of Emerson College tries suddenly to stand on his head and is immediately ill in a spreading plum-colored ectoplasm the dancers do not even try to evade the spread of, and Joelle applauds the Xtatic woman as well, because they are, Joelle admits freely, the paps, they are *attractive,* which in the Union is designated Compelling Within Compatible Relative Limits; Joelle has no problem seeing beauty approved, within compatible relative limits; she feels not empathy or maternal nurture any longer, just a desire to swallow every last drop of saliva she will ever manufacture and exit this vessel, have fifteen more minutes of Too Much Fun, eliminate her own map with the afflatus of the blind god of all doorless cages; and she lets herself slide forward from Méliès' lap, a tiny fall, leading with her lumpy purse and glass of matte apple juice toward the door beyond the lines of a becalmed conga and doorway'd huddles of a warm and well-felt theoretical party. And then, again, delays, dithers, and the easement to the bathroom is blocked. She is the only veiled woman here, and an academic generation ahead of most of these candidates, and rather feared, even though not many know she is an Aural Personality, feared for quitting instead of failing, and because of the connection of the memory of Jim, and she is given a certain wide social berth, allowed to delay and orbit and stand unengaged at the fringes of shifting groups, obliquely glanced at, veil going concave at each inbreath, waiting with hip-shot nonchalance for the bathroom off the bedroom to clear, Iaccarino the Chaplin-archivist and a jaundice-yellow older man have gone into Molly's bedroom and left the door ajar, waiting nonchalantly, ignoring the foreign academic who wishes to know where she works with that veil, turning from him, rudely, brain heaving in its bone-box, memorizing every detail like collecting empty shells, sipping cloudy juice under neatly lifted corners of veil, now looking at instead of through the translucent cloth, the Improbably Deformed's equivalent of closing the eyes in concentration on sound, letting the Very Last Party wash over her, passed gracefully by different mingling guests and once or twice almost touched, seeing only inrushing and then billowing white, listening to different mingling voices the way the unveiled young taste wine.

'This is a technologically constituted space.'

'— thing opens tight on Remington in a hideous grandfatherly flannel suit, b & w, straight full-frontal shot in this grainy b & w stuff Bouvier taught him to manipulate the *f*-stop to mimic that horrid old Super 8, straight full-frontal, staring past the camera, no attempt to disguise he's reading off a prompter, monotone and all, saying "Few foreigners realize that the German term *Berliner* is also the vulgate idiom for a common jelly doughnut, and thus that Kennedy's seminal *'Ich bein ein Berliner'* was greeted by the Teutonic crowds with a delight only apparently political," at which point he aims his thumb and finger at his own temple at which point his TA doubles the focal-length so there's this giant —'

'I would die to defend your constitutional right to error, friend, but in this one case you —'

'They used to be less beautiful but then Rutherford said to quit sleeping face-down.'

'No no I'm saying that *this,* this whole thing, what you and I are discoursing *within,* is a technologically constituted space.'

'*À du nous avons foi au poison.*'

'It's good cheese, but I've had better cheese.'

'Mainwaring, this is Kirby, Kirby here's in pain, he's been telling me about it and now he'd like to tell you about it.'

'— complete mystery why Eve Plumb didn't show, it's known she'd re-upped for the part, the whole rest of them were there, even Henderson and that Davis woman as Alice who had to be wheeled out under nurses' care, my God and Peter, looking as if he'd eaten nothing but pastry for the past forty years, Greg with that absurd hairpiece and snakeskin boots, yes but all the kids recognizable, underneath, somehow, this pre-digital insistence on continuity through time that was the project's whole magic and *raison,* you know this, you're current on pre-digital phenomenology and Brady-theory. And then but now here's this entirely incongruous *middle-aged black woman* playing Jan!'

'*De gustibus non est disputandum.*'

'Balls.'

'An incongruous central blackness could have served to accentuate the terrible whiteness that had been in ineluct —'

'The entire historical effect of a seminal program was horribly, horribly altered. Terribly altered.'

'Eisenstein and Kurosawa and Michaux walk into a bar.'

'You know those mass-market cartridges, for the masses? The ones that are so bad they're somehow perversely good? This was worse than that.'

'— so-called phantom, but real. And mobile. First the spine. Then not the spine but the right eye-socket. Then the old socket's fit as a fiddle but the thumb, the thumb doubles me over. It won't stay put.'

'Fucks with the emulsion's gradient so that all the tesseract's angles *appear* to be right-angled, except in —'

'So what I did I sat right up next to him, you see, so in a sense he didn't have room to stalk or draw a bead, Keck had said they needed a good ten m., so I cocked the hat just so, just ever so slightly, like so, just cocked it over to the side like so and sat down practically on the man's knee, asked after his show-carp, he keeps pedigreed carp, and of course you can imagine what —'

'— more interesting issue from a Heideggerian perspective is *a priori*, whether space as a concept is enframed by technology as a concept.'

'It has a mobile cunning, a kind of wraith- or phantom-like —'

'Because they're emotional more labile at that stage.'

' "So get dentures?" she said. "So get *dentures?*" '

'Who shot *The Incision?* Who did the cinematography on *The Incision?*'

'— way it can be film qua film. Comstock says if it even exists it has to be something more like an aesthetic pharmaceutical. Some beastly post-annular scopophiliacal vector. Suprasubliminals and that. Some kind of abstractable hypnosis, an optical dopamine-cue. A recorded delusion. Duquette says he's lost contact with three colleagues. He said a good bit of Berkeley isn't answering their phone.'

'I don't think anyone here would dispute that they're absolutely fetching tits, Melinda.'

'We had blinis with caviar. There were tartines. We had sweetbreads in mushroom cream sauce. He said it was all on him. He said he was treating. There was roast artichoke topped with a sort of sly aioli. Mutton stuffed with foie gras, double chocolate rum cake. Seven kinds of cheese. A kiwi glacé and brandy in snifters you needed two hands to swirl.'

'That coke-addled fag in his Morris Mini.'

The prosthetic film-scholar: 'Fans do not begin to keep it all in the Great Convexity. It creeps back in. What goes around, it comes back around. This your nation refuses to learn. It will keep creeping back in. You cannot give away your filth and prevent all creepage, no? Filth by its very nature it is a thing that is creeping always back. Me, I can remember when your Charles was café with cream. Look now at it. It is the blue river. You have a river outside you that is robin-egg's blue.'

'I think you mean Great Concavity, Alain.'

'I meant Great Convexity. I know what is the thing I meant.'

'And then it turned out he'd put ipecac in the brandy. It was the most horrible thing you've ever seen. Everyone, all over, spouting like whales. I'd heard the term *projectile vomiting* but I never thought that I — you could *aim*, the pressure was such that you could *aim*. And out come his grad technicians from under the tablecloth's like overhang, and he pulls out a canvas chair and clapper and begins filming the whole horrible staggering spouting groaning —'

'This ultimate cartridge-as-ecstatic-death rumor's been going around like a lazy toilet since Dishmaster, for Christ's sake. Simply make inquiries, mention some obscure foundation grant, obtain the thing through whatever shade of market the thing's alleged to be out in. Have a look. See that it's doubtless just high-concept erotica or an hour of rotating whorls. Or something like late Makavajev, something that's only entertaining after it's over, on reflection.'

The striated parallelogram of P.M. sunlight is elongating in transit across the coop's eastern wall, over bottle-laden sideboard and glass cabinet of antique editing equipment and louvered vent and shelves of art-cartridges in their dull black and dun cases. The mole-studded man in the equestrian helmet is either winking at her or has a tic. There's the pre-suicide's classic longing: Sit down one second, I want to tell you everything. My name is Joelle van Dyne, Dutch-Irish, and I was reared on family land east of Shiny Prize, Kentucky, the only child of a low-pH chemist and his second wife. I now have no accent except under stress. I am 1.7 meters tall and weigh 48 kilograms. I occupy space and have mass. I breathe in and breathe out. Joelle has never before today been conscious of the sustained volition required to just breathe in and breathe out, her veil recessing into nose and rounded mouth and then bowing out slightly like curtains over an opened pane.

'Convexity.'

'Con*cav*ity!'

'Con*vexity!*'

'*Concavity* damn your eyes!'

The bathroom has a hook and a mirrored medicine cabinet over the sink and is off the bedroom. Molly Notkin's bedroom looks like the bedroom of someone who stays in bed for serious lengths of time. A pair of pantyhose has been tossed onto a lamp. There are not crumbs but whole portions of crackers protruding from the gray surf of wopsed-up bedding. A photo of the phalloneurotic New Yorker with the same fold-out triangular support as the blank cartridge's anti-ad. A Ziploc of pot and EZ-Widers and seeds in the ashtray. Books with German and Cyrillic titles lie open in spine-cracking attitudes on the colorless rug. Joelle's never liked the fact that Notkin's father's photograph is nailed at iconic height to the wall above the headboard, a systems planner out of Knoxville TN, his smile the smile of a man who wears white loafers and a squirting carnation. And why are bathrooms always way brighter lit than whatever room they're off? On the private side of the bathroom door she's had to take two damp towels off the top of to close all the way, the same rotten old hook for a lock never quite ever seeming to want to fit its receptacle in the jamb, the party's music now some horrible collection of mollified rock classics with all soft rock's grim dental associations, the business side of the door is hung with a Selective Automation of Knoxville calendar from before Subsidized Time and cut-out photos of Kinski as Paganini and Léaud as Doinel and a borderless still of the crowd scene in what looks like Peterson's *The Lead Shoes* and rather curiously the offprinted page of J. van Dyne, M.A.'s one and only published film-theory monograph.[81] Joelle can smell, through her veil and own stale exhalations, the little room's complicated spice of sandalwood rubble in a little violet-ribboned pomander and deodorant soap and the sharp decayed-lemon odor of stress-diarrhea. Low-budget celluloid horror films created ambiguity and possible elision by putting *?* after *THE END,* is what pops into her head: *THE END?* amid the odors of mildew and dicky academic digestion? Joelle's mother's family had no indoor plumbing. It is all right. She represses all bathetic this-will-be-the-last-thing-I-smell thought-patterns. Joelle is going to have Too Much Fun in here. It was beyond all else so much *fun,* at the start. Orin had neither disapproved nor partaken; his urine was an open book because of football. Jim hadn't disapproved so much as been vacant with disinterest. His Too Much was neat bourbon, and he had lived life to the fullest, and then gone in for detoxification, again and again. This had been simply too much fun, at the start. So much better even than nasaling the Material up through rolled currency and waiting for the cold bitter drip at the back of your throat and cleaning the newly spacious apartment to within an inch of its life while your mouth twitches and writhes unbidden beneath the veil. The 'base frees and condenses, compresses the whole experience to the implosion of one terrible shattering spike in the graph, an afflated orgasm of the heart that makes her feel, truly, *attractive,* sheltered by limits, deviled and loved, observed and alone and sufficient and female, full, as if watched for an instant by God. She always sees, after inhaling, right at the apex, at the graph's spike's tip, Bernini's 'Ecstasy of St. Teresa,' behind glass, at the Vittoria, for some reason, the saint recumbent, half-supine, her flowing stone robe lifted by the angel in whose other hand a bare arrow is raised for that best descent, the saint's legs frozen in opening, the angel's expression not charity but the perfect vice of barb-headed love. The stuff had been not just her encaging god but her lover, too, fiendish, angelic, of rock. The toilet seat is up. She can hear a helicopter's chop somewhere overhead east, a traffic helicopter over Storrow, and Molly Notkin's shriek as an enormous glass crash sounds off in the living room, imagines her beard hanging aslant and her mouth ellipsed with champagne's foam as she waves off the breakage that signals good Party, can hear through the door the ecstatic Melinda's apologies and Molly's laugh, which sounds like a shriek:

'Oh everything falls off the wall sooner or later.'

Joelle has lifted her veil back to cover her skull like a bride. Since she threw away her pipes and bowls and screens again this A.M. she is going to have to be resourceful. On the counter of an old sink the same not-quite white as the floor and ceiling (the wallpaper is a maddening uncountable pattern of roses twined in garlands on sticks) on the counter are an old splay-bristled toothbrush, tube of Gleem rolled neatly up from the bottom, unsavory old NoCoat scraper, rubber cement, NeGram, depilatory ointment, tube of Monostat not squeezed from the bottom, phony-beard whiskerbits and curled green threads of used mint floss and Parapectolin and a wholly unsqueezed tube of diaphragm-foam and no makeup but serious styling gel in a big jar with no lid and hairs around the rim and an empty tampon box half-filled with nickels and pennies and rubber bands, and Joelle sweeps an arm across the counter and squunches everything over to the side under the small rod with a washcloth wrung viciously out and dried in the tight spiral of a twisted cord, and if some items do totter and fall to the floor it is all right because everything eventually has to fall. On the cleared counter goes Joelle's misshapen purse. The absence of veil dulls the bathroom's smells, somehow.

She's been resourceful before, but this is the most deliberate Joelle has been able to be about it in something like a year. From the purse she removes the plastic Pepsi container, a box of wooden matches kept dry in a resealable baggie, two little thick glycine bags each holding four grams of pharmaceutical-grade cocaine, a single-edge razor blade (increasingly tough to find), a little black Kodachrome canister whose gray lid she pops and discards to reveal baking soda sifted fine as talc, the empty glass cigar tube, a folded square of Reynolds Wrap foil the size of a playing card, and an amputated length of the bottom of a quality wire coat hanger. The overhead light casts shadows of her hands over what she needs, so she turns on the light over the medicine cabinet's mirror as well. The light stutters and hums and bathes the counter with cold lithium-free fluorescence. She undoes the four pins and removes the veil from her head and places it on the counter with the rest of the Material. Lady Delphina's little glycine baglets have clever seals that are green when sealed and blue and yellow when not. She taps half a glycine's worth into the cigar tube and adds half again as much baking soda, spilling some of the soda in a parenthesis of bright white on the counter. This is the most deliberate she's been able to be in at least a year. She turns the sink's C knob and lets the water get really cold, then cranks the volume back to a trickle and fills the rest of the tube to the top with water. She holds the tube up straight and gently taps on its side with a blunt unpainted nail, watching the water slowly darken the powders beneath it. She produces a double rose of flame in the mirror that illuminates the right side of her face as she holds the tube over the matches' flame and waits for the stuff to begin to bubble. She uses two matches, twice. When the tube gets too hot to hold she takes and folds her veil and uses it as a kind of oven-mitt over the fingers of her left hand, careful (from habit and experience) not to let the bottom corners get close enough to the flame to brown. After it's bubbled for just a second Joelle shakes out the matches with a flourish and tosses them in the toilet to hear that briefest of hisses. She takes up the black wire prod from the hanger and begins to stir and mash the just-bubbled stuff in the tube, feeling it thicken quickly and its resistance to the wire's tiny circles increase. It was when her hands started to tremble during this part of the cooking procedure that she'd first known she liked this more than anyone can like anything and still live. She is not stupid. The Charles rolling away far below the windowless bathroom is vividly blue, more mildly blue on top from the fresh rainwater that had made purple rings appear and widen, a deeper Magic Marker–type blue below the dilute layer, gulls stamped to the cleared sky, motionless as kites. A bulky thump sounds from behind the large flat-top Enfield hill on the river's south shore, a large but relatively shapeless projectile of drums wrapped in brown postal paper and belted with twine hurtling in a broad upward arc that bothers the gulls into dips and wheels, the brown package quickly a pinpoint in the yet-hazy sky to the north, where a yellow-brown cloud hangs just above the line between sky and terrain, its top slowly dispersing and opening out so that the cloud looks like a not very pretty sort of wastebasket, waiting. Inside, Joelle hears only a bit of the bulky thump, which could be anything. The only other thing besides what she's about to do too much of here right now she'd ever come close to feeling this way about: In Joelle's childhood, Paducah, not too bad a drive from Shiny Prize, still had a few public movie theaters, six and eight separate auditoria clustered in single honeycombs at the edges of inter-state malls. The theaters always ended in *-plex*, she reflected. The Thisoplex and Thatoplex. It had never struck her as odd. And she never saw even one film there, as a girl, that she didn't just about die with love for. It didn't matter what they were. She and her own personal Daddy up in the front row, they sat in the front rows of the narrow little overinsulated -plexes up in neck-crick territory and let the screen fill their whole visual field, her hand in his lap and their big box of Crackerjacks in her hand and sodapops secure in little rings cut out of the plastic of their seats' arms; and he, always with a wooden match in the corner of his mouth, pointing up into the rectangular world at this one or that one, performers, giant flawless 2D beauties irides-cent on the screen, telling Joelle over and over again how she was prettier than this one or that one right there. Standing in the placid line as he bought the -plex's paper tickets that looked like grocery receipts, knowing that she was going to love the celluloid entertainment no matter what it was, won-derfully innocent, still thinking *quality* referred to the living teddy bears in Qantas commercials, standing hand-held, eyes even with his wallet's back-pocket bulge, she'd never so much again as in that line felt so *taken care of,* destined for big-screen entertainment's unalloyed good fun, never once again until starting in with this lover, cooking and smoking it, five years back, before Incandenza's death, at the start. The punter never made her feel quite so *taken care of,* never made her feel about to be entered by something that didn't know she was there and yet was all about making her feel good anyway, coming in. Entertainment is blind.

The improbable thing of the whole thing is that, when the soda and water and cocaine are mixed right and heated right and stirred just right as the mix cools down, then when the stuff's too stiff to stir and is finally ready to come on out it comes out slick as shit from a goat, just an inverted-ketchup-bottle thump and out the son of a fucking whore slides, one molded cylinder hardened onto the black wire, its snout round from the glass tube's bottom. The average pre-chopped freebase rock looks like a .38 round. What Joelle now slides with three fillips from the cigar tube is a monstrous white wiener, a county-fair corn dog, its sides a bit rough, like mâché, a couple clots left on the inside of the tube that are what you forage and smoke before the Chore Boys and panties.

She is now a little under two deliberate minutes from Too Much Fun for anyone mortal to hope to endure. Her unveiled face in the dirty lit mirror is shocking in the intensity of its absorption. Out in the bedroom doorway she can hear Reeves Mainwaring telling some helium-voiced girl that life is essentially one long search for an ashtray. Too Much Fun. She uses the razor blade to cross-section chunks out of the freebase wiener. You can't whittle thin deli-shaved flakes off because they'll crumble back to powder right away and they anyway don't smoke as well as you'd think. Blunt chunks are S.O.P. Joelle chops out enough chunks for maybe twenty good-sized hits. They form a little quarry on the soft cloth of her folded veil on the counter. Her Brazilian skirt is no longer damp. Reeves Mainwaring's blond imperial often had little bits of food residue in it. 'The Ecstasy of St. Teresa' is on perpetual display at the Vittoria in Rome and she never got to see it. She will never again say *And Lo* and invite people to watch darkness dance on the face of the deep. 'The Face of the Deep' had been the title she'd suggested for Jim's unseen last cartridge, which he'd said would be too pretentious and then used that skull-fragment out of the *Hamlet* graveyard scene instead, which talk about pretentious she'd laughed. His frightened look when she'd laughed is for the life of her the last facial-expression memory she can remember of the man. Orin had referred to his father sometimes as Himself and sometimes as The Mad Stork and once in a slip as The Sad Stork. She lights one wooden match and blows it right out and touches the hot black head to the side of the plastic pop bottle. It melts right through and makes a little hole. The helicopter was probably a traffic helicopter. Somebody at their Academy had had some connection to some traffic helicopter that had had an accident. She can't for the life of her. No one out there knows she is in here getting ready to have Too Much. She can hear Molly Notkin calling through rooms about has anyone seen Keck. In her first theory seminar Reeves Mainwaring had called one film 'wretchedly ill-conceived' and another 'desperately acquiescent' and Molly Notkin had pretended to have a coughing fit and had had a Tennessee accent and that was how they met. The Reynolds Wrap is to make a screen that will rest in the bottle's open top. A regular dope screen is the size of a thimble, its sides spread like an opening bud. Joelle uses the point of some curved nail scissors on the back of the toilet to poke tiny holes in the rectangle of aluminum foil and shapes it into a shallow funnel large enough to siphon gasoline, narrowing its tip to fit in the bottle's mouth. She now owns a pipe with a monster-sized bowl and screen, now, and puts in enough chunklets to make five or six hits at once. The little rocks lie there piled and yellow-white. She puts her lips experimentally to the melted hole in the side of the bottle and draws, then, very deliberately, lights another match and extinguishes it and makes the hole bigger. The idea that she'll never see Molly Notkin or the cerebral Union or her U.H.I.D. support-brothers and -sisters or the YYY engineer or Uncle Bud on a roof or her stepmother in the Locked Ward or her poor personal Daddy again is sentimental and banal. The idea of what she's about in here contains all other ideas and makes them banal. Her glass of juice is on the back of the toilet, half-empty. The back of the toilet is lightly sheened with condensation of unknown origin. These are facts. This room in this apartment is the sum of very many specific facts and ideas. There is nothing more to it than that. Deliberately setting about to make her heart explode has assumed the status of just one of these facts. It was an idea but now is about to become a fact. The closer it comes to becoming concrete the more abstract it seems. Things get very abstract. The concrete room was the sum of abstract facts. Are facts abstract, or are they just abstract representations of concrete things? Molly Notkin's middle name is Cantrell. Joelle puts two more matches together and prepares to strike them, breathing rapidly in and out like a diver preparing for a long descent.

'I say is someone in there?' The voice is the young post-New Formalist from Pittsburgh who affects Continental and wears an ascot that won't stay tight, with that hesitant knocking of when you know perfectly well someone's in there, the bathroom door composed of thirty-six that's three times a lengthwise twelve recessed two-bevelled squares in a warped rectangle of steam-softened wood, not quite white, the bottom outside corner right here raw wood and mangled from hitting the cabinets' bottom drawer's wicked metal knob, through the door and offset 'Red' and glowering actors and calendar and very crowded scene and pubic spiral of pale blue smoke from the elephant-colored rubble of ash and little blackened chunks in the foil funnel's cone, the smoke's baby-blanket blue that's sent her sliding down along the wall past knotted washcloth, towel rack, blood-flower wallpaper and intricately grimed electrical outlet, the light sharp bitter tint of a heated sky's blue that's left her uprightly fetal with chin on knees in yet another North American bathroom, deviled, too pretty for words, maybe the Prettiest Girl Of All Time (Prettiest G.O.A.T.), knees to chest, slew-footed by the radiant chill of the claw-footed tub's porcelain, Molly's had somebody lacquer the tub in blue, lacquer, she's holding the bottle, recalling vividly its slogan for the last generation was The Choice of a Nude Generation, when she was of back-pocket height and prettier by far than any of the peach-colored titans they'd gazed up at, his hand in her lap her hand in the box and rooting down past candy for the Prize, more fun way too much fun inside her veil on the counter above her, the stuff in the funnel exhausted though it's still smoking thinly, its graph reaching its highest spiked prick, peak, the arrow's best descent, so good she can't stand it and reaches out for the cold tub's rim's cold edge to pull herself up as the white- party-noise reaches, for her, the sort of stereophonic precipice of volume to teeter on just before the speakers blow, people barely twitching and conversations strettoing against a ghastly old pre-Carter thing saying 'We've Only Just Begun,' Joelle's limbs have been removed to a distance where their acknowledgment of her commands seems like magic, both clogs simply gone, nowhere in sight, and socks oddly wet, pulls her face up to face the unclean medicine-cabinet mirror, twin roses of flame still hanging in the glass's corner, hair of the flame she's eaten now trailing like the legs of wasps through the air of the glass she uses to locate the de-faced veil and what's inside it, loading up the cone again, the ashes from the last load make the world's best filter: this is a fact. Breathes in and out like a savvy diver —

'Look here then who's that in there? Is someone in there? Do open up. I'm on one foot then the other out here. I say Notkin someone's been in here locked in and, well, sounding unwell, amid rather a queer scent.'

— and is knelt vomiting over the lip of the cool blue tub, gouges on the tub's lip revealing sandy white gritty stuff below the lacquer and porcelain, vomiting muddy juice and blue smoke and dots of mercuric red into the claw-footed trough, and can hear again and seems to see, against the fire of her closed lids' blood, bladed vessels aloft in the night to monitor flow, searchlit helicopters, fat fingers of blue light from one sky, searching.

○

Enfield MA is one of the stranger little facts that make up the idea that is metro Boston, because it is a township composed almost entirely of medical, corporate, and spiritual facilities. A kind of arm-shape extending north from Commonwealth Avenue and separating Brighton into Upper and Lower, its elbow nudging East Newton's ribs and its fist sunk into Allston, Enfield's broad municipal tax-base includes St. Elizabeth's Hospital, Franciscan Children's Hospital, The Universal Bleacher Co., the Provident Nursing Home, Shuco-Mist Medical Pressure Systems Inc., the Enfield Marine Public Health Hospital Complex, the Svelte Nail Co., half the metro Boston turbine and generating stations of Sunstrand Power and Light (the part that gets taxed is in incorporated Allston), corporate headquarters for 'The ATHSCME Family of Air-Displacement Effectuators' (meaning they make really big fans), the Enfield Tennis Academy, St. John of God Hospital, Hanneman Orthopedic Hospital, the Leisure Time Ice Company, a Dicalced monastery, the combined St. John's Seminary and offices for the RCC's Boston Archdiocese (partly in Upper Brighton; neither half taxed), convent headquarters of The Sisters for Africa, the National Cranio-Facial Pain Foundation, the Dr. George Roebling Runyon Memorial Institute for Podiatric Research, regional shiny-truck, land-barge, and catapult facilities for the O.N.A.N.-subsidized Empire Waste Displacement Co. (what the Québecois call *les trebuchets noirs,* spectacular block-long catapults that make a sound like a giant stamping foot as they fling great twine-bundled waste-vehicles into the subannular regions of the Great Concavity at a parabolic altitude exceeding 5 km.; the devices' slings are of alloy-belted elastic and their huge cupped vehicle-receptacles like catcher's mitts from hell, a half dozen or so of the catapults in this like blimp-hangarish thing with a selectively slide-backable roof, taking up a good six square blocks of Enfield's brachiform incursion into the Allston Spur, occasional school tours tolerated but not encouraged), and so on. W/ the whole flexed Enfield limb sleeved in a perimeter layer of light residential and mercantile properties. The Enfield Tennis Academy occupies probably now the nicest site in Enfield, some ten years after balding and shaving flat the top of the big abrupt hill that constitutes a kind of raised cyst on the township's elbow, the better part of 75 hectares of broad lawns and cloverleafing paths and topologically cutting-edge erections, 32 asphalt tennis courts and sixteen Har-Tru composition tennis courts and extensive underground maintenance and storage and athletic-training facilities and briers and calliopsis and pines mixed artfully in on the inclines with deciduous trees, the E.T.A. hilltop overlooking on one side, east, historic Commonwealth Avenue's acclivated migration out of the squalor of Lower Brighton — liquor stores and Laundromats and bars and palisades of somber and guano-dappled tenement facades, the huge and brooding Brighton Project high-rises with three-story-high orange I.D.-numerals on the sides, plus liquor stores, and pale men in leather and whole gangs of pale children in leather on the corners and Greek-owned pizza places with yellow walls and dirty corner markets owned by Orientals who try like heck to keep their sidewalks clean but can't, even with hoses, plus the quarter-hourly trundle and ding of the Green Line train's labor up the Ave.'s long rise to Boston College — into the spiky elegance of B.C. and the broad gentrification of Newton out to the west, where the haze-haloed Boston sun drops behind the last node in the four-km. sine wave that is collectively called the historic April Marathon's 'Heartbreak Hill,' the sun always setting fifteen minutes to the nanosecond after deLint turns on the courts' high-tower lights. To I think it must be the southwest, E.T.A. overlooks the steely gray tangle of Sunstrand's transformers and high-voltage grids and coaxial chokers strung with beads of ceramic insulators, with not one Sunstrand smokestack anywhere in sight but a monstrous mega-ohm insulator-cluster at the terminus of a string of signs trailing in from the northeast, each sign talking with many $\emptyset$'s about how many annular-generated amps are waiting underground for anyone who digs or in any way dicks around, with hair-raising nonverbal stick-figure symbols of somebody with a shovel going up like a Kleenex in the fireplace. There are smokestacks in the visual background slightly south of Sunstrand, though, from the E.W.D. hangars, each stack with a monstrous ATHSCME 2100-Series A.D.E. (fan) bolted behind it and blowing due north with an insistent high-pitched fury that is somehow soothing, aurally, at E.T.A.'s distance and height. From both the north and northeast tree-lines E.T.A. looks down its hill's steepest, best-planted decline into the complexly decaying grounds of Enfield Marine.

5 NOVEMBER — YEAR OF THE DEPEND ADULT UNDERGARMENT

The transparent phone sounded from somewhere under the hill of bedding[82] as Hal was on the edge of the bed with one leg up and his chin on its knee, clipping his nails into a wastebasket that sat several meters away in the middle of the room. It took four rings to find the receiver in the bedding and pull the antenna out.

'Mmmyellow.'

'Mr. Incredenza, this is the Enfield Raw Sewage Commission, and quite frankly we've had enough shit out of you.'

'Hello Orin.'

'How hangs it, kid.'

'God, please no, please O., not more Separatism questions.'

'Relax. Never crossed my mind. Social call. Shoot the breeze.'

'Interesting you should call just now. Because I'm clipping my toenails into a wastebasket several meters away.'

'Jesus, you know how I hate the sound of nail clippers.'

'Except I'm shooting seventy-plus percent. The little fragments of clipping. It's uncanny. I keep wanting to go out in the hall and get somebody in here to see it. But I don't want to break the spell.'

'The fragile magic-spell feel of those intervals where it feels you just can't miss.'

'It's definitely one of those can't-miss intervals. It's just like that magical feeling on those rare days out there playing. Playing out of your head, de-Lint calls it. Loach calls it The Zone. Being in The Zone. Those days when you feel perfectly calibrated.'

'Coordinated as God.'

'Some groove in the shape of the air of the day guides everything down and in.'

242

'When you feel like you couldn't miss if you tried to.'

'I'm so far away the wastebasket's mouth looks more like a slot than a circle. And yet in they go, ka-ching ka-ching. There went another one. Even the misses are near-misses, caroms off the rim.'

'I'm sitting here with the leg in a whirlpool in the bathroom of a Norwegian deep-tissue therapist's ranch-style house 1100 meters up in the Superstition mountains. Mesa-Scottsdale in flames far below. The bathroom's redwood-panelled and overlooks a precipice. The sunlight's the color of the bronze.'

'But you never know when the magic will descend on you. You never know when the grooves will open up. And once the magic descends you don't want to change even the smallest detail. You don't know what concordance of factors and variables yields that calibrated can't-miss feeling, and you don't want to soil the magic by trying to figure it out, but you don't want to change your grip, your stick, your side of the court, your angle of incidence to the sun. Your heart's in your throat every time you change sides of the court.'

'You start to get like a superstitious native. What's the word *propitiate* the divine spell.'

'I suddenly understand the gesundheit-impulse, the salt over the shoulder and apotropaic barn-signs. I'm actually frightened to switch feet right now. I'm clipping off the tiniest aerodynamically viable clippings possible, to prolong the time on this foot, in case the magic's a function of the foot. This isn't even the good foot.'

'These can't-miss intervals make superstitious natives out of us all, Hallie. The professional football player's maybe the worst superstitious native of all the sports. That's why all the high-tech padding and garish Lycra and complex play-terminology. The like self-reassuring display of high-tech. Because the bug-eyed native's lurking just under the surface, we know. The bug-eyed spear-rattling grass-skirted primitive, feeding virgins to Popogatapec and afraid of planes.'

'The new *Discursive O.E.D.* says the Ahts of Vancouver used to cut virgins' throats and pour the blood very carefully into the orifices of the embalmed bodies of their ancestors.'

'I can hear those clippers. Quit with the clippers a second.'

'The phone's no longer wedged under my jaw. I can even do it one-handed, holding the phone in one hand. But it's still the same foot.'

'You don't know from true bug-eyed athletic superstition till you hit the pro ranks, Hallie. When you hit the Show is when you'll understand *primitive*. Winning streaks bring the native bubbling up to the surface. Jock straps unwashed game after game until they stand up by themselves in the overhead luggage compartments of planes. Bizarrely ritualized dressing, eating, peeing.'

'Micturation.'

'Picture a 200-kilo interior lineman insisting on sitting down to pee. Don't even ask what wives and girlfriends have to suffer during a can't-miss winning streak.'

'I don't want to hear sexual stuff.'

'Then there are the players who write down exactly what they say to everybody before a game, so if it's a magical can't-miss-type game they can say exactly the same things to the same people in the same exact order before the next game.'

'Apparently the Ahts tried to fill up ancestors' bodies completely with virgin-blood to preserve the privacy of their own mental states. The apposite Aht dictum here being quote "The sated ghost cannot see secret things." The *Discursive O.E.D.* postulates that this is one of the earlier on-record prophylactics against schizophrenia.'

'Hey Hallie?'

'After a burial, rural Papineau-region Québecers purportedly drill a small hole down from ground level all the way down through the lid of the coffin, to let out the soul, if it wants out.'

'Hey Hallie? I think I'm being followed.'

'This is the big moment. I've totally exhausted the left foot finally and am switching to the right foot. This'll be the real test of the fragility of the spell.'

'I said I think I'm being followed.'

'Some men are born to lead, O.'

'I'm serious. And here's the weird part.'

'Here's the part that explains why you're sharing this with your estranged little brother instead of with anybody whose credulity you'd actually value.'

'The weird part is I think I'm being followed by . . . by handicapped people.'

'Two for three on the right foot, with one carom. Jury's still out.'

'Quit with the clipping a second. I'm not kidding. Take the other day. I strike up a conversation with a certain Subject in line in the post office. I notice a guy in a wheelchair behind us. No big deal. Are you listening?'

'What are you doing going to the post office? You hate snail-mail. And you quit mailing the Moms the pseudo-form-replies two years ago, Mario says.'

'But so the conversation goes well and hits it off, Seduction Strategies 12 and 16 are employed, which I'll tell you about sometime at length. The point is the Subject and I walk out together hitting it off and there's another guy in a wheelchair whittling in the shade of a shop-awning just down the street. OK. Still not necessarily any kind of deal. But now the Subject and I drive to her trailer park —'

'Phoenix has trailer parks? Not those silverish *metal* trailers.'

'So but we get out of the car, and across the park's lot here's yet *another* wheelchaired guy, trying to maneuver in the gravel and not making a very good job of it.'

'Doesn't Arizona have more than its share of the old and infirm?'

'But none of these handicapped guys were old. And they were all awfully burly for guys in wheelchairs. And three in an hour's kind of stretching it, I was thinking.'

'I always picture you having your little trysts in more domestic suburban settings. Or else tall motels with exotically shaped beds. Do women in metal trailers even have small children?'

'This one had very sweet little twin girls who played very quietly with blocks without supervision the whole time.'

'Cockle-warming, O.'

'And but so the point is I decamp the trailer like x number of hours later, and the guy's still there, mired in gravel. And in the distance I could swear he's got on some kind of domino-mask. And now everywhere I go the last several days there seems to be a statistically improbable number of wheel-chaired figures around, lurking, somehow just a little too nonchalantly.'

'Very shy fans, possibly? Some club of leg-dysfunctional people all ob-sessed in that shy-fan-like way with one of the first North American sports figures people think of in connection with the word *leg*?'

'It's probably my imagination. A dead bird fell in my jacuzzi.'

'But now let me ask you a couple questions.'

'This all wasn't even why I originally called.'

'But you brought up trailer parks and trailers. I need to confirm some suspicions — two points, right in there, ka-ching. Never having been in a trailer, and even the *Discursive O.E.D.* having pretty much of a lacuna where trailer-park trailers are concerned.'

'And this is the one supposedly nonbats family-member I call. This is who I reach out to.'

'It'd be *whom*, I think. But this trailer. This lady you met's trailer. Con-firm or deny the following. Its carpet was wall-to-wall and extremely thin, a kind of burnt yellow or orange.'

'Yes.'

'The living-room or like den area contained some or all of the following: a black velvet painting featuring an animal; a videophonic diorama on some sort of knickknack shelf; a needlepoint sampler with some kind of frothy biblical saw on it; at least one piece of chintz furniture with protective doi-lies on the arms; a Smoke-B-Gone air-filtration ashtray; the last couple years' *Reader's Digests* neatly displayed in their own special inclined maga-zine rack.'

'Check on velvet painting of leopard, sampler sofa with doilies, ashtray. No *Reader's Digests*. This isn't especially funny, Hallie. The Moms comes out in you in these odd little ways sometimes.'

'Last one. The trailer-person's name. Jean. May. Nora. Vera. Nora-Jean or Vera-May.'

'. . .'

'That was my question.'

'I guess I'll have to get back to you on that.'

'Boy, you really put the small r in *romance,* don't you.'

'But why I'm calling.'

'It's not clear whether the fragile can't-miss magic's still in force on the right foot. I'm seven for nine, but there's a whole different feel of somehow deliberately *trying* to get them in.'

'Hallie, I've got somebody from *Moment* fucking magazine out here doing a quote soft profile.'

'You've got what?'

'A human-interest thing. On me as a human. *Moment* doesn't do hard sports, this lady says. They're more people-oriented, human-interest. It's for something called quote People Right Now, a section.'

'*Moment*'s a supermarket-checkout-lane-display magazine. It's in there with the rodneys and gum. Lateral Alice Moore reads it. It's all over C.T.'s waiting room. They did a thing on the little blind Illinois kid Thorp thought so well of.'

'Hal.'

'I think Lateral Alice spends a lot of time in grocery-store checkout lanes, which if you think about it are almost the ideal environment for her.'

'Hal.'

'. . . Being that she can just locomote sideways right on through.'

'Hallie, this physically imposing *Moment* girl's asking all these soft-profilesque family-background questions.'

'She wants to know about Himself?'

'Everybody. You, the Mad Stork, the Moms. It's gradually emerging it's going to be some sort of memorial to the Stork as patriarch, everybody's talents and accomplishments profiled as some sort of refracted tribute to el Storko's careers.'

'He always did cast a long shadow, you said.'

'Of course and my first thought is to invite her to go piss up a string. But *Moment*'s been in touch with the team. The front office's indicated a soft profile would be positive for the team. Cardinal Stadium isn't exactly groaning under the weight of all the fannies, winning streak or no. I've also thought of referring her to Bain, let Bain rant at her or send her letters just trying to unparse for quotes'd take her a month.'

'*Her* as in female. Not your typical Orin-type subject. A hardened, fast-lane, gum-cracking, maybe even small-childless journalist-type female, in from New Youok on the red-eye. Plus you said imposing.'

'Not all that tough or hard, but physically imposing. Large but not un-erotic. A girl and a half in all directions.'

'A girl to dominate the space of any trailer she lives in.'

'Enough with the trailerisms.'

'The strained quality is me trying to speak and pick caromed toenail-parings up off the floor at the same time.'

'This girl's immune to most of your standard conversational distractions.'

'You're afraid you're losing your touch. An immune girl and a half.'

'I said distraction not seduction.'

'You kind of wisely avoid any female who you suspect could beat you up if things came down to that.'

'She's more imposing than like most of our starting backfield. But weirdly sexy. The linemen are gaga. The tackles keep making all these cracks about does she maybe want to see their hard profile.'

'Let's hope her prose is better than whoever did that human-interest thing on the blind kid last spring. Have you bounced this new fear of the handicapped off her?'

'Listen. You of all people should know I have zero intent of forthrightly answering any stained-family-linen-type questions from anybody, much less somebody who takes shorthand. Physical charms or no.'

'You and tennis, you and the Saints, Himself and tennis, the Moms and Québec and Royal Victoria, the Moms and immigration, Himself and annulation, Himself and Lyle, Himself and distilled spirits, Himself killing himself, you and Joelle, Himself and Joelle, the Moms and C.T., you v. the Moms, E.T.A., nonexistent films, et cetera.'

'But you can see how it's all going to get me thinking. How to avoid being forthright about the Stork material unless I know what the really forthright answers would be.'

'Everybody said you'd regret not coming to the funeral. But I don't think this is what they meant.'

'For example the Stork took himself down before C.T. moved in upstairs at HmH? or after?'

'. . .'

'. . .'

'This is you asking me?'

'Don't make this appalling for me, Hal.'

'I wouldn't dream of even trying.'

'. . .'

'Immediately before. Two, three days before. C.T. had had what's now deLint's room, next to Schtitt's, in Comm.-Ad.'

'And Dad knew they were . . . ?'

'Very close? I don't know, O.'

'You don't *know*?'

'Mario might know. Like to chew the fat with Booboo on this, O.?'

'Don't make this like this Hallie.'

'. . .'

'And Dad . . . the Mad Stork put his head in the oven?'

'. . .'

'. . .'

'The microwave, O. The rotisserie microwave over next to the fridge, on the freezer side, on the counter, under the cabinet with the plates and bowls to the left of the fridge as you face the fridge.'

'A microwave oven.'

'That is a Rog and Wilc, O.'

'Nobody ever said microwave.'

'I think it came out generally at the funeral.'

'I keep getting your point, if you're wondering.'

'. . .'

'So where was he found, then?'

'20 for 28 is what, 65%?'

'It's not like this is all that —'

'The microwave was in the kitchen I already explained, O.'

'All right.'

'All right.'

'So OK now, who would you say speaks most about the guy, keeps his memory alive, verbally, the most now: you, C.T., or the Moms?'

'I think it's a three-way tie.'

'So it's never mentioned. Nobody talks about him. It's taboo.'

'But you seem to be forgetting somebody.'

'Mario talks about him. About it.'

'Sometimes.'

'To what and/or who all this talking?'

'To me, for one, I suppose.'

'And so you *do* talk about it, but only to him, and only after he initiates it.'

'Orin I lied. I haven't even started on the right foot yet. I've been too afraid to change my angle of approach to the nails. The right foot's a whole different angle of approach. I'm afraid the magic is left-foot-dependent. I'm like your superstitious lineman. Talking about it's broken the spell. Now I'm self-conscious and afraid. I've been sitting here on the edge of the bed with my right knee up under my chin, poised, studying the foot, frozen with aboriginal terror. And lying about it to my own brother.'

'Can I ask you who it was who found him? His — who found him at the oven?'

'Found by one Harold James Incandenza, thirteen going on really old.'

'You were who found him? Not the Moms?'

'. . .'

'. . .'

'Listen, may I ask why this sudden interest after four years 216 days, and with two years of that not even once even calling?'

'I've already said I don't feel safe not answering Helen's questions if I haven't got a handle on what I'm not saying.'

'Helen. So you did.'

'Is why.'

'I'm still frozen, by the way. The self-consciousness that kills the magic is getting worse and worse. This is why Pemulis and Troeltsch always seem to let a lead slip away. The standard term is Tightening Up. The clippers are poised, blades on either side of the nail. I just can't achieve the unconsciousness to actually clip. Maybe it was cleaning up the few that missed. Suddenly the wastebasket seems small and far away. I've lost the magic by talking about it instead of just giving in to it. Launching the nail out toward the wastebasket now seems like an exercise in telemachry.'

'You mean telemetry?'

'How embarrassing. When the skills go they *go*.'

'Listen . . .'

'You know, why don't you go ahead and ask me whatever standard ghoulish questions you want not to answer. This may be your only shot. Usually I seem not to talk about it.'

'Was she there? The P.G.O.A.T.?'

'Joelle hadn't been around the grounds since you two split up. You knew about that. Himself met her at the brownstone, shooting. I'm sure you know way more about whatever it was they were trying to make. Joelle and Himself. Himself went underground too. C.T. was already doing most of the day-to-day administration. Himself was down in that little post-production closet off the lab for like a solid month. Mario'd bring food and . . . essentials down. Sometimes he'd eat with Lyle. I don't think he came up to ground level for at least a month, except for just one trip out to Belmont to McLean's for a two-day purge and detox. This was about a week after he came back. He'd flown off somewhere for three days, for what the impression I get was work-related business. Film-related. If Lyle didn't go with him Lyle went somewhere, because he wasn't in the weight room. I know Mario didn't go with him and didn't know what was up. Mario doesn't lie. It was unclear whether he'd finished whatever he was editing. Himself I mean. He stopped living on April First, if you weren't sure, was the day. I can tell you on April First he wasn't back by the time P.M. matches started, because I'd been around the lab door right after lunch and he wasn't back.'

'He went in for another detox you say. In what, March?'

'The Moms herself emerged and risked exterior transit and took him herself, so I gather it was urgent.'

'He quit drinking in January, Hal. It was something Joelle was real specific about. She called even after we'd agreed not to call and told me about it even after I said I didn't want to hear about him if she was going to still be in his things. She said he hadn't had a drop in weeks. It was her condition for letting him put her in what he was doing. She said he said he'd do anything.'

'Well, I don't know what to tell you. By this time it was hard to tell whether he'd been ingesting anything or not. Apparently at a certain point it stops making a difference.'

'Did he have film-related things with him when he flew somewhere? A film case? Equipment?'

'O., I didn't see him leave and didn't see him come back. He wasn't around by match-time, I know. Freer beat me badly and fast. It was 4 and 1, 4 and 2, something, and we were the first ones done. I came around HmH to do an emergency load of laundry before dinner. This was around 1630. I came over and came in and noticed something right away.'

'And found him.'

'And went to get the Moms, then changed my mind and went to get C.T., then changed my mind and went to get Lyle, but the first authority figure I ran into was Schtitt. Who was irreproachably brisk and efficient and sensible about everything and turned out to be just the authority figure to go get in the first place.'

'I didn't even think a microwave oven would go on unless the door was closed. What with microwaves oscillating all over, inside. I thought there was like a refrigerator-light or Read-Only-tab-like device.'

'You seem to be forgetting the technical ingenuity of the person we're talking about.'

'And you were totally shocked and traumatized. He was asphyxuated, irradiated, and/or burnt.'

'As we later reconstructed the scene, he'd used a wide-bit drill and small hacksaw to make a head-sized hole in the oven door, then when he'd gotten his head in he'd carefully packed the extra space around his neck with wadded-up aluminum foil.'

'Sounds kind of ad hoc and jerry-rigged and haphazard.'

'Everybody's a critic. This wasn't an aesthetic endeavor.'

'. . .'

'And there was a large and half-full bottle of Wild Turkey found on the counter not far away, with a large red decorative giftwrappish bow on the neck.'

'On the bottle's neck, you mean.'

'That is a Rog.'

'As in he hadn't been sober after all.'

'That would seem to follow, O.'

'And he left no note or living-will-type video or communiqué of any kind.'

'O, I know you know very well he didn't. You're now asking me stuff I know you know, besides criticizing him and making sobriety-claims when you weren't anywhere near the scene or the funeral. Are we just about through here? I've got a whole long-nailed foot waiting for me here.'

'As you reconstructed the scene, you just said.'

'Also it just hit me I've got a library book I was supposed to return. I'd forgotten all about it. Kertwang.'

' "Reconstructed the scene" as in the scene when you found him was somehow . . . deconstructed?'

'You of all people, O. You know that was the one word he hated more than —'

'So burned, then. Just say it. He was really really badly burned.'

'. . .'

'No, wait. Asphyxuated. The packed foil was to preserve the vacuum in a space that got automatically evacuated as soon as the magnitron started oscillating and generating the microwaves.'

'Magnitron? What do you know about magnitrons and oscillators? Aren't you the brother of mine who has to be reminded which way to turn the ignition key in a car?'

'Brief liaison with this one Subject who used to model at kitchen-appliance trade shows.'

'. . .'

'It was kind of a brutal brand of modelling. She'd stand there on a huge rotating Lazy Susan in a one-piece with one thigh turned in and a hand out palm-up, indicating the appliance next to her. Stood there smiling and spinning day after day. She'd stagger around half the evening trying to get her balance back.'

'Did this *subject* by any chance explain to you how microwaves actually cook things?'

'. . .'

'Or have you for example, say, ever like baked a potato in a microwave oven? Did you know you have to cut the potato open before you turn the oven on? Do you know why that is?'

'Jesus.'

'The B.P.D.[83] field pathologist said the build-up of internal pressures would have been almost instantaneous and equivalent in kg.s.cm. to over two sticks of TNT.'

'Jesus Christ, Hallie.'

'Hence the need to reconstruct the scene.'

'Jesus.'

'Don't feel bad. There's no guarantee anybody would have told you even if you'd popped in for, say, the memorial service. I for one wasn't exactly a jabberjaw at the time. I seemed to have been evincing shock and trauma throughout the whole funeral period. What I mostly recall is a great deal of quiet talk about my psychic well-being. It got so I kind of enjoyed popping in and out of rooms just to enjoy the quiet conversations stopping in mid-clause.'

'You must have been traumatized beyond fucking belief.'

'Your concern is much appreciated, believe me.'

'. . .'

'Trauma seems to have been the consensus. It turns out Rusk and the Moms had begun interviewing top-flight trauma- and grief-counselors for me within hours after it happened. I was shunted directly into concentrated grief- and trauma-therapy. Four days a week for over a month, right in the April-May gearing-up-for-summer-tour period. I lost two spots on the 14's ladder just because of all the P.M. matches I missed. I missed the Hard Court Qualies and would have missed Indianapolis if . . . if I hadn't finally figured out the grief- and trauma-therapy process.'

'But it helped. Ultimately. The grief-therapy.'

'The therapy ended up taking place in that Professional Building right up Comm. Ave. past the Sunstrand Plaza by Lake Street, the one with bricks the color of Thousand Island dressing we all run by four days a week. Who was to know one of the continent's top grief-men was right up the street.'

'The Moms didn't want the process going on too far from the old web, if need be, I'm sure.'

'This grief-counselor insisted I call him by his first name, which I forget. A large red meaty character with eyebrows at a demonic-looking synclinal angle and very small nubbly gray teeth. And a mustache. He always had the remains of a sneeze in his mustache. I got to know that mustache very well. His face had that same blood-pressure flush C.T.'s face gets. And let's not even go into the man's hands.'

'The Moms had Rusk shunt you to a top grief-pro so she wouldn't have to feel guilty about practically sawing the hole in the microwave door herself. Among other little guilt and antiguilt operations. She always did believe Himself was doing more with Joelle than work. Poor old Himself never had eyes for anybody but the Moms.'

'This was one tough hombré, O., this grief-counselor. He made a Rusk-session look like a day on the Adriatic. He wouldn't let up: "How did it feel, how does it feel, how do you feel when I ask how it feels." '

'Rusk always reminded me of a freshman fumbling with some Subject's bra, the way she'd sort of tug and fumble at your head.'

'The man was unsatisfiable and scary. Those eyebrows, that ham-rind face, bland little eyes. He never once turned his face away or looked away at anything but right at me. It was the most brutal six weeks of full-bore pro-fessional conversation anybody could imagine.'

'With fucking C.T. already moving his collection of platform shoes and unconvincing hairpieces and StairMaster in upstairs at HmH already.'

'The whole thing was nightmarish. I just could not figure out what the guy wanted. I went down and chewed through the Copley Square library's grief section. Not disk. The actual books. I read Kübler-Ross, Hinton. I slogged through Kastenbaum and Kastenbaum. I read things like Elizabeth Harper Neeld's *Seven Choices: Taking the Steps to New Life After Losing Someone You Love*,[84] which was 352 pages of sheer goo. I went in and presented with textbook-perfect symptoms of denial, bargaining, anger, still more denial, depression. I listed my seven textbook choices and vacillated plausibly between and among them. I provided etymological data on the word *acceptance* all the way back to Wyclif and 14th-century *langue-d'oc* French. The grief-therapist was having none of it. It was like one of those final exams in nightmares where you prepare immaculately and then you get there and all the exam questions are in Hindi. I even tried telling him Himself was miserable and pancreatitic and out of his tree half the time by then anyway, that he and the Moms were basically estranged, that even work and Wild Turkey weren't helping anymore, that he was despondent about something he was editing that turned out so bad he didn't want it released. That the . . . that what happened was probably kind of a mercy, in the end.'

'Himself didn't suffer, then. In the microwave.'

'The B.P.D. field pathologist who drew the chalk lines around Himself's shoes on the floor said maybe ten seconds tops. He said the pressure build-up would have been almost instantaneous. Then he gestured at the kitchen walls. Then he threw up. The field pathologist.'

'Jesus Christ, Hallie.'

'But the grief-therapist was having none of it, the at-least-his-suffering's-over angle that Kastenbaum and Kastenbaum said is basically a neon-bright sign of real acceptance. This grief-therapist hung on like a Gila monster. I even tried telling him I really didn't feel anything.'

'Which was a fiction.'

'Of course it was a fiction. What could I do? I was panic-stricken. This guy was a nightmare. His face just hung there over his desk like a hypertensive moon, never turning away. With this glistening mucoidal dew in his mustache. And don't even ask me about his hands. He was my worst nightmare. Talk about self-consciousness and fear. Here was a top-rank authority figure and I was failing to supply what he wanted. He made it manifestly clear I wasn't delivering the goods. I'd never failed to deliver the goods before.'

'You were our designated deliverer, Hallie, no question about it.'

'And here but here was this authority figure with top credentials in frames over every square cm. of his walls who sat there and refused even to define what the goods here would be. Say what you will about Schtitt and deLint: they let you know what they want in no uncertain terms. Flottman, Chawaf, Prickett, Nwangi, Fentress, Lingley, Pettijohn, Ogilvie, Leith, even the Moms in her way: they tell you on the very first day of class what they want from you. But this son of a bee right here: no dice.'

'You must have been in shock the whole time, too.'

'O., it got worse and worse. I dropped weight. I couldn't sleep. This was when the nightmares started. I kept dreaming of a face in the floor. I lost to Freer again, then to Coyle. I went three sets with Troeltsch. I got B's on two different quizzes. I couldn't concentrate on anything else. I'd become obsessed with the fear that I was somehow going to flunk grief-therapy. That this professional was going to tell Rusk and Schtitt and C.T. and the Moms that I couldn't deliver the goods.'

'I'm sorry I couldn't be there.'

'The odd thing was that the more obsessed I got, the worse I played and slept, the happier everybody got. The grief-therapist complimented me on how haggard I was looking. Rusk told deLint the grief-therapist'd told the Moms that it was starting to work, that I was starting to grieve, but that it was a long process.'

'Long and costly.'

'Roger. I began to despair. I began to foresee somehow getting left back in grief-therapy, never delivering the goods and it never ending. Having these Kafkaesque interfaces with this man day after day, week after week. It was now May. The Continental Clays I'd gotten all the way to the fourth round of the year before were coming up, and it became quietly clear that everybody felt I was at a crucial stage in the long costly grieving process and I wasn't going to get to go with the contingent to Indianapolis unless I could figure out some last-ditch way to deliver the emotional goods to this guy. I was totally desperate, a wreck.'

'So you schlepped on down to the weight room. You and the forehead paid a visit to good old Lyle.'

'Lyle turned out to be the key. He was down there reading *Leaves of Grass*. He was going through a Whitman period, part of grieving for Himself, he said. I'd never gone to Lyle before in any kind of supplicatory capacity, but he said he took one grief-stricken look at me flailing away down there working up a gourmet sweat and said he felt so moved by my additional suffering on top of having had to be the first of Himself's loved ones to experience the loss of Himself that he'd bend every cerebral effort. I assumed the position and let him at the old forehead and explained what had been happening and that if I couldn't figure out some way to satisfy this grief-pro I was going to end up in a soft quiet room somewhere. Lyle's key insight was that I'd been approaching the issue from the wrong side. I'd gone to the library and acted like a *student* of grief. What I needed to chew through was the section for grief-professionals *themselves*. I needed to prepare from the grief-pro's own perspective. How could I know what a professional wanted unless I knew what he was professionally required to want, etc. It was simple, he said. I needed to empathize with the grief-therapist, Lyle said, if I wanted to spread a broader breast than his own. It was such a simple obversion of my normal goods-delivery-preparation system that it hadn't once occurred to me, Lyle explained.'

'Lyle said all that? That doesn't sound like Lyle.'

'But a sort of soft light broke inside me for the first time in weeks. I called a cab, still in my towel. I jumped in the cab before it had even stopped at the gate. I actually said, "The nearest library with a cutting-edge professional grief- and trauma-therapy section, and step on it." Et cetera et cetera.'

'The Lyle my class knew wasn't a how-to-deliver-the-goods-to-authorities-type figure.'

'By the time I hit the grief-therapist's the next day I was a different man, immaculately prepared, unfazable. Everything I'd come to dread about the man — the eyebrows, the multicultural music in the waiting room, the implacable stare, the crusty mustache, the little gray teeth, even the hands — did I mention that this grief-therapist hid his hands under his desk at all times?'

'But you got through it. You grieved to everybody's satisfaction, you're saying.'

'What I did, I went in there and presented with anger at the grief-therapist. I accused the grief-therapist of actually inhibiting my attempt to process my grief, by refusing to validate my absence of feelings. I told him I'd told him the truth already. I used foul language and slang. I said I didn't give a damn if he was an abundantly credentialed authority figure or not. I called him a shithead. I asked him what the cock-shitting fuck he wanted from me. My overall demeanor was paroxysmic. I told him I'd told him that I didn't feel anything, which was the truth. I said it seemed like he wanted me to feel toxically guilty for not feeling anything. Notice I was subtly inserting certain loaded professional-grief-therapy terms like *validate, process* as a transitive verb, and *toxic guilt*. These were library-derived.'

'The whole difference was this time you were walking on-court oriented, with a sense of where the lines were, Schtitt would say.'

'The grief-therapist encouraged me to go with my paroxysmic feelings, to name and honor my rage. He got more and more pleased and excited as I angrily told him I flat-out refused to feel iota-one of guilt of any kind. I said what, I was supposed to have lost even more quickly to Freer, so I could have come around HmH in time to stop Himself? It wasn't my fault, I said. It was not my fault I found him, I shouted; I was down to black street-socks, I had legitimate emergency-grade laundry to do. By this time I was pounding myself on the breastbone with rage as I said that it just by-God was *not* my fault that —'

'That what?'

'That's just what the grief-therapist said. The professional literature had a whole bold-font section on Abrupt Pauses in High-Affect Speech. The grief-therapist was now leaning way forward at the waist. His lips were wet. I was in The Zone, therapeutically speaking. I felt on top of things for the first time in a long time. I broke eye-contact with him. That I'd been hungry, I muttered.'

'Come again?'

'That's just what he said, the grief-therapist. I muttered that it was nothing, just that it damn sure wasn't my fault that I had the reaction I did when I came through the front door of HmH, before I came into the kitchen to get to the basement stairs and found Himself with his head in what was left of the microwave. When I first came in and was still in the foyer trying to get my shoes off without putting the dirty laundry-bag down on the white carpet and hopping around and couldn't be expected to have any idea what had happened. I said nobody can choose or have any control over their first unconscious thoughts or reactions when they come into a house. I said it wasn't my fault that my first unconscious thought turned out to be —'

'Jesus, kid, what?'

' "*That something smelled delicious!*" I screamed. The force of my shriek almost sent the grief-therapist over backwards in his leather chair. A couple credentials fell off the wall. I bent over in my own nonleather chair as if for a crash-landing. I put a hand to each temple and rocked back in forth in the chair, weeping. It came out between sobs and screams. That it'd been four hours plus since lunchtime and I'd worked hard and played hard and I was starved. That the saliva had started the minute I came through the door. That golly something smells *delicious* was my first reaction!'

'But you forgave yourself.'

'I absolved myself with seven minutes left in the session right there in full approving view of the grief-therapist. He was ecstatic. By the end I swear his side of the desk was half a meter off the floor, at my grief-therapist-textbook breakdown into genuine affect and trauma and guilt and textbook earsplitting grief, then absolution.'

'Christ on a jet-ski, Hallie.'

'. . .'

'But you got through it. You really did grieve, and you can tell me what it was like, so I can say something generic but convincing about loss and grief for Helen for *Moment*.'

'But I'd omitted that somehow the single most nightmarishly compelling thing about this top grief-therapist was that his hands were never visible. The dreadfulness of the whole six weeks somehow coalesced around the issue of the guy's hands. His hands never emerged from underneath his desk. It was as if his arms terminated at the elbow. Besides mustache-material-analysis, I also spent large blocks of each hour trying to imagine the configurations and activities of those hands under there.'

'Hallie, let me just ask and then I'll never bring it back up again. You implied before that what was especially traumatic was that Himself's head had popped like an uncut spud.'

'Then on what turned out to be the last day of the therapy, the last day before the A squads were picked for Indianapolis, after I'd finally delivered the goods and my traumatic grief was professionally pronounced uncovered and countenanced and processed, when I put on my sweatshirt and got set to take my leave, and came up to the desk and put out my hand in a trembly grateful way he couldn't possibly have refused, and he stood and brought out the hand and shook my hand, I finally understood.'

'His hands were disfigured or something.'

'His hands were no bigger than a four-year-old girl's. It was surreal. This massive authoritative figure, with a huge red meaty face and thick walrus mustache and dewlaps and a neck that spilled over the rim of his shirt-collar, and his hands were tiny and pink and hairless and butt-soft, delicate as shells. The hands were the capper. I barely made it out of the office before it started.'

'The cathartic post-traumatic-like-reexperience hysteria. You reeled out of there.'

'I barely made it to the men's room down the hall. I was laughing so hysterically I was afraid all the periodontists and C.P.A.s on either side of the men's room would hear. I sat in a stall with my hands over my mouth, stamping my feet and beating my head against first one side of the stall and then the other in hysterical mirth. If you could have seen those hands.'

'But you got through it all, and you can thumbnail-sketch the overall feeling for me.'

'What I feel is myself gathering my resources for the right foot, finally. That magic feeling's back. I'm not lining up the vectors for the wastebasket or anything. I'm not even thinking. I'm trusting the feeling. It's like that celluloid moment when Luke removes his high-tech targeting helmet.'

'What helmet?'

'You know, of course, that human nails are the vestiges of talons and horns. That they're atavistic, like coccyges and hair. That they develop in-utero long before the cerebral cortex.'

'What's the matter?'

'That at some point in the first trimester we lose our gills but are now still now little more than a bladdery sac of spinal fluid and a rudimentary tail and hair-follicles and little microchips of vestigial talon and horn.'

'Is this to make me feel bad? Did this fuck you up, me probing for details after all this time? Did it reactivate the grief?'

'Just one more confirmation. The trailer's interior. There was some object or contiguous trio of objects with the following color scheme: brown, lavender, and either mint-green or jonquil-yellow.'

'I can call back when you're more yourself. The leg's starting to prune a bit from the whirlpool anyway.'

'I'll be right here. I've got a whole foot to yield to the magic with. I'm not going to alter the smallest particular. I'm just about ready to bear down on the clippers. It's going to feel right, I know.'

'A throw. Like an afghan throw, on the chintz sofa. The yellow was more fluorescent than jonquil.'

'And the word is *asphyxiated*. Kick some egg-shaped balls for all of us, O. The next sound you hear will be unpleasant,' Hal said, holding the phone down right next to the foot, his expression terrifically intense.

O

6 NOVEMBER
YEAR OF THE DEPEND ADULT UNDERGARMENT

White halogen off the green of the composite surface, the light out on the indoor courts at the Port Washington Tennis Academy is the color of sour apples. To the spectators at the gallery's glass, the duos of players arrayed and moving down below have a reptilian tinge to their skin, a kind of seasick-type pallor. This annual meet is mammoth: both academies' A and B teams for both Boys and Girls, both singles and doubles, in 14 and Unders, 16 and Unders, 18 and Unders. Thirty-six courts stretch out down away from one end's gallery under a fancy tri-domed system of permanent all-weather Lung.

A jr. tennis team has six people on it, with the highest-ranked playing #1 singles against the other team's best guy, the next-highest-ranked playing #2, and on down the line to #6. After the six singles matches there are three doubles, with a team's best two singles players usually turning around and also playing #1 doubles — with occasional exceptions, e.g. the Vaught twins, or the fact that Schacht and Troeltsch, way down on the B squad in 18's singles, play #2 doubles on E.T.A.'s 18's A team, because they've been a doubles team since they were incontinent toddlers back in Philly, and they're so experienced and smooth together they can wipe surfaces with the 18's A team's #3 and #4 singles guys, Coyle and Axford, who prefer to skip doubles altogether. It all tends to get complicated, and probably not all that interesting — unless you play.

But so a normal meet between two junior teams is the best out of nine matches, whereas this mammoth annual early-November thing between E.T.A. and P.W.T.A. will try to be the best out of 108. A 54-match-all conclusion is extremely unlikely — odds being 1 in 2^{27} — and has never happened in nine years. The meet's always down on Long Island because P.W.T.A. has indoor courts out the bazoo. Each year the academy that loses the meet has to get up on tables at the buffet supper afterward and sing a really silly song. An even more embarrassing transaction is supposed to take place in private between the two schools' Headmasters, but nobody knows quite what. Last year Enfield lost 57–51 and Charles Tavis didn't say one word on the bus-ride home and used the lavatory several times.

But last year E.T.A. didn't have John Wayne, and last year H. J. Incandenza hadn't yet exploded, competitively. John Wayne, formerly of Montcerf, Québec — an asbestos-mining town ten clicks or so from the infamously rupture-prone Mercier Dam — formerly the top-ranked junior male in Canada at sixteen as well as #5 overall in the Organization of North American Nations Tennis Association computerized rankings, was finally successfully recruited by Gerhardt Schtitt and Aubrey deLint last spring via the argument that two gratis years at an American academy would maybe let Wayne bypass the usual couple seasons of top college tennis and go pro immediately at nineteen with more than enough competitive tempering. This reasoning was not unsound, since the top four U.S. tennis academies' tournament schedules closely resemble the A.T.P. tour in terms of numbing travel and continual stress. John Wayne is currently ranked #3 in the O.N.A.N.T.A.'s Boys' 18's and #2 in the U.S.T.A. (Canada, under Provincial pressure, has disowned him as an emigrant) and has in this Year of the Depend Adult Undergarment reached the semis of both the Junior French and Junior U.S. Opens, and has lost to exactly nobody American in seven meets and a dozen major tournaments. He trails the #1 American kid, an Independent[85] down in Florida, Veach, by only a couple U.S.T.A. computer points, and they haven't yet met in sanctioned play this year, and the kid is well known to be hiding out from Wayne, avoiding him, staying down in Pompano Beach, allegedly nursing a like four-month groin-pull, sitting on his ranking. He's supposed to show at the WhataBurger Invitational in AZ in a couple weeks, this Veach, having won the 18's at age seventeen there last year, but he's got to know Wayne's coming down, and speculation is rife and complex. O.N.A.N.T.A.-wise, there's an Argentine kid that Mexico's Academia de Vera Cruz has got rat-holed away who's #1 and not about to lose to anybody, having this year taken three out of four legs of the Junior Grand Slam, the first time anybody's done that since a sepulchral Czech kid named Lendl, who retired from the Show and suicided well before the advent of Subsidized Time. But so there's Wayne at #1.

And it's been established that Hal Incandenza, last year a respectable but by no means to-write-home-about 43rd nationally and bouncing between

#4 and #5 on the Academy's A team in Boys' 16's singles, has made a kind of quantumish competitive plateaux-hop such that this year — the one nearly done, Kimberly-Clark Corp.'s Depend Absorbent Products Division soon to give way to the highest corporate bidder for rights to the New Year — Incandenza, mind you this year just seventeen, is 4th in the nation and #6 on the O.N.A.N.T.A. computer and playing A-#2 for E.T.A. in Boys' 18's. These competitive explosions happen sometimes. Nobody at the Academy talks to Hal much about the explosion, sort of the way you avoid a pitcher who's got a no-hitter going. Hal's delicate and spinny, rather cerebral game hasn't altered, but this year it seems to have grown a beak. No longer fragile or abstracted-looking on court, he seems now almost to hit the corners without thinking about it. His Unforced-Error stats look like a decimal-error.

Hal's game involves attrition. He'll probe, pecking, until some angle opens up. Until then he'll probe. He'd rather run his man ragged, wear him down. Three different opponents this past summer had to go to oxygen during breaks.[86] His serve yanks across at people as if on a hidden diagonal string. His serve, now, suddenly, after four summers of thousand-a-day serves to no one at dawn, is suddenly supposed to be one of the best left-handed kick serves the junior circuit has ever seen. Schtitt calls Hal Incandenza his 'revenant,' now, and sometimes points his pointer at him in an affectionate way from his observation crow's nest in the transom, during drills.

Most of the singles' A matches are under way. Coyle and his man on 3 are in an endless butterfly-shaped rally. Hal's muscular but unquick opponent is bent over trying to get his breath while Hal stands there and futzes with his strings. Tall Paul Shaw on 6 bounces the ball eight times before he serves. Never seven or nine.

And John Wayne's without question the best male player to appear at Enfield Academy in several years. He'd been spotted first by the late Dr. James Incandenza at age six, eleven summers back, when Incandenza was doing early and coldly conceptual Super-8 on people named John Wayne who were not the real thespio-historical John Wayne, a film Wayne's not-to-be-fucked-with papa eventually litigated the kid's segment out of because the film had the word *Homo* in the title.[87]

On 1, with John Wayne up at net, Port Washington's best boy throws up a lob. It's a beauty: the ball soars slowly up, just skirts the indoor courts' system of beams and lamps, and floats back down gentle as lint: a lovely quad-function of fluorescent green, seams whirling. John Wayne backpedals and flies back after it. You can tell — if you play seriously — you can tell just by the way the ball comes off a guy's strings whether the lob is going to land fair. There's surprisingly little thought. Coaches tell serious players what to do so often it gets automatic. John Wayne's game could be described as having a kind of automatic beauty. When the lob first went up he'd backpedaled from the net, keeping the ball in sight until it reached the top of its flight and its curve broke, casting many shadows in the tray of lights hung from the ceiling's insulation; then Wayne turned his back to the ball and sprinted flat-out for the spot where it will land fair. Would land. He doesn't have to locate the ball again until it's hit the green court just inside the baseline. By now he's come around the side of the bounced ball's flight, still sprinting. He looks mean in a kind of distant way. He comes around the side of the bounced ball's second ascent the way you come up around the side of somebody you're going to hurt, and he has to leave his feet and half-pirouette to get his side to the ball and whip his big right arm through it, catching it on the rise and slapping it down the line past the Port Washington boy, who's played the percentages and followed a beauty of a lob up to net. The Port Washington kid applauds with the heel of his hand against his strings in acknowledgment of a really nice get, even as he looks up at Port Washington's coaching staff in the gallery. The spectators' glass panel is at ground level, and the players play below it on courts that have been carved out of a kind of pit, dug long ago: some northeast clubs favor courts below ground, because earth insulates and keeps utility bills daunting instead of prohibitive, once the Lungs go up. The gallery panel stretches overhead behind Courts 1 through 6, but there's a decided spectatorial clumping at the part of the gallery that looks out over the Show Courts, Boys' 18's #1 and #2, Wayne and Hal and P.W.T.A.'s two best. Now after Wayne's balletic winner there's the sad sound of a small crowd behind glass's applause; on the courts the applause is muffled and compromised by on-court sounds, and sounds like the trapped survivors of something tapping for help at a great depth. The panel is like an aquarium's glass, thick and clean, and traps noise behind it, and to the gallery it seems that 72 well-muscled children are arrayed and competing in total silence in the pit. Almost everyone in the gallery is wearing tennis clothes and bright nylon warm-ups; some even wear wristbands, the tennis equivalent of a football fan's pennant and raccoon coat.

John Wayne's post-pirouette backward inertia has carried him into the heavy black tarpaulin that hangs several meters behind both sides of the 36 courts on a system of rods and rings not unlike a very ambitious shower-curtain, the tarps hiding from view the waterstained walls of puffy white-wrapped insulation and creating a narrow passage for players to get to their courts without crossing open court and interrupting play. Wayne hits the heavy tarp and kind of bounces off, producing a boom that resounds. The sounds on court in an indoor venue are huge and complex; everything echoes and the echoes then meld. In the gallery, Tavis and Nwangi bite their knuckles and deLint squashes his nose flat against the glass in anxiety as everyone else politely applauds. Schtitt calmly taps his pointer against the top of his boot at times of high stress. Wayne isn't hurt, though. Everybody goes into the tarp sometimes. That's what it's there for. It always sounds worse than it is.

The boom of the tarp sounds bad down below, though. The boom rattles Teddy Schacht, who's kneeling in the little passage right behind Court 1, holding M. Pemulis's head as Pemulis down on one knee is sick into a tall white plastic spare-ball bucket. Schacht has to haul Pemulis slightly back as Wayne's outline bulges for a moment into the billowing tarp and threatens to knock Pemulis over, plus maybe the bucket, which would be a bad scene. Pemulis, deep into the little hell of his own nauseous pre-match nerves, is too busy trying to vomit w/o sound to hear the mean sound of Wayne's winner or the boom of him against the heavy curtain. It's freezing back here in the little passage, up next to insulation and I-beams and away from the infrared heaters that hang over the courts. The plastic bucket is full of old bald Wilson tennis balls and Pemulis's breakfast. There is of course an odor. Schacht doesn't mind. He lightly strokes the sides of Pemulis's head as his mother had stroked his own big sick head, back in Philly.

Placed at eye-level intervals in the tarp are little plastic windows, archer-slit views of each court from the cold backstage passage. Schacht sees John Wayne walk to the net-post and flip his card as he and his opponent change sides. Even indoors, you change ends of the court after every odd-numbered game. No one knows why odd rather than even. Each P.W.T.A. court has, welded to its west net-post, another smaller post with a double set of like flippable cards with big red numerals from 1 to 7; in umpless competition you're supposed to flip your card appropriately at every change of sides, to help the gallery follow the score in the set. A lot of junior players neglect to flip their cards. Wayne is always automatic and scrupulous in his accounts. Wayne's father is an asbestos miner who at forty-three is far and away the seniorest guy on his shift; he now wears triple-thick masks and is trying to hold on until John Wayne can start making serious $ and take him away from all this. He has not seen his eldest son play since John Wayne's Québecois and Canadian citizenships were revoked last year. Wayne's card is on (5); his opponent has yet to flip a card. Wayne never even sits down to take the 60 seconds he's allowed on each change of sides. His opponent, in his light-blue flare-collared shirt with WILSON and P.W.T.A. on the sleeves, says something not unfriendly as Wayne brushes past him by the post. Wayne doesn't respond one way or the other. He just goes back to the baseline farthest from Schacht's little tarp-window and bounces a ball up and down in the air with the reticulate face of his stick as the Port Washington boy sits in his little canvas director's chair and towels the sweat off his arms (neither of which is large) and looks briefly up at the gallery behind the panel. The thing about Wayne is he's all business. His face on court is blankly rigid, with the hypertonic masking of schizophrenics and Zen adepts. He tends to look straight ahead at all times. He is about as reserved as they come. His emotions emerge in terms of velocity. Intelligence as strategic focus. His play, like his manner in general, seems to Schacht less alive than undead. Wayne tends to eat and study alone. He's sometimes seen with two or three expatriate E.T.A. Nucks, but when they're together they all seem morose. It's wholly unclear to Schacht how Wayne feels about the U.S. or his citizenship-status. He figures Wayne figures it doesn't much matter: he is destined for the Show; he will be an all-business entertainer, citizen of the world, everywhere undead, endorsing juice drinks and liniment ointment.

Pemulis has nothing left and is spasming dryly over the bucket, his covered Dunlop gut-strung sticks and gear tumbled just past Schacht's in the passage. They are the last guys to get out on court. Schacht is to play #3 singles on the 18's B team, Pemulis #6-B. They are undeniably tardy getting out there. Their opponents stand out on the baselines of Courts 9 and 12 waiting for them to come out and warm up, jittery, stretching out the way you do when you've already stretched out, dribbling fresh bright balls with their black Wilson widebody sticks. The whole Port Washington Tennis Academy student body gets free and mandatory Wilson sticks under an administrative contract. Nothing personal, but no way would Schacht let an academy tell him what brand of stick to swing. He himself favors Head Masters, which is regarded as bizarre and eccentric. The AMF-Head rep brings them out to him out of some cobwebby warehouse where they're kept since the line was discontinued during the large-head revolution many years back. Aluminum Head Masters have small, perfectly round heads and a dull blue plastic brace in the V of the throat and look less like weapons than toys. Coyle and Axford are always kibitzing that they've seen a Head Master for sale at like a flea market or garage sale someplace and Schacht better get down there quick. Schacht, who's historically tight with Mario and with Lyle down in the weight room (where Schacht, since the knee and the Crohn's Disease, likes to go even on off-days, to work off discomfort, and deLint and Loach are always on him about not getting musclebound), has a way of just smiling and holding his tongue when he's kibitzed.

'Are you okay?'

Pemulis says 'Blarg.' He wipes at his forehead in a gesture of completion and submits to being hauled to his feet and stands there on his own with his hands on his hips, slightly bent.

Schacht straightens and pulls some wrinkles out of the bandage around the brace on his knee. 'Take maybe another second. Wayne's already way up.'

Pemulis sniffs unpleasantly. 'How come this happens to me every time? This is not like me.'

'Happens to some people is all.'

'This hunched spurting pale guy is not any me I ever recognize.'

Schacht gathers gear. 'Some people their nerves are in their stomachs. Cisne, Yard-Guard, Lord, you: stomach men.'

'Teddy brother man I'm never *once* hung-over for a competitive thing. I take elaborate precautions. Not so much as a whippet. I'm always in bed the night before by 2300 all pink-cheeked and clean.'

As they pass the plastic window behind Court 2 Schacht sees Hal Incandenza try to pass his serve-and-volley guy with a baroque sideways slice down the backhand side and miss just wide. Hal's card's already flipped to (4). Schacht gives a little toodleoo-wave that Hal can't see to acknowledge. Pemulis is in front of him as they go down the cold passage.

'Hal's way up too. Another victory for the forces of peace.'

'Jesus I feel awful,' Pemulis says.

'Things could be worse.'

'Expand on that, will you?'

'This wasn't like that Atlanta stomach-incident. We were enclosed here. No one saw. You saw that glass; to Schtitt and deLint it's all a silent movie down here. Nobody heard thing one. Our guys'll think we were back here butting heads to get enraged or something. Or we can tell them I got a cramp. That was a freebie, in terms of stomach-incidents.'

Pemulis is a whole different person before competitive play.

'I'm fucking inept.'

Schacht laughs. 'You're one of the eptest people I know. Get off your own back.'

'Never remember getting sick as a kid. Now it's like I make myself sick just from worrying about getting sick.'

'Well then there you go. Just don't think anything thoracic. Pretend you don't have a stomach.'

'I have no stomach,' Pemulis says. His head stays still when he talks, at least, negotiating the passage. He carries four sticks, a rough white P.W.T.A. locker-room towel, an empty ball-can full of high-chlorine Long Island water, nervously zipping and unzipping the top stick's cover. Schacht only ever carries three sticks. His don't have covers on them. Except for Pemulis and Rader and Unwin and a couple others who favor gut strings and really need protection, nobody at Enfield uses racquet-covers; it's like an antifashion statement. People with covers make a point of telling you they're valid and for gut. A similar point of careful nonpride is never having their shirts tucked in. Ortho Stice used to drill in cut-off black jeans until Schtitt had Tony Nwangi go over and scream at him about it. Each academy has its own style or antistyle. The P.W.T.A. people, more or less a de facto subsidiary of Wilson, have unnecessary light-blue Wilson covers on all their courtside synthetic-strung sticks and big red W's stencilled onto their Wilson synth-gut strings. You have to let your company of choice spraypaint their logo on your strings if you want to be on their Free List for sticks, is the universal junior deal. Schacht's orange Gamma-9 synthetic strings have AMF-Head Inc.'s weird Taoist paraboloid logo sprayed on. Pemulis isn't on Dunlop's Free List[88] but gets the E.T.A. stringer to put Dunlop's dot-and-circumflex trademark on all his stick's strings, as a kind of touchingly insecure gesture, in Schacht's opinion.

'I played your guy in Tampa two years ago,' Pemulis says, sidestepping one of the old discolored drill-balls that always litter passages behind indoor tarps. 'Name escapes.'

'Le-something,' says Schacht. 'Yet another Nuck. One of those names that start with Le.' Mario Incandenza, in a pair of little Audern Tallat-Kelpsa's E.T.A. drill-sweats, is lurching noiselessly some ten m. behind them in the passage, his police-lock up and head uncamera'd; he's framing Schacht's back in a three-cornered box with his thumbs and long fingers, simulating the view through a lens. Mario's been authorized to travel with the squads to the WhataBurger Invitational for final footage for his short and upbeat annual documentary — brief testimonials and lighthearted moments and behind-the-scenes shots and emotional moments on court, etc. — that every year gets distributed to E.T.A. alumni and patrons and guests at the pre-Thanksgiving fundraising exhibition and formal fête. Mario is wondering how you could get enough light back here in a tarp-tunnel to film a tense cold pre-match gladiatorial march behind an indoor tarp, carrying tennis racquets in your arms like an obscene bouquet, without sacrificing the dim and diffuse and kind of gladiatorially doomed quality figures in the dim passage have. After Pemulis has mysteriously won, he'll tell Mario maybe a Marino 350 with a diffusion-filter on some kind of overhead cable you could winch along behind the figures at about twice the focal length, or else use fast film and station the Marino at the tunnel's very start and let the figures' backs gradually recede into a kind of doomed mist of low exposure.

'I remember your guy as one big forehand. Nothing but slice off the back. His VAPS never varies. If you kick the serve over to the backhand he'll slice it short. You can come in behind it at like will.'

'Worry about your own guy,' Schacht says.

'Your guy's got zero imagination.'

'And you've got an empty expanse where your stomach ought to be, remember.'

'I am a man with no stomach.'

They emerge through flaps in the tarp with hands upraised in slight apology to their opponents, walk out onto the warmer courts, the slow green eraserish footing of indoor composite. Their ears dilate into all the sounds in the larger space. Gasps and *thwaps* and *pocks* and sneakers' squeaks. Pemulis's court is almost down in female territory. Courts 13 to 24 are Girls' 18's A and B, all bobbing ponytails and two-handed backhands and high-pitched grunts that if girls could only hear what their own grunts sounded like they'd cut it out. Pemulis can't tell whether the very muffled applause way down up behind the gallery-panel is sardonic applause at his finally appearing after several minutes of vomiting or is sincerely for K. D. Coyle on Court 3, who's just smashed a sucker-lob so hard it's bounced up and racked 3's tray of hanging lights. Except for some rubber in his legs Pemulis feels stomachless and tentatively OK. This match is an all-out must-win for him in terms of the WhataBurger.

The infra-lit courts are warm and soft; the heaters bolted into both walls above the tarp's upper hem are the deep warm red of little square suns.

The Port Washington players all wear matching socks and shorts and tucked-in shirts. They look sharp but effete, a mannequinish aspect to them. Most of the higher-ranked E.T.A. students are free to sign on with different companies for no fees but free gear. Coyle is Prince and Reebok, as is Trevor Axford. John Wayne is Dunlop and Adidas. Schacht is Head Master sticks but his own clothes and knee-supports. Ortho Stice is Wilson and all-black Fila. Keith Freer is Fox sticks and both Adidas and Reebok until one of the two companies' NNE reps catches on. Troeltsch is Spalding and damn lucky to get that. Hal Incandenza is Dunlop and lightweight Nike hightops and an Air Stirrup brace for the dicky ankle. Shaw is Kennex sticks and clothes from Tachani's Big & Tall line. Pemulis's entrepreneurial vim has earned him complete freedom of choice and expense, though he's barred by deLint and Nwangi from shirts that mention the Sinn Fein or that extol Allston MA in any way, in competition.

Before going back to the baseline and warming up groundstrokes Schacht likes to take a little time courtside futzing around, hitting his heads' frames against strings and listening for the pitch of best tension, arranging his towel on the back of his chair, making sure his cards aren't still flipped from some previous match, etc., and then he prefers to sort of snuffle around his baseline for a bit, checking for dustbunnies of ball-fuzz and little divots or ridges from cold-weather heave, adjusting the brace on his ruined knee, putting his thick arms out cruciform and pulling them way back to stretch out the old pecs and cuffs. His opponent waits patiently, twirling his poly-butylene stick; and when they finally start to hit around, the guy's expression is pleasant. Schacht always prefers a pleasant match, one way or the other. He really doesn't care all that much whether he wins anymore, since first the Crohn's and then the knee at sixteen. He'd probably now describe his desire to win as a preference, nothing more. What's singular is that his tennis seems to have improved slightly in the two years since he stopped really caring. It's like his hard flat game stopped having any purpose beyond itself and started feeding on itself and got fuller, looser, its edges less jagged, though everybody else has been improving too, even faster, and Schacht's rank has been steadily declining since sixteen, and the staff has stopped talking even about a top-college ride. Schtitt's warmed to him, though, since the knee and the loss of any urge beyond the play itself, and treats Schacht now almost more like a peer than an experimental subject with something at stake. Schacht is already in his heart committed to a dental career, and he even interns twice a week for a root-specialist over at the National Cranio-Facial Pain Foundation, in east Enfield, when not touring.

It strikes Schacht as odd that Pemulis makes such a big deal of stopping all substances the day before competitive play but never connects the neurasthenic stomach to any kind of withdrawal or dependence. He'd never say this to Pemulis unless Pemulis asked him directly, but Schacht suspects Pemulis is physically 'drine-dependent, Preludin or Tenuate or something. It's not his business.

Schacht's supposedly French-Canadian guy is as broad as Schacht but shorter, his face dark and with a kind of Eskimoid structure to it, at eighteen his hairline recessed in the sort of way where you just know the kid's already got hair on his back, and he warms up with crazy spins, moony top off a western forehand and weird inside-out shit off a one-hand back, his knees dipping oddly whenever he makes contact and his follow-through full of the dancerly flourishes that characterize a case of nerves. A nervous spin-artist can be eaten more or less for lunch, if you hit as hard as Schacht does, and what Pemulis said is true: the guy's backhand is always sliced and lands shallow. Schacht looks over at Pemulis's guy, a grunter with a moody profile and the storky look of recent puberty. Pemulis is looking oddly sanguine and confident after a couple minutes futzing with the cans of water, rinsing out the oral cavity and so on. Pemulis is maybe going to win, too, despite himself. Schacht figures he can run in and get one of the twelve-year-olds he Big Buddies to go back into the passage and empty Pemulis's bucket on the sly before anybody coming off court sees it. Evidence of nervous incapacity of any kind gets noted and logged, at E.T.A., and Schacht's observed Pemulis having some kind of vested emotional interest in attending the WhataBurger Inv. over Thanksgiving. He thought Mario's lurking around in the cold passage scratching his poor big head over technical lighting problems was kind of funny. There will be no Lungs or tarps or dim passages at the WhataBurger: the Tucson tournament is outside, and Tucson cruised around 40° C even in November, and the sun there was a retinal horror-show on overheads and serves.

Though Schacht buys quarterly urine like the rest of them, it seems to Pemulis that Schacht ingests the occasional chemical that way grownups who sometimes forget to finish their cocktails drink liquor: to make a tense but fundamentally OK interior life interestingly different but no more, no element of relief; a kind of tourism; and Schacht doesn't even have to worry about obsessive training like Inc or Stice or get sick so often from the physical stress of constant 'drines like Troeltsch or suffer from thinly disguised psychological fallout like Inc or Struck or Pemulis himself. The way Pemulis and Troeltsch and Struck and Axford ingest substances and recover from substances and have a whole jargony argot based around various substances gives Schacht the creeps, a bit, but since the knee injury broke and remade him at sixteen he's learned to go his own interior way and let others go theirs. Like most very large men, he's getting comfortable early with the fact that his place in the world is very small and his real impact on other persons even smaller — which is a big reason he can sometimes forget to finish his portion of a given substance, so interested does he become in the way he's already started to feel. He's one of these people who don't need much, much less much more.

Schacht and his opponent warm up their groundstrokes with the fluid economy of years of warming up groundstrokes. They take turns feeding each other some volleys at net and then each take a 'couple up,' lobs, hitting loose easy overheads, slowly adjusting the idle from half-speed to three-quarter-speed. The knee feels fundamentally all right, springy. Slow indoor composite surfaces do not like Schacht's hard flat game, but they are kind to the knee, which after some days outside on hard cement swells to about the size of a volleyball. Schacht feels blandly happy down here on 9, playing in private, way down past the gallery's panel. There is a nourishing sense of pregnable space in a big indoor club that you never get playing outside, especially playing outside in the cold, when the balls feel hard and sullen and come off the stick's strung face with an echoless *ping*. Here everything cracks and booms, the grunts and shoe-squeaks and booming *pocks* of impact and curses unfolding across the white-on-green plane and echoing off each tarp. Soon they'll all go inside for the winter. Schtitt will yield and let them inflate the E.T.A. Lung over the sixteen Center Courts; it's like a barn-raising, inflation-day; it's communal and fun, and they'll take down the central fences and outdoor night-lamps and unbolt all the posts into sections and stack them and store them, and the TesTar and ATHSCME guys will come up in vans smoking cigarettes and squinting with weary expertise at tubes of plans in draftsman-blue, and there'll be one and sometimes two ATHSCME helicopters w/ slings and grappling hooks for the Lung's dome and nacelle; and Schtitt and deLint will let the younger E.T.A.s get the infrared indoor heaters out of the same corrugated shed the disassembled fences and lamps will go in, leaf-cutter-ant- or Korean-like armies of 14- and 16-year-olds carrying sections and heaters and Gore-Tex swatches and long halo-lithiated bulbs while the 18s get to sit on canvas chairs and kibitz because they did their leaf-cutter Lung-raising bits at 13-16 already. Two TesTar guys'll supervise Otis P. Lord and all this year's conspicuous tech-wonks in mounting the heaters and stringing the lights and running coaxial shunts with ceramic jacks between the Pump Room's main breaker and the Sunstrand grid and booting up the circulation-fans and pneumatic hoists that'll raise the Lung to the inflated shape of a distended igloo, sixteen courts in four rows of four, enclosed and warmed by nothing but fibrous Gore-Tex and AC current and an enormous ATHSCME Exhaust-Flow Effectuator that an ATHSCME crew in one of the ATHSCME helicopters will bring in in a sling and cable and mount and secure on the Lung's nipply nacelle at the top of the inflating dome. And that first night after Inflation, traditionally the fourth Monday of November, all the upperclass 18s so inclined will crank up the infrareds and get high and eat low-lipid microwave pizza and play all night, sweating magnificently, sheltered for the winter atop Enfield's level-headed hill.

Schacht stands back in the deuce court and lets his guy warm up his serves, oddly flat and low-margin for a nervous touch-artist. Schacht bloops each return up with severe backspin so the balls'll roll back to him and he can serve them back to his guy, also warming up. The warm-up routine has become automatic and requires no attention. Way up on #1, Schacht sees John Wayne just plaster a backhand cross-court. Wayne hits it so hard a little mushroom cloud of green fuzz hangs in the air where ball had met strings. Their cards were too far to read in the sour-apple light, but you could tell by the way Port Washington's best boy walked back to the baseline to take the next serve that his ass had already been presented to him. In a lot of junior matches everything past the fourth game or so is kind of a formality. Both players tend to know the overall score by then. The big picture. They'll have decided who's going to lose. Competitive tennis is largely mental, once you're at a certain plateau of skill and conditioning. Schtitt'd say *spiritual* instead of *mental*, but as far as Schacht can see it's the same thing. As Schacht sees it, Schtitt's philosophical stance is that to win enough of the time to be considered successful you have to both care a great deal about it and also not care about it at all.[89] Schacht does not care enough, probably, anymore, and has met his gradual displacement from E.T.A.'s A singles squad with an equanimity some E.T.A.'s thought was spiritual and others regarded as the surest sign of dicklessness and burnout. Only one or two people have ever used the word *brave* in connection with Schacht's radical reconfiguration after the things with the Crohn's Disease and knee. Hal Incandenza, who's probably as asymetrically hobbled on the care-too-much side as Schacht is on the not-enough, privately puts Schacht's laissez-faire down to some interior decline, some doom-gray surrender of his childhood's promise to adult gray mediocrity, and fears it; but since Schacht is an old friend and a dependable designated driver and has actually gotten pleasanter to be around since the knee — which Hal prays fervently that the ankle won't start being the size of a volleyball itself at the end of each outdoor day — Hal in a weird and deeper internal way almost somehow admires and envies the fact that Schacht's stoically committed himself to the oral professions and stopped dreaming of getting to the Show after graduation — an air of something other than failure about Schacht's not caring enough, something you can't quite define, the way you can't quite remember a word that you know you know, inside — Hal can't quite feel the contempt for Teddy Schacht's competitive slide that would be a pretty much natural contempt in one who cared so dreadfully secretly much, and so the two of them tend to settle for not talking about it, just as Schacht cheerfully wordlessly drives the tow truck on occasions when the rest of the crew are so incapacitated they'd have to hold one eye closed even to see an undoubled road, and consents w/o protest to pay retail for clean quarterly urine, and doesn't say a word about Hal's devolution from occasional tourist to subterranean compulsive, substance-wise, with his Pump Room visits and Visine, even though Schacht deep down believes that the substance-compulsion's strange apparent contribution to Hal's erumpent explosion up the rankings has got to be a temporary thing, that there's like a psychic credit-card bill for Hal in the mail, somewhere, coming, and is sad for him in advance about whatever's surely got to give, eventually. Though it won't be the Boards. Hal'll murder his Boards, and Schacht may well be among those jockeying to sit near him, he'd be the first to admit. On 2 Hal now kicks a second serve to the ad court with so much left-handed top on it that it almost kicks up over Port Washington's #2 guy's head. It's clearly carnage up there on Show Courts 1 and 2. Dr. Tavis will be irrepressible. The gallery is barely even applauding Wayne and Incandenza anymore; at a certain point it becomes like Romans applauding lions. All the coaches and staff and P.W.T.A. parents and civilians in the overhead gallery wear tennis outfits, the high white socks and tucked-in shirts of people who do not really play.

Schacht and his man play.

Both Pat Montesian and Gately's AA sponsor like to remind Gately how this new resident Geoffrey Day could end up being an invaluable teacher of patience and tolerance for him, Gately, as Ennet House Staff.

'So then at forty-six years of age I came here to learn to live by clichés,' is what Day says to Charlotte Treat right after Randy Lenz asked what time it was, again, at 0825. 'To turn my will and life over to the care of clichés. One day at a time. Easy does it. First things first. Courage is fear that has said its prayers. Ask for help. Thy will not mine be done. It works if you work it. Grow or go. Keep coming back.'

Poor old Charlotte Treat, needlepointing primly beside him on the old vinyl couch that just came from Goodwill, purses her lips. 'You need to ask for some gratitude.'

'Oh no but the point is I've already been fortunate enough to *receive* gratitude.' Day crosses one leg over the other in a way that inclines his whole little soft body toward her. 'For which, believe you me, I'm grateful. I cultivate gratitude. That's part of the system of clichés I'm here to live by. An attitude of gratitude. A grateful drunk will never drink. I know the actual cliché is "A grateful *heart* will never drink," but since organs can't properly be said to imbibe and I'm still afflicted with just enough self-will to decline to live by utter non sequiturs, as opposed to just good old clichés, I'm taking the liberty of light amendment.' He gives with this a look like butter wouldn't melt. 'Albeit grateful amendment, of course.'

Charlotte Treat looks over to Gately for some sort of help or Staff enforcement of dogma. The poor bitch is clueless. All of them are clueless, still. Gately reminds himself that he too is probably mostly still clueless, still, even after all these hundreds of days. 'I Didn't Know That I Didn't Know' is another of the slogans that looks so shallow for a while and then all of a sudden drops off and deepens like the lobster-waters off the North Shore. As Gately fidgets his way through daily A.M. meditation he always tries to remind himself daily that this is all an Ennet House residency is supposed to do: buy these poor yutzes some time, some thin pie-slice of abstinent time, till they can start to get a whiff of what's true and deep, almost magic, under the shallow surface of what they're trying to do.

'I cultivate it assiduously. I do special gratitude exercises at night up there in the room. Gratitude-Ups, you could call them. Ask Randy over there if I don't do them like clockwork. Diligently. Sedulously.'

'Well 'it's true is all,' Treat sniffs. 'About gratitude.'

Everybody else except Gately, lying on the old other couch opposite them, is ignoring this exchange, watching an old InterLace cartridge whose tracking is a little messed up so that staticky stripes eat at the screen's picture's bottom and top. Day is not done talking. Pat M. encourages newer Staff to think of residents they'd like to bludgeon to death as valuable teachers of patience, tolerance, self-discipline, restraint.

Day is not done talking. 'One of the exercises is being grateful that life is so much *easier* now. I used sometimes to think. I used to think in long compound sentences with subordinate clauses and even the odd polysyllable. Now I find I needn't. Now I live by the dictates of macramé samplers ordered from the back-page ad of an old *Reader's Digest* or *Saturday Evening Post*. Easy does it. Remember to remember. But for the grace of capital-g God. Turn it over. Terse, hard-boiled. Monosyllabic. Good old Norman Rockwell–Paul Harvey wisdom. I walk around with my arms out straight in front of me and recite these clichés. In a monotone. No inflection necessary. Could that be one? Could that be added to the cliché-pool? "*No inflection necessary*"? Too many syllables, probably.'

Randy Lenz says 'I ain't got time for this shit.'

Poor old Charlotte Treat, all of nine weeks clean, is trying to look primmer and primmer. She looks again over to Gately, lying on his back, taking up the living room's whole other sofa, one sneaker up on the sofa's square frayed fabric arm-thing, his eyes almost closed. Only Staff get to lie on the couches.

'Denial,' Charlotte finally says, 'is not a river in Egypt.'

'Hows about the both of you shut the fuck up,' says Emil Minty.

Geoffrey (not Geoff, Geoffrey) Day has been at Ennet House six days. He came from Roxbury's infamous Dimock Detox, where he was the only white person, which Gately bets must have been broadening for him. Day has a squished blank smeared flat face, one requiring like great self-effort to like, and eyes that are just starting to lose the nictitated glaze of early sobriety. Day is a newcomer and a wreck. A red-wine-and-Quaalude man who finally nodded out in late October and put his Saab through the window of a Malden sporting goods store and then got out and proceeded to browse until the Finest came and got him. Who taught something horseshit-sounding like social historicity or historical sociality at some jr. college up the Expressway in Medford and came in saying on his Intake he also manned the helm of a Scholarly Quarterly. Word for word, the House Manager had said: '*manned the helm*' and '*Scholarly*.' His Intake estimated that Day's been in and out of a blackout for most of the last several years, and his wiring is still as they say a bit frayed. His detox at Dimock, where they barely have the resources to give you a Librium if you start to D.T., must have been just real grim, because Geoffrey D. alleges it never happened: now his story is he just strolled into Ennet House on a lark one day from his home 10+ clicks away in Malden and found the place too hilariously egregulous to want to ever leave. It's the newcomers with some education that are the worst, according to Gene M. They identify their whole selves with their head, and the Disease makes its command headquarters in the head.[90] Day wears chinos of indeterminate hue, brown socks with black shoes, and shirts that Pat Montesian had described in the Intake as 'Eastern-European-type Hawaiian shirts.' Day's now on the vinyl couch with Charlotte Treat after breakfast in the Ennet House living room with a few of the other residents that either aren't working or don't have to be at work early, and with Gately, who'd pulled an all-night Dream Duty shift out in the front office till 0400, then got temp-relieved by Johnette Foltz so he could go to work janitoring down at the Shattuck Shelter till 0700, then came and hauled ass back up here and took back over so's that Johnette could go off to her NA thing with a bunch of NA people in what looked like a dune buggy if the dunes in question were in Hell, and is now, Gately, trying to unclench and center himself inside by tracing the cracks in the paint of the living room ceiling with his eyes. Gately often feels a terrible sense of loss, narcotics-wise, in the A.M., still, even after this long clean. His sponsor over at the White Flag Group says some people never get over the loss of what they'd thought was their one true best friend and lover; they just have to pray daily for acceptance and the brass danglers to move forward through the grief and loss, to wait for time to harden the scab. The sponsor, Ferocious Francis G., doesn't give Gately one iona of shit for feeling some negative feelings about it: on the contrary, he commends Gately for his candor in breaking down and crying like a baby and telling him about it early one A.M. over the pay phone, the sense of loss. It's a myth no one misses it. Their particular Substance. Shit, you wouldn't need help if you didn't miss it. You just have to Ask For Help and like Turn It Over, the loss and pain, to Keep Coming, show up, pray, Ask For Help. Gately rubs his eye. Simple advice like this does seem like a lot of clichés — Day's right about how it seems. Yes, and if Geoffrey Day keeps on steering by the way things seem to him then he's a dead man for sure. Gately's already watched dozens come through here and leave early and go back Out There and then go to jail or die. If Day ever gets lucky and breaks down, finally, and comes to the front office at night to scream that he can't take it anymore and clutch at Gately's pantcuff and blubber and beg for help at any cost, Gately'll get to tell Day the thing is that the clichéd directives are a lot more deep and hard to actually *do*. To try and live by instead of just say. But he'll only get to say it if Day comes and asks. Personally, Gately gives Geoffrey D. like a month at the outside before he's back tipping his hat to parking meters. Except who is Gately to judge who'll end up getting the Gift of the program v. who won't, he needs to remember. He tries to feel like Day is teaching him patience and tolerance. It takes great patience and tolerance not to want to punt the soft little guy out into the Comm. Ave. ravine and open up his bunk to somebody that really desperately wants it, the Gift. Except who is Gately to think he can know who wants it and who doesn't, deep down. Gately's arm is behind his head, up against the sofa's other arm. The old D.E.C. viewer is on to something violent and color-enhanced Gately neither sees nor hears. It was part of his gifts as a burglar: he can sort of turn his attention on and off like a light. Even when he was a resident here he'd had this prescient housebreaker's ability to screen input, to do sensory triage. It was one reason he'd even been able to stick out his nine residential months here with twenty-one other newly detoxed housebreakers, hoods, whores, fired execs, Avon ladies, subway musicians, beer-bloated construction workers, vagrants, indignant car salesmen, bulimic trauma-mamas, bunko artists, mincing pillow-biters, North End hard guys, pimply kids with electric nose-rings, denial-ridden housewives and etc., all jonesing and head-gaming and mokus and grieving and basically whacked out and producing nonstopping output 24-7-365.

At some point in here Day's saying 'So bring on the lobotomist, bring him on I say!'

Except Gately's own counselor when he was a resident here, Eugenio Martinez, one of the volunteer alumni counselors, a one-eared former boiler-room bunko man and now a cellular-phone retailer who'd hooked up with the House under the original founder Guy That Didn't Even Use His First Name, and had about ten years clean, Gene M. did — Eugenio'd lovingly confronted Gately early on about his special burglar's selective attention and about how it could be dangerous because how can you be sure it's you doing the screening and not The Spider. Gene called the Disease The Spider and talked about Feeding The Spider versus Starving The Spider and so on and so forth. Eugenio M. had called Gately into the House Manager's back office and said what if Don's screening input turned out to be Feeding The Old Spider and what about an experimental unscreening of input for a while. Gately had said he'd do his best to try and'd come back out and tried to watch a Spont-Dissem of the Celtics while two resident pillow-biters from the Fenway were having this involved conversation about some third fag having to go in and get the skeleton of some kind of fucking rodent removed from inside their butthole.[91] The unscreening experiment had lasted half an hour. This was right before Gately got his 90-day chip and wasn't exactly wrapped real tight or real tolerant, still. Ennet House this year is nothing like the freakshow it was when Gately went through.

Gately has been completely Substance-free for 421 days today.

Ms. Charlotte Treat, with a carefully made-up, ruined face, is watching the viewer's stripe-shot cartridge while she needlepoints something. Conversation between her and Geoffrey D. has mercifully petered out. Day is scanning the room for somebody else to engage and piss off so he can prove to himself he doesn't fit in here and stay separated off isolated inside himself and maybe get them so pissed off there's a beef and he gets bounced out, Day, and it won't be his fault. You can almost hear his Disease chewing away inside his head, feeding. Emil Minty, Randy Lenz, and Bruce Green are also in the room, sprawled in spring-shot chairs, lighting one gasper off the end of the last, their postures the don't-fuck-with-me slouch of the streets that here makes their bodies' texture somehow hard to distinguish from that of the chairs. Nell Gunther is sitting at the long table in the doorless dining room that opens out right off the old D.E.C. fold-out TP's pine stand, whitening under her nails with a manicure pencil amid the remains of something she's eaten that involved serious syrup. Burt F. Smith is also in there, way down by himself at the table's far end, trying to saw at a waffle with a knife and fork attached to the stumps of his wrists with Velcro bands. A long-time-ago former DMV Driver's License Examiner, Burt F. Smith is forty-five and looks seventy, has almost all-white hair that's waxy and yellow from close-order smoke, and finally got into Ennet House last month after nine months stuck in the Cambridge City Shelter. Burt F. Smith's story is he's making his like fiftieth-odd stab at sobriety in AA. Once devoutly R.C., Burt F.S. has potentially lethal trouble with Faith In A Loving God ever since the R.C. Church apparently granted his wife an annulment in like B.S.

'99 after fifteen years of marriage. Then for several years a rooming-house drunk, which on Gately's view is about like one step up from a homeless-person-type drunk. Burt F.S. got mugged and beaten half to death in Cambridge on Xmas Eve of last year, and left there to like freeze there, in an alley, in a storm, and ended up losing his hands and feet. Doony Glynn's been observed telling Burt F.S. things like that there's some new guy coming into the Disabled Room off Pat's office with Burt F.S. who's without not only hands and feet but arms and legs and even a head and who communicates by farting in Morris Code. This sally earned Glynn three days Full-House Restriction and a week's extra Chore for what Johnette Foltz described in the Log as 'XSive Cruetly.' There is a vague intestinal moaning in Gately's right side. Watching Burt F. Smith smoke a Benson & Hedges by holding it between his stumps with his elbows out like a guy with pruning shears is an adventure in fucking pathos as far as Gately's concerned. And Geoffrey Day cracks wise about There But for Grace. And forget about what it's like trying to watch Burt F. Smith try and light a match.

Gately, who's been on live-in Staff here four months now, believes Charlotte Treat's devotion to needlepoint is suspect. All those needles. In and out of all that thin sterile-white cotton stretched drum-tight in its round frame. The needle makes a kind of thud and squeak when it goes in the cloth. It's not much like the soundless pop and slide of a real cook-and-shoot. But still. She takes such great care.

Gately wonders what color he'd call the ceiling if forced to call it a color. It's not white and it's not gray. The brown-yellow tones are from high-tar gaspers; a pall hangs up near the ceiling even this early in the new sober day. Some of the drunks and tranq-jockeys stay up most of the night, joggling their feet and chain-smoking, even though there's no cartridges or music allowed after 0000h. He has that odd House Staffer's knack, Gately, already, after four months, of seeing everything in both living and dining rooms without really looking. Emil Minty, a hard-core smack-addict punk here for reasons nobody can quite yet pin down, is in an old mustard-colored easy chair with his combat boots up on one of the standing ashtrays, which is tilting not quite enough for Gately to tell him to watch out, please. Minty's orange mohawk and the shaved skull around it are starting to grow out brown, which is just not a pleasant sight in the morning at all. The other ashtray on the floor by his chair is full of the ragged little new moons of bitten nails, which has got to mean that the Hester T. that he'd ordered to bed at 0230 was right back down here in the chair going at her nails again the second Gately left to mop shit at the Shelter. When he's up all night Gately's stomach gets all tight and acidy, from either all the coffee maybe or just staying up. Minty's been on the streets since he was like sixteen, Gately can tell: he's got that sooty complexion homeless guys get where the soot has insinuated itself into the dermal layer and thickened, making Minty look somehow upholstered. And the big-armed driver for Leisure Time Ice, the quiet kid, Green, a garbage-head all-Substance-type kid, maybe twenty-one, face very slightly smunched in on one side, wears sleeveless khaki shirts and had lived in a trailer in that apocalyptic Enfield trailer park out near the Allston Spur; Gately likes Green because he seems to have got sense enough to keep his map shut when he's got nothing important to say, which is basically all the time. The tattoo on the kid's right tricep is a spear-pierced heart over the hideous name *MILDRED BONK,* who Bruce G. told him was a ray of living light and a dead ringer for the late lead singer of The Fiends in Human Shape and his dead heart's one love ever, and who took their daughter and left him this summer for some guy that told her he ranched fucking longhorn cows east of Atlantic City NJ. He's got, even by Ennet House standards, major-league sleep trouble, Green, and he and Gately play cribbage sometimes in the wee dead hours, a game Gately picked up in jail. Burt F.S. is now hunched in a meaty coughing fit, his elbows out and his forehead purple. No sign of Hester Thrale, nailbiter and something Pat calls Borderline. Gately can see everything without moving or moving his head or either eye. Also in here is Randy Lenz, who Lenz is a small-time organic-coke dealer who wears sportcoats rolled up over his parlor-tanned forearms and is always checking his pulse on the inside of his wrists. It's come out that Lenz is of keen interest to both sides of the law because this past May he'd apparently all of a sudden lost all control and holed up all of a sudden in a Charlestown motel and free-based most of a whole 100 grams he'd been fronted by a suspiciously trusting Brazilian in what Lenz didn't know was supposed to have been a D.E.A. sting operation in the South End. Having screwed both sides in what Gately secretly views as a delicious fuck-up, Randy Lenz has, since May, been the most wanted he's probably ever been. He is seedily handsome in the way of pimps and low-level coke dealers, muscular in the MP-ish way that certain guys' muscles look muscular but can't really lift anything, with complexly gelled hair and the little birdlike head-movements of the deeply vain. One forearm's hair has a little hairless patch, which Gately knows well spells knife-owner, and if there's one thing Gately's never been able to stomach it's a knife-owner, little swaggery guys that always queer a square beef and come up off the ground with a knife where you have to get cut to take it away from them. Lenz is teaching Gately reserved politeness to people you pretty much want to beat up on sight. It's pretty obvious to everybody except Pat Montesian — whose odd gullibility in the presence of human sludge, though, Gately needs to try to remember had been one of the reasons why he himself had got into Ennet House, originally — obvious that Lenz is here mostly just to hide out: he rarely leaves the House except under compulsion, avoids windows, and travels to the nightly required AA/NA meetings in a disguise that makes him look like Cesar Romero after a terrible accident;

and then he always wants to walk back to the House solo afterward, which is not encouraged. Lenz is seated low in the northeasternmost corner of an old fake-velour love seat he's jammed in the northeasternmost corner of the living room. Randy Lenz has a strange compulsive need to be north of everything, and possibly even northeast of everything, and Gately has no clue what it's about but observes Lenz's position routinely for his own interest and files. Lenz's leg, like Ken Erdedy's leg, never stops joggling; Day claims it joggles even worse in sleep. Another gurgle and abdominal chug for Don G., lying there. Charlotte Treat has violently red hair. As in hair the color of like a red crayon. The reason she doesn't have to work an outside menial job is she's got some strain of the Virus or like H.I.V. Former prostitute, reformed. Why do prostitutes when they get straight always try and get so prim? It's like long-repressed librarian-ambitions come flooding out. Charlotte T. has a cut-rate whore's hard half-pretty face, her eyes lassoed with shadow around all four lids. Her also with a case of the dermal-layer sooty complexion. The riveting thing about Treat is how her cheeks are deeply pitted in these deep trenches that she packs with foundation and tries to cover over with blush, which along with the hair gives her the look of a mean clown. The ghastly wounds in her cheeks look for all the world like somebody got at her with a woodburning kit at some point in her career path. Gately would rather not know.

Don Gately is almost twenty-nine and sober and just huge. Lying there gurgling and inert with a fluttery-eyed smile. One shoulder blade and buttock pooch out over the side of a sofa that sags like a hammock. Gately looks less built than poured, the smooth immovability of an Easter Island statue. It would be nice if intimidating size wasn't one of the major factors in a male alumni getting offered the male live-in Staff job here, but there you go. Don G. has a massive square head made squarer-looking by the Prince Valiantish haircut he tries to maintain himself in the mirror, to save $: room and board aside — plus the opportunity for Service — he makes very little as an Ennet House Staffer, and is paying off restitution schedules in three different district courts. He has the fluttery white-eyed smile now of someone who's holding himself just over the level of doze. Pat Montesian is due in at 0900 and Don G. can't go to bed until she arrives because the House Manager has driven Jennifer Belbin to a court appearance downtown and he's the only Staffer here. Foltz, the female live-in Staffer, is at a Narcotics Anonymous convention in Hartford for the long Interdependence Day weekend. Gately personally is not hot on NA: so many relapses and unhumble returns, so many war stories told with nondisguised bullshit pride, so little emphasis on Service or serious Message; all these people in leather and metal, preening. Rooms full of Randy Lenzes, all hugging each other, pretending they don't miss the Substance. Rampant newcomer-fucking. There's a difference between abstinence v. recovery, Gately knows. Except of course who's Gately to judge what works for who. He just knows what seems like it works for him today: AA's tough Enfield-Brighton love, the White Flag Group, old guys with suspendered bellies and white crew cuts and geologic amounts of sober time, the Crocodiles, that'll take your big square head off if they sense you're getting complacent or chasing tail or forgetting that your life still hangs in the balance every fucking day. White Flag newcomers so crazed and sick they can't sit and have to pace at the meeting's rear, like Gately when he first came. Retired old kindergarten teachers in polyresin slacks and a pince-nez who bake cookies for the weekly meeting and relate from behind the podium how they used to blow bartenders at closing for just two more fingers in a paper cup to take home against the morning's needled light. Gately, albeit an oral narcotics man from way back, has committed himself to AA. He drank his fair share, too, he figures, after all.

Exec. Director Pat M. is due in at 0900 and has application interviews with three people, 2F and 1M, who better be showing up soon, and Gately will answer the door when they don't know enough to just come in and will say Welcome and get them a cup of coffee if he judges them able to hold it. He'll get them aside and tip them off to be sure to pet Pat M.'s dogs during the interview. They'll be sprawled all over the front office, sides heaving, writhing and biting at themselves. He'll tell them it's a proved fact that if Pat's dogs like you, you're in. Pat M. has directed Gately to tell appliers this, and then if the appliers do actually pet the dogs — two hideous white golden retrievers with suppurating scabs and skin afflictions, plus one has Grand Mall epilepsy — it'll betray a level of desperate willingness that Pat says is just about all she goes by, deciding.

A nameless cat oozes by on the broad windowsill above the back of the fabric couch. Animals here come and go. Alumni adopt them or they just disappear. Their fleas tend to remain. Gately's intestines moan. Boston's dawn coming back on the Green Line this morning was chemically pink, trails of industrial exhaust blowing due north. The nail-parings in the ash-tray on the floor are, he realizes now, too big to be from fingernails. These bitten arcs are broad and thick and a deep autumnal yellow. He swallows hard. He'd tell Geoffrey Day how, even if they are just clichés, clichés are (a) soothing, and (b) remind you of common sense, and (c) license the universal assent that drowns out silence; and (4) silence is deadly, pure Spider-food, if you've got the Disease. Gene M. says you can spell the Disease DIS-EASE, which sums the basic situation up nicely. Pat has a meeting at the Division of Substance Abuse Services in Government Center at noon she needs to be reminded about. She can't read her own handwriting, which the stroke affected her handwriting. Gately envisions going around having to find out who's biting their fucking toenails in the living room and putting the disgusting toenail-bits in the ashtray at like 0500. Plus House regs prohibit bare feet anyplace downstairs. There's a pale-brown water stain on the ceiling over Day and Treat the almost exact shape of Florida. Randy Lenz has issues with Geoffrey Day because Day is glib and a teacher at a Scholarly Journal's helm. This threatens the self-concept of a Randy Lenz that thinks of himself as a kind of hiply sexy artist-intellectual. Small-time dealers never conceptualize themselves as just small-time dealers, kind of like whores never do. For *Occupation* on his Intake form Lenz had put *free lance script writer*. And he makes a show of that he reads. For the first week here in July he'd held the books upside-down in the northeast corner of whatever room. He had a gigantic Medical Dictionary he'd haul down and smoke and read until Annie Parrot the Asst. Manager had to tell him not to bring it down anymore because it was fucking with Morris Hanley's mind. At which juncture he quit reading and started talking, making everybody nostalgic for when he just sat there and read. Geoffrey D. has issues with Randy L., also, you can tell: there's a certain way they don't quite look at each other. And so now of course they're mashed together in the 3-Man together, since three guys in one night missed curfew and came in without one normal-sized pupil between them and refused Urines and got bounced on the spot, and so Day gets moved up in his first week from the 5-Man room to the 3-Man. Seniority comes quick around here. Past Minty, down at the dining-room table's end, Burt F.S.'s still coughing, still hunched over, his face a dusky purple, and Nell G. is behind him pounding him on the back so that it keeps sending him forward over his ashtray, and he's waving one stump vaguely over his shoulder to try and signal her to quit. Lenz and Day: a beef may be brewing: Day'll try to goad Lenz into a beef that'll be public enough so he doesn't get hurt but does get bounced, and then he can leave treatment and go back to Chianti and 'Ludes and getting assaulted by sidewalks and make out like the relapse is Ennet House's fault and never have to confront himself or his Disease. To Gately, Day is like a wide-open interactive textbook on the Disease. One of Gately's jobs is to keep an eye on what's possibly brewing among residents and let Pat or the Manager know and try to smooth things down in advance if possible. The ceiling's color could be called dun, if forced. Someone has farted; no one knows just who, but this isn't like a normal adult place where everybody coolly pretends a fart didn't happen; here everybody has to make their little comment.

Time is passing. Ennet House reeks of passing time. It is the humidity of early sobriety, hanging and palpable. You can hear ticking in clockless rooms here. Gately changes the angle of one sneaker, puts the other arm behind his head. His head has real weight and pressure. Randy Lenz's obsessive compulsions include the need to be north, a fear of disks, a tendency to constantly take his own pulse, a fear of all forms of timepieces, and a need to always know the time with great precision.

'Day man you got the time maybe real quick?' Lenz. For the third time in half an hour. Patience, tolerance, compassion, self-discipline, restraint.

Gately remembers his first six months here straight: he'd felt the sharp edge of every second that went by. And the freakshow dreams. Nightmares beyond the worst D.T.s you'd ever heard about. A reason for a night-shift Staffer in the front office is so somebody's there for the residents to talk at when — not if, when — when the freakshow dreams ratchet them out of bed at like 0300. Nightmares about relapsing and getting high, not getting high but having everybody think you're high, getting high with your alcoholic mom and then killing her with a baseball bat. Whipping the old Unit out for a spot-Urine and starting up and flames coming shooting out. Getting high and bursting into flames. Having a waterspout shaped like an enormous Talwin suck you up inside. A vehicle explodes in an enhanced bloom of sooty flame on the D.E.C. viewer, its hood up like an old pop-tab.

Day's making a broad gesture out of checking his watch. 'Right around 0830, fella.'

Randy L.'s fine nostrils flare and whiten. He stares straight ahead, eyes narrowed, fingers on his wrist. Day purses his lips, leg joggling. Gately hangs his head over the arm of the sofa and regards Lenz upside-down.

'That look on your map there mean something there, Randy? Are you like communicating something with that look?'

'Does anybody maybe know the time a little more *exactly* is what I'm wondering, Don, since Day doesn't.'

Gately checks his own cheap digital, head still hung over the sofa's arm. 'I got 0832:14, 15, 16, Randy.'

''ks a lot, D.G. man.'

So and now Day has that same flared narrow look for Lenz. 'We've been over this, friend. Amigo. Sport. You do this all the time with me. Again I'll say it — I don't have a digital watch. This is a fine old antique watch. It points. A memento of far better days. It's not a digital watch. It's not a cesium-based atomic clock. It points, with hands. See, Spiro Agnew here has two little arms: they point, they suggest. It's not a sodding stopwatch for life. Lenz, get a watch. Am I right? Why don't you just get a watch, Lenz. Three people I happen to know of for a fact have offered to get you a watch and you can pay them back whenever you feel comfortable about poking your nose out and investigating the work-a-world. Get a watch. Obtain a watch. A fine, digital, incredibly *wide* watch, about five times the width of your wrist, so you have to hold it like a falconer, and it treats time like pi.'

'Easy does it,' Charlotte Treat half-sings, not looking up from her needle and frame.

Day looks around at her. 'I don't believe I was speaking to you in any way shape or form.'

Lenz stares at him. 'If you're trying to fuck with me, brother.' He shakes his fine shiny head. 'Big mistake.'

'Oo I'm all atremble. I can barely hold my arm steady to read my watch.'

'Big big big *real* big mistake.'

'Peace on earth good will toward men,' says Gately, back on his back, smiling at the dun cracked ceiling. He's the one who'd farted.

They returned from Long Island bearing their shields rather than upon them, as they say. John Wayne and Hal Incandenza lost only five total games between them in singles. The A doubles had resembled a spatterpainting. And the B teams, especially the distaffs, had surpassed themselves. The whole P.W.T.A. staff and squad had had to sing a really silly song. Coyle and Troeltsch didn't win, and Teddy Schacht had, incredibly, lost to his squat spin-doctory opponent in three sets, despite the kid's debilitating nerves at crucial junctures. The fact that Schacht wasn't all that upset got remarked on by staff. Schacht and a conspicuously energized Jim Troeltsch rallied for the big win in 18-A #2 dubs, though. Troeltsch's disconnected microphone mysteriously disappeared from his gear bag during post-doubles showers, to the rejoicing of all. Pemulis's storky intense two-hands-off-both-sides opponent had gotten weirdly lethargic and then disoriented in the second set after Pemulis had lost the first in a tie-break. After the kid had delayed play for several minutes claiming the tennis balls were too pretty to hit, P.W.T.A. trainers had conducted him gently from the court, and the Peemster got 'V.D.,' which is jr.-circuit argot for a Victory by Default. The fact that Pemulis hadn't walked around with his chest out recounting the win for any E.T.A. females got remarked on only by Hal and T. Axford. Schacht was in too much knee-pain to remark on much of anything, and Schtitt had E.T.A.'s Barry Loach inject the big purple knee with something that made Schacht's eyes roll up in his head.

Then during the post-meet mixer and dance Pemulis's defaulted opponent ate from the hors d' oeuvres table without using utensils or at one point even hands, did a disco number when there wasn't any music going, and was finally heard telling the Port Washington Headmaster's wife that he'd always wanted to do her from behind. Pemulis spent a lot of time whistling and staring innocently up at the pre-fab ceiling.

The bus for all the 18's squads was warm and there were little nozzles of light over your seat that you could either have on to do homework or shut off and sleep. Troeltsch, left eye ominously nystagmic, pretended to recap the day's match highlights for a subscription audience, speaking earnestly into his fist. The C team's Stockhausen was pretending to sing opera. Hal and Tall Paul Shaw were each reading an SAT prep-guide. A good quarter of the bus was yellow-highlighting copies of E. A. Abbott's inescapable-at-

E.T.A. book *Flatland* for either Flottman or Chawaf or Thorp. An elongated darkness with assorted shapes melted by, plus long gauntlets, near exits, of tall Interstatish lamps laying down cones of dirty-looking sodium light. The ghastly sodium lamplight made Mario Incandenza happy to be in his little cone of white inside light. Mario sat next to K. D. Coyle — who was kind of mentally slow, especially after a hard loss — and they played rock-paper-scissors for two hundred clicks or more, not saying anything, engrossed in trying to locate patterns in each other's rhythms of choices of shapes, which they both decided there weren't any. Two or three upperclassmen in Levy-Richardson-O'Byrne-Chawaf's Disciplinary Lit. were slumped over Goncharov's *Oblomov*, looking very unhappy indeed. Charles Tavis sat way in the back with John Wayne and beamed and spoke nonstop in hushed tones to Wayne as the Canadian stared out the window. DeLint was with the 16's one bus back; he'd been ragging Stice's and Kornspan's asses since their doubles, which it looked like they practically gave away. The bus was Schtittless: Schtitt always found a private mysterious way back, then appeared at dawn drills with deLint and elaborate work-ups of everything that had gone wrong the day before. He was particularly shrill and insistent and negative after they'd won something. Schacht sat listing to port and didn't respond when hands were waved in front of his face, and Axford and Struck started kibitzing Barry Loach about their knees were feeling punk as well. The luggage rack over everyone's heads bristled with grips and coverless strings, and liniment and tincture of benzoin had been handed out and liberally applied, so the warm air became complexly spiced. Everybody was tired in a good way.

The homeward ride's camaraderie was marred only by the fact that someone near the back of the bus started the passing around of a Gothic-fonted leaflet offering the kingdom of prehistoric England to the man who could pull Keith Freer out of Bernadette Longley. Freer had been discovered by prorector Mary Esther Thode more or less Xing poor Bernadette Longley under an Adidas blanket in the very back seat on the bus trip to the East Coast Clays in Providence in September, and it had been a nasty scene, because there were some basic Academy-license rules that it was just unacceptable to flout under the nose of staff. Keith Freer was deeply asleep when the leaflet was getting passed around, but Bernadette Longley wasn't, and when the leaflet hit the front half where all the females now had to sit since September she'd buried her face in her hands and flushed even on the back of her pretty neck, and her doubles partner[92] came all the way back to where Jim Struck and Michael Pemulis were sitting and told them in no uncertain terms that somebody on this bus was so immature it was really sad.

Charles Tavis was irrepressible. He did a Pierre Trudeau impersonation no one except the driver was old enough to laugh at. And the whole mammoth travelling squad, three buses' worth, got to stop and have the Megabreakfast at Denny's, over next to Empire Waste, at like 0030, when they got in.

O

Hal's eldest brother Orin Incandenza got out of competitive tennis when Hal was nine and Mario nearly eleven. This was during the period of great pre-Experialist upheaval and the emergence of the fringe C.U.S.P. of Johnny Gentle, Famous Crooner, and the tumescence of O.N.A.N.ism. At late seventeen, Orin was ranked in the low 70s nationally; he was a senior; he was at that awful age for a low-70s player where age eighteen and the terminus of a junior career are looming and either: (1) you're going to surrender your dreams of the Show and go to college and play college tennis; or (2) you're going to get your full spectrum of gram-negative and cholera and amoebic-dysentery shots and try to eke out some kind of sad diasporic existence on a Eurasian satellite pro tour and try to hop those last few competitive plateaux up to Show-caliber as an adult; or (3) or you don't know what you're going to do; and it's often an awful time.[93]

E.T.A. tries to dilute the awfulness a little by letting eight or nine post-graduates stay on for two years and serve in deLint's platoon of prorectors[94] in exchange for room and board and travel expenses to small sad satellite tourneys, and Orin's being directly related to E.T.A. Administration obviously gave him kind of a lock on a prorector appointment if he wanted it, but a prorector's job was only for maybe at most a few years, and was regarded as sad and purgatorial . . . and then of course what then, what are you going to do after *that*, etc.

Orin's decision to attend college pleased his parents a great deal, though Mrs. Avril Incandenza, especially, had gone out of her way to make it clear that whatever Orin decided to do would please them because they stood squarely behind and in full support of him, Orin, and any decision his very best thinking yielded. But they were still in favor of college, privately, you could tell. Orin was clearly not ever going to be a professional-caliber adult tennis player. His competitive peak had come at thirteen, when he'd gotten to the 14-and-Under quarterfinals of the National Clays in Indianapolis IN and in the Quarters had taken a set off the second seed; but starting soon after that he'd suffered athletically from the same delayed puberty that had compromised his father when Himself had been a junior player, and having boys he'd cleaned the clocks of at twelve and thirteen become now seemingly overnight mannish and deep-chested and hairy-legged and starting now to clean Orin's own clock at fourteen and fifteen — this had sucked some kind of competitive afflatus out of him, broken his tennis spirit, Orin, and his U.S.T.A. ranking had nosedived through three years until it levelled off somewhere in the low 70s, which meant that by age fifteen he wasn't even qualifying for the major events' main 64-man draw. When E.T.A. opened, his ranking among the Boys' 18s hovered around 10 and he was relegated to a middle spot on the Academy's B-squad, a mediocrity that sort of becalmed his verve even further. His style was essentially that of a baseliner, a counterpuncher, but without the return of serve or passing shots you need to stand much of a chance against a quality net-man. The E.T.A. rap on Orin was that he lobbed well but too often. He did have a phenomenal lob: he could hug the curve of the dome of the Lung and three times out of four nail a large-sized coin placed on the opposite baseline; he and Marlon Bain and two or three other marginal counterpunching boys at E.T.A. all had phenomenal lobs, honed through spare P.M. devoted more and more to Eschaton, which by the most plausible account a Croatian-refugee transfer had brought up from the Palmer Academy in Tampa. Orin was Eschaton's first game-master at E.T.A., where in the first Eschaton generations it was mostly marginal and deafflatusized upperclassmen who played.

College was the comparatively obvious choice, then, for Orin, as the time of decision drew nigh. Oblique family pressures aside, as a low-ranked player at E.T.A. he'd had stiffer academic demands than did those for whom the real Show had seemed like a viable goal. And the Eschatonology helped a great deal with the math/computer stuff E.T.A. tended to be a bit weak in, both Himself and Schtitt being at that point pretty anti-quantitative. His grades were solid. His board-scores weren't going to embarrass anybody. Orin was basically academically sound, especially for a somebody with a top-level competitive sport on his secondary transcript.

And you have to understand that mediocrity is relative in a sport like junior tennis. A national ranking of 74 in Boys 18-and-Under Singles, while mediocre by the standards of aspiring pros, is enough to make most college coaches' chins shiny. Orin got a couple Pac-10 offers. Big 10 offers. U. New Mexico actually hired a mariachi band that established itself under his dorm-room's window six nights running until Mrs. Incandenza got Himself to authorize 'F. D. V.' Harde to electrify the fences. Ohio State flew him out to Columbus for such a weekend of 'prospective orientation' that when Orin got back he had to stay in bed for three days drinking Alka-Seltzer with an ice pack on his groin. Cal-Tech offered him an ROTC waiver and A.P. standing in their elite Strategic Studies program after *Decade Magazine* had run a short interest-piece on Orin and the Croate and Eschaton's applied use of c:\Pink$_2$.[95]

Orin chose B.U. Boston U. Not a tennis power. Not in Cal-Tech's league academically. Not the sort of place that hires bands or flies you out for Roman orgies of inducement. And only just about three clicks down the hill and Comm. Ave. from E.T.A., west of the Bay, around the intersection of Commonwealth and Beacon, Boston. It was kind of a joint Orin Incandenza/ Avril Incandenza decision. Orin's Moms privately thought it was important for Orin to be away from home, psychologically speaking, but still to be able to come home whenever he wished. She put everything to Orin in terms of worrying that her concern over what'd be best for him psychologically might prompt her to overstep her maternal bounds and speak out of turn or give intrusive advice. According to all her lists and advantage-disadvantage charts, B.U. was from every angle far and away O.'s best choice, but to keep ever from overstepping or lobbying intrusively the Moms actually for six weeks would flee any room Orin entered, both hands clapped over her mouth. Orin had this way his face would get when she'd beg him not to let her influence his choice. It was during this period that Orin had characterized the Moms to Hal as a kind of contortionist with other people's bodies, which Hal's never been able to forget. Himself, from his own experience, probably thought it'd be better for Orin to get the hell out of Dodge altogether, do something Midwest or PAC, but he kept his own counsel. He never had to struggle not to overstep. He probably figured Orin was a big boy. This was four years and 30-some released entertainments before Himself put his head in a microwave oven, fatally. Then it turned out Avril's adoptive-slash-half-brother Charles Tavis, who at this time was back chairing A.S.A. at Throppinghamshire,[96] turned out to be old minor-sport-athletic-administration-network friends with Boston University's varsity tennis coach. Tavis flew down special on Air Canada to set up a meet between the four of them, Avril and son and Tavis and the B.U. tennis coach. The B.U. tennis coach was a septuagenaric Ivy League guy, one of those emptily craggily handsome old patrician men whose profile looks like it ought to be on a coin, who liked his 'lads' to wear all white and actually literally vault the net, win or lose, after matches. B.U. had only had a couple nationally ranked players, like ever, and that had been in the A.D. 1960s, way before this fashion-conscious guy's tenure; and when the coach saw Orin play he about fell over sideways. Recall how mediocrity is contextual. B.U.'s players all hailed (literally) from New England country clubs and wore ironed shorts and those faggy white tennis sweaters with that blood-colored stripe across the chest, and talked without moving their jaw, and played the sort of stiff and patrician serve-and-volley game you play if you've had lots of summer lessons and club round-robins but had never ever had to get out there and kill or die, psychically. Orin wore cut-off jeans and deck-sneakers w/o socks and yawned compulsively as he beat B.U.'s immaculately groomed #1 Singles man 2 and 0, hitting something like 40 offensive lobs for winners. Then at the four-way meeting Tavis arranged, the old B.U. coach showed up in L.L. Bean chinos and a Lacoste polo shirt and got a look at the size of Orin's left arm, and then at Orin's Moms in a tight black skirt and levantine jacket with kohl around her eyes and a moussed tower of hair and about fell back over sideways the other way. She had this effect on older men, somehow. Orin was in a position to dictate terms limited only by the parameters of B.U.'s own sports-budget marginality.[97] Orin signed a Letter of Intent accepting a Full Ride to B.U., plus books and a Hitachi lap-top w/ software and off-campus housing and living expenses and a lucrative work-study job where his job was to turn on the sprinklers every morning at the B.U. football Terriers' historic Nickerson Field, sprinklers that were already on automatic timers — the sprinkler job was B.U.'s tennis team's one plum, recruitment-wise. Charles Tavis — who at Avril's urging that fall cashed in his Canadian return ticket and stayed on as Assistant Headmaster to assist Orin's father's oversight of the Academy[98] in a progressively more and more total capacity as both in- and external travels took J. O. Incandenza away from Enfield more and more often — said 3½ years later that he'd never really expected a Thank-You from Orin anyway, for liaisoning with the B.U. tennis apparatus, that he wasn't in this for the Thank-Yous, that a person who did a service *for* somebody's gratitude was more like a 2-D cutout image of a person than a bona fide person; at least that's what he thought, he said; he said what did Avril and Hal and Mario think? was he a genuine 3-D person? was he perhaps just rationalizing away some legitimate hurt? did Orin maybe resent him for seeming to move in just as he, Orin, moved out? though surely not for Tavis's assuming more and more total control of the E.T.A. helm as J. O. Incandenza spent increasingly long hiati either off with Mario on shoots or editing in his room off the tunnel or in alcohol-rehabilitative facilities (13 of them over those final three years; Tavis has the Blue Cross statements right here), and even more surely not for the final felo de se anyone with any kind of denial-free sensitivity could have predicted for the past 3½ years; but, C.T. opined on 4 July Y.D.P.A.H. after Orin, who now had plenty of free summer time, declined his fifth straight invitation back to Enfield and his family's annual barbecue and Wimbledon-Finals-InterLace-spontaneous-dissemination-watching, Orin might just be harboring a resentment over C.T. moving into the Headmaster's office and changing the door's '*TE OCCIDERE POSSUNT . . .*' before Himself's microwaved head had even cooled, even if it was to take over a Headmaster's job that had been positively *keening* to have someone sedulous and brisk take over. Incandenza Himself having eliminated his own map on 1 April of the Year of the Trial-Size Dove Bar just as spring Letters of Intent were due from seniors who'd decided to slouch off to college tennis, just as invitations for the European-dirt-circuit Invitationals were pouring in all over Lateral Alice Moore's paraboloid desk, just as E.T.A.'s tax-exempt status was coming up for review before the M.D.R.[99] Exemption Panel, just as the school was trying to readjust to new O.N.A.N.T.A.-accreditation procedures after years of U.S.T.A.-accreditation procedures, just as litigations with Enfield Marine Public Health Hospital over alleged damage from E.T.A.'s initial hilltop-flattening and with Empire Waste Displacement over the flight-paths of Concavity-bound displacement vehicles were reaching the appellate stage, just as applications and fellowships for the Fall term were in the final stages of review and response. Well *someone* had had to come in and fill the void, and that person was going to have to be someone who could achieve Total Worry without becoming paralyzed by the worry or by the absence of minimal Thank-Yous for inglorious duties discharged in the stead of a person whose replacement was naturally, *naturally* going to come in for some resentment, Tavis felt, since since you can't get mad at a dying man, much less at a dead man, who better to assume the stress of filling in as anger-object than that dead man's thankless inglorious sedulous untiring 3-D bureaucratic assistant and replacement, whose own upstairs room was right next to the HmH's master bedroom and who might, by some grieving parties, be viewed as some kind of interloping usurper. Tavis had been ready for all this stress and more, he told the assembled Academy in preparatory remarks before last year's Fall term Convocation, speaking through amplification from the red-and-gray-bunting-draped crow's nest of Gerhardt Schtitt's transom down into the rows of folding chairs arranged all along the base- and sidelines of E.T.A. Courts 6–9: he not only fully accepted the stress and resentment, he said he had worked hard and would continue, in his dull quiet unromantic fashion, to work hard to remain open to it, to this resentment and sense of loss and irreplaceability, even after four years, to let everyone who needed to get it out get it out, the anger and resentment and possible contempt, for their own psychological health, since Tavis acknowledged publicly that there was more than enough on every E.T.A.'s plate to begin with as it was. The Convocation assembly was outside, on the Center Courts that in winter are sheltered by the Lung. It was 31 August in the Year of Dairy Products from the American Heartland, hot and muggy. Upperclassmen who'd heard these same basic remarks for the past four years made little razor-to-jugular and hangman's-noose-over-imaginary-crossbeam motions, listening. The sky overhead was glassy blue between clots and strings of clouds moving swiftly north. On Courts 30–32 the Applied Music Chorus guys kept up a background of '*Tenabrae Factae Sunt*,' sotto v. Everybody had had on the black armbands everybody still wore for functions and assemblies, to keep from forgetting; and the cotton U.S. and crisp nylon O.N.A.N. flags flapped and clanked halfway down the driveway's poles in remembrance. The Sunstrand Plaza still as of that fall hadn't yet found a way to muffle its East Newton ATHSCME fans, and Tavis's voice, which even with the police bullhorn tended to sound distant and receding anyway, wove in and out of the sound of the fans and the whump of the E.W.D. catapults and locusts' electric screams and the exhaust-rich hot rush of the summer wind up off Comm. Ave. and the car-horns and Green Line's trundle and clang and the clank of the flags' poles and wires, and everybody but the staff and littlest kids up front missed most of Tavis's explanation that Salic law'd nothing to do with the fact that there was simply no way the late Headmaster's beloved spouse and E.T.A. Dean of Academic Affairs and of Females Mrs. Avril Incandenza could have become Headmaster: how would 'Headmistress' have sounded? and she had the females and female prorectors and Harde's custodians to oversee, and curricula and assignments and schedules, and complex new O.N.A.N.T.A. accreditation to finalize the Kafkan application for, plus daily HmH-sterilization and personal-ablution rituals and the constant battle against anthracnose and dry-climate blight in the dining room's Green Babies, plus of course E.T.A. teaching duties on top of that, with the addition of untold sleepless nights with the Militant Grammarians of Massachusetts, the academic PAC that watchdogged media-syntax and invited florid fish-lipped guys from the French Academy to come speak with trilled r's on prescriptive preservation, and held marathon multireadings of e.g. Orwell's 'Politics and the English Language,' and whose Avril-chaired Tactical Phalanx (MGM's) was then (unsuccessfully, it turned out) court-fighting the new Gentle administration's Title-II/G-public-funded-library-phaseout-fat-trimming initiative, besides of course being practically laid out flat with grief and having to do all the emotional-processing work attendant on working through that kind of personal trauma, on top of all of which assuming the administrative tiller of E.T.A. itself would have been simply an insupportable burden she's thanked C.T. effusively on more than one public occasion for leaving the plush sinecure of Throppinghamshire and coming down to undertake the stress-ridden tasks not only of bureaucratic administration and insuring as smooth a transition as possible but of being there for the Incandenza family itself, w/ or w/o Thank-Yous, and for helping support not only Orin's career and institutional decision-processes but also for being there supportively for all involved when Orin made his seminal choice not to go ahead and play competitive college tennis after all, at B.U.

What happened was that by the third week of his freshman year Orin was attempting an extremely unlikely defection from college tennis to college football. The reason he gave his parents — Avril made it clear that the very last thing she wanted was to have any of her children feel they had to justify or explain to her any sort of abruptly or even bizarrely sudden major decision they might happen to make, and it's not clear that The Mad Stork had even nailed down the fact that Orin was still in metro-Boston at B.U. in the first place, but Orin still felt the move demanded some kind of explanation — was that fall tennis practice had started and he'd discovered that he was an empty withered psychic husk, competitively, burned out.

Orin had been playing, eating, sleeping, and excreting competitive tennis since his racquet was bigger than he was. He said he realized he had at eighteen become exactly as fine a tennis player as he was ever destined to be. The prospect of further improvement, a crucial carrot that Schtitt and the E.T.A. staff were expert at dangling, had disappeared at a fourth-rate tennis program whose coach had a poster of Bill Tilden in his office and offered critique on the level of Bend Your Knees and Watch The Ball. This was all actually true, the burn-out part, and totally swallowable as far as the from-tennis- part went, but Orin had a harder time explaining the decision's -to-football component, partly because he had only the vaguest understanding of U.S. football's rules, tactics, and nonmetric venue; he had in fact never once even touched a real pebbled-leather football before and, like most serious tennis players, had always found the misshapen ball's schizoid bounces disorienting and upsetting to look at. In fact the decision had very little to do with football at all, or with the reason Orin ended up starting to give before Avril all but demanded that he stop feeling in any way pressured or compelled to do anything more than ask for their utter and unqualified support of whatever actions he felt his personal happiness required, which is what she did when he started a slightly lyrical thing about the crash of pads and Sisboomba of Pep Squad and ambience of male bonding and smell of dewy turf at Nickerson Field at dawn when he showed up to watch the sprinklers come on and turn the lemon-wedge of risen sun into plumed rainbows of refraction. The refracting-sprinklers part was actually true, and that he liked it; the rest had been fiction.

The real football reason, in all its inevitable real-reason banality, was that, over the course of weeks of dawns of watching the autosprinklers and the Pep Squad (which really did practice at dawn) practices, Orin had developed a horrible schoolboy-grade crush, complete with dilated pupils and weak knees, for a certain big-haired sophomore baton-twirler he watched twirl and strut from a distance through the diffracted spectrum of the plumed sprinklers, all the way across the field's dewy turf, a twirler who'd attended a few of the All-Athletic-Team mixers Orin and his strabismic B.U. doubles partner had gone to, and who danced the same way she twirled and invoked mass Pep, which is to say in a way that seemed to turn everything solid in Orin's body watery and distant and oddly refracted.

Orin Incandenza, who like many children of raging alcoholics and OCD-sufferers had internal addictive-sexuality issues, had already drawn idle little sideways 8's on the postcoital flanks of a dozen B.U. coeds. But this was different. He'd been smitten before, but not decapitated. He lay on his bed in the autumn P.M.s during the tennis coach's required nap-time, squeezing a tennis ball and talking for hours about this twirling sprinkler-obscured sophomore while his doubles partner lay way on the other side of the huge bed looking simultaneously at Orin and at the N.E. leaves changing color in the trees outside the window. The schoolboy epithet they'd made up to refer to Orin's twirler was the P.G.O.A.T., for the Prettiest Girl Of All Time. It wasn't the entire attraction, but she really was almost grotesquely lovely. She made the Moms look like the sort of piece of fruit you think you want to take out of the bin and but then once you're right there over the bin you put back because from close up you can see a much fresher and less preserved-seeming piece of fruit elsewhere in the bin. The twirler was so pretty that not even the senior B.U. football Terriers could summon the saliva to speak to her at Athletic mixers. In fact she was almost universally shunned. The twirler induced in heterosexual males what U.H.I.D. later told her was termed the Actaeon Complex, which is a kind of deep phylogenic fear of transhuman beauty. About all Orin's doubles partner — who as a strabismic was something of an expert on female unattainability — felt he could do was warn O. that this was the kind of hideously attractive girl you just knew in advance did not associate with normal collegiate human males, and clearly attended B.U.-Athletic social functions only out of a sort of bland scientific interest while she waited for the cleft-chinned ascapartic male-model-looking wildly-successful-in-business adult male she doubtless was involved with to telephone her from the back seat of his green stretch Infiniti, etc. No major-sport player had ever even orbited in close enough to hear the elisions and apical lapses of a mid-Southern accent in her oddly flat but resonant voice that sounded like someone enunciating very carefully inside a soundproof enclosure. When she danced, at dances, it was with other cheerleaders and twirlers and Pep Squad Terrierettes, because no male had the grit or spit to ask her. Orin himself couldn't get closer than four meters at parties, because he suddenly couldn't figure out where to put the stresses in the Charles-Tavis-unwittingly-inspired 'Describe-the-sort-of-man-you-find-attractive-and-I'll-affect-the-demeanor-of-that-sort-of-man' strategic opening that had worked so well on other B.U. Subjects. It took three hearings for him to figure out that her name wasn't Joel. The big hair was red-gold and the skin peachy-tinged pale and arms freckled and zygomatics indescribable and her eyes an extra-natural HD green. He wouldn't learn till later that the almost pungently clean line-dried-laundry scent that hung about her was a special low-pH dandelion attar decocted special by her chemist Daddy in Shiny Prize KY.

Boston University's tennis team, needless to say, had neither cheerleaders nor baton-twirling Pep Squads, which were reserved for major and large-crowd sports. This is pretty understandable.

The tennis coach took Orin's decision hard, and Orin had had to hand him a Kleenex and stand there for several minutes under the poster of an avuncular Big Bill Tilden standing there in WWII-era long white pants and ruffling a ballboy's hair, Orin watching the Kleenex soggify and get holes blown through it while he tried to articulate just what he meant by *burned out* and *withered husk* and *carrot*. The coach had kept asking if this meant Orin's mother wouldn't be coming down to watch practice anymore.

Orin's now former doubles partner, a strabismic and faggy-sweatered but basically decent guy who also happened to be heir to the Nickerson Farms Meat Facsmile fortune, had his cleft-chinned and solidly B.U.-connected Dad make 'a couple quick calls' from the back seat of his forest-green Lexus. B.U.'s Head Football Coach, the Boss Terrier, an exiled Oklahoman who really did wear a gray crewneck sweatshirt with a whistle on a string, was intrigued by the size of the left forearm and hand extended (impolitely but intriguingly) during introductions — this was Orin's tennis arm, roughly churn-sized; the other, whose dimensions were human, was hidden under a sportcoat draped strategically over the aspiring walk-on's right shoulder.

But you can't play U.S. football with a draped sportcoat. And Orin's only real speed was in tiny three-meter lateral bursts. And then it turned out that the idea of actually making direct physical contact with an opponent was so deeply ingrained as alien and horrific that Orin's tryouts, even at reserve positions, were too pathetic to describe. He was called a *dragass* and then a *mollygag* and then a *bona fried pussy*. He was finally told that he seemed to have some kind of empty swinging sack where his balls ought to be and that if he wanted to keep his scholarship he might ought to stick to minor-type sports where what you hit didn't up and hit you back. The Coach finally actually grabbed Orin's facemask and pointed to the mouth of the field's southern tunnel. Orin walked south off the field solo and disconsolate, helmet under his little right arm, with not even a wistful glance back at the Pep Squad's P.G.O.A.T. practicing baton-aloft splits in a heart-rendingly distant way beneath the Visitors' northern goalposts.

What metro Boston AAs are trite but correct about is that both destiny's kisses and its dope-slaps illustrate an individual person's basic personal powerlessness over the really meaningful events in his life:[100] i.e. almost nothing important that ever happens to you happens because you engineer it. Destiny has no beeper; destiny always leans trenchcoated out of an alley with some sort of *Psst* that you usually can't even hear because you're in such a rush to or from something important you've tried to engineer. The destiny-grade event that happened to Orin Incandenza at this point was that just as he was passing glumly under the Home goalposts and entering the shadow of the south exit-tunnel's adit a loud and ominously orthopedic cracking sound, plus then shrieking, issued from somewhere on the field behind him. What had happened was that B.U.'s best defensive tackle — a 180-kilo future pro who had no teeth and liked to color — practicing Special Teams punt-rushes, not only blocked B.U.'s varsity punter's kick but committed a serious mental error and kept coming and crashed into the little padless guy while the punter's cleated foot was still up over his head, falling on him in a beefy heap and snapping everything from femur to tarsus in the punter's leg with a dreadful high-caliber snap. Two Pep majorettes and a waterboy fainted from the sound of the punter's screams alone. The blocked punt's ball caromed hard off the defensive tackle's helmet and bounced crazily and rolled untended all the way back to the shadow of the south tunnel, where Orin had turned to watch the punter writhe and the lineman rise with a finger in his mouth and a guilty expression. The Defensive Line Coach disconnected his headset and dashed out and began blowing his whistle at the lineman at extremely close range, over and over, as the huge tackle started to cry and hit himself in the forehead with the heel of his hand. Since nobody else was close, Orin picked up the blocked punt's ball, which the Head Coach was gesturing impatiently for from his position at the midfield bench. Orin held the football (which he'd not been very good at it during tryouts, holding onto it), feeling its weird oval weight, and looked way upfield at the stretcher-bearers and punter and assistants and Coach. It was too far to try to throw, and there was just no way Orin was making another solo walk up the sideline and then back off the field again under the distant green gaze of the twirler who owned his CNS.

Orin, before that seminal moment, had never tried to kick any sort of ball before in his whole life, was the unengineered and kind of vulnerable revelation that ended up moving Joelle van Dyne way more than status or hang-time.

And but as of that moment, as whistles fell from lips and people pointed, and under that same green and sprinkler-hazed gaze Orin found for himself, within competitive U.S. football, a new niche and carrot. A Show-type career he could never have dreamed of trying to engineer. Within days he was punting 60 yards without a rush, practicing solo on an outside field with the Special Teams Assistant, a dreamy Gauloise-smoking man who invoked ideas of sky and flight and called Orin 'ephebe,' which a discreet phone call to his youngest brother revealed not to be the insult Orin had feared it sounded like. By the second week O. was up around 65 yards, still without a snap or rush, his rhythm clean and faultless, his concentration on the transaction between one foot and one leather egg almost frighteningly total. Nor, by the third week, was he much distracted by the ten crazed pituitary giants bearing down as he took the snap and stepped forward, the gasps and crunching and meaty splats of interpersonal contact around him, the cooly-type shuffle of the stretcher-bearers who came and went after the whistles blew. He'd been taken aside and the empty-scrotum crack apologized for, and it had been explained — complete with blow-ups of Rulebook pages — that regulations against direct physical contact with the punter were draconian, enforced by the threat of massive yardage and loss of possession. The rifle-shot sounds of the ex-punter's now useless leg were one-in-a-million sounds, he was assured. The Head Coach let Orin overhear him telling the defense that any man misfortunate enough to impact the team's new stellar punt-man might could just keep on walking after the play was over, all the way to the south tunnel and the stadium exit and the nearest transportation to some other institution of learning and ball.

It was, pretty obviously, the start of football season. Crisp air, everything half dead, burning leaves, hot chocolate, raccoon coats and halftime-twirling and something called the Wave. Crowds exponentially larger and more demonstrative than tennis-tournament crowds. HOME v. SUNY–Buffalo, HOME v. Syracuse, AT Boston College, AT Rhode Island, HOME v. the despised Minutemen of UMass–Amherst. Orin's average reached 69 yards per kick and was still improving, his eyes fixed on the twin inducements of a gleaming baton and a massive developmental carrot he hadn't felt since age fourteen. He punted the football better and better as his motion — a dancerly combination of moves and weight-transfers every bit as complex and precise as a kick serve — got more instinctive and he found his hamstrings and adductors loosening through constant and high-impact competitive punting, his left cleat finishing at 90° to the turf, knee to his nose, Rockette-kicking in the midst of crowd-noise so rabid and entire it seemed to remove stadiums' air, the one huge wordless orgasmic voice rising and creating a vacuum that sucked the ball after it into the sky, the leather egg receding as it climbed in a perfect spiral, seeming to chase the very crowd-roar it had produced.

By Halloween his control was even better than his distance. It wasn't by accident that the Special Teams Assistant described it as 'touch.' Consider that a football field is basically just a grass tennis court tugged unnaturally long, and that white lines at complex right angles still define tactics and movement, the very possibility of play. And that Orin Incandenza, who tennis-historically had had mediocre passing shots, had been indicted by Schtitt for depending way too often on the lob he'd developed as compensation. Like the equally weak-passing Eschaton-prodigy Michael Pemulis after him, Orin's whole limited game had been built around a preternatural lob, which of course a lob is just a higher-than-opponent parabola that ideally lands just shy of the area of play's rear boundary and is hard to retrieve and return. Gerhardt Schtitt and deLint and their depressed prorectors had had to sit eating butterless popcorn through only one cartridge of one B.U. game to understand how Orin had found his major-sport niche. Orin was still just only lobbing, Schtitt observed, illustrating with the pointer and a multiple-replayed fourth down, but now with the leg instead, the only punting, and now with ten armored and testosterone-flushed factota to deal with whatever return an opponent could muster; Schtitt posited that Orin had stumbled by accident on a way, in this grotesquely physical and territorial U.S. game, to legitimate the same dependency on the one shot of lob that had kept him from developing the courage to develop his weaker areas, which this unwillingness to risk the temporary failure and weakness for long-term gaining had been the real herbicide on the carrot of Orin Incandenza's tennis. Puberty *Schmüberty,* as the real reason for burning down the inside fire for tennis, Schtitt knew. Schtitt's remarks were nodded vigorously at and largely ignored, in the Viewing Room. Schtitt later told deLint he had several very bad feelings about Orin's future, inside.

But so by freshman Halloween Orin was regularly placing his punts inside the opponents' 20, spinning the ball off his cleats' laces so it either hit and squiggled outside the white sideline and out of play or else landed on its point and bounced straight up and seemed to squat in the air, hovering and spinning, waiting for some downfield Terrier to kill it just by touching. The Special Teams Assistant told Orin that these were historically called coffin-corner kicks, and that Orin Incandenza was the best natural coffin-corner man he'd lived to see. You almost had to smile. Orin's Full-Ride scholarship was renewed under the aegis of a brutaler but way more popular North American sport than competitive tennis. This was after the second home game, around the time that a certain Actaeonizingly pretty baton-twirler, invoking mass Pep during breaks in the action, seemed to begin somehow directing her glittering sideline routines at Orin in particular. So and then the only really cardiac-grade romantic relationship of Orin's life took bilateral root at a distance, during games, without one exchanged personal phoneme, a love communicated — across grassy expanses, against stadiums' monovocal roar — entirely through stylized repetitive motions — his functional, hers celebratory — their respective little dances of devotion to the spectacle they were both — in their different roles — trying to make as entertaining as possible.

But so the point was that the accuracy came after the distance. In his first couple games Orin had approached his fourth-down task as one of simply kicking the ball out of sight and past hope of return. The dreamy S.T. Assistant said this was a punter's natural pattern of growth and development. Your raw force tends to precede your control. In his initial Home start, wearing a padless uniform that didn't fit and a wide receiver's number, he was summoned when B.U.'s first drive stalled on the 40 of a Syracuse team that had no idea it was in its last season of representing an American university. A side-issue. College-sport analysts would later use the game to contrast the beginning and end of different eras. But a side-issue. Orin had a book-long of 73 yards that day, and an average hang of eight-point-something seconds; but that first official punt, exhilarated — the carrot, the P.G.O.A.T., the monovocal roar of a major-sport crowd — he sent over the head of the Orangeman back waiting to receive it, over the goalposts and the safety-nets behind the goalposts, over the first three sections of seats and into the lap of an Emeritus theology prof in Row 52 who'd needed opera glasses to make out the play itself. It went in the books at 40 yards, that baptismal competitive punt. It was really almost a 90-yard punt, and had the sort of hang-time the Special Teams Asst. said you could have tender and sensitive intercourse during. The sound of the podiatric impact had silenced a major-sport crowd, and a retired USMC flier who always came with petroleum-jelly samples he hawked to the knuckle-chapped crowds in the Nickerson stands told his cronies in a Brookline watering hole after the game that this Incandenza kid's first public punt had sounded just the way Rolling Thunder's big-bellied Berthas had sounded, the exaggerated WHUMP of incendiary tonnage, way larger than life.

After four weeks, Orin's success at kicking big egg-shaped balls was way past anything he'd accomplished hitting little round ones. Granted, the tennis and Eschaton hadn't hurt. But it wasn't all athletic, this affinity for the public punt. It wasn't all just high-level competitive training and high-pressure experience transported inter-sport. He told Joelle van Dyne, she of the accent and baton and brainlocking beauty, told her in the course of an increasingly revealing conversation after kind of amazingly *she* had approached *him* at a Columbus Day Major Sport function and asked him to autograph a squooshy-sided football he'd kicked a hole through in practice — the deflated bladder had landed in the Marching Terriers' sousaphone player's sousaphone and had been handed over to Joelle after extrication by the lardy tubist, sweaty and dumb under the girl's Actaeonizingly imploring gaze — asked him — Orin now also suddenly damp and blank on anything attractive to say or recite — asked him in an emptily resonant drawl to inscribe the punctured thing for her Own Personal Daddy, one Joe Lon van Dyne of Shiny Prize KY and she said also of the Dyne-Riney Proton Donor Reagent Corp. of nearby Boaz KY, and engaged him (O.) in a slowly decreasingly one-sided social-function-type conversation — the P.G.O.A.T. was pretty easy to stay in a one-to-one like tête-à-tête with, since no other Terrier could bring himself within four meters of her — and Orin gradually found himself almost meeting her eye as he shared that he believed it wasn't all athletic, punting's pull for him, that a lot of it seemed emotional and/or even, if there was such a thing anymore, spiritual: a denial of silence: here were upwards of 30,000 voices, souls, voicing approval as One Soul. He invoked the raw numbers. The frenzy. He was thinking out loud here. Audience exhortations and approvals so total they ceased to be numerically distinct and melded into a sort of single coital moan, one big vowel, the sound of the womb, the roar gathering, tidal, amniotic, the voice of what might as well be God. None of tennis's prim applause cut short by an umpire's patrician shush. He said he was just speculating here, ad-libbing; he was meeting her eye and not drowning, his dread now transformed into whatever it had been dread of. He said the sound of all those souls as One Sound, too loud to bear, building, waiting for his foot to release it: Orin said the thing he thought he liked was he literally could not hear himself think out there, maybe a cliché, but out there transformed, his own self transcended as he'd never escaped himself on the court, a sense of a presence in the sky, the crowd-sound congregational, the stadium-shaking climax as the ball climbed and inscribed a cathedran arch, seeming to take forever to fall. . . . It never even occurred to him to ask her what sort of demeanor she preferred. He didn't have to strategize or even scheme. Later he knew what the dread had been dread of. He hadn't had to promise her anything, it turned out. It was all for free.

By the end of his freshman fall and B.U.'s championship of the Yankee Conference, plus its nonvictorious but still unprecedented appearance at Las Vegas's dignitary-attended K-L-RMKI/Forsythia Bowl, Orin had taken his off-campus housing subsidy and moved with Joelle van Dyne the heart-stopping Kentuckian into an East Cambridge co-op three subway stops distant from B.U. and the all-new inconveniences of being publicly stellar at a major sport in a city where people beat each other to death in bars over stats and fealty.

Joelle had done the midnight Thanksgiving dinner at E.T.A., and survived Avril, and then Orin spent his first Xmas ever away from home, flying to Paducah and then driving a rented 4WD to kudzu-hung Shiny Prize, Kentucky, to drink toddies under a little white reusable Xmas tree with all red balls with Joelle and her mother and Personal Daddy and his loyal pointers, getting a storm-cellar tour of Joe Lon's incredible Pyrex collection of every solution in the known world that can turn blue litmus paper red, little red rectangles floating in the flasks for proof, Orin nodding a lot and trying incredibly hard and Joelle saying that Mr. van D.'s not once smiling at him was just His Way, was all, the way his own Moms had Her Way Joelle'd had trouble with. Orin wired Marlon Bain and Ross Reat and the strabismic Nickerson that he was by all indications in love with somebody.

Freshman New Year's Eve in Shiny Prize, far from the O.N.A.N.ite upheavals of the new Northeast, the last P.M. Before Subsidization, was the first time Orin saw Joelle ingest very small amounts of cocaine. Orin had exited his own substance-phase about the time he discovered sex, plus of course the N./O.N.A.N.C.A.A.-urine considerations, and he declined it, the cocaine, but not in a judgmental or killjoy way, and found he liked being with his P.G.O.A.T. straight while she ingested, he found it exciting, a vicariously on-the-edge feeling he associated with giving yourself not to any one game's definition but to yourself and how you unjudgmentally feel about somebody who's high and feeling even freer and better than normal, with you, alone, under the red balls. They were a natural match here: her ingestion then was recreational, and he not only didn't mind but never made a show of not minding, nor she that he abstained; the whole substance issue was natural and kind of free. Another reason they seemed star-fated was that Joelle had in her sophomore year decided to concentrate in Film/Cartridge, academically, at B.U. Either Film-Cartridge Theory or Film-Cartridge Production. Or maybe both. The P.G.O.A.T. was a film fanatic, though her tastes were pretty corporate: she told O. she preferred movies where 'a whole bunch of shit blows up.'[101] Orin in a low-key way introduced her to art film, conceptual and highbrow academic avant- and après-garde film, and taught her how to use some of InterLace's more esoteric menus. He blasted up the hill to Enfield and brought down The Mad Stork's own *Pre-Nuptial Agreement of Heaven and Hell,* which had a major impact on her. Right after Thanksgiving Himself let the P.G.O.A.T. understudy with Leith on the set of *The American Century as Seen Through a Brick* in return for getting to film her thumb against a plucked string. After an only mildly disappointing sophomore season O. flew with her to Toronto to watch part of the filming of *Blood Sister: One Tough Nun.* Himself would take Orin and his beloved out after dailies, entertaining Joelle with his freakish gift for Canadian-cab-hailing while Orin stood turtle-headed in his topcoat; and then later Orin would shepherd the two of them back to their Ontario Place hotel, stopping the cab to let them both throw up, fireman-carrying Joelle while he watched The Mad Stork negotiate his suite by holding on to walls. Himself showed them the U. Toronto Conference Center where he and the Moms had first met. This might have been the end's start, gradually, in hindsight. Joelle that summer declined a sixth summer at the Dixie Baton-Twirling Institute in Oxford MS and let Himself give her a stage name and use her in rapid succession in *Low Temperature Civics, (The) Desire to Desire,* and *Safe Boating Is No Accident,* travelling with Himself and Mario while Orin stayed in Boston recuperating from minor surgery on a hypertrophied left quadriceps at a Massachusetts General Hospital where no fewer than four nurses and P.T.s in the Sports Medicine wing filed for legal separation from their husbands, with custody.

The P.G.O.A.T.'s real ambitions weren't thespian, Orin knew, is one reason he hung in so long. Joelle when he'd met her already owned some modest personal film equipment, courtesy of her Personal Daddy. And she now had access to nothing if not serious digital gear. By Orin's sophomore year she no longer twirled or incited Pep in any way. In his first full season she stood behind various white lines with a little Bolex R32 digital recorder and BTL meters and lenses, including a bitching Angenieux zoom O.'d gone and paid for, as a gesture, and she shot little half-disk-sector clips of #78, B.U. Punter, sometimes with Leith in attendance (never Himself), experimenting with speed and focal length and digital mattes, extending herself technically. Orin, despite his interests in upgrading the P.G.O.A.T.'s commercial tastes, was himself pretty luke-warm on film and cartridges and theater and pretty much anything that reduced him to herd-like spectation, but he respected Joelle's own creative drives, to an extent; and he found out that he really did like watching the football footage of Joelle van Dyne, featuring pretty much him only, strongly preferred the little .5-sector clips to Himself's cartridges or corporate films where things blew up while Joelle bounced in her seat and pointed at the viewer; and he found them (her clips of him at play) way more engaging than the grainy overcluttered game- and play-celluloids the Head Coach made everybody sit through. Orin liked to adjust the co-op's rheostat way down when Joelle wasn't home and haul out the diskettes and make Jiffy Pop and watch her little ten-second clips of him over and over. He saw something different each time he rewound, something more. The clips of him punting unfolded like time-lapsing flowers and seemed to reveal him in ways he could never have engineered. He sat rapt. It only happened when he watched them alone. Sometimes he got an erection. He never masturbated; Joelle came home. Still in the last stages of a late puberty and the prettiness getting visibly worse day by day, Joelle had been maiden, still, when Orin met her. She'd been shunned theretofore, both at B.U. and Shiny Prize–Boaz Consolidated: the beauty had repelled every comer. She'd devoted her life to her twirling and amateur film. Disney Leith said she had the knack: her camera-hand was rock-steady; even the early clips from the start of the Y.W. season looked shot off a tripod. There'd been no audio in the sophomore clips, and you could hear the high-pitched noise of the cartridge in the TP's disk drive. A cartridge revolving at a digital diskette's 450 rpm sounds a bit like a distant vacuum cleaner. Late-night car-noises and sirens drifted in through the bars from as far away as the Storrow 500. Silence was not part of what Orin was after, watching. (Joelle housekeeps like a fiend. The place is always sterile. The resemblance to the Moms's housekeeping he finds a bit creepy. Except Joelle doesn't mind a mess or give anybody the creeps worrying about hiding that she minds it so nobody's feelings will be hurt. With Joelle the mess just disappears sometime during the night and you wake up and the place is sterile. It's like elves.) Soon after he started watching the clips in his junior year, Orin had blasted up Comm.'s hill and brought Joelle back a Bolex-compatible Tatsuoka recorder w/ sync pulse, a cardioid mike, a low-end tripod w/ a barney to muffle the Bolex's whir, a classy Pilotone blooper and sync-pulse cords, a whole auracopia. It took Leith three weeks to teach her to use the Pilotone. Now the clips had sound. Orin has trouble not burning the Jiffy Pop popcorn. It tends to burn as the foil top inflates; you have to take it off the stove before the foil forms a dome. No microwave popcorn for Orin, even then. He liked to dim the track-lights when Joelle was out and haul out the cartridge-rack and watch her little ten-second clips of his punts over and over. Here he is back against Delaware in the second Home game of Y.T.M.P. The sky is dull and pale, the five Yankee Conference flags — U. Vermont and UNH now history — are all right out straight with the gale off the Charles for which Nickerson Field is infamous. It's fourth down, obviously. Thousands of kilos of padded meat assume four-point stances and chuff at each other, poised to charge and stave. Orin is twelve yards back from scrimmage, his cleated feet together, his weight just ahead of himself, his mismatched arms out before him in the attitude of the blind before walls. His eyes are fixed on the distant grass-stained Valentine of the center's ass. His stance, waiting to receive the snap, is not unlike a diver's, he sees. Nine men on line, four-pointed, poised to stave off ten men's assault. The other team's deep back is back to receive, seventy yards away or more. The fullback whose sole job is to keep Orin from harm is ahead and to the left, bent at the knees, his taped fists together and elbows out like a winged thing ready to hurl itself at whatever breaches the line and comes at the punter. Joelle's equipment isn't quite pro-caliber but her technique is very good. By junior year there's also color. There's only one sound, and it is utter: the crowd's noise and its response to that noise, building. Orin's back against Delaware, ready, his helmet a bright noncontact white and his head's insides scrubbed free for ten seconds of every thought not connected to receiving the long snap and stepping martially forward to lob the leather egg beyond sight at an altitude that makes the wind no factor. Madame P.G.O.A.T. gets it all, zooming in from the opposite end zone. She gets his timing; a punt's timing is minutely precise, like a serve's; it's like a solo dance; she gets the ungodly WHUMP against and above the crowd's vowel's climax; she captures the pendular 180-arc of Orin's leg, the gluteal follow-through that puts his cleat's laces way over his helmet, the perfect right angle between leg and turf. Her technique is superb on the Delaware debacle Orin can just barely take reviewing, the one time all year the big chuffing center oversnaps and arcs the ball over Orin's upraised hands so by the time he's run back and grabbed the crazy-bouncing thing ten yards farther back the Delaware defense has breached the line, are through the line, the fullback supine and trampled, all ten rushers rushing, wanting nothing more than personal physical contact with Orin and his leather egg. Joelle gets him sprinting, a three-meter lateral burst as he avoids the first few sets of hands and the beefy curling lips and but is just about to get personally contacted and knocked out of his cleats by the Delaware strong safety flying in on a slant from way outside when the tiny .5-sector of digital space each punt's programmed to require runs out and the crowd-sound moos and dies and you can hear the disk-drive stalled at the terminal byte and Orin's chin-strapped plastic-barred face is there on the giant viewer, frozen and High-Def in his helmet, right before impact, zoomed in on with a quality lens. Of particular interest are the eyes.

14 NOVEMBER
YEAR OF THE DEPEND ADULT UNDERGARMENT

Poor Tony Krause had a seizure on the T. It happened on a Gray Line train from Watertown to Inman Square, Cambridge. He'd been drinking codeine cough syrup in the men's room of the Armenian Foundation Library in horrid central Watertown MA for over a week, darting out from cover only to beg a scrip from hideous Equus Reese and then dash in at Brooks Pharmacy, wearing a simply vile ensemble of synthetic-fiber slacks and suspenders and tweed Donegal cap he'd had to cadge from a longshoremen's union hall. Poor Tony couldn't dare wear anything comely, not even the Antitoi brothers' red leather coat, not since that poor woman's bag had turned out to have a heart inside. He had simply never felt so beset and overcome on all sides as the black July day when it fell to his lot to boost a heart. Who wouldn't wonder Why Me? He didn't dare dress expressive or ever go back to the Square. And Emil still had him marked for de-mapping as a consequence of that horrid thing with Wo and Bobby C last winter. Poor Tony hadn't dared show one feather east of Tremont St. or at the Brighton Projects or even Delphina's in backwater Enfield since last Xmas, even after Emil simply dematerialized from the street-scene; and now since 29 July he was *non grata* at Harvard Square and environs; and even the sight of an Oriental now gave him palpitations — say nothing of an Aigner accessory.

Thus Poor Tony had no way to cop for himself. He could trust no one enough to inject their wares. S. T. Cheese and Lolasister were no more trustworthy than he himself; he didn't even want them to know where he slept. He began drinking cough syrup. He managed to get Bridget Tenderhole and the strictly rough-trade Stokely Dark Star to cop for him on the wink for a few weeks, until Stokely died in a Fenway hospice and then Bridget Tenderhole was shipped by her pimp to Brockton under maddeningly vague circumstances. Then Poor Tony had read the dark portents and swallowed the first of his pride and hid himself even more deeply in a dumpster-complex behind the I.B.P.W.D.W.[102] Local #4 Hall in Fort Point downtown and resolved to stay hidden there for as long as he could swallow the pride to send Lolasister out to acquire heroin, accepting w/o pride or complaint the shameless rip-offs the miserable bitch perpetrated upon him, until a period in October when Lolasister went down with hepatitis-G and the supply of heroin dried horribly up and the only people even copping enough to chip were people in a position to dash here and there to great beastly lengths under an open public-access sky and no friend, no matter how dear or indebted, could afford to cop for another. Then, wholly friend- and connectionless, Poor Tony, in hiding, began to Withdraw From Heroin. Not just get strung out or sick. Withdraw. The words echoed in his neuralgiac and wigless head with the simply most awful sinister-footsteps-echoing-in-deserted-corridor quality. Withdrawal. The Wingless Fowl. Turkeyfication. Kicking. The Old Cold Bird. Poor Tony had never once had to Withdraw, not all the way down the deserted corridor of Withdrawal, not since he first got strung at seventeen. At the very worst, someone kind had always found him charming, if things got dire enough to have to rent out his charms. Alas thus about the fact that his charms were now at low ebb. He weighed fifty kilos and his skin was the color of summer squash. He had terrible shivering-attacks and also perspired. He had a sty that had scraped one eyeball as pink as a bunny's. His nose ran like twin spigots and the output had a yellow-green tinge he didn't think looked promising at *all*. There was an uncomely dry-rot smell about him that even he could smell. In Watertown he tried to pawn his fine auburn wig w/ removable chignon and was cursed at in Armenian because the wig had infestations from his own hair below. Let's not even mention the Armenian pawnbroker's critique of his red leather coat.

Poor Tony got more and more ill as he further Withdrew. His symptoms themselves developed symptoms, troughs and nodes he charted with morbid attention in the dumpster, in his suspenders and horrid tweed cap, clutching a shopping bag with his wig and coat and comely habiliments he could neither wear nor pawn. The empty Empire Displacement Co. dumpster he was hiding in was new and apple-green and the inside was bare dimpled iron, and it remained new and unutilized because persons declined to come near enough to utilize it. It took some time for Poor Tony to realize why this was so; for a brief interval it had seemed like a break, fortune's one wan smile. An E.W.D. land-barge crew set him straight in language that left quite a bit of tact to be wished for, he felt. The dumpster's green iron cover also leaked when it rained, and it contained already a colony of ants along one wall, which insects Poor Tony had ever since a neurasthenic childhood feared and detested in particular, ants; and in direct sunlight the quarters became a hellish living environment from which even the ants seemed to vanish.

With each step further into the black corridor of actual Withdrawal, Poor Tony Krause stamped his foot and simply refused to believe things could feel any worse. Then he stopped being able to anticipate when he needed to as it were visit the powder room. A fastidious gender-dysphoric's horror of incontinence cannot properly be described. Fluids of varying consistency began to pour w/o advance notice from several openings. Then of course they stayed there, the fluids, on the summer dumpster's iron floor. There they were, not going anywhere. He had no way to clean up and no way to cop. His entire set of interpersonal associations consisted of persons who did not care about him plus persons who wished him harm. His own late obstetrician father had rended his own clothing in symbolic shiva in the Year of the Whopper in the kitchen of the Krause home, 412 Mount Auburn Street, horrid central Watertown. It was the incontinence plus the prospect of 11/4's monthly Social Assistance checks that drove Poor Tony out for a mad scampering relocation to an obscure Armenian Foundation Library men's room in Watertown Center, wherein he tried to arrange a stall as comfortingly as he could with shiny magazine photos and cherished knickknacks and toilet paper laid down around the seat, and flushed repeatedly, and tried to keep true Withdrawal at some sort of bay with bottles of Codinex Plus. A tiny percentage of codeine gets metabolized into good old C_{17}-morphine, affording an agonizing hint of what real relief from The Bird might feel like. I.e. the cough syrup did little more than draw the process out, extend the corridor — it slowed up time.

Poor Tony Krause sat on the insulated toilet in the domesticated stall all day and night, alternately swilling and gushing. He held his high heels up at 1900h. when the library staff checked the stalls and turned off all the lights and left Poor Tony in a darkness within darkness so utter he had no idea where his own limbs were or went. He left that stall maybe once every two days, scampering madly to Brooks in cast-off shades and a kind of hood or shawl made pathetically of brown men's-room paper towels.

Time began to take on new aspects for him, now, as Withdrawal progressed. Time began to pass with sharp edges. Its passage in the dark or dim-lit stall was like time was being carried by a procession of ants, a gleaming red martial column of those militaristic red Southern-U.S. ants that build hideous tall boiling hills; and each vile gleaming ant wanted a minuscule little portion of Poor Tony's flesh in compensation as it helped bear time slowly forward down the corridor of true Withdrawal. By the second week in the stall time itself seemed the corridor, lightless at either end. After more time time then ceased to move or be moved or be move-throughable and assumed a shape above and apart, a huge, musty-feathered, orange-eyed wingless fowl hunched incontinent atop the stall, with a kind of watchful but deeply uncaring personality that didn't seem keen on Poor Tony Krause as a person at all, or to wish him well. Not one little bit. It spoke to him from atop the stall, the same things, over and over. They were unrepeatable. Nothing in even Poor Tony's grim life-experience prepared him for the experience of time with a shape and an odor, squatting; and the worsening physical symptoms were a spree at Bonwit's compared to time's black assurances that the symptoms were merely hints, signposts pointing up at a larger, far more dire set of Withdrawal phenomena that hung just overhead by a string that unravelled steadily with the passage of time. It would not keep still and would not end; it changed shape and smell. It moved in and out of him like the very most feared prison-shower assailant. Poor Tony had once had the hubris to fancy he'd had occasion really to shiver, ever, before. But he had never truly really shivered until time's cadences — jagged and cold and smelling oddly of deodorant — entered his body via several openings — cold the way only damp cold is cold — the phrase he'd had the gall to have imagined he understood was the phrase *chilled to the bone* — shard-studded columns of chill entering to fill his bones with ground glass, and he could hear his joints' glassy crunch with every slightest shift of hunched position, time ambient and in the air and entering and exiting at will, coldly; and the pain of his breath against his teeth. Time came to him in the falcon-black of the library night in an orange mohawk and Merry Widow w/ tacky Amalfo pumps and nothing else. Time spread him and entered him roughly and had its way and left him again in the form of endless gushing liquid shit that he could not flush enough to keep up with. He spent the longest morbid time trying to fathom whence all the shit came from when he was ingesting nothing at all but Codinex Plus. Then at some point he realized: time had become the shit itself: Poor Tony had become an hourglass: time moved through him now; he ceased to exist apart from its jagged-edged flow. He now weighed more like 45 kg. His legs were the size his comely arms had been, before Withdrawal. He was haunted by the word *Zuckung,* a foreign and possibly Yiddish word he did not recall ever before hearing. The word kept echoing in quick-step cadence through his head without meaning anything. He'd naïvely assumed that going mad meant you were not aware of going mad; he'd naïvely pictured madmen as forever laughing. He kept seeing his sonless father again — removing the training wheels, looking at his pager, wearing a green gown and mask, pouring iced tea in a pebbled glass, tearing his sportshirt in filial woe, grabbing his shoulder, sinking to his knees. Stiffening in a bronze casket. Being lowered under the snow at Mount Auburn Cemetery, through dark glasses from a distance. 'Chilled to the *Zuckung.*' When, then, even the funds for the codeine syrup were exhausted, he still sat on the toilet of the rear stall of the A.F.L. loo, surrounded by previously comforting hung habilements and fashion-magazine photographs he'd fastened to the wall with tape cadged on the way in from the Reference desk, sat for almost a whole nother night and day, because he had no faith that he could stem the flow of diarrhea long enough to make it anywhere — if anywhere to go presented itself — in his only pair of gender-appropriate slacks. During hours of lit operation, the men's room was full of old men who wore identical brown loafers and spoke Slavic and whose rapid-fire flatulence smelled of cabbage.

Toward the end of the day of the second syrupless afternoon (the day of the seizure) Poor Tony Krause began to Withdraw from the cough syrup's alcohol and codeine and demethylated morphine, now, as well as from the original heroin, yielding a set of sensations for which not even his recent experience had prepared him (the alcohol-Withdrawal especially); and when the true D.T.-type big-budget visuals commenced, when the first glossy and minutely hirsute army-ant crawled up his arm and refused ghost-like to be brushed away or hammered dead, Poor Tony threw his hygienic pride into time's porcelain maw and pulled up his slacks — mortifyingly wrinkled from 10+ days puddled around his ankles — made what slight cosmetic repairs he could, donned his tacky hat with Scotch-taped scarf of paper towels, and lit out in last-ditch desperation for Cambridge's Inman Square, for the sinister and duplicitous Antitoi brothers, their Glass-Entertainment-'N-Notions-fronted operations center he'd long ago vowed never again to darken the door of and but now figured to be his place of very last resort, the Antitois, Canadians of the Québec subgenus, sinister and duplicitous but when it came down to it rather hapless political insurgents he'd twice availed of services through the offices of Lolasister, now the only persons anywhere he could claim somehow owed him a kindness, since the affair of the heart.

In his coat and skallycap-over-scarf on Watertown Center's underground Gray Line platform, when the first hot loose load fell out into the baggy slacks and down his leg and out around his high heel — he still had only his red high heels with the crossing straps, which the slacks were long enough to mostly hide — Poor Tony closed his eyes against the ants formicating up and down his arms' skinny length and screamed a soundless interior scream of utter and soul-scalded woe. His beloved boa fit almost entirely in one breast pocket, where it stayed in the name of discretion. On the crowded train itself, then, he discovered that he'd gone in three weeks from being a colorful and comely albeit freakishly comely person to being one of those loathsome urban specimens that respectable persons on T-trains slide and drift quietly away from without even seeming to notice they're even there. His scarf of paper towels had come partly untaped. He smelled of bilirubin and yellow sweat and wore week-old eyeliner that simply did not fly if one needed a shave. There had been some negative urine-incidents as well, in the slacks, to round matters out. He had simply never in his life felt so unattractive or been so sick. He wept silently in shame and pain at the passage of each brightly lit public second's edge, and the driver ants that boiled in his lap opened needle-teethed little insectile mouths to catch the tears. He could feel his erratic pulse in his sty. The Gray Line was of the Green- and Orange-Line trundling-behemoth-type train, and he sat all alone at one end of the car, feeling each slow second take its cut.

When it descended, the seizure felt less like a separate distinct health-crisis than simply the next exhibit in the corridor of horrors that was the Old Cold Bird. In actual fact the seizure — a kind of synaptic firefight in Poor Tony's desiccated temporal lobes — was caused entirely by With-drawal not From Heroin but from plain old grain alcohol, which was Co-dinex Plus cough syrup's primary ingredient and balm. He'd consumed upwards of sixteen little Eighty-Proof bottles of Codinex per day for eight days, and so was cruising for a real neurochemical bruising when he just up and stopped. The first thing that didn't augur very well was a shower of spark-sized phosphenes from the ceiling of the swaying train, this plus the fiery violet aura around the heads of the respectables who'd quietly re-treated as far as possible from the various puddles in which he sat. Their clean pink faces looked somehow stricken, each inside a hood of violet flame. Poor Tony didn't know that his silent whimpers had ceased to be silent, was why everyone in the car had gotten so terribly interested in the floor-tiles between their feet. He knew only that the sudden and incongruous smell of Old Spice Stick Deodorant, Classic Original Scent — unbidden and unexplainable, his late obstetric Poppa's brand, not smelled for years — and the tiny panicked twitters with which Withdrawal's ants skittered glossily up into his mouth and nose and disappeared (each of course taking its tiny pincered farewell bite as it went) augured some new and vivider exhibit on the corridor's horizon. He'd become, at puberty, violently allergic to the smell of Old Spice. As he soiled himself and the plastic seat and floor once again the Classic Scent of times past intensified. Then Poor Tony's body began to swell. He watched his limbs become airy white dirigibles and felt them deny his authority and detach from him and float sluggishly up snout-first into the steel-mill sparks the ceiling rained. He suddenly felt nothing, or rather Nothing, a pre-tornadic stillness of zero sensation, as if he were the very space he occupied.

Then he had a seizure.[103] The floor of the subway car became the ceiling of the subway car and he was on his arched back in a waterfall of light, gagging on Old Spice and watching his tumid limbs tear-ass around the car's interior like undone balloons. The booming *Zuckung Zuckung Zuckung* was his high heels' heels drumming on the soiled floor's tile. He heard a rushing train-roar that was no train on earth and felt a vascular roaring rushing that until the pain hit seemed like the gathering of a kind of orgasm of the head. His head inflated hugely and creaked as it stretched, inflating. Then the pain (seizures *hurt,* is what few civilians have occasion to know) was the sharp end of a hammer. There was a squeak and rush of release inside his skull and something shot from him into the air. He saw Bobby ('C') C's blood misting upward in the hot wind of the Copley blower. His father knelt beside him on the ceiling in a well-rended sleeveless tee-, extolling the Red Sox of Rice and Lynn. Tony wore summer taffeta. His body flopped around without OK from HQ. He didn't feel one bit like a puppet. He thought of gaffed fish. The gown had 'a thousand flounces and a saucy bodice of lace crochet.' Then he saw his father, green-gowned and rubber-gloved, leaning to read the headlines off the skin of a fish a newspaper had wrapped. That had never happened. The largest-print headline said PUSH. Poor Tony flopped and gasped and pushed down inside and the utter red of the blood that feeds sight bloomed behind his fluttering lids. Time wasn't passing so much as kneeling beside him in a torn tee-shirt disclosing the rodent-nosed tits of a man who disdains the care of his once-comely bod. Poor Tony convulsed and drummed and gasped and fluttered, a fountain of light all around him. He felt a piece of nourishing and possibly even intoxicating meat in the back of his throat but elected not to swallow it but swallowed it anyway, and was immediately sorry he did; and when his father's bloody-rubbered fingers folded his teeth back to retrieve the tongue he'd swallowed he refused absolutely to bite down ungratefully on the hand that was taking his food, then without authorization he pushed and bit down and took the gloved fingers clean off, so there was rubber-wrapped meat in his mouth again and his father's head exploded into needled antennae of color like an exploding star between his gown's raised green arms and a call for *Zuckung* while Tony's heels drummed and struggled against the widening stirrups of light they were hoisted into while a curtain of red was drawn wetly up over the floor he stared down at, Tony, and he heard someone yelling for someone to Give In, Err, with a hand on his lace belly as he bore down to PUSH and he saw the legs in the stirrups they held would keep spreading until they cracked him open and all the way inside-out on the ceiling and his last worry was that red-handed Poppa could see up his dress, what was hidden.

O

7 NOVEMBER — YEAR OF THE DEPEND ADULT UNDERGARMENT

Each of the eight to ten prorectors at the Enfield Tennis Academy teaches one academic class per term, usually a once-a-week Saturday thing. This is mostly for certification reasons,[104] plus all but one of the prorectors are low-level touring professionals, with low-level professional tennis players in general being not exactly the most candent stars in the intellectual Orion. Because of all this, their classes tend to be not only electives but Academy jokes, and the E.T.A. Dean of Academic Affairs regards prorector-taught classes — e.g., in Fall Y.D.A.U., Corbett Thorp's 'Deviant Geometries,' Aubrey deLint's 'Introduction to Athletic Spreadsheets,' or the colon-mad Tex Watson's 'From Scarcity to Plenty: From Putrid Stuff Out of the Ground to the Atom in the Mirror: A Lay Look at Energy Resources from Anthracite to Annular Fusion,' etc. — as not satisfying any sort of quadrivial requirement. But the older E.T.A.s, with more latitude credit- and elective-wise, still tend to clamor and jostle for spots in the prorectors' seminars, not just because the classes can be passed by pretty much anybody who shows up and displays vital signs, but because most of the prorectors are (also like low-level tennis pros as a genus) kind of bats, and their classes are usually fascinating the way plane-crash footage is fascinating. E.g., although any closed room she's in soon develops a mysterious and overpowering vitamin-B stink he can just barely stand, E.T.A. senior Ted Schacht has taken Mary Esther Thode's perennially batsoid 'The Personal Is the Political Is the Psychopathological: the Politics of Contemporary Psychopathological Double-

306

Binds' all three times it's been offered. M. E. Thode is regarded by the upperclassmen as probably insane, by like clinical standards, although her coaching proficiency with the Girls' 16's is beyond dispute. A bit on the old side for an E.T.A. prorector, Thode had been a pupil of Coach G. Schtitt back at Schtitt's infamous old crop-and-epaulette Harry Hopman program in Winter Park FL and then for a couple years at the new E.T.A. as a top and Show-bound if kind of rabidly political and not too tightly wrapped female junior. Later blacklisted off both the Virginia Slims and Family Circle professional distaff circuits after trying to organize the circuits' more politically rabid and unwrapped players into a sort of radical post-feminist grange that would compete only in pro tournaments organized, subsidized, refereed, overseen, and even attended and cartridge-distributed exclusively to not only women or homosexual women, but only by, for, and to registered members of the infamously unpopular early-Interdependence-era Female Objectification Prevention and Protest Phalanx,[105] given the shoe, she'd come, practically with a bandanna-tied stick over her shoulder, back to Coach Schtitt, who for historico-national reasons has always had a soft place inside for anyone who seems even marginally politically repressed. Last spring's airless and B-redolent section of Thode's psycho-political offering, 'The Toothless Predator: Breast-Feeding as Sexual Assault,' had been one of the most disorientingly fascinating experiences of Ted Schacht's intellectual life so far, outside the dentist's chair, whereas this fall's focus on pathologic double-bind-type quandaries was turning out to be not quite as compelling but weirdly — almost intuitively — easy:

E.g., from today's:

The Personal Is the Political Is the Psychopathological: The Politics of
Contemporary Psychopathological Double-Binds
Midterm Examination
Ms. THODE
November 7, Yr. of D.A.U.

KEEP YOUR ANSWERS *BRIEF* AND *GENDER NEUTRAL*

ITEM *1*

(1a) You are an individual who, is pathologically kleptomaniacal. As a kleptomaniac, you are pathologically driven to steal, steal, steal. You must steal.

(1b) But, you are also an individual who, is pathologically agoraphobic. As an agoraphobic, you cannot so much as step off your front step of the porch of your home, without undergoing palpitations, drenching sweats, and feelings of impending doom. As an agoraphobic, you are driven to pathologically stay home and not leave. You cannot leave home.

(1c) But, from (1a) you are pathologically driven to go out and steal, steal, steal. But, from (1b) you are pathologically driven to not ever leave home. You live alone.

Meaning, there is no one else in your home to steal from. Meaning, you must go out, into the marketplace to satisfy your overwhelming compulsion to steal, steal, steal. But, such is your fear of the marketplace that you cannot under any circumstances, leave home. Whether your problem is true personal psychopathology, or merely marginalization by a political definition of 'psychopathology,' nevertheless, it is a Double-Bind.

(1d) Thus, respond to the question of, what do you do?

Schacht was just looping the d in *mail fraud* when Jim Troeltsch's pseudo-radio program, backed by its eustacian-crumpling operatic soundtrack, came over 112 West House's E.T.A.-intercom speaker up over the classroom clock. When no away-tournaments or meets were going on, WETA student-run 'radio' got to 'broadcast' E.T.A.-related news, sports and community affairs for ten or so minutes over the closed-circuit intercom every Tuesday and Saturday during the last P.M. class period, like 1435–1445h. Troeltsch, who's dreamed of a tennis-broadcast career ever since it became clear (very early) that he would be in no way Show-bound — the Troeltsch who spends every last fin his folks send him on his staggering InterLace/SPN-pro-match-cartridge library, and spends almost every free second calling pro action with his room's TP's viewer's volume down;[106] the kind of pathetic Troeltsch who shamelessly kiss-asses the InterLace/SPN sportscasters whenever he's on the scene of an I/SPN-recorded jr. event,[107] pestering the sportscasters and offering to get them doughnuts and joe, etc.; the Troeltsch who already owns a whole rack of generic blue blazers and practices combing his hair so that it has that glassy toupee-like look of a real sportscaster — Troeltsch's been doing the sports portion of WETA's weekly broadcast ever since Schacht's old man died of ulcerative colitis and Ted came up to join his old childhood doubles partner at the Academy in the fall of the Year of the Trial-Size Dove Bar, which had been four months after the late E.T.A. Headmaster's felo de se, when the flags were still at half-mast and everybody's bicep was banded in black cotton, which the mesomorphic Schacht got excused from because of biceps-size; Troeltsch'd already been doing WETA sports when he came, and he's been undislodgeable from the post ever since.

The sports portion of WETA's broadcast is mostly just reporting the outcomes and scores of whatever competitive events the E.T.A. squads have been in since the last broadcast.[108] Troeltsch, who approaches his twice-a-week duties with all possible verve, will say he feels like the hardest thing about his intercom-broadcasts is keeping things from getting repetitive as he goes through long lists of who beat whom and by how much. His quest for synonyms for *beat* and *got beat by* is never-ending and serious and a continual source of irritation to his friends. Mary Esther's exams were notorious no-brainers and automatic A's if you were careful with your third-person pronouns, and even while he listened closely enough to Troeltsch to be able to supply the audience-feedback that tonight's dinner-table would be inescapable without, Schacht was already on the test's third item, which concerned exhibitionism among the pathologically shy. 11/7's broadcast results were from E.T.A.'s 71–37 rout of Port Washington's A and B teams at the Port Washington annual thing.

'John Wayne at A-1 18's beat Port Washington's Bob Francis of Great Neck, New New York, 6–0, 6–2,' Troeltsch says, 'while A-2 Singles' Hal Incandenza defeated Craig Burda of Vivian Park, Utah, 6–2, 6–1; and while A-3 K. D. Coyle went down in a hard-fought loss to Port Wash's Shelby van der Merwe of Hempstead, Long Island 6–3, 5–7, 7–5, A-4 Trevor "The Axhandle" Axford crushed P.W.'s Tapio Martti out of Sonora, Mexico, 7–5, 6–2.'

And so on. By the time it's down to Boys A-14's, Troeltsch's delivery gets terser even as his attempts at verbiform variety tend to have gotten more lurid, e.g.: 'LaMont Chu disembowelled Charles Pospisilova 6–3, 6–2; Jeff Penn was on Nate Millis-Johnson like a duck on a Junebug 6–4, 6–7, 6–0; Peter Beak spread Ville Dillard on a cracker like some sort of hors d'oeuvre and bit down 6–4, 7–6, while 14's A-4 Idris Arslanian ground his heel into the neck of David Wiere 6–1, 6–4 and P.W.'s 5-man R. Greg Chubb had to be just about carried off over somebody's shoulder after Todd Possalthwaite moonballed him into a narcoleptic coma 4–6, 6–4, 7–5.'

Some of Corbett Thorp's class on geometric distortions a lot of kids find hard; likewise deLint's class, for the software-inept. And though Tex Watson's overall handle on Cold-Containment DT-annulation is shaky, his lay-physics survey of combustion and annulation has some sort of academic validity to it, especially because he some terms gets Pemulis to guest-lecture when he and Pemulis are in a period of détente. But the only really challenging prorected class ever for Hal Incandenza is turning out to be Mlle. Thierry Poutrincourt's 'Separatism and Return: Québecois History from Frontenac Through the Age of Interdependence,' which to be candid Hal'd never heard much positive about and had always deflected his Moms's suggestions that he might profitably take until finally this term's schedule-juggling got dicey, and which (the class) he finds difficult and annoying but surprisingly less and less dull as the semester wears on, and is actually developing something of a layman's savvy for Canadianism and O.N.A.N.ite politics, topics he'd previously found for some reason not only dull but queerly distasteful. The rub of this particular class's difficulty is that Poutrincourt teaches only in Québecois French, which Hal can get by in because of his youthful tour through Orin's real-French Pléiade Classics but has never all that much liked, particularly sound-wise, Québecois being a gurgly, glottal language that seems to require a perpetually sour facial expression to pronounce. Hal sees no way of Orin's knowing he was taking

Poutrincourt's 'Separatism and Return' when he called to ask for help with Separatism, which Orin's asking for help from him with anything was strange enough in itself.

'Bernadette Longley reluctantly bowed to P.W.'s Jessica Pearlberg at 18 A-1 Singles 6–4, 4–6, 6–2, though A-2 Diane Prins hopped up and down on the thorax of Port's Marilyn Ng-A-Thiep 7–6, 6–1, and Bridget Boone drove a hot thin spike into the right eye of Aimee Middleton-Law 6–3, 6–3'; and so on, in classroom after classroom, while instructors grade quizzes or read or tap a decreasingly patient foot, every Tues./Sat., while Schacht sketches prenatal dentition-charts in his exam's margins w/ a concentrated look, not wanting to embarrass Thode by handing the no-brainer exam in too soon.

Most of the early-Québec stuff about Cartier and Roberval and Cap Rouge and Champlain and flocks of Ursuline nuns with frozen wimples covered up to like U.N. Day Hal'd found mostly dry and repetitive, the wig-and-jerkin gentlemanly warfare stilted and absurd, like slow-motion slapstick, though everyone'd been sort of queasily intrigued by the way the English Commander Amherst had handled the Hurons by dispensing free blankets and buckskin that had been carefully coated with smallpox *variola*.

'14's A-3 Felicity Zweig went absolutely SACPOP on P.W.'s Kiki Pfefferblit 7–6, 6–1, while Gretchen Holt made PW's Tammi Taylor-Bing sorry her parents were ever even in the same room together 6–0, 6–3. At 5, Ann Kittenplan grimaced and flexed her way to a 7–5, 2–6, 6–3 win over Paisley Steinkamp, right next to where Jolene Criess at 6 was doing to P.W.'s Mona Ghent what a quality boot can do to a toadstool, 2 and 2.'

Saluki-faced Thierry Poutrincourt leans back in her chair and closes her eyes and presses her palms hard against her temples and stays like that all the way through every WETA broadcast, which always interrupts her last-period lecture and puts this section slightly and maddeningly behind Separation & Return's other section, resulting in two required lesson-preps instead of one. The sour Saskatchewanese kid next to Hal has been making impressive schematic drawings of automatic weaponry in his notebook all semester. The kid's assigned ROM-diskettes are always visible in his book-bag still in their wrapper, yet the Skatch kid always finishes quizzes in like five minutes. It had taken up to the week before Halloween to get through with the B.S. '67 Levesque-Parti-and-Bloc Québecois[109] and early Fronte de la Libération Nationale stuff and up to the present Interdependent era. Poutrincourt's lecture-voice has gotten quieter and quieter as history's approached its contemporary limit; and Hal, finding the stuff rather more high-concept and less dull than he'd expected — seeing himself as at his innermost core apolitical — nevertheless found the Québecois-Separatism mentality almost impossibly convoled and confused and impervious to U.S.

parsing,[110] plus was both com- and repelled by the fact that the contemporary-anti-O.N.A.N.-insurgence stuff provoked in him a queasy feeling, not the glittery disorientation of nightmares or on-court panic but a soggier, more furtively nauseous kind of sense, as if someone had been reading mail of Hal's that he thought he'd thrown away.

The proud and haughty Québecois had been harassing and even terrorizing the rest of Canada over the Separation issue for time out of mind. It was the establishment of O.N.A.N. and the gerrymandering of the Great Convexity (Poutrincourt's Canadian, recall) that turned the malevolent attention of Québec's worst post-F.L.N. insurgents south of the border. Ontario and New Brunswick took the continental *Anschluss* and territorial Reconfiguration like good sports. Certain far-right fringes in Alberta weren't too pleased, but not much pleases an Albertan far-rightist anyway. It was, finally, only the proud and haughty Québecois who whinged,[111] and the insurgent cells of Québec who completely lost their political shit.

Québec's anti-O.N.A.N. and thus -U.S. Séparatisteurs, the different terrorist cells formed when Ottawa had been the foe, proved to be not a very nice bunch at all. The earliest unignorable strikes involved a then-unknown terrorist cell[112] that apparently snuck down from the E.W.D.-blighted Papineau region at night and dragged huge standing mirrors across U.S. Interstate 87 at selected dangerous narrow winding Adirondack passes south of the border and its Lucite walls. Naïvely empiricist north-bound U.S. motorists — a good many of them military and O.N.A.N.ite personnel, this close to the Concavity — would see impending headlights and believe some like suicidal idiot or Canadian had transversed the median and was coming right for them. They'd flash their high beams, but to all appearances the impending idiot would just flash his high beams right back. The U.S. motorists — usually not to be fucked with in their vehicles, historically, it was well known — would brazen it out as long as anyone right-minded possibly could, but right before apparent impact with the impending lights they'd always veer wildly and leave shoulderless I-87 and put their arm over their head in that screaming pre-crash way and go ass-over-teakettle into an Adirondack chasm with a many-petaled bloom of Hi-Test flame, and the then-unknown Québecois terrorist cell would remove the huge mirror and truck off back up north via checkpointless back roads back into the blighted bowels of southern Québec until next time. There were fatalities this way well into the Year of the Tucks Medicated Pad before anyone had any idea they were diabolic-cell-related. For over twenty months the scores of burnt-out hulls piling up in Adirondack chasms were regarded as either suicides or inexplicable doze-behind-the-wheel-type single-car accidents by NNY State Troopers who had to detach their chinstraps to scratch under their big brown hats over the mysterious sleepiness that seemed to afflict Adirondack motorists at what looked to be high-adrenaline mountaintop passes. Chief of the new United States Office of Unspecified Services Rodney Tine pressed, to his later embarrassment, for a series of anti–driving-when-drowsy Public Service spots to be InterLace-disseminated in upstate New New York. It was an actual U.S. would-be suicide, a late-stage Valium-addicted Amway distributor from Schenectady who was at the end of her benzodioxane-rope and all over the road anyway, and who by historical accounts saw the sudden impending headlights in her northbound lane as Grace and shut her eyes and floored it right for them, the lights, never once veering, spraying glass and micronized silver over all four lanes, this unwitting civilian who 'SMASHED THE ILLUSION,' 'MADE THE BREAKTHROUGH' (media headlines), and brought to light the first tangible evidence of an anti-O.N.A.N. ill will way worse than anything aroused by plain old historical Separatism, up in Québec.

The first birth of the Incandenzas' second son was a surprise. The tall and eye-poppingly curvaceous Avril Incandenza did not show, bled like clockwork; no hemorrhoids or gland-static; no pica; affect and appetite normal; she threw up some mornings but who didn't in those days?

It was on a metal-lit November evening in the seventh month of a hidden pregnancy that she stopped, Avril, on her husband's long arm as they ascended the maple staircase of the Back Bay brownstone they were soon to leave, stopped, turned partly toward him, ashen, and opened her mouth in a mute way that was itself eloquent.

Her husband looked down at her, paling: 'What is it?'

'It's pain.'

It was pain. Broken water had made several steps below them gleam. She seemed to James Incandenza to sort of turn in toward herself, hold herself low, curl and sink to a stairstep she barely made the edge of, hunched, her forehead against her shapely knees. Incandenza saw the whole slow thing in a light like he was Vermeer: she sank steadily from his side and he bent to hers and she then tried to rise.

'Wait wait wait wait. Wait.'

'It's pain.'

A bit ragged from an afternoon of Wild Turkey and low-temperature holography, James had thought Avril was dying right before his eyes. His own father had dropped dead on a set of stairs. Luckily Avril's half-brother Charles Tavis was upstairs, using the portable StairMaster he'd brought with him for an extended and emotional-battery-recharging visit the preceding spring, after the horrible snafu with the video-scoreboard at Toronto's Skydome; and he heard the commotion and scuttled out and down and promptly took charge.

He had to be more or less scraped out, Mario, like the meat of an oyster from a womb to whose sides he'd been found spiderishly clinging, tiny and unobtrusive, attached by cords of sinew at both feet and a hand, the other fist stuck to his face by the same material.[113] He was a complete surprise and terribly premature, and withered, and he spent the next many weeks waggling his withered and contracted arms up at the Pyrex ceilings of incubators, being fed by tubes and monitored by wires and cupped in sterile palms, his head cradled by a thumb. Mario had been given the name of Dr. James Incandenza's father's father, a dour and golf-addicted Green Valley AZ oculist who made a small fortune, just after Jim grew up and fled east, by inventing those quote *X-Ray Specs!* that don't work but whose allure for mid-'60s pubescent comic-book readers almost compelled mail-order, then selling the copyrights to New England novelty-industry titan AcméCo, then promptly in mid-putt died, Mario Sr. did, allowing James Incandenza Sr. to retire from a sad third career as the Man From Glad[114] in sandwich-bag commercials during the B.S. 1960s and move back to the saguaro-studded desert he loathed and efficiently drink himself to a cerebral hemorrhage on a Tucson stairway.

Anyway, Mario II's incomplete gestation and arachnoidal birth left the kid with some lifelong character-building physical challenges. Size was one, he being in sixth grade about the size of a toddler and at 18+ in a range somewhere between elf and jockey. There was the matter of the withered-looking and bradyauxetic arms, which just as in a hair-raising case of Volk-mann's contracture[115] curled out in front of his thorax in magiscule S's and were usable for rudimentary knifeless eating and slapping at doorknobs un-til they sort of turned just enough and doors could be kicked open and forming a pretend lens-frame to scout scenes through, plus maybe toss-ing tennis balls very short distances to players who wanted them, but not for much else, though the arms were impressively — almost familial-dysautonomically — pain-resistant, and could be pinched, punctured, singed, and even compressed in a basement optical-device-securing viselike thing by Mario's older brother Orin without effect or complaint.

Bradypedestrianism-wise, Mario had not so much club feet as more like *block* feet: not only flat but perfectly square, good for kicking knob-fumbled doors open with but too short to be conventionally employed as feet: together with the lordosis in his lower spine, they force Mario to move in the sort of lurchy half-stumble of a vaudeville inebriate, body tilted way forward as if into a wind, right on the edge of pitching face-first onto the ground, which as a child he did fairly often, whether given a bit of a shove from behind by his older brother Orin or no. The fre-quent forward falls help explain why Mario's nose was squished severely in and so flared out to either side of his face but did not rise from it, with the consequence that his nostrils tended to flap just a bit, particularly during sleep. One eyelid hung lower than the other over his open eyes — good and gently brown eyes, if a bit large and protrusive to qualify as conventionally human eyes — the one lid hung like an ill-tempered windowshade, and his older brother Orin had sometimes tried to give the recalcitrant lid that smart type of downward snap that can unstick a dicky shade, but had succeeded only in gradually loosening the lid from its sutures, so that it eventually had to be refashioned and reattached in yet another blepharoplasty-procedure, because it was in fact not Mario's real eyelid — that had been sacrificed when the fist stuck to his face like a tongue to cold metal had been peeled away, at nativity — but an extremely advanced blepharoprosthesis of dermal fibropolymer studded with horsehair lashes that curved out into space well beyond the reach of his other lid's lashes and together with the lazy lid-action itself gave even Mario's most neutral expression the character of an oddly friendly pirate's squint. Together with the involuntarily constant smile.

This is probably also the place to mention Hal's older brother Mario's khaki-colored skin, an odd dead gray-green that in its corticate texture and together with his atrophic in-curled arms and arachnodactylism gave him, particularly from a middle-distance, an almost uncannily reptilian/dinosaurian look. The fingers being not only mucronate and talonesque but nonprehensile, which is what made Mario's knifework untenable at table. Plus the thin lank slack hair, at once tattered and somehow too smooth, that looked at 18+ like the hair of a short plump 48-year-old stress engineer and athletic director and Academy Headmaster who grows one side to girlish length and carefully combs it so it rides thinly up and over the gleaming yarmulke of bare gray-green-complected scalp on top and down over the other side where it hangs lank and fools no one and tends to flap back up over in any wind Charles Tavis forgets to carefully keep his left side to. Or that he's slow, Hal's brother is, technically, Stanford-Binet-wise, slow, the Brandeis C.D.C. found — but *not,* verifiably *not,* retarded or cognitively damaged or bradyphrenic, more like refracted, almost, ever so slightly epistemically bent, a pole poked into mental water and just a little off and just taking a little bit longer, in the manner of all refracted things.

Or that his status at the Enfield Tennis Academy — erected, along with Dr. and Mrs. I's marriage's third and final home at the northern rear of the grounds, when Mario was nine and Hallie eight and Orin seventeen and in his one E.T.A. year B-4 Singles and in the U.S.T.A.'s top 75 — that Mario's life there is by all appearances kind of a sad and left-out-type existence, the only physically challenged minor in residence, unable even to grip a regulation stick or stand unaided behind a boundaried space. That he and his late father had been, no pun intended, inseparable. That Mario'd been like an honorary assistant production-assistant and carried the late Incandenza's film and lenses and filters in a complex backpack the size of a joint of beef for most of the last three years of the late-blooming filmmaker's life, attending him on shoots and sleeping with multiple pillows in small soft available spaces in the same motel room as Himself and occasionally tottering out for a bright-red plastic bottle of something called Big Red Soda Water and taking it to the apparently mute veiled graduate-intern down the motel's hall, fetching coffee and joe and various pancreatitis-remedies and odds and ends for props and helping D. Leith out with Continuity when Incandenza wanted to preserve Continuity, basically being the way any son would be whose dad let him into his heart's final and best-loved love, lurching gamely but not pathetically to keep up with the tall stooped increasingly bats man's slow patient two-meter stride through airports, train stations, carrying the lenses, inclined ever forward but in no way resembling any kind of leashed pet.

When required to stand upright and still, like when videotaping an E.T.A.'s service motion or manning the light meters on the set of a high-contrast chiaroscuro art film, Mario in his forward list is supported by a NNYC-apartment-door-style police lock, a .7-meter steel pole that extends from a special Velcroed vest and angles about 40° down and out to a slotted piece of lead blocking (a bitch to carry, in that complicated pack) placed by someone understanding and prehensile on the ground before him. He stood thus buttressed on sets Himself had him help erect and furnish and light, the lighting usually unbelievably complex and for some parts of the crew sometimes almost blinding, sunbursts of angled mirrors and Marino lamps and key-light kliegs, Mario getting a thorough technical grounding in a cinematic craft he never even imagined being able to pursue on his own until Xmas of the Year of the Trial-Size Dove Bar, when a gaily wrapped package forwarded from the offices of Incandenza's attorney revealed that Himself had designed and built and legally willed (in a codicil) to be gaily wrapped and forwarded for Mario's thirteenth Xmas a trusty old Bolex H64 Rex 5[116] tri-lensed camera bolted to an oversized old leather aviator's helmet and supported by struts whose ends were the inverted tops of training-room crutches and curved nicely over Mario's shoulders, so the Bolex H64 required no digital prehensility because it fit over Mario's oversized face[117] like a tri-plated scuba mask and was controlled by a sewing-machine-adapted foot treadle, and but even then it took some serious getting used to, and Mario's earliest pieces of digital juvenilia are marred/enhanced by this palsied, pointing-every-which-way quality of like home movies shot at a dead run.

Five years hence, Mario's facility with the head-mount Bolex attenuates the sadness of his status here, allowing him to contribute via making the annual E.T.A. fundraising documentary cartridge, videotaping students' strokes and occasionally from over the railing of Schtitt's supervisory transom the occasional challenge-match — the taping's become part of the pro-instruction package detailed in the E.T.A. catalogue — plus producing more ambitious, arty-type things that occasionally find a bit of an à-clef-type following in the E.T.A. community.

After Orin Incandenza left the nest to first hit and then kick collegiate balls, there was almost nobody at E.T.A. or its Enfield-Brighton environs who did not treat Mario M. Incandenza with the casual gentility of somebody who doesn't pity you or admire you so much as just vaguely prefer it when you're around. And Mario — despite rectilinear feet and cumbersome police lock the most prodigious walker-and-recorder in three districts — hit the unsheltered area streets daily at a very slow pace, a halting constitutional, sometimes w/ head-mounted Bolex and sometimes not, and took citizens' kindness and cruelty the same way, with a kind of extra-inclined half-bow that mocked his own canted posture without pity or cringe. Mario's an especial favorite among the low-rent shopkeepers up and down E.T.A.'s stretch of Commonwealth Ave., and photographic stills from some of his better efforts adorn the walls behind certain Comm. Ave. deli counters and steam presses and Korean-keyed cash registers. The object of a strange and maybe kind of cliquey affection from Lyle the Spandexed sweat-guru, to whom he sometimes brings Caffeine-Free Diet Cokes to cut the diet's salt, Mario sometimes finds younger E.T.A.s referred to him by Lyle on really ticklish matters of injury and incapacity and character and rallying-what-remains, and never much knows what to say. Trainer Barry Loach all but kisses the kid's ring, since it's Mario who through coincidence saved him from the rank panhandling underbelly of Boston Common's netherworld and more or less got him his job.[118] Plus of course there's the fact that Schtitt himself constitutionalizes with him, of certain warm evenings, and lets him ride in his surplus sidecar. An object of some weird attracto-repulsive gestalt for Charles Tavis, Mario treats C.T. with the quiet deference he can feel his possible half-uncle wanting, and stays out of his way as much as possible, for Tavis's sake. Players at Denny's, when they all get to go to Denny's, almost vie to see who gets to cut up the cut-upable parts of Mario's under-12-size Kilobreakfast.

And his younger and way more externally impressive brother Hal almost idealizes Mario, secretly. God-type issues aside, Mario is a (semi-) walking miracle, Hal believes. People who're somehow burned at birth, withered or ablated way past anything like what might be fair, they either curl up in their fire, or else they rise. Withered saurian homodontic[119] Mario floats, for Hal. He calls him Booboo but fears his opinion more than probably anybody except their Moms's. Hal remembers the unending hours of blocks and balls on the hardwood floors of early childhood's 36 Belle Ave., Weston MA, tangrams and See 'N Spell, huge-headed Mario hanging in there for games he could not play, for make-believe in which he had no interest other than proximity to his brother. Avril remembers Mario still wanting Hal to help him with bathing and dressing at thirteen — an age when most unchallenged kids are ashamed of the very space their sound pink bodies take up — and wanting the help for Hal's sake, not his own. Despite himself (and showing a striking lack of insight into his Moms's psyche), Hal fears that Avril sees Mario as the family's real prodigy, an in-bent savant-type genius of no classifiable type, a very rare and shining thing, even if his intuition — slow and silent — scares her, his academic poverty breaks her heart, the smile he puts on each A.M. without fail since the suicide of their father makes her wish she could cry. This is why she tries so terribly hard to leave Mario alone, not to hover or wring, to treat him so less specially than she wants: it is for him. It is kind of noble, pitiable. Her love for the son who was born a surprise transcends all other experiences and informs her life. Hal suspects. It was Mario, not Avril, who obtained Hal his first copies of the unabridged O.E.D. at a time when Hal was still being shunted around for the assessment of possible damage, Booboo pulling them home in a wagon by his bicuspids over the fake-rural blacktop roads of upscale Weston, months before Hal tested out at Whatever's Beyond Eidetic on the Mnemonic Verbal Inventory designed by a dear and trusted colleague of the Moms at Brandeis. It was Avril, not Hal, who insisted that Mario live not in HmH with her and Charles Tavis but with Hal in an E.T.A. subdorm. But in the Year of Dairy Products From the American Heartland it was Hal, not she, who, when the veiled legate from the Union of the Hideously and Improbably Deformed showed up at the E.T.A. driveway's portcullis to discuss with Mario issues of blind inclusion v. visual estrangement, of the openness of concealment the veil might afford him, it was Hal, even as Mario laughed and half-bowed, it was Hal, brandishing his Dunlop stick, who told the guy to go peddle his linen someplace else.

30 APRIL / 1 MAY
YEAR OF THE DEPEND ADULT UNDERGARMENT

The sky of U.S.A.'s desert was clotted with blue stars. Now it was deep at night. Only above the U.S.A. city was the sky blank of stars; its color was pearly and blank. Marathe shrugged. 'Perhaps in you is the sense that citizens of Canada are not involved in the real root of the threat.'

Steeply shook the head in seeming annoyance. 'What's that supposed to mean?' he said. The lurid wig of him slipped when he moved the head with any abrupt force.

The first way Marathe betrayed anything of emotion was to smooth rather too fussily at the blanket on his lap. 'It is meaning that it will not of finality be Québecers making this kick to *l'aine des Etats Unis*. Look: the facts of the situation speak loudly. What is known. This is a U.S.A. production, this Entertainment cartridge. Made by an American man in the U.S.A. The appetite for the appeal of it: this also is U.S.A. The U.S.A. drive for spectation, which your culture teaches. This I was saying: this is why choosing is everything. When I say to you choose with great care in loving and you make ridicule it is why I look and say: can I believe this man is saying this thing of ridicule?' Marathe leaned slightly forward on his stumps, leaving the machine pistol to use both his hands in saying. Steeply could tell this was important to Marathe; he really believed it.

Marathe made small emphatic circles and cuts in the air while he spoke: 'These facts of situation, which speak so loudly of your *Bureau*'s fear of this *samizdat:* now is what has happened when a people choose nothing over themselves to love, each one. A U.S.A. that would die — and let its children die, each one — for the so-called perfect Entertainment, this film. Who would die for this chance to be fed this death of pleasure with spoons, in their warm homes, alone, unmoving: Hugh Steeply, in complete seriousness as a citizen of your neighbor I say to you: forget for a moment the Entertainment, and think instead about a U.S.A. where such a thing could be possible enough for your Office to fear: can such a U.S.A. hope to survive for a much longer time? To survive as a nation of peoples? To much less exercise dominion over other nations of other peoples? If these are other peoples who still know what it is to choose? who will die for something larger? who will sacrifice the warm home, the loved woman at home, their legs, their life even, for something more than their own wishes of sentiment? who would choose not to die for pleasure, alone?'

Steeply removed with cool deliberation another Belgian cigarette and lit it, this time on the first match. Waving the match out with a circular flourish and snap. All this took time of his silence. Marathe settled back. Marathe wondered why the presence of Americans could always make him feel vaguely ashamed after saying things he believed. An aftertaste of shame after revealing passion of any belief and type when with Americans, as if he had made flatulence instead of had revealed belief.

Steeply rested his one elbow on the forearm of the other arm across his prostheses, to smoke like a woman: 'You're saying that the administration wouldn't even be concerned about the Entertainment if we didn't know we were fatally weak. As in as a nation. You're saying the fact that we're worried speaks volumes about the nation itself.'

Marathe shrugged. 'Us, we will force nothing on U.S.A. persons in their warm homes. We will make only available. Entertainment. There will be then some choosing, to partake or choose not to.' Smoothing slightly at his lap's blanket. 'How will U.S.A.s choose? Who has taught them to choose with care? How will your Offices and Agencies protect them, your people?

By laws? By killing Québecois?' Marathe rose, but very slightly. 'As you were killing Colombians and Bolivians to protect U.S.A. citizens who desire their narcotics? How well did this work for your Agencies and Offices, the killing? How long was it before the Brazilians replaced the dead of Colombia?'

Steeply's wig had slipped hard to starboard. 'Rémy, no. Drug-dealers don't want you dead, necessarily; they just want your money. There's a difference. You people seem to want us dead. Not just the Concavity re-demised. Not just secession for Québec. The F.L.Q., maybe they're like the Bolivians. But Fortier wants us dead.'

'Again you pass over what is important. Why B.S.S. cannot understand us. You cannot kill what is already dead.'

'Just you wait and see if we're dead, paisano.'

Marathe made a gesture as if striking his own head. 'Again passing over the important. This appetite to choose death by pleasure if it is available to choose — this *appetite* of your people unable to choose appetites, *this* is the death. What you call the death, the collapsing: this will be the formality only. Do you not see? This was the genius of Guillaume DuPlessis, what M. DuPlessis taught the cells, even if F.L.Q. and les Fils did not understand. Much less the Albertans, all crazy inside their head. We of the A.F.R., we understand. This is why *this* cell of Québecers, *that* danger of Entertainment so fine it will kill the viewer, if so — the exact way does not matter. The exact time of death and way of death, this no longer matters. Not for your peoples. You wish to protect them? But you can only delay. Not save. The Entertainment exists. The attaché and gendarmes of the razzle incident — more proof. It is there, existing. The choice for death of the head by pleasure now exists, and your authorities know, or you would not be now trying to stop the pleasure. Your Sans-Christe Gentle was in this one part correct: "*Someone is to blame.*" '

'That had nothing to do with the Reconfiguration. The Reconfiguration was self-preservation.'

'That: forget it. There is the villain he saw you needed, all of you, to delay this splitting apart. To keep you together, the hating some other. Gentle is crazy in his head, but in this "*fault of someone*" he was correct in saying it. *Un ennemi commun.* But not someone outside you, this enemy. Someone or some people among your own history sometime killed your U.S.A. nation already, Hugh. Someone who had authority, or should have had authority and did not exercise authority. I do not know. But someone sometime let you forget how to choose, and what. Someone let your peoples forget it was the only thing of importance, choosing. So completely forgetting that when I say *choose* to you you make expressions with your face such as "*Herrrrrre we are going.*" Someone taught that temples are for fanatics only and took away the temples and promised there was no need for temples. And now there is no shelter. And no map for finding the shelter of a temple. And you all stumble about in the dark, this confusion of permissions. The without-end pursuit of a happiness of which someone let you forget the old things which made happiness possible. How is it you say: "*Anything is going*"?'

'And this is why we shudder at what a separate Québec would be like. Choose what we tell you, neglect your own wish and desires, sacrifice. For Québec. For the State.'

Marathe shrugged. '*L'état protecteur.*'

Steeply said 'Does this sound a little familiar, Rémy? The National Socialist Neofascist State of Separate Québec? You guys are worse than the worst Albertans. Totalitarity. Cuba with snow. Ski immediately to your nearest reeducation camp, for instructions on choosing. Moral eugenics. China. Cambodia. Chad. Unfree.'

'Unhappy.'

'There are no choices without personal freedom, Buckeroo. It's not us who are dead inside. These things you find so weak and contemptible in us — these are just the hazards of being free.'

'But what does this U.S.A. expression want to mean, this *Buckeroo?*'

Steeply turned to face away into the space they were above. 'And now here we go. Now you will say how free are we if you dangle fatal fruit before us and we cannot help ourselves from temptation. And we say "human" to you. We say that one cannot be human without freedom.'

Marathe's chair squeaked slightly as his weight shifted. 'Always with you this freedom! For your walled-up country, always to shout "Freedom! Freedom!" as if it were obvious to all people what it wants to mean, this word. But look: it is not so simple as that. Your freedom is the freedom-*from*: no one tells your precious individual U.S.A. selves what they must do. It is this meaning only, this freedom from constraint and forced duress.' Marathe over Steeply's shoulder suddenly could realize why the skies above the coruscating city were themselves erased of stars: it was the fumes from the exhaust's wastes of the moving autos' pretty lights that rose and hid stars from the city and made the city Tucson's lume nacreous in the dome's blankness of it. 'But what of the freedom-*to?* Not just free-*from*. Not all compulsion comes from without. You pretend you do not see this. What of freedom-*to*. How for the person to freely choose? How to choose any but a child's greedy choices if there is no loving-filled father to guide, inform, teach the person how to choose? How is there freedom to choose if one does not learn how to choose?'

Steeply threw away a cigarette and faced partly Marathe, from the edge: 'Now the story of the rich man.'

Marathe said 'The rich father who can afford the cost of candy as well as food for his children: but if he cries out "Freedom!" and allows his child to choose only what is sweet, eating only candy, not pea soup and bread and eggs, so his child becomes weak and sick: is the rich man who cries "Freedom!" the good father?'

Steeply made four small noises. Excitement of some belief made the American's electrolysis's little pimples of rash redden even in the milky dilute light of lume and low stars. The moon over the Mountains of Rincon was on its side, its color the color of a fat man's face. Marathe could believe he could hear some young U.S.A. voices shouting and laughing in a young gathering somewhere out on the desert floor below, but saw no headlights or young persons. Steeply stamped a high heel in frustration. Steeply said:

'But U.S. citizens aren't presumed by us to be children, to paternalistically do their thinking and choosing for them. Human beings are not children.'

Marathe pretended again to sniff.

'Ah, yes, but then you say: No?' Steeply said. 'No? you say, not children? You say: What is the difference, please, if you make a recorded pleasure so entertaining and diverting it is lethal to persons, you find a Copy-Capable copy and copy it and disseminate it for us to choose to see or turn off, and if we cannot choose to resist it, the pleasure, and cannot choose instead to live? You say what your Fortier believes, that we *are* children, not human adults like the noble Québecers, we are children, bullies but still children inside, and will kill ourselves for you if you put the candy within the arms' reach.'

Marathe tried to make his face expressive of anger, which was difficult for him. 'This is what happens: you imagine the things I will say and then say them for me and then become angry with them. Without my mouth; it never opens. You speak to yourself, inventing sides. This itself is the habit of children: lazy, lonely, self. I am not even here, possibly, for listening to.'

Unmentioned by either man was how in heaven's name either man expected to get up or down from the mountainside's shelf in the dark of the U.S. desert's night.

8 NOVEMBER
YEAR OF THE DEPEND ADULT UNDERGARMENT
INTERDEPENDENCE DAY
GAUDEAMUS IGITUR

Every year at E.T.A., maybe a dozen of the kids between maybe like twelve and fifteen — children in the very earliest stages of puberty and really abstract-capable thought, when one's allergy to the confining realities of the present is just starting to emerge as weird kind of nostalgia for stuff you never even knew[120] — maybe a dozen of these kids, mostly male, get fanatically devoted to a homemade Academy game called Eschaton. Eschaton is the most complicated children's game anybody around E.T.A.'d ever heard of. No one's entirely sure who brought it to Enfield from where. But you can pretty easily date its conception from the mechanics of the game itself. Its basic structure had already pretty much coalesced when Allston's Michael Pemulis hit age twelve and helped make it way more compelling. Its elegant complexity, combined with a dismissive-reenactment frisson and a complete disassociation from the realities of the present, composes most of its puerile appeal. Plus it's almost addictively compelling, and shocks the tall.

This year it's been Otis P. Lord, a thirteen-year-old baseliner and calculus phenom from Wilmington DE, who 'Wears the Beanie' as Eschaton's gamemaster and statistician of record, though Pemulis, since he's still around and is far and away the greatest Eschaton player in E.T.A. history, has a kind of unofficial emeritus power of correction over Lord's calculations and mandate.

Eschaton takes eight to twelve people to play, w/ 400 tennis balls so dead and bald they can't even be used for service drills anymore, plus an open expanse equal to the area of four contiguous tennis courts, plus a head for data-retrieval and coldly logical cognition, along with at least 40 megabytes of available RAM and wide array of tennis paraphernalia. The *vade-mecum*ish rulebook that Pemulis in Y.P.W. got Hal Incandenza to write — with appendices and sample c:\Pink$_2$\Mathpak\EndStat-path Decision-Tree diagrams and an offset of the most accessible essay Pemulis could find on applied game theory — is about as long and interesting as J. Bunyan's stupefying *Pilgrim's Progress from This World to That Which Is to Come,* and a pretty tough nut to compress into anything lively (although every year a dozen more E.T.A. kids memorize the thing at such a fanatical depth that they sometimes report reciting mumbled passages under light dental or cosmetic anesthesia, years later). But if Hal had a Luger pointed at him and were under compulsion to try, he'd probably start by explaining that each of the 400 dead tennis balls in the game's global arsenal represents a 5-megaton thermonuclear warhead. Of the total number of a given day's players,[121] three compose a theoretical *Anschluss* designated AMNAT, another three SOVWAR, one or two REDCHI, another one or two the wacko but always pesky LIBSYR or more formidable IRLIBSYR, and that the day's remaining players, depending on involved random considerations, can form anything from SOUTHAF to INDPAK to like an independent cell of Nuck insurgents with a 50-click Howitzer and big ideas. Each team is called a Combatant. On the open expanse of contiguous courts, Combatants are arrayed in positions corresponding to their location on the planet earth as represented in *The Rand McNally Slightly Rectangular Hanging Map of the*

World.[122] Practical distribution of total megatonnage requires a working knowledge of the Mean-Value Theorem for Integrals,[123] but for Hal's synoptic purposes here it's enough to say that megatonnage is distributed among Combatants according to an integrally regressed ratio of (a) Combatant's yearly military budget as percentage of Combatant's yearly GNP to (b) the inverse of stratego-tactical expenditures as percentage of Combatant's yearly military budget. In quainter days, Combatants' balls were simply doled out by throws of shiny red Yahtzee-dice. Quaint chance is no longer required, because Pemulis has downloaded Mathpak Unltd.'s elegant EndStat[124] stats-cruncher software into the late James Incandenza's fearsome idle drop-clothed D.E.C. 2100, and has shown Otis P. Lord how to dicky the lock to Schtitt's office at night with a dining-hall meal card and plug the D.E.C. into a three-prong that's under the lower left corner of the enormous print of Dürer's 'The Magnificent Beast' on the wall by the relevant edge of Schtitt's big glass desk, so Schtitt or deLint won't even know it's on, when it's on, then link it by cellular modem to a slick Yushityu portable with color monitor out on the courts' nuclear theater. AMNAT and SOVWAR usually end up with about 400 total megatons each, with the rest inconsistently divided. It's possible to complicate Pemulis's Mean-Value equation for distribution by factoring in stuff like historical incidences of bellicosity and appeasement, unique characteristics of perceived national interests, etc., but Lord, the son of not one but two bankers, is a straight bang-for-buck type of apportioner, a stance the equally bottom-line-minded Michael Pemulis endorses with both thumbs. Pieces of tennis gear are carefully placed within each Combatant's territories to mirror and map strategic targets. Folded gray-on-red E.T.A. T-shirts are MAMAs — Major Metro Areas. Towels stolen from selected motels on the junior tour stand for airfields, bridges, satellite-linked monitoring facilities, carrier groups, conventional power plants, important rail convergences. Red tennis shorts with gray trim are CONFORCONs — Conventional-Force Concentrations. The black cotton E.T.A. armbands — for when God forbid there's a death — designate the noncontemporary game-era's atomic power plants, uranium-/plutonium-enrichment facilities, gaseous diffusion plants, breeder reactors, initiator factories, neutron-scattering-reflector labs, tritium-production reactor vessels, heavy-water plants, semiprivate shaped-charge concerns, linear accelerators, and the especially point-heavy Annular Fusion research laboratories in North Syracuse NNY and Presque Isle ME, Chyonskrg Kurgistan and Pliscu Romania, and possibly elsewhere. Red shorts with gray trim (few in number because strongly disliked by the travelling squads) are SSTRACs — equally low-number but point-intensive Sites of Strategic Command. Socks are either missile installations or antimissile installations or isolated silo-clusters or Cruise-capable B2 or SS5 squadrons — let's draw the curtain of charity across any more MILABBREVs — depending on whether they're boys' tennis socks or boys' street-shoe socks or girls' tennis socks with the little bunny-tail at the heel or girls' tennis socks w/o the bunny-tail. Toe-worn cast-off corporate-supplied sneakers sit open-mouthed and serenely lethal, strongly suggesting the subs they stand for.

In the game, Combatants' 5-megaton warheads can be launched only with hand-held tennis racquets. Hence the requirement of actual physical targeting-skill that separates Eschaton from rotisserie-league holocaust games played with protractors and PCs around kitchen tables. The paraboloid transcontinental flight of a liquid-fuel strategic delivery vehicle closely resembles a topspin lob. One reason the E.T.A. administration and staff unofficially permit Eschaton to absorb students' attention and commitment might be that the game's devotees tend to develop terrific lobs. Pemulis's lobs can nail a coin on the baseline two out of three times off either side, is why it's idiotic that he rushes the net so much instead of letting the other guy come in more. Warheads can be launched independently or packed into an intricately knotted athletic supporter designed to open out in midflight and release Multiple Independent Reentry Vehicles — MIRVs. MIRVs, being a profligate use of a Combatant's available megatonnage, tend to get used only if a game of Eschaton metastasizes from a controlled set of Spasm Exchanges — SPASEX — to an all-out apocalyptic series of punishing Strikes Against Civilian Populations — SACPOP. Few Combatants will go to SACPOP unless compelled by the remorseless logic of game theory, since SACPOP-exchanges usually end up costing both Combatants so many points they're eliminated from further contention. A given Eschaton's winning team is simply that Combatant with the most favorable ratio of points for INDDIR — Infliction of Death, Destruction, and Incapacitation of Response — to SUFDDIR — self-evident — though the assignment of point-values for each Combatant's shirts, towels, shorts, armbands, socks, and shoes is statistically icky, plus there are also wildly involved corrections for initial megatonnage, population density, Land-Sea-Air delivery distributions, and EM-pulse-resistant civil-defense expenditures, so that the official victor takes three hours of EndStat number-crunching and at least four Motrin for Otis P. Lord to confirm.

Another reason why each year's master statistician has to be a special combination of tech-wonk and compulsive is that the baroque apparatus of each Eschaton has to be worked out in advance and then sold to a kind of immature and easily bored community of world leaders. A quorum of the day's Combatants has to endorse a particular simulated World Situation as Lord's stayed up well past several bedtimes to develop it: Land-Sea-Air force-distributions; ethnic, sociologic, economic, and even religious demographics for each Combatant, plus broadly sketched psych-profiles of all relevant heads of state; prevailing weather in all the map's quadrants; etc. Then everybody playing that day is assigned to a Combatant's team, and they all sit down over purified water and unfatted chips to hash out between Combatants stuff like mutual-defense alliances, humane-war pacts, facilities for inter-Combatant communication, DEFCON-gradients, city-trading, and so on. Since each Combatant's team knows only their own Situation-profile and total available megatonnage — and since even out in the four-court theater the stockpiled warheads are hidden from view inside the identical white plastic cast-off industrial-solvent buckets all academies and serious players use for drill-balls[125] — there can be a lot of poker-facing about response-resolve, willingness to go SACPOP, nonnegotiable interests, EM-pulse-immunity, distribution of strategic forces, and commitment to geopolitical ideals. You should have seen Michael Pemulis just about eat the whole world alive during pre-Eschaton summits, back when he played. His teams won most games before the first lob landed.

What often takes the longest to get a quorum on is each game's Triggering Situation. Here Lord, like many stellar statistics-wonks, shows a bit of an Achilles' heel imagination-wise, but he's got a good five or six years of Eschaton precedents to draw on. A Russo-Chinese border dispute goes tactical over Sinkiang. An AMNAT computracker in the Aleutians misreads a flight of geese as three SOVWAR SS10s on reentry. Israel moves armored divisions north and east through Jordan after an El Al airbus is bombed in midflight by a cell linked to both H'sseins. Black Albertan wackos infiltrate an isolated silo at Ft. Chimo and get two MIRVs through SOUTHAF's defense net. North Korea invades South Korea. Vice versa. AMNAT is within 72 hours of putting an impregnable string of antimissile satellites on line, and the remorseless logic of game theory compels SOVWAR to go SACPOP while it still has the chance.

On Interdependence Day, Sunday 11/8, game-master Lord's Triggering Situation unwinds nicely, on Pemulis's view. Explosions of suspicious origin occur at AMNAT satellite-receiver stations from Turkey to Labrador as three high-level Canadian defense ministers vanish and then a couple of days later are photographed at a Volgograd bistro hoisting shots of Stolichnaya with Slavic bimbos on their knee.[126] Then two SOVWAR trawlers just inside international waters off Washington are strafed by F16s on patrol out of Cape Flattery Naval Base. Both AMNAT and SOVWAR go from DEFCON 2 to DEFCON 4. REDCHI goes to DEFCON 3, in response to which SOVWAR airfields and antimissile networks from Irkutsk to the Dzhugdzhur Range go to DEFCON 5, in response to which AMNAT-SAC bombers and antimissile-missile silos in Nebraska and South Dakota and Saskatchewan and eastern Spain assume a Maximum Readiness posture. SOVWAR's bald and port-wine-stained premier calls AMNAT's wattle-chinned[127] president on the Hot Line and asks him if he's got Prince Albert in a can. Another pretty shady explosion levels a SOVWAR Big Ear monitoring station on Sakhalin. General Atomic Inc.'s gaseous diffusion uranium-enrichment facility in Portsmouth OH reports four kilograms of enriched uranium hexafluoride missing and then suffers a cataclysmic fire that forces evacuation of six downwind counties. An AMNAT minesweeper of the Sixth Fleet on maneuvers in the Red Sea is hit and sunk with REDCHI Silkworm torpedoes fired by LIBSYR MiG25s. Italy, in an apparently bizarre EndStat-generated development Otis P. Lord will only smile enigmatically about, invades Albania. SOVWAR goes apeshit. Apoplectic premier rings AMNAT's president, only to be asked if his refrigerator's running. LIBSYR shocks the Christian world by air-bursting a half-megaton device two clicks over Tel Aviv, causing deaths in the low six figures. Everybody and his brother goes to DEFCON 5. Air Force One leaves the ground. SOUTHAF and REDCHI announce neutrality and plead for cool heads. Israeli armored columns behind heavy tactical-artillery saturation push into Syria all the way to Abu Kenal in twelve hours: Damascus has firestorms; En Nebk is reportedly just plain gone. Several repressive right-wing regimes in the Third World suffer coups d'état and are replaced by repressive left-wing regimes. Tehran and Baghdad announce full dip-mil support of LIBSYR, thus reconstituting LIBSYR as IRLIBSYR. AMNAT and SOVWAR activate all civil defense personnel and armed forces reserves and commence evacuation of selected MAMAs. IRLIBSYR is today represented by Evan Ingersoll, whom Axford keeps growling at under his breath, Hal can hear. A shifty-eyed member of the U.S. Joint Chiefs of Staff vanishes and isn't photographed anywhere. Albania sues for terms. Crude and apparently amateur devices in the low-kiloton range explode across Israel from Haifa to Ashqelon. Tripoli is incommunicado after at least four thermonuclear explosions cause second-degree burns as far away as Médenine Tunisia. A 10-kiloton tactical-artillery device air-bursts over the Command Center of the Czech 3rd Army in Ostrava, resulting in what one Pentagon analyst calls 'a serious wienie roast.' Despite the fact that nobody but SOVWAR itself has anybody close enough to hit Ostrava from Howitzer-distance, SOVWAR stonewalls AMNAT's denials and regrets. AMNAT's president tries ringing SOVWAR's premier from the air and gets only the premier's answering machine. AMNAT is unable to determine whether the string of explosions at its radar installations all along the Arctic Circle are conventional or tactical. CIA/NSA reports that 64% of the civilian populations of SOVWAR's MAMAs have been successfully relocated below ground in hardened shelters. AMNAT orders evacuation of all MAMAs. SOVWAR MiG25s engage REDCHI aircraft over seas off Tientsin. Air Force Two tries to leave the ground and gets a flat tire. A single one-megaton SS10 evades antimissile missiles and detonates just over Provo UT, from which all communications abruptly cease. Eschaton's game-master now posits — but does not go so far as to actually assert — that EndStat's game-theoretic Decision Tree now dictates a SPASEX response from AMNAT.

Uninitiated adults who might be parked in a nearby mint-green adver-torial Ford sedan or might stroll casually past E.T.A.'s four easternmost tennis courts and see an atavistic global-nuclear-conflict game played by tanned and energetic little kids and so this might naturally expect to see fuzzless green warheads getting whacked indiscriminately skyward all over the place as everybody gets blackly drunk with thanatoptic fury in the crisp November air — these adults would more likely find an actual game of Es-chaton strangely subdued, almost narcotized-looking. Your standard round of Eschaton moves at about the pace of chess between adepts. For these devotees become, on court, almost parodically adult — staid, sober, hu-mane, and judicious twelve-year-old world leaders, trying their best not to let the awesome weight of their responsibilities — responsibilities to nation, globe, rationality, ideology, conscience and history, to both the living and the unborn — not to let the terrible agony they feel at the arrival of this day — this dark day the leaders've prayed would never come and have taken every conceivable measure rationally consistent with national strate-gic interest to avoid, to prevent — not to let the agonizing weight of respon-sibility compromise their resolve to do what they must to preserve their people's way of life. So they play, logically, cautiously, so earnest and delib-erate in their calculations they appear thoroughly and queerly adult, almost Talmudic, from a distance. A couple gulls fly overhead. A mint-green Ford sedan has passed through the gate's raised portcullis and is trying to parallel park between two dumpsters in the circular drive behind West House, which is behind and to the neck-straining left of the Gatorade pavilion. There's an autumnal tang to the air and a brittle gray shell of cloud-cover, plus the constant faraway hum of Sunstrand Plaza's ATHSCME fan-line.

Strategic acumen and feel for realism vary from kid to kid, of course. When IRLIBSYR's Evan Ingersoll starts lobbing warheads at SOVWAR's belt of Third-Wave reserve silos in the Kazakh, and it becomes pretty clear that AMNAT has won IRLIBSYR to its side by making sinister promises about the ultimate disposition of Israel, Israel, even though nobody's Israel out there today, seems in a fit of pique to have somehow persuaded SOUTHAF, who today is Brooklyn NY's little hard-ass Josh Gopnik — the same Josh Gopnik who by the way subscribes to *Commentary* — to expend all sixteen of its green fuzzy warheads in a debilitating enfilade against AM-NAT dams, bridges, and bases from Florida to Baja. Everybody involved orders total displacement of MAMA populations. Then, without any calcu-lation whatever, INDPAK, who today is J. J. Penn — a high-ranked thirteen-year-old but not exactly the brightest log on the Yuletide fire — dumps three poorly tied jockstraps' worth of MIRVs on Israel, landing most of the megatonnage in sub-Beersheba desert areas that didn't look much different before the blasts. When roundly kibitzed from the shelter of the Gatorade pavilion under Schtitt's tower by Troeltsch, Axford, and

Incandenza, Penn shrilly reminds them that Pakistan is a Muslim state and sworn foe to all infidelic enemies of Islam, but can do little but fiddle with the strings of his launcher when Pemulis cheerfully reminds him that nobody's Israel today and there isn't so much as a Combatant's sock on that part of the courts. It is not a matter of the principle of thing, ever, in Eschaton.

Except for the SOUTHAF flurry and INDPAK boner, 11/8's game proceeds with much probity and cold deliberation, with even more pauses and hushed, chin-stroking conferences today than tend to be the norm. The only harried-looking person on the 1300-m.^{2} map is Otis P. Lord, who has to keep legging it from one continent to another, pushing a rolling double-shelf stainless steel food cart purloined from St. John of God Hospital with a blinking Yushityu portable on one shelf and a 256-capacity diskette case about two-thirds full on the other, the shelves' sides hung with clattering clipboards, Lord having to dramatize manually the effortless dictates of real logic and necessity, verifying that command decisions are allowable functions of situation and capacity (he'd shrugged his shoulders in a neutral Whatever at SOUTHAF and INDPAK), locating necessary data for subterranean premiers and dictators and airsick presidents, removing vaporized articles of clothing from sites of devastating hits and just woppsing them up or folding them over at the sites of near-hits and fizzle yields, triangulating EM-pulse estimates from confirmed hits to authorize or deny communication-capacity, it's a nerve-racking job, he's more or less having to play God, tallying kill-ratios and radiation-levels and parameters of fallout, strontium-90 and iodine levels and the likelihood of conflagrations v. firestorms in MAMAs with different Mean-Value skyscraper-heights and combustible-capital indices. Despite chapped hands and a badly running nose, Lord's response-time to requests for data is impressive, thanks mainly to the sly D.E.C. hookup and the detailed decision-algorithm files Pemulis had authored three years back. Otis P. Lord informs SOVWAR and AMNAT that Peoria IL's topographic flatness ups the effective kill-radius for SOVWAR's 5-megaton direct hit to 10.1 clicks, meaning half of this MAMA-POP burns to death in evacuatory traffic jams out on Interstate 74. An AMNAT Minuteman can hold an absolute maximum of eight MIRVs *irregardless* of whether the titanic jockstrap little LaMont Chu promoted out of the sedated Teddy Schacht's gear bag on the bus Friday night can hold thirteen dead tennis balls. Given standard climatic conditions, the fire area from an air-burst will be 2π times larger than the blast area. Toronto has enough sub-code skyscrapers within its total area to guarantee a firestorm off a minimum of two strikes within

$$\frac{2\pi}{(1 \text{ / total Toronto area in m.}^2)}$$

of target center. Five megatons of heavy-hydrogen fusion yields at least 1,400,000 curies worth of strontium-90, meaning microcephalic kids in Montreal for roughly twenty-two generations, and yes wiseacre McKenna of AMNAT the world will probably notice the difference. Struck and Trevor Axford hoot loudly from under the green *GATORADE THIRST AID* awning of the open-air pavilion outside the fence along the south side of the East Courts, where (the pavilion) they and Michael Pemulis and Jim Troeltsch and Hal Incandenza are splayed on reticulate-mesh patio chairs in street clothes and with their street-sneakers up on reticulate-mesh foot-stools, Struck and Axford with suspiciously bracing Gatorades and what looks like a hand-rolled psychochemical cigarette of some sort being passed between them. 11/8 is an E.T.A. day of mandatory total R&R, though the public intoxicants are a bit much. Pemulis has a bag of red-skinned peanuts he hasn't eaten much of. Trevor Axford has overinhaled from the cigarette and is hunched coughing, his forehead purple. Hal Incandenza is squeezing a tennis ball and leaning out far to starboard to spit into a NASA glass on the ground and struggling with a strong desire to get high again for the second time since breakfast v. a strong distaste about smoking dope with/in front of all these others, especially out in the open in front of Little Buddies, which seems to him to violate some sort of issue of taste that he struggles to articulate satisfactorily to himself. A tooth way back on the upper left is twinging electrically in the cold air. Pemulis, though from his twitchy right eye he's clearly had recent recourse to some Tenuate (which helps explain the uneaten nuts), is currently abstaining and sitting on his hands for warmth, peanuts on the floor well away from Hal's NASA glass. The pavilion is open on all sides and compliments of Stokely-van Camp Corp. and little more than like a big fancy tent with a green felt cover over the expanse's real grass and white-iron patio furniture with reticulate plastic mesh; it's mostly used for civilians' spectation during exhibition matches on the East Show Courts 7, 8, 9; sometimes E.T.A.s cluster under it during drill-breaks in the summer in the heat of the day. The green awning gets taken down when they go into the Lung for the winter. Eschaton traditionally commandeers Courts 6–9, the really nice East Courts, unless there's legit tennis going on. All the upperclass spectators except Jim Struck are former Eschaton devotees, though Hal and Troeltsch were both marginal. Troeltsch, who's also pretty clearly had some Tenuate, is left-eye-nystagmic and is calling the action into a disconnected broadcast-headset, but Eschaton's tough to enliven, verbally, even for the stimulated. Being generally too slow and cerebral.

Struck is telling Axford to put his hands over his head and Pemulis is telling Axford to hold his breath. Now, in a stress-heightened voice, Otis P. Lord says he needs Pemulis to real quick come zip inside through the Cyclone-fence gate south of Court 12 and walk across the theater's four-court map to show Lord how to access the EndStat calculation that every thousand Roentgens of straight X and gamma produces 6.36 deaths per hundred POP and for the other 93.64 means reduced lifespans of

$$(\text{Total R} - 100)\,(.0636(\text{Total R}-100)^2)$$

years, meaning nobody's exactly going to have to be pricing dentures in Minsk, so to speak, in the future. And so on.

After about half the planet's extant megatonnage has been expended, things are looking pretty good for the AMNAT crew. Even though they and SOVWAR are SPASEXing back and forth with chilling accuracy — SOVWAR's designated launcher is the butch and suspiciously muscular Ann Kittenplan (who at twelve-and-a-half looks like a Belorussian shot-putter and has to buy urine more than quarter-annually and has a way more lush and impressive mustache than for instance Hal himself could raise, and who gets these terrible rages) but so Kittenplan's landed nothing worse than an indirect hit all afternoon, while AMNAT's launchman is Todd ('Postal Weight') Possalthwaite, an endomorphic thirteen-year-old from Edina MN whose whole infuriating tennis-game consists of nothing but kick serves and topspin lobs, and who's been the Eschaton MVL[128] for the last two years, and accuracy-wise has to be seen to be believed — still, both sides have artfully avoided the escalation to SACPOP that often takes both super-Combatants right out of the game; and AMNAT's president LaMont Chu has used the excuse of Gopnik's emotional strikes against the U.S. South, plus Penn's arational lobbing at an Israel that at the summit was explicitly placed under AMNAT's mutual-defense umbrella, has used these as golden tactical geese, racking up serious INDDIR-points against a SOUTHAF and INDPAK whose hasty defensive alliance and shaky aim produce nothing more than a lot of irradiated cod off Gloucester. Whenever there's a direct hit, Troeltsch sits up straight and gets to use the exclamation he's hit on for a kind of announcerial trademark: 'Ho-*ly CROW!*' But SOVWAR, beset from two vectors by AMNAT and IRLIBSYR (whose occasional lob Israel's way AMNAT, drawing a storm of diplomatic protest from SOUTHAF and INDPAK, keeps instructing Lord to log as 'regrettable mistargetings'), even with cutting-edge civil defense and EMP-resistant communications, poor old SOVWAR is absorbing such serious collateral SUFDDIR that it's being inexorably impelled by game-theoretic logic to a position where it's going to pretty much have no choice but to go SACPOP against AMNAT.

Now SOVWAR premier Timmy ('Sleepy T.P.') Peterson petitions O. P. Lord for capacity/authorization to place a scrambled call to Air Force One. 'Scrambled call' means they don't yell at each other publicly across the courts' map; Lord has to ferry messages from one side the other, complete with inclined heads and hushed tones etc. Premier and president exchange standard formalities. Premier apologizes for the Prince Albert crack. Hal, who's declining all public chemicals, he's decided, has a gander at Pemulis's rough tallies of Combatants' INDDIR/SUFDDIR ratios so far and agrees to bet Axford a U.S. finski no way AMNAT accepts SOVWAR's invitation to possible terms. During actionless diplomatic intervals like this, Troeltsch is reduced to saying 'What a beautiful day for an Eschaton' over and over and asking people for their thoughts on the game until Pemulis tells him he's cruising to get dope-slapped. There's pretty much nobody around: Tavis and Schtitt are off giving what are essentially recruiting-talks at indoor clubs in the west suburbs; Pemulis'd let Tall Paul Shaw take the multi-emblazoned tow truck to take Mario down to the Public Gardens to watch the public I.-Day festivities with the Bolex H64; the local kids often go home for the day; a lot of the rest like to lie in the Viewing Rooms barely moving all I. Day until the dinner gala. Lord tear-asses back and forth between Courts 6 and 8, food cart clattering (the food cart, which Pemulis and Axford picked up from a kind of a seedy-looking orderly at SJOG hospital that Pemulis knew from Allston, has one of those crazy left front wheels that e.g. seems always to afflict only *your* particular grocery cart in supermarkets, and makes a hell of a clattering racket when rushed), ferrying messages which the 18-and-Under guys can tell AMNAT and SOVWAR are making deliberately oblique and obtuse so Lord has to do that much more running: God is never a particularly popular role to have to play, and Lord this fall has already been the victim of several boarding-school-type pranks too puerile even to detail. J. A. L. Struck Jr., who as usual has made a swine of himself with the suspiciously bracing cups of Gatorade, is abruptly ill all over his own lap and then sort of slumps to one side in his patio-chair with his face slack and white and doesn't hear Pemulis's quick analysis that Hal might as well give Axhandle the $ right now, because LaMont Chu can parse a Decision Tree with the best of them, and the D. Tree's now indicating peace terms in whatever a D. Tree's version of neon letters is, because the biggest priority for AMNAT right at 1515h. is to avoid having to SACPOP with SOVWAR, since if the game stops right now AMNAT's probably won, whereas if they SACPOP with SOVWAR, trading massive infliction of INDDIR for massive body-shots of SUFDDIR, staying more or less even with each other, AMNAT'll still be the same number of points ahead of SOVWAR overall, but it'll have taken such heavy SUFDDIR debits that IRLIBSYR — never forget IRLIBSYR, brilliantly if obnoxiously Imam'd today by eleven-year-old eyebrowless Evan Ingersoll of Binghamton NNY — by staying out of the SACPOP-fest and lobbing sporadically at SOVWAR just often enough to rack up serious INDDIR but not quite enough to piss SOVWAR off enough to provoke the retaliatory SS10-wave that would mean significant SUFDDIR, could well have a serious shot at overtaking AMNAT for the overall Eschaton, especially when you factored in the $f(x)$ advantages for bellicosity and nonexistent civil defense. At some point Axford has passed the remainder of the cigarette back over toward Struck without looking to see that Struck is no longer in his chair, and Hal finds himself taking the proffered duBois and smoking dope in public without even thinking about it or having consciously decided to go ahead. Sure enough, poor red-faced runny-nosed Lord is making way too many clattering trips between Courts 6 and 8 for it to mean anything but peace terms. Evan Ingersoll is positively strip-mining his right nostril. Finally Lord stops with the running back and forth and positions himself in the ad service box of Court 7 and loads a new diskette into the Yushityu. Struck moans something in a possibly foreign tongue. All the other upperclass spectators have scooted their chairs well away from Struck. Troeltsch extends a blood-blistered palm and rubs the tips of the hand's fingers together at Hal, and Hal forks over the fin without handing the thin cigarette back over to Axford, somehow. Pemulis has leaned forward intently with his pointy chin in his hands; he seems completely absorbed.

Interdependence Day Y.D.A.U.'s Eschaton enters probably its most crucial phase. Lord, at his cart and portable TP, puts on the white beanie (n.b.: not the black or the red beanie) that signals a temporary cessation of SPASEX between two Combatants but allows all other Combatants to go on pursuing their strategic interests as they see fit. SOVWAR and AMNAT are thus pretty vulnerable right now. SOVWAR's Premier Peterson and Air Marshal Kittenplan, carrying their white janitorial stockpile-bucket between them, walk across Europe and the Atlantic to parley with AMNAT President Chu and Supreme Commander Possalthwaite in what looks to be roughly Sierra Leone. Various territories smolder quietly. The other players are mostly standing around beating their arms against their chests to stay warm. A few hesitant white flakes appear and swirl around and melt into dark stars the moment they hit court. A couple ostensible world leaders run here and there in a rather unstatesmanlike fashion with their open mouths directed at the sky, trying to catch bits of the fall's first snow. Yesterday it had been warmer and rained. Axford speculates about whether snow will mean Schtitt might consent to inflate the Lung even before the Fundraiser two weeks hence. Struck is threatening to fall out of his chair. Pemulis, leaning forward intently, wearing his Mr. Howell yachting cap, ignores everyone. He hates to type and keeps his tallies via pencil and clipboard à la deLint. The idling Ford sedan is conspicuous for the excruciated full-color old Nunhagen Aspirin ad on the green of its right rear door. Hal and Axford are passing what looks to the Combatants like a suckerless Tootsie-Roll stick back and forth between them, and occasionally to Troeltsch. Trevor ('The Axhandle') Axford has a total of only three-and-a-half digits on his right hand. From West House you can hear Mrs. Clarke and the time-and-a-half holiday kitchen staff preparing the Interdependence Day gala dinner, which always includes dessert.

Now REDCHI, itself quietly trying to rack up some unanswered

INDDIR, sends a towering topspin lob into INDPAK's quadrant, scoring what REDCHI claims is a direct hit on Karachi and what warheadless INDPAK claims is only an indirect hit on Karachi. It's an uneasy moment: a dispute such as this would never occur in the real God's real world, since the truth would be manifest in the actual size of the actual wienie roast in the actual Karachi. But God here is played by Otis P. Lord, and Lord is number-crunching so fiendishly at the cart's Yushityu, trying to confirm the veri-similitude of the peace terms AMNAT and SOVWAR are hashing out, that he can't even pretend to have seen where REDCHI's strike against INDPAK landed w/ respect to Karachi's T-shirt — which is admittedly kind of mashed and woppsed up, though this could be primarily from breezes and feet — and in his lapse of omniscience cannot see how he's supposed to allocate the relevant INDDIR- and SUFDDIR-points. Troeltsch doesn't know whether to say 'Holy CROW!' or not. Lord, vexed by a lapse it's tough to see how any mortal could have avoided, appeals over to Michael Pemulis for an independent ruling; and when Pemulis gravely shakes his white-hatted head, pointing out that Lord is God and either sees or doesn't, in Eschaton, Lord has an intense little crying fit that's made abruptly worse when now J. J. Penn of INDPAK all of a sudden gets the idea to start claim-ing that now that it's snowing the snow totally affects blast area and fire area and pulse-intensity and maybe also has fallout implications, and he says Lord has to now completely redo everybody's damage parameters be-fore anybody can form realistic strategies from here on out.

Pemulis's chairlegs shriek and make red-skin peanuts spill out in a kind of cornucopic cone-shape and he's up in his capacity as sort of eminence grise of Eschaton and ranging up and down just outside the theater's chain-link fencing, giving J. J. Penn the very roughest imaginable side of his tongue. Besides being real sensitive to any theater-boundary-puncturing threats to the map's integrity — threats that've come up before, and that as Pemulis sees it threaten the game's whole sense of animating realism (which realism depends on buying the artifice of 1300 m.² of composition tennis court representing the whole rectangular projection of the planet earth) — Pemulis is also a sworn foe of all Penns for all time: it had been J. J. Penn's much older brother Miles Penn, now twenty-one and flailing away on the grim Third-World Satellite pro tour, playing for travel-expenses in bleak dysenteric locales, who when Pemulis first arrived at E.T.A. at age eleven had christened him Michael Penisless and had had Pemulis convinced for almost a year that if he pressed on his belly-button his ass would fall off.[129]

'It's snowing on the goddamn *map,* not the *territory,* you *dick!*' Pemulis yells at Penn, whose lower lip is out and quivering. Pemulis's face is the face of a man who will someday need blood-pressure medication, a constitution the Tenuate doesn't help one bit. Troeltsch is sitting up straight and speak-ing very intensely and quietly into his headset. Hal, who in his day never wore the beanie, and usually portrayed some marginal nation somewhere out in the nuclear boondocks, finds himself more intrigued by Penn's map/territory faux pas than upset by it, or even amused.

Pemulis turns back to the pavilion and seems to be looking at Hal in some kind of appeal: '*Jaysus!*'

'Except is the territory the real world, quote unquote, though!' Axford calls across to Pemulis, who's pacing like the fence is between him and some sort of prey. Axford knows quite well Pemulis can be fucked with when he's like this: when he's hot he always cools down and becomes contrite.

Struck tries to yell out a Kertwang on Pemulis but can't get the megaphone he makes of his hands to fit over the mouth.

'The real world's what the map here *stands* for!' Lord lifts his head from the Yushityu and cries over at Axhandle, trying to please Pemulis.

'Kind of looks like real-world-type snow from here, M.P.,' Axford calls out. His forehead's still maroon from the coughing fit. Troeltsch is trying to describe the distinction between the symbolic map of the gear-littered courts and the global strategic theater it stands for using all and only sports-broadcast clichés. Hal looks from Axhandle to Pemulis to Lord.

Struck finally falls out of his chair with a clunk but his legs are still somehow entangled in the legs of the chair. It starts to snow harder, and dark stars of melt begin to multiply and then merge all over the courts. Otis Lord is trying to type and wipe his nose on his sleeve at the same time. J. Gopnik and K. McKenna are running around well outside their assigned quadrants with their tongues outstretched.

'Real-world snow isn't a factor if it's falling on the fucking *map!*'

Ann Kittenplan's crew-cutted head now protrudes from the kind of rugby-scrum AMNAT's and SOVWAR's heads of state form around Lord's computational food cart. 'For Christ's sake leave us alone!' she shrieks at Pemulis. Troeltsch is going 'Oh, *my*' into his headset. O. Lord is struggling with the cart's protective umbrella, his head's beanie's little white propeller rotating in a rising wind. A light dusting of snow is starting to appear in the players' hair.

'It's only real-world snow if it's already in the *scenario!*' Pemulis keeps directing everything at Penn, who hasn't said a word since his original suggestion and is busy sort of casually kicking the Karachi-shirt over into the Arabian Sea, clearly hoping the original detonation will get forgotten about in all the metatheoretical fuss. Pemulis rages along the East Courts' western fence. The combination of several Tenuate spansules plus Eschaton-adrenaline bring his blue-collar Irish right out. He's a muscular but fundamentally physically narrow guy: head, hands, the sharp little wad of cartilage at the tip of Pemulis's nose — everything about him seems to Hal to taper and come to a point, like a bad El Greco. Hal leans to spit and watches him pace like a caged thing as Lord works feverishly over EndStat's peace-terms decision-matrix. Hal wonders, not for the first time, whether he might deep down be a secret snob about collar-color issues and Pemulis, then whether the fact that he's capable of wondering whether he's a snob attenuates the possibility that he's really a snob. Though Hal hasn't had more than four or five total very small hits off the public duBois, this is a prime example of what's sometimes called 'marijuana thinking.' You can tell because Hal's leaned way over to spit but has gotten lost in a paralytic thought-helix and hasn't yet spit, even though he's right in bombing-position over the NASA glass. It also occurs to him that he finds the real-snow/unreal-snow snag in the Eschaton extremely abstract but somehow way more interesting than the Eschaton itself, so far.

IRLIBSYR's strongman Evan Ingersoll, all of 1.3 m. tall, warmed by babyfat and high-calorie cerebral endeavor, has been squatting on his heels like a catcher just west of Damascus, spinning his Rossignol launcher idly in his hand, watching the one-sided exchange between Pemulis and Ingersoll's roommate J. J. Penn, who's now threatening to quit and go in for cocoa if they can't for once play Eschaton without the big guys horning in again like always. There's a tiny whirring sound as Ingersoll's mental gears grind. From the duration of the little Sierra Leone summit and the studious blankness on everybody's face it's pretty clear that SOVWAR and AMNAT are going to come to terms, and the terms are likely to involve SOVWAR agreeing not to go SACPOP against AMNAT in return for AMNAT letting SOVWAR go SACPOP against Ingersoll's IRLIBSYR, because if SOVWAR goes SACPOP against an IRLIBSYR that can't have many warheads left in the old bucket by now (Ingersoll knows they know) then SOVWAR'll get to rack up a lot of INDDIR without much SUFDDIR, while inflicting such SUFDDIR on IRLIBSYR that IRLIBSYR'll be effectively eliminated as a threat to AMNAT's commanding lead in points, which is what has the most utility in the old game-theoretic matrix right now. The exact utility transformations are too oogly for an Ingersoll who's still grappling with fractions, but he can see clearly that this'd be the most remorselessly logical best-interest-conducive scenario for both LaMont Chu and especially the Sleepster, Peterson, who's hated Ingersoll for months now anyway without any good reason or cause or anything, Ingersoll can just somehow tell.

Hal, paralyzed and absorbed, watches Ingersoll bob on his haunches and shift his stick from hand to hand and cerebrate furiously and logically conclude, then, that IRLIBSYR's highest possible strategic utility lies in AMNAT and SOVWAR failing to come to terms.

Hal can almost visualize a dark lightbulb going on above Ingersoll's head. Pemulis is telling Penn that there's a critical distinction between horning in and letting asswipes like Jeffrey Joseph Penn run roughshod over the delimiting boundaries that are Eschaton's very life-blood. Chu and Peterson are nodding soberly at little things they're saying to each other while Kittenplan cracks her knuckles and Possalthwaite bounces a warhead idly on his strings.

So now Evan Ingersoll rises from his squat now only to bend again and take a warhead out of IRLIBSYR's ordnance-bucket, and Hal seems to be the only one who sees Ingersoll line up the vector very carefully with his slim thumb and take a lavish backswing and fire the ball directly at the little circle of super-Combatant leaders in West Africa. It's not a lob. It flies straight as if shot from a rifle and strikes Ann Kittenplan right in the back of the head with a loud *thock*. She whirls to face east, a hand at the back of her bristly skull, scanning and then locking on Damascus, her face a stony Toltec death-mask.

Pemulis and Penn and Lord and everyone else all freeze, shocked and silent, so there's just the weird glittered hiss of falling snow and the sounds of a couple crows interfacing in the pines over by HmH. The ATHSCME fans are silent, and four sweatsock-shaped clouds of exhaust hang motionless over the Sunstrand stacks. Nothing moves. No Eschaton Combatant has ever intentionally struck another Combatant's physical person with a 5-megaton thermonuclear weapon. No matter how frayed players' nerves, it's never made a lick of sense. A Combatant's megatonnage is too precious to waste on personal attacks outside the map. It's been like this unspoken but very basic rule.

Ann Kittenplan is so shocked and enraged that she stands there transfixed, quivering, her sights locked on Ingersoll and his smoking Rossignol. Otis P. Lord feels at his beanie.

Ingersoll now makes a show of examining the tiny nails of his left hand and casually suggests that IRLIBSYR has just scored a direct 5-megaton contact-burst against SOVWAR's entire launch capacity, namely Air Marshal Ann Kittenplan, and that plus also AMNAT's own launch capacity, plus both Combatants' ordnance and heads of state, all lie well within the blast's kill-radius — which by Ingersoll's rough calculations extends from the Ivory Coast to the doubles alley's Senegal. Unless of course that kill-radius is somehow altered by the possible presence of climatic snow, he adds, beaming.

Pemulis and Kittenplan now each let loose with a linear series of anti-Ingersoll invectives that drown each other out and make the trees' crows take slow flight.

But Otis Lord — who's watched the exchange, ashen, and has called up something relevant on EndStat's TREEMASTER metadecision subdirectory — now, to everyone's horror, removes from around his neck a shoelace with a little nickel-colored key and bends to the small locked solander box on the food cart's bottom shelf and as everyone watches in horror opens the box and with near-ceremonial care exchanges the white beanie on his head for the red beanie that signifies Utter Global Crisis. The dreaded red UGC beanie has been donned by an Eschaton game-master only once before, and that was over three years ago, when human input-error on EndStat tallies of aggregate SUFDDIR during a three-way SACPOP free-for-all yielded an apparent ignition of the earth's atmosphere.

Now a real-world chill descends over the grainily white-swirled landscape of the nuclear theater.

Pemulis tells Lord he cannot believe his *fucking* eyes. He tells Lord how dare he don the dreaded red beanie over such an obvious instance of map-not-territory equivocationary horseshit as Ingersoll's trying to foist.

Lord, bent to the cart's blinking Yushityu, responds that there seems to be a problem.

Ingersoll is whistling and pretending to do the Charleston between Abu Kemal and Es Suweida, using his racquet like a hoofer's cane.

Hal finally spits.

Under Pemulis's wild-eyed stare, Lord clears his throat and calls out to Ingersoll, tentatively positing that today's pre-game Triggering-Situation negotiations established no valid strategic target areas in the postage-stamp-sized nation of Sierra Leone.

Ingersoll calls back across the Mediterranean that target areas of keen strategic interest appeared in Sierra Leone at the exact moment the heads of state and total launch capacities of AMNAT and SOVWAR took it upon themselves to traipse into Sierra Leone. That Sierra Leone thenceforward as of that moment has, or rather had, he pretends to correct with a smile, become a de facto SSTRAC. If presidents and premiers wanted to leave the protection of their territories' defense-nets and hold cliquey little other-Combatant-excluding parleys in some hut somewhere that was up to them, but Lord had been wearing the white beanie that explicitly authorized the overexploited and underdeveloped defenders of the One True Faith of the world to keep on pursuing their strategic interests, and IRLIBSYR was now keenly interested in the aggregate INDDIR-points it had coming to them for just now vaporizing both super-Combatants' strategic capacities with one Flaming-Sword-of-The-Most-High-like strike.

Ann Kittenplan keeps taking a couple quivery steps toward Ingersoll and getting restrained and pulled back by LaMont Chu.

'Sleepy T.P.' Peterson, who always looks a little dazed even in the best of circumstances, asks Otis P. Lord to define *equivocationary* for him, causing Hal Incandenza to laugh out loud despite himself.

Just outside the theater's fence, Pemulis is bug-eyed with fury — not impossibly 'drine-aggravated — and is literally jumping up and down in one spot so hard that his yachting cap jumps slightly off his head with each impact, which Troeltsch and Axford confer and agree they have previously seen occur only in animated cartoons. Pemulis howls that Lord is in his vacillation appeasing Ingersoll in Ingersoll's effort to fatally fuck with the very breath and bread of Eschaton.[130] Players themselves can't be valid targets. Players aren't inside the goddamn game. Players are part of the *apparatus* of the game. They're part of the map. It's snowing on the players but not on the territory. They're part of the *map*, not the cluster-fucking *territory*. You can only launch against the *territory*. Not against the *map*. It's like the one ground-rule boundary that keeps Eschaton from degenerating into chaos. Eschaton gentlemen is about logic and axiom and mathematical probity and discipline and verity and *order*. You do not get points for hitting anybody real. Only the gear that *maps* what's real. Pemulis keeps looking back over his shoulder to the pavilion and screaming '*Jay*sus!'

Ingersoll's roommate J. J. Penn tries to claim that the vaporized Ann Kittenplan is wearing several articles of gear worth mucho INDDIR, and everyone tells him to shut up. The snow is now coming down hard enough to compose an environment, and everybody outside the sheltered pavilion looks gauzily shrouded, from Hal's perspective.

Lord is crunching madly away at the TP under the just-opened protection of an old beach umbrella a previous game-master had welded to the top of the food cart. Lord wipes his nose against the same shoulder that's clamping a phone to his ear, awkwardly, and reports he's checked the D.E.C.'s Eschaton-Axiom directory via $Pink_2$-capable modem and that unfortunately with all due respect to Ann and Mike it doesn't seem to explicitly say players with strategic functions can't become target-areas if they traipse around outside their defense-nets. LaMont Chu says how come point-values for actual players have never been assigned, then, for Pete's sake, and Pemulis shouts across that that's so totally beside the point it doesn't matter, that the reason players aren't explicitly exempted in the ESCHAX.DIR is that their exemption is what makes Eschaton and its axioms fucking possible in the *first* place. A kind of pale boat-wake of exhaust exits the idling Ford sedan off behind the pavilion and widens as it rises, dispersing. Pemulis says because otherwise use your heads otherwise nonstrategic emotions would get aroused and Combatants would be whacking balls at each other's physical persons all the time and Eschaton wouldn't even be possible in its icily elegant game-theoretical form. He's stopped jumping up and down, at least, Troeltsch observes. Players' exemption from strikes goes without saying, Pemulis says; it's like *pre*axiomatic. Pemulis tells Lord to consider what he's doing very carefully, because from where Pemulis is standing Lord looks to be willing to very possibly compromise Eschaton's map for all time. Girls 16's/18's prorector Mary Esther Thode putts from left to right behind the pavilion on the long driveway from the circular drive to the portcullis and halts her scooter and lifts her helmet's tinted visor and yells across for Kittenplan to put a hat on if she's going to play in the snow in a crew-cut. This even though Kittenplan isn't even strictly in Ms. Thode's like umbrella of authority, Axford observes to Troeltsch, who relays this fact into his headset. Hal moves his mouth around to try to gather up spit in a mouth that's gotten rather dry, which when you have a plug of Kodiak in is not very pleasant. Ann Kittenplan has been suffering from what look like almost Parkinsonian tremors for the last few minutes, her face writhing and her mustache almost standing right out straight. LaMont Chu repeats his claim that there's no way players even with strategic functions can ever be legit target-areas if no INDDIR/SUFDDIR values have been entered for them in EndStat's tally-function. Pemulis orders Chu not to distract Otis Lord from the incredibly potent and lethal ground Lord's letting Ingersoll lead them onto. He says none of them have ever even seen the true meaning of the word *crisis* yet. Ingersoll calls over to Pemulis that his emeritus veto-power is only over Lord's calculations, not over today's game's God's decisions about what's part of the game and what isn't. Pemulis invites Ingersoll to do something anatomically impossible. Pemulis asks LaMont Chu and Ann Kittenplan if they're just going to stand there with their thumbs in their bottoms and let Lord let Ingersoll eliminate Eschaton's map for keeps for one slimy cheesy victory in just one day's apocalypse. Kittenplan has been trembling and feeling at the back of her vein-laced head and looking across the Mediterranean at Ingersoll like somebody who knows they'll go to prison for what they want to do. Axford posits certain very unlikely physical conditions under which what Pemulis told Ingersoll to do to himself wouldn't be totally impossible. Hal spits thickly and gathers and tries to spit again, watching. Troeltsch broadcasts the fact that there's always a queer vague vitaminish stink about Mary Esther Thode that he never can quite place. There's the sudden tripartite whump of three Empire Waste Displacement vehicles being propelled above the cloud-cover to points far north. Hal identifies Thode's ambient odor as the stink of thiamine, which for reasons best known to Thode she takes a lot of; and Troeltsch broadcasts the datum and refers to Hal as a 'close source,' which strikes Hal as odd and somehow off in a way he can't quite name. Kittenplan shakes Chu's arm loose and darts over and extracts a warhead from SOVWAR's portable stockpile and shouts out that well OK then if players can be targets then in that case: and she fires a real screamer at Ingersoll's head, which Ingersoll barely blocks with his Rossignol and shrieks that Kittenplan can't launch anything at anything because she's been vaporized by a 5-megaton contact-burst. Kittenplan tells Ingersoll to write his congressman about it and over LaMont Chu's pleas for reasoned discussion takes several more theoretically valuable warheads out of the industrial-solvent bucket and gets truly serious about hitting Ingersoll, moving steadily east across Nigeria and Chad, causing Ingersoll to run due north across the courts' map at impressive speed, abandoning IRLIBSYR's ammo-bucket and tear-assing up through Siberia crying Foul. Lord's mewing ineffectually for order, but some of the other

Combatants' staffs have begun to smell that Evan Ingersoll's become fair game for cruelty — the way kids can seem to smell this sort of thing out with such uncanny acuity — and REDCHI's General Secretary and an AM-NAT vector-planning specialist and Josh Gopnik all start moving northeast over the map firing balls as hard as they can at Ingersoll, who's dropped his launcher and is shaking frantically at the chained gate on the fence's north side, where Mrs. Incandenza has decided she doesn't want kids exiting the East Courts and trampling her calliopsis; and these little kids can hit balls exceptionally hard. Hal is now unable to gather enough spit to spit. One warhead hits Ingersoll in the neck and another solidly in the meat of the thigh. Ingersoll begins to limp around in small circles holding his neck, crying in that slow-motion shuddery way little kids have when they're crying more at the fact of being hurt than at the hurt itself. Pemulis is walking backwards away from the south fence back toward the pavilion and has both arms up in either appeal or fury or something else. Axford tells Hal and Troeltsch he wishes he didn't feel the dark thrill he felt watching Ingersoll get pummeled. Some filmy red peanut-skin has gotten into Jim Struck's· hair as he lies there motionless. O. P. Lord attempts to rule that Ingersoll is no longer on the four courts of Eschaton's earth-map and so isn't even theoretically a valid target-area. It doesn't matter. Several kids close in on Ingersoll, triangulating their bombardment, T. Peterson on point. Ingersoll is hit several times, once right near the eye. Jim Troeltsch is up and running to the fence wanting to stop the thing, but Pemulis catches him by his headset's cord and tells him to let them all lie in their own bed. Hal, now leaning forward, steeple-fingered, finds himself just about paralyzed with absorption. Trevor Axford, fist to his chin, asks Hal if he's ever just simply fucking *hated* somebody without having any idea why. Hal finds himself riveted at something about the degenerating game that seems so terribly abstract and fraught with implications and consequences that even thinking about how to articulate it seems so complexly stressful that being almost incapacitated with absorption is almost the only way out of the complex stress. Now INDPAK's Penn and AMNAT's McKenna, who have long-standing personal bones to pick with Ann Kittenplan, peel off and gather ordnance and execute a pincer movement on Ann Kittenplan. She is hit twice from behind at close range. Ingersoll has long since gone down and is still getting hit. Lord is ruling at the top of his lungs that there's no way AMNAT can launch against itself when he gets tagged right on the breastbone by an errant warhead. Clutching his chest with one hand, with the other he flicks the red beanie's propeller, never before flicked, whose flicked spin heralds a worst-case-&-utterly-decontrolled-Armageddon-type situation. Timmy Peterson takes a ball in the groin and goes down like a sack of refined flour. Everybody's scooping up spent warheads and totally unrealistically refiring them. The fences shudder and sing as balls rain against them. Ingersoll now resembles some sort of animal that's been run over in the road. Troeltsch, who's looking for the first time at the idling sedan by West House's dumpsters and asking if anybody knew anybody who drove a Nunhagen-Aspirin-adverting Ford, is the only upperclass spectator who doesn't seem utterly silently engrossed. Ann Kittenplan has dropped her racquet and is charging McKenna. She takes two contact-bursts in the breast-area before she gets to him and lays McKenna out with an impressive left cross. LaMont Chu tackles Todd Possalthwaite from behind. Struck looks to have wet his pants in his sleep. J. J. Penn slips on a grounded warhead near Fiji and goes spectacularly down. The snowfall makes everything gauzy and terribly clear at the same time, eliminating all visual background so that the map's action seems stark and surreal. Nobody's using tennis balls now anymore. Josh Gopnik punches LaMont Chu in the stomach, and LaMont Chu yells that he's been punched in the stomach. Ann Kittenplan has Kieran McKenna in a headlock and is punching him repeatedly on the top of the skull. Otis P. Lord lets down the beach umbrella and starts pushing his crazy-wheeled food cart at a diskette-rattling clip toward 12's open south gate, still flicking furiously at the red beanie's propeller. Struck's hair is steadily accreting nut-skins. Pemulis is under cover but still standing, his legs well apart and his arms folded. The figure in the green Ford still hasn't moved once. Troeltsch says he for his own part wouldn't be just sitting and lying there if any of the Little Buddies under his personal charge were out there getting potentially injured, and Hal reflects that he does feel a certain sort of intense anxiety, but can't sort through the almost infinite-seeming implications of what Troeltsch is saying fast enough to determine whether the anxiety is over something about what he's seeing or something in the connection between what Troeltsch is saying and the degree to which he's absorbed in what's going on out inside the fence, which is a degenerative chaos so complex in its disorder that it's hard to tell whether it seems choreographed or simply chaotically disordered. LaMont Chu is throwing up into the Indian Ocean. Todd Possalthwaite has his hands to his face and is shrieking something about his 'doze.' It is now, beyond any argument or equivocation, snowing. The sky is off-white. Lord and his cart are now literally making tracks for the edge of the map. Evan Ingersoll hasn't moved in several minutes. Penn lies in a whitening service box with one leg bent beneath him at an impossible angle. Someone way off behind them has been blowing an athletic whistle. Ann Kittenplan begins to chase REDCHI's General Secretary south across the Asian subcontinent at top speed. Pemulis is telling Hal he hates to say he told them so. Hal can see Axford leaning way forward sheltering something tiny from the wind as he flicks at it with a spent lighter. It occurs to him this is the third anniversary of Axhandle losing a right finger and half his right thumb. Fierce little J. Gopnik is flailing at the air and telling whoever wants it to come on, come on. Otis P. Lord and his cart sail clattering across Indochina toward the southern gate. Hal is suddenly aware that Troeltsch and Pemulis are wincing but is not himself wincing and isn't sure why they are wincing and is looking out into the fray trying to determine whether he should be wincing when REDCHI's General Secretary, calling loudly for his mother and in full flight as he looks over his shoulder at Ann Kittenplan's contorted face, barrels directly into Lord's speeding food cart. There's a noise like the historical sum of all cafeteria accidents everywhere. 3.6-MB diskettes take flight like mad bats across what uncovered would be the baseline of Court 12. Different-colored beanies spill from the rolling solander box, whose lock's hasp is broken and protrudes like a tongue as it rolls. The TP's monitor and modem and Yushityu chassis, with most of Eschaton's nervous system on its hard drive, assume a parabolic southwest vector. The heavy equipment's altitude is impressive. An odd silent still moment hangs, the TP aloft. Pemulis bellows, his hands to his cheeks. Otis P. Lord hurdles the bent forms of food cart and General Secretary and sprints low over the court's map's snow, trying to save hardware that's now at the top of its rainbow's arc. It's clear Lord won't make it. It's a slow-motion moment. The snowfall's more than heavy enough now, Hal thinks, to excuse Lord's not seeing LaMont Chu directly before him, on his hands and knees, throwing up. Lord impacts Chu's arched form at about knee-level and is spectacularly airborne. The idling Ford reveals a sudden face at the driver's-side window. Axford is holding the lighter's chassis up to his ear and shaking it. Ann Kittenplan is ramming REDCHI's leader's face repeatedly into the mesh of the south fence. Lord's flight's parabola is less spectacular on the y-axis than the TP's has been. The Yushityu's hard-drive chassis makes an indescribable sound as it hits the earth and its brightly circuited guts come out. The color monitor lands on its back with its screen blinking ERROR at the white sky. Hal and everyone else can project Lord's flight's own terminus an instant before impact. For a brief moment that Hal will later regard as completely and uncomfortably bizarre, Hal feels at his own face to see whether he is wincing. The distant whistle patweets. Lord does indeed go headfirst down through the monitor's screen, and stays there, his sneakers in the air and his warm-up pants sagging upward to reveal black socks. There'd been a bad sound of glass. Penn flails on his back. Possalthwaite, Ingersoll, and McKenna bleed. The second shift's 1600h. siren down at Sunstrand Power & Light is creepily muffled by the no-sound of falling snow.

Boston AA is like AA nowhere else on this planet. Just like AA everyplace else, Boston AA is divided into numerous individual AA Groups, and each Group has its particular Group name like the Reality Group or the Allston Group or the Clean and Sober Group, and each Group holds its regular meeting once a week. But almost all Boston Groups' meetings are speaker meetings. That means that at the meetings there are recovering alcoholic speakers who stand up in front of everybody at an amplified podium and 'share their experience, strength, and hope.'[131] And the singular thing is that these speakers are not ever members of the Group that's holding the meeting, in Boston. The speakers at one certain Group's weekly speaker meeting are always from some other certain Boston AA Group. The people from the other Group who are here at like your Group speaking are here on something called a Commitment. Commitments are where some members of one Group commit to hit the road and travel to another Group's meeting to speak publicly from the podium. Then a bunch of people from the host Group hit the opposite lane of the same road on some other night and go to the visiting Group's meeting, to speak. Groups always trade Commitments: you come speak to us and we'll come speak to you. It can seem bizarre. You always go elsewhere to speak. At your own Group's meeting you're a host; you just sit there and listen as hard as you can, and you make coffee in 60-cup urns and stack polystyrene cups in big ziggurats and sell raffle tickets and make sandwiches, and you empty ashtrays and scrub out urns and sweep floors when the other Group's speakers are through. You never share your experience, strength, and hope on-stage behind a fiberboard podium with its cheap nondigital PA system's mike except in front of some *other* metro Boston Group.[132] Every night in Boston, bumper-stickered cars full of totally sober people, wall-eyed from caffeine and trying to read illegibly scrawled directions by the dashboard lights, crisscross the city, heading for the church basements or bingo halls or nursing-home cafeterias of other AA Groups, to put on Commitments. Being an active member of a Boston AA Group is probably a little bit like being a serious musician or like athlete, in terms of constant travel.

The White Flag Group of Enfield MA, in metropolitan Boston, meets Sundays in the cafeteria of the Provident Nursing Home on Hanneman Street, off Commonwealth Avenue a couple blocks west of Enfield Tennis Academy's flat-topped hill. Tonight the White Flag Group is hosting a Commitment from the Advanced Basics Group of Concord, a suburb of Boston. The Advanced Basics people have driven almost an hour to get here, plus there's always the problem of signless urban streets and directions given over the phone. On this coming Friday night, a small horde of White Flaggers will drive out to Concord to put on a reciprocal Commitment for the Advanced Basics Group. Travelling long distances on signless streets trying to parse directions like 'Take the second left off the rotary by the driveway to the chiropractor's' and getting lost and shooting your whole evening after a long day just to speak for like six minutes at a plywood podium is called 'Getting Active With Your Group'; the speaking itself is known as '12th-Step Work' or 'Giving It Away.' Giving It Away is a cardinal Boston AA principle. The term's derived from an epigrammatic description of recovery in Boston AA: 'You give it up to get it back to give it away.' Sobriety in Boston is regarded as less a gift than a sort of cosmic loan. You can't pay the loan back, but you can pay it *forward,* by spreading the message that despite all appearances AA works, spreading this message to the next new guy who's tottered in to a meeting and is sitting in the back row unable to hold his cup of coffee. The only way to hang onto sobriety is to give it away, and even just 24 hours of sobriety is worth doing anything for, a sober day being nothing short of a daily miracle if you've got the Disease like he's got the Disease, says the Advanced Basics member who's chairing this evening's Commitment, saying just a couple public words to the hall before he opens the meeting and retires to a stool next to the podium and calls his Group's speakers by random lot. The chairperson says he didn't used to be able to go 24 lousy *minutes* without a nip, before he Came In. 'Coming In' means admitting that your personal ass is kicked and tottering into Boston AA, ready to go to any lengths to stop the shit-storm. The Advanced Basics chairperson looks like a perfect cross between pictures of Dick Cavett and Truman Capote[133] except this guy's also like totally, almost flamboyantly bald, and to top it off he's wearing a bright-black country-western shirt with baroque curlicues of white Nodie-piping across the chest and shoulders, and a string tie, plus sharp-toed boots of some sort of weirdly imbricate reptile skin, and overall he's riveting to look at, grotesque in that riveting way that flaunts its grotesquerie. There are more cheap metal ashtrays and Styrofoam cups in this broad hall than you'll see anywhere else ever on earth. Gately's sitting right up front in the first row, so close to the podium he can see the tailor's notch in the chairperson's outsized incisors, but he enjoys twisting around and watching everybody come in and mill around shaking water off their outerwear, trying to find empty seats. Even on the night of the I.-Day holiday, the Provident's cafeteria is packed by 2000h. AA does not take holidays any more than the Disease does. This is the big established Sunday P.M. meeting for AAs in Enfield and Allston and Brighton. Regulars come every week from Watertown and East Newton, too, often, unless they're out on Commitments with their own Groups. The Provident cafeteria walls, painted an indecisive green, are tonight bedecked with portable felt banners emblazoned with AA slogans in Cub-Scoutish blue and gold. The slogans on them appear way too insipid even to mention what they are. E.g. 'ONE DAY AT A TIME,' for one. The effete western-dressed guy concludes his opening exhortation, leads the opening Moment of Silence, reads the AA Preamble, pulls a random name out of the Crested Beaut cowboy hat he's holding, makes a squinty show of reading it, says he'd like to call Advanced Basics' first random speaker of the evening, and asks if his fellow Group-member John L. is in the house, here, tonight.

John L. gets up to the podium and says, 'That is a question I did not used to be able to answer.' This gets a laugh, and everybody's posture gets subtly more relaxed, because it's clear that John L. has some sober time in and isn't going to be one of those AA speakers who's so wracked with self-conscious nerves he makes the empathetic audience nervous too. Everybody in the audience is aiming for total empathy with the speaker; that way they'll be able to receive the AA message he's here to carry. Empathy, in Boston AA, is called Identification.

Then John L. says his first name and what he is, and everybody calls Hello.

White Flag is one of the area AA meetings Ennet House requires its residents to attend. You have to be seen at a designated AA or NA meeting every single night of the week or out you go, discharged. A House Staff member has to accompany the residents when they go to the designated meetings, so they can be officially seen there.[134] The residents' House counselors suggest that they sit right up at the front of the hall where they can see the pores in the speaker's nose and try to Identify instead of Compare. Again, *Identify* means empathize. Identifying, unless you've got a stake in Comparing, isn't very hard to do, here. Because if you sit up front and listen hard, all the speakers' stories of decline and fall and surrender are basically alike, and like your own: fun with the Substance, then very gradually less fun, then significantly less fun because of like blackouts you suddenly come out of on the highway going 145 kph with companions you do not know, nights you awake from in unfamiliar bedding next to somebody who doesn't even resemble any known sort of mammal, three-day blackouts you come out of and have to buy a newspaper to even know what town you're in; yes gradually less and less actual fun but with some physical need for the Substance, now, instead of the former voluntary fun; then at some point suddenly just very little fun at all, combined with terrible daily hand-trembling need, then dread, anxiety, irrational phobias, dim siren-like memories of fun, trouble with assorted authorities, knee-buckling headaches, mild seizures, and the litany of what Boston AA calls Losses —

'Then come the day I lost my job to drinking.' Concord's John L. has a huge hanging gut and just no ass at all, the way some big older guys' asses seem to get sucked into their body and reappear out front as gut. Gately, in sobriety, does nightly sit-ups out of fear this'll all of a sudden happen to him, as age thirty approaches. Gately is so huge no one sits behind him for several rows. John L. has the biggest bunch of keys Gately's ever seen. They're on one of those pull-outable-wire janitor's keychains that clips to a belt loop, and the speaker jangles them absently, unaware, his one tip of the hat to public nerves. He's also wearing gray janitor's pants. 'Lost my damn job,' he says. 'I mean to say I still knew where it was and whatnot. I just went in as usual one day and there was some other fellow doing it,' which gets another laugh.

— then more Losses, with the Substance seeming like the only consolation against the pain of the mounting Losses, and of course you're in Denial about it being the Substance that's causing the very Losses it's consoling you about —

'Alcohol destroys *slowly* but *thoroughly* is what a fellow said to me the first night I Come In, up in Concord, and that fellow ended up becoming my sponsor.'

— then less mild seizures, D.T.s during attempts to taper off too fast, introduction to subjective bugs and rodents, then one more binge and more formicative bugs; then eventually a terrible acknowledgment that some line has been undeniably crossed, and fist-at-the-sky, as-God-is-my-witness vows to buckle down and lick this thing for good, to quit for all time, then maybe a few white-knuckled days of initial success, then a slip, then more pledges, clock-watching, baroque self-regulations, repeated slips back into the Substance's relief after like two days' abstinence, ghastly hangovers, head-flattening guilt and self-disgust, superstructures of additional self-regulations (e.g. not before 0900h. not on a worknight, only when the moon is waxing, only in the company of Swedes) which also fail —

'When I was drunk I wanted to get sober and when I was sober I wanted to get drunk,' John L. says; 'I lived that way for years, and I submit to you that's not livin, that's a fuckin death-in-life.'

— then unbelievable psychic pain, a kind of peritonitis of the soul, psychic agony, fear of impending insanity (why can't I quit if I so want to quit, unless I'm insane?), appearances at hospital detoxes and rehabs, domestic strife, financial free-fall, eventual domestic Losses —

'And then I lost my wife to drinking. I mean I still knew where she was and whatnot. I just went in one day and there was some other fellow doing it,' at which there's not all that much laughter, lots of pained nods: it's often the same all over, in terms of domestic Losses.

— then vocational ultimatums, unemployability, financial ruin, pancreatitis, overwhelming guilt, bloody vomiting, cirrhotic neuralgia, incontinence, neuropathy, nephritis, black depressions, searing pain, with the Substance affording increasingly brief periods of relief; then, finally, no relief available anywhere at all; finally it's impossible to get high enough to freeze what you feel like, being this way; and now you hate the Substance,

346

hate it, but you still find yourself unable to stop doing it, the Substance, you find you finally want to stop more than anything on earth and it's no fun doing it anymore and you can't believe you ever liked doing it and but you *still* can't stop, it's like you're totally fucking bats, it's like there's two yous; and when you'd sell your own dear Mum to stop and still, you find, can't stop, then the last layer of jolly friendly mask comes off your old friend the Substance, it's midnight now and all masks come off, and you all of a sudden see the Substance as it really is, for the first time you see the Disease as it really is, really has been all this time, you look in the mirror at midnight and see what owns you, what's become what you are —

'A fuckin livin death, I tell you it's not being near alive, by the end I was undead, not alive, and I tell you the idea of dyin was nothing compared to the idea of livin like that for another five or ten years and only *then* dyin,' with audience heads nodding in rows like a wind-swept meadow; *boy* can they ever Identify.

— and then you're in serious trouble, very serious trouble, and you know it, finally, deadly serious trouble, because this Substance you thought was your one true friend, that you gave up all for, gladly, that for so long gave you relief from the pain of the Losses your love of that relief caused, your mother and lover and god and compadre, has finally removed its smily-face mask to reveal centerless eyes and a ravening maw, and canines down to here, it's the Face In The Floor, the grinning root-white face of your worst nightmares, and the face is your own face in the mirror, now, it's *you,* the Substance has devoured or replaced and become *you,* and the puke-, drool- and Substance-crusted T-shirt you've both worn for weeks now gets torn off and you stand there looking and in the root-white chest where your heart (given away to It) should be beating, in its exposed chest's center and centerless eyes is just a lightless hole, more teeth, and a beckoning taloned hand dangling something irresistible, and now you see you've been had, screwed royal, stripped and fucked and tossed to the side like some stuffed toy to lie for all time in the posture you land in. You see now that It's your enemy and your worst personal nightmare and the trouble It's gotten you into is undeniable and you *still* can't stop. Doing the Substance now is like attending Black Mass but you still can't stop, even though the Substance no longer gets you high. You are, as they say, Finished. You cannot get drunk and you cannot get sober; you cannot get high and you cannot get straight. You are behind bars; you are in a cage and can see only bars in every direction. You are in the kind of a hell of a mess that either ends lives or turns them around. You are at a fork in the road that Boston AA calls your *Bottom,* though the term is misleading, because everybody here agrees it's more like someplace very high and unsupported: you're on the edge of something tall and leaning way out forward. . . .

If you listen for the similarities, all these speakers' Substance-careers seem to terminate at the same cliff's edge. You are now Finished, as a Substance-user. It's the jumping-off place. You now have two choices. You can either eliminate your own map for keeps — blades are the best, or else pills, or there's always quietly sucking off the exhaust pipe of your repossessable car in the bank-owned garage of your familyless home. Something whimpery instead of banging. Better clean and quiet and (since your whole career's been one long futile flight from pain) painless. Though of the alcoholics and drug addicts who compose over 70% of a given year's suicides, some try to go out with a last great garish Balaclavan gesture: one longtime member of the White Flag Group is a prognathous lady named Louise B. who tried to take a map-eliminating dive off the old Hancock Building downtown in B.S. '81 but got caught in the gust of a rising thermal only six flights off the roof and got blown cartwheeling back up and in through the smoked-glass window of an arbitrage firm's suite on the thirty-fourth floor, ending up sprawled prone on a high-gloss conference table with only lacerations and a compound of the collarbone and an experience of willed self-annihilation and external intervention that has left her rabidly Christian — rabidly, as in foam — so that she's comparatively ignored and avoided, though her AA story, being just like everybody else's but more spectacular, has become metro Boston AA myth. But so when you get to this jumping-off place at the Finish of your Substance-career you can either take up the Luger or blade and eliminate your own personal map — this can be at age sixty, or twenty-seven, or seventeen — or you can get out the very beginning of the Yellow Pages or InterNet Psych-Svce File and make a blubbering 0200h. phone call and admit to a gentle grandparentish voice that you're in trouble, deadly serious trouble, and the voice will try to soothe you into hanging on until a couple hours go by and two pleasantly earnest, weirdly calm guys in conservative attire appear smiling at your door sometime before dawn and speak quietly to you for hours and leave you not remembering anything from what they said except the sense that they used to be eerily like you, just where you are, utterly fucked, and but now somehow aren't anymore, fucked like you, at least they didn't seem like they were, unless the whole thing's some incredibly involved scam, this AA thing, and so but anyway you sit there on what's left of your furniture in the lavender dawnlight and realize that by now you literally have no other choices besides trying this AA thing or else eliminating your map, so you spend the day killing every last bit of every Substance you've got in one last joyless bitter farewell binge and resolve, the next day, to go ahead and swallow your pride and maybe your common sense too and try these meetings of this 'Program' that at best is probably just Unitarian happy horseshit and at worst is a cover for some glazed and canny cult-type thing where they'll keep you sober by making you spend twenty hours a day selling cellophane cones of artificial flowers on the median strips of heavy-flow roads. And

348

what defines this cliffish nexus of exactly two total choices, this miserable road-fork Boston AA calls your Bottom, is that at this point you feel like maybe selling flowers on median strips might not be so bad, not compared to what you've got going, personally, at this juncture. And this, at root, is what unites Boston AA: it turns out this same resigned, miserable, brainwash-and-exploit-me-if-that's-what-it-takes-type desperation has been the jumping-off place for just about every AA you meet, it emerges, once you've actually gotten it up to stop darting in and out of the big meetings and start walking up with your wet hand out and trying to actually personally meet some Boston AAs. As the one particular tough old guy or lady you're always particularly scared of and drawn to says, nobody ever Comes In because things were going really well and they just wanted to round out their P.M. social calendar. Everybody, but *everybody* Comes In dead-eyed and puke-white and with their face hanging down around their knees and with a well-thumbed firearm-and-ordnance mail-order catalogue kept safe and available at home, map-wise, for when this last desperate resort of hugs and clichés turns out to be just happy horseshit, for you. You are not unique, they'll say: this initial hopelessness unites every soul in this broad cold salad-bar'd hall. They are like Hindenburg-survivors. Every meeting is a reunion, once you've been in for a while.

And then the palsied newcomers who totter in desperate and miserable enough to Hang In and keep coming and start feebly to scratch beneath the unlikely insipid surface of the thing, Don Gately's found, then get united by a second common experience. The shocking discovery that the thing actually does seem to work. Does keep you Substance-free. It's improbable and shocking. When Gately finally snapped to the fact, one day about four months into his Ennet House residency, that quite a few days seemed to have gone by without his playing with the usual idea of slipping over to Unit #7 and getting loaded in some nonuremic way the courts couldn't prove, that several days had gone without his even *thinking* of oral narcotics or a tightly rolled duBois or a cold foamer on a hot day . . . when he realized that the various Substances he didn't used to be able to go a day without absorbing hadn't even like *occurred* to him in almost a week, Gately hadn't felt so much grateful or joyful as just plain shocked. The idea that AA might actually somehow *work* unnerved him. He suspected some sort of trap. Some new sort of trap. At this stage he and the other Ennet residents who were still there and starting to snap to the fact that AA might work began to sit around together late at night going batshit together because it seemed to be impossible to figure out just *how* AA worked. It did, yes, tentatively seem maybe actually to be working, but Gately couldn't for the life of him figure out how just sitting on hemorrhoid-hostile folding chairs every night looking at nose-pores and listening to clichés could work. Nobody's ever been able to figure AA out, is another binding commonality. And the folks with serious time in AA are infuriating about questions starting with *How*. You ask the scary old guys How AA Works and they smile their chilly smiles and say Just Fine. It just works, is all; end of story. The newcomers who abandon common sense and resolve to Hang In and keep coming and then find their cages all of a sudden open, mysteriously, after a while, share this sense of deep shock and possible trap; about newer Boston AAs with like six months clean you can see this look of glazed suspicion instead of beatific glee, an expression like that of bug-eyed natives confronted suddenly with a Zippo lighter. And so this unites them, nervously, this tentative assemblage of possible glimmers of something like hope, this grudging move toward maybe acknowledging that this unromantic, unhip, clichéd AA thing — so unlikely and unpromising, so much the inverse of what they'd come too much to love — might really be able to keep the lover's toothy maw at bay. The process is the neat reverse of what brought you down and In here: Substances start out being so magically great, so much the interior jigsaw's missing piece, that at the start you just know, deep in your gut, that they'll never let you down; you just know it. But they do. And then this goofy slapdash anarchic system of low-rent gatherings and corny slogans and saccharin grins and hideous coffee is so lame you just *know* there's no way it could ever possibly work except for the utterest morons . . . and then Gately seems to find out AA turns out to be the very loyal friend he thought he'd had and then lost, when you Came In. And so you Hang In and stay sober and straight, and out of sheer hand-burned-on-hot-stove terror you heed the improbable-sounding warnings not to stop pounding out the nightly meetings even after the Substance-cravings have left and you feel like you've got a grip on the thing at last and can now go it alone, you still don't try to go it alone, you heed the improbable warnings because by now you have no faith in your own sense of what's really improbable and what isn't, since AA seems, improbably enough, to be working, and with no faith in your own senses you're confused, flummoxed, and when people with AA time strongly advise you to keep coming you nod robotically and keep coming, and you sweep floors and scrub out ashtrays and fill stained steel urns with hideous coffee, and you keep getting ritually down on your big knees every morning and night asking for help from a sky that still seems a burnished shield against all who would ask aid of it — how can you pray to a 'God' you believe only morons believe in, still? — but the old guys say it doesn't yet matter what you believe or don't believe, Just Do It they say, and like a shock-trained organism without any kind of independent human will you do exactly like you're told, you keep coming and coming, nightly, and now you take pains not to get booted out of the squalid halfway house you'd at first tried so hard to get discharged from, you Hang In and Hang In, meeting after meeting, warm day after cold day . . . ; and not only does the urge to get high stay more or less away, but more general life-quality-type things —

350

just as improbably promised, at first, when you'd Come In — things seem to get progressively somehow better, inside, for a while, then worse, then even better, then for a while worse in a way that's still somehow better, realer, you feel weirdly unblinded, which is good, even though a lot of the things you now see about yourself and how you've lived are horrible to have to see — and by this time the whole thing is so improbable and unparsable that you're so flummoxed you're convinced you're maybe brain-damaged, still, at this point, from all the years of Substances, and you figure you'd better Hang In in this Boston AA where older guys who seem to be less damaged — or at least less flummoxed by their damage — will tell you in terse simple imperative clauses exactly what to do, and where and when to do it (though never How or Why); and at this point you've started to have an almost classic sort of Blind Faith in the older guys, a Blind Faith in them born not of zealotry or even belief but just of a chilled conviction that you have no faith whatsoever left in yourself;[135] and now if the older guys say Jump you ask them to hold their hand at the desired height, and now they've got you, and you're free.

Another Advanced Basics Group speaker, whose first name Gately loses in the crowd's big Hello but whose last initial is E., an even bigger guy than John L., a green-card Irishman in a skallycap and Sinn Fein sweatshirt, with a belly like a swinging sack of meal and a thoroughly visible ass to back it up, is sharing his hope's experience by listing the gifts that have followed his decision to Come In and put the plug in the jug and the cap on the phentermine-hydrochloride bottle[136] and stop driving long-haul truck routes in unbroken 96-hour metal-pedalled states of chemical psychosis. The rewards of his abstinence, he stresses, have been more than just spiritual. Only in Boston AA can you hear a fifty-year-old immigrant wax lyrical about his first solid bowel movement in adult life.

' 'd been a confarmed bowl-splatterer for yars b'yond contin'. 'd been barred from t'facilities at o't' troock stops twixt hair'n Nork for yars. T'wallpaper in de loo a t'ome hoong in t'ese carled sheets froom t'wall, ay till yo. But now woon dey . . . ay'll remaember't'always. T'were a wake to t'day ofter ay stewed oop for me ninety-dey chip. Ay were tray moents sobber. Ay were thar on t'throne a't'ome, yo new. No't'put too fain a point'on it, ay prodooced as er uzhal and . . . and ay war soo amazed as to no't'belaven' me yairs. 'Twas a sone so wonefamiliar at t'first ay tought ay'd droped me wallet in t'loo, do yo new. Ay tought ay'd droped me wallet in t'loo as Good is me wetness. So doan ay bend twixt m'knays and'ad a luke in t'dim o't'loo, and codn't belave me'yize. So gud paple ay do then ay drope to m'knays by t'loo an't'ad a *rail* luke. A loaver's luke, d'yo new. And friends t'were loavely past me pur poewers t'say. T'were a *tard* in t'loo. A *rail tard*. T'were farm an' teppered an' aiver so jaintly aitched. T'luked . . . *conestroocted* instaid've sprayed. T'luked as ay fel't'in me 'eart Good 'imsailf maint a tard t'luke. Me friends, this tard'o'mine practically had a poolse. Ay sted doan own m'knays an tanked me Har Par, which ay choose t'call me Har Par Good, an' ay been tankin me Har Par own m'knays aiver sin, marnin and natetime an in t'loo's'well, aiver sin.' The man's red-leather face radiant throughout. Gately and the other White Flaggers fall about, laugh from the gut, a turd that practically had a pulse, an ode to a solid dump; but the lightless eyes of certain palsied back-row newcomers widen with a very private Identification and possible hope, hardly daring to imagine. . . . A certain Message has been Carried.

Gately's biggest asset as an Ennet House live-in Staffer — besides the size thing, which is not to be discounted when order has to be maintained in a place where guys come in fresh from detox still in Withdrawal with their eyes rolling like palsied cattle and an earring in their eyelid and a tattoo that says BORN TO BE UNPLEASANT — besides the fact that his upper arms are the size of cuts of beef you rarely see off hooks, his big plus is he has this ability to convey his own experience about at first hating AA to new House residents who hate AA and resent being forced to go and sit up in nose-pore-range and listen to such limply improbable clichéd drivel night after night. Limp AA looks, at first, and actually limp it sometimes really is, Gately tells the new residents, and he says no way he'd expect them to believe on just his say-so that the thing'll work if they're miserable and desperate enough to Hang In against common sense for a while. But he says he'll clue them in on a truly great thing about AA: *they can't kick you out.* You're In if you say you're In. Nobody can get kicked out, not for any reason. Which means you can say *anything* in here. Talk about solid turds all you want. The molecular integrity of shit is small potatoes. Gately says he defies the new Ennet House residents to try and shock the smiles off these Boston AAs' faces. Can't be done, he says. These folks have literally heard it all. Enuresis. Impotence. Priapism. Onanism. Projectile-incontinence. Autocastration. Elaborate paranoid delusions, the grandiosest megalomania, Communism, fringe-Birchism, National-Socialist-Bundism, psychotic breaks, sodomy, bestiality, daughter-diddling, exposures at every conceivable level of indecency. Coprophilia and -phagia. Four-year White Flagger Glenn K.'s personally chosen Higher Power is *Satan,* for fuck's sake. Granted, nobody in White Flag much likes Glenn K., and the thing with the hooded cape and makeup and the candelabrum he carries around draw some mutters, but Glenn K. is a member for exactly as long as he cares to Hang In.

So say anything you want, Gately invites them. Go to the Beginner Meeting at 1930h. and raise your shaky mitt and tell the unlacquered truth. Free-associate. Run with it. Gately this morning, just after required A.M. meditation, Gately was telling the tatt-obsessed little new lawyer guy Ewell, with the hypertensive flush and little white beard, telling him how he, Gately, had perked up considerably at 30 days clean when he found he could raise his big mitt in Beginner Meetings and say publicly just how much he hates this limp AA drivel about gratitude and humility and miracles and how he hates it and thinks it's horseshit and hates the AAs and how they all seem like limp smug moronic self-satisfied shit-eating pricks with their lobotomized smiles and goopy sentiment and how he wishes them all violent technicolor harm in the worst way, new Gately sitting there spraying vitriol, wet-lipped and red-eared, *trying* to get kicked out, purposely *trying* to outrage the AAs into giving him the boot so he could quick-march back to Ennet House and tell crippled Pat Montesian and his counselor Gene M. how he'd been given the boot at AA, how they'd pleaded for honest sharing of innermost feelings and OK he'd honestly shared his deepest feelings on the matter of *them* and the grinning hypocrites had shaken their fists and told him to screw . . . and but so in the meetings the poison would leap and spurt from him, and how but he found out all that these veteran White Flaggers would do as a Group when he like vocally wished them harm was nod furiously in empathetic Identification and shout with maddening cheer 'Keep Coming!' and one or two Flaggers with medium amounts of sober time would come up to him after the meeting and say how it was so good to hear him share and holy *mackerel* could they ever Identify with the deeply honest feelings he'd shared and how he'd done them the service of giving them the gift of a real 'Remember-When'-type experience because they could now remember feeling just exactly the same way as Gately, when they first Came In, only they confess not then having the spine to honestly share it with the Group, and so in a bizarre improbable twist they'd have Gately ending up standing there feeling like some sort of AA hero, a prodigy of vitriolic spine, both frustrated and elated, and before they bid him orevwar and told him to come back they'd make sure to give him their phone numbers on the back of their little raffle tickets, phone numbers Gately wouldn't dream of actually calling up (to say *what*, for chrissakes?) but which he found he rather liked having in his wallet, to just carry around, just in case of who knew what; and then plus maybe one of these old Enfield-native White Flag guys with geologic amounts of sober time in AA and a twisted ruined old body and clear bright-white eyes would hobble sideways like a crab slowly up to Gately after a meeting in which he'd spewed vitriol and reach way up to clap him on his big sweaty shoulder and say in their fremitic smoker's croak that Well you at least seem like a ballsy little bastard, all full of piss and vinegar and whatnot, and that just maybe you'll be OK, Don G., just maybe, just Keep Coming, and, if you'd care for a spot of advice from somebody who likely spilled more booze in his day than you've even consumed in yours, you might try to just simply sit down at meetings and relax and take the cotton out of your ears and put it in your mouth and shut the fuck up and just listen, for the first time perhaps in your life really *listen,* and maybe you'll end up OK; and they don't offer their phone numbers, not the really old guys, Gately knows he'd have to eat his pride raw and actually *request* the numbers of the old ruined grim calm longtimers in White Flag, 'The Crocodiles' the less senior White Flaggers call them, because the old twisted guys all tend to sit clustered together with hideous turd-like cigars in one corner of the Provident cafeteria under a 16 X 20 framed glossy of crocodiles or alligators sunning themselves on some verdant riverbank somewhere, with the maybe-joke legend OLD-TIMERS CORNER somebody had magisculed across the bottom of the photo, and these old guys cluster together under it, rotating their green cigars in their misshapen fingers and discussing completely mysterious long-sober matters out of the sides of their mouths. Gately sort of fears these old AA guys with their varicose noses and flannel shirts and white crew cuts and brown teeth and coolly amused looks of appraisal, feels like a kind of low-rank tribal knucklehead in the presence of stone-faced chieftains who rule by some unspoken shamanistic fiat,[137] and so of course he hates them, the Crocodiles, for making him feel like he fears them, but oddly he also ends up looking forward a little to sitting in the same big nursing-home cafeteria with them and facing the same direction they face, every Sunday, and a little later finds he even enjoys riding at 30 kph tops in their perfectly maintained 25-year-old sedans when he starts going along on White Flag Commitments to other Boston AA Groups. He eventually heeds a terse suggestion and starts going out and telling his grisly personal story publicly from the podium with other members of White Flag, the Group he gave in and finally officially joined. This is what you do if you're new and have what's called The Gift of Desperation and are willing to go to any excruciating lengths to stay straight, you officially join a Group and put your name and sobriety-date down on the Group secretary's official roster, and you make it your business to start to get to know other members of the Group on a personal basis, and you carry their numbers talismanically in your wallet; and, most important, you get Active With Your Group, which here in Gately's Boston AA *Active* means not just sweeping the footprinty floor after the Lord's Prayer and making coffee and emptying ashtrays of gasper-butts and ghastly spit-wet cigar ends but also showing up regularly at specified P.M. times at the White Flag Group's regular haunt, the Elit (the final *e*'s neon's ballast's out) Diner next to Steve's Donuts in Enfield Center, showing up and pounding down tooth-loosening amounts of coffee and then getting in well-maintained Crocodilian sedans whose suspensions' springs Gately's mass makes sag and getting driven, wall-eyed with caffeine and cigar fumes and general public-speaking angst, to like Lowell's Joy of Living Group or Charlestown's Plug In The Jug Group or Bridgewater State Detox or Concord Honor Farm with these guys, and except for one or two other pale wall-eyed newcomers with The Gift of utter Desperation it's mostly Crocodiles with geologic sober time in these cars, it's mostly the guys that've stayed sober in White Flag for decades who still go on every single

354

booked Commitment, they go every time, dependable as death, even when the Celtics are on Spontaneous-Dis they hit the old Commitment trail, they remain rabidly Active With Their Group; and the Crocodiles in the car invite Gately to see the coincidence of long-term contented sobriety and rabidly tireless AA Activity as not a coincidence at all. The backs of their necks are complexly creased. The Crocodiles up front look into the rearview mirror and narrow their baggy bright-white eyes at Gately in the sagging backseat with the other new guys, and the Crocodiles say they can't even begin to say how many new guys they've seen Come In and then get sucked back Out There, Come In to AA for a while and Hang In and put together a little sober time and have things start to get better, head-wise and life-quality-wise, and after a while the new guys get cocky, they decide they've gotten 'Well,' and they get really busy at the new job sobriety's allowed them to get, or maybe they buy season Celtics tickets, or they rediscover pussy and start chasing pussy (these withered gnarled toothless totally post-sexual old fuckers actually say *pussy*), but one way or another these poor cocky clueless new bastards start gradually drifting away from rabid Activity In The Group, and then away from their Group itself, and then little by little gradually drift away from any AA meetings at all, and then, without the protection of meetings or a Group, in time — oh there's always plenty of time, the Disease is fiendishly patient — how in time they forget what it was like, the ones that've cockily drifted, they forget who and what they are, they forget about the Disease, until like one day they're at like maybe a Celtics-Sixers game, and the good old Fleet/First Interstate Center's hot, and they think what could just one cold foamer hurt, after all this sober time, now that they've gotten 'Well.' Just one cold one. What could it hurt. And after that one it's like they'd never stopped, if they've got the Disease. And how in a month or six months or a year they have to Come *Back* In, back to the Boston AA halls and their old Group, tottering, D.T.ing, with their faces hanging down around their knees all over again, or maybe it's five or ten years before they can get it up to get back In, beaten to shit again, or else their system isn't ready for the recurred abuse again after some sober time and they die Out There — the Crocodiles are always talking in hushed, 'Nam-like tones about *Out There* — or else, worse, maybe they kill somebody in a blackout and spend the rest of their lives in MCI-Walpole drinking raisin jack fermented in the seatless toilet and trying to recall what they did to get in there, Out There; or else, worst of all, these cocky new guys drift back Out There and have nothing sufficiently horrible to Finish them happen at all, just go back to drinking 24/7/365, to not-living, behind bars, undead, back in the Disease's cage all over again. The Crocodiles talk about how they can't count the number of guys that've Come In for a while and drifted away and gone back Out There and died, or not gotten to die. They even point some of these guys out — gaunt gray spectral men reeling on

355

sidewalks with all that they own in a trashbag — as the White Flaggers drive slowly by in their well-maintained cars. Old emphysemic Francis G. in particular likes to slow his LeSabre down at a corner in front of some jack-legged loose-faced homeless fuck who'd once been in AA and drifted cockily out and roll down his window and yell 'Live it up!'

Of course — the Crocodiles dig at each other with their knobby elbows and guffaw and wheeze — they say when they tell Gately to either Hang In AA and get rabidly Active or else die in slime of course it's only a *suggestion*. They howl and choke and slap their knees at this. It's your classic in-type joke. There are, by ratified tradition, no 'musts' in Boston AA. No doctrine or dogma or rules. They can't kick you out. You don't have to do what they say. Do exactly as you please — if you still trust what seems to please you. The Crocodiles roar and wheeze and pound on the dash and bob in the front seat in abject AA mirth.

Boston AA's take on itself is that it's a benign anarchy, that any order to the thing is a function of Miracle. No regs, no musts, only love and support and the occasional humble suggestion born of shared experience. A non-authoritarian, dogma-free movement. Normally a gifted cynic, with a keen bullshit-antenna, Gately needed over a year to pinpoint the ways in which he feels like Boston AA really is actually sub-rosa dogmatic. You're not supposed to pick up any sort of altering Substance, of course; that goes without saying; but the Fellowship's official line is that if you do slip or drift or fuck up or forget and go Out There for a night and absorb a Substance and get all your Disease's triggers pulled again they want you to know they not only invite but urge you to come on back to meetings as quickly as possible. They're pretty sincere about this, since a lot of new people slip and slide a bit, total-abstinence-wise, in the beginning. Nobody's supposed to judge you or snub you for slipping. Everybody's here to help. Everybody knows that the returning slippee has punished himself enough just being Out There, and that it takes incredible desperation and humility to eat your pride and wobble back In and put the Substance down again after you've fucked up the first time and the Substance is calling to you all over again. There's the sort of sincere compassion about fucking up that empathy makes possible, although some of the AAs will nod smugly when they find out the slippee didn't take some of the basic suggestions. Even newcomers who can't even start to quit yet and show up with suspicious flask-sized bulges in their coat pockets and list progressively to starboard as the meeting progresses are urged to keep coming, Hang In, stay, as long as they're not too disruptive. Inebriates are discouraged from driving themselves home after the Lord's Prayer, but nobody's going to wrestle your keys away. Boston AA stresses the utter autonomy of the individual member. Please say and do whatever you wish. Of course there are about a dozen basic suggestions,[138] and of course people who cockily decide they don't wish to abide

by the basic suggestions are constantly going back Out There and then wobbling back in with their faces around their knees and confessing from the
podium that they didn't take the suggestions and have paid full price for
their willful arrogance and have learned the hard way and but now they're
back, by God, and this time they're going to follow the suggestions to the
bloody *letter* just see if they don't. Gately's sponsor Francis ('Ferocious
Francis') G., the Crocodile that Gately finally got up the juice to ask to be
his sponsor, compares the totally optional basic suggestions in Boston AA
to, say for instance if you're going to jump out of an airplane, they 'suggest'
you wear a parachute. But of course you do what you want. Then he starts
laughing until he's coughing so bad he has to sit down.

The bitch of the thing is you have to *want* to. If you don't *want* to do as
you're told — I mean as it's suggested you do — it means that your own
personal will is still in control, and Eugenio Martinez over at Ennet House
never tires of pointing out that your personal will is the web your Disease
sits and spins in, still. The will you call your own ceased to be yours as of
who knows how many Substance-drenched years ago. It's now shot through
with the spidered fibrosis of your Disease. His own experience's term for the
Disease is: *The Spider*.[139] You have to Starve The Spider: you have to surrender your will. This is why most people will Come In and Hang In only
after their own entangled will has just about killed them. You have to want
to surrender your will to people who know how to Starve The Spider. You
have to want to take the suggestions, want to abide by the traditions of
anonymity, humility, surrender to the Group conscience. If you don't obey,
nobody will kick you out. They won't have to. You'll end up kicking *yourself* out, if you steer by your own sick will. This is maybe why just about
everybody in the White Flag Group tries so hard to be so disgustingly
humble, kind, helpful, tactful, cheerful, nonjudgmental, tidy, energetic, sanguine, modest, generous, fair, orderly, patient, tolerant, attentive, truthful.
It isn't like the Group makes them do it. It's more like that the only people
who end up able to hang for serious time in AA are the ones who willingly
try to be these things. This is why, to the cynical newcomer or fresh Ennet
House resident, serious AAs look like these weird combinations of Gandhi
and Mr. Rogers with tattoos and enlarged livers and no teeth who used to
beat wives and diddle daughters and now rhapsodize about their bowel
movements. It's all optional; do it or die.

So but like e.g. Gately puzzled for quite some time about why these AA
meetings where nobody kept order seemed so orderly. No interrupting, fist-
icuffery, no heckled invectives, no poisonous gossip or beefs over the tray's
last Oreo. Where was the hard-ass Sergeant at Arms who enforced these
principles they guaranteed would save your ass? Pat Montesian and Eugenio
Martinez and Ferocious Francis the Crocodile wouldn't answer Gately's
questions about where's the enforcement. They just all smiled coy smiles

357

and said to Keep Coming, an apothegm Gately found just as trite as 'Easy Does It!' 'Live and Let Live!'

How do trite things get to be trite? Why is the truth usually not just un- but *anti*-interesting? Because every one of the seminal little mini-epiphanies you have in early AA is always polyesterishly banal, Gately admits to residents. He'll tell how, as a resident, right after that one Harvard Square industrial-grunge post-punk, this guy whose name was Bernard but insisted on being called Plasmatron-7, right after old Plasmatron-7 drank nine bottles of NyQuil in the men's upstairs head and pitched forward face-first into his instant spuds at supper and got discharged on the spot, and got fireman-carried by Calvin Thrust right out to Comm. Ave.'s Green Line T-stop, and Gately got moved up from the newest guys' 5-Man room to take Plasmatron-7's old bunk in the less-new guys' 3-Man room, Gately had an epiphanic AA-related nocturnal dream he'll be the first to admit was banally trite.[140] In the dream Gately and row after row of totally average and non-unique U.S. citizens were kneeling on their knees on polyester cushions in a crummy low-rent church basement. The basement was your average low-rent church basement except for this dream-church's basement walls were of like this weird thin clean clear glass. Everybody was kneeling on these cheap but comfortable cushions, and it was weird because nobody seemed to have any clear idea why they were all on their knees, and there was like no tier-boss or sergeant-at-arms-type figure around coercing them into kneeling, and yet there was this sense of some compelling unspoken reason why they were all kneeling. It was one of those dream things where it didn't make sense but did. And but then some lady over to Gately's left got off her knees and all of a sudden stood up, just like to stretch, and the minute she stood up she was all of a sudden yanked backward with terrible force and sucked out through one of the clear glass walls of the basement, and Gately had winced to get ready for the sound of serious glass, but the glass wall didn't shatter so much as just let the cartwheeling lady sort of melt right through, and healed back over where she'd melted through, and she was gone. Her cushion and then Gately notices a couple other polyester cushions in some of the rows here and there were empty. And it was then, as he was looking around, that Gately in his dream looked slowly up overhead at the ceiling's exposed pipes and could now all of a sudden see, rotating slow and silent through the basement a meter above the different-shaped and -colored heads of the kneeling assembly, he could see a long plain hooked stick, like the crook of a giant shepherd, like the hook that appears from stage-left and drags bad acts out of tomato-range, moving slowly above them in French-curled circles, almost demurely, as if quietly scanning; and when a mild-faced guy in a cardigan happened to stand up and was hooked by the hooked stick and pulled ass-over-teakettle out through the soundless glass membrane Gately turned his big head as far as he could without leaving the cushion and could see, now, just outside the wall's clean pane, trolling with the big stick, an extraordinarily snappily dressed and authoritative figure manipulating the giant shepherd's crook with one hand and coolly examining the nails of his other hand from behind a mask that was simply the plain yellow smily-face circle that accompanied invitations to have a nice day. The figure was so impressive and trustworthy and casually self-assured as to be both soothing and compelling. The authoritative figure radiated good cheer and abundant charm and limitless patience. It manipulated the big stick in the coolly purposeful way of the sort of angler who you know isn't going to throw back anything he catches. The slow silent stick with the hook he held was what kept them all kneeling below the baroque little circumferences of its movement overhead.

One of Ennet House's live-in Staffers' rotating P.M. jobs is to be awake and on-call in the front office all night for Dream Duty — people in early recovery from Substances often get hit with real horror-show dreams, or else traumatically seductive Substance-dreams, and sometimes trite but important epiphanic dreams, and the Staffer on Dream Duty is required to be up doing paperwork or sit-ups or staring out the broad bay window in the front office downstairs, ready to make coffee and listen to the residents' dreams and offer the odd practical upbeat Boston-AA-type insight into possible implications for the dreamer's progress in recovery — but Gately had no need to clomp downstairs for a Staffer's feedback on this one, since it was so powerfully, tritely obvious. It had come clear to Gately that Boston AA had the planet's most remorselessly hard-ass and efficient sergeant at arms. Gately lay there, overhanging all four sides of his bunk, his broad square forehead beaded with revelation: Boston AA's Sergeant at Arms stood *outside* the orderly meeting halls, in that much-invoked Out There where exciting clubs full of good cheer throbbed gaily below lit signs with neon bottles endlessly pouring. AA's patient enforcer was always and everywhere Out There: it stood casually checking its cuticles in the astringent fluorescence of pharmacies that took forged Talwin scrips for a hefty surcharge, in the onionlight through paper shades in the furnished rooms of strung-out nurses who financed their own cages' maintenance with stolen pharmaceutical samples, in the isopropyl reek of the storefront offices of stooped old chain-smoking MD's whose scrip-pads were always out and who needed only to hear 'pain' and see cash. In the home of a snot-strangled Canadian VIP and the office of an implacable Revere A.D.A. whose wife has opted for dentures at thirty-five. AA's disciplinarian looked damn good and smelled even better and dressed to impress and his blank black-on-yellow smile never faltered as he sincerely urged you to have a nice day. Just one more last nice day. Just one.

And that was the first night that cynical Gately willingly took the basic suggestion to get down on his big knees by his undersized spring-shot Ennet

House bunk and Ask For Help from something he still didn't believe in, ask for his own sick Spider-bit will to be taken from him and fumigated and squished.

But and plus in Boston AA there is, unfortunately, dogma, too, it turns out; and some of it is both dated and smug. And there's an off-putting jargon in the Fellowship, a psychobabbly dialect that's damn near impossible to follow at first, says Ken Erdedy, the college-boy ad exec semi-new at Ennet House, complaining to Gately at the White Flag meeting's rafflebreak. Boston AA meetings are unusually long, an hour and a half instead of the national hour, but here they also have this formal break at about 45 minutes where everybody can grab a sandwich or Oreo and a sixth cup of coffee and stand around and chat, and bond, where people can pull their sponsors aside and confide some trite insight or emotional snafu that the sponsor can swiftly, privately validate but also place in the larger imperative context of the primary need not to absorb a Substance today, just today, no matter what happens. While everybody's bonding and interfacing in a bizarre system of catchphrases, there's also the raffle, another Boston idiosyncrasy: the newest of the White Flag newcomers trying to Get Active In Group Service wobble around with rattan baskets and packs of tickets, one for a buck and three for a fin, and the winner eventually gets announced from the podium and everyone hisses and shouts 'Fix!' and laughs, and the winner wins a Big Book or an *As Bill Sees It* or a *Came To Believe,* which if he's got some sober time in and already owns all the AA literature from winning previous raffles he'll stand up and publicly offer it to any newcomer who wants it, which means any newcomer with enough humble desperation to come up to him and ask for it and risk being given a phone number to carry around in his wallet.

At the White Flag raffle-break Gately usually stands around chainsmoking with the Ennet House residents, so that he's casually available to answer questions and empathize with complaints. He usually waits til after the meeting to do his own complaining to Ferocious Francis, with whom Gately now shares the important duty of 'breaking down the hall,' sweeping floors and emptying ashtrays and wiping down the long cafeteria tables, which F.F.G.'s function is limited because he's on oxygen and his function consists mostly of standing there sucking oxygen and holding an unlit cigar while Gately breaks down the hall. Gately rather likes Ken Erdedy, who came into the House about a month ago from some cushy Belmont rehab. Erdedy's an upscale guy, what Gately's mother would have called a yuppie, an account executive at Viney and Veals Advertising downtown his Intake form said, and though he's about Gately's age he's so softly good-looking in that soft mannequinish way Harvard and Tufts schoolboys have, and looks so smooth and groomed all the time even in jeans and a plain cotton sweater, that Gately thinks of him as much younger, totally un-grizzled, and refers to him mentally as 'kid.' Erdedy's in the House mainly for 'marijuana addiction,' which Gately has a hard time Identifying with anybody getting in enough trouble with weed to leave his job and condo to bunk in a room full of tattooed guys who smoke in their sleep, and to work like pumping gas (Erdedy just started his nine-month humility job at the Merit station down by North Harvard St. in Allston) for 32 minimum-wage hours a week. Or to have his leg be joggling like that all the time from tensions of Withdrawal: from fucking grass? But it's not Gately's place to say what's bad enough to make somebody Come In and what isn't, not for anybody else but himself, and the shapely but big-time-troubled new girl Kate Gompert — who mostly just stays in her bed in the new women's 5-Woman room when she isn't at meetings, and is on a Suicidality Contract with Pat, and isn't getting the usual pressure to get a humility job, and gets to get some sort of scrip-meds out of the meds locker every morning — Kate Gompert's counselor Danielle S. reported at the last Staff Meeting that Kate had finally opened up and told her she'd mostly Come In for weed, too, and not the lightweight prescription tranqs she'd listed on her Intake form. Gately used to treat weed like tobacco. He wasn't like some other narcotics addicts who smoked weed when they couldn't get anything else; he always smoked weed and could always get something else and simply smoked weed while he did whatever else he could get. Gately doesn't miss weed much. The shocker-type AA Miracle is he doesn't much miss the Demerol, either, today.

A hard November wind is spattering goopy sleet against the broad windows all around the hall. The Provident Nursing Home cafeteria is lit by a checkerboard array of oversized institutional bulbs overhead, a few of which are always low and give off fluttery strobes. The fluttering bulbs are why Pat Montesian and all the other photic-seizure-prone area AAs never go to White Flag, opting for the Freeway Group over in Brookline or the candyass Lake Street meeting up in West Newton on Sunday nights, which Pat M. bizarrely drives all the way up from her home down on the South Shore in Milton to get to, to hear people talk about their analysts and Saabs. There is no way to account for people's taste in AA. The White Flag hall is so brightly lit up all Gately can see out any of the windows is a kind of shiny drooling black against everybody's pale reflection.

Miracle's one of the Boston AA terms Erdedy and the brand-new and very shaky veiled girl resident standing over him complain they find hard to stomach, as in 'We're All Miracles Here' and 'Don't Leave Five Minutes Before The Miracle Happens' and 'To Stay Sober For 24 Hours Is A Miracle.'

Except the brand-new girl, either Joelle V. or Joelle D., who said she'd hit the occasional meeting in the past before her Bottom and had been roundly repelled, and is still pretty much cynical and repelled, she said on the way down to Provident under Gately's direct new-resident supervision, says she finds even the word *Miracle* preferable to the constant AA talk about 'the Grace of God,' which reminds her of wherever she grew up, where she's indicated places of worship were often aluminum trailers or fiberboard shacks and church-goers played with copperheads in the services to honor something about serpents and tongues.

Gately's also observed how Erdedy's also got that Tufts-Harvard way of speaking without seeming to move his lower jaw.

'It's as if it's its own country or something,' Erdedy complains, legs crossed in maybe a bit of a faggy schoolboy way, looking around at the raffle-break, sitting in Gately's generous shadow. 'The first time I ever talked, over at the St. E's meeting on Wednesday, somebody comes up after the Lord's Prayer and says "Good to hear you, I could really I.D. with that bottom you were sharing about, the isolating, the can't-and-can't, it's the greenest I've felt in months, hearing you." And then gives me this raffle ticket with his phone number that I didn't ask for and says I'm right where I'm supposed to be, which I have to say I found a bit patronizing.'

The best noise Gately produces is his laugh, which booms and reassures, and a certain haunted hardness goes out of his face when he laughs. Like most huge men, Gately has kind of a high hoarse speaking voice; his larynx sounds compressed. 'I still hate that right-where-you're-supposed-to-be thing,' he says, laughing. He likes that Erdedy, sitting, looks right up at him and cocks his head slightly to let Gately know he's got his full attention. Gately doesn't know that this is a requisite for a white-collar job where you have to show you're attending fully to clients who are paying major sums and get to expect an overt display of full attention. Gately is still not yet a good judge of anything about upscale people except where they tend to hide their valuables.

Boston AA, with its emphasis on the Group, is intensely social. The raffle-break goes on and on. An intoxicated street-guy with a venulated nose and missing incisors and electrician's tape wrapped around his shoes is trying to sing 'Volare' up at the empty podium microphone. He is gently, cheerfully induced offstage by a Crocodile with a sandwich and an arm around the shoulders. There's a certain pathos to the Crocodile's kindness, his clean flannel arm around the weatherstained shoulders, which pathos Gately feels and likes being able to feel it, while he says 'But at least the "Good to hear you" I quit minding. It's just what they say when somebody's got done speaking. They can't say like "Good job" or "You spoke well," cause it can't be anybody's place here to judge if anybody else did good or bad or whatnot. You know what I'm saying, Tiny, there?'

Tiny Ewell, in a blue suit and laser chronometer and tiny shoes whose shine you could read by, is sharing a dirty aluminum ashtray with Nell Gunther, who has a glass eye which she amuses herself by usually wearing so the pupil and iris face in and the dead white and tiny manufacturer's specifications on the back of the eye face out. Both of them are pretending to study the blond false wood of the tabletop, and Ewell makes a bit of a hostile show of not looking up or responding to Gately or entering into the conversation in any way, which is his choice and on him alone, so Gately lets it go. Wade McDade has a Walkman going, which is technically OK at the raffle-break although it's not a real good idea. Chandler Foss is flossing his teeth and pretending to throw the used floss at Jennifer Belbin. Most of the Ennet House residents are mingling satisfactorily. The couple of residents that are black are mingling with other blacks.[141] The Diehl kid and Doony Glynn are amusing themselves telling homosexuality jokes to Morris Hanley, who sits smoothing his hair with his fingertips, pretending to not even acknowledge, his left hand still bandaged. Alfonso Parias-Carbo is standing with three Allston Group guys, smiling broadly and nodding, not understanding a word anybody says. Bruce Green has gone downstairs to the men's head and amused Gately by asking his permission first. Gately told him to go knock himself out. Green has good big arms and no gut, even after all the Substances, and Gately suspects he might have played some ball at some point. Kate Gompert is totally by herself at a nonsmoking table over by a window, ignoring her pale reflection and making little cardboard tents out of her raffle tickets and moving them around. Clenette Henderson clutches another black girl and laughs and says 'Girl!' several times. Emil Minty is clutching his head. Geoff Day in his black turtleneck and blazer keeps lurking on the fringes of various groups of people pretending he's part of the conversations. No immediate sign of Burt F. Smith or Charlotte Treat. Randy Lenz, in his cognito white mustache and sideburns, is doubtless at the pay phone in the northeast corner of the Provident lobby downstairs: Lenz spends nearly unacceptable amounts of time either on a phone or trying to get in position to use a phone. 'Cause what I like,' Gately says to Erdedy (Erdedy really is listening, even though there's a compellingly cheap young woman in a brief white skirt and absurd black mesh stockings sitting with her legs nicely crossed — one-strap low-spike black Ferragamos, too — at the periphery of his vision, and the woman is with a large man, which makes her even more compelling; and also the veiled new girl's breasts and her hips' clefs are compelling and distracting, next to him, even in a long baggy loose blue sweater that matches the embroidered selvage around her veil), 'What I think I like is how "It was good to hear you" ends up, like, saying two separate things together.' Gately's also saying this to Joelle, who it's weird but you can tell she's looking at you, even through the linen veil. There's maybe half a dozen or so other veiled people in the White Flag hall tonight; a decent percentage of people in the 11-Step Union of the Hideously and Improbably Deformed are also in 12-Step fellowships for other issues besides hideous deformity. Most of the room's veiled AAs are women, though there is this one male veiled U.H.I.D. guy that's an active White Flagger, Tommy S. or F., who years ago nodded out on a stuffed acrylic couch with a bottle of Rémy and a lit Tiparillo — the guy now wears U.H.I.D. veils and a whole spectrum of silk turtlenecks and assorted hats and classy lambskin driving gloves. Gately's had the U.H.I.D.-and-veil philosophy explained to him in passing a couple times but still doesn't much get it, it seems like a gesture of shame and concealment, still, to him, the veil. Pat Montesian had said there's been a few other U.H.I.D.s who'd gone through Ennet House prior to the Year of Dairy Products From the American Heartland, which is when new resident Gately came wobbling in, but this Joelle van Dyne, who Gately feels he has zero handle on yet as a person or how serious she is about putting down Substances and Coming In to really get straight, this Joelle is the first veiled resident Gately's had under him, as a Staffer. This Joelle girl, that wasn't even on the two-month waiting list for Intake, got in overnight under some private arrangement with somebody on the House's Board of Directors, upscale Enfield guys into charity and directing. There'd been no Intake interview with Pat at the House; the girl just showed up two days ago right after supper. She'd been up at Brigham and Women's for five days after some sort of horrific O.D.-type situation said to have included both defib paddles and priests. She'd had real luggage and this like Chinese portable dressing-screen thing with clouds and pop-eyed dragons that even folded lengthwise took both Green and Parias-Carbo to lug upstairs. There's been no talk of a humility job for her, and Pat's counseling the girl personally. Pat's got some sort of privately directed arrangement with the girl; Gately's already seen enough private-type arrangements between certain Staffers and residents to feel like it's maybe kind of a character defect of Ennet House. A girl from the Brookline Young People's Group over in a cheerleader skirt and slut-stockings is ignoring all the ashtrays and putting her extra-long gasper out on the bare tabletop two rows over as she laughs like a seal at something an acne'd guy in a long camelhair car coat he hasn't taken off and sockless leather dance-shoes Gately's never seen at a meeting before says. And he's got his hand on hers as she grinds the gasper out. Something like putting a cigarette out against the wood-grain plastic tabletop, which Gately can already see the ragged black burn-divot that's formed, it's something the rankness of which would never have struck him one way or the other, before, until Gately took on half the break-down-the-hall-and-wipe-down-the-tables job at Ferocious Francis G.'s suggestion, and now he feels sort of proprietary about the Provident's tabletops. But it's not like he can go over and take anybody else's inventory and tell them how to behave. He settles for imagining the girl pinwheeling through the air toward a glass wall.

'When they say it it sort of means like what you said was good for them, it helped them out somehow,' he says, 'but plus now also I like saying it myself because if you think about it it also means it was good to be *able* to hear you. To really hear.' He's trying subtly to alternate and look at Erdedy and Joelle both, like he's addressing them both. It's not something he's good at. His head's too big to be subtle with. 'Because I remember for like the first sixty days or so I couldn't hear shit. I didn't hear nothing. I'd just sit there and Compare, I'd go to myself, like, "I never rolled a car," "I never lost a wife," "I never bled from the rectum." Gene would tell me to just keep coming for a while and sooner or later I'd start to be able to both listen and hear. He said it's hard to really hear. But he wouldn't say what was the difference between hearing and listening, which pissed me off. But after a while I started to really *hear*. It turns out — and this is just for me, maybe — but it turned out *hearing* the speaker means like all of a sudden hearing how fucking similar the way he felt and the way I felt were, Out There, at the Bottom, before we each Came In. Instead of just sitting here resenting being here and thinking how he bled from the ass and I didn't and how that means I'm not as bad as him yet and I can still be Out There.'

One of the tricks to being of real service to newcomers is not to lecture or give advice but only talk about your own personal experience and what you were told and what you found out personally, and to do it in a casual but positive and encouraging way. Plus you're supposed to try and Identify with the newcomer's feelings as much as possible. Ferocious Francis G. says this is one of the ways guys with just a year or two sober can be most helpful: being able to sincerely ID with the newly Sick and Suffering. Ferocious Francis told Gately as they were wiping down tables that if a Crocodile with decades of sober AA time can still sincerely empathize and Identify with a whacked-out bug-eyed Disease-ridden newcomer then there's something deeply fucked up about that Crocodile's recovery. The Crocodiles, decades sober, live in a totally different spiritual galaxy, inside. One long-timer describes it as he has a whole new unique interior spiritual castle, now, to live in.

Part of this new Joelle girl's pull for Ken Erdedy isn't just the sexual thing of her body, which he finds made way sexier by the way the overlarge blue coffee-stained sweater tries to downplay the body thing without being so hubristic as to try to hide it — sloppy sexiness pulls Erdedy in like a well-groomed moth to a lit window — but it's also the veil, wondering what horrific contrast to the body's allure lies swollen or askew under that veil; it gives the pull a perverse sideways slant that makes it even more distracting, and so Erdedy cocks his head a little more up at Gately and narrows his eyes to make his listening-look terribly intense. He doesn't know that there's an abstract distance in the look that makes it seem like he's studying a real bitch of a 7-iron on the tenth rough or something; the look doesn't communicate what he thinks his audience wants it to.

The raffle-break is winding down as everybody starts to want their own ashtray. Two more big urns of coffee emerge from the kitchen door over by the literature table. Erdedy is probably the second-biggest leg-and-foot-joggler in present residence, after Geoffrey D. Joelle v. D. now says something very strange. It's a very strange little moment, right at the end of the raffle-break, and Gately later finds it impossible to describe it in his Log entry for the P.M. shift. It is the first time he realizes that Joelle's voice — crisp and rich and oddly empty, her accent just barely Southern and with a strange and it turns out Kentuckian lapse in the pronunciation of all apicals except *s* — is familiar in a faraway way that both makes it familiar and yet lets Gately be sure he's never once met her before, Out There. She inclines the plane of her blue-bordered veil briefly toward the floor's tile (very bad tile, scab-colored, nauseous, worst thing about the big room by far), brings it back up level (unlike Erdedy she's standing, and in flats is nearly Gately's height), and says that she's finding it especially hard to take when these earnest ravaged folks at the lectern say they're 'Here But For the Grace of God,' except that's not the strange thing she says, because when Gately nods hard and starts to interject about 'It was the same for —' and wants to launch into a fairly standard Boston AA agnostic-soothing riff about the 'God' in the slogan being just shorthand for a totally subjective and up-to-you 'Higher Power' and AA being merely spiritual instead of dogmatically religious, a sort of benign anarchy of subjective spirit, Joelle cuts off his interjection and says that but that *her* trouble with it is that 'But For the Grace of God' is a subjunctive, a counterfactual, she says, and can make sense only when introducing a conditional clause, like e.g. 'But For the Grace of God I *would* have died on Molly Notkin's bathroom floor,' so that an indicative transposition like 'I'm here But For the Grace of God' is, she says, literally senseless, and regardless of whether she *hears* it or not it's meaningless, and that the foamy enthusiasm with which these folks can say what in fact means nothing at all makes her want to put her head in a Radarange at the thought that Substances have brought her to the sort of pass where this is the sort of language she has to have Blind Faith in. Gately looks at a rectangular blue-selvaged expanse of clean linen whose gentle rises barely allude to any features below, he looks at her and has no idea whether she's serious or not, or whacked, or trying like Dr. Geoff Day to erect Denial-type fortifications with some kind of intellectualish showing-off, and he doesn't know what to say in reply, he has absolutely nothing in his huge square head to Identify with her with or latch onto or say in encouraging reply, and for an instant the Provident cafeteria seems pin-drop silent, and his own heart grips him like an infant rattling the bars of its playpen, and he feels a greasy wave of an old and almost unfamiliar panic, and for a second it seems inevitable that at some point in his life he's going to get high again and be back in the cage all over again, because for a second the blank white veil levelled at him seems a screen on which might well be projected a casual and impressive black and yellow smily-face, grinning, and he feels all the muscles in his own face loosen and descend kneeward; and the moment hangs there, distended, until the White Flag raffle coordinator for November, Glenn K., glides up to the podium mike in his scarlet velour caparison and makeup and candelabrum with candles the same color as the floor tile and uses the plastic gavel to formally end the break and bring things back to whatever passes here for order, for the raffle drawing. The Watertown guy with middle-level sober time who wins the Big Book publicly offers it to any newcomer that wants it, and Gately is pleased to see Bruce Green raise a big hand, and decides he'll just turn it over and ask Ferocious Francis G. for feedback on subjunctives and countersexuals, and the infant leaves its playpen alone inside him, and the rivets of the long table his seat's attached to make a brief distressed noise as he sits and settles in for the second half of the meeting, asking silently for help to be determined to try to really hear or die trying.

NNYC's harbor's Liberty Island's gigantic Lady has the sun for a crown and holds what looks like a huge photo album under one iron arm, and the other arm holds aloft a product. The product is changed each 1 Jan. by brave men with pitons and cranes.

But it's funny what they'll find funny, AAs at Boston meetings, listening. The next Advanced Basics guy summoned by their gleamingly bald western-wear chairman to speak is dreadfully, transparently unfunny: painfully new but pretending to be at ease, to be an old hand, desperate to amuse and impress them. The guy's got the sort of professional background where he's used to trying to impress gatherings of persons. He's dying to be liked up there. He's performing. The White Flag crowd can see all this. Even the true morons among them see right through the guy. This is not a regular audience. A Boston AA is very sensitive to the presence of ego. When the new guy introduces himself and makes an ironic gesture and says, 'I'm told I've been given the Gift of Desperation. I'm looking for the exchange window,' it's so clearly unspontaneous, rehearsed — plus commits the subtle but cardinal Message-offense of appearing to deprecate the Program rather than the Self — that just a few polite titters resound, and people shift in their seats with a slight but signal discomfort. The worst punishment Gately's seen inflicted on a Commitment speaker is when the host crowd gets embarrassed for him. Speakers who are accustomed to figuring out what an audience wants to hear and then supplying it find out quickly that this particular audience does not want to be supplied with what someone else thinks it wants. It's another conundrum Gately finally ran out of cerebral steam on. Part of finally getting comfortable in Boston AA is just finally running out of steam in terms of trying to figure stuff like this out. Because it literally makes no sense. Close to two hundred people all punishing somebody by getting embarrassed for him, killing him by empathetically dying right there with him, for him, up there at the podium. The applause when this guy's done has the relieved feel of a fist unclenching, and their cries of 'Keep Coming!' are so sincere it's almost painful.

But then in equally paradoxical contrast have a look at the next Advanced Basics speaker — this tall baggy sack of a man, also painfully new, but this poor bastard here completely and openly nerve-racked, wobbling his way up to the front, his face shiny with sweat and his talk full of blank cunctations and disassociated leaps — as the guy speaks with terrible abashed chagrin about trying to hang on to his job Out There as his A.M. hangovers became more and more debilitating until he finally got so shaky and aphasiac he just couldn't bear to even face the customers who'd come knocking on his Department's door — he was, from 0800 to 1600h., the Complaint Department of Filene's Department Store —

— 'What I did finally, Jesus I don't know where I got such a stupid idea from, I brought this hammer in from home and brought it in and kept it right there under my desk, on the floor, and when somebody knocked at the door I'd just . . . I'd sort of *dive* onto the floor and crawl under the desk and grab up the hammer, and I'd start in to pounding on the leg of the desk, real hard-like, whacketa whacketa, like I was fixing something down there. And if they opened the door finally and came in anyhow or came in to bitch about me not opening the door I'd just stay out of sight under there pounding away like hell and I'd yell out I was going to be a moment, just a moment, emergency repairs, be with them momentarily. I guess you can guess how all that pounding felt, you know, under there, what with the big head I had every morning. I'd hide under there and pound and pound with the hammer till they finally gave up and went away, I'd watch from under the desk and tell when they finally went away, from I could see their feet from under the desk.'

— And about how the hiding-under-the-desk-and-pounding thing worked, incredibly enough, for almost the whole last year of his drinking, which ended around this past Labor Day, when one vindictive complainant finally figured out where in Filene's to go to complain about the Complaint Dept. — the White Flaggers all fell about, they were totally pleased and amused, the Crocodiles removed their cigars and roared and wheezed and stomped both feet on the floor and showed scary teeth, everyone roaring with Identification and pleasure. This even though, as the speaker's confusion at their delight openly betrays, the story wasn't meant to be one bit funny: it was just the truth.

Gately's found it's got to be the truth, is the thing. He's trying hard to really hear the speakers — he's stayed in the habit he'd developed as an Ennet resident of sitting right up where he could see dentition and pores, with zero obstructions or heads between him and the podium, so the speaker fills his whole vision, which makes it easier to really hear — trying to concentrate on receiving the Message instead of brooding on that odd old dark moment of aphasiac terror with this veiled like psuedo-intellectual-type girl who was probably just in some sort of complex Denial, or on whatever doubtlessly grim place he feels like he knows that smooth echoless slightly Southern voice from. The thing is it has to be the truth to really go over, here. It can't be a calculated crowd-pleaser, and it has to be the truth unslanted, unfortified. And maximally unironic. An ironist in a Boston AA meeting is a witch in church. Irony-free zone. Same with sly disingenuous manipulative pseudo-sincerity. Sincerity with an ulterior motive is something these tough ravaged people know and fear, all of them trained to remember the coyly sincere, ironic, self-presenting fortifications they'd had to construct in order to carry on Out There, under the ceaseless neon bottle.

This doesn't mean you can't pay empty or hypocritical lip-service, however. Paradoxically enough. The desperate, newly sober White Flaggers are always encouraged to invoke and pay empty lip-service to slogans they don't yet understand or believe — e.g. 'Easy Does It!' and 'Turn It Over!' and 'One Day At a Time!' It's called 'Fake It Till You Make It,' itself an oft-invoked slogan. Everybody on a Commitment who gets up publicly to speak starts out saying he's an alcoholic, says it whether he believes he is yet or not; then everybody up there says how Grateful he is to be sober today and how great it is to be Active and out on a Commitment with his Group, even if he's not grateful or pleased about it at all. You're encouraged to keep saying stuff like this until you start to believe it, just like if you ask somebody with serious sober time how long you'll have to keep schlepping to all these goddamn meetings he'll smile that infuriating smile and tell you just until you start to *want* to go to all these goddamn meetings. There are some definite cultish, brainwashy elements to the AA Program (the term *Program* itself resonates darkly, for those who fear getting brainwashed), and Gately tries to be candid with his residents re this issue. But he also shrugs and tells them that by the end of his oral-narcotics and burglary careers he'd sort of decided the old brain needed a good scrub and soak anyway. He says he pretty much held his brain out and told Pat Montesian and Gene M. to go ahead and wash away. But he tells his residents he's thinking now that the Program might be more like deprogramming than actual washing, considering the psychic job the Disease's Spider has done on them all. Gately's most marked progress in turning his life around in sobriety, besides the fact that he no longer drives off into the night with other people's merchandise, is that he tries to be just about as verbally honest as possible at almost all times, now, without too much calculation about how a listener's going to feel about what he says. This is harder than it sounds. But so that's why on Commitments, sweating at the podium as only a large man can sweat, his thing is that he always says he's Lucky to be sober today, instead of that he's Grateful today, because he admits that the former is always true, every day, even though a lot of the time he still doesn't feel Grateful, more like shocked that this thing seems to work, plus a lot of the time also ashamed and depressed about how he's spent over half his life, and scared he might be permanently brain-damaged or retarded from Substances, plus also usually without any sort of clue about where he's headed in sobriety or what he's supposed to be doing or about really anything at all except that he's not at all keen to be back Out There behind any bars, again, in a hurry. Ferocious Francis G. likes to punch Gately's shoulder and tell him he's right where he's supposed to be.

So but also know that causal attribution, like irony, is death, speaking-on-Commitments-wise. Crocodiles' temple-veins will actually stand out and pulse with irritation if you start trying to blame your Disease on some cause or other, and everybody with any kind of sober time will pale and writhe in their chair. See e.g. the White Flag audience's discomfort when the skinny hard-faced Advanced Basics girl who gets up to speak next to last posits that she was an eight-bag-a-day dope fiend *because* at sixteen she'd had to become a stripper and semi-whore at the infamous Naked I Club out on Route 1 (a number of male eyes in the audience flash with sudden recognition, and despite all willed restraint automatically do that crawly north-to-south thing down her body, and Gately can see every ashtray on the table shake from the force of Joelle V.'s shudder), and then but that she'd had to become a stripper at sixteen *because* she'd had to run away from her foster home in Saugus MA, and that she'd had to run away from home *because* . . . — here at least some of the room's discomfort is from the fact that the audience can tell the etiology is going to get head-clutchingly prolix and involved; this girl has not yet learned to Keep It Simple — . . . because, well, to begin with, she'd been adopted, and the foster parents also had their own biological daughter, and the biological daughter had, from birth, been totally paralyzed and retarded and catatonic, and the foster mother in the household was — as Joelle V. put it later to Gately — crazy as a Fucking Mud-Bug, and was in total Denial about her biological daughter's being a vegetable, and not only insisted on treating the invertebrate biological daughter like a valid member of the chordate phylum but also insisted that the father and the adopted daughter also treat It as normal and undamaged, and made the adopted daughter share a bedroom with It, bring It along to slumber parties (the speaker uses the term *It* for the invertebrate sister, and also to tell the truth uses the phrase 'drag It along' rather than 'bring It along,' which Gately wisely doesn't dwell over), and even to school with her, and softball practice, and the hairdresser's, and Campfire Girls, etc., where at whatever place she'd dragged It along to It would lie in a heap, drooling and incontinent under exquisite mother-bought fashions specially altered for atrophy and top-shelf Lancôme cosmetics that looked just *lurid* on It, and with only the whites of Its eyes showing, with fluid dribbling from Its mouth and elsewhere, and making unspeakable gurgly noises, completely pale and moist and stagnant; and then, when the adopted daughter now speaking turned fifteen, the rabidly Catholic wacko foster mother even announced that OK now that the adopted daughter was fifteen she could go out on dates, but only as long as It got to come along too, in other words that the only dates the fifteen-year-old adopted daughter could go out on were double dates with It and whatever submammalian escort the speaker could root up for It; and how this sort of stuff went on and on; and how the nightmarishness of Its continual pale soggy ubiquitousness in her young life would alone be more than sufficient to cause and explain the speaker's later drug addiction, she feels, but that also it so happened that the foster family's quiet smiling patriarch, who worked 0900 to 2100 as a claims processor for Aetna, it turned out that the cheerful smiling foster father actually made the wacko foster mother look like a Doric column of stability by comparison, because there turned out to be things about the biological daughter's utter paralytic pliability and catatonic inability to make anything except unspeakable gurgly noises that the smiling father found greatly to a certain very sick advantage the speaker says she has trouble openly discussing, still, even at thirty-one months sober in AA, being as yet still so retroactively Wounded and Hurting from it; but so in sum that she'd been ultimately forced to run away from the adoptive foster Saugus home and so become a Naked-I stripper and so become a raging dope fiend not, as in so many ununique cases, because she had been incestuously diddled, but because she'd been abusively forced to share a bedroom with a drooling invertebrate who by fourteen was *Itself* getting incestuously diddled on a nightly basis by a smiling biological claims processor of a father who — the speaker pauses to summon courage — who apparently liked to pretend It was Raquel Welch, the former celluloid sex goddess of the father's glandular heyday, and he even called It '*RAQUEL!*' in moments of incestuous extremity; and how, the New England summer the speaker turned fifteen and had to start dragging It along on double dates and then having to make sure to drag It back home again by 2300h. so It had plenty of time to be incestuously diddled, that summer the smiling quiet foster father even bought, had found somewhere, a cheesy rubber Raquel Welch full-head pull-on *mask*, with hair, and would now nightly come in in the dark and lift Its limp soft head up and struggle and lug to get the mask on and the relevant holes aligned for air, and then

371

would diddle his way to extremity and cry out 'RAQUEL!' and then but he would just clamber out and off and leave the dark bedroom smiling and sated and lots of times leave the mask still *on* It, he'd like forget, or not care, just as he seemed oblivious (But For the Grace of God, in a way) to the fetally curled skinny form of the adopted daughter lying perfectly still in the next bed, in the dark, pretending to sleep, silent, shell-breathing, with her hard skinny wounded pre-addiction face turned to the wall, in the room's next bed, her bed, the one without the collapsible crib-like hospital railings along the sides. . . . The audience is clutching its collective head, by this time only partly in empathy, as the speaker specifies how she was de facto emotionally all but like *forced* to flee and strip and swan-dive into the dark spiritual anesthesia of active drug addiction in a dysfunctional attempt to psychologically deal with one particular seminally scarring night of abject horror, the indescribable horror of the way It, the biological daughter, had looked up at her, the speaker, one particular final time on this one particular one of the frequent occasions the speaker had to get out of bed after the father had come and gone and tiptoe over to Its bed and lean over the cold metal hospital railing and remove the rubber Raquel Welch mask and replace it in a bedside drawer under some back issues of *Ramparts* and *Commonweal*, after carefully closing Its splayed legs and pulling down Its variously-stained designer nightie, all of which she made sure to do when the father didn't bother to, at night, so that the wacko foster mother wouldn't come in in the A.M. and find It in a rubber Raquel Welch mask with Its nightie hiked up and Its legs agape and put two and two together and get all kinds of deep Denial shattered about why the foster father always went around the foster house with a silent creepy smile, and flip out and make the invertebrate catatonic's father stop diddling It — because, the speaker figured, if the foster father had to stop diddling It it didn't exactly take Sally Jessy Raphael M.S.W. to figure out who was then probably going to get promoted to the role of Raquel, over in the next bed. The silent smiling claims-processor father never once acknowledged the adopted daughter's little post-incestuous tidyings-up. It's the kind of sick unspoken complicity characteristic of wildly dysfunctional families, confides the speaker, who's also proud she says to be a member of a splinter 12-Step Fellowship, an Adult-Child-type thing called Wounded, Hurting, Inadequately Nurtured but Ever-Recovering Survivors. But so she says it was this one particular night soon after she'd turned sixteen, after the father had come and gone and uncaringly just left Its mask on again, and over to Its bedside the speaker had to creep in the dark, to tidy up, and but this time it turned out there was a problem with the Raquel Welch mask's long auburn horsehair tresses having gotten twisted and knotted into the semi-living strands of Its own elaborately overmoussed coiffure, and the adopted daughter had to activate the perimeter of lights on Its bedside table's manybulbed vanity mirror to see to try to get the Raquel Welch wig untangled, and when she finally got the mask off, with the vanity mirror still blazing away, the speaker says how she was forced to gaze for the first time on Its lit-up paralytic post-diddle face, and how the expression thereon was most assuredly quite enough to force anybody with an operant limbic system[142] to leg it right out of her dysfunctional foster family's home, nay and the whole community of Saugus MA, now homeless and scarred and forced by dark psychic forces straight to Route 1's infamous gauntlet of neon-lit depravity and addiction, to try and forget, rasa the tabula, wipe the memory totally out, numb it with opiates. Voice trembling, she accepts the chairperson's proffered bandanna-hankie and blows her nose one nostril at a time and says she can almost see It all over again: Its expression: in the vanity's lights only Its eyes' whites showed, and while Its utter catatonia and paralysis prevented the contraction of Its luridly rouged face's circumoral muscles into any conventional human facial-type expression, nevertheless some hideously mobile and expressive layer in the moist regions below real people's expressive facial layer, some slow-twitch layer unique to It, had blindly contracted, somehow, to gather the blank soft cheese of Its face into the sort of pinched gasping look of neurologic concentration that marks a carnal bliss beyond smiles or sighs. Its face looked post-coital sort of the way you'd imagine the vacuole and optica of a protozoan looking post-coital after it's shuddered and shot its mono-cellular load into the cold waters of some really old sea. Its facial expression was, in a word, the speaker says, unspeakably, unforgettably ghastly and horrid and scarring. It was also the exact same expression as the facial expression on the stone-robed lady's face in this one untitled photo of some Catholic statue that hung (the photo) in the dysfunctional household's parlor right above the little teak table where the dysfunctional foster mother kept her beads and Hours and lay breviary, this photo of a statue of a woman whose stone robes were half hiked up and wrinkled in the most godawfully sensually prurient way, the woman reclined against uncut rock, her robes hiked and one stone foot hanging off the rock as her legs hung parted, with a grinning little totally psychotic-looking cherub-type angel standing on the lady's open thighs and pointing a bare arrow at where the stone robe hid her cold tit, the woman's face upturned and cocked and pinched into that exact same shuddering-protozoan look beyond pleasure or pain. The wacko foster mom knelt daily to that photo, in a beaded and worshipful posture, and also required daily that It be hoisted by the adopted daughter from Its never-mentioned wheelchair and held under Its arms and lowered so as to approximate the same knelt devotion to the photo, and while It gurgled and Its head lolled the speaker had gazed at the photo with a nameless revulsion each morning as she held Its dead slumped weight and tried to keep Its chin off Its chest, and now was being forced into seeing by mirror-light the exact same expression on the face of a catatonic who'd just been incestuously diddled, an expression at once reverent and greedy on a face connected by dead hair to the slack and flapping rubber visage of an old sex goddess's empty face. And to make a long story short (the speaker says, not trying to be funny as far as the Flaggers can see), the traumatically scarred adopted girl had legged it from the bedroom and foster house into the brooding North Shore teen-runaway night, and had stripped and semi-whored and IV-injected her way all the way to that standard two-option addicted cliff-edge, hoping only to Forget. That's what caused it, she says; that's what she's trying to recover from, a Day at a Time, and she's sure grateful to be here with her Group today, sober and courageously remembering, and newcomers should definitely Keep Coming. . . . As she's telling what she sees as etiological truth, even though the monologue seems sincere and unaffected and at least a B+ on the overall AA-story lucidity-scale, faces in the hall are averted and heads clutched and postures uneasily shifted in empathetic distress at the look-what-happened-to-poor-me invitation implicit in the tale, the talk's tone of self-pity itself less offensive (even though plenty of these White Flaggers, Gately knows, had personal childhoods that made this girl's look like a day at Six Flags Over the Poconos) than the subcurrent of explanation, an appeal to exterior *Cause* that can slide, in the addictive mind, so insidiously into *Excuse* that any causal attribution is in Boston AA feared, shunned, punished by empathic distress. The *Why* of the Disease is a labrynth it is strongly suggested all AAs boycott, inhabited as the maze is by the twin minotaurs of *Why Me?* and *Why Not?,* a.k.a. Self-Pity and Denial, two of the smily-faced Sergeant at Arms' more fearsome aides de camp. The Boston AA 'In Here' that protects against a return to 'Out There' is not about explaining what caused your Disease. It's about a goofily simple practical recipe for how to remember you've got the Disease day by day and how to treat the Disease day by day, how to keep the seductive ghost of a bliss long absconded from baiting you and hooking you and pulling you back Out and eating your heart raw and (if you're lucky) eliminating your map for good. So no whys or wherefores allowed. In other words check your head at the door. Though it can't be conventionally enforced, this, Boston AA's real root axiom, is almost classically authoritarian, maybe even proto-Fascist. Some ironist who decamped back Out There and left his meager effects to be bagged and tossed by Staff into the Ennet House attic had, all the way back in the Year of the Tucks Medicated Pad, permanently engraved his tribute to AA's real Prime Directive with a rosewood-handled boot-knife in the plastic seat of the 5-Man men's room's commode:

'Do not ask WHY
If you dont want to DIE
Do like your TOLD
If you want to get OLD[143]

30 APRIL / 1 MAY
YEAR OF THE DEPEND ADULT UNDERGARMENT

The choreography of interface had settled into the form of Steeply smok-ing, his bare arms crossed, going up and down slowly on the toes of his high heels, while Marathe hunched slightly in his metal chair, shoulders rounded and head slightly forward in a practiced position that allowed him almost to sleep while still attending to every detail of a conversation or wearisome surveillance. He (Marathe) had drawn his plaid blanket up to his chest. It was increasingly chilly at the altitude of the shelf. They could feel the re-mains of the U.S.A. Sonora Desert's heat rising past them into the clotted spangle of stars that were above them. The shirt Marathe wore beneath his windbreaker was not of Hawaiian type.

Marathe remained unsure in this time of what exactly it was that Hugh Steeply of U.S.O.U.S. wished to learn from him, or verify, through Mar-athe's betrayal. Near midnight Steeply had given him the datum that he (Steeply) had been on the personal Marital Leave over his recent divorce, and was now back in the field of duty, wearing prosthetic breasts and woman-journalist credentials, assigned to cultivate some of the Entertain-ment's alleged filmmaker's relatives and inner circles. Marathe had made gentle fun of the inoriginality of a journalistic cover, then later less gentle fun of Steeply's cover's false name, expressing humored doubts that the meaty electrolysized face of Steeply would be responsible of launching even one ship or vessel.

There'd been that first brutal winter night, early in the O.N.A.N.ite temporo-subsidized era, soon after the InterLace dissemination of *The Man Who Began to Suspect He Was Made of Glass,* that Himself emerged from the sauna and came to Lyle all sloppy-blotto and de-pressed over the fact that even the bastards in the avant-garde journals were complaining that even in his commercially entertaining stuff Incan-denza's fatal Achilles' heel was plot, that Incandenza's efforts had no sort of engaging plot, no movement that sucked you in and drew you along.[144] Mario and Ms. Joelle van Dyne are probably the only people who know that Found Drama[145] and anticonfluentialism both came out of this night with Lyle.

It's not like Boston AA recoils from the idea of responsibility, though. Cause: no; responsibility: yes. It seems like it all depends on which way the arrow of presumed responsibility points. The hard-faced adopted stripper had presented herself as the object of an outside Cause. Now the arrow comes back around as tonight's meeting's last and maybe best Advanced Basics speaker, another newcomer, a round pink girl with no eyelashes at all and a 'base-head's ruined teeth, gets up there and speaks in an *r*-less South Boston brogue about being pregnant at twenty and smoking Eightballs of freebase cocaine like a fiend all through her pregnancy even though she knew it was bad for the baby and wanted desperately to quit. She tells about having her water break and contractions start late one night in her welfare-hotel room when she was right in the middle of an Eightball she'd had to spend the evening turning unbelievably sordid and degrading tricks to pay for; she did what she had to do to get high, she says, even while pregnant, she says; and she says even when the pain of the contractions got to be too bad to bear she'd been unable to tear herself away from the 'base-pipe to go to the free clinic to deliver, and how she'd sat on the floor of the welfare-hotel room and freebased her way all through labor (that new Joelle girl's veil's billowing in and out with her breath, Gately sees, just like it also was during the last speaker's description of the statue's orgasm in the catatonic's dysfunctional Catholic mother's devotional photo); and how she'd finally delivered of a stillborn infant right there alone on her side like a cow on the rug of her room, all the time throughout still compulsively loading up the glass pipe and smoking; and how the infant emerged all dry and hard like a constipated turdlet, with no protective moisture and no afterbirth-material following it out, and how the emerged infant was tiny and dry and all withered and the color of strong tea, and dead, and also had no face, had in utero developed no eyes or nostrils and just a little lipless hyphen of a mouth, and its limbs were malformed and arachnodactylic, and there had been some sort of translucent reptilian like webbing between its mucronate digits; the speaker's mouth is a quivering arch of woe; her baby had been poisoned before it could grow a face or make any personal choices, it would have soon died of Substance-Withdrawal in the free clinic's Pyrex incubator if it had emerged alive anyway, she could tell, she'd been on such a bad 'base-binge all that pregnant year; and but so eventually the Eightball was consumed and then the screen and steel-wool ball in the pipe itself smoked and the cloth prep-filter smoked to ash and then of course likely-looking pieces of lint had been gleaned off the rug and also smoked, and the girl finally passed out, still umbilically linked to the dead infant; and how when she came to again in unsparing noonlight the next day and saw what still clung by a withered cord to her empty insides she got introduced to the real business-end of the arrow of responsibility, and as she gazed in daylight at the withered faceless stillborn baby she was so overcome with grief and self-loathing that she erected a fortification of complete and black Denial, like total Denial. She held and swaddled the dead thing just as if it were alive instead of dead, and she began to carry it around with her wherever she went, just as she imagined devoted mothers carry their babies with them everywhere they go, the faceless infant's corpse completely veiled and hidden in a little pink blanket the addicted expectant mother'd let herself buy at Woolworth's at seven months, and she also kept the cord's connection intact until her end of the cord finally fell out of her and dangled, and smelled, and she carried the dead infant everywhere, even when turning sordid tricks, because single motherhood or not she still needed to get high and still had to do what she had to do to get high, so she carried the blanket-wrapped infant in her arms as she walked the streets in her velvet fuchsia minipants and haltertop and green spike heels, turning tricks, until there began to be strong evidence, as she circled her block — it was August — let's just say compelling evidence that the infant in the stained cocoon of blanket in her arms was not a biologically viable infant, and passersby on the South Boston streets began to reel away white-faced as the girl passed by, stretch-marked and brown-toothed and lashless (lashes lost in a Substance-accident; fire hazard and dental dysplasia go with the freebase terrain) and also just hauntedly calm-looking, oblivious to the olfactory havoc she was wreaking in the sweltering streets, and but her August's trick-business soon fell off sharply, understandably, and eventually word that there was a serious infant-and-Denial problem here got around the streets, and her fellow Southie 'base-heads and street-friends came to her with not ungentle r-less remonstrances and scented hankies and gently prying hands and tried to reason her out of her Denial, but she ignored them all, she guarded her infant from all harm and kept it clutched to her — it was by now sort of stuck to her and would have been hard to separate from her by hand anyway — and she'd walk the streets shunned and trickless and broke and in early-stage Substance-Withdrawal, with the remains of the dead infant's tummy's cord dangling out from an unclosable fold in the now ominously ballooned and crusty Woolworth's blanket: talk about Denial, this girl was in some major-league Denial; and but finally a pale and reeling beat-cop phoned a hysterical olfactory alert in to the Commonwealth's infamous Department of Social Services — Gately sees alcoholic moms all over the hall cross themselves and shudder at the mere mention of D.S.S., every addicted parent's worst nightmare, D.S.S., they of the several different abstruse legal definitions of Neglect and the tungsten-tipped battering ram for triple-locked apartment doors; in a dark window Gately sees one reflected mom sitting over with the Brighton AAs that has her two little girls with her in the meeting and now at the D.S.S. reference clutches them reflexively to her bosom, one head per bosom, as one of the girls struggles and dips her knees in the little curtsies of impending potty — but so now D.S.S. was on the case, and a platoon of blandly efficient Wellesley-alum D.S.S. field personnel with clipboards and scary black Chanel women's businesswear were now on the prowl in the South Boston streets for the addicted speaker and her late faceless infant; and but finally around this time, during last year's awful late-August heat wave, evidence that the infant had a serious bio-viability problem started presenting itself so forcefully that even the Denial-ridden addict in the mother could not ignore or dismiss it — evidence which the speaker's reticence about describing (save to say that it involved an insect-attraction problem) makes things all the worse for the empathetic White Flaggers, since it engages the dark imaginations all Substance-abusers share in surplus — and so but the mother says how she finally broke down, emotionally and olfactorily, from the overwhelming evidence, on the cement playground outside her own late mother's abandoned Project building off the L Street Beach in Southie, and a D.S.S. field team closed in for the pinch, and she and her infant got pinched, and special D.S.S. spray-solvents had to be sent for and utilized in order to detach the Woolworth baby-blanket from her maternal bosom, and the blanket's contents were more or less reassembled and were interred in a D.S.S. coffin the speaker recalls as being the size of a Mary Kay makeup case, and the speaker was medically informed by somebody with a clipboard from D.S.S. that the infant had been involuntarily toxified to death somewhere along in its development toward becoming a boy; and the mother, after a painful D&C for the impacted placenta she'd carried inside, then spent the next four months on the locked ward of Metropolitan State Hospital in Waltham MA, psychotic with Denial-deferred guilt and cocaine-withdrawal and searing self-hatred; and how when she finally got discharged from Met State with her first S.S.I. mental-disability check she found she had no taste for chunks or powders, she wanted only tall smooth bottles whose labels spoke of Proof, and she drank and drank and believed in her heart she would never stop or swallow the truth, but finally she got to where she had to, she says, swallow it, the responsible truth; how she quickly drank her way to the old two-option welfare-hotel window-ledge and made a blubbering 0200h. phone call, and then so here she is, apologizing for going on so long, trying to tell a truth she hopes someday to swallow, inside. So she can just try and live. When she concludes by asking them to pray for her it almost doesn't sound corny. Gately tries not to think. Here is no Cause or Excuse. It is simply what happened. This final speaker is truly new, ready: all defenses have been burned away. Smooth-skinned and steadily pinker, at the podium, her eyes squeezed tight, she looks like she's the one that's the infant. The host White Flaggers pay this burnt public husk of a newcomer the ultimate Boston AA compliment: they have to consciously try to remember even to blink as they watch her, listening. I.D.ing without effort. There's no judgment. It's clear she's been punished enough. And it was basically the same all over, after all, Out There. And the fact that it was so good to hear her, so good that even Tiny Ewell and Kate Gompert and the rest of the worst of them all sat still and listened without blinking, looking not just at the speaker's face but into it, helps force Gately to remember all over again what a tragic adventure this is, that none of them signed up for.

They'd been the odd couple of libations, the muscled fitness-guru and the tall slope-shouldered optician/director, often down there in the weight room til all hours, sitting on the towel dispenser, drinking, Lyle with his Caffeine Free Diet Coke, Incandenza with his Wild Turkey. Mario literally standing by in case the ice bucket ran out or Himself needed moral support getting to the urinal. Mario often fell asleep as the hour got severe, drifted in and out, slept upright and leaning forward, weight borne by his police lock and lead receptacle.

James Incandenza was one of those profound-personality-change drinkers who seemed quiet and centered and almost affectless when he was sober but would move way out to one side or the other of the human emotional spectrum, when drunk, and seem to open up in a way that was almost injudicious.

Sometimes, libated late at night with Lyle in the newly outfitted E.T.A. weight room, Incandenza'd open up and pour his heart's thickest chyme right out there for all to be affected and potentially scarred by. E.g. one night Mario, leaning way forward into the police lock's support, drifted awake to the sound of his father saying that if he had to grade his marriage he'd give it a C−. This seems injudicious in the extreme, potentially, though Mario, like Lyle, tends to take data pretty much as it comes.

Lyle, who sometimes would start to get tipsy himself as Himself's pores began to excrete the bourbon, often brought some Blake out, as in William Blake, during these all-night sessions, and read Incandenza Blake, but in the voices of various cartoon characters, which Himself eventually started regarding as deep.[146]

O

If it's odd that Mario Incandenza's first halfway-coherent film cartridge — a 48-minute job shot three summers back in the carefully decorated janitor-closet of Subdorm B with his head-mount Bolex H64 and foot-treadle — if it's odd that Mario's first finished entertainment consists of a film of a puppet show — like a kids' puppet show — then it probably seems even odder that the film's proven to be way more popular with E.T.A.'s adults and adolescents than it is with the woefully historically underinformed children it had first been made for. It's proved so popular that it gets shown annually now every 11/8, Continental Interdependence Day, on a wide-beam cartridge projector and stand-up screen in the E.T.A. dining hall, after supper. It's part of the gala but rather ironic annual celebration of I.-Day at an Academy whose founder had married a Canadian, and it usually gets under way about 1930h., the film, and everybody gathers in the dining hall, and watches it, and by Charles Tavis's festive fiat[147] everybody gets to two-handed snack instead of squeezing tennis balls while they watch, and not only that but normal E.T.A. dietary regulations are for an hour completely suspended, and Mrs. Clarke, the dietician out in the kitchen — a former Four-Star dessert chef normally relegated here to protein-conveyors and ways to vary complex carbs — Mrs. Clarke gets to put on her floppy white chef's hat and just go sucrotically mad, out in West House's gleaming kitchen. Everybody's supposed to wear some sort of hat — Avril Incandenza positively towers in the same steeple-crowned witch's hat she teaches all her classes in every 10/31, and Pemulis wears the complex yachting cap and naval braid, and pale and blotchy Struck a toque with a kind of flitty aigrette, and Hal a black preacher's hat with a stern round downturned brim, etc. etc.[148] — and Mario, as director and putative author of the popular film, is encouraged to say a few words, like eight:

'Thanks everybody and I hope you like it,' is what he said this year, with Pemulis behind him making a show of putting a maraschino on top of the small twizzle of Redi-Whip that O. Stice had sprayed on the top of Mario's head-mount Bolex H64, which counts as a hat, when the dessert-course's zenith had gotten slightly out of control near the I.-Day gala supper's end. These few brief words and round of applause are Mario's big public yearly moment at E.T.A., and he neither likes the moment nor dislikes it — same with the untitled film itself, which really started out as just a kids' adaptation of *The ONANtiad,* a four-hour piece of tendentiously anticonfluential political parody long since dismissed as minor Incandenza by his late father's archivists. Mario's piece isn't really better than his father's; it's just different (plus of course way shorter). It's pretty obvious that somebody else in the Incandenza family had at least an amanuentic hand in the screenplay, but Mario did the choreography and most of the puppet-work personally — his little S-shaped arms and falcate digits are perfect for the forward curve from body to snout of a standard big-headed political puppet — and it was, without question, Mario's little square Hush Puppy on the H64's operant foot-treadle, the Bolex itself mounted on one of the tunnel's locked lab's Husky-VI TL tripods across the overlit closet, mops and dull-gray janitorial buckets carefully moved out past the frame's borders on either side of the little velvet stage.

Ann Kittenplan and two older crew-cut girls sit in identical snap-brim fedoras with their arms crossed, Kittenplan's right hand bandaged. Mary Esther Thode is grading midterms on the sly. Rik Dunkel has his eyes closed but is not asleep. Somebody's slapped an ad hoc Red Sox cap on the visiting Syrian Satellite pro, and the Syrian Satellite pro sits with most of the prorectors, looking confused, his shoulder taped up with a heatable compress, being polite about the comparative authenticity of Mrs. C.'s baklava.

Everyone gathers and all's quiet except for the sounds of saliva and chewing, and there's the yeasty-sweet smell of Coach Schtitt's pipe, and E.T.A.'s youngest kid Tina Echt in her giant beret gets to be in charge of the lights.

Mario's thing opens without credits, just a crudely matted imposition of fake-linotype print, a quotation from President Gentle's second Inaugural: 'Let the call go forth, to pretty much any nation we might feel like calling, that the past has been torched by a new and millennial generation of Americans,' against a full-facial still photo of a truly unmistakable personage. This is the projected face of Johnny Gentle, Famous Crooner. This is Johnny Gentle, né Joyner, lounge singer turned teenybopper throb turned B-movie mainstay, for two long-past decades known unkindly as the 'Cleanest Man in Entertainment' (the man's a world-class retentive, the late-Howard-Hughes kind, the really severe kind, the kind with the paralyzing fear of free-floating contamination, the either-wear-a-surgical-microfiltration-mask-or-make-the-people-around-you-wear-surgical-caps-and-masks-and-touch-doorknobs-only-with-a-boiled-hankie-and-take-fourteen-showers-a-day-only-they're-not-exactly-showers-they're-with-this-Dermalatix-brand-shower-sized-Hypospectral-Flash-Booth-that-actually-like-burns-your-outermost-layer-of-skin-off-in-a-dazzling-flash-and-leaves-you-baby's-butt-new-and-sterile-once-you-wipe-off-the-coating-of-fine-epidermal-ash-with-a-boiled-hankie kind) then in later public life a sterile-toupee-wearing promoter and entertainment-union bigwig, Vegas schmaltz-broker and head of the infamous Velvety Vocalists Guild, the tanned, gold-chained labor union that enforced those seven months of infamously dreadful 'Live

Silence,'[149] the total scab-free solidarity and performative silence that struck floor-shows and soundstages from Desert to NJ coast for over half a year until equitable compensation-formulae on certain late-millennial phone-order retrospective TV-advertised So-You-Don't-Forget-Order-Before-Midnight-Tonight-type records and CDs were agreed on by Management. Hence then Johnny Gentle, the man who brought GE/RCA to heel. And then thus, at the millennial fulcrum of very dark U.S. times, to national politics. The facial stills that Mario lap-dissolves between are of Johnny Gentle, Famous Crooner, founding standard-bearer of the seminal new 'Clean U.S. Party,' the strange-seeming but politically prescient annular agnation of ultra-right jingoist hunt-deer-with-automatic-weapons types and far-left macrobiotic Save-the-Ozone, -Rain-Forests, -Whales, -Spotted-Owl-and-High-pH-Waterways ponytailed granola-crunchers, a surreal union of both Rush L.– and Hillary R.C.–disillusioned fringes that drew mainstream-media guffaws at their first Convention (held in sterile venue), the seemingly LaRoucheishly marginal party whose first platform's plank had been Let's Shoot Our Wastes Into Space,[150] C.U.S.P. a kind of post-Perot national joke for three years, until — white-gloved finger on the pulse of an increasingly asthmatic and sunscreen-slathered and pissed-off American electorate — the C.U.S.P. suddenly swept to quadrennial victory in an angry reactionary voter-spasm that made the U.W.S.A. and LaRouchers and Libertarians chew their hands in envy as the Dems and G.O.P.s stood on either side watching dumbly, like doubles partners who each think the other's surely got it, the two established mainstream parties split open along tired philosophical lines in a dark time when all landfills got full and all grapes were raisins and sometimes in some places the falling rain clunked instead of splatted, and also, recall, a post-Soviet and -Jihad era when — somehow even worse — there was no real Foreign Menace of any real unified potency to hate and fear, and the U.S. sort of turned on itself and its own philosophical fatigue and hideous redolent wastes with a spasm of panicked rage that in retrospect seems possible only in a time of geopolitical supremacy and consequent silence, the loss of any external Menace to hate and fear. This motionless face on the E.T.A. screen is Johnny Gentle, Third-Party stunner. Johnny Gentle, the first U.S. President ever to swing his microphone around by the cord during his Inauguration speech. Whose new white-suited Office of Unspecified Services' retinue required Inauguration-attendees to scrub and mask and then walk through chlorinated footbaths as at public pools. Johnny Gentle, managing somehow to look presidential in a Fukoama microfiltration mask, whose Inaugural Address heralded the advent of a Tighter, Tidier Nation. Who promised to clean up government and trim fat and sweep out waste and hose down our chemically troubled streets and to sleep darn little until he'd fashioned a way to rid the American psychosphere of the unpleasant debris of a throw-away past, to restore the majestic ambers and purple fruits of a culture he now promises to rid of the toxic effluvia choking our highways and littering our byways and grungeing up our sunsets and cruddying those harbors in which televised garbage-barges lay stacked up at anchor, clotted and impotent amid undulating clouds of potbellied gulls and those disgusting blue-bodied flies that live on shit (first U.S. President ever to say *shit* publicly, shuddering), rusty-hulled barges cruising up and down petroleated coastlines or laying up reeky and stacked and emitting CO as they await the opening of new landfills and toxic repositories the People demanded in every area but their own. The Johnny Gentle whose C.U.S.P. had been totally up-front about seeing American renewal as an essentially aesthetic affair. The Johnny Gentle who promised to be the possibly sometimes unpopular architect of a more or less Spotless America that Cleaned Up Its Own Side of the Street. Of a new-era'd nation that looked out for Uno, of a one-time World Policeman that was now going to retire and have its blue uniform deep-dry-cleaned and placed in storage in triple-thick plastic dry-cleaning bags and hang up its cuffs to spend some quality domestic time raking its lawn and cleaning behind its refrigerator and dandling its freshly bathed kids on its neatly pressed mufti-pants' knee. A Gentle behind whom a diorama of the Lincoln Memorial's Lincoln smiled down benignly. A Johnny Gentle who was as of this new minute sending forth the call that 'he wasn't in this for a popularity contest' (Popsicle-stick-and-felt puppets in the Address's audience assuming puzzled-looking expressions above their tiny green surgical masks). A President J.G., F.C. who said he wasn't going to stand here and ask us to make some tough choices because he was standing here promising he was going to make them for us. Who asked us simply to sit back and enjoy the show. Who handled wild applause from camouflage-fatigue- and sandal-and-poncho-clad C.U.S.P.s with the unabashed grace of a real pro. Who had black hair and silver sideburns, just like his big-headed puppet, and the dusty brick-colored tan seen only among those without homes and those whose homes had a Dermalatix Hypospectral personal sterilization booth. Who declared that neither Tax & Spend nor Cut & Borrow comprised the ticket into a whole new millennial era (here more puzzlement among the Inaugural audience, which Mario represents by having the tiny finger-puppets turn rigidly toward each other and then away and then toward). Who alluded to ripe and available Novel Sources of Revenue just waiting out there, unexploited, not seen by his predecessors because of the trees (?). Who foresaw budgetary adipose trimmed with a really big knife. The Johnny Gentle who stressed above all — simultaneously pleaded for and promised — an end to atomized Americans' fractious blaming of one another for our terrible[151] internal troubles. Here bobs and smiles from both wealthily green-masked puppets and homeless puppets in rags and mismatched shoes and with used surgical masks, all made by E.T.A.'s fourth-

and fifth-grade crafts class, under the supervision of Ms. Heath, of matchsticks and Popsicle-stick shards and pool-table felt with sequins for eyes and painted fingernail-parings for smiles/frowns, under their masks.

The Johnny Gentle, Chief Executive who pounds a rubber-gloved fist on the podium so hard it knocks the Seal askew and declares that Dammit there just *must* be some people besides each other of us to blame. To unite in opposition to. And he promises to eat light and sleep very little until he finds them — in the Ukraine, or the Teutons, or the wacko Latins. Or — pausing with that one arm up and head down in the climactic Vegas way — closer to right below our nose. He swears he'll find us some cohesion-renewing Other. And then make some tough choices. Alludes to a whole new North America for a crazy post-millennial world. First U.S. President ever to use *boss* as an adjective. His throwing his surgical gloves into the miniature Inaugural crowd as souvenirs is Mario's own touch.

And Mario Incandenza's idea of representing President Gentle's cabinet as made up mostly of tall-coiffured black-girl puppets in shiny imbricate-sequin dresses is also of course historically inaccurate, though the honorary inclusion, in that cabinet's second year, of the Presidente of Mexico and the P.M. of Canada is both factual and of course seminal:

> PRES. MEX. AND P.M. CAN. [in unison and green-mask-muffled]: It is tremendously flattering to be invited to sit on the cabinet of the leadership of our beloved neighbor to the [choose one].
> GENTLE: Thanks, boys. You have gorgeous souls.

It's not the cartridge's strongest scene, heavy on stock phrases and two-handed handshakes. But the historical fact that the Presidente of Mexico and P.M. of Canada are honorarily appointed by President Gentle to be 'Secretaries' of Mexico and Canada (respectively) — as if the neighbors had already become sort of post-millennial American protectorates — is foreshadowed as ominous by a wavered D-minor on the soundtrack's organ — Mrs. Clarke's Wurlitzer, at home — but the two leaders' respectively dusky and Gallic expressions seem unperturbed, under their green masks, as more stock phrases are invoked.

Because budget and broom-closet constraints make artful transitions between scenes impractical, Mario has opted for the inter-scenic 'entr'acte' device of having Johnny Gentle, Famous Crooner doing some of his repertoire's bouncier numbers, with the cabinet-members undulating and harmonizing Motownishly behind him, and other puppets bouncing in tempo on- and offstage as the script requires. Audience-wise, most of the E.T.A.s under twelve, cortexes spangling with once-a-year sweets, have by now emigrated hyperactively under the long tables' tablecloths and met up on the dining-hall floor below and begun navigating on hands and knees the special children's second world of shins and chairlegs and tile that exists under long tablecloths, making various sorts of puerile trouble — investigations from last year's I. Day are still in progress w/r/t which kid or kids tied Aubrey deLint's shoelaces together and Krazy-Glued Mary Esther Thode's left buttock to the seat of her chair — but everyone glycemically mature enough to sit still and watch the cartridge is having a rousing good time, eating chocolate cannolis and twenty-six-layer baklava and Redi-Whip by itself if they want and homemade Raisinettes and little cream-filled caramel things and occasionally heckling or cheering ironically, every so often throwing sweets that stick to the screen, giving the smooth sterile Gentle a sort of carbuncular look that everyone approves. There is much cracking wise and baritone mimicry of a President roundly disliked for over two terms now. Only John Wayne and a handful of other Canadian students sit unhatted, chewing stolidly, faces blurred and distant. This American penchant for absolution via irony is foreign to them. The Canadian boys remember only hard facts, and the glass-walled Great Convexity whose southern array of ATHSCME Effectuators blow the tidy U.S.'s northern oxides north, toward home; and they feel with special poignancy on 11/8 the implications of their being down here, south of the border, training, in the land of their enemy-ally; and the less gifted among them wonder whether they'll ever get to go home again after graduation if a pro career or scholarship doesn't pan out. Wayne has a cloth hankie and keeps wiping his nose.

Mario's openly jejune version of his late father's take on the rise of O.N.A.N. and U.S. Experialism unfolds in little diffracted bits of real news and fake news and privately-conceived dialogue between the architects and hard-choice-makers of a new millennial era:

GENTLE: Another piece of pre-tasted cobbler, J.J.J.C.?

P.M. CAN.: Couldn't. Stuffed. Having trouble breathing. I would not say no to another beer, however.

GENTLE: . . .

P.M. CAN.: . . .

GENTLE: So we're sympatico on the gradual and subtle but inexorable disarmament and dissolution of NATO as a system of mutual-defense agreements.

P.M. CAN. [Less muffled than last scene because his surgical mask gets to have a prandial hole]: We are side by side and behind you on this thing. Let the EEC pay for their oown defendings henceforth I say. Let them foot some defensive budgets and then try to subsidize their farmers into undercutting NAFTA. Let them eat butter and guns for their oown for once in a change. Hey?

GENTLE: You said more than a mouthful right there, J.J. Now maybe we can all direct some cool-headed attention to our own infraternal affairs.

Our own internal quality of life. Refocusing priorities back to this crazy continent we call home. Am I being dug?

P.M. CAN: John, I am kilometers ahead of you. I happen to have my Term-In-Office-At-A-Glance book right with me here. Now that the big *frappeurs* are being put doown, we are wondering what is the date I can be pencilling in for the removals of NATO ICBM *frappeurs* from Manitoba.

GENTLE: Put that pencil away, you good-looking Canadian. I've got more long shiny trailer-rigs full of large men with very short haircuts and white suits than you can shake a maple leaf at heading for your silos right this very. Those complete totalities of Canada's strategic capacity'll be out of your hair toot sweet.

P.M. CAN: John, let me be the first world leader to call you a statesman.

GENTLE: We North Americans have to stick together, J.J.J.C., especially now, no? Am I off-base? We're interdependent. We're cheek to jowl.

P.M. CAN: It is a smaller world, today.

GENTLE: And an even smaller continent.

This segues into an entr'acte, with *continent* squeezed in for *world* in 'It's a Small World After All,' which enjambment doesn't do the rhythm section of doo-wopping cabinet girls a bit of good, but does usher in the start of a whole new era.

Though can any guru be held to a standard of like 100% exemption from the human pains of stunted desire? No. Not 100%. Regardless of level of transcendence, or diet.

Lyle, down in the dark Interdependence Day weight room, sometimes recalls an E.T.A. player from several years back whose first name was Marlon and whose last name Lyle never to his knowledge learned.[152]

The thing about this Marlon was that he was always wet. Arms purling, T-shirt darkly V'd, face and forehead ever gleaming. Orin's Academy doubles partner. It had had a lemony, low-cal taste, the boy's omniwetness. It wasn't exactly sweat, because you could lick off the forehead and more beads instantly replaced what you'd taken. None of real sweat's frustratingly gradual accretion. The kid was always in the shower, always doing his best to stay clean. There were powders and pills and electrical appliqués. And still this Marlon dripped and shone. The kid wrote accomplished juvenile verses about the dry clean boy inside, struggling to break the soggy surface. He shared extensively with Lyle. He confessed to Lyle one night in the quiet weight room that he'd gone in for high-level athletics mostly to have an excuse of some sort for being as wet as he was. It always looked like

Marlon had been rained on. But it wasn't rain. It's like Marlon hadn't been dry since the womb. It's like he leaked. It had been a tormenting but also in certain ways halcyon few years, in the past. A tormentingly unspecific hope in the air. Lyle had told this boy everything he had to tell.

It's raining tonight, though. As so often happens in autumn below the Great Concavity, P.M. snow has given way to rain. Outside the weight room's high windows a mean wind sweeps curtains of rain this way and that, and the windows shudder and drool. The sky is a mess. Thunder and lightning happen at the same time. The copper beech outside creaks and groans. Lightning claws the sky, briefly illuminating Lyle, seated lotus in Spandex on the towel dispenser, leaning forward to accept what is offered in the dark weight room. The idle resistance-machines look insectile in the lightning's brief light. The answer to some of the newer kids' complaints about what on earth Lyle can be doing down there at night in a locked empty weight room is that the nighttime weight room is rarely empty. The P.M. custodians Kenkle and Brandt do lock it up, but the door can be dickied by even the clumsiest insertion of an E.T.A. meal-card between latch and jamb. The kitchen crew always wonders why so many meal-cards' edges always look ravaged. Though the idle machines are scary and the room smells somehow worse in the dark, they come most at night, the E.T.A.s who are on to Lyle. They hit the saunas out by the cement stairs until they've got enough incentive on their skin, then they lurk, purled and shiny, in towels, by the weight room door, waiting to enter one by one, sometimes several E.T.A.s, dripping in towels, not speaking, some pretending to have other business down there, lurking in the eye-averted attitudes of like patients in the waiting room of an impotence clinic or shrink. They have to be real quiet and the lights stay off. It's like the administration'll turn a blind eye as long as you make it plausible to do so. From the dining hall, whose east wall of windows faces Comm.-Ad., you can hear very muffled laughter and kibitzing and the occasional scream from Mario's Interdependent puppet thing. A quiet slow small stream of yellow-slickered wet-shoed migrations back and forth between West House and the weight room — people know the slow parts, the times to duck out and go very briefly down to Lyle, to confer. They dicky the lock and go in one by one, in towels. Proffer beaded flesh. Confront the sorts of issues reserved for nighttime's gurutical tête-à-tête, whispers made echoless by rubberized floors and much damp laundry.

Sometimes Lyle will listen and shrug and smile and say 'The world is very old' or some such general Remark and decline to say much else. But it's the way he listens, somehow, that keeps the saunas full.

Lightning claws the eastern sky, and it's neat in the weight room's dark because Lyle is in a slightly different position and forward angle each time he's illuminated through the window up over the grip/wrist/forearm machines to his left, so it looks like there are different Lyles at different fulgurant moments.

LaMont Chu, glabrous and high-gloss in a white towel and wristwatch, haltingly confesses to an increasingly crippling obsession with tennis fame. He wants to get to the Show so bad it feels like it's eating him alive. To have his picture in shiny magazines, to be a wunderkind, to have guys in blue I/SPN blazers describe his every on-court move and mood in hushed broadcast clichés. To have little patches with products' names sewn onto his clothes. To be soft-profiled. To get compared to M. Chang, lately expired; to get called the next Great Yellow U.S. Hope. Let's not even talk about video magazines or the Grid. He confesses it to Lyle: he *wants* the hype; he *wants* it. Sometimes he'll pretend a glowing up-at-net action shot he's clipping out of a shiny magazine is of him, LaMont Chu. But then he finds he can't eat or sleep or sometimes even pee, so horribly does he envy the adults in the Show who get to have up-at-net action shots of themselves in magazines. Sometimes, he says, lately, he won't take risks in tournament matches even when risks are OK or even called for, because he finds he's too scared of losing and hurting his chances for the Show and hype and fame, down the road. A couple times this year the cold clenched fear of losing has itself made him lose, he believes. He's starting to fear that rabid ambition has more than one blade, maybe. He's ashamed of his secret hunger for hype in an academy that regards hype and the seduction of hype as the great Mephistophelan pitfall and hazard of talent. A lot of these are his own terms. He feels himself in a dark world, inside, ashamed, lost, locked in. LaMont Chu is eleven and hits with two hands off both sides. He doesn't mention the Eschaton or having been punched in the stomach. The obsession with future-tense fame makes all else pale. His wrists are so thin he wears his watch halfway up his forearm, which looks sort of gladiatorial.

Lyle has a way of sucking on the insides of his cheeks as he listens. Plates of old ridged muscle emerge and subside as he shifts his weight slightly on the raised towel dispenser. The dispenser's at about shoulder-height for someone like Chu. Like all good listeners, he has a way of attending that is at once intense and assuasive: the supplicant feels both nakedly revealed and sheltered, somehow, from all possible judgment. It's like he's working as hard as you. You both of you, briefly, feel unalone. Lyle will suck in first one side's cheek and then the other. 'You burn to have your photograph in a magazine.' 'I'm afraid so.' 'Why again exactly, now?' 'I guess to be felt about as I feel about those players with their pictures in magazines.' 'Why?' 'Why? I guess to give my life some sort of kind of meaning, Lyle.' 'And how would this do this again?' 'Lyle, I don't know. I do not know. It just does. Would. Why else would I burn like this, clip secret pictures, not take risks, not sleep or pee?' 'You feel these men with their photographs in magazines care deeply about having their photographs in magazines. Derive immense meaning.' 'I do. They must. I would. Else why would I burn like this to feel as they feel?' 'The meaning they feel, you mean. From the fame.' 'Lyle, don't they?' Lyle sucks his cheeks. It's not like he's condescending or stringing you along. He's thinking as hard as you. It's like he's you in the top of a clean pond. It's part of the attention. One side of his cheeks almost caves in, thinking. 'LaMont, perhaps they did at first. The first photograph, the first magazine, the gratified surge, the seeing themselves as others see them, the hagiography of image, perhaps. Perhaps the first time: *enjoyment*. After that, do you trust me, trust me: they do not feel what you burn for. After the first surge, they care only that their photographs seem awkward or unflattering, or untrue, or that their privacy, this thing you burn to escape, what they call their privacy is being violated. Something changes. After the first photograph has been in a magazine, the famous men do not *enjoy* their photographs in magazines so much as they fear that their photographs will cease to appear in magazines. They are trapped, just as you are.' 'Is this supposed to be good news? This is awful news.' 'LaMont, are you willing to listen to a Remark about what is true?' 'Okey-dokey.' 'The truth will set you free. But not until it is finished with you.' 'Maybe I ought to be getting back.' 'LaMont, the world is very old. You have been snared by something untrue. You are deluded. But this is good news. You have been snared by the delusion that envy has a reciprocal. You assume that there is a flip-side to your painful envy of Michael Chang: namely Michael Chang's enjoyable feeling of being-envied-by-LaMont-Chu. No such animal.' 'Animal?' 'You burn with hunger for food that does not exist.' 'This is good news?' 'It is the truth. To be envied, admired, is not a feeling. Nor is fame a feeling. There are feelings associated with fame, but few of them are any more enjoyable than the feelings associated with envy of fame.' 'The burning doesn't go away?' 'What fire dies when you feed it? It is not fame itself they wish to deny you here. Trust them. There is much fear in fame. Terrible and heavy fear to be pulled and held, carried. Perhaps they want only to keep it off you until you weigh enough to pull it toward yourself.' 'Would I sound ungrateful if I said this doesn't make me feel very much better at all?' 'La-Mont, the truth is that the world is incredibly, incredibly, unbelievably old. You suffer with the stunted desire caused by one of its oldest lies. Do not believe the photographs. Fame is not the exit from any cage.' 'So I'm stuck in the cage from either side. Fame or tortured envy of fame. There's no way out.' 'You might consider how escape from a cage must surely require, foremost, awareness of the fact of the cage. And I believe I see a drop on your temple, right . . . there. . . .' Etc.

The thunder's died down to a mutter, and the window's spatter's gone random and post-storm sad.

An E.T.A. female (female students wear two different towels, coming in), a breastless senior who can barely perspire at all, is troubled, whenever she has lunch with her fiancé, by the persistent whine of a mosquito that she can't see and no one else can hear. Summer and winter, indoors or alfresco. But only at lunch, and only with her fiancé. Remarks or advice are not always the point. Sometimes suffering's point is almost crying out in a high-pitched whine to be heard. As fitness gurus go, Lyle is results-oriented and can-do.[153] Ten-year-old Kent Blott, whose parents are Seventh-Day Adventists, isn't yet old enough to masturbate, but he hears quite a lot about it, not surprisingly, from his adolescent peers, in rather lush detail, masturbation, and is worried about what sorts of homemade-type potentially wicked and soul-sapping pornographic cartridges will run through his psychic projector as he masturbates, when he eventually can masturbate, and worries about whether different sorts of fantasy scenes and combinations herald different sorts of psychic dysfunction or turpi-tude, and wants to get a good jump on worrying about it. The sounds of the dining hall's gala are more frequent and convulsive without the sound of rain. Lyle tells Blott not to let the weight he would pull to himself exceed his own personal weight. Up to the left the storm's clouds' strag-glers run like ink in water between the window and the risen moon. Mario Incandenza's presidential puppet is just about to inaugurate Subsidized Time. 16-B's Anton Doucette's been driven to Lyle he says by an increas-ing self-consciousness about the big round dark raised mole on his upper-upper lip, just under his left nostril. It's only a mole but looks pretty dire, nasally. People who first meet him are always pulling him off to the side and handing him a Kleenex. Doucette lately wishes either the mole were gone or he were gone. Even if people don't stare at the mole it's like they're *intentionally* not staring at it. Doucette pounds himself in the chest and thigh, supposedly in frustration. He just cannot come to terms with how it must look. It's getting worse as puberty intensifies, the anxiety. Then in a vicious cycle the anxiety prompts the nervous tic on his face's right side. He's starting to suspect that some upperclassmen are referring to him behind his back as Anton ('Booger') Doucette. It's like he's frozen on this anxiety, unable to move on to more advanced anxieties. He can't see any way past this. The pounding is more a sign of intense unconscious self-hatred, though, Lyle knows. Doucette grimaces and says he's starting to want to play tennis with his hand over his nose and upper lip. But he has a two-handed backhand and it's too late to switch and there's no way they're going to let him switch to one hand just for aesthetic reasons. Lyle sends Anton Doucette packing off with directions to come on back with Mario Incandenza the minute the I.-Day gala lets out. Mario gets a fair number of aesthetic-self-consciousness referrals from Lyle. No type or rank of guru is above delegating. It's like a law. Doucette says it's like he's stuck. It's becoming all he thinks about. This is on his way out. His back's additional moles form no outline or shape. Lyle pops the tab to a C.F.D.C. Mario tends to bring down most evenings around suppertime. In between door-dickyings and visits Lyle does little isometric neck-stretches, for the tension.

Between Gerhardt Schtitt's pipe and Avril Incandenza's Benson & Hedges and certain cheeks full of chewing tobacco — plus the maddening cooking-smells of honey and chocolate and real high-lipid walnuts from the kitchen vents, plus over 150 very fit bodies only some of which have been showered on this day off — the dining hall is warm and close and multi-odored. Mario as *auteur* opts for his late father's parodic device of mixing real and fake news-summary cartridges, magazine articles, and historical headers from the last few great daily papers, all for a sort of time-lapse exposition of certain developments leading up to Interdependence and Subsidized Time and cartographic Reconfiguration and the renewal of a tight and considerably tidier Experialist U.S. of A., under Gentle:

UKRAINE, TWO MORE BALTIC STATES APPLY FOR NATO INCLUSION — 16-point bold Header;

SO THEN WHY A NATO? — Editorial Header;

E.E.C. SIDES WITH PACIFIC RIM, UPS TARIFFS IN RESPONSE TO U.S. QUOTAS — Header;

GENTLE ON WASTE STORAGE FROM DISMANTLED NATO THERMS: 'NOT IN MY NATION, BABE' — 12-point Subheader;

'Amid smiles and two-handed handshakes that belied the high tensions here, the leaders of twelve out of fifteen NATO nations today signed an accord effectively dismantling the Western Bloc's fifty-five-year-old defensive alliance.' — News-Summary Cartridge Voiceover;

U.S., CANADIAN SUPPORT CUTS DOOMED NATO SUMMIT FROM START, ICELANDIC POL DECLARES — Header;

SO THEN WHY NOT A CONTINENTAL ALLIANCE, NOW, MAYBE? — Editorial Header;

MEXICO SIGNS ON FOR 'ORGANIZATION OF NORTH AMERICAN NATIONS' CONTINENTAL ALLIANCE; BUT QUÉBEC SEPARATISTS RALLY AGAINST 'FINLANDIZATION' OF 'O.N.A.N.' ALLIANCE; BUT GENTLE TO CANADA: UNLESS 'O.N.A.N.' TREATY SIGNED, NAFTA NULL, MANITOBAN THERMS STAY PUT, INTRACONTINENTAL POLLUTION AND WASTE DISPOSAL EACH NATION'S 'INTERESTS TO PURSUE TO THE BEST THEY SEE FIT' — Header from Veteran but Methamphetamine-Dependent Headliner Finally Demoted after Repeated Warnings about Taking up Too Much Space;

FED WORKERS PROTEST RANDOM FINGERNAIL-HYGIENE SCREENS — 12-point Header;

GENTLE PROPOSES NATIONALIZATION OF INTERLACE TELENT — Header; SAYS GOVT IN LINE FOR 'PIECE OF THE ACTION' ON VIDEO, CARTRIDGE, DISK RENTALS — 8-point subheader;

BURGER KING'S PILLSBURY AWARDED RIGHTS TO NEW YEAR — Header; PIZZA HUT'S PEPSICO FILES BID-RIGGING COMPLAINT WITH IRS — 12-point Subheader; CALENDAR AND PRE-PRINTED CHECK INDUSTRIES STOCKS SOAR — 8-point subheader;

Three blue-jawed convicts in antiquated stripes dicky their cell's lock and run, backed by sirens and searchlights' crisscrossed play, not for the wall but straight to the Warden's empty nighttime office, where they sit rapt before his old dual-modem MacIntosh, slapping their knees and pointing to the monitor and elbowing each other in the ribs, nibbling at inexplicably-appeared boxes of popcorn, with a Voiceover: 'Cartridges by Modem! Just Insert a Blank Diskette! Break Free of the Confinement of Your Channel Selector!' — Some more of Ms. Heath's classes' puppets in a B-film parody of the InterLace TelEntertainment ads that the cable networks seemed so mysteriously suicidally to run all the time that last year of Unsubsidized Time;

O.N.A.N. PACT PENNED — 24-point Superheader;

CANADA 'NUCK'LES UNDER — Tabloidish NY Daily's 24-point Superheader;

ACID RAIN, LANDFILLS, BARGES, FUSION-TECH, MANITOBAN THERMS WERE 'BIG STICKS,' CHRÉTIEN ADMITS — 16-point Header;

SHORT-HAIRED MEN IN SHINY TRUCKS ARE NOT DISMANTLING MANITOBAN THERMS BUT INSTEAD MOVING THEM JUST OVER BORDER INTO TURTLE MTN. INDIAN RESERVATION, HORRIFIED N.D. GOV CHARGES — 12-point Subheader from Demoted Headliner Already in Dutch Down in the Subheader Dept., Now, Too;

EXCLUSIVE COLOR PHOTOS SHOW BRAVE DOCS FUTILELY FIGHTING TIME TO REMOVE RAILROAD SPIKE FROM CANADIAN PRIME MINISTER'S RIGHT EYE — Tabloidish NY Daily's 16-point Header;

PRESIDENT'S OFFICE IS 'A ANALLY RETENTIVE HORROR SHOW' SAYS THIS JUST RETIRED WHITE HOUSE CUSTODIAN — Tabloid Header with Photo of Old Guy with Basically One Eyebrow Running All the Way across His Forehead Holding up a Mammoth Plastic Barrel He Claims Held Just One Day's Haul of Dental Stimulators, Alcohol-Soaked Cotton Puffs, GI-X-Ray-Grade Colonic Purgative Bottles, Epidermal Ash, Surgical Masks and Gloves, Q-Tips, Kleenex, and Homeopathic Pruritis-Cream Containers;

U.S.O.U.S. CHIEF TINE: CHARGES OF AN OVAL OFFICE LITTERED WITH KLEENEX AND FLOSS A 'CLEAR CASE OF DIRTY TRICKS' — Respectable Daily Header;

OVERLOADED WASTE BARGES COLLIDE, CAPSIZE OFF GLOUCESTER — Boston Daily Header;

HUGE PUTRID SLICK EMPTIES BEACHES OFF BOTH SHORES, CAPE — Equally Large Subheader;

GENTLE SPEAKS OUT ON A U.S. 'CONSTIPATEDLY IMPACTED ON CONTINENTAL WASTE' AT U.N.L.V. COMMENCEMENT — Header;

AD COUNCIL REPORT: BOSTON'S VINEY & VEALS AGENCY'S LI-POSUCTION AND TONGUE-STICK CAMPAIGNS NOT TO BLAME FOR ABC HQ BOMB THREATS — *Advertising Age* Header;

'The Governors of Maine, Vermont, and New Hampshire today reacted strongly to President Gentle's establishment of a blue-ribbon panel of waste experts to investigate the feasibility of mass landfill and conversion sites in northern New England' — Respectable NY Daily's Lead 'Graph;

'WE ARE NOT THIS CONTINENT'S SIGMOID COLON,' GENTLE WARNS O.N.A.N. JOINT SESSION — Header;

BETHESDA MD'S: STRICKEN PRESIDENT CONFINED FOR 'HY-GIENIC STRESS' FOLLOWING INCOHERENT O.N.A.N. ADDRESS — Header;

HOLOGRAPHY MAKES ULTRA-TOXIC FUSION GAMBIT SAFE FOR WORKERS, COMMUNITY, D.O.E. REP ASSURES METHUEN P.T.A. — Boston Daily Header;

GENTLE OUT OF BETHESDA NAVAL HOSP CONFINEMENT, TO ADDRESS U.S. CONGRESS ON 'RECONFIGURATIVE OPTIONS' FOR 'TIGHT, TIDIER NATIONAL ERA' — Header,

all these twirling journalistically out from a black-acetate (one of O. Stice's old Fila warm-up tops) background in vintagely allusive old-b&w-film style, with a sonic background of that sad sappy Italianate stuff Scorsese had loved for his own montages, with the headlines lap-dissolving into transverse-angled shots of a modest, green-masked Gentle accepting tight-lipped handshakes from Mexican and Canadian officials in an agreement to make the U.S. President the first Chair of the Organization of North American Nations, with Mexican Presidente and new heavily guarded Canadian P.M. to be co-Vice Chairs. Gentle's first State of the O.N.A.N. Address, delivered before a triple-size Congress on the very last day of 'B.S.' solar time, holds out the promise of a whole bright spanking new millennium of sacrifices and rewards and Interdependence's 'not impossibly radically altered new look,' continent-wide.

Do not underestimate objects! Lyle says he finds it impossible to overstress this: do *not* underestimate objects. Partridge KS's serve-and-volley prodigy Ortho ('The Darkness') Stice, 16-A's very top man, whose sauna-fresh torso gleams the same color as the moonlight off the idle weights' metal, is being driven right to the edge by the fact that he goes to sleep with his bed against one wall and then but wakes up with his bed against a whole nother wall. Stice'd already had a whole series of beefs with roommate Kyle D. Coyle because he'd figured clearly Coyle was moving Stice's bed around in Stice's sleep. But then Coyle got put in the infirmary with a suspicious discharge, and he's been out of the room for the last two nights, Coyle, and here Stice is still waking up with his bed against a different wall. So then he thought like Axford or Struck was dickying his door with a meal-card and sneaking in really late and messing with Stice's bed out of obscure motives. So but last night Stice jammed a chair up against his door and piled empty tennis-ball cans on the chair to make a racket if there was any dickying, and lined up still more cans on the sills of all three windows, just to cover all bases; and but so the reason he's here is this A.M. he wakes up with his bed moved over against the chair by the door at an angle he didn't care for one bit and with all the ball-cans arranged in a neat pyramid in the dusty rectangle where his bed was supposed to normally be. Ortho Stice can think of only three possible explanations for what's going on, and he presents them to an attentive cheek-sucking Lyle in ascending order of grimness. One is that Stice is telekinetic, but only in his sleep. Two is that somebody else at E.T.A. is telekinetic and has it in for Stice and wants to drive him batsoid for some reason. Three is that Stice is like getting up in his sleep and rearranging the room without knowing it or remembering it, which means he's a severe fucking somnambulist, which means Lord only knows what all else he could get up and wander around and do in his sleep. He's got promise, the Staff say; he's got a quite legit shot at the Show when he graduates. Which he does not want to mess up with any sort of telekinetic or somnambulistical shenanigans. Stice offers up the planes of his torso and forehead. He wears one of his own personal towels, a black one. He is slim but wiry and beautifully muscled, and sweats freely and well. He says he knows too well he'd neglected Lyle's advice about the pull-down station two years back, and regrets it. He wholeheartedly apologizes for the time last spring he got Struck and Axford to distract Lyle and then Krazy-Glued Lyle's left buttock's Spandex to the wooden top of the towel dispenser. Stice says he realizes he's the last guy with any right to come to Lyle cap in hand after all the cracks about the diet and hairstyle and all. But here he is, cap in hand, or rather calotte in hand, offering up his sauna'd planes, asking for Lyle's input.

Lyle waves bygones away like a gnat you barely look at. He is completely engaged. The lightning now far off out over the Atlantic treats him like a weak strobe. *Do not underestimate objects,* he advises Stice. Do not leave objects out of account. The world, after all, which is radically old, is made up mostly of objects. Lyle leans in, waves Stice up even closer, and consents to tell Stice the story of this one man he once knew of. This man earned his living by going to various public sites where people congregated and were bored and impatient and cynical, he'd go in and bet people that he could stand on any chair in the place and then lift that chair up off the ground while standing on it. A bootstrap-type scenario. His M.O. is he climbs up on a chair and stands there and says publicly Hey, I can lift this chair I stand on. A bystander holds the bets. The idle bus-depot or DMV-waiting-area or hospital-lobby crowd is dumbstruck. They gaze up at a man who is standing 100% on top of a chair he has grabbed the back of and raised several m. off the ground. There is vigorous speculation about how the trick's done, which gives rise to side-bet action. A devoutly religious experimental oncologist dying of his own inoperable colorectal neoplastis moans Why oh why Lord do You give this man this idiotic picayune power and I no power over my own ravening colorectal cells. There are numerous silent variations on this sort of meditation in the crowd. The bet won, the $ finally forked over and handed up to him, the man Lyle says he once knew of now jumps back down to the floor, incidental change spraying from his pockets on impact, straightens his tie, and walks off, leaving behind a dumbfounded crowd still staring up at an object he had not underestimated.

Like most young people genetically hard-wired for a secret drug problem, Hal Incandenza also has severe compulsion-issues around nicotine and sugar. Because smoking will simply kill you during drills, only Bridget Boone, a steroidic Girls' 16 named Carol Spodek, and one or the other of the Vaught twins are masochistic enough to do it, though Teddy Schacht has been known to enjoy the occasional panatela. The nicotine craving Hal tries to mollify as best he can by dipping Kodiak Wintergreen Smokeless

Tobacco several times daily, spitting into either a cherished old childhood NASA glass or the empty can of Spiru-Tein High Protein Breakfast Beverage that even now sits — given a wide berth by all others — next to a small pile of the tennis balls the table's kids don't have to squeeze as long as they're eating. Hal's more serious problem is with sucrose — the Hope-smoker's ever-beckoning siren — because he craves it always and awfully, Hal does — sugar — but finds now lately that any sugar-infusion above the level of a 56-gram AminoPal High Energy Bar now induces odd and unpleasant emotional states that don't do him one bit of good on court.

Sitting here preacher-hatted, with a mouth full of multilayered baklava, Hal knows perfectly well that Mario gets his fetish for cartridges about puppets and entr'actes and audiences from their late father. Himself, during his anticonfluential middle period, went through this subphase of being obsessed with the idea of audiences' relationships with various sorts of shows. Hal doesn't even want to think about the grim one about the carnival of eyeballs.[154] But this one other short high-tech one was called 'The Medusa v. The Odalisque' and was a film of a fake stage-production at Ford's Theater in the nation's capital of Wash. DC that, like all his audience-obsessed pieces, had cost Incandenza a real bundle in terms of human extras. The extras in this one are a well-dressed audience of guys in muttonchops and ladies with paper fans who fill the place from first row to the rear of the balcony's boxes, and they're watching an incredibly violent little involuted playlet called 'The Medusa v. The Odalisque,' the relatively plotless plot of which is just that the mythic Medusa, snake-haired and armed with a sword and well-polished shield, is fighting to the death or petrification against L'Odalisque de Ste. Thérèse, a character out of old Québecois mythology who was supposedly so inhumanly gorgeous that anyone who looked at her turned instantly into a human-sized precious gem, from admiration. A pretty natural foil for the Medusa, obviously, the Odalisque has only a nail-file instead of a sword, but also has a well-wielded hand-held makeup mirror, and she and the Medusa are basically rumbling for like twenty minutes, leaping around the ornate stage trying to de-map each other with blades and/or de-animate each other with their respective reflectors, which each leaps around trying to position just right so that the other gets a glimpse of its own full-frontal reflection and gets instantly petrified or gemified or whatever. In the cartridge it's pretty clear from their milky-pixeled translucence and insubstantiality that they're holograms, but it's not clear what they're supposed to be on the level of the playlet, whether the audience is supposed to see/(not)see them as ghosts or wraiths or 'real' mythic entities or what. But it's a ballsy fight-scene up there on the stage — having been intricately choreographed by an Oriental guy Himself rented from some commercial studio and put up in the HmH, who ate like a bird and smiled very politely all the time and didn't have even a word to say to anybody, it seemed, except Avril, to whom the Oriental choreographer had cottoned right off — balletic and full of compelling little cornerings and near-misses and reversals, and the theater's audience is rapt and clearly entertained to the gills, because they keep spontaneously applauding, as much maybe for the film's play's choreography as anything else — which would make it more like spontaneously meta-applauding, Hal supposes — because the whole fight-scene has to be ingeniously choreographed so that both combatants have their respectively scaly and cream-complected backs[155] to the audience, for obvious reasons ... except as the shield and little mirror get whipped martially around and brandished at various strategic angles, certain members of the playlet's well-dressed audience eventually start catching disastrous glimpses of the combatants' fatal full-frontal reflections, and instantly get transformed into like ruby statues in their front-row seats, or get petrified and fall like embolized bats from the balcony's boxes, etc. The cartridge goes on like this until there's nobody left in the Ford's Theater seats animate enough to applaud the nested narrative of the fight-scene play, and it ends with the two aesthetic foils still rumbling like mad before an audience of varicolored stone. 'The Medusa v. The Odalisque' 's own audiences didn't think too much of the thing, because the film audience never does get much of a decent full-frontal look at what it is about the combatants that supposedly has such a melodramatic effect on the rumble's live audience, and so the film's audience ends up feeling teased and vaguely cheated, and the thing had only a regional release, and the cartridge rented like yesterday's newspapers, and it's now next to impossible to find. But that wasn't by any stretch of the imagination the James O. Incandenza film that audiences hated the most. The most hated Incandenza film, a variable-length one called The Joke, had only a very brief theatrical release, and then only at the widely scattered last remains of the pre-InterLace public art-film theaters in arty places like Cambridge MA and Berkeley CA. And InterLace never considered it for Pulse-Order rerelease, for obvious reasons. The art-film theaters' marquees and posters and ads for the thing were all required to say something like 'THE JOKE': You Are Strongly Advised NOT To Shell Out Money to See This Film, which art-film habitués of course thought was a cleverly ironic anti-ad joke, and so they'd shell out for little paper theater tickets and file in in their sweater vests and tweeds and dirndls and tank up on espresso at the concession stand and find seats and sit down and make those little pre-movie leg and posture adjustments, and look around with that sort of vacant intensity, and they'd figure the tri-lensed Bolex H32 cameras — one held by a tall stooped old guy and one complexly mounted on the huge head of the oddly forward-listing boy with what looked like a steel spike coming out of his thorax — the big cameras down by the red-lit EXITS on either side of the screen, the patrons figured, were there for like an ad or an anti-ad or a behind-the-scenes metafilmic documentary or something. That is, until the lights went down and the film started up and what was on the wide public screen was just a wide-angled binoculated shot of this very art-film theater's audience filing in with espressos and finding seats and sitting down and looking around and getting adjusted and saying knowledgeable little pre-movie things to their thick-lensed dates about what the Don't-Pay-To-See-This ad and Bolex cameras probably signified, artistically, and settling in as the lights dimmed and facing the screen (i.e. now themselves, it turns out) with the coolly excited smiles of highbrow-entertainment expectation, smiles which the cameras and screen's projection now revealed as just starting to drop from the faces of the audience as the audience saw row after row of itself staring back at it with less and less expectant and more and more blank and then puzzled and then eventually pissed-off facial expressions. *The Joke*'s total running time was just exactly as long as there was even one cross-legged patron left in the theater to watch his own huge projected image gazing back down at him with the special distaste of a disgusted and ripped-off-feeling art-film patron, which ended up being more than maybe twenty minutes only when there were critics or film-academics in the seats, who studied themselves studying themselves taking notes with endless fascination and finally left only when the espresso finally impelled them to the loo, at which point Himself and Mario would have to frantically pack up cameras and lens-cases and coaxials and run and totter like hell to catch the next cross-country flight from Cambridge to Berkeley or Berkeley to Cambridge, since they obviously had to be there all set up and Bolex'd for each showing at each venue. Mario said Lyle had said Incandenza had confessed that he'd loved the fact that *The Joke* was so publicly static and simple-minded and dumb, and that those rare critics who defended the film by arguing at convolved length that the simple-minded stasis was precisely the film's aesthetic thesis were dead wrong, as usual. It's still unclear whether it was the Eyeball-and-Sideshow thing or '*The Medusa v. . . .*' or *The Joke* that had metamorphosized into their late father's later involvement with the hostilely anti-Real genre of 'Found Drama,' which was probably the historical zenith of self-consciously dumb stasis, but which audiences never actually even got to hate, for a-priori reasons.

FREAK STATUE OF LIBERTY ACCIDENT KILLS FED ENGINEER — Header; BRAVE MAN ON CRANE CRUSHED BY 5 TON CAST IRON BURGER — 12-point Subheader;

GENTLE PROMISES SKEPTICAL CUB SCOUT CONVENTION 'YOU'LL BE ABLE TO EAT RIGHT OFF' TERRITORIAL U.S. BY END OF TERM'S FIRST YEAR — Header;

ANOTHER LOVE CANAL? — 24-point Superheader; TOXIC HOR-
ROR ACCIDENTALLY UNCOVERED IN UPSTATE NEW
HAMPSHIRE — 16-point Header-sized Subheader;

'New Hampshire environmental officials yesterday flatly denied that vast
collections of drums leaking industrial solvents, chlorides, benzenes and
oxins had been quote "stumbled on" by 18 federal EPA staffers playing a
casual game of softball east of Berlin, NH, claiming instead that the corroded receptacles had been placed there against statute by large men with
white body suits and short haircuts in long shiny trailer trucks with
O.N.A.N.'s official crest, a sombreroed eagle with a maple leaf in its
mouth, stencilled on the sides. In the nation's capital, a quote "full and
energetic investigation" has been promised by the Gentle administration
into claims by residents of Berlin, NH and Rumford, ME that the incidence of soft-skulled and extra-eyed newborns in the toxicly affected area
far exceeds the national average.' — $3.75 U.S. Nightly-Rental News Car-
tridge Anchor Lead;

SUB ROSA FUSION-IN-POISONOUS-ENVIRONMENT TEST SITE
ALLEGED AT MONTPELIER, VT — *Scientific North American* Header;

MY BABY HAS SIX EYES AND BASICALLY NO SKULL — Lurid Color
32-point Tabloid Header, Dateline Lancaster NH;

FED EPA SOFTBALLERS ALLEGE TWO MORE 'POISONOUS WASTE
HORRORFEST' ILLEGAL DUMP SITES 'STUMBLED OVER' NEAR
NORTH SYRACUSE, HISTORIC TICONDEROGA — NYC Daily
Header;

THE FINE ART OF FEDERAL STUMBLING: A WHOLE LOT OF
SOFTBALL GOING ON — Editorial Header in Syracuse NY's *Post-
Standard;*

CANADIAN P.M. DENIES SECRET MINIATURE GOLF OUTING
WITH OUTRAGED NEW ENGLAND GOVS — Surprisingly Small 3rd-
Page 10-point Header;

GENTLE SHOCKER — Pearl-Harbor-Sized 32-point Super-superheader
Almost Too Big to Read Clearly; MAYFLOWER, RED BALL, ALLIED,
U-HAUL STOCKS SOAR — 16-point Financial Daily Subheader;
TWO NORTHEAST GOVS HOSPITALIZED FOR INFARCTION,
ANEURISM — 10-point Subheader;

GENTLE DECLARES ALL U.S. TERRITORY NORTH OF LINE
FROM SYRACUSE TO TICONDEROGA, NY, TICONDEROGA, NY
TO SALEM, MA FEDERAL DISASTERS, OFFERS FEDERAL AID FOR

UPSTATE AND NEW ENGLAND RESIDENTS WISHING TO RE-
LOCATE, CLAIMS FUNDS FOR EPA CLEAN-UP 'ARE NOT
WITHIN THE MAP OF WHAT'S POSSIBLE' [*SIC*] — Header from
Chemically Over-Garrulous Headliner Eventually Fired Even from Sub-
header Dept. for Exceeding Verbal Parameters and Now Starting to
Get in the Same Hot Water All Over Again at a Much Less Prestigious
Daily Paper;

and so on and so forth. Himself's old optical editing lab has imposing Com-
pugraphic typesetting and matteing facilities: it's hard to tell which of the
headlines and other stuff are for real and which have been dickied with,
usually, if you're too young to recall the actual chronology. At least some of
the headlines are phony, the kids know; miniature golf indeed. But the accuracy of Mario's puppeteered account of the seminal meeting of what's come
to be known as 'The Concavity Cabinet' gets to stand uncontested by fact.
Nobody who wasn't actually there at the 16 January meeting knows just
what was said when or by whom, the Gentle administration being of the
position that extant Oval Office recording equipment was a veritable petri
dish of organisms. Gentle's claque of doo-wopping Motown cabinet-
puppets have purple dresses and matching lipstick and nail polish, and bouf-
fants so blindingly Afrosheened that there had been special lighting and
film-speed problems in the custodial closet:

SEC. TREAS.: You're looking vigorous and hale today, sir.
GENTLE: Hhhaaahh Hhhuuuhh Hhhaaahh Hhhuuuhh.
PRES. MEX./SEC. MEX./V-C O.N.A.N.: May I ask, Señor, why my distin-
guished co-Vice Chair of O.N.A.N. is not with us in attendance today.
GENTLE: Hhhaaahh Hhhuuuhh.
MR. RODNEY TINE, CHIEF, U.S. OFFICE OF UNSPECIFIED SERVICES: The
president's taking a little pure oxygen today, boys, and has authorized
me as his oral proxy on this may I say historically opportune day. The
Canadian P.M.'s in a bit of a snit. He prefers to whinge in the media
surrounded by Mounted Reserves and is off somewhere far from
Québec in a Kevlar vest doing whatever the Canadian word is for pout-
ing, doubtless poring over opinion polls prepared by chinless guys in
Canadian hornrims.
MEX. AND SOME OTHER SECS.: [Various puzzled apprehensive noises.]
TINE: I'm sure you've all been briefed on the unprecedented but not unop-
portune crisis that obtains north of the almost perfectly horizontal line
between Buffalo and Northeast Mass.
TINE arranges photos on seal-crested easels: a New Hampshire runoff-
ditch running off stuff a color nobody's quite ever seen before; a wide-
angle horizon-stretching vista of skull-embossed drums, with short-
haired guys in white body-suits walking around adjusting knobs and

reading dials on shiny hand-held devices; a very weird chemical sunrise, close in hue to the Cabinet members' lipstick, over some forests in southern Maine that look way taller and generally lusher than January forests ought properly to be; a couple indoor-lit snapshots of a multi-eyed infant crawling backwards, its ear to the carpet, dragging its shapeless head like a sack of spuds. The last display's a real heartstring-plucker.

ALL SECS.: [Various concerned and sympathetic noises.]

GENTLE: Hhhaaahh Hhhuuuhh.

TINE: Gentlemen, let the president just say that no one's prepared to say they're quite sure what's happened, or just which quote unquote loyal part of the Union or Organization might reasonably be said to be culpable, but it's not the administration's immediate concern to point the levelling finger of blame or aspersion just yet or right now. Our concern is to act, to respond, and act and respond decisively. Swiftly. And decisively.

SEC. INT.: We've come up with some extremely preliminary projections on the costs of detoxifying and/or deradiating the better part of four U.S. states, sir, and I have to tell you gentlemen that even with the atmosphere of uncertainty at this point in time of not yet having a definitive handle on just what kinds and combinations of compounds were — umm — found there and how wide your — not 'your' personally, sir, J.G., 'your' just being a shorthand way for — to say something like I suppose simply 'the' — how wide *the* dispersal- and toxicity-parameters are shaping up to look — umm — I have to relate that the figures we're looking at are almost staggeringly multi-zeroed, sir, gentlemen.

TINE: Tighten in and expand on *staggering* if you will, Blaine.

SEC. INT.: We're talking at bare minimum a staggering amount of Private-Sector-caliber guys in white suits and helmets, not unlike your own helmet, sir, with a commensurately massive tab for the suits and helmets, plus gloves and throwaway booties, and a lot of really shiny equipment with a great many knobs and dials. Sir.

GENTLE: Hhhaaahh Hhhuuuhh.

TINE: Gentlemen, let's pay the president the due tribute of proceeding right to the bone of the matter. I think the president's position is rendered patently clear by the pure oxygen he's been forced to take here with us today. No way we can possibly permit territory publicly exposed as this befouled and waste-impacted to continue to besmirch the already tight and tidier territory of a new era's U.S. of A. The president shudders at the mere thought. Just the mere thought of it forces him to resort to oxygen.

PRES. MEX./SEC. MEX./V-C O.N.A.N.: I do not anticipate what options your federal and our continental government might consider options to this permitting, señors.

OTHER SECS.: [Tentative puzzled nods and slightly off-key agreement-noises.]

TINE: Having been elected and conferred with a mandate on the clear and public anti-waste platform of the C.U.S.P., the president is inexorably driven to see the only viable option being to give it away.

SEC. STATE: Give it away?

TINE: Expressly.

SEC. STATE: You mean simply tell the truth? That Johnny's C.U.S.P. platform necessitates — given the unfeasibility of shooting national wastes into space, since NASA hasn't put a successful launch on in over a decade and the rockets simply fall over and blow up and become more waste — that — given the amount of additional waste annular fusion's start-up is going to start putting in circulation the minute start-up commences — that his platform all but necessitates the second-tier option of transforming certain vast stretches of U.S. territory into uninhabitable and probably barbed-wired landfills and fly-shrouded dumps and saprogenic magenta-fogged toxic-disposal sites? Concede publicly that those EPA softball games weren't casual or pick-up in the least? That you allowed Rod the God here to convince you[156] to authorize Unspecified Services to undertake massive toxic dumping and skull-softening against local statute for basically the same hard-choice, Greater-Good-of-the-Union reasons that prompted Lincoln to suspend the Constitution and jail Confederate activists without charge for the duration of the last great U.S. territorial crisis? And/or not least that these particular territories were chosen essentially because New Hampshire and Maine didn't let C.U.S.P. on their Independent ballots and the Mayor of Syracuse had the misfortune to sneeze on the president during a campaign swing? Give away the entire strategy the two of you have apparently huddled in some sterilized corner and mapped out? Can this be what you mean by *Give it away,* Rod?

TINE: Bôf. Don't be a maroon, Billingsley. The *it* in the president's *Give it away* signifies the territory.

GENTLE: Hhhaaaahhh.

TINE: We're going to give away the whole benighted smirch of ground.

SEC. INT.: Export it, one might venture to sally.

TINE: It's a novel and pro-active resource no prior statesman's had the vision or environmental cojones to envision. If there's one natural resource we've still got in spades, it's territory.

PRES. MEX./SEC. MEX./V-C O.N.A.N. AND SEVERAL OTHER SECS.: [Attempt to bring eyebrows back down below hairlines.]

TINE: President Gentle's decided we're going to reinvent not just government but history. Torch the past. Manifest a new destiny. Boys, we're going to institute some serious intra-O.N.A.N. interdependence.

GENTLE: Hhhaaahh hhhuuuhh.

TINE: Gentlemen, we're going to make an unprecedented intercontinental gift of certain newly expendable northeast American territories, in return for the *faute-de-mieux* continuation of U.S. waste-displacement access to those territories. Allow me to illustrate what Lur— just what the president means.

TINE places two large maps (also courtesy of Ms. Heath's crafts class) on Govt.-issue easels. They look both to be of the good old U.S.A.. The first map is your more or less traditional standard issue, with the U.S. looking really big in white and Mexico's northern fringes a tasteful ladies'-room pink and Canada's brooding bottom hem a garish, almost menacing red. The second North American map looks neither old nor all that good, traditionally speaking. It has a concavity. It looks sort of like some person or persons have taken a deep wicked canine-intensive bite out of its upper right bit, in which an ascending and then descending line has its near-right-angle at what looks to be the historic and now hideously befouled Ticonderoga NY; and the areas north of that jagged line look to be that pushy shade of Canadian red, now. Some little rubber practical-joke-type flies, the blue-bellied kind that live on filth, are stapled in a raisinesque dispersal over the red Concavity. TINE has a trademark telescoping weatherman's pointer that he plays with instead of using to point at much of anything.

SEC. STATE: A kind of ecological gerrymandering?

TINE: The president invites you gentlemen to conceive these two visuals as a sort of before-and-after representation of 'projected intra-O.N.A.N. territorial re-allocations,' or some public term like that. *Redemisement*'s probably too technical.

SEC. STATE: Still respectfully not quite sure we at State see how inhabited territories can be sold to the public as quote expendable when a decent slice of that public by all reports inhabits that territory, Rod.

GENTLE: Hhhaaahh.

TINE: The president's pro-actively chosen not to hedge that high-cost tough-choice possibly unpopular lonely-at-the-top fact one bit, guys. We've been moving forward full-bore on anticipating various highly involved relocation scenarios. Scenaria? Is it scenarios or scenaria?[157] Marty's on-task on the scenario front. Care to bring us to speed, Marty?

SEC. TRANSP.: We foresee a whole lot of people moving south really really fast. We foresee cars, light trucks, heavier trucks, buses, Winnebagos — Winnebaga? — commandeered vans and buses, and possibly commandeered Winnebagos or Winnebaga. We foresee

4-wheel-drive vehicles, motorcycles, Jeeps, boats, mopeds, bicycles, canoes and the odd makeshift raft. Snowmobiles and cross-country skiers and roller-skaters on those strange-looking roller-skates with only one line of wheels down each skate. We foresee backpack-type folks speed-walking in walking-shorts and boots and Tyrolean hats and a stick. We foresee some folks just outright running like hell, possibly, Rod. We foresee homemade wagons piled high with worldly goods. We foresee BMW war-surplus motorcycles with sidecars and guys in goggles and leather helmets. We foresee the occasional skateboard. We foresee a strictly temporary breakdown in the thin veneer of civilization over the souls of essentially frightened stampeding animals. We foresee looting, shooting, price-gouging, ethnic tensions, promiscuous sex, births in transit.

SEC. H.E.W.: Rollerblades I think you mean, Marty.

SEC. TRANSP.: All feedback and input welcome, Trent. Someone junior in the office foresaw hang-gliders. I don't foresee demographically significant hang-gliding, personally, at this juncture. Nor I need to stress do we foresee anything you could call true refugees.

GENTLE: Hhhaaahh *hhhuuuhhhhhhh*.

TINE: Absolutely not, Mart. No way a downer-association-rife term like *refugee* is going to be applicable here. I cannot overstress this too assertively. Eminent nondomain: yes. Renewal-grade brand of sacrifice: you bet. Heroes, new era's breed of new pioneers, striking in bravely for already-settled good old settled but unfoul American territory: *bien sûr*.

SEC. STATE: *Bien sûr?*

PRESS SEC. [w/ queer combination of bangs and bouffant and pair of bifocals on slim bead chain around neck and resting in cleavage]: Neil over in Spin has been poring through resource materials. Apparently the term *refugee* can be plausibly denied if both — I'm quoting direct from Neil's memo here — if both, a, no homemade wagons piled high with worldly goods are pulled by slow bovine animals with curvy horns, and b, if the percentage of children under six who are either, a, naked, or b, squalling at the top of their lungs, or c, both, is under 20% of the total number of children under six in transit. It's true that Neil's key resource here is Pol and Diang's *Totalitarian's Guide to Iron-Fisted Spin*, but they're thinking this fact can be spun away from without much to-do, over in Spin.

GENTLE: Hhhuuuhh.

TINE: Marty and Jay's staffs have been day-and-nighting on strategies to forestall anything like ostensible refugeeism.

PRESS SEC. [Holding brillantined head at that angle people in bifocals have to, to read]: Anything bovine with curvy horns gets shot on sight. Rod's top U.S.O. operatives in shiny trucks at strategic intervals handing out free toddler-wear courtesy of Sears' Winnie-the-Pooh line, to nip nakedness in the bud.

SEC. TREAS.: Still hammering out the boilerplate on the Sears agreement, Rod.

TINE: The president has every confidence, Chet. I believe Marty and Jay were just getting to the transportational coup de grâce.

SEC. TRANSP.: We're soliciting bids for signs for up there making it legal to drive really really fast in the breakdown lanes.

PRESS SEC.: South-bound breakdown lanes.

ALL SECS.: [Harmonic murmurs.]

SEC. STATE: Still don't see why not just retain cartographic title to the toxified areas, relocate citizenry and portable capital, use them as our own designated disposal area. Sort of the back of the hall closet or special wastebasket underneath the national kitchen sink as it were. Hammer out systems for delivering all national refuse and waste into the area, cordon it off, keep the rest of the nation edible-off as per Johnny's platform.

SEC. H.E.W.: Why cede vitally needed waste-disposal resources to a recalcitrant ally?

TINE: Billingsley, Trent, and yet who as I stated says we can't utilize these territories for just this purpose no matter whose nation's name they're in? Interdependence is as Interdependence does, after all.

PRES. MEX./SEC. MEX./V-C O.N.A.N.: ¿Qué?

GENTLE: Hhhaaahh?

TINE: Yet Billingsley's right that this kind of sprawling, depopulated, newly Canadian territory can accommodate the tidiness-needs of this whole great continental alliance for decades to come. After that, look out Yukon!

PRES. MEX./SEC. MEX./V-C O.N.A.N. [Face green and mask wetly dark over upper lip]: May I respectfully ask President Gentle how you are proposing to ask my newly succeeded Co-Vice Chair of our continental Organization to possibly be able to accept vast arenas of egregiously poisoned terrain on behalf of his peoples?

TINE: Valid question. Simple answer. Three answers. Statesmanship. Gamesmanship [counting, now, on fine strong white clean fingers]. Brinksmanship.

W/ now more — and rather more jejune — journalistic f/x spinning out of the black at high-camp speeds to a 45-rpm playing of custodian Dave ('F.D.V.') Harde's ⅓-rpm disc of 'Flight of the Bumblebee':

GENTLE TO CANADIAN PM: HAVE SOME TERRITORY — Header;

CANADIAN P.M. TO GENTLE: NO, REALLY, THANKS ANYWAY — Header;

GENTLE TO CANADIAN P.M.: BUT I INSIST — Header;

BLOC QUEBECOIS TO CANADIAN P.M.: ACCEPT TOXICLY CON-VEX ADDITION TO OUR PROVINCE AND WE ARE OUT OF HERE SO FAST YOUR HEAD WILL SPIN ALL THE WAY AROUND — Header from That Guy Again;

CANADIAN P.M. TO GENTLE: LOOK, WE'RE SWIMMING IN TER-RITORY ALREADY, HAVE A LOOK AT AN ATLAS WHY DON'T YOU, WE HAVE WAY MORE TERRITORY THAN WE KNOW WHAT TO DO WITH ALREADY, PLUS I DON'T MEAN TO BE RUDE EITHER BUT WE'RE ESPECIALLY UNKEEN ON ACCEPTING HOPE-LESSLY *BEFOULED* TERRITORY FROM YOU GUYS, INTERDE-PENDENCE RHETORIC OR NO, THERE'S REALLY JUST NO WAY — And Again;

abon26-MEMBER EEC ACCUSES U.S. OF 'EXPERIALIST DOM-INATION' — Header; THIRD-WORLD VEGETABLES HURLED IN U.N. IMBROGLIO — 10-point Subheader;

GENTLE TO P.M.: LOOK, BABE, TAKE THE TERRITORY OR YOU'RE GOING TO BE REALLY REALLY SORRY — Header;

SIN CITY SHRINK: NATION'S VELVETIEST VOCALIST WAS HOS-PITALIZED TWICE FOR MENTAL ILLNESS — Tabloid Header;

PRESIDENTIAL HISTORY OF 'EMOTIONAL INSTABILITY' AL-LEGED BY LAS VEGAS M.D. — Respectable Header;

MY GARDEN NOW'S GOT TOMATOES I COULDN'T LIFT EVEN IF I COULD HACK THROUGH THEIR VINES WITH A MACHETE TO EVEN REACH THEM — Tabloid Header, Dateline Montpelier VT, with Photo That Simply Has Got to Have Been Doctored;

F.E.C. CALLED TO INVESTIGATE C.U.S.P.s — Header; 'STRATEGIC MISREPRESENTATION' OF CANDIDATE'S PSYCH HISTORY HAS PUT NATION, CONTINENT AT RISK, DEMS CHARGE — 12-point Supersubheader;

TOP AIDES HUDDLE AS WORRIES OVER GENTLE'S 'PATHOLOG-ICAL INABILITY TO DEAL PROACTIVELY WITH ANY SORT OF REAL OR IMAGINED REJECTION' MOUNT IN FACE OF CANA-DIAN SHOWDOWN — Meth-Dependent Headliner, Now at Third Daily in 17 Months;

'Both financial and diplomatic communities have reacted with increasing concern to reports that President Gentle has isolated himself in a small private suite at Bethesda Naval Hospital with several thousand dollars' worth of sound and sterilization equipment and is spending all day every

406

day singing morose show-tunes in inappropriate keys to the U.S.M.C. Colonel who stands near the Dermalatix Hypospectral sterilization appliance handcuffed to the Black Box of United States nuclear codes. Unspecified Services Office spokespersons have declined to comment on reports of such erratic Executive directives as: ordering the Defense Department to commandeer department store giant Searsco's entire inventory of Winnie-the-Pooh toddler wear under National Security Emergency Proviso 414; requiring Armed Forces personnel to take target practice at cardboard silhouettes of what appear to be oxen, water buffalo, or Texas longhorn cattle; preparing the release of a Presidential Address to the Nation cartridge that purportedly consists entirely of the president seated at his desk with his head in his gloves intoning "What's the point of going on?" over and over; instructing silo personnel at all S.A.C. installations north of 44° to remove their missiles from the silos and then reinsert them upside-down; and ordering the installation of massive "air displacement effectuators" 28 km. south of each such silo, facing north.' — Anchor's Lead for Kind of Semi-Cheesy Weekly Lurid-News-Intensive Summary Cartridge;

'UNPRECEDENTED' WHOPPER REVENUES IN THIRD QUARTER CREDITED BY PILLSBURY/BK TO GENTLE'S 'CREATIVELY PRO-ACTIVE' RESUSCITATION OF POST-NETWORK ADVERTISING — *Ad Week* 14-point Full-Color Header;

GENTLE HAS COMPLETELY LOST MIND, CLAIMS CONFIDANT, O.U.S. CHIEF TINE AT PRESS CONFERENCE: THREATENS TO DETONATE UPSIDE-DOWN MISSILES IN U.S. SILOS, IRRADIATE CANADA W/ AID OF ATHSCME HELL-FANS — Header; 'WILLING TO ELIMINATE OWN MAP OUT OF SHEER PIQUE' IF CANADA NIXES RECONFIGURATIVE TRANSFER OF 'AESTHETICALLY UN-ACCEPTABLE' TERRAIN — Pretty Obviously Homemade Subheader.

This catastatic feature of the puppet-film's plot — that Johnny Gentle, Famous Crooner threatens to bomb his own nation and toxify neighbors in an insane pout over Canada's reluctance to take redemised title over O.N.A.N.'s very own vast dump — resonates powerfully with those members of the movie's E.T.A. audience who know that this whole parodic pseudo-ONANtiad scenario is actually a puppet-à-clef-type allusion to the dark legend of one Eric Clipperton and the Clipperton Brigade. In the very last couple years of solar, Unsubsidized Time, this kid Eric Clipperton appeared for the first time as an unseeded sixteen-year-old in East Coast regional tournament play. The little Town-or-Academy-Hailed-From slot after Clipperton's name on tournament draw-sheets just said 'Ind.,' presumably for 'Independent.' Nobody'd heard of him before or knew where he came from. He'd just sort of seepily risen, some sort of human radon, from someplace low and unknown, whence he lent the cliché 'Win or Die in the Attempt' grotesquely literal new levels of sense.

For the Clipperton legend derived from the fact that this Clipperton kid owned a hideous and immaculately maintained Glock 17 semiautomatic sidearm that came in a classy little leather-handled blond-wood case with German High-Gothic script on it and a velvet gun-shaped concavity inside where the Glock 17 lay nestled in plush velvet, gleaming, with another little rectangular divot for the 17-shot clip; and that he brought the gun-case and Glock 17 out on the court with him along with his towels and water-jug and sticks and gear bag, and from his very first appearance on the East Coast jr. tour made clear his intention to blow his own brains out publicly, right there on court, if he should lose, ever, even once.

Thus there came to be, in most every tournament with an initial draw of 64, a group of three boys, then four, and by the semifinals five, then finally six boys who for that tournament formed the Clipperton Brigade, players who'd had the misfortune to draw and meet Eric Clipperton and Clipperton's well-oiled Glock 17, and who understandably declined to be the player to cause Clipperton to eliminate his own map for keeps in public for something as comparatively cheesy as a tournament win over Clipperton. A win over Clipperton had no meaning because a *loss* to Clipperton had no meaning and didn't hurt anybody's regional and U.S.T.A. ranking, not once the guys in the U.S.T.A. computer center caught on to the Clipperton strategic M.O. Thus an early exit from a tournament because of a loss to Clipperton came to be regarded as sort of like a walk in baseball, stats-wise; and a boy who found himself in the Clipperton Brigade and defaulted his round tended to view that tournament as a kind of unexpected vacation, a chance to rest and heal, to finally get some sun on the chest and ankles, to work on chinks in his game's armor, to reflect a little on what it all might mean.

Clipperton's first meaningless victory ever came at sixteen, unseeded, at the Hartford Jr. Open, first round, against one Ross Reat, of Maddox OH and the just-opened Enfield Tennis Academy. For some reason it's Struck who sort of specializes in this story and never misses a chance to tell new E.T.A.s the tale of Clipperton v. Reat. Clipperton's an OK player, nothing spectacular but also not like absurdly out of place at a regional-grade tourney; but Reat is at fifteen seasoned and high-ranked, and the third seed at Hartford; and Reat is, for a while — as would be S.O.P. for a high seed in the first round — basically cleaning under his nails with this unseeded unknown Eric Clipperton. At 1–4 in the second set, Clipperton sits down at the side-change and, instead of toweling off, reaches into his gear bag and extracts his classy little blond-wood case and gets out the Glock 17. Fondles it. Takes out the clip and hefts it and rams it home in its slot at the base of the grip with a chillingly solid-sounding click. Caresses his left temple with the thing's blunt shiny barrel. Everybody watching the match agrees it is one ugly and all-business-looking piece of personal-defense hardware. Clipperton climbs up the rungs of the lifeguardish chair the umpire in his blue blazer[158] sits in and uses the umpire's mike to make public his intention of blowing his personal brains out all over the court with the hideous Glock, should he lose. The small first-round gallery stiffens and inhales and doesn't exhale for a long time. Reat audibly gulps. Reat is tall, densely freckled, a good kid, one of Incandenza's fair-haired boys, not too bright, with the Satellite Tour so clearly in his future that at only fifteen he's already starting cholera shots and mastering Third World exchange rates. And but for the remainder of the match (which lasts exactly eleven more games) Clipperton plays tennis with the Glock 17 held steadily to his left temple. The gun makes tossing kind of a hassle, on Clipperton's serve, but Reat is letting the serves go by untouched anyway. None of the E.T.A. staff has bothered to show up and coach Reat through what was supposed to be a standard first-round fingernail-cleaning, and so Reat is strategically and emotionally all alone out there, and he's opted for not even pretending to make an effort, given what the unseeded Clipperton seems willing to sacrifice for a win. Ross Reat was the first and last junior player ever to shake Clipperton's free hand at the end of a match, and the moment's captured in a *Hartford Courant* staff photo that some E.T.A. wiseacre'd later glued to the door of Struck's room with so much Elmer's all over the back that taking it off would gut the varnish, so the thing stays up for all in the hall to see, Reat here up at net on one knee, one arm over his eyes, the other hand extended upward to a Clipperton who'd simply obliterated him psychologically. And Ross Reat was never quite exactly the same ever again after that, both Schtitt and de Lint have assured all future potentially mercy-minded E.T.A. males.

And, the legend's story goes, Eric Clipperton never henceforth loses. No one is willing to beat him and risk going through life with the sight of the Glock going off on his conscience. Nobody ever knows where Clipperton comes from, to play. Never seen at airports or Interstate exit ramps or ever even spotted carb-loading at any Denny's between matches. He just starts materializing, always alone, at increasingly high-level junior tournaments, appears on draw-sheets with 'Ind.' by his name, plays competitive tennis with a Glock at his left temple;[159] and his opponents, unwilling to sacrifice Clipperton's hostage (Clipperton *même*), barely even try, or else they go for impossible angles and spins, or else talk on mobile phones while they play or try to hit every ball between their legs or behind their backs; and the matches' galleries tend to boo Clipperton just as much as they dare; and Clipperton sits and hefts his 17-shot clip and takes the brass-jacketed 9-mm. cartridges out sometimes and clicks a few together ruminatively in his hand in the sideline chair at all the odd-game breaks, and sometimes he tries little Western-gunslinger triggerguard-spins during the breaks; but when play resumes Clipperton's deadly serious once more and has the Glock 17 at his temple, playing, and mows through the lackadaisical Clipperton Brigade round by round, and wins the whole tournament by what is essentially psychic default, and then right after collecting his trophy vanishes like the ground itself inhaled him. His only even remote friend on the jr. tour is eight-year-old Mario Incandenza, whom Clipperton meets because, even though Disney Leith and an early prorector named Cantrell are shepherding the male tournament contingent (including a solid but sort of plateau-stuck and no longer much improving seventeen-year-old Orin Incandenza) that summer, E.T.A. Headmaster Dr. J. O. Incandenza shows up at quite a few of the events on the domestic circuit, doing under ostensible U.S.T.A. auspices a two-part documentary on jr. competitive tennis, stress, and light, and so Mario's tottering around with lens-cases and Tuffy tripods etc. at most of that late summer's meaningful events, and meets Clipperton, and finds Clipperton intriguing and in ways he can't be very articulate about hilarious, and is kind to him and seeks out his company, Clipperton's, or at any rate at least treats Clipperton like he *exists*, whereas by late July everybody else's attitude toward Clipperton resembled that kind of stiffly conspicuous nonrecognition that e.g. accompanies farts at formal functions. One of Himself's short test-cartridges — shot to check out transverse aberration at various sun-angles, the case's little adhesive sticker says — contains the only available footage of the late Eric Clipperton[160] — from the preponderance of salt-tablet dispensers and littered Pledge husks and Dade County ambulances it was pretty likely shot at the hideous Sunkist Jr. Inv. cramp-fest in August in Miami — just a couple overexposed meters of Clipperton, head down and hunched on a low orange bleacher, bony-shouldered, in no shirt and untied Nikes, his Gothic-scripted case in his lap, his elbows on his knees and his hands spidered across both cheeks, staring down between his feet and trying not to smile as a withered-toddler-sized and forward-listing Mario stands beside him, supported by his portable police lock, holding a light-meter and something else too halated to make out on the tape, open very wide for a homodontic laugh at something funny Clipperton has apparently just let slip.

Hal, having smoked cannabis on four separate occasions — twice w/ others — on this continental day of rest, plus still in a kind of guiltily sickening stomach-pit shock from the afternoon's Eschaton debacle and his failure to intervene or even get up out of his patio-chair, Hal has lost a bit of his grip and has just gotten on the outside of his fourth chocolate cannoli in half an hour, and is feeling the icy electric keening of some sort of incipient carie in the left-molar range, and also now as usual, after swinishness with sugar, finds himself sinking, emotionally, into a kind of distracted funk. The puppet-film is reminiscent enough of the late Himself that just about the only more depressing thing to pay attention to or think about would be advertising and the repercussions of O.N.A.N.ite Reconfiguration for the U.S. advertising industry. Mario's film executes some rather over-arty flash-cuts between the erections of Lucite fortifications and ATHSCME and E.W.D. displacement installations along the new U.S. border, on the one hand, and the shadowily implied Rodney-Tine-disastrous-love-interest element with the voluptuous puppet representing the infamous and enigmatic Québecois *fatale* known publicly only as 'Luria P———,' on the other. Tine's puppet's tiny brown felt hand is on Luria's voluptuously padded little Popsicle-stick knee in the famous Vienna, Virginia Szechuan steakhouse where, according to dark legend, Subsidized Time was conceived on the back of a chintzy Chinese-zodiac paper placemat, by R. Tine. Hal happens to know the fall and rise of millennial U.S. advertising exceptionally well, because one of the only two academic things he's ever written about anything even remotely filmic[161] was a mammoth research paper on the tangled fates of broadcast television and the American ad industry. This was the final and grade-determining project in Mr. U. Ogilvie's year-long Intro to Entertainment Studies in May of Y.P.W.; and Hal, a seventh-grader and only up to R in the *Condensed O.E.D.*, wrote about TV-advertising's demise with a reverent tone that sounded like the events had taken place at the misty remove of glaciers and guys in pelts instead of just four years prior, more or less overlapping with the waxing of the Gentle Era and Experialist Reconfiguration Mario's puppet-show makes fun of.

There's no question that the Network television industry — meaning, since PBS is a whole different kettle, the Big Three plus the fast-starting but low-endurance Fox — had already been in serious trouble. Between the exponential proliferation of cable channels, the rise of the total-viewer-control hand-held remotes known historically as zappers, and VCR-recording advances that used subtle volume- and hysterical-pitch-sensors to edit most commercials out of any program taped (here a rather chatty digression on legal battles between Networks and VCR-manufacturers over the Edit-function that Mr. O. drew a big red yawning skull next to, in the margin, out of impatience), the Networks were having problems drawing the kind of audiences they needed to justify the ad-rates their huge overhead's slavering maw demanded. The Big Four's arch-foe was America's 100-plus regional and national cable networks, which, in the pre-millennial Limbaugh Era of extraordinarily generous Justice Dept. interpretation of the Sherman statutes, had coalesced into a fractious but potent Trade Association under the stewardship of TCI's Malone, TBS's Turner, and a shadowy Albertan figure who owned the View-Out-the-Simulated-Window-of-Various-Lavish-Homes-in-Exotic-Locales Channel, the Yuletide-Fireplace Channel, CBC-

Cable's Educational Programming Matrix, and four of *Le Groupe Vidéo-tron*'s five big Canadian Shop-at-Home networks. Mounting an aggressive hearts-and-minds campaign that derided the 'passivity' of hundreds of millions of viewers forced to choose nightly between only four statistically pussified Network broadcasters, then extolled the 'empoweringly American choice' of 500-plus esoteric cable options, the American Council of Disseminators of Cable was attacking the Four right at the ideological root, the psychic matrix where viewers had been conditioned (conditioned, rather deliciously, by the Big Four Networks and their advertisers themselves, Hal notes) to associate the Freedom to Choose and the Right to Be Entertained with all that was U.S. and true.

The A.C.D.C. campaign, brilliantly orchestrated by Boston MA's Viney and Veals Advertising, was pummelling the Big Four in the fiscal thorax with its ubiquitous anti-passivity slogan *'Don't Sit Still for Anything Less'* when a wholly unintended coup de grâce to Network viability was delivered in the form of an unrelated Viney and Veals side-venture. V&V, like most U.S. ad agencies, greedily buttered its bread on every conceivable side when it could, and started taking advantage of the plummeting Big Four advertising rates to launch effective Network-ad campaigns for products and services that wouldn't previously have been able to afford national image-proliferation. For the obscure local Nunhagen Aspirin Co. of Framingham MA, Viney and Veals got the Enfield-based National Cranio-Facial Pain Foundation to sponsor a huge touring exhibition of paintings by artists with crippling cranio-facial pain about crippling cranio-facial pain. The resultant Network Nunhagen ads were simply silent 30-second shots of some of the exhibits, with NUNHAGEN ASPIRIN in soothing pale pastels at lower left. The paintings themselves were excruciating, the more so because consumer HDTV had arrived, at least in the very upscale Incandenza home. The ads with the more dental-pain-type paintings Hal doesn't even want to think back on, what with a fragment of cannoli wedged someplace upper-left he keeps looking around for Schacht to ask him to have an angle-mirrored look at. One he can recall was of an ordinary middle-class American guy's regular face, but with a tornado coming out of the right eyesocket and a mouth at the vortex of that tornado, screaming. And that was a mild one.[162] The ads cost next to nothing to produce. Nunhagen Aspirin sales went nationally roofward even as ratings-figures for the Nunhagen ads themselves went from low to abysmal. People found the paintings so excruciating that they were buying the product but recoiling from the ads. Now you'd think this wouldn't matter so long as the product itself was selling so well, this fact that millions of national viewers were zapping or surfing to a different channel with their remotes the moment a silent painted twisted face with a hatchet in its forehead came on. But what made the Nunhagen ads sort of fatally powerful was that they also compromised the ratings-figures for the ads that followed them and for the programs that enclosed the ads, and, worse, were disastrous because they were so violently unpleasing to look at that they awakened from their spectatorial slumbers literally millions of Network-devotees who'd hitherto been so numbed and pacified they usually hadn't bothered to expend the thumb-muscle-energy required to zap or surf away from anything on the screen, awakened legions of these suddenly violently repelled and disturbed viewers to the power and agency their thumbs actually afforded them.

Viney and Veals's next broadcast cash-cow, a lurid series of spots for a national string of walk-in liposuction clinics, reinforced the V&V trend of high product-sales but dreadful ad-ratings; and here the Big Four were really put on the spot, because — even though the critics and P.T.A.s and eating-disorder-oriented distaff PACs were denouncing the LipoVac spots' shots of rippling cellulite and explicit clips of procedures that resembled crosses between hyperbolic Hoover Upright demonstrations and filmed autopsies and cholesterol-conscious cooking shows that involved a great deal of chicken-fat drainage, and even though audiences' flights from the LipoVac spots themselves were absolutely gutting ratings for the other ads and the shows around them — Network execs' sweaty sleep infected with vivid REM-visions of flaccid atrophied thumbs coming twitchily to life over remote zap and surf controls — even though the spots were again fatally potent, the LipoVac string's revenues were so obscenely enhanced by the ads that LipoVac Unltd. could soon afford to pay obscene sums for 30-second Network spots, truly obscene, sums the besieged Four now needed in the very worst way. And so the LipoVac ads ran and ran, and much currency changed hands, and overall Network ratings began to slump as if punctured with something blunt. From a historical perspective it's easy to accuse the Network corporations of being greedy and short-sighted w/r/t explicit liposuction; but Hal argued, with a compassion Mr. Ogilvie found surprising in a seventh-grader, that it's probably hard to be restrained and far-sighted when you're fighting against a malignant invasive V&V-backed cable kabal for your very fiscal life, day to day.

In hindsight, though, the Big Four's spinal camel-straw had to have been V&V's trio of deep-focus b&w spots for a tiny Wisconsin cooperative firm that sold tongue-scrapers by pre-paid mail. These ads just clearly crossed some kind of psychoaesthetic line, regardless of the fact that they single-handedly created a national tongue-scraper industry and put Fond du Lac's NoCoat Inc. on the Fortune 500.[163] Stylistically reminiscent of those murderous mouthwash, deodorant, and dandruff-shampoo scenarios that had an antihero's chance encounter with a gorgeous desire-object ending in repulsion and shame because of an easily correctable hygiene deficiency, the NoCoat spots' chilling emotional force could be located in the exaggerated hideousness of the near-geologic layer of gray-white material coating the tongue of the otherwise handsome pedestrian who accepts a gorgeous meter maid's coquettish invitation to have a bit of a lick of the ice cream cone she's just bought from an avuncular sidewalk vendor. The lingering close-up on an extended tongue that must be seen to be believed, coat-wise. The slow-motion full-frontal shot of the maid's face going slack with disgust as she recoils, the returned cone falling unfelt from her repulsion-paralyzed fingers. The nightmarish slo-mo with which the mortified pedestrian reels away into street-traffic with his whole arm over his mouth, the avuncular vendor's kindly face now hateful and writhing as he hurls hygienic invectives.

These ads shook viewers to the existential core, apparently. It was partly a matter of plain old taste: ad-critics argued that the NoCoat spots were equivalent to like Preparation H filming a procto-exam, or a Depend Adult Undergarment camera panning for floor-puddles at a church social. But Hal's paper located the level at which the Big Four's audiences reacted, here, as way closer to the soul than mere tastelessness can get.

V&V's NoCoat campaign was a case-study in the eschatology of emotional appeals. It towered, a kind of Überad, casting a shaggy shadow back across a whole century of broadcast persuasion. It did what all ads are supposed to do: create an anxiety relievable by purchase. It just did it way more well than wisely, given the vulnerable psyche of an increasingly hygiene-conscious U.S.A. in those times.

The NoCoat campaign had three major consequences. The first was that horrible year Hal vaguely recalls when a nation became obsessed with the state of its tongue, when people would no sooner leave home without a tongue-scraper and an emergency backup tongue-scraper than they'd fail to wash and brush and spray. The year when the sink-and-mirror areas of public restrooms were such grim places to be. The NoCoat co-op folks traded in their B'Gosh overalls and hand-woven ponchos for Armani and Dior, then quickly disintegrated into various eight-figure litigations. But by this time everybody from Procter & Gamble to Tom's of Maine had its own brand's scraper out, some of them with baroque and potentially hazardous electronic extras.

The second consequence was that the Big Four broadcast Networks finally just plain fell off the shelf, fiscally speaking. Riding a crest of public disaffection not seen since the days Jif commercials had strangers shoving their shiny noses in your open jar, the Malone-Turner-and-shadowy-Albertan-led cable kabal got sponsors whose ads had been running as distant as seven or eight spots on either side of the NoCoat gaggers to jump ship to A.C.D.C. U.S. broadcast TV's true angels of death, Malone and Turner then immediately parlayed this fresh injection of sponsorial capital into unrefusable bids for the rights to the N.C.A.A. Final Four, the MLB World Series, Wimbledon, and the Pro Bowlers Tour, at which point the Big Four suffered further defections from Schick and Gillette on one side and

Miller and Bud on the other. Fox filed for Ch. 11 protection Monday after A.C.D.C.'s coup-announcements, and the Dow turned Grizzly indeed on G.E., Paramount, Disney, etc. Within days three out of the Big Four Networks had ceased broadcasting operations, and ABC had to fall back on old 'Happy Days' marathons of such relentless duration that bomb threats began to be received both by the Network and by poor old Henry Winkler, now hairless and sugar-addicted in La Honda CA and seriously considering giving that lurid-looking but hope-provoking LipoVac procedure a try. . . .

And but the ironic third consequence was that almost all the large slick advertising agencies with substantial Network billings — among these the Icarian Viney and Veals — went down, too, in the Big Four's maelstrom, taking with them countless production companies, graphic artists, account execs, computer-enhancement technicians, ruddy-tongued product-spokespersons, horn-rimmed demographers, etc. The millions of citizens in areas for one reason or another not cable-available ran their VCRs into meltdown, got homicidally tired of 'Happy Days,' and then began to find themselves with vast maddening blocks of utterly choiceless and unentertaining time; and domestic-crime rates, as well as out-and-out suicides, topped out at figures that cast a serious pall over the penultimate year of the millennium.

But these consequences' own consequence — with all the Yankee-ingenious irony that attends true resurrections — comes when the now-combined Big Four, muted and unseen, now, but with its remaining creditor-proof assets now supporting only those rapaciously clever executive minds that can survive the cuts down to a skeleton of a skeleton staff, rises from the dust-heap and has a collective last hurrah, ironically deploying V&V's old pro-choice/anti-passivity appeal to obliterate the A.C.D.C. that had just months before obliterated the Big Four, bringing TCI's Malone down on a golden bell-shaped 'chute and sending TBS's Turner into self-imposed nautical exile:

Because enter one Noreen Lace-Forché, the USC-educated video-rental mogulette who in the B.S. '90s had taken Phoenix's Intermission Video chain from the middle of the Sun Belt pack to a national distribution second only to Blockbuster Entertainment in gross receipts. The woman called by Microsoft's Gates 'The Killer-App Queen' and by Blockbuster's Huizenga 'The only woman I personally fear.'

Convincing the rapacious skeletal remains of the Big Four to consolidate its combined production, distribution, and capital resources behind a front company she'd had incorporated and idling ever since she'd first foreseen broadcast apocalypse in the Nunhagen ads' psycho-fiscal fallout — the front an obscure-sounding concern called InterLace TelEntertainment — Lace-Forché then went and persuaded ad-maestro P. Tom Veals — at that time mourning his remorse-tortured partner's half-gainer off the Tobin

Bridge by drinking himself toward pancreatitis in a Beacon Hill brownstone — to regather himself and orchestrate a profound national dissatisfaction with the 'passivity' involved even in D.S.S.-based *cable*-watching:

What matter whether your 'choices' are 4 or 104, or 504? Veals's campaign argued. Because here you were — assuming of course you were even cable-ready or dish-equipped and able to afford monthly fees that applied no matter what you 'chose' each month — here you were, sitting here accepting only what was pumped by distant A.C.D.C. fiat into your entertainment-ken. Here you were consoling yourself about your dependence and passivity with rapid-fire zapping and surfing that were starting to be suspected to cause certain rather nasty types of epilepsy over the longish term. The cable kabal's promise of 'empowerment,' the campaign argued, was still just the invitation to choose which of 504 visual spoon-feedings you'd sit there and open wide for.[164] And so but *what if,* their campaign's appeal basically ran, what if, instead of sitting still for choosing the least of 504 infantile evils, the vox- and digitus-populi could choose to make its home entertainment literally and essentially *adult?* I.e. what if — according to InterLace — what if a viewer could more or less *100% choose what's on at any given time?* Choose and rent, over PC and modem and fiber-optic line, from tens of thousands of second-run films, documentaries, the occasional sport, old beloved non–'Happy Days' programs, wholly new programs, cultural stuff, and c., all prepared by the time-tested, newly lean Big Four's mammoth vaults and production facilities and packaged and disseminated by InterLace TelEnt. in convenient fiber-optic pulses that fit directly on the new palm-sized 4.8-mb PC-diskettes InterLace was marketing as 'cartridges'? Viewable right there on your trusty PC's high-resolution monitor? Or, if you preferred and so chose, jackable into a good old premillennial wide-screen TV with at most a coaxial or two? Self-selected programming, chargeable on any major card or on a special low-finance-charge InterLace account available to any of the 76% of U.S. households possessed of PC, phone line, and verifiable credit? What if, Veals's spokeswoman ruminated aloud, what if the viewer could become her/his *own* programming director; what if s/he could *define* the very entertainment-happiness it was her/his right to pursue?

The rest, for Hal, is recent history.

By the time not only second-run Hollywood releases but a good many first-run films, plus new sitcoms and crime-dramas and near-live sports, plus now also big-name-anchor nightly newscasts, weather, art, health, and financial-analysis cartridges were available and pulsing nicely onto cartridges everywhere, the ranks of A.C.D.C.'s own solvent program-pumpers had been winnowed back to the old-movie-and-afternoon-baseball major-metro regional systems of more like the B.S. '80s. Passive pickings were slim now. American mass-entertainment became inherently pro-active, consumer-driven. And because advertisements were now out of the tele-visual question — any halfway-sensitive Power-PC's CPU could edit out anything shrill or ungratifying in the post-receipt Review Function of an entertainment-diskette — cartridge production (meaning by now both the satellitic 'spontaneous dissemination' of viewer-selected menu-programming and the factory-recording of programming on packaged 9.6 mb diskettes available cheap and playable on any CD-ROM-equipped system) yes cartridge production — though tentacularly controlled by an InterLace that had patented the digital-transmission process for moving images and held more stock than any one of the five Baby Bells involved in the InterNet fiber-optic transmission-grid bought for .17 on the dollar from GTE after Sprint went belly-up trying to launch a primitively naked early mask- and Tableauxless form of videophony — became almost Hobbes-ianly free-market. No more Network reluctance to make a program too entertaining for fear its commercials would pale in comparison. The more pleasing a given cartridge was, the more orders there were for it from viewers; and the more orders for a given cartridge, the more InterLace kicked back to whatever production facility they'd acquired it from. Simple. Personal pleasure and gross revenue looked at last to lie along the same demand curve, at least as far as home entertainment went.

And as InterLace's eventual outright purchase of the Networks' produc-tion talent and facilities, of two major home-computer conglomerates, of the cutting-edge Froxx 2100 CD-ROM licenses of Aapps Inc., of RCA's D.S.S. orbiters and hardware-patents, and of the digital-compatible patents to the still-needing-to-come-down-in-price-a-little technology of HDTV's visually enhanced color monitor with microprocessed circuitry and $2^{(\sqrt{area})}$! more lines of optical resolution — as these acquisitions allowed Noreen Lace-Forché's cartridge-dissemination network to achieve vertical integration and economies of scale, viewers' pulse-reception- and cartridge-fees went down markedly;[165] and then the further increased revenues from consequent increases in order- and rental-volume were plowed presciently back into more fiber-optic-InterGrid-cable-laying, into outright purchase of three of the five Baby Bells InterNet'd started with, into extremely attractive rebate-offers on special new InterLace-designed R.I.S.C.[166]-grade High-Def-screen PCs with mimetic-resolution cartridge-view motherboards (re-cognizably renamed by Veals's boys in Recognition 'Teleputers' or 'TPs'), into fiber-only modems, and, of course, into extremely high-quality enter-tainments that viewers would freely desire to choose even more.[167]

But there were — could be — no ads of any kind in the InterLace pulses or ROM cartridges, was the point Hal's presentation kept struggling to re-turn to. And so then besides e.g. a Turner who kept litigating bitterly via shortwave radio from his equatorial yacht, the true loser in the shift from

A.C.D.C. cable to InterLace Grid was an American advertising industry already reeling from the death of broadcast's Big Four. No significant markets seemed in any hurry to open up and compensate for the capping of TV's old gusher. Agencies, reduced to skeletal cells of their best and most rapacious creative minds, cast wildly about for new pulses to finger and niches to fill. Billboards sprouted with near-mycological fury alongside even rural two-laners. No bus, train, trolley, or hack went unfestooned with high-gloss ads. Commercial airliners began for a while to trail those terse translucent ad-banners usually reserved for like Piper Cubs over football games and July beaches. Magazines (already endangered by HD-video equivalents) got so full of those infuriating little fall-out ad cards that Fourth-Class postal rates ballooned, making the e-mail of their video-equivalents that much more attractive, in another vicious spiral. Chicago's once-vaunted Sickengen, Smith and Lundine went so far as to get Ford to start painting little domestic-product come-ons on their new lines' side-panels, an idea that fizzled as U.S. customers in Nike T-shirts and Marlboro caps perversely refused to invest in 'cars that sold out.' In contrast to just about the whole rest of the industry, a certain partnerless metro-Boston ad agency was doing so well that it was more out of ennui and a sense of unlikely challenge that P. Tom Veals consented to manage PR for the fringe candidacy of a former crooner and schmaltz-mogul who went around swinging a mike and ranting about literally clean streets and creatively refocused blame and rocketing people's waste into the forgiving chill of infinite space.[168]

30 APRIL / 1 MAY
YEAR OF THE DEPEND ADULT UNDERGARMENT

Marathe did not quite sleep. They had remained on the shelf for some hours. He thought it a bit of much that Steeply refused even for a brief time to sit down upon the ground. If his persona's skirt rode up above his weapon, what was the difference? Were grotesque and humiliating undergarments also involved? Marathe's wife had been in an irreversible coma for fourteen months. Marathe was able to refresh himself without quite sleeping. It was not a state of fugue or neural relaxation, but a type of detachment. He had learned this in the months after losing his legs to a U.S.A. train. Part of Marathe floated off and hovered somewhere just above him, crossing its legs, nibbling at his consciousness as does a spectator at popcorn.

At some times on the outcropping Steeply went farther than crossing his arms, almost embracing himself, chilled but unwilling to comment on the chill. Marathe noted that the gesture of self-embrace appeared convincingly feminine and unconscious. Steeply's preparations for his returning field-assignment had been disciplined and effective. The feature of complete un-swallowability about M. Steeply as a U.S.A. female journalist — even a massive and unfortunate-looking U.S.A. female journalist — was his feet. These were broad and yellow-nailed, hairy and trollesque, the ugliest feet Marathe had observed anywhere south of 60° N, and the ugliest supposedly female feet of his experience.

Both men were strangely reluctant, somehow, to broach the subject of plans for getting down off the shelf in the utter dark. Steeply didn't even waste time wondering how Marathe could have gotten up (or down) there in the first place, short of some sort of helicopter drop, which capricious winds and the proximity of the mountainside made unlikely. The dogma around Unspecified Services was that if *Les Assassins des Fauteuils Rollents* had one Achilles' heel it was their penchant for showing off, making a spec-tacle of denying any kind of physical limitation, etc. Steeply had field-interfaced with Rémy Marathe once on a rickety-feeling Louisiana oil plat-form 50-plus clicks out of Caillou Bay, covered the whole time by armed Cajun sympathizers. Marathe always disguised the boggling size of his arms under a long-sleeved windbreaker. His eyelids were half-closed whenever Steeply turned to look. If he (Marathe) were a cat he would be purring. One hand stayed below the blanket at all times, Steeply noted. Steeply himself had a small and unregistered Taurus PT9 taped to his shaved inner thigh, which was the main reason he was reluctant to sit down on the outcrop-ping's stone; the weapon was unsafetied.

In the faint lume- and starlight Marathe found the four-limbed Ameri-can's high-heeled feet compellingly grotesque, like loaves of soft processed U.S.A. bread being slowly squeezed and mangled by the footwear's straps. The meaty compression of the toes at the shoes' open tips, the leather faintly creaking as he bobbed up and down, hugging himself chillily in the sleeve-less summer dress, his fleshy bare arms webbed redly with mottle in the chill, one arm luridly scratched. The received wisdom among Québecois anti-O.N.A.N. cells was that there was something latent and sadistic in the *Bureau des Services sans Spécificité*'s assignments of fictional personae for its field-operatives — casting men as women, women as longshoremen or Orthodox rabbinicals, heterosexual men as homosexual men, Caucasians as Negroes or caricaturesque Haitians and Dominicans, healthy males as degenerative-nerve-disease-sufferers, healthy women operatives as hydro-cephalic boys or epileptic public-relations executives, nondeformed U.S.O.U.S. personnel made not only to pretend but sometimes to actually suffer actual deformity, all for the realism of their field-personae. Steeply, silent, rose and fell absently on the toes of these feet. The feet were also visibly unused to high U.S.A. women's heels, for they were mangled-looking, deprived of flowing blood and abundantly blistered, and the smallest toes' nails were blackening and preparing, Marathe noted, in the future to fall off.

But Marathe knew also that something within the real M. Hugh Steeply did need the humiliations of his absurd field-personae, that the more grotesque or unconvincing he seemed likely to be as a disguised persona the more nourished and actualized his deep parts felt in the course of preparation for the humiliating attempt to portray; he (Steeply) used the mortification he felt as a huge woman or pale Negro or palsied twit of a degenerate musician as fuel for the assignments' performance; Steeply welcomed the subsumption of his dignity and self in the very *rôle* that offended his dignity of self ... the psychomechanics became too confusing for Marathe, who had not the capacity for abstractions of his A.F.R. superiors Fortier and Broullîme. But he knew this was why Steeply was one of *Services sans Spécificité*'s finest field-operatives, once spending the better part of a year in magenta robes, sleeping three hours nightly and allowing his large head to be shaved and teeth removed, shaking a tambourine in airports and selling plastic flowers on median strips to infiltrate a cult-fronted 3-amino-8-hydroxytetralin[169]-import ring in the U.S.A. city Seattle.

Steeply said 'Because this is the thing about the A.F.R. that really gives them the fantods, if you're talking about fear and what to fear.' He spoke either quietly or not, that Marathe could determine. The empty expanse they both faced off the shelf sucked all resonance, causing every sound to sound self-enclosed and every utterance to seem flatly soft and somehow overintimate, almost post-coital. The sounds of things said beneath blankets, winter beating at the log walls. Steeply himself appeared frightened, perhaps, or confused. He continued: 'This disinterest, by you guys, it seems, in anything but the harm itself. Just getting the Entertainment out there to hurt us.'

'The naked aggression by us.'

Muscles beneath the nylons of the calves bulged and receded as Steeply bobbed. 'The boys in Behavioral Science say they can't see any sort of positive political goal the A.F.R. even wants. Anything DuPlessis was having your Fortier work toward.'

'The U.S.A. *fantods* are meaning fear, confusion, standing hair.'

'The F.L.Q. and Montcalmists — shit, even the most whacked out of Alberta's ultra-rightists —'

M. DuPlessis had once studied beneath radical Edmonton Jesuits, Marathe reflected.

'— them we can begin to understand, as political bodies. Them we can more or less get a feel for dealing with.'

'Their aggression is clothed in agenda, the Bureau of you perceives.'

Steeply's was a thinking face now, in apparent puzzlement. 'They at least have aims. Real desires.'

'For themselves.'

Steeply appeared convincingly to ruminate. 'It's like there's a context for the whole game, then, with them. We know where where we stand differs from where they stand. There's a sort of playing field of context.'

Causing the chair to squeak, Marathe again rotated two fingers of a hand in the air, which for Québecers signifies impatience. 'Rules of play. Rules of engagement.' The other hand was with the Sterling UL machine pistol beneath the blanket.

'Even historically — the 60s bomb-tossers, the Spic Separatists, the Ragheads —'

'Very charming. These are attractive terms.'

'Ragheads, Colombians, Brazilians — they had positive objectives.'

'Desires for self which you could understand.'

'Even if the objectives were nothing more than things we could file, pin to the board under "STATED OBJECTIVES" — the pathetic Spics. They wanted certain things. There was a context. A compass for maneuvers against them.'

'Your guardians of National Security could understand these positive desires of self-interest. Look at them and "relate" as one says, at least. Knowing where you stand on the field of play.'

Steeply slowly nodded, as if to only himself. 'There wasn't just pure malice. There was never the sense that here were some people who had just all of a sudden let the air out of your tires for no reason.'

'You allege we disperse our resources deflating automobile tires?'

'A figure of speech. Or for example a serial killer. A sadist. Somebody who wants you down just for the deviant sake of wanting you down. A deviant.'

Far south, a blinking system of tri-colored lights described a spiral over the airport's tower's pulsing tip — this was a landing aircraft.

Steeply lit another cigarette off the butt of his previous and then tossed the butt, peering over the shelf's edge to watch its spiralled fall. Marathe was looking up and right. Steeply said:

'Because politics are one thing. Even way-out-far-in-the-distance fringe politics are one thing. Your Fortier doesn't seem to care much about Reconfiguration, territory, redemisement, cartography, tariffs, Finlandization, O.N.A.N.ite Anschluss or toxic-waste displacement.'

'Experialism.'

Steeply said 'Or so-called Experialism. Even Separatism. None of the other cells' agendas seem to drive you people. Most of the Office sees it as just sheer malice with you. No agenda or story.'

'And for you there is something appalling.'

Steeply pursed his lips, as if trying to blow something off them. 'But when there are delineatable strategic political goals and objectives. When there's some set of ends we can make sense of the malice with. Then it's just business.'

'Nothing of persons.' Marathe was looking up. Some of the stars seemed to flutter, others to burn with more steadiness.

'We know which end is up when it's business. We've got a field and a compass.' He regarded Marathe directly in a way that was not accusing. 'This seems personal,' he said.

Marathe could not think of descriptions for the way Steeply regarded him. Neither was it sad nor inquisitive nor quite ruminative. There were small flickers and shadows of movements around the flickers of the celebratory fire down far away on the floor of the desert. Marathe could not determine whether Steeply was truly revealing emotions about himself. The flickers continually went out. Small shreds of young laughter drifted up to them in the vacuous silence. There were also sometimes rustles in the hillside's scrub, of gravel or small living nightly things. Or whether perhaps Steeply was trying to give him something, let him know something and determine whether it went back to M. Fortier. Marathe's arrangement with the Office of Unspecified Services seemed most often to consist in submitting himself to numerous tests and games of truth and betrayal. He felt often with U.S.O.U.S. like a caged rodent being regarded blandly by bland men in white coats.

Marathe shrugged. 'U.S.A. has previously been hated. Richly so. Shining Path and your Maxwell House company. The trans-Latin cocaine cartels and the poor late M. Kemp with his exploding home. Did not both Iraq and Iran call U.S.A. the Very Large Satan? As you hatefully say they have Heads of Rags?'

Steeply exhumed smoke quickly to reply. 'Yes but there were still contexts and ends. Revenue, religion, spheres of influence, Israel, petroleum, neo-Marxism, post-Cold-War power-jockeying. There was always a third thing.'

'Some desire.'

'Some piece of business. Some third thing between them and us — it wasn't just *us* — it was something they wanted from us, or wanted us out of.' Steeply seemed earnestly to say it. 'The third thing, the goal or desire — it mediated the ill will, abstracted it somehow.'

'For this is how one who is sane proceeds,' Marathe said, paying great concentration to aligning the blanket's hems against his chest and wheels; 'some desire of self, and efforts expending to meet that desire.'

'Not just wanting negatives,' Steeply said, shaking the lurid head. 'Not just wanting some other's harm for no purpose.'

Marathe again found himself pretending to sniff with the congestion. 'And a U.S.A. purpose, desires?' This he asked quietly; its sound was strange against stone.

Steeply was pinching yet a next particle of tobacco from his lipstick. He said 'This you can't generalize on with most of us, since our whole system is founded on your individual's freedom to pursue his own individual desires.' His mascara had now cooled in the formations of its past running. Marathe kept silent and fussed with the blanket as Steeply sometimes regarded him. A whole minute passed this way. Finally Steeply said:

'Me, for me personally, as an American, Rémy, if you're really serious, I think it's probably your standard old basic American dreams and ideals. Freedom from tyranny, from excessive want, fear, censorship of speech and thought.' He was looking with seriousness, even in this wig. 'The old ones, tested by time. Relative plenty, meaningful work, adequate leisure-time. The ones you might call corny.' His smiling revealed to Marathe lipstick upon one incisor. 'We want choice. A sense of efficaciousness and choice. To be loved by someone. To freely love who you happen to love. To be loved irregardless of whether you can tell them Classified stuff about your job. To have them just trust you and trust that you know what you're doing. To feel valued. Not to be agendalessly despised. To have good neighborly relations. Cheap and abundant energy. Pride in your work and family, and home.' The lipstick had been smeared onto the tooth when the finger had removed the grain of tobacco. He was *'faisait monter la pression'*:[170] 'The little things. Access to transport. Good digestion. Work-saving appliances. A wife who doesn't mistake your job's requirements for your own fetishes. Reliable waste-removal and disposal. Sunsets over the Pacific. Shoes that don't cut off circulation. Frozen yogurt. A tall lemonade on a squeak-free porch swing.'

Marathe's face, it showed nothing. 'The loyalty of a domestic pet.'

Steeply pointed the cigarette. 'There you go, friend.'

'High-quality entertainment. High value for the dollar of leisure and spectation.'

Steeply laughed agreeably, exhaling a shaped sausage of smoke. In response to this, Marathe smiled. There was some silence for thinking until Marathe finally said, looking up and off to think: 'This U.S.A. type of person and desires appears to me like almost the classic, how do you say, *utilitaire.*'

'A French appliance?'

'Comme on dit,' Marathe said, '*utilitarienne*. Maximize pleasure, minimize displeasure: result: what is good. This is the U.S.A. of you.'

Steeply pronounced the U.S.A. English word for Marathe, then. Then a sustained pause. Steeply rose and fell upon his toes. A bonfire of young persons was burning some k. down away on the desert floor, the flames burning in a seeming ring instead of a sphere.

Marathe said 'But yes, but precisely whose pleasure and whose pain, in this personality type's equation of what is good?'

When Steeply removed a particle of the cigarette from the lip he would then roll it absently between his first finger and thumb; this did not appear womanly. 'Come again?'

Marathe scratched inside the windbreaker. 'I am wondering, me, in the equations of this U.S.A. type: the best good is each individual U.S.A. person's maximum pleasure? or it is the maximum pleasure for all the people?'

Steeply nodded in a way that indicated willing patience with someone whose wits were not too speedy. 'But there you go, but this question itself shows how our different types of national character part ways from each other, Rémy. The American genius, our good fortune is that someplace along the line back there in American history them realizing that each American seeking to pursue his maximum good results together in maximizing *everyone's* good.'

'Ah.'

'We learn this as early as grade school, as kids.'

'I am seeing.'

'This is what lets us steer free of oppression and tyranny. Even your Greekly democratic howling-mob-type tyranny. The United States: a community of sacred individuals which reveres the sacredness of the individual choice. The individual's right to pursue his own vision of the best ratio of pleasure to pain: utterly sacrosanct. Defended with teeth and bared claws all through our history.'

'Bien sûr.'

Steeply for the first time seemed to be feeling with his hand his wig's disorder. He was attempting to straightly reposition it without removing the wig. Marathe tried not to envision what his B.S.S. had done to the natural brown male hair of Steeply, to accommodate the complex wig. Steeply said: 'It might be hard for you to quite understand what's so precious about this for us, from across this chasm of different values that separates our peoples.'

Marathe flexed his hand. 'Perhaps because it is so general and abstracted. In practice, however, you may force me to understand.'

'We don't force. It's exactly about *not*-forcing, our history's genius. You are entitled to your values of maximum pleasure. So long as you don't fuck with mine. Are you seeing?'

'Perhaps help me see by practical evidence. An instance. Suppose you are able at one moment to increase your own pleasure, but the cost of this is the displeasuring pain of another? Another sacred individual's displeasing pain.'

Steeply said: 'Well now this is precisely what gives us the fantods about the A.F.R., why it's so important I think to remember how we come from different cultures and value systems, Rémy. Because in our U.S. value system, anybody who derives an increase in pleasure from somebody else's pain is a deviant, a sadistic sicko, and is thereby excluded from the community of everybody's right to pursue their own best pleasure-to-pain ratio.

Sickos deserve compassion and the best treatment feasible. But they're not part of the big picture.'

Marathe willed himself not to rise on his stumps again. 'No, but not another's pain as a pleasurable end in itself. I did not mean where my pleasure is in your pain. How to say better. Imagine there arises a situation in which your deprivation or pain is merely the consequence, the price, of my own pleasure.'

'You mean you're talking a tough-choices, limited-resources-type situation.'

'But in the simplest of examples. The most child-like case.' Marathe's eyes momentarily gleamed with enthusiasm. 'Suppose that you and I, we both wish to enjoy a hot bowl of the Habitant *soupe aux pois*.'

Steeply said 'You mean. . .'

'But yes. French-Canadian-type pea soup. *Produit du Montréal. Saveur Maison. Prête à Servir.*'[171]

'What *is* it with you people and this stuff?'

'In this case imagining both you and I are in the worst way craving for Habitant Soup. But there is one can only, of the small and well-known Single-Serving Size.'

'An American invention, by the way, the 3-S, let's insert.'

The part of Marathe's mind that hovered above and watched coldly, it could not know whether Steeply was being deliberately parodically dense and annoying, to arouse Marathe to some revealing passion. Marathe made his rotary gesture of impatience, slowly. 'But OK,' he said neutrally. 'It is simple here. We both want the soup. So me, my pleasure from eating the Habitant *soupe aux pois* has the price of your pain at not eating soup when you badly crave it.' Marathe was patting his pockets for something. 'And the reverse, if you are who eats this serving. By the U.S.A. genius of for each "*pursuivre le bonheur*,"[172] then, who can decide who may receive this soup?'

Steeply stood with weight on one leg. 'Example's a bit oversimplified. We bid on the soup, maybe. We negotiate. Maybe we divide the soup.'

'No, for the ingenious Single-Serving Size of serving is notoriously for only one, and we are both large and vigorous U.S.A. individuals who have spent the afternoon watching huge men in pads and helmets hurl themselves at one another in the High Definition of InterLace, and we are both ravenous for the satiation of a complete hot bowl's serving. Half the bowl would only torment this craving I have.'

The fast shadow of pain across the face of Steeply showed Marathe's choice of example was witty: the divorced U.S.A. man has much experience with the small size of Single-Serving products. Marathe said:

'OK. OK, yes, why should I, as the sacred individual, give you half of my soup? My *own* pleasure over torment is what is good, for I am a loyal U.S.A., a genius of this individual desire.'

The bonfire slowly was filling out. Another cross of colored lights circled the airport area of Tucson. Steeply's movements of smoothing the wig and twisting fingers through the snarls of hair became perhaps more abrupt and frustrated. Steeply said 'Well whose soup is it legally? Who actually bought the soup?'

Marathe shrugged. 'Not relevant for my question. Suppose a third party, now unfortunately deceased. He appears at our flat with a can of *soupe aux pois* to eat while watching recorded U.S.A. sporting and suddenly is clutching his heart and falls to the carpeting deceased, holding the soup we are now both so wishing.'

'Then we bid on the soup. Whoever's got the most desire for the soup and is willing to fork over the higher price buys out the other's half, then the other just jogs on down — jogs or rolls on down to Safeway and buys himself some more soup. Whoever's willing to put his money where his hunger is gets the dead guy's soup.'

Marathe shook his head without any heat. 'The Safeway store and bidding, these are also not relevant to my question I hope the example of pea soup to raise. Which perhaps this is a dull-witted question.'

Steeply was at the wig with both hands, for repair. Former perspiration had mashed its form inward on one side, as well as small clots and small burrs from the falls of his descent to the outcropping. Presumably there was no comb or brushes in his small evening's-wear purse. The rear of his dress was dirty. The straps of his prostheses' brassiere dug cruelly into the meat of his back and shoulders. Again there was for Marathe the picture of something soft being slowly throttled.

Steeply was responding 'No, I know what you want to raise all right. You want to talk politics. Scarcity and allocating and tough choices. All right. Politics we can understand. All right. Politics we can discuss. I bet I know where you're — you want to raise the question of what prevents 310 million individual American happiness-pursuers from all going around bonking each other over the head and taking each other's soup. A state of nature. My own pleasure and to hell with all the rest.'

Marathe had his handkerchief out. 'What does this wish to mean, this *bonking?*'

'Because this simplistic example shows just how far apart across the chasm our people's values are, friend.' Steeply was saying this. 'Because a certain basic amount of respect for the wishes of other people is required, is in my interest, in order to preserve a community where my own wishes and interests are respected. OK? My total and overall happiness is maximized by respecting your individual sanctity and not simply kicking you in the knee and running off with the soup.' Steeply watched Marathe blow one nostril into the handkerchief. Marathe was one of the rare types who did not examine the hankie after he blew. Steeply said:

'And but then I can anticipate somebody on your side of the chasm retorting with something like, quote, Yes my very good *ami,* but what if your rival for the pleasurable soup is some individual *outside* your community, for example, you'll say, let's just make the example that it a hapless Canadian, foreign, *"un autre,"* separated from me by a chasm of history and language and value and deep respect for individual freedom — then in this wholly random instance there would be no community-minded constraints on my natural impulse to bonk your head and commandeer the desired soup, since the poor Canadian is outside the equation of *"pursuivre le bonheur"* of each individual, since he is not a part of the community whose environment of mutual respect I depend on for pursuing my interest of maximal pleasure-to-pain.'

Marathe, during this time, was smiling up and to the left, north, rolling his head like a blind person. His favorite personal place of off-duty in the U.S.A.'s city Boston was in the Public Garden of summer, a broad and treeless declivity leading down to the *mare des canards,* the duck pond, a grassy wedge facing south and west so that the grass of the slope turns pale green and then gold as the sun circles over the head, the pond's water cool and muddy green and overhung with impressionist willows, persons beneath the willows, also pigeons, and ducks with tight emerald heads gliding in circles, their eyes round stones, moving as if without effort, gliding upon the water as if legless below. Like films' idylls in cities the moment before the nuclear blast, in old films of U.S.A. death and horror. He was missing this time in U.S.A. Boston MA of refilling the pond for the ducks' return, the willows greening, the winelight of a northern sunset curving gently in to land without explosion. Children flew taut kites and adults lay supine on the slope absorbing the suntan, eyes closed as if in concentration. He was giving out a small and desolate smile, as of fatigue. His wrist's watch was unilluminated. Steeply threw a butt without turning away from Marathe to watch it fall.

'And you'll accuse me of you'll say I won't only poke him in the eye and commandeer the whole serving of soup for myself,' Steeply said, 'but will, after eating it, I'll give him the dirty bowl and spoon and maybe even the no-deposit Habitant can to have to deal with, saddle him with my greed's waste, all under some sham-arrangement of quote Interdependence that's really just a crude nationalist scheme to indulge my own U.S. individual pleasure-lust without the complications or annoyance of considering some neighbor's own desires and interests.'

Marathe said 'You will notice that I do not with sarcasm say "*And herrrrrrrrre we go off together once more,*" which you enjoy saying.'

Steeply's use of the body to shelter the lighting match for his smoking was not feminine, either. His parody of Marathe's accent sounded guttural and U.S.A.-Cajun with the cigarette in the mouth. He looked up past the flame. 'But no? Am I off-base?'

Marathe had an almost Buddhist way of studying the blanket on his lap.

For some seconds he behaved as if almost asleep, nodding very smally with the rise and fall of his lungs. The ponderous rectangles of moving light within Tucson's nightly spread were 'Barges of Land' ministering to nests of dumpsters in the deep part of night. Part of Marathe always felt almost a desire to shoot persons who anticipated his responses and inserted words and said they were from Marathe, not letting him speak. Marathe suspected Steeply of knowing this, sensing this in Marathe. All two of Marathe's older brothers from childhood had engaged in this, arguing every side and silencing Rémy by inserting his words. Both had kissed trains head-on before reaching marriageable age;[173] Marathe had been part of the audience for the death of the better one. Some of the Barges of Land's waste would be vectored into the Sonora region of Mexico, but much would be shipped north for displacement-launch into the Convexity. Steeply was regarding him.

'No, Rémy? Am I off-base in terms of what you'd say?'

The smile around Marathe's mouth cost him all his training in restraint. 'The cans containing Habitant, they say boldly "*Veuillez Recycler Ce Contenant.*" You are not false, maybe. But I think I am asking less for nations' arguing and more for the example of you and me only, we two, if we pretend we are both of your U.S.A. type, each separate, both sacred, both desiring *soupe aux pois.* I am asking how is community and your respect part of my happiness in this moment, with the soup, if I am a U.S.A. person?'

Steeply worked a finger under one strap of the brassiere to relieve the throttling pressure. 'I don't get you.'

'Well. We both crave badly the entire recyclable Single-Serving can of this Habitant.' Marathe sniffed. 'In my mind I know it is true that I must not simply make a bonking of your head and take away the soup, because my overall happiness of pleasure of the long term needs a community of "*rien de bonk.*"[174] But this is the long term, Steeply. This is down the road of my happiness, this respecting of you. How do I calculate this distant road of long term into my action of this moment, now, with our dead comrade clutching the soup and both of us with spittle on our chins as we regard the soup? My question is trying to say: if the most pleasure right now, *en ce moment,* is in the whole serving of Habitant, how is my self able to put aside this moment's desire to make bonk on you and take this soup? How am I able to think past this soup to the future of soup down my road?'

'In other words delayed gratification.'

'Good. This is well. Delayed gratification. How is my U.S.A. type able in my mind to calculate my long-term overall pleasure, then decide to sacrifice this intense soup-craving of this moment to the long term and overall?'

Steeply sent out two hard tusks of smoke from the nostrils of his nose. His expression was one of patience together with polite impatience. 'I think it's called simply being a mature and adult American instead of a childish and immature American. A term we might use might be "enlightened self-interest." '

'*D'éclaisant.*'

Steeply, he did not smile back. 'Enlightened. For example your example from before. The little kid who'll eat candy all day because it's what tastes best at each individual moment.'

'Even if he knows inside his mind that it will hurt his stomach and rot his little fangs.'

'Teeth,' Steeply corrected. 'But see that here it can't be a Fascist matter of screaming at the kid or giving him electric shocks each time he overindulges in candy. You can't induce a moral sensibility the same way you'd train a rat. The kid has to learn by his own experience how to learn to balance the short- and long-term pursuit of what he wants.'

'He must be *freely* enlightened to self.'

'This is the crux of the educational system you find so appalling. Not to teach what to desire. To teach how to be free. To teach how to make knowledgeable choices about pleasure and delay and the kid's overall down-the-road maximal interests.'

Marathe farted mildly into his cushion, nodding as if with thought.

'And I know what you'll say,' Steeply said, 'and no, the system isn't perfect. There is greed, there is crime, there are drugs and cruelty and ruin and infidelity and divorce and suicide. Murder.'

'To bonk the head.'

Steeply again dug at this strap. He would snap open the purse and then pause to move the brassiere's tight strap and then dig into the purse, which sounded femininely full and cluttered. He said 'But this is just the price. This is the price of the free pursuit. Not everybody learns it in childhood, how to balance his interests.'

Marathe tried to envision thin men with horn-rim spectacles and natural-shoulder sportcoats or white coats of the laboratory, carefully packing with clutter the purse of a field-operative to create the female effect. Now Steeply had his pack of Flanderfumes cigarettes and his finger of pinkie in the pack's hole, evidently trying to gauge how many were left. Venus was low in the northeast rim. When Marathe's wife was born as an infant without a skull, there had been at first suspicion that the cause was that her parents smoked cigarettes as a habit. The light of the stars and moon had become sullen. The moon had not yet set. It seemed as if sometimes the bonfire of youthful mafficking was there and then when the eyes were averted in the next moment it was not there. Time was passing in a silence. Steeply was using a nail to extract slowly one of the cigarettes. Marathe, as a small child and with legs, had always disliked persons who made comments about how much others smoked. Steeply now had learned here just how he must stand to keep the match alive. Some wind had died down, but there were scattered chill gusts that it seemed came from nowhere. Marathe sniffed so deeply that it became a sigh. The struck match sounded loud; there was no echo.

Marathe sniffed again and said:

'But of these types of your persons — the different types, the mature who see down the road, the puerile type that eats the candy and soup in the moment only. *Entre nous,* here on this shelf, Hugh Steeply: which do you think describes the U.S.A. of O.N.A.N. and the Great Convexity, this U.S.A. you feel pain that others might wish to harm?' Hands which shake out matches act always as if they are burned, this motion of snapping. Marathe sniffed. 'Are you understanding? I am asking between only us. How could it be that A.F.R. malice could hurt all of the U.S.A. culture by making available something as momentary and free as the choice to view only this one Entertainment? You know there can be no forcing to watch a thing. If we disseminate the *samizdat,* the choice will be free, no? Free from force, no? Yes? Freely chosen?'

M. Hugh Steeply of B.S.S. was standing then with his weight on one hip and looked his most female when he smoked, with his elbow in his arm and the hand to his mouth and the back of this hand to Marathe, a type of fussy ennui that reminded Marathe of women in hats and padded shoulders in black-and-white films, smoking. Marathe said:

'You believe we are underestimating to see all you as selfish, decadent. But the question has been raised: are we cells of Canada alone in this view? Aren't you afraid, you of your government and gendarmes? If not, your B.S.S., why work so hard to prevent dissemination? Why make a simple Entertainment, no matter how seducing its pleasures, a *samizdat* and forbidden in the first place, if you do not fear so many U.S.A.s cannot make the enlightened choices?'

This now was the closest large Steeply had come, to stand over Marathe to look down, looming. The rising astral body Venus lit his left side of the face to the color of pallid cheese. 'Get real. The Entertainment isn't candy or beer. Look at Boston just now. You can't compare this kind of insidious enslaving process to your little cases of sugar and soup.'

Marathe smiled bleakly into the chiaroscuro flesh of this round and hairless U.S.A. face. 'Perhaps the facts are true, after the first watching: that then there seems to be no choice. But to decide to be this pleasurably entertained in the first place. This is still a choice, no? Sacred to the viewing self, and free? No? Yes?'

During that last pre-Subsidized year, after each tournament's perfunctory final, at the little post-final award-presentations and dance, Eric Clipperton would attend unarmed and eat maybe a little shaved turkey from the buffet and mutter out of the side of his slot-like mouth to Mario Incandenza, and would stand there expressionless and receive his outsized first-place trophy amid witheringly slight and scattered applause, and would melt into the crowd soon after and dematerialize back to wherever he lived and trained and target-practiced. Clipperton by this time must have had a whole mantel plus bookcase's worth of tall U.S.T.A. trophies, each U.S.T.A. trophy a marbled plastic base with a tall metal boy on top arched in mid-serve, looking rather like a wedding-cake groom with a very good outside slider. Clipperton must have been just broke out in brass and plastic, but he had no official ranking whatsoever: since his Glock 9 mm. and public intentions were instantly legendary, he was regarded by the U.S.T.A. as never having had a legitimate victory, or even a legit match, in sanctioned play. People on the jr. tour sometimes asked tiny Mario if that's why Eric Clipperton always seemed so terrifically glum and withdrawn and made such a big deal out of materializing and dematerializing at tournaments, that the very tactic that let him win in the first place kept the wins, and in a way Clipperton himself, from being treated as real.

All this until the erection of O.N.A.N. and the inception, in Clipperton's eighteenth summer, of Subsidized Time, the adverted Year of the Whopper, when the U.S.T.A. became the O.N.A.N.T.A, and some Mexican systems analyst — who barely spoke English and had never once even fondled a ball and knew from exactly zilch except for crunching raw results-data — this guy stepped in as manager of the O.N.A.N.T.A. computer and ranking center in Forest Lawn NNY, and didn't know enough not to treat Clipperton's string of six major junior-tournament championships that spring as sanctioned and real. And when the first biweekly issue of the trilingual *North American Junior Tennis* that's replaced *American Junior Tennis* comes out, there's one E. R. Clipperton, Home Town 'Ind.,' ranked #1 in Boys' Continental 18-and-Unders; and competitive eyebrows ascend at all latitudes; and but everyone at E.T.A., from Schtitt on down, is highly amused, and some of them wonder whether maybe now Eric Clipperton will put down his psychic cuirass and take his unarmed competitive chances with the rest of them, now that he's got what he's surely been burning over and holding himself hostage for all along, a real and sanctioned #1; and the Continental Jr. Clay-Courts are coming up the following week, in Indianapolis IN, and little Michael Pemulis of Allston takes his PowerBook and odds-software and makes a killing on vig in the frenzy of locker-room wagering over whether Clipperton'll even bother to materialize at Indy now that he's extorted himself to the sanctioned top he must have craved so terribly, or whether he'll retire from the tour now and lie around masturbating over the Glock in one hand and the latest issue of *NAJT* in the other.[175] And so everyone's taken aback when Eric Clipperton of all people suddenly appears at the E.T.A. front gate's portcullis on a rainy warm late A.M. two days before the Clays, wearing a flap-frayed trench-type coat and toe-abraded sneakers and a five-day growth of armpitty adolescent beard, but without any sticks or anything in the way of competitive gear, not even his Glock 17's custom-made wooden case, and he makes the cold-eyed part-time portcullis attendant from the halfway place down the hill just about lean on the intercom-buzzer, pleading for entry and counsel — he's in a terrible way, is the portcullis attendant's intercom diagnosis — and rules about nonenrolled jr. players being on academies' grounds are strict and complex, and but little Mario Incandenza sways down the steep path to the portcullis in the warm rain and interfaces with Clipperton through the bars and has the attendant hold the intercom-button down for him and personally requests that Clipperton be admitted under a special nonplay codicil to the regulations, saying the kid is truly in desperate psychic straits, Mario speaking first to Lateral Alice Moore and then to this prorector Cantrell and then to the Headmaster himself as Clipperton stares wordlessly up at the little wrought-iron racquet-heads that serve as spikes at the top of the portcullis and fencing around E.T.A., his expression so blackly haunted that even the hard-boiled attendant told some of the people back at the halfway place later that the spectral trench-coated figure had given him sobriety's worst fantods, so far; and J. O. Incandenza finally lets Clipperton in over Cantrell's and then Schtitt's vehement objections when it's established that Clipperton wants only a few private minutes to obtain the counsel of Incandenza Sr. himself — of whom I think we can presume Mario's spoken glowingly to Clipperton — and Incandenza, while not quite strictly sober, is lucid, and has a very low melting-point of compassion for traumas connected with early success; and so up goes the portcullis, and the Clipperton and the two Incandenzas go at high noon up to an unused top-floor room in Subdorm C of East House, the structure nearest the front gate, for some sort of psycho-existential CPR-session or something — Mario has never spoken of what he got to sit in on, not even at night to Hal when Hal's trying to go to sleep. But it's a matter of record that at some point first E.T.A. counselor Dolores Rusk was beeped by Himself at her Winchester home and then her beep was canceled and Lateral Alice Moore was beeped and asked with due speed to get Lyle up from the weight room/sauna and over to East House ASAP, and that at some point while Lyle was delotusing from the dispenser and making his way with sideways Lateral Alice to this emergency-type huddle, at some point in this interval — in front of Dr. James O. Incandenza and a Mario whose tiny borrowed head-clamped Bolex H128 Incandenza required Clipperton to consent to having digitally record the whole crisis-conversation, to protect E.T.A. from the O.N.A.N.T.A.'s Kafkaesque rules on unregistered recipients of any sort of counsel at U.S. academies — at some point, w/ Lyle in transit, Clipperton pulls out of various pockets in his wet complicated coat an elaborately altered copy of NAJT's biweekly ranking report, a sepia'd snapshot of some whey-faced Midwestern couple's wedding, and the hideous blunt-barreled Glock 17 9 mm. semiautomatic, which even as both

Incandenzas reach for the sky Clipperton places to his right — not left — temple, as in with his good right stick-hand, closes his eyes and scrunches up his face and blows his legitimated brains out for real and all time, eradicates his map and then some; and there's just an ungodly subsequent mess in there, and the Incandenzas respectively stagger and totter from the room all green-gilled and red-mist-stained, and — because reports of Lyle's appearance outside the weight room upright and walking across the grounds have spread and caused enormous excitement and student-snapshots — it's because it was just as Lyle and L. A. Moore hit the upstairs hallway that they reeled out of the room in a miasma of cordite and ghastly mist that they're preserved in various snapshots as resembling miners of some sort of really grisly coal.

People in the competitive jr. tennis community somehow regarded it as healthy that Mario Incandenza's perfectly even smile never faltered even through tears at Clipperton's funeral. The funeral was poorly attended. It turned out Eric Clipperton had hailed from Crawfordsville, Indiana, where his Ma was a late-stage Valium addict and his ex-soybean-farmer Pa, blinded in the infamous hailstorms of B.S. '94, now spent all day every day playing with one of those little wooden paddles with a red rubber ball attached by elastic string, paddle-ball, with an understandable lack of success; and the tranquilized and sightless Clippertons had had no clue about where Eric had even disappeared off to most weekends, and bought his explanation that all the tall trophies came from an after-school job as a freelance tennis-trophy designer, the parents apparently being not exactly the two brightest bulbs in the great U.S. parental light-show. They held the interment under a threat of rain in Veedersburg IN, where there's a budget cemetery, and Himself skipped Indianapolis and took Mario to the first of his life's two funerals so far; and it was probably moving that Incandenza acceded to Mario's request that nothing get filmed or documented, at the funeral, for Himself's jr.-tennis documentary. Mario probably told Lyle all about everything, back down in the weight room, but he sure never told Hal or the Moms; and Himself was already in and out of rehabs and hardly a credible source on much of anything by this point. But Incandenza did let Mario insist that no one else get to clean up the scene in Subdorm C after Enfield's Finest had come and peered around and drawn a chalk ectoplasm around Clipperton's sprawled form and written things down in little spiral notebooks which they kept checking against one another with maddening care, and then EMTs had zipped Clipperton up in a huge rubber bag and taken him down and out on a wheeled stretcher with retractable legs they had to retract on all the stairs. Lyle was long gone by this time. It took the bradykinetic Mario all night and two bottles of Ajax Plus to clean the room with his tiny contractured arms and square feet; the 18's girls in the rooms on either side could hear him falling around in there and picking himself up, again and again; and the finally spotless room in question had been locked ever since, with its tasteless sign — except G. Schtitt holds a special key, and when an E.T.A. jr. whinges too loudly about some tennis-connected vicissitude or hardship or something, he's invited to go chill for a bit in the Clipperton Suite, to maybe meditate on some of the other ways to succeed besides votaried self-transcendence and gut-sucking-in and hard daily slogging toward a distant goal you can then maybe, if you get there, live with.

It was Ennet House's Assistant Director Annie P. who coined the phrase that Don Gately 'sunlights on the side.' Five A.M.s a week, whether he's just getting off all-night Staff duty or not, he has to be on the Inbound Green Line by 0430h. to then catch two more trains to his other job at the Shattuck Shelter For Homeless Males down in bombed-out Jamaica Plain. Gately has become, in sobriety, a janitor. He mops down broad cot-strewn floors with anti-fungal delousing solvents. Likewise the walls. He scrubs toilets. The relative cleanliness of the Shattuck's toilets might seem surprising until you head into the shower area, with your equipment and facemask. Half the guys in the Shattuck are always incontinent. There's human waste in the showers on a daily fucking basis. Stavros lets him attach an industrial hose to a nozzle and spray the worst of the shit away from a distance before Gately has to go in there with his mop and brushes and solvents, and his mask.

Cleaning the Shattuck only takes three hours, since he and his partner got the routine down tight. Gately's partner is also the guy that owns the company that contracts with the Commonwealth for the Shattuck's maintenance, a guy like forty or fifty, Stavros Lobokulas, a troubling guy with a long cigarette-filter and an enormous collection of women's-shoes catalogues he keeps piled behind the seats in the cab of his 4×4.

So at like 0800 usually they're done and by vendor's contract still get to bill for eight hours (Stavros L. only pays Gately for three, but it's sub-table), and Gately heads back to Government Center to take the westbound Greenie back up Commonwealth to Ennet House to put on his black eyepatch mask thing and sleep till 1200h. and the afternoon shift. Stavros L. himself gets a couple hours off to footwear-browse (Gately very much needs to assume that's all he does with the catalogues, is browse), then has to head over to Pine Street Inn, the biggest and foulest homeless shelter in all of Boston, where Stavros and two other broke and desperate yutzes from another of the halfway houses Stavros cruises for cheap labor will spend four hours cleaning and then bill the state for six.

The inmates at the Shattuck suffer from every kind of physical and psychological and addictive and spiritual difficulty you could ever think of, specializing in ones that are repulsive. There are colostomy bags and projectile vomiting and cirrhotic discharges and missing limbs and misshapen heads and incontinence and Kaposi's Sarcoma and suppurating sores and all different levels of enfeeblement and impulse-control-deficit and damage. Schizophrenia is like the norm. Guys in D.T.s treat the heaters like TVs and leave broad spatter-paintings of coffee over the walls of the barrackses. There are industrial buckets for A.M. puking that they seem to treat like golfers treat the pin on like a golf course, aiming in its vague direction from a distance. There's one sort of blocked off and more hidden corner, over near the bank of little lockers for valuables, that's always got sperm moving slowly down the walls. And way too much sperm for just one or two guys, either. The whole place smells like death no matter what the fuck you do. Gately gets to the shelter at 0459.9h. and just shuts his head off as if his head has a kind of control switch. He screens input with a fucking vengeance the whole time. The barrackses's cots reek of urine and have insect-activity observable. The state employees who supervise the shelter at night are dead-eyed and watch soft-core tapes behind the desk and are all around Gately's size and build, and he's been approached to maybe work there himself, nights, supervising, more than once, and has said Thanks Anyway, and always screws right out of there at 0801h. and rides the Greenie back up the hill with his Gratitude-battery totally recharged.

Janitoring the Shattuck for Stavros Lobokulas was the menial job Gately had landed with only three days to go on his month's deadline to find some honest job, as a resident, and he's kept it ever since.

The males in the Shattuck are supposed to be up and out by 0500h. regardless of weather or D.T.s, to let Gately and Stavros L. clean. But some never screw out of there on time — and these're always the worst guys, the ones you don't want anyplace near you, these ones that won't leave. They'll clump behind Gately and watch him jet feces off the shower-tiling, treating it like a sport and yelling encouragement and advice. They'll cringe and ass-kiss when the supervisor heaves himself on by to tell them to get out and then when he leaves not get out. A couple have those little shaved patches on their arms. They'll lie in the cots and hallucinate and thrash and scream in the cots and knock army blankets off onto the floors Gately's trying to mop. They'll skulk back over to the little dark spermy corner the minute Gately's got done scrubbing the night's sperm off and has backed away and started again to inhale.

Maybe the worst is that there's almost always one or two guys in the Shattuck who Gately knows personally, from his days of addiction and B&E, from before he got to the no-choice point and surrendered his will to staying straight at any cost. These guys are always 25–30 and look 45–60 and are a better ad for sobriety at any cost than any ad agency could come up with. Gately'll slip them a finski or a pack of Kools and maybe sometimes try and talk a little AA to them, if they seem like maybe they're ready to give up. With everybody else in the Shattuck Gately adopts this expression where he lets them know he's ignoring them totally as long as they keep their distance, but it's a look that says *Street* and *Jail* and not to fuck with him. If they get in his way, Gately will stare hard at a point just behind their heads until they move off. The protective face-mask helps.

Stavros Lobokulas's great ambition — which he goes on about regularly to Gately when they're cleaning the same barracks — Stavros's dream is to utilize his unique combination of entrepreneurial drives and janitorial savvy and flairs for creative billing and finding desperate recovering halfway-house guys who'll scrub shit for next to nothing, to pile up enough $ to open a women's shoe store in some mobilely upward part of Boston where the women are healthy and upscale and have good feet and can afford to take care of their feet. Gately spends a lot of the time around Stavros nodding and not saying really much of anything. Because what is there to really say about ambitious career-dreams involving feet? But Gately'll be paying court-scheduled restitution well into his thirties if he stays straight, and needs the work. Foot-thing or no foot-thing. Stavros has allegedly been clean for eight years, but Gately has his private doubts about the spiritual quality of the sobriety involved. E.g. like Stavros gets easily aggravated at the Shattuck guys that can't get up and out like they're supposed to and clear out, and almost daily he'll make a production of throwing down his mop in the middle of the floor and throwing his head back to scream: "Why don't you sorry motherfucks just *go home?*" which so far for over thirteen months he hasn't quit finding hilarious, his own witticism, Stavros.

But the whole Clipperton saga highlights the way there are certain very talented jr. players who just cannot keep the lip stiff and fires stoked if they ever finally do achieve a top ranking or win some important event. Next to Clipperton, the most historically ghastly instance of this syndrome involved a kid from Fresno, in Central CA, also an unaffiliated kid (his dad, an architect or draftsman or something, functioned as his coach; his dad had played for UC-Davis or -Irvine or one of those; all the E.T.A. staff really emphasize is that again here was a kid w/o academy-support and -perspective), who, after upsetting two top seeds and winning the Pacific Coast Hardcourt Boys 18's and getting toasted wildly at the post-tourney ceremony and ball and carried off on the shoulders of his dad and Fresno teammates, came home late that night and drank a big glass of Nestlé's Quik laced with the sodium cyanide his Dad kept around for ink for drafting, drinks cyanitic Quik in his family's home's redecorated kitchen, and keels over dead, blue-faced and still with a ghastly mouthful of lethal Quik, and apparently his dad hears the thump of the kid keeling over and rushes into the kitchen in his bathrobe and leather slippers and tries to give the kid mouth-to-mouth resuscitation, and but gets the odd bit of NaCN-laced Quik in his own mouth, from the kid, and also keels over and turns bright blue, and dies, and then the mom rushes in in a mud-mask and fluffy slippers and sees them both lying there bright blue and stiffening, and she tries giving the architect dad mouth-to-mouth and is of course in short order also lying there keeled over and blue, wherever she's not mud-colored, from the mask, and but anyway dead as a rivet. And since the family has six more various-aged kids who as the night wears on come in from dates or patter down the stairs in little pajamas with adorable little pajama-feet attached to them, drawn by the noise of all the cumulative keeling over, plus I should mention the odd agonized gurgle-sound, and but since all six kids had gone through a four-hour Rotary-sponsored CPR course at Fresno's YMCA, by the end of the night the whole family's lying there blue-hued and stiff as posts, with incrementally tinier amounts of lethal Quik smeared around their rictus-grimaced mouths; and in sum this whole instance of unprepared-goal-attaintment-trauma is unbelievably gruesome and sad, and it's one historical reason why all accredited tennis academies have to have a Ph.D.-level counselor on full-time staff, to screen student athletes for their possibly lethal reactions to ever actually reaching the level they've been pointed at for years. E.T.A.'s staff counselor is the bird-of-prey-faced Dr. Dolores Rusk, M.S., Ph.D., and she's regarded by the kids as whatever's just slightly worse than useless. You go in there with an Issue and all she'll do is make a cage of her hands and look abstractly over the cage at you and take the last dependent clause of whatever you say and repeat it back to you with an interrogative lilt — 'Possible homosexual attraction to your doubles partner?' 'Whole sense of yourself as a purposive male athlete messed with?' 'Uncontrolled boner during semis at Cleveland?' 'Drives you bats when people just parrot you instead of responding?' 'Having trouble keeping from twisting my twittery head off like a game-hen's?' — all with an expression she probably thinks looks blandly deep but which really looks exactly the way a girl's face looks when she's dancing with you but would really rather be dancing with just about anyone else in the room. Only the very newest E.T.A. players ever go to Rusk, and then not for long, and she spends her massive blocks of free time in her Comm.-Ad. office doing involved acrostics and working on some sort of pop-psych manuscript the first four pages of which Axford and Shaw dickied her lock and had a look at and counted 29 appearances of the prefix *self-*. Lyle, a dewimpled Carmelite who works the kitchen day-shift, occasionally Mario Incandenza, and many times Avril herself take up most of the psychic slack, for practical purposes, among E.T.A.s in the know.

It's possible that the only jr. tennis players who can win their way to the top and stay there without going bats are the ones who are already bats, or else who seem to be just grim machines à la John Wayne. Wayne's sitting low on his spine in the dining hall with the other Canadian kids, watching the screen and squeezing a ball without any readable expression. Hal's eyes are fevered and rolling around in his head. And actually by this time a lot of the eyes in the I.-Day audience have lost a bit of that festive sparkle. Though there's a certain chortle-momentum left over from the film's self-felonious Gentle/Clipperton comparisons, the Rodney-Tine-Luria-P.-love-rumor-and-Tine-as-Benedict-Arnold thing seems brow-clutchingly slow and digressive.[176] Plus there's some retroactive puzzlement, because the advent of Subsidized Time is historically known to have been a revenue-response to the heady costs of the U.S.'s Reconfigurative giveaway, which means it must have come after formal Interdependence, and indeed in the film it does come after, but then the chronology of some of the end makes it seem like Tine sold Johnny Gentle on his whole Sino-temporal-endorsement revenue scheme sometime in Orin Incandenza's first major-sport year at Boston U., which ended in the Year of the Whopper, pretty obviously a Subsidized year. By this time the E.T.A.s are eating more slowly, playing in that idle post-prandial way with the orts on their plates, and people's hats are making some people's heads itch, and plus everybody's sugar-crashing a bit; and one of the really small E.T.A. kids crawling around with a bottle of adhesive under the tables has whacked his head on the sharp edge of an institutional chair and is in Avril I.'s lap crying with a desolate late-day hysteria that makes everybody feel jagged.

GENTLE AT LARGE! — Superheader; TOURS NEW 'NEW-NEW' ENGLAND BORDER AMID TIGHT SECURITY — Header; WHACKS CHAMPAGNE BOTTLES AGAINST MASSIVE LUCITE WALLS SOUTH OF WHAT USED TO BE SYRACUSE, CONCORD NH, SALEM MA. — 10-point Subheader;

GENTLE MORE OR LESS AT LARGE: WATCHES FROM OXY-GENATED PORTABUBBLE AS CLEMSON DOWNS BOSTON U IN LAS VEGAS'S FORSYTHIA BOWL — Header from That Guy Who's Now Reduced to Laying out Headlines for the Rantoul IL *Eagle;*

CRANIALLY CHALLENGED, ACROMEGALIC INFANTS LOST IN EXPERIALIST SHUFFLE? — Editorial Header in Ithaca NY's *Daily Odyssean;*

GENTLE CABINET TO DRAFT BUDGET OVERHAUL IN LIGHT OF WALL STREET ANGST OVER COSTS OF 'TERRITORIAL RECONFIGURATION' — Header; ADMINISTRATION HEADS PUT TOGETHER ON MISSILE INVERSION EXPENDITURES, RELOCATION COSTS, LOSS OF REVENUE FROM BETTER PART OF FOUR STATES — Subheader.

GENTLE [substantially muffled by both Fukoama microfiltration mask and oxygenated Lucite portabubble]: Boys.

ALL SECS EXCEPT SEC. MEX. & SEC. CAN. [the Cabinet's Motown-girl puppets, decked out for climactic camp, are all in wicked three-piecers with slicked-back-straight hair and enormous robber-baron steer-horn mustaches, which mustaches could be straighter but are on the whole pretty impressive mustaches, for female puppets]: Chief.

SEC. DEF.: So then how was the big game, Mr. President?

GENTLE: Ollster, boys: seminal, visionary. An outstanding experience. I now say things like *outstanding* instead of *boss*. But also seminal. Ollie, men, I saw something outstandingly visional and seminary yesterday. I do not refer to the football game. I normally don't much get into football. All that grunting. Mud everywhere. Not my scene ordinarily. The most diverting single thing of the game was one of the two teams' punters. This one slim cat with an outsized leg and slightly less outsized arm. Never saw punts I could hear before. *Whoom. Blam.* I ate an entire wiener stem to stern while one punt was in the air. People stood around conferring and making a racket and going to the restroom and coming back and eating concessions, all while this one cat's punts were still in the air. What was that cat's name again, R.T.?

SEC. INT.: May I respectfully ask whether this is to be a lunch meeting, Mr. President? Is that why these Chinese-calendar-zodiac-Year-of-the-Tiger-and-like-Rat Szechuan-restaurant paper placemats are at all our places next to our water-pitchers? Are we going to get to tuck into some Chinese takeout, Chief?

[Mario's aural background becomes something with a brisk cornet, and there's some glove-muffled finger-snapping from J.G.F.C., who's lapsed into a visionary reverie.]

SEC. TRANSP.: Always been partial to the General Tsu's Chicken, if we're —

RODNEY TINE, CHIEF, UNITED STATES OFFICE OF UNSPECIFIED SERVICES: President Gentle's asked us all here this morning to put our collective expertise together on an issue about which we in Unspecified Services believe he's been hit with a truly seminal set of creative insights.

GENTLE: Gentlemen, we're both pleased and concerned to report that our seminal experiment in the Territorial Reconfiguration of O.N.A.N.[177] has been a thoroughgoing logistical coup. More or less. Delaware's looking a bit crowded, and one or two curvy-horned animals apparently got by the tactical squads, and there's rather less overall good sportsmanship in downstate New New York than we'd like to see, but overall I think 'thoroughgoing coup' would not be out of line as a term to describe this sort of success.

TINE: Now it's time to think about how to pay for it.

ALL SECS.: [Stiff turns to look at each other, tie- and mustache-straightenings, gulping sounds.]

GENTLE: Rod informs me Marty's got the preliminary figures on gross costs, while Chet's boys have provided us with some projections on gross revenue-losses from the Reconfiguration of taxable territories and households and businesses and that there.

SEC. TRANSP. & SEC. TREAS.: [Pass around thick bound folders, each emblazoned with the yawning red skull that emblazons all bad-news memos in the Gentle administration. Folders opened and scanned by ALL SECS. Sounds of jaws hitting the tabletop. A couple mustaches fall off altogether. One SEC. heard to ask whether there's even a name for a figure with this many zeroes. GENTLE's portabubble on-screen is hit right over his plastic-wrapped corsage by a half-chewed Raisinette, to half-hearted audience cheers. Another cross-dressed Motown puppet is throwing a tiny string noose over a beam at the back of the velvet-lined Cabinet Room.]

GENTLE: Boys. Men. Before anybody needs oxygen here [holding a placative hand up against the bubble's glass], let Rod here explain that despite a quantitative downer-type quality to these figures, all we merely have here is just what Rod might call an exaggerated example of a quadrennial problem any administration with vision is going to have to face eventually anyway. By the way, the unfamiliar but welcome face on my left here is Mr. P. Tom Veals, of Veals Associates Advertising, Boston, USA, N.A.

ALL SECS.: [Not terribly placated-sounding mutterings of salutation to Veals.]

MR. P. TOM VEALS [A tiny little caucasoid Tootsie-Pop-stick-puppet body and enormous face that's mostly front teeth and spectacles]: Yo.

TINE: And to Tom's own left may I also present the charming and delightful Ms. Luria P——— [indicating with pointer a puppet simply beyond pulchritudinous belief; the Cabinet Room's conference table seems to ascend ever so slightly as Luria P——— cocks a well-pencilled eyebrow].

STILL TINE: Gentlemen, what the president is articulating is that what we face here is a microsmic exemplar of the infamous Democratic Triple Bind faced by visionarians from FDR and JFK on down. The American electorate, as is its every right, on one hand demands the sort of millennial statesmanship and vision — decisive action, tough choices, lots of programs and services — see for instance the Territorial Reconfiguration for example — that will lead a renewed community into a whole new era of interdependent choice and freedom.

GENTLE: The rhetorical chapeau's off to you, babe.

TINE [Rising, eyes now two glittery red points in his round face's felt, the eyes two tiny smoke-detector bulbs run off a single AAA cell taped to the back of the puppet's surgical gown]: Now, speaking in the very most general terms, if the president's vision dictates the tough choice of cutting certain programs and services, our statistical people predict with reasonable inductive certainty that the American electorate will whinge.

VEALS: Whinge?

LURIA P——— [TO TINE]: This is a Canadian idiom, cheri.

VEALS: And who is this chick?

TINE [Looking momentarily blank]: Sorry Tom. Canadian idiom. Whinge. Complain. Petition for redress. Assemble. March in those five-abreast demonstrating lines. Shake upraised fists in unison. Whinge [indicating photos on easels behind him of various historical pressure- and advocacy groups whingeing].

SEC. TREAS.: And we already have an all-too-good idea of what will happen if we attempt any sort of conventional revenue enhancements.

SEC. STATE: Tax revolt.

SEC. H.E.W.: A whingeathon, Chief.

SEC. DEF.: Tea-party.

GENTLE: Bullseye. Whingeville. Political whingeocide. A serious drag-caliber lapse in mandate. We've already promised no new enhancements. I told them on Inauguration Day. I said look into my eyes: no new enhancements. I pointed at my eyes up there and said that was one tough choice that was not going to rain on anybody's program. Rod and Tom and I had that three-planked platform-exhibit. One: waste. Two: no new enhancements. Three: find somebody outside the borders of our community selves to blame.

TINE: So then a double bind, so far, with potential whingeing on both flanks.

SEC. TREAS.: And yet the financial communities demand a balanced federal budget. The Reserve Board all but insists on a balanced budget. Our balance of trade with the handful of nations we're still trading with requires a stable buck and so a balanced budget.

TINE: The third flank, Chet, of the Triple Bind. Outflows required, inflows restricted, balance demanded.

GENTLE: The classic executive-branch Cerberus-horned dilemma. The thorn in the Achilles' tendon of democratic process. Does anybody here by the way hear a sort of high pitch?

ALL SECS.: [Blank glances at one another.]

VEALS: [Blows nose at high volume.]

GENTLE [Knocking experimentally on interior surfaces of portabubble]: Sometimes I hear a pitch at a high range beyond most people's hearing, admittedly, but this seems like a different type of high pitch.

ALL SECS. [Necktie-knot-adjusting, polished-tabletop-studying.]

GENTLE: That would be a no on the pitch, then.

VEALS: Could this all be moved along up to at least a canter, guys?

TINE: Perhaps it's the distinctive high pitch that sometimes precedes your getting ready to announce some seminal, visionary insight you've achieved into the previously intractable Triple Bind, sir.

GENTLE: Babe, Rod, again a direct hit. Gentlemen: have a gander at these restaurant exhibits of the Sino-epithetic calendrical scheme.

TINE: Meaning of course these placemats right here, bearing directly on the president's revenue vision.

GENTLE: Gentlemen, as you all know I've just returned, at extremely high speeds, burping up the taste of wieners I'm pretty sure were just crawling with every sort of microbe that makes publicly vended concessions a scourge and menace that —

TINE: [Ixnayish hand-signal]

GENTLE: But so gentlemen I'm fresh back from a goodwill appearance at a post-collegiate bowl game. At which I ingested the pre-mentioned franks. But the real point is: do any of you guys happen to know the *name* of that collegiate bowl game?

SEC. H.U.D.: We thought you'd said it was the Forsythia Bowl, Chief.

GENTLE: That, Mr. Sivnik, is because that's what I was thinking its name in fact was, en route, when we'd all interfaced on the old scrambler. That's what the name was when I did the anthem there in '91.

LURIA P——— [Holding up zodiacalized placemat with a slight grease-corona'd spot of Hot and Sour Soup in the upper left corner]: Perhaps you would care now to tell your cabinet what ze contest of football calls itself, M. Président.

GENTLE [With a showmanlike look at VEALS, who's probing the gap between his mammoth incisors with the business cards of the CEOs of Pillsbury and Pepsico]: Boys, I heard punts, burped redhots, smelled beer-foam and recoiled from public urinals at the Ken-L-Ration-Magnavox-Kemper-Insurance-Forsythia Bowl.

O

YEAR OF THE DEPEND ADULT UNDERGARMENT

On a White Flag Group Commitment to the Tough Shit But You Still Can't Drink Group down in Braintree this past July, Don G., up at the podium, revealed publicly about how he was ashamed that he still as yet had no real solid understanding of a Higher Power. It's suggested in the 3rd of

Boston AA's 12 Steps that you to turn your Diseased will over to the direction and love of 'God as you understand Him.' It's supposed to be one of AA's major selling points that you get to choose your own God. You get to make up your own understanding of God or a Higher Power or Whom-/Whatever. But Gately, at like ten months clean, at the TSBYSCD podium in Braintree, opines that at this juncture he's so totally clueless and lost he's thinking that he'd maybe rather have the White Flag Crocodiles just grab him by the lapels and just tell him what AA God to have an understanding of, and give him totally blunt and dogmatic orders about how to turn over his Diseased will to whatever this Higher Power is. He notes how he's observed already that some Catholics and Fundamentalists now in AA had a childhood understanding of a Stern and Punishing–type God, and Gately's heard them express incredible Gratitude that AA let them at long last let go and change over to an under-standing of a Loving, Forgiving, Nurturing–type God. But at least these folks started out with *some* idea of Him/Her/It, whether fucked up or no. You might think it'd be easier if you Came In with 0 in the way of denominational background or preconceptions, you might think it'd be easier to sort of invent a Higher-Powerish God from scratch and then like erect an understanding, but Don Gately complains that this has not been his experience thus far. His sole experience so far is that he takes one of AA's very rare specific suggestions and hits the knees in the A.M. and asks for Help and then hits the knees again at bedtime and says Thank You, whether he believes he's talking to Anything/-body or not, and he somehow gets through that day clean. This, after ten months of ear-smoking concentration and reflection, is still all he feels like he 'understands' about the 'God angle.' Publicly, in front of a very tough and hard-ass-looking AA crowd, he sort of simultaneously confesses and com-plains that he feels like a rat that's learned one route in the maze to the cheese and travels that route in a ratty-type fashion and whatnot. W/ the God thing being the cheese in the metaphor. Gately still feels like he has no access to the Big spiritual Picture. He feels about the ritualistic daily *Please* and *Thank You* prayers rather like like a hitter that's on a hitting streak and doesn't change his jock or socks or pre-game routine for as long as he's on the streak. W/ sobriety being the hitting streak and whatnot, he explains. The whole church basement is literally blue with smoke. Gately says he feels like this is a pretty limp and lame understanding of a Higher Power: a cheese-easement or unwashed athle-tic supporter. He says but when he tries to go beyond the very basic rote automatic get-me-through-this-day-please stuff, when he kneels at other times and prays or meditates or tries to achieve a Big-Picture spiritual under-standing of a God as he can understand Him, he feels Nothing — not nothing but *Nothing,* an edgeless blankness that somehow feels worse than the sort of unconsidered atheism he Came In with. He says he doesn't know if any of this is coming through or making any sense or if it's all just still symptomatic of a thoroughgoingly Diseased will and quote 'spirit.' He finds himself telling the Tough Shit But You Still Can't Drink audience dark doubtful thoughts he wouldn't have fucking ever dared tell Ferocious Francis man to man. He can't even look at F.F. in the Crocodile's row as he says that at this point the God-understanding stuff kind of makes him want to puke, from fear. Something you can't see or hear or touch or smell: OK. All right. But something you can't even *feel?* Because that's what he feels when he tries to understand something to really sincerely pray to. Nothingness. He says when he tries to pray he gets this like image in his mind's eye of the brainwaves or whatever of his prayers going out and out, with nothing to stop them, going, going, radiating out into like space and outliving him and still going and never hitting Anything out there, much less Something with an ear. Much *much* less Something with an ear that could possibly give a rat's ass. He's both pissed off and ashamed to be talking about this instead of how just completely good it is to just be getting through the day without ingesting a Substance, but there it is. This is what's going on. He's no closer to carrying out the suggestion of the 3rd Step than the day the Probie drove him over to his halfway house from Peabody Holding. The idea of this whole God thing makes him puke, still. And he is afraid.

And the same fucking thing happens again. The tough chain-smoking TSBYSCD Group all stands and applauds and the men give two-finger whistles, and people come up at the raffle-break to pump his big hand and even sometimes try and hug on him.

It seems like every time he forgets himself and publicizes how he's fucking up in sobriety Boston AAs fall all over themselves to tell him how good it was to hear him and to for God's sake Keep Coming, for them if not for himself, whatever the fuck that means.

The Tough Shit But You Still Can't Drink Group seems to be over 50% bikers and biker-chicks, meaning your standard leather vests and 10-cm. boot heels, belt-buckles with little spade-shaped knives that come out of a slot in the side, tattoos that are more like murals, serious tits in cotton halters, big beards, Harleywear, wooden matches in mouth-corners and so forth. After the Our Father, as Gately and the other White Flag speakers are clustered smoking outside the door to the church basement, the sound of high-cc. hawgs being kick-started is enough to rattle your fillings. Gately can't even start to guess what it would be like to be a sober and drug-free biker. It's like what would be the point. He imagines these people polishing the hell out of their leather and like playing a lot of really precise pool.

This one sober biker that can't be much older than Gately and is nearly Gately's size — though with a really small head and a tapered jaw that makes him look kind of like a handsome mantis — as they're massed around the door he brings a car-length chopper up alongside Gately. Says it was good to hear him. Shakes his hand in the complex way of Niggers and Harleyheads. He introduces his name as Robert F., though on the lapel of his leather vest it says BOB DEATH. A biker-chick's got her arms around his waist from behind, as is SOP. He tells Gately it was good to hear somebody new share from the heart about his struggles with the God component. It's weird to hear a biker use the Boston AA word *share*, much less *component* or *heart*.

The other White Flaggers have stopped talking and are watching the two men sort of just awkwardly stand there, the biker embraced from behind and straddling his throbbing hawg. The guy's got on leather spats and a leather vest with no shirt, and Gately notices the guy's got a jailhouse tatt of AA's weird little insignia of a triangle inside a circle on one big shoulder.

Robert F./Bob Death asks Gately if by any chance he's heard the one about the fish. Glenn K. in his fucking robe overhears, and of course he's got to put his own oar in, and breaks in and asks them all if they've heard the one What did the blind man say as he passed by the Quincy Market fish-stall, and without waiting says He goes 'Evening, Ladies.' A couple male White Flaggers fall about, and Tamara N. slaps at the back of Glenn K.'s head's pointy hood, but without real heat, as in like what are you going to do with this sick fuck.

Bob Death smiles coolly (South Shore bikers are required to be extremely cool in everything they do) and manipulates a wooden match with his lip and says No, not that fish-one. He has to assume a kind of bar-shout to clear the noise of his idling hawg. He leans in more toward Gately and shouts that the one he was talking about was: This wise old whiskery fish swims up to three young fish and goes, 'Morning, boys, how's the water?' and swims away; and the three young fish watch him swim away and look at each other and go, 'What the fuck is water?' and swim away. The young biker leans back and smiles at Gately and gives an affable shrug and blatts away, a halter top's tits mashed against his back.

Gately's forehead was wrinkled in emotional pain all the way up Rte. 3 home. They were in the back of Ferocious Francis's old car. Glenn K. was trying to ask what was the difference between a bottle of 15-year-old Hennessey and a human female vagina. Crocodile Dicky N. up riding shotgun told Glenn to try to fucking remember there was ladies present. Ferocious Francis kept moving the toothpick around in his mouth and looking at Gately in the rearview. Gately wanted to both cry and hit somebody. Glenn's cheap pseudo-demonic robes had the faint rank oily smell of a dish towel. There was no smoking in the car: Ferocious Francis had a little oxygen tank he had to carry around and a little thin pale-blue plastic-like tube thing that lay under his nose and was taped there and sent oxygen up his nose. All he'd ever say about the tank and the tube is that they were not his personal will but that he'd submitted to advice and now here he was, still sucking air and staying rabidly Active.

Something they seem to omit to mention in Boston AA when you're new and out of your skull with desperation and ready to eliminate your map and they tell you how it'll all get better and better as you abstain and recover: they somehow omit to mention that the way it gets better and you get better is through pain. Not around pain, or in spite of it. They leave this out, talking instead about Gratitude and Release from Compulsion. There's serious pain in being sober, though, you find out, after time. Then now that you're clean and don't even much want Substances and feeling like you want to both cry and stomp somebody into goo with pain, these Boston AAs start in on telling you you're right where you're supposed to be and telling you to remember the pointless pain of active addiction and telling you that at least this sober pain now has a purpose. At least this pain means you're going somewhere, they say, instead of the repetitive gerbil-wheel of addictive pain.

They neglect to tell you that after the urge to get high magically vanishes and you've been Substanceless for maybe six or eight months, you'll begin to start to 'Get In Touch' with why it was that you used Substances in the first place. You'll start to feel why it was you got dependent on what was, when you get right down to it, an anesthetic. 'Getting In Touch With Your Feelings' is another quilted-sampler-type cliché that ends up masking something ghastly deep and real, it turns out.[178] It starts to turn out that the vapider the AA cliché, the sharper the canines of the real truth it covers.

Near the end of his Ennet residency, at like eight months clean and more or less free of any chemical compulsion, going to the Shattuck every A.M. and working the Steps and getting Active and pounding out meetings like a madman, Don Gately suddenly started to remember things he would just as soon not have. Remembered. Actually *remembered*'s probably not the best word. It was more like he started to almost reexperience things that he'd barely even been there to experience, in terms of emotionally, in the first place. A lot of it was undramatic little shit, but still somehow painful. E.g. like when he was maybe eleven, pretending to watch TV with his mother and pretending to listen to her P.M. nightly monologue, a litany of complaint and regret whose consonants got mushier and mushier. To the extent it's Gately's place to diagnose anybody else as an alcoholic, his mom was pretty definitely an alcoholic. She drank Stolichnaya vodka in front of the TV. They weren't cable-ready, for reasons of $. She drank little thin glasses with cut-up bits of carrot and pepper that she'd drop into the vodka. Her maiden name was Gately. Don's like organic father had been an Estonian immigrant, a wrought-iron worker, which is like sort of a welder with ambition. He'd broken Gately's mother's jaw and left Boston when Gately was in his mother's stomach. Gately had no brothers or sisters. His mother was subsequently involved with a live-in lover, a former Navy M.P. who used to beat her up on a regular schedule, hitting her in the vicinities between groin and breast so that nothing showed. A skill he'd picked up as a brig guard and Shore Patrol. At about 8–10 Heinekens he used to all of a sudden throw his *Readers' Digest* against the wall and get her down and beat her with measured blows, she'd go down on the floor of the apartment and he'd hit her in the hidden vicinity, timing the blows between her arms' little waves — Gately remembered she tried to ward off the blows with a fluttered downward motion of her arms and hands, as if she were beating out flames. Gately still hasn't ever quite gotten over to look at her in State Care in the Long-Term-Care Medicaid place. The M.P.'s tongue was in the corner of his mouth and his little-eyed face wore a look of great concentration, as if he were taking something delicate apart or putting it together. He'd be on one knee knelt over her with his look of sober problem-solving, timing his shots, the blows abrupt and darting, her writhing and trying to kind of shoo them away. The darting blows. Out of the psychic blue, very detailed memories of these fights surfaced one afternoon as he was getting ready to mow the Ennet House lawn for Pat in May Y.D.A.U., when Enfield Marine P.H.H. withheld maintenance services in reprisal for late utilities. After the little Salem decayed beach-cottage with Herman the Ceiling That Breathed, the little like tract house by Mrs. Waite's tract house in Beverly's good dining room chairs had fluted legs and Gately had scratched *Donad* and *Donold* in each leg with a pin, low down. Higher up on the legs, the scratches became correctly spelled. It's like a lot of memories of his youth sank without bubbles when he quit school and then later only in sobriety bubbled back up to where he could Get In Touch with them. His mother used to call the M.P. a *bastuhd* and sometimes go *oof* when he landed one in the vicinity. She drank vodka with vegetables suspended in it, a habit she'd picked up from the missing Estonian, whose first name, Gately read on a torn and then fucked-uppedly Scotch-taped paper out of her jewelry box after his mother's cirrhotic hemorrhage, was Bulat. The Medicaid Long-Term place was way the fuck out the Yirrell Beach bridge in Point Shirley across the water from the Airport. The former M.P. delivered cheese and then later worked in a chowder factory and kept weights in the Beverly house's garage and drank Heineken beer, and logged each beer he drank carefully in a little spiral notebook he used to monitor his intake of alcohol.

His mom's special couch for TV was nubbly red chintz, and when she shifted from seated upright to lying on her side with her arm between her head and the little protective doily on the couch's armrest and the glass held tilting on the little space her breasts left at the cushion's edge, it was a sign she was going under. Gately at like ten or eleven used to pretend to listen and watch TV on the floor but really be dividing his attention between how close his Mom was to unconsciousness and how much Stolichnaya was left in the bottle. She would only drink Stolichnaya, which she called her Comrade in Arms and said Nothing but the Comrade would do. After she went under for the evening and he'd carefully taken the tilted glass out of her hand, Don'd take the bottle and mix the first couple vodkas with Diet Coke and drink a couple of those until it lost its fire, then drink it straight. This was like a routine. Then he'd put the near-empty bottle back next to her glass with its vegetables darkening in the undrunk vodka, and she'd wake up on the couch in the morning with no idea she hadn't drank the whole thing. Gately was careful to always leave her enough for a wake-up swallow. But this gesture of leaving some, Gately's now realized, wasn't just filial kindness on his part: if she didn't have the wake-up swallow she wouldn't get off the red couch all day, and then there would be no new bottle that night.

This was at age ten or eleven, as he now recalls. Most of the furniture was wrapped in plastic. The carpet was burnt-orange shag that the landlord kept saying he was going to take up and go to wood floors. The M.P. worked nights or else most nights went out, and then she'd take the plastic off the couch.

Why the couch had little protective doilies on the arms when it usually had a plastic cover on it Gately cannot recall or explain.

For a while in Beverly they had Nimitz the kitty.

This all came burpling greasily up into memory in the space of two or three weeks in May, and now more stuff steadily like dribbles up, for Gately to Touch.

Sober, she'd called him Bimmy or Bim because that's what she heard his little friends call him. She didn't know the neighborhood cognomen came from an acronym for 'Big Indestructible Moron.' His head had been huge, as a child. Out of all proportion, though with nothing especially Estonian about it, that he could see. He'd been very sensitive about it, the head, but never told her not to call him Bim. When she was drunk and conscious she called him her Doshka or Dochka or like that. Sometimes, well in the bag himself, when he turned off the uncabled set and covered her with the afghan, easing the mostly empty Stoly bottle back onto the little *TV Guide* table by the bowl of darkening chopped peppers, his unconscious Mom would groan and titter and call him her Doshka and good sir knight and last and only love, and ask him not to hit her anymore.

In June he Got In Touch with memories that their front steps in Beverly were a pocked cement painted red even in the pocks. Their mailbox was part of a whole tract-housing complex's honeycomb of mailboxes on a like small pole, brushed-steel and gray with a postal eagle on it. You needed a little key to get your mail out, and for a long time he thought the sign on it said 'US MAIL,' as in *us* instead of *U.S.* His mom's hair had been dry blond-white with dark roots that never lengthened or went away. No one tells you when they tell you you have cirrhosis that eventually you'll all of a sudden start choking on your own blood. This is called a *cirrhotic hemorrhage.* Your liver won't process any more of your blood and it quote *shunts* the blood and it goes up your throat in a high-pressure jet, is what they told him, is why he'd first thought the M.P.'d come back and cut his Mom or stabbed her, when he first came in, after football, his last season, at age seventeen. She'd been Diagnosed for years. She'd go to Meetings[179] for a few weeks, then drink on the couch, silent, telling him if the phone rang she wasn't home. After a few weeks of this she'd spend a whole day weeping, beating at herself as if on fire. Then she'd go back to Meetings for a while. Eventually her face began to swell and make her eyes piggy and her big breasts pointed at the floor and she turned the deep yellow of quality squash. This was all part of the Diagnosis. At first Gately just couldn't go out to the Long-Term place, couldn't see her out there. Couldn't deal. Then after some time passed he couldn't go because he couldn't face her and try and explain why he hadn't come before now. Ten-plus years have gone like that. Gately hadn't probably consciously thought of her once for three years, before getting straight.

Right after their neighbor Mrs. Waite got found by the meter-guy dead, so he must have been nine, when his Mom was first Diagnosed, Gately had gotten the Diagnosis mixed up in his head with King Arthur. He'd ride a mop-handle horse and brandish a trashcan-lid and a batteryless plastic Light-Saber and tell the neighborhood kids he was Sir Osis of Thuliver, most fearsomely loyal and fierce of Arthur's vessels. Since the summer now, when he mops Shattuck Shelter floors, he hears the Clopaclopaclop he used to make with his big square tongue as Sir Osis, then, riding.

And his dreams late that night, after the Braintree/Bob Death Commitment, seem to set him under a sort of sea, at terrific depths, the water all around him silent and dim and the same temperature he is.

VERY LATE OCTOBER Y.D.A.U.

Hal Incandenza had this horrible new recurring dream where he was losing his teeth, where his teeth had become like shale and splintered when he tried to chew, and fragmented and melted into grit in his mouth; in the dream he was going around squeezing a ball and spitting fragments and grit, getting more and more hungry and scared. Everything in there loosened by a great oral rot that the nightmare's Teddy Schacht wouldn't even look at, saying he was late for his next appointment, everyone Hal saw seeing Hal's crumbling teeth and looking at their watch and making vague excuses, a general atmosphere of the splintering teeth being a symptom of something way more dire and distasteful that no one wanted to confront him about. He was pricing dentures when he woke. It was about an hour before dawn drills. His keys were on the floor by the bed with his College Board prep books. Mario's great iron bed was empty and made up tight, all five pillows neatly stacked. Mario'd been spending the last few nights over at HmH, sleeping on an air mattress in the living room in front of Tavis's Tatsuoka receiver, listening to WYYY–109 into the wee hours, weirdly agitated about Madame Psychosis's unannounced sabbatical from the '60 Minutes +/−' midnight thing where she'd been an unvarying M-F presence for several years, it seemed like. WYYY had been evasive and unforthcoming about the whole thing. For two days some alto grad student had tried to fill in, billing herself as Miss Diagnosis, reading Horkheimer and Adorno against a background of Partridge Family slowed down to a narcotized slur. At no time had anyone of managerial pitch or timbre mentioned Madame Psychosis or what her story was or her date of expected return. Hal'd told Mario that the silence was a positive sign, that if she'd left the air for good the station would have had to say something. Hal, Coach Schtitt, and the Moms had all remarked Mario's odd mood. Mario was usually next to impossible to agitate.[180]

Now WYYY was back to running 'Sixty Minutes More or Less' without anybody at all at the helm. For the past several nights Mario has lain there in a sarcophagally tapered sleeping bag of GoreTex and fiberfill and listened to them run the weird static ambient musics Madame Psychosis uses for background, but now without any spoken voice as foreground; and the static, momentumless music as subject instead of environment is somehow terribly disturbing: Hal listened to a few minutes of the stuff and told his brother it sounded like somebody's mind coming apart right before your ears.

9 NOVEMBER
YEAR OF THE DEPEND ADULT UNDERGARMENT

The Enfield Tennis Academy has an accredited capacity of 148 junior players — of whom 80 are to be male — but an actual Fall Y.D.A.U. population of 95 paying and 41 scholarship students, so 136, of which 72 are female, right now, for some reason, meaning that while there's room for twelve more (preferably full-tuition) junior players, there ought ideally to be fully sixteen more males than there are, meaning Charles Tavis and Co. are wanting to fill all twelve available spots with males — plus they wouldn't exactly mind, is the general scuttlebutt, if a half dozen or so of the better girls left before graduation and tried for the Show, simply because housing more than 68 girls means putting some in the male dorms, which creates tensions and licensing- and conservative-parent-problems, given that coed hall bathrooms are not a good idea what with all the adolescent glands firing all over the place.

It also means that, since there are twice as many male prorectors as female, A.M. drills have to be complexly staggered, the boys in two sets of 32, the girls in three of 24, which creates problems in terms of early-P.M. classes for the lowest-ranked C-squad girls, who drill last.

Matriculations, gender quotas, recruiting, financial aid, room-assignments, mealtimes, rankings, class v. drill schedules, prorector-hiring, accommodating changes in drill schedule consequent to a player's movement up or down a squad. It's all the sort of thing that's uninteresting unless you're the one responsible, in which case it's cholesterol-raisingly stressful and complex. The stress of all the complexities and priorities to be triaged and then weighted against one another gets Charles Tavis out of bed in the Headmaster's House at an ungodly hour most mornings, his sleep-swollen face twitching with permutations. He stands in leather slippers at the living-room window, looking southeast past West and Center Courts at the array of A-team players assembling stiffly in the gray glow, carrying gear with their heads down and some still asleep on their feet, the first bit of snout of the sun protruding through the city's little skyline far beyond them, the aluminum glints of river and sea, east, Tavis's hands working nervously around the cup of hazelnut decaf that steams upward into his face as he holds it, hair unarranged and one side hanging, high forehead up against the window's glass so he can feel the mean chill of the dawn just outside, his lips moving slightly and without sound, the thing it's not entirely impossible he may have fathered asleep up next to the sound system with its claws on its chest and four pillows for bradypnea-afflicted breathing that sounds like soft repetitions of the words *sky* or *ski,* making no unnecessary sound, not eager to wake it and have to interface with it and have it look up at him with a terrible calm and accepting knowledge it's quite possible is nothing but Tavis's imagination, so lips moving w/o sound but breath and cup's steam spreading on the glass, and little icicles from the rainy melt of yesterday's snow hanging from the anodized gutters just above the window and seen by Tavis as a distant skyline upside-down. In the lightening sky the same two or three clouds seem to move back and forth like sentries. The heat comes on with a distant whoom and the glass against his forehead trembles slightly. A hiss of low static from the speaker it had fallen into sleep without turning off. The A-team's array keeps shifting and melding as they await Schtitt. Permutations of complications.

Tavis watches the boys stretch and confer and sips from the cup with both hands, the concerns of the day assembling themselves in a sort of tree-diagram of worry. Charles Tavis knows what James Incandenza could not have cared about less: the key to the successful administration of a top-level junior tennis academy lies in cultivating a kind of reverse-Buddhism, a state of Total Worry.

So the best E.T.A. players' special perk is they get hauled out of bed at dawn, still crusty-eyed and pale with sleep, to drill in the first shift.

Dawn drills are of course alfresco until they erect and inflate the Lung, which Hal Incandenza hopes is soon. His circulation is poor because of tobacco and/or marijuana, and even with his DUNLOP-down-both-legs sweatpants and a turtleneck and thick old white alpaca tennis jacket that had been his father's and has to be rolled up at the sleeves, he's sullen and chilled, Hal is, and by the time they've run the pre-stretch sprints up and down the E.T.A. hill four times, swinging their sticks madly in all directions and (at A. deLint's dictate) making various half-hearted warrior-noises, Hal is both chilled and wet, and his sneakers squelch from dew as he hops in place and looks at his breath, wincing as the cold air hits the one bad tooth.

By the time they're all stretching out, lined up in rows along the service- and baselines, flexing and bowing, genuflecting to nothing, changing postures at the sound of a whistle, by this time the sky has lightened to the color of Kaopectate. The ATHSCME fans are idle and the E.T.A.s can hear birds. Smoke from the stacks of the Sunstrand complex is weakly sunlit as it hangs in plumes, completely still, as if painted on the air. Tiny cries and a repetitive scream for help come up from someplace downhill to the east, presumably Enfield Marine. This is the one time of day the Charles doesn't look bright blue. The pines' birds don't sound any happier than the players. The grounds' non-pines are bare and canted at circuitous hillside angles all up and down the hill when they sprint again, four more times, then on bad days another four, maybe the most hated part of the day's conditioning. Somebody always throws up a little; it's like the drills' reveille. The river at dawn is a strip of foil's dull side. Kyle Coyle keeps saying it's co-wo-*wold*. All the lesser players are still abed. Today there's multiple retching, from last night's sweets. Hal's breath hangs before his face until he moves through it. Sprints produce the sick sound of much squelching; everyone wishes the hill's grass would die.

Twenty-four girls are drilled in groups of six on four of the Center Courts. The 32 boys (minus, rather ominously, J. J. Penn) are split by rough age into fours and take a semi-staggered eight of the East Courts. Schtitt is up in his little observational crow's nest, a sort of apse at the end of the iron transom players call the Tower that extends west to east over the centers of all three sets of courts and terminates w/ the nest high above the Show Courts. He has a chair and an ashtray up there. Sometimes from the courts you can see him leaning over the railing, tapping the edge of the bullhorn with his weatherman's pointer; from the West and Center Courts the rising sun behind him gives his white head a pinkish corona. When he's seated you just see misshapen smoke-rings coming up out of the nest and moving off with the wind. The sound of the bullhorn is scarier when you can't see him. The waffled iron stairs leading up to the transom are west of the West Courts, all the way across from the nest, so sometimes Schtitt paces back and forth along the transom with his pointer behind his back, his boots ringing out on the iron. Schtitt seems immune to all weather and always dresses the same for drills: the warm-ups and boots. When the E.T.A.s' strokes or play's being filmed for study, Mario Incandenza is positioned on the railing of Schtitt's nest, leaning way out and filming down, his police lock protruding into empty air, with somebody beefy assigned to stand behind him and grip the back of the Velcro vest: it always scares hell out of Hal because you can never see Dunkel or Nwangi behind Mario and it always looks like he's leaning way out to dive Bolex-first down onto Court 7's net.

Except during periods of disciplinary conditioning, alfresco A.M. drills work like this. A prorector is at each relevant court with two yellow Ball-Hopper-brand baskets of used balls, plus a ball machine, which machine looks like an open footlocker with a blunt muzzle at one end pointed across the net at a quartet of boys and connected by long orange industrial cords to a three-prong outdoor outlet at the base of each light-pole. Some of the light-poles cast long thin shadows across the courts as soon as the sun is strong enough for there to be shadows; in summertime players try to sort of huddle in the thin lines of shade. Ortho Stice keeps yawning and shivering; John Wayne wears a small cold smile. Hal hops up and down in his capacious jacket and plum turtleneck and looks at his breath and tries à la Lyle to focus very intently on the pain of his tooth without judging it as bad or good. K. D. Coyle, out of the infirmary after the weekend, opines that he doesn't see why the better players' reward for hard slogging to the upper rungs is dawn drills while for instance Pemulis and the Vikemeister et al. are still horizontal and sawing logs. Coyle says this every morning. Stice tells him he's surprised at how little they've missed him. Coyle is from the small Tucson AZ suburb of Erythema and claims to have thin desert blood and special sensitivity to the wet chill of Boston's dawn. The WhataBurger Jr. Invitational is a sort of double-edged Thanksgiving homecoming for Coyle, who at thirteen was lured from Tucson's own Rancho Vista Golf and Tennis Academy by promises of self-transcendence from Schtitt.

Drills work like this. Eight different emphases on eight different courts. Each quartet starts at a different court and rotates around. The top four traditionally start drills on the first court: backhands down the line, two boys to a side. Corbett Thorp lays down squares of electrician's tape at the court's corners and they are strongly encouraged to hit the balls into the little squares. Hal hits with Stice, Coyle with Wayne; Axford's been sent down with Shaw and Struck for some reason. Second court: forehands, same deal. Stice consistently misses the square and gets a low-pH rejoinder from Tex Watson, hatless and pattern-balding at twenty-seven. Hal's tooth hurts and his ankle is stiff and the cold balls come off his strings with a dead sound like *chung*. Tiny bratwursts of smoke ascend rhythmically from Schtitt's little nest. Third court is 'Butterflies,' a complex VAPS deal where

Hal hits a backhand down the line to Stice while Coyle forehands it to Wayne and then Wayne and Stice cross-court the balls back to Hal and Coyle, who have to switch sides without bashing into each other and hit back down the line now to Wayne and Stice, respectively. Wayne and Hal amuse themselves by making their cross-court balls collide on every fifth exchange or so — this is known around E.T.A. as 'atom-smashing' and is understandably hard to do — and the collided balls sprong wildly out onto the other practice courts, and Rik Dunkel is less amused than Wayne and Hal are, so, nicely warm now and arms singing, they're shunted quickly onto the fourth court: volleys for depth, then for angle, then lobs and overheads, which latter drill can be converted into a disciplinary Puker if a prorector's feeding you the lobs: the overhead drill's called 'Tap & Whack': Hal pedals back, terribly ankle-conscious, jumps, kicks out, nails Stice's lob, then has to sprint up and tap the net's tape with his Dunlop's head as Stice lobs deep again, and Hal has to backpedal again and jump and kick and hit it, and so on. Then Hal and Coyle, both sucking wind after twenty and trying to stand up straight, feed lobs to Wayne and Stice, neither of whom is fatiguable as far as anyone can tell. You have to kick out on overheads to keep your balance in the air. Overhead, Schtitt uses an unamplified bullhorn and careful enunciation to call out for everyone to hear that Mr. revenant Hal Incandenza was letting the ball get the little much behind him on overheads, fears of the ankle maybe. Hal raises his stick in acknowledgment without looking up. To hang in past age fourteen here is to become immune to humiliation from staff. Coyle tells Hal between the lobs they send up he'd love to see Schtitt have to do twenty Tap & Whacks in a row. They're all flushed to a shine, all chill washed off, noses running freely and heads squeaking with blood, the sun well above the sea's dull glint and starting to melt the frozen slush from I.-Day's snow and rain that night-custodians had swept into little wedged lines up against the lengthwise fences, which grimy wedges are now starting to melt and run. There's still no movement in the Sunstrand stacks' plumes. The watching prorectors stand easy with their legs apart and their arms crossed over their racquets' faces. The same three or four booger-shaped clouds seem to pass back and forth overhead, and when they cover the sun people's breath reappears. Stice blows on his racquet-hand and cries out thinly for the inflation of the Lung. Mr. A. F. deLint ranges behind the fence with his clipboard and whistle, blowing his nose. The girls behind him are too bundled up to be worth watching, their hair rubber-banded into little bouncing tails.

Fifth court: serves to both corners of both boxes, catching each others' serves and serving them back. First serves, second serves, slice serves, shank serves, and back-snapping American Twist serves that Stice begs off of, telling the prorector — Neil Hartigan, who's 2 m. tall and of so few words everybody fears him by default — he's having lower spasms from a mispositioned bed. Then Coyle — he of the weak bladder and suspicious discharge — gets excused to go back into the eastern tree-line out of sight of the distaffs and pee, so the other three get a minute to jog over to the pavilion and stand with their hands on their hips and breathe and drink Gatorade out of little conic paper cups you can't put down til they're empty. The way you flush out a cottony mouth between drills is you take a mouthful of Gatorade and puff out your cheeks to make a globe of liquid that you mangle with your teeth and tongue, then lean out and spit out into the grass and take another drink for real. The sixth court is returns of serve down the line, down the center, cross-court for depth, then for placement, then for deep placement, w/ more taped squares; then chipped center- and cross-returns against a server who follows his serve to the net. The server practices half-volleys off the chips, although Wayne and Stice are so fast that they're on top of the net by the time the return gets to them and they can volley it away at chest-height. Wayne drills with the casual economy of somebody who's in about second gear. The urns' dispensers' cups can't stand up, their bottoms are pointy and they'll spill any liquid still in them, is why you have to empty them. Between squads Harde's guys will sweep the pavilion of dozens of cones.

Then, blessedly, on the seventh court, physically undemanding Finesse drills. Drops, drops for angles, topspin lobs, extreme angles, drops for extreme angles, then restful microtennis, tennis inside the service lines, very soft and precise, radical angles much encouraged. Touch- and artistry-wise nobody comes close to Hal in microtennis. By this time Hal's turtleneck is soaked through under the alpaca jacket, and exchanging it for a sweatshirt out of the gear bag is a kind of renewal. What wind there is down here is out of the south. The temperature is now probably in the low 10's C.; the sun's been up an hour, and you can almost see the light-pole and transom shadows rotating slowly northwest. The Sunstrand stacks' plumes stand there cigarette-straight, not even seeming to spread at the top; the sky is going a glassy blue.

No (tennis) balls required on the final court. Wind sprints. Probably the less said about wind sprints the better. Then more Gatorade, which Hal and Coyle are breathing too hard to enjoy, as Schtitt comes slowly down from the transom. It takes a while. You can hear his steel-toed boots hit each iron step. There is something creepy about a very fit older man, to say nothing of jackboots w/ Fila warm-ups of claret-colored silk. He's coming this way, both hands behind his back and the pointer poking out to the side. Schtitt's crew cut and face are nacreous as he moves east in the yellowing A.M. light. This is sort of the signal for all the quartets to gather at the Show Courts. Behind them the girls are still hitting groundstrokes in baroque combinations, much high-pitched grunting and the lifeless *chung* of cold hit balls. Three 14's are made to squeegee the more extrusive melt back into the little banks of frozen leaves along the fence. At the horizon to the north a bulbous cone of picric clouds that gets taller by the hour as the Methuen–Andover border's mammoth effectuators force northern MA's combined oxides north against some sort of upper-air resistance, it looks like. You can see little bits of glitter from broken monitor-glass in the frozen stuff up by the fences behind 6–9, and one or two curved shards of floppy disk, and they're a troubling sight, Penn being absent amid troubling leg-rumors, Postal-Weight with two black eyes and his nose covered with horizontal bandages that are starting to loosen and curl at the edges from sweat, and Otis P. Lord alleged to have come back from the emergency room at St. Elizabeth's last night with the Hitachi monitor over his head, still, its removal, with all the sharp teeth of the broken screen's glass pointing at key parts of Lord's throat, apparently calling for the sort of esoteric expertise you have to fly in by private medical jet, according to Axford.

They all get on the outside of three cones of Gatorade, bent or squatting, sucking wind, while Schtitt stands at a sort of Parade Rest with his weather-man's pointer behind his back and shares overall impressions with the players on the morning's work thus far. Certain players are singled out for special mention or humiliation. Then more wind sprints. Then a brief like strategy-clinic-thing from Corbett Thorp on how approach shots down the line aren't always the very best tactic, and why. Thorp's a first-rate tennis mind, but his terrible stutter makes the boys so uncomfortable they have a hard time listening.[181]

The whole first shift's on the eighth court for the final conditioning drills.[182] First are Star Drills. A dozen-plus boys on either side of the net, behind the baselines. Form a line. Go one at a time. Go: run up the side line, touch the net with your stick; then backwards to the outside corner of the service box and then forward to touch the net again; backward to the middle of the service box, forward to touch net; back to the baseline's little jut of centerline, up to net; service box's other outside corner, net, baseline's corner, net, then turn and run like hell for the corner you started from. Schtitt has a stopwatch. There's a janitorial bucket[183] placed in the doubles alley by the finish point, for potential distress. They each do the Star Drill three times. Hal has 41 seconds and 38 and 48, which is average both for him and for any seventeen-year-old with a resting pulse rate in the high 50s. John Wayne's low of 33 occurs on his third Star, and he stops dead at the finish point and always just stands there, never bending or walking it off. Stice gets a 29 and everyone gets very excited until Schtitt says he was slow starting the watch: the arthritis in a thumb. Everyone but Wayne and Stice uses the retch-bucket in a sort of pro forma way. Sixteen-year-old Petropolis Kahn, a.k.a. 'W.M.' for 'Woolly Mammoth' because he's so hairy, gets a 60 and then a 59 and then pitches forward onto the hard surface and lies very still. Tony Nwangi tells people to walk around him.

The cardiovascular finale is Side-to-Sides, conceived by van der Meer in the B.S. '60s and demonic in its simplicity. Again split into fours on eight courts. For the top 18's, prorector R. Dunkel at net with an armful of balls and more in a hopper beside him, hitting fungoes, one to the forehand corner and then one to the backhand corner and then farther out to the forehand corner and so on. And on. Hal Incandenza is expected at least to get a racquet on each ball; for Stice and Wayne the expectations are higher. A very unpleasant drill fatigue-wise, and for Hal also ankle-wise, what with all the stopping and reversing. Hal wears two bandages over a left ankle he shaves way more often than his upper lip. Over the bandages goes an Air-Stirrup inflatable ankle brace that's very lightweight but looks a bit like a medieval torture-implement. It was in a stop-and-reverse move much like Side-to-Sides[184] that Hal tore all the soft left-ankle tissue he then owned, at fifteen, in his ankle, at Atlanta's Easter Bowl, in the third round, which he was losing anyway. Dunkel goes fairly easy on Hal, at least on the first two go-arounds, because of the ankle. Hal's going to be seeded in at least the top 4 at the WhataBurger Inv. in a couple weeks, and woe to the prorector who lets Hal get hurt the way Hal let some of his Little Buddies get hurt yesterday.

What's potentially demonic about Side-to-Sides is that the duration of the drill and pace and angle of the fungoes to be chased down from side to side are entirely at the prorector's discretion. Prorector Rik Dunkel, a former 16's-doubles runner-up at Jr. Wimbledon and a decent enough guy, the son of some kind of plastic-packaging-systems tycoon on the South Shore, tied with Thorp for brightest of the prorectors (more or less by default), regarded as kind of a mystic because he refers people sometimes to Lyle and has been observed sitting at community gatherings with his eyes closed but not sleeping . . . but the point is a decent enough guy but not much into any kind of exchange of quarter. He seems to have received instructions to put the particular hurt on Ortho Stice this time, and by his third go-around Stice is trying to weep without breath and mewing for his aunts.[185] But anyway everybody goes through Sides-to-Sides three times. Even Petropolis Kahn staggers through them, who after Stars had had to be sort of lugged over by Stephan Wagenknecht and Jeff Wax with his Nikes dragging behind him and his head swinging free on his neck and given kind of a swingset-shove to get started. Hal feels for Kahn, who's not fat but is in the Schacht-type mold, very thick and solid, except also carrying extra weight in terms of leg-and-back-hair, and who always tires easily no matter how hard he conditions. Kahn makes it through but stays bent over the distress-bucket long after the third go-around, staring into it, and stays that way while everybody else removes more soaked bottom layers of clothing and accepts clean towels from a halfway-house part-time black girl with a towel cart, and picks up balls.[186]

It is 0720h. and they are through with the active part of dawn drills. Nwangi, at the edge of the hillside, is whistling the next shift over for opening sprints. Schtitt shares more overall impressions as minimum-wage aides dispense Kleenex and paper cones. Nwangi's reedy voice carries; he's telling the B's he wishes to see nothing but assholes and elbows on these sprints. It's unclear to Hal what this might connote. The A-players have formed those ragged rows behind the baseline again, and Schtitt paces back and forth.

'Am seeing sluggish drilling, by sluggards. Not meaning insults. This is the fact. Motions are gone through. Barely minimal efforts. Cold, yes? The cold hands and nose with mucus? Thoughts on getting through, going in, hot showers, water very hot. A meal. The thoughts are drifting toward the comfort of ending. Too cold to demand the total, yes? Master Chu, too cold for tennis at the high level, yes?'

Chu: 'It does seem pretty cold out, sir.'

'Ah.' Pacing back and forth with about-faces at every tenth step, stopwatch around his neck, pipe and pouch and pointer in his hands behind his back, nodding to himself, clearly wishing he had a third hand so he could stroke his white chin, pretending to ruminate. Every A.M. essentially the same, except when Schtitt does the females and the males get dressed down by deLint. All the older boys' eyes are glazed with repetition. Hal's tooth gives off little electric shivers with each inbreath, and he feels slightly unwell. When he moves his head slightly the monitor-glass bits' glitter shifts and dances along the opposite fence in a sort of sickening way.

'Ah.' Turns crisply toward them, looking briefly skyward. 'And when is hot? Too pretty hot for the total self on the court? The other hand of the spectrum? Ach. Is always something that is *too*. Master Incandenza who cannot quickly get behind lob's descent so weight can move *forvart* into overhand,[187] please tell your thinking: it is always hot or cold, yes?'

A small smile. ''s been our general observation out there, sir.'

'So then then so, Master Chu, from California's temperance regions?'

Chu brings down his hankie. 'I guess we have to learn to adjust to conditions, sir, I believe is what you're saying.'

A full sharp half-turn to face the group. 'Is what I am *not* saying, young LaMont Chu, is why you cease to seem to give total effort of self since you begin with the clipping pictures of great professional figures for your adhesive tape and walls. No? Because, privileged gentlemen and boys I am saying, is always something that is *too*. Cold. Hot. Wet and dry. Very bright sun and you see the purple dots. Very bright hot and you have no salt. Outside is wind, the insects which like the sweat. Inside is smell of heaters, echo, being jammed in together, tarp is overclose to baseline, not enough of room, bells inside clubs which ring the hour loudly to distract, clunk of machines vomiting sweet cola for coins. Inside roof too low for the lob. Bad lighting, so. Or outside: the bad surface. Oh no look no: crabgrass in cracks along baseline. Who could give the total, with crabgrass. Look here is low net high net. Opponent's relatives heckle, opponent cheats, linesman in semifinal is impaired or cheats. You hurt. You have the injury. Bad knee and back. Hurt groin area from not stretching as asked. Aches of elbow. Eyelash in eye. The throat is sore. A too pretty girl in audience, watching. Who could play like this? Big crowd overwhelming or too small to inspire. Always something.'

His turns as he paces are crisp and used to punctuate. 'Adjust. Adjust? Stay the *same*. No? Is not stay the same? It is cold? It is wind? Cold and wind is the world. Outside, yes? On the tennis court the you the player: this is not where there is cold wind. I am saying. Different world *in*side. World built inside cold outside world of wind breaks the wind, shelters the player, you, if you stay the same, stay inside.' Pacing gradually faster, the turns becoming pirouettic. The older kids stare straight ahead; some of the younger follow every move of the pointer with wide eyes. Trevor Axford is bent at the waist and moving his head slightly, trying to get the sweat dripping off his face to spell something out on the surface. Schtitt is silent for two fast about-faces, ranging before them, tapping his jaw with the pointer. 'Not ever I think this adjusting. To what, this adjusting? This world inside is the same, always, if you stay there. This is what we are making, no? New type citizen. Not of cold and wind outside. Citizens of this sheltering second world we are working to show you every dawn, no? To make your introduction.' The Big Buddies translate Schtitt into accessible language for the littler kids, is a big part of their assignment.

'Borders of court for singles Mr. Rader are what.'

'Twenty-four by eight sir,' sounding hoarse and thin.

'So. Second world without cold or purple dots of bright for you is 23.8 meters, 8 I think .2 meters. Yes? In that world is joy because there is shelter of *something else,* of purpose past sluggardly self and complaints about uncomfort. I am speaking to not just LaMont Chu of the temperance world. You have a chance to *occur,* playing. No? To make for you this second world that is always the same: there is in this world you, and in the hand a tool, there is a ball, there is opponent with his tool, and always only two of you, you and this other, inside the lines, with always a purpose to keep this world alive, yes?' The pointer-motions through all this become too orchestral and intricate to describe. 'This second world inside the lines. Yes? Is this *adjusting?* This is not adjusting. This is not adjusting to *ignore* cold and wind and tired. Not ignoring "as if." *Is* no cold. *Is* no wind. No cold wind where you *occur.* No? Not "adjust to conditions." Make this second world inside the world: here there *are* no conditions.'

Looks around.

'So put a lid on it about the fucking cold,' says deLint, with his clipboard under his arm and his strangler-sized hands in his pockets, hopping a little in place.

Schtitt is looking around. Like most Germans outside popular entertainment, he gets quieter when he wants to impress or menace. (There are very few shrill Germans, actually.) 'If it is hard,' he says softly, hard to hear because of the rising wind, 'difficult, for you to move between the two worlds, from cold hot wind and sun to this inside place inside the lines where is always the same,' he says, seeming now to study the weatherman's pointer he holds down and out with both hands, 'it can be arranged for you gentlemen not to leave, ever here, this world inside the lines of court. You know. Can stay here until there is citizenship. Right here.' The pointer is pointed at the spots they're standing at breathing and blotting their faces and blowing their noses. 'Can today put up Testar Lung, for world's shelter. Sleep bags. Meals brought to you. Never across the lines. Never leave the court. Study here. A bucket for hygienic needs. At Gymnasium Kaiserslautern where I am privileged boy who whining about cold wind, we live inside tennis court for months, to learn to live inside. Very lucky days when they bring us meals. Not possible to cross a line for months of living.'

Left-hander Brian van Vleck picks a bad moment to break wind.

Schtitt shrugs, half-turning away from them to look off somewhere. 'Or else leave here into large external world where is cold and pain without purpose or tool, eyelash in eye and pretty girl — not worry anymore about how to *occur*.' Looks around. 'No one is a prisoner here. Who would like to escape into large world? Master Sweeny?'

Little eyes down.

'Mr. Coyle, with always too co-wold to give total?'

Coyle studies the vasculature on the inside of his elbow with deep interest as he shakes his head. John Wayne is joggling his head around like a Raggedy-Andy-head, stretching out the neck hardware. John Wayne is notoriously tight and can't touch anything below the knee with straight legs during stretches.

'Mr. Peter Beak with always the weeping to home on the telephone?'

The twelve-year-old says Not Me Sir several times.

Hal very subtly shoots in a small plug of Kodiak. Aubrey deLint has his arms crossed over the clipboard and is looking around beadily like a crow. Hal Incandenza has an almost obsessive dislike for deLint, whom he tells Mario he sometimes cannot quite believe is even real, and tries to get to the side of, to see whether deLint has a true z coordinate or is just a cutout or projection. The kids of the next shift are walking downhill and sprinting back up and walking down, warrior-whooping without conviction. The other male prorectors are drinking cones of Gatorade, clustered in the little pavilion, feet up on patio-chairs, Dunkel's and Watson's eyes closed. Neil Hartigan, in his traditional Tahitian shirt and Gaugin-motif sweater, has to stay sitting down to fit under the Gatorade awning.

'Simple,' Schtitt shrugs, so that the upraised pointer seems to stab at the sky. 'Hit,' he suggests. 'Move. Travel lightly. Occur. Be *here*. Not in bed or shower or over baconschteam, in the mind. Be *here* in total. Is nothing else. Learn. Try. Drink your green juice. Perform the Butterfly exercises on all eight of these courts, please, to warm down. Mr. deLint, please to bring them back down, make sure of stretching the groins. Gentlemen: hit tennis balls. Fire at your will. Use a head. You are not arms. Arm in the real tennis is like wheels of vehicles. Not engine. Legs: not either. Where is where you apply for citizenship in second world Mr. consciousness of ankle Incandenza, our revenant?'

Hal can lean out and spit in a way that isn't insolent. 'Head, sir.'

'Excuse?'

'The human head, sir, if I got your thrust. Where I'm going to occur as a player. The game's two heads' one world. One world, sir.'

Schtitt sweeps the pointer in an ironic morendo arc and laughs aloud: 'Play.'

Part of Don Gately's live-in Staff job is that he hurtles here and there on selected Ennet House errands. He cooks the communal supper on weekdays,[188] which means he does the House's weekly shopping, which means that at least a couple times a week he gets to take Pat Montesian's black 1964 Ford Aventura and drive to the Purity Supreme Market. The Aventura is an antique variant of the Mustang, the sort of car you usually only see waxed and static in car shows with somebody in a bikini pointing at it. Pat's is functional and mint-reconditioned — her shadowy husband with something like ten years sober being big into cars — with such a wicked nice multilayer paint job that its black has the bottomless quality of water at night. It has two different alarm systems and a red metal bar you're supposed to lock across the steering wheel when you get out. The engine sounds more like a jet engine than a piston engine, plus there's a scoop poking periscopically from the hood, and for Gately the vehicle's so terrifically tight and sleek it's like being strapped into a missile and launched at the site of a domestic errand. He can barely fit in the driver's seat. The steering wheel is about the size of an old video-arcade game's steering wheel, and the thin canted six-speed shift is encased in a red leather baglet that smells strongly of leather. The height of the car's roof compromises Gately's driving-posture, and his right ham like exceeds the seat and squeezes against the gearshift so that shifting pinches his hip. He does not care. Some of the profoundest spiritual feelings of his sobriety so far are for this car. He'd drive this car if the driver's seat was just a sharp pointy spike, he told Johnette Foltz. Johnette Foltz is the other live-in Staffer, though between ultra-rabid Commitment-activity in NA and a somehow damaged NA fiancé she spends a lot of time pushing around places in a wicker wheelchair, she's around Ennet House less and less now, and there are rumblings about a possible replacement, which Gately and the heterosexual male residents pray daily will be the leggy alumna and part-time counselor Danielle Steenbok, who's rumored also to attend Sex and Love Addicts Anonymous, which engages everyone's imagination to the max.

It's a mark of serious regard and questionable judgment that Director Pat M. lets Don Gately drive her priceless Aventura, even just to like the Metro Food Bank or Purity Supreme, because Gately lost his license more or less permanently back in the Year of the Whisper-Quiet Maytag Dishmaster for getting pinched on a DUI in Peabody on a license that had already been suspended for a previous DUI in Lowell. This was not the only Loss Don Gately incurred as his chemical careers moved toward their life-reversing climax. Once every couple months now, still, he has to put on his brown dress slacks and slightly irregular green sportcoat from Brighton Budget Large 'N Tall Menswear and take the commuter rail up to selected District Court venues on the North Shore and meet with his various P.D.s and P.O.s and caseworkers and sometimes appear briefly up in front of Judges and Review Boards to review the progress of his sobriety and reparations. When he first came to Ennet House last year, Gately had Bad-Check and Forgery issues, he had a Malicious Destruction of Property issue, plus two D&Ds and a bullshit Public Urination out of Tewksbury. He had a Break-and-Enter from a silent-alarmed Peabody mansion where he and a colleague got pinched before anything could get promoted. He had a Possession With Intent from 38 50-mg. tablets of Demerol[189] in a Pez container which he'd shoved down into the crack of the Peabody Finest's cruiser's back seat, but which got found anyway on the routine post-transport cruiser-search all cops perform when the arrestee's pupils are unresponsive both to light and to head-slaps.

There was, too, of course, a certain darker issue, vis-à-vis a certain upscale Brookline home whose late owner had been eulogized at terrifying length and headline-size in both the *Globe* and *Herald*. After eight months of indescribable psychic cringing, waiting for the legal footwear to drop on the Nuck-VIP issue — toward the end of his drug-use Gately'd gotten sloppy and crazy and stuck idiotically with a method of straight meter-shunting that he'd learned up at MCI-Billerica and was pretty sure now constituted a signature Gately M.O., since the older guy that'd taught it to him in the Billerica metal-shop had subsequently got out and gone to Utah and died of a morphine overdose (and like who on earth hopes to get reliable morphine in fucking *Utah?*) over two years ago — after eight months of cringing and nail-biting, the last couple months of the torment in Ennet House — even though the House's D.S.A.S.-license put it legally off-limits to all constabulary without Pat Montesian's physical presence and notarized permission — after he was down to the cuticles on all ten digits, Gately had very discreetly approached a certain Percodan-devoted court stenographer an old girlfriend had once dealt to, and had the guy make equally discreet inquiries, and found that the potential Murder–2 investigation of the botched burglary[190] had been taken over — *pace* the loud howls of a certain remorseless Revere A.D.A. — by something federal the addled stenographer called 'Non-Specific Services Bureau,' whereupon the case vanished from any sort of investigative scene the stenographer could make inquiries about, though quiet rumor had it that current suspicions were being directed at certain shadowy Nucko-political bodies all the way up in Quebec, far north of the Enfield MA where Gately had been cringing his way to nightly AA meetings with his fingers in his mouth.

Most of the cases Gately had had pending his P.D. had gotten Closed Without Finding,[191] contingent on Gately's entering long-term treatment and maintaining chemical abstinence and submitting to random urinalyses and making biweekly reparation payments out of the pathetic paychecks he earned cleaning shit and sperm under Stavros Lobokulas and now also cooking and live-in-Staffing at Ennet House. The only issue not resolved on a Blue-File deferral was the business of driving with a DUI-suspended license. In the Commonwealth of MA, this issue carries a mandatory 90-day bit, as in like the penalty's written right into the statute; and the case's P.D. has been up-front with Gately about it's only a matter of the time of the wheels' slow judicial grind before some judge Red-Files the issue and the case and Gately has to do the bit at someplace MCI-Minimum like Concord or Deer Island. Gately isn't too hinked about 90 inside. At twenty-four he'd done 17 months at Billerica for assaulting two bouncers in a nightclub — it was more like he'd beaten the second bouncer bloody with the unconscious body of the first — and he knew quite well he could get by in a Commonwealth lockdown. He was too big to fuck or fuck with and not interested in fucking with anyone else: he did his time stand-up and gave nobody any provoking cause; and when the first couple hard guys had come after him for his canteen cigarettes he'd laughed it off with ferocious jolliness, and when they came back a second time Gately beat them half to death in the corridor behind the weight room where he could be sure plenty of other guys could hear it, and after that one incident was out of the way he could simply get by and not get fucked with. Gately now was hinked only about the prospect of getting just one or two AA meetings a week in jail — the only meetings sober inmates get are when an area Group comes in on an Institutional Commitment, which Gately's been on — when Demerol and Talwin and good old weed are almost easier to get in jail than in the outside world. Gately cringed now only at the thought of the Sergeant at Arms, the distinguished-looking shepherd guy. Going back to ingesting Substances had become his biggest fear. Even Gately can tell this is a major psychic turn-around. He tells the newer residents right up front that AA's somehow gotten him by the mental curlies: he'll now go to literally Any Lengths to stay clean.

He'll tell them right out that he'd first come to Ennet House only to keep out of jail, and hadn't had much interest or hope about actually staying clean for any length of time; and he'd been up-front with Pat Montesian about this during his application interview. The grim honesty about his disinterest and hopelessness was one reason Pat even let such a clearly bad-news specimen into the House on nothing but a lukewarm referral from a P.O. up at the 5th District office in Peabody. Pat told Gately that grim honesty and hopelessness were the only things you need to start recovering from Substance-addiction, but that without these qualities you were totally up the creek. Desperation helped also, she said. Gately scratched at her dog's stomach and said he wasn't sure if he was desperate about anything except wanting to somehow stop getting in trouble for things he usually afterward couldn't even remember he did them. The dog trembled and shuddered and its eyes rolled up as Gately, who hadn't been told about Pat's thing about wanting her dogs petted, rubbed its scabby stomach. Pat had said like well that was enough, that desire for the shitstorm to end.[192] Gately said her dog sure did like having its stomach rubbed, and Pat explained that the dog was epileptic, and said that just a desire to stop blacking out was more than enough to start with. She pulled some Commonwealth Substance-Abuse study in a black plastic binder off a long black plastic bookshelf filled with black plastic binders. It turned out Pat Montesian liked the color black a lot. She was dressed — really kind of overdressed, for a halfway house — in black leather pants and a black shirt of silk or something silky. Outside the bay window a Green Line train was laboring up the first Enfield hill in the late-summer rain. The downhill view from the bay window over Pat's black lacquer or enamelish desk was like the only spectacular thing about Ennet House, which was otherwise a wicked awful dump. Pat made a sound against the binder with a Svelte nail-extension and said that in this state study right here, conducted in the Year of the Tucks Medicated Pad, over 60% of the inmates serving Life sentences in hellish MCI-Walpole and not disputing that they'd done what they'd done to get in there nevertheless had no memory of having done it, whatever got them in there. For Life. None. Gately had to have her run it by him a couple times before he isolated her point. They'd been in blackouts. Pat said a blackout was where you continued to function — sometimes disastrously — but weren't aware later of what you did. It's like your mind wasn't in possession of your body, and it was usually brought on by alcohol but could also be brought on by chronic use of other Substances, synthetic narcotics among them. Gately said he couldn't recall ever having a real blackout, and Pat M. got it but didn't laugh. The dog was heaving and quivering with its legs spronged out to all points of the compass and kind of spasming, and Gately didn't know whether to quit rubbing on it. To be honest he didn't know what epilepsy was but suspected Pat was not referring to the woman's leg-shaver thing his totally alcoholic past girlfriend Pamela Hoffman-Jeep used to scream in the bathroom when she used. Everything mental for Gately was kind of befogged and prone to misprision for well into his first year clean.

Pat Montesian was both pretty and not. She was in maybe her late thirties. She'd supposedly been this young and pretty and wealthy socialite out on the Cape until her husband had divorced her for being a nearly full-blown alcoholic, which seemed like abandonment and didn't improve her subsequent drinking one jot. She'd been in and out of rehabs and halfway places in her twenties, but then it wasn't until she'd almost died from a stroke during the D.T.s one A.M. that she'd been able to Surrender and Come In with the requisite hopeless desperation, etc. Gately didn't wince when he heard about Pat's stroke because his mom hadn't had D.T.s or a classic stroke, but rather a cirrhotic hemorrhage that made her choke and deprived her brain of oxygen and had irreparably vegetabilized her brain. The two cases were totally, like, apart in his mind. Pat M. was never in any way a mother-figure for Gately. Pat liked to smile and say, when residents pissed and moaned about their own addictions' Losses during the weekly House Community Meeting, she'd nod and smile and say that for her, the stroke had been far and away the best thing that's ever happened to her because it enabled her to finally Surrender. She'd come to Ennet House in an electric wheelchair at thirty-two and been unable to communicate except via like Morse-Code blinks or something for the first six months,[193] but had even without use of her arms demonstrated a willingness to try and eat a rock when the founding Guy Who Didn't Even Use His First Name told her to, using her torso and neck to like chop downwardly at the rock and chipping both incisors (you can still see the caps at the corners), and had gotten sober, and remarried a different and older South Shore like trillionaire with what sounded like psychotic kids, and but regained an unexpected amount of function, and had been working at the House ever since. The right side of her face was still pulled way over in this sort of rictus, and her speech took Gately some getting used to — it sounded like she was still loaded all the time, a kind of overenunciated slurring. The half of her face that wasn't rictusized was very pretty, and she had very long pretty red hair, and a sexually credible body even though her right arm had atrophied into a kind of semi-claw[194] and the right hand was strapped into this black plastic brace to keep its nail-extensioned fingers from curling into her palm; and Pat walked with a dignified but godawful lurch, dragging a terribly thin right leg in black leather pants behind her like something hanging on to her that she was trying to get away from.

During his residency, she'd gone personally with Gately on most of his bigger court-dates, driving him up to the North Shore in the killer Aventura with its Handicapped plates — she because of the neurological right-leg thing literally had a lead foot, and drove all the time like a maniac, and Gately had usually almost wet himself on Rte. 1 — and she'd throw all Ennet House's substantial respect and clout behind him with Judges and Boards, until every issue that could be resolved without finding was Blue-Filed. Gately still couldn't figure out why all the personal extra attention and help. It was like he'd been Pat M.'s biggest favorite among the residents last year. She did have favorites and nonfavorites; it was probably unavoidable. Annie Parrot and the counselors and House Manager always had their particular favorites, too, so it all tended to work out square.

About four months into his Ennet House residency, the agonizing desire to ingest synthetic narcotics had been mysteriously magically removed from Don Gately, just like the House Staff and the Crocodiles at the White Flag Group had said it would if he pounded out the nightly meetings and stayed minimally open and willing to persistently ask some extremely vague Higher Power to remove it. The desire. They said to get creakily down on his mammoth knees in the A.M. every day and ask God As He Understood Him to remove the agonizing desire, and to hit the old knees again at night before sack and thank this God-ish figure for the Substanceless day just ended, if he got through it. They suggested he keep his shoes and keys under the bed to help him remember to get on his knees. The only times Gately had ever been on his knees before were to throw up or mate, or shunt a low-on-the-wall alarm, or if somebody got lucky during a beef and landed one near Gately's groin. He didn't have any God- or J.C.-background, and the knee-stuff seemed like the limpest kind of dickless pap, and he felt like a true hypocrite just going through the knee-motions that he went through faithfully every A.M. and P.M., without fail, motivated by a desire to get loaded so horrible that he often found himself humbly praying for his head to just finally explode already and get it over with. Pat had said it didn't matter at this point what he thought or believed or even said. All that mattered was what he *did*. If he did the right things, and kept doing them for long enough, what Gately thought and believed would magically change. Even what he said. She'd seen it happen again and again, and to some awfully unlikely candidates for change. She said it had happened to her. The left side of her face was very alive and kind. And Gately's counselor, an ex-coke and -phone-bunko guy whose left ear had been one of his Losses, had hit Gately early on with the infamous Boston AA cake analogy. The grizzled Filipino had met with the resident Don G. once a week, driving Gately around Brighton-Allston in aimless circles in a customized Subaru 4×4 just like the ones Gately used to hotwire and promote to use for burgling. Eugenio Martinez had this eccentric thing where he maintained he could only be in touch with his own

Higher Power when he was driving. Down near E.W.D.'s barge-docks off the Allston Spur one night he invited Gately to think of Boston AA as a box of Betty Crocker Cake Mix. Gately had smacked himself in the forehead at yet another limp oblique Gene M. analogy, which Gene had already bludgeoned him with several insectile tropes for thinking about the Disease. The counselor had let him vent spleen for a while, smoking as he crawled along behind land-barges lined up to unload. He told Gately to just imagine for a second that he's holding a box of Betty Crocker Cake Mix, which represented Boston AA. The box came with directions on the side any eight-year-old could read. Gately said he was waiting for the mention of some kind of damn insect inside the cake mix. Gene M. said all Gately had to do was for fuck's sake give himself a break and relax and for once shut up and just follow the directions on the side of the fucking box. It didn't matter one fuckola whether Gately like *believed* a cake would result, or whether he *understood* the like fucking baking-chemistry of *how* a cake would result: if he just followed the motherfucking directions, and had sense enough to get help from slightly more experienced bakers to keep from fucking the directions up if he got confused somehow, but basically the point was if he just followed the childish directions, a cake would result. He'd have his cake. The only thing Gately knew about cake was that the frosting was the best part, and he personally found Eugenio Martinez a smug and self-righteous prick — plus he'd always distrusted both Orientals and spics, and Gene M. managed to seem like both — but he didn't screw out of the House or quite do anything they could Discharge him for, and he went to meetings nightly and told the more or less truth, and he did the shoe-under-bed knee thing every A.M./P.M. 24/7, and he took the suggestion to join a Group and get rabidly Active and clean up ashtrays and go out speaking on Commitments. He had nothing in the way of a like God-concept, and at that point maybe even less than nothing in terms of interest in the whole thing; he treated prayer like setting an oven-temp according to a box's direction. Thinking of it as talking to the ceiling was somehow preferable to imagining talking to Nothing. And he found it embarrassing to get down on his knees in his underwear, and like the other guys in the room he always pretended his sneakers were like way under the bed and he had to stay down there a while to find them and get them out, when he prayed, but he did it, and beseeched the ceiling and thanked the ceiling, and after maybe five months Gately was riding the Greenie at 0430 to go clean human turds out of the Shattuck shower and all of a sudden realized that quite a few days had gone by since he'd even thought about Demerol or Talwin or even weed. Not just merely getting through those last few days — Substances hadn't even *occurred* to him. I.e. the Desire and Compulsion had been Removed. More weeks went by, a blur of Commitments and meetings and gasper-smoke and clichés, and he still didn't feel anything like his old need to get high. He was, in a way,

Free. It was the first time he'd been out of this kind of mental cage since he was maybe ten. He couldn't believe it. He wasn't Grateful so much as kind of suspicious about it, the Removal. How could some kind of Higher Power he didn't even believe in magically let him out of the cage when Gately had been a total hypocrite in even asking something he didn't believe in to let him out of a cage he had like zero hope of ever being let out of? When he could only get himself on his knees for the prayers in the first place by pretending to look for his shoes? He couldn't for the goddamn *life* of him understand how this thing worked, this thing that was working. It drove him bats. At about seven months, at the little Sunday Beginners' Mtg., he actually cracked one of the Provident's fake-wood tabletops beating his big square head against it.[195]

White Flagger ('Ferocious') Francis Gehaney, one of the most ancient and gnarled of the Crocodiles, had a white crew cut and skallycap and suspenders over the flannel shirt that encased his gut, and an enormous cucumber-shaped red schnoz you could actually see whole arteries in the skin of, and brown stumpy teeth and emphysema and a portable little oxygen-tank thing whose blue tube was held under the schnoz with white tape, and the very clear bright eye-whites that went along with the extremely low resting pulse-rate of a guy with geologic amounts of sober AA time. Ferocious Francis G., whose mouth was never without a toothpick and who had on his right forearm a faded martini-glass-and-naked-lady tattoo of Korean-War-vintage, who'd gotten sober under the Nixon administration and who communicated in the obscene but antiquated epigrams the Crocs all used[196] — F.F. had taken Gately out for eye-rattling amounts of coffee, after the incident with the table and the head. He'd listened with the slight boredom of detached Identification to Gately's complaint that there was no way something he didn't understand enough to even start to believe in was seriously going to be interested in helping save his ass, even if He/She/It did in some sense exist. Gately still doesn't quite know why it helped, but somehow it helped when Ferocious Francis suggested that maybe anything minor-league enough for Don Gately to understand probably wasn't going to be major-league enough to save Gately's addled ass from the well-dressed Sergeant at Arms, now, was it?

That was months ago. Gately usually no longer much cares whether he understands or not. He does the knee-and-ceiling thing twice a day, and cleans shit, and listens to dreams, and stays Active, and tells the truth to the Ennet House residents, and tries to help a couple of them if they approach him wanting help. And when Ferocious Francis G. and the White Flaggers presented him, on the September Sunday that marked his first year sober, with a faultlessly baked and heavily frosted one-candle cake, Don Gately had cried in front of nonrelatives for the first time in his life. He now denies that he actually did cry, saying something about candle-fumes in his eye. But he did.

Gately is an unlikely choice for Ennet House chef, having fed for most of the last twelve years on sub-shop subs and corporate snack foods consumed amid some sort of motion. He is 188 cm. and 128 kg. and had never once eaten broccoli or a pear until last year. Chef-wise, he offers up an exceptionless routine of: boiled hot dogs; dense damp meat loaf with little pieces of American cheese and half a box of cornflakes on top, for texture; Cream of Chicken soup over spirochete-shaped noodles; ominously dark, leathery Shake 'N Bake chicken legs; queasily underdone hamburgs; and hamburg-sauce spaghetti whose pasta he boils for almost an hour.[197] None but the most street-hardened Ennet residents would ever hazard an open crack about the food, which appears nightly at the long dinner table still in the broad steaming pans it was cooked in, with Gately's big face hovering lunarly above it, flushed and beaded under the floppy chef's hat Annie Parrot had given him as a dark joke he hadn't got, his eyes full of anxiety and hopes for everyone's full enjoyment, basically looking like a nervous bride serving her first conjugal dish, except this bride's hands are the same size as the House's dinner plates and have jailhouse tatts on them, and this bride seems to need no oven-mitts as he sets down massive pans on the towels that have to be laid down to keep the plastic tabletop from searing. Any sort of culinary comments are always extremely oblique. Randy Lenz up at the northeast corner likes to raise his can of tonic and say that Don's food is the kind of food that helps you really appreciate whatever you're drinking along with it. Geoffrey Day talks about what a refreshing change it is to leave a dinner table not feeling bloated. Wade McDade, a young hard-core flask-alkie from Ashland KY, and Doony Glynn, who's still woozy and infirm from some horrendous Workers Comp. scam gone awry last year, and is constantly sickly and who's probably going to get Discharged soon for losing his menial job at Brighton Fence & Wire and not even pretending to look for another one — the two have this bit they do on spaghetti night where McDade comes into the living room right before chow and goes 'Some of that extra-fine spay-ghetti tonight, Doonster,' and Doony Glynn goes 'Ooo, will it be all lovely and soft?' and McDade goes 'Leave your teeth at home, boy' in the voice of a Kentucky sheriff, leading Glynn to the table by the hand as if Glynn were a damaged child. They take care to do the bit while Gately's still in the kitchen tossing salad and worrying about course-presentation. Though Tiny Ewell never fails to thank Gately for the meal, and April Cortelyu is lavish in her praises, and Burt F. Smith always rolls his eyes with pleasure and makes yummy-noises whenever he can get a fork to his mouth.

PRE-DAWN, 1 MAY — Y.D.A.U.
OUTCROPPING NORTHWEST OF TUCSON AZ U.S.A., STILL

'Do you remember hearing,' U.S.O.U.S.'s Hugh Steeply said, 'in your own country, in the late I think B.S. '70s, of an experimental program, a biomedical experiment, involving the idea of electro-implantations in the human brain?' Steeply, at the shelf's lip, turned to look. Marathe merely looked back at him. Steeply said: 'No? Some sort of radical advance. Stereo-taxy. Epilepsy-treatment. They proposed to implant tiny little hair-thin electrodes in the brain. Some leading Canadian neurologist — Elder, Elders, something — at the time had hit on evidence that certain tiny little stimulations in certain brain-areas could prevent a seizure. As in an epileptic seizure. They implant electrodes — hair-thin, just a few millivolts or —'

'Briggs electrodes.'

'Beg pardon?'

Marathe coughed slightly. 'Also the type used in pacemakers of the heart.'

Steeply felt his lip. 'I'm thinking I'm recalling a tentative Bio-entry saying your father had had a pacemaker.'

Marathe touched his own face absently. 'The plutonium-239 pack of power. The Briggs electrode. The Kenbeck DC circuit. I am recalling terms and instructions. Avoid all microwaving ovens and many transmitters. Cremation for burial forbidden — this is because of plutonium-239.'

'So but you know of this old program with epileptics? Experiments they thought could avoid ablative surgery for severe epilepsy?'

Marathe said nothing and made what might be seen as slightly shaking the head.

Steeply turned back to face the east with his hands clasped before his back, wishing to speak of it one way or another way, Marathe could tell.

'I can't remember if I read about it or heard a lecture or what. The implantation was a pretty inexact science. It was all experimental. A whole lot of electrodes had to be implanted in an incredibly small area in the temporal lobe to hope to find the nerve-terminals that involved epileptic seizures, and it was trial and error, stimulating each electrode and checking the reaction.'

'Temporal lobes of the brain,' Marathe said.

'What happened was that Olders and the Canadian neuroscientists happened to find, during all the trial and error, that firing certain electrodes in certain parts of the lobes gave the brain intense feelings of pleasure.' Steeply looked back over his shoulder at Marathe. 'I mean we're talking about *intense* pleasure, Rémy. I'm remembering Olders called these little strips of stimulatable pleasure-tissue *p*-terminals.'

' "*P*" wishing to mean "the pleasure." '

'And that their location seemed maddeningly inexact and unpredictable, even within brains of the same species — a *p*-terminal'd turn out to be right up next to some other neuron whose stimulation would cause pain, or hunger, or God knows what.'

'The human brain is very dense; it is the truth.'

'The whole point is they weren't doing it on humans yet. It was regarded as radically experimental. They used animals and animal-lobes. But soon the pleasure-stimulation phenomenon was its own separate radical experiment, while the second-string neuro-team stuck with the epileptic animals. Older — or Elder, some Anglo-Canadian name — headed the team to map these what he called quote "Rivers of Reward," the *p*-terminals in the lobes.'

Marathe idly felt at the little pills of cotton in his windbreaker's cotton pockets, pleasantly nodding. 'An experimental program of Canada, you stated.'

'I even remember. The Brandon Psychiatric Center.'

Marathe pretended to cough in the recognition of this. 'This is a mental hospital. The far north of Manitoba. Forbidding wastelands. The center of nothing.'

'Because they were theorizing that these quote "rivers" or terminals were also the brain's receptors for things like beta-endorphins, L-dopa, Q-dopa, serotonin, all the various neurotransmitters of pleasure.'

'The Department of Euphoria, so to speak, within the human brain.'

There was no hint or suggestion yet of dawn or light.

'But not humans yet,' Steeply said. 'Older's earliest subject were rats, and the results were apparently sobering. The Nu— the Canadians found that if they rigged an auto-stimulation lever, the rat would press the lever to stimulate his *p*-terminal over and over, thousands of times an hour, over and over, ignoring food and female rats in heat, completely fixated on the lever's stimulation, day and night, stopping only when the rat finally died of dehydration or simple fatigue.'

Marathe said 'Not of the pleasure itself, however.'

'I think dehydration. I'm fuzzy on just what the rat died of.'

Marathe shrugged. 'But the envy of all experimental rats everywhere, this rat, I think.'

'Then likewise implantations and levers for cats, dogs, swine, monkeys, primates, even a dolphin.'

'Up the evolving scale, *p*-terminals for each. Each died?'

'Eventually,' Steeply said, 'or else they had to be lobotomized. Because I remember even if the pleasure-electrode was removed, the stimulation-lever removed, the subject'd run around pressing anything that could be pressed or flipped, trying to get one more jolt.'

'The dolphin, probably it swam about and did this, I think.'

'You seem amused by this, Rémy. This was totally a Canadian show, this little neuroelectric adventure.'

'I am amused while you make a way toward your point so slowly.'

'Because then eventually Elder and company of course wanted to try human subjects, to see whether the human lobe had p-terminals and so on; and because of the sobering consequences for the subject-animals in the program they couldn't legally use prisoners or patients, they had to try to secure volunteers.'

'Because of a risk,' Marathe said.

'The whole thing was apparently a nightmare of Canadian legalities and statutes.'

Marathe pursed the lips: 'I have doubts in my mind: Ottawa could easily have asked your then CIA for, what is the term, "Persons of Expendability" from Southeast Asia or Negroes, the subjects expended for your inspiring U.S.A.'s MK-Ultra.'[198]

Steeply elected ignoring this, rummaging in the purse. 'But what apparently happened was that somehow word of the p-terminal discovery and experiments had gotten out up in Manitoba — some low-level worker at Brandon had broken security and leaked word.'

'Very little else to do in northern Manitoba besides leaking and gossiping.'

'. . . And suddenly the neuro-team at Brandon pull in to work one day and find human volunteers lining up literally around the block outside the place, able-bodied and I should remember to recall mostly young Canadians, lining up and literally trampling each other in their desire to sign up as volunteers for p-terminal-electrode implantation and stimulation.'

'In full knowledge of the rat's and dolphin's death, from pressing the lever.'

Marathe's father had always assigned it to Rémy, his youngest, to go first inside some public restaurant or shop to check for the presence of a microwave or GC-type of transmitter. Of special concerns were stores with instruments for thwarting a shoplifter, the shrieking instruments at doors.

Steeply said 'And of course this eagerness for implantation put a whole new disturbing spin on the study of human pleasure and behavior, and a whole new Brandon Hospital team was hastily assembled to study the psych-profiles of all these people willing to trample one another to undergo invasive brain surgery and foreign-object implantation —'

'To become some crazed rats.'

'— All just for the chance at this kind of pleasure, and the M.M.P.I.s and

Millon's and Approception tests on all these hordes of prospective volunteers — the hordes were told it was part of the screening — the scores came out fascinatingly, chillingly average, normal.'

'In other words not any *deviants*.'

'Nonabnormal along every axis they could see. Just regular young people — Canadian young people.'

'Volunteering for fatal addiction to the electrical pleasure.'

'But Rémy, apparently the purest, most refined pleasure imaginable. The neural distillate of, say, orgasm, religious enlightenment, ecstatic drugs, shiatsu, a crackling fire on a winter night — the sum of all possible pleasures refined into pure current and deliverable at the flip of a hand-held lever. Thousands of times an hour, at will.'

Marathe gave him a bland look.

Steeply examined a cuticle. 'By free choice, of course.'

Marathe assumed an expression that lampooned a dullard's hard thought. 'Thus, but how long before these leaks and rumors of *p*-terminals reach the Ottawa of government and public weal, for Canada's government reacts with horror at the prospect of this.'

'Oh, and not just Ottawa,' Steeply said. 'You can see the implications if a technology like Elder's really became available. I know Ottawa informed Turner, Bush, Casey, whoever it was at the time, and everyone at Langley bit their knuckle in horror.'

'The CIA chewed a hand?'

'Because surely you can see the implications for any industrialized, market-driven, high-discretionary-spending society.'

'But it would be illegalized,' Marathe said, noting to remember the various routines of movements Steeply made for keeping warm.

'Stop with the babe-in-woods charade,' Steeply said. 'There was still the prospect of an underground market exponentially more pernicious than narcotics or LSD. The electrode-and-lever technology looked expensive at the time, but it was easy to foresee enormous widespread demand bringing it down to where electrodes'd be no more exotic than syringes.'

'But yes, but surgery, this would be a different matter to implant.'

'Plenty of surgeons were already willing to perform illegal procedures. Abortions. Electric penile implants.'

'The MK-Ultra surgeries.'

Steeply laughed without mirth. 'Or off-the-record amputations for daring young train-cultists, no?'

Marathe blew just one nostril of his nose. This was the Québecois way: one of the nostrils at a time. Marathe's father's generation, they had used to bend and blow the one nostril out into the gutter in the street.

Steeply said 'Picture millions of average nonabnormal North Americans, all implanted with Briggs electrodes, all with electronic access to their own personal *p*-terminals, never leaving home, thumbing their personal stimulation levers over and over.'

'Lying upon their divans. Ignoring females in rutting. Having rivers of reward without earning reward.'

'Bug-eyed, drooling, moaning, trembling, incontinent, dehydrated. Not working, not consuming, not interacting or taking part in community life. Finally pitching forward from sheer —'

Marathe said 'Giving away their souls and lives for *p*-terminal stimulation, you are saying.'

'You can maybe see the analogy,' Steeply said, over the shoulders to smile in a wry way. 'In Canada, my friend, this was.'

Marathe made a very slight version of his rotary motion of impatience: 'From the A.D. 1970s of time. This never has come to be. There would have been no development of the Happy Patch . . .'

'We both went in. Both our nations.'

'In secret.'

'Ottawa first cutting the Brandon program's funding, which Turner or Casey or whoever howled at — our old CIA wanted the procedure developed and perfected, then Classified — military use or something.'

Marathe said 'But the civilian guardians of the weal of the public felt differently.'

'I think I'm remembering Carter was President. Both our combined nations made it a Security priority, shutting it down. Our old N.S.A., your old C7 with the R.C.M.P.s.'

'Bright red jackets and hats with wide brims. In the 1970s still on horses.'

Steeply held his mouth of the purse half up to the faint lights of Tucson, peering for something. 'I recall they went in directly. As in guns drawn. Boomed the doors. Dismantled the labs. Mercy-killed dolphins and goats. Olders disappeared somewhere.'

Marathe's slow circular gesture. 'Your point finally is Canadians also, we would choose dying for this, the total pleasure of a passive goat.'

Steeply turned, fiddling with an emery board. 'But you don't see a more specific analogy with the Entertainment?'

Marathe tongued the inside of his cheek. 'You are saying the Entertainment, a somehow optical stimulation of the *p*-terminals? A way to bypass Briggs electrodes for orgasm-and-massage pleasures?'

The dry rasp of the emerying a nail. 'All I'm saying is analogy. A precedent in your own nation.'

'Us, our nation is the Québec nation. Manitoba is —'

'I'm saying that if he could get past the blind desire for harm against the U.S., your M. Fortier might be induced to see just what it is he's proposing to let out of the cage.' His training was such that he could emery without watching the procedure. For Steeply's most effective interviewing tactic was this long looking down into the face without emotion of any kind. For Marathe felt more uncomfortable not knowing whether Steeply believed a thing than if Steeply's emotion of face showed he did not believe.

Then tonight, at the prospect of boiled hot dogs, the two newest residents had pulled the typically standard new-resident princess-and-pea special-food-issue thing: the new-today girl Amy J. that just sits there on the vinyl couch shaking like an aspen and having people bring her coffee and light her gaspers and with just short of a like *HELPLESS VICTIM: PLEASE CODDLE* sign hung around her neck now claiming Red Dye #4 gives her 'cluster migraines' (Gately gives this girl like a week tops before she's a vapor trail back to the Xanax[199]; she has that look), and the weirdly-familiar-but-Southernish-sounding girl Joelle van D. with the past-believing bod and the linen face announcing she was a vegetarian and would 'rather eat a bug' than even get downwind of a boiled frank. And but in an incredible move Pat M. has asked Gately, at like 1800h., to blast down to the Purity Supreme down in Allston and pick up some eggs and peppers so the two new delicate-tummied newcomers can make themselves quiche or whatever. To Gately's way of thinking, this looks like catering to just the sort of classic addict's claim of special uniqueness that it's supposed to be Pat's job to help break down. The Joelle v.D. girl seems to have like inordinate immediate weight and pet-status with Pat, who's already making noises about exempting the girl from the menial-job requirement, and wants Gately to look for some kind of weird Big Red Soda Water tonic for the girl, who's apparently still dehydrated. It's sure a long way from making somebody chew feldspar. Gately has long since quit trying to figure Pat Montesian out.

It's a weird-weather evening, both thundering and spitting snow. Gately had finally become able to distinguish genuine thunder from the Enfield sounds of ATHSCME fans and E.W.D. catapults, this after nine months of wearing a Goodwill rain-slicker every morning on the 0430 Green Line.

One of the possible weak spots in Gately's AA recovery-program of rigorous personal honesty is that once he's jammed himself into a black-as-water Aventura and watched the spoiler throb as he turns over the carnivorous engine, etc., he often finds himself taking a little bit less of a direct route to a given Ennet-errand-site than he probably could. If he had to come right down to the heart of the issue he likes to cruise around town in Pat's car. He's able to minimize the suspicious time any particular bit of extra cruising adds to his errands by basically driving like a lunatic: ignoring lights, cutting people off, scoffing at One-Ways, veering wildly in and out, making pedestrians drop things and lunge curbward, leaning on a horn that sounds more like an air-raid siren. You'd think this would be judicially insane, in terms of not having a license and facing a no-license jail-bit anyway, but the fact is that this sort of on-the-way-to-the-E.R.-with-a-passenger-in-labor driving doesn't usually raise so much as an eyebrow among Boston's Finest, since they have more than enough other stuff to attend to, in these troubled times, and since everybody else in metro Boston drives exactly the same sociopathic way, including the Finest themselves, so that the only real risk Gately's running is to his own sense of rigorous personal honesty. One cliché he's found especially serviceable w/r/t the Aventura issue is that Recovery is about Progress Not Perfection. He likes to make a stately left onto Commonwealth and wait to get out of view of the House's bay window and then produce what he imagines is a Rebel Yell and open her up down the serpentine tree-lined boulevard of the Ave. as it slithers through bleak parts of Brighton and Allston and past Boston U. and toward the big triangular CITGO neon sign and the Back Bay. He passes The Unexamined Life club, where he no longer goes, at 1800h. already throbbing with voices and bass under its ceaseless neon bottle, and then the great gray numbered towers of the Brighton Projects, where he definitely no longer goes. Scenery starts to blur and distend at 70 kph. Comm. Ave. splits Enfield-Brighton-Allston from the downscale north edge of Brookline on the right. He passes the meat-colored facades of anonymous Brookline tenements, Father & Son Market, a dumpster-nest, Burger Kings, Blanchard's Liquors, an InterLace outlet, a land-barge alongside another dumpster-nest, corner bars and clubs — Play It Again Sam's, Harper's Ferry, Bunratty's, Rathskeller, Father's First I and II — a CVS, two InterLace outlets right next to each other, the ELLIS THE RIM MAN sign, the Marty's Liquors that they rebuilt like ants the week after it burned down. He passes the hideous Riley's Roast Beef where the Allston Group gathers to pound coffee before Commitments. The giant distant CITGO sign's like a triangular star to steer by. He's doing 75 k down a straightaway, keeping abreast of an Inbound Green Line train ramming downhill on the slightly raised track that splits Comm.'s lanes into two and two. He likes to match a Green train at 75 k all the way down Commonwealth's integral ς and see how close he can cut beating it across the tracks at the Brighton Ave. split. It's a vestige. He'd admit it's like a dark vestige of his old low-self-esteem suicidal-thrill behaviors. He doesn't have a license, it's not his car, it's a priceless art-object car, it's his boss's car, who he owes his life to and sort of maybe loves, he's on a vegetable-run for shattered husks of newcomers just out of detox whose eyes are rolling around in their heads. Has anybody mentioned Gately's head is square? It's almost perfectly square, massive and boxy and mysticetously blunt: the head of somebody who looks like he likes to lower his head and charge. He used to let people open and close elevator doors on his head, break things across his head. The '*Indestructible*' in his childhood cognomen referred to the head. His left ear looks a bit like a prizefighter's left ear. The head's nearly flat on top, so that his hair, long in back but with short Prince Valiant bangs in front, looks sort of like a carpet remnant someone's tossed on the head and let slide slightly back but stay.[200] Nobody that lives in these guano-spotted old brown buildings along Comm. with bars on the low floors' windows[201] ever goes inside, it seems like. Even in thunder and little asterisks of snow, all kinds of olive Spanish and puke-white Irish are on every corner, bullshitting and trying to look like they're just out there waiting for something important and drinking out of tallboys wrapped tight in brown bags. A strange nod to discretion, the bags, wrapped so tight the outline of the cans can't be missed. A Shore boy, Gately'd never used a paper bag around streetcorner cans: it's like a city thing. The Aventura can do 80 kph in third gear. The engine never strains or whines, just eventually starts to sound hostile, is how you to know to hurt your hip and shift. The Aventura's instrument panel looks more like the instrument panel of military aircraft. Something's always blinking and Indicating; one of the blinking lights is supposed to tell you when to shift; Pat has told him to ignore the panel. He loves to make the driver's-side window go down and rest his left elbow on the jamb like a cabbie.

He's caught behind a bus whose big square ass is in both lanes and he can't get around it in time to beat the train across the split, though, and the train crosses in front of the bus with a blast of its farty-sounding horn and what Gately sees as a kind of swagger to its jiggle on the street-level track. He can see people bouncing around inside the train, holding on to straps and bars. Below the split on Comm. it's Boston U., Kenmore and Fenway, Berklee School of Music. The CITGO sign's still off in the distance ahead. You have to go a shocking long way to actually get to the big sign, which everybody says is hollow and you can get up inside there and stick your head out in a pulsing neon sea but nobody's ever personally been up in there.

Arm out like a hack's arm, Gately blasts through B.U. country. As in backpack and personal-stereo and designer-fatigues country. Soft-faced boys with backpacks and high hard hair and seamless foreheads. Totally lineless untroubled foreheads like cream cheese or ironed sheets. All the storefronts here are for clothes or TP cartridges or posters. Gately's had lines in his big forehead since he was about twelve. It's here he especially likes making people throw their packages in the air and dive for the curb. B.U. girls who look like they've eaten nothing but dairy products their whole lives. Girls who do step-aerobics. Girls with good combed long clean hair. Nonaddicted girls. The weird *hopelessness* at the heart of lust. Gately hasn't had sex in almost two years. At the end of the Demerol he physically couldn't. Then in Boston AA they tell you not to, not in your first year clean, if you want to be sure to Hang In. But they like omit to tell you that after that year's gone by you're going to have forgotten how to even talk to a girl except about Surrender and Denial and what it used to be like Out There in the cage. Gately's never had sex sober yet, or danced, or held somebody's hand except to say the Our Father in a big circle. He's gone back to having wet dreams at age twenty-nine.

Gately's found he can get away with smoking in the Aventura if he opens the passenger window too and makes sure no ashes go anywhere. The cross-wind through the open car is brutal. He smokes menthols. He'd switched to menthols at four months clean because he couldn't stand them and the only people he knew that smoked them were Niggers and he'd figured that if menthols were the only gaspers he let himself smoke he'd be more likely to quit. And now he can't stand anything but menthols, which Calvin T. says are even worse for you because they got little bits of asbestosy shit in the filter and whatnot. But Gately had been living in the little male live-in Staffer's room down in the basement by the audio pay phone and tonic machines for like two months before it turned out the Health guy came and inspected and said all the big pipes up at the room's ceiling were insulated in ancient asbestos that was coming apart and asbestosizing the room, and Gately had to move all his shit and the furniture out into the open basement and guys in white suits with oxygen tanks went in and stripped everything off the pipes and went over the room with what smells like it was a flamethrower. Then hauled the decayed asbestos down to E.W.D. in a welded drum with a skull on it. So Gately figures menthol gaspers are probably the least of his lung-worries at this point.

You can get on the Storrow 500[202] off Comm. Ave. below Kenmore via this long twiny overpass-shadowed road that cuts across the Fens. Basically the Storrow 500 is an urban express route that runs along the bright-blue Chuck all the way along Cambridge's spine. The Charles is vivid even under gloomy thundering skies. Gately has decided to buy the newcomers' om-elette stuff at Bread & Circus in Inman Square, Cambridge. It will explain delay, and will be a subtle nonverbal stab at unique dietary requests in general. Bread & Circus is a socially hyperresponsible overpriced grocery full of Cambridge Green Party granola-crunchers, and everything's like micro-biotic and fertilized only with organic genuine llama-shit, etc. The Aventura's low driver's seat and huge windshield afford your thinking man maybe a little more view of the sky than he'd like. The sky is low and gray and loose and seems to hang. There's something *baggy* about the sky. It's impossible to tell whether snow is still actually falling or whether just a little snow that's already fallen is blowing around. To get to Inman Square you veer over three lines to get off the Storrow 500 on Prospect St.'s Ramp of Death and slalom between the sinkholes and go right, north, and take Prospect through Central Square and all the way north through heavy ethnicity up almost into Somerville.

Inman Square, too, is someplace Gately rarely goes anymore, because it's in Cambridge's Little Lisbon, heavily Portuguese, which means also Brazilians in the antiquated bellbottoms and flare-collared leisure suits they've never let go of, and where there are disco-ized Brazilians can cocaine and narcotics ever be far away. The district's Brazilians are another solid rationale for driving at excessive rates of speed, for Gately. Plus Gately's solidly pro-American, and north of Central Square's clot and snarl Prospect St.'s a copless straight shot through eerily alien lands: billboards in Spanish, plaster madonnas in fenced front yards, intricately latticed grape arbors looking seized and clutched at, now, by networks of finger-thick bare woody vines; ads for lottery tickets in what isn't quite Spanish, all the houses gray, more bright plastic madonnas in nunnish getups on peeling front porches, stores and bodegas and low-suspension cars triple-parked, an all-out full-cast crèche-type scene hung from a second-floor balcony, clotheslines hanging between houses, gray houses in rows squished right up next to each other in long rows with tiny toy-strewn yards, and tall, the houses, like being squished in from either side distends them. A couple Canadian and Nuck-owned stores mashed in here and there, between the propinquous Spanish three-deckers, looking subjugated and exiled and etc. The street shitty with litter and holes. Indifferent drainage. Big-assed girls stuffed like stuffed sausage into cigarette jeans in always trios in the twilight with that weird blond-brown hair Portuguese girls dye their hair to. A store in good old English advertising Chickens Fresh Killed Daily. Ryle's Jazz Club's upscale pub-type bar, guys in tweed caps and briar pipes in mouths at angles taking all day on a pint of warm stout. Gately's always thought dark beer tasted like cork. An intriguing single-decker medical-looking bldg. with a sort of tympanum over the smoked-glass door with an ad that says COMPLETE DESTRUCTION OF CONFIDENTIAL RECORDS that Gately's always wanted to poke the old head in and have a look at what on earth they might be up to in there. Little Portuguese markets with food in there you can't even tell what species it's from. Once at a Portuguese take-out at Inman Square's east end a coke-whore tried to get Gately to eat something that had tentacles. He had a sub instead. Gately now simply blows through Inman, heading for B&C over on the upscale northwest side nearer to Harvard, every light suddenly green and kind, the Aventura's ten-cylinder backwash raising an odd little tornado of discarded ad-leaflets and glassine bags and corporate-snack bags and a syringe's husk and filterless gasper-butts and general crud and a flattened Millennial Fizzy cup, like from a stand, which whirls in his exhaust, the tornado of waste does, moving behind him as the last pearly curve of the sun through baggy clouds is eaten by the countless Sancta Something and then whitewashed WASP church roofs' finials farther west, nearer Harvard, at 60 k but sustained in its whirl by the strong west breeze as the last of the sun goes and a blue-black shadow quietly fills the canyon of Prospect, whose streetlights don't work for the same municipal reasons the street is in such crummy repair; and one piece of the debris Gately's raised and set spinning behind him, a thick flattened M.F. cup, caught by a sudden gust as it falls, twirling, is caught at some aerodyne's angle and blown spinning all the way to the storefront of one 'Antitoi Entertainent'[203] on the street's east side, and hits, its waxed bottom making a clunk, hits the glass pane in the locked front shop door with a sound for all the world like the rap of a knuckle, so that in a minute a burly bearded thoroughly Canadian figure in one of those Canadianly inevitable checked-flannel shirts appears out of the dim light in the shop's back room and wipes its mouth on first one sleeve then the other and opens up the front door with a loud hinge-squeak and looks around a bit, viz. for who knocked, looking not overly pleased at being interrupted at what his sleeves betray as a foreign supper, and also, below that harried expression, looking edgy and emotionally pale, which might explain the X of small-arms ammo-belts across his checked chest and the rather absurdly large .44 revolver tucked and straining in the waistband of his jeans. Lucien Antitoi's equally burly partner and brother Bertraund — currently still back there in the little back room where they sleep on cots with serious weaponry underneath and listen to CQBC radio and scheme and smoke killer U.S.A. hydroponic dope and cut and mount glass and sew flags and cook over sterno in L.L. Bean upscale survivalist cookware, he's back there eating Habitant *soupe aux pois* and bread with Bread & Circus molasses and some sort of oblong blue-veined patties of a meat your thinking American wouldn't even want to try to identify — Bertraund's forever laughing in Québecois and telling Lucien he looks forward with humorous anticipation to the day Lucien forgets to check the big Colt's safety before he jams it into the waistband of his pants and goes lumbering around the shop in his hobnail boots making every reflective and blown-glass item in the place tinkle and clink. The unautomatic revolver, it is a souvenir of affiliation. Once or twice doing work of affiliation with the Separatist/Anti-O.N.A.N. F.L.Q., they are for the most part a not very terrifying insurgent cell, the Antitois, more or less loners, self-contained, a monomitotic cell, eccentric and borderline-incompetent, protected gently by their late regional patron M. Guillaume DuPlessis of the Gaspé Peninsula, spurned by F.L.Q. after DuPlessis's assassination and also ridiculed by the more malignant anti-O.N.A.N. cells. Betraund Antitoi is in charge, the brains of the outfit, pretty much by default, since Lucien Antitoi is one of the very few natives of *Notre Rai Pays* ever who cannot understand French, just never caught on, and so has very limited veto-powers, even when it comes to such harebrained Bertraund-schemes as hanging a sword-stemmed fleur-de-lis flag from the nose of a U.S.A. Civic War hero's Boylston St. statue when it would simply be cut down by bored O.N.A.N.ite *chiens-courants* gendarmes the next morning, or taping bricks to the return-postage-paid solicitation cards of *Sans-Christe* Gentle's C.U.S.P. party, or fashioning Astroturf doormats with a likeness of *Sans-Christe* Gentle on them and distributing them gratis to home-supply outlets throughout their insurgency-grid — puerile and on the whole rather sad little gestures that M. DuPlessis would have interdicted with a merry laugh and a friendly hand on Bertraund's bowling ball of a shoulder. But M. DuPlessis had been martyred, an assassination only O.N.A.N. would be stupid enough to believe Command would be stupid enough to believe was merely an unfortunate burglary-and-mucus mishap. And Bertraund Antitoi, after DuPlessis's death and F.L.Q.'s rejection left to his own conceptual devices for the first time since their all-terrain vehicle was packed with quality Van Buskirk of Montreal exotic reflective glasswares and glass-blowing hardware and broom and ordnance and survivalist cookware and hip postcards and black-lather gag soap and cheesy old low-demand InterLace 3rd-Grid cartridges and hand-buzzers and fraudulent but seductive X-ray spectacles and they were sent through the remains of Provincial Autoroute 55/ U.S.A. 91 in protective garb they'd shed and buried just south of the Convexity's Bellow's Falls VT O.N.A.N.ite checkpoint, sent as a kind of primitive two-celled organism to establish a respectable front and abet more malignant cells and to insurge and terrorize in small sad anti-experialist ways, now Bertraund has shown a previously DuPlessis-restrained flair for stupid wastes of time, including this branching out into harmful pharmaceuticals as an attack on the fiber of New New England's youth — as if the U.S.A. youth were not already more than fiberless enough, in Lucien's mute opinion. Bertraund had actually been credulous enough with a wrinkled long-haired person of advanced years in a paisley Nehru jacket also of great age and a puzzling cap with a skeleton playing at the violin emblazoned upon it, on the front, wearing also the most stupid-appearing small round wire spectacles with salmon-colored lenses, and also continually forming the letter of V with fingers of his hand and directing this letter of V at Bertraund and Lucien — Bertraund felt the gesture was a subtle affirmation of solidarity with patriotic Struggle everywhere and stood for *Victoire,* but Lucien suspected a U.S.A. obscenity laughingly flashed at persons who would not comprehend its insult, just as one of Lucien's sadistic *école-spéciale* tutors back in Ste.-Anne-des-Monts had spent weeks in Second Form teaching Lucien to say '*Va chier, putain!*' which he (the tutor) claimed meant 'Look Maman I can speak French and thus finally express my love and devotion to you' — Bertraund had been starry-eyed enough to agree to barter the person an antique blue lava-lamp and a lavender-tinged apothecary's mirror for eighteen unexceptional-looking and old lozenges the long-haired old person had claimed in a jumble of West-Swiss-accented French were 650 mg. of a trop-formidable harmful pharmaceutical no longer available and guaranteed to make one's most hair-raising psychedelic experience look like a day on the massage-tables of a Basel hot-springs resort, throwing in as well a kitchen-can waste bag filled with crusty old mossy boot-and-leg Read-Only cartridges, sans any labels, that appeared to have been stored in a person's rear yard and then run through a gaseous dryer of clothes, as if Lucien did not have already more than plenty of crusty old cartridges which Bertraund removed from Inter-Lace dumpsters or was cheated in barters for and brought back to the shop for Lucien's job to view and label and organize the cartridges for storing and were never bought except the occasional cartridge in Portuguese, or pornographical. And the aged person had flopped off in his cap and sandals with a lamp and an apothecary's mirror to which Lucien had been personally much attached, particularly to the lavender mirror, flashing this covert obscenity of V and with smiles urging the brothers to write their name and address on the palm of their hands with the drenching-sweat-proof ink before they dropped any of the so-called '*tu-sais-quoi*,' if they were going to be the persons who ingested these lozenges.

The front door squeaks loudly of the hinge and Lucien recloses it and drives the bolt home: *squeak*. The upper hinge squeaks no matter the oil, as the shop drives Lucien crazy by becoming again dusty each time the door is opened to the street's grit, and from the dust of the alley with so many dumpsters behind the back room which Bertraund refuses not to open the iron service door of, to spit. The squeak functions in the place of a customer-bell, however. The front knock of the closed door clearly is once again big-bottomed Brazilian children playing at unamusing pranks. He does not pull the window shade, but he does grab the stout trusty home-made broom he sweeps the shop all day with and stands there, chewing anxiously the nail of a thumb, looking out. Lucien Antitoi enjoys standing at the door's glass pane and looking blankly out at the light snow of dust bright against the blue-shadowed twilight eating the American street outside. The door continues to squeak faintly even after he's driven home the bolt. He can stand here happily for hours, leaning on the sturdy broom he'd carved from a snow-snapped limb as a boy during the Gaspé's terrible blizzards of Québec of A.D. 1993 and bound broom-corn onto and sharpened the tip of, as a sort of domestic weapon, even then, before O.N.A.N.ite experialist impost made any sort of struggle or sacrifice remotely necessary, as a silent boy, keenly interested in weapons and ammunitions of all the different sorts. Which along with the size thing helped with the teasing. He could and does stand here for hours, complexly backlit, transparently reflected, looking at alien traffic and commerce. He has that rare spinal appreciation for beauty in the ordinary that nature seems to bestow on those who have no native words for what they see. 'Squeak.' The visual bulk of the shoproom of Antitoi Entertainent is devoted to glass: they have set curved and planar mirrors at studied angles whereby each part of the room is reflected in every other part, which flusters and disorients customers and keeps haggling to a minimum. In a sort of narrow fashioned corridor behind one gauntlet of angled glass is their stock of gags, notions, ironic postcards, and unironic sentimental greeting cards as well.[204] Flanking another are shelf after shelf of used and bootleg InterLace and independent and even homemade digital entertainment cartridges, in no discernible order, since Bertraund handles acquisition and Lucien's in charge of inventory and order. Nevertheless, once he's viewed it even once, he can identify any used cartridge in stock and will point it out to the rare customer with the sharpened whitewood tip of his homemade broom. Some of the cartridges do not even have labels, they're so obscure or illicit. To keep up with Bertraund, Lucien must watch new acquisitions on the small cheap viewer beside the manual cash register as he sweeps the shop with the imposing broom he has loved and kept sharpened and polished and floor-fuzz-free since adolescence, and which he sometimes imagines he is conversing with, very quietly, telling it to *va chier putain* in tones surprisingly gentle and kind for such a large terrorist. The viewer's screen has something wrong with its Definition and there is a wobble that makes all cartridge performers on the left section of it appear to have Tourette's syndrome. The pornographical cartridges he finds nonsensical and views them in Fast Forward to get them over with as quickly as possible. So but he knows all but the most recent acquisitions' colors and visual plots, but some still have no labels. He still has not gotten to see and shelve many of the massive assortment Bertraund lugged home and out of the all-terrain vehicle in Saturday's chilling rain, several old exercise and film cartridges a small Back Bay TelEntertainment outlet was discarding as outdated. Also there were one or two Bertraund claimed he had picked up literally on the street downtown from the site of the flag-draped Shaw statue from untended commercial displays that stupidly contained detachable cartridges anyone could detach and lug home in the rain. The displays' cartridges he had immediately viewed, for though they were unlabelled save for a commercialed slogan in tiny raised letters of IL NE FAUT PLUS QU'ON PURSUIVE LE BONHEUR — which to Lucien Antitoi signified zilch — each was stamped also with a circle and arc that resembled a disembodied smile, which made Lucien himself smile and pop them in right away, to find to his disappointment and impatience with Bertraund that they were blank, without even HD static, just as the old rude person's bartered tapes he had removed from the waste bag of their storage for viewing had proved, blank beyond static, to the satisfaction of Lucien's disgust.[205] Through the door's window, passing headlights illumine a disabled person in a wheelchair laboring along the rutted walk outside the Portuguese grocery opposite Antitoi Entertainent's storefront. Lucien forgets he was eating bread with upscale molasses and *soupe aux pois;* he forgets he is eating the moment the food's taste leaves his mouth. His mind is usually as clean and transparent as anything in the shop. He sweeps a little, absently, in front of the pane, watching his face's reflection bob against the blackening night outside. Light snowfall almost is bouncing back and forth between sides of Prospect's canyon. The broom's bristles say 'Hush, hush.' The tin-and-static sound of CQBC has been silenced, he can hear Bertraund moving about rattling some pans and dropping one, and Lucien works his sharp-pointed broom against the chipped Portuguese tile of the nonwood floor. He is a gifted domestic, the best 125-kilo domestic ever to wear a beard and suspenders of small-arms ordnance. The shop, crammed to the acoustic-tile ceiling and dustless, resembles a junkyard for anal retentives. He bobs and sweeps, and bobbing shafts of mirror-light gleam and dance, backed by night, in the locked door's pane. The figure in the wheelchair still labors at his wheels, but appears, queerly, still to be where he was before, in front of the Portuguese grocery. Moving closer to the pane, so that his face's transparent image fills the glass and he can now see clearly beyond it, Lucien sees that what it is is it's a different figure in a different wheelchair from the one before, this new figure's face also downcasted and queerly masked, laboring around the sidewalk's jagged holes; and that not too far behind this seated figure is yet another figure in a wheelchair, coming this way; and as Lucien Antitoi twists his head and presses his hairy cheek to the glass of the squeaking door — except but now how can a door's upper hinge loudly squeak when the door is tightly closed and the bolt driven home with the solid *snick* of a .44 bullet slipping home in a revolver's chamber? — looking due southeast up Prospect, Lucien can see the variegated glints of passing low-chassis headlights off a whole long single-file column of polished metal wheels stolidly turning, being turned by swarthy hands in fingerless wheelchair-gloves. 'Squeak.' *'Squeak.'* Lucien has been hearing squeaks for several minutes from what he had naïvely like the babe assumed was the door's upper hinge. This hinge does truly squeak.[206] But Lucien now hears whole systems of squeaks, slow and soft but not stealthy squeaks, the squeaks of weighted wheelchairs moving slow, implacable, calm and businesslike and yet menacing, moving with the indifference of things at the very top of the food-chain; and, now, turning, heart loud in his head, can now see, in the carefully placed display mirrors' angles, spikes of light off rotary metal rotating at a height about waist-level to a huge standing man w/ broom clutched to barrel chest, there are great quiet numbers of persons in wheelchairs moving in the room with him, in the shoproom, moving calmly into position behind waist-high glass counters full of wacky notions. The street outside is flanked on both sidewalks by defiles of wheelchaired, blanket-lapped persons whose faces are obscured by what look like large and snow-dotted leaves, and the shades of the Portuguese grocery have been drawn and a ROPAS sign hung by a circumflex of twine in the pane of the front door. Wheelchair Assassins. Lucien has been taught the glyph of a profiled wheelchair with an enormous bone-crossed skull below. It is the worst possible scenario; it is worse than

O.N.A.N.ite gendarmes by far: A.F.R. Whimpering to his broom, Lucien disengages the mammoth Colt from his pants and finds that a length of black thread from the denim panel that surrounds his zipper has gotten looped around the barrel's sight-blade and comes ripping out with a long high squeak from the pants with the convulsive force of his drawing the weapon, so that his pants split open alongside the zipper and the force of his mammoth Canadian gut extends the tear all up and down the front so that the snap unsnaps and the jeans burst open and fall immediately to his ankles, puddling around his hobnail boots, revealing red union-suit under-wear beneath and forcing Lucien to take tiny undignified shuffling steps frantically toward the back room as he tries with the thread-snagged Colt to cover every piece of fragmented waist-high motion the mirror's shards of light reveal in the shoproom while scuttling as fast as the fallen jeans allow toward the back room to alert, nonverbally, using the sort of demon-eyed tongue-protruded neck-corded tortured rigid bug-eyed face a small child makes when he is playing *Le Monstre,* to alert Bertraund that *They* have come, not Bostonian gendarmes or white-suited O.N.A.N.ite chiens but *They, Them, Les Assassins des Fauteuils Rollents,* A.F.R.s, the ones who come always in the twilight, implacably squeaking, and cannot be reasoned with or bargained with, feel no pity or remorse, or fear (except a rumored fear of steep hills), and now they're all in here all over the shoproom like faceless rats, the devil's own hamsters, moving with placid squeaks just be-yond view of the shop's mirrored peripheries, regally serene; and Lucien, with the big broom in one hand and the thread-webbed Colt in the other, tries to cover his little-stepped flight with a thunderous shot that goes high and shatters an angled full-length planar door-mirror, spraying anodized glass and replacing the reflection of a blanket-lapped A.F.R. wearing a plas-tic fleur-de-lis-with-sword-stem mask on his face with a jagged stelliform hole, with glittered shards and glass-dust in the air all over the place and the unperturbable squeaks — 'squeak *squeak* squeak squeak,' it is awful — sounding right through clatter and tinkle and frantic hobnailed bootfalls, and through the flying glass, aiming every which way behind him, Lucien bursts almost falling through the curtains, bug-eyed and corded and webbed in thread, to alert Bertraund facially that the shot had signified A.F.R.s and to break out the sub-cot weaponry and prepare to bunker for encirclement, only to horrifically see the shop's rear service door standing agape in a gritty breeze and Bertraund still at the card table they use for their supper — used — with pea soup and troubling meat-patty still on his ration-tray, sit-ting, squinting piratically straight ahead, with a railroad spike in his eye. The spike, its tip is both domed and squared, also rusty, and it protrudes from the socket of his brother's former blue right eye. There are maybe about six or nine A.F.R. here in the drafty back room, silent as ever, seated with motionless wheels, flannel blankets obscuring an absence of the legs, also of course flannel-shirted, masked in synthetic-blend heraldic-flag irises with flaming transperçant stems at the chin and slits for eyes and round utter holes for mouths — all except for one particular of the A.F.R., in an unpretentious sportcoat and tie and the worst mask of all, a plain yellow polyresin circle with an obscenely simple smily-face in thin black lines, who is speculatively dipping a baguette's heel in Bertraund's metal soup-cup and popping the bread into his mask's mouth's cheery hole with an elegantly cerise-gloved hand. Lucien, staring goggle-eyed at the only brother he's ever had, is standing very still, face still unwittingly teratoid, the broom at an angle in his hand, the Colt dangling at his side, and the long black zipper-thread he's pulled from his zipper caught somehow now and wrapped around his thumb and hung trailing on the spotless floor with slack between gun and thumb, his pants woppsed around his red woolen ankles, when he hears a quick efficient *squeak* and feels from behind a tremendous wallop on the backs of his knees that drives him down to his knees on the floor, the .44 bucking as it discharges by reflex into the wood-pattern Portuguese tile, so that he's down in a supplicant's posture on his red knees, encircled by *fauteuils des rollents,* still holding his broom but now down near the broomcorn's wire binding; his face is now of equal height to the yellow empty smiling chewing face of the A.F.R. as this leader — everything about him radiates pitiless and remorseless command — rotates a right wheel to bring himself about and with three squeakless rotations has his hideous blank black smile within cm. of Lucien Antitoi's face. The A.F.R. bids him *''n soir, 'sieur,'* which means nothing to Lucien Antitoi, whose chin has caved and lips are quivering, though his eyes are not what you would call jacklighted or terrified eyes. Lucien's brother's pierced and rigid profile is visible over the leader's left shoulder. The man still has some soup-sopped bread in his glove's left hand.

'*Malheureusement, ton collégue est décédé. Il faisait une excellente soupe aux pois.*' He looks amused. '*Non? Ou c'était toi, faisait-elle?*' The leader leans forward in the graceful way people who always sit can lean, revealing wiry hair and a small and strangely banal bald-spot, and gently removes the hot revolver from Lucien's hand. He engages the safety without having to look at the revolver. Spanish-language music is thinly audible from somewhere up above the alley. The A.F.R. looks warmly into Lucien's eyes for a moment, then with a professionally vicious backhanded motion pegs the gun at Bertraund's profiled head, striking Bertraund in the side of the head; and Bertraund rocks away and then toward and forward and slides forward-left off the rickety camping-chair and with a ghastly and moist thump comes to rest chairless but upright, his left hip on the floor, the eye's sturdy railroad spike's thick tip caught on the edge of the card table and tilted up as the table tilts downward and cookery slides nautically off and onto the tile as the weight of Bertraund's large upper body is somehow held by the spike and tilted table. His brother's face is now turned away from Lucien, and his overall posture is of some person crumpled with hilarity or regret, maybe beer — a man overcome. Lucien, who never has apprehended what the safety-switch is or where, thinks it a small miracle that the Colt .44 with its tail of thread does not discharge again as it wangs off Bertraund's temple and hits the slick tile and slides from sight under a cot. Somewhere in the tall house next door a toilet flushes, and the back room's pipes sing. The black thread has remained snagged on the Colt's sight-blade and in the middle caught somewhere on Bertraund's ear; the other remains also attached to Lucien by a persistent hangnail on his well-gnawed right thumb, so that a black filament still connects the knelt Lucien to his hidden revolver, with a surreal angled turn at the ear of his overcome *frère*.

The happy-masked A.F.R. leader, politely ignoring the fact that Lucien's sphincter has failed them all in the small room, after complimenting them both on the craftsmanship of some of the front's blown-glass notions, pulls his velvet gloves tighter and tells Lucien that it has fallen to him, Lucien, to direct their attention without delay to an entertainment item they have come here to acquire. And require, this Copy-Capable item. They are here on business, *ne pas plaisanter*, this is not the social call. They will acquire this thing and then *iront paître*. They have no wish to disturb anyone's repast, but the A.F.R. fears that it is fearfully urgent and key, this Master item they now require without delay or dissembly from Lucien — *entend-il?*

The vigor with which Lucien shakes his head at the leader's meaningless sounds can't help but be misinterpreted, probably.

Does this shop have the 585-rpm-drive TP somewhere about here, for running Masters?

Same vigorous negative-looking denial of comprehension.

Can a mask's drawn smile widen?

From the front of the shop come whole symphonies of squeaks and low trilled *r*'s and the sounds of a densely packed area being swiftly dismantled and searched. A few legless thick-armed men climb the shelves by hand and hang up near the drop-ceiling by special climbing equipment and suction-cups fitted to their stumps, brown arms busy in the upper shelving, dismantling and searching upside-down like obscene industrious bugs. The outline of Lucien's quivering mouth is being traced by a mammoth-torso'd A.F.R. in a Jesuitical collar who holds Lucien's own trusty broom inverted and leans in his chair to caress Lucien's full Gaspé-provincial lips (the lips are quivering) with the handle's wicked tip, which is sharply white, whittled free of the sienna glaze of broomstick-varnish that patinas the rest of the big stick's length. Lucien's lips are quivering not so much from fear — although there is certainly fear — but not from fear so much as in an attempt to form words.[207] Words that are not and can never be words are sought by Lucien here through what he guesses to be the maxillofacial movements of speech, and there is a childlike pathos to the movements that perhaps the rigid-grinned A.F.R. leader can sense, perhaps that is why his sigh is sincere, his complaint sincere when he complains that what will follow will be *inutile*, Lucien's failure to assist will be *inutile*, there will be no point serviced, there are several dozen highly trained and motivated wheelchaired personnel here who will find whatever they seek and more, anyhow, perhaps it is sincere, the Gallic shrug and fatigue of the voice through the leader's mask-hole, as Lucien's leonine head is tilted back by a hand in his hair and his mouth opened wide by callused fingers that appear overhead and around the sides of his head from behind and jack his writhing mouth open so wide that the tendons in his jaws tear audibly and Lucien's first sounds are reduced from howls to a natal gargle as the pale wicked tip of the broom he loves is inserted, the wood piney-tasting then white tasteless pain as the broom is shoved in and abruptly down by the big and collared A.F.R., thrust farther in rhythmically in strokes that accompany each syllable in the wearily re-peated '*In-U-Tile*' of the technical interviewer, down into Lucien's wide throat and lower, small natal cries escaping around the brown-glazed shaft, the strangled impeded sounds of absolute aphonia, the landed-fish gasps that accompany speechlessness in a dream, the cleric-collared A.F.R. driving the broom home now to half its length, up on his stumps to get downward leverage as the fibers that protect the esophagal terminus resist and then give with a crunching pop and splat of red that bathes Lucien's teeth and tongue and makes of itself in the air a spout, and his gargled sounds now sound drowned; and behind fluttering lids the aphrasiac half-cellular insurgent who loves only to sweep and dance in a clean pane sees snow on the round hills of his native Gaspé, pretty curls of smoke from chimneys, his mother's linen apron, her kind red face above his crib, homemade skates and cider-steam, Chic-Choc lakes seen stretching away from the Cap-Chat hillside they skied down to Mass, the red face's noises he knows from the tone are tender, beyond crib and rimed window Gaspésie lake after lake after lake lit up by the near-Arctic sun and stretching out in the southeastern distance like chips of broken glass thrown to scatter across the white Chic-Choc country, gleaming, and the river Ste.-Anne a ribbon of light, unspeakably pure; and as the culcate handle navigates the inguinal canal and sigmoid with a queer deep full hot tickle and with a grunt and shove completes its passage and forms an obscene erectile bulge in the back of his red sopped johns, bursting then through the wool and puncturing tile and floor at a police-lock's canted angle to hold him upright on his knees, completely skewered, and as the attentions of the A.F.R.s in the little room are turned from him to the shelves and trunks of the Antitois' sad insurgents' lives, and Lucien finally dies, rather a while after he's quit shuddering like a clubbed muskie and seemed to them to die, as he finally sheds his body's suit, Lucien finds his gut and throat again and newly whole, clean and unimpeded, and is free, catapulted home over fans and the Convexity's glass palisades at desperate speeds, soaring north, sounding a bell-clear and nearly maternal alarmed call-to-arms in all the world's well-known tongues.

O

PRE-DAWN, 1 MAY Y.D.A.U.
OUTCROPPING NORTHWEST OF TUCSON AZ U.S.A., STILL

M. Hugh Steeply spoke quietly, after a prolonged silence of both operatives alone with their thoughts, upon this mountain. Steeply faced still out, standing on the outcropping's lip, bare arms around him for some warmth, his dress's soiled back to Marathe. Around the bonfire, far out below upon the desert floor, rotated a ring of smaller and palsied fires, persons carrying torches or fires.

'Do you ever think of viewing it?'

Marathe did not reply. It was not impossible that the young persons carrying the torches were dancing.

'Whether or not the A.F.R. ever even recover this alleged Master copy from the DuPlessis burglary,' Steeply said quietly; 'still, you guys have a Read-Only copy, at least one, you've told us, no?'

'Yes.'

'Nobody has this mysterious Master, but we've all got Read-Only's — all the anti-O.N.A.N. cells have at least one Read-Only, we're pretty sure.'

Marathe said, 'M. Brullîme, he tells Fortier he thinks the CPCP of Alberta do not have any copy.'

'Fuck the Albertans,' Steeply said. 'Who's worried about the Albertans? The Albertans' idea of a blow to the U.S. plexus is they blow up rangeland in Montana. They're wackos.'

'I have not been tempted,' Marathe said.

Steeply's sound appeared as if he did not hear. 'We have more than one. Copies. Sure we can assume your boys know this.'

Marathe dryly laughed. 'Confiscated from razzles of Berkeley, Boston. But who can know what is on them? Who can study the Entertainment while detached?'

Steeply's scratch on the arm had become overnight puffed, and there were cross-hatches of his scratching. 'But just between us two, though. Tête to tête. You've never been even slightly tempted? I mean personally. You the person. Wife's condition be damned. Kids be damned. Just for a second, slip into wherever you guys keep it and load it and have a quick look? To see what's all the fuss, the irresistible pull of the thing?' He pivoted on one heel and looked, and cocked his head in a way of cynicism that seemed to Marathe consummately U.S.A.

Marathe coughed softly into his fist. His own dead father's Kenbeck pacemaker, it had been damaged accidentally by a videophonic pulse of waves. This from a telephone call from the telephone company, a video call, advertising the videophony. M. Marathe had picked up the ringing telephone; the videophonic pulse, it had come; M. Marathe had fallen, still holding a telephone Rémy had never been instructed to answer first, to check. The advertisement, which was recorded, played its audible portion out upon the floor beside his father's ear, audible between Marathe's mother's cries.

Steeply raised and lowered himself on his shoes' toes. 'Us, Rod the God Tine's got Tom Flatto's I/O boys running tests around the clock. 24-dash-7.'

'Flatto, Thomas M., B.S.S. director of Input/Output testing, resident of Falls Church's community, a widower with three children, one child with cystic fibrosis.'

'Funny as an impacted follicle, Rémy. And no doubt the insurgent cells are all each doing work of your own, you guys with your own Dr. Brullent or whomever, trying to find out what the Entertainment's appeal could be without sacrificing any of your own.' Steeply again turned; he did this for emphasis. 'Or maybe you're willingly sacrificing your own. Yes? Willing volunteers in chairs. Sacrificing self for the Greater and all that. By adult choice and all that. Just for the sake of causing us harm. Wouldn't even want to *think* about how the A.F.R.'s conducting tests of the thing.'

'*C'est ça.*'

'But not so much for content,' Steeply said. 'Input/Output's exhaustive testing. Flatto's got them working on conditions and environments for possible nonlethal viewing. Certain departments in Virginia, the developing theory is that it's holography.'

'The *samizdat.*'

'The filmmaker'd been a cutting-edge optics man. Holography, diffraction. He'd used holography a couple times before, and in the context of a kind of filmed assault on the viewer. He was of the Hostile School or some such shit.'

'Also a maker of reflecting panels for thermal weapons, and an important *Annulateur,* also, and amasser of the capital from opticals, before hostility and film,' Marathe said.

Steeply embraced himself. 'Tom Flatto's personal theory is the appeal's got something to do with density. The visual compulsion. Theory's that with a really sophisticated piece of holography you'd get the neural density of an actual stage play without losing the selective realism of the viewer-screen. That the density plus the realism might be too much to take. Dick Desai in Data Production wants to go in with ALGOL and see if there are Fourier Equations in the root code's ALGOL, which would signify holo-grammatical activity going on.'

'M. Fortier finds the theories of content irrelevant.'

Steeply cocked his head sometimes in a way that was both feminine and birdlike. He did this most often during silences. Also he again removed something small from his painted lip. Also he spoke with more feminine inflection. Marathe committed all this to his memories.

WINTER, B.S. 1963, SEPULVEDA CA

I remember[208] I was eating lunch and reading something dull by Bazin when my father came into the kitchen and made himself a tomato juice beverage and said that as soon as I was finished he and my mother needed my help in their bedroom. My father had spent the morning at the commercial studio and was still all in white, with his wig with its rigid white parted hair, and hadn't yet removed the television makeup that gave his real face an orange cast in daylight. I hurried up and finished and rinsed my dishes in the sink and proceeded down the hall to the master bedroom. My mother and father were both in there. The master bedroom's valance curtains and the heavy lightproof curtain behind them were all slid back and the venetian blinds up, and the daylight was very bright in the room, the decor of which was white and blue and powder-blue.

My father was bent over my parents' large bed, which was stripped of bedding all the way down to the mattress protector. He was bent over, pushing down on the bed's mattress with the heels of his hands. The bed's sheets and pillows and powder-blue coverlet were all in a pile on the carpet next to the bed. Then my father handed me his tumbler of tomato juice to hold for him and got all the way on top of the bed and knelt on it, pressing down vigorously on the mattress with his hands, putting all his weight into it. He bore down hard on one area of the mattress, then let up and pivoted slightly on his knees and bore down with equal vigor on a different area of the mattress. He did this all over the bed, sometimes actually walking around on the mattress on his knees to get at different areas of the mattress, then bearing down on them. I remember thinking the bearing-down action looked very much like emergency compression of a heart patient's chest. I remember my father's tomato juice had grains of pepperish material floating on the surface. My mother was standing at the bedroom window, smoking a long cigarette and looking at the lawn, which I had watered before I ate lunch. The uncovered window faced south. The room blazed with sunlight.

491

'Eureka,' my father said, pressing down several times on one particular spot.

I asked whether I could ask what was going on.

'Goddamn bed squeaks,' he said. He stayed on his knees over the one particular spot, bearing down on it repeatedly. There was now a squeaking sound from the mattress when he bore down on the spot. My father looked up and over at my mother next to the bedroom window. 'Do you or do you not hear that?' he said, bearing down and letting up. My mother tapped her long cigarette into a shallow ashtray she held in her other hand. She watched my father press down on the squeaking spot.

Sweat was running in dark orange lines down my father's face from under his rigid white professional wig. My father served for two years as the Man from Glad, representing what was then the Glad Flaccid Plastic Receptacle Co. of Zanesville, Ohio, via a California-based advertising agency. The tunic, tight trousers, and boots the agency made him wear were also white.

My father pivoted on his knees and swung his body around and got off the mattress and put his hand at the small of his back and straightened up, continuing to look at the mattress.

'This miserable cock-sucking bed your mother felt she needed to hang on to and bring with us out here for quote sentimental value has started squeaking,' my father said. His saying 'your mother' indicated that he was addressing himself to me. He held his hand out for his tumbler of tomato juice without having to look at me. He stared darkly down at the bed. 'It's driving us fucking nuts.'

My mother balanced her cigarette in her shallow ashtray and laid the ashtray on the windowsill and bent over from the foot of the bed and bore down on the spot my father had isolated, and it squeaked again.

'And at night this one spot here we've isolated and identified seems to spread and metastisate until the whole Goddamn bed's replete with squeaks.' He drank some of his tomato juice. 'Areas that gibber and squeak,' my father said, 'until we both feel as if we're being eaten by rats.' He felt along the line of his jaw. 'Boiling hordes of gibbering squeaking ravenous rapacious rats,' he said, almost trembling with irritation.

I looked down at the mattress, at my mother's hands, which tended to flake in dry climates. She carried a small bottle of moisturizing lotion at all times.

My father said, 'And I have personally had it with the aggravation.' He blotted his forehead on his white sleeve.

I reminded my father that he'd mentioned needing my help with something. At that age I was already taller than both my parents. My mother was taller than my father, even in his boots, but much of her height was in her legs. My father's body was denser and more substantial.

My mother came around to my father's side of the bed and picked the bedding up off the floor. She started folding the sheets very precisely, using both arms and her chin. She stacked the folded bedding neatly on top of her dresser, which I remember was white lacquer.

My father looked at me. 'What we need to do here, Jim, is take the mattress and box spring off the bed frame under here,' my father said, 'and expose the frame.' He took time out to explain that the bed's bottom mattress was hard-framed and known uniformly as a box spring. I was looking at my sneakers and making my feet alternately pigeon-toed and then penguin-toed on the bedroom's blue carpet. My father drank some of his tomato juice and looked down at the edge of the bed's metal frame and felt along the outline of his jaw, where his commercial studio makeup ended abruptly at the turtleneck collar of his white commercial tunic.

'The frame on this bed is old,' he told me. 'It's probably older than you are. Right now I'm thinking the thing's bolts have maybe started coming loose, and that's what's gibbering and squeaking at night.' He finished his tomato juice and held the glass out for me to take and put somewhere. 'So we want to move all this top crap out of the way, entirely' — he gestured with one arm — 'entirely out of the way, get it out of the room, and expose the frame, and see if we don't maybe just need to tighten up the bolts.'

I wasn't sure where to put my father's empty glass, which had juice residue and grains of pepper along the inside's sides. I poked at the mattress and box spring a little bit with my foot. 'Are you sure it isn't just the mattress?' I said. The bed's frame's bolts struck me as a rather exotic first-order explanation for the squeaking.

My father gestured broadly. 'Synchronicity surrounds me. Concord,' he said. 'Because that's what your mother thinks it is, also.' My mother was using both hands to take the blue pillowcases off all five of their pillows, again using her chin as a clamp. The pillows were all the overplump polyester fiberfill kind, because of my father's allergies.

'Great minds think alike,' my father said.

Neither of my parents had any interest in hard science, though a great uncle had accidentally electrocuted himself with a field series generator he was seeking to patent.

My mother stacked the pillows on top of the neatly folded bedding on her dresser. She had to get up on her tiptoes to put the folded pillowcases on top of the pillows. I had started to move to help her, but I couldn't decide where to put the empty tomato juice glass.

'But you just want to hope it isn't the mattress,' father said. 'Or the box spring.'

My mother sat down on the foot of the bed and got out another long cigarette and lit it. She carried a little leatherette snap-case for both her cigarettes and her lighter.

My father said, 'Because a new frame, even if we can't get the bolts squared away on this one and I have to go get a new one. A new frame. It wouldn't be too bad, see. Even top-shelf bed frames aren't that expensive. But new mattresses are outrageously expensive.' He looked at my mother. 'And I mean fucking *outrageous*.' He looked down at the back of my mother's head. 'And we bought a new box spring for this sad excuse for a bed not five years ago.' He was looking down at the back of my mother's head as if he wanted to confirm that she was listening. My mother had crossed her legs and was looking with a certain concentration either at or out the master bedroom window. Our home's whole subdivision was spread along a severe hillside, which meant that the view from my parents' bedroom on the first floor was of just sky and sun and a foreshortened declivity of lawn. The lawn sloped at an average angle of 55° and had to be mowed horizontally. None of the subdivision's lawns had trees yet. 'Of course that was during a seldom-discussed point in time when your mother had to assume the burden of assuming responsibility for finances in the household,' my father said. He was now perspiring very heavily, but still had his white professional toupee on, and still looked at my mother.

My father acted, throughout our time in California, as both symbol and spokesman for the Glad F.P.R. Co.'s Individual Sandwich Bag Division. He was the first of two actors to portray the Man from Glad. He was inserted several times a month in a mock-up of a car interior, where he would be filmed in a tight trans-windshield shot receiving an emergency radio summons to some household that was having a portable-food-storage problem. He was then inserted opposite an actress in a generic kitchen-interior set, where he would explain how a particular species of Glad Sandwich Bag was precisely what the doctor ordered for the particular portable-food-storage problem at issue. In his vaguely medical uniform of all white, he carried an air of authority and great evident conviction, and earned what I always gathered was an impressive salary, for those times, and received, for the first time in his career, fan mail, some of which bordered on the disturbing, and which he sometimes liked to read out loud at night in the living room, loudly and dramatically, sitting up with a nightcap and fan mail long after my mother and I had gone to bed.

I asked whether I could excuse myself for a moment to take my father's empty tomato juice glass out to the kitchen sink. I was worried that the residue along the inside sides of the tumbler would harden into the kind of precipitate that would be hard to wash off.

'For Christ's sake Jim just put the thing down,' my father said.

I put the tumbler down on the bedroom carpet over next to the base of my mother's dresser, pressing down to create a kind of circular receptacle for it in the carpet. My mother stood up and went back over by the bedroom window with her ashtray. We could tell she was getting out of our way.

My father cracked his knuckles and studied the path between the bed and the bedroom door.

I said I understood my part here to be to help my father move the mattress and box spring off the suspect bed frame and well out of the way. My father cracked his knuckles and replied that I was becoming almost frighteningly quick and perceptive. He went around between the foot of the bed and my mother at the window. He said, 'I want to let's just stack it all out in the hall, to get it the hell out of here and give us some room to maneuver.'

'Right,' I said.

My father and I were now on opposite sides of my parents' bed. My father rubbed his hands together and bent and worked his hands between the mattress and box spring and began to lift the mattress up from his side of the bed. When his side of the mattress had risen to the height of his shoulders, he somehow inverted his hands and began pushing his side up rather than lifting it. The top of his wig disappeared behind the rising mattress, and his side rose in an arc to almost the height of the white ceiling, exceeded 90°, toppled over, and began to fall over down toward me. The mattress's overall movement was like the crest of a breaking wave, I remember. I spread my arms and took the impact of the mattress with my chest and face, supporting the angled mattress with my chest, outspread arms, and face. All I could see was an extreme close-up of the woodland floral pattern of the mattress protector.

The mattress, a Simmons Beauty Rest whose tag said that it could not by law be removed, now formed the hypotenuse of a right dihedral triangle whose legs were myself and the bed's box spring. I remember visualizing and considering this triangle. My legs were trembling under the mattress's canted weight. My father exhorted me to hold and support the mattress. The respectively sharp plastic and meaty human smells of the mattress and protector were very distinct because my nose was mashed up against them.

My father came around to my side of the bed, and together we pushed the mattress back up until it stood up at 90° again. We edged carefully apart and each took one end of the upright mattress and began jockeying it off the bed and out the bedroom door into the uncarpeted hallway.

This was a King-Size Simmons Beauty Rest mattress. It was massive but had very little structural integrity. It kept curving and curling and wobbling. My father exhorted both me and the mattress. It was flaccid and floppy as we tried to jockey it. My father had an especially hard time with his half of the mattress's upright weight because of an old competitive-tennis injury.

While we were jockeying it on its side off the bed, part of the mattress on my father's end slipped and flopped over and down onto a pair of steel reading lamps, adjustable cubes of brushed steel attached by toggle bolts to the white wall over the head of the bed. The lamps took a solid hit from the mattress, and one cube was rotated all the way around on its toggle so that its open side and bulb now pointed at the ceiling. The joint and toggle made a painful squeaking sound as the cube was wrenched around upward. This was also when I became aware that even the reading lamps were on in the daylit room, because a faint square of direct lamplight, its four sides rendered slightly concave by the distortion of projection, appeared on the white ceiling above the skewed cube. But the lamps didn't fall off. They remained attached to the wall.

'God damn it to hell,' my father said as he regained control of his end of the mattress.

My father also said, 'Fucking son of a . . .' when the mattress's thickness made it difficult for him to squeeze through the doorway still holding his end.

In time we were able to get my parents' giant mattress out in the narrow hallway that ran between the master bedroom and the kitchen. I could hear another terrible squeak from the bedroom as my mother tried to realign the reading lamp whose cube had been inverted. Drops of sweat were falling from my father's face onto his side of the mattress, darkening part of the protector's fabric. My father and I tried to lean the mattress at a slight supporting angle against one wall of the hallway, but because the floor of the hallway was uncarpeted and didn't provide sufficient resistance, the mattress wouldn't stay upright. Its bottom edge slid out from the wall all the way across the width of the hallway until it met the baseboard of the opposite wall, and the upright mattress's top edge slid down the wall until the whole mattress sagged at an extremely concave slumped angle, a dry section of the woodland floral mattress protector stretched drum-tight over the slumped crease and the springs possibly damaged by the deforming concavity.

My father looked at the canted concave mattress sagging across the width of the hall and moved one end of it a little with the toe of his boot and looked at me and said, 'Fuck it.'

My bow tie was rumpled and at an angle.

My father had to walk unsteadily across the mattress in his white boots to get back to my side of the mattress and the bedroom behind me. On his way across he stopped and felt speculatively at his jaw, his boots sunk deep in woodland floral cotton. He said 'Fuck it' again, and I remember not being clear about what he was referring to. Then my father turned and started unsteadily back the way he had come across the mattress, one hand against the wall for support. He instructed me to wait right there in the hallway for one moment while he darted into the kitchen at the other end of the hall on a very brief errand. His steadying hand left four faint smeared prints on the wall's white paint.

My parents' bed's box spring, though also King-Size and heavy, had just below its synthetic covering a wooden frame that gave the box spring structural integrity, and it didn't flop or alter its shape, and after another bit of difficulty for my father — who was too thick through the middle, even with the professional girdle beneath his Glad costume — after another bit of difficulty for my father squeezing with his end of the box spring through the bedroom doorway, we were able to get it into the hall and lean it vertically at something just over 70° against the wall, where it stayed upright with no problem.

'That's the way she wants doing, Jim,' my father said, clapping me on the back in exactly the ebullient way that had prompted me to have my mother buy an elastic athletic cranial strap for my glasses. I had told my mother I needed the strap for tennis purposes, and she had not asked any questions.

My father's hand was still on my back as we returned to the master bedroom. 'Right, then!' my father said. His mood was now elevated. There was a brief second of confusion at the doorway as each of us tried to step back to let the other through first.

There was now nothing but the suspect frame left where the bed had been. There was something exoskeletal and frail-looking about the bed frame, a plain low-ratio rectangle of black steel. At each corner of the rectangle was a caster. The casters' wheels had sunk into the pile carpet under the weight of the bed and my parents and were almost completely submerged in the carpet's fibers. Each of the frame's sides had a narrow steel shelf welded at 90° to its interior's base, so that a single rectangular narrow shelf perpendicular to the frame's rectangle ran all around the frame's interior. This shelf was obviously there to support the bed's occupants and King-Size box spring and mattress.

My father seemed frozen in place. I cannot remember what my mother was doing. There seemed to be a long silent interval of my father looking closely at the exposed frame. The interval had the silence and stillness of dusty rooms immersed in sunlight. I briefly imagined every piece of furniture in the bedroom covered with sheets and the room unoccupied for years as the sun rose and crossed and fell outside the window, the room's daylight becoming staler and staler. I could hear two power lawnmowers of slightly different pitch from somewhere down our subdivision's street. The direct light through the master bedroom's window swam with rotating columns of raised dust. I remember it seemed the ideal moment for a sneeze.

Dust lay thick on the frame and even hung from the frame's interior support-shelf in little gray beards. It was impossible to see any bolts anywhere on the frame.

My father blotted sweat and wet makeup from his forehead with the back of his sleeve, which was now dark orange with makeup. 'Jesus will you look at that mess,' he said. He looked at my mother. 'Jesus.'

The carpeting in my parents' bedroom was deep-pile and a darker blue than the pale blue of the rest of the bedroom's color scheme. I remember the carpet as more a royal blue, with a saturation level somewhere between moderate and strong. The rectangular expanse of royal blue carpet that had been hidden under the bed was itself carpeted with a thick layer of clotted dust. The rectangle of dust was gray-white and thick and unevenly layered, and the only evidence of the room's carpet below was a faint sick bluish cast to the dust-layer. It looked as if dust had not drifted under the bed and settled on the carpet inside the frame but rather had somehow taken root and grown on it, upon it, the way a mold will take root and gradually cover an expanse of spoiled food. The layer of dust itself looked a little like spoiled food, bad cottage cheese. It was nauseous. Some of the dust-layer's uneven topography was caused by certain lost- and litter-type objects that had found their way under the bed — a flyswatter, a roughly *Variety*-sized magazine, some bottletops, three wadded Kleenex, and what was probably a sock — and gotten covered and textured in dust.

There was also a faint odor, sour and fungal, like the smell of an over-used bathmat.

'Jesus, there's even a smell,' my father said. He made a show of inhaling through his nose and screwing up his face. 'There's even a fucking *smell*.' He blotted his forehead and felt his jaw and looked hard at my mother. His mood was no longer elevated. My father's mood surrounded him like a field and affected any room he occupied, like an odor or a certain cast to the light.

'When was the last time this got cleaned under here?' my father asked my mother.

My mother didn't say anything. She looked at my father as he moved the steel frame around a little with his boot, which raised even more dust into the window's sunlight. The bed frame seemed very lightweight, moving back and forth noiselessly on its casters' submerged wheels. My father often moved lightweight objects absently around with his foot, rather the way other men doodle or examine their cuticles. Rugs, magazines, telephone and electrical cords, his own removed shoe. It was one of my father's ways of musing or gathering his thoughts or trying to control his mood.

'Under what presidential administration was this room last deep-cleaned, I'm standing here prompted to fucking muse out loud,' my father said.

I looked at my mother to see whether she was going to say anything in reply.

I said to my father, 'You know, since we're discussing squeaking beds, my bed squeaks, too.'

My father was trying to squat down to see whether he could locate any bolts on the frame, saying something to himself under his breath. He put his hands on the frame for balance and almost fell forward when the frame rolled under his weight.

'But I don't think I even really noticed it until we began to discuss it,' I said. I looked at my mother. 'I don't think it bothers me,' I said. 'Actually, I think I kind of like it. I think I've gradually gotten so used to it that it's become almost comforting. At this juncture,' I said.

My mother looked at me.

'I'm not complaining about it,' I said. 'The discussion just made me think of it.'

'Oh, we hear your bed, don't you worry,' my father said. He was still trying to squat, which drew his corset and the hem of his tunic up and allowed the top of his bottom's crack to appear above the the waist of his white pants. He shifted slightly to point up at the master bedroom's ceiling. 'You so much as turn over in bed up there? We hear it down here.' He took one steel side of the rectangle and shook the frame vigorously, sending up a shroud of dust. The bed frame seemed to weigh next to nothing under his hands. My mother made a mustache of her finger to hold back a sneeze.

He shook the frame again. 'But it doesn't aggravate us the way this rodential son of a whore right here does.'

I remarked that I didn't think I'd ever once heard their bed squeak before, from upstairs. My father twisted his head around to try to look up at me as I stood there behind him. But I said I'd definitely heard and could confirm the presence of a squeak when he'd pressed on the mattress, and could verify that the squeak was no one's imagination.

My father held a hand up to signal me to please stop talking. He remained in a squat, rocking slightly on the balls of his feet, using the rolling frame to keep his balance. The flesh of the top of his bottom and crack-area protruded over the waist of his pants. There were also deep red folds in the back of his neck, below the blunt cut of the wig, because he was looking up and over at my mother, who was resting her tailbone on the sill of the window, still holding her shallow ashtray.

'Maybe you'd like to go get the vacuum,' he said. My mother put the ashtray down on the sill and exited the master bedroom, passing between me and the dresser piled with bedding. 'If you can . . . if you can remember where it is!' my father called after her.

I could hear my mother trying to get past the King-Size mattress sagging diagonally across the hall.

My father was rocking more violently on the balls of his feet, and now the rocking had the sort of rolling, side-to-side quality of a ship in high seas. He came very close to losing his balance as he leaned to his right to get a handkerchief from his hip pocket and began using it to reach out and flick dust off something at one corner of the bed frame. After a moment he pointed down next to a caster.

'Bolt,' he said, pointing at the side of a caster. 'Right there's a bolt.' I leaned in over him. Drops of my father's perspiration made small dark coins in the dust of the frame. There was nothing but smooth lightweight black steel surface where he was pointing, but just to the left of where he was pointing I could see what might have been a bolt, a little stalactite of clotted dust hanging from some slight protrusion. My father's hands were broad and his fingers blunt. Another possible bolt lay several inches to the right of where he pointed. His finger trembled badly, and I believe the trembling might have been from the muscular strain on his bad knees, trying to hold so much new weight in a squat for an extended period. I heard the telephone ring twice. There had been an extended silence, with my father pointing at neither protrusion and me trying to lean in over him.

Then, still squatting on the balls of his feet, my father placed both hands on the side of the frame and leaned out over the side into the rectangle of dust inside the frame and had what at first sounded like a bad coughing fit. His hunched back and rising bottom kept me from watching him. I remember deciding that the reason the frame was not rolling under his hands' pressure was that my father had so much of his weight on it, and that maybe my father's nervous system's response to heavy dust was a cough-signal instead of a sneeze-signal. It was the wet sound of material hitting the dust inside the rectangle, plus the rising odor, that signified to me that, rather than coughing, my father had been taken ill. The spasms involved made his back rise and fall and his bottom tremble under his white commercial slacks. It was not too uncommon for my father to be taken ill shortly after coming home from work to relax, but now he seemed to have been taken really ill. To give him some privacy, I went around the frame to the side of the frame closest to the window where there was direct light and less odor and examined another of the frame's casters. My father was whispering to himself in brief expletive phrases between the spasms of his illness. I squatted easily and rubbed dust from a small area of the frame and wiped the dust on the carpet by my feet. There was a small carriage-head bolt on either side of the plating that attached the caster to the bed frame. I knelt and felt one of the bolts. Its round smooth head made it impossible either to tighten or loosen. Putting my cheek to the carpet and examining the bottom of the little horizontal shelf welded to the frame's side, I observed that the bolt seemed threaded tightly and completely through its hole, and I decided it was doubtful that any of the casters' platings' bolts were producing the sounds that reminded my father of rodents.

Just at this time, I remember, there was a loud cracking sound and my area of the frame jumped violently as my father's illness caused him to faint and he lost his balance and pitched forward and lay prone and asleep over his side of the bed frame, which as I rolled away from the frame and rose to my knees I saw was either broken or very badly bent. My father lay facedown in the mixture of the rectangle's thick dust and the material he'd brought up from his upset stomach. The dust his collapse raised was very thick, and as the new dust rose and spread it attenuated the master bedroom's daylight as decisively as if a cloud had moved over the sun in the window. My father's professional wig had detached and lay scalp-up in the mixture of dust and stomach material. The stomach material appeared to be mostly gastric blood until I recalled the tomato juice my father had been drinking. He lay face-down, with his bottom high in the air, over the side of the bed frame, which his weight had broken in half. This was how I accounted for the loud cracking sound.

I stood out of the way of the dust and the window's dusty light, feeling along the line of my jaw and examining my prone father from a distance. I remember that his breathing was regular and wet, and that the dust mixture bubbled somewhat. It was then that it occurred to me that when I'd been supporting the bed's raised mattress with my chest and face preparatory to its removal from the room, the dihedral triangle I'd imagined the mattress forming with the box spring and my body had not in fact even been a closed figure: the box spring and the floor I had stood on did not constitute a continuous plane.

Then I could hear my mother trying to get the heavy canister vacuum cleaner past the angled Simmons Beauty Rest in the hall, and I went to help her. My father's legs were stretched out across the clean blue carpet between his side of the frame and my mother's white dresser. His feet's boots were at a pigeon-toed angle, and his bottom's crack all the way down to the anus itself was now visible because the force of his fall had pulled his white slacks down even farther. I stepped carefully between his legs.

'Excuse me,' I said.

I was able to help my mother by telling her to detach the vacuum cleaner's attachments and hand them one at a time to me over the width of the slumped mattress, where I held them. The vacuum cleaner was manufactured by Regina, and its canister, which contained the engine, bag, and evacuating fan, was very heavy. I reassembled the vacuum and held it while my mother made her way back across the mattress, then handed the vacuum cleaner back to her, flattening myself against the wall to let her pass by on her way into the master bedroom.

'Thanks,' my mother said as she passed.

I stood there by the slumped mattress for several moments of a silence so complete that I could hear the street's lawnmowers all the way out in the hall, then heard the sound of my mother pulling out the vacuum cleaner's retractable cord and plugging it into the same bedside outlet the steel reading lamps were attached to.

I made my way over the angled mattress and quickly down the hall, made a sharp right at the entrance to the kitchen, crossed the foyer to the staircase, and ran up to my room, taking several stairs at a time, hurrying to get some distance between myself and the vacuum cleaner, because the sound of vacuuming has always frightened me in the same irrational way it seemed a bed's squeak frightened my father.

I ran upstairs and pivoted left at the upstairs landing and went into my room. In my room was my bed. It was narrow, a twin bed, with a headboard of wood and frame and slats of wood. I didn't know where it had come from, originally. The frame held the narrow box spring and mattress much higher off the floor than my parents' bed. It was an old-fashioned bed, so high off the floor that you had to put one knee up on the mattress and clamber up into it, or else jump.

That is what I did. For the first time since I had become taller than my parents, I took several running strides in from the doorway, past my shelves' collection of prisms and lenses and tennis trophies and my scale-model magneto, past my bookcase, the wall's still-posters from Powell's *Peeping Tom* and the closet door and my bedside's high-intensity standing lamp, and jumped, doing a full swan dive up onto my bed. I landed with my weight on my chest with my arms and legs out from my body on the indigo comforter on my bed, squashing my tie and bending my glasses' temples slightly. I was trying to make my bed produce a loud squeak, which in the case of my bed I knew was caused by any lateral friction between the wooden slats and the frame's interior's shelf-like slat-support.

But in the course of the leap and the dive, my overlong arm hit the heavy iron pole of the high-intensity standing lamp that stood next to the bed. The lamp teetered violently and began to fall over sideways, away from the bed. It fell with a kind of majestic slowness, resembling a felled tree. As the lamp fell, its heavy iron pole struck the brass knob on the door to my closet, shearing the knob off completely. The round knob and half its interior hex bolt fell off and hit my room's wooden floor with a loud noise and began then to roll around in a remarkable way, the sheared end of the hex bolt stationary and the round knob, rolling on its circumference, circling it in a spherical orbit, describing two perfectly circular motions on two distinct axes, a non-Euclidian figure on a planar surface, i.e., a cycloid on a sphere:

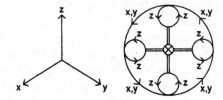

The closest conventional analogue I could derive for this figure was a cycloid, L'Hôpital's solution to Bernoulli's famous Brachistochrone Problem, the curve traced by a fixed point on the circumference of a circle rolling along a continuous plane. But since here, on the bedroom's floor, a circle was rolling around what was itself the circumference of a circle, the cycloid's standard parametric equations were no longer apposite, those equations' trigonometric expressions here becoming themselves first-order differential equations.

Because of the lack of resistance or friction against the bare floor, the knob rolled this way for a long time as I watched over the edge of the comforter and mattress, holding my glasses in place, completely distracted from the minor-D shriek of the vacuum below. It occurred to me that the movement of the amputated knob perfectly schematized what it would look like for someone to try to turn somersaults with one hand nailed to the floor. This was how I first became interested in the possibilities of annulation.

The night after the chilly and sort of awkward joint Interdependence Day picnic for Enfield's Ennet House Drug and Alcohol Recovery House, Somerville's Phoenix House, and Dorchester's grim New Choice juvenile rehab, Ennet House staffer Johnette Foltz took Ken Erdedy and Kate Gompert along with her to this one NA Beginners' Discussion Meeting where the focus was always marijuana: how every addict at the meeting had gotten in terrible addictive trouble with it right from the first duBois, or else how they'd been strung out on harder drugs and had tried switching to grass to get off the original drugs and but then had gotten in even terribler trouble with grass than they'd been in with the original hard stuff. This was supposedly the only NA meeting in metro Boston explicitly devoted to marijuana. Johnette Foltz said she wanted Erdedy and Gompert to see how completely nonunique and unalone they were in terms of the Substance that had brought them both down.

There were about maybe two dozen beginning recovering addicts there in the anechoic vestry of an upscale church in what Erdedy figured had to be either west Belmont or east Waltham. The chairs were arranged in NA's traditional huge circle, with no tables to sit at and everybody balancing ashtrays on their knees and accidentally kicking over their cups of coffee. Everybody who raised their hand to share concurred on the insidious ways marijuana had ravaged their bodies, minds, and spirits: marijuana destroys *slowly* but *thoroughly* was the consensus. Ken Erdedy's joggling foot knocked over his coffee not once but twice as the NAs took turns concurring on the hideous psychic fallout they'd all endured both in active marijuana-dependency and then in marijuana-detox: the social isolation, anxious lassitude, and the hyperself-consciousness that then reinforced the withdrawal and anxiety — the increasing emotional abstraction, poverty of affect, and then total emotional catalepsy — the obsessive analyzing, finally the paralytic stasis that results from the obsessive analysis of all possible implications of both getting up from the couch and not getting up from the couch — and then the endless symptomatic gauntlet of Withdrawal from delta-9-tetrahydrocannabinol: i.e. pot-detox: the loss of appetite, the mania and insomnia, the chronic fatigue and nightmares, the impotence and cessation of menses and lactation, the circadian arrhythmia, the sudden sauna-type sweats and mental confusion and fine-motor tremors, the particularly nasty excess production of saliva — several beginners still holding institutional drool-cups just under their chins — the generalized anxiety and foreboding and dread, and the shame of feeling like neither M.D.s nor the hard-drug NAs themselves showed much empathy or compassion for the 'addict' brought down by what was supposed to be nature's humblest buzz, the benignest Substance around.

Ken Erdedy noticed that nobody came right out and used the terms *melancholy* or *anhedonia* or *depression,* much less *clinical depression;* but this worst of symptoms, this logarithm of all suffering, seemed, though unmentioned, to hang fog-like just over the room's heads, to drift between the peristyle columns and over the decorative astrolabes and candles on long prickets and medieval knockoffs and framed Knights of Columbus charters, a gassy plasm so dreaded no beginner could bear to look up and name it. Kate Gompert kept staring at the floor and making a revolver of her forefinger and thumb and shooting herself in the temple and then blowing pretend-cordite off the barrel's tip until Johnette Foltz whispered to her to knock it off.

As was his custom at meetings, Ken Erdedy said nothing and observed everybody else very closely, cracking his knuckles and joggling his foot. Since an NA 'Beginner' is technically anybody with under a year clean, there were varying degrees of denial and distress and general cluelessness in this plush upscale vestry. The meeting had the usual broad demographic cross-section, but the bulk of these grass-ravaged people looked to him urban and tough and busted-up and dressed without any color-sense at all, people you could easily imagine smacking their kid in a supermarket or lurking with a homemade sap in the dark of a downtown alley. Same as AA. Motley disrespectability was like the room norm, along with glazed eyes and excess spittle. A couple of the beginners still had the milky plastic I.D. bracelets from psych wards they'd forgotten to cut off, or else hadn't yet gotten up the drive to do it.

Unlike Boston AA, Boston NA has no mid-meeting raffle-break and goes for just an hour. At the close of this Monday Beginners' Meeting everybody got up and held hands in a circle and recited the NA-Conference-Approved 'Just For Today,' then they all recited the Our Father, not exactly in unison. Kate Gompert later swore she distinctly heard the tattered older man beside her say 'And lead us not into Penn Station' during the Our Father.

Then, just as in AA, the NA meeting closed with everybody shouting to the air in front of them to Keep Coming Back because It Works.

But then, kind of horrifically, everyone in the room started milling around wildly and hugging each other. It was like somebody'd thrown a switch. There wasn't even very much conversation. It was just hugging, as far as Erdedy could see. Rampant, indiscriminate hugging, where the point seemed to be to hug as many people as possible regardless of whether you'd ever seen them before in your life. People went from person to person, arms out and leaning in. Big people stooped and short people got up on tiptoe. Jowls ground into other jowls. Both genders hugged both genders. And the male-to-male hugs were straight embraces, hugs minus the vigorous little thumps on the back that Erdedy'd always seen as somehow requisite for male-to-male hugs. Johnette Foltz was almost a blur. She went from person to person. She was racking up serious numbers of hugs. Kate Gompert had her usual lipless expression of morose distaste, but even she gave and got some hugs. But Erdedy — who'd never particularly liked hugging — moved way back from the throng, over up next to the NA-Conference-Approved-Literature table, and stood there by himself with his hands in his pockets, pretending to study the coffee urn with great interest.

But then a tall heavy Afro-American fellow with a gold incisor and perfect vertical cylinder of Afro-American hairstyle peeled away from a sort of group-hug nearby, he'd spotted Erdedy, and the fellow came over and established himself right in front of Erdedy, spreading the arms of his fatigue jacket for a hug, stooping slightly and leaning in toward Erdedy's personal trunk-region.

Erdedy raised his hands in a benign No Thanks and backed up further so that his bottom was squashed up against the edge of the Conference-Approved-Literature table.

'Thanks, but I don't particularly like to hug,' he said.

The fellow had to sort of pull up out of his pre-hug lean, and stood there awkwardly frozen, with his big arms still out, which Erdedy could see must have been awkward and embarrassing for the fellow. Erdedy found himself trying to calculate just what remote sub-Asian locale would be the maximum possible number of km. away from this exact spot and moment as the fellow just stood there, his arms out and the smile draining from his face.

'Say what?' the fellow said.

Erdedy proffered a hand. 'Ken E., Ennet House, Enfield. How do you do. You are?'

The fellow slowly let his arms down but just looked at Erdedy's proffered hand. A single styptic blink. 'Roy Tony,' he said.

'Roy, how do you do.'

'What it is,' Roy said. The big fellow now had his handshake-hand behind his neck and was pretending to feel the back of his neck, which Erdedy didn't know was a blatant dis.

'Well Roy, if I may call you Roy, or Mr. Tony, if you prefer, unless it's a compound first name, hyphenated, "Roy-Tony" and then a last name, but well with respect to this hugging thing, Roy, it's nothing personal, rest assured.'

'Assured?'

Erdedy's best helpless smile and an apologetic shrug of the GoreTex anorak. 'I'm afraid I just don't particularly like to hug. Just not a hugger. Never have been. It was something of a joke among my fam—'

Now the ominous finger-pointing of street-aggression, this Roy fellow pointing first at Erdedy's chest and then at his own: 'So man what you say you saying I'm a hugger? You saying you think I go around like to hug?'

Both Erdedy's hands were now up palms-out and waggling in a like bonhommic gesture of heading off all possible misunderstanding: 'No but see the whole point is that I wouldn't presume to call you either a hugger or a nonhugger because I don't know you. I only meant to say it's nothing personal having to do with you as an individual, and I'd be more than happy to shake hands, even one of those intricate multiple-handed ethnic handshakes if you'll bear with my inexperience with that sort of handshake, but I'm simply uncomfortable with the whole idea of hugging.'

By the time Johnette Foltz could break away and get over to them, the fellow had Erdedy by his anorak's insulated lapels and was leaning him way back over the edge of the Literature table so that Erdedy's waterproof lodge boots were off the ground, and the fellow's face was right up in Erdedy's face in a show of naked aggression:

'You think I fucking *like* to go around hug on folks? You think *any* of us *like* this *shit*? We fucking do what they tell us. They tell us Hugs Not Drugs in here. We done motherfucking *surrendered* our wills in here,' Roy said. 'You little faggot,' Roy added. He wedged his hand between them to point at himself, which meant he was now holding Erdedy off the ground with just one hand, which fact was not lost on Erdedy's nervous system. 'I done had to give four hugs my first night here and then I gone ran in the fucking can and fucking puked. *Puked*,' he said. 'Not *com*fortable? Who the *fuck* are you? Don't *even* try and tell me I'm coming over feeling *com*fortable about trying to hug on your James-River-Traders-wearing-Calvin-Klein-aftershave-smelling-goofy-ass motherfucking ass.'

Erdedy observed one of the Afro-American women who was looking on clap her hands and shout '*Talk* about it!'

'And now you go and disre*spect* me in front of my whole clean and sober *set* just when I gone risk sharing my vulner*abi*lity and dis*com*fort with you?'

Johnette Foltz was sort of pawing at the back of Roy Tony's fatigue jacket, shuddering mentally at how the report of an Ennet House resident assaulted at an NA meeting she'd personally brought him to would look written up in the Staff Log.

'*Now*,' Roy said, extracting his free hand and pointing to the vestry floor with a stabbing gesture, 'now,' he said, 'you gone risk vulnerability and discomfort and hug my ass or do I gone fucking rip your head off and *shit* down your neck?'

Johnette Foltz had hold of the Roy fellow's coat now with both hands and was trying to pull the fellow off, Keds scrabbling for purchase on the smooth parquet, saying 'Yo Roy T. man, easy there Dude, Man, Esse, Bro, Posse, Crew, Homes, Jim, Brother, he's just new is all'; but by this time Erdedy had both arms around the guy's neck and was hugging him with such vigor Kate Gompert later told Joelle van Dyne it looked like Erdedy was trying to climb him.

'We've lost a couple already,' Steeply admitted. 'During the testing. Not just volunteers. Some idiot intern in Data Analysis yielded to temptation and wanted to see what all the fuss was for and got hold of Flatto's I/O lab's clearance card and went in and viewed.'

'From among the many Read-Only copies of your stock of the Entertainment.'

'No great tragic loss in itself — lose some idiot-child intern. *C'est la guerre.* The real loss was that his supervisor tried to go in after him and pull him out. Our head of Data Analysis himself.'

'Hoyne, Henri or pronounce "Henry," middle initial of F., with the wife, with his adult diabetes he controls.'

'*Did* control. Twenty-year man, Hank. Damn good man. He was a friend. He's in four-point restraints now. Nourishment through a tube. No desire or even basic survival-type will for anything other than more viewing.'

'Of it.'

'I tried to visit.'

'With your sleeveless skirt and different breasts.'

'I couldn't even stand to be in the same room, see him like that. Begging for just even a few seconds — a trailer, a snatch of soundtrack, anything. His eyes wobbling around like some drug-addicted newborn. Break your fucking heart. In the next bed, restrained, the idiot intern: *this* was the sort of undisciplined selfish child you like to talk about, Rémy. But Hank Hoyne was no child. I watched this man put down all sugar and treats when he first got diagnosed. Just put them down and walked away. Not even a whimper or backward glance.'

'A will of steel.'

'An American adult of exemplary self-control and discretion.'

'The *samizdat* is not to be played crazily about with, so. We too have lost persons. It is serious.'

The legs of the constellation of Perseus were amputated by the earth's horizon. Perseus, he wore the hat of a jongleur or pantalone. Hercules' head, this head was square. It was not long to dawn also because at 32° N Pollux and Castor became visible. They were over Marathe's left shoulder, as if giants were looking over his shoulder, one of Castor's legs inbent in a feminine manner.

'But do you ever consider?' Steeply lit another cigarette.

'Fantasize, you are meaning.'

'If it's that consuming. If it somehow addresses desires that total,' Steeply said. 'Not even sure I can imagine what desires that total and utter even are.' Up and down upon the toes. Turning above the waist only to look back at Marathe. 'You ever think of what it'd be like, speculate?'

'Us, we think of what ends the Entertainment may serve. We find its efficacy tempting. You and we are tempted in different ways.' Marathe could identify no other Southwest U.S.A. constellations except the Big Dipper, which at this latitude appeared attached to the Great Bear to form something resembling the 'Big Bucket' or the 'Great Cradle.' The chair gave small squeaks when he shifted his weight upon it.

Steeply said 'Well I can't say I've been tempted in the strictest sense of *tempted*.'

'Perhaps we are meaning different things by this.'

'Frankly, when I think of it I'm as much terrified as I am intrigued. Hank Hoyne is an empty shell. The iron will, the analytic savvy. His love of a fine cigar. All gone. His world's as if it has collapsed into one small bright point. Inner world. Lost to us. You look in his eyes and there's nothing you can recognize in them. Poor Miriam.' Steeply kneaded a bare shoulder. 'Willis, on the I/O night-shift, came up with a phrase for their eyes. "Empty of intent." This appeared in a memo.'

Marathe pretended to sniff. 'The temptation of the passive Reward of terminal *p*, this all seems complex to me. Terror seems part of the temptation for you. Us of Québec's cause, we have never felt this temptation for the Entertainment, or knowing. But we respect its power. Thus, we do not fool crazily about.'

It was not that the sky was lightening so much as that the stars' light had paled. There became a sullenness about their light. Now, also, strange-looking U.S.A. insects whirred actively past from time to time, moving jaggedly and making Marathe think of many windblown sparks.

10 NOVEMBER
YEAR OF THE DEPEND ADULT UNDERGARMENT

The following things in the room were blue. The blue checks in the blue-and-black-checked shag carpet. Two of the room's six institutional-plush chairs, whose legs were steel tubes bent into big ellipses, which wobbled, so that while the chairs couldn't really be rocked in they could be sort of bobbed in, which Michael Pemulis was doing absently as he waited and scanned a printout of Eschaton's highly technical core ESCHAX directory, i.e. bobbing in his chair, which produced a kind of rapid rodential squeaking that gave Hal Incandenza the howling fantods as he sat there kittycorner from Pemulis, also waiting. The printout kept rotating in Pemulis's hands. Each chair had a 105-watt reading lamp attached to the back on a flexible metal stalk that let the reading lamp curve out from behind and shine right down on whatever magazine the waiting person was looking at, but since the curved lamps induced this unbearable sensation of somebody feverish right there reading over your shoulder, the magazines (some of whose covers involved the color blue) tended to stay unread, and were fanned neatly out on a low ceramic coffeetable. The carpet was a product of something called Antron. Hal could see streaks of lividity where somebody'd vacuumed against the grain.

Though the magazines' coffeetable was nonblue — a wet-nail-polish red with *E.T.A.* in a kind of gray escutcheon — two of the unsettlingly attached lamps that kept its magazines unread and neatly fanned were blue, although the two blue lamps were not the lamps attached to the two blue chairs. Dr. Charles Tavis liked to say that you could tell a lot about an administrator by the decor of his waiting room. The Headmaster's waiting room was part of a little hallway in the Comm.-Ad. lobby's southwest corner. The premie violets in an asymmetrical sprig in a tennis-ball-shaped vase on the coffeetable were arguably in the blue family. And also the overenhanced blue of the wallpaper's sky, which the wallpaper scheme was fluffy cumuli arrayed patternlessly against an overenhancedly blue sky, incredibly disorienting wallpaper that was by an unpleasant coincidence also the wallpaper in the Enfield offices of a Dr. Zegarelli, D.D.S., which Hal's just come back from, after a removal: the left side of his face still feels big and dead, with this persistent sensation that he's drooling without being able to feel it or stop it. No one's sure what C.T.'s choice of this wallpaper is supposed to communicate, especially to parents who come with prospective kids in tow to scout out E.T.A., but Hal loathes sky-and-cloud wallpaper because it makes him feel high-altitude and disoriented and sometimes plummeting.

The sills and crosspieces of the waiting room's two windows have always been dark blue. There was a nautical-blue border of braid around the bill of Michael Pemulis's jaunty yachting cap. Hal was confident Pemulis would remove the insouciant hat the minute they were called in on what was presumably going to be the carpet.

Also blue: the upper-border slices of sky in the framed informal photos of E.T.A. students that hung on the walls;[209] the chassis of Alice Moore's Intel 972 word processor w/ modem but no cartridge-capability; also Ms. Moore's fingertips and lips. The E.T.A. Headmaster's receptionist and administrative assistant is known to the players as Lateral Alice Moore. In her youth Lateral Alice Moore had been a helicopter pilot and airborne traffic reporter for a major Boston radio station until a tragic collision with another station's airborne traffic-report helicopter — plus then the cataclysmic fall to the rush hour's Jamaica Way six-laner below — had left her with chronic oxygen debt and a neurological condition whereby she was able to move only from side to side. So hence the sobriquet Lateral Alice Moore. An effective time-killer while sitting there waiting for whatever administrator's summoned you is to have Lateral Alice Moore drum rapidly on her chest and give imitations of her old Boston rush-hour traffic reports in a stuttered helicopterish reporter-voice. Neither Hal, continually checking his chin for drool, nor Pemulis, scanning and bobbing, nor Ann Kittenplan nor Trevor Axford — about whom there was today not even a hint of the color blue — are in the mood for this right now, awaiting what they presume to be some kind of administrative fallout from Sunday's horrendous Eschaton fiasco. The presumption is based on who's been summoned here, to wait.

The two different-sized offices that open off the waiting room (through the open and only other door of which the dusky blue Mannington shag of the Comm.-Ad. lobby is visible) belong to Dr. Charles Tavis and to Mrs. Avril Incandenza. Tavis's office's outer door is real oak and has his name and degree and title in (nonblue) letters so big that the total I.D. crowds the door's margins. There's also an inner door.

Avril, whose feelings about enclosure are well known, has no door on her office. Her office is bigger than C.T.'s, though, and has a seminar table it's always been obvious he covets. Avril's office's blue-and-black-checkered shag is deeper than the waiting room's shag, so that the border between the two is like a mowed v. unmowed lawn. Avril serves (pro bono) as E.T.A.'s Dean of Academic Affairs and Dean of Females. She's in there unenclosed right now with pretty much every E.T.A. female under thirteen except Ann Kittenplan, whose tattooed knuckles are bruised and who looks somehow cross-dressed in a dress and (nonblue) barrette. Avril has vividly white hair — as of the last few months before Himself's felo de se — that looks like it never went through the gray stage (it mostly didn't) and legs whose taper you can see T. Axford is appraising with the frankness of adolescence as she paces a bit in front of the crowded seminar table, in full if kind of oblique-angled view of the people in the waiting room.[210] Though it's not technically in the waiting room with Hal, the plastic fine-tip felt pen Avril taps professionally against her incisors as she paces and considers is: blue.

Administrative diddle-checks have been required at all North American tennis academies since the infamous case of coach R. Bill ('Touchy') Phiely at California's Rolling Hills Academy, whose hair-raising diary and collection of telephotos and tiny panties — discovered only after his disappearance into the Humboldt County hill country with a thirteen-year-old companion — created what might be conservatively termed a climate of concern among the continent's tennis parents. At the Enfield Tennis Academy, for the last four years, Dr. Dolores Rusk is supposed to hold a kind of distaff community meeting with all female players judged naïve and moppetish enough to be potential diddlees — the youngest of these is Rhode Island's pint-sized Tina Echt, just seven but a true cannibal off the backhand side — to interface in a discreet but nurturingly empowering group setting, etc., and nip any potential Phielyisms in the bud. Monthly diddle-checks are in Rusk's contract because they're in E.T.A.'s O.N.A.N.T.A. accreditation-charter.

Dean of Females Avril M. Incandenza presides over the diddle-check when Dr. Rusk is otherwise engaged, and Rusk is so very rarely legitimately engaged that the fact that it's the Moms doing diddle-prevention duty today leads Hal to fear that Rusk is maybe in there in the Headmaster's office getting ready to be in on the upcoming disciplinary scene: C.T. would have to be really upset to want to have Rusk included; Rusk might be there more for C.T. than for any studential psyches.

Axhandle has his eyes closed and is repeating a mnemonic limerick about Brewster's Angle for the Leith-taught Quadrivial colloquium 'Reflections on Refraction.' Michael Pemulis is still scanning a serrated scroll of EndStat-axiomatic $Pink_2$, which looks to be all math and spiky brackets, and bobbing, ignoring Ann Kittenplan's murderous looks and tubercular throat-clearings at the squeaking of his bobbing blue chair. You can tell Pemulis really is studying because he keeps turning something upside-down and then rightside-up. Hal declines to share his Rusk-being-in-there-with-Tavis worries with Michael Pemulis, not just because Hal avoids ever mentioning Rusk's name but also because Pemulis loathes Rusk with a hard and gem-like flame, and though he'd never admit it is already clearly nauseated with worry that he's going to get the lion's share of the blame for damage to Lord and Possalthwaite and not only receive corrective on-court discipline but maybe get denied a spot on the trip to Tucson's WhataBurger, or worse.[211]

Avril is indirect but syntactically crisp with the couple dozen little girls in there, probing. The girls' outfits involve blue at many levels of hue and intensity in varied combination. Avril Incandenza's voice is higher on the register than one would expect from a woman so imposingly tall. It is high and sort of airy. Oddly insubstantial, is the E.T.A. consensus. Orin says one reason Avril dislikes music is that whenever she hums along she sounds insane.

The absence of a door to the Moms's office means you might as well be in there, in terms of being able to hear what's going on. She has little sense of spatial privacy or boundary, having been so much alone so much when a child. Lateral Alice Moore wears a sort of surreal combination of black Lycra Spandex and filmy green tulle. The portable-stereo headphones she wears — entering what appear to be Response-macros for 80+ received invitations to next week's WhataBurger Invitational — are powder-blue. Her typing is clearly in synch with something's backbeat. Her lips and cheek-points are the vague robin's-egg of cyanosis.

Just why Michael Pemulis hates Dr. Rusk is unclear and seems free-floating; Hal gets a different answer from Pemulis every time. Hal himself feels uncomfortable around Dolores Rusk and avoids her but isn't aware of any particular reason for being uncomfortable around her. But Pemulis positively detests Rusk. It was Pemulis who'd dickied in at night and hooked a Delco battery up to the inside brass knob of her locked office door, at age fifteen, Rusk's office door, the first door over in the other little hallway at the lobby's NE corner, next to the shift-nurses' office and infirmary, then exiting Rusk's office by a window and thorny hedge, which Pemulis was extremely fortunate no one but Hal and Schacht and maybe Mario knew he authored the hot knob, because the whole scheme turned quickly disastrous, because it was an elderly Brighton-Irish cleaning lady who got to the hot knob first, at like 0500h., and it turned out Pemulis had seriously undercalculated the brass-conducted Delco voltage involved, and if the cleaning lady hadn't been wearing yellow rubber cleaning-lady gloves she would have ended up with way worse than the permanent perm and irreversible crossed eyes she regained consciousness with, and the cleaning lady's Ward Boss was upper Brighton's infamous F. X. ('Follow That Ambulance') Byrne, rapacious personal-injury J.D., and the Academy's Workman's Comp. premiums had skyrocketed, and the whole thing was still in litigation.

Avril had eschewed an office door even before the cleaning-lady kert-wang, for simple enclosure-reasons.

Recrossed legs and closer inspection reveal that Trevor Axford's left sock, though not his right sock, is blue.

Sinistral, his right hand missing digits from a fireworks accident three Interdependence Days past, Axhandle is several cm. shorter than Hal Incandenza and is a true redheaded person, with copper-colored hair and that moist white freckle-chocked skin that even through two layers of summer Pledge only reddens and peels, plus there's the matter of the enormous and forever chapped lips; and as a tennis player he is like a less effective version of John Wayne — he does nothing but blast from the baseline, w/o discernible spin. He's a junior from Short Beach CT and under enormous family pressure to continue the male Axford tradition of attending Yale and is academically so marginal that he knows his only chance to go to Yale is to play tennis for Yale, which would effectively blow any chance at a Show-level future, and is high-ranked but has set his competitive sights on nothing past a Ride-offer to Yale. Though Ingersoll's informally in Hal's Big Buddy contingent, he's technically in Axhandle's, they're both aware; and Hal's a little uncomfortable about his relief that none of the real Eschaton casualties were technically his Buddies.[212] The only real thing Axford and Hal have in common on the court is a curious habit of refusing to ask for help from other courts when their balls go astray.[213]

Pemulis has finally quit with the bobbing and folded the printout scroll of Pink$_2$ into a big ragged square and has sidled over to Lateral Alice Moore's horseshoe-shaped desk and is bantering with her very casually, looking all around him as he banters, trying subtly to feel her out re whether maybe one of these WhataBurger Jr. Invitational invitations stacked cruciform, female athwart male, in Lateral Alice's IN box concerns anybody with the male initials M.M.P., by any chance. Pemulis and Moore would be less tight if she knew he dickied in at night and used her WATS and modem, though she's very laid-back and easygoing and not at all like the little framed thing by her name plaque with a scowling woman saying I'VE GOT ONE NERVE LEFT AND YOU'RE GETTING ON IT. The little cartoon is just a standard like office-worker gag. She'd summoned them out of Sixth Hour with the same ancient intercom-and-mike system Troeltsch et al. get to commandeer for Saturdays' WETA (Troeltsch has had to be prohibited from playing with her chair), and her transmitted voice had not been ungentle. Hal's face's left side feels queerly inflated, but then when he runs his right hand over it it's always regulation-size. Administrative assistants worth their health benefits are synaptically evolved to the point where they can banter, accept compliments on a Spandex-and-tulle ensemble, effortlessly deflect unauthorized info-probes, listen to something bass-intensive on personal-stereo headphones, and word-process effortlessly to the headphones' backbeat, all simul-taneously. Lateral Alice Moore's bluish fingertips make her painted nails ten little sunsets. Lateral Alice Moore's desk's chair's wheels fit on a track with an electrified third rail, so she can slide from one corner of the horseshoe's arc to the other — more or less laterally — at the touch of a cerise desktop button. For post-Delco-incident legal reasons, the name-plaque on her re-ception desk has **DANGER: THIRD RAIL** instead of the name Lateral Alice Moore.

Hal can hear Avril saying 'Now. If I speak to all of you very gently about being touched by a tall person in an uncomfortable way, will you know what I mean? Have any of you been kissed or nuzzled or hugged or rubbed or pinched or probed or fondled or in any way touched by a tall person in a way that's made you uncomfortable?' Hal can see one of his Moms's stock-inged legs, terminating in a trim ankle and a very white Reebok, extruding from stage-right into the frame of the empty doorway, the Reebok tapping patiently, and one arm crossed over Avril's chest, and the other arm's elbow resting on that arm and fluttering in and out of view as Avril taps at her teeth with a blue pen.

'Gramma pinches my cheek,' one girl volunteers. She'd actually raised her hand to be called on, her wrist with its touching little (blue) terry wrist-band. Hal hasn't seen so many pigtails and button noses and small berry-shaped mouths convened in one indoor place in who knows how long. Very few of the sneakered feet reach all the way to the thick shag in there. Much leg-dangling and absent uncomfortable sneaker-swinging. A couple fingers in nostrils in absent contemplation. Ann Kittenplan, in her blue chair, is coolly appraising the little wash-offable tattoos she applies daily to the knuckles of her hands.

'Not quite what we're trying to speak of together right now, Erica,' from someplace above the tapping foot and in-and-out arm. Hal knows the register and inflections of his mother's voice so well it almost makes him uncomfortable. His left ankle gives a sick squeak when he flexes it. Cords in his left forearm stand out and subside as he squeezes his tennis ball. The left side of his face feels like something far away that means him harm and is coming gradually closer. He can make out just the whistly fricatives of Charles Tavis's distant voice from behind his double office doors; it sounds somehow like he's speaking to more than one person in there. Charles Tavis's office's inner door also has the I.D. *DR. CHARLES TAVIS* on it, and below that his E.T.A. motto about the man who knows his limitations having none.

'She does it really hard,' rebuts what must be Erica Siress.

'I've seen her do it,' what sounds like Jolene Criess confirms.

Another: 'I hate that.'

'I hate it when some adult pats my head like I'm a schnauzer.'

'The next adult that calls me adorable is in for a really unpleasant surprise let me tell you.'

'I hate it when my hair is tousled or smoothed in any way.'

'Kittenplan's tall. Kittenplan gives Indian rub-burns after lights-out.'

Avril gives them verbal space, tries gently to steer the topic closer to true Phielyism; she's subtle and very good with small children.

'. . . that my daddy gives me these small little shoves in the small of the back when he wants me to go into rooms. It's like he *influences* me into rooms from behind. This tiny little irritating push, that makes me want to let him have it in the shin.'

'Mmmmmm-hmm,' Avril muses.

It's impossible not to overhear, because things out in the waiting room right now are so comparatively silent except for the tinny hiss of Lateral Alice Moore's disengaged headphones and the conspiratorial murmur of Michael Pemulis trying to get her to drum on her chest and describe I-93 South's Neponset exit-ramp as one very long thin parking lot. Things are so quiet because the anxiety level in Tavis's waiting room is high.

'You're all in for some serious Pukers is my prediction,' Ann Kittenplan had said to Pemulis as they all first answered the intercom's summons, which was also about the time that Pemulis started in with the rodential chair-squeaking that made one half of Kittenplan's face spasm.

One of the tricky and sinister things about corrective discipline at a tennis academy is that punishments can take the form of what might look like straight-out athletic conditioning. Q.v. the drill sergeant telling the recruit to drop and give him fifty, etc. So but this is why Gerhardt Schtitt and his prorectors are way more feared than Ogilvie or Richardson-Levy-O'Byrne-Chawaf or any of the regular academics. It's not just that Schtitt's corporal reputation preceded him here. It's that Schtitt and deLint make out the daily schedules for A.M. drills and P.M. matches and resistance-training and conditioning runs. But especially the A.M. drills. Certain drills are well known to be nothing more than attitude-adjusters, designed to do nothing but dramatically lower life-quality for a few minutes. Too brutal to be assigned on the daily basis that would contribute to genuine aerobic conditioning, drills like the disciplinary version of Tap & Whack[214] are known to the kids simply as Pukers. Puker-drills are really meant to do nothing but hurt you and make you think long and hard before repeating whatever you did to merit them; but they're still to all outward appearances exempt from any kind of VIII-Amendment protest or sniveling calls home to parents, insidiously, since they can be described to parents and police[215] alike as just drills assigned for your overall cardiovascular benefit, with all the actual sadism completely sub rosa.

Kittenplan's prediction that the upperclassmen are going to wear the whole brown helmet for the Eschaton free-for-all is hopefully rebuttable by Pemulis's observation that Eschaton's extracurricular impulse and structure had been firmly in place before any of them'd even enrolled. All Michael Pemulis had done was codify basic principles and impose a sort of matrix of decidable strategy. Maybe helped create a mythology and established, mostly through personal example, a certain level of expectation. All Hal'd done was act as amanuensis on a lousy manual. The I.-Day Combatants had been out there of their own volition. Pemulis and Axford'd gotten Hal to write out most of all this in maximally rhetorical diction, which Pemulis had then embedded in a Pink$_2$ printout so he could carry it around and study it and have it all nailed down before Tavis tried any boom-lowering. The strategy is to let Pemulis do all the talking but let Hal interject at will, the voice of reason, good-cop/bad. Axford's been instructed to count the Antron fibers between his shoes the whole time they're in there.

Hal has no idea what it might signify that the Headmaster's summons hasn't come for almost 48 hours. It might be odd that it hadn't once occurred to him to see Tavis personally, or to go to HmH and ask the Moms for intercession or info. It's not like he had the urge but resisted it; it hadn't even occurred to him.

For somebody who not only lives on the same institutional grounds as his family but also has his training and education and pretty much his whole overall raison-d'être directly overseen by relatives, Hal devotes an unusually small part of his brain and time ever thinking about people in his family *qua* family-members. Sometimes when he'll be chatting with somebody in the endless registration-line for a tournament or at a post-meet dance or something and somebody'll say something like 'How's Avril getting along?' or 'I saw Orin kicking the everliving shit out of the ball on an O.N.A.N.F.L. highlights cartridge last week,' there will be this odd tense moment where Hal's mind will go utterly blank and his mouth slack and flabby, working soundlessly, as if the names were words on the tip of his tongue. Except for Mario, about whom Hal will talk your ear off, it's almost like some ponderous creaky machine has to get up and running for Hal even to think about members of his immediate family as standing in relation to himself. It's a possible reason Hal avoids Dr. Dolores Rusk, who always wants to probe him on issues of space and self-definition and something she keeps calling the 'Coatlicue Complex.'[216]

Hal's maternal half-uncle Charles Tavis is a little like the late Himself in that Tavis's C.V. is a back-and-forth but not indecisive mix of athletics and hard science. A B.A. and doctorate in engineering, an M.B.A. in athletics administration — in his professional youth Tavis had put them together as a civil engineer, his specialty the accommodation of stress through patterned dispersal, i.e. distributing the weight of gargantuan athletic-spectatorial crowds. I.e., he'd say, he'd handled large live audiences; he'd been in his own small way a minor pioneer in polymer-reinforced cement and mobile fulcra. He'd been on design teams for stadia and civic centers and grandstands and micological-looking superdomes. He'd admit up-front that he'd been a far better team-player engineer than out there up-front stage-center in the architectural limelight. He'd apologize profusely when you had no idea what that sentence meant and say maybe the obfuscation had been unconsciously deliberate, out of some kind of embarrassment over his first and last limelighted architectural supervision, up in Ontario, before the rise of O.N.A.N.ite Interdependence, when he'd designed the Toronto Blue Jays' novel and much-ballyhooed SkyDome ballpark-and-hotel complex. Because Tavis had been the one to take the lion's share of the heat when it turned out that Blue Jays' spectators in the stands, many of them innocent children wearing caps and pounding their little fists into the gloves they'd brought with hopes of nothing more exotic than a speared foul ball, that spectators at a distressing number of different points all along both foul-lines could see right into the windows of guests having various and sometimes exotic sex in the hotel bedrooms over the center-field wall. The bulk of the call for Tavis's rolling head had come, he'd tell you, when the cameraman in charge of the SkyDome's Instant-Replay-Video Scoreboard, disgruntled or professionally suicidal or both, started training his camera on the bedroom windows and routing the resultant multi-limbed coital images up onto the 75-meter scoreboard screen, etc. Sometimes in slow motion and with multiple replays, etc. Tavis will admit his reluctance to talk about it, still, after all this time. He'll confess that his usual former-career-summary is to say just that he'd specialized in athletic venues that could safely and comfortably seat enormous numbers of live spectators, and that the market for his services had bottomed out as more and more events were designed for cartridge-dissemination and private home-viewing, which he'll point out is not technically untrue so much as just not entirely open and forthcoming.

Lateral Alice Moore is printing out WhataBurger RSVPs. The Intel 972 is cutting-edge, but she clings to a hideous old dot-matrix printer she refuses to replace as long as Dave Harde can keep it going. It's the same with the intercom system and its antiquated iron stand-up mike that Troeltsch says is an affront to the whole broadcasting profession. Lateral Alice has queer eccentric pockets of intransigence and Ludditism, due possibly to her helicopter-crash and neurologic deficits. The printer's needly sound fills the waiting room. Hal finds he can be confident of his face's symmetry and saliva only when he sits there with his right hand over his left cheek. Each line of Alice's printed response sounds like some sort of supposedly unrippable fabric getting ripped, over and over, a dental and life-denying sound.

For Hal, the general deal with his maternal uncle is that Tavis is terribly shy around people and tries to hide it by being very open and expansive and wordy and bluff, and that it's excruciating to be around. Mario's way of looking at it is that Tavis is very open and expansive and wordy, but so clearly uses these qualities as a kind of protective shield that it betrays a frightened vulnerability almost impossible not to feel for. Either way, the unsettling thing about Charles Tavis is that he's possibly the openest man of all time. Orin and Marlon Bain's view was always that C.T. was less like a person than like a sort of cross-section of a person. Even the Moms Hal could remember relating anecdotes about how as a teenager, when she'd taken the child C.T. or been around him at Québecois functions or gatherings involving other kids, the child C.T. had been too self-conscious and awkward to join right in with any group of the kids clustered around, talking or plotting or whatever, and so Avril said she'd watch him just kind of drift from cluster to cluster and lurk around creepily on the fringe, listening, but that he'd always say, loudly, in some lull in the group's conversation, something like 'I'm afraid I'm far too self-conscious really to join in here, so I'm just going to lurk creepily at the fringe and listen, if that's all right, just so you know,' and so on.

But so the point is that Tavis is an odd and delicate specimen, both ineffectual and in certain ways fearsome as a Headmaster, and being a relative guarantees no special predictive insight or quarter, unless certain maternal connections are exploited, the thought of doing which literally does not occur to Hal. This odd blankness about his family might be one way to manage a life where domestic and vocational authorities sort of bleed into each other. Hal squeezes his tennis ball like a madman, sitting there in the needly printout-noise, right palm against his left cheek and elbow hiding his mouth, wanting very much to go first to the Pump Room and then to brush vigorously with his portable collapsible Oral-B. A quick chew of Kodiak is out of the question for several reasons.

The only other time this year that Hal was officially summoned to the Headmaster's waiting room had been in late August, right before Convocation and during Orientation period, when Y.D.A.U.'s new kids were coming in and wandering around clueless and terrified, etc., and Tavis had wanted Hal to take temporary charge of a nine-year-old kid coming in from somewhere called Philo IL, who was allegedly blind, the kid, and apparently had cranium-issues, from having originally been one of the infantile natives of Ticonderoga NNY evacuated too late, and had several eyes in various stages of evolutionary development in his head but was legally blind, but still an extremely solid player, which is all kind of a long tale in itself, given that his skull was apparently the consistency of a Chesapeake crabshell but the head itself so huge it made Booboo look microcephalic, and the kid apparently had on-court use of only one hand because the other had to pull around beside him a kind of rolling IV-stand appliance with a halo-shaped metal brace welded to it at head-height, to encircle and support his head; but anyway Tex Watson and Thorp had broken C.T. down over the kid's admission and tuition-waver, and C.T. now figured the kid would need to say the least some extra help getting oriented (literally), and he wanted Hal to be the one to take him in hand (again literally). It turned out a couple days later that the kid had some kind of either family or cerebro-spinal-fluid crisis at home in rural IL and wasn't matriculating now till the Spring term. But back in August Hal had sat in the very chair Trevor Axford is now nodding off in, very late in the day, like dusk, having had an informal exhibition match with a visiting Latvian Satellite pro go an encouraging three sets that P.M. so that he'd missed Mrs. C.'s stuffed peppers at supper, his stomach making those where's-the-food noises from around the transverse colon, alone in the blue room, waiting, the chair bobbing reflexively, with Lateral Alice Moore gone home to her long apartment with rooms only 2 m. wide in Newton and an opaque plastic dust-thing wrapped tight over her Intel processor and intercom-console and the little red danger-light on her **DANGER: THIRD RAIL** plaque unlit, and the only lights besides the weak dusk outside were the hot 105W of his chairback's creepy blue-shaded magazine-lamp, plus the multiple lamps on in Charles Tavis's office (Tavis has a phobic thing about overhead lighting) as Tavis was doing a late-day Intake interview on impossibly tiny little Tina Echt, who just matriculated this fall at age seven. His doors were open because it was a brutal August and F. D. V. Harde had somehow rigged Lateral Alice's air-conditioner vent in the waiting room so it really put out. Tavis's office's outer door opened out while the inner door opened in, which gave his little inter-door vestibule kind of a jaw-like quality, when exposed.

August Y.D.A.U. had been when Hal's chronic left ankle had been almost the worst it's ever been, after an erumpent but grueling summer tour of getting to at least the Quarters of just about everything, mostly on hard asphalt,[217] and he could feel his pulse in the vessels in the raw ligaments of the ankle as he sat flipping the shiny pages of a new *World Tennis* and watching the little ad-cards fall out and flutter; but he also couldn't help exploiting the open-jawed view of a substantial section of Charles Tavis at his office desk, looking as usual oddly foreshortened and small and with his hands together on the massive desktop across from a partial-profile view of a girl who looked like she couldn't be much more than five or six, preparing to receive Intake papers as she listened to Tavis. There'd been no Echt parents or guardians anywhere in view. Some kids just get dropped off. Sometimes the parents' cars barely even stop, just slow down, throw gravel as they accelerate away. Tavis's desk drawers have squeaky casters. Jim Struck's folks' Lincoln hadn't even much slowed. Struck had been helped to his feet and taken immediately to the locker room to shower the gravel out of his hair. Hal had been in charge of his Orientation, too, when Struck transferred, booted out of Palmer Academy after his pet tarantula (named Simone — another long story) escaped and wouldn't even have *dreamed* of biting the Headmaster's wife if she hadn't screamed and passed out and fallen right on it, Struck explained as Hal helped pick up suitcases tumbled all over the drive.

Like many gifted bureaucrats, Hal's mother's adoptive brother Charles Tavis is physically small in a way that seems less endocrine than perspectival. His smallness resembles the smallness of something that's farther away from you than it wants to be, plus is receding.[218] This weird appearance of recessive drift, together with the compulsive hand-movements that followed his quitting smoking some years back, helped contribute to the quality of perpetual frenzy about the man, a kind of locational panic that it's easy to see explains not only Tavis's compulsive energy — he and Avril, pretty much the Dynamic Duo of compulsion, between them, sleep, in their second-floor rooms in the Headmaster's House — separate rooms — tend to sleep, between them, about as much as any one normal insomniac — but maybe also contributes to the pathological openness of his manner, the way he thinks out loud about thinking out loud, a manner Ortho Stice can imitate so eerily that he's been prohibited by the male 18's from doing his Tavis-impression in front of the younger players, for fear that the littler kids will find it impossible to take the real Tavis seriously at the times he needs to be taken seriously.

As for the older kids, Stice can make them all double up now merely by shielding his eyes with his hand and assuming a horizon-scan expression whenever Tavis heaves into view, seeming to recede even as he bears down.

C.T. as Headmaster always has a number of introductory questions for matriculants, and Hal, now, in November, can't remember which one of these Tavis opened with with Echt, but he remembers seeing the little girl's sucker-stick sweep the air and a plastic Mr. Bouncety-Bounce[219] no-pierce earring swing wildly as she shook her head. Hal'd marvelled at her size. How high could somebody this little be ranked, even regionally, in 12's?

And then yes the sumptuous squeak of Tavis's big seagrass chair coming back forward as his elbows took his weight and he laced his fingers together out across meters of polymer-reinforced shale desktop, custom-designed. The Headmaster's smile as he leaned back, though hidden from Hal because of the shadow of the office's enormous StairBlaster,[220] was nevertheless audible because of the thing with Charles Tavis's teeth, about which maybe the less said the better. Looking discreetly in, Hal had felt an involuntary rush of affection for C.T. His maternal uncle's hair was straight and very precisely combed over, and his little mustache was never quite symmetrical. One eye was also set at a slightly different angle than the other, so that besides holding his hand up to scan Stice would also cock his head slightly to the side whenever C.T. came near. Hal's involuntary grin is lopsided and only half-felt, now, remembering. The Axhandle's sitting there slumped, with his fist to his chin, a posture that he thinks makes him look meditative but that really makes him look *in utero,* and Kittenplan is chewing at her knuckles' tattoos, which is what she does instead of washing them off.

Then Ortho Stice had entered the hot waiting room, shirt wet and crew cut matted from the courts and toting his Wilsons, and made right for the AC-vent's downdraft outside Tavis's little vestibule. Stice's clothes were comped by Fila and when he played any sort of match he wore all black, and at E.T.A. and on the tour was known as The Darkness. He had a crew cut and the beginnings of jowls. He and Hal exchanged the very slight sorts of nods people use when they like each other past all need for politeness. They had similar games, although most of Stice's touch was at the net. Stice raised one hand to his eyes and cocked his head slightly in the direction of the office's lamplight.

'The little guy going to be a long time in there?'

'You have to ask?'

Tavis was saying 'What actually we do for you here is to break you down in very carefully selected ways, take you apart as a little girl and put you back together again as a tennis player who can take the court against any little girl in North America without fear of limitation. With a perspective unmarred by the eyelashes of whatever pockets you brought here. A little girl now who can regard the court as a mirror whose reflection holds no illusions or fear for you.'

'Now the thing with the skull,' Stice said. Hal had watched gooseflesh rise on Stice's arms and legs as he stood under the cold air and faced up and breathed, hugging his gear to his chest.

'One possible way of couching it is to choose to say that we will take apart your skull very gently and reconstruct a skull for you that will have a highly developed bump of clarity and a slight concave dent where the fear-instinct used to be. I'm doing my best to cast all this in terms the you you are right now can be comfortable with, Tina. Though I need to tell you I feel uncomfortable adjusting a presentation toward or down toward anyone in any way, since I'm terribly vain, both as a man and an educator, about my reputation for candor,' Tavis said. The audible smile. 'It is one of my limitations.'

Stice withdrew without even having to say goodbye to Hal. They were at complete ease with one another. It had been a bit different the year before, when Hal was still in Boys' 16's. Hal heard Stice say something to somebody out in the lobby. Part of C.T.'s impression of distance just past the eye's focal length was the fact that the two sides of his face didn't quite go together. It wasn't as drastic as a stroke-victim's face or a deformity; the subtlety of it was part of it, the essential vagueness about himself that Tavis fought by sort of peeling his skull back and exposing his brain to you without any sort of warning or invitation; it was part of the man's preoccupied frenzy.

Between Ortho Stice's exit and the Moms's entry Hal had been flexing the ankle and watching the swelling shift slightly under the multiple socks. He stood and put his weight on the ankle experimentally a couple times and then sat back down and flexed it, watching the swelling very intently. The way he knew suddenly that he was going to go down and get high in secret in the Pump Room before showering was that it hadn't occurred to him to ask The Darkness about making some sort of arrangements to eat together, since Stice had missed supper too. His viscera were putting out the sound of one of those teakettles that doesn't have a whistle and so just rumbles as it boils. A competitive athlete cannot skip meals without terrific metabolic distress.

After a little while Avril Incandenza, E.T.A.'s Dean of Academic Affairs, had lowered her head under the waiting room's jamb and come in, looking fresh and totally untouched by the heat. She had one of the Orientation packets in its customary red-and-gray binder.

The Moms always had this way of establishing herself in the *exact center* of any room she was in, so that from any angle she was somehow in the line of all sight. It was part of her, and so to that extent dear to Hal, but it was noticeable and kind of unsettling. His brother Orin, during a late-night round of Family Trivia, had once described Avril as The Black Hole of Human Attention. Hal had been pacing, rising up on the toes of the left foot, trying to gauge the exact level of physical discomfort he was feeling. That's when she'd come in. Hal and the Moms always greeted each other kind of extravagantly. When Avril entered a room, any sort of pacing reduced to orbiting, and Hal's pacing became vaguely circular around the waiting room's perimeter as Avril rested her tailbone on the receptionist's desk and crossed her ankles and produced her cigarette case. Her manner always became very casual and almost sort of male when she and Hal were alone in a room.

She watched him walk. 'The ankle?'

He hated himself for exaggerating the limp even slightly. 'Tender. Sore at the very worst. More like tender.'

'No, now, now no need to *cry*,' C.T. was exclaiming as he knelt at the side of the chair from which little legs dangled and were spasming around. 'I didn't mean *literally* break, as in break open your *head*, Tina. Please let me acknowledge that this is *totally* my fault my dear for presenting what we'll be up to here in just *exactly* the wrong sort of light.'

Avril had casually produced a 100-mm. rodney from the flat brass case and tamped it on an unlined knuckle. Hal produced no lighter. Neither of them had looked toward Tavis's office's maw. Avril's smock-type dress was blue cotton, with a kind of scalloped white doily around the shoulders and white stockings and painfully white Reebok cross-trainers.

'I am *horrified* that I've made you cry like this.' Tavis's voice had assumed that stressed character of issuing from the end of a long corridor. 'Just please know that a totally unthreatening lap is available if you want a lap, is all I can think of to say.'

Avril always smoked with her smoking-arm up and elbow resting in the crook of the other arm. She would frequently hold a rodney just this same way without lighting it or even putting it in her mouth. She permitted herself to smoke only in her E.T.A. office and HmH study and one or two other venues outfitted with air-filtration equipment. Her posture, that night, with her coccyx against something and looking down the length of her legs, was awfully close to the way Himself used to stand around. She indicated C.T.'s door with her head.

'I gather he's been in there a while.'

Hal despised even the very slight suggestion of whine that came in: 'I've been waiting here coming up on an hour.' And that he liked it a little that she looked pained for him as her tiny eyebrows (unplucked, just naturally tiny and arched) went up.

'You've had nothing to eat, then, yet?'

'I was *summoned*.'

Tavis's voice in there: 'I'll invite you right here and now to sit in my lap and let me make such soothing sounds as There There There.'

'Want my Mommy and *Daddy*.'

Avril said, 'That's the old tum making those sounds then, and not the air conditioner?' with that smile that was also a kind of wince.

'Couldn't even *start* to describe the sounds coming from down there, like that whistleless kettle Himself used to leave on when —'

An apple appeared from a deep pocket in her smock. 'Happen to have a spare Granny Smith here, to tack body to soul while we wait.'

He smiled tiredly at the big green apple. 'Moms, that's your apple. That's all you're going to eat between 12 and 23, I happen to know.'

Avril made a distended gesture. 'Stuffed. Huge lunch with a set of parents not three hours ago. I've been staggering around since.' Looking at the apple like she had no idea where it'd even come from. 'I'll probably pitch this out.'

'You will not.'

'Please,' rising from the desk's edge without seeming to use muscles, apple held out like something distasteful, cigarette down at her side where it would be putting a hole in the smock if lit. 'You'd be doing us both a favor.'

'This drives me bats. You know this drives me bats.'

Orin and Hal's term for this routine is Politeness Roulette. This Moms-thing that makes you hate yourself for telling her the truth about any kind of problem because of what the consequences will be for her. It's like to report any sort of need or problem is to mug her. Orin and Hal had this bit, during Family Trivia sometimes: 'Please, I'm not using this oxygen anyway.' 'What, this old limb? Take it. In the way all the time. Take it.' 'But it's a *gorgeous* bowel movement, Mario — the living room rug *needed* something, I didn't know what til right this very moment.' The special fantodish chill of feeling both complicit and obliged. Hal despised the way he always reacted, taking the apple, pretending to pretend his reluctance to eat her supper was a pre-tense. Orin believed she did it all on purpose, which was way too easy. He said she went around with her feelings out in front of her with an arm around the feelings' windpipe and a Glock 9 mm. to the feelings' temple like a terrorist with a hostage, daring you to shoot.

The Moms held the red binder out to Hal without moving. 'Have you seen Alice's new packets?' The apple was good-sour but perfumy from the pocket of the Moms's smock, and it stimulated a torrent of saliva. The binder had different little informal and action photos from the waiting-room walls, and offprints of clippings, and three rings for the packet of guidelines and Honor-Code pledges, all done up by Moore in a Gothic ital.

Hal looked up from the binder, indicating C.T.'s office with his head. 'You're taking the girl around yourself?'

'We're encouragingly short-staffed. Thierry and Donni won their qualify-ing round at Hartford, so they're staying over.' She leaned way forward and looked in at C.T. so he could see she was out here. She smiled.

Hal followed her look. 'The girl's name's Tina something and she'll come up to about your knee.'

'Echt,' Avril said, looking at something on a printout.

Hal looked at her while he chewed. 'You don't like her already?'

'Tina Echt. Pawtucket. Father apparently some sort of unleavened baker, mother a public relations person for the Red Sox A.A.A. baseball there.'

Hal had to wipe his chin as he smiled. 'Triple-A. Not A.A.A.'

Avril was leaning forward at the waist with the binder to her breast the way females hold flat things, still trying to catch the Headmaster's eye.

Hal said 'Troeltsch finally has some competition in the repulsive-last-name department.'

'Lord she is a small one isn't she.'

'I can't see her being more than maybe five.'

'Oh golly let's see: age seven, high I.Q., somewhat impoverished-looking M.M.P.I., played out of Providence Racquet and Bath in East Providence. Ranked thirty-first in Eastern 12's as of June.'

'She can't be much taller than her damn stick out there, when she plays. Schtitt's going to keep her here what, twelve years?'

'The girl's father has been calling about admission for her for over two years, Charles said.'

'He was doing that thing about taking skulls apart and she yelled bloody murder.'

Avril's laugh's onset was high-pitched and alarming and distinctive, so now at least C.T. would for sure know the Moms was out here waiting and would wind things up and maybe get to Hal so Hal could go get high in secret. 'Well good for her,' Avril said.

The orbit took him around Lateral Alice Moore's desk in a kind of thick ellipse. Every time his left foot came down he either dipped down or raised up briefly to tip-toe, flexing the ankle. 'Ten years here and she'll lose her mind. If she starts at seven she'll either be ready for the Show at fourteen or by fourteen she'll start getting that burned-out look that makes you want to wave your hand in front of her face.'

There was the sound of Tavis's squeaky right Nunn Bush pacing faster, which meant real conclusion. 'I'm going to predict it's probably hard to see yourself as a great athlete at this stage, Tina, not being able to see over the net yet, but possibly even harder to see yourself as providing entertainment, engaging people's attention. As a high-velocity object people can project themselves onto, forgetting their own limitations in the face of the nearly limitless potential someone as young as yourself represents.'

The apple generated tremendous amounts of saliva. 'He'll put her in the Show before menses, there'll be another enormous fuss and high-rental cartridges of a girl no larger than her racquet beating up on hairy Slavic lesbians, and then by fourteen she'll be like old coal in the bottom of a backyard grill.' Some old military joke about apples kept running through. Eat the Apple, Fuck the Core. Hal couldn't remember what it was supposed to signify.

The Moms was snapping her fingers silently and working her forehead. 'There's some term for coals reduced to residue after all day in a grill. I'm trying to think.'

Hal hates this. 'Clinkers,' he said instantly. 'From *klinker* low German and *klinckaerd* old Dutch, to sound, ring, nominated to substantive around 1769: a hard mass formed by the fusion of the earthy impurities of like coal, iron ore, limestone.' He hated it that she could even dream he'd be taken in by the aphasiac furrowing and finger-snapping, and then that he's always so pleased to play along. Is it showing off if you hate it?

'Clinker.'

'A grill wouldn't have clinkers. Charcoal's refined to burn right down to dust. Clinkers are sort of metallic, I think. See for example the ring-dash-sound etymology.'

'I like to suspect this is why so many of our older players like to project me into this carnival-barker persona with tiny balance sheets revolving in my eyes, that I'm up-front with every incoming addition to our family that this is where the resources come from for professional tennis, and for the North American junior development system for gifted children who want to scale the heights to professionalism or to a competitive college career, and so ultimately for an Academy like this one's considerable operating expenses, and for scholarships like the partial one we're so happy to be able to offer your parents for you.'

'So then perhaps you'd care to join us for dinner. We'll also have Ms. Echt if she can stay up that long.'

The core made a very-muffled-cymbal sound in the bottom of Lateral Alice's wastebasket. 'I can't get out of dawns. Wayne and I are supposed to play Slobodan[221] and Hartigan at some corporate-spectacle thing at Auburndale right after lunch.'

'Have you had Barry speak to Gerhardt about the ankle not getting better?'

'The clay'll be good to it. Schtitt knows all about the ankle.'

'Well best of British luck to you both.' Avril's purse looked more like soft luggage than like a purse. 'May I lend you the key to the kitchen, then.'

It's always the Moms's left shoulder Hal looks over, whenever he orbits, and his plans emerged between Avril's invitations to accept some sort of politeness-act. 'The Darkness and I were going to blast down the hill and grab something if and when I ever get out of here.'

'Oh.'

Then he wondered with dread what Stice might have said to her on her way in, re supper. 'Maybe Pemulis too, I think Pemulis said.'

'Well do not, under any circumstances, enjoy yourself.'

Echt and Tavis were both standing, now, in there. Their handshake looked, for the first split-second he looked, like C.T. was jacking off and the little girl was going *Sieg Heil*. Hal thought he was maybe starting to lose his mind. Even the meat of the Granny Smith smelled like perfume.

Three months later, earlier today, before being again summoned, at the dentist's, the dentist's office had had a weird sharp clean sweet smell about it, the olfactory equivalent of fluorescent light. Hal had felt the cold stab in the gum and then the slow radial freeze, his face ballooning to become one of the frozen cumuli against the aftershave-blue of the dental wallpaper's sky. Zegarelli D.D.S. had dry dark green eyes that bulged above his mint-blue mask, as in like olives where eyes should be, as he leaned in to proceed, his dental overhead light's corona giving him one of those malperspectived medieval halos that seem to stand on end. Even masked, Zegarelli's breath is infamous — E.T.A.s forced for the first time by their E.T.A. Group Plan to recline below Zegarelli are counselled on how to respire, to inhale when Zegarelli inhales and exhale right back out with him, to avoid doubling the amount of suffering Hal's already gone through, just today.

Charles Tavis is not a buffoon. The thing that's keeping things so tensely quiet out here amid all this waiting-room blue is that there are historically at least two Charles Tavises, the three older boys know. The openly cross-sectional and free-associating and arms-waving-on-the-perspectival-horizon dithering hand-wringing Total-Worry persona is really Tavis's version of social composure, his way of trying to get along with you. But just ask Michael Pemulis, whose sneakers have been on Tavis's carpet so often they've left an unvacuumable impression in the checked Antron: when Tavis loses his composure, when the integrity or smooth function of the Academy or his unquestioned place at the E.T.A. tiller is God forbid threatened, Hal's openly adjustable uncle becomes a different man, one not to be fucked with. It's not necessarily pejorative to compare a cornered bureaucrat to a cornered rat. The danger-sign to watch out for is if Tavis suddenly gets very quiet and very still. Because then he seems, perspectivally, to grow. He seems, sitting there, to rush in at you, dopplering in at a whisper. Almost looming over you from across the huge desk. If shit meets administrative fan, kids coming out of his mandible-doored office come out pale and rubbing their eyes, not from tears but from this depth-perspective skewing that C.T. suddenly effects, when there's shit.

Another alert is when Lateral Alice Moore gets formally buzzed to bring you and the others in, instead of the office doors ever opening from inside, and when she gets up and edges over to show you in like you're some sort of hat-holding salesman, without once meeting your eye, as if there's shame. One big family.

The diddle-check seems like it's degenerated into the girls all getting very excited and exchanging data on what kinds of animals members of their own biologic families either imitate or physically resemble, and Avril's out of sight and silent and apparently letting them go with it for a while and vent stress. Hal keeps checking for jaw-drool with the back of his hand. Pemulis, in a cyrillic-lettered T-shirt, takes off the hat and looks around himself and makes reflexive tie-straightening movements, taking one last look at his lines on the printout while Axford stands there needing three tries to work the outside door's knob. Ann Kittenplan, on the other hand, wears an expression of almost regal calm, and precedes them through the inner door like someone stepping down off a dais.

And it also seems somehow sinister that she's apparently been in here all this time, this Clenette person, one of the nine-month temps from down the hill, pretty-eyed and so black she's got a bluish cast, with hair ironed straight and then pinned up and the standard E.T.A.-custodial teal-blue zip-upable jumpsuit, emptying Tavis's personal brass wastebaskets into her big cart with its gray canvas sides. The way she stares at a point just to the side of Hal's own stare as she and her cart wait at C.T.'s inner door for Hal and the others to be ushered sideways through by Lateral Alice Moore. The cart, like poor Otis Lord's own game-master's cart, has a crazy wheel, and clatters a bit even buried in shag, trying to maneuver around Moore as she reverses back along the vestibule's wall. Neither Schtitt nor deLint is in here, but from the hiss of Pemulis's inhale Hal can tell that Dr. Dolores Rusk is in the room even before he takes his eyes from a C.T. who's sitting pulsing with swollen proximity in his seagrass swivel-chair and almost done coolly bending a giant paper clip into a sort of cardioid or else sloppy circle: Tavis's window-lit shadow now reaches all the way past the StairBlaster to the red-and-gray-fabric ottoman along the east wall, in which sits sure enough Rusk, her hose laddered and face betraying nothing; and then next to her is poor old Otis P. Lord, the Hitachi monitor still over his head like the sallet of some grotesque high-tech knight, slumped and with his sneakers pointing at each other in the blue and black shag, hands in his lap, two crude eye-holes cut into the black plastic casing of the monitor's base, Lord not meeting Pemulis's eye, and wicked hanging shards of glass from the screen he fell through pointing — some nearly touching, even — his slim neck and throat, so he has to hold his head very still, despite the heavings of his shallow chest, with the day-shift E.T.A. nurse standing behind him and inclined over the back of the sofa to hold the monitor very carefully in place, the incline producing cleavage which Hal would gladly choose to be the sort of person not to note. Lord's eyes move to Hal and blink dolefully through the holes, and he can be heard sniffing moistly in there, complexly muffled; and Pemulis is just finishing moving his feet precisely into their familiar impressions in the office carpet when C.T., seeming direly to rise from his chair without getting up, quietly asks the room's last occupant — the scrubbed young button-nosed urologist in an O.N.A.N.T.A. blazer, severely underdue at E.T.A., seated back in the shadow of the open inner door in the room's southeast corner, so he's hidden right behind them from the start and there's the opportunity for this stagy incriminating-type whirl-and-kertwang-face from Axford and Hal as they hear Charles Tavis addressing the urine expert behind them, asking him very quietly please to close both doors.

'You can't say it's only a U.S. thing,' Steeply said again. 'I went through school when multiculturalism was inescapable. We read about the Japanese and Indonesians, for example, having a mythic figure. I forget its name. Oriental myth. It's a woman covered with long blond hair. Entirely. Her whole body with blond down all over it.'

'This type of passive temptation, part of it seems to include a felt lack. A perceived deprivation. Orientals are not bodily a hairy culture.'

'These multicultural Oriental myths always had young Oriental men happening upon her by some body of water combing her body-hair and singing. And they have sex with her. Apparently she's simply too exotic and intriguing or seductive to resist. Even the young Oriental men who know of the myths can't resist, according to the myths.'

'And are rendered paralyzed with stasis by this intimate act,' Marathe said. When now he dreamt of his father, it was of the two skating, young Marathe and M. Marathe, at a St. Remi-d'Amherst outdoor rink, M. Marathe's breath visible and his pacemaker a boxy bulge in his Brunswickian cardigan.

'Killed outright, usually. The pleasure's too intense. No mortal can stand it. Kills them. *M-o-r-t-s.*'

Marathe sniffed.

'The analogous part is how even the ones who know the pleasure of it will kill them, they go ahead anyway.'

Marathe coughed.

Some of the insects flying had multiple pairs of wings and were bioluminescent. They seemed very intent, flying past the outcropping and darting jaggedly off on a course, on their way to something urgent. The sound of them, the insects, made Marathe think of playing cards in the bicycle spokes of the bicycle of a boy with legs. Both men were silent. This is the time of false dawns. Venus moved east away from them. The softest light imaginable seeped into the desert and spread into the strange tan vistas around them, something heating just below the ring of night. His blanket of the lap was covered in burrs and small spiked seeds of some species. The U.S.A. desert began to rustle with life of which most remained hidden. In the American sky, the stars fluttering like banked flames above a low-resolution seepage of glow. But none of the pinkening of genuine dawn.

Both the U.S.A. Office of Unspecified Services and *les Assassins des Fauteuils Rollents* looked forward to these meetings of Marathe and Steeply. They accomplished little. It was their sixth or seventh. Meeting. Steeply had volunteered to be liaison with Marathe's betrayal, despite language.[222] The A.F.R. believed Marathe functioned as a triple agent, pretending to betray his nation for his wife, memorizing every detail of the meetings with B.S.S. According to Steeply, Steeply's B.S.S. superiors did not know that Fortier knew that Steeply knew he (Fortier) knew Marathe was here. Steeply held this fact back from his superiors. It satisfied some U.S.A. desire to hold some small thing back from one's superiors, Marathe felt. Unless Steeply was deceiving Marathe about this. Marathe did not know. M. Fortier did not know Marathe had reached the internal choice that he loved his skull-deprived and heart-defective wife Gertraud Marathe more than he loved the Separatist and anti-O.N.A.N. cause of the nation Québec, making Marathe no better than M. Rodney 'the God' Tine. If Fortier knew of this, he would understandably drive a railroad spike through Gertraud's boneless right eye, killing her and Marathe both.

The real Marathe gestured outward at the glowing but unpink east. 'A false dawn.'

'No,' Steeply said, 'but your own francophone myth of your Odalisk of Theresa.'

'*L'Odalisque de Sainte Thérèse.*' Marathe rarely yielded to the temptation to correct Steeply, whose horrid pronunciation and the syntax as well Marathe could never determine for sure either was or was not an intentional irritant, intended to discomfit Marathe.

Steeply said 'The multicultural myth being that the Odalisk's so beautiful that mortal Québecois eyes can't take it. Whoever looks at her turns into a diamond or gem.'

'In most versions an opal.'

'A Medusa in reverse, one might say.'

Both men, well versed in this, mirthlessly laughed.[223]

Marathe said 'The Greeks, they did not fear beauty. They feared ugliness. Hence I think beauty and pleasure, these were not fatal temptations for the Greek type.'

'Or like a combination of Medusa and Circe, your Odalisk' said Steeply. He was smoking either his last or one of his purse's pack's last cigarettes — the American's habit to throw the butts off the outcropping had prevented Marathe from counting the consumed butts. Marathe knew that Steeply knew that filters of cigarettes did not biodegrade for the environment. The two men, by this juncture of time, each knew the other.

A hidden bird twittered.

'The Greek mythic personality, it had also pregnancy by rain and rape by fowl.'

'And haven't we come a long way,' Steeply said ironically.

'This irony and contempt for selves. These also are part of your U.S.A. type's temptation, I think.'

'Whereas your type's a man of only actions, ends,' Steeply said, with Marathe could not tell whether irony or maybe not.

The desert floor was brightening by imperceptible degrees, its surface the color of overtanned hide. The saguaro cactus reptile-hued. Potentially young forms in down sleeping bags of coffinous shape were now discernible around the black remains of the night's bonfire. The air smelled of green wood. A tasteless odor of dust. The distant construction site's payloaders were urine-colored and appeared frozen in the middle of various actions. It was still chill. Marathe's teeth had a palpable film on them, of perhaps a paste of dust, especially the front teeth. No sun's top arc was appearing, and Marathe could cast no shadow yet on the shale behind them.

Rémy Marathe's resting pulse rate was very low: no legs to require blood from the heart. He very rarely felt phantom pains, and then only in the stump of the left. All A.F.R.s have enormous arms, particularly upper arms. Marathe was left-handed. Steeply manipulated his cigarette with his left hand and used his right arm to cradle the left elbow. But Marathe knew quite well that Steeply was right-handed. The little wens of his field-persona's electrolysis were now brightly pink against the pallor of Steeply's face, which appeared both puffy and drawn.

The cloudless sky above the east's Mountains of Rincon range was the faint sick pink of an unhealed burn. The whole imperceptibly lightening scene of the vistas had a stillness about it that suggested photography. Marathe had long ago placed his watch in his windbreaker's pocket, to keep from continually checking. Steeply enjoyed imagining that his interface dictated its own period and time; Marathe had chosen to indulge this.

Marathe realized about himself that some of his pretended sniffing was for the purpose of alerting Steeply to the breaking of a silence. 'You could seat yourself briefly, if you have fatigue. The shoes' straps . . .' He gestured slightly.

Steeply made a show of looking down and prodding at the tan stone's dust with the toes of his shoe. 'It looks like there might be things.'

'I must soon leave.' Marathe's hand was imprinted with the texture of the Sterling's pebbled grip. 'It has been good to be in the air for a night. Soon I must leave.'

'Crawling around. The skirt, it makes one sensitive about simply plopping down wherever you wish. Possibility of things . . . crawling up.' He looked up at Marathe. He appeared sad. 'I'd never realized.'

'Didn't know whether to shit or shout Dixie after it went off. And the *look* on his face.'

'One of the times for me was I'm in some bar in Lowell with some guys I'm crewing around with and we were there with some other guys, just fucking Lowell knuckleheads, your young drunks that are just getting to be your young working-type drunks that stop off after work for just a couple and don't make it home til closing. Just putting away boilermakers and playing darts and this and that. And this one guy on the crew starts making moves on this one guy's girl, this real ordinary-looking guy's in there with his girl and one of our guys starts saying this and that to her, trying to pick her up, and her date got pissed off, you know, who can blame him, and there was words exchanged and so on and so forth, and we was all there with this first guy, in our like group, he was the one talking the shit to this guy's girl but he was our boy, we're all in the crew, so we all crew up on this girl's date and push him around somewhat, you know how it is, say he's talking shit to our boy, he gets a little bit of a beating, dope-slaps, nothing like extreme or blood, and we kick his ass around a little bit and toss him out of this bar and get this girl to drink boilermakers with us and the one guy that was making the moves on her in the first place gets her to start playing strip-darts, like taking off bits of clothes for points in darts, which the keep isn't too like thrilled but these boys are his customers, it's like family. We're all real drunk and playing strip-darts.'

'I get the picture. Sounds like a real nice picture.'

'Except when I got a little smarter later I learned you never in a neighborhood bar fu— you don't ever mess with a local guy with a girl and make him look small in front of the girl and then stay there where it happened if he leaves, because it's this kind of guy always comes back.'

'You learned to leave.'

'Because this guy like a half-hour later on he comes back packing. *Packing* means there's a Item involved, now, see.'

'Item?'

'A gun. This wasn't a big one, I'm remembering a .25 somewhat, in that range, but in he comes and comes straight over to the dart game and the girl

531

that's down to her slip and pulls it out and without saying nothing up and comes right over and shoots our boy, that'd taken his girl and made him look small, shoots him right in the head, right in the back of the head.'

'Boy was crazy as a shithouse rat.'

'Well Joelle he'd got made small in front of his girl, and we stayed, and he came back and plugged him in the back of the head.'

'And killed him dead.'

'Not right away he didn't die. The negativest part for me is what we do. All us guys with the guy that was shot. We are all very fucked up by this point in time. I remember it not seeming real. The keep's busy calling the Finest, the guy drops the Item and the keep grabbed him and covered him with the bar piece and called the Finest and kept the guy back behind the bar, I think mostly now to keep us from eliminating his map right there, out of payback. We're all blotto-zombie drunk by this juncture. The girl, there was blood all down the side of her slip. And here our boy's shot in the head, the guy'd shot him right through the back of the head from the side, and blood's all over. You always maybe think of individuals bleeding in this one way, like steady. But your serious bleeding comes with the pulse, if you didn't know. It like shoots out and dies down and shoots out.'

'Don't have to tell me.'

'Well I don't know you, Joelle, am I right? I don't know what you seen or know.'

'I saw an old boy cut his hand off with a chainsaw cutting back brush back of the Cumberland when I was fishing with my Daddy. Like to have bled to death right there. My Daddy had to use his belt. Before he got it tied off the blood came like that, with the pulse. My Daddy got him to the hospital in his car, like to saved his life. He'd had some training. He could save lives like that.'

'I tell you, what still gets me is we was so drunk we didn't even somehow take it seriously, because everything seemed like a movie when I got real drunk. I still wish we'd thought to take him to the hospital right away. We could of piled him in. He wasn't dead yet even though he didn't look good. We didn't even lay him down, we got this idea, one of the guys started walking him around. We all walked him around in circles like some kind of O.D., thought if we could keep him walking til the wagon came he'd be OK. By the end we was dragging him, I think then he was dead. Blood all over everybody. The gun wasn't more than an old .25. People was yelling at us to pile him in and take him to the hospital, but we'd got this walking-him-around idea into our heads, to hold him up and walk him in circles, the girl's screaming and trying to put her stockings on and we're yelling to the guy that'd shot him how we were going to off with his map and so on and so forth, till the keep called an ambulance and they came and he was dead as a stick.'

'Gately that's really bad.'

'Why are you even up, don't have to work.'

'...'

'...'

'I like it when it snows real early like this. This is the best window. But you learned a lesson.'

'His name was Chuck or Chick. The one that got shot that time.'

'Did you hear that McDade person at supper? You know how some folks have one of their legs shorter than the other?'

'I don't listen to those guys' crap.'

'It was down at the far end of the table at supper. He was telling Ken and me how he had a counselor when he was in Juvenile in Jamaica Plain, he had this counselor he said she had this condition where each leg was shorter than the other.'

'...'

'...'

'I don't think I follow you, Joelle.'

'Each of the woman's legs was shorter than the other.'

'How can a leg that's shorter than the other leg have the other leg shorter than it?'

'He was having us on. He said the point was an AA point, that it defied sense and explaining and you just had to accept it on faith. That creepy Randy guy with the white wig was backing him up with a very straight face. McDade said she walked like a metronome. He was making fun of us, but I still thought it was funny.'

'Maybe tell me about this veil of yours, then, Joelle, if we're talking about defied sense.'

'Waaaay out to one side. Then waaaay out to the other side.'

'Really. Let's really interface if you're in here. How come with the veil?'

'Bridal thing.'

'...'

'Aspiring Muslim.'

'I didn't mean to pry in. You can just tell me if you don't want to talk about the veil.'

'I'm also in another fellowship, with almost four years in.'

'U.H.I.D.'

'It's the Union of the Hideously and Improbably Deformed. The veil is a sort of fellowship caparison.'

'What's it compared to?'

'We all wear one. Almost all of us, with some time in.'

'But if you don't mind, how come you're in it? U.H.I.D.? How're you supposed to be deformed? It's nothing that sticks way out, if I can say it. Are you, like, missing something?'

'There's a brief ceremony. It's a bit like giving out chips over at the Better Late Than Never meeting, for Varying Lengths. The new U.H.I.D.s stand and receive the veil and don the veil and stand there and recite that the veil they've donned is a Type and a Symbol, and that they are choosing freely to be bound to wear it always — a day at a time — both in light and darkness, both in solitude and before others' gaze, and as with strangers so with familiar friends, even Daddies. That no mortal eye will see it withdrawn. That they hereby declare openly that they wish to hide from all sight. Unquote.'

'. . .'

'I've also got a membership card that spells out everything you could ever want to know, and more.'

'Except I've asked Pat and Tommy S. and still the thing I don't get is why join a fellowship just to hide? I can see if somebody is like — you know, hideously — and they've been hiding away in the dark all their life, and they want to Come In and join a fellowship where everybody's equal and everybody can Identify because they all spent their whole life hiding also, and you join a fellowship so you can step out of the dark and into the group and get support and finally show yourself minus eyes or with three ti— arms or whatever and be accepted by people that know just what it's like, and like in AA they say they'll love you till you can like love yourself and accept yourself, so you don't care what people see or think anymore, and you can finally step out of the cage and quit hiding.'

'That's AA?'

'Kind of, a little bit, I think.'

'Well Mr. Gately what people don't get about being hideously or improbably deformed is that the urge to hide is offset by a gigantic sense of shame about your urge to hide. You're at a graduate wine-tasting party and improbably deformed and you're the object of stares that the people try to conceal because they're ashamed of wanting to stare, and you want nothing more than to hide from the covert stares, to erase your difference, to crawl under the tablecloth or put your face under your arm, or you pray for a power failure and for this kind of utter liberating equalizing darkness to descend so you can be reduced to nothing but a voice among other voices, invisible, equal, no different, hidden.'

'Is this like this thing they talked about about people hating their faces on videophones?'

'But Don you're still a human being, you still want to live, you crave connection and society, you know intellectually that you're no less worthy of connection and society than anyone else simply because of how you appear, you know that hiding yourself away out of fear of gazes is really giving in to a shame that is not required and that will keep you from the kind of life you deserve as much as the next girl, you know that you can't help how you look but that you are supposed to be able to help how much you *care* about how you look. You're supposed to be strong enough to exert some control over how much you want to hide, and you're so desperate to feel some kind of control that you settle for the *appearance* of control.'

'Your voice gets different when you talk about this shit.'

'What you do is you *hide* your deep need to hide, and you do this out of the need to *appear* to other people as if you have the strength not to care how you *appear* to others. You stick your hideous face right in there into the wine-tasting crowd's visual meatgrinder, you smile so wide it hurts and put out your hand and are extra gregarious and outgoing and exert yourself to appear totally unaware of the facial struggles of people who are trying not to wince or stare or give away the fact that they can see that you're hideously, improbably deformed. You feign acceptance of your deformity. You take your desire to hide and conceal it under a mask of acceptance.'

'Use less words.'

'In other words you hide your hiding. And you do this out of shame, Don: you're ashamed of the fact that you want to hide from sight. You're ashamed of your uncontrolled craving for shadow. U.H.I.D.'s First Step is admission of powerlessness over the need to hide. U.H.I.D. allows members to be open about their essential need for concealment. In other words we don the veil. We don the veil and wear the veil proudly and stand very straight and walk briskly wherever we wish, veiled and hidden, and but now completely up-front and unashamed about the fact that how we appear to others affects us deeply, about the fact that we want to be shielded from all sight. U.H.I.D. supports us in our decision to hide openly.'

'You seem like you drift in and out of different ways of talking. Sometimes it's like you don't want me to follow.'

'Well I've got a brand-new life, just out of the wrapper, which you all say'll take some time to fit.'

'So they teach you how to accept your nonacceptance, the Union, you're saying.'

'You followed very well. You didn't need fewer words at all. If you don't mind my saying so, my sense is that you think you're not bright but you're not.'

'Not bright?'

'I put that poorly. You're not *not* bright. As in you're incorrect in thinking you have nothing upstairs.'

'It's a self-esteem issue, then, you're seeing in me after like three days here, then. I feel low esteem about how I think I'm not bright enough for some people.'

'Which is fine, U.H.I.D. would say, to illustrate the U.H.I.D. take versus an apparently more AA take. U.H.I.D.'d say it's fine to feel inadequate and ashamed because you're not as bright as some others, but that the cycle becomes annular and insidious if you begin to be *ashamed* of the fact that being unbright shames you, if you try to hide the fact that you feel mentally inadequate, and so go around making jokes about your own dullness and acting as if it didn't bother you at all, pretending you didn't care whether others perceived you as unbright or not.'

'This makes the front of my head hurt, trying to follow this.'

'Well you've been up all night.'

'Then now I have to go to my other fucking job.'

'You're way brighter than you think, Don G., although I doubt anything anyone else says can get in there into the gnawed ragged place where you're afraid you're slow and dull.'

'And what makes you think I think I'm not bright, unless it's you're saying it's obvious to anybody I'm not bright?'

'I didn't mean to pry. Just tell me if you don't want to speak to someone you barely know about it.'

'Now you're being sarcastic on what I said before.'

'. . .'

'I got kicked off of football my tenth-grade year for flunking English.'

'You played American football?'

'I was good til I got kicked off. They gave me a tutor and I still flunked.'

'I used to twirl a baton at halftimes. I went to a special camp six summers running.'

'. . .'

'But a lot of the forms of self-hatred there is no veil for. U.H.I.D.'s taught a lot of us to be grateful that there's at least a veil for our form.'

'So the veil's a way to not hide it.'

'To hide openly, is more like it.'

'. . .'

'I'm already seeing it's very different from the drug-recovery agenda, the AA and NA program.'

'Can I ask how you're deformed?'

'The best is when the sun's coming up right through the snow and everything looks so white.'

'. . .'

'I almost forgot why I came on in, that that Kate girl said Ken E. like to get killed by some son of a bitch last night at that Waltham NA thing and they want somebody to tell Johnette not to make them go back again if they don't want.'

'. . .'

'. . .'

'One is Kate and Ken can talk for themselves with Johnette and I don't need to pry in and you *sure* don't need to pry in and rescue nobody else. Two is you're all of a sudden talking different again, and when you were talking about the veil you didn't sound like you to me. And three is don't think I can't see you're coming out sideways all over the place about when I asked can I ask what deformity you're not hiding the fact that you're hiding under that thing. The Staff part of me wants to say if you don't want to answer it just say so, but don't try and go around the side and think you can distract me into forgetting I asked it.'

'The U.H.I.D. in me would say you're trapped in shame about the shame, in response, and that the shame-circle keeps you from really being *present* for your Staff job, Don. You're more bugged by the possibility that I'm treating you as unbright and distractable than you are about a resident's inability to come right out and openly exercise her right to refuse to answer an incredibly private and drug-unrelated question.'

'And now she's back to talking like a fucking English teacher again. But ignore that. That's not the point. Look at how you're trying to get our dialogue all distracted up in shame and me again instead of saying Yes or No to me asking Will you tell me what you're missing behind that veil.'

'Oh you're good at hiding Mr. G. you're *good*. The minute we start to poke at any inadequacies you're ashamed of, see, you drop behind your own protective mask of House Staff and start probing areas that you now *know* I can't bring myself to be open about — since you got me to tell you all about U.H.I.D.'s philosophy of hiding — so that your own sense of inadequacy gets either buried or used as a backlight to illuminate my own inability to be open and straightforward. The best defense is a good offense isn't it Mr. Football Player.'

'Aspirin-time, now, with all the words. You win. Go watch the snow come down someplace else.'

'The thing is, Mr. Staff, I've already just completely opened up about my shame and my inability to be open and straightforward about this. You're exposing something I've already held up to view. It's your shame about being ashamed of what you're afraid might be seen as a lack of brightness that's getting to stay buried under this dead horse of my deformity that you're trying to whip.'

'And then meantime you still didn't say a straight-on Yes or No to Can I ask what's up behind there, are you cross-eyed or have a like beard, or do you have like really bad skin under there even though your skin everyplace that isn't hidden looks —'

'Looks what? My unhidden skin is what?'

'See, this is you keep trying to sidetrack instead of just saying No to Can I ask. Just say No. Try it. It's OK. Nothing bad'll happen. Just try it straight out.'

'Perfect. You were going to say every visible expanse of my skin is just drop-dead creamy perfect.'

'Jesus, why am I even here? Why don't you just interface with yourself if you think you know all my issues and shames and everything I'm going to say? Why not take the suggestion to say No? Why come in here? Did I come to you, to talk? Was I just sitting in here trying to keep awake and do the Log and getting ready to go mop shit with a shoe-freak and did or didn't you waltz on in and sit down and come to me?'

'Don, I'm perfect. I'm so beautiful I drive anybody with a nervous system out of their fucking mind. Once they've seen me they can't think of anything else and don't want to look at anything else and stop carrying out normal responsibilities and believe that if they can only have me right there with them at all times everything will be all right. Everything. Like I'm the solution to their deep slavering need to be jowl to cheek with perfection.'

'Now with the sarcasm.'

'I am so beautiful I am deformed.'

'Now with the nonrespectful acting-out of treating me like I'm stupid for trying to get her to walk through her fear to give a straight-out No, which she isn't willing.'

'I am deformed with beauty.'

'You want to see my professional Staff face here's my Staff face. I nod and smile, I treat you like somebody I have to humor by nodding and smiling, and behind the face I'm going with my finger around and around my temple like What a fucking yutz, like Where's the net.'

'Believe what you want. I'm powerless over what you believe, I know.'

'See the professional Staffer writing in the Meds Log: "Six extra-strong-kind aspirin for Staff after sarcasm and sideways refusal to walk through fears and sarcastic acting out by newcomer who thinks she knows everybody else's issues.'

'What position did you play?'

'. . . that the Staffer wonders how come she's even here in treatment then, if she knows so much.'

It is starting to get quietly around Ennet House that Randy Lenz has found his own dark way to deal with the well-known Rage and Powerlessness issues that beset the drug addict in his first few months of abstinence.

The nightly AA or NA meetings get out at 2130h. or 2200h., and curfew isn't until 2330, and every Ennet resident mostly carpools back to the House with whatever residents have cars, or some of them go out in cars for massive doses of ice cream and coffee.

Lenz is one of the ones with a car, a heavily modified old Duster, white with what look like 12-gauge blasts of rust over the wheelwells, with oversized rear tires and an engine so bored-out for heavy-breathing speed it's a small miracle he still has a license.

Lenz sets loafer one outside Ennet House only after sunset, and then only in his white toupee and mustache and billowing tall-collared topcoat, and goes only to the required nightly meetings; and the thing is that he'll never drive his own car to the meetings. He always thumbs along with somebody else and adds to the crowd in their car. And then he always has to sit in the northernmost seat in the car, for some reason, using a compass and napkin to plot out what the night's major direction of travel'll be and then figuring out what seat he'll have to be in to stay maximally north. Both Gately and Johnette Foltz have had to make a nightly routine of telling the other residents that Lenz is teaching them valuable patience and tolerance.

But then after the meeting lets out, Lenz never thumbs back with anybody. He always walks back to the House after meetings. He says it's that he needs the air, what with being shut up in the crowded House all day and avoiding doors and windows, hiding from both sides of the Justice System.

And then one Wednesday after the Brookline Young People's AA up Beacon by Chestnut Hill it takes him right up to 2329 to get home, almost two hours, even though it's like a half-hour walk and even Burt Smith did it in September in under an hour; and Lenz gets back just at curfew and without saying a word to anybody books right up to his and Glynn's and Day's room, Polo topcoat flapping and powdered wig shedding powder, and sweating, and making an unacceptable classy-shoed racket running up the men's side's carpetless stairs, which Gately didn't have time to go up and address because of having to deal with Bruce Green and Amy J. separately both missing curfew.

Lenz abroad in the urban night, solo, on almost a nightly basis, sometimes carrying a book.

Residents who seem to make it a point to go off alone a lot are red-flagged at Thursday's All-Staff Meeting in Pat's office as clear relapse-risks. But they've pulled spot-urines on Lenz five times, and the three times the lab didn't fuck up the E.M.I.T. test Lenz's urine's come back clean. Gately's basically decided to just let Lenz be. Some newcomers' Higher Power is like Nature, the sky, the stars, the cold-penny tang of the autumn air, who knows.

So Lenz abroad in the night, unaccompanied and disguised, apparently strolling. He's mastered the streets' cockeyed grid around Enfield-Brighton-Allston. South Cambridge and East Newton and North Brookline and the hideous Spur. He takes side-streets home from meetings, mostly. Low-rent dumpster-strewn residential streets and Projects' driveways that become alleys, gritty passages behind stores and dumpsters and warehouses and loading docks and Empire Waste Displacement's mongo hangars, etc. His loafers have a wicked shine and make an elegant dancerly click as he walks along with his hands in his pockets and open coat flared wide, scanning. He scans for several nights before he even becomes aware of why or what he might be scanning for.[224] He moves nightly through urban-animal territory. Liberated housecats and hard-core strays ooze in and out of shadows, rustle in dumpsters, fuck and fight with hellish noises all around him as he walks, senses very sharp in the downscale night. You got your rats, your mice, your stray dogs with tongues hanging and countable ribs. Maybe the odd feral hamster and/or raccoon. Everything slinky and furtive after sunset. Also non-stray dogs that clank their chains or bay or lunge, when he goes by yards with dogs. He prefers to move north but will move east or west on the streets' good sides. His shoes' fine click precedes him by several hundred meters on cement of varying texture.

Sometimes near drainage pipes he sees serious rats, or sometimes near cat-free dumpsters. The first conscious thing he did was a rat that this one time he came on some rats in a wide W-E alley by the loading dock out behind the Svelte Nail Co. just east of Watertown on N. Harvard St. What night was that. It'd been coming back from East Watertown, which meant More Will Be Revealed NA with Glynn and Diehl instead of St. E.'s Better Late Than Never AA with the rest of the House's herd, so a Monday. So on a Monday he'd been strolling through this one alley, his steps echoing trebled back off the cement sides of the docks and the north left wall he hugged, scanning without knowing what he was scanning for. Up ahead there was the Stegosaurus-shape of a Svelte Co. dumpster as versus your lower slimmer E.W.D.-type dumpster. There were dry skulky sounds issuing from the dumpster's shadow. He hadn't consciously picked anything up. The alley's surface was coming apart and Lenz barely broke his dancerly stride picking a kilo-sized chunk of tar-shot concrete. It was rats. Two big rats were going at a half-eaten wiener in a mustardy paper tray from a Lunchwagon in a recess between the north wall and the dumpster's barge-hitch. Their hideous pink tails were poking out into the alley's dim light. They didn't move as Randy Lenz came up behind them on the toes of his loafers. Their tails were meaty and bald and like twitched back and forth, twitching in and out of the dim yellow light. The big flat-top chunk came down on most of one rat and a bit of the other rat. There'd been godawful twittering squeaks, but the major hit on the one rat also made a very solid and significant noise, some aural combination of a tomato thrown at a wall and a pocketwatch getting clocked with a hammer. Material came out of the rat's anus. The rat lay on its side in a very bad medical way, its tail twitching and anus material and there were little beads of blood on its whiskers that looked black, the beads, in the sodium security-lights along the Svelte Nail Co. roof. Its side heaved; its back legs were moving like it was running, but this rat wasn't going anywhere. The other rat had vanished under the dumpster, dragging its rear region. There were more chunks of dismantled street lying all over. When Lenz brought another down on the head of the rat he consciously discovered what he liked to say at the moment of issue-resolution was: '*There.*'

Demapping rats became Lenz's way of resolving internal-type issues for the first couple weeks of it, walking home in the verminal dark.

Don Gately, House chef and shopper, buys these huge econo-size boxes of Hefty[225] bags that get stored under the kitchen sink for whoever's got Trash for their weekly chore. Ennet House generates serious waste.

So after vermin started to get a little ho-hum and insignificant, Lenz starts cabbaging a Hefty bag out from under the sink and taking it with him to meetings and walking back home with it. He keeps a trashbag neatly folded in an inside pocket of his topcoat, a billowing top-collared Lauren-Polo model he loves and uses a daily lint-roller on. He also takes along a little of the House's Food-Bank tunafish in a Zip-loc baggie in another pocket, which your average drug addict has expertise in rolling baggies into a cylinder so they're secure and odor-free.

The Ennet House residents call Hefty bags 'Irish Luggage' — even McDade — it's a street-term.

Randy Lenz found that if he could get an urban cat up close enough with some outstretched tuna he could pop the Hefty bag over it and scoop up from the bottom so the cat was in the air in the bottom of the bag, and then he could tie the bag shut with the complimentary wire twist-tie that comes with each bag. He could put the closed bag down next to the vicinity's northernmost wall or fence or dumpster and light a gasper and hunker down up next to the wall to watch the wide variety of changing shapes the bag would assume as the agitated cat got lower on air. The shapes got more and more violent and twisted and mid-air with the passage of a minute. After it stopped assuming shapes Lenz would dab his butt with a spitty finger to save the rest for later and get up and untie the twist-tie and look inside the bag and go: '*There.*' The '*There*' turned out to be crucial for the sense of brisance and closure and resolving issues of impotent rage and pow-erless fear that like accrued in Lenz all day being trapped in the northeastern portions of a squalid halfway house all day fearing for his life, Lenz felt.

There evolved for Lenz a certain sportsman's hierarchy of types of cats and neighborhoods of types of your abroad cats; and he becomes a connois-seur of cats the same way a deep-sea sportsman knows the fish-species that fight most fiercely and excitatingly for their marine lives. The best and most fiercely alive cats could usually claw their way out of a Hefty bag, though, which created this conundrum where the ones most worth watching assum-ing bagged shapes were the ones Lenz risked maybe not getting his issues resolved on. Watching a spike-furred hissing cat run twisting away still half wrapped in a plastic bag made Lenz admire the cat's fighting spirit but still feel unresolved.

So the next stage is Lenz gives Ms. Charlotte Treat or Ms. Hester Thrale some of his own $ when they go down to the Palace Spa or Father/Son to buy smokes or LifeSavers and has them start to get him special Hefty Steel-Sak[226] trashbags, fiber-reinforced for your especially sharp or uncooperative waste needs, described by Ken E. as 'Irish Guccis,' extra resilient and a businesslike gunmetal-gray in tone. Lenz has such a panoply of strange compulsive habits that a request for SteelSaks barely raises a brow on anybody.

And then he doubles them, the special reinforced bags, and employs industrial-growth pipe-cleaners as twist-ties, and then now the grittiest most salutary cats make the doubled bags assume all manners of wickedly abstract twisting shapes, even sometimes moving the closed bags a couple dozen m. down the alley in a haphazard hopping-like fashion, until finally the cat runs out of gas and resolves itself and Lenz's issues into one nightly shape.

Lenz's interval of choice for this is the interval 2216h. to 2226h. He doesn't consciously know why this interval. Anchovies turn out to be even more effective than tuna. A Program of Attraction, he recalls coolly, strolling along. His northern routes back to the House are restricted by the priority to keep Brighton Best Savings Bank's rooftop digital Time and Temperature display in view as much as possible. B.B.S.B. displays both EST and Greenwich Mean, which Lenz approves of. The liquid-crystal data sort of melts upward into view on the screen and then disappears from the bottom up and is replaced by new data. Mr. Doony R. Glynn said at the House's Community Meeting Monday once that one time in B.S. 1989 A.D. after he'd done a reckless amount of a hallucinogen he'd refer to only as 'The Madame' he'd gone around for several subsequent weeks under a Boston sky that instead of a kindly curved blue dome with your clouds and your stars and sun was a flat square coldly Euclidian grid with black axes and a thread-fine reseau of lines creating grid-type coordinates, the whole grid the same color as a D.E.C. HD viewer-screen when the viewer's off, that sort of dead deepwater gray-green, with the DOW Ticker running up one side of the grid and the NIKEI Index running down the other, and the Time and Celsius Temp to like serious decimal points flashing along the bottom axis of the sky's screen, and whenever he'd go to a real clock or get a *Herald* and check the like DOW the skygrid would turn out to have been totally accurate; and that several unbroken weeks of this sky overhead had sent Glynn off first to his mother's Stoneham apartment's fold-out couch and then into Waltham's Metropolitan State Hospital for a month of Haldol[227] and tapioca, to get out from under the empty-grid accurate sky, and says it makes his ass wet to this day to even think about the grid-interval; but Lenz had thought it sounded wicked nice, the sky as digital timepiece. And also between 2216 and 2226 the ATHSCME giant fans off up at the Sunstrand Plaza within earshot were typically shut off for daily de-linting, and it was quiet except for the big Ssshhh of a whole urban city's vehicular traffic, and maybe the odd E.W.D. airborne deliverer catapulted up off Concavityward, its little string of lights arcing northeast; and of course also sirens, both the Eurotrochaic sirens of ambulances and the regular U.S.-sounding sirens of the city's very Finest, Protecting and Serving, keeping the citizenry at bay; and the winsome thing about sirens in the urban night is that unless they're right up close where the lights bathe you in red-blue-red they always sound like they're terribly achingly far away, and receding, calling to you across an expanding gap. Either that or they're on your ass. No middle distance with sirens, Lenz reflects, walking along and scanning.

Glynn hadn't come right out and said *Euclidian,* but Lenz had gotten the picture all right. Glynn had thin hair and an invariant three-day growth of gray stubble and diverticulitis that made him stoop somewhat over, and remaining physique-type issues from a load of bricks falling on his head from a Workers Comp scam gone rye that included crossed eyes that Lenz overheard the veiled girl Joe L. tell Clenette Henderson and Didi Neaves the man was so cross-eyed he could stand in the middle of the week and see both Sundays.

Lenz has gotten high on organic cocaine two or three, maybe half a dozen times tops, secretly, since he came into Ennet House in the summer, just enough times to keep him from going totally out of his fucking mind, utilizing lines from the private emergency stash he kept in a kind of rectangular bunker razor-bladed out of three hundred or so pages of Bill James's gargantuan Large-Print *Principles of Psychology and The Gifford Lectures on Natural Religion.* Such totally occasional Substance-ingestions in a run-down sloppy-clocked House where he's cooped up and under terrible stress all day every day, hiding from threats from two different legal directions, with, upstairs at all times, calling to him, a 20-gram stash from the under-reported South End two-way attempted scam whose very bad luck had forced him into hiding in squalor and rooming with the likes of fucking Geoffrey D. — cocaine-ingestion this occasional and last-resort is such a marked reduction of Use & Abuse for Lenz that it's a bonerfied miracle and clearly constitutes as much miraculous sobriety as total abstinence would be for another person without Lenz's unique sensitivities and psychological makeup and fucking intolerable daily stresses and difficulty unwinding, and he accepts his monthly chips with a clear conscience and a head unmuddled by doubting: he knows he's sober. He's smart about it: he's never ingested cocaine on his solo walks home from meetings, which is where the Staff'd expect him to ingest if he was going to ingest. And never in Ennet House itself, and only once in the forbidden #7 across the roadlet. And anybody with half a clue can beat an E.M.I.T. urine-screen: a cup of lemon juice or vinegar down the hatch'll turn the lab's reading into gibberish; a trace of powdered bleach on the fingertips and let the stream play warmly over the fingertips on its way into the cup while you banter with Don G. A Texas catheter's a pain to get piss for and put on, plus the obscene size of the thing's receptacle for his Unit gives Lenz inadequacy-issues, and he's only used it twice, both times when Johnette F. took the urine and he could embarrass her into turning away. Lenz owns a Texas Cathy from his last halfway house in Quincy, in what Lenz recalls as the Year of the Maytag Quietmaster.

And then it turned out, when a cat aggrieved Lenz by scratching his wrist in a particularly hostile fashion on the way into the receptacle, that doubled Hefty SteelSaks were such quality-reinforced products they could hold something razor-clawed and frantically in-motion and still survive a direct swung hit against a NO PARKING sign or a telephone pole without splitting open, even when what was inside split nicely open; and so that technique got substituted around United Nations Day, because even though it was too quick and less meditative it allowed Randy Lenz to take a more active role in the process, and the feeling of (temporary, nightly) issues-resolution was more definitive when Lenz could swing a twisting ten-kilo burden hard against a pole and go: 'There,' and hear a sound. On banner nights the doubled bag would continue for a brief period of time to undergo a subtle flux of smaller, more subtle and connoisseur-oriented shapes, even after the melony sound of hard impact, along with further smaller sounds.

Then it was discovered that resolving them directly inside the yards and porches of the people that owned them provided more adrenal excitation and thus more sense of what Bill James one time called a *Catharsis* of resolving, which Lenz felt he could agree. A small can of oil in its own little baggie, for squeaky gates. But because SteelSak trashbags — and then also tunafish mixed with anchovies and Raid ant poison from behind the Ennet residents' fridge — caused too much resultant noise to allow for lighting a gasper and hunkering down to meditatively watch, Lenz developed the habit of setting the resolution in motion and then booking on out of the yard into the urban night, his Polo topcoat billowing, hurdling fences and running over the hoods of cars and etc. For a period during the two-week interval of give-them-poison-tuna-and-run Lenz had brief recourse to a small Caldor-brand squeeze-bottle of kerosene, plus of course his lighter; but a Wednesday night on which the alight cat ran (as alight cats will, like hell) but ran after *Lenz*, seemingly, leaping the same fences Lenz hurdled and staying on his tail and not only making an unacceptable attention-calling racket but also illuminating Lenz to the scopophobic view of passing homes until it finally decided to drop to the ground and expire and smolder thereupon — Lenz considered this his only really close call, and took an enormous and partly non-north route home, with every siren sounding up-close and on his personal ass, and barely got in by 2330h., and ran right up to the 3-Man room. This was the night Lenz had to have another recourse to the hollowed-out cavity in his *Principles of Psychology and The Gifford Lectures on Natural Religion* after just beating curfew home, which who wouldn't need a bit of an un-winder after a stressful close-call-type situation with a flaming cat chasing you and screaming in a way that made porch lights go on all up and down Sumner Blake Rd.; except but instead of an unwinder the couple or few lines of uncut Bing proved to be on this occasion an *un*-unwinder — which happens, sometimes, depending on one's like spiritual condition when ingesting it through a rolled dollar bill off the back of the john in the men's can — and Lenz barely made it through switching his car's parking spot at 2350h. before the verbal torrent started, and after lights-out had only gotten up to age eight in the oral autobiography that followed in the 3-Man when Geoff D. threatened to go get Don G. and have Lenz forcibly stifled, and Lenz was scared to go downstairs to find somebody to listen and so for the rest of the night he had to lie there in the dark, mute, with his mouth twisting and writhing — it always twisted and writhed on the times the Bing proved to be a rev-upper instead of a rough-edge-smoother — and pretending to be asleep, with phosphenes like leaping flaming shapes dancing behind his quivering lids, listening to Day's moist gurgles and Glynn's apnea and think-ing that each siren abroad out there in the urban city was meant for him and coming closer, with Day's illuminated watchface in his fucking tableside drawer instead of out where anybody with some stress and anxiety could check the time from time to time.

So after the incident with the flaming cat from hell and before Halloween Lenz had moved on and up to the Browning X444 Serrated he even had a shoulder-holster for, from his previous life Out There. The Browning X444 has a 25-cm. overall length, with a burl-walnut handle with a brass butt-cap and a point Lenz'd sharpened the clip out of when he got it and a single-edge Bowie-style blade with .1-mm. serrations that Lenz owns a hone for and tests by dry-shaving a little patch of his tan forearm, which he loves.

The Browning X444, combined with blocks of Don Gately's highly portable cornflake-garnish meatloaf, were for canines, which your urban canines tended to be nonferal and could be found within the confinement of their pet-owners' fenced yards on a regularer basis than the urban-cat species, and who are less suspicious of food and, though more of a per-sonal-injury risk to approach, do not scratch the hand that feeds them.

For when the dense square of meatloaf is taken out and unwrapped from the Zip-loc and proffered from the edgelet of yard out past the fence by the sidewalk, the dog at issue invariably stops with the barking and/or lunging and its nose flares and it becomes totally uncynical and friendly and comes to the end of its chain or the fence Lenz stands behind and makes interested noises and if Lenz holds the meat-item just up out of reach the dog if its rope or chain will permit it it'll go up on the hind legs and sort of play the fence with its front paws, jumping eagerly, as Lenz dangles the meat.

Day had had some Recovery-Issue paperback he was reading that Lenz had a look at one P.M. in their room when Day was downstairs with Ewell and Erdedy telling each other their windbagathon stories, lying on Day's mattress with his shoes on and trying to fart into the mattress as much as possible: some line in the book had arrested Lenz's attention: something about the more basically Powerless an individual feels, the more the likelihood for the propensity for violent acting-out — and Lenz found the observation to be sound.

The only serious challenge to using the Browning X444 is that Lenz has to make sure to get around behind the dog before he cuts the dog's throat, because the bleeding is far-reaching in its intensity, and Lenz is now on his second R. Lauren topcoat and third pair of dark wool slacks.

Then once near Halloween in an alley behind Blanchard's Liquors off Allston's Union Square Lenz comes across a street drunk in a chewed-looking old topcoat in the deserted alley taking a public leak against the side of a dumpster, and Lenz envisualizes the old guy both cut and on fire and dancing jaggedly around hitting at himself while Lenz goes 'There,' but that's as close as Lenz comes to that kind of level of resolution; and it's maybe to his credit that he's a little off his psychic feed for a few days after that close call, and inactive with pets circa 2216h.

Lenz has nothing much against his newer fellow resident Bruce Green, and when one Sunday night after the White Flag Green asks can he walk along with Lenz on the walk back after the Our Father Lenz says Whatever and lets Green walk with him, and is inactive during this night's 2216 interval as well. Except after a couple nights of Green strolling home along with him, first from the White Flag and then from St. Columbkill's on Tuesday and a double 1900–2200 shot of St. E.'s Sharing and Caring NA and then BYP on Wed., Green following him around like a terrier from mtg. to mtg. and then home, it begins to like emerge on Lenz that Bruce G. is starting to treat this walking-through-the-urban-P.M.-with-Randy-Lenz thing as like a regular fucking thing, and Lenz starts to jones about it, the unresolved Powerless Rage issues that the thing is now he's gotten so he's used to resolving them on a more or less nightly basis, so that being unable to be freely alone to be active with the Browning X444 or even a SteelSak during the 2216–2226h. interval causes this pressure to build up like almost a Withdrawal-grade pressure. But on the other side of the hand, walking with Green has its positive aspects as well. Like that Green doesn't complain about lengthy detours to keep a mainly north/northeastern orientation to the walks when possible. And Lenz enjoys a sympathetic and listening ear to have around; he has numerous aspects and experiences to mull over and issues to organize and mull, and (like many people hardwired for organic stimulants) talking is sort of Lenz's way of thinking. And but most of the ears of the other residents at Ennet House are not only unsympathetic but are attached to great gaping flapping oral mouths which keep horning into the conversation with the mouths' own opinions and issues and aspects — most of the residents are the worst listeners Lenz has ever seen. Bruce Green, on the hand's positive side, hardly says anything. Bruce Green is quiet the way certain stand-up type guys you want to have there with you beside you if a beef starts going down are quiet, like self-contained. Yet Green is not so quiet and unresponding that it's like with some silent people where you start to wonder if he's listening with a sympathizing ear or if he's really drifting around in his own self-oriented thoughts and not even listening to Lenz, etc., treating Lenz like a radio you can tune in or out. Lenz has a keen antenna for people like this and their stock is low on his personal exchange. Bruce Green inserts low affirmatives and 'No shit's and 'Fucking-A's, etc., at just the right places to communicate his attentions to Lenz. Which Lenz admires.

So it's not like Lenz just wants to blow Green off and tell him to go peddle his papers and let him the fuck alone after Meetings so he can solo. It would have to be handled in a more diplomatic fashion. Plus Lenz finds himself nervous at the prospect of offending Green. It's not like he's scared of Green in terms of physically. And it's not like he's concerned Green would be the Ewell- or Day-type you have to stressfully worry about maybe going and ratting out on Lenz's place of whereabouts to the Finest and everything like that. Green has a strong air of non-rat about him which Lenz admires. So it's not like he's frightened to blow Green off; it's more like very tense and tightly wound.

Plus it agitates Lenz that he has the feeling that it really wouldn't be any big deal to Green that much one way or the other, and that Lenz feels like he's spending all this stress tensely worrying about his side of something that Green would barely think about for more than a couple seconds, and it enrages Lenz that he can know in his head that the tense worry about how to diplomatize Green into leaving him alone is unnecessary and a waste of time and tension and yet still not be able to stop worrying about it, which all only increases the sense of Powerlessness that Lenz is impotent to resolve with his Browning and meatloaf as long as Green continues to walk home with him.

And the schizoid cats with clotted fur that lurk around Ennet House cringing and neurotic and afraid of their own shadow are too risky, for the female residents are always formulating attachments to them. And Pat M.'s Golden Retrievers would be tattlemount to legal suicide. On a Saturday c. 2221h., Lenz found a miniature bird that had fallen out of some nest and was sitting bald and pencil-necked on the lawn of Unit #3 flapping ineffectually, and went in with Green and ducked Green and went back outside to #3's lawn and put the thing in a pocket and went in and put it down the garbage disposal in the kitchen sink of the kitchen, but still felt largely impotent and unresolved.

Except for Pat Montesian's bay-windowed front office and the House Manager's phone-booth-sized back office and the two live-in Staff bedrooms down in the basement, none of the doors inside Ennet House have locks, for predictable reasons.

EARLY NOVEMBER
YEAR OF THE DEPEND ADULT UNDERGARMENT

The only bona fide blackmailable thing about Rodney Tine, Chief, U.S. Office of Unspecified Services: his special metric ruler. In a locked drawer of his bathroom cabinets at home on Connecticut Ave. NW in the District is kept a special metric ruler, and Tine measures his penis every A.M., like clockwork; has since twelve; still does. Plus a special telescoping travelling model of the ruler he travels with, for on-the-road-A.M.-penis-measurement. President Gentle has no N.S.A.[228] as such. Tine's in metro Boston because of the N.S. implications of what they'd first come to Unspecified Services about two summers past, both the head of D.E.A. and the Chair of the Academy of Digital Arts and Sciences, now both here standing on one foot and then the other and twidgelling the brims of their hats. This unwatchable underground Entertainment-cartridge that at first seemed to be just popping haphazardly up in random locales: a film with certain he's given to understand from briefings quote 'qualities' such that whoever saw it wanted nothing else ever in life but to see it again, and then again, and so on. It had popped up in Berkeley NCA, in the home of a film-scholar and his male companion, neither of whom had appeared for appointments for days; and now lost to meaningful human activity henceforward, by all appearances, were the scholar and companion, the two cops dispatched to the Berkeley home, the six cops dispatched after the two cops never followed up their Code-Five, the watch sergeant and partner dispatched after them — seventeen police, paramedics, and teleputer-technicians in all, until the lethality of whatever they'd caught sight of presented itself with enough clarity for somebody to think to go around back and kill the Berkeley home's power. The Entertainment had popped up in New Iberia LA. Tempe AZ had lost two-thirds of the attendees of an avant-garde film festival in Arizona State U.'s Entertainment Studies amphitheater before a level-headed custodian killed the building's whole grid. J. Gentle had been apprised about the thing only after it had popped up and taken out a diplomatically immune Near Eastern medical attaché and a dozen incidentals here in Boston MA late last spring. These persons now all in wards. Docile and continent but blank, as if on some deep reptile-brain level pithed. Tine had toured a ward. The persons' lives' meanings had collapsed to such a narrow focus that no other activity or connection could hold their attention. Possessed of roughly the mental/spiritual energies of a moth, now, according to a diagnostician out of C.D.C. The Berkeley cartridge had vanished from an S.F.P.D. Evidence Room an electron-microscopy toss of which had revealed flannel fibers. The D.E.A. had lost four field researchers and a consultant before they'd bowed to the intractable problems involved in trying to have somebody view the confiscated Tempe cartridge and articulate the thing's lethal charms. The strongest possible language had been necessary to restrain a certain Famous Crooner from attempting a personal review of the thing's qualities. Neither C.D.C. nor the entertainment pros wanted any part of any controlled-viewing tests. Three members of the Academy of D.A.S. had received unlabelled copies in the mail, and the one who'd actually sat down to have a look now needed a receptacle under his chin at all times. Reports of the thing popping up yet again in metro Boston MA remain unsubstantiated. Tine's been dispatched here in part to coordinate substantiation. There's also the special pocket-Franklin-Planner-sized chart he charts the daily A.M. penis-measurement in, daily, though to the uninitiated the little leather notebook could look like almost anything statistical at all. By now several U.S.O. test-subjects, volunteers from the federal and military penal systems, have been lost in attempts to produce a description of the cartridge's contents. The Tempe and New Iberia cartridges are in custody, vaulted. A sociopathic and mentally retarded Lance Corporal at Leavenworth, strapped down with electrode appliqués and headset-recorder, was able to report that the thing apparently opens with an engaging and high-quality cinematic shot of a veiled woman going through a large building's revolving doors and catching a glimpse of someone else in the revolving doors, somebody the sight of whom makes her veil billow, before the subject's mental and spiritual energies abruptly declined to a point where even near-lethal voltages through the electrodes couldn't divert his attention from the Entertainment. Tine's staff had sifted through dozens of entries before deciding that the intelligence community's terse little name for the allegedly enslaving Entertainment would be 'the *samizdat*.' P.E.T.s on sacrificed subjects revealed unexceptional wave-activity, with not near enough alpha to indicate hypnosis or induced dopamine-surges. Attempts to trace the matrix of the *samizdat* without viewing it — from induction on postal codes, e-microscopies on the brown padded mailers, immolation and chromatography on the unlabelled cartridge-cases, extensive and maddening interviews of those civilians exposed — place the likely dissemination-point someplace along the U.S. north border, with routing hubs in metro Boston/New Bedford and/or somewhere in the desert Southwest. The U.S.'s Canadian Problem is U.S.O.U.S. Anti-Anti-O.N.A.N. Activities' Agency's[229] special province. So to speak. The possibility of Canadian involvement in the lethally compelling Entertainment's dissemination is what has brought to metro Boston Rodney Tine, his retinue, and his ruler.

LATE P.M., MONDAY 9 NOVEMBER
YEAR OF THE DEPEND ADULT UNDERGARMENT

For reasons that Pemulis couldn't for the life of him, Ortho Stice seemed to be in there in Dr. Dolores Rusk's office, interfacing with Dr. Rusk well after regular hours. Pemulis paused at the door on his way by.

'— nical assessment, after our work together on your fear of weights, would be that your presenting maladjustment, Ortho, like many males and athletes, is that you're suffering from counterphobia.'

'Fear of linoleum?' It was unmistakably the flat twang of The Darkness in there through the door's wood.

'On the level of objects and a projective infantile omnipotence where you experience magical thinking about your thoughts and the behavior of objects' relation to your narcissistic wishes, the counterphobia presents as the delusion of some special agency or control to compensate for some repressed wounded inner trauma having to do with absence of control.'

'Over linoleum?'

'My suggestion might be to forget linoleum and objects in general. In for instance an analytic model, the types of traumas counterphobic reactions cover are almost always pre-Oedipal, at which stage objects' cathexis is Oedipal and symbolic. For example small children's dolls and Action-Figurines.'

'I don't play with no goddamn Action-Figurines.'

'GI Joe typically being cathected as an image of the potent but antagonistic father, the "military" man, with "GI" representing at once the "General Issue" of a "weapon" the Oedipal child both covets and fears *and* a well-known medical acronym for the gastro-intestinal tract, with all the attendant anal anxieties that require repression in the Oedipal phase's desire to control the bowels in order to impress or quote "win" the mother, of whom the Barbie might be seen as the most obviously reductive and phallocentric reduction of the mother to an archetype of sexual function and availability, the Barbie as image of the Oedipal mother *as image.*'

'So you're saying I'm *over*estimating objects?'

'I'm saying there's a very young Ortho in there with some very real abandonment-issues who needs some nurturing and championing from the older Ortho instead of indulging in fantasies of omnipotence.'

'I ain't omnipotent and I don't want to X no Goddamn Barbiedoll.' Then Dark's voice went way up and cracked as he said something about his bed.

Dr. Rusk's office door had a nonconducting rubberized sheath on the knob, and Dr. Rusk's name and degrees and title, and a needlepoint sampler with a little heart inside a big heart and a cursive exhortation to *Champion An Inner Child Today,* which the little kids at E.T.A. find puzzling and upsetting. Pemulis, pausing by habit first at the silent locked infirmary door and then Rusk's bottom-crack-lit door on his way across the Comm.-Ad. lobby, was wearing the most insolent ensemble he could throw together. He wore maroon paratrooper's pants with green stovepipe stripes down the sides. The pants' cuffs were tucked into fuchsia socks above ancient and radically uncool Clark's Wallabies with dirty soles of eraserish gum. He wore an orange fake-silk turtleneck under an English-cut sportcoat in a purple-and-tan windowpane check. He wore naval shoulder-braid at the level of ensign. He wore his yachting cap, but with the bill bent up at a bumpkinish angle. He looked less insolent than just extremely poorly dressed, really. Dr. Rusk's door was cool against his ear. Jim Troeltsch had been coming down B's hall just as Pemulis was leaving and said Pemulis looked like a hangover. Through the door, Rusk was urging Stice to name his anger and Stice was proposing to name his anger Horace after his old man's late pointer that had got into some coyote bait when The Darkness was nine and was much missed by the whole Stice brood, back in Kansas. The old Wallabies were from Pemulis's older brother's incomplete public-school career and had boogerish little greebles of dirty gum all around the soles' perimeter. The socks belonged to Jennie Bash and she made it explicit she wanted them back laundered. The sportcoat's checked arms were several cm. too short and exposed ribbed cuffs of shiny orange acetate esters.

The Community & Administration Bldg.'s downstairs was real quiet. It was like 2100h., supposedly mandatory Study Period, and Harde's crew had gone home but the custodial graveyard shift hadn't come on yet. Pemulis moved noiselessly NE-SW across the lobby's shag. Except for lines of lamplight from under a couple doors the E.T.A. lobby was pitch-black, and the outer Academy doors locked. There was an odd vehicular shape near the north wall's trophy case that Pemulis didn't pause to investigate. He lifted up slightly to keep the little SW hall's door from squeaking as he opened it and entered the administrative reception area, snapping his fingers softly to himself. A loose music played in his head. Tavis's reception area was empty and dim, the wallpaper's clouds now stormy-dark. It wasn't totally quiet. Light came from Mrs. Inc's doorway and from the crack under Tavis's inner door. Lateral Alice Moore had gone home. Pemulis activated her Third Rail and played with her chair as he made a very quick survey of the material on her desk. Activating the P.A. mike was out of all question. Two of her five drawers were still locked. Pemulis scanned behind him and popped another breath mint and sat quietly for a moment as Moore's chair slid back and forth along the rail, his fingers in a steeple under his nose, considering.

Light shone from the crack of Tavis's inner door because the outer door stood open. Pemulis didn't even have to put any kind of ear to the wood of the inside door. He could hear the hiss and high-speed grind of Tavis's StairBlaster, and Tavis's breathless recessive voice. You could tell there was nobody else in there. You could tell Tavis had no shirt on and an E.T.A. towel around his neck and his hair a sweaty curtain down one side of his little head as he ran to keep up with what reminded everybody of a Satanishly-possessed Filene's escalator. He was exhorting himself in a kind of fast rhythmic chant that sounded to Pemulis like either 'Total worry total worry' or 'No don't worry no don't worry' and c. Pemulis could envision Tavis's round belly and little titties of fat bouncing with the action of the StairBlaster. You could hear the sudden muffling when he probably brought the towel up to dab at his slanted mustache. Tavis's doorknob had no insulating rubber sheath, Pemulis noticed.

Pemulis's ensemble's belt was a plastic thing with chintzy fake-Navajo beading, purchased by little Chip Sweeny at one of last fall's WhataBurger's souvenir stands and subsequently transferred to Pemulis during a Big Buddy tennis-as-game-of-chance exercise. The beading-patterns were in Gila-monster orange and black, the orange a different shade than Pemulis's turtleneck.

He could never resist biting down once a mint'd melted to a certain size and texture.

The doorless Dean of Academic Affairs's office was a blazing rectangle of light. The light didn't spill very far into the reception area, however. At close-range, sounds issued from the office, but not exactly words. Pemulis checked his fly and snapped his fingers under his own nose and assumed a businesslike stride and rapped firmly on the doorless jamb without breaking stride. The heavier blue shag of the office itself slowed him down a bit. He stopped once he was all the way in. 18-A John Wayne and Hal's Mumsly-Wumsly were both in the front of the office. They were about maybe two meters apart. The room was lit overhead and by four standing lamps. The seminar table and chairs cast a complicated shadow. Two homemade pom-poms of shredded paper and what looked like the amputated handles of wooden tennis racquets were on the seminar table, which was otherwise bare. John Wayne wore a football helmet and light shoulderpads and a Russell athletic supporter and socks and shoes and nothing else. He was down in the classic three-point stance of U.S. football. Inc's incredibly tall and well-preserved mother Dr. Avril Incandenza wore a little green-and-white cheerleader's outfit and had one of deLint's big brass whistles hanging around her neck. She was blowing on the whistle, which appeared to be minus the little inside pellet because no whistling sound resulted. She was about two meters from Wayne, facing him, doing near-splits on the heavy shag, one arm up and pretending to blow the whistle while Wayne produced the classic low-register growling sounds of U.S. football. Pemulis made rather a show of pushing the bumpkin-billed yachting hat back to scratch his head, blinking. Mrs. Inc was the only one looking at him.

'I probably won't even waste everybody's time asking if I'm interrupting,' Pemulis said.

Mrs. Inc seemed frozen in place. Her one hand was still up in the air, fine fingers splayed. Wayne craned his neck to look over at Pemulis from under his helmet without changing his three-point stance. The football-noises trailed off. Wayne's got a narrow nose and close-set witchy eyes. He wore a plastic mouthguard. The musculature of his legs and buttocks was clearly outlined as he squatted forward with his weight on his knuckles. There was way less time passing in the office than there seemed to be.

'Hoping for a second of your time,' Pemulis told Mrs. Inc. He was standing schoolboy-straight, hands clasped demurely over his fly, which on Pemulis this posture did look insolent.

Wayne straightened up and moved toward his clothing with no little dignity. His sweats were neatly folded on the Dean's desk at the rear of the office. The mouthguard was attached to the facemask and hung from it when removed. The chin strap had several snaps Wayne had to undo.

'Nice-looking helmet,' Pemulis told him.

Wayne, pulling hard on his sweatpants' cuffs to fit them over a shoe, didn't reply. He was so fit that his supporter's straps didn't even dent his buttocks.

Mrs. Incandenza removed the mute whistle. She was still split down on the floor. Pemulis made rather a show of not looking south of her face. She pursed her lips to chuff hair out of her eyes.

'I predict this'll take about two minutes at most,' Pemulis said, smiling.

WEDNESDAY 11 NOVEMBER
YEAR OF THE DEPEND ADULT UNDERGARMENT

Lenz wears a worsted topcoat and dark slacks and Brazilian loafers with a high-wattage shine and a disguise that makes him look like Andy Warhol with a tan. Bruce Green wears a cheesy off-the-rack leather jacket of stiff cheap leather that makes the jacket creak when he breathes.

'This is when you man this is when you find out your like what like true character, is when it's pointed right at you and some bugeyed fucking spic's not five mitts[230] away pointing it, and I strangely I get real calm see and said I said Pepito I said I Pepito man you go on and do what you need to do man go on and shoot but man you *better* I mean fucking *better* kill me with the first shot man or you won't get another one I said. Not even bullshitting man I'm serious it's like I found right then I meant it. You know what I'm saying?' Green lights both their smokes. Lenz exhales with that hiss of people in a rush to drive their point home. 'You know what I'm saying?'

'I don't know.'

It's an urban November P.M.: very last leaves down, dry gray hairy grass, brittle bushes, gap-toothed trees. The rising moon looks like it doesn't feel very well. The click of Lenz's loafers and the crunchy thud of Green's old asphalt-spreader's boots with the thick black soles. Green's little noises of attention and assent. He says he's been broken by life, is all he'll personally say. Green. Life has kicked his ass, and he's regrouping. Lenz likes him, and there's always this slight hangnail of fear, like clinging, whenever he likes somebody. It's like something terrible could happen at any time. Less fear than a kind of tension in the region of stomach and ass, an all-body wince. Deciding to go ahead and think somebody's a stand-up guy: it's like you drop something, you give up all of your power over it: you have to stand there impotent waiting for it to hit the ground: all you can do is brace and wince. It kind of enrages Lenz to like somebody. There would be no way to say any of this out loud to Green. As it gets past 2200h. and the meatloaf in his pocket's baggie's gotten dark and hard from disuse the pressure to exploit the c. 2216 interval for resolution builds to a terrible pitch, but Lenz still can't yet quite get it up to ask Green to walk back some other way at least once in a while. How does he do it and still have Green know he thinks he's OK? But you don't come right out there and let somebody hear you say you think they're OK. When it's a girl you're just trying to X it's a different thing, straightforwarder; but like for instance where do you look with your eyes when you tell somebody you like them and mean what you say? You can't look right at them, because then what if their eyes look at you as your eyes look at them and you lock eyes as you're saying it, and then there'd be some awful like voltage or energy there, hanging between you. But you can't look away like you're nervous, like some nervous kid asking for a date or something. You can't go around giving that kind of thing of yourself away. Plus the knowing that the whole fucking thing's not worth this kind of wince and stress: the whole thing's enraging. The afternoon of tonight earlier at circa 1610h. Lenz'd sprayed RIJID-brand male hairspray in the face of a one-eyed Ennet House stray cat that had wandered by mischance into the men's head upstairs, but the result: unsatisfying. The cat had just run away downstairs, clunking into the bannister only once. Lenz then got diarrhea, which always disgusts him, and he had to stay in the head and open the little warped frosted-glass window and run the shower on C until the smell's evidence cleared, with fucking Glynn pounding on the door and attracting attention howling about who's flailing the whale in there all this time is it by any chance Lenz. But then how would he be supposed to act henceforward toward Green if he blows him off and says to let him walk solo home? How would he be supposed to act if it'd seemed like he'd like spurned Green? What does he henceforward say if he and Green pass each other in the aisle at Saturday Night Lively or both reach for the same sandwich at the raffle-break at White Flag, or get caught standing there half-naked in towels in the hall waiting for somebody to get out of the shower? What if he like spurns Green and Green ends up in the 3-Man room while Lenz is still in there and they have to room together and interface constantly? And if Lenz tries to temper the spurning by telling Green he likes him, where the fuck is he supposed to look when he says it? If trying to X a female species Lenz would have nullo problemo with where to look. He'd have no problem with looking deep into some bitch's eyes and looking so sincere it's like he's dying inside him. Or if like assuring a bad-complected Brazilian he hadn't stepped on a half-kilo three separate times with Inositol.[231] Or if high: zero problem. If he got high, he'd have no problem telling somebody he liked him even if he really did. For it'd give his spirits a voltage that'd more than overweigh whatever upsetting voltage might hang in the air between somebody. A few lineskers and there'd be no stress-issues about telling Bruce G. with all due respects to screw, go peddle his papers, go play in the freeway, go play with a chain saw, go find a short pier, that no disrespect but Lenz needed to fly solo in the urban night. So after the incident with the cat and diarrhea and some hard words with D. R. Glynn, who was slumped holding his abdomen down against the south wall of the upstairs hall, Lenz decides enough is enough and goes and gets a little square of foil off the industrial roll Don G. keeps under the Ennet sink and goes and takes a half-gram, maybe a gram at most out of the emergency stash out of the vault-thing he's razored out of the *Principles of Natural Lectures*. Far from your scenario of relapsing, the Bing is medicinal support for assertively sharing his need for aloneness with Green, so that issues of early sobriety can get resolved before standing in the way of spiritual growth — Lenz will use cocaine in the very interests of sobriety and growth itself.

So then like strategically, at the Brookline Young People's Mtg. over on Beacon near the Newton line on a Wednesday, at the raffle-break, at 2109h., Lenz moistens his half-gasper and puts it carefully back in the pack and yawns and stretches and does a quick pulse-check and gets up and saunters casually into the Handicapped head with the lockable door and the big sort of crib built around the shitter itself for crippled lowering onto the toilet and does like maybe two, maybe three generous lines of Bing off the top of the toilet-tank and wipes the tank-top off both before and after with wet paper towels, ironically rolling up the same crisp buck he'd brought for the meeting's collection and utilizing it and cleaning it thoroughly with his finger and rubbing his gums with the finger and then putting his head way back in the mirror to check the kidney-shaped nostrils of his fine aqua-line nose for clinging evidence in the trim hair up there and tasting the bitter drip in the back of his frozen throat and taking the clean rolled buck and back-rolling it and smoothing it out and hammering it with his fist on the lip of the sink and folding it neatly into half of half its original Treasury Dept. size so that all evidence anybody ever even had a passing thought of rolling the buck into a hard tight tube is, like, *anileated*. Then sauntered back out like butter wouldn't soften anywhere on his body, knowing just where to look at all times and casually hefting his balls before he sat back down.

And then aside from the every so often hemispasm of the mouth and right eye he hides via the old sunglasses and pretend-cough tactic the second half of the mtg.'s endless oratory goes fine, he supposes, even though he did smoke almost a whole expensive pack of gaspers in 34 minutes, and the holier-than-you Young-People AAs over in what were supposed to be the Nonsmoking rows of chairs against the east wall to his right shot him over some negative-type looks when perchance he happened to find he had one going in the little tin ashtray and two at once going in his mouth, but Lenz was able to play the whole thing off with insousistent aplomb, sitting there in his aviator sunglasses with his legs crossed and his topcoated arms resting out along the backs of the empty chairs on either side.

The night-noises of the metro night: harbor-wind skirling on angled cement, the shush and sheen of overpass traffic, TPs' laughter in interior rooms, the yowl of unresolved cat-life. Horns blatting off in the harbor. Receding sirens. Confused inland gulls' cries. Broken glass from far away. Car horns in gridlock, arguments in languages, more broken glass, running shoes, a woman's either laugh or scream from who can tell how far, coming off the grid. Dogs defending whatever dog-yards they pass by, the sounds of chains and risen hackles. The podiatric click and thud, the visible breath, gravel's crunch, creak of Green's leather, the *snick* of a million urban lighters, the gauzy far-off humming ATHSCMEs pointing out true plumb north, the clunk and tinkle of stuff going into dumpsters and rustle of stuff in dumpsters settling and skirl of wind on the sharp edges of dumpsters and unmistakable clanks and tinkles of dumpster-divers and can-miners going after dumpsters' cans and bottles, the district Redemption Center down in West Brighton and actually even boldly sharing a storefront with Liquor World liquor store, so the can-miners can do like one-stop redeeming and shopping. Which Lenz finds repellent to the maximus, and shares the feelings with Green. Lenz observes to Green how myriadly ironic are the devices by which the Famous Crooner's promise to Clean Up Our Urban Cities has come to be kept. The noises parallaxing in from out over the city's winking grid, at night. The wooly haze of monoxides. You got your faint cuntstink of the wind off the Bay. Planes' little crucifi of landing lights well ahead of their own noise. Crows in trees. You got your standard crepuscular rustles. Ground floors' lit windows laying little rugs of light out into their lawns. Porch lights that go on automatically when you stroll by. A threnody of sirens somewhere north of the Charles. Bare trees creaking in the wind. The State Bird of Massachusetts, he shares to Green, is the police siren. To Project and to Swerve. The cries and screams from out across who knows how many blocks, who knows the screams' intent. Sometimes the end of the scream is at the sound of the start of the scream, he opines. The visible breath and the rainbowed rings of streetlights and headlights through that breath. Unless the screams are really laughing. Lenz's own mother's laugh had sounded like she was being eaten alive.

Except — after the maybe five total lines hoovered in a totally purposive medicinal nonrecreational spirit — except then instead of assuring Green he's a blue-chip commodity on Lenz's Exchange but to please screw and let Lenz stroll home solo with his meatloaf and agenda, it eventuates that Lenz has again miscalculated the effect the Bing's hydrolysis[232] will have, he always like previsions the effect as cool nonchalant verbal sangfroid, but instead Lenz on the way home finds himself under huge hydrolystic compulsion to have Green right there by his side — or basically anyone who can't get away or won't go away — right there with him, and to share with Green or any compliant ear pretty much every experience and thought he's ever had, to give each datum of the case of R. Lenz shape and visible breath as his whole life (and then some) tear-asses across his mind's arctic horizon, trailing phosphenes.

He tells Green that his phobic fear of timepieces stems from his stepfather, an Amtrak train conductor with deeply unresolved issues which he used to make Lenz wind his pocketwatch and polish his fob daily with a chamois cloth and nightly make sure his watch's displayed time was correct to the second or else he'd lay into the pint-sized Randy with a rolled-up copy of *Track and Flange,* a slick and wicked-heavy coffee-table-sized trade periodical.

Lenz tells Green how spectacularly obese his own late mother had been, using his arms to dramatically illustrate the dimensions involved.

He breathes between about every third or fourth fact, ergo about once a block.

Lenz tells Green the plots of several books he's read, confabulating them.

Lenz doesn't notice the way Green's face sort of crumples blankly when Lenz mentions the issue of late mothers.

Lenz euphorically tells Green how he once got the tip of his left finger cut off in a minibike chain once and how but within days of intensive concentration the finger had grown back and regenerated itself like a lizard's tail, confounding doctoral authorities. Lenz says that was the incident in youth after which he got in touch with his own unusual life-force and *energois de vivre* and knew and accepted that he was somehow not like the run of common men, and began to accept his uniqueness and all that it entailed.

Lenz clues Green in on it's a myth the Nile crocodile is the most dreaded species of crocodile, that the dreaded Estuarial crocodile of saltwater habits is a billion times more dreaded by those in the know.

Lenz theorizes that his compulsive need to know the time with microspic precision is also a function of his stepfather's dysfunctional abuse regarding the pocketwatch and *Track and Flange*. This segues into an analysis of the term *dysfunction* and its revelance to the distinctions between, say, psychology and natural religion.

Lenz tells how once in the Back Bay on Boylston outside Bonwit's a pushy prosthesis-vendor gave him a hard time about a glass-eye item of jewelry and got his issues' juices flowing and then down the prosthesis-vendor line another vendor simply would not take No of any sort about a bottle of A.D.A.-Approved Xero-Lube Saliva Substitute with a confabulated celeb-endorsement from J. Gentle F. Crooner on it and Lenz utilized akido to break the man's nose with one blow and then drive the bone's shards and fragments up into the vendor's brain with the follow-up heel of his hand, a maneuver known by a secret ancient Chinese term meaning The Old One-Two, eliminating the saliva guy's map on the spot, so that Lenz had learned about the lethality of his whatever-was-beyond-black belt in akido and his hands' deadliness as weapons when his issues were provoked and tells Green how he'd taken a solemn vow right there, running like hell down Boylston for the Auditorium T-Stop to evade prosecution, vowed never to use his lethally adept akido skills except in the most compulsory situation of defending the innocent and/or weak.

Lenz tells Green how once he was at a Halloween party where a hydro-cephalic woman wore a necklace made of dead gulls.

Lenz shares about this recurring dream where he's seated under a tropical ceiling fan in a cane chair wearing an L.L. Bean safari hat and holding a wickerware valise in his lap, and that's all, and that's the recurring dream.

On the 400 block of W. Beacon, around 2202h., Lenz demonstrates for Bruce Green the secret akido 1-2 with which he'd demapped the saliva-monger, breaking the move down into slo-mo constituent movements so that Green's untrained eye could follow. He says there's another recurring nightmare about a clock with hands frozen eternally at 1830 that's so trouser-foulingly scary he won't even burden Green's fragile psychology with the explicits of it.

Green, lighting both their smokes, says he either doesn't remember his dreams or doesn't dream.

Lenz adjusts his white toupee and mustache in a darkened InterLace outlet's window, does the odd bit of t'ai-chi stretching, and blows his nose into W. Beacon's cluttered gutter Euro-style, one nostril at a time, arching to keep his coatfront well back from what he expels.

Green's one of these muscle-shirt types that carries his next gasper tucked up over his ear, which the use of RIJID or other brands of quality hair-fixative makes impossible for the reason that residues of spray on the cigarette cause it to burst unexpectedly into flame at points along its length. Lenz regales how at that Halloween Party with the necklace of birds there'd been allegedly a Concavity-refugee infant there, at the party, at the home of a South Boston orthodontist that dealt Lidocaine to Bing-retailers on the prescriptional dicky,[233] a normal-size and unferal infant but totally without a skull, lying in a kind of raised platform or dais by the fireplace with its shapeless and deskulled head-region supported and, like (shuddering), *contained* in a sort of lidless plastic box, and its eyes were sunk way down in its face, which was the consistency of like quicksand, the face, and its nose concave and its mouth hanging out over either side of the boneless face, and the total head had like *conformed* to the inside of the containing box it was contained in, the head, and appeared roughly square in overall outline, the head, and the woman with the lei of gull-heads and other persons in costumes had ingested hallucinogens and drank mescal and ate the little worms in the mescal and had performed circled rituals around the box and platform around 2355h., worshipping the infant, or as they termed it simply *The Infant,* as if there were only One.

Green lets Lenz know the time at roughly two-minute intervals, maybe once a block, from his cheap but digital watch, when the critical B.B.S.B. liquid-crystal sign is obscured by the urban night's strolling skyline.

Lenz's labial writhing occurs worst on diphthongs involving o-sounds.

Lenz clues Green in that AA/NA works all right but there's no fucking question it's a cult, he and Green've apparently got themselves to the point where the only way out of the addictive tailspin is to enlist in a fucking cult and let them try and brainwash your ass, and that the first person tries to lay a saffron robe or tambourine on Lenz is going to be one very sorry cableyarrow indeed, is all.

Lenz claims to remember some experiences which he says happened to him *in vitro*.

Lenz says the Ennet graduates who often come back and take up livingroom space sitting around comparing horror stories about former religious cults they'd tried joining as part of their struggle to try to quit with the drugs and alcohol are not w/o a certain naïve charm but are basically naïve. Lenz details that robes and mass weddings and head-shaving and pamphleteering in airports and selling flowers on median strips and signing away inheritances and never sleeping and marrying whoever they tell you and then never seeing who you marry are small potatoes in terms of bizarre-cult criterion. Lenz tells Green he knows individuals who've heard shit that would blow Green's mind out his ear-sockets.

At lunchtime, Hal Incandenza was lying on his bunk in bright sunlight through the window with his hands laced over his chest, and Jim Troeltsch poked his head in and asked Hal what he was doing, and Hal told him photosynthesizing and then didn't say anything else until Troeltsch went away.

Then, 41 breaths later, Michael Pemulis stuck his head in where Troeltsch's had been.

'Did you eat yet?'

Hal made his stomach bulge up and patted it, still looking at the ceiling. 'The beast has killed and gorged and now lies in the shade of the Baobob tree.'

'Gotcha.'

'Surveying his loyal pride.'

'*I* gotcha.'

Over 200 breaths later, John ('N.R.') Wayne opened up the ajar door a little more and put his whole head in and stayed like that, with just his head in. He didn't say anything and Hal didn't say anything, and they stayed like that for a while, and then Wayne's head smoothly withdrew.

Under a streetlamp on Faneuil St. off W. Beacon, Randy Lenz shares a vulnerable personal thing and tilts his head back to show Bruce Green where his septum used to be.

Randy Lenz reguiles Bruce Green about certain real-estate cults in S. Cal. and the West Coast. Of Delawareans that still believed Virtual-Reality pornography even though it'd been found to cause bleeding from the eye-corners and real-world permanent impotence was still the key to Shrangi-la and believed that some sort of perfect piece of digito-holographic porn was circulating somewhere in the form of a bootleg Write-Protect-notched software diskette and devoted their cultic lives to snuffling around trying to get hold of the virtual kamasupra diskette and getting together in dim Wilmington-area venues and talking very obliquely about rumors of where and just what the software was and how their snufflings for it were going, and watching Virtual fuckfilms and mopping the corner of their eyes, etc. Or of something called Stelliform Cultism that Bruce Green isn't even near ready to hear about, Lenz opines. Or like e.g. of a suicidal Nuck cult of Nucks that worshipped a form of Russian Roulette that involved jumping in front of trains and seeing which Nuck could come the closest to the train's front without getting demapped.

What sounds like Lenz chewing gum is really Lenz trying to talk and grind his teeth together at the same time.

Lenz recalls orally that his stepfather's blue-vested gut had preceded the conductor into rooms by several seconds, fob glinting above the watch-pocket's sinister slit. How Lenz's mother back in Fall River had made it a point of utilizing Greyhound for voyages and sojourns, basically to piss her stephusband off.

Lenz discusses how a serious disadvantage to dealing Bing retail is the way customers'll show up pounding on your door at 0300 sporting lint in the terms of resources and putting their arms around your shins and ankles and begging for just a half-gram or tenth of a gram and offering to give Lenz their kids, like Lenz wants to fucking deal with anybody's kids, which these scenes were always constant drags on his spirits.

Green, who's hoovered his share, says cocaine always seemed like it grabbed you by the throat and just didn't let go, and he could relate to why the Boston AAs call Bing the 'Express Elevator To AA.'

In a dumpster-lined easement between Faneuil St. and Brighton Ave., Brighton, right after Green almost steps in what he's pretty sure is human vomit, Lenz proves logically why it's all too likely that Ennet House resident Geoffrey D. is a closet poofta.

Lenz reports how he's been approached in the past to male-model and act, but that the male-model and acting profession is pretty much crawling with your closet pooftas, and it's no kind of work for a man that's confronted the ins and outs of his own character.

Lenz speculates openly on how there are purportaged to be whole packs and herds of feral animals operating in locust-like fashion in the rhythmic lushness of parts of the Great Concavity to the due northeast, descended reputedly from domestic pets and abandoned during the relocational transition to an O.N.A.N.ite map, and how teams of pro researchers and amateur explorers and intrepid hearts and cultists have ventured northeast of Checkpoints along the Lucited ATHSCMulated walls and never returned, vanishing in toto from the short-wave E.M. bands, as in like dropping off the radar.

Green turns out to have no conceptions or views on the issues of fauna of the Concavity at all. He literally says he's never given it one thought one way or the other.

Whole NNE cults and stelliform subcults Lenz reports as existing around belief systems about the metaphysics of the Concavity and annular fusion and B.S.-1950s-B-cartridge-type-radiation-affected fauna and overfertilization and verdant forests with periodic oasises of purportaged desert and whatever east of the former Montpelier VT area of where the annulated Shawshine River feeds the Charles and tints it the exact same tint of blue as the blue on boxes of Hefty SteelSaks and the ideas of ravacious herds of feral domesticated housepets and oversized insects not only taking over the abandoned homes of relocated Americans but actually setting up house and keeping them in model repair and impressive equity, allegedly, and the idea of infants the size of prehistoric beasts roaming the overfertilized east Concavity quadrants, leaving enormous scat-piles and keening for the abortive parents who'd left or lost them in the general geopolitical shuffle of mass migration and really fast packing, or, as some of your more Limbaugh-era-type cultists sharingly believe, originating from abortions hastily disposed of in barrels in ditches that got breached and mixed ghastly contents with other barrels that reanimated the abortive feti and brought them to a kind of repelsive oversized B-cartridge life thundering around due north of where yrstruly and Green strolled through the urban grid. Of one local underground stelliform offshoot from the Bob Hope–worshipping Rastafarians who smoked enormous doobsters and wove their negroid hair into clusters of wet cigars like the Rastafarians but instead of Rastafarians these post-Rastas worshipped the Infant and every New Year donned tie-dyed parkas and cardboard snowshoes and ventured northward, trailing smoke, past the walls and fans of Checkpoint Pongo into the former areas of VT and NH, seeking *The Infant* they called it, as if there were only One, and toting paraphernalia for performing a cultish ritual referred to in oblique tones only as *Propitiating The Infant,* whole posses of these stelliform pot-head reggae-swaying Infant-cultists disappearing forever off the human race's radar every winter, never heard or smelled again, regarded by fellow cultists as martyrs and/or lambs, possibly too addled by blimp-sized doobsters to find their way back out of the Concavity and freezing to death, or enswarmed by herds of feral pets, or shot by property-value-conscious insects, or ... (face plum-colored, finally breathing) worse.

Lenz shudders just at the thought of the raging Powerlessness he'd feel, he shares, lost and disorientated, wandering in circles in blinding white frozen points due north of all domesticated men, forget the time not even knowing what fucking *date* it was, his breath an ice-beard, with just his tinder and wits and character to live by, armed just with a Browning blade.

Green opines that if Boston AA is a cult that like brainwashes you, he guesses he'd got himself to the point where his brain needed a good brisk washing, which Lenz knows is not an original view, being exactly what big blockheaded Don Gately repeats about once a diem.

SELECTED SNIPPETS FROM THE INDIVIDUAL-RESIDENT-INFORMAL-INTERFACE MOMENTS OF D. W. GATELY, LIVE-IN STAFF, ENNET HOUSE DRUG AND ALCOHOL RECOVERY HOUSE, ENFIELD MA, ON AND OFF FROM JUST AFTER THE BROOKLINE YOUNG PEOPLE'S AA MTNG. UP TO ABOUT 2329H., WEDNESDAY 11 NOVEMBER Y.D.A.U.

'I don't know why all this shit about wanting to hear about the football all the time. And I'm not going to make my goddamn muscle. It's stupid.'

'Okey-doke.'

'It's *inappropriate,* since you like words like that.'

'But this Sharing and Caring Commitment guy, the Chair, the Sudbury Half-Measures Avail Us Nothing Group, he had a power about him. The Chair, he said he used to be a nuclear auditor. For the Defense industry. This man who was very quiet and broken-seeming and fatherly and strange. There was this kind of broken authority about him.'

'I know what you mean. I can I.D.'

'. . . that seemed *fatherly* somehow.'

'The sponsor type. My sponsor's like that, Joelle, in White Flag.'

'Can I ask? Is your own personal Daddy still alive?'

'I dunno.'

'Oh. Oh. My mother's dead. Worm-farming. My own personal Daddy's still sucking air, though. That's how he puts it — still sucking air. In Kentucky.'

'. . .'

'My mother's a worm-farmer from way back, though.'

'But so what about this Half Measures guy hit you so hard?'

'*Harrd. Harrrrrd.* Sound it out.'

'Real funny.'

'Don well it started out as that he spoke about himself like he used to be somebody else. Like a whole different person. He said he used to wear a four-piece suit and the fourth piece was him.'

'An Allston Group guy says that all the time, that joke.'

'He had on a real nice white thick-weave cotton shirt opened at the throat and wheat-colored pants and loafers without socks, which I'm up here ten years Don and I still can't follow this thing up here about y'all all wearing nice shoes and then wrecking them by wearing them without socks.'

'Joelle, you're maybe about the last person to be taking somebody's inventory about weird ways they dress, under there, maybe.'

'Kiss my rosy red ass, maybe.'

'Remind me to Log how it's real positive to see you coming out of this shell of yours.'

'Well and I got reservations on this Don but Diehl and Ken are telling me to come in to you with this issue of what's like occurring out there which Erdedy says it's a Staff-type issue and duh-duh duh-duh.'

'Had a little coffee tonight have we Foss?'

'Well Don and like you know and duh-duh.'

'Take a second. Inhale and blow out. I'm not going anywheres.'

'Well Don I hate a cheese-nibbler much as the next man but Geoff D. and Nell G. are out in the living room going around to all the new people asking them to think about if their Higher Power is omni-potent enough to make a suitcase that's too heavy for him to lift. They're doing it to everybody that's new. And that skittery kid Dingley —'

'Tingley. The new kid.'

'Well Don he's sitting in the linen closet with his legs sticking out of the linen closet with his eyes bugging out with like smoke coming out his ears and duh-duh duh-duh going like He Can but He Can't but He Can, respecting the suitcase and duh-duh, and Diehl says it's a matter for Staff, it's a negative thing Day's doing and Erdedy says I'm Senior Res. and to go to Staff with it and eat cheese.'

'Shit.'

'Diehl said a case this negative and duh-duh, no way it's like ratting.'

'No, I appreciate. It ain't ratting.'

'Plus I brought in this really good like tollhouse-butterscotch cookie thing Hanley made a plate of, which Erdedy said it's not like kissing ass so much as commonplace decency.'

'Erdedy's a community pillar. I got to stay in here with the phone. Maybe you could tell Geoff and Nell to like waltz on in if they can take time out from torturing the new people.'

'I'll probably leave out the torturing part if it's OK with you, Don.'

'Which by the way here I am looking at this cookie still in your hand, notice.'

'Jesus, the cookie. Jesus.'

'Try and relax a little, kid.'

'I got to stay down with the phones till 2200. Try a plunger and let me know and I can call Services.'

'I'm thinking it'd be doing a favor if Staff clued in anybody new that comes in on the fact that the H-faucet in the shower that its H really stands for *Holy Cow That's Cold.*'

'Are you saying in a sideways way there's some trouble with the water-temp in the head, McDade?'

'Don, I'm saying just what I came in here to say. And can I say by the way nice shirt. My dad used to bowl, too, when he still had a thumb.'

'I don't care what the sick bastard told you, Yolanda. Getting on your knees in the A.M. to Ask For Help does not mean getting on your knees in the A.M. while this sick yutz stands in front of you and unzips his fly and you Ask For Help into his fly. I'm praying this is not a male resident said this. This is the sort of thing why same-sex sponsors only are a suggestion. Is that there's some sick bastards around the rooms, you get me? Any AA tells a new female in the Program to use his Unit for her Higher Power, I'd give that guy a wide detour. You get what I'm saying?'

'And I didn't even tell you yet how he suggested I should thank the Higher Power at night.'

'I'd cross a broad street to avoid an AA like this guy, Yolanda.'

'And how he said how I always have to be on the south of him, like stay on his south side, and I have to buy a digital watch.'

'Holy Christ this is Lenz. Is this Lenz you're telling me about?'

'I ain't use no names in here. All I say he seemed real friendly and fly at first, and helpful, when I first came, this dude I ain't say no name.'

'You have trouble with the part of the Second Step that's about insanity and you've been using *Randy Lenz* for a sponsor?'

'This is a nomonous Program, you know what I'm saying?'

'Jesus, kid.'

Orin ('O.') Incandenza stands embracing a putatively Swiss hand-model in a rented room. They embrace. Their faces become sexual faces. It seems clear evidence of a kind of benign fate or world-spirit that this incredible specimen had appeared at Sky Harbor Int. Airp. just as Orin stood with his fine forehead against the glass of the Gate overlooking the tarmac after actually volunteering to drive Helen Steeply all the night-marish way down I-17/-10 to the ghastly glittering unnavigable airport and the Subject seemed, in the car, not only not especially grateful, and hadn't let him so much as place a friendly and supportive palm on her incredible quadricep during the ride, but had been irritatingly all-business and had continued to pursue lines of family-linen inquiry he'd all but begged her to quit subjecting him to the inappropriateness of[234] — that, as he stood there after having received little other than a cool smile and a promise to try to say hello to Hallie, with his forehead against the glass of the Weston back door — or rather the Delta gate window — this incredible specimen had — unbidden, unStrategized — come up to him and started a lush foreign-accented conversation and revealed professionally lovely hands as she rooted in her tripolymer bag to ask him to autograph for her *toddler-age son* a Cardinal-souvenir football she had *right there* (!) in her bag, along with her Swiss passport — as if the universe were reaching out a hand to pluck him from the rim of the abyss of despair that any real sort of rejection or frustration of his need for some Subject he'd picked out always threatened him with, as if he'd been teetering with his arms windmilling at a great height without even idiotic red wings strapped to his back and the universe were sending this lovely steadying left hand to pull him gently back and embrace him and not so much console him as remind him of who and what he was about, standing there embracing a Subject with a sexual face for his sexual face, no longer speaking, the football and pen on the neatly made bed, the two of them embracing between the bed and the mirror with the woman facing the bed so that Orin can see past her head the large hanging mirror and the small framed photos of her Swiss family arrayed along the wood-grain dresser below the window,[235] the tubby-faced man and Swiss-looking kids all smiling trustingly into a nothing somewhere up and to their right.

They have shifted into a sexual mode. Her lids flutter; his close. There's a concentrated tactile languor. She is left-handed. It is not about consolation. They start the thing with each other's buttons. It is not about conquest or forced capture. It is not about glands or instincts or the split-second shiver and clench of leaving yourself; nor about love or about whose love you deep-down desire, by whom you feel betrayed. Not and never love, which kills what needs it. It feels to the punter rather to be about hope, an immense, wide-as-the-sky hope of finding a something in each Subject's fluttering face, a something the same that will propitiate hope, somehow, pay its tribute, the need to be assured that for a moment he *has* her, now has *won* her as if from someone or something else, something other than he, but that he *has* her and is what she sees and all she sees, that it is not conquest but surrender, that he is both offense and defense and she neither, nothing but this one second's love of her, *of*-her, spinning as it arcs his way, not his but *her* love, that he has *it,* this love (his shirt off now, in the mirror), that for one second she loves him too much to stand it, that she *must* (she feels) have him, *must* take him inside or else dissolve into worse than nothing; that all else is gone: that her sense of humor is gone, her petty griefs, triumphs, memories, hands, career, betrayals, the deaths of pets — that there is now inside her a vividness vacuumed of all but his name: O., O. That he is the One.

(This is why, maybe, one Subject is never enough, why hand after hand must descend to pull him back from the endless fall. For were there for him just one, now, special and only, the One would be not he or she but what was between them, the obliterating trinity of You and I into We. Orin felt that once and has never recovered, and will never again.)

And about contempt, it is about a kind of hatred, too, along with the hope and need. Because he needs them, needs her, because he needs her he fears her and so hates her a little, hates all of them, a hatred that comes out disguised as a contempt he disguises in the tender attention with which he does the thing with her buttons, touches the blouse as if it too were part of her, and him. As if it could feel. They have stripped each other neatly. Her mouth is glued to his mouth; she is his breath, his eyes shut against the sight of hers. They are stripped in the mirror and she, in a kind of virtuoso jitterbug that is 100% New World, uses O.'s uneven shoulders as support to leap and circle his neck with her legs, and she arches her back and is supported, her weight, by just one hand at the small of her back as he bears her to bed as would a waiter a tray.

'*Hoompf.*'

'*Herrmmp.*'

'Well in excess of a thousand pardons for my collision.'

'Arslanian? Is that you?'

'It is I, Idris Arslanian. Who is this other?'

'It's Ted Schacht, Id. Why the blindfold?'

'Where have I come, please. I became disoriented upon a set of stairs. I became panicked. I nearly removed my blindfold. Where are we? I detect many odors.'

'You're just off the weight room, in the little hall off the tunnel that isn't the little hall that goes to the sauna. Why the blindfold, though?'

'And the origin of this sound of hysterical weeping and moans, this is —?'

'It's Anton Doucette in there. He's in there clinically depressed. Lyle's trying to buck him up. Some of the crueler guys are in there watching like it's entertainment. I got disgusted. Somebody in pain isn't entertainment. I did my sets, now I'm a vapor-trail.'

'You exude vapor?'

'Always nice running into you, Id.'

'Await. Please conduct me upstairs or into the locker for a lavatory visit. The blindfold I am wearing is experimental on the part of Thorp. You are told of the visually challenged player who will matriculate?'

'The blind kid? From like Nowheresburg, Iowa? Dempster?'

'Dymphna.'

'He's not coming in til next term. He delayed, Inc said they said. Dural edema or something.'

'Though age only nine, he is in his Midwest region's ranking of Twelve and Belows highly ranked. Coach Thorp tells this.'

'Well, I'd say for a blind, soft-skulled kid he's real high-ranked, Id, yeah.'

'But Dymphna, I hear Thorp tell that the highness of the ranking may be due to the blindness itself. Thorp and Texas Watson were who scouted this player.'

'I wouldn't mention the name *Watson* near that weight room in there if I were you.'

'Thorp tells that his excellence of play is scouted by them to be his anticipation. As in the player Dymphna arrives at the necessary location well before the opponent player's ball, through anticipation.'

'I know what anticipation is, Id.'

'Thorp tells to me that this excellence in anticipation in the blind is because of hearing and sounds, because sounds are merely . . . here. Please read the comment I have carefully notated upon this folded piece of paper.'

' "Sound Merely 'Variations In Intensity' — Throp." Throp?'

'It was meaning *Thorp,* in excitement. He tells that one may, perforce, judge the opponent player's VAPS[236] in more detail by the ear than the eye. This is experimental theory of Thorp. This is explaining why the highly ranked Dymphna appears to always have floated by magic to the necessary spot where a ball is soon to land. Thorp tells this in a convincing manner.'

'Perforce?'

'That this blind person is able to judge the necessary spot of landing by the intensity of the sound of the ball against the opponent player's string.'

'Instead of watching the contact and then imaginatively extending the beginning of its flight, like those of us hobbled by sight.'

'I, Idris Arslanian, am compelled with Thorp's telling.'

'Which helps explain the blindfold.'

'I therefore experiment with volunteer blindness. Training the ear in degrees of intensity in play. Today versus Whale I was wearing the blindfold to play.'

'How'd it go?'

'Not as well as hoped. I frequently faced the wrong direction for play. I frequently judged by the intensity of balls struck on adjacent courts and ran onto adjacent courts, intruding on play.'

'We sort of wondered what all the ruckus was down there at the 14's end.'

'Thorp tells that training the ear is a process of time, in encouragement.'

'Well, later, Id.'

'Stop. Wait before leaving. Please conduct me to a lavatory. Ted Schacht? Are you as yet there?'

'. . .'

'Are you as yet there? I very —'

'*Whuffff* watch where you're going kid for Christ's sake.'

'Who is this please.'

'Troeltsch, James L., slightly doubled over.'

'It is I, Idris Arslanian, wearing a rayon handkerchief as a blindfold over my features. I am disoriented and wishing badly for a lavatory. Wondering also what is ensuing inside the weight room, where Schacht alleges you are all watching Doucette weep in clinical depression.'

'Kert*wannnggg!* Just kidding, Ars. It's really Mike Pemulis.'

'Then you, Mike Pemulis, may even now be questioning why is this blindfold upon Idris Arslanian.'

'What blindfold? Ars, no, you're wearing a fucking blindfold too?'

'You, Mike Pemulis, are also wearing a blindfold?'

'Just kertwanging on you, brother.'

'I became disoriented on a stairway, then conversed with Ted Schacht. I am suspecting I do not trust your sense of laughter enough to conduct me back upstairs.'

'You should feel your way in and just for one second see the amount of high-stress sweat Lyle's taking off Anton ("The Booger") Doucette in there, Ars.'

'Doucette is the two-hand player whose mole appears to be material from a nostril, clinically depressing Doucette at its appearance.'

'Rog on the mole. Except that's not what's depressing the Booger this time. This one we decided we'd describe him as more like anxiously depressed than depressed.'

'One can be depressed of different types?'

'Boy are you young, Ars. The Booger's got himself convinced he's going to get the academic Boot. He's been on proby this whole year, since apparently some trouble last year with Thorp's cubular trig —'

'I am sympathizing with this in toto.'

'— and but except now he claims he's close to flunking in Watson's laughable Energy survey class, which would obviously mean the old Boot at term's end, if he really does flunk. He's thought himself into a brainlock of anxiety. He's in there clutching his skull with Lyle and Mario, and some of the like less kind guys in there have a pool going on whether Lyle can pull him back from the brink.'

'Texas Watson the prorector, teaching of energy in models of resource-scarcity and resource-plenty.'

'Ars, I'm nodding in confirmation. Fossil fuels all the way up to annular fusion/fission cycles, DT-lithiumization, so on and so forth. All on a real superficial-type level, since Watson's basically got like a little liquid-filled nubbin at the top of his spine where his brain ought to be.'

'Texas Watson does not overwhelm with brightness, it is true.'

'But Doucette's got himself convinced he's got this insurmagulate conceptual block that keeps him from grasping annulation, even superficially.'

'After we converse you will conduct me to micturate, please.'

'It's the same sort of block some people get with the Mean-Value

Theorem. Or in Optics when we get to color fields. At a certain level of abstraction it's like the brain recoils.'

'Causing pain of impact within the skull, resulting in clutching the head.'

'Watson's gone the extra click with him. Watson's good-hearted if nothing else. He's tried flash-cards, mnemonic rhymes, even claymation filmstrips from over at Rindge-Latin Remedial.'

'You are saying without avail.'

'I'm saying apparently the Boogster just sits there in class, eyes bugging out, stomach in fucking knots, dope-slapped by anxiety. I'm saying frozen.'

'You are saying recoiling.'

'The right side of his face frozen in this anxiety-tic. Envisioning any possible tennis career as with these little wings on it, flying off. Talking all kinds of crazy self-injuring anxious-depression talk. It all started with him and Mario and me in the sauna, him breaking down, me and Mario trying to talk him out of the crazy washed-up-at-fifteen-type depressed talk, Mario exploiting a previous like therapeutic bond with the kid from about the mole, then with me putting DT-annulation in broad-stroke terms a freaking *invertebrate* could have understood for Christ's sake. Just about passing out from the sauna all through this. Finally taking him in to Lyle even with the 18's still doing circuits in there. Lyle's working with the Booger now. Between the anxiety and the marathon sauna-time it's a real feeding frenzy for old Lyle let me tell you.'

'I too confess experiences of anxiety for annulation with Tex Watson, though I am Trivially thirteen and not yet required to grapple in hard science.'

'Mario in the sauna kept telling Doucette to just imagine somebody doing somersaults with one hand nailed to the ground, which what the fuck is that, and lo and surprise didn't help the Booger a whole lot.'

'Did not part the veil of Maya.'

'Didn't do jack.'

'Annular energy cycles are intensively abstract, my home nation believes.'

'But my whole message to Boog was that DT-cycles aren't all that fucking hard if you don't paralyze your brain with career-with-wings brain-cartoons. The extra-hot breedering and lithiumization stuff gets hairy, but the whole fusion/fission waste-annulation thing in toto you can imagine as nothing but a huge right triangle.'

'You are presaging to give the thumbnail lecture.'

'Commit this one simple model to your little Pakistani RAM-cells, and you'll tapdance right through Watson's kiddie-physics and up into Optics, which is where the abstracto-conceptual fur really flies, kid, let me tell you.'

'I am one of the seldom of my home nation whose talents are weak in science, unhappily.'

'This is why God also gave you quick hands and a wicked lob off the backhand, though. Just picture a kind of massive pseudocartographic right triangle.[237] You've got your central, impregnately-guarded O.N.A.N.- Sunstrand waste-intensive fusion facility up in what used to be Montpelier in what used to be Vermont, in the Concavity. From Montpelier the process's waste's piped to two sites, one of which is that blue glow at night up by the Methuen Fan-Complex, just south of the Concavity, right flush up against the Wall and Checkpoint Pongo —'

'Which our tall and sleep-depriving fans in our area point at to blow away from the south.'

'— Roger that, where the toxo-fusion's waste's plutonium fluoride's refined into plutonium-239 and uranium-238 and fissioned in a standard if somewhat hot and risky breeder-system, much of the output of which is waste U-239, which gets piped or catapulted or long-shiny-trucked way up to what used to be Loring A.F.B. — Air Force Base near what used to be Presque Isle Maine — where it's allowed to decay naturally into neptunium-239 and then plutonium-239 and then added to the UF_4 fractional waste also piped up from Montpelier, then fissioned in a purposely ugly way in such a way as to create like hellacious amounts of highly poisonous radioactive wastes, which are mixed with heavy water and specially heated-zirconium-piped through special heavily guarded heated zirconium pipes back down to Montpelier as raw matériel for the massive poisons needed for toxic lithiumization and waste-intenseness and annular fusion.'

'My head is spinning on its axis.'

'Just a moving right-triangular cycle of interdependence and waste-creation and -utilization. See? And when are we going to get you out on the old Eschaton map for a little geopolitical sparring, Ars, what with those hands and wicked lob? Incidentally, the arrhythmic meaty whacking sound is Booger hitting himself in the thigh and chest in there, which self-abuse is a textbook symptom of an anxiously depressed episode.'

'With this I can create sympathy. For, confusingly to me, fusion produces no waste. This we are taught in the science of my home nation. This is the very essence of the promise of the attraction of fusion for a densely populous and waste-impacted nation such as mine, we are taught fusion to be self-sufficient and wasteless perpetuation. Alas, my need to visit the lavatory is becoming distended.'

'But except no, although this was the very roadblock that'd stymied annulation, and what had to be overcome, and was overcome, though in a way so unintuitive and abstracto-conceptual that this is where your Third World educational system's real sadly in need of like a massive up-to-date-textbook airlift or something. It's also at just this point in the fusion-wastelessness problem where our own glorious optical Founder, Inc's ex-Da, Mrs. Inc's poor cuc —'

'I know who you refer.'

'The man himself, at just this point, makes his final lasting contribution to state science after he quit designing neutron-diffusion reflectors for Defense. You've seen the coprolite placque in Tavis's office. This is from the A.E.C., for the Incster's Da's, like, lasting contribution to the energy of waste.'

'The purpose for which I was upon the stairs and became disoriented was to visit a lavatory. This was long ago.'

'Hold your water one second is all this'll take. You wouldn't even fucking *be* here without Inc's Da, you know. What the guy did was he helped design these special holographic conversions so the team that worked on annulation could study the behavior of subatomics in highly poisonous environments. Without getting poisoned themselves.'

'They thus are studying holographic conversions of the poisons instead of the poisons.'

'Men's Sanity in Corporate Sterno, Ars. Like an optical glove-box. The ultimate prophylactic.'

'Please conduct me.'

'Like but for instance did your nation know that the whole annular theory behind a type of fusion that can produce waste that's fuel for a process whose waste is fuel for the fusion: the whole theory behind the physics of it comes out of medicine?'

'This means what? A bottle of medicine?'

'The study of medicine, Ars. Your part of the world takes annular medicine for granted now, but the whole idea of treating cancer by giving the cancer cells themselves cancer was anathematic just a couple decades back.'

'Anathematic?'

'As in like radical, fringe. Wacko. Laughed out of town on a rail by quote mainstream established science. Whose idea of treatment was to like poison the whole body and see what was left. Though annular chemotherapy did start out kind of wacko. You can see these early microphotos Schacht's got that poster of that he won't take down even after you're sick of it, the early microphotos of cancer cells getting force-fed micromassive quantities of overdone beef and diet soda, forced to chain-smoke microsized Marlboros near tiny little cellular phones —'238

'I am standing first upon one foot then upon another foot.'

'— except and corollarying out of the micromedical model was this equally radical idea that maybe you could achieve a high-waste annulating fusion by bombarding highly toxic radioactive particles with massive doses of stuff even more toxic than the radioactive particles. A fusion that feeds on poisons and produces relatively stable plutonium fluoride and uranium tetra-fluoride. All you turn out to need is access to mind-staggering volumes of toxic material.'

'Therefore placing the natural fusion site in the Great Concavity.'

'Roger and *Jawohl*. Here things get abstractly furry and I'll just skim through the fact that the only kertwang in the whole process environmentally is that the resultant fusion turns out so greedily efficient that it sucks every last toxin and poison out of the surrounding ecosystem, all inhibitors to organic growth for hundreds of radial clicks in every direction.'

'Hence the eastern Concavity of anxiety and myth.'

'You end up with a surrounding environment so fertilely lush it's practically unlivable.'

'A rain forest on sterebolic anoids.'

'Close enough.'

'Therefore rapacial feral hamsters and insects of Volkswagen size and infantile giganticism and the unmacheteable regions of forests of the mythic eastern Concavity.'

'Yes Ars and you find you need to keep steadily dumping in toxins to keep the uninhibited ecosystem from spreading and overrunning more ecologically stable areas, exhausting the atmosphere's poisons so that everything hyperventilates. And thus and such. So this is why E.W.D.'s major catapulting is from the metro area due north.'

'Into the eastern Concavity, keeping it at bay.'

'See how it all comes together?'

'Mr. Thorp will evince keen disappointment if I resort to remove my blindfold to locate a lavatory.'

'Ars, I hear you. I hear fine. You don't need to go on and on. The thing to keep in mind for if you have to take Watson is the cyclic effects of the waste-delivery and fusion. Major catapulting is on what days?'

'The dates which are in each month prime numbers, until midnight.'

'Which eradicates the overgrowth until the toxins are fused and utilized. The satellite scenario is that the eastern part of Grid 3 goes from overgrown to wasteland to overgrown several times a month. With the first week of the month being especially barren and the last week being like nothing on earth.'

'As if time itself were vastly sped up. As if nature itself had desperately to visit the lavatory.'

'Accelerated phenomena, which is actually equivalent to an incredible *slowing down* of time. The mnemonic rhyme Watson tried to get the Boog to remember here is "Wasteland to lush: time's in no rush." '

'Decelerated time, I have got you.'

'And this is what the Boog's saying is eating him alive the worst, conceptually. He says he's toast if he can't wrap his head around the concept of time in flux, conceptually. It jacklights him for the whole annular model overall. Granted, it's abstract. But you should see him. One half of the face is like spasming around while the half with the mole just like hangs there staring like a bunny you're about to run over. Lyle's trying to walk him real slowly through the most basic kiddie-physical principles of the relativity of time in extreme organic environments. In between Booger's trips back to the sauna. The irony for the Boogerman is you don't really even have to know that much about the temporal-flux stuff, since Watson's forehead gets all mottled and pruny-looking when he thinks about it himself.'

'Do not please necessitate begging from me, Idris Arslanian.'

'The eastern Concavity of course being a whole different kettle of colored horses from what Inc calls the barren Eliotical wastes of the western Concavity, let me tell you.'

'I will let you tell me anything as long as it is told to me over the porcelain of a lavatory.'

'Interesting step you're doing there, Id, I have to say.'

'I beg without frequency. My home culture views begging as low-caste.'

'Hmm. Ars, I'm standing here thinking we could work something out, maybe.'

'I commit no illegal or degrading acts. But I will, if forced, beg.'

'Forget that. I'm just thinking. You're Muslimic, isn't that right?'

'Devoutly. I pray five times daily in the prescribed fashion. I eschew representational art and carnality in all its four-thousand-four-hundred-and-four forms and guises.'

'Body a temple and suchlike?

'I eschew. Neither stimulants nor depressing compounds pass my lips, as is prescribed in the holy teachings of my faith.'

'I'm wondering if you had any specific plans for this urine you're so anxious to get rid of, Ars, then.'

'I am not following.'

'What say we hash it all out over some porcelain, then, brother.'

'Mike Pemulis, you are in motion a prince and in repose a sage.'

'Brother, it'll be a cold day in a warm climate when this kid right here's in repose.'

It was strange upon strange; it was almost as if the legless and pathologically shy punting-groupies were somehow afraid of *Moment*'s Junoesque Ms. Steeply — Orin had seen his last wheelchair the day before she came up, and now (he realized, driving) it was only hours after she'd left that they were now back, with their shy ruses. The Excitement-Hope-Acquisition-Contempt cycle of seduction always left Orin stunned and wrung out and not at his quickest on the uptake. It was only after he'd cleaned up and dressed and exchanged the standard compliments and assurances, taken the elevator's glass pod down the tall hotel's round glass core into the lobby, gone out through the pressurized revolving door into the scalp-crackling gust of Phoenix heat, waited for the car's directional AC to render the steering wheel touchable, and then injected himself into the teeming arteries of Rt. 85 and Bell Rd. west, back out toward Sun City, ruminating as he drove, that it kertwanged on him that the handicapped man at the hotel room's door had had a wheelchair, that it was the first wheelchair he'd seen since Hal'd hit him with his theory, and that the legless surveyer had had (stranger) the same Swiss accent as the hand-model.

En route, R. Lenz's mouth writhes and he scratches at the little rhynophemic rash and sniffs terribly and complains of terrible late-autumn leaf-mold allergies, forgetting that Bruce Green knows all too well what coke-hydrolysis's symptoms are from having done so many lines himself, back when life with M. Bonk was one big party.

Lenz details how the vegetarian new Joel girl's veil is because of this condition people get where she's got only one eye that's right in the middle of her forehead, from birth, like a seahorse, and asks Green not even to think of asking how he knows this fact.

While Green acts as lookout while Lenz relieves himself against a Market St. dumpster, Lenz swears Green to secrecy about how poor old scarred-up diseased Charlotte Treat had sworn him to secrecy about her secret dream in sobriety was to someday get her G.E.D. and become a dental hygienist specializing in educating youngsters pathologically frightened of dental anesthesia, because her dream was to help youngsters, and but how she feared her Virus has placed her secret dream forever out of reach.[239]

All the way up the Spur's Harvard St. toward Union Square, in a barely NW vector, Lenz consumes several minutes and less than twenty breaths sharing with Green some painful Family-Of-Origin Issues about how Lenz's mother Mrs. Lenz, a thrice-divorcée and Data Processor, was so unspeakably obese she had to make her own mumus out of brocade drapes and cotton tablecloths and never once did come to Parents' Day at Bishop Anthony McDiardama Elementary School in Fall River MA because of the parents had to sit in the youngsters' little liftable-desktop desks during the Parents' Day presentations and skits, and the one time Mrs. L. hove her way down to B.A.M.E.S. for Parents' Day and tried to seat herself at little Randall L.'s desk between Mrs. Lamb and Mrs. Leroux she broke the desk into kindling and needed four stocky cranberry-farmer dads and a textbook-dolly to arise back up from the classroom floor, and never went back, fabricating thin excuses of busyness with Data Processing and basic disinterest in Randy L.'s schoolwork. Lenz shares how then in adolescence (his), his mother died because one day she was riding a Greyhound bus from Fall River MA north to Quincy MA to visit her son in a Commonwealth Youth Corrections facility Lenz was doing research for a possible screenplay in, and during the voyage on the bus she had to go potty, and she was in the bus's tiny potty in the rear of the bus going about her private business of going potty, as she later testified, and even though it was the height of winter she had the little window of the potty wide open, for reasons Lenz predicts Green doesn't want to hear about, on the northbound bus, and how this was one of the last years of Unsubsidized ordinational year-dating, and the final fiscal year that actual maintenance-work had ever been done on the infernous six-lane commuter-ravaged Commonwealth Route 24 from Fall River to Boston's South Shore by the pre-O.N.A.N.ite Governor Claprood's Commonwealth Highway Authority, and the Greyhound bus encountered a poorly marked UNDER CONSTRUCTION area where 24 was all stripped down to the dimpled-iron sheeting below and was tooth-rattlingly striated and chuckholed and torn up and just in general basically a mess, and the poorly marked and unflag-manned debris plus the excessive speed of the northbound bus made it jounce godawfully, the bus, and swerve violently to and forth, fighting to maintain control of what there was of the road, and passengers were hurled violently from their seats while, meanwhile, back in the closet-sized rear potty, Mrs. Lenz, right in the process of going potty, was hurled from the toilet by the first swerve and proceeded to do some high-velocity and human-waste-flinging pinballing back and forth against the potty's plastic walls; and when the bus finally regained total control and resumed course Mrs. Lenz had, freakishly enough, ended up her human pinballing with her bare and unspeakably huge backside wedged tight in the open window of the potty, so forcefully ensconced into the recesstacle that she was unable to extricate, and the bus continued on its northward sojourn the rest of the way up 24 with Mrs. Lenz's bare backside protruding from the ensconcing window, prompting car horns and derisive oratory from other vehicles; and Mrs. Lenz's plaintiff shouts for Help were unavailed by the passengers that were arising back up off the floor and rubbing their sore noggins and hearing Mrs. Lenz's mortified screams from behind the potty's locked reinforced plastic door, but were unable to excretate her because the potty's door locked from the interior by sliding across a deadbolt that made the door's outside say OCCUPIED/OCCUPADO/OCCUPÉ, and the door was locked, and Mrs. Lenz was wedged beyond the reach of arm-length and couldn't reach the deadbolt no matter how plaintiffly she reached out her mammoth fat-wattled arm; and, like fully 88% of all clinically obese Americans, Mrs. Lenz was diagnosed clinically claustrophobic and took prescription medication for anxiety and ensconcement-phobias, and she ended up successfully filing a Seven-Figure suit against Greyhound Lines and the almost-defunct Commonwealth Highway Authority for psychiatric trauma, public mortification, and second-degree frostbite, and received such a morbidly obese settlement from the Dukakis-appointed 18th-Circus Civil Court that when the check arrived, in an extra-long-size envelope to accommodate all the zeroes, Mrs. L. lost all will to Data Process or cook or clean, or nurture, or finally even move, simply reclining in a custom-designed 1.5-meter-wide recliner watching InterLace Gothic Romances and consuming mammoth volumes of high-lipid pastry brought on gold trays by a pastry chef she'd had put at her individual 24-hour disposal and outfitted with a cellular beeper, until four months after the huge settlement she ruptured and died, her mouth so crammed with peach cobbler the paramedics were hapless to administer C.P.R., which Lenz says he knows, by the way — C.P.R.

By the time they hit the Spur, their northwest tacking has wheeled broadly right to become more truly north. Their route down here is a Mondrian of alleys narrowed to near-defiles from all the dumpsters. Lenz goes first, blaze-trailing. Lenz gives these sort of smoky looks to every female that passes within eyeshot. Their vector is now mostly N/NW. They stroll through the rich smell of dryer-exhaust from the backside of a laundromat off Dustin and Comm. The city of metro Boston MA at night. The ding and trundle of the B and C Greenie trains heading up Comm. Ave.'s hill, west. Street-drunks sitting with their backs to sooted walls, seeming to study their laps, even the mist of their breath discolored. The complex hiss of bus-brakes. The jagged shadows distending with headlights' passage. Latin music drifting through the Spur's Projects, twined around some 5/4 'shine stuff from a boombox over off Feeny Park, and in between these a haunting plasm of Hawaiian-type music that sounds at once top-volume and far far away. The zithery drifting Polynesian strains make Bruce Green's face spread in a flat mask of psychic pain he doesn't even feel is there, and then the music's gone. Lenz asks Green what it's like to work with ice all day at Leisure Time Ice and then himself theorizes on what it must be like, he'll bet, with your crushed ice and ice cubes in pale-blue plastic bags with a staple for a Twistie and dry ice in wood tubs pouring out white smoke and then your huge blocks of industrial ice packed in fragrant sawdust, the huge blocks of man-sized ice with flaws way inside like trapped white faces, white flames of internal cracks. Your picks and hatchets and really big tongs, red knuckles and rimed windows and thin bitter freezer-smell with runny-nosed Poles in plaid coats and kalpacs, your older ones with a chronic cant to one side from all the time lugging ice.

They crunch through iridescent chunks of what Lenz I.D.s as a busted windshield. Lenz shares feelings on how between three ex-husbands and feral attorneys and a pastry-chef that used pastry-dependence to warp and twist her into distorting a testament toward the chef and Lenz's being through red-tape still in Quincy's Y.C.A. hold and in a weak litigational vantage, the ruptured Mrs. L.'s will had left him out in the cold to self-fend by his urban wits while ex-husbands and patissiers lay on Riviera beach-furniture fanning themselves with high-denomination currency, about all which Lenz says he grapples with the Issues of on a like daily basis; leaving

Green a gap to make understanding sounds. Green's jacket creaks as he breathes. The windshield-glass is in an alley whose fire escapes are hung with what look like wet frozen tarps. The alley's tight-packed dumpsters and knobless steel doors and the dull black of total grime. The blunt snout of a bus protrudes into the frame of the alley's end, idling.

Dumpsters' garbage doesn't have just one smell, depending. The urban lume makes the urban night only semidark, as in licoricey, a luminescence just under the skin of the dark, and swelling. Green keeps them updated re time. Lenz has begun to refer to Green as 'brother.' Lenz says he has to piss like a racehorse. He says the nice thing about the urban city is that it's one big commode. The way Lenz pronounces *brother* involves one *r*. Green moves up to stand in the mouth of the alley, facing out, giving Lenz a little privacy several dumpsters behind. Green stands there in the start of the alley's shadow, in the bus's warm backwash, his elbows out and hands in the jacket's little pockets, looking out. It's unclear whether Green knows Lenz is under the influence of Bing. All he feels is a moment of deep wrenching loss, of wishing getting high was still pleasurable for him so he could get high. This feeling comes and goes all day every day, still. Green takes a gasper from behind his ear and lights it and puts a fresh one on-deck behind the ear. Union Square, Allston: Kiss me where it smells, she said, so I took her to Allston, unquote. Union Square's lights throb. Whenever somebody stops blowing their horn somebody else starts blowing their horn. There's three Chinese women waiting at the light across the street from the guy with the lobsters. Each of them's got a shopping bag. An old VW Bug like Doony Glynn's VW Bug idling mufflerless outside Riley's Roast Beef, except Doony's Bug's engine is exposed where the back hood got removed to expose the Bug's guts. It's like impossible to ever spot a Chinese woman on a Boston street that's under sixty or over 1.5 m. or not carrying a shopping bag, except never more than one bag. If you close your eyes on a busy urban sidewalk the sound of everybody's different footwear's footsteps all put together sounds like something getting chewed by something huge and tireless and patient. The searing facts of the case of Bruce Green's natural parents' deaths when he was a toddler are so deeply repressed inside Green that whole strata and substrata of silence and mute dumb animal suffering will have to be strip-mined up and dealt with a Day at a Time in sobriety for Green even to remember how, on his fifth Xmas Eve, in Waltham MA, his Pop had taken the hydrant-sized little Brucie Green aside and given him, to give his beloved Mama for Xmas, a gaily Gauguin-colored can of Polynesian Mauna Loa-brand[240] macadamia nuts, said cylindrical can of nuts then toted upstairs by the child and painstakingly wrapped in so much foil-sheen paper that the final wrapped present looked like an oversized dachshund that had required first bludgeoning and then restraint at both ends with two rolls each of Scotch tape and garish fuchsia ribbon to be subdued and wrapped and placed under the gaily lit pine, and even then the package seemed mushily to struggle as the substrata of paper shifted and settled.

Bruce Green's Pop Mr. Green had at one time been one of New England's most influential aerobics instructors — even costarring once or twice, in the decade before digital dissemination, on the widely rented *Buns of Steel* aerobics home-video series — and had been in high demand and very influential until, to his horror, in his late twenties, the absolute prime of an aerobics instructor's working life, either one of Mr. Green's legs began spontaneously to grow or the other leg began spontaneously to retract, because within weeks one leg was all of a sudden nearly six inches longer than the other — Bruce Green's one unrepressed visual memory of the man is of a man who progressively and perilously *leaned* as he hobbled from specialist to specialist — and he had to get outfitted with a specialized orthopedic boot, black as a cauldron, that seemed to be 90% sole and resembled an asphalt-spreader's clunky boot, and weighed several pounds, and looked absurd with Spandex leggings; and the long and short of it was that Brucie Green's Pop was aerobically washed up by the leg and boot, and had to career-change, and went bitterly to work for a Waltham novelty or notions concern, something with 'N in the name, Acme Novelties 'N Notions or some such, where Mr. Green designed sort of sadistic practical-joke supplies, specializing in the Jolly Jolt Hand Buzzer and Blammo Cigar product-lines, with a sideline in entomological icecubes and artificial dandruff, etc. Demoralizing, sedentary, character-twisting work, is what an older child would have been able to understand, peering from his nightlit doorway at an unshaven man who clunkily paced away the wee hours on a nightly basis down in the living room, his gait like a bosun's in heavy seas, occasionally breaking into a tiny tentative gluteal-thruster squat-and-kick, almost falling, muttering bitterly, carrying a Falstaff tallboy.

Something touching about a gift that a toddler's so awfully overwrapped makes a sickly-pale and neurasthenic but doting Mrs. Green, Bruce's beloved Mama, choose the mugged-dachshund-foil-sheen-cylinder present first, of course, to open, on Xmas morning, as they sit before the crackling fireplace in different chairs by different windows with views of Waltham sleet, with bowls of Xmas snacks and Acme-'N-logoed mugs of cocoa and hazelnut decaf and watch each other taking turns opening gifts. Brucie's little face aglow in the firelight as the unwrapping of the nuts proceeds through layer and stratum, Mrs. Green a couple times having to use her teeth on the rinds of tape. Finally the last layer is off and the gay-colored can in view. Mauna Loa: Mrs. Green's favorite and most decadent special-treat food. World's highest-calorie food except for like pure suet. Nuts so yummy they should be spelled S-I-N, she says. Brucie excitedly bobbing in his chair, spilling cocoa and Gummi Bears, a loving toddler, more excited about his gift's receipt than what he's going to get himself. His mother's clasped hands before her sunken bosom. Sighs of delight and protest. And an EZ-Open Lid, on the can.

Which the contents of the macadamia-labelled can is really a coiled cloth snake with an ejaculatory spring. The snake sprongs out as Mrs. G. screams, a hand to her throat. Mr. Green howls with bitterly professional practical-gag mirth and clunks over and slaps little Bruce on the back so hard that Brucie expels a lime Gummi Bear he'd been eating — this too a visual memory, contextless and creepy — which arcs across the living room and lands in the fireplace's fire with a little green *siss* of flame. The cloth snake's arc has terminated at the imitation-crystal chandelier overhead, where the snake gets caught and hangs with quivering spring as the chandelier swings and tinkles and Mr. Green's thigh-slapping laughter takes a while to run down even as Brucie's Mama's hand at her delicate throat becomes claw-shaped and she claws at her throat and gurgles and slumps over to starboard with a fatal cardiac, her cyanotic mouth still open in surprise. For the first couple minutes Mr. Green thinks she's putting them on, and he keeps rating her performance on an Acme interdepartmental 1-8 Gag Scale until he finally gets pissed off and starts saying she's drawing the gag out too long, that she's going to scare their little Brucie who's sitting there under the swinging crystal, wide-eyed and silent.

And Bruce Green uttered not another out-loud word until his last year of grade school, living by then in Winchester with his late mother's sister, a decent but Dustbowly-looking Seventh-Day Adventist who never once pressed Brucie to speak, probably out of sympathy, probably sympathizing with the searing pain the opaque-eyed child must have felt over not only giving his Mama a lethal Xmas present but over then having to watch his widowed asymetrical Pop cave psycho-spiritually in after the wake, watching Mr. Green pace-and-clunk around the living room all night every night after work and an undermicrowaved supper-for-two, in his Frankensteinian boot, clunking around in circles, scratching slowly at his face and arms until he looked less scourged than brambled, and in loosely associated mutters cursing God and himself and Acme Nuts 'N Serpents or whatever, and leaving the fatal snake up hanging from the fake-crystal fixture and the fatal Xmas tree up in its little red metal stand until all the strings of lights went out and the strings of popcorn got dark and hard and the stand's bowl of water evaporated so the tree's needles died and fell brownly off onto the rest of the still-unopened Xmas presents clustered below, one of which was a package of Nebraska corn-fed steaks whose cherub-motif wrapping was beginning ominously to swell . . . ; and then finally the even more searing childhood pain of the public arrest and media-scandal and Sanity Hearing and Midwest trial as it was established after the fact that the post-Xmas Mr. Green — whose one encouraging sign of holding some tattered remnants of himself together after the funeral had been the fact that he still went faithfully every day to work at Acme Inc. — had gone in and packed a totally random case of the company's outgoing Blammo Cigars with vengefully lethal tetryl-based high explosives, and a V.F.W., three Rotarians, and 24 Shriners had been grotesquely decapitated across Southeastern Ohio before the federal A.T.F. traced the grisly forensic fragments back to B. Green Sr.'s Blammo lab, in Waltham; and then the extradition and horribly complex Sanity Hearing and trial and controversial sentencing; and then the appeals and deathwatch and Lethal Injection, Bruce Green's aunt handing out poorly reproduced W. Miller tracts to the crowds outside the Ohio prison as the clock ticked down to Injection, little Bruce in tow, blank-faced and watching, the crowd of media and anti-Capital activists and Defarge-like picnickers milling and roiling, many T-shirts for sale, and the red-faced men in sportcoats and fezzes, oh their rage-twisted faces the same red as their fezzes as the men careened this way and that in their little cars, formations of motorized Shriners buzzing the gates of the O.D.C.-Maximum facility and shouting *Burn Baby Burn* or the more timely *Get Lethally Injected Baby Get Lethally Injected,* Bruce Green's aunt with her center-parted hair visibly graying under the pillbox hat and face obscured for three Ohio months behind the black mesh veil that fluttered from the pillbox hat, clutching little Bruce's head to her underwired bosom day after day until his blank face was smooshed in on one side. . . . Green's guilt, pain, fear and self-loathing have over years of unprescribed medication been compressed to the igneous point where he now knows only that he compulsively avoids any product or service with 'N in its name, always checks a palm before a handshake, will go blocks out of his way to avoid any parade involving fezzes in little cars, and has this silent, substratified fascination/horror gestalt about all things even remotely Polynesian. It's probably the distant and attenuated luau-music echoing erratically back and forth through angled blocks of Allston cement that causes Bruce Green to wander as if mesmerized out of Union Square and all the way up Comm. Ave. into Brighton and up to like the corner of Comm. Ave. and Brainerd Road, the home of The Unexamined Life nightclub with its tilted flickering bottle of blue neon over the entrance, before he realizes that Lenz is no longer beside him asking the time, that Lenz hadn't followed him up the hill even though Green had stood there outside the Union Square alley way longer than anybody could have needed to take a legitimate whiz.

He and Lenz have become separated, he realizes. Now way southwest of Union on Comm., Green looks around at traffic and T-tracks and bar-patrons and T.U.L.'s huge bottle's low-neon flutter. He wonders whether he's somehow blown Lenz off or whether Lenz's blown him off, and that's all he wonders, that's the total complexity the speculation assumes, that's his thought for the minute. It's like the whole nut-can-and-cigar traumas drained into some psychic sump at puberty, sank and left only an oily slick that catches the light in distorted ways. The warbly Polynesian music's way clearer up here. He starts up the steep hill on Brainerd Rd., which terminates at the Enfield line. Maybe Lenz can't move straightforwardly south at all past a certain time. The acclivity is not kind to asphalt-spreader's boots. After the initial crazed-gerbil-in-brain phase of early Withdrawal and detox, Bruce Green has now returned to his normal psychorepressed cerebral state where he has about one fully developed thought every sixty seconds, and then just one at a time, a thought, each materializing already fully developed and sitting there and then melting back away like a languid liquid-crystal display. His Ennet House counselor, the extremely tough-loving Calvin T., complains that listening to Green is like listening to a faucet with a very slow drip. His rap is that Green seems not serene or detached but totally shut down, disassociated, and Calvin T. tries weekly to draw Green out by pissing him off. Green's next full thought is the realization that even though the hideous Hawaiian music had sounded like it was drifting up northward from down at the Allston Spur, it's somewhat louder now the farther west he moves toward Enfield's Cambridge St. dogleg and St. Elizabeth's Hospital. Brainerd between Commonwealth and Cambridge St. is a sine wave of lung-busting hills through neighborhoods Tiny Ewell had described as Depressed Residential, unending rows of crammed-together triple-decker houses with those tiny sad architectural differences that seem to highlight the essential sameness, with sagging porches and psoriatic paint-jobs or aluminum siding gone carbuncular from violent temperature-swings, yard-litter and dishes and patchy grass and fenced pets and children's toys lying around in discarded attitudes and eclectic food-smells and wildly different-patterned curtains or blinds in a house's different windows due to these old houses are carved up inside into apartments for like alienated B.U. students or Canadian and Concavity-displaced families or even more alienated B.C. students, or probably it looks like the bulk of the lease-holders are Green-and-Bonkesque younger blue-collar hard-partying types that have posters of the Fiends In Human Shape or Choosy Mothers or Snout or the Bioavailable Five[241] in the bathroom and black lights in the bedroom and oil-change stains in the driveway and that throw their supper dishes into the yard and buy new dishes at Caldor instead of washing their dishes and that still, in their twenties, ingest Substances nightly and use *party* as a verb and put their sound-systems' speakers in their apartments' windows facing out and crank the volume out of sheer high-spirit obnoxiousness because they still have their girlfriends to pound beers with and do shotguns of dope into the mouth of and do lines of Bing off various parts of the naked body of, and still find pounding beers and doing bongs and lines fun and get to have fun on a nightly after-work basis, cranking the tunes out into the neighborhood air. The street's bare trees are densely limbed, they're a certain type of tree, they look like inverted brooms in the residential dark, Green doesn't know his tree-names. The Hawaiian music is what's pulled him southwest, it emerges: it's originating from someplace in this very neighborhood somewhere around W. Brainerd, and Green moves upriver toward what sounds like the source of the sound with a blankly horrified fascination. Most of the yards are fenced in stainless-steel chain-link fencing, and occasional yard-dogs whine or more commonly bark and snarl and leap territorially at Green from behind their fences, the fences shivering from the impact and the chain-link stuff dented outward from previous impacts from previous passersby. The thought that he isn't scared of dogs develops and recedes in Green's midbrain. His jacket creaks with every step. The temperature is steadily dropping. The fenced front yards are the toy-and-beer-can-strewn type where the brown grass grows in uneven tufts and the leaves haven't been raked and are piled in wind-blown lines of force along the base of the fence and unpruned hedges and overfull wastebaskets and untwisted trash-bags are on the sagging porch because nobody's gotten around to taking them down to the E.W.D. dumpster at the corner and garbage from the overfull receptacles blows out into the yard and mixes with the leaves along the fences' base and some gets out into the street and is never picked up and eventually becomes part of the composition of the street. A nonpeanut M&M box is like intaglioed into the concrete of the sidewalk under Green, so bleached by the elements it's turned bone-white and is only barely identifiable as a nonpeanut M&M box, for instance. And, looking up from identifying the M&M box's make, Green now espies Randy Lenz. Green has happened upon Lenz, way up here on Brainerd, now strolling briskly alone up ahead of Green, not close but visible under a functioning streetlight about a block farther uphill on Brainerd. There's some disincentive to call out. The incline on this block isn't bad. It's cold enough now so his breath looks the same whether he's smoking or not. The tall curved streetlamps here look to Green just like the weaponish part of the Martian vessels that fired fatal rays in their conquest of the planet in an ancient cartridge Tommy Doocy'd never tired of that he labelled the case 'War of the Welles.' The Hawaiian music dominates the aural landscape by this point, now, coming from someplace up near where he sees the back of Lenz's coat. Someone has put Polynesian-music speakers in their window, pretty clearly. Creepy slack-key steel guitar balloons across the dim street, booms off the sagging facades opposite, it's Don Ho and the Sol Hoopi Players, the grass-skirt-and-foamy-breakers sound that makes Green put his fingers in his ears while at the same time he moves more urgently toward the Hawaiian-music source, a pink or aqua three-decker with a second-floor dormer and red-shingled roof with a blue and white Quenucker flag on a pole protruding from a window in the dormer and serious JBL speakers facing outward in the two windows on either side of the flag, with the screens off so you can see the woofers throbbing like brown bellies hula-ing, bathing the 1700 block of W. Brainerd in dreadful ukuleles and hollow-log percussives. All the blunt fingers in his ears do is add the squeak of Green's pulse and the underwater sound of his respiration to the music, though. Figures in plaid-flannel or else floral Hawaiian shirts and those flower necklaces melt in and out of lit view behind and over the window-speakers with the oozing quality of large-group chemical fun and dancing and social intercoursing. The lit windows make slender rectangles of light out across the yard, which the yard is a sty. Something about Randy Lenz's movements up ahead, the high-kneed tiptoed skulk of a vaudeville fiend up to no good at all, keeps Green from calling out to him even if he could have made himself heard over what to him is a roar of blood and breath and Ho. Lenz moves through the one operative streetlight's cone across the sidewalk and over to the stainless chain-link of the same Quenucker house, holding something out to a Shetland-sized dog whose leash is attached to a fluorescent-plastic clotheslisey thing by a pulley, and can slide. It's cold and the air is thin and keen and his fingers are icy in his ears, which ache with cold. Green watches, rapt on levels he doesn't know he has, drawn slowly forward, moving his head from side to side to keep from losing Lenz in the fog of his breath, not calling out, but transfixed. Green and Mildred Bonk and the other couple they'd shared a trailer with T. Doocy with had gone through a phase one time where they'd crash various collegiate parties and mix with the upper-scale collegiates, and once in one February Green found himself at a Harvard U. dorm where they were having a like Beach-Theme Party, with a dumptruck's worth of sand on the common-room floor and everybody with flower necklaces and skin bronzed with cream or UV-booth-salon visits, all the towheaded guys in floral untucked shirts walking around with lockjawed *noblest oblige* and drinking drinks with umbrellas in them or else wearing Speedos with no shirts and not one fucking pimple anyplace on their back and pretending to surf on a surfboard somebody had nailed to a hump-shaped wave made of blue and white papier mâché with a motor inside that made the fake wave sort of undulate, and all the girls in grass skirts oozing around the room trying to hula in a shimmying way that showed their thighs' LipoVac scars through the shimmying grass of their skirts, and Mildred Bonk had donned a grass skirt and bikini-top out of the pile by the keggers and even though almost seven months pregnant had oozed and shimmied right into the mainstream of the swing of things, but Bruce Green had felt awkward and out of place in his cheap leather jacket and haircut he'd dyed orange with gasoline in a blackout and the EAT THE RICH patch he'd perversely let Mildred Bonk sew onto the groin of his police-pants, and then they'd finally got tired of the 'Hawaii Five-0' theme and started in with the Don Ho and Sol Hoopi CDs, and Green had gotten so uncomfortably fascinated and repelled and paralyzed by the Polynesian tunes that he'd set up a cabana-chair right by the kegs and had sat there overworking the pump on the kegs and downing one plastic cup after another of beer-foam until he got so blind drunk his sphincter had failed and he'd not only pissed but also actually *shit* his pants, for only the second time ever, and the first public time ever, and was mortified with complexly layered shame, and had to ease very gingerly into the nearest-by head and remove his pants and wipe himself off like a fucking baby, having to shut one eye to make sure which him he saw was him, and then there'd been nothing to do with the fouled police-pants but crack the bathroom door and reach a tattooed arm out with the pants and bury them in the living room's sand like a housecat's litterbox, and then of course what was he supposed to put on if he ever wanted to leave that head or dorm again, to get home, so he'd had to hold one eye shut and reach one arm out again and like strain to reach the pile of grass skirts and bikini-tops and snatch a grass skirt, and put it on, and slip out of the Hawaiian dorm out a side door without letting anybody see him, and then ride the Red Line and C-Greenie and then a bus all the way home in February in a cheap leather jacket and asphalt-spreader's boots and a grass skirt, the grass of which rode up in the most horrifying way, and he'd spent the next three days not leaving the trailer in the Spur, in a paralyzing depression of unknown etiology, lying on Tommy D.'s crusty-stained sofa and drinking Southern Comfort straight out of the bottle and watching Doocy's snakes not move once in three days, in their tank, and Mildred had given him two days of high-volume shit for first sulking antisocially by the keg and then screwing out and abandoning her at seven months gone to a sandy room full of tanly anomic blondes who said catty things about her tattoos and creepy boys who talked without moving their lower jaw and asked her things like where she 'summered' and kept offering her advice on no-load funds and inviting her upstairs to check out their Dürer prints and saying they found overweight girls terribly compelling in their defiance of culturo-ascetic norms, and Bruce Green lay there with a head full of Hoopi and unresolved pain and didn't say a word or even have a fully developed thought for three days, and had hidden the grass skirt under the dustruffle of the couch and later savagely torn it to shreds and sprinkled the clippings over Doocy's hydroponic-marijuana development in the tub, for mulch. Lenz goes in and out of Green's focus several times within a dozen andante strides, still out in front of the Canadian-refugee-type house that's drawn Green on, Lenz holding a little can of something up over one side of the fence's gate and dribbling something onto the gate, holding something else that suddenly engages the dog's full attention. For some reason Green thinks to check his watch. The pink or orange clothesline quivers as the leash's pulley runs along it as the dog comes up to meet Lenz inside the gate he's slowly opened. The huge dog seems neither friendly nor unfriendly toward Lenz, but his attention is engaged. The leash and pulley could never hold him if he decided Lenz was food. There's bitter-smelling material from his ear on Green's finger, which he can't help but sniff. He's forgotten and left the other finger in his ear. He's now pretty close, standing in a van's shadow just outside the pyramid of sodium light from the streetlight, like two houses down from the source of the grisly sound, which all of a sudden is in the silence between cuts of Ho's early *Don Ho: From Hawaii With All My Love,* so that Green can hear baritone Canadianese party-voices through the open windows and also the low lalations of baby-talk of some sort from Lenz, 'Pooty ooty doggy woggy' and whatnot, presumably directed at the dog, who's coming over to Lenz in a sort of neutrally cautious but attentive way. Green has no clue what kind of dog it is, but it's big. Green can remember not the sight but the two very different sounds of the footfalls of his Pop the late Mr. Green pacing the Waltham living room, the crinkle of the paper bag around the tallboy in his hand. It's well after 2245h. The dog's leash slides hissing to the end of the Day-Glo line and stops the dog a couple paces from the inside of the gate, where Lenz is standing, inclined in the slight forward way of somebody who's talking baby-talk to a dog. Green can see that Lenz has a slightly gnawed square of Don G.'s hard old meatloaf out in front of him, holding it toward the straining dog. Lenz has the blankly intent look of a short-haired man with a Geiger counter. The hideously compelling Ho starts again with the total abruptness that makes CDs so creepy. Green's got one finger in one ear, shifting around slightly to keep Lenz's lampshadow from blocking the view. The music balloons and booms. The Nucks have turned it way up for 'My Lovely Launa-Una Luau Lady,' a song that's always made Green want to put his head through a window. Part of the instrumentals sounds like a harp on acid. The hollow-log percussives are like a heart in your extremest-type terror. Green fancies he can see windows in the houses opposite vibrate from the horrific vibration. Green's having way more than one thought p.m. now, the squeak of the gerbil-wheel starting to crank deep inside. The undulating shiver is a slack-steel guitar that fills little Brucie's head with white sand and undulating tummies and heads that resemble New Year's subsidized parade balloons, huge soft shiny baggy wrinkled grinning heads nodding and bobbing as they slowly inflate to the shape of a giant head, tilted forward, straining at the ropes they're pulled by. Green hasn't watched a New Year's parade since the Year of the Tucks Medicated Pad's, which had been obscene. Green's close enough to see that the Hawaiianized Nuck house is 412 W. Brainerd. Blue-collar-type cars and 4×4s and vans are all up and down the street packed in in a somehow partyish attitude, as in parked in a hurry, some of them with Canadian lettering on the plates. Fleur-de-lis stickers and slogans in Canadian on some of the windows also. An old Montego cammed out into a slingshot dragster is parked square in front of 412 in a sort of menacing way with two wheels up on the curb and a circle of flowers hung jauntily over the antenna, and the ellipses of dull fade in the paintjob of the hood that show the engine's been bored out and the hood gets real hot, and Lenz has gotten down on one knee and breaks off some of the meatloaf and tosses it underhand to the ground inside the leash's range. The dog goes over and lowers its head to the meat. The distinctive sound of Gately's meatloaf getting chewed plus the ghastly music's zithery warbling roar. Lenz now rises and his movements in the yard have a melting and wraithlike quality in the different shades of shadow. The lit window farthest from the limp flag has solid swarthy guys in beards and loud shirts passing back and forth snapping their fingers under their elbows with flower-strewn females in tow. Many of the heads are thrown back and attached to Molson bottles. Green's jacket creaks as he tries to breathe. The snake had leapt from the can with a sound like: *spronnnnng*. His aunt at the Winchester breakfast nook, in dazzling winter dawnlight, quietly doing a word-search puzzle. Two dormer windows are half-blocked by the throbbing rectangles of the JBLs. Green's the type that can recognize a JBL speaker and Molson-green bottle from way far away.

A developed thought coheres: Ho's voice has the quality of a type of: *ointment*.

Any displaced and shaggy Nuck head in these windows chancing to look out into the yard now would be able to probably see Lenz depositing another chunk of meat in front of the pet and removing something from up near his shoulder under his topcoat as he's melting stealthily all the way around behind the dog to sort of straddle the big dog from the rear, easing the last of the loaf down in front of the dog, the big dog hunched, the crunch of Don's cornflake topping and the goopy sound of a dog eating institutional meat. The arm comes out from under the coat and goes up with something that looks like it would glitter if the windows' yardlight reached far enough. Bruce Green keeps trying to wave his breath out of the way. Lenz's fine coat billows around the dog's flanks as Lenz braces and leans and gathers the hunched thing's scruff in one hand and straightens up with a mighty grunting hoist that brings the animal up onto its hind legs as its front legs dig frantically at empty air, and the dog's whine brings a lei-and-flannel shape to the lit space above one speaker overhead. Green doesn't even think of calling out from his shadowed spot, and the moment hangs there with the dog upright and Lenz behind it, bringing the upraised hand down in front and hard across the dog's throat. There's a lightless arc from the spot Lenz's hand crossed; the arc splatters the gate and the sidewalk outside it. The music balloons without cease but Green hears Lenz say what sounds like 'How *dare* you' with great emphasis as he drops the dog forward onto the yard as there's a high-pitched male sound from the form at the window and the dog goes down and hits the ground on its side with the meaty crunch of a 32-kilo bag of Party-Size Cubelets, all four legs dog-paddling uselessly, the dark surface of the lawn blackening in a pulsing curve before its jaws that open and close. Green has moved unthinking out of the vanshadow toward

Lenz and now thinks and stops between two trees by the street in front of 416 wanting to call to Lenz and feeling the strangled aphasia people feel in bad dreams, and so just stands there between the treetrunks with a finger in one ear, looking. The way Lenz stands over the hull of the big dog is like you stand over a punished child, at full height and radiating authority, and the moment hangs there distended like that until there's the shriek of long-shut windows opening against the Ho and the dire sound of numerous high-tempo logger's boots rushing down stairs inside 412. The creepily friendly bachelor that lived next to his aunt had had two big groomed dogs and when Bruce passed the house the dogs' toenails would scrabble on the wood of the front porch and run with their tails up to the anodized fence as Bruce came by and jump up and like sort of *play* the metal fence with their paws, excited to see him. To just like set eyes on him. Lenz's arm with the knife is up again and ungleaming in the streetlight's light as Lenz uses his other hand on the top of the fence to vault the fence sideways and tear-ass uphill up Brainerd Rd. in the southwest direction of Enfield, his loafers making a quality sound on the pavement and his open coat filling like a sail. Green retreats to behind one of the trees as beefy flannel forms with leis shedding petals, their speech grunty-foreign and unmistakably Canadian, a couple with ukuleles, spill out like ants over the sagging porch and into the yard, mill and jabber, a couple kneel by the form of the former dog. A bearded guy so huge a Hawaiian shirt looks tight on him has picked up the meat-loaf's baggie. Another guy without very much hair picks what looks like a white caterpillar out of the dark grass and holds it up delicately between his thumb and finger, looking at it. Yet another huge guy in suspenders drops his beer and picks up the limp dog and it lies across his arms on its back with its head way back like a swooned girl, dripping and with one leg still going, and the guy is either screaming or singing. The original massive Nuck with the baggie clutches his head to signal agitation as he and two other Nucks run heavily to the slingshot Montego. A first-floor light in the house across Brainerd lights up and backlights a figure in a sort of suit and metal wheel-chair sitting right up next to the window in the sideways way of wheelchairs that want to get right up next to something, scanning the street and Nuck-swarmed yard. The Hawaiian music has apparently stopped, but not abruptly, it's not like somebody took it off in the middle. Green has retreat-ed to behind a tree, which he sort of one-arm-hugs. A thick girl in a hor-rible grass skirt is saying 'Dyu!' several times. There are obscenities and heavily accented stock phrases like 'Stop!' and 'There he goes!,' with point-ing. Several guys are running up the sidewalk after Lenz, but they're in boots, and Lenz is way ahead and now disappears as he cuts like a tailback left and disappears down either an alley or a serious driveway, though you can still hear his fine shoes. One of the guys actually shakes his fist as he gives chase. The Montego with the twin cam reveals muffler problems and clunks down off the curb and lays two parentheses as it 180s professionally around in the middle of the street and peels out up in Lenz's direction, a very low and fast and no-shit car, its antenna's gay lei tugged by speed into a strained ellipse and leaving a wake of white petals that take forever to stop falling. Green thinks his finger might be frozen to his ear's inside. Nobody seems to be gesticulating about anything about maybe an accomplice. There's no evidence they're looking around for any other unwittingly guilty accessory-type party. Another wheelchaired form has appeared just behind and to the right of the first seated backlit form across the street, and they're both in a position to see Green up against the tree with his hand to his ear so it looks like he's maybe receiving communiqués from some kind of earpiece. The Nucks are still milling around the yard in a way that's indescribably foreign as the one Nuck staggers in circles under the weight of the expired dog, saying something to the sky. Green is getting to know this one tree very well, spread out against its lee side and breathing into the bark of the tree so his exhaled breath won't plume out from behind the tree and be seen as an accomplice's breath, potentially.

Mario Incandenza's nineteenth birthday will be Wednesday 25 November, the day before Thanksgiving. His insomnia worsens as Madame Psychosis's hiatus enters its third week and WYYY tries bringing back poor Miss Diagnosis again, who's started in on a Pig-Latin reading of the Revelation of John that makes you so embarrassed for her it's uncomfortable. For a couple nights in the HmH living room he tries falling asleep to WODS, an AM-fringe outfit that plays narcotizing orchestral arrangements of old Carpenters songs. It makes things worse. It's weird to feel like you miss someone you're not even sure you know.

He gets a serious burn on his pelvis leaning against a hot steel stove talking to Mrs. Clarke. His hip is swaddled in bandages under Orin's old corduroys, and there's a sucking sound of salve when he walks, late at night, unable to sleep. The birth-related disability that wasn't even definitively diagnosed until Mario was six and had let Orin tattoo his shoulder with the red coil of an immersion heater is called Familial Dysautonomia, a neurological deficit whereby he can't feel physical pain very well. A lot of the E.T.A.s kid him about they should have such problems, and even Hal's sometimes felt a twinge of envy about it, but the defect is a serious hassle and actually very dangerous, see for instance the burnt pelvis, which wasn't even discovered until Mrs. Clarke thought she smelled her eggplant overcooking.

At HmH he lies on the air mattress in a tight down bag on the edge of the violet plant-light with the wind rattling the big east window, listening to buttery violins and what sounds like a zither. There's sometimes a scream upstairs, shrill and drawn out, from where C.T.'s and the Moms's rooms are. Mario listens closely for whether the sound ends up as Avril laughing or Avril screaming. She gets night terrors, which are like nightmares but worse, and which afflict small children and apparently also adults who eat the day's biggest meal right before bed.

His nighttime prayers take almost an hour and sometimes more and are not a chore. He doesn't kneel; it's more like a conversation. And he's not crazy, it's not like he hears anybody or anything conversing back with him, Hal's established.

Hal had asked him when he'll start coming back to their room to sleep, which made Mario feel good.

He keeps trying to imagine Madame Psychosis — whom he imagines as being very tall — lying in an XL beach chair on a beach smiling and not saying anything for days, resting. But it doesn't work very well.

He can't tell if Hal is sad. He is having a harder and harder time reading Hal's states of mind or whether he's in good spirits. This worries him. He used to be able to sort of preverbally know in his stomach generally where Hal was and what he was doing, even if Hal was far away and playing or if Mario was away, and now he can't anymore. Feel it. This worries him and feels like when you've lost something important in a dream and you can't even remember what it was but it's important. Mario loves Hal so much it makes his heart beat hard. He doesn't have to wonder if the difference now is him or his brother because Mario never changes.

He hadn't told the Moms he was going to walk around after he left her office after their interface: Avril usually tries in a nonintrusive way to discourage Mario from taking walks at night, because he doesn't see well at night, and the areas around the E.T.A. hill are not the best neighborhood, and there's no skirting the fact that Mario would be easy prey for just about anybody, physically. And, though one perk of Familial Dysautonomia is a relative physical fearlessness,[242] Mario keeps to a pretty limited area during insomniacal strolls, out of deference to Avril's worry.[243] He'll sometimes walk around the grounds of the Enfield Marine P.H.H. at the bottom of the hill's east side because they're pretty much enclosed, the grounds are, and he knows a couple of the E.M. Security officers from when his father got them to portray Boston police in his whimsical *Dial C for Concupiscence;* and he likes the E.M. grounds at night because the different brick houses' window-light is yellow lamplight[244] and he can see people on the ground floors all together playing cards or talking or watching TP. He also likes whitewashed brick regardless of its state of upkeep. And a lot of the people in the different brick houses are damaged or askew and lean hard to one side or are twisted into themselves, through the windows, and he can feel his heart going out into the world through them, which is good for insomnia. A woman's voice, calling for help without any real urgency — not like the screams that signify the Moms laughing or screaming at night — sounds from a darkened upper window. And across the little street that's crammed with cars everybody has to move at 0000h. is Ennet's House, where the Headmistress has a disability and had had a wheelchair ramp installed and has twice invited Mario in during the day for a Caffeine-Free Millennial Fizzy, and Mario likes the place: it's crowded and noisy and none of the furniture has protective plastic wrap, but nobody notices anybody else or comments on a disability and the Headmistress is kind to the people and the people cry in front of each other. The inside of it smells like an ashtray, but Mario's felt good both times in Ennet's House because it's very real; people are crying and making noise and getting less unhappy, and once he heard somebody say *God* with a straight face and nobody looked at them or looked down or smiled in any sort of way where you could tell they were worried inside.

People from the public can't be in there after 2300, though, because they have a Curfew, so Mario just totters past on the broken sidewalk and looks in the ground windows at all the different people. Every window is lit up with light and some are slid partly open, and there is the noise of being outside a house full of people. From one of the upstairs windows facing the street comes a voice going 'Give it here, give it here.' Someone is crying and someone else is either laughing or coughing very hard. An irritable man's voice from a kitchen window at the side says something to somebody else that just said something like 'So get dentures,' followed by curse words. Another upstairs window, over at the side by the wheelchair ramp and the kitchen window where the ground is soft enough to take the stress of a police lock and lead block nicely, the upper window has a billowing lengthwise flag for a curtain and an old bumper sticker on the glass half scraped off so it says *ONE DAY A* in cursive, and Mario is arrested by the quiet but unmistakable sound of a recording of a broadcast of 'Sixty Minutes More or Less with Madame Psychosis,' which Mario has never taped a show of because he feels it wouldn't be right for him but is strangely thrilled to hear someone in Ennet's thinking enough of to tape and replay. What's coming from behind the open window with a billowing flag for a curtain is one of the old ones, from the Year of the Wonderchicken, Madame's inaugural year, when she'd sometimes talk all hour and had an accent. A hard east wind blows Mario's thin hair straight back off his head. His standing angle is 50°. A female girl in a little fur coat and uncomfortable-looking bluejeans and tall shoes clicks past on the sidewalk and goes up the ramp into Ennet's back door without indicating she saw somebody with a really big head standing braced by a police lock on the lawn outside the kitchen window. The lady had had on so much makeup she'd looked unwell but the wake of her passage smells very good. For some reason Mario felt like the person behind the flag in the window was also a female. Mario thinks it might not be out of the question that she might lend tapes to a fellow listener if he could ask. He usually checks etiquette questions with Hal, who is incredibly knowledgeable and smart. When he thinks of Hal his heart beats and his forehead's thick skin becomes wrinkled. Hal will also know the term for private tapes made of broadcast things on the air. Perhaps this lady owns multiple tapes. This one is from 'Sixty Minutes +/−' 's first year, when Madame still had a slight accent and often spoke on the show as if she were talking exclusively to one person or character who was very important to her. The Moms revealed that if you're not crazy then speaking to someone who isn't there is termed *apostrophe* and is valid art. Mario'd fallen in love with the first Madame Psychosis programs because he felt like he was listening to someone sad read out loud from yellow letters she'd taken out of a shoebox on a rainy P.M., stuff about heartbreak and people you loved dying and U.S. woe, stuff that was real. It is increasingly hard to find valid art that is about stuff that is real in this way. The older Mario gets, the more confused he gets about the fact that everyone at E.T.A. over the age of about Kent Blott finds stuff that's really real uncomfortable and they get embarrassed. It's like there's some rule that real stuff can only get mentioned if everybody rolls their eyes or laughs in a way that isn't happy. The worst-feeling thing that happened today was at lunch when Michael Pemulis told Mario he had an idea for setting up a Dial-a-Prayer telephone service for atheists in which the atheist dials the number and the line just rings and rings and no one answers. It was a joke and a good one, and Mario got it; what was unpleasant was that Mario was the only one at the big table whose laugh was a happy laugh; everybody else sort of looked down like they were laughing at somebody with a disability. The whole issue was far above Mario's head, and he was unable to understand Lyle's replies when he tried to bring the confusion up. And Hal was for once no help, because Hal seemed even more uncomfortable and embarrassed than the fellows at lunch, and when Mario brought up real stuff Hal called him Booboo and acted like he'd wet himself and Hal was going to be very patient about helping him change.

A lot of people are appearing out of the dark and walking by to go in for the Curfew. They all seem afraid and scowl to pretend they're not shy. The men have their hands in their coat pockets and the females have their hands at their coats' throats, keeping them shut. One young person Mario's never seen sees him struggling with the police lock and helps him disengage the bar and get the lead block into his backpack. Just that little bit of help that makes the difference. Mario is suddenly so sleepy he's not sure he can get up the hill to go home. The musics that played at the beginning of Madame Psychosis's career are the exact same that played to the end, what sounds so unacceptable without her there.

Mario's forward list is perfect for walking up hills, however. His pelvis's salve makes a sound but doesn't hurt. In the big protruding window of Ennet's House's Headmistress's office that the window overlooks the Avenue and the train tracks and the Ngs' clean Father and Son Grocery, where they give Mario yellow tea in the A.M. when he comes by when it's cold, the last thing Mario can see, before the hillside's trees close behind him and reduce the Ennet House to shattered yellow lighting, is a wide square-headed boy bent over something he's writing at the Headmistress's black desk, licking a pencil-end and hunched all uncomfortably with one arm curled out around what he's writing in, like a slow boy over a class theme at Rindge and Latin Special.

Live-in Staffers' evening duties are divided pretty evenly between the picayune and the unpleasant. Somebody has to hit the area meetings to verify residents' attendance, while somebody else has to miss a nightly meeting to man the empty House and phones and do the picayune Daily Log. After the meetings let out, Gately's supposed to do a head-count every hour and make a Log-entry on who all's there and what's going on. Gately has to do a Chore-patrol and Log-entry on Chore-performance and nail down tomorrow's Chore-assignments off the weekly sheet. The residents need to have everything expected of them spelled out in advance so they can't bitch if they get popped for something. Then people who haven't performed on their Chore have to be told they're on a week's Restriction, which tends to be unpleasant. Gately has to unlock Pat's cabinets and get the key to the meds locker and open the meds locker. Residents on meds respond to the sound of the meds locker the way a cat will respond to the sound of a can-opener. They just like materialize. Gately has to dispense oral insulin and Virus-meds and pimple medicine and antidepressants and lithium to the residents who materialize for meds, and then he has to enter everything in the Medical Log, which the M. Log is an incredible fucking mess. He has to get out Pat's Week-At-A-Glance book and print out her next day's appointments on a sheet of paper in block letters, because Pat finds her own palsied handwriting impossible to read. Gately has to confer with Johnette Foltz about how different residents conducted themselves at St. E.'s Sharing and Caring and Brookline's B.Y.P. and a Women's NA Step down in East Cambridge they let a couple of the senior females go to, and then Log all the data. Gately has to go up and check on Kate G., who claimed to be too sick to hit AA again tonight and has been in bed in her room more or less steadily for three days, reading somebody called Sylvia Plate. Going up onto the women's side of the upstairs is an incredible pain in the ass because he has to unlock a little steel cage over a little button at the bottom of their stairway by the back office and press the button to sound an upstairs buzzer and shout up the stairs 'Male on the floor' and then give the female residents as much time as they need to get decent or whatever before he can come up.

Going up there has been educational for Gately because he'd always had this idea that women's areas were essentially cleaner and pleasanter than men's areas. Having to verify the Chore in the women's two bathrooms smashed his longstanding delusion that women didn't go to the bathroom with the same appalling vigor that men did. Gately'd done a fair amount of cleaning up after his mother, but he'd never much thought of her as a woman. So the whole unpleasant thing's been an education.

Gately has to check on Doony Glynn, who has recurrent diverticulitis and has to lie fetal on his bunk when he gets an attack and has to be brought Motrin and a SlimFast shake that Gately had to make with 2% milk because there was no skim left, and then Food Bank crackers and a tonic out of the basement's machine when Glynn can't drink the 2% shake, and then Log Glynn's comments and condition, neither of which are good.

Somebody has made those disgusting marshmallowy Rice Krispie things in the kitchen and then not cleaned up after themselves, and Gately has to clomp around finding out who's responsible and get them to clean it up, and the code about ratting among the residents is such that you'd think he was a narc all of a sudden. The daily bullshit here is hip-deep and not so much annoying as soul-sucking; a double-shift here now empties him out by dawn, just in time to clean real shit. It hadn't been this way at the start, the soul-sucking aspect, and Gately every couple minutes wonders again what he'll end up doing when his year's Staff term is up and his soul is sucked out and he's sober but without any money and still clueless and has to leave here and do something back Out There.

Kate Gompert, when he buzzed and went up to the 5-Woman room to look in, had made a possible sideways comment about hurting herself,[245] and Gately has to call Pat at home about it, and she's out or not picking up, so then he has to call the House Manager and relay the verbatim comment and let her interpret it and tell Gately what action to take and how the comment stands in relation to Gompert's Suicide Contract and how the whole thing should be Logged. A resident at Ennet had hung herself from a heating pipe in the basement a couple years before Gately arrived, and there are now baroque procedures for monitoring ideation among residents with psych issues. The number of 5-East at St. Elizabeth's is on a red card in Pat's Rolodex.

Gately has to collect the previous week's counselor-reports and collate them and get the residents' files together and get any updates or changes printed out and into the files for tomorrow's All-Staff Meeting, where the Staff gets together in Pat's office and interfaces on how each resident seems to be doing. Residents have a pretty good idea that their alumni counselors basically rat them out in toto at each Staff meeting, which is why counselling sessions tend to be so incredibly dull that only really grateful giving Ennet alumni are willing to serve as counselors. Filing-organization is picayune, and for Gately using the back office's TP array to print stuff out is unpleasant, mostly because each of his fingers covers almost three keys of the keyboard and he has to hit each key carefully with the tip of a pen, which sometimes he forgets to retract the nub of, leaving blue smears on the keys that the House Manager always gives him an ass-chewing for.

And Gately has to have each newer resident in to the office for at least a couple minutes to like touch base and see how they're doing and make it clear they're regarded as existing so they can't just melt into the living room's decor and disappear. The newest guy's still sitting in the linen closet claiming he's comfortablest there with the door open and the new 'helpless' Amy Johnson hasn't come back yet. A brand-new Court-Ordered female, Ruth van Cleve, who looks like one of those people you see in pictures of African famine, has to fill out Intake forms and go through Orientation, and Gately goes over the House rules with her and gives her a copy of the Ennet House Survival Guide, which some resident years gone had written for Pat.

Gately has to answer the phone and tell people who call the office for a resident that residents can receive calls only on the pay phone in the basement, which he has to say yes is frequently busy all the time. The House prohibits cellular/mobiles and has a Boundary about the office phone for residents. Gately has to kick residents off down there when other residents in line come and complain they've exceeded their five minutes. This also tends to be unpleasant: the pay phone down there is undigital and un-shutoffable and a constant source of aggravation and beefs; every conversation is life-and-death; crisis down there 24/7. There's a special way to kick somebody off a pay phone that's respectful and nonshaming but also firm. Gately has gotten good at assuming a blank but not passive expression when residents are abusive. There's this look of weary expertise the House Staffers cultivate, then have to flex their face to get rid of when they're off-duty. Gately's gotten so stoic in the face of abuse that a resident has to mention actual unnatural acts in connection with his name for Gately to Log the abuse and give out a Restriction. He's respected and well-liked by almost all the residents, which the House Manager says causes the veteran Staff some concern, because Gately's job is not to be these people's friend all the time.

Then in the kitchen with the fucking Krispie-treat bowls and pans still a fucking mess Wade McDade and some other residents were standing around waiting for various things to toast and boil and McDade was using his finger and pushing the tip of his nose up so that his nostrils faced straight out at everybody. He was looking piggishly around and asking if people knew any people where their nose looked like this right here, and some people said yes, sure, why. Gately checked the fridge and again saw evidence that his special meatloaf had a secret admirer, it looked like, another big rectangle cut out of the leftovers he'd carefully wrapped and laid out on the sturdiest shelf in there. McDade, who Gately struggles daily with the urge to hit McDade so hard there'd be nothing but eyes and a nose down over the tops of his cowboy boots, McDade's telling everybody he's constructing a Gratitude List at Calvin T.'s tough-love suggestion and he says he's decided one of the things he's grateful for is his nose don't look like this here. Gately tries not to judge on the basis of who laughs and who doesn't. When Pat's phone rings and Gately leaves, McDade's squunching his upper lip up in his hand and asking people about acquaintance with cleft palates.

Gately has to monitor the like emotional barometer in the House and put a wet finger to the wind for potential conflicts and issues and rumors. A subtle art here is maintaining access to the residents' gossip-grapevine and keeping on top of rumors without seeming like you're inducing a resident to cross the line and actually eat cheese on another resident. The only thing a resident is actually encouraged to rat out another resident on here is picking up a Substance. All other-type issues it's supposed to be Staff's job to glean and ferret out etc., to decoct legitimate infractions out of the tides of innuendo and bullshit complaint 20+ bored crammed-together street-canny people in detox from wrecked lives can generate. Rumors that so-and-so blew so-and-so on the couch at 0300, that thus-and-such's got a knife, that X was using what had to be some kind of code on the pay phone, that Y's gone back to carrying a beeper, that so-and-so's making book on football out of the 5-Man room, that Belbin had led Diehl to believe she'd clean up if he made Krispie Treats and then she weaseled out, and etc. Almost all of it's picayune and, over time, as it accretes, unpleasant.

Rarely a feeling of outright unalloyed sadness as such, afterward — just an abrupt loss of hope. Plus there is the contempt he belies so well with gentleness and caring during that post-coital period of small sounds and adjustments.

Orin can only give, not receive, pleasure, and this makes a contemptible number of them think he is a wonderful lover, almost a dream-type lover; and this fuels the contempt. But he cannot show the contempt, since this would pretty clearly detract from the Subject's pleasure.

Because the Subject's pleasure in him has become his food, he is conscientious in the consideration and gentleness he shows after coitus, making clear his desire to stay right there very close and be intimate, when so many other male lovers, the Subjects say, seem afterward to become uneasy, contemptuous, or distant, rolling over to stare at the wall or tamping down a smoke before they've even stopped twitching.

The hand-model told him very softly how the photograph's big pink Swiss husband after coitus hove himself off her and lay there stunned under his stomach's weight, his eyes narrowed to piggy slits and the faint smirk on his face that of a gorged predator: not like the punter: uncaring. As was S.O.P. with Subjects she became then briefly stricken and anxious and said *no one* must ever know, she could lose her children. Orin administered the standard assurances in a very soft intimate voice. Orin was resoundingly gentle and caring afterward, as she could somehow just intuitively *tell* he would be. It was true. It gave him real pleasure to give the impression of care and intimacy in this interval; if someone asked about his favorite part of the anticlimactic time after the Subject lay back and glisteningly opened and he could see her eyes holding him whole, Orin would say his #2 favorite is this post-seminal interval of clingy vulnerability on the Subject's part and gentle intimate care on his own.

When the knock on the room door came it seemed like a further grace, for the Subject had been up on an elbow in bed, exhaling slim tusks of cigarette-smoke from her nose and starting to ask him to tell her things about his own family, and Orin was stroking her very tenderly and watching the twin curves of smoke pale and spread and trying not to shudder at the thought of what the inside of the Subject's fine nose must look like, what gray-white tangles of necrotic snot must hang and twine up in there, from the smoke, whether she had the stomach to look at a hankie she'd used or whether she balled the thing up and flung it from her with the sort of shudder O. knew *he'd* feel; and when the brisk action of male knuckles sounded against the room's door he watched her face whiten from the forehead down as she pleaded that no one must know of her whoever was there and stabbed out her butt and dove beneath the blankets as he called out for patience to the door and veered to the bathroom to wrap a towel around him before he went to it, the sort of bland hotel door you used a card and not a key for. The defiled, guilty, and frightened married hand-model's wrist and hand protruded for a moment from the edge of the bedding and felt the floor for shoes and clothes, the hand moving like a blind spider and sucking things up under the blankets. Orin didn't ask who it was at the door; *he* had nothing to hide. His mood at the door became extraordinarily fine. When the wife and mother had erased all evidence of herself and heaped the bedding over her so she could lie there sniffing grayly and imagining that she was hidden from view, just one lumpy part of a celibate napper's dishevelled bed, Orin checked the door's fish-eye peeper, saw only the hallway's claret-colored wall opposite, and opened the door with a smile he felt all the way down to his bare soles. Swiss cuckolds, furtive near-Eastern medical attachés, zaftig print-journalists: he felt ready for anything.

The man in the hall at the door was handicapped, challenged, in a wheelchair, looking up at him from well below peephole-range, bushy-haired and mostly nose and looking up into the swell of Orin's pectorals, making no attempt to see around him into the room. One of the disabled. Orin looked down and felt both let down and almost touched. The little fellow's wheelchair shiny and his lap blanketed and his string tie half-hidden by the clipboard he held to his chest with a curled and motherly arm.

'Survey,' the man said, nothing else, joggling the clipboard a little like an infant, presenting it as evidence.

Orin imagined the terrified Subject lying there hidden and trying to hear, and despite a sort of mild disappointment he felt touched at whatever this shy ruse of an excuse for proximity to his leg and autograph might be. He felt for the Subject the sort of clinical contempt you feel for an insect you've looked down and seen and know you're going to torture for a while. From the way she smoked and performed certain other manual operations, Orin'd noted she was left-handed.

He said to the man in the wheelchair, 'Goody.'

'Plus or minus three percent sample.'

'Eager to cooperate in any way.'

The man cocked his head in that way people in wheelchairs do. 'Scholarly academic study.'

'Pisser.' Leaning against the jamb with arms crossed, watching the man try to process the dissimilarity in the size of his limbs. No shins or extremities, however withery, extended below the wheelchair's blanket's hem. The guy was like totally legless. Orin's rising heart went out.

'Chamber of Commerce survey. Concerned veterans' group systematic inquiry. Consumer advocacy polling operation. Three percentage points error on either of two sides of the issue.'

'Bully.'

'Consumer-advocacy group opinion sweep. Very little time involved. Government study. Ad council demographic assessment. Sweeps. Random anonymity. Minimum in terms of time or trouble.'

'I'm clearing my mind to be of maximum help.'

When the man had taken out his pen with a flourish and looked down at his board Orin got a look at the yarmulke of skin in the center of the seated man's hair. There was something almost unbearably touching about a bald spot on a handicapped man.

'What do you miss, please?'

Orin smiled coolly. 'Very little, I like to think.'

'Backtrack. U.S.A. citizen?'

'Yes.'

'You have how many years?'

'Age?'

'You have which age?'

'Age is twenty-six.'

'Over twenty-five?'

'That'd follow.' Orin was waiting for the ruse involving the pen that'd get him to sign something so the very shy fan club'd get their autograph. He tried to remember from Mario's childhood how long under blankets before it got unbearably hot and you started to smother and thrash.

The man pretended to notate. 'Employed, self-employed, unemployed?'

Orin smiled. 'The first.'

'Please list what you miss.'

The whisper of the vent, hush of the wine-colored hallway, vaguest whisper of rustling sheets behind, imagining the growing bubble of CO^2 under the sheets.

'Please list lifestyle elements of your U.S.A. lifetime you recall, and/or at present lack, and miss.'

'I'm not sure I follow.'

The man flipped a page over to check. 'Pine, yearn, winsome, nostalgia. Lump of throat.' Flipping one more sheet. 'Wistful, as well.'

'You mean childhood memories. You mean like cocoa with half-melted marshmallows floating on top in a checker-tiled kitchen warmed by an enamel gas range, that sort of thing. Or omnissent doors at airports and Star Markets that somehow knew you were there and slid open. Before they disappeared. Where did those doors go?'

'*Enamel* is with the *e*?'

'And then some.'

Orin's gaze now was up at the ceiling's acoustic tile, the little blinking disk of the hall's smoke detector, as if memories were always lighter than air. The seated man stared blandly up at the throb of Orin's internal jugular vein. Orin's face changed a little. Behind him, under the blankets, the non-Swiss woman lay very calmly and patiently on her side, breathing silently into the portable O_2-mask w/ canister from the purse beside her, one hand in the purse on the Schmeisser GBF miniature machine pistol.

'I miss TV,' Orin said, looking back down. He no longer smiled coolly.

'The former television of commercial broadcast.'

'I do.'

'Reason in several words or less, please, for the box after *REASON*,' displaying the board.

'Oh, man.' Orin looked back up and away at what seemed to be nothing, feeling at his jaw around the retromandibular's much tinier and more vulnerable throb. 'Some of this may sound stupid. I miss commercials that were louder than the programs. I miss the phrases "Order before midnight tonight" and "Save up to fifty percent and more." I miss being told things were filmed before a live studio audience. I miss late-night anthems and shots of flags and fighter jets and leathery-faced Indian chiefs crying at litter. I miss "Sermonette" and "Evensong" and test patterns and being told how many megahertz something's transmitter was broadcasting at.' He felt his face. 'I miss sneering at something I love. How we used to love to gather in the checker-tiled kitchen in front of the old boxy cathode-ray Sony whose reception was sensitive to airplanes and sneer at the commercial vapidity of broadcast stuff.'

'Vapid ditty,' pretending to notate.

'I miss stuff so low-denominator I could watch and know in advance what people were going to say.'

'Emotions of mastery and control and superiority. And pleasure.'

'You can say that again, boy. I miss summer reruns. I miss reruns hastily inserted to fill the intervals of writers' strikes, Actors' Guild strikes. I miss Jeannie, Samantha, Sam and Diane, Gilligan, Hawkeye, Hazel, Jed, all the syndicated airwave-haunters. You know? I miss seeing the same things over and over again.'

There were two muffled sneezes from the bed behind him that the hand-icapped man didn't even acknowledge, pretending to write, brushing his string tie's dangle away again and again as he wrote. Orin tried not to imag-ine the topography of the sheets the Subject'd sneezed into. He no longer cared about the ruse. He did feel tender, somehow, toward him.

The man tended to look up at him like people with legs look up at build-ings and planes. 'You can of course view entertainments again and again without surcease on TelEntertainment disks of storage and retrieval.'

Orin's way of looking up as he remembered was nothing like the seated guy's way of looking up. 'But not the same. The choice, see. It ruins it somehow. With television you were *subjected* to repetition. The familiarity was inflicted. Different now.'

'Inflicted.'

'I don't think I exactly know,' Orin said, suddenly dimly stunned and sad inside. The terrible sense as in dreams of something vital you've forgotten to do. The inclined head's bald spot was freckled and tan. 'Is there a next item?'

'Things to tell me you do not miss.'

'For symmetry.'

'Balance of opinion.'

Orin smiled. 'Plus or minus.'

'Just so,' the man said.

Orin resisted an urge to lay his hand tenderly over the arc of the disabled man's skull. 'Well how much time do we have here?'

The skyscraper-gawking aspect was only when the man's gaze went higher than Orin's neck. They were not shy or indirect or even the eyes of someone in any way disabled, was what struck Orin later as odd — besides the Swiss accent, the absence of a signature-ruse, the Subject's patience with the wait and the absence of gasping when O. pulled the covers abruptly back, later. The man had looked up at Orin and flicked his eyes slightly past him, at the room behind with pantyless floor and humped covers. Orin was meant to see the glance past him. 'Can return at later time which we specify. You are, *comme on dit,* engaged?'

Orin's smile wasn't as cool as he thought as he told the seated figure that that was a matter of opinion.

As at all D.S.A.S.-certified halfway facilities, Ennet House's resident curfew is 2330h. From 2300 to 2330, the Staffer on night-duty has to do head-counts and sit around like somebody's mom waiting for different residents to come in. There's always ones that always like to cut it close and play with the idea of getting Discharged for something picayune so it won't be their fault. Tonight Clenette H. and the deeply whacked-out Yolanda W. come back in from Footprints[246] around 2315 in purple skirts and purple lipstick and ironed hair, tottering on heels and telling each other what a wicked time they just had. Hester Thrale undulates in in a false fox jacket at 2320 as usual even though she has to be up at like 0430 for the breakfast-shift at the Provident Nursing Home and sometimes eats breakfast with Gately, both of their faces nodding down perilously close to their Frosted Flakes. Chandler Foss and the spectrally thin April Cortelyu come in from someplace with postures and expressions that arouse comments and force Gately to Log a possible issue about an in-House relationship. Gately has to bid goodnight to two craggy-faced brunette ex-residents who've been planted on the couch all night talking cults. Emil Minty and Nell Gunther and sometimes Gavin Diehl (who Gately did three weeks of a municipal bit with, once, at Concord Farm) make a nightly point of going to smoke outside on the front porch and coming in only after Gately says twice he's got to lock the door, just as some limp rebellious gesture. Tonight they're closely followed by a mustacheless Lenz, who sort of oozes through the door just as Gately's going through his keys to get the key to lock it, and kind of brushes by and goes up to the 3-Man without a word, which he's been doing a lot lately, which Gately has to Log, plus the fact that it's now after 2330 and he can't account for either the semi-new girl Amy J. or — more upsetting — Bruce Green. Then Green knocks at the front door at 2336 — Gately has to Log the exact time and then it's his call whether to unlock the door. After curfew Staff doesn't have to unlock the door. Many a bad-news resident gets effectively bounced this way. Gately lets him in. Green's never come close to missing curfew before and looks godawful, skin potato-white and eyes vacant. And a big quiet kid is one thing, but Green looks at the floor of Pat's office like it's a loved one while Gately gives him the required ass-chewing; and Green takes the standard dreaded week's Full House Restriction[247] in such a vacantly hangdog way, and is so lamely vague when Gately asks does he want to tell him where he's been at and why he couldn't make 2330 and whether there's anything that's an issue that he might want to share with Staff, so unresponsive that Gately feels like he has no choice but to pull an immediate spot-urine on Green, which Gately hates doing not only because he plays cribbage with Green and feels like he's taken Green under the old Gately wing and is probably the closest thing to a sponsor the kid's got but also because urine samples taken after Unit #2's clinic's closed[248] have to be stored overnight in the little Staff miniature fridgelette in Don Gately's basement room — the only fridge in the House that no resident could conceivably dicky into — and Gately hates to have a warm blue-lidded cup of somebody's goddamn urine in his fridgelette with his pears and Polar seltzer, etc. Green submits to Gately's cross-armed presence in the men's head as Green produces a urine so efficiently and with so little bullshit that Gately is able to take the lidded cup between gloved thumb and finger and get it downstairs and tagged and Logged and down in the fridgelette in time to not be late for getting the residents' cars moved, the night-shift's biggest pain in the ass; but then his final head-count at 2345 reminds Gately that Amy J. isn't back, and she hasn't called, and Pat has told him the decision to Discharge after a missed curfew is his call, and at 2350 Gately makes the decision, and has to get Treat and Belbin to go up into the 5-Woman room and pack the girl's stuff up in the same Irish Luggage she'd brought it in Monday, and Gately has to put the trashbags on the front porch with a quick note explaining the Discharge and wishing the girl good luck, and has to call Pat's answering device down in Milton and leave word of a mandatory Curfew-Discharge at 2350h., so Pat can hear about it first thing in the A.M. and schedule interviews to fill the available bed ASAP, and then with a hissed curse Gately remembers the anti-big-hanging-gut situps he's sworn to himself to do every night before 0000, and it's 2356, and he has time to do only 20 with his huge discolored sneakers wedged under the frame of the office's black vinyl couch before it's unavoidably time to supervise moving the residents' cars around.

Gately's predecessor as male live-in Staff, a designer-narcotics man who's now (via Mass Rehab) learning to repair jet engines at East Coast AeroTech, once described residents' vehicles to Gately as a continuing boil on the ass of night Staff. Ennet House lets any resident with a legally registered vehicle and insurance keep their car at the House, if they want, during residency, to use for work and nightly meetings, etc., and the Enfield Marine Public Health Hospital goes along, except they put authorized parking for all the Units' clients out in the little street right outside the House. And since metro Boston's serious fiscal troubles in the third year of Subsidized Time there's been this hellish municipal deal where only one side of any street is legal for parking, and the legal side switches abruptly at 0000h., and cruisers and municipal tow trucks prowl the streets from 0001h. on, writing $95.00 tickets and/or towing suddenly-illegally-parked vehicles to a region of the South End so blasted and dangerous no cabbie with anything to live for will even go there. So the interval 2355h.–0005h. in Boston is a time of total but not very spiritual community, with guys in skivvies and ladies in mud-masks staggering out yawning into the crowded midnight streets and disabling their alarms and revving and all trying to pull out and do a U and find a parallel-parking place facing the other way. There's nothing very mysterious about the fact that metro Boston's battery- and homicide-rates during this ten-minute interval are the highest per diem, so that ambulances and paddy wagons are especially aprowl at this hour, too, adding to the general clot and snarl.

Since the E.M.P.H.H. Units' catatonics and enfeebled people rarely own registered vehicles, it's generally pretty easy to find places along the little road to switch to, but it's a constant sore point between Pat Montesian and the E.M.P.H.H. Board of Regents that Ennet House residents don't get to park overnight in the big off-street lot by the condemned hospital building — the lot's spaces are reserved for all the different Units' professional staff starting at 0600h., and E.M. Security got sick of staffs' complaints about drug addicts' poorly maintained autos still sitting there taking up their spots in the A.M. — and that Security won't consider changing the little E.M. streetlet's nightly side-switch to 2300h., before Ennet Houses's D.S.A.S.-required curfew; E.M.'s Board claims it's a municipal ordinance that they can't be expected to mess with just to accommodate one tenant, while Pat's memos keep pointing out that the Enfield Marine Hospital complex is state- not city-owned, and that Ennet House residents are the only tenants who face the nightly car-moving problem, since just about everyone else is catatonic or enfeebled. And so on.

But so every P.M. at like 2359 Gately has to lock up the lockers and Pat's cabinets and desk drawers and the door to the front office and put the phone console's answering machine on and personally escort all residents who own cars out post-curfew outside into the little nameless streetlet, and for somebody with Gately's real limited managerial skills the headaches involved are daunting: he has to herd the vehicular residents together just inside the locked front door; he has to threaten the residents he's herded together into staying together by the door while he clomps upstairs to get the one or two drivers who always forget and fall asleep before 0000 — and this straggler-collecting is a particular pain in the ass if the straggler's a female, because he has to unlock and press the Male Coming Up button by the kitchen, and the 'buzzer' sounds more like a klaxon, and wakes the edgiest female residents up with an ugly surge of adrenaline, and Gately as he clomps up the stairs gets roundly bitched out by all the mud-masked heads sticking out into the female hall, and he by regulation can't go into the sleeper's bedroom but has to pound on the door and keep shouting out his gender and get one of the straggler's roommates to wake her up and get her dressed and to the bedroom door; so he has to retrieve the stragglers and chew them out and threaten them with both a Restriction and a possible tow while herding them quick-walking down the staircase to join the main car-owner herd as quickly as possible before the main herd can like disperse. They'll always disperse if he takes too long getting stragglers; they'll get distracted or hungry or need an ashtray or just get impatient and start looking at the whole car-moving-after-curfew thing as an imposition on their time. Their early-recovery Denial makes it impossible for them to imagine their own car getting towed instead of, say, somebody else's car. It's the same Denial Gately can see at work in the younger B.U. or -C. students when he's driving Pat's Aventura to the Food Bank or Purity Supreme when they'll fucking walk right out in the street against the light in front of the car, whose brakes are fortunately in top shape. Gately's snapped to the fact that people of a certain age and level of like life-experience believe they're immortal: college students and alcoholics/addicts are the worst: they deep-down believe they're exempt from the laws of physics and statistics that ironly govern everybody else. They'll piss and moan your ear off if somebody else fucks with the rules, but they don't deep down see themselves subject to them, the same rules. And they're constitutionally unable to learn from anybody else's experience: if some jaywalking B.U. student does get splattered on Comm. or some House resident does get his car towed at 0005, your other student's or addict's response to this will be to ponder just what imponderable difference makes it possible for that other guy to get splattered or towed and not him, the ponderer. They never doubt the difference — they just ponder it. It's like a kind of idolatry of uniqueness. It's unvarying and kind of spirit-killing for a Staffer to watch, that the only way your addict ever learns anything is the hard way. It has to happen to *them* to like upset the idolatry. Eugenio M. and Annie Parrot always recommend letting everybody get towed at least once, early on in their residency, to help make believers out of them in terms of laws and rules; but Gately for some reason on his night-shifts can't do it, cannot fucking *stand* to have one of his people get towed as long as there's something he can do to prevent it, and then plus if they do get towed there's the nail-chewing hassle of arranging their transport to the South End's municipal lot the next day, fielding calls from bosses and supplying verification of residents' carlessness in terms of getting to work without letting the boss know that the carless employee is a resident of a halfway house, which is totally sacred private residents' private information to give out or not — Gately breaks a full-body sweat just thinking about the managerial headaches involved in a fucking tow, so he'll spend time herding and regathering and chewing the absentminded asses of residents who Gene M. says have such calloused asses still it's a waste of Gately's time and spirit: you have to let them learn for themselves.[249]

Gately alerts Thrale and Foss and Erdedy and Henderson,[250] and Morris

Hanley, and drags the new kid Tingley out of the linen closet, and Nell Gunther — who's fucking sacked out slack-mouthed on the couch, in violation — and lets them all get coats and herds them together by the locked front door. Yolanda W. says she left personal items in Clenette's car and can she come. Lenz owns a car but doesn't answer Gately's yell up the stairs. Gately tells the herd to stay put and that if anybody leaves the herd he's going to take a personal interest in their discomfort. Gately clomps up the stairs and into the 3-Man room, plotting different fun ways to wake Lenz up without bruises that'd show. Lenz is not asleep but is wearing personal-stereo headphones, plus a jock strap, doing handstand-pushups up against the wall by Geoffrey Day's rack, his bottom only inches from Day's pillow and farting in rhythm to the pushups' downstrokes, as Day lies there in pajamas and Lone Ranger sleep mask, hands folded over his heaving chest, lips moving soundlessly. Gately's maybe a little rough about grabbing Lenz's calf and lifting him off his hands and using his other big hand on Lenz's hip to twirl him around upright like a drill-team's rifle, but Lenz's cry is of over-ebullient greeting, not pain, but it sends both Day and Gavin Diehl bolt-upright in their racks, and then they curse as Lenz hits the floor. Lenz starts saying he'd let time completely get away from him and didn't know what time it was. Gately can hear the herd down by the front door at the bottom of the stairs stamping and chuffing and getting ready to maybe disperse.

Up this close, Gately doesn't even need his Staffer's eerie seventh sense to sense that Lenz is clearly wired on either 'drines or Bing. That Lenz has been visited by the Sergeant at Arms. Lenz's right eyeball is wobbling around in its socket and his mouth writhing in that way and he has that Nietzschean supercharged aura of a wired individual, and all the time he's throwing on slacks and topcoat and incognitoizing wig and getting almost pitched head-first down the stairs by Gately he's telling this insane breathless whopper about his finger once getting cut off and then spontaneously regentrifying itself back on, and his mouth is writhing in that fish-on-a-gaff way distinctive of a sustained L-Dopa surge, and Gately wants to pull an immediate urine, *immediate,* but meanwhile the cars' herd's edges are just starting to widen in that way that precedes distraction and dispersal, and they're angry not at Lenz for straggling but at Gately for even bothering with him, and Lenz pantomimes the akido Serene But Deadly Crane stance at Ken Erdedy, and it's 0004h. and Gately can see tow trucks aprowl way down on Comm. Ave., coming this way, and he jangles his keys and unlocks all three curfew-locks on the front door and gets everybody out in the scrotum-tightening November cold and out down the walk to the line of their cars in the little street and stands there on the porch watching in just orange shirtsleeves, making sure Lenz doesn't bolt before he can pull a spot-urine and extract an admission and Discharge him officially, feeling a twinge of conscience at so looking forward to giving Lenz the administrative shoe, and Lenz jabbers nonstop to whoever's closest all the way to his Duster, and everybody goes to their car, and the backwash around Gately from the open House door is hot and people in the living room provide loud feedback on the draft from the open door, the sky overhead immense and dimensional and the night so clear you can see stars hanging in a kind of lacteal goo, and out on the streetlet a couple car doors are squeaking and slamming and some people are conversing and delaying just to make Staff have to stand there in shirtsleeves on the cold porch, a small nightly sideways ball-busting rebellious gesture, when Gately's eye falls on Doony R. Glynn's specialty-disembowelled old dusty-black VW Bug parked with the other cars on the now-illicit street-side, its rear-mount engine's guts on full glittered display under the little street's lights, and Glynn's upstairs in bed tonight legitimately prostrate with diverticulitis, which for insurance reasons means Gately has to go back in and ask some resident with a driver's license to come move Glynn's VW across the street, which is humiliating because it means admitting publicly to these specimens that he, Gately, doesn't have a valid license, and the sudden heat of the living room confuses his goosepimples, and nobody in the living room will admit to have a driver's license, and it turns out the only licensed resident who's still vertical and downstairs is Bruce Green, who's in the kitchen expressionlessly stirring a huge amount of sugar into a cup of coffee with his bare blunt finger, and Gately finds himself having to ask for managerial assistance from a kid he likes and has just bitched out and extracted urine from, which Green minimizes the humiliation of the whole thing by volunteering to help the second he hears the words *Glynn* and *fucking car,* and goes to the living room closet to get out his cheap leather jacket and fingerless gloves, and but Gately now has to leave the residents outside still unsupervised for a second to go clomping upstairs and verify that it's kosher with Glynn for Bruce Green to move his car.[251] The 2-Man seniorest males' bedroom has a bunch of old AA bumper-stickers on it and a calligraphic poster saying EVERYTHING I'VE EVER LET GO OF HAS CLAW MARKS ON IT, and the answer to Gately's knock is a moan, and Glynn's little naked-lady bedside lamp he brought in with him is on, he's in his rack curled on his side clutching his abdomen like a kicked man. McDade is illicitly sitting on Foss's rack reading one of Foss's motorcycle magazines and drinking Glynn's Millennial Fizzy with stereo headphones on, and he hurriedly puts out his cigarette when Gately enters and closes the little drawer in the bedside table where Foss keeps his ashtray just like everybody else.[252] The street outside sounds like Daytona — a drug addict is like physically unable to start a car without gunning the engine. Gately looks quickly out the west window over Glynn's rack to verify that all the unsupervised headlights going down the little street are Uing and coming back the right way to repark. Gately's forehead is wet and he feels the start of a greasy headache, from managerial stress. Glynn's crossed eyes are glassy and feverish and he's softly singing the lyrics to a Choosy Mothers song to a tune that isn't the song's tune.

'Doon,' Gately whispers.

One of the cars is coming back down the street a little fast for Gately's taste. Anything involving residents that happens on the grounds after curfew is his responsibility, the House Manager's made clear.

'Doon.'

It's the bottom eye, grotesquely, that rolls up at Gately. 'Don.'

'*Doon.*'

'Don Doon the witch is dead.'

'Doon, I need to let Green move your car.'

'Vehicle's black, Don.'

'*Brucie Green* needs your keys so's we can switch your car over, brother, it's midnight.'

'My Black Bug. My baby. The Roachmobile. The Doonulater's wheels. His mobility. His exposed baby. His slice of the American Pie. Simonize my baby when I'm gone, Don Doon.'

'Keys, Doony.'

'Take them. Take it. Want you to have it. One true friend. Brought me Ritz crackers and a Fizz. Treat it like a roachlady. Shiny, black, hard, mobile. Needs Premium and a weekly wax.'

'Doon. You got to show me where's the keys, brother.'

'And the bowel. Gotta weekly shine the pipes in the bowel. Exposed to view. With a soft cloth. The mobile roach. The bowelmobile.'

The heat coming off Glynn is face-tightening.

'You feel like you got a fever, Doon?' At one point elements of Staff thought Glynn might be playing sick to get out of looking for a job after losing his menial job at Brighton Fence & Wire. All Gately knows about diverticulitis is that Pat said it's intestinal and alcoholics can get it in recovery from impurities in bottom-shelf blends that the body's trying to expel. Glynn's had physical complaints all through his residency, but nothing like this here. His face is gray and waxy with pain and there's a yellowish crust on his lips. Glynn's got a real severe adtorsion, and the bottom eye is rolled up at Gately with a terrible delirious glitter, the top eye rolling around like a cow's eye. Gately still cannot bring himself to feel another man's forehead. He settles for punching Glynn very lightly on the shoulder.

'You think we need to take you over to St. E.'s to get your intestine looked at, Doon, do you think?'

'Hoits, Don.'

'You think you —?'

Because he's worrying about what if a resident comas or dies on his shift, and then feeling shame that this is his worry, the squeal of brakes and raised voices' noises down out front hasn't registered on Gately right away, but Hester Thrale's unmistakable high-B# scream does — i.e. register — and now serious feet running up the stairs:

Green's face in the doorway, red in round patches high on his cheeks: 'Come out.'

'The fuck's the problem out —'

Green: 'Come *now* Gately.'

Glynn sotto: 'Mother.'

Gately doesn't get to even ask Green what the fuck again on the stairs because Green is down ahead out the door so fast; the damn front door's been open all this time. A watercolor of a retrieverish dog cants and then falls from the wall on the staircase from the vibrations of Gately taking two stairs down at a time. He doesn't take time to grab his coat off Pat's couch. All he's got on is a donated orange bowling shirt with the name *Moose* cursive-stitched on the breast and SHUCO-MIST M.P.S. in ghastly aqua blocks across the back,[253] and he feels every follicle on his body hump up again as the cold encases him on the front porch and the wheelchair-ramp down to the little walkway. The night is cold and glycerine-clear and quite still. Very distant sounds of car horns and raised voices down on Comm. Green's receding at a run off up the little streetlet into a glare of highbeams that diffracts in the clouds of Gately's breath, so even as Gately walks briskly[254] in Green's leather-smelling backwash toward a rising hubbub of curses and Lenz's high-speed voice and Thrale's glass-shattering cries and Henderson and Willis talking shit angrily to somebody and the sound of Joelle v.D.'s veiled head in an upstairs window that isn't the 5-Women room's shouting something down to Gately as he appears in the street, even as he closes in it takes a while for the scene to decoct out of the fog of his breath and its shifting spears of color against the headlights. He passes Glynn's disembowelled and illegally parked Bug. Several of the residents' cars are idling at haphazard angles of mid-U-turn in the middle of the street, and in front of them is a modified dark Montego with highbeams and jacked rear wheels and a turbo's carnivorous idle. Two almost Gately-sized bearded guys in loose like bowling-wear shirts with flowers or suns on them and what look like big faggy necklaces of flowers around what would be their necks if they had necks turn out to be chasing Randy Lenz around this Montego car. Yet another guy with a necklace and a plaid Donegal is holding the rest of the residents at bay on the lawn of #4 with a nasty-looking Item[255] expertly held. Everything now slightly slows down; at the sight of an Item held on his residents there's almost a kind of mechanistic click as Gately's mind shifts into a different kind of drive. He gets very cool and clear and his headache recedes and his breathing slows. It's not so much that things slow as break into frames.

The ruckus has aroused the old nurse in #4 who Asks For Help, and her spectral figure is splayed in a nightie against an upstairs #4 window yelling *'Eeeeeeeyelp!'* Hester Thrale now has her pink-nailed hands over her eyes and is screaming over and over for nobody to hurt nobody especially her. It's the Bulldog Item that holds the attention. The two guys chasing Lenz around the Montego are unarmed but look coldly determined in a way Gately recognizes. They're not wearing coats either but they don't look cold. All this appraisal's taking only seconds; it only takes time to list it. They have vaguely non-U.S. beards and are each about ⅘ Gately's size. They take turns coming around the car and running past the headlights' glare and Gately can see they have similar froggy lippy pale foreign faces. Lenz is talking at the guys nonstop, mostly imprecating. They're all three going around and around the car like a cartoon. Gately's still walking up as he sees all this. It's obvious to appraisal the foreignish guys aren't real bright because of they're chasing Lenz in tandem instead of heading around the car in opposite directions to trap him in like a pincer. They all three stop and start, Lenz across the car from them. Some of the at-bay residents are yelling to Lenz. Like most coke-dealers Lenz is quick on his feet, his topcoat billowing and then settling whenever he stops. Lenz's voice is nonstop — he's alternately inviting the guy to perform impossible acts and advancing baroque arguments for how whatever they think he did there's no way he was even in the same area code as whatever happened that they think he did. The guys keep speeding up like they want to catch Lenz just to shut him up. Ken Erdedy has his hands up and his car keys in his hand; his legs look like he's about to wet himself. Clenette and the new black girl, clearly veterans at gunpoint-etiquette, are prone on the lawn with their fingers laced behind their heads. Nell Gunther's assumed Lenz's old martial-arts Crane stance, hands twisted into flat claws, eyeing the guy's .44, which pans coolly back and forth over the residents. This smaller guy gets the most frames the slowest. He's got on a plaid hunting cap that keeps Gately from seeing if he's foreign also. But the guy's holding the weapon in the classic Weaver stance of somebody that can really shoot — left foot slightly forward, slightly hunched, a two-handed grip with the right arm cocked elbow-out so the Item's held high up in front of the guy's face, up to his sighting eye. This is how policemen and Made Guys from the North End shoot. Gately knows weapons way better than sobriety, still. And the Item — if the guy trig-pulls on some resident that resident's going down — the Item's some customized version of a U.S. .44 Bulldog Special, or maybe a Nuck or Brazilian clone, blunt and ugly and with a bore like the mouth of a cave. The stout alcoholic kid Tingley has both hands to his cheeks and is 100% at bay. The piece's been modified, Gately can appraise. The barrel's been vented out near the muzzle to cut your Bulldog's infamous recoil, the hammer's bobbed, and the thing's got a fat Mag Na Port or -clone grip like the metro Finest favor. This is not a weekend-warrior or liquor-store-holdup type Item; it's one that's made real specifically for putting projectiles into people. It's not a semiauto but is throated for a fucking speed-loader, which Gately can't see if the guy's got a speed-loader under the loose floral shirt but needs to assume the guy's got near-unlimited shots with a speed-loader. The North Shore Finest on the other hand wrap their grips in this like colored gauze that wicks sweat. Gately tries to recall a past associate's insufferable ammo-lectures when under the influence — your Bulldog and clones can take anything from light target loads and wadcutter to Colt SofTip dum-dums and worse. He's pretty sure this thing could put him down with one round; he's not sure. Gately's never been shot but he's seen guys shot. He feels something that is neither fear nor excitement. Joelle van D. is shouting stuff you can't make out, and Erdedy at bay on the lawn's calling out to her to get her head out of the whole picture. Gately's been bearing down this whole brief time, both seeing his breath and hearing it, beating his arms across his chest to keep some feeling in his hands. You could almost call what he feels a kind of jolly calm. The unAmerican guys chase Lenz and then stop across the car facing him for a second and then get furious again and chase him. Gately guesses he ought to be grateful the third guy doesn't come over and just shoot him. Lenz puts both hands on whatever part of the car he stops at and sends language out across the car at the two guys. Lenz's white wig is askew and he's got no mustache, you can see. E.M. Security, normally so scrupulous with their fucking trucks at 0005h., is nowhere around, lending weight to yet another cliché. If you asked Gately what he was feeling right this second he'd have no idea. He's got a hand up shading his eyes and closes on the Montego as things further clarify. One of the guys now you can see has Lenz's disguise's mustache in two fingers and keeps holding it up and brandishing it at Lenz. The other guy issues stilted but colorful threats in a Canadian accent, so it emerges on Gately it's Nucks, the trio Lenz has managed to somehow enrage is Nucks. Gately cops a black surge of Remember-Whenning, the babbling little football-head Québecer he'd killed by gagging a man with a bad cold. This line of thinking is intolerable. Joelle's overhead shout to for Christ's sake somebody call Pat mixes in and out of the Help lady's cries. It occurs to Gately that the Help lady has cried Wolf for so many years that real shouts for real help are all going to be ignored. The residents all look to Gately as he crosses the street directly into the Montego's wash of light. Hester Thrale screams out Look out there's a Item. The plaid-hat Nuck pans stiffly to sight at Gately, his elbow up around his ear. It occurs to Gately if you fire with an Item right up to your sighting-eye like that won't you get a face full of cordite. There's a break in the circular action around the throbbing car as Lenz shouts *Don* with great gusto just as the Help lady shouts for Help. The Nuck with the Item has backed up several steps to keep the residents in his peripheral vision while he sights square on Gately as the massive Nuck holding the mustache across the car tells Gately if he was him he'd return to whence he came, him, to avoid the trouble. Gately nods and beams. Nucks really do pronounce *the* with a *z*. Both the car and Lenz are between Gately and the large Nucks, Lenz's back to Gately. Gately stands quietly, wishing he felt different about potential trouble, less almost jolly. Late in Gately's Substance and burglary careers, when he'd felt so low about himself, he'd had sick little fantasies of saving somebody from harm, some innocent party, and getting killed in the process and getting eulogized at great length in bold-faced *Globe* print. Now Lenz breaks away from the hood of the car and dashes Gately's way and around behind him to stand behind him, spreading his arms wide to put a hand on each of Gately's shoulders, using Don Gately like a shield. Gately's stance has the kind of weary resolution of like You'll Have to Go Through Me. The only anxious part of him can see the Log entry he'll have to make if residents come to physical grief on his shift. For a moment he can almost smell the smells of the penitentiary, armpits and Pomade and sour food and cribbage-board-wood and reefer and mopwater, the rich piss stink of a zoo's lion house, the smell of the bars you lace your hands through and stand there, looking out. This line of thinking is intolerable. He's neither goosepimpled nor sweating. His senses haven't been this keen in over a year. The stars in their jelly and dirty sodium lamplight and stark white steer-horns of headlights splayed at residents' different angles. Star-chocked sky, his breath, faraway horns, low trill of ATHSCMEs way to the north. Thin keen cold air in his wide-open nose. Motionless heads at #5's windows.

The Nuck duo with flowers chasing Lenz come around this side and now break away from the car toward them. Now Hester Thrale at Gately's right periphery breaks away from the cluster and runs for it off into the night across the lawn and behind #4, waving her arms and screaming, and Minty and McDade and Parias-Carbo and Charlotte Treat appear out of Ennet House's back door across the hedge and mill and jostle amid the mops and old furniture on Ennet's back porch, watching, and a couple of the more mobile catatonics appear on the porch of the Shed across the little street, staring at the spect-op, all this flummoxing the smaller one so he keeps swinging the Item stiffly this way and that way, trying to keep way more people at potential bay. The two alien foreigners that want Lenz's map bear down slowly across the Montego's headlights toward where Lenz is holding Gately like a shield. The larger one that's so large his luauish shirt won't even button all the way holding out the mustache adopts the overly reasonable tone that always precedes a serious-type beef. He reads Gately's bowling shirt in the headlight and says reasonably that Moose still has a chance to keep out of what they've got no beef with him, them. Lenz is pouring a diarrheatic spatter of disclaimers and exhortations into Gately's right ear. Gately shrugs at the Nucks like he's got no choice but to be here. Green's just looking at them. It occurs to Gately by White Flag suggestion that who gives a fuck how it'd look, he ought to hit his knees right here on the headlit blacktop and ask for guidance on this from a Higher Power. But he stands there, Lenz chattering in his shadow. The fingernails of Lenz's hand on Gately's shoulder have horseshoes of dried blood in the creases between nail and finger, and there's a coppery smell off Lenz that isn't just fear. It occurs to Gately that if he'd pulled the instant spot-urine he'd wanted on Lenz this whole snafu wouldn't maybe be happening. The one Nuck is holding Lenz's disguise's mustache out at them like a blade. Lenz hasn't asked the time once, notice. Then the other Nuck's got his hand down at his side and a real blade's gleam appears in that hand with the familiar *snick*. At the blade's sound the situation becomes even more automatic and Gately feels adrenaline's warmth spread through him as his subdural hardware clicks deeper into a worn familiar long-past track. Having no choice now not to fight and things simplify radically, divisions collapse. Gately's just one part of something bigger he can't control. His face in the left headlight has dropped into its fight-expression of ferocious good cheer. He says he's responsible for these people on these private grounds tonight and is part of this whether he wants to be or not, and can they talk this out because he doesn't want to have to fight them. He says twice very distinctly that he does not want to fight them. He's no longer divided enough to think about whether this is true. His eyes are on the two men's maple-leaf belt buckles, the part of the body where you can't get suckered by a feint. The guys shake their manes and say they're going to unembowel this craven *bâtard* here like this *sans-Christe bâtard* killed somebody they call either Pépé or Bébé, and if Moose has any self-interest he'll backpedal away from there's no way it is his duty to get frapped or fropped for this sick gutless U.S.A. *bâtard* in his womanly wig. Lenz, apparently thinking they're Brazilian, pops his head around Gately's flank and calls them *maricones* and tells them they can suck his *bâtard* is what they can do. Gately has just division enough to almost wish he didn't feel such a glow of familiar warmth, a surge of almost sexual competence, as the two shriek at Lenz's taunts and split and curve in at them an arm's length apart, walking gradually faster, like unstoppable inertia, but stupidly too close together. At two meters off they charge, shedding petals and unisonly bellowing something in Canadian.

It's always that everything always speeds up and slows down both. Gately's smile broadens as he's shoved slightly forward by Lenz as Lenz recoils backward off him to run from the guys' shrieking charge. Gately takes the shove's momentum and bodychecks the enormous Nuck holding the mustache into the Nuck holding the blade, who goes down with an *euf* of expelled air. The first Nuck has hold of Gately's bowling shirt and rips it and punches Gately in the forehead and audibly breaks his hand, letting go of Gately to grab his hand. The punch makes Gately stop thinking in any sort of spiritual terms at all. Gately takes the man's broken hand's arm he's holding out and with his eyes on the ground's other Nuck breaks the arm over his knee, and as the guy goes down on one knee Gately takes the arm and pirouettes around twisting the broken arm behind the guy's back and plants his sneaker on the guy's floral back and forces him forward so there's a sick crack and he feels the arm come out of the socket, and there's a high foreign scream. The Nuck with the blade who was down slashes Gately's calf through his jeans as the guy rolls gracefully left and starts to rise, up on one knee, knife out front, a guy that knows his knives and can't be closed with while he's got the blade up. Gately feints and takes one giant step and gets all his weight into a Rockette kick that lands high up under the Nuck's beard's chin and audibly breaks Gately's big toe in the sneaker and sends the man curving out back into the dazzle of the highbeams, and there's a metallic boom of him landing on the Montego's hood and the click and skitter of the blade landing somewhere on the street beyond the car. Gately on one foot, holding his toe, and his slashed calf feels hot. His smile is broad but impersonal. It's impossible, outside choreographed entertainment, to fight two guys together at once; they'll kill you; the trick to fighting two is to make sure and put one down for long enough that he's out of the picture long enough to put the other guy down. And this first larger one with the extreme arm-trouble is clutching himself as he rolls, trying to rise, still perversely holding the white mustache. You can tell this is a real beef because nobody's saying anything and the sounds from everybody else have receded to the sounds stands' crowds make and Gately hops over and uses the good foot to kick the Nuck twice in the side of the big head and then without a thought in his head moves down the guy and lines it up and drops to one knee with all his weight on the guy's groin, resulting in an indescribable sound from the guy and a shout from J.v.D. overhead and a flat crack from the lawn and Gately's punched so hard in the shoulder he's spun around on one knee and almost goes over backwards and the shoulder goes hotly numb, which tells Gately he's gotten shot instead of punched in the shoulder. He never got shot before. **SHOT IN SOBRIETY** in bold headline caps goes across his mind's eye like a slow train as he sees the third Nuck with his cap pushed back and Nuck face contorted with cordite in his good stance with elbow back up drawing a second bead on Don's big head from #4's lawn with the bore's lightless eye and a little pubic curl of smoke coming up from the vented muzzle, and Gately can't move and forgets to pray, and then the bore zagging up and away as it blooms orange as good old Bruce Green's got the Nuck from behind in a half-nelson with his hand in the necklace of flowers and with the other hand is forcing the cocked elbow down and the Item skyward away from Gately's head as it blooms with that flat crack of a vented muzzle. The first thing somebody's who's shot wants to do is throw up, which by the way the larger Nuck with the breezeblocked crotch under Gately's doing all over his beard and flower necklace and Gately's leg's thigh as Gately weaves on one knee on the guy's groin still. The lady yells for Help. Now a meaty thwack as Nell Gunther on the lawn leaps several twirling meters and kicks the Nuck Green's half-nelsoning in the face with her paratrooper-boot's heel, and the guy's hat flies off and his head snaps back and hits Green's face, and there's the pop of Green's nose breaking but he doesn't let go, and the guy's slumped forward in the Parkinsonian half-bow of a guy in a quality half-nelson, with the guy's Item-hand's arm still up in the air with Green's arm like they're dancing, and good old Green doesn't even let go to hold his spurting nose, and now that the Nuck's restrained, notice, here comes Lenz barrelling in howling from the hedge's shadows and leaping and he tackles the Nuck and Green both, and they're a roil of clothes and legs on the lawn, the Item not in sight. Ken Erdedy still has his hands up. Gately, still kneeling shot on the Nuck's sickeningly softened groin, Gately hears the second Nuck trying to slide himself off the hood of the Montego and hops and wobbles over. Joelle v.D. keeps yelling something monosyllabic from what can't be her window. Don goes to the Montego's front bumper and punches the large man carefully in the kidneys with his good arm and takes him by the thick foreign hair and slides him back up the hood and begins banging his head off the Montego's windshield. He remembers how he'd stay in luxury furnished North Shore apts. with G. Fackelmann and T. Kite and they'd gradually strip the place and sell the appointments off until they were sleeping in a totally bare apartment. Green has risen bloody-faced, and Lenz is on the lawn with his heaving topcoat covering him and the third Nuck, and Clenette H. and Yolanda W. are now up and not at bay and circling them and getting solid high-heel kicks into the Nuck's and sometimes hopefully Lenz's ribs, reciting 'Mothafucka' and landing a kick each time they get to fu. Gately, canted way over to the side, methodically beats his Nuck's shaggy head against the windshield so hard that spidered stars are appearing in the shatterproof glass until something in the head gives with a sort of liquid crunch. Petals from the guy's necklace are all over the hood and Gately's torn shirt. Joelle v.D. in her terry robe and gauze veil and still clutching a toothbrush has climbed out onto the little balcony outside the 5-Woman's window and into a skinny ailanthus beside it and is coming down, showing about two meters of spectacularly undeformed thigh, shouting Gately's name by the first name, which he likes. Gately leaves the largest Nuck prone on the idling hood, his head resting in a shatter-frosted head-shaped recession in the windshield. It occurs to Ken Erdedy, looking up into the oak past his upraised hands, that this deformed veiled girl likes Don Gately in an extracurricular way, it would seem. Gately, toe and shoulder or no, has looked strictly all-business this whole time. He's projected a sort of white-collar attitude of cheery competence and sangfroid. Erdedy's found he rather likes standing there with his hands up in a gesture of noncombatant status while the Afro-American girls curse and kick and Lenz continues to roll around with the unconscious man hitting him and going 'There, *there*,' and Gately moves backward between the second fellow in the windshield and the first fellow he'd originally disarmed, his smile now as empty as a pumpkin's grin. Chandler Foss is trying on the third fellow's plaid hunting cap. There's a sound in #4 of somebody trying to force a warped window. An Empire W.D.V. is launched with a kind of spronging thud and whistles overhead, climbing, its warning-light wrap of like Xmas lights winking red and green as Don Gately starts to come over in the direction of the lawn and the fellow who appears to have winged him and then veers drunkenly and changes direction and in three one-foot hops is over to the vomit-covered first Nuck, the one who'd called Gately Moose and punched him in the forehead. There's the slow trundle of the Green T and exhortations from Minty as Gately begins stomping on the supine face of the Nuck with the heel of his good foot as if he were killing cockroaches. The guy's movable arm is waggling pathetically in the air around Gately's shoe as it rises and falls. Gately's hideous torn orange shirt's whole right side is dark and his right arm drips blackly and seems weirdly set in its socket. Lenz is up and adjusting his wig and brushing off. The veiled girl has hit a rough part some three meters up and is hanging from a limb and kicking, Erdedy staring Copernicanly up her flapping robe. The new Tingley kid sits cross-legged in the grass and rocks as the black ladies continue stomping the inert Nuck. You can hear Emil Minty and Wade McDade exhorting Yolanda W. to use the spike heel. Charlotte Treat is reciting the Serenity Prayer over and over. Bruce Green has his head back and his finger held like a mustache under his nostrils. Hester Thrale can still be heard way off down Warren Street, receding, as Gately wobbles back from the Nuck's map and sits heavily down in the little street, in shadow except for his huge head in the Nucks' car's lights, sitting there with his head on his knees. Lenz and Green move in toward him the cautious way you approach a big animal that's hurt. Joelle van Dyne lands on her feet. The lady at the high warped window shouts for Helphelphelphelp*help*. Minty and McDade come down off the back porch, finally, McDade for some reason wielding a mop. Everybody except Lenz and Minty looks unwell.

Joelle runs just like a girl, Erdedy notes.[256] She gets out through the many-angled cars into the street just as Gately decides to lie down.

It's not like passing out. It's just a decision Gately makes to like lie back with his knees bent and pointing up into the sky's depth, which seems to bulge and recede with the pulse in his right shoulder, which has now gone dead cold, which means there will very soon be pain, he predicts.

He waves off concern with the left hand and goes 'Flesh-wound' the second Joelle's bare feet and robe's hem are in view.

'Son of a fucking *bitch*.'

'Flesh-wound.'

'Are you ever *bleeding*.'

'Thanks for the feedback.'

You can hear Henderson and Willis off in the background still going '*fu*.'

'I think you can tell them he's probably subdued,' Gately pointing off in what he thinks is #4's lawn's direction. His lying flat gives him a double-chin, he can feel, and pulls his big face into a smile. His big present fear is throwing up in front of and maybe partly on Joelle v.D., whose calves he's noted.

Now Lenz's lizard-skin loafers with grass stains at the toes. 'Don what can I say.'

Gately struggles to sit back up. 'You got fucking armed *Nucks* wanting your ass too?'

Revealing a kind of blackly kimonoish thing under, Joelle has taken off the terry robe and folds the robe into a kind of trapezoidal pad and is kneeling over Gately's shoulder, straddling his arm, pressing down on the pad with the heels of her hands.

'Owie.'

'Lenz he's really bleeding bad here.'

'I'm groping to even know what to begin to say, Don.'

'You owe me urine, Lenz.'

'I think there's two of them, like, desisted.' Wade McD.'s unlaced high-tops, his voice breathy with awe.

'He's bleeding really bad I said.'

'You mean deceased.'

'There's one of their shoes in one of them's fucking eye.'

'Tell Ken to put his hands down for Christ's sake.'

'Oh fucking *God*.'

Gately can feel his eyes crossing and uncrossing by themselves.

'He soaking right through it man look at that shit.'

'This man needs an ambulance.'

Somebody else female says God again and Gately's hearing warbles a bit as Joelle snaps at her to shut up. She leans down and in, so Gately can see up at what looks like a regular human female chin and makeupless lower lip under the veil's billowing hem. 'Whom should we call?' she asks him.

'Call Pat's machine and Calvin. You have to dial 9. Tell them to come down.'

'I'm going to be sick.'

'Airdaddy!' Minty is shouting at Ken E.

'Tell her to call Annie and the E.M. office down there and do some like strategic thing.'

'Where the fuck is Security when it isn't just innocent recovering cars to get towed?'

'And call Pat,' Gately says.

A forest of footwear and bare feet and shins all around him, and heads too high to see. Lenz screaming back to somebody in the House: 'Call a fucking *am*bulance already.'

'Regulate the voice, man.'

'Fucking call about *five* ambulances is more like it.'

'Motha*fu*cka.'

'Ssshh.'

'I just never saw anything *like* that.'

'Nuh-uh,' Gately gasps, trying to rise and deciding he just likes it better lying down. 'Don't call one for me.'

'This is the straight and narrow?'

'By doze is fide.'

'He doesn't *want* one he said.'

Green's and Minty's boots, Treat's purple plastic shower-thongs. Somebody has on Clearasil, he can smell.

'Seen some righteous ass-kickings in my past, brother, but —'

Somebody male screams back off to the right.

'Just don't try and walk me around,' Gately grins up.

'Dipshit.'

'He can't go in no E.R. with a gunshot,' Minty says to Lenz, whose shoes keep moving to get himself north of everybody.

'Somebody turn off the car will you?'

'I wouldn't touch nothing.'

Gately focuses at where the Joelle girl's eyes would be. Her thighs are forked way wide to straddle his arm, which is numb and doesn't feel like his. She's bearing down on him. She smells strange but good. She's got all her weight on her bathrobe's pad. She weighs roughly nothing. The first threads of pain are starting to radiate out of the shoulder and down the side and into the neck. Gately hasn't looked down at the shoulder, on purpose, and he tries to wedge his left hand's finger under the shoulder to see if anything went through. The night's so clear the stars shine right through people's heads.

'Green.'

'I'b dot touchig dothig, dud worry.'

'Look at his *head*.'

Her kimono's shoulders are humped and glassy black in the Montego's light. Gately's brain keeps wanting to go away inside himself. When you start to feel deeply cold that's shock and blood-loss. Gately sort of wills himself to stay right here, looks over past Joelle's hand at Lenz's fine shoes. 'Lenz. You and Green. Get me inside.'

'Green!'

The circle of stars' heads' faces above are all faceless from the headlights' shadows. Some car engines have shut off and some haven't. One of the cars has a twittering fan-belt. Somebody's suggesting to call the genuine Finest — Erdedy — which everybody greets with scorn at his naïveté. Gately's figuring Staff from the Shed or #4 has called them or at least dialed down to Security. By the time he was ten only his pinkie-finger would fit in the dialer's holes of his mother's old princess phone; he exerts will to un-cross his eyes and stay right here; he in the worst way does not want to be lying here with a gunshot in shock trying to deal with the Finest.

'I think one of these guys is, like, expired.'

'No shit Shylock.'

'*Nobody call.*' Gately yells it up and out. He's afraid he's going to vomit when they stand him up. 'Nobody call nobody til you get me in.' He can smell Green's leather jacket overhead. Bits of grass and whatnot drifting down onto him from where Lenz is still brushing off his clothes, and coins of blood on the street from Green's nose. Joelle tells Lenz if he doesn't cut something out she's going to hand him his ass. Gately's whole right side had gone deadly cold. To Joelle he says, 'I'm Supervised. I'll go to jail sure.'

'You got fucking eyewitnesses out the ass behind you Don man,' either McDade or Glynn says, but it can't be Glynn, for some reason he tries to bring up inside him. And it seems like Charlotte T.'s voice saying Ewell's trying to get in Pat's office to call but Gately locked Pat's door.

'Nobody call *anyone!*' Joelle shouts up and out. She smells good.

'They're calling!'

'Get him off the phone! Say prank for Christ's sake! You hear me?' Her kimono smells good. Her voice has a Staff-like authority. The scene out here has changed: Gately's down, Madame Psychosis is in charge.

'We're going to get him up and we're going to get him inside,' she says to the circle. 'Lenz.'

There's impending static-crackle and the sound of a serious set of keys.

Her voice is that one Madame lady's voice on no-subscription radio, from out of nowhere he's all of a sudden sure, is where he heard that odd empty half-accented voice before.

'Secyotty! Hold it *right* thaah.' It's at least luckily one of the ex-football E.M. Security guys, that spends half his shift down at the Life and then goes up and down the streetlet all night playing with his service baton and sing-ing sea chanties off-key, that's just impressively qualified to Come In to AA with them.

Joelle: 'Erdedy — deal with him.'

'Pardon me?'

'It's the drunk,' Gately gets out.

Joelle's looking up at presumably Ken E. 'Go over and look high-income and respectable at him. Verbalize at him. Distract him while we get him inside before the real ones come.'

'How am I supposed to explain all these prone figures draped over cars?'

'For Christ's sake Ken he's not a mental titan — distract him with something shiny or something. Get your thumb out of your ass and move.'

Gately's smile has reached his eyes. 'You're Madame on the FM, is how I knew you.'

Erdedy's squeaky shoe and the obese guy's radio and keys. 'Who hold it? As in desist?'

'Se*cyotty* I said *halt!*'

Green and Lenz bending in, white breath all over and Green's dripping nose the same copper smell as Lenz.

'I knew I knew you,' Gately says to Joelle, whose veil remains inscrutable.

'If I could ask you to specify halt from what.'

'Get his back up here first,' Green tells Lenz.

'Not crazy about all this blood,' Lenz is saying.

Many hands slide under his back; the shoulder blooms with colorless fire. The sky looks so 3-D you could like dive in. The stars distend and sprout spikes. Joelle's warm legs shift with her weight to keep pressure on the pad. The squishing sound Gately knows means the robe's soaked through. He wants somebody to congratulate him for not having thrown up. You can tell some of the stars are nearer and some far, down there. What Gately's always thought of as the Big Question Mark is really the Big Dipper.

'I'm *oddering* desist until who's in chahge that I can repot the si*chation*.' The Security guy's hammered, his name's Sidney or Stanley and he wears his Security-hat and baton shopping in the Purity Supreme and always asks Gately how it's hanging. His shoes' uppers are blasted along the feet's insides the way fat men that have to walk a lot's are; his ex-ballplayer's collops and big hanging gut are one of Gately's great motivators for nightly situps. Gately turns his head to throw up a little on both Green and Joelle, who both ignore it.

'Oh sorry. Oh shit I hate that.'

Joelle v.D. runs a hand down Gately's wet arm that leaves a warm wake, the hand, and then gently squeezes as much of the wrist as she can get her hand around. 'And Lo,' she says softly.

'Jesus his leg's all bloody too.'

'Boy do I know guys loved that show you did.' A tiny bit more throwing up.

'Now we're going to lift him very gently and get the feet under.'

'Here Green man get over here on the south why don't you.'

'I'm oddering the whole sitchation halt it *right* thaah whe*yaah*.'

Lenz and Green's shoes coming together and moving apart at either side of Gately, faces coming down in a fish-eye lens, lifting:

'Ready?'

<h1 style="text-align:center">O</h1>

Year of the Depend Adult Undergarment: InterLace TelEntertainment, 932/1864 R.I.S.C. power-TPs w/ or w/o console, Pink$_2$, post-Primestar D.S.S. dissemination, menus and icons, pixel-free InterNet Fax, tri- and quad-modems w/ adjustable baud, post-Web Dissemination-Grids, screens so high-def you might as well be there, cost-effective videophonic conferencing, internal Froxx CD-ROM, electronic couture, all-in-one consoles, Yushityu ceramic nanoprocessors, laser chromatography, Virtual-capable media-cards, fiber-optic pulse, digital encoding, killer apps; carpal neuralgia, phosphenic migraine, gluteal hyperadiposity, lumbar stressae. Half of all metro Bostonians now work at home via some digital link. 50% of all public education disseminated through accredited encoded pulses, absorbable at home on couches. Ms. Tawni Kondo's immensely popular exercise program spontaneously disseminated daily in all three O.N.A.N. time zones at 0700h., a combination of low-impact aerobics, Canadian Air Force calisthenics, and what might be termed 'cosmetic psychology' — upwards of 60 million North Americans daily kicking and genuflecting with Tawni Kondo, a mass choreography somewhat similar to those compulsory A.M. tai chi slo-mo exercise assemblies in post-Mao China — except that the Chinese assemble publicly together. One-third of those 50% of metro Bostonians who still leave home to work could work at home if they wished. And (get this) 94% of all O.N.A.N.ite paid entertainment now absorbed at home: pulses, storage cartridges, digital displays, domestic decor — an entertainment-market of sofas and eyes.

Saying this is bad is like saying traffic is bad, or health-care surtaxes, or the hazards of annular fusion: nobody but Ludditic granola-crunching freaks would call bad what no one can imagine being without.

But so very much private watching of customized screens behind drawn curtains in the dreamy familiarity of home. A floating no-space world of personal spectation. Whole new millennial era, under Gentle and Lace-Forché. Total freedom, privacy, choice.

Hence the new millennium's passion for standing live witness to things. A whole sub-rosa schedule of public spectation opportunities, 'spect-ops,' the priceless chance to be part of a live crowd, watching. Thus the Gapers' Blocks at traffic accidents, sewer-gas explosions, muggings, purse-snatchings, the occasional Empire W.D.V. with an incomplete vector splatting into North Shore suburbs and planned communities and people leaving their front doors agape in their rush to get out and mill around and spectate at the circle of impacted waste drawing sober and studious crowds, milling in rings around the impact, earnestly comparing mental notes on just what it is they all see. Hence the apotheosis and intricate pecking-order of Boston street musicians, the best of whom now commute to work in foreign autos. The nightly chance to crank back the drapes and face out into the streets at 0000h., when all street-parked vehicles have to switch sides and everyone goes nuts and mills, either switching or watching. Street fights, supermarket-checkout confrontations, tax-auctions, speeders stopped for ticketing, coprolaliac Touretters on downtown corners, all drawing liquid crowds. The fellowship and anonymous communion of being part of a watching crowd, a mass of eyes all not at home, all out in the world and pointed the same way. Q.v. the crowd-control headaches at crime-scenes, fires, demonstrations, rallies, marches, displays of Canadian insurgency; crowds brought together now so quickly, too quickly even to see them, a kind of visual inversion of watching something melt, the crowds collect and are held tight by an almost seemingly nucleic force, watching together. Almost anything can do it. Street vendors are back. Homeless vets and twisted figures in wheelchairs with hand-lettered signs outlining entitlement. Jugglers, freaks, magicians, mimes, charismatic preachers with portable PAs. Hardcore panhandlers stem like they're selling nostrums to small crowds; the best panhandling now verges on stand-up comedy, and is rewarded by watching crowds. Cultists in saffron with much percussion and laser-jet leaflets. Even some old-style Eurobeggars, black-browed persons in striped leggings, mute and aloof. Even local candidates, activists, advocates and grass-roots aides have returned full-circle to the public stump — the bunting-hung platform, the dumpster-lid, vehicles' roofs, awnings, anything overhead, anything raised to a crowd-collecting public view: people climb and declaim, drawing crowds.

One top Back Bay public spect-op every November is watching expressionless men in federal white and municipal cadet-blue drain and scrub the Public Gardens' man-made duck pond for the upcoming winter. They drain it sometime in November every year. It's publicly unannounced; there's no fixed schedule; long shiny trucks just all of a sudden appear in a ring at pond's rim; it's always a weekday c. mid-November; it's also always somehow a gray raw sad windy Boston day, gulls cartwheeling in a sky the color of dirty glass, people mufflered and with new gloves on. Not your ideal sylvan-type day for conventional lounging or public spectation. But a massive crowd always collects and thickens in a dense ring along the banks of the Public Gardens' pond. The pond has ducks. The pond is perfectly round, its surface roughened to elephant skin by the wind, geometrically round and banked with lawn-quality grass and shrubbery in even-spaced clumps, with park-type benches between the shrubs overhung by white-barked willows who've now wept their yellow autumn grit onto the green benches and grass banks where an arc of crowd now forms and thickens, watching duly designated authorities commence to drain the pond. Some of the pond's flightier ducks have already decamped for points south, and more leave on some phylogenic cue just as the shiny trucks pull up, but the main herd remains. Two private planes fly in lazy ellipses just under the cloud-cover overhead, banners strung out behind them advertising four different levels of comfort and protection from Depend. The wind keeps blowing the banners sideways, möbiusizing them and then straightening them back out with the loud pop of flags unfurling. From the ground the engines and banners' pops are too faint to hear above the crowd-noise and ducks and wind's mean whistle. The swirling groundwind's so bad that U.S. Chief of Unspecified Services Rodney Tine, standing with his hands at the small of his back at a window on the eighth floor of the State House Annex on Beacon and Joy Sts., looking southwest and down at the concentric rings of pond and crowd and trucks, can see wind-driven leaves and street-grit swirling right outside and pecking at this very window he stands before, massaging his coccyx.

Dr. James O. Incandenza, filmmaker and almost a scopophile about spect-ops and crowds, never once missed this spectacle, when alive and in town. Hal and Mario have both been to a few. So have several Ennet residents, though some of them weren't in much of a position to remember. It seems as if everyone in metro Boston's seen at least one pond-draining. It's always the same sort of grim windy Northeast November day where if you were at home you'd be eating earth-tone soups in a warm kitchen, listening to the wind and glad of home and hearth. Every year Himself came was the same. The deciduous trees were always skeletal, the pines palsied, the willows wind-whipped and nubbly, the grass dun and crunchy underfoot, the water-rats always seeing the big drainage-picture first and gliding like night to the cement sides to flee. Always a crowd in thickening rings. Always rollerblades on the Gardens' paths, lovers joined at the hand, Frisbee in the distance on the rim of the Gardens' other side's hillside's slope, which faces away from the pond.

U.S. Office of Unspecified Services Chief Rodney Tine stands at the unclean window for much of the morning, ruminative, his posture a martial at-ease. A stenographer and an aide and a Deputy Mayor and the Director of the Massachusetts Division for Substance Abuse Services, and Unspecified Services Regional Operatives Rodney Tine Jr.[257] and Hugh Steeply[258] all sit silently in the conference room behind him, the stenographer's Gregg pen poised in mid-dictation. The eighth-floor window's purview goes all the way to the ridge of the hillside at the Gardens' other end. Two Frisbees and what looks like a disembowelled ring of Frisbee float back and forth along this ridge, dreamily floating back and forth, sometimes dipping below the ridge and lost, for a moment, to the specular vision of Tine.

Trying at the same time to give his bad skin some quality UV and a good chill's chap, the grad-work-study engineer of M.I.T.'s WYYY-109 lies bare-chested on a silvery NASA-souvenir space blanket, supine and cruciform at about the angle of a living-room recliner on the Public Gardens' far hillside. This is out by Arlington St., in the Gardens' southwest corner, hidden by its ridge from the pond's basin and tourism booth and pavilion and the hub of radial paths and the giant verdigrised statues of ducklings in a row commemorating Robert McCloskey's beloved and timeless *Make Way for Ducklings*. The Gardens' only other slope is now the bowl of the former pond. The hillside's grassy decline, not too steep, runs at a wedge's angle down toward Arlington St. and is one broad greensward, free of dog droppings because dogs won't go to the bathroom on inclined terrain. Frisbees float on the ridge behind the engineer's head, and four lithe boys on the ridge play a game with a small beanbaggy ball and bare blue feet. It is 5° C. The sun has the attenuated autumn quality of seeming to be behind several panes of glass. The wind is bitter and keeps flopping unmoored sections of NASA blanket over parts of the engineer's body. Goose-pimples and real pimples jostle each other for space on his exposed flesh. The student engineer's is the hillside's only metallic space blanket and bare torso. He lies there splayed, wholly open to the weak sun. The WYYY student engineer is one of roughly three dozen human forms scattered over the steep slope, a human collection without pattern or cohesion or anything to bind them, looking rather like firewood before it's been gathered. Wind-bronzed sooty men in zipperless parkas and mismatched shoes, some of the Gardens' permanent residents, sleeping or in stupors of various origin. Curled on their sides, knees drawn up, unopen to anything. In other words huddled. From the great height of one of Arlington St.'s office buildings, the forms look like things dumped onto the hillside from a great height. An overhead veteran'd be apt to see a post-battle-battlefield aspect to the array of forms. Except for the WYYY engineer, all the men are textured in urban scuz, unshaven, yellow-fingered and exposure-bronzed. They have coats and bedrolls for blankets and old twine-handle shopping bags and Glad bags for recyclable cans and bottles. Also huge camper's packs without any color to them. Their clothes and appurtenances are the same color as the men, in other words. A few have steel supermarket-carts filled with possessions and wedged by their owners' bodies against a downhill roll. One of the cart-owners has vomited in his sleep, and the vomit has assumed a lava-like course toward the huddled form of another man curled just downhill. One of the shopping carts, from upscale Bread & Circus, has an ingeniously convenient little calculator on its handlebar, designed to let shoppers subtotal their groceries as they select them. The men have sepia nails and all somehow look toothless whether they have teeth or not. Every so often a Frisbee lands among them. The loose ball makes a beanbaggy sound against players' feet above and behind them. Two skinny and knit-capped boys descend very close to the engineer, chanting very softly 'Smoke,' ignoring all the other forms, which anyone could tell are undercapitalized for purchasing Smoke. When his eyes are open he's the only one on the hillside to see the round bellies of ascending ducks pass low overhead, catching a thermal off the hillside and rising to wheel away left, due south. His WYYY-109 T-shirt and inhaler and glasses and M. Fizzy and spine-split copy of *Metallurgy of Annular Isotopes* are just off the edge of the reflecting blanket. His torso is pale and ribby, his chest covered with tough little buttons of acne scar. The hillside's grass is still pretty viable. One or two of the scattered fetal forms have black cans of burnt-out Sterno beside them. Bits of the hillside are reflected in Arlington's storefronts and office windows and the glass of passing cars. An unexceptional white Dodge or Chevy-type van pulls out of Arlington's traffic and does some pretty impressive parallel parking along the curb at the hillside's bottom. A man in an ancient NATO-surplus wool greatcoat is up on his hands and knees to the engineer's lower left, throwing up. Bits of chyme hang from his mouth and refuse to detach. There's little bloody threads in it. His hunched form looks somehow canine on the uneven slope. The fetal figure wedged unconscious under the front wheels of the shopping cart nearest the engineer has only one shoe, and that shoe's without laces. The exposed sock is ash-colored. Besides the HANDI-CAPPED license plate, the only exceptional things about the van now idling at the curb far below are the tinted windows and the fact that the van is spotless and twinkly with wax to about halfway up its panelled side, but above that line dirty and rust-saucered and shamefully neglected-looking. The engineer has been turning his head this way and that, trying to tan evenly along his whole jawline. The curbside van idles at a distant little point between his heels. Some of the hillside's forms have curled themselves around bottles and pipes. A smell comes off them, rich and agricultural. The student engineer doesn't usually try to sun and chap his skin at the same time, but chapping-ops have lately been scarce: since Madame Psychosis of '60+/−' took her sudden leave of medical absence, the student engineer hasn't once had the heart to sit out on the Union's convoluted roof and monitor the substitute shows.

The engineer moves his upturned face back and forth. First, Madame was replaced by a Mass Comm. graduate student who proved a crushing disappointment as a Miss Diagnosis; then Madame was publicly deemed irreplaceable by management, and the engineer is now paid simply to cue her background music and then sit monitoring a live mike for a noiseless 60 minutes, which means he has to stay in his booth maintaining 0-levels with a live mike and can't ascend with his receiver and cigarettes even if he wanted to. The station's student manager's given the engineer written instructions on just what to say when people phone in during the hour to inquire and wish Psychosis a speedy recovery from whatever might ail her. At once denying and encouraging rumors of suicide, institutionalization, spiritual crisis, silent retreat, pilgrimage to the snow-capped East. The disappearance of someone who's been only a voice is somehow worse instead of better. A terrible silence now, weeknights. A different silence altogether from the radio-silence-type silence that used to take up over half her nightly show. Silence of presence v. silence of absence, maybe. The silences on the tapes are the worst. Some listeners have actually come in and down through the deep cortex and into the cold pink studio itself, to inquire. Some to allay this firm conviction that Madame was still actually still showing up and sitting there by the mike but not saying anything. Another of the men sleeping nearby keeps punching at the air in his sleep. Almost all the personal wee-hour inquiries are from listeners somehow bent, misshapen, speech-defective, vacantly grinning, damaged in some way. The type whose spectacles have been repaired with electrician's tape. Shyly inquiring. Apologies for bothering someone they can clearly see is not even there. Before the student manager's written instructions, the student engineer'd wordlessly directed their attention to Madame's triptych screen with no silhouette behind it. Another white Dodge van, just as unevenly clean and opaque-windowed, has appeared on the ridge above and behind the hillside's littered forms. It casts no visible shadow. A Frisbee-ring caroms off the clean grille of its snout. It idles, its panel door facing the declivity and the other white van's panel door far below. One hideous little inquirer had had a hat with a lens on it and seemed about to fall forward into the engineer's lap. His attendant wanting some address where they might send something supportive and floral. The NASA blanket's micronized aluminumoid coating is designed to refract every possible UV ray into the student engineer's bare skin. The engineer knows about the ambulance and the Brigham and Women's ICU and five-day rehab ward from the thick swart girl Notkin, the one with the disreputable hat and Film-Dept. I.D. who came down via the Basilar elevator late at night to retrieve some old tapes of the program for the Madame's personal listening use, she said, and was fortunate enough to know the Madame in private life, she said. The term is *Treatment*, Madame Psychosis is in long-term *Treatment* at something the bearded girl in the sooty hat obliquely described as only half a house in some unbelievably unpleasant and low-rent part of the metro-area. This is the precise total of what the WYYY engineer knows. He is shortly to have occasion to wish he knew a great deal more. Q.v. the dimpled steel ramp now protruding from the squeakily opened panel door of the van on the ridge above and behind him. Q.v. the utter darkness inside the idling van down along the Arlington St. curb, whose side panel's also been slid open from within. The southwest hillside is copless: the Gardens' platoon of M.D.C. Finest are all in their souped-up golf carts over at the drained pond, throwing curved sections of glazed doughnut into the ducks' shrubbery and telling a largely-dispersed-already crowd to please move along. The ridge's Frisbees and hackysackers have abruptly vanished; there's now an eerie stillness like a reef when a shark cruises through; the ridge's van's idling maw open and black, silver-tongued.

Q.v. also the wheelchair that now all of a sudden shoots down the hillside's van's ramp as a madly squeaking brass-colored blur, a snowplow-like scoop-type thing welded to it and out front skimming the ground and throwing off chaff from the swath of grass it's mowing, moving terrifically fast, brakes unapplied, the legless figure up on burly stumps in the chair fleur-de-lis-with-sword-stem-masked and bent far forward for a skier's pure speed, the huddled fetal hillside figures the speeding chair slaloms, the dim glittered movements of arrangement for reception deep within the curbside van way at the bottom of the steep grade, the engineer arching his neck way out to capture sun on the scarred hollows under his jaw, the shopping cart with the calculator clipped by a squeaking rubberized wheel at an angle and sent clattering off down the hillside, spraying possessions, the homeless shoe to which it had been roped skittering empty behind it and the cart's now shoeless unconscious owner just waving at the air in front of his face in sleep as if at a bad D.T.-dream of lost shoe and worldly goods, the calculating cart whumping into the side of the hunched man vomiting and flipping over and bouncing several times and the vomiting man rolling and yelping, vulgarities echoing, the WYYY engineer now to be seen hiking himself up on a chill-reddened elbow with a start and starting to turn and look above and behind him up at the ridge just as the speeding wheelchair with the hunched figure reaches him and the chair's shovel scoops the engineer and his NASA blanket and shirt and book up and runs over the glasses and bottle of M. Fizzy with one wheel and bears the engineer in the scoop up and away and down the steep grade toward the idling van at the bottom, a van whose own angled ramp now slides out like a tongue or Autoteller's transaction-receipt, the NASA blanket blowing away from the scooped engineer's flailing form about halfway down and suddenly aloft in a hillside thermal and blown far out over Arlington St. traffic by the keen November wind, the madly squeaking wheelchair aloft over hillside moguls and coming back down and up again, the snatched engineer in the chair's scoop appearing to the hillside's roused figures mostly as a hallucinatory waggle of bare limbs and strangely wheezy shrieks for Help or at least to Look Out Below, all as the modified chair squeaks frantically straight down the hillside's most efficient downward line toward the van with the ramp now idling in gear, its pipe's exhaust beating the street in high-rpm idle, the NASA blanket twisting coruscant in the air high above the street, and the shriek-roused figures on the hillside lying there still bent in and barely moving, stiff with cold and general woe, except for the hunched man, the unwell man who'd been hit by the dislodged cart, who's rolled to a stop and is thrashing, holding the parts that were hit.

1810h., 133 kids and thirteen assorted staff sitting down at suppertime, the E.T.A. dining hall taking most of the first floor of West House, a sort of airy atrium-like commons, broad and knotty-pine-panelled, the east wall hugely fenestrated and columns running the length of the room at center, with ceiling fans high overhead circulating the rich and slightly sour smell of bulk-prepared food, the oceanic sound of 20 different tables' conversation, the flat clink of utensils on plates, much chewing, the clank and tinkle of the dish-washer's conveyor belt behind the tray-bus window with its sign saying *YR MOTHER DOES NOT LIVE HERE; BUS YR TRAY*, the muffled shouts of kitchen workers in steam. The top upperclassmen get the best table, an un-spoken tradition, the one nearest the gas fireplace in winter and the AC venting in July, the one whose chairs' legs are all pretty much even, both seats and backs with thin corduroy cushions in E.T.A. red and gray. The prorectors have their own permanent table near the carbs bar; the Syrian Satelliter and enormous peasant-skirted *Moment* soft-profiler are with them.

The players can all do some very serious eating, some of them still in sweaty sweats with salt-stiff hair, too hungry after three-set P.M.s to shower before refueling. Coed tables are quietly discouraged. The Boys 18's and the cream of the 16's are all at the best table. Ortho ('The Darkness') Stice, E.T.A.'s 16's A-1, has just this P.M. gone three sets with Hal Incandenza, seventeen, E.T.A.'s second-best overall boy, taking Hal all the way to 7–5 in the third in an off-record nonchallenge exhibitionish engagement Schtitt had them play out on the West Courts that afternoon for reasons no one has yet pinned down. The match's audience had grown steadily as other chal-lenges got done and people came up from the weight room and showers. News that Stice had very nearly beaten an Inc nobody but John Wayne has been able to beat has made its figure-eight way around the tables and serv-ing line and salad bar, and lots of younger kids keep looking to the best table and Stice, sixteen, crew-cutted and still in his black Fila sweats with no shirt under the unzipped top, assembling a complex sandwich on his plate, and they let their eyes widen and postures sag to communicate awe: R.H.I.P.

Stice, oblivious, bites into his sandwich like it's the wrist of an assailant. The only sound at the table for the first few minutes is of forkwork and mastication and the slight gasping sounds of people trying to breathe while they eat. You rarely speak for the first few minutes here, eating. Supper is deadly-serious. Some of the kids even start in on their trays while still in line at the milk dispenser. Now Coyle bites in. Wayne has made his entree into a sandwich and lowers and bites. Keith Freer's eyes are half closed as his jaw muscles bulge and slacken. Some of the players' inclined heads are hard to see over the height of their food. Struck and Schacht, side by side, bite in sync and chew. The only one at the table not eating like a refugee is Trevor Axford, who as a small child back in Short Beach CT once fell off his bike onto his head and received a tiny lesion-type brain injury after which all food everywhere tastes horrible to him. His clearest explanation of the way food tastes to him is that it tastes the way vomit smells. He's discouraged from speaking at meals and holds his nose while he eats and eats with the neutral joyless expression of somebody dispensing fuel into his car. Hal Incandenza dismantles the stelliform-mold shape E.T.A. mashed potatoes come in, mixing baby-boileds in with the mashed. Petropolis Kahn and Eliot Kornspan eat with such horrible P.O.W.ish gusto that nobody else will sit with them — they're by themselves at a small table behind Schacht and Struck, utensils glittering amid a kind of fine mist or spray. Jim Troeltsch keeps holding a clear tumbler of milk up to the ceiling's full-spectrum lights and swirling the milk around in the light, looking at it. Pemulis chews with his mouth open, producing moist noises, a habit so family-of-origin-ingrained no amount of peer pressure can break him of it.

Eventually The Darkness clears his throat to speak. In the showers he'd gotten up to the middle of an Xmas story about one of his parents' epic rows. His parents had met and fallen in love in a Country/Western bar in Partridge KS — just outside Liberal KS on the Oklahoma border — met and fallen in star-crossed love in a bar playing this popular Kansas C/W-bar-game where they put their bare forearms together and laid a lit cigarette in the little valley between the two forearms' flesh and kept it there till one of them finally jerked their arm away and reeled away holding their arm. Mr. and Mrs. Stice each discovered somebody else that wouldn't jerk away and reel away, Stice explained. Their forearms were still to this day covered with little white slugs of burn-scar. They'd toppled like pines for each other from the git-go, Stice explained. They'd been divorced and remarried four or five times, depending on how you defined certain juris-prudential precepts. When they were on good domestic terms they stayed in their bedroom for days of squeaking springs with the door locked except for brief sallies out for Beefeater gin and Chinese take-out in little white cardboard pails with wire handles, with the Stice children wandering ghostlike through the clapboard house in sagging diapers or woolen underwear subsisting on potato chips out of econobags bigger than most of them were, the Stice kids. The kids did somewhat physically better during periods of nuptial strife, when a stony-faced Mr. Stice slammed the kitchen door and went off daily to sell crop insurance while Mrs. Stice — whom both Mr.

Stice and The Darkness called 'The Bride' — while The Bride spent all day and evening cooking intricate multicourse meals she'd feed bits of to The Brood (Stice refers to both himself and his six siblings as 'The Brood') and then keep warm in quietly rattling-lidded pots and then hurl at the kitchen walls when Mr. Stice came home smelling of gin and of cigarette-brands and toilet-eau not The Bride's own. Ortho Stice loves his folks to distraction, but not blindly, and every holiday home to Partridge KS he memorizes highlights of their connubial battles so he can regale the E.T.A. upperclassmen with them, mostly at meals, after the initial forkwork and gasping have died down and people have returned to sufficient levels of blood-sugar and awareness of their surroundings to be regaled. Some of them listen, drifting in and out. Troeltsch and Pemulis are arguing about whether E.T.A.'s kitchen staff has started trying to slip them powdered milk on the sly. Freer and Wayne are still hunched and chewing, very intent. Hal's making some sort of structure out of his food. Struck keeps both elbows on the table at all times and utensils in his clenched fists like a parody of a man eating. Pemulis always listens to Stice's tales, often repeating little phrases, shaking his head in admiration.

'I'm just going to go up and refuse to eat one more thing with a utensil that's gone down the disposal.' Schacht is holding up a fork with crazy tines. 'Just look at it. Who could eat with something like that.'

'The old man is a son of a bitch that is cool under fire, in terms of The Bride,' Stice says, leaning in to bite and chew. The tendency at E.T.A. is to take the entree and unless it's a wet entree to take wheat bread and make it a sandwich, for the extra carbs. It's like Pemulis can't really taste his food unless he mashes it against his palate. The Academy's wheat bread is bicycled in by guys in Birkenstock sandals from Bread & Circus Quality Provisions in Cambridge, because it's got to be not only sugarless but low in glutens, which Tavis and Schtitt believe promote torpor and excess mucus. Axford, who lost to Tall Paul Shaw in straight sets and if he loses to him again tomorrow goes down to #5-A, stares stonily into space, his motions less like somebody eating than like somebody miming eating. Hal's made an intricate fortification-structure of his food, complete with turrets and archer-slits, and even though he's not much eating or drinking his six cranberry juices he keeps swallowing a lot, studying his structure. As the eating slows down at the best table the more observant of them give Hal and Axford tiny sideways looks, the players' different CPUs humming through Decision Trees on whether a still-publicly-undiscussed but much-rumored showdown with Dr. Tavis and the O.N.A.N.T.A. urology guy, plus now this loss to Shaw and near-loss to Ortho Stice, might not have shaken Inc and Axhandle along some psychic competitive fault-line, different guys with different rankings calculating the permuted advantages to themselves of Hal and Axford having a deeply distracted and anxious week. Though Michael

Pemulis, the other rumored O.N.A.N.T.A. urine-scannee, ignores Axford's expression and Hal's excessive swallowing altogether, though possibly studiously ignoring them, staring meditatively at the squeegees[259] taken down off the wall and leaning against the unlit fireplace, fingers steepled before his lips, hearing out Troeltsch, who blows his nose with one hand and rattles his tumbler of half-drunk milk on the tabletop with the other.

Pemulis shakes his head very seriously at Troeltsch. 'Not a chance, brother.'

'I'm telling you man this milk is powdered.' Troeltsch peering down into the tumbler, probing the milk's surface with a thick finger. 'Me I can tell from powdered. I have growing-up domestic confirmed traumas around powdered. The day Mother announced milk was too heavy to keep lugging back from the store and switched to powdered, with Father's OK. Father knuckling under like Roosevelt at Yalta. My big sister ran away from *home*, and the rest of us were traumatized around it, this switch to powdered, which is unmistakable if you know what to look for.'

Freer makes a snoring noise.

'And do I ever know what to look for, to verify.' Troeltsch is hoarse, and one of these people who speaks to more than one person at once by looking from one person to one person to one person; he's not a born public speaker. 'Namely your telltale residues along the sides of the glass, when swished.' W/ great flourished swishings of the milk.

'Except Troeltsch you can turn around and see them fucking loading the bags into the dispenser every twenty minutes. Bags of milk. That say *MILK* on them, the bags. Liquid, sloshy, hard to handle. It's milk.'

'You see bags, you see the word *MILK*. They're counting on the packaging. Image management. Sensory management.' Responding to Pemulis but looking at Struck. 'Part of some larger overall kertwang. Possible punishment for the Eschaton thing.' Eyes going briefly to Hal. 'Covert vitamins possibly next. Let's not even mention saltpeter. Put aside deductions from bags a second. I'm sticking to facts. Fact: this is verifiably powdered milk.'

'You're saying they mix powdered milk and then try and pour it into milk-bags, all to allay?'

Schacht clears his mouth and swallows mightily. 'Tavis can't even regrout tile in the locker room without calling a Community Meeting or appointing a committee. The Regrouting Committee's been dragging along since May. Suddenly they're pulling secret 0300 milk-switches? It doesn't ring true, Jim.'

'And Troeltsch has a cold, he said,' Freer observes, indicating the little bottle of Seldane next to Troeltsch's squeezing-ball, by his plate. 'You can't even taste, Troeltsch, if you got a real cold.'

'Trevor should have the cold, Axhandle, no?' Schacht says, tapping carminative capsules onto his palm from his own amber bottle.

With supper they can choose milk or else cranberry juice, that most carb-caloric of juices, which froths redly in its own clear dispenser by the salad bar. The milk dispenser stands alone against the west wall, a big huge 24-liter three-bagger, the milk inserted in ovaloid mammarial bags into its refrigerated cabinet of brushed steel, with three receptacles for tumblers and three levers for controlled dispensing. There's two levers for skim and one for supposedly high-lecithin chocolate skim, which every new E.T.A. tries exactly once and discovers tastes like skim with a brown crayon melted into it. There's a sign in a kitchen-staffer's crude black block caps taped to the dispenser's façade that says MILK IS FILLING; DRINK WHAT YOU TAKE. The sign used to say MILK IS FILLING, DRINK WHAT YOU TAKE until the comma was semicolonized by the insertion of a blue dot by a fairly obvious person.[260] The line for seconds on entrees now stretches out past the milk dispenser. The best thing about satiation and slowing down on the eating is leaning back and feeling autolysis start in on what you ate and tending to your teeth while you gaze around the airy room at crowds and clumps of kids, observing behaviors and pathologies with a clear and sated head. The littler kids running in tight circles trying to follow the shadow of the ceiling fan. Girls laughing crumpled against their seatmates' shoulders. People protecting their plates. The blurred sexuality and indecisive postures of puberty. Two marginal male 16's have their heads directly in the bowls in the salad bar, and some of the surrounding females are commenting. Different kids are illustrating points with different gestures. John Wayne and Keith Freer stroll purposefully through the serpentine crowd and up to the front of the Seconds line and insert themselves in front of a little boy who's tearing at a held bagel with great violent movements of head and neck. The 18-A's get free buttinskis: R.H.I. literal P., at E.T.A. Jim Struck spears one of the cherry tomatoes out of Hal's salad bowl with a savage fork-gesture; Hal makes no comment.

Troeltsch has run his thick finger around the inside of the tumbler and is holding the digit out at different guys around the table. 'Note a certain bluish cast to it. Traces and remains. Suspicious foam. Minute grains of not quite altogether dissolved particulate powdered stuff. Powdered always leaves its telltale signs.'

'Your fucking head is a minute grain, Troeltsch.'

'Put that finger away.'

'Tryna *eat* here.'

'Paranoia,' Pemulis says, scooping up stray peas with the flat of his knife.

'Base tuition of 21,700 scooters, not counting,' Troeltsch says, moving the finger back and forth in the air — the stuff drying on the finger does not, admittedly, exactly look appetite-whetting — 'and yet let's note how the Lung's not up in spite of rampant weather and Achilles'-complaints, and today's lunch a total déjà vu of yesterday's lunch, and the bread and bagels they've started getting us Day-Old with the yellow stickers on the bags, and there's dinette sets in the tunnels and acoustic tiles in the halls and lawn-mowers in the kitchen and tripods in the grass and squeegees on the wall and Stice's bed moves around, and there's a *ball machine* in the girls' lockers, Longley reports, that for this kind of tuition none of this stuff the staff can get around to cleaning up bef—'

Stice's head has jerked up, a trace of mashed potato on his nose. 'Who says my bed moves? How's it you know anything about any beds moving?'

But it's true. The Husky VI tripod of Mario's near-fatal encounter with the U.S.S. Millicent Kent was only the beginning. Starting with the myste-rious and continuing fall of acoustic ceiling-tiles from their places in the subdorms' drop ceilings, inanimate objects have either been moved into or just out of nowhere appearing in wildly inappropriate places around E.T.A. for the past couple months in a steadily accelerating and troubling cycle. Last week a grounds-crew lawnmower sitting clean and silent and somehow menacing in the middle of the dawn kitchen gave Mrs. Clarke the fantods and resulted in Eggplant Parmesan for two suppers in a row, which sent shock waves. Yesterday A.M. there'd been a cannonesque ball machine — no small feat to move around anywhere or get through doors — in the Females' Sauna, which machine some of the upperclass girls had found and screamed at when they went in for the dawn saunas that help alleviate some vague female-type problem that none of the guys quite fathom. And two black girls on the breakfast crew reportedly found a set of squeegees on the dining hall's north wall, several meters up and hung crossed in a kind of saltire, placed there by parties unknown. F. D. V. Harde's A.M. groundsmen reportedly took the things down, and now they're leaning by the fireplace. The inappropriate found objects have had a tektitic and sinister aspect: none of the cheery odor of regular pranksterism; they're not funny. To varying degrees they've given everyone the fantods. Mrs. Clarke had taken the morning off again, was why the repeat-lunch. Stice's eyes are back on his plate, which is nearly clean. Unmentioned is the fact that Schacht and Tall Paul Shaw at lunch went over the whole part of the north wall the black girls said they found the squeegees on and could find neither nails nor holes from nails, as in no visible means of attachment. The whole thing's been studiously not talked about, adding to everybody's discomfort at Troeltsch's hoarse complaints about tuition, which vary in specifics but are otherwise routine.

'And then now the ultimate dietary cluster-fuck: attempted powdered milk.'

'Trying to foist it you're saying.'

'I'm saying and look at us and what do we do?'

'Fake a cold and stay in bed playing sportscaster with the TP, in protest?' says Pemulis.

Troeltsch uses the bottle of Seldane to point for emphasis. 'We don't want to hear about it. We look the other way with our heads in the sand.'

'Sounds fucking painful.'

'Go find some fucking synonyms for *beat*.'

Stice swallows hugely: 'Never open your eyes underground: my old man's dictum.'

'And so we distract ourselves,' Troeltsch says; 'we yuck it up.'

Pemulis makes a k-sound. 'Here's the real question: how dumb is Troeltsch?'

'Troeltsch's so dumb he thinks a manila folder's a Filipino contortionist.'

'Troeltsch, who's buried in Grant's Tomb?'

Kyle Coyle says surely they've all heard the one about what do Canadian girls put behind their ears to attract boys. John Wayne gives him not a look. Wayne's peering inside his own tumbler, where there does seem to be some sort of residue. There are fragments of lettuce in his eyelashes. Ortho Stice's cheeks are ballooned with food, his eyes on his own salad's remains, expression abstract and furrowed. A terrible kind of community energy in the whole dining hall, a kind of anxious sound-carpet under the surf of voices and the tinkle of flatware, and The Darkness is at some vague center of this energy, somehow, you can feel. Neither Wayne nor Hal's been approachable all fall, on-court. Kids at other tables say low-toned things to their seatmates, and then the seatmate looks covertly over at Stice's table. Forehead purply crumpled, Stice stares hard at his salad and tries to block input from his phenomenal peripheral vision. Two 14's are contending over toast. Petropolis Kahn is preparing to catapult a chickpea at somebody. Jim Struck points out Bridgette Boone and the U.S.S. Millicent Kent returning for what Struck counts as Fourths, and Stice blocks the sight out. The sad pretty sunset out over the hilltops of Newton cannot be seen because the room's big windows face east, out over the hillside and the Enfield Marine complex that the Academy has bathed in shadow, so E.M.'s porch lights are already on, and tall cubist bits of the old metropolis beyond that, east, with shadows encroaching. The afternoon just past was a glory, scrubbed and cool and windless, cloud-free, the sun a disk, the sky a dome, soaked in light, even the northern horizons bell-clear against a faint green-yellow cast. Schacht has about eight amber bottles of various medicines for his Crohn's Disease, and a whole ritual of administration. A couple of the black girls who work kitchen and custodial day-shifts can be seen against the shadowy tree-line, making their way down the steep hillside's unauthorized path back down to the halfway-house thing for wretched people who come up here to work short-time. The girls' bright cheap jackets are vivid in the shadow and trees' tangle. The girls are having to hold hands against the grade, walking sideways and digging heavily in at each step. The black girl Clenette Hal had read fear in as she left C.T.'s office with his litter now has a bulging backpack on her back, as in bulging maybe with dumpster-pilferage,[261] her arms strung way out between the other black girl Didi and the trees she grabs and digging in sideways with each step, the hesitancy of steep dark slopes, rooty and shot through with briers.

A girl with bangs rises and tings her tumbler with a spoon to make an announcement; nobody pays any attention.

Now Kahn's by custom allowed to come over and sit with them at the best table, post-prandially.

Wayne and Stice both shiver at the same time as the overhead lighting suddenly becomes the big room's primary light.

There's a brief and sort of ignorant discussion on why girls who hit backhands one-handed seem prone to having different-sized breasts. Hal recalls his brother's late-in-college thing of seeing if he could take a girl out somewhere public and then meet and have covert sex with a whole different girl while still out with the first girl. This was after the girl Orin had been wildly in love with and Himself had compulsively used in films had been disfigured. Orin kept a record of Subjects that was sort of a cross between a chart and a journal. He used to come home and leave it out just pleading to be read. This was back when his brother Orin needed only to have sexual intercourse with them instead of getting them to fall so terribly in love with him they'd never be able to want anyone else. He'd taken obscure massage and psych courses and read tantric books whose illustrations seemed about as sexy to Hal as Twister.

Coyle says 'Their ankles'; everybody ignores him. Wayne's already left the table.

Little 14-C Bernard Makulic, two tables over from the milk dispenser and constitutionally delicate and not long for E.T.A., throws up in a silky tan cataract onto the floor by his chair, and there is the shriek of the feet of other chairs being scooted in a star pattern away from the table, and the protracted vowels of repulsed children.

Struck, Pemulis, Schacht and Freer have all had sexual intercourse. Coyle's a probable, but reticent. Axford has trouble even publicly showering, much less submitting nude to a female's inspection. Hal is maybe the one male E.T.A. for whom lifetime virginity is a conscious goal. He sort of feels like O.'s having enough acrobatic coitus for all three of them. Freer even has a like souvenir-colposcope bolted to the inside of his locker door where a pin-up'd have been in days of yore, and Pemulis and Struck have allegedly patronized the Combat Zone after the fiscally pressed city'd buckled and rehung the Combat Zone's red lights, east of the Common. But Jim Troeltsch and sex: no way. And with Wayne and Stice the question seems somehow beside the point. Hal's mouth feels like it's overflowing with spit. He should by all rights have lost to Stice today, and he knows it. Stice was in physical control of the third set. Stice choked it away only because he didn't believe he could beat Hal yet, deep down, since Hal's competitive explosion. But the crisis of faith that cost Stice the match had concerned a different Hal, Hal can tell. It's now a whole new Hal, a Hal who does not get high, or hide, a Hal who in 29 days is going to hand his own personal urine over to authority figures with a wide smile and exemplary posture and not a secretive thought in his head. No one except Pemulis and Axford know it's a whole new and chemical-free Hal who should by all rights have lost to a 16-year-old out there in public on what ended up a gorgeous NNE autumn day.

Wayne had gotten up and bussed his tray in the middle of the jejune breast thing. Ortho ('The Darkness') Stice is still staring into his salad. If you could open Stice's head you'd see a wheel inside another wheel, gears and cogs being widgeted into place. Stice has a secret suspicion about a secret that has more to do with the actual table than with the people at the table. A lot of the guys interpret his intense distraction as Stice's still being in the magic can't-miss Zone from this P.M.'s match.

'The idea being that Nuck girls can only attract guys by being really easy to X, is the joke,' Coyle says into the noise.

Then there's a brief rippling lull in the whole dining hall as little Evan Ingersoll emerges from the Entree Line's end on crutches, his cast new and sailor-hat-white, unsigned, prorector Tony Nwangi behind him with his hatchet-face stony, carrying the kid's tray for him. The hall's unease is almost visible, a corona around Ingersoll and the ruptured patellar tendon that'll cost him at least six months of competitive development. Penn, whose femoral fracture'll cost him a year, isn't even back yet from St. E.'s orthopedic. But at least Ingersoll's back. Hal gets up to go over, Troeltsch rising to accompany him after a long look at Trevor Axford, Ingersoll's B.B. of record, who's sitting in his chair with his eyes shut tight, unable to make any sort of conciliatory gesture. A match-sore Hal not limping but stiff-legged and shoulders slightly rolling as he and Troeltsch move serpentine around tables, steering way clear of the custodian and dull-steel bucket on rollers and the mop spreading and diluting Makulic's chyme out in a thinning circle that clears three tables, which Hal and Troeltsch avoid with practiced curves around tables whose layout they all know well, Hal to say Hey and How's the Limb, Troeltsch to say Hey and be basically relieved he's away from a discussion of females as sexual objects. Troeltsch's never come close to even dating anybody. Some guys here never do. It's the same at all the academies, this asexual contingent. Some junior players don't have the emotional juice left over after tennis to face what dating requires. Bold nerveless guys on the court who go slack and pale at the thought of approaching a female in any social context. Certain things not only can't be taught but can be retarded by other stuff that can be taught. The whole Tavis/Schtitt program here is supposedly a progression toward self-forgetting; some find the whole girl-issue thing brings them face to face with something in themselves they need to believe they've left far behind in order to hang in and develop. Troeltsch, Shaw, Axford: any sort of sexual tension makes them feel like they need more oxygen than is available right then. A couple of the girls at E.T.A. are kind of slutty, and some of the more aggressive Freer-type guys can break some of the girls down and get them to have sex — there's nothing if not time and proximity here. But E.T.A. is mostly a comparatively unsexual place, maybe almost surprisingly so, considering the constant roar and gurgle here of adolescent glands, the emphasis on physicality, the fears of mediocrity, the back-and-forth struggles with ego, the loneliness and close proximity. There's scattered homosexuality, much of it emotional and unconsummated. Keith Freer's pet theory is that the bulk of E.T.A. females are nascent lesbians who don't know it yet. That like any serious female athletes they're basically vigorously male inside, and so Sapphic-tending. The ones that get to the W.T.A.[262] Show'll probably be the only ones who find out that they are, he believes — dykes that is. The rest will marry and spend a lifetime by the club pool wondering why the hair on their husbands' backs makes them shudder. E.g. the U.S.S. Millicent Kent, sixteen and phenomenal on the incline bench-press, with breasts like artillery and a butt like two bulldogs in a bag (Stice's term, which caught on), already looks like a Penal Matron, Freer likes to observe. And no one likes the fact that Carol Spodek's carried and prized the same single large-grip Donnay stick for going on five straight years.

Ortho Stice of southwest Kansas looks briefly up at Hal and Troeltsch's departure before returning his attention to a certain cherry tomato perched somehow halfway up the shallow incline of his salad bowl. It's possible that the cherry tomato is attached halfway up the incline by an adhesive bit of yogurt dressing rather than just sitting there defying gravity on its own. Stice doesn't use a finger to move the tomato and check this. He's using only his concentrated will. He's trying to will the cherry tomato to roll of its own objectile power down the incline and into the bowl's center. He stares at the cherry tomato with enormous concentration, chewing his tri-level skinless-chicken-fillet sandwich. The chewing makes overlapping plates of muscle all the way up one side of his face and crew-cut scalp bulge and roll. He's trying to flex some kind of psychic muscle he's not sure he even has. The crew cut lends his head an anvil-like aspect. Complete concentration makes his round red fleshy face look crumpled. Stice is one of those athletes whose body you know is an unearned divine gift because its conjunction with his face is so incongruous. He resembles a poorly spliced photo, some superhuman cardboard persona with a hole for your human face. A beautiful sports body, lithe and tapered and sleekly muscled, smooth — like a Polycleitos body, Hermes or Theseus before his trials — on whose graceful neck sits the face of a ravaged Winston Churchill, broad and slab-featured, swart, fleshy, large-pored, with a mottled forehead under the crew cut's

V-shaped hairline, and eye-pouches, and jowls that hang and whenever he moves suddenly or lithely make a sort of meaty staccato sound like a wet dog shaking itself dry. Tony Nwangi is saying something acerbic to Hal, who looks like he's kneeling penitent before Ingersoll, everyone at the surrounding tables inclined very subtly away from Hal. Troeltsch is signing Ingersoll's cast as he speaks into his fist. Off the court, Ortho Stice's flattop crew cut and penchant for cuff-rolled bluejeans and button-down short-sleeves with a checkered pattern are strictly from hick. The facial scrunching that attends concentration adds crevices and seams and an uneven flush to the bulldog face. His cheeks are ballooned with food as he stares at the perched cherry tomato, trying to respect this object with all his might. Summoning the sort of coercive reverence he'd felt this P.M. as several balls' sudden anomalous swerves against wind and their own vectors half convinced Stice they'd become sensitive to his inner will, at crucial times. He'd mishit one cross-court volley and seen the thing head for an area wide even of the doubles sideline and then curve like a drenched spitter back to land just inside the singles corner, and this at a time when the grounds' pines behind Hal Incandenza were breeze-leaning in the exact opposite direction. Hal had given Stice a little bit of a look on that one. Stice couldn't finally tell whether Hal noticed anything amiss in the mysterious curves and downdrafts that seemed to favor The Darkness alone; Hal had played with the wide-eyed but unfocused look of a tennis player right on the verge of falling apart out there, and yet strangely affectless, as if deep inside some well of his own private troubles; and Stice wills himself again not to wonder what had passed with the Headmaster and the O.N.A.N.T.A. urologist, whose lab-equipped van's unscheduled appearance in the E.T.A. parking lot yesterday afternoon had caused a tsunami of panic just before supper, especially since Pemulis and his supply of lab-ready Visine bottles were nowhere to be found.

Even among the small circle who know Hal gets secretly high, it doesn't make much sense that Hal's misery'd be Tavis- or urine-related, since Pemulis has never seemed blither than today; and if anyone were going to get the boot, chemically or otherwise, it was not going to be the E.T.A. administration's relative and second-best boy.

Hal and his brother Mario both know that the skim milk at E.T.A. has been pre-mixed powdered milk since Charles Tavis assumed the helm four years back and told Mrs. Clarke he wanted the kids' animal-fat intake halved in a month by any and all means. The kitchen's grave-yard shift power-mixes it in enormous steel bowls and then strains out the foam and pours the milk into real-milk milk-dispenser bags for a kind of placebo effect; it's mostly just the *concept* of powdered milk that gags people.

Struck has traded his shiny clean plate for the absent Incandenza's fortification-structured plate of uneaten fillets, low-gluten bread, corn-bread, baby boileds, a pea-chickpea-based olla, half a fresh squash, mashed potatoes packed in a stelliform gelatin mold, and a shallow bowl of dessert-tsimmes featuring mostly it seemed like plums. Hal is still down on one knee by Ingersoll's chair, his elbows on his knee, listening across Ingersoll and a blindfolded Idris Arslanian to Tony Nwangi. Keith Freer remarks blandly on how Hal seems like he's feeling sort of punk this evening, checking Stice for a reaction. Struck utters truisms about wasting food and global hunger through a full mouth. Struck is wearing a Sox cap to the side so the bill shadows half his face. The bread is unkind to his braces. Freer is wearing the leather vest with no shirt under, which is what he favors after weights have pumped his torso full of air. Stice had had a traumatic psychic experience at fourteen when he'd set the weight on the pull-down station too high, and Dr. Dolores Rusk has authorized his exemption from all but very basic weights, pending resolution of his fear of weights. The joke around E.T.A. is that Stice, who's surely Show-bound after graduation, has no fear of heights, but does fear weights. Keith Freer, though kind of a second-rank junior player, does look beautiful in his calfskin vest — his face and body match. Troeltsch wants a sportscasting career, but Freer is the E.T.A. with looks InterLace would favor. Freer's from inland Mary-land, originally, his family's riches nouveaux, a family Amway business that hit big in the B.S. '90s with his now-deceased father's invention of a Pet-Rockish novelty that was ubiquitous in stockings for two straight pre-millennial Xmases — the so-called Phoneless Cord. Stice dimly recalls his old man getting a Phoneless Cord in his stocking, ostentatiously pack-aged, on Ortho's first recallable Xmas, back in Partridge KS, the old man cocking an eyebrow and The Bride laughing and slapping her big knee. Nobody now much even gets the remembered gag, though, so few things needing cords anymore. But Freer's old man had invested his windfall shrewdly.

1 MAY Y.D.A.U.
OUTCROPPING NORTHWEST OF TUCSON AZ U.S.A.

'My own father,' Steeply said. Steeply again faced outward, one hip out and a hand on that hip. The scratch on his triceps was now ugly and puffed. Also, an area of Steeply's left finger was whiter than the skin around it. The removal of a university ring, or more probably a wedding band. It seemed curious to Marathe that Steeply would undergo electrolysis but not take trouble to fix his finger's annular pallor.

Steeply said 'My own father, sometime around midlife. We watched him get consumed with a sort of entertainment. It wasn't pretty. I was never sure how it started or what it was about.'

'You are now imparting a personal anecdote of you,' Marathe stated.

Steeply did not shrug. He was pretending to study something particular out on the floor of the desert. 'But nothing like this sort of Entertainment — a plain old television program.'

'Television of broadcasting and — how did one express it? — the passivity.'

'Yes. Broadcast television. The program in question was called "M*A*S*H." The title was an acronym, not a command. As a boy I can recall some confusion on this point.'

'I am knowing of the U.S.A. historical broadcast television comedy program "M*A*S*H," ' Marathe stated.

'The fucking thing ran forever, it seemed. The program that would not die. B.S. '70s and '80s before it finally died, mercifully. Set in a military hospital during the U.N.'s action on Korea.'

Marathe remained without expression. 'Police Action.'

Many small birds of the mountain of the outcropping had begun to whistle and twitter somewhere off above and behind them. Also maybe the tentative rattle of some serpent. Marathe pretended to search for the watch in his pocket.

Steeply said 'Now, nothing prima facie exceptional about getting attached to a show. God knows I was attached to my share of shows. That's all it started as. An attachment or habit. Thursday nights at 2100h. "Nine O'Clock Eastern, Eight O'Clock Central and Mountain." They used to broadcast this, to alert you to when to watch, or if you were going to tape it.' Marathe watched the big man shrug from behind. 'So the show was important to him. So, fine. OK. So he took pleasure in the program. God knows the guy was entitled — he'd worked like a dog his whole life. So OK, so at the start he scheduled his Thursday around the show, to an extent. It was hard to pinpoint anything wrong or consumptive. He was, yes, always home from work by 2050 on Thursdays. And he always had his supper watching the program. It seemed almost cute. Mummykins used to tease him, think it was adorable.'

'Cuteness in fathers, this is rare.' There was no way Marathe was going to touch the evident U.S.A. childhood expression *Mummykins*.

'My old man worked for a heating-oil distributorship. Home heating-oil. Have your files got this? A tidbit for M. Fortier: U.S.O.U.S.'s Steeply, H.H.: late father a heating-oil-delivery dispatcher, Cheery Oil, Troy, New York.'

'State of New York, U.S.A., prior to Reconfiguration.'

Hugh Steeply turned around but not all the way, scratching absently at his wens. 'But then: syndication. "M*A*S*H." The show was incredibly popular, and after a few years of Thursday nights it started also to run daily, during the day, or late at night, sometimes, in what I remember all too well was called *syndication,* where local stations bought old episodes and chopped them up and loaded them with ads, and ran them. And this, note, was while all-new episodes of the show were still appearing on Thursdays at 2100. I think this was the start.'

'The cuteness, it was over.'

'My old man started to find the syndicated reruns extremely important to him, too. As in like not to be missed.'

'Even though he had viewed and enjoyed them before, these reruns.'

'The fucking show ran on two different local stations in the Capital District. Albany and environs. For a while, this one station even had a "M*A*S*H" hour, two of them, back to back, every night, from 2300. Plus another half an hour in the early P.M., for the unemployed or something.'

Marathe said 'Virtually a bombardment of this U.S.A. broadcast comedy program.'

After a brief pause of attention to some wens of the face, Steeply said 'He started to keep a small television down at work. Down at the distributorship.'

'For the broadcast of afternoon.'

Steeply appeared to Marathe uncalculating in his statements. 'Broadcast TVs, toward the end they made some of them really small. Kind of a pathetic try at keeping cable down. Some as small as like wrist-size. You'd be too young to remember.'

'I remember well a pre-digital television.' Marathe, if Steeply's anecdote of himself had a political point or communiqué, Marathe could not yet determine this.

Steeply moved his foul Belgian cigarette into his right hand to flick it out into the space below. 'It progressed very slowly. The gradual immersion. The withdrawal from life. I remember guys from his bowling league calling, that he'd quit. Our Mummykins found out he'd dropped out of Knights of Columbus. Thursdays the jokes and cuteness stopped — him all hunched in front of the set, barely even eating from his tray. And every night late at night, for the nightly hour, the old man too wide awake, and hunched over weirdly, head out, as if pulled toward the screen.'

'I too have seen this posture of viewing,' Marathe grimly said, recalling his second-oldest of brothers and the Canadiens of the N.L. of H.

'And he got anxious, ugly, if something made him miss even one. Even one episode. And he'd get ugly if you pointed out he'd already seen most of them about seven times before. Mummykins began to have to lie to get them out of engagements that would have infringed. Neither of them talked about it. I don't remember any of us trying to name the thing out loud — this dark shift in his attachment to the program "M*A*S*H." '

'The organism of family simply shifted to accommodate.'

'Which it wasn't even all that consuming an entertainment,' Steeply said. He sounded to Marathe uncalculated and somewhat younger. 'I mean it was OK. But it was broadcast TV. Broad comedy and canned laughter.'

'I am remembering well this rerunning program, do not worry about me,' said Marathe.

'It was at some point during this gradual shift the notebook first appeared. He began writing notes in a notebook as he viewed. But only when viewing "M*A*S*H." And he never left the notebook lying around where you could get any kind of look at it. He wasn't openly secretive about it; you couldn't even point to that and say something was wrong. The "M*A*S*H" notebook just never seemed to be lying around.'

With the hand that was not below the blanket still gripping the Sterling UL35, Marathe was holding his thumb and forefinger up against the smear of red which was just over the Mountains of Rincon and craning his neck to see his shadow behind them on the hillside.

Steeply changed the hip which was out, in his standing, to his other hip. 'As a child, this is when it became impossible to ignore the odor of obsession about the whole thing. The secrecy about the notebook, and the secrecy about the secrecy. The scrupulous recording of tiny details, in careful order, for purposes you could just tell were both urgent and furtive.'

'This is unbalance,' Marathe concurred. 'This attaching of excessive importance.'

'Jesus, you don't know the half of it.'

'And for you also,' Marathe said, 'excessive unbalance. For your father progresses downhill in this obsessing, but always so slowly that always you could question yourself, whether you were maybe yourself the one out of balance, attaching too much importance to any one thing — a notebook, a posture. Crazy making.'

'And the toll on Mummykins.'

Marathe had turned the chair to a slight angle to be able to see his shadow, which appeared blunt and deformed by the topography of the steep hillside above the outcropping, and in general pathetic and small. There would be no titanic or menacing *Bröckengespenstphänom* with the sunrise of dawn. Marathe said 'The whole organism of family becomes out of balance, questioning its perceptions.'

'The old man — then he started developing this habit of quoting little lines and scenes from "M*A*S*H," to illustrate some idea, make some point in conversation. At the beginning of the habit he seemed casual about it, as if the little bits and scenes simply occurred to him. But this changed, but slowly. Plus I remember he started seeking out feature films that also featured the television program's actors.'

Marathe pretended to sniff.

'Then at some point it was as if he was no longer able to converse or communicate on any topic without bringing it back to the program. The topic. Without some system of references to the program.' Steeply gave small indications of paying attention to the small squeaks as Marathe turned his chair slightly this way and that way, achieving different angles of sight on his small shadow. Steeply exhaled air through the nostrils with a forceful sound. 'Though it wasn't as though he was wholly uncritical of it.'

It sometimes from somewhere blue occurred to Marathe that he did not dislike this Steeply, though *like* or *respect* would be too far in going, to say.

'It was not that type of obsession with it, it, you are saying.'

'It was gradual and slow. He started at some point I remember to refer to the kitchen as the Mess Tent and his den as the Marsh or Swamp. These were fictional locations on the show. He began renting films with even crowd-extra or cameo appearances by the program's actors. He bought what was then called a Betamixer,263 a kind of early magnetic-video recorder. He began a practice of magnetically recording each week's 29 broadcasts and reruns. He stored the tapes, organizing them in baroque systems of cross-reference that had nothing discernible to do with dates of recording. I remember Mummykins didn't say anything when he moved his bedding and began to sleep at night in the easy chair in his den, the Swamp. Or pretend to. Sleep.'

'But you had your suspicions of not real sleeping.'

'It was gradually obvious he was viewing his magnetic recordings of the program "M*A*S*H" throughout the night, probably over and over again, using a crude white plastic earplug to hide the noise, scribbling feverishly in his notebook.'

In contrast with the violence and *transperçant* puncturing of the sunset, the dawn sun seemed slowly exhaled from the more rounded salience of the Mountains of Rincon, its heat a moister heat and the light the vague red of a type of fond sentiment; and U.S.O.U.S.'s Steeply's standing shadow was cast back over the outcropping toward Marathe behind him, close enough that Marathe might reach his arm out and touch the shadow.

'You can tell I don't have a good recall of the exact progression of the thing,' Steeply said.

'The gradual.'

'I do know that Mummykins, I remember one day in the garbage can out behind the house she found a number of letters addressed to a "M*A*S*H" character named — this I fucking-A sure remember — Major Burns. She found them.'

Marathe did not allow himself the chuckle. 'While searching inside the can of waste in the back. For evidence of unbalance.'

Steeply waved Marathe off. He was incapable of amused. 'She didn't search through the garbage. Mumkinsky had too much class. She probably forgot and threw away the day's *Troy Record* before she'd clipped her food-coupons. She was an inveterate coupon-clipper.'

'This was prior to the days of North American laws of recircling[264] of newspapers.'

Steeply did not wave off or give a glare. He wore the look of concentrating. 'This character — this I remember, too well — was portrayed by I remember the actor Maury Linville, a plain old employee of 20th Century Fox.'

'Which later upstarted the fourth network of the Large Four.'

Steeply's luridly run makeup from the heat of the day before had now over the night hardened into a configuration of almost horror. 'But the letters, the letters were addressed to Major Burns. Not to Maury Linville. And not c/o Fox Studios or wherever, but addressed to an involved military address, with a Seoul routing code.'

'In the South Korea of history.'

'The letters were hostile, savage, and lavishly descriptive. He'd come to think the show's character Major Burns embodied some type of cataclysmic, Armageddon-type theme that was slowly assembling itself on the program and progressively being hinted at and emerging in the gradual succession of seasons of this "M*A*S*H."' Steeply felt at his lip. 'I remember Mummykins never mentioned the letters. From the garbage. She just left them around where my kid sister and I would see them.'

'You are not meaning your sister was a goat.'

Steeply was not provokable into some different emotion, however, Marathe observed. 'Younger sister. But my old man, the progression of the program from fun to obsession — crucial distinctions had collapsed, I think, now. Between the fictional Burns and this Linville who portrayed Burns.'

Marathe raised a brow for concurring: 'This is signifying a severe loss of balance.'

'I remember something about he seemed to believe the name of the character Burns also somehow hiddenly signified the English verb for the promise of the consuming fire of apocalypse.'

Marathe looked puzzled or else squinted because of a rising sun. 'But he threw the letters into the waste receptacle, you stated, instead of the Snail's Mail.'

'He'd already started missing whole weeks at a time from work. He'd been at Cheery for decades. He was only a few years from retirement.'

Marathe was looking at his lap's blanket's brightening colors of plaid.

'Mo Cheery and the old man — they'd bowled together, they were in Knights of Columbus together. Missing all the weeks of work made things awkward. Mo didn't want to can the old man. He wanted the old man to see somebody.'

'A professional person.'

'A lot of this I wasn't even there for. The "M*A*S*H" thing. I was at college by the time the really crucial distinctions had collapsed.'

'Studying the multiple cultures.'

'My kid sister had to keep me abreast of developments during the term. Good old Mo Cheery'd come by the house, view magnetic tapes of the show with the old man a while, listen to the old man's theories and views, then on his way out he'd collar Mummykins and take her out into the garage and talk to her very quietly about the fact that the old man was in a high-angle psychic nose-dive and needed with all due regard in his opinion to see somebody in the direst fucking way. My kid sister said the Mumkinsky always acted like she had no idea what Mo Cheery was talking about.'

Marathe smoothed at his blanket.

'*Mumkinsky* being a type of pet family name,' Steeply said, looking a little bit of embarrassed.

Marathe nodded.

'I'm trying to reconstruct this out of memory,' Steeply said. 'The old man is by this time pretty much unable to converse about anything except the television program "M*A*S*H." The theory of the theme of this Burns-slash-*Burn*ing apocalypse now sort of spreads out to become huge and complex theories about wide-ranging and deeply hidden themes having to do with death and time, on the show. Like evidence of some sort of coded communication to certain viewers about an end to our familiar type of world-time and the advent of a whole different order of world-time.'

'Your mother continues to play-act at normalcy, however.'

'I'm trying to reconstruct things that weren't even clear at the time,' Steeply said, his wet and then dried makeup now grotesque in his concentration in the sunrise, like a mask of a mentally ill clown. He said 'One theory involved the fact, which the old man found extremely significant, that the historical Korean Police Action of the U.N. lasted only roughly two-odd years, but that "M*A*S*H" itself was by then into something like its seventh year of new episodes. Some characters of the program were getting gray hair, receding hair, face-lifts. The old man was convinced this signified intentional themes. According to my kid sister, who bore the brunt of time spent with him, watching,' Steeply said, 'the old man's theories were almost inconceivably complex and wide-ranging. As the years of new seasons went on and some actors retired and characters were replaced by other characters, the old man generated baroquoco theories about what it was that had quote-underline "*really*" happened to the absent characters. Where they'd gone, where they were, what it all augured. Then the next thing was one or two of the letters started to appear, canceled and returned, stamped as undeliverable, or to addresses that were not just nonexistent but absurd.'

'Unbalanced letters were no longer being discarded as waste, but now mailed.'

'And Mummykins was uncomplaining throughout. It was enough to break your heart. She was a rock. She did, granted, begin taking prescription anti-anxiety medication.'

Land of the freely brave: Marathe did not say this aloud. He looked at his pocket's watch and was trying to remember a time when he had ever with Steeply had to consider the tact of departing.

Steeply, at this time, gave the impression somehow of having several cigarettes going at one time. 'Somewhere along late in the progression the old man let it be known he was working on a secret book that revised and explicated much of the world's military, medical, philosophical and religious history by analogies to certain subtle and complex thematic codes in "M*A*S*H."' Steeply would stand on one foot to raise the other foot to look at a shoe's inflicted damage, all the time smoking. 'Even when he went in to work, there were problems. Heating-oil customers who called for deliveries or information or whatever began to complain that the old man kept trying to engage them in bizarre theoretical discussions of the thematics of "M*A*S*H."'

'Because it is necessary that I leave soon, a central point must be soon emerging,' Marathe worked in as gracefully as possible.

Steeply seemed not to hear this other man. He seemed not only uncalculated and self-enmeshed; his demeanor itself seemed more young, that of some young person. This unless this was part of some performance beyond Marathe, Marathe knew he must consider.

'Then the double blow,' Steeply said. 'In B.S. 1983. My memory's clear on this. The Mumkinsky opened an alarming letter from attorneys for CBS and 20th Century Fox. Certain letters had been apparently rerouted by do-goodnik military postal clerks to Fox. The old man'd been trying to correspond with different past and present "M*A*S*H" personas in letters the family never saw get mailed but whose content, the attorneys said, raised quote grave concern and could quote constitute grounds for strenuous legal action.' Steeply raised the foot to look, his face in pain. He said, 'Then the program's final episode ran. Late autumn of B.S. 1983. I was on an ROTC marching-band trip to Fort Ticonderoga. My kid sister, who'd by this time left home herself, and who could blame the kid, she reported that the Mumkinsky was talking very casually and uncomplainingly of the old man's now refusing to leave his den.'

'This, the final enclosing isolation of obsession.'

Steeply looked over his shoulder on one awkward foot to look slightly at Marathe. 'As in even to go to the bathroom, now, the not leaving.'

'Your mother's prescriptions prevented some episodes of great anxiety, I think.'

'He'd gotten a special A.C.D.C. cable hook-up that brought in extra syndication. When reruns weren't running, the video-magnetic tapes ran constantly. He was haggard and spectral and his easy chair was all but unrecognizable. Cheery Oil was keeping him on the books until he could get his thirty years in at age sixty. My kid sister and I started reluctantly discussing intervening on Mummykins to intervene on the old man and force him to see somebody.'

'Yourselves, you could not reach him.'

'He died just before his birthday. He died in his easy chair, set at full Recline, watching an episode in which Alda's Hawkeye can't stop sleep-walking and fears he's going out of his fucking mind until a professional military therapist reassures him, I remember.'

'Me, I too have seen this episode rerunning, in my childhood.'

'All I can recall of it is the army professional telling Alda not to worry, that if he was truly crazy he'd sleep like a newborn, as did the notorious Burns-slash-Linville.'

'The program's character of Burns slept exceptionally well, I remember.'

'His secret book's manuscript filled scores of notebooks. This is what the notebooks turned out to be. One closet in the den had to be forced open. All these notebooks tumbled out. The whole thing was written in a kind of medical-slash-military-looking code, though, indecipherable — Sis and her first husband and I spent some time trying to decode them. After his death in the chair.'

'His unbalance of temptation cost him life. An otherwise harmless U.S.A. broadcast television program took his life, because of the consuming obsession. This is your anecdote.'

'No. It was a transmural infarction. Blew out a whole ventricle. His whole family had a history: the heart. The pathologist said it was amazing he'd lasted this long.'

Marathe shrugged. 'The obsessed frequently endure.'

Steeply shook the head. 'It must have been hell on the poor old Mumkinsky.'

'She never complained, however.'

Already the sun was up and pulsing. Light ran over everything in a sick-ening yellow way like gravy. All birds and living animals had been silenced, stunned already by heat, and the site's bright loaders had not yet been started in movement. All was calm. All was bright. Steeply's shadow on the shelf was squat and blunt, already shorter than the living figure of Steeply himself, who was leaning outward to try to find a spot far below to litter with a crumpled Belgian packing with one prayed no more finally to smoke.

Marathe took his watch from out of the windbreaker's pocket.

Steeply shrugged. 'I think you're right, that it's part of both the horror and the pull. When I'm east and thinking of Flatto's lab and I sort of look up and find myself tempted.'

'About the Entertainment of now.'

'And I kind of half-picture Hank Hoyne in the old man's old recliner, hunched and scribbling feverishly.'

'In military coding.'

'His eyes, they got like that, too, the old man's, like Hoyne's. Periodically.'

Heat began to shimmer, as well, off the lionhide floor of a desert. The mesquite and cactus wobbled, and Tucson AZ resumed once more the appearance of the mirage, as it had appeared when Marathe had first arrived and found his shadow so entrancing in its size and reach. The sun of A.M. had no radial knives of light. It appeared brutal and businesslike and harmful to look upon. Marathe allowed himself a few diverting seconds of watching the Mountains of the Rincons' widening shadows melt slowly backward into the base of the Mountains of the Rincons. Steeply hawked and spat, still holding the last crumpled pack of Flanderfumes.

'My time is sharply finite to remain.' Marathe said this. Every change of his postures brought small squeaks of leather and metal. 'I would feel gratitude if you departed first.'

Steeply figured Marathe wanted him to have no idea how he got up and down, in and out. To no real purpose; a personal point of pride. Steeply squatted for adjusting the straps of his high heels. His prostheses were still not quite aligned. He spoke with the faintly breathless quality of large men trying to bend:

'Well. Rémy, but I don't think Dick Willis's "empty of intent" quite does it. Captures it. The eye-factor. Hoyne, the Arab internist. The old man. Not for eyes like that.'

'You would say it does not capture these eyes' expression.'

Looking up while squatting, this made Steeply's neck appear thick. He stared past Marathe, at the shale. He said 'The expressions seem more like — fuck, how to say it. Fuck,' Steeply said in concentration.

'Petrified,' Marathe said. 'Ossified. Inanimate.'

'No. Not inanimate. More like the opposite. More as if . . . *stuck* in some way.'

Marathe's neck itself was stiff from so much time looking out and down from a height. 'What is it this wishes here to mean? Glued?'

Steeply was doing something to a toenail's cracked polish. 'Stuck. Fixed. Held. Trapped. As in trapped in some sort of middle. Between two things. Pulled apart in different directions.'

Marathe's eyes searched the sky, which this was already too light blue for his pleasure, filmed with a sort of eggy plura of heat. 'Meaning between different cravings of great intensity, this.'

'Not even cravings so much. Emptier than that. As if he were stuck wondering. As if there was something he'd forgotten.'

'Misplaced. Lost.'

'Misplaced.'

'Lost.'

'Misplaced.'

'As you wish.'

13 NOVEMBER
YEAR OF THE DEPEND ADULT UNDERGARMENT

0245h., Ennet House, the hours that are truly wee. Eugenio M., voluntarily filling in for Johnette Foltz on Dream Duty, is out in the office playing some sort of hand-held sports game that blips and tweets. Kate Gompert and Geoffrey Day and Ken Erdedy and Bruce Green are in the living room with the lights mostly out and the old jumpy-picture D.E.C. viewer on. Cartridges not allowed after 0000h., to encourage sleep. Sober cocaine- and stimulant-addicts sleep pretty well by the second month, straight alcoholics by the fourth. Abstinent pot- and tranq-addicts can pretty much forget about sleep for the first year. Though Bruce Green is asleep and would be in violation of the no-lying-on-the-couch rule if his legs weren't twisted over and his feet on the floor. All the Ennet House viewer gets on Spontaneous Dissemination is basic InterLace, and from 0200 to 0400 InterLace NNE downloads for the next dissemination-day and cuts all transmissions except one line's four straight redissemms of 'The Mr. Bouncety-Bounce Daily Program,' and when Mr. Bouncety-Bounce appears in his old cloth-and-safety-pin diaper and paunch and rubber infant-head mask he is not a soothing or pleasant figure at all, for the sleepless adult. Ken Erdedy has started to smoke cigarettes and sits smoking, joggling one leather slipper. Kate Gompert and Geoffrey Day are on the nonleather couch. Kate Gompert sits cross-legged on the couch with her head all the way forward so her forehead touches her foot. It looks like some kind of spiritually advanced yoga position or stretching exercise, but it's really just the way Kate Gompert has been sitting on the sofa all night every night since Wednesday's free-for-all unpleasantness with Lenz and Gately in the streetlet, from which the whole House is still reeling and spiritually palsied. Day's bare calves are completely hairless and look sort of absurd with dress shoes and black socks and a velour bathrobe, but Day's proven kind of admirably resistant to caring what other people think, in a way.

'Like you really care.' Kate Gompert's voice is toneless and hard to hear because it issues from out of the circle formed by her crossed legs.

'It isn't a question of caring or not caring,' Day says quietly. 'I meant only that I identify to an extent.'

648

Gompert's sarcastic chuff of air raises a section of her unwashed bangs.

Bruce Green doesn't snore, even with his nose broken and cross-hatched in white tape. Neither he nor Erdedy is listening to them.

Day speaks softly and doesn't cross his legs to incline over to the side toward her. 'When I was a little boy —'

Gompert chuffs air again.

'— just a boy with a violin and a dream and special roundabout routes to school to avoid the boys who took my violin case and played keep-away over my head with it, one summer afternoon I was upstairs in the bedroom I shared with my younger brother, alone, practicing my violin. It was very hot, and there was an electric fan in the window, blowing out, acting as an exhaust fan.'

'I know from exhaust fans, believe you me.'

'The direction of flow is beside the point. It was on, and its position in the window made the glass of the upraised pane vibrate somehow. It produced an odd high-pitched vibration, invariant and constant. By itself it was strange but benign. But on this one afternoon, the fan's vibration combined with some certain set of notes I was practicing on the violin, and the two vibrations set up a resonance that made something happen in my head. It is impossible really to explain it, but it was a certain quality of this resonance that produced it.'

'A thing.'

'As the two vibrations combined, it was as if a large dark billowing shape came billowing out of some corner in my mind. I can be no more precise than to say *large, dark, shape,* and *billowing,* what came flapping out of some backwater of my psyche I had not had the slightest inkling was there.'

'But it was inside you, though.'

'Katherine, Kate, it was total horror. It was all horror everywhere, distilled and given form. It rose in me, out of me, summoned somehow by the odd confluence of the fan and those notes. It rose and grew larger and became engulfing and more horrible than I shall ever have the power to convey. I dropped my violin and ran from the room.'

'Was it triangular? The shape? When you say *billowing,* do you mean like a triangle?'

'Shapeless. Shapelessness was one of the horrible things about it. I can say and mean only *shape, dark,* and either *billowing* or *flapping.* But because the horror receded the moment I left the room, within minutes it had become unreal. The shape and horror. It seemed to have been my imagination, some random bit of psychic flatulence, an anomaly.'

A mirthless laugh into the ankle. 'Alcoholics Anomalous.'

Day hasn't switched legs or moved, and he isn't looking at her ear or her scalp, which are in view. 'In just the way any child will probe a wound or pick at a scab I returned shortly to the room and the fan and picked up the violin again. And produced the resonance again immediately. And immediately again the black flapping shape rose in my mind again. It was a bit like a sail, or a small part of the wing of something far too large to be seen in totality. It was total psychic horror: death, decay, dissolution, cold empty black malevolent lonely voided space. It was the worst thing I have ever confronted.'

'But you still forgot and went back up there and brought it back. And it was inside you.'

Completely incongruously, Ken Erdedy says 'His head's shaped like a mushroom.' Day has no idea what he was referring to or talking about.

'Set free somehow by that one-day-only resonance of violin and fan, the dark shape began rising out of my mind's corner on its own. I dropped the violin again and ran from the room once again, clutching my head at the front and back, but this time it did not recede.'

'The triangular horror.'

'It was as if I'd awakened it and now it was active. It came and went for a year. I lived in horror of it for a year, as a child, never knowing when it would rise up billowing and blot out all light. After a year it receded. I think I was ten. But not all the way. I'd awakened it somehow. Every so often. Every few months it would rise inside me.'

It isn't like a real interface or conversation. Day doesn't seem to be addressing anybody in particular. 'The last time it ever rose up billowing was my second year of college. I attended Brown University in Providence RI, graduating *magna cum laude*. One sophomore night it came up out of nowhere, the black shape, for the first time in years.'

'But there was an inevitability-feeling about it, too, when it came.'

'It is the most horrible feeling I have ever imagined, much less felt. There is no possible way death can feel as bad. It rose up. It was worse now that I was older.'

'Tell me all about it.'

'I thought I'd have to hurl myself out of my dormitory's window. I simply could not live with how it felt.'

Gompert's head isn't all the way up, but now it's about halfway up; her forehead has a major red impression-spot from her ankle-bone. She's looking roughly halfway between straight ahead and Day beside her. 'And there was this idea underneath that you'd brought it on, that you'd wakened it up. You went back up to the fan that second time. You like despised yourself for waking it up.'

Day is looking straight ahead. Mr. Bouncety-Bounce's head is in no way mushroom-shaped, though it is large and — in the rubber infant-mask — apt to appear to the adult viewer kind of grotesque. 'Some boy I hardly knew in the room below mine heard me staggering around whimpering at the top of my lungs. He came up and sat up with me until it went away. It took most of the night. We didn't converse; he didn't try to comfort me. He spoke very little, just sat up with me. We didn't become friends. By graduation I'd forgotten his name and major. But on that night he seemed to be the piece of string by which I hung suspended over hell itself.'

Green in his sleep cries out something that sounds like 'For God's sake no Mr. Ho don't light it!' His swollen black eyes and R.E.M.'s non sequiturs, plus the capering 130-kilo infant on the viewer, plus Day and Gompert conversing while both staring into space, all backed by the blurps and wonks of Gene M.'s hand-held game in the office, give the dark living room a dreamy and almost surreal atmosphere.

Day finally uncrosses his legs and switches them. 'It's never come back. Over twenty years. But I've not forgotten. And the worst times I have felt since then were like a day at the foot-masseur's compared to the feeling of that black sail or wing rising inside me.'

'Billowing.'

'Not the nuts Jesus God not the *nutsss*.'

'I understood the term *hell* as of that summer day and that night in the sophomore dormitory. I understood what people meant by *hell*. They did not mean the black sail. They meant the associated feelings.'

'Or the corner it came up out of, inside, if they mean a place.' Kate Gompert is now looking at him. Her face doesn't look better but does look different. Her neck's clearly stiff from having been contorted.

'From that day, whether I could articulate it satisfactorily or not,' Day says, holding the knee of the leg just crossed, 'I understood on an intuitive level why people killed themselves. If I had to go for any length of time with that feeling I'd surely kill myself.'

'Time in the shadow of the wing of the thing too big to see, rising.'

'Oh God please,' Green says very distinctly.

Day says: 'There is no way it could feel worse.'

11 NOVEMBER
YEAR OF THE DEPEND ADULT UNDERGARMENT

Apparently some higher-up had sent Mary Esther Thode out on her little yellow Vespa with the order for their match; she'd pulled up alongside Stice and Wayne just as they cleared the Hammond golf course, Hal a good half km. behind them with galumphers Kornspan and Kahn. Schtitt was inscrutable about the whole thing. The match wasn't like a ladder-challenge; Stice and Hal were in different age-divisions this year. The match was more like maybe an exhibition, and by the second set, as people got done with the weight room and showers, it was attended like one. The match. Helen Steeply of *Moment,* possessed of a certain thuggish allure but hardly the pericardium-piercer that Orin had made her sound like, to Hal, sat through the whole thing, accompanied for the first set by Aubrey deLint before Thierry Poutrincourt stole his spot on the bleacher. It was the first high-caliber junior tennis she'd ever seen, she said, the massive journalist. They played on #6, the best of the east Show Courts. Also the scene of some of the recent Eschaton's worst carnage. It was a conditioning-heavy day, a very light schedule of matches. Bags of smoke burped steadily up from Schtitt's crow's nest high overhead, and sometimes you could hear the weatherman's pointer tapping absently on the transom's iron. The only other thing nearby was down on #10, a challenge in Girls' 14's, two baseliners sending parabolas back and forth: ponytails, an air of baseline attrition, the ball's high heavy arc that of a loogy spat for distance. Shaw and Axford were also way out on #23, warming up. No one paid them or the 14's much mind. The bleachers behind the Show Court filled steadily up. Schtitt had Mario film the whole first set from above, leaning way out over the transom's railing with Watson braced and gripping his vest from behind, Mario's police lock protruding and casting a weird needly shadow slanted northeast of Court 9's net.

'This is the first real match I've seen, after hearing so much about the junior tour,' Helen Steeply told deLint, trying to cross her legs on a cramped bleacher a few tiers from the top. Aubrey deLint's smile was notoriously bad, his face seeming to break into crescents and shards, wholly without cheer. It was almost more like a grimace. Orders that deLint keep the mammoth soft-profiler in direct sight at all times were explicit and emphatic. Helen Steeply had a notebook, and deLint was filling in both players' names on performance charts Schtitt won't ever let anyone look at.

The P.M. was moving fast from a chilly noon cloud-cover into blue autumn glory, but in the first set it was still very cold, the sun still pale and seeming to flutter as if poorly wired. Hal and Stice didn't have to stretch and barely warmed up at all, after the run. They'd changed clothes and were both expressionless. Stice was in all-black, Hal in E.T.A. sweats with his left shoe's upper bulging distended around his AirStirrup brace.

A born net-man, Ortho Stice played with a kind of rigid, liquid grace, like a panther in a back-brace. He was shorter than Hal but better-built and with quicker feet. A southpaw with factory-painted W's on his Wilson Pro Staff 5.8 si's.

Hal was left-handed too, which complicated strategy and percentages hideously, deLint told the journalist beside him.

The Darkness's service motion was in the McEnroe-Esconja tradition, legs splayed, feet parallel, a figure off an Egyptian frieze, side so severely to the net he's almost facing away. Both arms out straight and stiff on the serve's downswing. Hal bobbed on his feet's balls a little in the ad court, waiting. Stice started his service-motion motion in little segments — it looks a little like bad animation — then grimaced, tossed, pivoted netward and served it with a hard flat *spang* way out to Hal's forehand, pulling Hal wide. The finish of Stice's pivot lets his momentum carry him naturally up to net, following the serve. Hal lunged for the serve and chipped a little forehand return down the line and scrambled right to get back into court. The return was lucky, a feeble chip that just cleared the net's tape, so shallow that Stice had to half-volley it at the service line, still moving in, his backhand two-handed and clumsy for half-volleys; he had to sort of scoop it and hit up soft so it wouldn't float out deep. Axiom: the man who has to hit up from the net is going to get passed. And Stice's half-volley landed in the ad court squishy and slow and sat up for Hal, who was waiting for it. Hal's stick was back for the forehand, waiting, and there was a moment of total mentation as the ball hung there. Statistically, Hal was book to pass a left-handed volleyer cross-court off a ball this ripe, though he also always loved a good humiliating topspin lob, and Stice's fractional chance at saving the point was to guess what Hal would do — Stice couldn't crowd the net because Hal would put it up over him; he stayed a couple stick-lengths off the net, leaning for a cross. Everything seemed to hang distended in air now so clear it seemed washed, after the clouds. The bleachers' people could feel Hal feel Stice letting the point go, inside, figuring it lost, knowing he could only guess and stab, hoping. Little hope of Hal fucking up: Hal Incandenza does not fuck up passes off floater half-volleys. Hal's forehand's wind-up was nicely disguised, prepped for either lob or pass. When he hit it so hard his forearm's musculature stood starkly out it was a pass but not cross-court; he went inside-out on it, a flat forehand as hard as he could from the baseline's center back toward Stice's deuce-sideline. Stice had finally guessed lob at the start of the stroke and had half-turned to sprint back for where it would land, and the inside-out pass wrong-footed him; he could do no more than stand there flat-footed and watching as the fresh ball landed a meter fair to get Hal back to deuce in the fifth game. There was applause off thirty hands for the point as a whole, which was faultless and on Hal's part imaginative, anti-book. One of very few total inspired points from Incandenza, deLint's chart would show. Neither player's face moved as a couple people shouted for Hal. The basic ten-level R.A.S.U.[265] from the Universal Bleacher Co. sat right behind the court. At the start it was mostly staff and the A's who were running alongside when Thode brought Stice and Hal the directive to play. But the stands gradually filled as word got down to the locker rooms that The Darkness was playing 18's A-2 dead-even in the first set of something Schtitt had actually dispatched a scooter to order. The bleachers' E.T.A.s hunched forward with hands warmed in the crease between hamstrings and calves, or else gloved and layered and stretched out with their heads and bottoms and heels on three different levels, watching both sky and play. The lozenges of shadow from the court's mesh fences elongated as the sun wheeled southwest to west. Several sets of legs and sneakers hung swinging from the transom above. Mario allowed himself several reaction-shots from staff and partisans in the bleachers. Aubrey deLint spent the set with the punter's cathected profiler, who allegedly came to see Hal only about Orin but whom Charles Tavis won't let see Hal yet, even chaperoned, Tavis's reasons for the reticence too detailed for Helen Steeply to understand, probably, but she was watching from the Show-bleachers' top row, poised over a notebook, wearing a fuchsia ski cap with a rooster-comb top instead of a pompom top, blowing into her fist, her weight making the bleacher below her bow and inclining deLint oddly toward her. For the spectators not perched on the transom overhead, the players looked waffle-cut by the chain-link fencing. The green windscreens that wrecked spectation were used only in the spring in the weeks right after the Lung's disassembly. DeLint hadn't stopped talking into the big lady's ear.

All the E.T.A. players loved the Show Courts 6–9 because they loved to be watched, and also hated the Show Courts because the transom's crow's-nested shadow covered the north halves of the courts around noon and all through the P.M. wheeled around gradually east like some giant hooded shadowed moving presence, brooding. Sometimes just the sight of Schtitt's little head's shadow could make a younger kid on the Show Courts clutch and freeze. By Hal and Stice's seventh game, the sky was cloudless, and the transom's monolithic shadow, black as ink, gave everyone watching the fantods as it elongated along the nets, completely obscuring Stice when he followed a serve in. Another advantage of the Lung was that it afforded no overhead view, which was one more reason why staff waited as long as possible before its erection. There was no indication Hal even saw it, the shadow, hunched and waiting for Stice.

The Darkness splayed out stiff on the deuce side of the center line, ratcheting slowly into his service motion. He overhit the first serve long and Hal angled it softly off-court, moving two steps in for the second ball. Stice hit his second serve as hard as he could again and netted it, and pursed his thick lips a little as he walked into the net's shadow to retrieve the ball, and Hal jogged over to the fence behind the next court to get the ball he'd angled over. DeLint was putting a pejorative hieroglyphic in a box on his chart marked STICE.

At just this moment, @1200 meters east and downhill and one level below ground, Ennet House live-in Staff Don Gately lay deeply asleep in his Lone-Rangerish sleeping mask, his snores rattling the deinsulated pipes along his little room's ceiling.

Four-odd clicks to the northwest in the men's room of the Armenian Foundation Library, right near the onion-domed Watertown Arsenal, Poor Tony Krause hunched forward in a stall in his ghastly suspenders and purloined cap, his elbows on his knees and his face in his hands, getting a whole new perspective on time and the various passages and personae of time.

M. M. Pemulis and J. G. Struck, wet-haired after their P.M. runs, had blarneyed their way past the library-attendant at the B.U. School of Pharmacy 2.8 clicks down Commonwealth on Comm. and Cook St. and were seated at a table in Reference, Pemulis's yachting cap pushed way back to accommodate his rising eyebrows, licking his finger to turn pages.

H. Steeply's green sedan with its neuralgiac full-front Nunhagen ad on the side sat in an Authorized Guest parking spot in the E.T.A. lot.

Between appointments,[266] in an office whose west windows yielded no view of the match, Charles Tavis had his head mashed up against the upholstered seat-rail of his sofa, his arm under the gray-and-red ruffle and sweeping back and forth for the bathroom scale he keeps under there.

Avril Incandenza's whereabouts on the grounds were throughout this interval unknown.

At just this moment M.S.T., Orin Incandenza was once again embracing a certain 'Swiss' hand-model before a wall-width window in a rented suite halfway up a different tall hotel (from before) in Phoenix AZ. The windowlight was fiery with heat. Way below, tiny cars' roofs glared so bright with reflected light their colors were obscured. Pedestrians hunched and sprinted between different areas of shade and refrigeration. The cityscape's glass and metal twinkled but seemed to sag — the whole vista looked somehow stunned. The cool air through the room's vent whispered. They'd put down their glasses of ice and come together upright and embraced. The embrace was not like a hug. There was no talking — the only sound was the vent and their breath. Orin's linen knee probed the deltoid fork of the hand-model's parted legs. He let the 'Swiss' woman grind against the muscular knee of his good leg. They got so close no light shone between them, and ground together. Her lids fluttered; his closed; their breath became somehow coded. Again the concentrated tactile languor of the sexual mode. Again they stripped each other to the waist and she, in that same kind of jitterbug jape they didn't have the breath to laugh at, she hopped up at him and forked her legs the same way over his shoulders and arched back until his arm stopped her fall and he supported her like that, the left hand horned with old callus at the small of her satiny back, and bore her.

Sometimes it's hard to believe the sun's the same sun over all different parts of the planet. The NNE sun was at this same moment the color of hollandaise and gave off no heat. Between points, both Hal and Stice switched their sticks to their right hands and clamped their left hands tight under their arms to keep from losing sensation in the chill. Stice was double-faulting more than his average because he was trying to get enough on his second serve to follow it credibly to net. DeLint estimated he was charting Stice at one double-fault per 1.3 games, and his a./d.f. ratio[267] was an undistinguished .6, but he, deLint, told Helen Steeply of *Moment,* spread way out next to him on the third row from the top and using Gregg shorthand, deLint told this Ms. Steeply that Stice was nevertheless wise to crank the second serve and eat the occasional double-fault. Stice wound up to serve so stiff, his motion so sprocketed and serial, that the journalist told deLint Stice looked to her as if he'd learned to serve by studying still photos of the motion's different stages, no offense intended. There was none of real high-speed motion's liquid flow until the very end, when Stice pivoted toward the net and seemed to sort of fall out into the court, his tennis racquet whirling behind his back and snapping upward to impact the yellow ball hanging at just the height of his maximum reach, and there was a solid *pock* as this Stice cracked it flat into Orin's brother's body, handcuffing Hal at such speeds the ball's movement presented only as afterimage, the creamy retinal trail of something too fast to track. Hal's awkward return had too much slice, and floated, and Stice hurtled forward to volley it chest-high, blocking it acute into open court for a clean winner. There was mild applause. DeLint invited Helen Steeply to note that The Darkness really won that point on the serve itself. Hal Incandenza walked to the fence to retrieve the ball, impassive, wiping his nose against his sweatshirt's sleeve; ad-in. Hal was up 5–4 in the first and had saved three ads off Stice's fifth service game, two off double-faults; but deLint still maintained Stice was wise.

'Hal's got to the point in the last year here where a kid's only real chance is to totally press, attack at all times, whale the serve, haul ass to the net, assume the aggressor role.'

'Does Herr Schtitt wear eye makeup?' Helen Steeply asked him. 'I was noticing.'

'You stay back against this Hal kid, you try to out-think him and move him around, he'll yank you back and forth and chew you up and spit you out and step on the remains. We've spent years getting him to this point. Nobody stays back and out-controls Incandenza anymore.'

Pretending to flip to a fresh page, Helen Steeply dropped her pen, which fell into the bleachers' struts and supports and clattered as only something dropped into a system of metal bleachers can clatter. The prolonged noise made Stice take some extra bounces before he served. He bounced the ball several times, leaning forward, lined up splayed and violently sideways. He went into his odd segmented windup; Helen Steeply produced another pen from the pocket of her fiberfill parka; Stice cracked it flat down the center, aiming for an ace on the service lines' T. It went by Hal unplayable and literally too close to call. There are no linesmen for internal E.T.A. matches. Hal looked down the line at where the thing hit and skidded, pausing before indicating his call, the hand to his cheek indicating deliberation. He shrugged and shook his head and laid a hand out flat in the air before him to signify to Stice he was calling the serve good. This meant game Stice. The Darkness was walking toward the net, kneading his neck, looking at where Hal was still standing.

'We can go on and play two,' Stice said. 'Didn't see it neither.'

Hal was coming in closer to Stice because he was going to the net-post for his towel. 'Not your job to see it.' He looked unhappy and tried to smile. 'You hit it too hard to see, you deserve the point.'

Stice shrugged and nodded, chewing. 'You take the next gimme then.' He sliced two balls soft so they ended their roll down near the opposite base-line, where Hal could use them to serve. The Darkness still made huge man-dibular chewing faces on-court even though he hadn't been allowed to chew gum in play since he accidentally inhaled gum and had to be Heimliched by his opponent in the semis of last spring's Easter Bowl.

'Ortho's saying how the next debatable call goes immediately to Hal; they don't take two,' deLint said, darkening in half-squares on the two charts.

'Take two?'

'Play a let, babe. Do it over. Two serves: one point.' Aubrey deLint was a lightly pockmarked man with thick yellow hair in an anchorman's helmety style and a hypertensive flush, and eyes, oval and close-set and lightless, that seemed like a second set of nostrils in his face. 'Do a whole lot of sports at *Moment* do you?'

'So they're being sporting,' Steeply said. 'Generous, fair.'

'We inculcate that as a priority here,' deLint said, gesturing vaguely at the space around them, head bent to his charts.

'They seem like friends.'

'The angle here for *Moment* might be the good-friends-off-the-court-and-remorseless-pitiless-foes-on-court angle.'

'I mean they seem like friends even playing,' Helen Steeply said, watching Hal dry off his leather grip with a white towel as Stice jumped up and down in place back at his deuce corner, one hand in his armpit.

DeLint's laugh sounded to Steeply's keen ear like the laugh of a much older and less fit man, the mucoidal fist-at-chest laugh of a lap-blanketed old man in a lawn chair on his gravel backyard in Scottsdale AZ, hearing his son say his wife claimed no longer to know who he was. 'Don't kid yourself, babe,' de Lint got out. The Vaught twins on the bleacher below looked up and around and pretended to shush him, the left mouth grinning, deLint with that bad cold-eyed shard of a smile back at them as Hal Incandenza bounced the ball three times and went into his own service motion.

Several little boys were strung busily out along the sides of a small utility tunnel twenty-six meters below the Show Courts.

Steeply's face looked as if the journalist were trying to think of pithy images for a motion as unexceptional and fluid as Hal Incandenza's serve. At the start a violinist maybe, standing alert with his sleek head cocked and racket up in front and the hand with the ball at the racket's throat like a bow. The down-together-up-together of the downswing and toss could be a child making angels in the snow, cheeks rosy and eyes at the sky. But Hal's face was pale and thoroughly unchildlike, his gaze somehow extending only half a meter in front of him. He looked nothing like the punter. The service motion's middle might be a man at a precipice, falling forward, giving in sweetly to his own weight, and the serve's terminus and impact a hammering man, the driven nail just within range at the top of his tiptoed reach. But all these were only parts, and made the motion seem segmented, when the smaller crew-cutted jowly boy was the one with the stuttered motion, the man of parts. Steeply had played tennis only a couple times, with his wife, and had felt ungainly and simian out there. The punter's discourses on the game had been lengthy but not much use. It was unlikely that any one game figured much in the Entertainment.

Hal Incandenza's first serve was a tactically aggressive shot but not immediately identifiable as such. Stice wanted to serve so hard he could set himself up to put the ball away on the next shot, up at net. Hal's serve seemed to set in motion a much more involved mechanism, one that took several exchanges to reveal itself as aggressive. His first serve hadn't Stice's pace, but it had depth, plus a topspin Hal achieved with an arched back and faint brushing action over the back of the ball that made the serve curve visibly in the air, egg-shaped with spin, to land deep in the box and hop up high, so that Stice couldn't do more than send back a deep backhand chip from shoulder-height, and then couldn't come in behind a return that'd been robbed of all pace. Stice moved to the baseline's center as the chip floated back to Hal. Hal's pivot moved him right so he could take it on the forehand,[268] another looper dripping with top, right back in the same corner he'd served to, so that Stice had to stop and sprint back the same way he'd come. Stice drove this backhand hard down the line to Hal's forehand, a blazing thing that made the audience inhale, but as the *samizdat*'s director's other son glided a few strides left Steeply could see that he now had a whole open court to hit cross-court into, Stice having hit so hard he'd backpedalled a bit off the shot and was now scrambling to get back out of the deuce corner, and Hal hit the flat textbook drive cross-court into green lined space, hard but not flamboyantly so, and the diagonal of the ball kept it travelling out wide after it hit Stice's ad sideline, carrying it away from the boy in black's outstretched racquet, and for a second it looked as if Stice at a dead run might get his strings on the ball, but the ball stayed tantalizingly just out of reach, still travelling at a severe cross-court diagonal, and it passed Stice's racquet half a meter past its rim, and Stice's momentum carried him almost halfway into the next court. Stice slowed to a jog to go retrieve the ball. Hal stood slightly hipshot on the ad side, waiting for Stice to get back and let him serve again. DeLint, whose peripheral vision's acuity and disguise was an E.T.A. legend, observed the big journalist chew her nib for a second and then put down nothing more than the Gregg ideogram for *pretty*, shaking her fuchsia cap.

'Wasn't that pretty,' he said blandly.

Steeply rooted for a hankie. 'Not exactly.'

'Hal's in essence a torturer, if you want his essence as a player, instead of a straight-out killer like Stice or the Canadian Wayne,' deLint said. 'This is why you don't stay back or play safe against Hal. This way of the ball seeming just in reach, to keep you trying, running. He yanks you around. Always two or three shots ahead. He won that point on the deep forehand after the serve — the second he had Stice wrong-footed you could see the angle open up. Though the serve set the whole thing up in advance, and without the risk of much pace on it. The kid doesn't need pace, we've helped him find.'

'When might I get a chance to talk to him?'

'Incandenza took a lot of bringing along. He didn't used to quite have the complete game to be able to do this. Slice the court up into sections and chinks, then all of a sudden you see light through one of the chinks and you see he's been setting up the angle since the start of the point. It makes you think of chess.'

The journalist blew her red nose. ' "Chess on the run." '

'Nice term.'

Hal went into his service motion to the ad court.

'Do the students play chess here?'

A mirthless chuckle. 'No time.'

'Do you play chess?'

Stice hit a backhand winner off Hal's second serve; mild applause.

'I don't have time to play anything,' deLint said, filling in a square.

You could tell by the sound that the other boy's racquet was strung tighter than Hal's.

'When do I get to sit down with Hal directly?'

'I don't know. I don't think you do.'

The journalist's rapid head-movement reconfigured the flesh of her neck. 'Pardon me?'

'It's not my decision. My guess is you don't. Dr. Tavis didn't already tell you?'

'I really couldn't tell what he was telling me.'

'We've never had a kid here interviewed. The Founder let you guys on the grounds, versus Tavis this is an exception your even getting in.'

'I'm here for background only, for your alumnus, the punter.'

DeLint was making his lips look like he was whistling even though no whistling-sound was emerging. 'We've never let somebody do any kind of interview on a kid here while he's still in training and inculcation.'

'Does the student have some sort of say in who he talks to and why? What if the boy wants to chat with me about his brother's transition from tennis to football?'

DeLint kept his concentration on the match and the chart in a way that was supposed to let you know you had very little of his attention. 'Talk to Tavis about it.'

'I was in there for over two hours.'

'You pick up how to do questions with him after a while. Tavis you have to back into a Yes-No corner where you can finally say I need a Yes or a No. It takes about twenty minutes if you're sharp. This is your whole business, getting answers out of people. The answer's not for me to officially say, but I'm guessing a No. The Boston press guys come around after a big event, they get match results and physical stats and hometowns and nothing more.'

'*Moment* is a national magazine for and about exceptional people, not some sportswriter with a cigar and a deadline.'

'It's a command-decision, babe. I'm not in command. I know they teach us to teach that this place is about seeing instead of being seen.'

'I'm here only for the human-interest perspective of a talented boy on his talented brother's bold transition to a major sport where he's shown himself to be even more talented. One exceptional brother on another. Hal is not the profile's focus.'

'Get Tavis in the right corner and he'll tell you about seeing and being seen. These kids, the best of them are here to learn to see. Schtitt's thing is self-transcendence through pain. These kids —' gesturing at Stice running madly up for a drop-volley that stopped rolling well inside the service line; mild applause — 'they're here to get lost in something bigger than them. To have it stay the way it was when they started, the game as something bigger, at first. Then they show talent, start winning, become big fish in their ponds out there in their hometowns, stop being able to get lost inside the game and see. Fucks with a junior's head, talent. They pay top dollar to come here and go back to being little fish and to get savaged and feel small and see and develop. To forget themselves as objects of attention for a few years and see what they can do when the eyes are off them. They didn't come here to get read about as some soft-news item or background. Babe.'

DeLint read Steeply's expression as some kind of tic. The tiniest tuft of nostril-hair protruded from one of her nostrils, which deLint found repellent. She said, 'Were you ever written about, as a player?'

DeLint smiled coolly at his charts. 'Never had the sort of ranking or promise this issue'd even come up for me.'

'But some of these do. Hal's brother did.'

DeLint felt along his lip's outline with his pencil, sniffed. 'Orin was OK. Orin was essentially a one-trick pony as a player. And between you and me and the fence he was kind of a head-case. His game left here on the downswing. Now his little brother's got a future in tennis if he wants. And Ortho. Wayne for sure. A couple of the girls — Kent, Caryn and Sharyn here,' indicating the Vaught-apparition below them. 'The really gifted ones, the ones that make it out of here still on the upswing, if they get to the Show — '

'Meaning professional you mean.'

'In the Show they'll get all they want of being made into statues to be looked at and poked at and discussed, and then some. For now they're here to get to be the ones who look and see and forget getting looked at, for now.'

'But even you call it "The Show." They'll be entertainers.'

'You bet your ass they will be.'

'So audiences will be the whole point. Why not also prepare them for the stresses of entertaining an audience, get them used to being seen?'

The two boys were at the near net-post, Stice blowing his nose into a towel. DeLint made kind of a show of putting his clipboard down. 'Assume wrongly for a second that I can speak for the Enfield Academy. I say you do not get it. The point here for the best kids is to inculcate their sense that it's never about being seen. It's never. If they can get that inculcated, the Show won't fuck them up, Schtitt thinks. If they can forget everything but the game when all of you out there outside the fence see only them and want only them and the game's incidental to you, for you it's about entertainment and personality, it's about the statue, but if they can get inculcated right they'll never be slaves to the statue, they'll never blow their brains out after winning an event when they win, or dive out a third-story window when they start to stop getting poked at or profiled, when their blossom starts to fade. Whether or not you mean to, babe, you chew them up, it's what you do.'

'We chew statues?'

'Whether you mean to or no. You, *Moment, World Tennis, Self,* Inter-Lace, the audiences. The crowds in Italy fucking *literally.* It's the nature of the game. It's the machine they're all dying to throw themselves into. They don't know the machine. But we do. Gerhardt's teaching them to see the ball out of a place inside that can't be chewed. It takes time and total focus. The man's a fucking genius. Profile Schtitt, if you want to profile somebody.'

'And I'm not going to be allowed even to ask the students what it looks like, this inside chew-proof place. It's a secret place.'

Hal mishit a second serve and it flew off his frame and way down to where the girls were sending each other squeaks and lobs, and Stice had now broken him to go up 6–5, and the murmurs in the bleachers were like a courtroom at an unpleasant revelation. DeLint rounded his lips and made a kind of bovine sound in Ortho Stice's direction. Hal chipped his balls out along the baseline and made some small adjustments in his cross-hatched strings as he walked around for the side-change. A couple of the nastier kids applauded Hal's mishit a little.

'Get sardonic with me all you want. I already said it's not my command-decision. I wouldn't get sardonic with Tavis, though.'

'But if it were. Your command.'

'Lady, if it was me you'd be pressing your nose between the bars of the gate down there is as far in as you'd get. You're coming into a little slice of space and/or time that's been carved out to protect talented kids from exactly the kind of activities you guys come in here to do. Why Orin, anyway? The kid appears four times a game, never gets hit, doesn't even wear pads. A one-trick pony. Why not John Wayne? A more dramatic story, geopolitics, privation, exile, drama. A better player than Hal even. A more complete game. Aimed like a fucking missile at the Show, maybe the Top Five if he doesn't fuck up or burn down. Wayne's your ideal food-group. Which is why we'll keep you off him as long as he's here.'

The soft-profiler looked around at the scalps and knees in the stands, the bags of gear and a couple incongruous cans of furniture polish. 'Carved out of what, though, this place?'

From the Desk of Helen Steeply
Contributing Editor
Moment Magazine
13473 Blasted Expanse Blvd.
Tucson, AZ, 857048787/2

Mr. Marlon K. Bain
Saprogenic Greetings, Inc.
BPL-Waltham Bldg.
1214 Totten Pond Road
Waltham, MA, 021549872/4.
November Y.D.A.U.

Dear Mr. Bain:

In Phoenix on other business, it has been my good fortune to meet your adolescent friend, Mr. Orin J. Incandenza, and to have become intrigued with the possibilities of a profile of the Incandenza family and its accomplishments in not only sports but wide-ranging topics such as independent film circa metropolitan Boston, past and present.

I am writing to ask for your cooperation in contacting you with questions which you could answer in writing, as I am informed by Mr. Orin Incandenza you dislike to meet people outside your home and office.

I am hoping to hear from you in response to this request at your earliest convenience,

Etc. etc. etc.

Saprogenic Greetings*

WHEN YOU CARE ENOUGH TO LET A PROFESSIONAL SAY IT FOR YOU

*a proud member of the ACMÉ Family of Gags 'N Notions,
Pre-Packaged Emotions, Jokes and Surprises and Wacky Disguises

Ms. Helen Steepley
And So On
November Y.D.A.U.

Dear Ms. Steepley:

Fire away.

                          V.D.,

                          MK Bain
                          Saprogenic Greetings/ACMÉ

From the Desk of Helen Steeply
Contributing Editor
Moment Magazine
13473 Blasted Expanse Blvd.
Tucson, AZ, 857048787/2

Mr. MK Bain
Saprogenic Greetings Inc.
BPL-Waltham Bldg.
1214 Totten Pond Road
Waltham, MA, 021549872/4.
November Y.D.A.U.

Dear Mr. Bain:

    Q, Q, Q (Q, Q[Q], Q, Q, Q), Q, Q (Q), Q, Q.[269]

Carved out of sedimentary shale and ferrous granite and generic morphic crud — at more or less the same time the hilltop's bulge was shaved off and rolled and impacted level for tennis — are E.T.A.'s abundant tunnels. There are access tunnels and hallway tunnels, with rooms and labs and Pump Room's Lung-nexus off both sides, utility tunnels and storage tunnels and little blunt off-tunnels connecting tunnels to other tunnels. Maybe about sixteen different tunnels in all, in a shape that's more generally ovoid than anything else.

11/11, 1625h., LaMont Chu, Josh Gopnik, Audern Tallat-Kelpsa, Philip Traub, Tim ('Sleepy T.P.') Peterson, Carl Whale, Kieran McKenna — the bulk of the ambulatory sub-14 male Eschatonites — plus ten-year-old Kent Blott — are 26 meters directly below the Hal/Darkness match's Show Court with Glad Handle-Tie[270] trashbags and B.P. low-diffusion compact mercuric flashlights. Plus Chu has a clipboard with a pen attached to its clamp with twine. The sounds of competitive sneaker-movement and spectatorial bleacher-squeaks on the surface, travelling down through meters of compacted crud and polymerized cement tunnel-ceiling w/ parget-layer, sound rather like the stealthy dry scuttle of rodents, vermin. And this heightens the excitement that's part of why they're really down here.

One part of the reason they're down here is that small U.S. boys seem to have this fetish for getting down in the enclosed fundaments underneath things — tunnels, caves, ventilator-shafts, the horrific areas beneath wooden porches — rather the way older U.S. boys like great perspectival heights and spectacular views encompassing huge swaths of territory, this latter fetish accounting for why E.T.A.'s hilltop site is one of its trump-cards in the recruiting war with Port Washington and other Eastern-seaboard academies.

Another part is a semi-punitive shit detail in which certain players — judged to have been involved in the recent Eschaton nonstrategic-combat debacle, but who are uninjured[271] and not in the much severer hot water that the Big Buddies on the scene are in — have been punitively remanded below ground in P.M. shifts on what's supposed to constitute an unpleasant chore, to scout out the tunnelled route the TesTar All-Weather Inflatable Structures Corp.'s professional guys will have to take as they haul out from the Lung-Storage Room the fiberglass struts and crosspieces and dendriurethane folds that compose the Lung, for erection of the Lung, when the E.T.A. administration finally decides that the late-fall weather has gone beyond character-building and become an impediment to development and morale. This will be soon. Because the prorectors live in rooms off the larger tunnels and F. D. V. Harde's Physical Plant and Maintenance guys have their offices and supplies down here, and because Dr. James Incandenza's old optics and editing facilities are down here off one of the main tunnels and get used for Leith/Ogilvie classes in entertainment production and for optical science tutorials etc., and because a couple of the secondary and off-tunnels are used for temporary storage by departing seniors who can't tote eight or more years' worth of accumulated stuff in one post-graduate load — especially if they jet off to some novitiate-pro Satellite circuit for the summer, because that means air travel, two bags plus gear, max — some of the tunnels become badly littered in the warm season with trash-type material. And sometimes there's bulky-possession-type overflow from the little curved storage tunnels off the prorectors' hallway. Smaller kids are perfect for recons into low narrow tunnels partly blocked with dross, and even though it's no secret around E.T.A. that the smaller boys spend a fair amount of time down in the tunnels anyway, a retributive aspect is lent to this recon-detail by making the kids take down Handle-Tie trashbags to clear away littered exam papers and lab-handouts, calculator-batteries and banana peels and Kodiak smokeless-tobacco tins and spirals of synthetic-gut racquet-string, and Maintenance guys' hideous cigar-butts — Sleepy T.P. finds two bright Trojan wrappers just off the prorectors' hallway-tunnel, and then a couple meters farther along the floor the vermiform gleam of an actual condom, and there's some high-register debate about whether it's a used condom or not, and poor old Kent Blott is finally put in charge of picking it up and putting it in a trashbag, just in case it's a used condom — and empty boxes of complimentary corporate gear, and full boxes of faggy or poorly-absorbent gear nobody wants, and Habitant can-wrappers, and senior trunks and dorm-sized fridgelettes, etc.; and also to move whatever boxes they can heft, clear them out of the TesTar guys' access-route into the Lung-Storage and Pump Rooms; and LaMont Chu is supposed to note the location of any boxes or objects too bulky for them to move out of the way, and beefy custodial guys will be dispatched to handle them as they see fit.

This is why a fair number of the smaller E.T.A. males don't see Stice take a set off Hal Incandenza and nearly beat him, is that they were remanded down here by Neil Hartigan right after post-conditioning showers.

As noted already, they don't much mind it, being down here, now in one of the child-size-diametered off-tunnels between the prorectors' hallway and the Lung-Storage Room. The Eschatonites are down here quite a lot anyway. In fact the sub-14 E.T.A.s historically have a kind of Tunnel Club. Like many small boys' clubs, the Tunnel Club's unifying raison d'être is kind of vague. Tunnel Club activities mostly involve congregating informally in the better-lit main tunnels and hanging out and catching each other in lies about their lives and careers before E.T.A., and recapitulating the most recent Eschaton (usually only about five a term); and the Club's only formal activity is sitting around with a yellowed copy of *Robert's Rules* endlessly refining and amending the rules for who can and can't join the Tunnel Club. A true boy-type club, the Tunnel Club's least vague raison d'être has to do with exclusion. The vital No-Girls exclusion is the only ironclad part of the Tunnel Club's charter.[272] With the exception of Kent Blott, every boy down here on this detail is an Eschatonite and a member of the Tunnel Club. Kent Blott, ineligible for Eschaton because he's a humanities-type kid and hasn't even taken quadrivial Algebra yet, and excluded from the Club under every incarnation of the eligibility requirements thus far, is down here solely because he was heard to maintain at lunch that he was in the north part of the main tunnel between the Comm.-Ad. locker rooms and the subterranean laundry room this A.M., short-cutting back to his room in West House after drills and a sauna, and claimed to have espied — scuttling out of his mercuric light toward one of the secondary tunnels to Subdorms C and D and the East Courts and this same general tunnel-area they're now in — to have sighted what was either a rat or, he said, what looked even more like a Concavitated feral hamster. So the Eschatonites are also enthusiastic to be down here for potential rodent-recon, checking out Blott's claim, and they've brought what's either a very nervous or very excited Blott down with them, so they can trace the possible routes Blott said he saw the rodent maybe take, filling their Glad Handle-Ties and noting heavy items along the way, and also so they can immediately encircle and discipline Kent Blott if it turns out he was yanking people's chains.

Plus they make Blott be the one to take full trashbags and tie their plastic handles together and drag them back to where the expedition started — the entrance to the large smooth main tunnel by the boys' sauna — since none of them enjoys dragging full trashbags solo through dark tunnels with the rodential squeaking of match play and spectation far above. Chu holds a penlight in his teeth and writes heavy stuff down. They've filled several bags and gotten the lighter shit stacked off back enough to create a narrow route almost all the way to the Pump Room, around which Room hangs a strange sweet stale burny smell that none of them can place. The applause as Hal Incandenza barely takes the first set above sounds down here like faraway rain. The off-tunnel's dark as a pocket, but warm and dry, and there's surprisingly little dust. Ducts and coaxials running along the low ceiling make Whale and Tallat-Kelpsa have to crouch as they walk Point, clearing boxes and trying unsuccessfully to move fridgelettes back out of the way. There are several pockets of small but heavy dorm-size Maytag fridgelettes, the kind of thing no graduate takes with him, panelled in dark wood-grain plastic, some of them old models with three-prong plugs instead of chargers. Some of the empty fridgelettes have been indifferently scrubbed out and have their doors partway open and smell stale. Most of Chu's inventory for beefy-adult removal are either fridgelettes or locked trunks full of what sound like magazines and eight-year accumulations of pennies. The muffled rodential squeak of sneakers far overhead excites the Tunnel Club boys and puts them on edge. Philip Traub keeps making little squeaky noises and secretly tickling the back of people's necks, causing enormous excitement and much stopping and starting and tightly-enclosed whirling around, until Kieran McKenna captures Traub tickling Josh Gopnik in the bright beam of his P.B. light and Gopnik punches Traub in the radial nerve, and Traub clutches his arm and weeps and says he's quitting and going topside — Traub's the youngest kid here except for Blott and is a probationary second-string launcher in most Eschatons — and they have to stop and let Chu note and mark two discarded fridgelettes while Peterson and Gopnik try to distract and amuse Traub into staying and not retreating back up to Nwangi and making a high-pitched stink.

Discarded fridgelettes, empty boxes, immovable and complexly-address-labelled trunks, used athletic tape and Ace bandages, the occasional empty Visine bottle (which Blott stashes in his sweatshirt-pouch, for Mike Pemulis's next contest), Optics I & II lab reports, broken ball machines and stray tennis balls too dead even for the repressurization machine, broken or discarded TP cartridges of stroke-analysis filmings or worn-out entertainments, an anomalous set of parfait glasses, fruit peels and AminoPal energy-bar-wrappers that the Club itself had left down here after meetings, discarded curls of grip and tensile string, several incongruous barrettes, several old broadcast televisions some older kids used to like to keep around to watch the static, and, along the seam of wall and floor, brittle limb-shaped husks of exfoliated Pledge, expanses of arm and leg already half-decayed into fragrant dust — this comprising the bulk of the crud down here, and the kids don't much mind scanning and inventorying and bagging it, because their minds are diverted by something else very exciting, a kind of possible raison d'être for the Club itself, unless Blott had been tweaking their Units, in which case look out Blott, is the consensus.

Gopnik to a sniffling Traub, while Peterson shines his flashlight on the clipboard for Chu: 'Mary had a little lamb, its fleece electrostatic / And everywhere that Mary went, the lights became erratic.'

Carl Whale pretends to be immensely fat and moves along the wall with a blimpish splay-legged waddle.

Peterson to Traub, while Gopnik holds the light: 'Eighteen-year-old top-ranked John Wayne / Had sex with Herr Schtitt on a train / They had sex again / And again and again / And again and again and again,' which the slightly older kids find more entertaining than Traub does.

Kent Blott asks why a wispy-dicked blubberer like Phil gets to be in the Tunnel Club while his own applications get turned down, and Tallat-Kelpsa cuts him short by doing something to him in the dark that makes Blott shriek.

It's utterly dark except for the dime-sized discs of their low-diffusion B.P.s, because they've left the tunnels' strings of bare overhead bulbs off, because Gopnik, who's originally from Brooklyn and knows from rodents, says only a complete booger-eating moron would do rat-reconnaissance in the light, and it seems reasonable to assume that feral hamsters, also, have a basically ratty attitude toward light.

Chu has Blott see whether he can lift a bulky old doorless microwave oven that's lying on its side up next to one wall, and Blott tries and barely lifts it, and pules, and Chu marks the oven down for the adults to lift and tells Blott to drop it, which invitation Blott takes literally, and the crash and tinkle infuriate Gopnik and McKenna, who say that scanning for rodents with Blott is like fly-fishing with an epileptic, which cheers Traub up quite a bit.

Feral hamsters — bogey-wise right up there with mile-high toddlers, skull-deprived wraiths, carnivorous flora, and marsh-gas that melts your face off and leaves you with exposed gray-and-red facial musculature for the rest of your ghoulish-pariah life, in terms of late-night hair-raising Concavity narratives — are rarely sighted south of the Lucite walls and ATH-SCME'd checkpoints that delimit the Great Concavity, and only once in a blue moon anywhere south of like the new-border burg of Methuen MA, whose Chamber of Commerce calls it 'The City That Interdependence Rebuilt,' and anyway *pace* Blott are hardly ever seen solo, being the sort of rapacious locust-like mass-movement creature that Canadian agronomists call 'Piranha of the Plains.' An infestation of feral hamsters in the waste-rich terrain of metro Boston, to say nothing of the clutter-tunnelled E.T.A. grounds, would be an almost grand-scale public-health disaster, would cause simply no end of adult running-in-circles and knuckle-biting, and would consume megacalories of displaced pre-adolescent stress for the E.T.A. players. Every ear-cocked eye-peeled bag-toting kid in the off-tunnel this afternoon is hoping hamster in a big way, except for Kent Blott, who's hoping simply and fervently for some sort of rodential sighting or scat-sample that'll keep him from being disciplinarily hung upside-down in a lavatory stall to shriek until a staff-member finds him. He reminds the Tunnel Clubbers that it's not like he'd claimed he espied the thing actually *heading* in this direction, he'd only seen the thing scuttling in a way that seemed to suggest a *tendency* or like *probability* of heading in this direction.

One whole box on its side with its frayed strapping tape split has spilled part of a load of old TP-cartridges, old and mostly unlabelled, out onto the tunnel floor in a fannish pattern, and Gopnik and Peterson complain that the cartridge-cases' sharp edges put holes in their Glad bags, and Blott is dispatched with three bags of cartridges and fruit rinds, each only about half full, back to the lit vestibule outside the Comm.-Ad. tunnel's start, where a serious pile of bags is starting to pile fragrantly up.

Plus a confirmed feral-hamster sighting, Chu and Gopnik and 'S.T.P.'

Peterson have agreed, could well distract the Headmaster's office from post-Eschaton reprisals against Big Buddies Pemulis, Incandenza and Axford, whom the Club's Eschatonite faction doesn't want to see reprised against, particularly, though the consensus is nobody would much mind seeing the malefic Ann Kittenplan hung out to dry in a serious way. Plus hamster-incursions could be posited to account for the occult appearance of large and incongruous E.T.A. objects in inappropriate places, which started in August with the thousands of practice balls found scattered all over the blue lobby carpeting and the carefully arranged pyramid of AminoPal energy bars found on Court 6 at dawn drills in mid-September and has gained momentum in a way no one cares for one bit — feral hamsters being notorious draggers and rearrangers of stuff they can't eat but feel compelled to fuck with anyway, somehow — and so ease the communal near-hysteria the objects have caused among aboriginal blue-collar staff and sub-16 E.T.A. alike. Which would make the Tunnel Club guys something like heroes, foreseeably.

They move along the tunnel, their mercuric lights Xing and separating and forming jagged angles, colored faintly pink.

But even a confirmed rat would be a coup. Dean of Academic Affairs Mrs. Inc has a violent phobic thing about vermin and waste and insects and overall facility hygiene, and Orkin men with beer-bellies and playing cards with naked girls in high-heeled shoes on the backs (McKenna's claim) spray the bejeesus out of the E.T.A. grounds twice a semester. None of the younger E.T.A. boys — who have the same post-latency fetish for vermin they have about subterranean access and exclusive Clubs — none of them has ever once gotten to see or trap a rat or roach or even so much as a lousy silverfish anyplace around here. So the unspoken consensus is that a hamster'd be optimal but they'd settle for a rat. Just one lousy rat could give the whole Club a legit *raison*, an explicable reason for congregating underground — all of them are a bit uneasy about liking to congregate underground for no good or clear reason.

'Sleeps, you think you could lift that and carry it?'

'Chu man I wouldn't even get up next to whatever that is much less touch it.'

Blott's footfalls and tuneless whistling can be heard from far away, returning, and the distant squeak of overhead sneakers.

Gopnik stops and his light pans, playing on faces. 'OK. Somebody farted.'

'What's this up next to it, Sleeps?' Chu backing up to widen his light's beam on something broad and squat and dark.

'Could I get some lights over here on this you guys?'

'Because did somebody go ahead and *cut one* in this little unventilated space?'

'Chu, it's a room fridge, that's all.'

'But it's bigger than the room fridges.'

'But it's not as big as a real fridge.'

'It's in-between.'

'I do smell something, though, Gop, I admit.'

'There *is* a smell. If somebody farted, speak up.'

'Otherwise it's a *smell*.'

'Don't try to describe it.'

'Sleeps, that's no human fart I've ever smelled.'

'It's too powerful for a fart.'

'Maybe Teddy Schacht was having an attack and staggered down here just to cut one.'

Peterson trains his light on the midsized brown fridge. 'You don't possibly think . . .'

Chu says 'No way. No way.'

'*What?*' Blott says.

'Don't even think it,' Chu says.

'I don't even think any kind of *mammal* could fart that bad, Chu.'

Peterson's looking at Chu, both of their faces pale in the mercuric light. 'No *way* somebody'd graduate and leave and put their fridge down here without taking the food out.'

Blott goes 'Is that the smell?'

'Was this Pearson's fridge last year?'

Sleepy T.P. turns around. 'Who smells a, like, a like decay-element?'

Lights on the tunnel ceiling from upraised hands.

'Quorum on decay-type odor.'

'Should we check?' Chu says. 'Blott's hamster might be in there.'

'Gnawing on something unspeakable, maybe.'

'You mean open it?'

'Pearson had a bigger than usual fridge.'

'*Open* it?'

Chu scratches behind his ear. 'Me and Gop'll light it up, Peterson opens it.'

'Why me?'

'You're closest, Sleeps. Hold your breath.'

'Jesus. Well back off up here so I can jump way back if anything like flies out.'

'Nobody could be so low. Who would go off and leave a full fridge?'

'Happy to back way, way off,' says Carl Whale, his light receding.

'Not even Pearson could be that low, leaving food in an unplugged fridge.'

'This could explain rodent-attraction and then some.'

'Now look out . . . ready? . . . *hummph*.'

'Ow! Get off!'

'Put the light ov— oh my God.'

'Eeeeeeeyu.'

'Hhhhwwwww.'

'Oh my *God*.'

'Bllaaaaarrr.'

'Such a smell I'm smelling!'

'There's *mayonnaise!* He left *mayonnaise* in there.'

'Why the bulge in the top of the lid?'

'The ballooning carton of orange juice!'

'Nothing could live in that, rodent or otherwise.'

'So why's that sandwich-meat moving?'

'Maggots?'

'Maggots!'

'Shut it! Sleeps! Kick it shut!'

'This right here is exactly as close as I'm ever getting to that fridge ever again, Chu.'

'The smell's expanding!'

'I can smell it from here!': Whale's tiny distant voice.

'I'm not enjoying this at all.'

'This is Death. Woe unto those that gazeth on Death. The Bible.'

'What're maggots?'

'Should we just run really fast the other way?'

'Second that.'

'This is probably what the rat or hamster smelled,' Blott ventures.

'Run!'

High receding voices, bobbing lights, Whale's light way out front.

After Stice and Incandenza split the first two sets and Hal dashed into the locker room at the break to put Collyrium-brand eyewash in eyes that were bothering him and deLint made warped crashing sounds on the tiers as he walked down the bleachers and over to have a word with Stice, who was squatting against the net-post holding his left arm up like a scrubbed surgeon and applying a towel to the arm, deLint's place up next to Helen Steeply was taken by female prorector Thierry Poutrincourt, freshly showered, long-faced, a non-U.S. citizen, a tall Québecer former Satellite pro in rimless specs and a violetish ski cap just enough of a shade away from the journalist's hat to make the people behind them pretend to shield their eyes from the clash. The putative newshound introduced herself and asked Poutrincourt who the heavy-browed kid was at the end of the top bleacher behind them, hunched over and gesturing and speaking into his empty fist.

'James Troeltsch of Philadelphia is better to leave alone to play the broadcaster to himself. He is a strange and unhappy,' Poutrincourt said, her face long and cavern-cheeked and not terribly happy-looking itself. Her slight shrugs and way of looking elsewhere while speaking were not unlike Rémy Marathe's. 'When we hear you are the journalist for shiny perfumed magazines of fad and trend we are told be unfriendly, but me, I think I am friendly.' Her smile was rictal and showed confused teeth. 'My family's loved ones also are large of size. It is difficult to be large.'

Steeply's pre-assignment decision was to let all size-references pass as if there was some ability to screen out any reference to size or girth, originating possibly in adolescence. 'Your Mr. deLint certainly held himself aloof.'

'DeLint, when we prorectors are suggested to do a thing, he asks to himself only: how can I perfectly do this thing so the superiors will smile with pleasure at deLint.' Poutrincourt's right forearm was almost twice the size of her left. She wore white sneakers and a Donnay warmup of a deep glowing neutron-blue that clashed hideously with both their caps. The circles beneath her eyes were also blue.

'Why the instructions to be unfriendly?'

Poutrincourt always nodded for a while before she replied to anything, as if things had to go through various translation-circuits. She nodded and scratched at her long jaw, thinking. 'You are here to make publicity a child player, one of our *étoiles*,[273] and Dr. Tavis, he is how you say quantified — '

'Quarantined. Suspicious. Guarded.'

'No. . . .'

'Confused. Torn. In a quandary.'

'*Quandary* is how. Because this is a good place, and Hal is good, better since before the present, perhaps now he is *étoile*.' A shrug, long arms akimbo. Hal reemerged from Comm.-Ad. and, ankle-brace or no, displayed a slow loose thoroughbred trot past the pavilion and bleachers and to the gate in #12's southern fence, acting as if unwatched by people in bleachers, and tapped two of his big-headed tennis racquets together to listen for the strings' pitch, exchanging some neutral words with deLint, who was standing with Stice at the edge of the transom's shadow, Stice breaking into a half-laugh at something, twirling his racquet and walking back to serve as Hal retrieved a ball along the north fence. Both players' racquets had large heads and thick frames. Thierry Poutrincourt said 'And by nature who does not wish the shiny attention, that the magazines with cologne on their pages say this is *étoile*, Enfield Tennis Academy it is good?'

'I'm here to do a soft inoffensive profile on his brother, with Hal mentioned only as part of an American family exceptional in several respects. I don't see what's quandariacal for Dr. Tavis about this.' The tiny plump officious man who seemed to have a phone tucked under his chin at all times, the kind of frenzied over-cooperation that's a technical interviewer's worst nightmare for an interrogation; the little man's monologue had done to Steeply's brain kind of what a flashbulb does to your eyes, and if he'd explicitly denied him access to the brother then the denial had been slipped in after he'd worn Steeply down.

There was the slight shaken-saw wobble of bleachers as deLint walked back up, stacked charts against his chest like a schoolgirl's books, his smile at the Québecois player in his seat as if he'd never met her before, settling in heavily on Steeply's other side, glancing down at where the profiler'd bracketed notes on the possible sounds a string-hit ball sounds like in cold air: *cut, king, ping, pons, pock, cop, thwa, thwat.*

The *samizdat* Entertainment's director's other son chipped a return that caught the tape and sat there a moment and fell back.

"*Veux que nous nous parlons en français? Serait plus facile, ça?*" This invitation because Poutrincourt's eyes had gone hooded the minute the de-Lint person joined them.

Poutrincourt's shrug was blasé: Francophones are never impressed that anyone else can speak French. 'Very well then look:' she said (Poutrincourt did, in Québecois), 'pubescent stars are nothing new to this sport. Lenglen, Rosewall. In A.D. 1887 a fifteen-year-old girl won Wimbledon, she was the first. Evert in the semifinals of the US Open at sixteen, '71 or '2. Austin, Jaeger, Graff, Sawamatsu, Venus Williams. Borg. Wilander, Chang, Treffert, Medvedev, Esconja. Becker of the A.D. '80s. Now this new Argentinean Kleckner.'

Steeply lit a Flanderfume that made deLint's face spread with distaste. 'You compare it is like gymnastics, figure skating, competitive to-swim.'

Poutrincourt made no comment on Steeply's syntax. 'Just so, then. Good.'

Steeply was adjusting the long peasant skirt and crossing legs so he was inclined away from deLint, gazing at a kind of translucent mole on Poutrincourt's long cheek. Poutrincourt's thick rimless specs were like a scary nun's. She looked more male than anything, long and hard and breastless. Steeply tried to exhale away from everyone. 'The world-plateau tennis not being required to have neither the size and muscle of the hockey nor the basketball nor the American football, for example.'

Poutrincourt nodded. 'But yes, nor the millimetric precision of your baseball's hitting, nor how the Italians say the *senza errori,* the never-miss consistency, that keeps the golfers from true mastery until they have thirty or more years.' The prorector switched for just a moment to English, possibly for deLint's benefit: 'Your French is Parisian but possible. Me, mine is Québecois.'

Steeply now got to give that same sour Gallic shrug. 'You're saying to me serious tennis doesn't need of an athlete anything already adolescents do not possess, if they are exceptional for it.'

'The medicinists of sports science know well what top tennis requires,' Poutrincourt said, back in French. 'Too well, which are the agility, the reflexes,[274] the short-range speed, the balance, some coordination between the hand and the eye, and very much endurance. Some strength, with particular importance for the male. But all these are achievable by the period of puberty, for some. But yes, but wait,' she said, putting a hand on the notebook as Steeply started to pretend to inscribe. 'The thing you have put as the question to me. This is why the quandary. The young players, they have the advantage in psyche, also.'

'The edge of mentality,' Steeply said, trying to ignore the boy speaking into his hand several seats over. DeLint seemed to be ignoring everything around him, engrossed in the match and his statistics. The Canadian prorector's hands moved in small circles out front to indicate engagement in the conversation. Americans' conversational hands sit like lumps of dough most of the time, Rémy Marathe had pointed out once.

'But yes, so, the formidable mental edge that their psyches are still not yet adult in all ways — therefore, so, they do not feel the anxiety and pressure in the way it is felt by adult players. This is every story of the teenager appearing from no location to upset the famous adult in professional play — the ephebic, they do not feel the pressure, they can play with abandon, they are without fear.' A cold smile. Sunlight blazed on her lenses. 'At the beginning. At the beginning they are without pressure or fear, and they *burst* from seemingly no location onto the professional stage, instant *étoiles,* phenomenal, fearless, immunized to pressure, numb to anxiety — at first. They seem as if they are like the adult players only better — better in emotion, more abandoned, not human to the stress or fatigue or the airplaning without end, to the publicity.'

'The English expression of the child in the store of candy.'

'Seemingly unfeeling of the loneliness and alienation and everyone wants a thing from the *étoile.*'

'The money, also.'

'But it is soon you start to see the burning out which the place like ours is hoping to prevent. You remember Jaeger, burned out at sixteen, Austin at twenty. Arias and Krickstein, Esconja and Treffert, too injured to play on by their late teenage years. The much-promising Capriati, the well-known tragedy. Pat Cash of Australia, fourth on earth at eighteen, vanished by the twenties of age.'

'Not to be mentioning the large money. The endorsings and appearings.'

'Always so, for the young *étoile*. And now worse in today, that the sponsors have no broadcasting to advertise with. Now the ephebe who is famous *étoile,* who is in magazines and the sports reports *aux disques,* he is pursued to become the *Billboard Who Walks.* Use this, wear this, for money. Millions thrown at you before you can drive the cars you buy. The head swells to the size of a balloon, why not?'

'But can pressure be far behind the back?' Steeply said.

'Many times the same. Winning two and three upset matches, feeling suddenly so loved, so many talking to you as if there is love. But always the same, then. For then you awaken to the fact that you are loved for winning only. The two and three wins created you, for people. It is not that the wins made them recognize something that existed unrecognized before these up-set wins. The from-noplace winning *created* you. You must keep winning to keep the existence of love and endorsements and the shiny magazines wanting your profile.'

'Enter the pressure,' Steeply said.

'Pressure such as one could not imagine, now that to maintain you must win. Now that winning is the *expected*. And all alone, in the hotels and the airplanes, with any other player you could speak to of the pressure to exist wanting to beat you, wanting to be exist above and not below. Or the others, wanting from you, and only so long as you play with abandon, winning.'

'Hence the suicides. The burn-out. The drugs, the self-indulging, the spoilage.'

'What is the instruction if we shape the ephebe into the athlete who can win fearlessly to be loved, yet we do not prepare her for the time after fear comes, no?'

'Therefore the terrible pressure here. They are being tempered. Oven-toughened.'

Hal served wide and this time followed it in, the serve, taking a stutter-step at the service line. Stice's body seemed to elongate as he reached and got the stick up over the return, driving a forehand. Hal volleyed it too short and took a couple steps off the net as Stice came in, winding up for an easy pass. Hal guessed a direction and started to his left, and The Darkness chipped a lob right over him and hit the heel of his hand against his strings as Hal gave it up halfway back, Stice not rubbing it in but exhorting himself. Hal's sweat was way heavier than the Kansan's, but Stice's face was almost maroon with flush. Each player twirled his stick in his hand as Hal walked back to retrieve the ball. Stice took his position in the deuce court, pulling up his socks.

'Still smart for Hal to follow the serve in once a game or so,' deLint said into Steeply's ear.

And irritating throughout was the heavy-browed red-nostriled kid James Troeltsch at the very end of the top bleacher, speaking into his fist, coming at the fist from first one angle and then another, pretending to be two people:

'Incandenza the controller. Incandenza the tactician.

'Rare tactical lapse for Incandenza, following the serve in when he's just finally started establishing control from the baseline.

'Have a look at Incandenza standing there waiting for Ortho Stice to finish futzing with his socks so he can serve. The resemblance to statues of

Augustus of Rome. The regal bearing, the set of the head, the face impassive and emanating command. The chilly blue eyes.

'The chilly reptilian film of concentration in the cold blue eyes, Jim.

'The Halster's been having some trouble controlling his volleys.

'Personally, Jim, I think he'd be better off with his old midsized graphite stick than that large head the creepy Dunlop guy got him to switch to.

'Stice being the younger player out there, he's grown up with the extra-large head. A large head is all The Darkness knows.

'You could say Stice was born with a large head, and that Incandenza's a man who's adapted his game to a large head.

'Hal's career dating back to before your polycarbonate resins changed the whole power-matrix of the junior game, too, Jim.

'And what a day for tennis.

'What a day for family fun of all kinds.

'This Bud's for the Whole Family. It's the Bud Match of the Week. Brought to you.

'Incandenza even reported to have modified his grip, all to accommodate the large head.

'And by the Multiphasix family of fine graphite-reinforced polycarbonate resins, Ray.

'Jim, Ortho Stice — impossible to even visualize Stice without his trusty large head.

'It's all they know, these kids.'

DeLint hiked back onto an elbow on the tier above and told James Troeltsch to regulate the volume or he was going to take a personal interest in seeing Troeltsch suffer.

Hal bounced the ball three times, tossed, rocked farther back on the toss, and absolutely crunched the serve, spinless and wickedly angled out wide, Stice grotesquely off-balance, lunging too far and hitting the backhand cramped, down the line and shallow. Hal moved in to the service line for it, hunched and with his stick cocked up behind him, looking somehow insectile. Stice stood in the middle of the baseline awaiting pace and was helpless when Hal shortened the stroke and dribbled it at an angle cross-court, barely clearing the net and distorted with backspin and falling into the half-meter of fair space the acuteness of the angle allowed.

'Hal Incandenza has the greater tennis brain,' Poutrincourt said in English.

Hal aced Stice down the center to go up either 2–1 or 3–2 in the third.

'The thing you want to know about Hal, babe, is he's got a complete game,' deLint said as the boys changed ends of the court, Stice holding two balls out before him on the face of his racquet. Hal went to the towel again. The children along the bottom tier were leaning left and then right in tandem, amusing themselves. The apparition with the lens and metal pole was gone, overhead.

678

'What you want to know, watching juniors at this level,' deLint says, still back on an elbow so his upper body was out of sight and he was just legs and a voice in Steeply's cold ear. 'They all have different strengths, areas of the game they're better at, and you can drown in profiling a match or a player in terms of the different strengths and the number of individual strengths.'

'I am not here to profile the boy,' Steeply said, but in French again.

DeLint ignored him. 'It's not just the strengths or the number of strengths. It's do they come together to make a game. How complete is a kid. Has he got a game. Those kids at lunch you got to meet.'

'But not speak to.'

'The kid in the idiotic hat, Pemulis, Mike's got great, great volleys, he's a natural at net, great, great hand-eye. Mike's other strength is he's got the best lob in East Coast juniors bar none. These are his strengths. The reason both of these kids you're looking at out here right now can beat the living shit out of Pemulis is Pemulis's strengths don't give him a complete game. Volleys're an offensive shot. A lob's a baseliner's weapon, counterpuncher. You can't lob from the net or volley from the baseline.'

'He says Michael Pemulis's abilities cancel each other out,'[275] Poutrin-court said in the other ear.

DeLint made the small salaam of iteration. 'Pemulis's strengths cancel each other out. Now Todd Possalthwaite, the littler kid with the bandage on his nose from the soap-and-shower-slipping thing, Possalthwaite's also got a great lob, and while Pemulis'd take him right now on pure age and power Possalthwaite's the technically superior player with the better future, because Todd's built a complete game out of his lob.'

'This deLint is wrong,' Poutrincourt said in Québecois, smiling rictally across Steeply at deLint.

'Because Possalthwaite won't come in to net. Possalthwaite hangs back at any cost, and unlike Pemulis he works to develop the groundstrokes to let him stay back and draw the other guy in and use that venomous lob.'

'Which means at fourteen his game, it will never change or grow, and if he grows strong and wishes to attack he will never be able,' Poutrincourt said.

DeLint displayed so little curiosity about what Poutrincourt inserted that Steeply wondered if he had some French on the sly, and made a private ideogram to this effect. 'Possalthwaite's a pure defensive strategist. He's got a gestalt. The term we use here for a complete game is either *gestalt* or *complete game*.'

Stice aced Hal out wide on the ad court again, and the ball got stuck in an intersticial diamond in the chain-link fencing, and Hal had to put his stick down and use both hands to force the thing out.

'Maybe for your article, though, the poop on this kid, the punter's brother — Hal can't lob half as good as even Possalthwaite, and compared to Ortho or Mike his net-play's pedestrian. But unlike his brother when he was here, see, Hal's strengths have started to fit together. He's got a great serve, a great return of serve, and great, great groundstrokes, with great control and great touch, great command of touch and spin; and he can take a defensive player and yank the kid around with his superior control, and he can take an attacking player and use the guy's own pace against him.'

Hal passed Stice off the backhand down the line and the ball looked sure to land fair, and then at the last possible second it veered out, an abrupt tight curve out of bounds as if some freak gust came out of nowhere and blew it out, and Stice looked more surprised than Hal did. The punter's brother's face registered nothing as he stood at the ad corner, adjusting something on his strings.

'But perhaps one does attain this, to win. Imagine you. You become just what you have given your life to be. Not merely very good but the best. The good philosophy of here and Schtitt — I believe this philosophy of Enfield is more Canadian than American, so you may see I have prejudice — is that you must have also — so, leave to one side for a moment the talent and work to become best — that you are doomed[276] if you do not have also within you some ability to transcend the goal, transcend the success of the best, if you get to there.'

Steeply could see, off in the parking lot behind the hideous bulging neo-Georgian cube of the Community and Administration Building, several small boys carrying and dragging white plastic bags to the nest of dumpsters that abutted the pines at the parking lot's rear, the children pale and wild-eyed and conferring among themselves and casting anxious looks across the grounds at the crowd behind the Show Court.

'Then,' Poutrincourt said, 'and for the ones who do become the *étoiles,* the lucky who become profiled and photographed for readers and in the U.S.A. religion *make it,* they must have something built into them along the path that will let them transcend it, or they are doomed. We see this in experience. One sees this in all obsessive goal-based cultures of pursuit. Look at the *Japonois,* the suicide rates of their later years. This task of us at the Enfield is more delicate still, with the *étoiles.* For, you, if you attain your goal and cannot find some way to transcend the experience of having that goal be your entire existence, your *raison de faire,*[277] so, then, one of two things we see will happen.'

Steeply had to keep breathing on the pen to keep the point thawed.

'One, one is that you attain the goal and realize the shocking realization that attaining the goal does not complete or redeem you, does not make everything for your life "*OK*" as you are, in the culture, educated to assume it will do this, the goal. And then you face this fact that what you had thought would have the meaning does not have the meaning when you get it, and you are impaled by shock. We see suicides in history by people at

680

these pinnacles; the children here are versed in what is called the saga of Eric Clipperton.'

'With two *p*'s?'

'Just so. Or the other possibility of doom, for the *étoiles* who attain. They attain the goal, thus, and put as much equal passion into celebrating their attainment as they had put into pursuing the attainment. This is called here the Syndrome of the Endless Party. The celebrity, money, sexual behaviors, drugs and substances. The glitter. They become celebrities instead of players, and because they are celebrities only as long as they feed the culture-of-goal's hunger for the *make-it,* the winning, they are doomed, because you cannot both celebrate and suffer, and play is always suffering, just so.'

'Our best boy is better than Hal, you'll see him play tomorrow if you want, John Wayne. No relation to the real John Wayne. A fellow compatriot of Terry here.' Aubrey deLint was sitting back up beside them, the cold giving his pitted cheeks a second flush, two feverish harlequin ovals. 'John Wayne's got a gestalt because Wayne's simply got everything, and everything with him's got the sort of pace that a touch-artist and thinker like Hal just can't handle.'

'This was the Founder's philosophy, too, of doom, the punter Incandenza's father, who also I am being told dabbled in filming?' Steeply asked the Canadian.

Poutrincourt's shrug could have meant too many things to note. 'I came after. M. Schtitt, his different goal for the *étoiles* is to walk between these.' Nor did Steeply quite notice the woman's shifts between dialects. 'To map out some path between needing the success and mockery-making of the success.'

DeLint leaned in. 'Wayne's got everything. Hal's strength has become knowing he doesn't have everything, and constructing a game as much out of what's missing as what's there.'

Steeply pretended to arrange the cap but was really adjusting the wig. 'It all sounds awfully abstract for something so physical.'

Poutrincourt's shrug pushed her glasses slightly up. 'It is contradictory. Two selves, one not there. M. Schtitt, when the Academy Founder died . . .'

'The punter's father, who dabbled in films.' Steeply's raglan sweater had been his wife's.

Again nodding blandly, Poutrincourt: 'This academic Founder, M. Schtitt tells that this Founder was a student of types of sight.'

DeLint said 'Wayne's only possible limits being also his strength, the tungsten-steel will and resolve, the insistence on imposing his game and his will on his man, totally unwilling to change the pace of his game if he's not doing good. Wayne's got the touch and the lobs to hang back on an off-day, but he won't — if he's down or things aren't going his way, he just hits harder. His pace is so overwhelming he can get away with being uncompromising about attack against North American juniors. But in the Show, which Wayne'll go pro maybe as soon as next year, in the Show flexibility is more important, he'll find. What do you call, a humility.'

Poutrincourt was looking at Steeply almost too carelessly, it almost seemed. 'The studying was not so much how one sees a thing, but this relation between oneself and what one sees. He translated this numerously across different fields, M. Schtitt tells.'

'The son described his father as quote "genre-dysphoric."''

Poutrincourt cocked her head. 'This does not sound like Hal Incandenza.'

DeLint sniffed meatily. 'But Wayne's gestalt's chief edge over Hal is the head. Wayne is pure force. He doesn't feel fear, pity, remorse — when a point's over, it might as well have never happened. For Wayne. Hal actually has finer groundstrokes than Wayne, and he could have Wayne's pace if he wanted. But the reason Wayne is Three continentally and Hal's Six is the head. Hal looks just as perfectly dead out there, but he's more vulnerable in terms of, like, emotionally. Hal remembers points, senses trends in a match. Wayne doesn't. Hal's susceptible to fluctuations. Discouragement. Set-long lapses in concentration. Some days you can almost see Hal like flit in and out of a match, like some part of him leaves and hovers and then comes back.'

The Troeltsch person said 'Holy *crow*.'

'So to survive here for later is, finally, to have it both ways,' Thierry Poutrincourt said quietly, in nearly accentless English, as if to herself.

'This emotional susceptibility in terms of forgetting being more commonly a female thing. Schtitt and I think it's a will issue. Susceptible wills are more common to the top girls here. We see it in Longley, we see it in Millie Kent and Frannie Unwin. We don't see this forgetful will in the Vaughts, or in Spodek, who you can watch if you want.'

The Troeltsch person said 'Could we see that again, Ray, do you think?'

Steeply was looking at the side of Poutrincourt's face as deLint on the other side was saying 'But the one we see this most in is Hal.'

14 NOVEMBER
YEAR OF THE DEPEND ADULT UNDERGARMENT

The Man o' War Grille on Prospect: Matty sat in the hot clatter of the Portuguese restaurant with his hands in his lap, looking at nothing. A waiter brought his soup. The waiter had bits of either bloodstain or soup on his apron, and for no discernible reason wore a fez. Matty ate his soup without once slurping. He'd been the neat eater in the family. Matty Pemulis was a prostitute and today he was twenty-three.

The Man o' War Grille is on Prospect Street in Cambridge and its front windows overlook the heavy foot traffic between Inman and Central Squares. As Matty waited for his soup he'd seen across the restaurant and out the front's glass a bag-lady-type older female in several clothing-layers lift her skirts and lower herself to the pavement and move her scaggly old bowels right there in full view of passersby and diners both, then gather all her plastic shopping bags together and walk stolidly out of view. The pile of bowel movement sat there on the pavement, steaming slightly. Matty'd heard the college kids at the next table say they didn't know whether to be totally illed or totally awed.

A big rangy kid, with a big sharp face and tight short hair and a smile and a shave-twice jaw since he was fourteen. Now balding smoothly back from a high clear forehead. A permanent smile that always seemed like he was trying not to but just couldn't help it. His Da always formerly saying to Wipe it off.

Inman Square: Little Lisbon. The soup has bits of calamari that make the muscles in his face flex, chewing.

Now two Brazilians in bellbottoms and tall shoes along the sidewalk across the window over the diners' heads, what might be a brewing street-fight, one walking forward and one walking backward, facing off as they move, each missing the dollop of bowel-movement on the walk, speaking high-volume street-Portuguese muffled by windows and hot clatter, but each looking around and then pointing at his own chest like: 'You saying this shit to *me?*' Then the forward man's sudden charge carrying them both past the window's right frame.

Matty's Da'd come over on a boat from Louth in Lenster in 1989. Matty'd been three or four. Da'd worked on the Southie docks, coiling lengths of rope as big around as phone poles into tall cones, and had died when Matty was seventeen, of pancreatic complaints.

Matty looked up from the roll he was dipping in the soup and saw two underweight interracial girls moving across the window, one a nigger, neither even looking at the shit everyone's stepping around; and then a few seconds behind them Poor Tony Krause, who because of the trousers and cap Matty didn't even recognize as Poor Tony Krause until he'd looked back down and then up again: Poor Tony Krause looked godawful: sucked-out, hollow-eyed, past ill, grave-ready, his face's skin the greenish white of extreme-depth marine life, looking less alive than undead, identifiable as poor old Poor Tony only by the boa and red leather coat and the certain way he held his hand to his throat's hollow as he walked, that way Equus Reese always said always reminded him of black-and-white-era starlets descending curved stairs into some black-tie function, Krause never so much walking as making an infinite series of grand entrances into pocket after pocket of space, a queenly hauteur now both sickening and awesome given

Krause's spectral mien, passing across the Grille's window, his eyes either on or looking right through the two skinny girls plodding ahead of him, following them out of the window's right-hand side.

His Da'd begun fucking Matty up the ass when Matty was ten. A *fook in t'boom*. Matty had complete recall of the whole thing. He'd seen sometimes where persons that had unpleasant things happen to them as children blocked the unpleasantness out in their mentality as adults and forgot it. Not so with Matty Pemulis. He remembered every inch and pimple of every single time. His father outside the little room Matt and Micky slept in, late at night, the cat's-eye sliver of lit hallway through the crack in the door Da'd opened, the door on well-oiled hinges opening with the implacable slowness of a rising moon, Da's shadow lengthening across the floor and then the man his very self weaving in behind it, crossing the moonlit floor in darned socks and that smell about him that later Matty'd know was malt liquor but at that age he and Mickey called something else, when they smelled it. Matty lay and pretended to sleep; he didn't know why tonight he pretended not to know the man was there; he was afraid. Even the first time. Micky just five. All the times were the same. Da drunk. Tacking across the bedroom floor. A certain stealth. Managing somehow never to break his neck on the toy trucks and tiny cars scattered on the floor, left there that first time by accident. Sitting on the edge of the bed so his weight changed the bed's angle. A big man smelling of tobacco and something else, his breath always audible when drunk. Sitting on the edge of the bed. Shaking Matty 'awake' to the point where Matty'd have to pretend to wake up. Asking if he'd been asleep, sleeping, there, was he. Tenderness, caresses that were somehow just over the line from true ethnic-Irish fatherly affection, the emotional largesse of a man without a Green Card who daily broke his back for his family's food. Caresses that were in some vague way just over the line from that and from the emotional largesse of something else, drunk, when all the rules of mood were suspended and you never knew from minute to minute whether you were to be kissed or hit — impossible to say how or even know how they were just over those lines. But they were, the caresses. Tenderness, caresses, low soft oversweet hot bad breath, soft apologies for some flash of savagery or discipline from the day. A way of cupping the pillow-warm cheek and jaw in the hollow of the hand, the huge pinkie finger tracing the hollow between throat and jaw. Matty'd shrink away: shy are we sone scared are we? Matty'd shrink away even after he knew the shrinking fear was part of what brought it on, for Da'd get angry: who are we scared of, then? Then who are we, a sone, to be scared so of our own Da? As if the Da that broke daily his back were nothing more than a. Can't a Da show his son some love without being taken for a. As if Matty could lie here with his food inside him under bedding he'd paid for and think his Da were no better than a. Is it a fookin you're scared of, then. You think a Da what comes in to speak to his sone and holds him as a Da has nought on his mind but a fook? As if the sone were some forty-dollar whore off the docks? As if the Da were a. Is that what you take me for. Is that what you take me for then. Matty shrinking back into a flattening pillow the Da'd paid for, the springs of the convertible bed singing with his fear; he shook. Why then so then I've a mind to give you just what you're thinking t'fear. Take me for. Matty knew early on that his being afraid fueled the thing somehow, made his Da want to. He was unable not to be afraid. He tried and tried, cursed himself for a coward and deserving, all but calling his father a. It was years before he snapped to the fact that his Da'd have *fooked him in t'boom* no matter what he'd done. That the event was laid out before the first slim line of doorlight broadened, and whatever Matty'd felt or betrayed made no difference. An advantage to not blocking it out is you can snap to things later, with maturer perspective; you can come to see no sone on the planet could in any way ask for that, regardless. At a certain later age he started lying there when his Da shook him and pretended to sleep on, even when the shakes got to where his teeth clacked together in a mouth that wore the slight smile Matty'd decided truly sleeping people's faces always wore. The harder his father shook him, the tighter Matty'd shut his eyes and the more set the slight smile and the louder the rasps of the cartoon snores he alternated with exhaled whistles. Mickey over in the cot by the window always silent as a tomb, on his side, face to the wall and hidden. Never a word between them about anything more than the chances of being kissed v. hit. Finally Da'd grab both his shoulders and flip him over with a sound of disgust and frustration. Matty thought just the smell of the fear was maybe enough to deserve it, until (later on) he got some maturer perspective. He remembered the oval sound of the cap coming off the jar of petroleum jelly, that special stone-in-pond plop of a Vaseline cap (not Child-Proof even in an era of Child-Proof caps), hearing his Da muttering as he applied it to himself, feeling the ice-cold awful cold finger between him as his Da smeared the stuff roughly around Matty's rosebud, his dark star.

It was only the maturer perspective of years and experience that let Matty find something to be thankful for, that the Da'd at least used a lube. The origins of the big man's clear familiarity with the stuff and its nighttime use not even adult perspective could illuminate, let Matty snap to, still, now, at twenty-three.

One hears, say, *cirrhosis* and *acute pancreatitis* and thinks of the subject clutching his middle like an old film's gutshot actor and slumping quietly over to eternal rest with lids shut and face composed. Matty's Da'd died choking on aspirated blood, a veritable fountain of the darkest possible blood, Matty coated a spray-paint-russet as he held the man's yellow wrists and Mum lumbered off down the ward in search of a crash-cart team. Particles aspirated so terribly fine, like almost atomized, so that they hung in the air like the air itself over the cribbed bed as the man expired, cat-yellow eyes wide open and face screwed into the very most godawful rictusized grin of pain, his last thoughts (if any) unknowable. Matty still toasted the man's final memory with his first shot, whenever he indulged.[278]

11 NOVEMBER
YEAR OF THE DEPEND ADULT UNDERGARMENT

First thing after supper Hal drops around to Schtitt's room off the Comm.-Ad. lobby to go through the motions of getting some input on just what had gone so terribly wrong against Stice. Also to get maybe some kind of bead on why he'd had to play The Darkness publicly in the first place, so close to the WhataBurger. I.e. like what the exhibition might have signified. This endless tension among E.T.A.s about how the coaches are seeing you, gauging your progress — is your stock going up or down. But A. deLint's the only one in there, working on some sort of oversized spreadsheetish chart, lying prone and shirtless on the bare floor with his chin in his hand and a pungent Magic Marker, and says Schtitt has gone off on the cycle somewhere after confections, but to sit down. Presumably meaning in a chair. So Hal's subjected to several minutes of deLint's take on the match, complete with stats out of the prorector's head. DeLint's back is pale and constellated with red pits of old pimples, though the back's nothing compared to Struck's or Shaw's back. There's a cane chair and a wood chair. DeLint's liquid-crystal laptop screen pulses grayly on the floor next to him. Schtitt's room's overlit and there's no dust anywhere, not even in the very corners. Schtitt's sound system's lights are on but nothing's playing. Neither Hal nor deLint mentions Orin's profiler's presence in the match's stands, nor the big lady's long interchange with Poutrincourt, which had been conspicuous. Stice's and Wayne's names are at the top of the huge chart on the floor, but Hal's name isn't. Hal says he can't tell whether he'd made some sort of basic tactical error or whether he just wasn't quite up to snuff this afternoon or what.

'You just never quite occurred out there, kid,' deLint apprises him. He has regressed certain figures to back this up, this nonoccurrence. His choice of words chills Hal to the root.

After which, during what's supposed to be mandatory P.M. Study Period, and despite the three chapters of Boards-prep his Boards-prep schedule calls for, Hal sits alone up in Viewing Room 6, the bad leg out along the couch in front of him, flexing the bad ankle idly, holding the other leg's knee to his chest, squeezing a ball but with the hand he doesn't play with, chewing Kodiak and spitting directly into an unlined wastebasket, his expression

686

neutral, watching some cartridges of his late father's entertainments. Anyone else looking at him in there tonight would call Hal depressed. He watches several cartridges all in a row. He watches *The American Century as Seen Through a Brick* and *Pre-Nuptial Agreement of Heaven and Hell* and then part of *Valuable Coupon Has Been Removed,* which is maddening because it's all a monologue from some bespectacled little contemporary of Miles Penn and Heath Pearson who was almost as ubiquitous as Reat and Bain in Himself's work but whose name right now Hal can't for the life of him recall. He watches parts of *Death in Scarsdale* and *Union of Publicly Hidden in Lynn* and *Various Small Flames* and *Kinds of Pain.* The Viewing Room has insulated panelling behind the wallpaper and is essentially soundproof. Hal watches half of the '*Medusa v. Odalisque*' thing but takes it out abruptly when people in the audience start getting turned to stone.

Hal tortures himself by imagining swarthy leering types threatening to torture various loved ones if Hal can't come up with the name of the kid in *Valuable Coupon* and *Low-Temperature Civics* and *Wave Bye-Bye to the Bureaucrat.*

There are two cartridges on V.R. 6's glass shelves of Himself getting interviewed in various arty Community-Access-cable-type forums, which Hal declines to watch.

The lights' slight flicker and subtle change in the pressure of the room is from the E.T.A. furnaces kicking on way down in the tunnels below Comm.-Ad. Hal shifts uneasily on the couch, spitting into the wastecan. The very faint smell of burnt dust is also from the furnace.

A minor short didactic one Hal likes and runs twice in a row is *Wave Bye-Bye to the Bureaucrat.* A bureaucrat in some kind of sterile fluorescent-lit office complex is a fantastically efficient worker when awake, but he has this terrible problem waking up in the A.M., and is consistently late to work, which in a bureaucracy is idiosyncratic and disorderly and wholly unacceptable, and we see this bureaucrat getting called in to his supervisor's pebbled-glass cubicle, and the supervisor, who wears a severely dated leisure suit with his shirt-collar flaring out on either side of its rust-colored lapels, tells the bureaucrat that's he's a good worker and a fine man, but that this chronic tardiness in the A.M. is simply not going to fly, and if it happens one more time the bureaucrat is going to have to find another fluorescent-lit office complex to work in. It's no accident that in a bureaucracy getting fired is called 'termination,' as in ontological erasure, and the bureaucrat leaves his supervisor's cubicle duly shaken. That night he and his wife go through their Bauhaus condominium collecting every alarm clock they own, each one of which is electric and digital and extremely precise, and they festoon their bedroom with them, so there are like a dozen timepieces with their digital alarms all set for 0615h. But that night there's a power failure, and all the clocks lose an hour or just sit there blinking 0000h. over and over,

687

and the bureaucrat still oversleeps the next A.M. He wakes late, lies there for a moment staring at a blinking 0000. He shrieks, clutches his head, throws on wrinkled clothes, ties his shoes in the elevator, shaves in the car, blasting through red lights on the way to the commuter rail. The 0816 train to the City pulls in to the station's lower level just as the crazed bureaucrat's car screeches into the station's parking lot, and the bureaucrat can see the top of the train sitting there idling from across the open lot. This is the very last temporally feasible train: if the bureaucrat misses this train he'll be late again, and terminated. He hauls into a Handicapped spot and leaves the car there at a crazy angle, vaults the turnstile, and takes the stairs down to the platform seven at a time, sweaty and bug-eyed. People scream and dive out of his way. As he careers down the long stairway he keeps his crazed eyes on the open doors of the 0816 train, willing them to stay open just a little longer. Finally, filmed in a glacial slo-mo, the bureaucrat leaps from the seventh-to-the-bottom step and lunges toward the train's open doors, and right in mid-lunge smashes headlong into an earnest-faced little kid with thick glasses and a bow-tie and those nerdy little schoolboy-shorts who's tottering along the platform under a tall armful of carefully wrapped packages. Kerwham, they collide. Bureaucrat and kid both stagger back from the impact. The kid's packages go flying all over the place. The kid recovers his balance and stands there stunned, glasses and bow-tie askew.[279] The bureaucrat looks frantically from the kid to the litter of packages to the kid to the train's doors, which are still open. The train thrums. Its interior is fluorescent-lit and filled with employed, ontologically secure bureaucrats. You can hear the station's PA announcer saying something tinny and garbled about departure. The stream of platform foot-traffic opens around the bureaucrat and the stunned boy and the litter of packages. Ogilvie'd once lectured for a whole period on this kid's character as an instance of the difference between an antagonist and a deuteragonist in moral drama; he'd mentioned the child-actor's name over and over. Hal tries whacking himself just over the right eye several times, to dislodge the name. The film's bureaucrat's buggy eyes keep going back and forth between the train's open doors and the little kid, who's looking steadily up at him, almost studious, his eyes big and liquid behind the lenses. Hal doesn't remember who played the bureaucrat, either, but it's the kid's name that's driving him bats. The bureaucrat's leaning away, inclined way over toward the train doors, as if his very cells were being pulled that way. But he keeps looking at the kid, the gifts, struggling with himself. It's a clear internal-conflict moment, one of Himself's films' very few. The bureaucrat's eyes suddenly recede back into their normal places in his sockets. He turns from the fluorescent doors and bends to the kid and asks if he's OK and says it'll all be OK. He cleans the kid's spectacles with his pocket handkerchief, picks the kid's packages up. About halfway through the packages the PA issues something final and the train's doors close with a pressurized hiss. The bureaucrat gently loads the kid back up with packages, neatens them. The train pulls out. The bureaucrat watches the train pull out, expressionless. It's anybody's guess what he's thinking. He straightens the kid's bow-tie, kneeling down the way adults do when they're ministering to a child, and tells him he's sorry about the impact and that it's OK. He turns to go. The platform's mostly empty now. Now the strange moment. The kid cranes his neck around the packages and looks up at the guy as he starts to walk away:

'Mister?' the kid says. 'Are you Jesus?'

'Don't I wish,' the ex-bureaucrat says over his shoulder, walking away, as the kid shifts the packages and frees one little hand to wave Bye at the guy's topcoat's back as the camera, revealed now as mounted on the 0816's rear, recedes from the platform and picks up speed.

Wave Bye-Bye to the Bureaucrat remains Mario's favorite of all their late father's entertainments, possibly because of its unhip earnestness. Though to Mario he always maintains it's basically goo, Hal secretly likes it, too, the cartridge, and likes to project himself imaginatively into the ex-bureaucrat's character on the leisurely drive home toward ontological erasure.

As a kind of weird self-punishment, Hal also plans to subject himself to the horrific *Fun with Teeth* and *Baby Pictures of Famous Dictators,* then finally to one of Himself's posthumous hits, a cartridge called *Blood Sister: One Tough Nun* that he'd always found kind of gratuitously nasty and overwrought, but which Hal has no idea that this piece of entertainment actually germinated out of James O. Incandenza's one brief and unpleasant experience with Boston AA, in the B.S. mid-'90s, when Himself lasted two and a half months and then drifted gradually away, turned off by the simplistic God-stuff and covert dogma. Bob-Hopeless, Hal spits way more than is his norm, now, and also likes having the wastecan right nearby in case he might throw up. That afternoon he'd had zilch in the way of a kinesthetic sense: he couldn't feel the ball on his stick. His nausea has nothing to do with watching his father's cartridges. For the last year his arm's been an extension of his mind and the stick an extension of the arm, acutely sensitive. Each of the cartridges is a carefully labelled black diskette; they're all signed neatly out on the clipboard by the egg-shaped glass bookshelf and are loaded in the cueing slots and waiting to drop, in order, and be digitally decoded.

14 NOVEMBER
YEAR OF THE DEPEND ADULT UNDERGARMENT

P. T. Krause: N. Cambridge: that infamous deceptive post-seizure feeling of well-being. That broken-fever, reversal-of-fortune-type highhearted feeling after a neuroelectric event. Poor Tony Krause awoke in the ambulance lizardless and continent and feeling right as rain. Lay there and flirted with the blue-jawed paramedic leaning over him, certain bawdy entendres on expressions like *vital signs* and *dilation* until the paramedic radioed ahead to Cambridge City's E. Room to cancel the crash-cart. Manipulated his skinny arms in a parodic Minimal Mambo, lying there. Fiddle-de-dee'd the paramedic's warning that post-seizure feelings of well-being were notoriously deceptive and transient.

And then also the little-mentioned advantage to being destitute and in possession of a Health Card that's expired and not even in your name: hospitals show you a kind of inverted respect; a place like Cambridge City Hospital bows to your will not to stay; they all of a sudden defer to your subjective diagnostic knowledge of your own condition, which post-seizure condition you feel has turned the corner toward improvement: they bow to your quixotic will: it's unfortunately not a free hospital but it is a free country: they honor your wishes and compliment your mambo and say Go with God.

It's a good thing you can't see what you look like, though.

And the serendipity of Cambridge City Hospital being just an eight-block stroll east on Cambridge St. and then south on Prospect, through mentholated autumn air, through Inman Square and up to Antitoi Entertainment, maybe the one last place where a renewed, post-seizure, on-the-diagnostic-upswing if still slightly shaky young gender-dysphoric might yet expect a bit of kindness, pharmacological credit, since the affairs of Wo and Copley Library and heart.

The big brick cake of the hospital behind Krause in purple twilight. The brisk click of his heels on pavement, boa semi-formally loose on his shoulders and down beneath each arm, hand holding red leather collar closed at the throat, head up and staying that way on its own, steady eyes meeting with blasé dignity the eyes of whoever passes. The dignity of a man risen by will from the ashes of Withdrawal and now on the upswing and with places to go and potentially considerate Canadians to see. A charming and potentially once again in the not-too-distant future gorgeous creature with the renewed wherewithal to now meet the eyes of Inman Sq. pedestrians veering sharply away from the residual smells of men's room stall and subway vomit, the ashes from which he's been rescued and risen once again, feeling righter than rain. A rind of moon hanging cocked above a four-spired church. And the emergent stars are yo-yos, you feel, after a seizure: Poor Tony feels as if he could cast them out, draw them in again at will.

The way Poor Tony Krause, Lolasister, and Susan T. Cheese became mercenary adjuncts to something dour Bertraund Antitoi had invited them to call the 'Front-Contre-O.N.A.N.isme' was that, for a heavily cut bundle to split six ways, Lolasister, Susan T. Cheese, P. T. Krause, Bridget Tenderhole, Equus Reese, and the late Stokely ('Dark Star') McNair had had to wear identical red leather coats and auburn wigs and spike heels and go and hang around the lobby of Harvard Square's Sheraton Commander Hotel with six mannish-looking women in the same wigs and coats while an androgynous Québecer insurgent who filled out h/his red leather coat in a way that made Bridget Tenderhole dig his nails into his palms in sheer green envy came through the Commander's revolving Lucite doors and strode purposefully into the crowded Epaulet Ballroom and threw foul semi-liquid violet waste from a souvenir miniature waste-displacement barrel in the face of the Canadian Minister of Inter-O.N.A.N. Trade, who was addressing the U.S. press from a leaf-shaped rostrum. The decoys were then required to mill hysterically in the lobby, all twelve of them, and then hit the revolving doors and disperse in a dozen different vectors as the androgynous waste-wielding Québecer legged it out of the Epaulet Ballroom and lobby pursued by white-suited men with earplugs and Cobray M–11 subautomatics, so the security guys'd see identical epicene figures high-heeling it away in different directions and get fuddled about who to chase. Susan T. Cheese and Poor Tony'd met the Antitoi Bros. — only one of whom could or would speak, and who'd been in charge of the diversionary aspects of the Sheraton Commander operation, and had clearly been subordinate to still other Québecers of way higher I.Q. — Krause and S.T.C. had met them at Inman Square's Ryle's Tavern, which had Gender-Dysphoric Night every second Wednesday, and attracted comely and unrough trade, and which Poor Tony passed now (Ryle's), just after the Man o' War Grille, now only a block or so from the Antitois' glass-and-novelty-shop front, feeling not so much quite ill again as just deeply tired, after only five or so blocks — that post-fever, sleep-for-a-week-type cellular fatigue — and is debating with himself about whether to have a go at the purses of the two young and unstriking women walking just a few steps ahead, both of their purses hanging only by the flimsiest of evening-gown-width straps from slumped shoulders, the duo interracial, rare and disquieting in metro Boston, the black girl talking a click a minute and the white one not responding, her weary stolid plod and air of inattention fairly begging for a purse-snatch, both of them with an air about them of routine victimization, the sort of demoralized lassitude Poor Tony felt always guaranteed a minimum of protest or pursuit — though the white girl wore formidable-looking running shoes under her tartan skirt. So intent was Poor Tony Krause on the logistics and implications of the possible purses dangled as if by God right before him — how different to hit the Antitois' doorstep with liquid assets, to request a transaction rather than bare charity, more almost a social call than a contemptible Withdrawn snivel for compassion — so intent as he sidestepped an impressive pile of dog-droppings and passed across the broad windows of the Man o' War that he never saw his old former crewmate Mad Matty Pemulis, a sure source of compassion, looking up and out and down and back up, aghast in recognition of what Poor Tony has come through the corridor to resemble.

Geoffrey Day's noted the way most of the male residents of Ennet House have special little cognomens for their genitals. E.g. 'Bruno,' 'Jake,' 'Fang' (Minty), 'The One-Eyed Monk,' 'Fritzie,' 'Russell the Love Muscle.' He speculates this could be a class thing: neither he nor Ewell nor Ken Erdedy have named their Units. Like Ewell, Day enters a certain amount of comparative-class data in his journal. Doony Glynn called his penis 'Poor Richard'; Chandler Foss confessed to the moniker 'Bam-Bam.' Lenz had referred to his own Unit as 'the Frightful Hog.' Day would die before admitting he missed either Lenz or his soliloquies about the Hog, which had been frequent. The penis in question had been that curious two or three shades darker than the rest of Lenz that people's penises sometimes are. Lenz had brandished it at his roommates whenever he wished to emphasize a point. It had been short and thick and blunt, and Lenz described the Hog as a primo example of what he called the Polish Curse, viz. undistinguished length but sobering circumference: 'Easy on the bottom but tears hell out of the sides, brother.' This had been his description of the Polish Curse. A surprising amount of Day's Recovery Journal is filled with quotations from R. Lenz. Lenz's discharge had moved the tax-attorney Tiny Ewell up into the 3-Man room with Day. Ewell was the one man here with whom a conversation of anything remotely approaching depth could be held, so Day was nonplussed when he found himself, after a couple long nights, almost missing Lenz, his obsession with time, his patter, his way of leaning up against the wall upside-down in his briefs, or brandishing the Hog.

And re Ennet House resident Kate Gompert and this depression issue: Some psychiatric patients — plus a certain percentage of people who've gotten so dependent on chemicals for feelings of well-being that when the chemicals have to be abandoned they undergo a loss-trauma that reaches way down deep into the soul's core systems — these persons know firsthand that there's more than one kind of so-called 'depression.' One kind is low-grade and sometimes gets called *anhedonia*[280] or *simple melancholy*. It's a kind of spiritual torpor in which one loses the ability to feel pleasure or attachment to things formerly important. The avid bowler drops out of his league and stays home at night staring dully at kick-boxing cartridges. The gourmand is off his feed. The sensualist finds his beloved Unit all of a sudden to be so much feelingless gristle, just hanging there. The devoted wife and mother finds the thought of her family about as moving, all of a sudden, as a theorem of Euclid. It's a kind of emotional novocaine, this form of depression, and while it's not overtly painful its deadness is disconcerting and . . . well, depressing. Kate Gompert's always thought of this anhedonic state as a kind of radical abstracting of everything, a hollowing out of stuff that used to have affective content. Terms the undepressed toss around and take for granted as full and fleshy — *happiness, joie de vivre, preference, love* — are stripped to their skeletons and reduced to abstract ideas. They have, as it were, denotation but not connotation. The anhedonic can still speak about happiness and meaning et al., but she has become incapable of feeling anything in them, of understanding anything about them, of hoping anything about them, or of believing them to exist as anything more than concepts. Everything becomes an outline of the thing. Objects become schemata. The world becomes a map of the world. An anhedonic can navigate, but has no location. I.e. the anhedonic becomes, in the lingo of Boston AA, Unable To Identify.

It's worth noting that, among younger E.T.A.s, the standard take on Dr. J. O. Incandenza's suicide attributes his putting his head in the microwave to this kind of anhedonia. This is maybe because anhedonia's often associated with the crises that afflict extremely goal-oriented people who reach a certain age having achieved all or more than all than they'd hoped for. The what-does-it-all-mean-type crisis of middle-aged Americans. In fact this is in fact not what killed Incandenza at all. In fact the presumption that he'd achieved all his goals and found that the achievement didn't confer meaning or joy on his existence says more about the students at E.T.A. than it says about Orin's and Hal's father: still under the influence of the deLint-like carrot-and-stick philosophies of their hometown coaches rather than the more paradoxical Schtitt/Incandenza/Lyle school, younger athletes who can't help gauging their whole worth by their place in an ordinal ranking use the idea that achieving their goals and finding the gnawing sense of worthlessness still there in their own gut as a kind of psychic bogey, something that they can use to justify stopping on their way down to dawn drills to smell flowers along the E.T.A. paths. The idea that achievement doesn't automatically confer interior worth is, to them, still, at this age, an abstraction, rather like the prospect of their own death — 'Caius Is Mortal' and so on. Deep down, they all still view the competitive carrot as the grail. They're mostly going through the motions when they invoke anhedonia. They're mostly small children, keep in mind. Listen to any sort of sub-16 exchange you hear in the bathroom or food line: 'Hey there, how are you?' 'Number eight this week, is how I am.' They all still worship the carrot. With the possible exception of the tormented LaMont Chu, they all still subscribe to the delusive idea that the continent's second-ranked fourteen-year-old feels exactly twice as worthwhile as the continent's #4.

Deluded or not, it's still a lucky way to live. Even though it's temporary. It may well be that the lower-ranked little kids at E.T.A. are proportionally happier than the higher-ranked kids, since we (who are mostly not small children) know it's more invigorating to *want* than to *have,* it seems. Though maybe this is just the inverse of the same delusion.

Hal Incandenza, though he has no idea yet of why his father really put his head in a specially-dickied microwave in the Year of the Trial-Size Dove Bar, is pretty sure that it wasn't because of standard U.S. anhedonia. Hal himself hasn't had a bona fide intensity-of-interior-life-type emotion since he was tiny; he finds terms like *joie* and *value* to be like so many variables in rarified equations, and he can manipulate them well enough to satisfy everyone but himself that he's in there, inside his own hull, as a human being — but in fact he's far more robotic than John Wayne. One of his troubles with his Moms is the fact that Avril Incandenza believes she knows him inside and out as a human being, and an internally worthy one at that, when in fact inside Hal there's pretty much nothing at all, he knows. His Moms Avril hears her own echoes inside him and thinks what she hears is him, and this makes Hal feel the one thing he feels to the limit, lately: he is lonely.

It's of some interest that the lively arts of the millennial U.S.A. treat anhedonia and internal emptiness as hip and cool. It's maybe the vestiges of the Romantic glorification of *Weltschmerz,* which means world-weariness or hip ennui. Maybe it's the fact that most of the arts here are produced by world-weary and sophisticated older people and then consumed by younger people who not only consume art but study it for clues on how to be cool, hip — and keep in mind that, for kids and younger people, to be hip and cool is the same as to be admired and accepted and included and so Unalone. Forget so-called peer-pressure. It's more like peer-*hunger.* No? We enter a spiritual puberty where we snap to the fact that the great transcendent horror is loneliness, excluded encagement in the self. Once we've hit this age, we will now give or take anything, wear any mask, to fit, be part-of, not be Alone, we young. The U.S. arts are our guide to inclusion. A how-to. We are shown how to fashion masks of ennui and jaded irony at a young age where the face is fictile enough to assume the shape of whatever it wears. And then it's stuck there, the weary cynicism that saves us from gooey sentiment and unsophisticated naïveté. Sentiment equals naïveté on this continent (at least since the Reconfiguration). One of the things sophisticated viewers have always liked about J. O. Incandenza's *The American Century as Seen Through a Brick* is its unsubtle thesis that naïveté is the last true terrible sin in the theology of millennial America. And since sin is the sort of thing that can be talked about only figuratively, it's natural that Himself's dark little cartridge was mostly about a myth, viz. that queerly persistent U.S. myth that cynicism and naïveté are mutually exclusive. Hal, who's empty but not dumb, theorizes privately that what passes for hip cynical transcendence of sentiment is really some kind of fear of being really human, since to be really human (at least as he conceptual-izes it) is probably to be unavoidably sentimental and naïve and goo-prone and generally pathetic, is to be in some basic interior way forever infantile, some sort of not-quite-right-looking infant dragging itself anaclitically around the map, with big wet eyes and froggy-soft skin, huge skull, gooey drool. One of the really American things about Hal, probably, is the way he despises what it is he's really lonely for: this hideous internal self, inconti-nent of sentiment and need, that pules and writhes just under the hip empty mask, anhedonia.[281]

The American Century as Seen Through a Brick's main and famous key-image is of a piano-string vibrating — a high D, it looks like — vibrating, and making a very sweet unadorned solo sound indeed, and then a little thumb comes into the frame, a blunt moist pale and yet dingy thumb, with disreputable stuff crusted in one of the nail-corners, small and unlined, clearly an infantile thumb, and as it touches the piano string the high sweet sound immediately dies. And the silence that follows is excruciating. Later in the film, after much mordant and didactic panoramic brick-following, we're back at the piano-string, and the thumb is removed, and the high sweet sound recommences, extremely pure and solo, and yet now somehow, as the volume increases, now with something rotten about it underneath, there's something sick-sweet and overripe and potentially putrid about the one clear high D as its volume increases and increases, the sound getting purer and louder and more dysphoric until after a surprisingly few seconds we find ourselves right in the middle of the pure undampered sound longing and even maybe praying for the return of the natal thumb, to shut it up.

Hal isn't old enough yet to know that this is because numb emptiness isn't the worst kind of depression. That dead-eyed anhedonia is but a rem-ora on the ventral flank of the true predator, the Great White Shark of pain. Authorities term this condition *clinical depression* or *involutional depres-sion* or *unipolar dysphoria*. Instead of just an incapacity for feeling, a dead-ening of soul, the predator-grade depression Kate Gompert always feels as she Withdraws from secret marijuana is *itself* a feeling. It goes by many names — *anguish, despair, torment,* or q.v. Burton's *melancholia* or Yev-tuschenko's more authoritative *psychotic depression* — but Kate Gompert, down in the trenches with the thing itself, knows it simply as *It.*

It is a level of psychic pain wholly incompatible with human life as we know it. *It* is a sense of radical and thoroughgoing evil not just as a feature but as the essence of conscious existence. *It* is a sense of poisoning that pervades the self at the self's most elementary levels. *It* is a nausea of the cells and soul. *It* is an unnumb intuition in which the world is fully rich and animate and un-map-like and also thoroughly painful and malignant and antagonistic to the self, which depressed self *It* billows on and coagulates around and wraps in *Its* black folds and absorbs into *Itself,* so that an almost mystical unity is achieved with a world every constituent of which means painful harm to the self. *Its* emotional character, the feeling Gompert describes *It* as, is probably mostly indescribable except as a sort of double bind in which any/all of the alternatives we associate with human agency — sitting or standing, doing or resting, speaking or keeping silent, living or dying — are not just unpleasant but literally horrible.

It is also lonely on a level that cannot be conveyed. There is no way Kate Gompert could ever even begin to make someone else understand what clinical depression feels like, not even another person who is herself clinically depressed, because a person in such a state is incapable of empathy with any other living thing. This anhedonic Inability To Identify is also an integral part of *It*. If a person in physical pain has a hard time attending to anything except that pain,[282] a clinically depressed person cannot even perceive any other person or thing as independent of the universal pain that is digesting her cell by cell. Everything is part of the problem, and there is no solution. It is a hell for one.

The authoritative term *psychotic depression* makes Kate Gompert feel especially lonely. Specifically the *psychotic* part. Think of it this way. Two people are screaming in pain. One of them is being tortured with electric current. The other is not. The screamer who's being tortured with electric current is not psychotic: her screams are circumstantially appropriate. The screaming person who's not being tortured, however, is psychotic, since the outside parties making the diagnoses can see no electrodes or measurable amperage. One of the least pleasant things about being psychotically depressed on a ward full of psychotically depressed patients is coming to see that none of them is really psychotic, that their screams are entirely appropriate to certain circumstances part of whose special charm is that they are undetectable by any outside party. Thus the loneliness: it's a closed circuit: the current is both applied and received from within.

The so-called 'psychotically depressed' person who tries to kill herself doesn't do so out of quote 'hopelessness' or any abstract conviction that life's assets and debits do not square. And surely not because death seems suddenly appealing. The person in whom *Its* invisible agony reaches a certain unendurable level will kill herself the same way a trapped person will eventually jump from the window of a burning high-rise. Make no mistake about people who leap from burning windows. Their terror of falling from a great height is still just as great as it would be for you or me standing speculatively at the same window just checking out the view; i.e. the fear of falling remains a constant. The variable here is the other terror, the fire's flames: when the flames get close enough, falling to death becomes the slightly less terrible of two terrors. It's not desiring the fall; it's terror of the flames. And yet nobody down on the sidewalk, looking up and yelling 'Don't!' and 'Hang on!', can understand the jump. Not really. You'd have to have personally been trapped and felt flames to really understand a terror way beyond falling.

But and so the idea of a person in the grip of *It* being bound by a 'Suicide Contract' some well-meaning Substance-abuse halfway house makes her sign is simply absurd. Because such a contract will constrain such a person only until the exact psychic circumstances that made the contract necessary in the first place assert themselves, invisibly and indescribably. That the well-meaning halfway-house Staff does not understand *Its* overriding terror will only make the depressed resident feel more alone.

One fellow psychotically depressed patient Kate Gompert came to know at Newton-Wellesley Hospital in Newton two years ago was a man in his fifties. He was a civil engineer whose hobby was model trains — like from Lionel Trains Inc., etc. — for which he erected incredibly intricate systems of switching and track that filled his basement recreation room. His wife brought photographs of the trains and networks of trellis and track into the locked ward, to help remind him. The man said he had been suffering from psychotic depression for seventeen straight years, and Kate Gompert had had no reason to disbelieve him. He was stocky and swart with thinning hair and hands that he held very still in his lap as he sat. Twenty years ago he had slipped on a patch of 3-In-1-brand oil from his model-train tracks and bonked his head on the cement floor of his basement rec room in Wellesley Hills, and when he woke up in the E.R. he was depressed beyond all human endurance, and stayed that way. He'd never once tried suicide, though he confessed that he yearned for unconsciousness without end. His wife was very devoted and loving. She went to Catholic Mass every day. She was very devout. The psychotically depressed man, too, went to daily Mass when he was not institutionalized. He prayed for relief. He still had his job and his hobby. He went to work regularly, taking medical leaves only when the invisible torment got too bad for him to trust himself, or when there was some radical new treatment the psychiatrists wanted him to try. They'd tried Tricyclics, M.A.O.I.s, insulin-comas, Selective-Serotonin-Reuptake Inhibitors,[283] the new and side-effect-laden Quadracyclics. They'd scanned his lobes and affective matrices for lesions and scars. Nothing worked. Not even high-amperage E.C.T. relieved *It*. This happens sometimes. Some cases of depression are beyond human aid. The man's case gave Kate Gompert the howling fantods. The idea of this man going to work and to Mass and building miniaturized railroad networks day after day after day while feeling anything like what Kate Gompert felt in that ward was simply beyond her ability to imagine. The rationo-spiritual part of her knew this man and his wife must be possessed of a courage way off any sort of known courage-chart. But in her toxified soul Kate Gompert felt only a paralyzing horror at the idea of the squat dead-eyed man laying toy track slowly and carefully in the silence of his wood-panelled rec room, the silence total except for the sounds of the track being oiled and snapped together and laid into place, the man's head full of poison and worms and every cell in his body screaming for relief from flames no one else could help with or even feel.

The permanently psychotically depressed man was finally transferred to a place on Long Island to be evaluated for a radical new type of psychosurgery where they supposedly went in and yanked out your whole limbic system, which is the part of the brain that causes all sentiment and feeling. The man's fondest dream was anhedonia, complete psychic numbing. I.e. death in life. The prospect of radical psychosurgery was the dangled carrot that Kate guessed still gave the man's life enough meaning for him to hang onto the windowsill by his fingernails, which were probably black and gnarled from the flames. That and his wife: he seemed genuinely to love his wife, and she him. He went to bed every night at home holding her, weeping for it to be over, while she prayed or did that devout thing with beads.

The couple had gotten Kate Gompert's mother's address and had sent Kate an Xmas card the last two years, Mr. and Mrs. Ernest Feaster of Wellesley Hills MA, stating that she was in their prayers and wishing her all available joy. Kate Gompert doesn't know whether Mr. Ernest Feaster's limbic system got yanked out or not. Whether he achieved anhedonia. The Xmas cards had had excruciating little watercolor pictures of locomotives on them. She could barely stand to think about them, even at the best of times, which the present was not.

14 NOVEMBER
YEAR OF THE DEPEND ADULT UNDERGARMENT

Ms. Ruth van Cleve's first day off new residents' three-day House Restriction. Allowed now to hit meetings outside Enfield if accompanied by some more senior resident the Staff judges safe. Ruth van Cleve in spike heels walking alongside a psychotically depressed Kate Gompert on Prospect just south of Inman Square, Cambridge, a little after 2200h., yammering nonstop.

Ruth van Cleve is shaping up to be excruciating for Kate Gompert to be around. Ruth van Cleve hails from Braintree on the South Shore, is many kilos underweight, wears brass-colored lipstick, and has dry hair teased out in the big-hair fashion of decades past. Her face has the late-stage Ice[284]-addict's concave long-jawed insectile look. Her hair is a dry tangled cloud, with tiny little eyes and bones and projecting beak underneath. Joelle v.D.'d said it almost looked like Ruth van Cleve's hair grew her head instead of the other way around. Kate Gompert's hair is butcher-block cut and has recognizable color, at least.

Kate Gompert hasn't slept in four nights, and her slumped progress up the Prospect sidewalk resembles the lazy tack of a boat in no rush. Ruth van Cleve talks nonstop into her right ear. It's around 2200h. on Saturday and the sodium streetlights keep going off and then on again with a stuttered hum, some connection in them loose somewhere. Foot-traffic is dense, and the undead and drunks who live in the streets around Inman Square also crowd the sidewalk's edges, and if Kate G. looks at the images of passersby in the darkened shop windows they become (pedestrians and undead stem-artists) just heads that seem to float across each window unconnected to anything. As in disconnected floating heads. In doorways by shops are incomplete persons in wheelchairs with creative receptacles where limbs should be and hand-lettered invitations to help them.

An oral narrative begins to emerge. Ms. Ruth v.C. has been remanded to Ennet House by D.S.S. and Family Court after her newborn baby was discovered in a Braintree MA alley swaddled in WalMart advertising circulars whose Harvest Moon Value Specials had expired 11/01, a Sunday. Ruth van Cleve had rather unshrewdly left the hospital I.D. bracelet with its D.O.B. and her own name and Health Card # on the discarded infant's wrist. The infant is apparently now in a South Shore hospital incubator, attached to machines and tapering off the Clonidine[285] it received for in-utero addictions to substances Kate Gompert can only speculate about.[286] The father of Ruth van Cleve's child, she reports, is under the protection and care of the Norfolk County Correctional Authority, awaiting sentencing for what Ruth van Cleve describes several times as operating a pharmaceutical company without a license.

What's remarkable to Kate Gompert is that she seems to be able to move forward without any sort of conscious moving-forward-type volitions. She puts her left foot in front of her right foot and then her right foot in front of her left foot, and she's moving forward, her whole self, when all she's capable of concentrating on is one foot and then the other foot. Heads glide by in the darkened windows. Some of the Latino males in the vicinity do a kind of sexual checking-out as they pass — even though underweight and dry-haired and kind of haggish, Ruth van Cleve's manner and attire and big hair broadcast that she's all about sexuality and sex.

A negative thing about opting for recovery in NA instead of AA is availability and location of meetings. In other words fewer NA meetings. On a Saturday night you could stand on the roof of Ennet House in Enfield and be hard-pressed to spit in any direction without hitting some AA venue nearby. Whereas the closest Saturday-P.M. NA meeting is N. Cambridge's Clean and Serene Group, infamous for cross-talk and chair-throwing, and the thing's Beginner's Mtng. goes from 2000 to 2100h. and the regular from 2100 to 2200h., purposely late, to offset the Saturday-night jones so many drug addicts suffer weekly, Saturday still being the week's special mythic Party-Night even for persons who long ago ceased to be able to do anything but Party 24/7/365. But from Inman Square back to Ennet House is a ghastly hike — hoof up Prospect to Central Sq. and take the Red Line all the way to Park Street station and then the maddening Green Line B Train forever west on Comm. Ave. — and it's now after 2215h., meaning Kate Gompert has 75 minutes to get herself and this hideous, despair-producing, slutty and yammering newcomer beside her back for Curfew. Ruth van Cleve's chatter is as listener-interest-independent as anything Kate Gompert's heard since Randy Lenz got invited to ingest Substances and abuse animals elsewhere, and left, which was who knows how many days or weeks ago.

The two move in and out of cones of epileptic light from fluttering street-lamps. Kate Gompert is trying not to shudder as Ruth van Cleve asks her if she knows someplace you can pick up a good toothbrush cheap. Kate Gompert's entire spiritual energy and attention are focused on first her left foot and then her right foot. One of the heads she does not see, floating in the windows with her own unrecognizable head and Ruth van Cleve's cloud of hair, is the gaunt and spectral hollow-eyed head of Poor Tony Krause, who's several steps behind them and matching their slightly serpentine course step for step, eyeing string purses he imagines contain more than just train-fare and NA Newcomers' keychains.

The vaporizer chugs and seethes and makes the room's windows weep as Jim Troeltsch inserts a pro-wrestling cartridge in the little TP's viewer and dons his tackiest sportcoat and wet-combs his hair down smooth so it looks toupeeish and settles back on his bunk, surrounded by Seldane-bottles and two-ply facial tissue, preparing to call the action. His roommates have long since seen what was coming, and screwed.

Standing on tiptoe in Subdorm B's curved hallway, using the handle of an inverted tennis racquet whose vinyl cover he can absently zip and unzip as he moves the handle around, Michael Pemulis is gently raising one of the panels in the drop-ceiling and shifting it on its aluminum strut, the panel, changing its lie on the strut from square-shaped to diamond-shaped, being careful not to let it fall.

Lyle hovers cross-legged just a couple mm. above the top of the towel dispenser in the unlit weight room, eyes rolled up white, lips barely moving and making no sound.

Coach Schtitt and Mario tear-ass downhill on W. Commonwealth on Schtitt's old BMW, bound for Evangeline's Low-Temperature Confections in Newton Center, right at the bottom of what usually gets called Heartbreak Hill, Schtitt intense-faced and leaning forward like a skier, his white scarf whipping around and whipping Mario's face, in the sidecar, as Mario too leans way forward into their downhill flight, preparing to whoop when they bottom out.

Ms. Avril Incandenza, seeming somehow to have three or four cigarettes all going at once, secures from Information the phone and e-mail #s of a journalistic business address on East Tucson AZ's Blasted Expanse Blvd., then begins to dial, using the stern of a blue felt pen to stab at the console's keys.

'*AIYEE!*' cries the man, rushing at the nun, wielding a power tool.

The tough-looking nun yells '*AIYEE!*' right back as she kicks at him expertly, her habit's skirts whipping complexly around her. The combatants circle each other warily in the abandoned warehouse, both growling. The nun's wimple is askew and soiled; the back of her hand, held out in a bladish martial-art fist, displays part of a faded tattoo, some wicked-clawed bird of prey. The cartridge opens like this, in violent medias res, then freezes in the middle of the nun's leaping kick, and its title, *Blood Sister: One Tough Nun*, gets matte-dissolved in and bleeds lurid blood-colored light down into the performance credits rolling across the screen's bottom. Bridget Boone and Frances L. Unwin have come in uninvited and joined Hal in V.R. 6 and are curled up against the arms of the room's other recumbency, their feet touching at the soles, Boone eating unauthorized frozen yogurt from a cylindrical carton. Hal's turned the rheostat down low, and the film's title and credits make their faces glow redly. Bridget Boone extends the confection-carton over in Hal's direction in an inviting way, and by way of declining Hal points to the lump of Kodiak in his cheek and makes a display of leaning out to spit. He appears to be studying the scrolling credits very closely.

'So what is this?' Fran Unwin says.

Hal looks over at her very slowly, then even more slowly raises his right arm and points around the tennis ball he's squeezing at the monitor, where the cartridge's 50-point title is still trickling redly over the credits and frozen scene.

Bridget Boone gives him a look. 'What's up your particular butt?'

'I'm isolating. I came in here to be by myself.'

She has this way that gets to Hal of digging the chocolate yogurt out with the spoon and then inverting the spoon, turning the spoon over, so that it always enters her mouth upside-down and her tongue gets to contact the confection immediately, without the mediation of cold spoon, and for some reason this has always gotten under Hal's skin.

'So then you should've locked the door.'

'Except there aren't locks on the V.R. doors,[287] as you quite well know.'

Round-faced Frannie Unwin says 'Sshhh.'

Then too sometimes Boone plays with the laden spoon, makes it fly around in front of her face like a child's plane before inverting it and sticking it in. 'Maybe this is partly because this is a public room, for everybody, that your thinking person probably wouldn't choose to isolate in.'

Hal leans over to spit and lets the spit hang for a while before he lets it go, so it hangs there slowly distending.

Boone withdraws the clean spoon just as slowly. 'No matter how sullen and pouty that person is over that person's play or near-loss in full view of a whole crowd that day, I hear.'

'Bridget, I forgot to tell you I saw that Rite Aid's having an enormous clearance on emetics. If I were you I'd scoot right over.'

'You are vile.'

Bernadette Longley sticks her long boxy head in the door and sees Bridget Boone and says 'I *thought* I heard you in here' and comes in uninvited with Jennie Bash in tow.

Hal whimpers.

Jennie Bash looks at the large screen. The cartridge's theme-music is female-choral and very heavy and ironic on the descants. Bernadette Longley looks at Hal. 'You know there's a totally huge lady cruising the halls looking for you, with a notebook and a very determined expression.'

Boone banks the spoon back and forth absently. 'He's isolating. He won't respond and is spitting extra repulsively to get across the point.'

Jennie Bash says 'Haven't you got a huge paper due for Thierry tomorrow? There was moaning coming from Struck and Shaw's room.'

Hal packs chew down with his tongue. 'Done.'

'Figures,' Bridget Boone says.

'Done, redone, formatted, printed, proofed, collated, stapled.'

'Proofed to within its life,' Boone says, barrel-rolling the spoon. Hal can tell she's done a couple one-hitters. He's looking straight at the wall's screen, squeezing the ball so hard his forearm keeps swelling to twice its size.

'Plus I hear your best friend in the whole world did something really funny today,' Longley says.

'She means Pemulis,' Fran Unwin tells Hal.

Bridget Boone makes dive-bomber sounds and swoops the spoon around.

'Sounds like too good a story not to save and let my craving for it build and build until finally it's like I have to hear it or die right on the spot.'

'What is up his butt?' Jennie Bash asks Fran Unwin. Fran Unwin's a sort of hanuman-faced girl with a torso and trunk about twice as long as her legs, and a scuttly, vaguely simian style of play. Bernadette Longley wears knee-length candy-cane trousers and a sweatshirt with the fleecy inside out. All the girls are now in socks. Hal notes that girls always seem to slip out of their shoes when they assume any kind of spectatorial posture. Eight empty white sneakers now sit mute and weird at various points, slightly sunk in carpet pile. No two of the shoes face quite the same exact direction. Male players, on the other hand, tend to leave the footwear on when they come in and sit down somewhere. Girls literally embody the idea of making yourself at home. Males, when they come in somewhere and sit down, project an air of transience. Remain suited up and mobile. It's the same whenever Hal comes in and sits down someplace where people are already gathered. He's aware that they sense he's somehow there only in a very technical sense, that he's got an air of moment's-notice readiness to leave about him. Boone extends her carton of TCBY[288] toward Longley in an inviting way, even tilting it invitingly back and forth. Longley puffs her cheeks and blows air out with a fatigued sound. At least three different smells of cologne and skin-cream struggle for primacy in here. Bridget Boone's free LA Gear shoes are both on their sides from the force of having been almost kicked off her feet. Hal's spit makes a sound against the bottom of the wastebasket. Jennie Bash has bigger arms than Hal. The Viewing Room is redly dim. Bash asks Unwin what they're watching.

Blood Sister: One Tough Nun, one of Himself's few commercial successes, wouldn't have made near the money it made if it hadn't come out just as InterLace was starting to purchase first-run features for its rental menus and hyping the cartridges with one-time Spontaneous Disseminations. It was the sort of sleazy-looking shocksploitation film that would have had a two-week run in multiplex theaters 8 and above and then gone right to the featureless brown boxes of magnetic-video limbo. Hal's critical take on the film is that Himself, at certain dark points when abstract theory-issues seemed to provide an escape from the far more wrenching creative work of making humanly true or entertaining cartridges, had made films in certain commercial-type genre modes that so grotesquely exaggerated the formulaic schticks of the genres that they became ironic metacinematic parodies on the genres: 'sub/inversions of the genres,' cognoscenti taken in were wont to call them. The metacinematic-parody idea itself was aloof and over-clever, to Hal's way of thinking, and he's not comfortable with the way Himself always seemed to get seduced by the very commercial formulae he was trying to invert, especially the seductive formulae of violent payback, i.e. the cathartic bloodbath, i.e. the hero trying with every will-fiber to eschew the generic world of the stick and fist and but driven by unjust circumstance back to the violence again, to the cathartic final bloodbath the audience is brought to applaud instead of mourn. Himself's best in this vein was *The Night Wears a Sombrero*, a Langesque metaWestern but also a really good Western, with chintzy homemade interior sets but breathtaking exteriors shot outside Tucson AZ, an ambivalent-but-finally-avenging-son story played out against dust-colored skies and big angles of flesh-colored mountain, plus with minimal splatter, shot men clutching their chests and falling deliciously sideways, all hats staying on at all times. *Blood Sister: One Tough Nun* was a supposedly ironic lampoon of the avenging-cleric splatter-films of the late B.S. '90s. Nor did Himself make any friends on either side of the Concavity, trying to shoot the thing in Canada.

Hal tries to imagine the tall slumped tremulous stork-shape of Himself inclined at an osteoporotic angle over digital editing equipment for hours on end, deleting and inserting code, arranging *Blood Sister: One Tough Nun* into subversive/inversion, and can't summon one shadowy idea of what Himself might have been feeling as he patiently labored. Maybe that was the point of the thing's metasilliness, to have nothing really felt going on.[289]

Jennie Bash has left V.R. 6's door agape, and Idris Arslanian and Todd ('Postal Weight') Possalthwaite and Kent Blott all drift in and sit Indian-style in a loose hemisphere on the thick carpet between the girls' recumbency and Hal's recumbency, and are more or less considerately quiet. They all keep their sneakers on. Postal Weight's nose is a massive proboscoid bandaged thing. Kent Blott wears a sportfisherman's cap with an extremely long bill. That queer faint smell of hot dogs that seems to follow Idris Arslanian around begins to insinuate itself into the room's colognes. He isn't wearing the rayon handkerchief as a blindfold but does have it tied around his neck; no one asks him about it. All the littler kids are consummate spectators and are sucked immediately into *Blood Sister*'s unfolding narrative, and the older females seem to take some kind of psychic cue from the little boys and subside, too, and watch, until after a while Hal's the only person in the room who isn't 100% absorbed.

The entertainment's uptake is that a tough biker-chick-type girl from the mean streets of Toronto is found O.D.'d, beaten up, molested, and robbed of her leather jacket outside the portcullis of a downtown convent and is rescued, nursed, befriended, spiritually guided, and converted — '*saved*' is the weak entendre made much of in the first act's dialogue — by a tough-looking older nun who it turns out, she reveals (the tough older nun), had herself been hauled up out of a life of Harleys, narcotics-dealing and -addiction by an even tougher even older nun, a nun who had *herself* been saved by a tough ex-biker nun, and so on. The latest saved biker-chick becomes a tough and street-smart nun in the same urban order, and is known on the mean streets as Blood Sister, and wimple or not still rides her Hawg from parish to parish and still knows akido and is not to be fucked with, is the word on the streets.

The motivational crux here being that almost this whole order of nuns is staffed by nuns who'd been saved from Toronto's mean, dead-end streets by other older tougher saved nuns. So, endless novenas later, Blood Sister eventually feels this transitive spiritual urge to go out and find a troubled adolescent female of her own, to 'save' and bring into the order, thereby discharging her soul's debt to the old tough nun who'd saved *her*. Through processes obscure (a Toronto troubled-but-savable-adolescent-girl-directory of some sort? Bridget Boone cuts wise), Blood Sister eventually takes on a burn-scarred, deeply troubled adolescent punker-type Toronto girl who is sullen and, yes, reasonably tough, but is also vulnerable and emotionally tormented (the girl's pink shiny burn-scarred face tends to writhe in misery whenever she thinks Blood Sister's not looking) by the terrible depredations she's endured as a result of her rapacious and unshakable addiction to crank cocaine, the kind you have to convert and cook up yourself, and with ether, which is highly combustible, and which people used before somebody found out baking soda and temperature-flux would do the same thing, which dates the film's B.S. time-period even more clearly than the tough tortured punk girl's violet stelliform coiffure.[290]

But so Blood Sister eventually gets the girl clean, by nurturing her through Withdrawal in a locked sacristy; and the girl becomes less sullen by degrees that almost have audible clicks to them — the girl stops trying to dicky the lock of the sacramental-wine cabinet, stops farting on purpose during matins and vespers, stops going up to the Trappists who hang around the convent and asking them for the time and other sly little things to try to make them slip up and speak aloud, etc. A couple times the girl's face writhes in emotional torment and vulnerability even *when* Blood Sister's looking. The girl gets a severe and somewhat lesbianic haircut, and her roots establish themselves as softly brown. Blood Sister, revealing biceps like nobody's business, beats the girl at arm-wrestling; they both laugh; they compare tattoos: this marks the start of a brutally drawn-out Getting-to-Know-and-Trust-You montage, a genre-convention, this montage involving Harley-rides at such speeds that the girl has to keep her hand on Blood Sister's head to keep B.S.'s wimple from flying off, and long conversational walks filmed at wide-angle, and protracted and basically unwinnable games of charades with the Trappists, plus some quick scenes of Blood Sister finding the girl's Marlboros and dildo-facsimile lighter in the wastebasket, of the girl doing chores unsullenly under B.S.'s grudgingly approving eye, of candle-lit scripture-study sessions with the girl's finger under each word she reads, of the girl carefully snipping the last bits of split violet ends from her soft brown hair, of the more senior tough nuns punching Blood Sister's shoulder approvingly as the girl's eyes start to get that impending-conversion gleam in them, then, finally, of Blood Sister and the girl habit-shopping, the girl's burned lantern jaw and hairless Promethean brow frozen in a sunlit montage-climax shot under a novitiate wimple's gull-wings — all accompanied by — no kidding — 'Getting to Know You,' which Hal imagines the Stork justified to himself as subversively saccharine. This all takes about half an hour. Bridget Boone, of the Indianapolis arch-diocese, begins to declaim briefly on *Blood Sister: One Tough Nun*'s ironic anti-Catholic subthesis — that the deformed addicted girl's 'salvation' here seemed simply the exchange of one will-obliterating 'habit' for another, sub-stituting one sort of outlandish head-decoration for another — and gets pinched by Jennie Bash and shushed by just about everyone in the room but Hal, who could pass for asleep except for the brief lists to port over the wastebasket, to spit, and in fact is experiencing some of the radical loss of concentration that attends THC-Withdrawal and is thinking about another, even more familiar J. O. Incandenza cartridge even while he watches this one with the other E.T.A.s. This other attention-object is the late Himself's so-called 'inversion' of the corporate-politics genre, *Low-Temperature Civics,* an executive-suite soap opera filled with power plays, position-jockeyings, timid adulteries, martinis, and malignantly pretty female execu-tives in elegant tight-fitting dress-for-successwear who eat their paunched and muddled male counterparts for political lunch. Hal knows that *L-TC* wasn't an inversion or lampoon at all, but derived right from the dark B.S. '80s period when Himself had changed careers from government service to private entreprenurism, when a sudden infusion of patent-receipts left him feeling post-carrot anhedonic and existentially unmoored, and Himself took an entire year off to drink Wild Turkey and watch broadcast-television tycoon-operas like Lorimar's *Dynasty* et al. in a remote spa off Canada's Northwest coast, where he supposedly met and bonded with Lyle, now of the E.T.A. weight room.

What's intriguing but unknown to everyone in V.R. 6 is the way Boone's take on Himself's take on the substitution-of-one-crutch-for-another inter-pretation of substituting Catholic devotion for chemical dependence is very close to the way many not-yet-desperate-enough newcomers to Boston AA see Boston AA as just an exchange of slavish dependence on the bottle/pipe for slavish dependence on meetings and banal shibboleths and robotic piety, an 'Attitude of Platitude,' and use this idea that it's still slavish dependence as an excuse to stop trying Boston AA, and to go back to the original slavish Substance-dependence, until that dependence has finally beaten them into such a double-bound desperation that they finally come back in with their faces hanging off their skulls and beg to be told just what platitudes to shout, and how high to adjust their vacant grins.

Some Substance-dependent persons, though, have already been so broken by the time they first Come In that they don't care about stuff like substitution or banality, they'll give their left nut to trade their original dependence in for robotic platitudes and pep-rally cheer. They're the ones with the gun to their head, the ones who stick and Hang. It remains to be determined whether Joelle van Dyne, whose first appearance in a James O. Incandenza project occurred in this very *Low-Temperature Civics*, is one of these people who've come into AA/NA shattered enough to stick, but she's starting to I.D. more and more with the Commitment speakers she hears who did come in shattered enough to know it's get straight or die. A click and a half straight downhill from E.T.A., Joelle is hitting the Reality Is For People That Can't Handle Drugs Group, a meeting of the NA-splinter Cocaine Anonymous,[291] mostly because the meeting's in the St. Elizabeth's Hospital Grand Rounds Auditorium, just a couple floors down from where Don Gately, whom she just got done visiting and mopping the massive unconscious forehead of, is lying in the Trauma Wing in a truly bad way. CA meetings have a long preamble and endless little Xeroxed formalities they read aloud at the start, is one reason Joelle avoids CA, but the opening stuff is done by the time she gets down and comes in and gets some burnt urn-bottom coffee and finds an available seat. The only empty seats are in the meeting's back row — 'Denial Aisle,' the back rows are usually called — and Joelle is surrounded by catexic newcomers crossing and uncrossing their legs every few seconds and sniffing compulsively and looking like they're wearing everything they own. Plus there's the row of standing men — there's a certain hard-faced type of male in Boston fellowships who refuses ever to sit for meetings — standing behind the back row, legs set wide and arms crossed and talking to each other out the sides of their mouths, and she can tell the standing men are looking at her bare knees over her shoulder, making little comments about the knees and the veil. She thinks with fearful sentiment[292] of Don Gately, a tube down his throat, torn by fever and guilt and shoulder-pain, offered Demerol by well-meaning but clueless M.D.s, in and out of delirium, torn, convinced that certain men with hats wished him ill, looking at his room's semi-private ceiling like it would eat him if he dropped his guard. The big blackboard up on the stage says the Reality Is For People That Can't Handle Drugs Group welcomes tonight's Commitment speakers, the Freeway Access Group from Mattapan, which is deep in the colored part of Boston where Cocaine Anonymous tends to be most heavily concentrated. The speaker just starting in at the podium when Joelle sits down is a tall yellowish colored man with a weightlifter's build and frightening eyes, sloe and a kind of tannin-brown. He's been in CA seven months, he says. He eschews the normal CA drugologue's macho war-stories and gets right to his Bottom, his jumping-off place. Joelle can tell he's trying to tell the truth and not just posturing and performing the way so many CAs seem like they do. His story's full of colored idioms and those annoying little colored hand-motions and gestures, but to Joelle it doesn't seem like she cares that much anymore. She can Identify. The truth has a kind of irresistible unconscious attraction at meetings, no matter what the color or fellowship. Even Denial Aisle and the standing men are absorbed by the colored man's story. The colored man says his thing is he'd had a wife and a little baby daughter at home in Mattapan's Perry Hill Projects, and another baby on the way. He'd managed to hang on to his menial riveter's-assistant job at Universal Bleacher right up the street from here in Enfield because his addiction to crank cocaine wasn't everyday; he smoked on your binge-type basis, mostly weekends. Hellacious, psychopathic, bank-account-emptying binges, though. Like getting strapped to a Raytheon missile and you don't stop till that missile stops, Jim. He says his wife had got temp work cleaning houses, but when she worked they had to put their little girl in a day-care that just about ate her day's pay. So his paycheck was like their total float, and his weekend binges with the glass pipe caused them no end of Financial Insecurity, which he mispronounces. Which brings him to his last binge, the Bottom, which, predictably, occurred on a payday. This check just *had* to go for groceries and rent. They were two months back, and there was not jackshit in the house in the way of to eat. At a smoke-break at Universal Bleacher he'd made sure and bought just one single vial, for just a tensky, for a Sunday-night treat after a weekend of abstinence and groceries and quality time with his pregnant wife and little daughter. The wife and little daughter were to meet him after work right off the bus stop at Brighton Best Savings, right under the big clock, to 'help' him deposit the paycheck right then and there. He'd let his wife stipulate the meeting at the bank because he knew in a self-disgusted way even then that there was this hazard of paycheck-type incidents from binges he'd pulled in the past, and their Financial Insecurity was now whatever word's past the word *deep shit,* and he knew god*damn* well he could not afford to fuck up this time.

He says that's how he used to think of it to himself: fucking up.

He didn't even make it to the bus after clocking out, he said. Two other Holmeses[293] in Riveting had three vials each, which vials they had, like, *brandished* at him, and he'd kicked in his one vial because two-and-a-third vials v. one thin-ass Sunday-night vial was only a fucking fool way out of touch with the whole seize-the-opportunity concept could pass that shit up. In short it was the familiar insanity of money in the pocket and no defense against the urge, and the thought of his woman holding his little girl in her little knit cap and mittens standing under the big clock in cold March dusk didn't so much get pushed aside as somehow shrink to a tiny locket-size picture in the center of a part of him he and the Holmeses had set out busily to kill, with the pipe.

He says he never made the bus. They passed a bottle of rye around the old Ford Mystique one of the Holmeses profiled, and fired up, right in the car, and after he once fired up with $ in his pocket the fat woman with the little helmet with horns on it done already like fucking *sang*, Jim.[294]

The man's hands grip the sides of the podium and he rests his weight on his elbow-locked arms in a way that conveys both abjection and pluck. He invites the CAs to let's just draw the curtain of charity over the rest of the night's scene, which after the check-cashing stop got hazy with missile-exhaust anyhow; but so he finally did get home to Mattapan the next morning, Saturday morning, sick and green-yellow and on that mean post-crank slide, dying for more and willing to kill for more and yet so mortified and ashamed of having done fucked up (again) that just going up the elevator to their apartment was maybe the bravest thing he'd ever done, up to that point, he felt.

It was like 0600 in the A.M. and they weren't there. There was nobody home, and in the sort of way where the place's emptiness pulsed and breathed. An envelope was slid under the door from the B.H.A.,[295] not the salmon color of an Eviction Notice but a green Last Warning re rent. And he went into the kitchen and opened up the fridge, hating himself for hoping there was a beer. In the fridge was a jar of grape jelly near-empty and a half a can of biscuit mix, and that, plus a sour empty-fridge odor, was all, Jim. A little plastic jar of labelless Food-Bank peanut butter so empty its insides had knife-scrapes on the sides and a little clotted box of salt was all there was in the whole rest of the kitchen.

But what sent his face clear down off his skull and broke him in two, though, was he said when he saw the Pam-shiny empty biscuit pan on top of the stove and the plastic rind of the peanut butter's safety-seal wrap on top of the wastebasket's tall pile. The little locket-picture in the back of his head swelled and became a sharp-focused scene of his wife and little girl and little unborn child eating what he now could see they must have eaten, last night and this morning, while he was out ingesting their groceries and rent. This was his cliff-edge, his personal intersection of choice, standing there loose-faced in the kitchen, running his finger around a shiny pan with not one little crumb of biscuit left in it. He sat down on the kitchen tile with his scary eyes shut tight but still seeing his little girl's face. They'd ate some charity peanut butter on biscuits washed down with tapwater and a grimace.

Their apartment was six floors up in Perry Hill's Bldg. 5. The window didn't open but could be broke through with a running start.

He didn't kill himself, though, he says. He just got up and walked out. He didn't leave his wife a note. Not nothing. He went and walked the whole four clicks to Shattuck Shelter in Jamaica Plain. He felt like for sure they'd of been better off without him, he said. But he said he didn't know why but he didn't kill himself. But he didn't. He figures there was some God-involvement, sitting there on the floor. He just decided to go to Shattuck and

Surrender and get straight and never ever have his little girl's grimacing face in his hung-over head ever again, James.

And Shattuck Shelter — by coincidence — that usually had a waiting list every March until it got warm, they'd just kicked out some sorry-ass specimen for defecating in the shower, and they took him, the speaker. He asked for a CA Meeting right away. And a Shattuck Staff guy called somebody Afro-American with a lot of clean recovered time, and the speaker got taken to his first CA Meeting. That was 224 days ago tonight. That night, when the colored CA Crocodile dropped him off back at the Shattuck — after he'd wept in front of other colored men at his first meeting and told men he didn't know from shit about the big clock and glass pipe and paycheck and the biscuits and his little girl's face — and after he come back to the Shattuck and got buzzed through and the buzzer sounded for supper, it turned out — by coincidence — that the Saturday-night Shattuck supper was coffee and peanut butter sandwiches. It was the end of the week and the Shelter's donated food had run out, they only had PB on cheap-ass white bread and Sunny Square instant coffee, the cheap shit that doesn't even quite dissolve all the way.

He's got your autodidactic orator's way with emotional dramatic pauses that don't seem affected. Joelle makes another line down the Styrofoam coffee cup with her fingernail and chooses consciously to believe it isn't affected, the story's emotive drama. Her eyes feel sandy from forgetting to blink. This always happens when you don't expect it, when it's a meeting you have to drag yourself to and are all but sure will suck. The speaker's face has lost its color, shape, everything distinctive. Something has taken the tight ratchet in Joelle's belly and turned it three turns to the good. It's the first time she's felt sure she wants to keep straight no matter what it means facing. No matter if Don Gately takes Demerol or goes to jail or rejects her if she can't show him the face. It's the first time in a long time — tonight, 11/14 — Joelle's even considered possibly showing somebody the face.

After the pause the speaker says all the other sorry motherfuckers in the Shattuck Shelter in there started in to bitching about what was this shit, peanut butter sandwiches for fucking supper. The speaker says how whatever he silently thanked for just that particular sandwich he held and chewed, washing it down with gritty Sunny Square coffee, that thing became his Higher Power. He's now seven-plus months clean. Universal Bleacher let him go, but he's got steady work at Logan, pushing a third-shift mop, and a Holmes on his crew's also in the Program — by coincidence. His pregnant wife, it turned out, had gone to a Unwed Mothers Shelter with Shantel, that night. She was still in there. D.S.S. still wouldn't let him appeal his wife's Restraining Order and see Shantel, but he got to talk to his little girl on the phone just last month. And he's now straight, from Giving Up and joining the Freeway Access Group and getting Active and taking the voluntary suggestions of the Fellowship of Cocaine Anonymous. His wife was due to have her baby around Xmas. He said he didn't know what was going to happen to him or his family. But he says he has received certain promises from his new family — the Freeway Access Group of Cocaine Anonymous — and so he had certain hope-type emotions about the future, inside. He didn't so much conclude or make obligatory reference to Gratitude or any of that usual shit as grip the lectern and shrug and say he'd started feeling just last month that the choice he made on the kitchen floor was the right choice, personally speaking.

Entertainment-wise, things take a rapid turn for the splattery once the tough girl Blood Sister seemed to have saved is found bluely dead in her novitiate's cot, her habit's interior pockets stuffed with all kinds of substances and paraphernalia and her arm a veritable forest of syringes. Tight shot of B.S., face working purply, staring down at the ex-ex-punker. Suspecting foul play instead of spiritual recidivism, Blood Sister, disregarding first the Other-Cheek pieties and then the impassioned pleas and then the direct orders of the Vice-Mother Superior — who happens now to be the tough nun who'd saved Blood Sister, way back — begins reverting to her former Toronto-mean-street pre-salvation tough-biker-chick ways: demufflering her Harley Hawg, hauling an age-faded stud-covered leather bike-jacket out of storage and squeezing it over her pectoral-swollen habit, unbandaging her most lurid tattoos, shaking down former altar boys for information, flipping off motorists who get in her bike's way, meeting old street-contacts in dim saloons and tossing back jiggers with even the most cirrhotic of them, beating, bludgeoning, akido-ing, disarming thugs of power tools, avenging the desalvation and demapping of her young charge, determined to prove that the girl's death was no accident or backslide, that Blood Sister had not failed with the soul she'd chosen to save to discharge her own soul's debt to the tough old Vice-Mother Superior who'd saved her, Blood Sister, so far back. Several thuggish stuntmen and countless liters of potassium thiocyanate[296] later, the truth does out: the novitiate girl had been murdered by the Mother Superior, the order's top and toughest nun. This M.S. is the nun who'd saved the Vice-M.S. who'd saved Blood Sister, meaning, ironically, that the evidence Blood Sister needs to prove that her salvation-debt really was discharged is also evidence inimical to the legal interests of the tough nun to whom Blood Sister's own saviour is obligated, so Blood Sister gets increasingly tortured and ill-tempered as evidence of the Mother Superior's guilt accretes. In one scene she says *fuck*. In another she swings a censer like a mace and brains an old verger who's one of the Mother Superior's stooges, knocking his toothless head clean off. Then, in

Act III, a veritable orgy of retribution follows the full emergence of the sordid truth: it seems that the tough old Vice-Mother Superior, viz. the nun who'd saved Blood Sister, had in fact *not* been saved, truly, after all — had in fact, during 20+ years of exemplary novena-saying and wafer-baking, been suffering a kind of hidden degenerative recidivist soul-rot, and had resumed, the Vice-M.S., at about the time Blood Sister had donned the habit of full nunhood, had not only resumed Substance-dependence but had started actually dealing in serious weights of whatever at the time was most profitable (which after 20+ years had changed from Marseillese heroin to Colombian freebaseable-grade Bing Crosby) to support her own hidden habit, covertly operating a high-volume retail operation out of the order's Community Outreach Rescue Mission's little-used confessionals. This nun's superior, the top tough Mother Superior nun, stumbling onto the drug-operation after the now-demapped verger informed her that a suspicious number of limousines were discharging gold-chained and not very penitent-looking persons into the order's Community Outreach Rescue Mission, and disastrously unable to summon the pious humility to accept the fact that she'd failed, it seemed, at truly and forever saving the ex-dealer whose salvation the Mother Superior required to discharge the debt to the now-retired octogenarian nun who'd saved *her* — this Mother Superior herself is the one who murdered Blood Sister's ex-punk novitiate, to silence the girl. What emerges is that Blood Sister's addicted punk-girl's Substance-copping venue, when she was Out There pre-salvation, had been nothing other than the Vice-Mother Superior's infamous Community Outreach Rescue Mission. In other words, the nun who'd saved Blood Sister but had herself been secretly unsaved had been the tough girl's Bing-dealer, is why the tough non-Catholic girl'd been so mysteriously adept at the Confiteor. The order's Mother Superior had figured that it was only a matter of time before the girl's conversion and salvation reached the sort of spiritual pitch where her guarded silence broke and she told Blood Sister the seamy truth about the nun she (Blood Sister) thought had saved her (Blood Sister). So she (the Mother Superior) had eliminated the girl's map — ostensibly, she (the Mother Superior) told her lieutenant, the Vice-Mother Superior, to save her (the Vice-Mother Superior) from exposure and excommunication and maybe worse, if the girl weren't silenced.[297]

This narratively prolix and tangled stuff all gets explicated at near-Kabuki volume during an appalling free-for-all in the office of the Mother Superior who hadn't saved the Vice-M.S. who'd saved Blood Sister, with the two senior nuns — who'd been tough and unsaved back in the Ontarian days when men were men and so were drug-addicted bike-chicks — teaming up and kicking Blood Sister's ass, the fight-scene a blur of swirling habiteaments and serious martial arts against the spot-lit backdrop of the wall's huge decorative mahogany crucifix, with Blood Sister giving a good account of herself but still getting her wimple beat in and finally, after several whirling kicks to the forehead, starting to bid adieu to her corporeal map and commend herself to the arms of God; until the unsaved recidivist Vice-Mother Superior nun who'd saved Blood Sister, wiping blood from her eyes after a head-butt and seeing the Mother Superior about to decapitate Blood Sister with the souvenir Champlain-era tomahawk the Huron nun who'd been saved by the original founder of the Toronto tough-girl-saving order had used to decapitate Jesuit missionaries before she (the tough Huron nun) had been saved, seeing the tomahawk raised with both arms before the normally pious-eyed old Mother Superior's face — a face now rendered indescribable in aspect by the absence of humility and the passion for truth-silencing that add up to pure and radical evil — seeing now the upraised hatchet and demonized face of the M.S., the unsaved Vice-nun has a moment of epiphanic anti-recidivist spiritual clarity, and averts Blood Sister's demapping by leaping across the office and cold-cocking the Mother Superior with a large decorative mahogany Christian object so symbolically obvious it needn't even be named, the object's symbolic unsubtlety making both Hal and Bridget Boone cringe. Now Blood Sister has the Champlain-era hatchet, and the unsaved nun who'd saved her has an unnamed object whose mahogany's no match for a hatchet, and they stand facing each other over the prone Mother Superior's puddle of skirts, chests heaving, and the Vice-M.S. has a writhing expression under her askew wimple like *Go ahead, make the circle of recidivist retribution against the nun you thought had saved you but ultimately couldn't even save herself complete, complete the lapsarian circuit* or whatever. They stare at each other for countless frames, the office wall behind them cruciformly pale where the unnamed object'd hung. Then Blood Sister shrugs in resignation and drops the tomahawk, and turns and with an ironic little obeisance walks out the Mother Superior's office door and through the little sacristy and over the altar and down the little convent nave (bike boots echoing on the tile, emphasizing the silence) and out the big doors whose tympanum overhead is carved with a sword and a ploughshare and a syringe and a soup-ladle and the motto *CONTRARIA SUNT COMPLEMENTA,* the heaviness of which makes Hal cringe so severely it's Boone who has to supply the translation Kent Blott asks for.[298] On-screen, we're still following the tough nun (or ex-nun). The fact that the hatchet she resignedly dropped fetched the prone Mother Superior a pretty healthy knock is presented as clearly accidental . . . because she (Blood Sister) is still walking away from the convent, moving emphatically and in a gradually deepening focus. Limping toughly eastward into the twittering Toronto dawn. The cartridge's closing sequence shows her astride her Hawg on Toronto's meanest street. About to lapse? Backslide back into her tough pre-saved ways? It's unclear in a way that's supposed to be rich: her expression is agnostic at best, but the huge sign of a discount Harley-muffler outlet juts just at the horizon she's roaring toward. The closing credits are the odd lime-green of bugs on a windshield.

It's hard to tell whether Boone and Bash's applause is sarcastic. There's that post-entertainment flurry of changed positions and stretched limbs and critical sallies. Out of nowhere Hal remembers: Smothergill. Possalthwaite says he and the Id-man brought Blott in to speak to Hal about something disturbing they encountered during their disciplinary shit-detail in the tunnels that P.M. Hal holds up a hand for the kids to hang on, flipping through cartridge cases to see whether *Low-Temperature Civics* is up here. All the cases are clearly labelled.

The apparition receded, the red of its coat shrinking against the swinging view of Prospect St. and pavement and dumpsters and looming storefronts, Ruth van Cleve on its lurid tail and receding also, screaming bits of urban argot that became less faint than swallowed. Kate Gompert held her hurt head and heard it roar. Ruth van Cleve's pursuit was slowed by her arms, which were waving around as she screamed; and the apparition was swinging their purses to clear a path on the sidewalk before it. Kate Gompert could see pedestrians leaping out into the street way up ahead to avoid getting clocked. The whole visual scene seemed tinged in violet.

A voice under a storefront awning right nearby somewhere said: 'Seen it!'

Kate Gompert leaned over again and held the part of her head that surrounded her eye. The eye was palpably swelling shut, and her whole vision was queerly violet. A sound in her head like a drawbridge being drawn up, implacable trundle and squeaks. Hot watery spit was flooding her mouth, and she kept swallowing against nausea.

'Seen it? Bet your ever-living goddamn *life* I seen it!' A kind of gargoyle seemed to detach itself from a storefront hardware display and moved in, its motions oddly jerky, as in a film missing frames. 'Seen the whole thing!' it said, then repeated it. 'I'm a witness!' it said.

Kate Gompert put her other arm out against the lightpost and hauled herself mostly upright, looking at it.

'Witnessed the whole *god*damn thing,' it said. In the eye that wasn't swelling shut the thing resolved violetly into a bearded man in an army coat and a sleeveless army coat over that coat, spittle in his beard. One eye had a system of exploded arteries in it. He shook like an old machine. There was a smell involved. The old man got right up close, looming in, so that pedestrians had to curve out around both of them together. Kate Gompert could feel her pulse in her eye.

'Witness! *Eye*witness! The whole thing!' But he was looking someplace else, like more around at people passing. 'Seen it? *I'm* him!' Not clear who

714

he was shouting at. It wasn't her, and the passersby were paying that studious, urban kind of no-attention as they broke and melted around them at the lightpost and then reformed. Kate Gompert had the idea that supporting herself against the lightpost would keep her from throwing up. *Concussion* is really another word for a bruised brain. She tried not to think about it, that the impact had maybe sent one part of her brain slamming against her skull, and now that part was purply swelling, mashed up against the inside of her skull. The lightpost she held herself up with was what had hit her.

'Fellow? *I'm* your fellow. Witness? Saw it all!' And the old fellow was holding a trembling palm up just under Kate Gompert's face, as if he wanted it thrown up into. The palm was violet, with splotches of some sort of possible fungal decay, and with dark branching lines where the pink palm-lines of people who don't live in dumpsters usually are, and Kate Gompert studied the palm abstractly, and the weather-bleached GIGABUCKS[299] ticket on the pavement below it. The ticket seemed to recede into a violet mist and then move back up. Pedestrians barely glanced at them and then looked studiously elsewhere: a drunk-looking pale girl and a street bum showing her something in his hand. 'Witnessed the whole thing being committed,' the man remarked to a passerby with a cellular on his belt. Kate Gompert couldn't summon the juice to tell him to go screw. That's the way it was said down here in the real city, Go Screw, with a deft little thumb-gesture. She couldn't even say Go Away, though the smell involved in the man made it worse, the nausea. It seemed terribly important not to vomit. She could feel her pulse in the eye the pole had hit. As if the strain of vomiting could aggravate the spongy purpling of the part of her brain the pole had bruised. The thought made her want to vomit in this horrid palm that wouldn't stay still. She tried to reason. If the man had witnessed the whole thing then how could he think she'd have change to put in his hand. Ruth van Cleve had been listing some of her baby's jailed father's wittier aliases when Kate Gompert had felt a hand strike her back and close around the strap of her purse. Ruth van Cleve had cried out as the apparition of just about the most unattractive woman Kate Gompert had ever seen crashed forward between them, knocking them apart. Ruth van Cleve's vinyl purse's strap gave right away, but Kate Gompert's thin but densely macramé'd strap held around her shoulder and she was pulled wrenchingly forward by the womanly apparition's momentum as it tried to sprint up Prospect St., and the red hag-like figure was yanked wrenchingly back as the quality Filene's all-cotton French-braidedly macramé'd purse-strap held, and Kate Gompert had got a whiff of something danker than the dankest municipal sewage and a glimpse of what looked like a five-day facial growth on the hag's face as street-tough Ruth van Cleve got a grip on her/his/its red leather coat, proclaiming the thief a son of a mafun ho. Kate Gompert was staggering forward, trying to get her arm out of the strap's loop. They all three moved forward together this way. The apparition spun itself violently around, trying to shake off Ruth van Cleve, and her/its spin with her purse took the strap-attached Kate Gompert (who didn't weigh very much) out around in a wide circle (she'd had a flashback of reminiscence back to Crack-the-Whip at the Wellesley Hills Skating Club's rink's 'Wee Blades' Toddler Skating Hour, as a child), gaining speed; and then a rust-pocked curbside lightpost rotated toward her, also gaining speed, and the sound was somewhere between a *bonk* and a *clang*, and the sky and the sidewalk switched places, and a violet sun exploded outward, and the whole street turned violet and swung like a clanging bell; and then she was alone and purseless and watching the two recede, both seeming to be shrieking for help.

14 NOVEMBER
YEAR OF THE DEPEND ADULT UNDERGARMENT

A disadvantage of your nasally ingested cocaine being that at a certain point somewhere past the euphoric crest — if you haven't got the sense left to stop and just ride the crest, and instead keep going, nasally — it takes you into regions of almost interstellar cold and nasal numbness. Randy Lenz's sinuses were frozen against his skull, numb and hung with crystal frost. His legs felt like they ended at the knees. He was trailing two very small-sized Chinese women as they lugged enormous paper shopping bags east on Bishop Allen Dr. under Central. His heart sounded like a shoe in the Ennet House basement's dryer. His heart was beating that loud. The Chinese women scuttled at an amazing rate, given their size and the bags' size. It was c. 2212:30–40h., smack in the middle of the former Interval of Issues-Resolution. The Chinese women didn't walk so much as scuttle with a kind of insectile rapidity, and Lenz was heart-pressed to both keep up and seem to casually saunter, numb from the knee down and the nostril back. They made the turn onto Prospect St. two or a few blocks below Central Square, moving in the direction of Inman Square. Lenz followed ten or thirty paces behind, eyes on the twine handles of the shopping bags. The Chinese women were about the size of fire hydrants and moved like they had more than the normal amount of legs, conversing in their anxious and high-pitched monkey-language. Evolution proved your Orientoid tongues were closer to your primatal languages than not. At first, on the brick sidewalks of the stretch of Mass. Ave. between Harvard and Central, Lenz had thought *they* might be following *him* — he'd been followed a great deal in his time, and like the well-read Geoffrey D. he knew only too well thank you that the most fearsome surveillance got carried out by unlikely-looking people that followed you by walking in front of you with small mirrors in their glasses' temples or elaborate systems of cellular communicators for reporting to the Command Center — or else also by helicopters, also, that flew too high to see, hovering, the tiny chop of their rotors disguised as your own drumming heart. But after he'd had success at successfully shaking the Chinese women twice — the second time so successfully he'd had to tear-ass around through alleys and vault wooden fences to pick them up again a couple blocks north on Bishop Allen Dr., scuttling along, jabbering — he'd settled down in his conviction about who was trailing who, here. As in just who had the controlling discretion over the general situation right here. The ejection from the House, which the ejection had at first seemed like the kiss of a death sentence, had turned out to maybe be just the thing. He'd tried the Straight On Narrow and for his pains had been threatened and dismissively sent off; he'd given it his best, and for the most part impressively; and he had been sent Away, Alone, and at least now could openly hide. R. Lenz lived by his wits out here, deeply disguised, on the amonymous streets of N. Cambridge and Somerville, never sleeping, ever moving, hiding in bright-lit and public plain sight, the last place They would think to find him.

Lenz wore fluorescent-yellow snowpants, the slightly shiny coat to a long-tailed tux, a sombrero with little wooden balls hanging off the brim, oversize tortoise-shell glasses that darkened automatically in response to bright light, and a glossy black mustache promoted from the upper lip of a mannequin at Lechmere's in Cambridgeside — the ensemble the result of bold snatch-and-sprints all up and down the nighttime Charles, when he'd first gone Overground northeast from Enfield several-odd days back. The absolute blackness of the mannequin's mustache — very securely attached with promoted Krazy Glue and made even glossier by the discharge from a nose Lenz can't feel running — gives his pallor an almost ghostly aspect in the sombrero's portable shade — another both advantage and disadvantage of nasal cocaine is that eating becomes otiose and optional, and one forgets to for extended periods of time, to eat — in his gaudy pastiche of disguise he passes easily for one of metro Boston's homeless and wandering mad, the walking dead and dying, and is given a wide berth by all comers. The trick, he's found, is to not sleep or eat, to stay up and moving at all times, alert in all six directions at all times, heading for under the cover of T-station or enclosed mall whenever the invisible rotors' cardiac chop betrayed surveillance at altitude.

He'd got quickly familiarized with Little Lisbon's networks of alleys and transoms and back trash-lots, and its (dwindling) population of feral cats and dogs. The area was fertile in overhead clocks of banks and churches, dictating movements. He carried his Browning X444 Serrated in its shoulder-holster strapped inside his one sock just above the spats of the formal footwear he'd taken off the same A Formal Affair, Ltd. sidewalk display as the tux's coat. His lighter was in a fluorescent zip-uppable slash pocket;

quality trashbags were plentiful in dumpsters and Land Barges stopped at lights. The *James Principles of the Gifford Lectures,* its razored-out receptacled heart now quite a bit closer to empty than Lenz would be comfortable thinking about directly, he had in his hand tucked up under one formal arm. And the Chinese women scuttled centipedishly abreast, their mammoth shopping bags held in a right hand and left, respective, so the bags were side by side between them. Lenz was closing the gap behind them, but gradually and with no little nonchalant stealth, considering it was hard to walk stealthily when one couldn't feel one's feet, and when one's eyeglasses darkened automatically whenever one went under a streetlight and then took their time lightening up again, after, so that no less than two of Lenz's vital sensory street-senses were disorientated; but he still managed both stealth and nonchalance both. He had no clue how he really looked. Like many of the itinerant mad of metro Boston, he tended to confuse a wide berth with invisibility. The shopping bags looked heavy and impressive, their weight making the Chinese women lean in slightly toward each other. Call it 2214:10h. The Chinese women and then Lenz all passed a gray-faced woman squatting back between two dumpsters, her multiple skirts hiked up. Vehicles were packed bumper-flush all along the curb, with myriad double parking also. The Chinese women passed a man lined up at the curb with a toy bow and arrows, and when the glasses undarkened Lenz could see him as well as he passed also — the guy wore a rat-colored suit and was shooting a suction-cup arrow at the side of a For Lease building and then going up and drawing a miniature chalk circle on the brick around the arrow, and then another circle around that circle, and etc., as in a what's the word. The women paid him no Orientoid mind. The suit's string tie was also brown in tone, unlike a rat's tail. His wall's chalk was more pinkish. One of the women said something high-pitched, like an exclamation to the other. Your monkey-languages' exclamatories have an explosive ricocheting sound to them. As in a component of *boing* to every word. A window up across the street was producing *The Star-Spanned Banner* all this time. The man had a string tie and fingerless little gloves, and he stepped back from the wall to examine his pink circles and almost collided with Lenz, and they both looked at each other and shook their heads like Look at this poor son of an urban bitch I'm on the same street with.

It was universally well known that your basic Orientoid types carried their earthly sum-total of personal wealth with them at all times. As in on their person while they scuttled around. The Orientoid religion prohibited banks, and Lenz had seen mammoth double-width twine-handled shopping bags in too many tiny Chinese women's hands not to have deducted that the Chinese female species of Oriental used shopping bags to carry their personal wealth. He felt the energy required for the snatch-and-sprint increasing now with each stride, drawing nonchalantly closer, able now to distinguish different patterns in the clear like plastic flags they wrapped their little hair in. The Chinese women. His heartrate speedened to a steady warming gallop. He began to feel his feet. Adrenaline about what would shortly occur dried his nose and helped his mouth stop moving around on his face. The Frightful Hog was not and never numb, and now it stirred in the snowpants slightly with excitement of wits and the thrill of the hunt. Far from cutting-edge surveillance: the shoe was on the other foot: the unwitting Oriental women had no idea who they were dealing with, behind them, no idea he was back there surveilling them and closing the nonchalant gap, stumbling only slightly after each streetlight's light. He was in total control of this situation. And they did not even know there was a situation. Bull's-eye. Lenz straightened the mustache with one finger and gave a tiny little Yellow-Brick-Road stutter-skip of pure controlling glee, his adrenaline invisible for all to see.

There were two ways of going, and *Les Assassins des Fauteuils Rollents* were prepared to pursue both these. Less better was the indirect route: surveillance and infiltrating the surviving associates of the Entertainment's *auteur,* its actress and rumored performer, relatives — if necessary, taking them and subjecting them to technical interview, leading with hope to the original *auteur*'s cartridge of the Entertainment. This had risks and exposures and was held *abeyant* until the directer route — to locate and secure a Master copy of the Entertainment on their own — had been exhausted. It was this way that thus they were now still here, in the Antitois' shop of Cambridge, to — *comme on dit* — be turning all the stones.

14 NOVEMBER
YEAR OF THE DEPEND ADULT UNDERGARMENT

The secret to sprinting in high heels, Poor Tony Krause knew, was to run on one's toes, inclined way forward, with so much forward momentum that one stayed well up on her toes and the heels never came into play. Evidently the wretched Creature behind him knew this trade-secret too. They careered up Prospect, the Creature's clutching hand just mm. away from the trailing boa. Poor Tony held the two purses together tucked away against his side like a football in U.S. football. Pedestrians moved artfully aside, long-practiced. Poor Tony saw the pedestrians' faces very clearly as his odor preceded him like a shock-wave. A man in a car coat made a smell-face and did a kind of artful veronica to let the two of them career past. Poor Tony's breath came in great ragged stitchy gasps. He had not banked on victim-pursuit. He felt the Creature's hand grope for purchase on the remains of his boa. The Donegal cap flew off and was not mourned. The Thing's own breathing was also ragged, but the obscenities she hurled still came from the diaphragm, with conviction and vigor. The other Thing had impacted a pole with a meaty sound Tony had shuddered to hear. His own father had struck himself about the head and shoulders as he grieved for his symbolically dead son. The moment after the impact and the strap gave way, Tony was up on his toes and in full flight, not banking on pursuit from the other one, this black Creature screaming and just off his tail. For the first couple blocks the Creature had shouted for *Help* and to *Stop The Bitch*, and Poor Tony, then with a decent lead, had countered by also yelling *Help!* and *For God's Sake Stop Her*, flummoxing any would-be citizens. An ancient trade-device among Harvard Square crews. But now the black Creature had closed to within mm., and now it had real hold of the boa as they careered breathing at full speed on their toes, and Krause unlooped the thing from his neck with a flourish and sacrificed the boa to the Thing, but the loathsome Creature's hand came right back, clutching at the air just over his leather collar, its ragged breath in his ear, cursing him. Poor Tony grieved in mid-stride at the thought that the Thing had doubtless just tossed the boa carelessly aside into the street or gutter. Their shoes' toes formed complex and variable rhythms on the pavement; sometimes their footfalls were in sync, then they were not. The Thing stayed agonizingly just behind. Bold-print signs for FRESH-KILLED CHICKEN and COMPLETE DESTRUCTION flashed past; Antitoi Entertainment was just over two long north-south blocks distant. Krause and pursuer both jay-ran through a gridlocked intersection. Poor Tony shouted *Help!* and *Please!* The hand and hissed breath just behind him was like one of those simply horrid dreams where something unimaginable is chasing you for km. after km. and just before its talons close on the back of your collar you wake up sitting bolt upright; except this horrid Creature's-clutching-hand-just-behind-him scenario went on and on, storefront and curb and leaping pedestrians all melting together at the periphery due right. Antitoi Ent.'s discreet back door was accessible by a parking alley that cut west off Prospect just before Broadway and went west to intersect a smaller and dumpster-lined north-south alley, one of whose dumpsters (in which Poor Tony had occasionally slept, when out late and short of train-fare) was within underhand-toss distance of the Canadian brothers' rear exit. Poor Tony, purses under arm and the other hand clamped tight to the wig, calculated that if he could get a reasonable lead on the Creature by the time they hit the smaller alley the dumpsters would keep It from seeing just which hopefully unlocked rear door P.T. sought basic human kindly refuge behind. He feinted around a bodega's sidewalk fruit display and shot a quick look back, hoping the Creature would crash itself ass-over-teakettle into the stacked fruit. It did not. It was still right there, breathing. Its stutter-step around two cardboard tiers of Cape cranberries was discouragingly deft. This Thing had all too clearly chased persons before. Its breath had a ragged implacability about it. It was all too clearly in this for the long haul. It was no longer shouting *Stop* or gutterish obscenities. Poor Tony's breaths felt flamish. It sounded as if he were weeping, almost. He tried to shout Help! and could not; he hadn't the breath to spare; black specks floated upward through his vision; only certain of the streetlamps worked; his heartbeat was *zuckungzuckungzuckung*. Poor Tony hurdled a queerly placed cardboard display for something wheelchaired and heard the Creature vault it also and land lightly on its toes. Its uppers were not straps and could not dig like the fine Aigners; Tony felt blood on his feet. The entrance to the parking alley west was between a Tax Preparer's and something else; it was right around here; Krause squinted; the black specks were tiny rings with opaque centers and floated upward through his sight like balloons, lazily; Poor Tony was post-seizure, infirm, not to mention Withdrawn; his breath came in stitches and half-sobs; he could barely stay on his toes; he had not consumed food since before the library's men's room stall, which was how many days; he scanned the blurred storefronts ripping past; an elderly person went down with a noise as the Creature stiff-armed him; somewhere a rape-whistle blew; the Tax Preparer's had the odd storefront announcement ON PARLE LE POR-TUGAIS ICI. Its hand's finger knocked the rim of Tony's leather collar with each footfall until it moved up and Poor Tony could feel its fingers in the hair of the chignon he held clamped to his head with a hand. Poor Tony's father used to come home to 412 Mount Auburn Street Watertown at the completion of a long day of cesareans and sit in a chair in the darkening kitchen, scratching at his head where his mask's green strings had dug into the head. Its doubtlessly luridly long-nailed fingers were twining for purchase in his wig's hair when they hit the Preparer's and Tony cut a sharp right, breaking a heel on the pivot but gaining several steps toward a lead as the Creature's momentum carried it past the alley's recessed mouth. Krause whimpered raggedly and flew west, up on his bloody toes, hearing his breath off both alley walls, negotiating broken glass and the homeless supine, hearing it back behind him several steps crying a tight-echoed Stop Motherfucking *Stop!*, with a supine person Krause vaulted lifting a decayed head from the alley floor to counter with: *Go*.

Having traced — through the strenuous technical interview of the sar-torially eccentric cranio-facial-pain-specialist, whom they had traced through the regrettably fatal technical interview of the young burglar[300] whose electrical-surge-tolerance proved considerably lower than that of his room's computer's machinery — having traced their best chances at a copy to the hapless Antitois' establishment, it had taken the A.F.R. then several days to find it there, the real Entertainment.

A.F.R.'s U.S.A. cell's leader, Fortier, the son of a Glen Almond glass-blower, had allowed none of the mirrors to be broken or dismantled. In all other respects, the search had been methodical and thorough. It was a neat search and also orderly, with time taken. Because the viewer of the shop was visually dysfunctional, a consumer TP had been purchased and set up for volunteer viewing in the room of storage off the shop's back room. Each cartridge of the shop's exhaustive shelves was sampled by a volunteer, then discarded in one of the huge metal *coffre d'amas* in the alley outside the shop's rear door. A detail had been assigned to roll the extinguished Antitoi brothers in construction-plastic and place them in a room of storage off the back room. This was for hygienic purposes. A detail also had procured an oilskin windowshade for the front door's glass, also some printed signs which read CLOSED, ROPAS, and RELACHE. No person had knocked at the door after the first hours, thus.

Quickly, on the first day, in a liquor box which was damp and smelled, they had found an example of the rival F.L.Q.'s tactical street-display cartridges, with its crudely stamped smiling face and the 'IL NE FAUT PLUS QU'ON PURSUIVE LE BONHEUR' embossed upon it. And young Tassigny, with characteristic valor, volunteered to be rolled into the room of storage and strapped in, in order to verify this, and Fortier allowed this. All had drunk the gesture of a toast to Tassigny and promised to look after his aged father and fur-traps, and M. Fortier had embraced the young volunteer and kissed both his face's cheeks as he was rolled in and fitted by M. Broullîme with EEG wires and strapped in before the viewer placed in the room of storage.

Then the cartridge of the street-display turned out to be blank, void. Then another from this box, also wet: also blank. Two blanks. *Donc. D'accord.* Fortier, philosophical, counselled against disappointment or damage from a frustration — he and Marathe had counselled all along that the F.L.Q. displays of the Entertainment and the wheelchaired man were probably the hoax, instilling of terror only. The fact of the displays which featured wheelchairs, a smack to the testicles of A.F.R. — this was ignored. A.F.R. wanted only to repossess this copy of the Entertainment. As well, chiefly, now to determine: could this copy of DuPlessis itself be copied? This was the real objective: a Master cartridge.[301] Unlike the F.L.Q., *les Assassins des Fauteuils Rollents* had no interest in blackmail or cartographic extortings for the Convexity's return. Not in re-Reconfiguration of O.N.A.N. or even its charter's dissolution. The A.F.R. were interested only in dealing the sort of testicular *frappe* to the underbelly of U.S.A. self-interests that would render Canada itself unwilling to face the U.S.A. retaliation for this — if A.F.R. could secure, copy, and disseminate the Entertainment, Québec would be not so much allowed as required by Ottawa to secede, to face on its own the wrath of a neighbor struck down by its own inability to say 'Non' to fatal pleasures.[302]

Fortier bid the A.F.R. methodically to continue the search. Younger volunteers were rolled into the room of storage on a rotating basis to sample each set of cartridges. Aside from some bickering over the Portuguese pornography, the rotation proceeded with valor and care. The plastic-wrapped cadavers began to swell, but the plastic maintained hygienic conditions adequately for viewing samples of the many cartridges in the room of storage. The search and inventory proceeded in a painstaking and slow fashion.

M. Fortier was required to absent himself for a period, in the search's middle, to help facilitate Southwest ops, the infiltration of that relative of the *auteur* felt most strongly (according to Marathe) to have knowledge or possession of a duplicable copy. There was reason to think M. DuPlessis had received his original copies from this relative, an athlete. Marathe felt U.S.B.S.S. felt this person may have borne responsibility for the razzles and dazzles of Berkeley and Boston, U.S.A. The Americans' field-operative, jutting with prostheses, had been clinging to this person like a bad odor.

The nation U.S.A. treated wheelchaired persons with the solicitude that the weak substitute for respect. As if he were a sickly child, Fortier. Buses knelt, smooth ramps flanked steps, attendants pushed him aboard flights in full solicitous view of those standing upon legs. Fortier owned attachable legs of flesh-tone polymer resins whose interior circuitry was responsive to large-bundle neural stimuli from his stumps, which with metal crutches whose bracelets locked to his wrists allowed a sort of swirling parody of perambulation. But Fortier, he rarely wore the prostheses, not in U.S.A., and never for public transit. He preferred the condescension, the pretense of institutional 'sensitivity' to his 'right' of the 'equal access'; it honed the edge of his senses of purpose. Like all of them, Fortier was willing to sacrifice.

14 NOVEMBER
YEAR OF THE DEPEND ADULT UNDERGARMENT

After so long not caring, and then now the caring crashes back in and turns so easily into obsessive worry, in sobriety. A few days before the debacle in which Don Gately got hurt, Joelle had begun to worry obsessively about her teeth. Smoking 'base cocaine eats teeth, corrodes teeth, attacks the enamel directly. Chandler Foss had explained all this to her at supper, showing her his corroded stumps. In her Latin cloth purse now she carried a traveller's brush and expensive toothpaste with alleged enamel-revitalizers and anti-corrosives. Several of the Ennet House residents who'd hit bottom with the glass pipe had no teeth or blackened and disintegrating teeth; the sight of Wade McDade's or Chandler Foss's teeth gave Joelle the fantods like nothing at meetings could. The toothpaste was only recently available over the counter and was a whole level of power and expense above standard smoker's polish.

As she lies on her side beside Kate Gompert's empty bunk, her veil's selvage tucked secure between pillow and jaw, and Charlotte Treat also asleep across the lit room, Joelle dreams that Don Gately, unhurt and mid-South-accented, is ministering to her teeth. He is bibbed in dental white, humming softly to himself, his big hands deft as he plucks instruments from the gleaming chair-side tray. Her chair is dental and canted back, yielding her face up to him, her legs shut tight and stretching up and out before her. Dr. Don's eyes are abstractly kind, concerned for her teeth; and his thick fingers, as he inserts things to hold her open, are gloveless and taste warm and clean. Even the light seems sterilely clean. There is no assistant; the dentist is solo, leaning in above her, humming absent chords as he probes. His head is massive and vaguely square. In the dream she is concerned for her teeth and feels Gately shares her concern. She feels good that he makes no chitchat and probably doesn't know her name. There's very little eye-contact. He is completely intent on her teeth. He is there to help if possible, is his whole demeanor's message. His bib hangs by a necklace of tiny steel balls and could not be whiter, his head haloed with a strap and a polished metal disk attached to the strap just above his eyes, a tiny mirror of stainless steel, clean as the instruments' tray; and the dream's yielding and trustful quality of calm is undercut only by the view of her face in the halo's mirror, the disk like a third eye in Gately's broad clean forehead: because she can see her face, convexly distorted and ravaged by years of cocaine and not caring, her face all bug-eyes and sunken cheeks, lampblack-smudges beneath the pop-eyes; and as the dentist's warm thick fingers gently draw her lips back she looks up into his head's mirror at long rows of all canine teeth, tapered and sharp, with then more rows of canines behind them, in reserve. The countless rows of the teeth are all sharp and strong and unblackened but tinged at the tips with an odd kind of red, as of old blood, the teeth of a creature that carelessly tears at meat. These are teeth that have been up to things she hasn't known about, she tries to say around the fingers. The dentist hums, probing. In the dream Joelle looks up into Don Gately's forehead's dental mirror's disk and is seized with a fear of her teeth, a terror, and as her spread mouth spreads farther to cry out in fear all she can see in the little round mirror are endless red-stained rows of teeth leading back and away down a pitch-black pipe, and the image of all these rows of teeth in the disk blots out the big dentist's good face as he probes with a hook and says he assures her that these can be saved.

Then, by the time Fortier was able to return to the dismantled shop, they had located a third cartridge emblazoned with the embossed smile and letters disclaiming need of happy pursuit, and, after some regretful losses, they had secured and verified it, the *samizdat* cartridge of Entertainment burglared from the death of DuPlessis.

Fortier was told the story. The cell's young Desjardins had been taking his turn in the viewing rotation, seated with young Tassigny in the room of storage during the hours of early morning, sampling the dregs of unshelved entertainments found in kitchen-can waste bags in the same closet the Antitois' cadavers were swelling within. Desjardins had just moments before complained of the wasted time of cartridges scheduled for the coffre d'amas.

Tassigny, who had been in the room of storage with Desjardins, then was saved by the need to leave this room to change the bag of his partial colostomy. But, Marathe reported, they had lost Desjardins, and the older and valued Joubet also, who rolled against orders into the room of storage to see why Desjardins had not been sending out the tapes for more tapes to sample. Both were lost. They had not lost more only because someone had thought to wake up Broullîme, whom Fortier had briefed with care on procedures for if the actual Entertainment was found by this viewing. But two were lost — Joubet the red-bearded workhorse, who loved to pop wheelies, and young Desjardins, so filled with the idealism and so young as to be still feeling the phantom pains in his stumps. Rémy Marathe reported that the two had been made comfortable since their loss, allowed to remain in the locked room of storage and view the Entertainment again and again, silent behind the door except when the watch-detail reported the hearing of cries of impatience at the player's rewinder, to rewind. Marathe reported they had declined to come out for water or food, or Joubet — who was diabétique — for his insulin. M. Broullîme estimated that it would be a matter of hours now for Joubet, perhaps maybe one day or two days for Desjardins. Fortier had sadly said 'Bôf' and acceptingly shrugged: all knew the sacrifices that might have been required: all viewing details had taken their chances at random in the rotation of viewing.

On Fortier's return, Marathe delivered also the expected bad news of the finding of it: there was no need yet for high-rpm hardware of duplication: the found copy was Read-Only.[303]

Philosophical, Fortier reminded the A.F.R. that they did now encouragingly know the Entertainment of such power did truly exist, for themselves, and could thus gird their courage and fortitude for the more indirect task of forfeiting hopes of securing a Master copy and instead striving to secure the original Master, the *auteur*'s own cartridge, from which all Read-Only copies had presumably been copied.

Thus, he said, now the more arduous and risky task of taking for technical interview known persons associated with the Entertainment and locating the original maker's duplicable Master copy. None of this would have been worthy of the risk had they not now determined, through the heroic sacrifices of Joubet and Desjardins, that the device for extending O.N.A.N.'s self-destructing logic to its final conclusion lay within their arduous grasp.

Fortier gave numerous orders. The platoon of A.F.R. remained in the closed Antitoi Entertainent shop, behind their lingual window shade. Surveillance on the hated F.L.Q.'s *bureau centrale,* in the poorly disciplined house on Allston's Rue de Brainerd — this was suspended, the A.F.R. personnel pulled in and relocated to this commandeered Inman Square shop, where Fortier and Marathe and M. Broullîme coordinated phases of activity in this next more arduous and indirect phase, and reviewed tactics also.

The deceased *auteur*'s colleagues and relations were under consistent surveillance. Their concentration of place worked in the favor of this. An employee at the Academy of Tennis of Enfield had been recruited and joined the Canadian instructor and student already inside for closer work of surveillance. In the Desert, the redoubtable Mlle. Luria P—— was winning necessary confidences with her usual alacrity. An expensive source in the Subject's former department of the M.I.T. University had reported the Entertainment's probable performer's last known employment — the small Cambridge radio station which Marathe and Beausoleil had pronounced *Weee* — where she had donned the defacing veil of O.N.A.N.ite deformity.

Attentions were to be focused on the cartridge's performer and on the Academy of Tennis of the *auteur*'s estate. The fact that the players of the Academy were to play a provincially-selected team from Québec would have been easier to exploit had the A.F.R. possessed a tennis player of talent and lower extremities. Inquiries into the composition and travel of the Québecois team were under way from sources at home in Papineau.

On the day of Fortier's return also, the performer's radio program's technical engineer of radio had been acquired in a public but low-risk operation whose success had raised hopeful spirits for the acquisitions of more directly related persons to the Entertainment in this next phase. This person of U.S.A. radio had divulged all he professed to know under the mere descriptive threat of technical-interview procedures. Marathe, the best lay judge of Americans' veracity which the cell possessed, believed the veracity of the engineer; but nevertheless a formal technical interview had proceeded, justified in order to verify. The young and eruption-studded person's report remained consistent two levels past average U.S.A. endurance, the only variance involving several curious claims that the Massachusetts Institute of Technology was defensive in bed.

Today, Fortier himself, and Marathe, young Balbalis, R. Ossowiecke — all those with the better English — were thus now therefore making the rounds of all Substance-Difficulty-Rehabilitation facilities in hospitals, psychiatric institutions, and *demi-maisons* within a 25-km. radius. Procedures for expanding the radius of inquiry by factors of two and three had been preformulated, teams assembled, lines rehearsed. Joubet and then Desjardins had succumbed and been transported north by van as well with the remains of the Antitois' remains. The U.S.A. student radio engineering person, the veracity of whose limited statements of the Subject's whereabouts Broullîme had verified to within +/− (.35) of assurance well before debriefing-levels incompatible with physical existence, had been allowed several hours to recover, then had become of service as the A.F.R.'s first Subject in field-tests of the *samizdat* cartridge's motivational range. The room of storage again was utilized for this. His head immobilized with some straps, the test Subject had viewed the Entertainment twice at gratis, without the application of any motivational inquiry. For inquiry into the degree of motivation the cartridge will induce, M. Broullîme had rolled himself blindfolded into the room of storage holding an orthopedic saw and informed the Subject of the test that, as of beginning now, each subsequent reviewing of the Entertainment now would have the price of one digit from the Subject's extremities. And handed the Subject the orthopedic saw in question, also. Broullîme's explanation to Fortier was that thus a matrix could be created to compute the statistical relation between (n) the number of times the Subject replayed the Entertainment and (t) the amount of time he took to decide and remove a digit for each subsequent (n + 1) viewing. The goal was to confirm with statistical assurance the Subject's desire for viewing and reviewing as incapable of satiation. There could be no index of diminishing satisfaction as in the econometrics of normal U.S.A. commodities. For the *samizdat* Entertainment's allure to be macro-politically lethal, the ninth digit of extremities had to come off as quickly and willingly as the second. Broullîme, personally he had some skepticism about this. But this was Broullîme's function in his role in the cell: expertise in combination with skepticism *de coeur.*

And then naturally also a wider range of field-test Subjects would then be required, to verify that this Subject's responses were not merely subjective and typical only of a certain sensibility of entertainment-consumer. The bus window yielded a faint and ghostly reflection of Fortier, and, through that faint view, the lights of urban life outside the bus. Somerville Massachusetts U.S.A.'s Phoenix House administrative person had listened to Fortier's delivery with shows of great compassion, then explained with patience that they were unable to admit addicted persons for whom English was the secondary language. *D'accord,* though he was pretending disappointment. Fortier had been able to see the admitted addicts of Phoenix House holding a gathering in the room of living outside the office door: no person among them wore a veil of facial concealment, and so *c'est ça.* Four small teams were at this moment rolling through the streets and small streets and alleys of the unpleasant district of the Antitoi establishment, for the purpose of acquiring additional Subjects for M. Broullîme for the time when the Subject's digits were expended. The Subjects for suitability had to be passively undefended enough to be acquired publicly with quiet, yet not damaged in the brains or under the influence of the many of the district's intoxicant compounds. The A.F.R. were highly trained in patience and to be disciplined.

The southbound bus, empty and (which he detested) fluorescently lit, climbs a thin hill off Winter Park, north Cambridge, heading for the Squares Inman and Central. Fortier looks out at the lights passing. He can smell snow coming; it soon will snow. He sees in his imagination two-thirds of NNE's largest urban city inert, sybaritically entranced, staring, without bodily movement, home-bounded, fouling their divans and the chairs which may recline. He sees the district of business's towers of buildings and luxury apartments striated as two of every three floors is darkened to lightless black. With here and there the vaguely blue flicker of expensive digital entertainment equipment flickering through darkened windows. He imagines M. Tine holding the hand holding the pen of President J. Gentle as the O.N.A.N.ite President signs declaring War. He imagines teacups clinking thinly beneath trembling hands in the interior sanctums of Ottawa's sanctum of power. He adjusts his sportcoat's lapel over his sweater and smooths the wiry hair that tends to bulge unsmoothly around the bare spot. He watches the back of the bus driver's neck as the driver stares straight ahead.

Sure enough the Chinkette women had been strengthless and lightweight, flew aside like dolls, and their bags were indeed treasure-heavy, hard to heft; but as Lenz cut left down the north-south alley he could hold the bags by their twine handles out slightly before him, so their weight's momentum kind of pulled him along. The cruciform alleys through the blocks between Central and Inman in Little Lisbon were a kind of second city. Lenz ran. His breath came easy and he could feel himself from scalp to sole. Green and green-with-red dumpsters lined both walls and made the going narrow. He vaulted two sitting figures in khaki sharing a can of Sterno on the alley floor. He glided through the foul air above them, untouched by it. The sounds behind him were his footfalls' echo off dumpsters and fire-escapes' iron. His left hand ached nicely from holding both a bag's handle and his large-print volume. A dumpster up ahead had been hitched to an E.W.D. truck and just left to sit: probably quitting time. The Empire guys had an incredible union. In the recess of the hitch's bar a small blue light flickered and died. This was a dozen dumpsters up ahead. Lenz slowed to a brisk walk. His topcoat had slipped slightly off one of his shoulders but he had no free hand to fix it and wasn't going to take time to put a bag down. His left hand felt cramped. It was somewhere vague between 2224 and 2226h. The alley was dark as a pocket. A tiny crash off somewhere south down the network of alleys was actually Poor Tony Krause rolling the steel waste-barrel that tripped up Ruth van Cleve. The tiny blue flame came on, hung still, flickered, moved, hung there, went back out. Its glow was dark blue against the back of the huge E.W.D. truck. Empire trucks were unstrippable, hitches were valuable but locked down with a Kryptonite device thing you needed welding stuff to cut through. From the recess of the hitch there were small sounds. When the lighter lit again Lenz was almost on them, two boys on the hitch and two squatting down by the hitch facing them, four of them, a fire-escape's pull-ladder distended like a tongue and hanging just above them. None of the boys was over like twelve. They used a M. Fizzy bottle instead of a pipe, and the smell of burnt plastic hung mixed with the sicksweet smell of overcarbonated rock. The boys were all small and slight and either black or spic, greedily hunching over the flame; they looked ratty. Lenz kept them in peripheral view as he strode briskly by, carrying his bags, spine straight and extruding dignified purpose. The lighter went out. The boys on the hitch eyed Lenz's bags. The squatting boys turned their heads to look. Lenz kept them in peripheral view. None of them wore watches. One of them wore a knit cap and watched steadily. He locked eyes with Lenz's left eye, made a gun of his thin hand, pretended to draw a slow bead. Like performing for the others. Lenz walked by with urban dignity, like he both saw them and didn't. The smell was intense but real local, of the rock and bottle. He had to veer out to miss the Empire truck's side mirror on its steel strut. He heard them say things as the truck's grille fell behind, and unkind laughter, and then something called out in a minority agnate he didn't know. He heard the lighter's flint. He thought to himself Assholes. He was looking for someplace empty and a bit more lit, to go through the bags. And cleaner than this one north-south alley here, which smelled of ripe waste and rotting skin. He would separate the bags' valuables from the nonvaluables and transfer the valuables to a single bag. He would fence the nonnegotiable valuables in Little Lisbon and refill the receptacle in his medical dictionary, and buy some attractiver shoes. The alley was devroid of cats and rodents both; he did not stop to reflect why. A rock or bit of brick courtesy of the junior crack-jockeys back there landed behind him and skittered past and rang out against something, and someone cried out aloud, a sexless figure lying back against a maybe duffel bag or pack against a dumpster, its hand moving furiously in its groin and its feet pointed out into the alley and turned out like a dead body's, its shoes two different shoes, its hair a clotted mass around its face, looking up over at Lenz going past in the faint start of light from a broader alley's intersection ahead, chanting softly what Lenz could hear as he stepped gingerly over the rot-smelling legs as 'Pretty, pretty, pretty.' Lenz whispered to himself 'Jesus what a lot of fucked-up ass-eating fucking *losers*.'

'Our cult burned money for fuel.'
'As in like currency.'
'We used Ones. The Semi Divine One advocated thrift. We'd bring them

to Him at the stove. There was one stove. We had to bring them to Him on our knees with no part of our feet could touch the floor. He sat by the stove in our blankets and fed it Ones. We got an extra slap if the currency was new.'

'As in like crisp and new.'

'It was a cleansing. Somebody always played a drum.'

'Our cult's Divinely Chosen Leader drove a Rolls. In neutral. We pushed him wherever he was Called to like be at. He never turned it on. The Rolls. I got all muscled up.'

'In summer then they made us slither on our bellies. We had to embrace our snake-nature. It was a cleansing.'

'As in like slithering.'

'Serious slithering. They took wire and bound our arms and legs.'

'At least your wire wasn't barbed.'

'I finally felt too cleansed to stay.'

'Meaning over-pure, I can I.D. totally.'

'It was too much love somehow to take.'

'I'm like feeling the Identification all over, this is —'

'Plus I was up to three bags a day, at the end.'

'And then our Divinely Chosen's Love Squads made us chop wood with our teeth when it got cold. As in like subzero wintertime.'

'Yours let you keep your teeth?'

'Only the ones for gnawing. See?'

'Sheesh.'

'Just the ones for gnawing.'

Rémy Marathe sat veiled and blanket-lapped in the much crowded living room evening of this Ennet House Drug and Alcohol Recovery House, the last *demi-maison* on his portion of the list for this day. The hills of upper Enfield, they were *de l'infere* of difficulty, but the *demi-maison* itself had a ramp. A person with authority was conducting interviews to fill some vacancies of recent time in the place's Office, of which its locked door was visible from this sitting. Marathe and others were invited to sit in the living room with a cup of unpleasant coffee. Urged to smoke if he liked. Everyone else was smoking. The living room smelled like an ashtray, and its ceiling was yellow like the fingers of long smokers. Also the living room evening resembled an anthill which had been stirred with a stick; it was too full of persons, all of them restless and loud. There were *demi-maison* patients viewing a cartridge of martial arts conflict, former patients and persons of the upper Enfield area cohabiting on the furniture, conversing. A damaged woman, also in a *fauteuil de rollent* like Marathe, slumped *inutile* next to the cartridge's viewer, while a male person of advanced pallor mimed the kicks and thrusts of martial arts at her motionless head, trying to force the woman to twitch or cry out. Also a man without hands and feet trying to negotiate the stairway. Other persons, presumably addicted, waiting in the room to seek admittance to the Recovery House. The room was loud and hot. Marathe could hear a person who will seek admittance vomiting in the shrubberies just outside the window. Marathe's chair was locked down next to a divan's arm and directly before a window. The window, one could wish it was open more than a crack, he felt. Upon the dull-colored carpet a tormented-appearing man scuttling like the crab while two hooligans in leather played a cruel game of jumping over him. Persons reading cartoon books and painting the nails of their extremities. A tall-haired woman brought her foot to her mouth to blow upon her toes. Another young girl seemed to remove her eye from her head and placed it in her mouth. No other in the room wore the veil of the Entertainment's performer's organization U.H.I.D. The smell of the U.S.A. cigarettes permeated his veil and made Marathe's eyes water, and he thought of vomiting also. Two additional windows were open, but the room lacked all air.

During the time of his sitting, several persons approached Marathe, but they would say to him only the whispers 'Pet the dogs' or 'Make sure and pet the dogs.' This idiomatic expression was not in Marathe's knowledge of U.S.A. idiom.

Also one person approached of a face whose skin seemed that it was rotting away from him in some way and asked him if he, Marathe, was *court-ordered.*

Marathe was one of few persons not smoking. He noted that none of the room's persons appeared to regard the cheesecloth veil he wore over his face as unusual or curious or to be questioned. The old sportcoat he wore over a turtleneck sweater of Desjardin's made Marathe more formally dressed than other of the applicants for treatment. Two of the Ennet House *demi-maison* current patients wore neckties, however. Marathe kept pretending to sniff; he did not know why. He sat up next to a divan of false velour at whose end beside him two women who had sought previous treatment of addiction in religious cults were meeting and speaking together of their unenjoyable existences when in cults.

To whomever approached, Marathe carefully recited the introductory lines he and M. Fortier quickly had developed: 'Good night, I am addicted and deformed, seeking residential treatment for addiction, desperately.' Persons' responses to his introductory lines were difficult to interpret. One of the older two men in neckties who had approached, he had clapped a hand to his soft face's cheek and responded 'How extraordinarily nice for you,' in which Marathe could detect sarcasm. The two women of cult experience were inclined closely toward each other upon the divan. They touched each other's arms several times in a kind of excitement as they conversed. When they laughed in delight they seemed to chew at the air. One's laughter involved also a snorting noise. A clatter and two shrieks: these came from one end of the dining room, in the *demi-maison*'s floor plans a large kitchen.

The sounds were then followed by a roiling cloud of steam, with repeated obscenities from unseen persons. A bald large black man in a white cotton undershirt's laughing became coughing that would not cease. The two patients in neckties and the girl whose eye could be removed spoke together intensively and also audibly at the end of one other divan.

'But consider this quality of portability with respect to, say, a car. Is a car portable? With respect to a car it's more as though *I'm* portable.'

'They're portable when they're on one of them semis where they got new cars stacked on with prices in the windows like a good couple dozen on them semis that swing all to fuck all over I-93 and make you think the cars are going to start falling out all over the road when you're wanting to try and pass.'

The plump one who had been ironic toward Marathe, he was nodding: 'Or, say, too, with respect to a tow truck or wrecker, if you suffer a breakdown. One might be in a position to say that a deactivated car can be quote portable, but that with respect to a functional car it is I who am portable.'

The girl's nod caused the particular eye to wheel queasily in the socket of it. 'I'll buy that, Day.'

'If we're jot-and-tittling with all possible precision regarding *portable*, that is.'

The other man continually rubbed at his shine of the shoes with a facial tissue, causing his necktie to touch the floor.

These conversers formed this triad on an unevenly sloped divan of leather-colored plastic across the room, which was now more airless yet from the roiling steam from the kitchen, infiltrating. Directly facing Marathe in a yellow chair against the wall by these conversers' divan most directly across the living room from Marathe was an addicted man waiting for seeking treatment by admission. This one, he appeared to have several cigarettes burning at one time. He held a metal ashtray in his lap and jiggled the boot of his crossed leg with vigor. For Marathe, it was not difficult to ignore the fact that the addicted man was glaring at him. He noted it, and did not understand because of what the man glared, but he was unconcerned. Marathe was prepared to die violently at any time, which rendered him free to choose among emotions. U.S.A.'s B.S.S.'s M. Steeply had verified that U.S.A.s did not comprehend this or appreciate it; it was foreign to them. The veil allowed Marathe the liberty of staring calmly back at the addicted man without the man's knowledge, which Marathe found he enjoyed. Marathe felt sick to his body, from the smoky room's smoke. Marathe had once, as a child, with legs, bent himself over and overturned a decaying log in the forests of the Lac de Deux Montaignes region of his four-limbed childhood, before *Le Culte du Prochain Train*.[304] The pallor of the things which had writhed and scuttled beneath the wet log was the pallor of this addicted man, who wore a square of the facial hair between lower lip and chin and

732

had also a needle run through the flesh of the top of an ear, which the needle, it glistened and did not glisten rapidly in succession as it vibrated with the jiggle of the jiggling boot. Marathe gazed at him calmly through the veil while rehearsing his prepared lines within his head. The more idiomatic would be that the needle jiggled sympathetically with the jiggle of the boot, which was dull black and square-heeled, the motorcycle boot of persons who did not own motorcycles but wore the boots of those who did.

The addicted man rose slowly and carried the burning ashtray with him nearer to Marathe, trying to kneel. His Blue Jeans of Levi #501 were strangely torn in spots with tattered white strings which showed the pallor of the knees; the torn holes had the size and perimeter-damage of holes that Marathe recognized had been made by shotgun-blasts of the high gauge. Marathe was mentally memorizing every detail of all things, for both his reports. The addicted man kneeling before him, he leaned in closer, trying to remove something he believed was on his lip. Close in, the expression that through the veil had appeared as glaring corrected itself: the expression was more truly that the man's eyes had the vacant intensity of those who have violently died.

The man whispered: 'You real?' Marathe looked through the veil at his facial square. 'Are you real?' again the man whispered. All the time leaning more and more in, slowly.

'You're real I can tell ain't you,' the man whispered. Quickly he looked behind him at the uproaring room before leaning once more in. 'Listen then.'

Marathe kept his hands calmly in his lap, his machine pistol holstered securely to his right stump beneath the blanket. The whispering man's searching fingers were leaving small bits of filth on the lip.

''s these poor fuckers' — the man gestured slightly with indicating the room — 'most of them ain't real. So watch your six. Most of these fuckers are —: metal people.'

'I am Swiss," Marathe experimentally said. It was the second of his lines of introduction.

'Walking around, make you think they're alive.' The addicted man had the way with subtleness of looking all around himself which Marathe associated with intelligence professionals. One of his eyes had an exploded vein within it. 'But that's just the layer,' he said. He leaned in so far Marathe could see pores through the veil. 'There's a micro-thin layer of skin. But underneath, it's metal. Heads full of parts. Under a organic layer that's micro-thin.' The eyes of men violently dead were also the eye of a fish in a vendor's crushed ice, studying nothing. The man's smell suggested livestock on a hot day, a goatish, even through the smoke of the room. Trans-3-methyl-2 hexenoic acid was a material, M. Broullîme had lectured to pass times in long surveillances, a chemical material in the sweat of grave mental illness. Marathe, he had no trouble timing his breath so his exhalation matched the addicted man's, who leaned more in.

'There's one way to tell,' he said. 'Get right up close. Like right up flush next to: you can hear a whir. Micro-faint. This whirring. It's the processors' gears. It's their flaw. Machines always whir. They're good. They can quiet down the whir.'

'I have no six.'

'But they can't — can *not* — eliminate it.'

'I am Swiss, seeking residential treatment with desperation.'

'Not under no micro-thin tissue-layer they can't.' If the gaze were not vacant the gaze would be grim, frightened. Marathe distantly remembered the emotion fear.

'Did you hear what she said?' the ironic man on the divan laughed. '*Potable* means drinkable. It's not even the same *root*. Did you hear what she said?'

The man's breath, it smelled of trans-3-methyl acid as well. 'I'm clueing y'in,' he whispered. 'They're there to fool you. The real ones of us're getting *fooled*. Nine-nine-plus per cent of the time.' The flesh of the knees through the holes in the Blue Jeans was the white of long death. 'But you, I could tell you were real.' He indicated the veil. 'No micro-thin layer. The metal ones — have faces.' The smoke of his cigarette in the ashtray rose in a motion of corkscrewing. 'Which this is why' — feeling the lip — 'why the ones on the T or in the street — they won't let you right up close. Try it. They'll never let you right up close. It's programming. They know to look scared and — like — offended and back away and move to another seat. The real advanced ones, they'll give you change, even, to let 'em back off. Try it. Get right — up — like this — close.' Marathe sat calmly behind the veil, feeling the veil move with the man's breath, waiting patiently to inhale. The women with experiences in cults had smelled the odor of the man's trans-3 odor and relocated farther away upon the divan. The man's face smiled with one knowing side only of his mouth, acknowledging their movement away. He was so close that the nose of him touched the veil when Marathe finally inhaled. Marathe was prepared for death in all forms. The smells were trans-3-methyl-2 and of digested cheese and the under of an arm, from the facial skin. Marathe ignored impulses to impale the eyesockets with one two-finger motion. The man had his hand to his ear in a mime of to listen closely. His smile disclosed what might have once been teeth. 'Nothing,' he smiled. 'I knew. Not a sound.'

'The Swiss, we are a quiet people, and reserved. In addition, I am deformed.'

The man waved his cigarette with impatience. 'Listen up. This is why. You're how come I was here. I only thought it was the habit. They can *fool* you.' He scrubbed at the lip of his mouth. 'I'm here to tell you. Listen. You ain't here.'

'I have emigrated from my native Swiss.'

Still whispering: 'You ain't *here*. These fuckers are *metal*. Us — us that are real — there's not many — they're *fooling* us. We're all in one room. The real ones. One room all the time. Everything's pro — jected. They can do it with machines. They pro — ject. To fool us. The pictures on the walls change so's we think we're going places. Here and there, this and that. That's just they change the pro — jections. It's all the same place all the time. They fool your mind with machines to think you're moving, eating, cooking up, doing this and that.'

'I have come desperately here.'

'The real world's one room. These so-called people, so-called' — with again the flourish — 'they're everybody you know. You've met 'em before, hunnerts times, with different faces. There's only 26 total. They play differ-ent characters, that you think you know. They wear different faces with different pictures they pro — ject on the wall. You get me?'

'This Recovery House was recommended highly.'

'You follow? Count. Coincidence? There's 26 here, counting the one without feet on the stairs. Coincidence? Chance? This here's every machine that's played everbody you ever met. Are you hearin' me? They fool us. They take the machines in the back room and they — like —'

The visible door of the locked Office opened and an addicted patient emerged with a person in authority holding a clipboard. The addicted pa-tient limped and leaned far to a side, though was attractive in the blond stereotype of the U.S.A. image-culture.

'— *change them*. The thin organic layers. All the different people you know. So-called. They're the *same machines*.'

'Physically challenged foreign person with unpronounceable name!' the authority called with the clipboard.

'I am being indicated,' Marathe said, bending to release the clamps on his *fauteuil*'s wheels.

'— why I'm in this pro — jection, to clue you. So that now you know.'

Marathe manipulated the *fauteuil* to the right with its trusty left wheel. 'I must be excused to plead for treatment.'

'Get right up close.'

'Good night,' over his left shoulder. The *inutile* woman seemed to twitch slightly in her heavy *fauteuil* as he passed.

'You only think you're goin' someplace!' the addicted man called, still one-half kneeling.

Marathe rolled up to the person in authority as slowly as possible, hunched deep into the sportcoat and pathetically tacking. With significance, the large and clipboarded woman seemed without faze at the veil of U.H.I.D. Marathe extended a large hand in greeting which he made tremble. 'Good night.'

The insane-smelling man on the carpet called out after: 'Make sure and pet the dogs!'

Joelle used to like to get really high and then clean. Now she was finding she just liked to clean. She dusted the top of the fiberboard dresser she and Nell Gunther shared. She dusted the oval top of the dresser's mirror's frame and cleaned off the mirror as best she could. She was using Kleenex and stale water from a glass by Kate Gompert's bed. She felt oddly averse to putting on socks and clogs and going down to the kitchen for real cleaning supplies. She could hear the noise of all the post-meeting nighttime residents and visitors and applicants down there. She could feel their voices in the floor. When the dental nightmare tore her upright awake her mouth was open to scream out, but the scream was Nell G. down in the living room, whose laugh always sounds like she's being eviscerated. Nell preempted Joelle's own scream. Then Joelle cleaned. Cleaning is maybe a form of meditation for addicts too new in recovery to sit still. The 5-Woman's scarred wood floor had so much grit all over she could sweep a pile of grit together with just an appliquéd bumper sticker she'd won at B.Y.P. Then she could use damp Kleenex to get up most of the pile. She had only Kate G.'s little bedside lamp on, and she wasn't listening to any YYY tapes, out of consideration for Charlotte Treat, who was unwell and missed her Saturday Night Lively Mtng. on Pat's OK and was now asleep, wearing a sleep mask but not her foam earplugs. Expandable foam earplugs were issued to every new Ennet resident, for reasons the Staff said would clarify for them real quick, but Joelle hated to wear them — they shut out exterior noise, but they made your head's pulse audible, and your breath sounded like someone in a space suit — and Charlotte Treat, Kate Gompert, April Cortelyu, and the former Amy Johnson had all felt the same way. April said the foam plugs made her brain itch.

It had started with Orin Incandenza, the cleaning. When relations were strained, or she was seized with anxiety at the seriousness and possible impermanence of the thing in the Back Bay's co-op, the getting high and cleaning became an important exercise, like creative visualization, a preview of the discipline and order with which she could survive alone if it came to that. She would get high and visualize herself solo in a dazzlingly clean space, every surface twinkling, every possession in place. She saw herself being able to pick, say, dropped popcorn up off the rug and ingest it with total confidence. An aura of steely independence surrounded her when she cleaned the co-op, even with the little whimpers and anxious moans that exited her writhing mouth when she cleaned high. The place had been provided nearly gratis by Jim, who said so little to Joelle on their first several meetings that Orin kept having to reassure her that it wasn't disapproval — Himself was missing the part of the human brain that allowed for being aware enough of other people to disapprove of them, Orin had said — or dislike. It was just how The Mad Stork was. Orin had referred to Jim as 'Himself' or 'The Mad Stork' — family nicknames, both of which gave Joelle the creeps even then.

It'd been Orin who introduced her to his father's films. The Work was then so obscure not even local students of serious film knew the name. The reason Jim kept forming his own distribution companies was to ensure distribution. He didn't become notorious until after Joelle'd met him. By then she was closer to Jim than Orin had ever been, part of which caused part of the strains that kept the brownstone co-op so terribly clean.

She'd barely thought consciously of any Incandenzas for four years before Don Gately, who for some reason kept bringing them bubbling up to mind. They were the second-saddest family Joelle'd ever seen. Orin felt Jim disliked him to the precise extent that Jim was even aware of him. Orin had spoken about his family at length, usually at night. On how no amount of punting success could erase the psychic stain of basic fatherly dislike, failure to be seen or acknowledged. Orin'd had no idea how banal and average his same-sex-parent-issues were; he'd felt they were some hideous exceptional thing. Joelle'd known her mother didn't much like her from the first time her own personal Daddy'd told her he'd rather take Pokie to the pictures alone. Much of the stuff Orin said about his family was dull, gone stale from years of never daring to say it. He credited Joelle with some strange generosity for not screaming and fleeing the room when he revealed the banal stuff. *Pokie* had been Joelle's family nickname, though her mother'd never called her anything but Joelle. The Orin she knew first felt his mother was the family's pulse and center, a ray of light incarnate, with enough depth of love and open maternal concern to almost make up for a father who barely existed, parentally. Jim's internal life was to Orin a black hole, Orin said, his father's face any room's fifth wall. Joelle had struggled to stay awake and attentive, listening, letting Orin get the stale stuff out. Orin had no idea what his father thought or felt about anything. He thought Jim wore the opaque blank facial expression his mother in French sometimes jokingly called *Le Masque*. The man was so blankly and irretrievably hidden that Orin said he'd come to see him as like autistic, almost catatonic. Jim opened himself only to the mother. They all did, he said. She was there for them all, psychically. She was the family's light and pulse and the center that held tight. Joelle could yawn in bed without looking like she was yawning. The children's name for their mother was 'the Moms.' As if there were more than one of her. His younger brother was a hopeless retard, Orin had said. Orin recalled the Moms used to tell him she loved him about a hundred times a day. It nearly made up for Himself's blank stare. Orin's basic childhood memory of Jim had been of an expressionless stare from a great height. His mother had been really tall, too, for a girl. He'd said he'd found it secretly odd that none of the brothers were taller. His retarded brother was stunted to about the size of a fire hydrant, Orin reported. Joelle cleaned behind the filthy room's radiator as far as she could reach, being careful not to touch the radiator. Orin described his childhood's mother as his emotional sun. Joelle remembered her own personal Daddy's Uncle T.S. talking about how her own personal Daddy'd thought his own Momma 'Hung the God Damn Moon,' he'd said. The radiators on Ennet House's female side stayed on at all times, 24/7/365. At first Joelle had thought Mrs. Avril Incandenza's high-watt maternal love had maybe damaged Orin by bringing into sharper relief Jim's remote self-absorption, which would have looked, by comparison, like neglect or dislike. That it had maybe made Orin too emotionally dependent on his mother — why else would he have been so traumatized when a younger brother had suddenly appeared, specially challenged from birth and in need of even more maternal attention than Orin? Orin, late one night on the co-op's futon, recalled to Joelle his skulking in and dragging a wastebasket over and inverting it next to his infant brother's special crib, holding a heavy box of Quaker Oats high above his head, preparing to brain the needy infant. Joelle had gotten an A- in Developmental Psych. the semester before. And also dependent psychologically, Orin, it seemed, or even metaphysically — Orin said he'd grown up, first in a regular house in Weston and then at the Academy in Enfield, grown up dividing the human world into those who were open, readable, trustworthy, v. those so closed and hidden that you had no clue what they thought of you but could pretty damn well imagine it couldn't be anything all that marvelous or else why hide it? Orin had recounted that he'd started to see himself getting closed and blank and hidden like that, as a tennis player, toward the end of his junior career, despite all the Moms's frantic attempts to keep him from hiddenness. Joelle had thought of B.U.'s Nickerson Field's 30,000 voices' openly roared endorsement, the sound rising with the punt to a kind of amniotic pulse of pure positive noise. Versus tennis's staid and reserved applause. It had all been so easy to figure and see, then, listening, loving Orin and feeling for him, poor little rich and prodigious boy — all this was before she came to know Jim and the Work.

Joelle scrubbed at the discolored square of fingerprints around the light-switch until the wet Kleenex disintegrated into greebles.

Never trust a man on the subject of his own parents. As tall and basso as a man might be on the outside, he nevertheless sees his parents from the perspective of a tiny child, still, and will always. And the unhappier his childhood was, the more arrested will be his perspective on it. She's learned this through sheer experience.

Greebles had been her own mother's word for the little bits of sleepy goo you got in your eyes' corners. Her own personal Daddy called them 'eye-boogers' and used to get them out for her with the twisted corner of his hankie.

Though it's not as if you could trust parents on the subject of their memory of their children either.

The cheap glass shade over the ceiling's light was black with interior grime and dead bugs. Some of the bugs looked like they might have been from long-extinct species. The loose grime alone filled half an empty Carefree box. The more stubborn crud would take a scouring pad and ammonia. Joelle put the shade aside for until she'd shot down to the kitchen to toss out different boxes of crud and wet Kleenex and grab some serious Chore-type supplies from under the sink.

Orin had said she was the third-neatnikest person he knew after his Moms and a former player he'd played with with Obsessive Compulsive Disorder, a dual diagnosis with which the U.H.I.D. membership was rife. But at the time the import had missed her. At that time it had never occurred to her that Orin's pull toward her could have had anything either pro or con to do with his mother. Her biggest worry was that Orin was pulled only by what she looked like, which her personal Daddy'd warned her the sweetest syrup draws the nastiest flies, so to watch out.

Orin hadn't been anything like her own personal Daddy. When Orin was out of the room it had never seemed like a relief. When she was home, her own Daddy never seemed to be out of the room for more than a few seconds. Her mother said she hardly even tried to talk to him when his Pokie was home. He kind of trailed her around from room to room, kind of pathetically, talking batons and low-pH chemistry. It was like when she exhaled he inhaled and vice versa. He was all through the house. He was real present at all times. His presence penetrated a room and outlasted him there. Orin's absence, whether for class or practice, emptied the co-op out. The place seemed vacuumed and buffed sterile before the cleaning even started, when he went. She didn't feel lonely in the place without him, but she did feel alone, what alone was going to feel like, and she, no one's fool,[305] was erecting fortifications real early into it.

It was Orin, of course, who'd introduced them. He'd had this stubborn idea that Himself would want to use her. In the Work. She was too pretty for somebody not to want to arrange, capture. Better Himself than some weak-chinned academic. Joelle'd protested the whole idea. She had a brainy girl's discomfort about her own beauty and its effect on folks, a caution intensified by the repeated warnings of her personal Daddy. Even more to the immediate point, her filmic interests lay behind the lens. She'd do the capturing thank you very much. She wanted to make things, not appear in them. She had a student filmmaker's vague disdain for actors. Worst, Orin's idea's real project was developmentally obvious: he thought he could somehow get to his father through her. That he pictured himself having weighty, steeple-fingered conversations with the man, Joelle's appearance and performance the subjects. A three-way bond. It made her real uneasy. She theorized that Orin unconsciously wished her to mediate between himself and 'Himself,' just as it sounded like his mother had. She was uneasy about the excited way Orin predicted that his father wouldn't be able to *'resist using'* her. She was extra uneasy about how Orin referred to his father as 'Himself.' It seemed painfully blatant, developmental-arrest-wise. Plus she felt — only a little less than she made it sound, on the futon at night, protesting — she'd felt uneasy at the prospect of any sort of connection with the man who had hurt Orin so, a man so monstrously tall and cold and remotely hidden. Joelle heard a howl and a crash from the kitchen, followed by McDade's tubercular laugh. Twice Charlotte Treat sat up in sleep, glistening with fever, and said in a flat dead voice something that sounded for all the world like 'Trances in which she did not breathe,' and then fell back, out. Joelle was trying to pin down a queer rancid-cinnamon smell that came from the back of a closet stuffed with luggage. It was especially hard to clean when you weren't supposed to be allowed to touch any other resident's stuff.

She might have known from the Work. The man's Work was amateurish, she'd seen, when Orin had had his brother — the unretarded one — lend them some of The Mad Stork's Read-Only copies. Was *amateurish* the right word? More like the work of a brilliant optician and technician who was an amateur at any kind of real communication. Technically gorgeous, the Work, with lighting and angles planned out to the frame. But oddly hollow, empty, no sense of dramatic *towardness* — no narrative movement toward a real story; no emotional movement toward an audience. Like conversing with a prisoner through that plastic screen using phones, the upperclassman Molly Notkin had said of Incandenza's early oeuvre. Joelle thought them more like a very smart person conversing with himself. She thought of the significance of the moniker 'Himself.' Cold. *Pre-Nuptial Agreement of Heaven and Hell* — mordant, sophisticated, campy, hip, cynical, technically mind-bending; but cold, amateurish, hidden: no risk of empathy with the Job-like protagonist, whom she felt like the audience was induced to regard like somebody sitting atop a dunk-tank. The lampoons of 'inverted' genres: archly funny and sometimes insightful but with something provisional about them, like the finger-exercises of someone promising who refused to really sit down and play something to test that promise. Even as an under-grad Joelle'd been convinced that parodists were no better than camp-followers in ironic masks, satires usually the work of people with nothing new themselves to say.[306] *'The Medusa v. the Odalisque'* — cold, allusive, inbent, hostile: the only feeling for the audience one of contempt, the meta-audience in the film's theater presented as objects long before they turn to blind stone.

But there had been flashes of something else. Even in the early oeuvre, before Himself made the leap to narratively anticonfluential but unironic melodrama she helped prolong the arc of, where he dropped the technical fireworks and tried to make characters move, however inconclusively, and showed courage, abandoned everything he did well and willingly took the risk of appearing amateurish (which he had). But even in the early Work — flashes of something. Very hidden and quick. Almost furtive. She noticed them only when alone, watching, without Orin and his rheostat's dimmer, the living room's lights up high like she liked them, liked to see herself and everything else in the room with the viewer — Orin liked to sit in the dark and enter what he watched, his jaw slackening, a child raised on multi-channel cable TV. But Joelle began — on repeated viewing whose original purpose was to study how the man had blocked out scenes, for an Advanced Storyboard course she went the extra click in — she began to see little flashes of something. The *M v. O.*'s three quick cuts to the sides of the gorgeous combatants' faces, twisted past recognition with some kind of torment. Each cut to a flash of pained face had followed the crash of a petrified spectator toppling over in her chair. Three split-seconds, no more, of glimpses of facial pain. And not pain at wounds — they never touched each other, whirling with mirrors and blades; the defenses of both were impenetrable. More like as if what their beauty was doing to those drawn to watch it ate them alive, up there on stage, the flashes seemed to suggest. But just three flashes, each almost subliminally quick. Accidents? But not one shot or cut in the whole queer cold film was accidental — the thing was clearly s-boarded frame by frame. Must have taken hundreds of hours. Astounding technical anality. Joelle kept trying to Pause the cartridge on the flashes of facial torment, but these were the early days of InterLace cartridges, and the Pause still distorted the screen just enough to keep her from seeing what she wanted to study. Plus she got the creepy feeling the man had upped the film-speed in these few-frame human flashes, to thwart just such study. It was like he couldn't help putting human flashes in, but he wanted to get them in as quickly and unstudyably as possible, as if they compromised him somehow.

Orin Incandenza had been only the second boy ever to approach her in a male-female way.[307] The first had been shiny-chinned and half blind on Everclear punch, an All-Kentucky lineman for the Shiny Prize Biting Shoats team back in Shiny Prize KY, at a cookout to which the Boosters had invited the Pep and Baton girls; and the lineman had looked like a little shy boy as he confessed, by way of apologizing for almost splashing her when he threw up, that she was just too Goddamn-all petrifyingly pretty to approach any other way but liquored up past all horror. The lineman'd confessed the whole team's paralyzing horror of the prettiness of varsity Pep's top twirler, Joelle. Orin confessed to his private name for her. The memory of that H.S. afternoon remained real strong. She could smell the mesquite smoke and the blue pines and the YardGuard spray, hear the squeals of the stock they butchered and cleaned in symbolic prep for the opener against the

N. Paducah Technical H.S. Rivermen. She could still see the swooning line-man, wet-lipped and confessing, keeping himself upright against an imma-ture blue pine until the blue pine's trunk finally gave with a snap and crash.

Until that cookout and confession she'd somehow thought it was her own personal Daddy, somehow, discouraging dates and male-female ap-proaches. The whole thing had been queer, and lonely, until she'd been approached by Orin, who made no secret of the fact that he had balls of unrejectable steel where horrifyingly pretty girls were concerned.

But it wasn't even the subjective identification she felt, watching, she felt, somehow, for the flashes and seeming non-seqs that betrayed something more than cold hip technical abstraction. Like e.g. the 240-second motion-less low-angle shot of Gianlorenzo Bernini's 'Ecstasy of St. Teresa,' which — yes — ground *Pre-Nuptial* . . . 's dramatic movement to an annoy-ing halt and added nothing that a 15- or 30-second still shot wouldn't have added just as well; but on the fifth or sixth reviewing Joelle started to see the four-minute motionless shot as important for what was absent: the whole film was from the alcoholic sandwich-bag salesman's POV,[308] and the alco-holic sandwich-bag salesman — or rather his head — was on-screen every moment, even when split-screened against the titanic celestial marathon seven-card-stud-with-Tarot-cards game — his rolling eyes and temples' dents and rosary of upper-lip sweat was imposed nonstop on the screen and viewer . . . except for the four narrative minutes the alcoholic sandwich-bag salesman stood in the Vittorio's Bernini room, and the climactic statue filled the screen and pressed against all four edges. The statue, the sensuous pres-ence of the thing, let the alcoholic sandwich-bag salesman escape himself, his tiresome ubiquitous involuted head, she saw, was the thing. The four-minute still shot maybe wasn't just a heavy-art gesture or audience-hostile herring. Freedom from one's own head, one's inescapable P.O.V. — Joelle started to see here, oblique to the point of being hidden, an emotional thrust, since the mediated transcendence of self was just what the appar-ently decadent statue of the orgasmic nun claimed for itself as subject. Here then, after studious (and admittedly kind of boring) review, was an un-ironic, almost *moral* thesis to the campy abstract mordant cartridge: the film's climactic statue's stasis presented the theoretical subject as the emo-tional effect — self-forgetting as the Grail — and — in a covert gesture al-most moralistic, Joelle thought as she glanced at the room-lit screen, very high, mouth writhing as she cleaned — presented the self-forgetting of alco-hol as inferior to that of religion/art (since the consumption of bourbon made the salesman's head progressively swell, horrendously, until by the film's end its dimensions exceeded the frame, and he had a nasty and humili-ating time squeezing it through the front door of the Vittorio).

It didn't much matter once she'd met the whole family anyhow, though. The Work and reviewings were just an inkling — usually felt on the small manageable bits of coke that helped her see deeper, harder, and so maybe not even objectively accessible in the Work itself — a lower-belly intuition that the punter's hurt take on his father was limited and arrested and maybe unreal.

With Joelle makeupless and stone-sober and hair up in a sloppy knot, the introductory supper with Orin and Himself at Legal Seafood up in Brookline[309] betrayed nothing much at all, save that the director seemed more than able to resist 'using' Joelle in any capacity — she saw the tall man slump and cringe when Orin told him the P.G.O.A.T. majored in F&C[310] — Jim'd told her later she'd seemed too conventionally, commercially pretty to consider using in any of that period's Work, part of whose theoretical project was to militate against received U.S. commercial-prettiness-conventions — and that Orin was so tense in 'Himself' 's presence that there wasn't room for any other real emotion at the table, Orin gradually beginning to fill up silences with more and faster nonstop blather until both Joelle and Jim were embarrassed at the fact that the punter hadn't touched his steamed grouper or given anyone else space for a word of reply.

Jim later told Joelle that he simply didn't know how to speak with either of his undamaged sons without their mother's presence and mediation. Orin could not be made to shut up, and Hal was so completely shut down in Jim's presence that the silences were excruciating. Jim said he suspected he and Mario were so easy with each other only because the boy had been too damaged and arrested even to speak to until he was six, so that both he and Jim had got a chance to become comfortable in mutual silence, though Mario did have an interest in lenses and film that had nothing to do with fathers or needs to please, so that the interest was something truly to share, the two of them; and even when Mario was allowed to work crew on some of Jim's later Work it was without any of the sort of pressures to interact or bond via film that there'd been with Orin and Hal and tennis, at which Jim (Orin informed her) had been a late-blooming junior but a top collegian.

Jim referred to the Work's various films as 'entertainments.' He did this ironically about half the time.

In the cab (that Jim had hailed for them), on the way back home from Legal Seafood, Orin had beaten his fine forehead against the plastic partition and wept that he couldn't seem to communicate with Himself without his mother's presence and mediation. It wasn't clear how the Moms mediated or facilitated communication between different family-members, he said. But she did. He didn't have one fucking clue how Himself felt about his abandoning a decade's tennis for punting, Orin wept. Or about Orin's being truly great at it, at something, finally. Was he proud, or jealously threatened, or judgmental that Orin had quit tennis, or what?

The 5-Woman's room's mattresses were too skinny for their frames, and the rims of the frames between the slats were appallingly clotted with dust, with female hair entwined and involved in the dust, so that it took one Kleenex just to wet the stuff down, several dry ones to wipe the muck out. Charlotte Treat had been too sick to shower for days, and her frame and slats were hard to be near.

At Joelle's first interface with the whole sad family unit — Thanksgiving, Headmaster's House, E.T.A., straight up Comm. Ave. in Enfield — Orin's Moms Mrs. Incandenza ('Please do call me Avril, Joelle') had been gracious and warm and attentive without obtruding, and worked unobtrusively hard to put everyone at ease and to facilitate communication, and to make Joelle feel like a welcomed and esteemed part of the family gathering — and something about the woman made every follicle on Joelle's body pucker and distend. It wasn't that Avril Incandenza was one of the tallest women Joelle had ever seen, and definitely the tallest pretty older woman with immaculate posture (Dr. Incandenza slumped something awful) she'd ever met. It wasn't that her syntax was so artless and fluid and imposing. Nor the near-sterile cleanliness of the home's downstairs (the bathroom's toilet seemed not only scrubbed but waxed to a high shine). And it wasn't that Avril's graciousness was in any conventional way fake. It took a long time for Joelle even to start to put a finger on what gave her the howling fantods about Orin's mother. The dinner itself — no turkey; some politico-familial in-joke about no turkey on Thanksgiving — was delicious without being grandiose. They didn't even sit down to eat until 2300h. Avril drank champagne out of a little fluted glass whose level somehow never went down. Dr. Incandenza (no invitation to call him Jim, she noticed) drank at a tri-faceted tumbler of something that made the air above it shimmer slightly. Avril put everyone at ease. Orin did credible impressions of famous figures. He and little Hal made dry fun of Avril's Canadian pronunciation of certain diphthongs. Avril and Dr. Incandenza took turns cutting up Mario's salmon. Joelle had a weird half-vision of Avril hiking her knife up hilt-first and plunging it into Joelle's breast. Hal Incandenza and two other lopsidedly muscular boys from the tennis school ate like refugees and were regarded with gentle amusement. Avril dabbed her mouth in a patrician way after every bite. Joelle wore girl-clothes, her dress's neckline very high. Hal and Orin looked vaguely alike. Avril directed every fourth comment to Joelle, to include her. Orin's brother Mario was stunted and complexly deformed. There was a spotless doggie-dish under the table, but no dog, and no mention was ever made of a dog. Joelle noticed Avril also directed every fourth comment to Orin, Hal, and Mario, like a cycle of even inclusion. There was New York white and Albertan champagne. Dr. Incandenza drank his drink instead of wine, and got up several times to freshen his drink in the kitchen. A massive hanging garden behind Avril's and Hal's captains' chairs cut complex shadows into the UV light that made the table's candles' glow a weird bright blue. The director was so tall he seemed to rise forever, when he rose with his tumbler. Joelle had the queerest indefensible feeling that Avril wished her ill; she kept feeling different areas of hair stand up. Everybody Please-and-Thank-You'd in a way that was sheer Yankee WASP. After his second trip to the kitchen, Dr. Incandenza molded his twice-baked potatoes into an intricate futuristic cityscape and suddenly started to discourse animatedly on the 1946 breakup of Hollywood's monolithic Studio system and the subsequent rise of the Method actors Brando, Dean, Clift et al., arguing for a causal connection. His voice was mid-range and mild and devoid of accent. Orin's Moms had to be over two meters tall, way taller than Joelle's own personal Daddy. Joelle could somehow tell Avril was the sort of female who'd been ungainly as a girl and then blossomed and but who'd only become really beautiful later in life, like thirty-five. She'd decided Dr. Incandenza looked like an ecologically poisoned crane, she told him later. Mrs. Incandenza put everyone at ease. Joelle imagined her with a conductor's baton. She never did tell Jim that Orin called him The Mad or Sad Stork. The whole Thanksgiving table inclined very subtly toward Avril, very slightly and subtly, like heliotropes. Joelle found herself doing it too, the inclining. Dr. Incandenza kept shading his eyes from the UV plant-light in a gesture that resembled a salute. Avril referred to her plants as her Green Babies. At some point out of nowhere, little Hal Incandenza, maybe ten, announced that the basic unit of luminous intensity is the Candela, which he defined for no one in particular as the luminous intensity of 1/600,000 of a square meter of a cavity at the freezing-temperature of platinum. All the table's males wore coats and ties. The larger of Hal's two tennis partners passed out dental stimulators, and no one made fun of him. Mario's grin seemed both obscene and sincere. Hal, whom Joelle wasn't crazy about, kept asking wasn't anybody going to ask him the freezing-temperature of platinum. Joelle and Dr. Incandenza found themselves in a small conversation about Bazin, a film-theorist Himself detested, making a tormented face at the name. Joelle intrigued the optical scientist and director by explaining Bazin's disparagement of self-conscious directorial expression as historically connected to the neo-Thomist Realism of the 'Personalistes,' an aesthetic school of great influence over French Catholic intellectuals circa 1930–1940 — many of Bazin's teachers had been eminent *Personalistes*. Avril encouraged Joelle to describe rural Kentucky. Orin did a long impression of late pop-astronomer Carl Sagan expressing televisual awe at the cosmos' scale. 'Billions and billions,' he said. One of the tennis friends burped just awfully, and no one reacted to the sound in any way. Orin said '*Billions* and *billions* and *billions*' in the voice of Sagan. Avril and Hal had a brief good-natured argument about whether the term *circa* could modify an interval or only a specific year. Then Hal asked for several examples of something called Haplology. Joelle kept fighting urges to slap the sleek little show-offy kid upside the head so hard his bow-tie would spin. 'The universe:' — Orin continued long after the wit had worn thin — 'cold, immense, incredibly universal.' The subjects of tennis, baton-twirling, and punting never came up: organized sports were never once mentioned. Joelle noticed that nobody seemed to look directly at Dr. Incandenza except her. A curious flabby white mammarial dome covered part of the Academy's grounds outside the dining room's window. Mario plunged his special fork into Dr. Incandenza's potato-cityscape, to general applause and certain grating puns on the term *deconstruction* from the insufferable Hal kid. Everyone's teeth were dazzling in the candlelight and UV. Hal wiped Mario's snout, which seemed to run continuously. Avril invited Joelle by all means to make a Thanksgiving call home to her family in rural Kentucky if she wished. Orin said the Moms was herself originally from rural Québec. Joelle was on her seventh glass of wine. Orin's fingering his half-Windsor kept looking more and more like a signal to somebody. Avril urged Dr. Incandenza to find a way to include Joelle in a production, since she was both a film student and a now a heartily welcome honorary addition to the family. Mario, reaching for the salad, fell out of his chair, and was helped up by one of the tennis players amid much hilarity. Mario's deformities seemed wide-ranging and hard to name. Joelle decided he looked like a cross between a puppet and one of the big-headed carnivores from Spielberg's old special-effects orgies about reptiles. Hal and Avril hashed out whether *misspoke* was a bona fide word. Dr. Incandenza's tall narrow head kept inclining toward his plate and then slowly rising back up in a way that was either meditative or tipsy. Deformed Mario's broad smile was so constant you could have hung things from the corners of it. In a fake Southern-belle accent that was clearly no jab at Joelle, more like a Scarlett O'Hara accent, Avril said she did declare that Albertan champagne always gave her 'the vapors.' Joelle noticed that pretty much everybody at the table was smiling, broadly and constantly, eyes shiny in the plants' odd light. She was doing it herself, too, she noticed; her cheek muscles were starting to ache. Hal's larger friend kept pausing to use his dental stimulator. Nobody else was using their dental stimulator, but everyone held one politely, as if getting ready to use it. Hal and the two friends made odd spasmic one-handed squeezing motions, periodically. No one seemed to notice. Not once in Orin's presence did anyone mention the word *tennis*. He had been up half the previous night vomiting with anxiety. Now he challenged Hal to name the freezing-point of platinum. Joelle couldn't for the life of her remember either of the names of poor old Spielberg's old computer-enhanced celluloid dinosaur things, though her own Daddy'd personally taken her to each one. At some point Orin's father got up to go freshen his drink and never returned.

Just before dessert — which was on fire — Orin's Moms had asked whether they could perhaps all join hands secularly for a moment and simply be grateful for all being together. She made a special point of asking

Joelle to include her hands in the hand-holding. Joelle held Orin's hand and Hal's smaller friend's hand, which was so callused up it felt like some sort of rind. Dessert was Cherries Jubilee with gourmet New Brunswick ice cream. Dr. Incandenza's absence from the table went unmentioned, almost unnoticed, it seemed. Both Hal and his nonstimulating friend pleaded for Kahlua, and Mario flapped pathetically at the tabletop in imitation. Avril made a show of gazing at Orin in mock-horror as he produced a cigar and clipper. There was also a blancmange. The coffee was decaf with chickory. When Joelle looked over again, Orin had put his cigar away without lighting it.

The dinner ended in a kind of explosion of goodwill.

Joelle'd felt half-crazed. She could detect nothing fake about the lady's grace and cheer toward her, the goodwill. And at the same time felt sure in her guts' pit that the woman could have sat there and cut out Joelle's pancreas and thymus and minced them and prepared sweetbreads and eaten them chilled and patted her mouth without batting an eye. And unremarked by all who leaned her way.

On the way back home, in a cab whose company's phone-number Hal had summoned from memory, Orin hung his leg over Joelle's crossed legs and said that if anybody could have been counted on to see that the Stork needed to use Joelle somehow, it was the Moms. He asked Joelle twice how she'd liked her. Joelle's cheek muscles ached something awful. When they got back to the brownstone co-op on that last pre-Subsidized Thanksgiving was the first historical time Joelle intentionally did lines of cocaine to keep from sleeping. Orin couldn't ingest anything during the season even if he wanted to: B.U.'s major-sport teams Tested randomly. So Joelle was awake at 0400, cleaning back behind the refrigerator for the second time, when Orin cried out in the nightmare she'd somehow felt should have been hers.

Shaking to the confidence of his judgment of these persons, the one Marathe had believed a desperate addict was revealed as the woman in authority for the *demi-maison* of Ennet. The clipboarded woman was a mere subaltern. Marathe very seldom misjudged persons or their roles.

The woman in authority was negative on the telephone. 'No, no. No,' she said into the telephone. 'No.'

'I am sorry,' she spoke to Marathe over the telephone's speaker without placing the hand of privacy over the speaker. 'This won't take a second. No she *can't*, Mars. Promises don't matter. She's promised before. How many times. No. Mars, because it'll end up hurting us again and just enabling her.' The other side's man's voice came loudly, and the authority stopped a sobbing with the back of her wrist, then stiffened. Marathe watched expressionlessly. He had the great fatigue, a time at which English was straining.

There were dogs upon the floor. 'I know, but no. For today, no. Next time she calls, ask her to call me here. Yes.'

She deactivated this transmission and stared at her top of the desk for a moment. Two dogs lay on the floor between her chair and Marathe's *fauteuil*, one dog of which was licking its private organs. Marathe stifled a shudder and pulled up his blanket slightly, hunching to minimalize the musculature of health of his upper torso, also.

'Good night . . . ,' Marathe began.

'Well, don't go,' the woman of authority ejaculated from coming out of her reverie of sadness, giving her seat the rotation to face him. She tried to smile in the professional manner of U.S.A. 'After you waited all that time out there. I saw you sharing with Selwyn. Selwyn tends to show up whenever we're doing group intakes.'

'Me, I think he suffers with mental illness.' Marathe noticed one leg of the woman was thinner by far of her other leg. He was being driven distracted also by this habit to pretend to sniff. The false sniffs came from nowhere.

She crossed these legs. Two autos' horns mightily blew upon the avenue far beyond the concave window of her desk.

'This Selwyn, he advised me to stroke your animals, which I have regret but I will not.'

This woman quietly laughed and leaned forward above the crossed legs. In addition, one of the dogs had flatulence. 'You listed your citizenship as Swiss.'

'I am a residing alien addicted to smack, to scag, and to H, seeking desperately the residential treatment.'

'But legally residing? With a Green Card? An O.I.N.S.[311] Residency Code?'

Marathe from his sportcoat produced the documents M. DuPlessis had arranged with foresight in the long past.

'Disabled, also. Also deformed,' Marathe said, shrugging stoically, inclining his veil at the dark carpet.

The woman was examining his O.I.N.S. documents with the pursed mouth and face for poker of O.N.A.N. authorities in all places. One of her hands was twisted in the manner of a claw. 'We all come in with issues, Henry,' she said.

'Henri. Pardon. Hen*ri*.'

Some woman just outside the door near the *demi-maison*'s front door, she laughed in the manner of an automatic weapon. Wet sounds were audible from beneath the rear leg of the dog with private organs, of which the head hid beneath the raised leg. The woman of authority had to support the body by placing the hands on the desk to rise and unlock and lift the door of a black metal cabinet over her TP and console of her desk. The door of old black metal lifted outward. Marathe committed to memory the model numbers of this teleputer, which was Indonesian and of cheap cost.

'Well Henri, Ennet House, in the years I've been on Staff here, we've had aliens, resident aliens, E.S.L.'s whose English was worse than yours by a long shot.' She stood on the thicker leg to reach into this cabinet deeply for some item. Marathe took the opportunity of her inattention to commit to his memory the office's facts. The office's door had a decoration of a triangle within a circle, and no bolt of death for locking, but merely a sadly cheap recess-lock in the knob. Nowhere the small nozzle of standard 10.525 GHz microwave alarming. The large windows had no small ends of wires about their frames. This left the possibility only of a magnet-contact alarm, which if so was difficult to jumper but also possible. Marathe felt himself missing his wife intensely, which always signalled his deep fatigue. Twice he sniffed.

The woman was speaking into the cabinet to him: '. . . get you to sign some releases for me so we can make copies of your O.I.N.S. proofs and get an Outtake faxed from your detox, which was in . . . ?'

'The Chit Chat Farms Rehabilitation of Pennsylvania State. Last month.' The A.F.R.'s data liaison in Montreal had promised to arrange all records without some delay.

'In, what, Wernersdale, something?'

Marathe cocked his veiled head ever so slightly. 'Wernersberg of Pennsylvania.'

'Well we know Chit Chat, we've had some Chit Chat graduates come through the House. Highest . . . respect.' Her head was inside the cabinet, with an arm. It appeared difficult for her to rummage inside the cabinet and keep at the same time her balance. Deciding the bay windows were the optimal office's entry if required, Marathe looked at the woman's attempt to balance and the old cabinet. Then he blinked slowly. In this cabinet visibly, in twin stacks near the front of the open cabinet, were many cartridges of TP entertainment.

The woman said 'And we've been Disabled-Accessible since the beginning. One of only a handful of Houses in the metro area that are fully equipped to take disabled clients, I assume they told you down at Chit Chat.' The wall banged with the impact of boisterousness in the outside room, and somebody either laughed or was in pain. Marathe sniffed. The woman was continuing to speak: '. . . why I got to come here in the first place. Which I came in in a chair, too, originally, by the way.' She teetered back out from the cabinet with a folder of Manila. 'At the time I declared up and down I was too disabled to kneel and pray, to give you an idea of where I was at.' She laughed gaily. She was attractive.

'Me,' Marathe responded, 'I will attempt to pray at a moment's order.' Aiding the ruse of application, he and Fortier discovered, was that U.S.A. recovery from the addictions was somewhat paramilitary in nature. There were orders and the obeying of orders. The A.F.R. had reviewed cartridges of antique U.S.A. programming, which they had found through luck in the inventory of Antitoi, and had watched to learn many things. But casting his veiled face desperately upward while saying allowed that Marathe could scan along the plastic cases of cartridges' spines. Among the small-of-font titles such as *Focal Length Parameters X-XL* and *Drop Volley Ex. II* were two cases of plain brown plastic, blank, except for — this was why his veil, it remained tilted upward for so much longer that he was concerned that this woman of authority — except for — but it was difficult of sureness, for the office's light was the deadening fluorescence of U.S.A., and the cabinet's mouth in the shadow of the lid and the cheesecloth veil made less his focus — except maybe for tiny round faces of embossed smiles upon the brown cases. Marathe felt suddenly the excitement of himself — M. Hugh Steeply's wording for this had been *from somewhere blue*.

The authority spoke also: 'Not to mention U.H.I.D. members, you might want to know.' Gesturing then at the veil of Marathe neither was mentioning. The woman attempted to affix a sheet of faint toner to a board with a clip. 'In fact we have a U.H.I.D. member in early residency right now.'

Marathe blinked twice more. He said 'I am deformed, me.'

'She might be able to help you adjust, identify. Be good for her, too.'

Marathe had begun locking down in RAM every detail of every moment since his entering the Ennet House *demi-maison*. He in another part of his brain considered whether he would report truly first to M. Fortier or to the Steeply of U.S.B.S.S., whose contact number had always the prefix of 8000, he had jested. In another part was whether to seem eager for meeting the Entertainment's performer here now, a fellow veil. To think of what a desperate addict would have eagerness in. Marathe was throughout this thinking smiling largely at the woman, forgetting she could not witness it. 'This is happy,' finally he said.

'Your facial issues —' the person stated, leaning in over the crossed legs in her chair. 'Are they connected to your use and abuse? Did they work with you on progression and Y.E.T.s[312] and owning consequences at Chit Chat?'

Marathe was in little hurry now to leave for returning to chez Antitoi. He utilized his abilities to recite complex lines of covering-story on addiction while also at the time reviewed locking down the face and locations of every person at the Ennet House he had regarded. For they would come here again, the A.F.R., and maybe Services Without Specificity of Steeply and Tine, as well. He had the ability of splitting his mind's thinking along several parallel tracks.

'The legs — I do an overdose in Berne, which is in my home of Switzerland, while alone, and I fall down face-down while my legs, they remain how you say tangle, tangled in the chair on which occurred this injection, fix. A stupid. I lie down without conscious or to move for many days, and my legs, they — *comment-on-dit?* — they are sleepy, lose the circulating, suffer gangrene, become infectious.' Marathe sniffed while stoically shrugging. 'As well the nose and mouth, from facial squishing of lying face-down in a position without conscious for days. I die almost. All is amputated, for my life. I withdraw from the scag, smack, and H, in *l'infirmière*. A result of abuse of the drugs.'

'This is your story. This is your first step.'

Marathe shrugged. 'My legs, my nose and oral. All as a consequence of the progression. At the Chit Chat, I admit all the things, I realize I am addicted desperately.' Marathe was trying to decide if to find ways to make the authority woman briefly leave the office, so that Marathe might rapidly arm-climb up to the cabinet to regard the smiling cases of cartridge closely before the cabinet's locking. Or instead also to return on pretext to remain and hang roundly in the living room for waiting persons, to find a glimpse of who is this mentioned resident with her female U.H.I.D. veil; for this is the purpose of coming to *demi-maisons* M. Fortier gave. Marathe could give the fact of the cartridges to Fortier and the veiled girl to Steeply, or oppositely. The fatigue returned. But Steeply, before committing to overt action, will wish for confirmation that those in the cabinet were items of the true Entertainment, not the blank and joking F.L.Q. displays. There was truly a faint whirring noise coming from the head, he imagined. Marathe's sidearm sat in its holster under the seat of him, hidden by the plaid-colored blanket of his lap. To easily kill the person in authority was *inutile* at this time of not glimpsing the girl, he had decided, plus impractical of surrounding witness. Marathe's *fauteuil* could travel 45 kph on a level surface over short distance. The authority figure liked to comb at the bright hair with her claw of the deformed hand. She was telling Marathe the false addict that she found his honesty encouraging and saying to sign these forms, for releasing. As Marathe signed slowly the name of a deceased Health-Benefits administrator at the *Caisse de Dépôt et Placement,*[313] the woman began to ask about what lengths he believed he was willing to go to.

The whole family was lousy with secrets, she'd decided, was part of the nonturkey dinner's sadness. From each other, themselves, itself. A big one being this pretense that overt eccentricity was the same as openness. I.e. that they were all 'exactly as crazy as they seem' — the punter's phrase.

We're all a lot more intuitive about our lovers' families than we are about our own families, she knew. Charlotte Treat's face glistened; her cheek's deep scars were a more violent red than the rest. Her ribs under the wet Michelob Dry T-shirt were starting to stand out, her neck to get that skinny stemmy look of katexia. She looked like a ravaged fowl. Kate Gompert's bed sat unmade, a copy of some yellow paperback called *Feeling Good* open face-down on the mattress and starting to curl. Joelle had this weird fear that Gompert, who made Joelle extremely nervous at the best of times, would come home and walk in and find Joelle cleaning with her hair in a kerchief and veil damply clinging. She used the last of the room's Kleenex dusting all five bedside tables, wiping in careful rings around objects she wasn't to touch.

There was then some trickiness in the situation when the *demi-maison*'s woman offered the extension of a place for Marathe. Desperately addicted Henri the Swiss could sleep upon the Convertisofa in the rear office this very P.M., she said, if he was willing to endure the mess and sometimes insects of the rear office. The woman had a ripe spot of *sympathique* for the disableds, Marathe could see. For trickiness in the situation, no lines had been pre-pared by Fortier to defer this offer of the extension of the spot of treatment in the *demi-maison*. The woman in authority smiled that she could see in his playing with the *fauteuil*'s wheels the addicted struggle between desperation and denial, she said. Marathe was rapidly calculating should he falsely ac-cept and remain here for one night to observe for himself the description of the veiled patient from U.H.I.D., against should he exit and roll like no person's business to the nearest place of private telephoning to alert the A.F.R. at the shop that here at this *demi-maison* were of possibility real cartridges of the Entertainment, perhaps including a duplicatable Master or the anti-*samizdat* remedy cartridge of F.L.Q.'s allegation, to return to chez Antitoi and return later in squeaking force to the *demi-maison* and acquire both the cartridges and the veiled performer, if the U.H.I.D. patient of treat-ment is revealed as the disguised performer. The engineer of radio had spo-ken volubly of this person's veil and screen. Or calculating also whether to telephone not Antitoi Entertainent but the 24-hour costless prefix of M./Mlle. Steeply and convey the very same information instead, finally, first, to *Bureau des Services sans Spécificité*, placing bets on O.N.A.N. and against Fortier, casting his lots finally with one side only, conveying his restenotic wife and entertainment-hungry children down from St.-Remi-d'Amherst's Convexity-ravaged wastes to live with him the rest of their lives down here among U.S.A.'s confusion of choices, demanding hidden protec-tion from Steeply and high-income medical care for the heart- and head-difficulties of beloved Gertraude.

Or to tell this figure of medical authority to look out behind for a large spider and thereupon snap her slim neck with one hand and use the tele-phone console in this office to summon Fortier and an A.F.R. elite detail directly to this *demi-maison*. Or else to summon directly Steeply and the white-suiting forces of O.N.A.N.. The authority made a spire of her fingers beneath her chin and gazed at Marathe's cocked head with a face of respect and sympathy but not solicitude, also which made snapping her neck with one hand seem a sad choice for Marathe. He pretended that it was necessary to sniff. Mssrs. Fortier and Broullîme, the A.F.R. others he had known well since the days of when they stood together tensed at the crossings of many trains, beneath the sky's moon — none of them sensed truly that Marathe has lost the belly for this type of work. That Marathe, he must fight the nausea of the stomach as he pushed the sharpened handle of the *manche à balai* broomstick through the Antitoi's insides during the technical interview of the Antitoi, and later had vomited out into the alley under secrecy. One of the Office's dogs chewed at its haunch with great ferocity, in misery. In the U.S.A. of O.N.A.N., M./Mlle. Hugh/Helen Steeply of the clandestine U.S.O.U.S./U.S.B.S.S. would hide the family of Marathe in obscure suburban locales, with papers of identity fashioned by specialists in above reproach and no suspicion; and Marathe, his familiarity with the knowledge of Québecois insurgency would be comfortably rewarded once *Notre Rai Pays* seceded to alone draw down the wrath of *chanteur-fou* Gentle's anger. The A.F.R.'s triumph of dissemination of the lethal Entertainment would ensure Marathe's valuable welcome by Gentle and his wife's beloved treatments for the ventricle and lack of skull. Marathe pictured Gertraude with a helmet and hook of gold, breathing easily through expensive tubes. The variable of calculus was how long to remain and work for dissemination against when to jump to the safety of American welcome. Fortier's wrath would be implacable at Marathe's '*perdant son coeur*,'[314] and it may be far wiser of waiting until Québec had been evicted and the A.F.R. were fully engaged to reveal his quadrupling for O.N.A.N., Marathe.

Knocking at the Office's door at the same time as entering came a young girl with missing teeth, radiating coldness from the exterior outside the *demi-maison*, leaning only her upper half of the body into the office through the doorway she had opened.

'Clocking in, boss,' the young girl stated in the flat nasality of Boston U.S.A.

The woman in authority smiled in return. 'Two more to interview, Johnette, then I'm off.'

'Pisser.'

'Can you let the people in from the shed when they come for Mrs. Lopate?'

The young and inclined girl nodded her slim head. In a nostril a generic diaper-pin was *transpercé*, which glittered in the fluorescence of the light as she nodded. 'And Janice says she's screwing out of here now and any message for her before she goes.' The authority negated with her head at this. The young girl in the door looked down upon Marathe and said 'Hey' or

'Eh' in a greeting of neutral emotions. Marathe smiled with desperation and pretended to sniff. Visible smoke's odor came through the open door from the noisy salon beyond it. Marathe decided firmly against the snapping of any necks upon this visit, because of bodies leaning with suddenness into the office unexpectedly. The torso of the person began to withdraw as suddenly the authority looked up and stated 'Oh and Johnette?'

The door swung more open once more as the returned upper half replied 'Yo.'

'Do me a favor? Clenette H. brought some donie-cartridges down from E.T.A. this afternoon?'

'Let me guess.'

'The natives are restless.' The authority laughed aloud. 'Something new.'

The torso laughed as well. 'Did you see McDade's watching that Korean thing *again* out here?'

'So can you just run them through after lights-out, as many as you can, check and make sure they're appropriate?'

'No skin, no substances, light drinking only,' the young girl said in the manner of reviewing the rehearsal of something learned.

'As many as you can get through, and leave them on Janice's desk, and I'll have her put them out at the start of the day-shift tomorrow.'

The young girl of substitute authority made a curious circle with two of her fingers in the air of the doorway. Some kind of signal of the hand to the chief authority. Every finger of the hand of the girl wore a ring of different type. 'The natives'll be grateful, for once.'

'They're in the cabinet with the intakes,' the authority told her.

'I'll watch them during Dream Duty, as many as there's time.'

'And Johnette?'

Once more the torso reextended inward.

The woman with authority said 'And keep Emil and Wade from tormenting David K., will you please?'

Marathe smiled largely as the door closed entirely and the authority made a small motion of apologies for being interrupted. 'I do not have these meanings *donie* and *natives,* if I may boldly ask,' he said. 'Nor *etier.*'

A laugh of friendliness. It occurred to Marathe that this was a happy person. 'Donies are donated goods. Which we depend on more than we'd like. The residents and alums are always on the lookout. Sometimes we call the current residents the natives; we mean it as affectionate. That was Johnette, she's living[315] staff. We've got two living staff, alums of the house. One's under the weather, but Johnette's — you'll like Johnette. Johnette's a keeper. *E.T.A.* is letters, E-T-A.'

Marathe pretended to laugh aloud. 'I beg a pardon, for I thought some *etier* in the pronunciation of my native Swiss.'

The authority smiled with understanding. 'E.T.A.'s a private school. We usually get some residents on up there, part-time. It's just up the hill.' Seeing the deep intake of veil which his inhaling caused for one moment only, the authority expressed surprise of the face and said 'But you did know Ennet's a working house. Residents have a month to find work, normally.'

Exhaling with care, Marathe gestured faintly as in But of course.

11 NOVEMBER
YEAR OF THE DEPEND ADULT UNDERGARMENT

Part of Mario's footage for the documentary they're letting him do on this fall's E.T.A. consists of Mario just walking around different parts of the Academy with the Bolex H64 camera strapped to his head and joined by co-ax cable to the foot-treadle, which he holds against his sweatered chest with one hand and operates with the other. At 2100 at night it's cold out. The Center Courts are brightly lit, but only one court is being used, Gretchen Holt and Jolene Criess still winding up some sort of marathon challenge from the P.M. session, the hands around their grips bluish and sweaty hair frozen into electrified spikes, pausing between points to blow noses on sleeves, wearing so many layers of sweats they look barrel-bodied out there, and Mario doesn't bother with the change in film-speed he'd need to record them through the steamed window of Schtitt's room, where he is. The room's noise is deafening.

Coach Schtitt's room is 106, next to his office on the first floor of Comm.-Ad., past Dr. Rusk's office and down a two-corner hall from the lobby.

It's a big empty room, built for its stereo. Hardwood floor in need of sanding, a wooden chair and a cane chair, an army cot. A little low table just big enough for Schtitt's pipe rack. A folding card table folded up and leaning against the wall. Acoustic damping-tile on all the walls and nothing decorative hanging or mounted on the walls. Acoustic tiling on the ceiling also, with a bare overhead light with a long chain mounted in a dirty ceiling fan with a short chain. The fan never rotates but sometimes emits a sound of faulty wiring. There's a faint odor of Magic Marker in the room. There is nothing upholstered, no pillow on the cot, nothing soft to absorb or deflect the sound of the equipment stacked on the floor, the black Germanness of a top-shelf sound system, a Mario-sized speaker in each corner of the room with the cloth cover removed so each woofer's cone is exposed and mightily throbbing. Schtitt's room is soundproofed. The window faces the Center Courts, the transom and observatory directly overhead and mangling the shadows of the courts' lights. The window is right over the radiator, which when the stereo is off makes odd hollow ringing clanky clunks as if someone deep underground were having at the pipes with a hammer. The cold window over the radiator is steamed and trembles slightly with Wagnerian bass.

Gerhardt Schtitt is asleep in the cane chair in the middle of the empty room, his head thrown back and arms hanging, hands treed with arteries you can see his slow pulse in. His feet are stolidly on the floor, his knees spread way out wide, the way Schtitt always has to sit, on account of his varicoceles. His mouth is partly open and a dead pipe hangs at an alarming angle from its corner. Mario records him sleeping for a little while, looking very old and white and frail, yet also obscenely fit. What's on and making the window shiver and condensed droplets gather and run in little bullet-headed lines down the glass is a duet that keeps climbing in pitch and emotion: a German second tenor and a German soprano are either very happy or very unhappy or both. Mario's ears are extremely sensitive. Schtitt sleeps only amid excruciatingly loud European opera. He's shared with Mario several different tales of grim childhood experiences at a BMW-sponsored 'Quality-Control-Orientated' Austrian Akademie to account for his REM-peculiarities. The soprano leaves the baritone and goes up to a high D and just hangs there, either shattered or ecstatic. Schtitt doesn't stir, not even when Mario falls twice, loudly, trying to get to the door with his hands over his ears.

The Community-Administration stairwells are narrow and no-nonsense. Red railings of cold iron whose red is one coat of primer. Steps and walls of raw-colored rough cement. The sort of sandy echo in there that makes you take stairs as fast as possible. The salve makes a sucking sound. The upper halls are empty. Low voices and lights from under the doors on the second floor. 2100 is still mandatory Study Period. There won't be serious movement till 2200, when the girls will drift from room to room, congregating, doing whatever packs of girls in robes and furry slippers do late at night, until deLint kills all the dormitory lights at the dorms' main breaker around 2300. Isolated movement: a door down the hall opens and shuts, the Vaught twins are heading down the hall to the bathroom at the far end, wearing only an enormous towel, one of their heads in curlers. One of the falls in Mr. Schtitt's room had been on the burnt hip, and squunched salve from the bandage is starting to darken the corduroys at that side of the pelvis, though there is zero pain. Three tense voices behind Carol Spodek and Shoshana Abram's door, lists of degrees and focal lengths, a study group for Mr. Ogilvie's 'Reflections on Refraction' exam tomorrow. A girl's voice from he can't tell which room says 'Steep hot beach sea' twice very distinctly and then is still. Mario is leaning back against a wall in the hallway, panning idly. Felicity Zweig emerges from her door by the stairwell carrying a soap-dish and wearing a towel tied at that breast-level, as if there were breasts, moving toward Mario on her way to the head. She puts her hand out straight at his head's camera, a kind of distant stiff-arm as she passes:

'I'm wearing a towel.'

'I understand,' Mario says, using his arms to turn himself around and pointing the lens at the bare wall.

'I'm wearing a *towel*.'

Brisk controlled sounds of retching from behind Diane Prins's door. Mario gets a couple seconds of Zweig hurrying away in the towel, tiny little bird steps, looking terribly fragile.

The stairwells smell like the cement they're made of.

Behind 310, Ingersoll and Penn's door, is the faint rubbery squeak of somebody moving around on crutches. Someone in 311 is yelling 'Boner check! Boner check!' A lot of the third floor is for boys under fourteen. The hall carpet up here is ectoplasmically stained, the expanses of wall between doors hung with posters of professional players endorsing gear. Someone has drawn a goatee and fangs on an old Donnay poster of Mats Wilander, and the poster of Gilbert Treffert is defaced with anti-Canadian slurs. Otis Lord's door has *Infirmary* next to his name on the door's name-card. Penn's room's door's card's name also had *Infirmary*. Sounds of someone talking low to someone who's sobbing from Beak, Whale, and Virgilio's room, and Mario resists an impulse to knock. LaMont Chu's door next door is completely covered with magazines' action-shots of matches. Mario is leaning back to get footage of the door when LaMont Chu exits the bathroom at this end in a terry robe and thongs and wet hair, literally whistling 'Dixie.'

'Mario!'

Mario gets him bearing down, his calves hairless and muscular, hair-water dripping onto his robe's shoulders with each step. 'LaMont Chu!'

'What's happening?'

'Nothing's happening!'

Chu stands there just within conversation-range. He's only slightly taller than Mario. A door down the hall opens and a head sticks out and scans and then withdraws.

'Well.' Chu squares his shoulders and looks into the camera atop Mario's head. 'You want me to say something for posterity?'

'Sure!'

'What should I say?'

'You can say anything you want!'

Chu draws himself way up and looks penetrating. Mario checks the meter on his belt and uses the treadle to shorten the focal length and adjust the angle of the camera's lens slightly downward, right at Chu, and there are tiny grinding adjustment-sounds from the Bolex.

Chu's still just standing there. 'I can't think what to say.'

'That happens to me all the time.'

'The minute your invitation became official my mind went blank.'

'That can happen.'

'There's just this staticky blank field in there now.'

'I know just what you mean.'

They stand there silent, the camera's mechanism emitting a tiny whir.

Mario says 'You just got out of the shower, I can tell.'

'I was talking with good old Lyle downstairs.'

'Lyle's terrific!'

'I was going to just whip right over into the showers, but the locker room's got this, like, odor.'

'It's always great to talk with good old Lyle.'

'So I came up here.'

'Everything you're saying is very good.'

LaMont Chu stands there a moment looking at Mario, who's smiling and Chu can tell wants to nod furiously, but can't, because he needs to keep the Bolex steady. 'What I was doing, I was filling Lyle in on the Eschaton debacle, telling him about the lack of hard info, the conflicted rumors that are going around, about how Kittenplan and some of the Big Buds are going to get blamed. About disciplinary action for the Buds.'

'Lyle's just an outstanding person to go to with concerns,' Mario says, fighting not to nod furiously.

'Lord's head and Penn's leg, the Postman's broken nose. What's going to happen to the Incster?'

'You're acting perfectly natural. This is very good.'

'I'm asking if you've heard from Hal what they're going to do, if he's in on the blame from Tavis. Pemulis and Kittenplan I can see, but I'm having trouble with the idea of Struck or your brother taking discipline for what happened out there. They were strictly from spectation for the whole thing. Kittenplan's Bud is Spodek, and she wasn't even out there.'

'I'm getting all this, you'll be glad to know.'

Chu is now looking at Mario, which for Mario is weird because he's looking through the viewfinder, a lens-eye view, which means when Chu looks down from the lens to look at Mario it looks to Mario like he's looking down south somewhere along Mario's thorax.

'Mario, I'm asking if Hal's told you what they're going to do to anybody.'

'Is this what you're saying, or are you asking me?'

'Asking.'

Chu's face looks slightly oval and convex through the lens's fish-eye, a jutting aspect. 'So what if I want to use this that you're saying for the documentary I've been asked to make?'

'Jesus, Mario, use whatever you want. I'm just saying I have conscience-trouble with the idea of Hal and Troeltsch. And Struck didn't even seem like he was conscious for the debacle itself.'

'I should tell you I feel like we're getting the totally real LaMont Chu here.'

'Mario, camera to one side, I'm standing here dripping asking you for Hal's impressions of when Tavis called them in, as in did he give you impressions. Van Vleck at lunch said he yesterday saw Pemulis and Hal coming out of Tavis's office with the Association urine-guy holding them both by the ear. Van Vleck said Hal's face was the color of Kaopectate.'

Mario directs the lens at Chu's shower-thongs so he can look over the viewfinder at Chu. 'Are you saying this, or is this what happened?'

'That's what I'm asking *you*, Mario, if Hal told you what happened.'

'I follow what you're saying.'

'So you asked whether I was asking, and I'm asking you about it.'

Mario zooms in very tight: Chu's complexion is a kind of creamy green, with not one follicle in view. 'LaMont, I'm going to find you and tell you whatever Hal tells me, this is so good.'

'So then you haven't talked to Hal?'

'When?'

'Jesus, Mario, it's like trying to talk to a rock with you sometimes.'

'This is going very well!'

Someone gargling. Guglielmo Redondo's voice going through the rosary, it sounds like, just inside his and Esteban Reynes's door. The Clipperton Suite in East House had had a bright-yellow strip of B.P.D. plastic for over a month, he remembers. The Boys Room door a different kind of wood than the room doors. The Clipperton Suite had a glued picture of Ross Reat pretending to kiss Clipperton's ring at the net. The roar of a toilet and a stall door's squeak. The Academy's plumbing is high-pressure. It takes Mario longer to walk down a set of stairs than to walk up. Red primer stains his hand, he has to hold the railing so tight.

The special hush of lobby carpet, and smells of Benson & Hedges brand cigarettes in the reception area off the lobby. The little hall doors that are always closed and never locked. The rubber sheaths on the knobs. Benson & Hedges cost $5.60 O.N.A.N. a pack at Father & Son grocery down the hill. Lateral Alice Moore's desk's plaque's DANGER: THIRD RAIL light is unilluminated, and her word-processing setup wears its cover of frosted plastic. The blue chairs have the faint imprints of people's bottoms. The waiting room is empty and dim. Some light from the lit courts outside. From under double doors is lamplight, much attenuated by double doors, from the Headmaster's office, which Mario doesn't explore; Tavis is unnerved into such gregarity around Mario it's awkward for all parties.[316] If you asked Mario whether he got on with his Uncle C.T. he'd say: Sure. The Bolex's light-meter is in the No Way range. Most of the waiting area's available light comes from the doorless Dean of Females's office. Meaning the Moms is: In.

Heavy shag carpet is especially treacherous for Mario when he's top-heavy with equipment. Avril Incandenza, a fiend for light, has the whole bank of overheads going, two torchères and some desk lamps, and a B&H cigarette on fire in the big clay ashtray Mario'd made her at Rindge and Latin School. She is swivelled around in her swivel-chair, facing out the big window behind her desk, listening to someone on the phone, holding the transmitter violin-style under her chin and holding up a stapler, checking its load. Her desk has what looks like a skyline of stacks of file folders and books in neat cross-hatched stacks; nothing teeters. The open book on top facing Mario is Dowty, Wall and Peters's seminal *Introduction to Montague Semantics,*[317] which has very fascinating illustrations that Mario doesn't look at this time, trying to film the cock of the Moms's head and the phone's extended antenna against the cumulus of her hair from behind, capturing her back unawares.

But the sound of Mario entering even a shag-carpeted room is unmistakable, plus she can see his reflection in the window.

'Mario!' Her arms go up in a V, stapler open in one hand, facing the window.

'The Moms!' It's a good ten meters past the seminar table and viewer and portable blackboard to the far part of the office where the desk is, and each step on the deep shag is precarious, Mario resembling a very old brittle-boned man or someone carrying a load of breakables down a slick hill.

'Hello!' She's addressing his reflection in the quartered window, watching him put the treadle down carefully on the desk and struggle with the pack on his back. 'Not you,' she tells the phone. She points the stapler at the image of the Bolex on the image of his head. 'Are we On-Air?'

Mario laughs. 'Would you like to be?'

She tells the phone she's still here, that Mario's come in.

'I don't want to intercept your call.'

'Don't be absurd.' She talks past the phone at the window. She rotates her swivel-chair to face Mario, the receiver's antenna describing a half moon and now pointing up at the window behind her. There are two blue chairs like the reception-area chairs in front of her desk; she doesn't indicate to Mario to sit. Mario's most comfortable standing and leaning into the support of the police lock he's trying to detach from his canvas plastron and lower, shucking the pack off his back at the same time. Avril looks at him like the sort of stellar mother where just looking at her kid gives her joy. She doesn't offer to help him get the lock's lead brace out of the pack because she knows he'd feel completely comfortable asking for her help if he needed it. It's like she feels these two sons are the people in her life with whom so little important needs to be said that she loves it. The Bolex and support-yoke and viewfinder over his forehead and eyes give Mario an underwater look. His movements, setting and bracing his police lock, are at once grace-less and deft. The lit Center Courts, now empty, are visible out the left side of Avril's window, if you lean far forward and look. Someone has forgotten a gear bag and pile of sticks out by the net-post of Court 17.

Silences between them are totally comfortable. Mario can't tell if the person on the phone is still talking or if Avril just hasn't put the dead phone down. She still holds the black stapler. Its jaws are open and it looks alligatorish in her hand.

'Is this you passing through the neighborhood poking a head in to say hello? Or am I a subject, tonight?'

'You can be a subject, Moms.' He moves the big head around in a weary circle. 'I get tired from wearing this.'

'It gets heavy. I've held it.'

'It's good.'

'I remember his making that. He took such care making that. It's the last time I believe he enjoyed himself on something, thoroughly.'

'It's terrific!'

'He took weeks putting everything together.'

He likes to look at her, too, leaning in and letting her know he likes looking. They are the two least embarrassable people either of them knows. She's rarely here this late; she has a big study at the HmH. The only thing that ever shows she's tired is that her hair gets a sort of huge white cowlick, like a rolling ocean comber of hair, and just on one side, the side with the phone, sticking up and touching the antenna. Her hair has been pure white since Mario can first remember seeing her looking down at him through the incubator's glass. Pictures of her own father's hair were like that. It goes down the middle of her back against the chair and down both arms, hanging off the arms near the elbow. Its part shows her pink scalp. She keeps the hair very clean and well-combed. She has one of Mr. deLint's big whistles around her neck. The big cowlick casts a bent shadow on the sill of the window. There's a maple-leaf flag and a 50-star U.S.A. flag hanging limp off brass poles on either side of the window; in an extreme corner are fleur-de-lis pennons on tall sharp polished sticks. C.T.'s office has an O.N.A.N. flag and a 49-star U.S.A. flag.[318]

'I had quality interface dialogue with LaMont Chu upstairs. But I made the girl Felicity, the really thin one — she got upset. She said only a towel.'

'Felicity will be just fine. So you're just strolling. Peripatetic footage.' She refuses to adjust syntax, to speak in any way down to him, it'd be beneath him, though he seems not to mind when most people do it, speak down.

Nor will she ask about the burn on his pelvis unless he brings it up. She's careful to keep her oar out of Mario's health stuff unless he brings things up, out of concern that it might be taken as intrusive or smothering.

'I saw your lights. Why is the Moms here, still, I thought to myself.'

She made as if to clutch her head. 'Don't ask. I'll starting whingeing. Tomorrow's going to be hellishly busy.' Mario didn't hear her say goodbye to the man as she put down the phone so the antenna now points at Mario's chest. She's putting out the nub of the Benson & Hedge against the rooster-comb holder he'd squeezed and karate-chopped and put down the bowl's center, when he made it, after she'd said she wanted it to be an ashtray. 'You give me such pleasure standing there, all outfitted for work,' she said. '*Aprowl*.' She ground individual sparks out in the bowl. She had the idea that her smoking around Mario made him worry, though he'd never said anything about it one way or the other. 'I have a breakfast engagement at 07, which means I have to do final swotting and whacking for morning classes now, so I just lurched back over here to do it instead of carrying everything back and forth.'

'Are you tired?'

She just smiled at him.

'This is off.' Pointing at his head. 'I turned it off.'

To look at them, you'd never guess these two persons were related, one sitting and one standing canted forward.

'Will you eat with us? I hadn't even thought of dinner until I saw you. I don't even know what there might be for dinner. Many Wonders.[319] Turkey cartilage. Your bag is by the radio. Will you stay again? Charles is still in conference, I believe, he said.'

'About the debracle with the Eschaton and the Postman's nose?'

'A person from a magazine has come to do a piece of reportage on your brother. Charles is speaking to her in lieu of any of the students. You may speak to her about Orin if you like.'

'She's been *aprowl* for Hal, Ortho said.'

Avril has a certain way of cocking her fine head at him.

'Your poor Uncle Charles has been with Thierry and this magazine person since this afternoon.'

'Have you talked to him?'

'I've been trying to buttonhole your brother. He's not in your room. The Pemulis person was seen by Mary Esther taking their truck before Study Period. Is Hal with him, Mario?'

'I haven't seen Hal since lunchtime. He said he'd had a tooth thing.'

'I didn't even find out he'd been to see Zeggarelli until today.'

'He asked about how the burn on my pelvis is.'

'Which I won't ask about unless you'd care to discuss how it's coming along.'

'It's fine. Plus Hal said he wishes I'd come back and sleep there.'

'I left two messages asking him to let me know how the tooth was. Love-o, I feel bad I wasn't there for him. Hal and his teeth.'

'Did C.T. tell what happened? Was he upset? Was that C.T. on the phone you were with?' Mario can't see why the Moms would call C.T. on the phone when he was in there right across the hall behind his doors. When she didn't smoke a lot of the time she held a pen in her mouth; Mario didn't know why. Her college mug has about a hundred blue pens in it, on the desk. She likes to square herself in her chair, sitting up extra straight and grasping the chair's arms in a commanding posture. She looks like something Mario can't place when she does this. He keeps thinking the word *typhoon*. He knows she's not trying to consciously be commanding with him.

'How was your own day, I want to hear.'

'Hey Moms?'

'I determined years ago that my position needs to be that I trust my children, and I'd never traffic in third-party hearsay when the lines of communication with my children are as open and judgment-free as I'm fortunate they are.'

'That seems like a really good position. Hey Moms?'

'So I have no problem waiting to hear about Eschaton, teeth, and urine from your brother, who'll come to me the moment it's appropriate for him to come to me.'

'Hey Moms?'

'I'm right here, Love-o.'

Tycoon is the term her commanding way of sitting suggests, grasping her chair, a pen clamped in her teeth like a businessman's cigar. There were other carpet-prints in the heavy shag.

'Moms?'

'Yes.'

'Can I ask you a thing?'

'Please do.'

'This is off,' again indicating the silent apparatus on his head.

'Is this a confidential thing, then?'

'There isn't any secret. My day was I was wondering about something. In my mind.'

'I'm right here for you anytime day or night, Mario, as you are for me, as I am for Hal and we all are for each other.' She gestures in a hard-to-describe way. 'Right here.'

'Moms?'

'I am right here with my attention completely focused on you.'

'How can you tell if somebody's sad?'

A quick smile. 'You mean whether someone's sad.'

A smile back, but still earnest: 'That improves it a lot. *Whether* someone's sad, how can you tell so you're sure?'

Her teeth are not discolored; she gets them cleaned at the dentist all the time for the smoking, a habit she despises. Hal inherited the dental problems from Himself; Himself had horrible dental problems; half his teeth were bridges.

'You're not exactly insensitive when it comes to people, Love-o,' she says.

'What if you, like, only *suspect* somebody's sad. How do you reinforce the suspicion?'

'Confirm the suspicion?'

'In your mind.' Some of the prints in the deep shag he can see are shoes, and some are different, almost like knuckles. His lordotic posture makes him acute and observant about things like carpet-prints.

'How would I, for my part, confirm a suspicion of sadness in someone, you mean?'

'Yes. Good. All right.'

'Well, the person in question may cry, sob, weep, or, in certain cultures, wail, keen, or rend his or her garments.'

Mario nods encouragingly, so the headgear clanks a little. 'But say in a case where they don't weep or rend. But you still have a suspicion which they're sad.'

She uses a hand to rotate the pen in her mouth like a fine cigar. 'He or she might alternatively sigh, mope, frown, smile halfheartedly, appear downcast, slump, look at the floor more than is appropriate.'

'But what if they don't?'

'Well, he or she may act out by seeming distracted, losing enthusiasm for previous interests. The person may present with what appears to be laziness, lethargy, fatigue, sluggishness, a certain passive reluctance to engage you. Torpor.'

'What else?'

'They may seem unusually subdued, quiet, literally "low." '

Mario leans all his weight into his police lock, which makes his head jut, his expression the sort of mangled one that expresses puzzlement, an attempt to reason out something hard. Pemulis called it Mario's Data-Search Face, which Mario liked.

'What if sometime they might act even less low than normal. But still these suspicions are in your mind.'

She's about the same height sitting as Mario upright and leaning forward. Now neither of them is quite looking at the other, both just a couple degrees off. Avril taps the pen against her front teeth. Her phone light is blinking, but there's no ringing. The thing's handset's antenna still points at Mario. Her hands are not her age. She hoists the executive chair back slightly to cross her legs.

'Would you feel comfortable telling me whether we're discussing a particular person?'

'Hey Moms?'

'Is there someone specific in whom you're intuiting sadness?'

'Moms?'

'Is this about Hal? Is Hal sad and for some reason not yet able to speak about it?'

'I'm just saying how to be generally sure.'

'And you have no idea where he is or whether he left the grounds this evening sad?'

Lunch today was the exact same as lunch yesterday: pasta with tuna and garlic, and thick wheaty bread, and required salad, and milk or juice, and pears in juice in a dish. Mrs. Clark had taken a Sick Morning off because when she came in this morning Pemulis at lunch said one of the breakfast girls had said there'd been brooms on the wall in an X of brooms, out of nowhere, on the wall, when she'd come in very early to fire up the Wheatina-cauldron, and nobody knowing how the brooms were there or why or who glued them on had upset Mrs. Clarke's nerves, who'd been with the Incandenzas since long before E.T.A., and had nerves.

'I didn't see Hal since lunchtime. He had an apple he cut into chunks and put peanut butter on, instead of pears in juice.'

Avril nods with vigor.

'LaMont didn't know either. Mr. Schtitt is asleep in his chair in his room. Hey Moms?'

Avril Incandenza can switch a Bic from one side of her mouth to the other without using her hand; she never knows she's doing it when she's doing it. 'Whether or not we're discussing anyone in particular, then.'

Mario smiles at her.

'Hypothetically, then, you may be picking up in someone a certain very strange type of sadness that appears as a kind of disassociation from itself, maybe, Love-o.'

'I don't know *disassociation*.'

'Well, love, but you know the idiom "not yourself" — "He's not himself today," for example,' crooking and uncrooking fingers to form quotes on either side of what she says, which Mario adores. 'There are, apparently, persons who are deeply afraid of their own emotions, particularly the painful ones. Grief, regret, sadness. Sadness especially, perhaps. Dolores describes these persons as afraid of obliteration, emotional engulfment. As if something truly and thoroughly felt would have no end or bottom. Would become infinite and engulf them.'

'*Engulf* means *obliterate*.'

'I am saying that such persons usually have a very fragile sense of themselves as persons. As existing at all. This interpretation is "existential," Mario, which means vague and slightly flaky. But I think it may hold true in certain cases. My own father told stories of his own father, whose potato farm had been in St. Pamphile and very much larger than my father's. My grandfather had had a marvelous harvest one season, and he wanted to invest money. This was in the early 1920s, when there was a great deal of money to be made on upstart companies and new American products. He apparently narrowed the field to two choices — Delaware-brand Punch, or an obscure sweet fizzy coffee substitute that sold out of pharmacy soda fountains and was rumored to contain smidgeons of cocaine, which was the subject of much controversy in those days. My father's father chose Delaware Punch, which apparently tasted like rancid cranberry juice, and the manufacturer of which folded. And then his next two potato harvests were decimated by blight, resulting in the forced sale of his farm. Coca-Cola is now Coca-Cola. My father said his father showed very little emotion or anger or sadness about this, though. That he somehow couldn't. My father said his father was frozen, and could feel emotion only when he was drunk. He would apparently get drunk four times a year, weep about his life, throw my father through the living room window, and disappear for several days, roaming the countryside of L'Islet Province, drunk and enraged.'

She's not been looking at Mario this whole time, though Mario's been looking at her.

She smiled. 'My father, of course, could himself tell this story only when *he* was drunk. He never threw anyone through any windows. He simply sat in his chair, drinking ale and reading the newspaper, for hours, until he fell out of the chair. And then one day he fell out of the chair and didn't get up again, and that was how your maternal grandfather passed away. I'd never have gotten to go to University had he not died when I was a girl. He believed education was a waste for girls. It was a function of his era; it wasn't his fault. His inheritance to Charles and me paid for university.'

She's been smiling pleasantly this whole time, emptying the butt from the ashtray into the wastebasket, wiping the bowl's inside with a Kleenex, straightening straight piles of folders on her desk. A couple odd long crinkly paper strips of bright red hung over the side of the wastebasket, which was normally totally empty and clean.

Avril Incandenza is the sort of tall beautiful woman who wasn't ever quite world-class, shiny-magazine-class beautiful, but who early on hit a certain pretty high point on the beauty scale and has stayed right at that point as she ages and lots of other beautiful women age too and get less beautiful. She's 56 years old, and Mario gets pleasure out of just getting to look at her face, still. She doesn't think she's pretty, he knows. Orin and Hal both have parts of her prettiness in different ways. Mario likes to look at Hal and at their mother and try to see just what slendering and spacing of different features makes a woman's face different from a man's, in attractive people. A male face versus a face you can just tell is female. Avril thinks she's much too tall to be pretty. She'd seemed much less tall when compared to Himself, who was seriously tall. Mario wears small special shoes, almost perfectly square, with weights at the heel and Velcro straps instead of laces, and a pair of the corduroys Orin Incandenza had worn in elementary school, which Mario still favors and wears instead of brand-new pants he's given, and a warm crewneck sweater that's striped like a flea.

'My point here is that certain types of persons are terrified even to poke a big toe into genuinely felt regret or sadness, or to get angry. This means they are afraid to live. They are imprisoned in something, I think. Frozen inside, emotionally. Why is this. No one knows, Love-o. It's sometimes called "suppression," ' with the fingers out to the sides again. 'Dolores believes it derives from childhood trauma, but I suspect not always. There may be some persons who are born imprisoned. The irony, of course, being that the very imprisonment that prohibits sadness's expression must itself feel intensely sad and painful. For the hypothetical person in question. There may be sad people right here at the Academy who are like this, Mario, and perhaps you're sensitive to it. You are not exactly insensitive when it comes to people.'

Mario scratches his lip again.

She says 'What I'll do' — leaning forward to write something on a Post-It note with a different pen than the one she has in her mouth — 'is to write down for you the terms *disassociation, engulfment,* and *suppression,* which I'll put next to another word, *repression,* with an underlined unequal sign between them, because they denote entirely different things and should not be regarded as synonyms.'

Mario shifts slightly forward. 'Sometimes I get afraid when you forget you have to talk more simply to me.'

'Well then I'm both sorry for that and grateful that you can tell me about it. I do forget things. Particularly when I'm tired. I forget and just get going.' Lining the edges up and folding the little sticky note in half and then half again and dropping it into the wastebasket without having to look for where the wastebasket is. Her chair is a fine executive leather swivelling chair but it shrieks a little when she leans back or forward. Mario can tell she's making herself not look at her watch, which is all right.

'Hey Moms?'

'People, then, who are sad, but who can't let themselves feel sad, or express it, the sadness, I'm trying rather clunkily to say, these persons may strike someone who's sensitive as somehow just not quite right. Not quite there. Blank. Distant. Muted. Distant. *Spacey* was an American term we grew up with. Wooden. Deadened. Disconnected. Distant. Or they may drink alcohol or take other drugs. The drugs both blunt the real sadness and allow some skewed version of the sadness some sort of expression, like throwing someone through a living room window out into the flowerbeds she'd so very carefully repaired after the last incident.'

'Moms, I think I get it.'

'Is that better, then, instead of my maundering on and on?'

She's risen to pour herself coffee from the last black bit in the glass pot. So her back is almost to him as she stands there at the little sideboard. An old folded pair of U.S.A. football pants and a helmet are on top of one of the file cabinets by the flag. Her one memento of Orin, who won't talk to them or contact them in any way. She has an old mug with a cartoon of someone in a dress small and perspectivally distant in a knee-high field of wheat or rye, that says TO A WOMAN OUTSTANDING IN HER

FIELD. A blue blazer with an O.N.A.N.T.A. insignia is hung very neatly and straight on a wooden hanger from the metal tree of the coatrack in the corner. She's always had her coffee out of the *OUTSTANDING FIELD* mug, even in Weston. The Moms hangs up stuff like shirts and blazers neater and more wrinkle-free than anyone alive. The mug has a hair-thin brown crack down one side, but it's not dirty or stained, and she never gets lipstick on the rim the way other ladies over fifty years old pinken cups' rims.

Mario was involuntarily incontinent up to his early teens. His father and later Hal had changed him for years, never once judging or wrinkling their face or acting upset or sad.

'But except hey Moms?'

'I'm still right here.'

Avril couldn't change diapers. She'd come to him in tears, he'd been seven, and explained, and apologized. She just couldn't handle diapers. She just couldn't deal with them. She'd sobbed and asked him to forgive her and to assure her that he understood it didn't mean she didn't love him to death or find him repellent.

'Can you be sensitive to something sad even though the person isn't not himself?'

She especially likes to hold the coffee's mug in both hands. 'Pardon me?'

'You explained it very well. It helped a lot. Except what if it's that they're almost like even *more* themselves than normal? Than they were before? If it's not that he's blank or dead. If he's himself even more than before a sad thing happened. What if that happens and you still think he's sad, inside, somewhere?'

One thing that's happened as she got over fifty is she gets a little red sideways line in the skin between her eyes when she doesn't follow you. Ms. Poutrincourt gets the same little line, and she's twenty-eight. 'I don't follow you. How can someone be too much himself?'

'I think I wanted to ask you that.'

'Are we discussing your Uncle Charles?'

'Hey Moms?'

She pretends to knock her forehead at being obtuse. 'Mario Love-o, are *you* sad? Are you trying to determine whether I've been sensing that you *yourself* are sad?'

Mario's gaze keeps going from Avril to the window behind her. He can activate the Bolex's foot-treadle with his hands, if necessary. The Center Courts' towering lights cast an odd pall up and out into the night. The sky has a wind in it, and dark thin high clouds whose movement's pattern has a kind of writhing weave. All this is visible out past the faint reflections of the lit room, and up, the tennis lights' odd small lumes like criss-crossing spots.

'Though of course the sun would leave my sky if I couldn't assume you'd

768

simply come and tell me you were sad. There would be no need for intuition about it.'

And plus then to the east, past all the courts, you can see some lights in houses in the Enfield Marine Complex below, and beyond that Commonwealth's cars' headers and store lights and the robed lit lady's downcast-looking statue atop St. Elizabeth's Hospital. Out the right to the north over lots of different lights is the red rotating tip of the WYYY transmitter, its spin's ring of red reflected in the visible Charles River, the Charles tumid with rain and snowmelt, illumined in patches by headlights on Memorial and the Storrow 500, the river unwinding, swollen and humped, its top a mosaic of oil rainbows and dead branches, gulls asleep or brooding, bobbing, head under wing.

The dark had a distanceless shape. The room's ceiling might as well have been clouds.

'Skkkkk.'

'Booboo?'

'Skk-kkk.'

'Mario.'

'Hal!'

'Were you asleep there, Boo?'

'I don't think I was.'

'Cause I don't want to wake you up if you were.'

'Is it dark or is it me?'

'The sun won't be up for a while, I don't think.'

'So it's dark then.'

'Booboo, I just had a wicked awful dream.'

'You were saying "Thank you Sir may I have another" several times.'

'Sorry Boo.'

'Numerous times.'

'Sorry.'

'I think I slept right through it.'

'Jesus, you can hear Schacht snoring all the way across. You can feel the snores' vibrations in your midsection.'

'I slept right through it. I didn't hear you even come in.'

'Quite a nice surprise to come in and see the good old many-pillowed Mario-shape in his rack again.'

'. . .'

'I hope you didn't move the bag back here just because it sounded like I might have been asking you. To.'

'I found somebody with tapes of old Psychosis, for until the return. I need you to show me how to ask somebody I don't know to borrow tapes, if we're both devoted.'

'. . .'

'Hey Hal?'

'Booboo, I dreamed I was losing my teeth. I dreamed that my teeth dry-rotted somehow into shale and splintered when I ate or spoke, and I was jettisoning fragments all over the place, and there was a long scene where I was pricing dentures.'

'All night last night people were coming up going where is Hal, have you seen Hal, what happened with CT and the urine doctor and Hal's urine. Moms asked me where's Hal, and I was surprised at that because of how she makes it a big point never to check up.'

'Then, without any sort of dream-segue, I'm sitting in a cold room, naked as a jaybird, in a flame-retardant chair, and I keep receiving bills in the mail for teeth. A mail carrier keeps knocking on the door and coming in without being invited and presenting me with various bills for teeth.'

'She wants you to know she trusts you at all times and you're too trust-worthy to worry about or check up on.'

'Only not for any teeth of mine, Boo. The bills are for somebody *else's* teeth, not my teeth, and I can't seem to get the mail carrier to acknowledge this, that they're not for my teeth.'

'I promised LaMont Chu I'd tell him whatever information you told me, he was so concerned.'

'The bills are in little envelopes with plasticized windows that show the addressee part of the bills. I put them in my lap until the stack gets so big they start to slip off the top and fall to the floor.'

'LaMont and me had a whole dialogue about his concerns. I like LaMont a lot.'

'Booboo, do you happen to remember S. Johnson?'

'S. Johnson used to be the Moms's dog. That passed away.'

'And you remember how he died, then.'

'Hey Hal, you remember a period in time back in Weston when we were little that the Moms wouldn't go anywhere without S. Johnson? She took him with her to work, and had that unique car seat for him when she had the Volvo, before Himself had the accident in the Volvo. The seat was from the Fisher-Price Company. We went to Himself's opening of *Kinds of Light* at the Hayden[320] that wouldn't let in cigarettes or dogs and the Moms brought S. Johnson in a blind dog's harness-collar that went all the way around his chest with the square bar on the leash thing and the Moms wore those sunglasses and looked up and to the right the whole time so it looked like she was legally blind so they'd let S.J. into the Hayden with us, because he had to be there. And how Himself just thought it was a good one on the Hayden, he said.'

'I keep thinking about Orin and how he stood there and lied to her about S. Johnson's map getting eliminated.'

'She was sad.'

'I've been thinking compulsively about Orin ever since C.T. called us all in. When you think about Orin what do you think, Boo?'

'The best was remember when she had to fly and wouldn't put him in a cagey box and they wouldn't even let a blind dog on the plane, so she'd leave S. Johnson and leave him out tied to the Volvo and she'd make Orin put a phone out there with its antenna up during the day out by where S. Johnson was tied to the Volvo and she'd call on the phone and let it ring next to S. Johnson because she said how S. Johnson knew her unique personal ring on the phone and would hear the ring and know that he was thought about and cared about from afar, she said?'

'She was unbent where that dog was concerned, I remember. She bought some kind of esoteric food for it. Remember how often she bathed it?

'. . .'

'What was it with her and that dog, Boo?'

'And the day we were out rolling balls in the driveway and Orin and Marlon were there and S. Johnson was there lying there on the driveway tied to the bumper with the phone right there and it rang and rang and Orin picked it up and barked into it like a dog and hung it up and turned it off?'

'. . .'

'So she'd think it was S. Johnson? The joke that Orin thought was such a good one?'

'Jesus, Boo, I don't remember any of that.'

'And he said we'd get Indian Rub-Burns down both arms if we didn't pretend how we didn't know what she was talking about if and when she asked us about the bark on the phone when she got home?

'The Indian Rub-Burns I remember far too well.'

'We were supposed to shrug and look at her like she was minus cards from her deck, or else?'

'Orin lied with a really pathological intensity, growing up, is what I've been remembering.'

'He made us laugh really hard a lot of times, though. I miss him.'

'I don't know whether I miss him or not.'

'I miss Family Trivia. Do you remember four times he let us sit in on when they played Family Trivia?'

'You've got a phenomenal memory for this stuff, Boo.'

'. . .'

'You probably think I'm wondering why you don't ask me about the thing with C.T. and Pemulis and the impromptu urine, after the Eschaton debacle, where the urologist took us right down to the administrative loo and was going to watch personally while we filled his cups, like watch it go in, the urine, to make sure it came from us personally.'

'I think I especially have a phenomenal memory for things I remember that I liked.'

'You can ask, if you like.'

'Hey Hal?'

'The key datum is that the O.N.A.N.T.A. guy didn't actually extract urine samples from us. We got to hold on to our urine, as the Moms no doubt knows quite well, don't kid yourself, from C.T.'

'I have a phenomenal memory for things that make me *laugh* is what I think it is.'

'That Pemulis, without self-abasement or concession of anything compromising, got the guy to give us thirty days — the Fundraiser, the WhataBurger, Thanksgiving Break, then Pemulis, Axford and I pee like racehorses into whatever-sized receptacles he wants, is the arrangement we made.'

'I can hear Schacht, you're right. Also the fans.'

'Boo?'

'I like the fans' sound at night. Do you? It's like somebody big far away goes like: it'sOKit'sOKit'sOKit'sOK, over and over. From very far away.'

'Pemulis — the alleged weak-stomached clutch-artist — Pemulis showed some serious brass under pressure, standing there over that urinal. He played the O.N.A.N.T.A. man like a fine instrument. I found myself feeling almost proud for him.'

'. . .'

'You might think I'm wondering why you aren't asking me why thirty days, why it was so important to extract thirty days from the blue-blazered guy before a G.C./M.S. scan. As in what is there to be afraid of, you might ask.'

'Hal, pretty much all I do is love you and be glad I have an excellent brother in every way, Hal.'

'Jesus, it's just like talking to the Moms with you sometimes, Boo.'

'Hey Hal?'

'Except with you I can feel you mean it.'

'You're up on your elbow. You're on your side, facing my way. I can see your shadow.'

'How does somebody with your kind of Panglossian constitution determine whether you're ever being lied to, I sometimes wonder, Booboo. Like what criteria brought to bear. Intuition, induction, reductio, what?'

'You always get hard to understand when you're up on your side on your elbow like this.'

'Maybe it just doesn't occur to you. Even the possibility. Maybe it's never once struck you that something's being fabricated, misrepresented, skewed. Hidden.'

'Hey Hal?'

'And maybe that's the key. Maybe then whatever's said to you is so completely believed by you that, what, it becomes sort of true in transit. Flies through the air toward you and reverses its spin and hits you true, however mendaciously it comes off the other person's stick.'

'. . .'

'You know, for me, Boo, people seem to lie in different but definite ways, I've found. Maybe I can't change the spin the way you can, and this is all I've been able to do, is assemble a kind of field guide to the different kinds of ways.'

'. . .'

'Some people, from what I've seen, Boo, when they lie, they become very still and centered and their gaze very concentrated and intense. They try to dominate the person they lie to. The person to whom they're lying. Another type becomes fluttery and insubstantial and punctuates his lie with little self-deprecating motions and sounds, as if credulity were the same as pity. Some bury the lie in so many digressions and asides that they like try to slip the lie in there through all the extraneous data like a tiny bug through a windowscreen.'

'Except Orin used to end up telling the truth even when he didn't think he was.'

'Would that that were a trait family-wide, Boo.'

'Maybe if we call him he'll come to the WhataBurger. You can see him if you want to if you ask, maybe.'

'Then there are what I might call your Kamikaze-style liars. These'll tell you a surreal and fundamentally incredible lie, and then pretend a crisis of conscience and retract the original lie, and then offer you the lie they really want you to buy instead, so the real lie'll appear as some kind of concession, a settlement with truth. That type's mercifully easy to see through.'

'The merciful type of lie.'

'Or then the type who sort of overelaborates on the lie, buttresses it with rococo formations of detail and amendment, and that's how you can always tell. Pemulis was like that, I always thought, til his performance over the urinal.'

'*Rococo*'s a pretty word.'

'So now I've established a subtype of the over-elaborator type. This is the liar who used to be an over-elaborator and but has somehow snapped to the fact that rococo elaborations give him away every time, so he changes and now lies tersely, sparely, seeming somehow bored, like what he's saying is too obviously true to waste time on.'

'. . .'

'I've established that as a sort of subtype.'

'You sound like you can always tell.'

'Pemulis could have sold that urologist land in there, Boo. It was an incredibly high-pressure moment. I never thought he had it in him. He was nerveless and stomachless. He projected a kind of weary pragmatism the urologist found impossible to discount. His face was a brass mask. It was almost frightening. I told him I never would have believed he had that kind of performance in him.'

'Psychosis live on the radio used to read an Eve Arden beauty brochure all the time where Eve Arden says: "The importance of a mask is to increase your circulation," quote.'

'The truth is nobody can *always* tell, Boo. Some types are just too good, too complex and idiosyncratic; their lies are too close to the truth's heart for you to tell.'

'I can't ever tell. You wanted to know. You're right. It never crosses my mind.'

'. . .'

'I'm the type that'd buy land, I think.'

'You remember my hideous phobic thing about monsters, as a kid?'

'Boy do I ever.'

'Boo, I think I no longer believe in monsters as faces in the floor or feral infants or vampires or whatever. I think at seventeen now I believe the only real monsters might be the type of liar where there's simply no way to tell. The ones who give nothing away.'

'But then how do you know they're monsters, then?'

'That's the monstrosity right there, Boo, I'm starting to think.'

'Golly Ned.'

'That they walk among us. Teach our children. Inscrutable. Brass-faced.'

'Can I ask you how it is being in that thing?'

'Thing?'

'You *know*. Don't play *dumb* and *embarrass* me.'

'A wheelchair is a thing which: you prefer it or do not prefer, it is no distance. Difference. You are in the chair even if you do not prefer it. So it is better to prefer, no?'

'I can't believe I'm *drinking*. There's all these people in the House they're always worried they're going to *drink*. I'm in there for *drugs*. I've never had more than a beer *ever* in my *life*. I only came in here to throw up from getting *mugged*. Some street guy was offering to be a witness and he would *not* leave me alone. I didn't even have any *money*. I came in here to *vomit*.'

'I know what it is you are meaning.'

'What's your name one more time?'

'I call myself Rémy.'

'This is a *beautiful thing* as Hester would say. I don't feel horrid anymore. Ramy I feel *better* than I feel, felt in ever so I don't know *how long*. This is like *novocaine of the soul*. I'm like: why was I spending all that time doing one-hitters when *this* is really what *I* call feeling *better*.'

'Us, I do not take any drugs. I drink infrequently.'

'Well you're *making up for lost time* I have to say.'

'When I drink I have many drinks. This is how it is for my people.'

'My mom won't even have it in the *house*. She said it's what made her father drive into *concrete* and wipe out his *entire family*. Which like I'm so tired of hearing it. I came in here — what is this place?'

'This, it is Ryle's Inman Square Club of Jazz. My wife is dying at home in my native province.'

'There's this thing in the *Big Book* they make us every Sunday we have to *drag* ourselves out of bed at the absolute crack of *dawn* and sit in a circle and read out of it and half the people can barely even *read* and it's *excruciating* to listen to!'

'You should make your voice lower, for in the hours of no jazz they enjoy low voices, coming in for quiet.'

'And there's a thing about a car salesman trying to quit drinking, it's about the they call it the insanity of the first one, drink — he comes in a bar for a sandwich and a glass of milk — are you hungry?'

'Non.'

'What am I saying I don't have any *money*. I don't even have my *purse*. This stuff makes you stupid but it makes you feel quite a bit *improved*. He wasn't thinking of a drink and then all of a sudden he thinks of a drink. This guy.'

'Out of a blue place, in one flashing instant.'

'*Exactly*. But the insanity is after all this time in *hospitals* and losing his *business* and his *wife* because of *drinking* he suddenly gets it into his head that one drink won't hurt him if he puts it in a glass of *milk*.'

'Crazy in his head.'

'So when this absolutely *reptilian* character you *saved* me from by sitting down, rolling over, whatever. *Sor*-ry. When he says can he buy me a drink the book flashes in my mind and for sort of as it felt like a *joke* I ordered Kahlua and milk.'

'Me, I come in for nights I am tired, after the music has packed away, for the quiet. I use the telephone here as well, sometimes.'

'I mean even before the mugging I was walking along soberly deciding how to kill myself, so it seems a little silly to worry about drinking.'

'You have a certain expression of resemblance of my wife.'

'Your wife is *dying*. Jesus I'm sitting here *laughing* and your wife is *dying*. I think it's that I haven't felt *decent* in so *freaking* long, do you know what I'm saying? I'm not talking like *good*, I'm not talking like *pleasure*, I wouldn't want to go overboard with this thing, but at least at like *zero*, even, what do they call it Feeling No Pain.'

'I know of this meaning. I am spending a day to find someone I think my friends will kill, all the time I am awaiting the chance to betray my friends, and I come here and telephone to betray them and I see this bruised person who strongly resembles my wife. I think: Rémy, it is time for many drinks.'

'Well *I* think you're *nice*. I think you just about saved my *life*. I've spent like nine weeks feeling so bad I wanted to just about *kill myself*, both getting high and not. Dr. Garton never mentioned *this*. He talked plenty about *shock* but he never even freaking *mentioned* Kahlua and milk.'

'Katherine, I will tell you a story about feeling so bad and saving a life. I do not know you but we are drunk together now, and will you hear this story?'

'It's not about Hitting Bottom ingesting any sort of Substance and trying to Surrender, is it?'

'My people, we do not hit the bottoms of women. I am, shall we say, Swiss. My legs, they were lost in the teenage years being struck by a train.'

'That must have *smarted*.'

'I would have temptation to say you have no idea. But I am sensing you have an idea of hurting.'

'You have no *idea*.'

'I am in early twenty years, without the legs. Many of my friends also: without legs.'

'Must have been an *awful* train crash.'

'Also my own father: dead when his Kenbeck pacemaker came within range of a misdialed number of a cellular phone far away in Trois Rivières, in a freakish occurrence of tragedy.'

'My dad emotionally abandoned us and moved to Portland, which is in Oregon, with his therapist.'

'Also in this time, my Swiss nation, we are a strong people but not strong as a nation, surrounded by strong nations. There is much hatred of our neighbors, and unfairness.'

'It all started when my mom found a picture of his therapist in his wallet and goes "What's *that* doing in here?" '

'It is, for me, who I am weak, so painful to be without legs in the early twenty years. One feels grotesque to people; one's freedom is restricted. I have no chances now for jobs in the mines of Switzerland.'

'The Swiss have gold mines.'

'As you say. And much beautiful territory, which the stronger nations at the time of losing my legs committed paper atrocities to my nation's land.'

'Frucking *bastards*.'

'It is a long story to the side of this story, but my part of the Swiss nation is in my time of no legs invaded and despoiled by stronger and evil hated and neighboring nations, who claim as in the *Anschluss* of Hitler that they are friends and are not invading the Swiss but conferring on us gifts of alliance.'

'Total *dicks.*'

'It is to the side, but for my Swiss friends and myself without legs it is a dark period of injustice and dishonor, and of terrible pain. Some of my friends roll themselves off to fight against the invasion of paper, but me, I am too painful to care enough to fight. To me, the fight seems without point: our own Swiss leaders have been subverted to pretend the invasion is alliance; we very few legless young cannot repel an invasion; we cannot even make our government admit that there is an invasion. I am weak and, in pain, see all is pointless: I do not see the meaning of choosing to fight.'

'You're *depressed* is what you are.'

'I see no point and do no work and belong to nothing; I am alone. I think of death. I do nothing but frequently drink, roll around the despoiled countryside, sometimes dodging falling projectiles of invasion, thinking of death, bemoaning the depredation of the Swiss land, in great pain. But it is myself I bemoan. I have pain. I have no legs.'

'I'm Identifying every step of the way with you, Ramy. Oh *God,* what did I *say?*'

'And us, our Swiss countryside is very hilly. The fauteuil, it is hard to push up many hills, then one is braking with all the might to keep from flying out of control on the downhill.'

'Sometimes it's like that walking, too.'

'Katherine, I am, in English, *moribund.* I have no legs, no Swiss honor, no leaders who will fight the truth. I am not alive, Katherine. I roll from skiing lodge to tavern, frequently drinking, alone, wishing for my death, locked inside my pain in the heart. I wish for my death but have not the courage to make actions to cause death. I twice try to roll over the side of a tall Swiss hill but cannot bring myself. I curse myself for cowardice and inutile. I roll about, hoping to be hit by a vehicle of someone else, but at the last minute rolling out of the path of vehicles on Autoroutes, for I am unable to will my death. The more pain in my self, the more I am inside the self and cannot will my death, I think. I feel I am chained in a cage of the self, from the pain. Unable to care or choose anything outside it. Unable to see anything or feel anything outside my pain.'

'The billowing shaped black sailing wing. I am so totally Identifying it's not even *funny.*'

'My story it was one day at the top of a hill I had drunkenly labored for many minutes to roll to the crest, and looking out over the downhill slope I see a small hunched woman in what I am thinking is a metal hat far below at the bottom, attempting the crossing of the Swiss Provincial Autoroute at the bottom, in the middle of the Provincial Autoroute, this woman, standing and staring in the terror at one of the hated long and shiny many-wheeled trucks of our paper invaders, bearing down upon her at high speeds in the hurry to come despoil part of the Swiss land.'

'Like one of those Swiss metal helmets? Is she scrambling crazily to get out of the way?'

'She is standing transfixed with horror of the truck — identically as I had been motionless and transfixed by horror inside me, unable to move, like one of the many moose of Switzerland transfixed by the headlights of one of the many logging-trucks of Switzerland. The sunlight is reflecting madly on her metal hat as she is shaking her head in terror and she is clutching her — pardon me, but her female bosom, as if the heart of her would explode from the terror.'

'And you think, Oh *fuck me*, just great, another horrible thing I'm going to have stand here and witness and then go feel pain over.'

'But the great gift of this time today at the hilltop above the Provincial Autoroute is I do not think of me. I do not know this woman or love her, but without thinking I release my brake and I am careening down the downhill, almost wipe-outing numerous places on the bumps and rocks of the hill's slope, and as we say in Switzerland I *schüssch* at enough speed to reach my wife and sweep her up into the chair and roll across the Provincial Autoroute into the embanking ahead just ahead of the nose of the truck, which had not slowed.'

'Hang me upside-down and fuck me in both *ears*. You pulled yourself out of a clinical depression by being a freaking *hero*.'

'We rolled and tumbled down the embanking on the Autoroute's distant side, causing my chair to tip and injuring a stump of me, and knocking away her thick metal hat.'

'You saved somebody's freaking *life*, Ramy. I'd give my left nut for a chance to pull myself out of the shadow of the wing that way, Ramy.'

'You are not seeing this. It was this frozen with the terror woman, she saved my life. For this saved my life. This moment broke my moribund chains, Katherine. In one instant and without thought I was allowed to choose something as more important than my thinking of my life. Her, she allowed this will without thinking. She with one blow broke the chains of the cage of pain at my half a body and nation. When I had crawled back to my fauteuil and placed my tipped fauteuil aright and I was again seated I realized the pain of inside no longer pained me. I became, then, adult. I was permitted leaving the pain of my own loss and pain at the top of Switzerland's Mont Papineau.'

'Because suddenly you gazed at the girl without her metal hat and felt a rush of passion and fell madly in love enough to get married and roll together off into the s—'

'She had no skull, this woman. Later I am learning she had been among the first Swiss children of southwestern Switzerland to become born without a skull, from the toxicities in association of our enemy's invasion on paper. Without the confinement of the metal hat the head hung from the shoulders like the half-filled balloon or empty bag, the eyes and oral cavity greatly distended from this hanging, and sounds exiting this cavity which were difficult to listen.'

'But still, something about her moved you to fall madly in love. Her gratitude and humility and acceptance and that kind of quiet dignity really horribly handic— birth-defected people usually have.'

'It was not mad. I had already chosen. The unclamping of the brakes of the fauteuil and *schüssch*ing to the Autoroute — this was the love. I had chosen loving her above my lost legs and this half a self.'

'And she looked at your missing limbs and didn't even see them and chose you right back — result: passionate love.'

'There was for this woman in the embanking no possible choosing. Without the containing helmet all energies in her were committed to the shaping of the oral cavity in a shape that allowed breathing, which was a task of great enormity, for her head it had also neither muscles nor nerves. The special hat had found itself dented in upon one side, and I had not the ability to shape my wife's head into a shape that I could stuff the sac of her head into the hat, and I chose to carry her over my shoulders in a high-speed rolling to the nearest Swiss hôpital specializing in deformities of grave nature. It was there I learned of the other troubles.'

'I think I'd like a couple more Kahlua and milks.'

'There was the trouble of the digestive tracking. There were seizures also. There were progressive decays of circulation and vessel, which calls itself restenosis. There were the more than standard accepted amounts of eyes and cavities in many different stages of development upon different parts of the body. There were the fugue states and rages and frequency of coma. She had wandered away from a public institution of Swiss charitable care. Worst for choosing to love was the cerebro-and-spinal fluids which dribbled at all times from her distending oral cavity.'

'And but your passionate love for each other dried up her cerebro-spinal drool and ended the seizures and there were certain hats she looked so good in it just about drove you mad with love? Is that it?'

'Garçon!'

'Is the madly-in-love part coming up?'

'Katherine, I had too believed there was no love without passion. Pleasure. This was part of the pain of the no legs, this fear that for me there would be no passion. The fear of the pain is many times worse than the pain of the pain, n'est ce —?'

'Ramy I don't think I'm like thinking this is a feel-better story at *all*.'

'I tried to leave the soft-head and cerebro-spinally incontinent woman, m'épouse au future, behind at the hôpital of grave nature and to wheel off into my new life of uncaged acceptance and choice. I would roll into the fraying of battle for my despoiled nation, for now I saw the point not of winning but of choosing merely to fight. But I had travelled no more than several revolutions of the fauteuil when the old despair of before choosing this no-skull creature rose up once again inside me. Within several revolutions there was no point again and no legs, and only fear of the pain that made me not choose. Pain rolled me backwards to this woman, my wife.'

'You're saying this is *love?* This isn't love. I'll know when it's love because of the way it'll *feel.* It won't be about spinal fluid and despair believe you *me,* Bucko. It'll be about your eyes meet across someplace and both your knees give out and from that second forward you know you're not going to be *alone* and in *hell.* You're not half the guy I started to think you might have been, Ray.'

'I had to face: I had chosen. My choice, this was love. I had chosen I think the way out of the chains of the cage. I needed this woman. Without her to choose over myself, there was only pain and not choosing, rolling drunkenly and making fantasies of death.'

'This is love? It's like you were *chained* to her. It's like if you tried to get on with your own life the pain of the clinical depression came back. It's like the clinical depression was a shotgun nudging you down the wedding aisle. Was there a wedding aisle? Could she even get down a wedding aisle?'

'My wife's wedding helmet was of the finest nickel mined and molded by friends in the nickel mines of southwest Switzerland. Each of us, we were rolled down the aisle in special conveyings. Hers with special pans and drains, for the fluids. It was the happiest day ever for me, since the train. The cleric asked did I choose this woman. There was a long time of silence. My whole very being came to a knifelike point in that instant, Katherine, my hand holding tenderly the hook of my wife.'

'*Hook?* As in *hand-hook?*'

'I have been knowing since the wedding night her death was coming. Her restenosis of the heart, it is irreversible. Now my Gertraude, she has been in a comatose and vegetating state for almost one year. This coma has no exit, it is said. The advanced Jaarvik IX Exterior Artificial Heart is said by the public-aid cardiologists of Switzerland to be her chance for life. With it they say my wife can live for many more years in a comatose and vegetated state.'

'So you're down here like pressing your case to the Jaarvik IX people at Harvard or wherever.'

'It is for her I betray my friends and cell, the cause of my nation, which now that victory and independence of the neighbors is possible I am betraying it.'

'You're spying and betraying Switzerland to try and keep alive somebody with a hook and spinal fluid and no skull in an irreversible coma? And I thought *I* was disturbed. You're making me totally reorient my idea of *disturbed,* mister.'

'I am not telling for disturbing you, poor Katherine. I am telling of pain and saving a life, and love.'

'Well, Ray, far be it from far for me, but that's not love: that's low self-esteem and self-abuse and Settling For Less, choosing a coma over your comrades. Assuming you're even not totally lying to get me into the *hay* or some fucked-up disturbed sicko shit like that.'

'This —'

'Which I've got to tell you, saying I *remind* you of her isn't exactly the way to sweep my feet off, you know what I'm saying here?'

'This is what is hard to tell. To ask any person to see. It is no choice. It is not choosing Gertraude over the A.F.R., my companions. Over the causes. Choosing Gertraude to love as my wife was necessary for the others, these other choices. Without the choice of her life there are no other choices. I tried leaving at the commencement. I got only very few revolutions of the fauteuil.'

'Sounds more like a *gun to your head* than a choice. If you can't choose the other way, there's no choice.'

'No, but this choice, Katherine: I made it. It chains me, but the chains are of my choice. The other chains: no. The others were the chains of not choosing.'

'Do you have a twin that just came in and sat down just to the left of you but is also like about one-third overlapping on you?'

'You are merely drunk. This will happened quickly if unused to alcohol. Nausea often accompanies this. Do not be alarmed if there is visual doubling, losing balance, and nausea of the stomach.'

'The price of a like complete normal human digestive tract. I used to throw up every morning without drinking. Rain and shine both.'

'You think there is no love without the pleasure, the no-choice compelling of passion.'

'I appreciate the *drinks* and all, but I don't think I'm going to like memorize a lecture on *love* from somebody who marries somebody with cerebro-fluid spewing out of their *mouth,* no offense intended.'

'As you say. My opinions are only that the love you of this country speak of yields none of the pleasure you seek in love. This whole idea of the pleasure and good feelings being what to choose. To give yourself away to. That all choice for you leads there — this pleasure of not choosing.'

'Don't grudge me a little feeling good, of all people, Ray, asshole, shit-puddle, Swisshead.'

'. . .'

'Is it better to throw up right away or try to wait before you throw up, Mr. Drinking Expert?'

'I am thinking: what if I were to claim we might leave and I could lead you only three streets from here and show you something with this promise: you would feel more good feeling and pleasure than ever before for you: you would never again feel sorrow or pity or the pain of the chains and cage of never choosing. I am thinking of this offer: you would reply to me what?'

'*I voot make ze hreply zat* I've heard that one before, asshole, and from . . . from guys with a little more to them south of the waist, if you follow.'

'I do not understand.'

'What I'd reply is I'm a *shitty lay*. As in *sex-partner*. I've only ever been sexual twice, and both times it was awful, and Brad Anderson when I called and said why didn't you call again Brad Anderson you know what he said? He said I was a *lousy lay* and my *snatch* was sure awful *big* for somebody with such a *little flat ass,* Brad Anderson said.'

'No. No. You are not understanding.'

'That's just what *I* said.'

'You would say No Thank You, you are saying, but this is because you would not believe my claim.'

'. . .'

'If my claim, it was true, you would say yes, Katherine, no?'

'. . .'

'Yes?'

'Now you're not on your side anymore, Hal, I can see. When you're on your back you don't have a shadow.'

'. . .'

'Hey Hal?'

'Yes, Mario.'

'I'm sorry if you're sad, Hal. You seem sad.'

'I smoke high-resin Bob Hope in secret by myself down in the Pump Room off the secondary maintenance tunnel. I use Visine and mint toothpaste and shower with Irish Spring to hide it from almost everyone. Only Pemulis knows the true extent.'

'. . .'

'I'm not the one C.T. and the Moms want gone. I'm not the one they suspect. Pemulis publicly dosed his opponent at Port Washington. It was impossible to miss. The kid was a devout Mormon. The dose was impossible to miss. Sales of Visine bottles of pre-adolescent urine during quarterly tests have been noted, it turns out, and classed as a Pemulis production.'

'Selling Visine bottles?'

'I'd be immune to expulsion anyway, obviously, as the Moms's relative. But I'm suspected of nothing other than ill-considered moral paralysis out there on I. Day. My urine and Axhandle's urine are just to establish a context of objectivity for Pemulis's urine. It's Pemulis they want. I'm almost positive they're going to give Pemulis the Shoe by the end of the term. I don't know whether Pemulis knows this or not.'

'Hey Hal?'

'Normally they're after steroids, endocrine synthetics, mild 'drines, when they test. The O.N.A.N.T.A. guy gave indications this one'll be a full-spectrum scan. Gas chromatography followed by electron-bombardment, with spectrometer readings on the resultant mass-fragments. The real Mc-Coy. The kind the Show uses.'

'Hey Hal?'

'Mike stands there and says what if hypothetically somebody was down-wind from substances and got exposed and so on. Claimed vague memories of a poppy-seed bagel. Not at all Pemulis's normal rococo type of lie. This one had a kind of weary earnestness. The guy in the blazer said he'd go ahead and give us thirty days before a full-spectrum scan. Mike had pointed out that there was an enormous lady from *Moment* due to arrive and snuffle around, making it a really unfortunate time for any outside-chance inadvertent scandals for anybody. It was like the guy needed hardly any prodding to give us time to clean out the system. O.N.A.N.T.A. doesn't want to catch anybody, really. Good clean fun and so on and so forth.'

'. . .'

'The ingenious layer to the lie was that the guy thought the thirty days' grace was for Pemulis. That it was what Pemulis needed. Pemulis could pass a urine test hanging upside down in a high wind. Guy watching or not. He has a whole unpleasant catheterization technique you don't want to hear about. He's checked it. And Tenuates are apparently the Indy-type car of 'drines, he says; his own urine can be all innocent and pale with two days' warning, as long as he stays off the Bob.'

'. . .'

'Booboo, the thirty days was actually for me, and Mike let me stand there with my Unit out and not say anything while he sold the urologist land and magazine subscriptions and Ginsu knives. He did it for me, and I'm not even the one they want.'

'You can tell me whatever you said.'

'What I do in secret, Boo, Mike says no more than thirty days to get it all out for sure. Cranberry juice, Calli tea, vinegar in water. Plus or minus a couple days. The Bob Hope I smoke and hide, Boo, it's fat-soluble. It stays in there, in the body's fat.'

'Mrs. Clarke told Bridget the human brain is high in fat, Bridget said.'

'Mario, if I get caught. If I come up dirty-urined in front of O.N.A.N.T.A., what could C.T. do? It's not just that I'd lose my even year in 18's. He'd have to give me the Shoe if he'd brought O.N.A.N.T.A. into it. And what about Himself's memory? I'm directly related to Himself. Not to mention Orin. And meanwhile here's this *Moment* lady lumbering around looking for family linen.'

'Troeltsch says she all she wants to do is soften Orin's profile.'

'The hideous thing is how brightly it'd come out, if I flunk a urine. E.T.A.'ll be publicly hurt. Hence Himself's memory, hence Himself.'

'...'

'And it'd *kill* the Moms, Mario. It'd be a terrible kertwang on the Moms. Not so much the Hope. The *secrecy* of it. That I hid it from her. That she'll feel I had to hide it from her.'

'Hey Hal?'

'Something terrible will happen if she finds out I hid it from her.'

'Thirty days is one calendar month of Calli tea and juice, you're saying.'

'Of tea and vinegar and total abstinence. Of no substances whatsoever. Of abrupt and total withdrawal while I try to justify my seed at the WhataBurger and maybe get offered up to Wayne at the Fundraiser. And then your birthday in two weeks.'

'Hey Hal?'

'Jesus and then the SAT's in December, I'll have to finish prepping for the Boards and then take the Boards while still in abrupt withdrawal.'

'You'll get a perfect score. Everybody's betting you get a perfect score. I've heard them.'

'Marvelous. That's just exactly what I need to hear.'

'Hey Hal?'

'And of course you're hurt, Boo, that I've tried to hide all of it from you.'

'I'm zero percent hurt, Hal.'

'And of course you're wondering why I didn't just tell you when of course you knew anyway, knew something, the times hanging upside-down in the weight room with a forehead Lyle didn't even want to get near. You sitting there letting me say I was just really really tired and nightmare-ridden.'

'I feel like you always tell me the truth. You tell me when it's right to.'

'Marvelous.'

'I feel like you're the only one who knows when it's right to tell. I can't know for you, so why should I be hurt.'

'Be a fucking human *being* for once, Boo. I room with you and I hid it from you and let you worry and be hurt that I was trying to hide it.'

'I wasn't hurt. I don't want you to be sad.'

'You can get hurt and mad at people, Boo. News-flash at almost fucking nineteen, kid. It's called being a person. You can get mad at somebody and it doesn't mean they'll go away. You don't have to put on a Moms-act of total trust and forgiveness. One liar's enough.'

'You're scared your pee might still flunk after one calendar month.'

'Jesus it's like talking to a big poster of some smily-faced guy. Are you *in* there?'

'And you can't use a Visine bottle of pee because the man will be right there looking at your penis, and Trevor and Pemulis's penises.'

'. . .'

'The sun's thinking about coming up in the window. You can see it.'

'It's been like forty hours without Bob Hope and already I'm bats inside and I can't sleep without more of the horror-show dreams. I feel like I'm stuck halfway down a chimney.'

'You beat Ortho, and your toothache's gone.'

'Pemulis and Axhandle say a month'll be tit. Pemulis's only concern is is this DMZ he got for the WhataBurger detectable. He goes to the library and pores. He's fully alert and functional.[321] It seems different with me, Boo. I feel a hole. It's going to be a huge hole, in a month. A way more than Hal-sized hole.'

'So what do you think you should do?'

'And the hole's going to get a little bigger every day until I fly apart in different directions. I'll fly apart in midair. I'll fly apart in the Lung, or at Tucson at 200 degrees in front of all these people who knew Himself and think I'm different. Whom I've lied to, and liked it. It'll all come out anyway, clean pee or no.'

'Hey Hal?'

'And it'll kill her. I know it will. It will kill her dead, Booboo, I'm afraid.'

'Hey Hal? What are you going to do?'

'. . .'

'Hal?'

'Booboo, I'm up on my elbow again. Tell me what you think I should do.'

'Me tell you?'

'I'm just two big aprick ears right here, Boo. Listening. Because I do not know what to do.'

'Hal, if I tell you the truth, will you get mad and tell me be a fucking?'

'I trust you. You're smart, Boo.'

'Then Hal?'

'Tell me what I should do.'

'I think you just did it. What you should do. I think you just did.'

'. . .'

'Do you see what I mean?'

17 NOVEMBER
YEAR OF THE DEPEND ADULT UNDERGARMENT

In Don Gately's medical absence, Johnette F. had worked five straight night shifts on Dream Duty and was in the front office just after 0830 writing up the previous night in the Log, trying to think of synonyms for *boredom* and periodically dipping a finger in her scalding coffee to stay awake, plus listening to distant toilets flush and showers hiss and residents clunking sleepily around in the kitchen and dining room and everything like that, when somebody all of a sudden starts knocking at the House's front door, which meant that the person was like a newcomer or stranger, since people in the Ennet House recovery community know that the front door's unlocked at 0800 and always completely open to all but the Law as of 0801.

The residents these days all know not to answer any knocks at the door themselves.

So Johnette F. at first thought it might be some more of those kind of police[322] that wore suits and ties, come to depose more residents as witnesses on the Lenz-and-Gately-and-Canadian fuck-up and everything like that; and Johnette got out the clipboard with the names of all the residents with unresolved legal issues who needed to be put upstairs out of sight before any police were let on the premises. A couple of the residents on the list were in the dining room in full view, eating cereal and smoking. Johnette carried the clipboard as a kind of emblem of authority as she went to the window by the front door to check out the knocking party and everything like that.

And but the kid at the door there was no way he was police or court-personnel, and Johnette opened the unlocked door and let him in, not bothering to explain that nobody had to knock. It was an upscale kid about Johnette's own age or slightly less, coughing against the foyer's pall of A.M. smoke, saying he wanted to speak in comparative private to someone in whatever passed here for authority, he said. This kid he had the sort of cool aluminum sheen of an upscale kid, a kid with either a weird tan or a weird windburn on top of a tan, and just the whitest Nike hightops Johnette had ever seen, and ironed jeans, as in with like a crease down the front, and a weird woolly-white jacket with A.T.E. in red up one sleeve and in gray up the other, and slicked-back dark hair that was wet, as in showered and not oil, and had half frozen, the hair, in the early outside cold and was standing up straight and frozen in front, making his dark face look small. His ears looked inflamed from the cold. Johnette appraised him coolly, digging at her ear with a pinkie. She watched the boy's face as David Krone came scuttling over like a crab and blinked at the boy upside-down a few times and scuttled around and up the stairs, his forehead clunking against each stair. It was pretty obvious the boy wasn't any resident's like homey or boyfriend come to give somebody a ride to work or like that. The way the boy looked and stood and talked and everything like that radiated high-maintenance upkeep and privilege and schools where nobody carried weapons, pretty much a whole planet of privilege away from the planet of Johnette Marie Foltz of South Chelsea and then the Right Honorable Edmund F. Heany Facility for Demonstrably Incorrigible Girls down in Brockton; and in Pat's office, with the door only half shut, Johnette gave her face the blandly hostile expression she wore around upscale boys with no tatts and all their teeth that outside of

786

NA wouldn't have interest in her or might view her lack of front teeth and nose-pin as evidence of they were like better than her and like that, somehow. It emerged this kid didn't seem like he had enough emotional juice to be interested in judging anybody or even noticing them, however. His talking had a burbly, oversalivated quality Johnette knew all too wicked well, the quality of somebody who'd just lately put down the pipe and/or bong. The kid's hair was starting to melt in the heat of Pat's office and drip and settle on his head like a slashed tire, causing that his face got bigger. He looked a little like what the fourth Mrs. Foltz had called green around the gills. The boy stood there very straight with his hands behind his back and said he lived nearby and had for some time been interested in sort of an idle, largely speculative way in considering maybe dropping in on some sort of Substance Anonymous meeting and everything like that, basically as just something to do, the exact same roundabout Denial shit as persons without teeth, and said but he didn't know where any were, any Meetings, or when, and but knew The Ennet House[323] was nearby, that dealt directly with Anonymous organizations of this sort, and was wondering whether he maybe could have — or borrow and Xerox and promptly return by either e- or fax or First-Class mail, whichever they might prefer — some sort of relevant meeting schedule. He apologized for intruding and said but he didn't know whom else to call. The sort of guy like Ewell and Day and snotty look-right-through-you-if-you-weren't-a-fucking-covergirl Ken E. that knew how to long-divide and say *whom* but didn't even know how to look up shit in the Yellow Pages.

Much later, in subsequent events' light, Johnette F. would clearly recall the sight of the boy's frozen hair slowly settling, and how the boy had said *whom,* and the sight of clear upscale odor-free saliva almost running out over his lower lip as he fought to pronounce the word without swallowing.

324

Technical interviewers under Chief of Unspecified Services R. ('the G.') Tine [325] really do do this, bring a portable high-watt lamp and plug it in and adjust its neck so the light shines down directly on the face of the interview's subject, whose homburg and shade-affording eyebrows had been removed by polite but emphatic request. And it was this, the harsh light on her fully exposed post-Marxist face, more than any kind of tough *noir*-informed grilling from R. Tine Jr. and the other technical interviewer, that prompted M.I.T. A.B.D.-Ph.D. Molly Notkin, fresh off the N.N.Y.C. high-speed rail, seated in the Sidney Peterson–shaped directorial chair amid dropped luggage in her co-op's darkened and lock-dickied living room, to spill her guts, roll over, eat cheese, sing like a canary, tell everything she believed she knew:[326]

— Molly Notkin tells the U.S.O.U.S. operatives that her understanding of the après-garde Auteur J. O. Incandenza's lethally entertaining *Infinite Jest* (V or VI) is that it features Madame Psychosis as some kind of maternal instantiation of the archetypal figure Death, sitting naked, corporeally gorgeous, ravishing, hugely pregnant, her hideously deformed face either veiled or blanked out by undulating computer-generated squares of color or anamorphosized into unrecognizability as any kind of face by the camera's apparently very strange and novel lens, sitting there nude, explaining in very simple childlike language to whomever the film's camera represents that Death is always female, and that the female is always maternal. I.e. that the woman who kills you is always your next life's mother. This, which Molly Notkin said didn't make too much sense to her either, when she heard it, was the alleged substance of the Death-cosmology Madame Psychosis was supposed to deliver in a lalating monologue to the viewer, mediated by the very special lens. She may or may not have been holding a knife during this monologue, and the film's big technical hook (the Auteur's films always involved some sort of technical hook) involved some very unusual kind of single lens on the Bolex H32's turret,[327] and it was unquestionably an f/x that Madame Psychosis looked pregnant, because the real Madame Psychosis had never been visibly pregnant, Molly Notkin had seen her naked,[328] and you can always tell if a woman's ever carried anything past the first trimester if you look at her naked.[329]

— Molly Notkin tells them that Madame Psychosis's own mother had killed herself in a truly ghastly way with an ordinary kitchen garbage disposal on the evening of Thanksgiving Day in the Year of the Tucks Medicated Pad, four-odd months before the film's Auteur himself had killed himself, also with a kitchen appliance, also ghastlyly, which she says though any Lincoln-Kennedy-type connections between the two suicides will have to be ferreted out by the interviewers on their own, since as far as Molly Notkin knew the two different parents didn't even know of each other's existence.

— That the lethal cartridge's digital Bolex H32 camera — already a Rube-Goldbergesque amalgam of various improvements and digital adaptations to the already modification-heavy classic Bolex H16 Rex 5 — a Canadian line, by the way, favored throughout his whole career by the Auteur because its turret could accept three different C-mount lenses and adapters — that *Infinite Jest* (V) or (VI)'s had been fitted with an extremely strange and extrusive kind of lens, and lay during filming on either the floor or like a cot or bed, the camera, with Madame Psychosis as the Death-

Mother figure inclined over it, parturient and nude, talking *down* to it — in both senses of the word, which from a critical perspective would introduce into the film a kind of synesthetic double-entendre involving both the aural and visual perspectives of the subjective camera — explaining to the camera as audience-synecdoche that this was why mothers were so obsessively, consumingly, drivenly, and yet somehow narcissistically loving of you, their kid: the mothers are trying frantically to make amends for a murder neither of you quite remember.

— Molly Notkin tells them she could be far more helpful and forthcomingly detailed if only they'd switch that beastly lamp off or train it someplace else, which is a brass-faced falsehood and dismissed as such by R. Tine Jr., and so the light stays right on Molly Notkin's glabrous unhappy face.

— That Madame Psychosis and the film's Auteur had not been sexually enmeshed, and for reasons beyond the fact that the Auteur's belief in a finite world-total of available erections rendered him always either impotent or guilt-ridden. That in fact Madame Psychosis had loved and been sexually enmeshed only with the Auteur's son, who, though Molly Notkin never encountered him personally and Madame Psychosis had taken care never to speak ill of him, was clearly as thoroughgoing a little rotter as one would find down through the whole white male canon of venery, moral cowardice, emotional chicanery, and rot.

— That Madame Psychosis had been present neither at the Auteur's suicide nor at his funeral. That she'd missed the funeral because her passport had expired. That nor had Madame Psychosis been present at the reading of the late Auteur's will, despite the fact that she was one of the beneficiaries. That Madame Psychosis had never mentioned the fate or present disposition of the unreleased cartridge entitled either *Infinite Jest* (V) or *Infinite Jest* (VI), and had described it only from the perspective of the experience of performing in it, nude, and had never seen it, but had a hard time believing it was even entertaining, let alone lethally entertaining, and tended to believe it had represented little more than the thinly veiled cries of a man at the very terminus of his existential tether — the Auteur having apparently been extremely close to his own mother, in childhood — and had no doubt been recognized as such by the Auteur — who though not exactly the psychic sea's steadiest keel had been in many respects an acute reader and critic of film, and would have been able to distinguish the real filmic McCoy from pathetic cries veiled as film no matter how wildly his nautical compass was spinning around, on its tether, and would in all probability have destroyed the Master Print of the failed piece of art, the same way he'd reportedly destroyed the first four or five failed attempts at the same piece, which pieces had admittedly featured actresses of lesser mystique and allure.

— That the Auteur's funeral had purportedly taken place in the L'Islet

Province of Nouveau Québec, the birth-province of the Auteur's widow, featuring an interrment and not a cremation.

— That far be it from her to tell the U.S. Office of Unspecified Services its business, but why not simply go to J.O.I.'s widow and verify directly the existence and location of the purported cartridge?

— . . .

— That it seemed pretty unlikely to her, Molly Notkin, that the Auteur's widow had any connections to any anti-American groups, cells, or movements, no matter what the files on her indiscreet youth might suggest, since from everything Molly Notkin's heard the woman didn't have much interest in any agendas larger than her own individually neurotic agendas, even though she came on to Madame Psychosis all sweet and solicitous. That Madame Psychosis had confessed to Molly Notkin that the widow struck her as very possibly Death incarnate — her constant smile the rictal smile of some kind of thanatoptic figure — and that it had struck Madame Psychosis as bizarre that it was she, Madame Psychosis, whom the Auteur kept casting as various feminine instantiations of Death when he had the real thing right under his nose, and eminently photogenic to boot, the widow-to-be, apparently a real restaurant-silencer-type beauty even in her late forties.

— That the Auteur had stopped ingesting distilled spirits as Madame Psychosis's personal condition for consenting to appear in what she knew to be her but did not know to be the J.O.I.'s final film-cartridge, and that the Auteur had, apparently, incredibly,[330] kept his side of the bargain — possibly because he'd been so deeply moved at M.P.'s consent to appear before the camera again even after her terrible accident and deformation and the little rotter of a son's despicable abandonment of the relationship under the excuse of accusing Madame Psychosis of being sexually enmeshed with their — here Molly Notkin said that she of course had meant to say *his* — father, the Auteur. And that the Auteur had apparently remained alcohol-free for the whole next three-and-a-half months, from Xmas of the Year of the Tucks Medicated Pad to 1 April of the Year of the Trial-Size Dove Bar, the date of his suicide.

— That the completely secret and hidden substance-abuse problem, the one that had now landed Madame Psychosis in an elite private dependency-treatment facility so elite that not even M.P.'s closest friends knew where it was beyond knowing only that it was someplace far, very far away, that the abuse-problem could have been nothing but a consequence of the terrible guilt Madame Psychosis felt over the Auteur's suicide, and constituted a clear unconscious compulsion to punish herself with the same sort of substance-abuse activity she had coerced the Auteur into stopping, merely substituting narcotics for Wild Turkey, which Molly Notkin could attest was some very gnarly-tasting liquor indeed.

— No, that Madame Psychosis's guilt over the Auteur's *felo de self* had nothing to do with the purportedly lethal *Infinite Jest* (V) or (VI), which as far as Madame Psychosis had determined from the filming itself was little more than an olla podrida of depressive conceits strung together with flashy lensmanship and perspectival novelty. That, no, rather the consuming guilt had been over the condition that the Auteur suspend the ingestion of spirits, which it turned out, M.P. had claimed in deluded hindsight, had been all that was keeping the man's tether ravelled, the ingestion, such that without it he was unable to withstand the psychic pressures that pushed him over the edge into what Madame Psychosis said she and the Auteur had sometimes referred to as quote 'self-erasure.'

— That it did not strike her, Molly Notkin, as improbable that the special limited-edition turkey-shaped gift bottle of Wild Turkey Blended Whiskey-brand distilled spirits with the cerise velveteen gift-ribbon around its neck with the bow tucked under its wattles on the kitchen counter next to the microwave oven before which the Auteur's body had been found so ghastlyly inclined had been placed there by the spouse's widow-to-be — who may well have been enraged by the fact that the Auteur had never been willing to give up spirits quote 'for her' but had apparently been willing to give them up quote 'for' Madame Psychosis and her nude appearance in his final opus.

— That the by all reports exceptionally attractive Madame Psychosis had suffered an irreparable facial trauma on the same Thanksgiving Day that her mother had killed herself with a kitchen-appliance, leaving her (Madame Psychosis) hideously and improbably deformed, and that her membership in the Union of the Hideously and Improbably Deformed's 13-Step self-help organization was no kind of metaphor or ruse.

— That the intolerable stresses leading to the Auteur's self-erasure had probably way less to do with film or digital art — this Auteur's anti-confluential approach to the medium having always struck Molly Notkin as being rather aloof and cerebrally technical, to say nothing of naïvely post-Marxist in its self-congratulatory combination of anamorphic fragmentation and anti-Picaresque[331] narrative stasis — or with having allegedly spawned some angelic monster of audience-gratification — anyone with a nervous system who watched much of his oeuvre could see that fun or entertainment was pretty low on the late filmmaker's list of priorities — but rather much more likely to do with the fact that his widow-to-be was engaging in sexual enmeshments with just about everything with a Y-chromosome, and had been for what sounded like many years, including possibly with the Auteur's son and Madame's craven lover, as a child, seeing as it sounded like the little rotter had enough malcathected issues with his mother to keep all of Vienna humming briskly for quite some time.

— That thus — with the Promethean-guilt angle on the Auteur's suicide cast into serious doubt — there was little question in A.B.D.-Dr. Notkin's mind that the entire perfect-entertainment-as-*Liebestod* myth surrounding the purportedly lethal final cartridge was nothing more than a classic illustration of the antinomically schizoid function of the post-industrial capitalist mechanism, whose logic presented commodity as the escape-from-anxieties-of-mortality-which-escape-is-itself-psychologically-fatal, as detailed in perspicuous detail in M. Gilles Deleuze's posthumous *Incest and the Life of Death in Capitalist Entertainment,* which she'd be happy to lend the figures standing up somewhere above the lamp's white fire, one of them tapping something irritatingly against the lamp's conic metal shade, if they'd promise to return it and not mark it up.

— That — in response to respectful but pointed requests to keep the responses on some sort of factual track and spare them all the eggheaded abstractions — Madame Psychosis's deforming trauma, in its combination of coincidence and malefic intention, had been like something right out of the Auteur's most ghastly and unresolvable proto-incestuous disaster films, e.g. *The Night Wears a Sombrero, Dial C for Concupiscence,* and *The Unfortunate Case of Me.* That Madame Psychosis, an only child, had been extremely and heart-warmingly close to her father, a low-pH chemist for a Kentucky reagent outfit, who'd apparently had an extremely close only-child and watching-movies-together-based relationship with his own mother and seemed to reenact the closeness with Madame Psychosis, taking her to movies on a near-daily basis, in Kentucky, and driving her all over the mid-South for various junior baton-twirling competitions while his wife, Madame Psychosis's mother, a devoutly religious but wounded and neurasthenic woman with a fear of public spaces, stayed home on the family farm, canning preserves and seeing to the administration of the farm, etc. But that things had gotten first strange and then creepy as Madame Psychosis entered puberty, apparently; specifically the low-pH father had gotten creepy, seeming to behave as if Madame Psychosis were getting younger instead of older: taking her to increasingly child-rated films at the local Cineplex, refusing to acknowledge issues of menses or breasts, strongly discouraging dating, etc. Apparently issues were complicated by the fact that Madame Psychosis emerged from puberty as an almost freakishly beautiful young woman, especially in a part of the United States where poor nutrition and indifference to dentition and hygiene made physical beauty an extremely rare and sort of discomfiting condition, one in no way shared by Madame Psychosis's toothless and fireplug-shaped mother, who said not a word as Madame Psychosis's father interdicted everything from brassieres to Pap smears, addressing the nubile Madame Psychosis in progressively puerile baby-talk and continuing to use her childhood diminutive like *Pookie* or *Putti* as he attempted to dissuade her from accepting a scholarship to a Boston University whose Film and Film-Cartridge Studies Program was, he apparently maintained, full of quote Nasty Pootem Wooky Bam-Bams, unquote, whatever family-code pejorative this signified.

— That — to cut to a chase which the interviewers' hands-on-hip attitudes and replacement of the lamp's bulb with a much higher wattage signified they'd very much like to see cut to — as is often the case, it wasn't until Madame Psychosis got to college and gradually acquired some psychic distance and matter for emotional comparison that she even began to see how creepy her reagent-Daddy's regression had been, and not until a certain major-sport-star son's autograph on a punctured football inspired more e-mailed suspicion and sarcasm than gratitude from home in KY that she began even to suspect that her lack of social life throughout puberty might have had as much to do with her Daddy's intrusive discouragement as with her actaeonizing pubescent charms. That — pausing briefly to spell *actaeonizing* — the shit had hit the intergenerational psychic fan when Madame Psychosis brought the Auteur's little rotter of a son home to the KY spread for the third time, for Thanksgiving in the Year of the Tucks Medicated Pad, and witnessing her Daddy's infantilizing conduct of her and her mother's wordless compulsive canning and cooking, not to mention the terrific tension that resulted when Madame Psychosis attempted to move some of the stuffed animals out of her room to make room for the Auteur's son, in short experiencing her home and Daddy through the comparative filter of enmeshment with the Auteur's son brought Madame Psychosis to the crisis that precipitates Speaking the Unspeakable; and that it had been at Thanksgiving Dinner, at midday on 24 November Y.T.M.P., when the low-pH Daddy began not only cutting up Madame Psychosis's plate's turkey for her but mashing it into puree between the tines of his fork, all under the raised comparative eyebrows of the Auteur's son, that Madame Psychosis finally aired the unspoken question of why, with her now of legal age and living with a male and retired from childhood's twirling and carving out an adult career on one and potentially two sides of the film-camera, did her own personal Daddy seem to feel she needed help to chew? Molly Notkin's secondhand take on the emotional eruptions that ensued is not detailed, but she feels she can state w/ confidence that it's plausibly a case of any kind of system that's been under enormous silent pressure for some time, that when the system finally blows the accreted pressure's such that it's almost always a full-scale eruption. The low-pH Daddy's enormous stress had apparently erupted, right there at the table, with his grown daughter's white meat between his tines, in the confession that he'd been secretly, silently in love with Madame Psychosis from way, way back; that the love had been the real thing, pure, unspoken, genuflectory, timeless, impossible; that he never touched her, wouldn't, nor ogle, less out of a horror of being the sort of mid-South father who touched and ogled than out of the purity of his doomed love for the little girl he'd escorted to the movies as proudly as any beau, daily; that the repression and disguisability of his pure love hadn't been all that hard when Madame Psychosis had been juvenile and sexless, but that at the onset of puberty and nubility the pressure'd become so great that he could compensate only by regressing the child mentally to an age of incontinence and pre-mashed meat, and that his awareness of how creepy his denial of her maturation must have seemed — even though neither the daughter nor mother, even now wordlessly chewing a candied yam, had remarked on it, the denial and creepiness, although the man's beloved pointers were given to whimper and scratch at the door when the denial had gotten especially creepy (animals being way more sensitive than humans to emotional anomalies, in Molly Notkin's experience) — had raised his internal limbic system's pressure to near intolerable foot-kilo levels, and that he'd been hanging on for dear life for the past nigh on now a decade, but that now that he'd had to actually stand witness to the removal of Pooky and Urgle-Bear et al. from her ballerina-wallpapered room to make space for a nonrelated mature male whose physical vigor through the peephole the Daddy'd exerted every gram of trembling will he'd possessed trying not to drill the hole in the bathroom wall just above the mirror over the sink whose pipes made the wall behind the headboard of Madame Psychosis's room's bed sing and clunk, and through which, late at night — claiming to Mother a case of skitters from all the holiday nibbles — hunched atop the sink, every night since Madame Psychosis and the Auteur's son had first arrived to sleep together in the unstuffed-animaled bed of a childhood through which he'd been all but tortured by the purity of his impossible love for the —

— That it had been at this point that Madame Psychosis's mother's fork and then whole plate had clattered to the floor, and that amid the sounds of the pointers under the table fighting over that plate the mother's own denial-system's pressure blew, and she freaked, announcing publicly at the table that she and the Daddy had not once known each other as man and wife since Madame Psychosis had first menstruated, that she'd known something incredibly creepy was going on but had denied it, evacuated her suspicions and placed them under great pressure in the bell-jar of her own denial, because, she admits — *admits* is probably less accurate than something like *keens* or *shrieks* or *jabbers* — that her own father — an itinerant camp-meeting preacher — had molested her and her sister all through childhood, ogled and touched and worse, and that this had been why she'd married at just sixteen, to escape, and that now it was clear to her that she'd married the exact same kind of monster, the kind who spurns his ordained mate and wants his daughter.

— That she'd said maybe it was her, she, the mother, who was the monster, which if so she was tired of hiding it and appearing falsely before God and man.

— That whereupon she'd reeled from her place and hurdled three pointers and run down to the Daddy's acid-lab in the cellar, to disfigure herself with acid.

— That the Daddy'd kept a world-class collection of various acids in Pyrex-brand flasks on wooden shelves down in the cellar.

— That the Daddy, the rotter of a son, and finally a shock-slowed Madame Psychosis had all run down the stairs after the mother and hit the cellar just as the mother had removed the stopper of a Pyrex flask with an enormous half-eaten-away skull on the side, which along with the flaming scarlet piece of litmus paper afloat inside signified an incredibly low-pH and corrosive type of acid.

— That Madame Psychosis's name was in reality Lucille Duquette, and the Daddy's name either Earl or Al Duquette of extreme southeast KY, way down near TN and VA.

— That, despite the little rotter's professions of self-recrimination for allowing the deformity to take place and claim that the swirling systems of guilt and horror and denial-informed forgiveness made a committed relationship with Madame Psychosis increasingly untenable, it didn't take an expert in character-disorders and weaknesses to figure out why the fellow'd given Madame Psychosis the boot within months of the traumatic deformity, now did it.

— That, right on the hysterical cusp where internalized rage can so easily shift to externalized rage, the mother had hurled the low-pH flask at the Daddy, who'd reflexively ducked; and that the rotter, one *Orin*, right behind, a former tennis champion with superb upper-body reflexes, had instinctively ducked also, leaving Madame Psychosis — dazed and bradykinetic from the sudden venting of so many high-pressure repressive family systems — open for a direct facial hit, resulting in the traumatic deformity. And that it had been everyone's failure to press any charges that had liberated the mother from Southeast-KY custody and allowed her access once again to her home's kitchen, where, apparently despondent, she committed suicide by putting her extremities down the garbage disposal — first one arm and then, kind of miraculously if you think about it, the other arm.

332

The most distant and obscure Tuesday P.M. Meeting listed in the little white Metro-Boston Recovery Options[333] booklet the incisorless nostril-pierced girl down at The Ennet House had given him looked to be a males-only thing at 1730h. out in Natick, almost in Framingham, at something with a location on Route 27 that the M.B.R.O. booklet listed only as

'Q.R.S.–32A.' Hal, who had no last class period, rushed through P.M.'s, dispatching Shaw 1 and 3 by the time the regular P.M.'s were even warming up, then skipping left-leg circuits in the weight room, and was also forgoing tonight's lemon chicken with potato rolls, all to blast out to Natick in time to check this anti-Substance-fellowship-Meeting business out. He wasn't sure why, since it didn't seem to be any kind of slobbering inability to abstain that was the problem — he hadn't had so much as a mg. of a Substance of any kind since the 30-day urological condonation of last week. The issue's the horrific way his head's felt, increasingly, since he abruptly Abandoned All Hope.[334] It wasn't just nightmares and saliva. It was as if his head perched on the bedpost all night now and in the terribly early A.M. when Hal's eyes snapped open immediately said Glad You're UP I've Been Wanting To TALK To You and then didn't let up all day, having at him like a well-revved chain-saw all day until he could finally try to fall unconscious, crawling into the rack wretched to await more bad dreams. 24/7's of feeling wretched and bereft.

Dusk was coming earlier. Hal signed out at the portcullis and blasted down the hill and took the tow truck up Comm. Ave. to the C.C. Reservoir and then south on Hammond, the same deadening route as the E.T.A. conditioning run, except when he hit Boylston St. he turned right and struck out west. Once it cleared West Newton, Boylston St. became shunpike Rte. 9, the major west-suburb-commuter alternative to the suicidal I–90, and 9 suburb-hopped serpentine all the way west to Natick and Rte. 27.

Hal crawled through traffic on a major-flow road that had once been a cowpath. By the time he was in Wellesley Hills, the sky's combustionish orange had deepened to the hellish crimson of a fire's last embers. Darkness fell with a clunk shortly after, and Hal's spirits with it. He felt pathetic and absurd even going to check this Narcotics Anonymous Meeting thing out.

Everybody always flashed his or her brights at the tow truck because the headlamps were set so senselessly high on the truck's grille.

The little portable disk player had been detached by either Pemulis or Axford and not returned. WYYY was a ghostly thread of jazz against a sea of static. AM had only corporate rock and reports that the Gentle administration had scheduled and then cancelled a special Spontaneous-Disseminated address to the nation on subjects unknown. NPR had a kind of roundtable on potential subjects — George Will's laryngectomy-prosthesis sounded hideous. Hal preferred silence and traffic-sounds. He ate two of three $4.00 bran muffins he'd whipped in for at a Cleveland Circle gourmet bakery, grimacing as he swallowed because he'd forgotten a tonic to wash them down, then put in a mammoth plug of Kodiak and spat periodically into his special NASA glass, which fit neatly in the cup-holder down by the transmission, and passed the last fifteen minutes of the dull drive considering the probable etymological career of the word *Anonymous,* all the way he supposed from the Æolic ὄνμγα through Thynne's B.S. 1580s reference to 'anonymall Chronicals'; and whether it was joined way back somewhere at the Saxonic taproot to the Olde English *on-áne,* which supposedly meant All as One or As One Body and became Cynewulf's eventual standard inversion to the classic *anon,* maybe. Then called up on his mnemonic screen the developmental history since B.S. '35 of the initial Substance group AA, on which there'd been such a lengthy entry in the *Discursive O.E.D.* that Hal hadn't had to hit any sort of outside database to feel more or less factually prepared to drop into its spin-off NA and at least give the thing an appraising once-over. Hal can summon a kind of mental Xerox of anything he'd ever read and basically read it all over again, at will, which talent the Abandonment of Hope hasn't (so far) compromised, the withdrawal's effects being more like emotional/salivo-digestive.

The rock faces on either side of the truck when 27 goes through blasted hills of rock, the very fringes of the Berkshires' penumbra, are either granite or gneiss.

Hal for a while also practices saying 'My name's Mike.' 'Mike. Hi.' 'Hey there, name's Mike,' etc., into the truck's rearview.

By 15 minutes east of Natick it becomes obvious that the little booklet's terse *Q.R.S.* designates a facility called Quabbin Recovery Systems, which is easy to find, roadside ad-signs starting to announce the place several clicks away, each sign a little different and designed to form a little like narrative of which actual arrival at Q.R.S. would be the climax. Even Hal's late father was too young really to remember Burma-Shave signs.

Quabbin Recovery Systems is set far back from Rte. 27 on a winding groomed-gravel road flanked all the way up by classy old-time standing lanterns whose glass shades are pebbled and faceted like candy dishes and seem more for mood than illumination. Then the actual building's driveway's an even more winding little road that's barely more than a tunnel through meditative pines and poor-postured Lombardy poplars. Once off the highway the whole nighttime scene out here in exurbia — Boston's true boonies — seems ghostly and circumspect. Hal's tires crunch cones in the road. Some sort of bird shits on his windshield. The driveway broadens gradually into a like delta and then a parking lot of mint-white gravel, and the physical Q.R.S. is right there, cubular and brooding. The building's one of these late-model undeformed cubes of rough panel-brick and granite quoins. Illuminated moodily from below by more classy lanterns, it looks like a building-block from some child-titan's toy-chest. Its windows are the smoky brown kind that in daylight become dark mirrors. Hal's late father had publicly repudiated this kind of window-glass in an interview in *Lens & Pane* when the stuff first came out. Right now, lit from inside, the windows have a sort of bloody, polluted aspect.

A good two-thirds of the lot's parking places say RESERVED FOR

STAFF, which strikes Hal as odd. The tow truck tends to diesel and chuff after deignition, finally subsiding with a shuddering fart. It's dead quiet except for the hiss of light traffic down on 27 past all the trees. Only TP-link workers and marathon-type commuters live in exurban Natick. It's either way colder out here or else a front's been coming in while Hal drove. The lot's piney air has the ethyl sting of winter.

Q.R.S.'s big doors and lintel are more of that reflector-shade glass. There's no obvious bell, but the doors are unlocked. They open in that sort of pressurized way of institutional doors. The savanna-colored lobby is broad and still and has a vague medical/dental smell. Its carpet's a dense low tan Dacronyl weave that evacuates sound. There's a circular high-countered nurse's station or reception desk, but nobody's there.

The whole place is so quiet Hal can hear the squeak of blood in his head.

The *32A* that follows *Q.R.S.* in the girl's little white booklet is presumably a room number. Hal has on a non-E.T.A. jacket and carries the NASA glass he spits in. He'd have to spit even if he didn't have chew in; the Kodiak's almost like a cover or excuse.

There is no map or You-Are-Here-type directory on view in the lobby. The lobby's heat is intense and close but kind of porous; it's in a sort of uneasy struggle with the radiant chill of all the smoked glass of the entrance. The lamps out in the lot and off along the driveway are blobs of sepia light through the glass. Inside, cove-lighting at the seams of walls and ceiling produce an indirect light that's shadowless and seems to rise from the room's objects themselves. It's the same lighting and lion-colored carpeting in the first long hall Hal tries. The room numbers go up to 17 and then after Hal turns a sharp corner start at 34A. The room doors are false blond wood but look thick and private, flush in their frames. There's also the smell of stale coffee. The walls' color scheme is somewhere between puce and mature eggplant-skin, kind of nauseous against the sandy tan of the carpet. All buildings with any kind of health-theme to them have this thin sick sweet dental sub-odor to them. Q.R.S. also seems to have some sort of balsamy air-freshener going in the ventilation system, too, but it doesn't quite cover the sweet medical stink or the bland sour smell of institutional food.

Hal hasn't heard one human sound since he came in. The place's silence has that glittery sound of total silence. His footfalls make no sound on the Dacronyl. He feels furtive and burglarish and holds the NASA glass down at his side and the NA booklet higher up and cover-out as a sort of explanatory I.D. There are computer-enhanced landscapes on the walls, little low tables with glossy pamphlets, a framed print of Picasso's 'Seated Harlequin,' and nothing else that wasn't just institutional bullshit, visual Muzak. Without any sound to his footfalls it's like the gauntlets of doors just glide by. The quiet has a kind of menace. The whole cubular building seems to Hal to hold the tensed menace of a living thing that's chosen to hold itself still. If you asked Hal to describe his feelings as he looked for room 32A the best he could do would be to say he wished he were somewhere else and feeling some way besides how he felt. His mouth pours spit. The glass's one-third full and heavy in his hand and not much fun to look at. He's missed the glass a couple of times and marred the tan carpet with dark spit. After two 90° turns it's clear the hallway's run is a perfect square around the cube's ground level. He's seen no stairs or entrances to stairways. He empties the NASA glass rather gooily into a potted rubber tree's dirt. Q.R.S.'s building may be one of those infamous Rubikular cubes that looks topologically undeformed but is actually impossible to negotiate on the inside. But the numbers after the third corner start at 18, and now Hal can hear either very distant or very muffled voices. He carries the NA booklet in front of him like a crucifix. He has about $50 U.S. and another $100 in eagle-, leaf-, and broom-emblemized O.N.A.N. scrip, having had no idea what sort of introductory costs might be involved. Q.R.S. didn't purchase prime Natick acreage and the cutting-edge services of a São-Paulo-School Geometric-Minimalist architect with just altruistic goodwill, that was for sure.

Room 32A's wood-grain door was just as emphatically shut as all the others, but the muffled voices were behind this one. The Meeting was listed in the book as starting at 1730, and it was only around 1720, and Hal thought the voices might signify some sort of pre-Meeting orientation for people who've come for the first time, sort of tentatively, just to scout the whole enterprise out, so he doesn't knock.

He still has this intractable habit of making a move like he's straightening a bow tie before he enters a strange room.

And except for the thin rubber sheaths, the doorknobs on the Quabbin Recovery Systems doors are the same as at E.T.A. — flat bars of brass toggle-bolted to the latch mechanism, so you have to push the bar down instead of turning anything to open the door.

But the Meeting is under way, apparently. It isn't near big enough to create a mood of anonymity or casual spectation. Nine or ten adult middle-class males are in the warm room on orange plastic chairs with legs of molded steel tubing. Every one of the men has a beard, and each wears chinos and a sweater, and they all sit the same way, that Indian cross-legged style with their hands on their knees and their feet under their knees, and they all wear socks, with no footwear or winter jackets anywhere in sight. Hal eases the door shut and sort of slinks along the wall to an empty chair, all the time conspicuously brandishing the Meeting booklet. The chairs are placed in no discernible order, and their orange clashes nastily with the room's own colors, walls and ceiling the color of Thousand Island dressing — a color-scheme with unplaceable but uneasy associations for Hal — and more of the lionskin Dacronyl carpet. And the warm air in 32A is stuffy with CO_2 and unpleasantly scented with the aroma of soft male middle-aged bodies not wearing footwear, a stale meaty cheesy smell, more nauseous even than the E.T.A. locker room after a Mrs. Clarke Tex-Mex fiesta.

The only guy in the Meeting to acknowledge Hal's entrance is at the front of the room, a man Hal would have to call almost morbidly round, his body nearly Leith-sized and globularly round and the smaller but still large globe of a head atop it, his socks plaid and his legs not all the way crossable so it looks like he might pitch disastrously backward in his chair any minute, smiling warmly at Hal's winter coat and NASA glass as Hal slinks and sits and slumps down low. The round man's chair is positioned under a small white Magic Marker blackboard, and all the other chairs approximately face it, and the man holds a Magic Marker in one hand and holds what looks quite a bit like a teddy bear to his chest with the other, and wears chinos and a cable-knit Norwegian sweater the color of toast. His hair is that waxy sort of blond, and he's got the blond eyebrows and creepy blond eyelashes and violently flushed face of a true Norwegian blond, and his little beard is an imperial so sharply waxed it looks like a truncated star. The morbidly round blond man's pretty clearly the leader of the Meeting, possibly a high-ranking official of Narcotics Anonymous, whom Hal could casually approach about tracts and texts to buy and study, afterward.

Another middle-aged guy up near the front is crying, and he too holds what looks like a bear.

The blond brows hike up and down as the leader says 'I'd like to suggest we men all hold our bears tight and let our Inner Infant nonjudgmentally listen to Kevin's Inner Infant expressing his grief and loss.'

They're all at subtly different angles to Hal, who's slumped low over by the wall in the second-to-last row, but it turns out after some subtle casual neck-craning that, sure enough, all these middle-class guys in at least their thirties are sitting there clutching teddy bears to their sweatered chests — and identical teddy bears, plump and brown and splay-limbed and with a little red corduroy tongue protruding from the mouths, so the bears all look oddly throttled. The room is menacingly quiet now except for the sibilance of the heating vents and the sobbing guy Kevin, and the plip of Hal's saliva hitting the bottom of the empty glass rather more loudly than he might have wished.

The back of the crying guy's neck is turning redder and redder as he clutches his bear and rocks on his hams.

Hal sits with his leg crossed good-ankle-on-knee and joggles his white hightop and looks at his callused thumb and listens to the Kevin guy sob and snuffle. The guy wipes his nose with the heel of his hand just like the littler Buddies at E.T.A. Hal figures the tears and bears have something to do with giving up drugs, and that the Meeting is probably on the verge of coming around to talking explicitly about drugs and how to give up drugs for a certain period without feeling indescribably wretched and bereft, or maybe at least some data on how long one might expect the wretchedness of giving up drugs to continue before the old nervous system and salivary glands returned to normal. Even though *Inner Infant* sounds uncomfortably close to Dr. Doloros Rusk's dreaded *Inner Child*, Hal'd be willing to bet that here it's some sort of shorthand Narcotics Anonymous sobriquet for like 'limbic component of the CNS' or 'the part of our cortex that's not utterly wretched and bereft without the drugs that up to now have been pulling us through the day, secretly' or some affirming, encouraging thing like that. Hal wills himself to stay objective and not form any judgments before he has serious data, hoping desperately for some sort of hopeful feeling to emerge.

The diglobular leader has made a cage of his hands and rested his hands on his teddy bear's head and is breathing slowly and evenly, watching Kevin kindly from under the blond eyebrows, looking more than anything like some sort of Buddha-as-California-surfer-dude. The leader inhales gently and says 'The energies I'm feeling in the group are energies of unconditional love and acceptance for Kevin's Inner Infant.' Nobody else says anything, and the leader doesn't seem to need anybody to say anything. He looks down at the cage his hands have made on the bear and keeps subtly changing the shape of the cage. The guy Kevin, whose neck is now not only beet-red but shiny with embarrassed sweat between his shirt-collar and hair's hem, sobs even harder at the affirmation of love and support. The round leader's high hoarse voice had the same blandly kind didactic quality as Rusk's, as if always speaking to a not-too-bright child.

After some more cage-play and deep breathing the leader looks up and around and nods at nothing and says 'Maybe we could all name our feelings right now for Kevin and share how much we're caring for him and his Inner Infant right now, in his pain.'

Various bearded cross-legged guys speak up:

'I love you, Kevin.'

'I'm not judging you, Kevin.'

'Know just how you and the I.I. feel.'

'I'm feeling really close to you.'

'I'm feeling a lot of love for you right now, Kevin.'

'You're crying for two, guy.'

'Kevin Kevin Kevin Kevin Kevin.'

'I'm not feeling like your crying is one bit unmanly or pathetic, fella.'

It's at this point that Hal begins truly to lose his willed objectivity and open-mindedness and to get a bad personal feeling about this Narcotics Anonymous ('NA') Meeting, which seems already deeply under way and isn't one bit like he's imagined an even remotely hopeful antidrug Meeting would be like. It seems more like some kind of cosmetic-psychology encounter thing. Not one Substance or symptom of Substance-deprivation has been mentioned so far. And none of these guys looks like they've ever been engaged with anything more substantial than an occasional wine cooler, if he had to guess.

Hal's grim mood deepens as the round man up front now leans precariously over and down and opens a sort of toy-box under the blackboard by his chair and produces a cheap plastic portable CD laser-scanner and sets it on top of the toy-box, where it begins to issue a kind of low treacly ambient shopping-mall music, mostly cello, with sporadic harps and chimes. The stuff spreads through the hot little room like melted butter, and Hal sinks lower in his orange chair and looks hard at the space-and-spacecraft emblem on his NASA glass.

'Kevin?' the leader says over the music. 'Kevin?' The sobbing man's hand lies over his face like a spider, and he doesn't even start to look up until the leader has said several times very blandly and kindly 'Kevin, do you feel okay about looking at the rest of the group?'

Kevin's red neck wrinkles as he looks up at the blond leader through his fingers.

The leader's made the cage again on his poor bear's squashed head. 'Can you share what you're feeling, Kevin?' he says. 'Can you name it?'

Kevin's voice is muffled by the hand he hides behind. 'I'm feeling my Inner Infant's abandonment and deep-deprivation issues, Harv,' he says, drawing shuddering breaths. His mauve sweater's shoulders tremble. 'I'm feeling my Inner Infant standing holding the bars of his crib and looking out of the bars . . . bars of his crib and crying for his Mommy and Daddy to come hold him and nurture him.' Kevin sobs twice in an apneated way. One arm holds his lap's bear so tight Hal thinks he can see a little stuffing start to come out of its mouth around its tongue, and a stalactite of that clear thin weepy-type mucus hangs from Kevin's nose just mm. over the throttled bear's head. 'And nobody's *coming!*' he sobs. 'Nobody's coming. I feel alone with my bear and plastic airplane-mobile and teething ring.'

Everybody's nodding in an affirming and pained way. No two beards are exactly the same fullness and design. A couple other sobs break out across the room. Everyone's bear stares blankly ahead.

The leader's nod is slow and meditative. 'And can you share your needs with the group right now, Kevin?'

'Please share, Kevin,' says a slim guy over by a black filing cabinet who sits like he's a veteran at sitting Indian-style in hard plastic chairs.

The music's still going, going absolutely nowhere, like Philip Glass on Quaaludes.

'The work we're here to do,' the leader says over the music, one hand now pressed pensively to the side of his big face, 'is to work on our dysfunctional passivity and tendency to wait silently for our Inner Infant's needs to be magically met. The energy I feel in the group now is that the group is supportively asking Kevin to nurture his Inner Infant by naming and sharing his needs out loud with the group. And I'm feeling how aware we all are how risky and vulnerable need-naming-out-loud must feel for Kevin right now.'

Everybody looks deadly serious. A couple guys are rubbing their bears' bellies pregnantly. The only really Infantile thing Hal can feel inside him is the inguinal gurgle of two heavy bran muffins swallowed at high speeds w/o liquid. The string of mucus from Kevin's nose trembles and swings. The slender guy who'd asked Kevin please to share is now waggling the arms of his teddy bear in an infantile way. Hal feels a wave of nausea flood his mouth with fresh saliva.

'We're asking you to name what your Inner Infant wants right now more than anything in the world,' the leader's saying to Kevin.

'*To be loved and held!*' Kevin keens, sobbing harder. His lachrymucus is now a thin silver string joining his nose and the fuzzy top of his bear's head. The bear's expression is seeming creepier to Hal by the second. Hal wonders what the etiquette is in NA about getting up and leaving right in the middle of somebody's Infantile revelation of need. Meanwhile Kevin is saying that his Inner Infant inside him had always hoped that some day his Mom and Dad would be there for him, to hold him and love him. He says but right from the start they'd never been there for him, leaving him and his brother with Hispanic nannies while they devoted themselves to their jobs and various types of psychotherapy and support groups. This takes a while to say, given all the snuffles and wracked spasms. Then Kevin says but then by the time he was eight they were gone altogether, dead, smooshed by a dysfunctionally falling radio traffic helicopter on the Jamaica Way on the way to Couples Counselling.

At this Hal's slumped head jerks up, his mouth oval with horror. He's all of a sudden realized that this guy who's seated at such an angle that Hal's been able to see only the obliquest portion of his profile is in fact Kevin Bain, his brother Orin's old E.T.A. doubles and chemical-mischief partner Marlon Bain's older brother, Kevin Bain, of Dedham MA, who the last Hal had heard had gotten his M.B.A. at Wharton and cleaned up with a string of Simulated Reality arcades all up and down the South Shore, back during the pre-Subsidized-Time Simulated Reality craze, before InterLace viewers and digital cartridges let you do your own customized Simulating right at home and the novelty wore off.[335] The Kevin Bain whose childhood hobby was memorizing IRS capital-depreciation schedules and whose adult idea of a wild time[336] had been putting extra marshmallows in his nightly cocoa, and who wouldn't have known a recreational drug if it walked up and poked him in the eye. Hal begins to scan for possible exits. The only door was the one he'd come in, which is in full view of most of the room. There are no windows at all.

Hal's chilled by multiple realizations. This is no NA or anti-Substance Meeting. This is one of those men's-issues-Men's-Movement-type Meetings K. D. Coyle's stepdad went to and Coyle liked to mimic and parody during drills, making his stick's grip poke out between his legs and yelling 'Nurture this! Honor getting in touch with this!'

Kevin Bain is wiping his nose with his poor teddy bear's head and saying it didn't look like his Inner Infant would ever get its wish. The gooey music's cello sounds like some sort of cow mooing in distress, maybe at what it's in the middle of.

Sure enough, the round man, whose hand's left a print on his soft cheek, asks poor old Kevin Bain to honor and name his I.I.'s wounded wish anyway, to say 'Please, Mommy and Daddy, come love and hold me,' out loud, several times, which Kevin Bain goes ahead and does, rocking a little in his chair, his voice now with an edge of good old adult mortified embarrassment to it, along with the racking sobs. A couple of the other men in the room are wiping at their bright-white drug-free eyes with the arms of their teddy bears. Hal is painfully reminded of the rare Ziplocs of Humboldt County hydroponic marijuana that Pemulis occasionally scored via FedEx from his mercantile counterpart at the Rolling Hills Academy, the curved tawny buds so big and plump with high-Delta-9 resin the Ziplocs had looked like bags of little teddy-bear arms. The moist sounds right behind him turn out to be a mild-faced older man eating yogurt out of a plastic cup. Hal keeps rechecking the Meeting data in the little M.B.R.O. booklet the girl had given him. He notes that the booklet has broad chocolate thumbprints on several of the pages, and that two pages are stuck firmly together with what Hal fears is an ancient dried booger, and now that the booklet's cover is dated January in the Year of Dairy Products from the American Heartland, i.e. nearly two years past, and that it's not impossible that the blandly hostile toothless girl at The Ennet facility had kertwanged him by giving him a dated and useless M.B.R.O. guide.

Kevin Bain keeps repeating 'Please, Mommy and Daddy, come love me and hold me' in a kind of monotone of pathos. The gradually intensifying lisp in *Please* is apparently a performative invocation of the old Inner Infant. Tears and other fluids flow and roll. The warm round leader Harv's own eyes are a moist glassy blue. The CD scanner's cello is now into some sort of semi-jazzy pizzicato stuff that seems oxymoronic against the room's mood. Hal keeps catching whiffs of a hot sick-sweet civety smell that signifies somebody nearby has some athlete's-foot issues to confront, under his socks. Plus it's mystifying that 32A has no windows, given all the smoky-brown fenestration Hal'd seen from outside the Q.R.S. cube. The man eating yogurt's beard is one of those small rectangular ones that's easy to keep clear of the cup's rim. The back and side of Kevin Bain's hair has separated into spiky sweat-soaked strands, from the room's heat and the Infant's emotions.

All through his own infancy and toddlerhood, Hal had continually been held and dandled and told at high volume that he was loved, and he feels like he could have told K. Bain's Inner Infant that getting held and told you were loved didn't automatically seem like it rendered you emotionally whole or Substance-free. Hal finds he rather envies a man who feels he has something to explain his being fucked up, parents to blame it on. Not even Pemulis blamed his late father Mr. Pemulis, who hadn't exactly sounded like the Fred MacMurray of U.S. fathers. But then Pemulis didn't consider himself fucked up or unfree w/r/t Substances.

The blond and Buddhic cable-knit Harv, dandling his bear on his knee now, calmly asks Kevin Bain if it feels to his Inner Infant like Mommy and Daddy were ever going to appear cribside to meet his needs.

'No,' Kevin says very quietly. 'No, it doesn't, Harv.'

The leader is idly arranging his bear's splayed arms in different positions, so it looks like the bear's either waving or surrendering. 'Do you suppose you would be able to ask someone in the group here tonight to love and hold you instead, Kevin?'

The back of Kevin Bain's head doesn't move. Hal's whole digestive tract spasms at the prospect of watching two bearded adult males in sweaters and socks engage in surrogate Infant-hugging. He begins asking himself why he doesn't just fake a hideous coughing fit and flee Q.R.S.-32A with his fist over his face.

Harv's now waggling the bear's arms back and forth and making his voice high and cartoon-characterish and pretending to have his bear ask Kevin Bain's bear if it would maybe point to the man in the group Kevin Bain would most like to have hold and nurture and love him *in loco parentis*. Hal's spitting quietly down the side of his glass and brooding wretchedly at the fact that he's driven fifty supperless clicks to listen to a globular man in plaid socks pretend his teddy bear's speaking Latin when he looks up from the glass and is chilled to see that Kevin Bain has wiggled his Indian-style way around in his chair and is holding his bear way up by its underarms, just the way a father holds a toddler up for a public spect-op or parade, turning the throttled-looking bear this way and that, scanning the room — as Hal covers part of his face with a hand, pretending to scratch an eyebrow, praying not to be recognized — and finally manipulating the bear's arm so the plump brown fuzzy fingerless hand of the bear's pointing right in Hal's direction. Hal doubles over in a coughing spasm only half-faked, running decision-trees on various ruses for flight.

Just like his younger brother Marlon Bain, Kevin Bain is a short thick person with a dark swart face. He looks sort of like an overdeveloped troll. And he has the same capacity for constant incredible sweating that always made Marlon Bain look to Hal, both on-court and off-, like a toad hunched moist and unblinking in humid shade. Except Kevin Bain's little glittery

Bain eyes are also red and swollen with public weeping, and he's balding back from the temples in a way that gives him a widow's peak like nobody's business, and doesn't seem to recognize a post-pubescent Hal, and is pointing his bear's blunt hand Hal realizes finally after almost swallowing his plug of Kodiak not at Hal but at the mild-faced square-bearded older guy behind him, who's holding a spoon of vividly pink yogurt in front of his bear's open mouth, just touching its protruding tongue's red corduroy, pretending to be feeding the bear. Hal very casually puts the NASA glass between his legs and gets both hands under his chair-seat and hops the chair bit by bit over and out of the lines of sight and transit between Kevin Bain and the yogurt man. Harv, up front, is making a complex hand-signal to the yogurt man not to speak or move from his back-row orange chair no matter what; and then, as Kevin Bain wriggles cross-legged back around to face front again, Harv smoothly turns the hand-signal into a motion like he's smoothing his hair. The motion then becomes sincere and ruminative as the leader breathes deeply a couple of times. The music's settled back into its original nodding narcosis.

'Kevin,' Harv says, 'since this is a group exercise in passivity and Inner-Infant needs, and since you've selected Jim as the member of the group you need something from, we need you to ask Jim out loud to meet your needs. Ask him to come up and hold you and love you, since your parents aren't ever coming. Not ever, Kevin.'

Kevin Bain makes a mortified sound and reclamps a hand over his big swart face.

'Go for it, Kev,' somebody over near the Bly poster calls out.

'We affirm and support you,' says the guy by the filing cabinet.

Hal now starts scrolling through an alphabetical list of the faraway places he'd rather be right now. He's not even up to Addis Ababa when Kevin Bain acquiesces and begins very softly and hesitantly asking the mild-faced Jim, who's put aside his yogurt but not the bear, to please come up and love him and hold him. By the time Hal's envisioned himself tumbling over American Falls at the Concavity's southwest rim in a rusty old noxious-waste-displacement drum, Kevin Bain has asked Jim eleven progressively louder times to come nurture and hold him, to no avail. The older guy just sits there, clutching his yogurt-tongued bear, his expression somewhere between mild and blank.

Hal has never actually seen projectile-weeping before. Bain's tears are actually exiting his eyes and projecting outward several cm. before starting to fall. His facial expression is the scrunched spread one of a small child's total woe, his neck-cords standing out and face darkening so that it looks like some sort of huge catcher's mitt. A bright cape of mucus hangs from his upper lip, and his lower lip seems to be having some kind of epileptic fit. Hal finds the tantrum's expression on an adult face sort of compelling. At a certain point hysterical grief becomes facially indistinguishable from hysterical mirth, it appears. Hal imagines watching Bain weep on a white beach through binoculars from the balcony of a cool dim Aruban hotel room.

'He's not *coming!*' Kevin Bain finally keens to the leader.

Harv the leader nods, scratching an eyebrow, and confirms that that seems to be the case. He pretends to stroke his imperial in puzzlement and asks rhetorically what might be the problem, why mild-faced Jim isn't automatically coming when called.

Kevin Bain's just about vivisecting his poor bear out of mortified frustration. He seems deeply into his Infant persona now, and Hal rather hopes these guys have procedures for getting Bain at least back to sixteen before he has to try to drive home. At some point a timpani has gotten involved in the CD's music, and a rather saucy cornet, and the music's finally started moving a little, toward what's either a climax or the end of the disk.

By now various men in the group have started crying out to Kevin Bain that his Inner Infant wasn't getting its needs met, that sitting there passively asking for nurture to get up and come to him wasn't getting the needs met, that Kevin owed it to his Inner Infant to come up with some sort of active way to meet the Infant's needs. Somebody shouted out 'Honor that Infant!' Somebody else called 'Meet those needs!' Hal is mentally strolling down the Appian Way in bright Eurosunlight, eating a cannoli, twirling his Dunlop racquets by the throats like six-shooters, enjoying the sunshine and cranial silence and a normal salivary flow.

Pretty soon the men's supportive exhortations have distilled into everybody in the room except Harv, Jim and Hal chanting 'Meet Those Needs! Meet Those Needs!' in the same male-crowd-exhortative meter as 'Hold That Line!' or 'Block That Kick!'

Kevin Bain wipes his nose on his sleeve and asks humongous Harv the leader what he's supposed to do to get his Infant's needs met if the person he's chosen to meet those needs won't come.

The leader has folded his hands over his belly and sat back, by this time, smiling, cross-legged, holding his tongue. His bear sits atop the protrusion of belly with its little blunt legs straight out, the way you'll see a bear sitting on a shelf. It seems to Hal that the O_2 in 32A is now getting used up at a ferocious clip. Not at all like the cool, sheep-scented breezes of Ascension Island in the South Atlantic. The men in the room are still chanting 'Meet Those Needs!'

'What you're saying is I need to actively go over to Jim myself and ask him to hold me,' Kevin Bain says, grinding at his eyes with his knuckles.

The leader smiles blandly.

'Instead of you're saying passively trying to get Jim to come to me,' says Kevin Bain, whose tears have largely stopped, and whose sweat has taken on the clammy shine of true fear-sweat.

Harv emerges as one of these people who can heft one eyebrow and not the other. 'It would take real courage and love and commitment to your Inner Infant to take the risk and go actively over to somebody that might give you what your Infant needs,' he says quietly. The CD player has at some point shifted into an all-cello instrumental of 'I Don't Know (How to Love Him)' from an old opera Lyle sometimes borrowed people's players and listened to at night in the weight room. Lyle and Marlon Bain had been particularly tight, Hal recalls.

The trimeter of the men's chant has reduced to a one-foot low-volume 'Needs, Needs, Needs, Needs, Needs' as Kevin Bain slowly and hesitantly uncrosses his legs and rises from his orange chair, turning to face Hal and the motionless guy behind him, this Jim. Bain begins to move slowly toward them with the tortured steps of a mime miming walking against a tornadic gale. Hal's picturing himself doing a lazy backstroke in the Azores, spouting glassy water up out of his mouth in a cytological plume. He's leaning almost out of his chair, as far as possible out of Kevin Bain's line of transit, studying the brown suspension in the bottom of his glass. His prayer not to be recognized by a regressive Kevin Bain is the first really desperate and sincere prayer Hal can remember offering since he'd stopped wearing pajamas with feet in them.

'Kevin?' Harv calls softly from the front of the room. 'Is it you moving actively toward Jim, or should it be the Infant inside you, the one with the needs?'

'Needs, Needs, Needs,' the bearded men are chanting, some rhythmically raising their manicured fists in the air.

Bain's looking back and forth between Harv and Jim, chewing his finger indecisively.

'Is this how an Infant moves towards its needs, Kevin?' Harv says.

'Go for it, Kevin!' a full-bearded man calls out.

'Let the Infant out!'

'Let your Infant do the walking, Kev.'

So Hal's most vivid full-color memory of the non-anti-Substance Meeting he drove fifty oversalivated clicks to by mistake will become that of his older brother's doubles partner's older brother down on all fours on a Dacronyl rug, crawling, hampered because one arm was holding his bear to his chest, so he sort of dipped and rose as he crawled on three limbs toward Hal and the needs-meeter behind him, Bain's knees leaving twin pale tracks in the carpet and his head up on a wobbly neck and looking up and past Hal, his face unspeakable.

O

The ceiling was breathing. It bulged and receded. It swelled and settled. The room was in St. Elizabeth's Hospital's Trauma Wing. Whenever he looked at it, the ceiling bulged and then deflated, shiny as a lung. When Don was a massive toddler his mother had put them in a little beach house just back of the dunes off a public beach in Beverly. The place was affordable because it had a big ragged hole in the roof. Origin of hole unknown. Gately's outsized crib had been in the beach house's little living room, right under the hole. The guy that owned the little cottages off the dunes had stapled thick clear polyurethane sheeting across the room's ceiling. It was an attempt to deal with the hole. The polyurethane bulged and settled in the North Shore wind and seemed like some monstrous vacuole inhaling and exhaling directly over little Gately, lying there, wide-eyed. The breathing polyurethane vacuole had seemed like it developed a character and personality as winter deepened and the winds grew worse. Gately, age like four, had regarded the vacuole as a living thing, and had named it Herman, and had been afraid of it. He couldn't feel the right side of his upper body. He couldn't move in any real sense of the word. The hospital room had that misty quality rooms in fevers have. Gately lay on his back. Ghostish figures materialized at the peripheries of his vision and hung around and then dematerialized. The ceiling bulged and receded. Gately's own breath hurt his throat. His throat felt somehow raped. The blurred figure in the next bed sat up very still in bed in a sitting position and seemed to have a box on its head. Gately kept having a terrible repetitious ethnocentric dream that he was robbing the house of an Oriental and had the guy tied to a chair and was trying to blindfold him with quality mailing twine from the drawer under the Oriental's kitchen phone. The Oriental kept being able to see around the twine and kept looking steadily at Gately and blinking inscrutably. Plus the Oriental had no nose or mouth, just a smooth expanse of lower-facial skin, and wore a silk robe and scary sandals, and had no hair on its legs.

What Gately perceived as light-cycles and events all out of normal sequence was really Gately going in and out of consciousness. Gately did not perceive this. It seemed to him more like he kept coming up for air and then being pushed below the surface of something. Once when Gately came up for air he found that resident Tiny Ewell was seated in a chair right up next to the bed. Tiny's little slim hand was on the bed's crib-type railing, and his chin rested on the hand, so his face was right up close. The ceiling bulged and receded. The room's only light was what spilled in from the nighttime hall. Nurses glided down the hall and past the door in subsonic footwear. A tall and slumped ghostish figure appeared to Gately's left, off past the blurred seated square-head boy's bed, slumped and fluttering, appearing to rest its tailbone on the sill of the dark window. The ceiling rounded on down and then settled back flat. Gately rolled his eyes up at Ewell. Ewell had shaved off his blunt white goatee. His hair was so completely clean and white it took a faint pink cast from the pink of his scalp below. Ewell had been discoursing to him for an unknown length of time. It was Gately's first full night in St. Elizabeth's Hospital's Trauma Wing. He didn't know what night of the week it was. His circadian rhythm was the least of the personal rhythms that had been scrambled. His right side felt encased in a kind of hot cement. Also a sick throb in what he assumed was a toe. He wondered dimly about going to the bathroom, if and when. Ewell was right in the middle of speaking. Gately couldn't tell if Ewell was whispering. Nurses glided across the doorway's light. Their sneakers were so noiseless the nurses seemed to be on wheels. A stolid shadow of somebody in a hat was cast obliquely across the hall's tile floor just outside the room, as if a stolid figure were seated just outside the door, against the wall, in a hat.

'My wife's personal term for soul is *personality*. As in "There's something incorrigibly dark in your personality, Eldred Ewell, and Dewars brings it out." '

The hall floor was pretty definitely white tile, with a cloudy overwaxed shine in the bright fluorescence out there. Some kind of red or pink stripe ran down the center of the hall. Gately couldn't tell if Tiny Ewell thought he was awake or unconscious or what.

'It was in the fall term of third grade as a child that I found myself fallen in with the bad element. They were a group of tough blue-collar Irish lads bussed in from the East Watertown projects. Runny noses, home-cut hair, frayed cuffs, quick with their fists, sports-mad, fond of sneaker-hockey on asphalt,' Ewell said, 'and yet, strangely, I, unable to do even one pull-up in the President's Physical Fitness Test, quickly became the leader of the pack we all fell into. The blue-collar lads all seemed to admire me for attributes that were not clear. We formed a sort of club. Our uniform was a gray skallycap. Our clubhouse was the dugout of a Little League diamond that had fallen into disuse. Our club was called the Money-Stealers' Club. At my suggestion we went with a descriptive name as opposed to euphemistic. The name was mine. The Irish lads acquiesced. They viewed me as the brains of the operation. I held them in a kind of thrall. This was due in large part to my capacity for rhetoric. Even the toughest and most brutish Irish lad respects a gilded tongue. Our club was formed for the express purpose of undertaking a bunko operation. We went around to people's homes after school, ringing the doorbell and soliciting donations for Project Hope Youth Hockey. There was no such organization. Our donation-receptacle was a Chock Full O' Nuts can with PROJECT HOPE YOUTH HOCKEY written on a strip of masking tape wrapped around the can. The lad who made the receptacle had spelled *PROJECT* with a G in the first draft. I ridiculed him for the error, and the whole club pointed at him and laughed.

810

Brutally.' Ewell kept staring at the crude blue jailhouse square and canted cross on Gately's forearms. 'Our only visible credentials were kneepads and sticks we'd purloined from the P.E. stockroom. By my order, all were held carefully to conceal the *PPTY W. WTTN ELEM SCH* emblazoned down the side of every stick. One lad had a goalie mask on under his skallycap, the rest kneepads and carefully held sticks. The kneepads were turned inside-out for the same reason. I couldn't even skate, and my mother absolutely forbade rough play on asphalt. I wore a necktie and combed my hair carefully after each solicitation. I was the spokesperson. The mouthpiece, the bad lads called me. They were Irish Catholics all. Watertown from east to west is Catholic, Armenian, and Mixed. The Eastside boys all but genuflected to my gift for bullshit. I was exceptionally smooth with adults. I rang doorbells and the lads arrayed themselves behind me on the porch. I spoke of disadvantaged youth and team spirit and fresh air and the meaning of competition and alternatives to the after-school streets' bad element. I spoke of mothers in support-hose and war-injured older brothers with elaborate prostheses cheering disadvantaged lads on to victory against far better-equipped teams. I discovered that I had a gift for it, the emotional appeal of adult rhetoric. It was the first time I felt personal power. I was unrehearsed and creative and moving. Hard-case homeowners who came to the door in sleeveless Ts holding tallboys of beer with stubble and expressions of minimal charity were often weeping openly by the time we left their porch. I was called a fine lad and a good kid and a credit to me Mum and Da. My hair was tousled so often I had to carry a mirror and comb. The coffee can became hard to carry back to the dugout, where we hid it behind a cinderblock bench-support. We'd netted over a hundred dollars by Halloween. This was a serious amount in those days.'

Tiny Ewell and the ceiling kept receding and then looming in, bulging roundly. Figures Gately didn't know from Adam kept popping in and out of fluttery view in different corners of the room. The space between his bed and the other bed seemed to distend and then contract with a slow sort of boinging motion. Gately's eyes kept rolling up in his head, his upper lip mustached with sweat. 'And I was revelling in the fraud of it, the discovery of the gift,' Ewell was saying. 'I was flushed with adrenaline. I had tasted power, the verbal manipulation of human hearts. The lads called me the gilded blarneyman. Soon the first-order fraud wasn't enough. I began secretly filching receipts from the club's Chock Full O' Nuts can. Embezzling. I persuaded the lads it was too risky to keep the can in the open-air dugout and took personal charge of the can. I kept the can in my bedroom and persuaded my mother that it contained Christmas-connected gifts and must under no circumstances be inspected. To my underlings in the club I claimed to be rolling the coins and depositing them in a high-interest savings account I'd opened for us in the name Franklin W. Dixon. In fact I was buying myself Pez and Milky Ways and *Mad* magazines and a Creeple Peeple-brand Deluxe Oven-and-Mold Set with six different colors of goo. This was in the early 1970s. At first I was discreet. Grandiose but discreet. At first the embezzlement was controlled. But the power had roused something dark in my personality, and the adrenaline drove it forward. Self-will run riot. Soon the club's coffee can was empty by each weekend's end. Each week's haul went toward some uncontrolled Saturday binge of puerile consumption. I doctored up flamboyant bank statements to show the club, in the dugout. I got more loquacious and imperious with them. None of the lads thought to question me, or the purple Magic Marker the bank statements were done in. I was not dealing with intellectual titans here, I knew. They were nothing but malice and muscle, the worst of the school's bad element. And I ruled them. Thrall. They trusted me completely, and the rhetorical gift. In retrospect they probably could not conceive of any sane third-grader with glasses and a necktie trying to defraud them, given the inevitably brutal consequences. Any *sane* third-grader. But I was no longer a sane third-grader. I lived only to feed the dark thing in my personality, which told me any consequences could be forestalled by my gift and grand personal aura.

'But then of course eventually Christmas hove into view.' Gately tries to stop Ewell and say 'hove?' and finds to his horror that he can't make any sounds come out. 'The meaty Catholic Eastside bad-element lads now wanted to tap their nonexistent Franklin W. Dixon account to buy support-hose and sleeveless Ts for their swarthy blue-collar families. I held them off as long as I could with pedantic blather on interest penalties and fiscal years. Irish Catholic Christmas is no laughing matter, though, and for the first time their swarthy eyes began to narrow at me. Things at school grew increasingly tense. One afternoon, the largest and swarthiest of them assumed control of the can in an ugly dugout coup. It was a blow from which my authority never recovered. I began to feel a gnawing fear: my denial broke: I realized I'd gradually embezzled far more than I could ever make good. At home, I began talking up the merits of private-school curricula at the dinner table. The can's weekly take fell off sharply as holiday expenses drained homeowners of change and patience. This bear-market in giving was attributed by some of the club's swarthier lads to my deficiencies. The whole club began muttering in the dugout. I began to learn that one could perspire heavily even in a bitterly cold open-air dugout. Then, on the first day of Advent, the lad now in charge of the can produced childish-looking figures and announced the whole club wanted their share of the accrued booty in the Dixon account. I bought time with vague allusions to co-signatures and a misplaced passbook. I arrived home with chattering teeth and blood-less lips and was forced by my mother to swallow fish-oil. I was consumed with puerile fear. I felt small and weak and evil and consumed by dread of my embezzlement's exposure. Not to mention the brutal consequences. I claimed intestinal distress and stayed home from school. The telephone began ringing in the middle of the night. I could hear my father saying "Hello? *Hello?*" I did not sleep. My personality's dark part had grown leathery wings and a beak and turned on me. There were still several days until Christmas vacation. I'd lie in bed panicked during school hours amid piles of ill-gotten *Mad* magazines and Creeple Peeple figures and listen to the lonely handheld bells of the Salvation Army Santas on the street below and think of synonyms for *dread* and *doom*. I began to know shame, and to know it as grandiosity's aide-de-camp. My unspecific digestive illness wore on, and teachers sent cards and concerned notes. On some days the door-buzzer would buzz after school hours and my mother would come upstairs and say "How *sweet,* Eldred," that there were swarthy and cuff-frayed but clearly good-hearted boys in gray skallycaps on the stoop asking after me and declaring that they were *keenly* awaiting my return to school. I began to gnaw on the bathroom's soap in the morning to make a convincing case for staying home. My mother was alarmed at the masses of bubbles I vomited and threatened to consult a specialist. I felt myself moving closer and closer to some cliff-edge at which everything would come out. I longed to be able to lean into my mother's arms and weep and confess all. I could not. For the shame. Three or four of the Money-Stealers' Club's harder cases took up afternoon positions by the nativity scene in the churchyard across from our house and stared stonily up at my bedroom window, pounding their fists in their palms. I began to understand what a Belfast Protestant must feel. But even more prospectively dreadful than pummellings from Irish Catholics was the prospect of my parents' finding out my personality had a dark thing that had driven me to grandiose wickedness and left me there.'

Gately has no idea how Ewell feels about him making no responses, whether Ewell doesn't like it or even notices it or what. He can breathe OK, but something in his raped throat won't let whatever's supposed to vibrate to speak vibrate.

'Finally, on the day before my gastroenterologist appointment, when my mother was down the street at a speculum party, I crept downstairs from my sick bed and stole over a hundred dollars from a shoebox marked I.B.E.W. LOCAL 517 PETTY SLUSH in the back of my father's den's closet. I'd never dreamed of resorting to the shoebox before. Stealing from my own parents. To remit funds I'd stolen from dull-witted boys with whom I'd stolen them from adults I'd lied to. My feelings of fear and despicability only increased. I now felt ill for real. I lived and moved in the shadow of something dark that hovered just overhead. I vomited without aid of emetic, now, but secretly, so I could return to school; I couldn't face the prospect of a whole Christmas vacation of swarthy sentries pounding their palms outside the house. I converted my father's union's bills to small change and paid off the Money-Stealers' Club and got pummelled anyway. Apparently on general bad-element principles. I discovered the latent rage in followers, the fate of the leader who falls from the mob's esteem. I was pummelled and given a savage wedgie and hung from a hook in my school locker, where I remained for several hours, swollen and mortified. And going home was worse; home was no refuge. For home was the scene of the third-order crime. Of theft cubed. I couldn't sleep. I tossed and turned. There were night terrors. I was unable to eat, no matter how long after supper I had to stay at the table. The more worried about me my parents became, the greater my shame. I felt a shame and personal despicability no third-grader should have to feel. The holidays were not jolly. I looked back over the autumn and failed to recognize anyone named Eldred K. Ewell Jr. It no longer seemed a question of insanity or dark parts of me. I had stolen from neighbors, slum-children, and family, and bought myself sweets and toys. Under any tenable definition of *bad*, I was bad. I resolved to toe the virtuous line from then on. The shame and horror was too awful: I had to remake myself. I resolved to do whatever was required to see myself as good, remade. I never knowingly committed another felony. The whole shameful interval of the Money-Stealers' Club was moved to mental storage and buried there. Don, I'd forgotten it ever happened. Until the other night. Don, the other night, after the fracas and your display of reluctant *se offendendo*,[337] after your injury and the whole aftermath ... Don, I dreamed the whole mad repressed third-grade interval of grandiose perfidy all over again. Vividly and completely. When I awoke, I was somehow minus my goatee and my hair was center-parted in a fashion I haven't favored for forty years. The bed was soaked, and there was a gnawed-looking cake of McDade's special anti-acne soap in my hand.'

Gately starts to short-term recall that he was offered I.V.-Demerol for the pain of his gunshot wound immediately on admission to the E.R. and has been offered Demerol twice by shift-Drs. who haven't bothered to read the HISTORY OF NARCOTICS DEPENDENCY NO SCHEDULE C-IV+ MEDIC. that Gately'd made Pat Montesian swear she'd make them put in italics on his file or chart or whatever, first thing. Last night's emergency surgery was remedial, not extractive, because the big pistol's ordnance had apparently fragmented on impacting and passed through the meters of muscle that surrounded Gately's Humorous ball and Scalpula socket, passing through and missing bone but doing great and various damage to soft tissues. The E.R.'s Trauma Specialist had prescribed Toradol-IM[338] but had warned that the pain after the surgery's general anesthetic wore off was going to be unlike anything Gately had ever imagined. The next thing Gately knew he was upstairs in a Trauma Wing room that trembled with sunlight and a different Dr. was speculating to either Pat M. or Calvin T. that the invasive foreign body had been treated with something unclean, beforehand, possibly, because Gately's developed a massive infection, and they're monitoring him for something he heard as *Noxzema* but is really toxemia. Gately also wanted to protest that his body was 100% American, but he seemed temporarily unable to vocalize aloud. Later it was nighttime and Ewell was there, intoning. It was totally unclear what Ewell wanted from Gately or why he was choosing this particular time to share. Gately's right shoulder was almost the same size as his head, and he had to roll his eyes up and over like a cow to see Ewell's hand on the railing and his face floating above it.

'And how will I administer the Ninth Step when it comes time to make amends? How can I start to make reparations? Even if I could remember the homes of the citizens we defrauded, how many could still be there, living? The club lads have doubtless scattered into various low-rent districts and dead-end careers. My father lost the I.B.E.W.[339] account under the Weld administration and has been dead since 1993. And the revelations would kill my mother. My mother is very frail. She uses a walker, and arthritis has twisted her head nearly all the way around on her neck. My wife jealously protects my mother from all unpleasant facts regarding me. She says someone has to do it. My mother believes right this minute I'm at a nine-month Banque-de-Genève-sponsored tax-law symposium in the Alsace. She keeps sending me knitted skiwear that doesn't fit, from the rest home.

'Don, this buried interval and the impost I've carried ever since may have informed my whole life. Why I was drawn to tax law, helping wealthy suburbanites two-step around their fair share. My marriage to a woman who looks at me as if I were a dark stain at the back of her child's trousers. My whole descent into somewhat-heavier-than-normal drinking may have been some instinctive attempt to bury third-grade feelings of despicability, submerge them in an amber sea.

'I don't know what to do,' Ewell said.

Gately was on enough Toradol-IM to make his ears ring, plus a saline drip with Doryx.[340]

'I don't want to remember despicabilities I can do nothing about. If this is a sample of the "More Will Be Revealed," I hereby lodge a complaint. Some things seem better left submerged. No?'

And everything on his right side was on fire. The pain was getting to be emergency-type pain, like scream-and-yank-your-charred-hand-off-the-stove-type pain. Parts of him kept sending up emergency flares to other parts of him, and he could neither move nor call out.

'I'm scared,' from what seemed somewhere overhead and rising, was the last thing Gately heard Ewell whisper as the ceiling bulged down toward them. Gately wanted to tell Tiny Ewell that he could totally fucking I.D. with Ewell's feelings, and that if he, Tiny, could just hang in and tote that bale and put one little well-shined shoe in front of the other everything would end up all right, that the God of Ewell's Understanding would find some way for Ewell to make things right, and then he could let the despicable feelings go instead of keeping them down with Dewars, but Gately couldn't connect the impulse to speak with actual speech, still. He settled for trying to reach his left hand across and pat Ewell's hand on the railing. But his own breadth was too far to reach across. And then the white ceiling came all the way down and made everything white.

He seemed to sort of sleep. He fever-dreamed of dark writhing storm clouds writhing darkly and screaming on down the beach at Beverly MA, the winds increasing over his head until Herman the polyurethane vacuole burst from the force, leaving a ragged inhaling maw that tugged at Gately's XXL Dr. Dentons. A blue stuffed brontosaurus was sucked upward out of the crib and disappeared into the maw, spinning. His mother was getting the shit beaten out of her by a man with a shepherd's crook in the kitchen and couldn't hear Gately's frantic cries for help. He broke through the crib's bars with his head and went to the front door and ran outside. The black clouds up the beach lowered and roiled, funnelling sand, and as Gately watched he saw a tornado's snout emerge from the clouds and slowly lower. It looked as if the clouds were either giving birth or taking a shit. Gately ran across the beach to the water to escape the tornado. He ran through the crazed breakers to deep warm water and submerged himself and stayed under until he ran out of breath. It was now no longer clear if he was little Bimmy or the grown man Don. He kept coming up briefly for a great sucking breath and then going back under where it was warm and still. The tornado stayed in one place on the beach, bulging and receding, screaming like a jet, its opening a breathing maw, lightning coming off the funnel-cloud like hair. He could hear the tiny tattered sounds of his mother calling his name. The tornado was right by the beach house and the whole house trembled. His mother came out the front door, wild-haired and holding a bloody Ginsu knife, calling his name. Gately tried to call for her to come into the deep water with him, but even he couldn't hear his calls against the scream of the storm. She dropped the knife and held her head as the funnel pointed its pointy maw her way. The beach house exploded and his mother flew through the air toward the funnel's intake, arms and legs threshing, as if swimming in wind. She vanished into the maw and was pulled spinning up into the tornado's vortex. Shingles and boards followed her. No sign of the shepherd's crook of the man who'd hurt her. Gately's right lung burned horribly. He saw his mother for the last time when lightning lit up the funnel's cone. She was whirling around and around like something in a drain, rising, seeming to swim, bluely backlit. The burst of lightning was the white of the sunlit room when he came up for air and opened his eyes. His mother's tiny rotating imago faded against the ceiling. What seemed like heavy breathing was him trying to scream. The skinny bed's sheets were soaked and he needed a piss something bad. It was daytime and his right side was in no way numb, and he was immediately nostalgic for the warm-cement feeling of when it was numb. Tiny Ewell was gone. His every pulse was an assault on his right side. He didn't think he could stand it for even another second. He didn't know what would happen, but he didn't think he could stand it.

Later somebody who was either Joelle van D. or a St. E's nurse in a U.H.I.D. veil was running a cold washcloth over his face. His face was so big it took some time to cover it all. It seemed too tender a touch on the cloth for a nurse, but then Gately heard the clink of I.V. bottles being changed or R.N.ishly messed with somewhere overhead behind him. He was unable to ask about changing the sheets or going to the bathroom. Some time after the veiled lady left, he just gave up and let the piss go, and instead of feeling wet heat he heard the rising metallic sound of something filling up somewhere near the bed. He couldn't move to lift the covers and see what he was hooked up to. The blinds were up, and the room was so bright-white in the sunlight everything looked bleached and boiled. The guy with either the square head or the box on his head had been taken off some-place, his bed unmade and one crib-railing down. There were no ghostish figures or figures in mist. The hallway was no brighter than the room, and Gately couldn't see any shadows of anybody in a hat. He didn't even know if last night had been real. The pain kept making his lids flutter. He hadn't cried over pain since he was four. His last thought before letting his lids stay shut against the brutal white of the room was that he'd maybe been cas-trated, which was how he'd always heard the term *catheterized*. He could smell rubbing alcohol and a kind of vitamin stink, and himself.

At some point a probably real Pat Montesian came in and got her hair in his eye when she kissed his cheek and told him if he could just hang in and concentrate on getting well everything would be fine, that everything at the House was back to normal, more or less, and essentially fine, that she was so sorry he'd had to handle a situation like that alone, without support or counsel, and that she realized full well Lenz and the Canadian thugs hadn't given him enough time to call anybody, that he'd done the very best he could with what he'd had to work with and had nothing to feel horrid about, to let it go, that the violence hadn't been relapse-type thrill-seeking violence but simply doing the best he could at that moment and trying to stand up for himself and for a resident of the House. Pat Montesian was dressed as usual entirely in black, but formally, as in for taking somebody to court, and her formalwear looked like a Mexican widow's. She really had said the words *thug* and *horrid*. She said not to worry, the House was a community and it took care of its own. She kept asking if he was sleepy. Her hair's red was a different and less radiant red than the red of Joelle van D.'s hair. The left side of her face was very kind. Gately had very little understanding of what she was talking about. He was kind of surprised the Finest hadn't come calling already. Pat didn't know about the remorseless A.D.A. or the suffocated Nuck: Gately'd tried hard to share openly about the wreckage of his past, but some issues still seemed suicidal to share about. Pat said that Gately was showing tremendous humility and willingness sticking to his resolution about nothing stronger than non-narcotic painkillers, but that she hoped he'd remember that he wasn't in charge of anything except putting himself in his Higher Power's hands and following the dictates of his heart. That codeine or maybe Percoset[341] or maybe even Demerol wouldn't be a relapse unless his heart of hearts that knew his motives thought it would be. Her red hair was down and looked uncombed and mashed in on the side; she looked frazzled. Gately wanted very much to ask Pat about the legal fallout of the other night's thug-fracas. He realized she kept asking if he was sleepy because his attempts to speak looked like yawns. His inability to still speak was like speechlessness in bad dreams, airless and hellish, horrid.

What made the whole interface with Pat M. possibly unreal was that right at the end for no reason Pat M. burst into tears, and for no reason Gately got so embarrassed he pretended to pass out, and slept again, and probably dreamed.

Almost certainly dreamed and unreal was the interval when Gately came up with a start and saw Mrs. Lopate, the objay dart from the Shed that they come and install next to the Ennet House viewer some days, sitting there in a gunmetal wheelchair, face contorted, head cocked, hair stringy, looking not at him but more like seemingly at whatever array of I.V. bottles and signifying monitors hung above and behind his big crib, so not speaking or even looking at him but still in some sense being there *with* him, somehow. Even though there was no way she could have really been there, it was the first time Gately realized that the catatonic Mrs. L. had been the same lady he'd seen touching the tree in #5's front lawn late at night, some nights, when he'd first come on Staff. That they were the same person. And that this realization was real even though the lady's presence in the room was not, the complexities of which made his eyes roll up in his head again as he passed back out again.

Then at some later point Joelle van Dyne was sitting in a chair just outside the railing of the bed, veiled, wearing sweatpants and a sweater that was starting to unravel, in a pink-bordered veil, not saying anything, probably looking at him, probably thinking he was unconscious with his eyes open, or delirious with Noxzema. The whole right side of himself hurt so bad each breath was like a hard decision. He wanted to cry like a small child. The girl's silence and the blankness of her veil frightened him after a while, and he wished he could ask her to come back later.

Nobody'd offered him anything to eat, but he wasn't hungry. There were

I.V. tubes going into the backs of both hands and the crook of his left elbow. Other tubing exited him lower down. He didn't want to know. He kept trying to ask his heart if just codeine would be a relapse, according to the heart, but his heart was declining to comment.

Then at some point Ennet House alum and senior counselor Calvin Thrust came roaring in and pulled up a chair and straddled it backwards like a slow-tease stripper, slumping and draping his arms over the back of the chair, gesturing with an unlit rodney as he spoke. He told Gately that man he looked like shit something heavy had fell on. But he told Gately he should get a gander of the other guys, the Nucks in Polynesian-wear. Thrust and the House Manager had got there before E.M.P.H.H. Security could drag the Finest away from issuing midnight street-side citations down on Comm. Ave., he told Gately. Lenz and Green and Alfonso Parias-Carbo had dragged/carried the passed-out Gately inside and laid him on the black vinyl couch in Pat's office, where Gately had come to and told them ixnay on the ambulanceay and to please wake him up in five more minutes, and then passed out for serious real. Parias-Carbo seemed like he'd suffered a mild intestinal hernia from dragging/carrying Gately, but he was being a man about it and had refused codeine downstairs at the E.R. and was expressing gratitude for the growth experience, and the thoracic lump was receding nicely. Calvin Thrust's breath smelled of smoke and old scrambled eggs. Gately had once seen a cheap bootleg cartridge of a young Calvin Thrust having sex with a lady with only one arm on what looked like a crude homemade trapeze. The cartridge's lighting and production values had been real low-quality, and Gately had been in and out of a Demerol-nod, but he was 98% sure it had been the young Calvin Thrust. Calvin Thrust said how right there over Gately's unconscious form in the office Randy Lenz had begun womaning right off how of course he, Randy Lenz, was going to somehow get blamed for Gately and the Nucks getting fucked up and why didn't they just get it over with and give him the administrative Shoe right now without going through the sham motions of deliberating. Bruce Green had rammed Lenz up against Pat's cabinets and shaken him like a margarita, but refused to rat out Lenz or say why irate Canadians might think a specimen as dickless as Lenz might have demapped their friend. The matter was under investigation, but Thrust confessed to a certain admiration for Green's refusal to eat cheese. Brucie G. had suffered a broken nose in the beef and now had a terrific set of twin shiners. Calvin Thrust said both he, Calvin Thrust, and the House Manager had immediately on arrival pegged Lenz as either coked up or 'drined to the gills on some 'drine, and Thrust said he summoned every Oreida of self-control sobriety'd blessed him with and had quietly taken Lenz out of the office into the special Disabled Bedroom next door and over the sound of Burt F. Smith coughing up little pieces of lung in his sleep he said he'd real controlledly given Lenz the choice of voluntarily resigning his Ennet residency on the spot or submitting to a spot-urine and a room-search and everything like that, plus to questioning by the Finest, who were pretty doubtless even now on route with the fleet of ambulances for the Nucks. Meanwhile, Thrust said — gesturing with the gasper and occasionally leaning forward to see whether Gately was still conscious and to tell him he looked like shit, meanwhile — Gately had been lying there passed out, wedged with two full filing cabinets to keep him from rolling off the couch he was wider than, and was bleeding in a very big way, and nobody knew how to, like, *affix* a turnipcut to a shoulder, and the good-bodied new girl with the cloth mask was bending over the arm of the couch applying pressure to towels on Gately's bleeding, and her partly-open robe was yielding a view that even brought Alfonso P.-C. around from his herniated fetal posture on the floor, and Thrust and the House Manager were taking turns Asking for Help to intuitively know what they ought to do with Gately, because it was well known that he was on Probie against a real serious bit, and with all due trust and respect to Don it wasn't clear at that point from the scattered damaged Canadian forms still in different prone positions out in the street who'd done what to who in defense of whatever or not, and the Finest tend to take a keen interest in huge guys who come into E.R.'s with spectacular gunshot wounds, and but then when Pat M. pulled up in the Aventura laying rubber a couple minutes later she'd screamed rather unserenely at Thrust for not having already rikky-ticked Don Gately over to St. E.'s on his own already. Thrust said he'd let go of Pat's screaming like water off a duck, revealing that Pat M. had been under felony-weight domestic stress at home, he knew. He said and but so Gately was too heavy to carry unconscious for more than a few meters, even with the masked girl filling in for Parias-Carbo, and they'd just barely got Gately outside still in his wet bowling shirt and laid him briefly on the sidewalk and covered him with Pat's black suede car-coat while Thrust maneuvered his beloved Corvette up as close to Gately as possible. The sounds of sirens on the way up Comm. Ave. mixed with the sounds of severely fucked-up Canadians returning to whatever passed with Nucks for consciousness and calling for what they called *medecins,* and with the crazed-squirrel sound of Lenz trying to start his rusted-out brown Duster, which had a bad solenoid. They'd heaved Gately's dead weight in the 'Vette and Pat M. drove interference like a madwoman in her turbocharged Aventura. Pat let the masked girl ride shotgun with her because the masked girl wouldn't quit asking her to let her come too. The House Manager stayed behind to represent Ennet House to E.M.P.H.H. Security and the somewhat less bullshittable BPD-Finest. The sirens got steadily closer, which added to the confusion because senile and mobile-vegetable residents of both Unit #4 and the Shed had been drawn out on the frozen lawns by the freakas, and the mix of several kinds of sirens didn't do them a bit of good, and they started flapping and shrieking and running around and adding to the medical confusion of the whole scene, which by the time him and Pat pulled out of there was a fucking millhouse and everything like that. Thrust asks rhetorically how much does Don fucking *weigh,* anyway, because moving the front buckets way up to where like dwarfs put them and putting Gately's carcass across the back seat of the 'Vette had required all available hands and even Burt F.S.'s stumps, had been like trying to get something humongous through a door that's way smaller than the humongous thing was and everything like that. Thrust occasionally tapped his gasper like he thought it was lit. The first squad cars had come fishtailing around the Warren-Comm. corner just as they all came out of the E.M. driveway onto Warren. Pat in her car up ahead had made an arm-motion that could have been either waving coolly at the passing Finest or uncoolly clutching her head. Thrust said had he mentioned Gately's blood? Gately'd bled all over Pat M.'s vinyl couch and filing cabinets and carpet, the little E.M. streetlet, the sidewalk, Pat M.'s black suede car-coat, pretty much everybody's winter coats, and the beloved upholstery of Thrust's beloved Corvette, which upholstery Thrust might add had been new, and dear. But he said not to worry about it, Thrust said: the fucking blood was the least of the problems. Gately didn't like the sound of that at all, and started trying to blink at him in a kind of crude code, to get his attention, but Thrust either didn't notice it or thought it was like a post-operative tic. Thrust's hair was always combed straight back like a mobster. Thrust said at the St. E.'s E.R. how the E.R. crew had been quick and ingenious about getting Gately out of the 'Vette and onto a double-width gurney, though they did have some trouble lifting the gurney so they could get the legs with wheels set up under it so the guys in white could roll him in with more guys in white walking briskly alongside of him and leaning over him and applying pressure and barking little orders in terse code like they always do in E.R.s and everything like that, in emergencies. Thrust says he couldn't tell if they could tell right away it was a spectacular gunshot wound, nobody used the G-word or anything like that. Thrust had babbled something about a chain-saw while Pat nodded furiously. The chief two things Gately kept blinking rhythmically to try to find out were: did anybody end up getting killed, meaning the Nucks; and has this one certain A.D.A.-type figure that always wore a hat come in from Essex County or given any sign of getting wind of Gately's whereabouts or involvement; and — so really three things — and will any of the Ennet House residents that were right there on the scene from start to finish look respectable enough on paper to have credibility as like legal witnesses. Plus he wouldn't mind knowing what the fuck Thrust was thinking of, scaring Lenz off and letting him screw off into the urban night leaving Gately maybe holding the statutory bag. Most of Calvin Thrust's legality-experience was filmic and petty-vice. Thrust eventually describes that one of the House

Manager's key coups of quick thinking was doing a quick TP-scan and finding out which of the residents out there milling around with the catatonics on the street had up-in-the-air legal issues such that they needed to be secloistered in the protected area of the House out of legal sight by the time the BPD's Finest hit the scene. He says in his view it was lucky for Gately that he (Gately) was such a massive son of a bitch and had so much blood, because even so Gately'd lost huge volumes of blood all over people's upholstery and was in shock and everything like that by the time they got him on the double-width gurney, his face cheese-colored and his lips blue and muttering all this shock-type stuff, but even so here he (Gately) was, not exactly ready for a *GQ* cover but still sucking air. Thrust said in the waiting room at the E.R., where they wouldn't let a working man smoke down there either, he said then the arrogant new girl resident in the white veil had up and tried to take Thrust's inventory for letting Randy L. resign and decamp before his part in Gately's legal embryoglio could be nailed down, and Pat M. had been pretty unconditionally loving about it but it was obvious she wasn't thrilled with Thrust's tactics either and everything like that. Gately blinked furiously to signify his agreement with Joelle's position. Calvin Thrust gestured stoically with his cigarette and said he'd told Pat M. the truth: he always told the truth, no matter how unpleasant for himself, today: he said he'd said he'd encouraged Lenz to rikky-tick out of there because otherwise he was afraid that he (Thrust) was going to eliminate Lenz's map on the spot, out of rage. Lenz's solenoid appeared to have been on the permanent dicky, because the rusty Duster was seen by new resident Amy J. real early the next A.M. getting towed from its wrong-side-of-the-street spot in front of #3 when Amy J. slunk back to the House all jonesy and hungover to get her Hefty bag full of evicted personal shit, Lenz apparently having abandoned his wheels and fleen off by foot during all the Finest's confusion and static with the ambulance drivers that who could blame them didn't want to take Canadians because of horrible paperwork for Health Card reimbursement for Nucks. The House Manager had gone so far as planting herself out in front of the House's locked front door with her not-all-that-small arms and legs spread out, blocking the door, assertively stating at whatever Finest tried to enter that Ennet House was court-mandated Protected by the Commonwealth of MA and could only be entered with a Court Order and three working days' mandated time for the House to file an injunction and wait for a ruling, and the Finest and even the boogereating morons from E.M.P.H.H. Security were successfully held in bay and kept out, therefore, by her, alone, and Pat M. was considering rewarding the House Manager's coolness under fire by promoting her to Assistant Director next month when the present Assistant Director left to go get certified in jet-engine maintenance at East Coast Aerotech on a Mass Rehab grant.

Gately's eyes keep rolling up in his head, only partly from pain.

Unless he actually had a lit gasper going, Calvin Thrust always has this way of being only technically wherever he was. There was always this air of imminent departure about him, like a man whose beeper was about to sound. It's like a lit gasper was psychic ballast for him or something. Everything he said to Gately seemed like it was going to be the last thing he said right before he looked at his watch and slapped his forehead and left.

Thrust said whatever that Nuck that the residents allege shot him shot him with was serious ordnance, because there'd been bits of Gately's shoulder and bowling shirt all over the complex's little street. Thrust pointed at the huge bandage and asked whether they'd talked to Gately yet about was he going to get to keep what was left of the mutilated shoulder and arm. Gately found that the only audible sound he could make sounded like a run-over kitten. Thrust mentioned that Danielle S.'d been over to Mass Rehab with Burt F.S. and had reported how they were doing miraculous things with prosfeces these days. Gately's eyes were rolling around in his head and he was making pathetic little scared aspirated sounds as he pictured himself with a hook and parrot and patch making piratical 'Arr Matey' sounds from the AA podium. He felt a terrible certainty that the whole nerve-assembly network that connected the human voice-box to the human mind and let somebody ask for crucial legal and medical feedback must run through the right human shoulder. All kinds of fucking shunts and crazy interconnections with nerves, he knew. He imagined himself with one of those solar-cell electric shaver voice-box prosfeces he has to hold up to his throat (maybe with his hook), trying to Carry the Message with it from the podium, sounding like an automatic teller or ROM-audio interface. Gately wanted to know what day the next day was and whether any of Lenz's Nucks had been demapped, and what the official capacity of the guy was in the hat who'd been sitting just outside the door to the room either last night or the night before, his hat's shadow cast in a kind of parallelogram across the open doorway, and if the guy was still there, assuming the sight of the guy's hatted shadow had been valid and not phantasmic, and he wondered how they went about cuffing you if one of your arms' shoulders was mutilated and the size of your head. If Gately took anything deeper than a half-breath, a mind-bending sheet of pain goes down his right side. He even breathed like a sick kitten, more like throbbing than breathing. Thrust said Hester Thrale had apparently disappeared sometime during the freakas and never came back. Gately could remember her running screaming off into the urban night. Thrust said her Alfa Romeo got towed the next A.M. right along with Lenz's bum Duster, and her stuff's been duly bagged and is on the porch and everything familiar like that. Thrust said they found this mysteriously huge stash of high-quality Irish Luggage during the Staff's search of Lenz's room, and the House looks to be fixed for trash- and eviction-bags for the next fiscal year. Discharged residents' bagged possessions stay on the porch for three days, and Gately's trying to calculate the present date from this fact. Thrust says Emil Minty got a Full House Restriction for getting observed removing one of Hester Thrale's undergarments from her bag on the porch, for reasons nobody much wants to speculate about. Kate Gompert and Ruth van Cleve supposedly went to hit an NA meeting in Inman Square and got supposedly mugged and separated, and then only Ruth van Cleve showed up back at the House, and Pat's sworn out a P.C. warrant for Gompert because of the girl's other psych and suicide issues. Gately discovers he doesn't even all that much care whether anybody thought to call Stavros L. at the Shattuck about Gately's day job. Thrust smoothed his hair back and said what else let's see. Johnette Foltz is so far covering Gately's shifts and said to say he's in her prayers. Chandler Foss finished out his nine months and graduated but came back the next morning and hung around for Morning Meditation, which has to be a good sign sobriety-wise for the old Chandulator. Jennifer Belbin did get indicted on the bad-check issue up in Wellfleet Circuit Court, but they're going to let her finish out her residency at the House before anything goes to trial, which her P.D. said graduating the House is guaranteed to get her bit cut in at least half. The Asst. Director had gone up to court with Belbin on her own time. Doony Glynn's still laid up with the diveritis thing, and can be neither coaxed nor threatened out of his fetal position in bed, and the House Manager's trying to breastwork through the red tape at Health to get them to OK him admission to St. E.'s even though he's got insurance fraud on his yellow sheet, part of his own past-wreckage. A guy that had gone through the House back when Thrust did and had stayed sober in AA for four solid years had suddenly out of nowhere slipped up and took The First Drink the same day as the Lenz freakas, and predictably ended getting totally shitfaced, and went and fell off the end of the Fort Point pier — like literally took a long walk on a short pier, apparently — and sank like a rock, and the memorial service is today, which is why Thrust is going to have to take off in a second here, he says. The new kid Tingley's coming out of the linen closet for up to an hour at a time and is taking solid food and Johnette's quit lobbying to have the kid sent over to Met State. The even newer new guy now that's come in to take Chandler Foss's spot's name is Dave K. and is one grim story to behold, Thrust assures him, a junior executive guy at ATHSCME Air Displacement, an upscale guy with a picket house and kids and a worried wife with tall hair, who this Dave K.'s bottom was he drank half a liter of Cuerva at some ATHSCME Interdependence Day office party and everything like that and got in some insane drunken limbo-dance challenge with a rival executive and tried to like limbo under a desk or a chair or something insanely low, and got his spine all fucked up in a limbo-lock, maybe permanently: so the newest new guy scuttles around the Ennet House living room like a crab, his scalp brushing the floor and his knees trembling with effort. Danielle S.

thinks Burt F.S. might have batorial ammonia or some kind of chronic lung thing, and Geoff D.'s trying to get the other residents to sign a petition to get Burt barred from the kitchen and dining room because Burt can't cover his mouth when he coughs, understandably. Thrust says Clenette H. and Yolanda W. are taking meals in their room and are under orders not to come down or go near any windows, because of what happened to the map of the Nuck they allegedly stomped and everything like that. Gately mews and blinks like mad. Thrust says everybody's being real supportive of Jenny B. and encouraging her to turn the Wellfleet indictment over to her Higher Power. The Shed staff are still rolling the catatonic lady's wheelchair over from the Shed to the House on scheduled A.M.'s, and Thrust says Johnette had to write up Minty and Diehl for putting one of those gag-arrows that are curved in the middle and look like there's an arrow through your head over the catatonic lady's paralyzed head yesterday and leaving her slumped by the TP like that all day. Plus Thrale's panties; so suddenly in twelve hours Minty's just one more offense away from getting the Shoe, which Thrust is already personally shining the tip of his very sharpest shoe, in hopes. The biggest issue at the House Bitch and Complaint meeting was that earlier this week it turns out Clenette H. had brung in this whole humongous shitload of cartridges she said they were getting ready to throw in the dumpster up at the swank tennis school up the hill she works at, and she promoted them and hauled them down to the House, and the residents all have a wild hair because Pat says Staff has to preview the cartridges for suitability and sex before they can be put out for the residents, and the residents are all bitching that this'll take forever and it's just the fucking Staff hoarding the new entertainment when the House's TP's just about on its hands and knees in the entertainment desert starving for new entertainment. McDade bitched at the meeting that if he had to watch *Nightmare on Elm Street XXII: The Senescence* one more time he was going to take a brody off the House's roof.

Plus Thrust says Bruce Green hasn't shared word one to Staff about his feelings about anything to do with Lenz or Gately's embryoglio; that he just sits around waiting for somebody to read his mind; that his roommates have complained that he thrashes and shouts about nuts and cigars in his sleep.

Calvin Thrust, four years sober, straddling the backwards chair, keeps inclining himself ever more forward in the posture of a man who's at any moment going to push up off out of the chair and leave. He reports how something deep in the previously hopelessly arrogant-seeming 'Tiny' Ewell seems like it's broken and melted, spiritually speaking: the guy shaved off his Kentucky Chicken beard, was heard weeping in the 5-Man head, and was observed by Johnette taking out the kitchen trash in secret even though his Chore this week was Office Windows. Thrust had discovered fine dining in sobriety, and has the beginning of chins. His hair is slicked back with odorless stuff at all times, and he has a more or less permanent sore on his upper lip. Gately for some reason keeps imagining Joelle van Dyne dressed as Madame Psychosis sitting in a plain chair in the 3-Woman room eating a peach and looking out the open window at the crucifix atop St. Elizabeth's Hospital's prolix roof. The crucifix isn't big, but it's up so high it's visible from most anywhere in Enfield-Brighton. Sees Joelle delicately pulling the veil out to get the peach up under it. Thrust says Charlotte Treat's T-cell count is down. She's needlepointing Gately some kind of GET BETTER A DAY AT A TIME ASSUMING THAT'S GOD'S WILL doily, but it's been slow going, because Treat's developed some kind of goopy Virus-related eye infection that's got her bumping into walls, and her counselor Maureen N. at the Staff Meeting wanted Pat to consider having her transferred to an HIV halfway house up in Everett that's got some recovering addicts in there. Morris Hanley, speaking of T-cells, has baked some cream-cheese brownies for Gately as a nurturing gesture, but then the twats at the Trauma Wing's nurses' station, like, impounded them from Thrust when he came up, but he'd had a couple on the way over in the bloodstained 'Vette and he could assure Don that Hanley's brownies were worth killing a loved one for and everything like that. Gately feels a sudden rush of anxiety over the issue of who's cooking the House supper in his absence, like will they know to put corn flakes in the meat loaf, for texture. He finds Thrust insufferable and wishes he'd just fucking go already, but has to admit he's less conscious of the horrific pain when somebody's there, but that that's mostly because the drowned panic of not being able to ask questions or have any input into what somebody's saying is so awful it sort of dwarfs the pain. Thrust puts his unlit gasper behind his ear where Gately predicts hair-tonic will render it unsmokable, looks conspiratorially around back over each shoulder, leans in so his face is visible between two bars of the bed's side-railing, and bathes Gately's face in old eggs and smoke as he leans in and quietly says that Gately'll be psyched to hear that all the residents that were at the embryoglio — except Lenz and Thrale and the ones that aren't in a legal position to step forward and like that, he says — he says they've most of them all come forward and filed depositions, that the BPD's Finest, plus some rather weirder Federal guys with goofy-looking archaic crew cuts, probably involved because of the like inter-O.N.A.N. element of the Nucks — here Gately's big heart skips and sinks — have come around and been voluntarily admitted inside, on Pat's written OK, and they took depositions, which is like testifying on paper, and the depositions look to be basically 110% behind Don Gately and support a justifiable señorio of either self-defense or Lenz-defense. Several testimonies indicate the Nucks gave the impression of being under the influence of aggressive-type Substances. The single biggest problem right now, Thrust says Pat says, is the missing alleged Item. As in the .44 Item Gately was plugged with's whereabouts are missing, Thrust says. The last resident to depose to seeing it was

Green, who says he took it away from the Nuck the nigger girls stomped, whereupon he, Green, says he dropped it on the lawn. Whereupon it liked vanished from legal view. Thrust says that in his legal view the Item's the thing that makes the difference between a señorio of ironshod self-defense and one of just maybe a huge fucking beef in which Gately got mysteriously plugged at some indefinite point while rearranging a couple Canadian maps with his huge bare hands. Gately's heart is now somewhere around his bare hairy shins, at the mention of Federal crewcuts. His attempted plea for Thrust to come out and say did he actually kill anybody *did he* sounds like that crushed kitten again. The pain of the terror is past standing, and it helps him surrender and quit trying, and he relaxes his legs and decides Thrust gets to not say whatever he wants, that the reality right this second is that he's mute and powerless over Thrust. Thrust leans in and hugs the back of the chair and says Clenette Henderson and Yolanda Willis are on Full House Restriction in their room to keep them from coming down and maybe fucking themselves over legally in a deposition. Because the Nuck with the plaid hat with the ear-flaps and the missing alleged Item had expired on the spot from a spike heel through the right eye, as he was getting the shit stomped out of him as only female niggers can stomp, and everything like that, and Yolanda Willis had very shrewdly left the shoe and spike heel right there protruding from the guy's map with her toe-prints all over its insides — meaning presumably the shoe's — so producing the Item was going to be in her strong legal interests too, as well, as Thrust analyzes the legal landscape. Thrust says Pat's limped around and appealed to every single resident personally, and everybody's submitted more or less voluntarily to a room- and property-search and everything like that, and still no large-caliber Item has turned up, though Nell Gunther's hidden Oriental-knife collection sure made an impression. Thrust predicts it'll be strongly in Gately's lego-judicial interest and everything like that to ransack his brain and mind for where and with who he last saw the alleged gun. The sun was starting to go down over the West Newton hills through the double-sealed windows, now, trembling slightly, and the windowlight against the far wall was ruddled and bloody. The heater vents kept making a sound like a distant parent gently shushing. When it starts to get dark out is when the ceiling breathes. And everything like that.

Sometime later, at night, backlit by the light of the hall, is the figure of resident Geoffrey Day, sitting where Thrust had sat but with the chair turned around the right way and with his legs primly crossed, eating a cream-cheese brownie he reports they're passing out free to people down at the nurses' station. Day says Johnette F. is certainly no Don Gately in the culinary arena. She seems to enjoy some sort of collusive kickback-type relationship with the manufacturers of Spam, Day says, is his theory. It might be a whole different night. The nighttime ceiling no longer bulges convexly with Gately's own shallow breaths, and the improved sounds he can now make have evolved from feline to more like bovine. But his right side hurts so bad he can barely hear. It's gone from a fiery pain to cold dead deep tight pain with a queer flavor of emotional loss to it. From deep inside he can hear the pain laughing at the 90 mg. of Toradol-IM they've got in the I.V. drip. As with Ewell, when Gately comes up out of sleep there's no way to tell how long Day's been there, or quite why. Day is plowing through a long story it seems about his relationship growing up with his younger brother. Gately has a hard time imagining Day being blood-related to anybody. Day says his brother was developmentally challenged in some way. He had enormous red wet loose lips and wore eyeglasses so thick his eyes had looked like an ant's eyes, growing up. Part of his challenge was that Day's brother had had a crippling phobic fear of leaves, apparently. As in ordinary leaves, from trees. Day's been sucker-punched by an emergent sober memory of how he used to emotionally abuse his little brother simply by threatening to touch him with a leaf. Day has this way of holding his cheek and jaw when he talks like cutout photos of the late J. Benny. It's not at all evident why Day's choosing to share this stuff with a mute and feverishly semiconscious Gately. It seems like Don G.'s gotten way more popular as somebody to talk to since he's become effectively paralyzed and mute. The ceiling's behaving itself, but in the room's gray Gately could still make out a tallly insubstantial ghostish figure appearing and disappearing in the mist of his vision's periphery. There was some creepy relationship between the figure's postures and the passing nurses' noiseless glide. This figure pretty definitely seemed to prefer night to day, though by this point Gately could well have been asleep again, as Day began to describe different species of hand-held leaves.

A recurring bad dream Gately's had ever since he gave up and Came In and got straight consists simply of a tiny acne-scarred Oriental woman looking down at him. Nothing else happens; she's just looking down at Gately. Her acne scars aren't even all that bad. The thing is that she's tiny. She's one of those tiny little anonymous Oriental women you see all over metro Boston, always seeming to be carrying multiple shopping bags. But in the recurring dream she's looking *down* at him, from his perspective he's looking up and she's looking down, which means Gately in the dream is either (a) lying down on his back looking vulnerably up at her or (b) is himself even more incredibly tiny than the woman. Involved in the dream also in a menacing way somehow is a dog standing rigidly in the distance past the Oriental woman, motionless and rigid, in profile, standing there still and straight as a toy. The Oriental woman has no particular expression and never says anything, though her face's scars have a certain elusive pattern to them that seems like it wants to mean something. When Gately opens his eyes again Geoffrey Day's gone, and his hospital bed with its railings and I.V. bottles on stands has been moved way over so that it's right up next to the bed of whoever the person in the room's other bed is, so it's like Gately and this unknown patient are a sexless old couple sleeping together but in separate beds, and Gately's mouth goes oval and his eyes bug out with horror, and his effort at yelling hurts enough to wake him up, and his eyelids shoot up and rattle like old windowshades, and his hospital bed's back where it's always been, and a nurse is giving the anonymous guy in the other bed some sort of late-night-type shot you could tell was narcotic, and the patient, who has a very deep voice, is crying. Then somewhere later in the couple of hours before midnight's parking-switch symphony on Washington St. outside is an unpleasantly detailed dream where the ghostish figure that's been flickering in and out of sight around the room finally stays in one spot long enough for Gately to really check him out. In the dream it's the figure of a very tall sunken-chested man in black-frame glasses and a sweatshirt with old stained chinos, leaning back sort of casually or else morosely slumped, resting its tailbone against the window sill's ventilator's whispering grille, with its long arms hanging at its sides and its ankles casually crossed so that Gately can even see the detail that the ghostly chinos aren't long enough for its height, they're the kind kids used to call 'Highwaters' in Gately's childhood — a couple of Bimmy Gately's savager pals would corner some pencil-necked kid in those-type too-short trousers on the playground and go like 'Yo little brother where's the fucking *flood?*' and then lay the kid out with a head-slap or chest-shove so the inevitable violin went skittering ass-over-teakettle across the blacktop, in its case. The creepy ghostish figure's arm sometimes, like, vanishes and then reappears at the bridge of its nose, pushing the glasses up in a weary unconscious morose gesture, just like those kids in the Highwater pants on the playground always did in a weak morose way that always somehow made Gately himself want to shove them savagely in the chest. Gately in the dream experienced a painful adrenal flash of remorse and entertained the possibility that the figure represented one of the North Shore violin-playing kids he'd never kept his savage pals from abusing, now come in an adult state when Gately was vulnerable and mute, to exact some kind of payback. The ghostly figure shrugged its thin shoulders and said But no, it was nothing of the sort, it was just a plain old wraith, one without any sort of grudge or agenda, just a generic garden-variety wraith. Gately sarcastically in the dream thought that Oh well then if it was just a garden-variety *wraith*, is all, geez what a fucking *relief*. The wraith-figure smiled apologetically and shrugged, shifting its tailbone on the whispering grille a bit. There was an odd quality to its movements in the dream: they were of regulation speed, the movements, but they seemed oddly segmented and deliberate, as if more effort than necessary were going into them somehow. Then Gately considered that who knew what was necessary or normal for a self-proclaimed generic wraith in a pain-and-fever dream. Then he considered that this was the only dream he could recall where even in the dream he knew that it was a dream, much less lay there considering the fact that he was considering the up-front dream quality of the dream he was dreaming. It quickly got so multilevelled and confusing that his eyes rolled back in his head. The wraith made a weary morose gesture as if not wanting to bother to get into any sort of confusing dream-v.-real controversies. The wraith said Gately might as well stop trying to figure it out and just capitalize on its presence, the wraith's presence in the room or dream, whatever, because Gately, if he'd bothered to notice and appreciate it, at least didn't have to speak out loud to be able to interface with the wraith-figure; and also the wraith-figure said it was by the way requiring incredible patience and fortitude for him (the wraith) to stay in one position long enough for Gately to really see him and interface with him, and the wraith was making no promises about how many more months he (the wraith) could keep it up, since fortitude had never seemed to have been his long suit. The city's aggregate nighttime lights lightened the sky through the room's window to the same dark rose shade you see when you close your eyes, adding to the dream-of-dream-type ambiguity. Gately in the dream tried the test of pretending to lose consciousness so the wraith would go away, and then somewhere during the pretense lost consciousness and really did sleep, for a bit, in the dream, because the tiny pocked Oriental woman was back and looking wordlessly down at him, plus the creepy rigid dog. And then the sedated patient in the next bed woke Gately back up, in the original dream, with some kind of narcotized gurgle or snore, and the so-called wraith-figure was still there and visible, only now it was standing on top of the railing at the side of Gately's bed, looking down at him now from a towering railing-plus-original-tallness height, having to exaggerate his shoulders' natural slump in order to clear the ceiling. Gately got a clear view of an impressive thatch of nostril-hair, looking up into the wraith's nostrils, and also a clear lateral look at the wraith's skinny ankles' like ankle-bones bulging in brown socks below the cuffs of the Highwater chinos. As much as his shoulder, calf, toe, and whole right side were hurting, it occurred to Gately that you don't normally think of wraiths or ghostish phantasms as being tall or short, or having bad posture, or wearing certain-colored socks. Much less having anything as specific as extrusive nostril-hair. There was a degree of, what, *specificness* about this figure in this dream that Gately found troubling. Much less having the unpleasant old-Oriental-woman dream *inside* this dream right here. He began to wish again that he could call out for assistance or to wake himself up. But now not even moos or mews would come, all he could seem to do was *pant* real hard, as if the air was like totally missing his vocal box, or like his vocal box was totally demapped from nerve-damage in his shoulder and now just sort of hung there all withered and dry like an old hornet nest while air rushed out Gately's throat all around it. His throat still didn't feel right. It was exactly the suffocated speechlessness in dreams, nightmares, Gately realized. This was both terrifying and reassuring, somehow. Evidence for the dream-element and so on and so forth. The wraith was looking down at him and nodding sympathetically. The wraith could empathize totally, it said. The wraith said Even a garden-variety wraith could move at the speed of quanta and be anywhere anytime and hear in symphonic toto the thoughts of animate men, but it couldn't ordinarily affect anybody or anything solid, and it could never speak right to anybody, a wraith had no out-loud voice of its own, and had to use somebody's like internal brain-voice if it wanted to try to communicate something, which was why thoughts and insights that were coming from some wraith always just sound like your own thoughts, from inside your own head, if a wraith's trying to interface with you. The wraith says By way of illustration consider phenomena like intuition or inspiration or hunches, or when someone for instance says 'a little voice inside' was telling them such-and-such on an intuitive basis. Gately can now take no more than a third of a normal breath without wanting to throw up from the pain. The wraith was pushing his glasses up and saying Besides, it took incredible discipline and fortitude and patient effort to stay stock-still in one place for long enough for an animate man actually to see and be in any way affected by a wraith, and very few wraiths had anything important enough to interface about to be willing to stand still for this kind of time, preferring ordinarily to whiz around at the invisible speed of quanta. The wraith says It doesn't really matter whether Gately knows what the term *quanta* means. He says Wraiths by and large exist (putting his arms out slowly and making little quotation-mark finger-wiggles as he said *exist*) in a totally different Heisenbergian dimension of rate-change and time-passage. As an example, he goes on, normal animate men's actions and motions look, to a wraith, to be occurring at about the rate a clock's hour-hand moves, and are just about as interesting to look at. Gately was thinking for fuck's sake what was this, now even in unpleasant fever-dreams now somebody else is going to tell him their troubles now that Gately can't get away or dialogue back with anything about his own experience. He normally couldn't ever get Ewell or Day to sit down for any kind of real or honest mutual sharing, and now that he's totally mute and inert and passive all of a sudden everybody seems to view him as a sympathetic ear, or not even a sympathetic *real* ear, more like a wooden carving or statue of an ear. An empty confessional booth. Don G. as huge empty confessional booth. The wraith disappears and instantly reappears in a far corner of the room, waving Hi at him. It was slightly reminiscent of 'Bewitched' reruns from Gately's toddlerhood. The wraith disappears again and again just as instantly reappears, now holding one of Gately's Ennet House basement fleabaggy Staff bedroom's cut-out-and-Scotch-taped celebrity photos, this one an old one of U.S. Head of State Johnny Gentle, Famous Crooner, on stage, wearing velour, twirling a mike, from back in the days before he went to a copper-colored toupee, when he used a strigil instead of a UV flash-booth and was just a Vegas crooner. Again the wraith disappears and instantly reappears holding a can of Coke, with good old Coke's distinctive interwoven red and white French curls on it but alien unfamiliar Oriental-type writing on it instead of the good old words *Coca-Cola* and *Coke*. The unfamiliar script on the Coke can is maybe the whole dream's worst moment. The wraith walks jerkily and overdeliberately across the floor and then up a wall, occasionally disappearing and then reappearing, sort of fluttering mistily, and ends up standing upside-down on the hospital room's drop ceiling, directly over Gately, and holds one knee to its sunken chest and starts doing what Gately would know were pirouettes if he'd ever once been exposed to ballet, pirouetting faster and faster and then so fast the wraith's nothing but a long stalk of sweatshirt-and-Coke-can-colored light that seems to extrude from the ceiling; and then, in a moment that rivals the Coke-can moment for unpleasantness, into Gately's personal mind, in Gately's own brain-voice but with roaring and unwilled force, comes the term *PIROUETTE,* in caps, which term Gately knows for a fact he doesn't have any idea what it means and no reason to be thinking it with roaring force, so the sensation is not only creepy but somehow violating, a sort of lexical rape. Gately begins to consider this hopefully nonrecurring dream even more unpleasant than the tiny-pocked-Oriental-woman dream, overall. Other terms and words Gately knows he doesn't know from a divot in the sod now come crashing through his head with the same ghastly intrusive force, e.g. *ACCIAC-CATURA* and *ALEMBIC, LATRODECTUS MACTANS* and *NEUTRAL DENSITY POINT, CHIAROSCURO* and *PROPRIOCEPTION* and *TESTUDO* and *ANNULATE* and *BRICOLAGE* and *CATALEPT* and *GERRYMANDER* and *SCOPOPHILIA* and *LAERTES* — and all of a sudden it occurs to Gately the aforethought *EXTRUDING, STRIGIL* and *LEXICAL* themselves — and *LORDOSIS* and *IMPOST* and *SINISTRAL* and *MENISCUS* and *CHRONAXY* and *POOR YORICK* and *LUCULUS* and *CERISE MONTCLAIR* and then *DE SICA NEO-REAL CRANE DOLLY* and *CIRCUMAMBIENTFOUNDDRAMALEVIRATEMAR-RIAGE* and then more lexical terms and words speeding up to chipmunkish and then *HELIATED* and then all the way up to a sound like a mosquito on speed, and Gately tries to clutch both his temples with one hand and scream, but nothing comes out. When the wraith reappears, it's seated way up behind him where Gately has to let his eyes roll way back in his head to see him, and it turns out Gately's heart is being medically monitored and the wraith is seated up on the heart monitor in a strange cross-legged posture with his pantcuffs pulled up so high Gately could see the actual skinny hairless above-the-sock skin of the wraith's ankles, glowing a bit in the spilled light of the Trauma Wing hall. The Oriental can of Coke now rests on Gately's broad flat forehead. It's cold and smells a little funny, like low tide, the can. Now footsteps and the sound of bubblegum in the hall. An orderly shines a flashlight in and plays it over Gately and the narcotized roommate and environs, and makes marks on a clipboard while blowing a small orange bubble. It's not like the light passes through the wraith or anything dramatic — the wraith simply disappears the instant the light hits the heart monitor and reappears the instant it moves away. Gately's unpleasant dreams definitely don't normally include specific gum-color and intense physical discomfort and invasions of lexical terms he doesn't know from shinola. Gately begins to conclude it's not impossible that the garden-variety wraith on the heart monitor, though not conventionally real, could be a sort of epiphanyish visitation from Gately's personally confused under-standing of God, a Higher Power or something, maybe sort of like the leg-endary Pulsing Blue Light that AA founder Bill W. historically saw during his last detox, that turned out to be God telling him how to stay sober via starting AA and Carrying The Message. The wraith smiles sadly and says something like Don't we both wish, young sir. Gately's forehead wrinkling as his eyes keep rolling up makes the foreign can wobble coldly: of course there's also the possibility that the tall slumped extremely fast wraith might represent the Sergeant at Arms, the Disease, exploiting the loose security of Gately's fever-addled mind, getting ready to fuck with his motives and per-suade him to accept Demerol just once, just one last time, for the totally legitimate medical pain. Gately lets himself wonder what it would be like, able to quantum off anyplace instantly and stand on ceilings and probably burgle like no burglar'd ever dreamed of, but not able to really affect any-thing or interface with anybody, having nobody know you're there, having people's normal rushed daily lives look like the movements of planets and suns, having to sit patiently very still in one place for a long time even to have some poor addled son of a bitch even be willing to entertain your maybe being there. It'd be real free-seeming, but incredibly lonely, he imag-ines. Gately knows a thing or two about loneliness, he feels. Does *wraith* mean like a ghost, as in dead? Is this a message from a Higher Power about sobriety and death? What would it be like to try and talk and have the person think it was just their own mind talking? Gately could maybe Iden-tify, to an extent, he decides. This is the only time he's ever been struck dumb except for a brief but nasty bout of pleuritic laryngitis he'd had when he was twenty-four and sleeping on the cold beach up in Gloucester, and he doesn't like it a bit, the being struck dumb. It's like some combination of invisibility and being buried alive, in terms of the feeling. It's like being strangled somewhere deeper inside you than your neck. Gately imagines himself with a piratical hook, unable to speak on Commitments because he can only gurgle and pant, doomed to an AA life of ashtrays and urns. The wraith reaches down and removes the can of un-American tonic from Gately's forehead and assures Gately he can more than Identify with an animate man's feelings of communicative impotence and mute strangulation. Gately's thoughts become agitated as he tries to yell mentally that he never said a fucking thing about im*potence*. He's got a way clearer and more direct view of the wraith's extreme nostril-hair situation than he'd prefer to. The wraith hefts the can absently and says age twenty-eight seems old enough for Gately to remember U.S. broadcast television's old network situation comedies of the B.S. '80s and '90s, probably. Gately has to smile at the wraith's cluelessness: Gately's after all a fucking drug addict, and a drug addict's second most meaningful relationship is always with his domestic entertainment unit, TV/VCR or HDTP. A drug addict's maybe the only human species whose own personal vision has a Vertical Hold, for Christ's sake, he thinks. And Gately, even in recovery, can still summon great verbatim chunks not only of drug-addicted adolescence's 'Seinfeld' and 'Ren and Stimpy' and 'Oo Is 'E When 'E's at 'Ome' and 'Exposed Northerners' but also the syndicated 'Bewitched' and 'Hazel' and ubiquitous 'M*A*S*H' he grew to monstrous childhood size in front of, and especially the home-town ensemble-casted 'Cheers!,' both the late-network version with the stacked brunette and the syndicated older ones with the titless blond, which Gately even after the switch over to InterLace and HDTP dissemination felt like he had a special personal relationship with 'Cheers!,' not only because everybody on the show always had a cold foamer in hand, just like in real life, but because Gately's big childhood claim to recognition had been his eerie resemblance to the huge neckless simian-browed accountant Nom who more or less seemed to live at the bar, and was unkind but not cruel, and drank foamer after foamer without once hitting anybody's Mom or pitching over sideways and passing out in vomit somebody else had to clean up, and who'd looked — right down to the massive square head and Neanderthal brow and paddle-sized thumbs — eerily like the child D. W. ('Bim') Gately, hulking and neckless and shy, riding his broom handle, Sir Osis of Thuliver. And the wraith on the heart monitor looks pensively down at Gately from upside-down and asks does Gately remember the myriad thespian extras on for example his beloved 'Cheers!,' not the center-stage Sam and Carla and Nom, but the nameless patrons always at tables, filling out the bar's crowd, concessions to realism, always relegated to back- and foreground; and always having utterly silent conversations: their faces would animate and mouths move realistically, but without sound; only the name-stars at the bar itself could audibilize. The wraith says these fractional actors, human scenery, could be seen (but not heard) in most pieces of filmed entertainment. And Gately remembers them, the extras in all public scenes, especially like bar and restaurant scenes, or rather remembers how he doesn't quite remember them, how it never struck his addled mind as in fact surreal that their mouths moved but nothing emerged, and what a miserable fucking bottom-rung job that must be for an actor, to be sort of human furniture, *figurants* the wraith says they're called, these surreally mute background presences whose presence really revealed that the camera, like any eye, has a perceptual corner, a triage of who's important enough to be seen and heard v. just seen. A term from ballet, originally, *figurant,* the wraith explains. The wraith pushes his glasses up in the vaguely snivelling way of a kid that's just got slapped around on the playground and says he personally spent the vast bulk of his own former animate life as pretty much a figurant, furniture at the periphery of the very eyes closest to him, it turned out, and that it's one heck of a crummy way to try to live. Gately, whose increasing self-pity leaves little room or patience for anybody else's self-pity, tries to lift his left hand and wiggle his pinkie to indicate the world's smallest viola playing the theme from *The Sorrow and the Pity,* but even moving his left arm makes him almost faint. And either the wraith is saying or Gately is realizing that you can't appreciate the dramatic pathos of a figurant until you realize how completely *trapped* and *encaged* he is in his mute peripheral status, because like say for example if one of 'Cheers!' 's bar's figurants suddenly decided he couldn't take it any more and stood up and started shouting and gesturing around wildly in a bid for attention and nonperipheral status on the show, Gately realizes, all that would happen is that one of the audibilizing 'name' stars of the show would bolt over from stage-center and apply restraints or the Heineken Maneuver or CPR, figuring the silent gesturing figurant was choking on a beer-nut or something, and that then the whole rest of that episode of 'Cheers!' would be about jokes about the name star's life-saving heroics, or else his fuck-up in applying the Heineken Maneuver to somebody who wasn't choking on a nut. No way for a figurant to win. No possible voice or focus for the encaged figurant. Gately speculates briefly about the suicide statistics for bottom-rung actors. The wraith disappears and then reappears in the chair by the bed's railing, leaning forward with its chin on its hands on the railing in what Gately's coming to regard as the classic tell-your-troubles-to-the-trauma-patient-that-can't-interrupt-or-get-away position. The wraith says that he himself, the wraith, when animate, had dabbled in filmed entertainments, as in making them, cartridges, for Gately's info to either believe or not, and but in the entertainments the wraith himself made, he says he goddamn bloody well made sure that either the whole entertainment was silent or else if it wasn't silent that you could bloody well hear every single performer's voice, no matter how far out on the cinematographic or narrative periphery they were; and that it wasn't just the self-conscious overlapping dialogue of a poseur like Schwulst or Altman, i.e. it wasn't just the crafted imitation of aural chaos: it was real life's real egalitarian babble of figurantless crowds, of the animate world's real agora, the babble[342] of crowds every member of which was the central and articulate protagonist of his own entertainment. It occurs to Gately he's never had any sort of dream where somebody says anything like *vast bulk,* much less *agora,* which Gately interprets as a kind of expensive sweater. Which was why, the wraith is continuing, the complete unfigured egalitarian aural realism was why party-line entertainment-critics always complained that the wraith's entertainments' public-area scenes were always incredibly dull and self-conscious and irritating, that they could never hear the really meaningful central narrative conversations for all the unfiltered babble of the peripheral crowd, which they assumed the babble(/babel) was some self-conscious viewer-hostile heavy-art directorial pose, instead of radical realism. The wraith's grim smile almost disappears before it appears. Gately's slight tight smile back is the way you can always tell he's not really listening. He's remembering that he used to pretend to himself that the unviolent and sarcastic accountant Nom on 'Cheers!' was Gately's own organic father, straining to hold young Bimmy on his lap and letting him draw finger-pictures in the condensation-rings on the bartop, and when he was pissed off at Gately's mother being sarcastic and witty instead of getting her down and administering horribly careful U.S.-Navy-brig-type beatings that hurt like hell but would never bruise or show. The can of foreign Coke has left a ring on his forehead that's colder than the feverish skin around it, and Gately tries to concentrate on the cold of the ring instead of the dead cold total ache on his whole right side — *DEXTRAL* — or the sober memory of his mother Mrs. Gately's ex-significant other, the little-eyed former M.P. in khaki skivvies hunched drunk over his notebook's record of his Heinekens for the day, his tongue in the corner of his mouth and his eyes scrunched as he tries to see a unitary enough notebook to write in, Gately's mother on the floor trying to crawl off toward the lockable bathroom quietly enough so the M.P. wouldn't notice her again.

The wraith says Just to give Gately an idea, he, the wraith, in order to appear as visible and interface with him, Gately, he, the wraith, has been sitting, still as a root, in the chair by Gately's bedside for the wraith-equivalent of *three weeks,* which Gately can't even imagine. It occurs to Gately that none of the people that've dropped by to tell him their troubles has bothered to say how many days he's even been in the Trauma Wing now, or what day it's going to be when the sun comes up, and so Gately has no idea how long he's gone now without an AA meeting. Gately wishes his sponsor Ferocious Francis G. would hobble by instead of Ennet Staff that want to talk about prosfeces and residents who come just to share remembered wreckage with somebody they don't even think can even hear them, sort of the way a little kid confides to a dog. He doesn't let himself even contemplate why no Finest or federally crew-cut guys have visited yet, if he's been in here a while, if they've been all over the House like hamsters on wheat already, as Thrust had said. The seated shadow of somebody in a hat is still there out there in the hall, though if the whole interlude was a dream it isn't and has never been there, Gately realizes, squinting a little to try to make sure the shadow is the shadow of a hat and not a fire-extinguisher box on the hall wall or something. The wraith excuses himself and disappears but then reappears two slow blinks later, back in the same position. 'That was worth an Excuse Me?' Gately thinks at the wraith dryly, almost laughing. The sheet of pain from the near-laugh send his eyes way up back up in his head. The chassis of the heart monitor doesn't look broad enough to support even a wraith's ass. The heart monitor's the silent kind. It's got the moving white line with big speed bumps moving across it for Gately's pulse, but it doesn't make the sterile beeping that old hospital-drama monitors did. Patients in hospital-dramas were frequently unconscious figurants, Gately reflects. The wraith says he'd just paid a small quantumish call to the old spotless Brighton two-decker of one Ferocious Francis Gehaney, and from the way the old Crocodile's shaving and putting on a clean white T-shirt, the wraith says, he predicts F.F. will be visiting the Trauma Wing soon to offer Gately unconditional empathy and fellowship and acerbic Crocodilian counsel. Unless this was just Gately himself thinking this up to keep a stiff upper attitude, Gately thinks. The wraith pushes his glasses up sadly. You never think of a wraith looking sad or unsad, but this dream-wraith displays the whole affective range. Gately can hear the horns and raised voices and U-turn squeals way down below on Wash. that indicate it's around 0000h., the switching hour. He wonders what something as brief as a car-horn-honk sounds like to a figurant that has to sit still for three weeks to be seen. Wraith, not figurant, Gately meant, he corrects himself. He's lying here correcting his thoughts like he was talking. He wonders if his brain-voice talks fast enough for the wraith not to have to like tap its foot and look at its watch between words. Are they words if they're only in your head, though? The wraith blows its nose in a hankie that's visibly seen better epochs and says he, the wraith, when alive in the world of animate men, had seen his own personal youngest offspring, a son, the one most like him, the one most marvelous and frightening to him, becoming a figurant, toward the end. His end, not the son's end, the wraith clarifies. Gately wonders if it offends the wraith when he sometimes refers to it mentally as *it*. The wraith opens and examines the used hankie just like an alive person can never help but do and says No horror on earth or elsewhere could equal watching your own offspring open his mouth and have nothing come out. The wraith says it mars the memory of the end of his animate life, this son's retreat to the periphery of life's frame. The wraith confesses that he had, at one time, blamed the boy's mother for his silence. But what good does that kind of thing do, he said, making a blurred motion that might have been shrugging. Gately remembers the former Navy M.P. telling Gately's mother why it was her fault he lost his job at the chowder plant. 'Resentment Is The #1 Offender' is another Boston AA cliché Gately'd started to believe. That blame's a shell-game. Not that he wouldn't mind a private couple of minutes alone in a doorless room with Randy Lenz, once he was up and capable again, though.

The wraith reappears slumped back in the chair with his weight on his tailbone and his legs crossed in that Erdedyish upscale way. He says Just imagine the horror of spending your whole itinerant lonely Southwest and West Coast boyhood trying unsuccessfully to convince your father that you even existed, to do something well enough to be heard and seen but not so well that you became just a screen for his own (the Dad's) projections of his own failure and self-loathing, failing ever to be really seen, gesturing wildly through the distilled haze, so that in adulthood you still carried the moist flabby weight of your failure ever to make him hear you really *speak,* carried it on through the animate years on your increasingly slumped shoulders — only to find, near the end, that your very own child had himself become blank, inbent, silent, frightening, mute. I.e. that his son had become what he (the wraith) had feared as a child he (the wraith) was. Gately's eyes roll up in his head. The boy, who did everything well and with a natural unslumped grace the wraith himself had always lacked, and whom the wraith had been so terribly eager to see and hear and let him (the son) know he was seen and heard, the son had become a steadily more and more *hidden* boy, toward the wraith's life's end; and no one else in the wraith and boy's nuclear family would see or acknowledge this, the fact that the graceful and marvelous boy was disappearing right before their eyes. They looked but did not see his invisibility. And they listened but did not hear the wraith's warning. Gately has that slight tight absent smile again. The wraith says the nuclear family had believed he (the wraith) was unstable and was confusing the boy with his own (the wraith's) boyhood self, or with the wraith's father's father, the blank wooden man who according to family mythology had 'driven' the wraith's father to 'the bottle' and unrealized potential and an early cerebral hemorrhage. Toward the end, he'd begun privately to fear that his son was experimenting with Substances. The wraith keeps having to push its glasses up. The wraith says almost bitterly that when he'd stand up and wave his arms for them all to attend to the fact that his youngest and most promising son was disappearing, they'd thought all his agitation meant was that he had gone bats from Wild Turkey–intake and needed to try to get sober, again, one more time.

This gets Gately's attention. Here at last could be some sort of point to the unpleasantness and confusion of the dream. 'You tried to get sober?' he thinks, rolling his eyes over to the wraith. 'More than once, you tried? Was it White-Knuckle?[343] Did you ever Surrender and Come In?'

The wraith feels along his long jaw and says he spent the whole sober last ninety days of his animate life working tirelessly to contrive a medium via which he and the muted son could simply *converse.* To concoct something

838

the gifted boy couldn't simply master and move on from to a new plateau. Something the boy would love enough to induce him to open his mouth and come *out* — even if it was only to ask for more. Games hadn't done it, professionals hadn't done it, impersonation of professionals hadn't done it. His last resort: entertainment. Make something so bloody compelling it would reverse thrust on a young self's fall into the womb of solipsism, anhedonia, death in life. A magically entertaining toy to dangle at the infant still somewhere alive in the boy, to make its eyes light and toothless mouth open unconsciously, to laugh. To bring him 'out of himself,' as they say. The womb could be used both ways. A way to say I AM SO VERY, VERY SORRY and have it *heard*. A life-long dream. The scholars and Foundations and disseminators never saw that his most serious wish was: *to entertain*.

Gately's not too agonized and feverish not to recognize gross self-pity when he hears it, wraith or no. As in the slogan 'Poor Me, Poor Me, Pour Me A Drink.' With all due respect, pretty hard to believe this wraith could stay sober, if he needed to get sober, with the combination of abstraction and tragically-misunderstood-me attitude he's betraying, in the dream.

He'd been sober as a Mennonite quilter for 89 days, at the very tail-end of his life, the wraith avers, now back up on the silent heart monitor, though Boston AA had a humorless evangelical rabidity about it that had kept his attendance at meetings spotty. And he never could stand the vapid clichés and disdain for abstraction. Not to mention the cigarette smoke. The atmosphere of the meeting rooms had been like a poker game in hell, had been his impression. The wraith stops and says he bets Gately's struggling to hide his curiosity about whether the wraith succeeded in coming up with a figurantless entertainment so thoroughly engaging it'd make even an in-bent figurant of a boy laugh and cry out for more.

Father-figure-wise, Gately's tried his best these last few sober months to fend off uninvited memories of his own grim conversations and interchanges with the M.P.

The wraith on the monitor now bends sharply at the waist, way over forward so his face is upside-down only cm. from Gately's face — the wraith's face is only about half the size of Gately's face, and has no odor — and responds vehemently that No! *No! Any* conversation or interchange is better than none at all, to trust him on this, that the worst kind of gut-wrenching intergenerational interface is better than withdrawal or hiddenness on either side. The wraith apparently can't tell the difference between Gately just thinking to himself and Gately using his brain-voice to sort of think *at* the wraith. His shoulder suddenly sends up a flare of pain so sickening Gately's afraid he might shit the bed. The wraith gasps and almost falls off the monitor as if he can totally empathize with the dextral flare. Gately wonders if the wraith has to endure the same pain as Gately in order to hear his brain-voice and have a conversation with him. Even in a dream, that'd be a higher price than anybody's ever paid to interface with D. W. Gately. Maybe the pain's supposed to lend credibility to some Diseased argument for Demerol the wraith's going to make. Gately feels somehow too self-conscious or stupid to ask the wraith if it's here on behalf of the Higher Power or maybe the Disease, so instead of thinking at the wraith he simply concentrates on pretending to wonder to himself why the wraith is spending probably months of aggregate wraith-time flitting around a hospital room and making pirouetted demonstrations with crooner-photos and foreign tonic-cans on the ceiling of some drug addict he doesn't know from a rock instead of just quantuming over to wherever this alleged youngest son is and holding very still for wraith-months and trying to have an interface with the fucking *son*. Though maybe thinking he was seeing his late organic dad as a ghost or wraith would drive the youngest son bats, though, might be the thing. The son didn't exactly sound like the steadiest hand on the old mental joystick as it was, from what the wraith's shared. Of course this was assuming the mute figurant son even existed, this was assuming this wasn't all some roundabout way of the Disease starting to talk Gately into succumbing to a shot of Demerol. He tries to concentrate on all this instead of remembering what Demerol's warm rush of utter well-being felt like, remembering the comfortable sound of the clunk of his chin against his chest. Or instead of remembering any of his own interchanges with his mother's live-in retired M.P. One of the highest prices of sobriety was not being able to keep from remembering things you didn't want to remember, see for instance Ewell and the fraudulent-grandiosity thing from his wie-nieish childhood. The ex-M.P. had referred to small children and toddlers as 'rug-rats.' It was not a term of gruff affection. The M.P. had made the toddler Don Gately return empty Heineken bottles to the neighborhood packy and then haul-ass on back with the bottle-deposits, timing him with a U.S.N.-issue chronometer. He never laid a hand on Gately personally, that Don could recall. But he'd still been afraid of the M.P. The M.P.'d beaten his mother up on an almost daily basis. The most hazardous time for Gately's mother was between eight Heinekens and ten Heinekens. When the M.P. threw her on the floor and knelt down very intently over her, picking his spots and hitting her very intently, he'd looked like a lobsterman pulling at his outboard's rope. The M.P. was slightly shorter than Mrs. Gately but was broad and very muscular, and proud of his muscles, going shirtless whenever possible. Or in like sleeveless khaki military T's. He had bars and weights and benches, and had taught the child Don Gately the fundamentals of free-weight training, with special emphasis on control and form as opposed to just sloppily lifting as much weight as possible. The weights were old and greasy and their poundage pre-metric. The M.P. was very precise and controlled in his approach to things, in a way Gately has somehow come to associate with all blond-haired men. When Gately, at age ten, began to be able to bench-press more weight than the M.P., the M.P. had not taken it in a good spirit and began refusing to spot him on his sets. The M.P. entered his own weights and repetitions carefully in a little notebook, pausing to do this after each set. He always licked the point of the pencil before he wrote, a habit Gately still finds repellent. In a different little note-book, the M.P. noted the date and time of each Heineken he consumed. He was the sort of person who equated incredibly careful record-keeping with control. In other words he was by nature a turd-counter. Gately had realized this at a very young age, and that it was bullshit and maybe crazy. The M.P. was very possibly crazy. The circumstances of his leaving the Navy were like: shadowy. When Gately involuntarily remembers the M.P. now he also remembers — and wonders why, and feels bad — that he never once asked his mother about the M.P. and why the fuck was he even there and did she actually love him, and why did she love him when he flang her down and beat her up on a more or less daily basis for fucking years on end. The intensifying rose-colors behind Gately's closed lids are from the hospital room lightening as the light outside the window gets licoricey and pre-dawn. Gately lies below the unoccupied heart-monitor snoring so hard the railings on either side of his bed shiver and rattle. When the M.P. was sleep-ing or out of the house, Don Gately and Mrs. Gately never once talked about him. His memory is clear on this. It wasn't just that they never dis-cussed him, or the notebooks or weights or chronometer or his beating up Mrs. Gately. The M.P.'s name was never even mentioned. The M.P. worked nights a lot — driving a cheese-and-egg delivery truck for Cheese King Inc. until he was terminated for embezzling wheels of Stilton and fencing them, then for a time on a mostly automated canning line, pulling a lever that sent New England chowder out of hundreds of spigots into hundreds of lidless cans with an indescribable plopping sound — and the Gately home was like a different world when the M.P. was working or out: it was like the very idea of the M.P. walked out the door with him, leaving Don and his mother not just behind but alone, together, at night, she on the couch and he on the floor, both gradually losing consciousness in front of broadcast TV's final seasons. Gately tries especially hard now not to explore why it never oc-curred to him to step in and pull the M.P. off his mother, even after he could bench-press more than the M.P. The precise daily beatings had always seemed in some strangely emphatic way not his business. He rarely even felt anything, he remembers, watching him hit her. The M.P. was totally unshy about hitting her in front of Gately. It was like everybody unspokenly agreed the whole thing was none of Bimmy's beeswax. When he was a toddler he'd flee the room and cry about it, he seems to recall. By a certain age, though, all he'd do is raise the volume on the television, not even both-ering to look over at the beating, watching 'Cheers!' Sometimes he'd leave the room and go into the garage and lift weights, but when he left the room it was never like he was fleeing the room. When he'd been small he'd sometimes hear the springs and sounds from their bedroom sometimes in the A.M. and worry that the M.P. was beating her up on their bed, but at a certain point without anybody taking him aside and explaining anything to him he realized that the sounds then didn't mean she was getting hurt. The similarity of her hurt sounds in the kitchen and living room and her sex-sounds through the asbestos fiberboard bedroom wall troubles Gately, though, when he remembers now, and is one reason why he fends off remembering, when awake.

Shirtless in the summer — and pale, with a blond man's dislike for the sun — the M.P. would sit in the little kitchen, at the kitchen table, feet flat on the wood-grain tiling, with a patriotic-themed bandanna wrapped around his head, recording Heinekens in his little notebook. A previous tenant had thrown something heavy through the kitchen window once, and the window's screen was fucked up and not quite flush, and houseflies came and went more or less at will. Gately, when small, would be in there in the kitchen with the M.P. sometimes; the tile was better for his little cars' suspensions than nubbly carpet. What Gately remembers, in pain, bubbling just under the lid of sleep, is the special and precise way the M.P. would handle the flies that came into the kitchen. He used no swatter or rolled cone of *Herald*. He had fast hands, the M.P., thick and white and fast. He'd whack them as they lit on the kitchen table. The flies. But in a controlled way. Not hard enough to kill them. He was very controlled and intent about it. He'd whack them just hard enough to disable them. Then he'd pick them up real precisely and remove either a wing or like a leg, something important to the fly. He'd take the wing or leg over to the beige kitchen wastebasket and very deliberately hike the lid with the foot-pedal and deposit the tiny wing or leg in the wastebasket, bending at the waist. The memory is unbidden and very clear. The M.P.'d wash his hands at the kitchen sink, using green generic dishwashing liquid. The maimed fly itself he'd ignore and allow to scuttle in crazed circles on the table until it got stuck in a sticky spot or fell off the edge onto the kitchen floor. The conversation with the M.P. that Gately reexperiences in minutely dreamed detail was the M.P., at about five Heinekens, explaining that maiming a fly was way more effective than killing a fly, for flies. A fly was stuck in a sticky spot of dried Heineken and agitating its wing as the M.P. explained that a well-maimed fly produced tiny little fly-screams of pain and fear. Human beings couldn't hear a maimed fly's screams, but you could bet your fat little rug-rat ass other flies could, and the screams of their maimed colleagues helped keep them away. By the time the M.P. would put his head on his big pale arms and grab a little shut-eye among the Heineken bottles on the sun-heated table there'd often be several flies trapped in goo or scuttling in circles on the table, sometimes giving odd little hops, trying to fly with one wing or no wings. Possibly in Denial, these flies, as to their like condition. The ones that fell to the floor Gately would hunch directly over on hands and knees, getting one big red ear down just as close to the fly as possible, listening, his big pink forehead wrinkled. What makes Gately most uncomfortable now as he starts to try to wake up in the lemonlight of true hospital morning is that he can't remember putting the maimed flies out of their misery, ever, after the M.P. passed out, can't mentally see himself stepping on them or wrapping them in paper towels and flushing them down the toilet or something, but he feels like he must have; it seems somehow real vital to be able to remember his doing something more than just hunkering blankly down amid his Transformer-cars and trying to see if he could hear tiny agonized screams, listening very intently. But he can't for the life of him remember doing more than trying to hear, and the sheer cerebral stress of trying to force a more noble memory should have awakened him, on top of the dextral hurt; but he doesn't come all the way awake in the big crib until the memory's realistic dream bleeds into a nasty fictional dream where he's wearing Lenz's worsted topcoat and leaning very precisely and carefully over the prone figure of the Hawaiian-dressed Nuck whose head he's whacked repeatedly against the hood's windshield, he's supporting his inclined weight on his good left hand against the warm throbbing hood, bent in real close to the maimed head, his ear to the bleeding face, listening very intently. The head opens its red mouth.

The wet start Gately finally wakes with jars his shoulder and side and sends a yellow sheet of pain over him that makes him almost scream into the window's light. For about a year once at age twenty in Malden he'd slept most nights in a home-built loft in the dorm of a certain graduate R.N.-nursing program in Malden, with a ragingly addicted R.N.-nursing student, in the loft, which you needed a five-rung ladder to get up into this loft and the thing was only a couple of feet under the ceiling, and every A.M. Gately'd awake out of some bad dream and sit up with a jolt and thwack his head against the ceiling, until after some time there was a permanent concavity in the ceiling and a flattish spot in the curve of the top of his forehead he can still feel, lying here blinking and holding his head with his good left hand. For a second, blinking and red with A.M. fever, he thinks he sees Ferocious Francis G. in the bedside chair, chin freshly shaved and dotted with bits of Kleenex, posture stolid, his old man's saggy little tits rising slowly under a clean white T-, smiling grimly around blue tubes and an unlit cigar between his teeth and saying 'Well kid at least you're still on this side of the fuckin' sod, I guess there's something to be said for that there. And are you as yet sober, then?' the Crocodile says coolly, disappearing and then not reappearing after several blinks.

The forms and sound in the room is really only three White Flaggers

Gately's never known or connected with that well, but are apparently here stopping in on their way to work, to show empathy and support, Bud O. and Glenn K. and Jack J. Glenn K. in daytime wears the gray jumpsuit and complex utility-belt of a refrigeration technician.

'And who's the fellow in the hat outside?' he's asking.

Gately grunts in a frantic way that suggests the phoneme *ü*.

'Tall, well-dressed, grumpy, cocky-looking, piggy-eyed, wearing a hat. Civil-Service-looking. Black socks and brown shoes,' Glenn K. says, pointing out toward the door where there's sometimes been the ominous shadow of a hat.

Gately's teeth taste long-unbrushed.

'Looking settled in for a stay, surrounded with sports pages and the take-out foods of many cultures, Laddie,' says Bud O., who the story from before Gately's time goes once hit his wife so hard in the blackout that made him Come In he broke her nose and bent it over flat against her face, which he asked her never to have repaired, as a daily visual reminder of the depths drink sunk him to, so Mrs. O. had gone around with her nose bent over flat against her left cheek — Bud O.'d tagged her with a left cross — until U.H.I.D. referred her to Al-Anon, which eventually nurtured and supported Mrs. O. into eventually telling Bud O. to take a flying fuck to the moon and getting her nose realigned back out front and leaving him for a male Al-Anon in Birkenstock sandals. Gately's bowels have gone watery with dread: he has all-too-clear memories of a certain remorseless Revere A.D.A.'s brown shoes, piggy eyes, Stetson w/ feather, and penchant for Third World takeout. He keeps grunting pathetically.

Unsure how to be supportive, for a while the Flaggers try to cheer Gately up by telling him CPR jokes. 'CPR' is their term for Al-Anon, which is known to Boston AAs as the 'Church of Perpetual Revenge.'

'What's an Al-Anon Relapse?' asks Glenn K.

'It is a twinge of compassion,' says Jack J., who has a kind of a facial tic.

'But what is an Al-Anon Salute?' Jack J. asks back.

The three all pause, and then Jack J. puts the back of his hand to his brow and flutters his lashes martyrishly at the drop-ceiling. They all three of them laugh. They have no clue that if Gately actually laughs he'll tear his shoulder's sutures. One side of Jack J.'s face goes in and out of a tortured grimace that doesn't affect the other side of his face one bit, something that's always given Gately the fantods. Bud O. is waggling his finger disapprovingly at Glenn K., to signify an Al-Anon Handshake. Glenn K. gives a lengthy impression of an Al-Anon mom watching her alcoholic kid marching in some parade and getting more and more outraged at how everybody's out of step except her kid. Gately closes his eyes and moves his chest up and down a few times in a dumbshow of polite laughter, so they'll think they've cheered him up and screw. The little thoracic movements make his dextral regions make him want to bite the side of his hand in pain. It's like a big wooden spoon keeps pushing him just under the surface of sleep and then spooning him up for something huge to taste him, again and again.

19 NOVEMBER
YEAR OF THE DEPEND ADULT UNDERGARMENT

After Rémy Marathe and Ossowiecke, and Balbalis also, they all reported back negatively for all signs of this veiled performer, M. Fortier and Marathe threw into an effect this finally most drastic of the operations for the locating of the Master Entertainment. This was to acquire members of the immediate family of the *auteur,* perhaps in public.

Marathe was charged with this operation's details, for M. Broullîme was now thrust into technical trouble-killing on the furthering field-tests of viewer willingness; for one of the newly acquired test-subjects — this was an eccentrically dressed and extremely irritating without-home man of the streets in a white wig appropriated with large bags filled of foreign cookware and extremely small-in-size ladies' undergarments — was discovered to have been being severing and pushing beneath the room of storage's closed door the severed digits of the second of the newly acquired test-subjects — this was a mis-dressed and severely weakened or addicted man dressed in the clothing of a gauche woman, carrying multiple purses of suspicious nature — rather than his own digits, marring the statistics of Broullîme's field-experiment to such the extent that M. Fortier was forced to consider whether to allow Broullîme to conduct a lethal technical interview of the wigged substituter of digits for reasons of anger only. Substantially, a technical interview of more importance was to be conducted in the city Phoenix far across the U.S. to the south, a city's name Fortier had amusement from, and departed before incoming weather to attend Mlle. Luria P—— in this conducting, leaving the trusted Rémy Marathe to charge details of the preliminary acquisition.

Marathe, who had made his decision and call, did what he could. A direct assault upon the Academy of Tennis itself was impossible. A.F.R.s fear nothing in this hemisphere except tall and steep hillsides. Their attack must not be direct. Thus the preliminary was to acquire and replace the tennis children of Québec, known by the A.F.R. to be even then en route to U.S.A. soil for gala competition with the tennis children of this Academy. Marathe selected young Balbalis, the one still with both the legs — albeit paralyzed and stickishly withered, them — to lead the A.F.R. field-detail which must intercept the provincial players. Marathe, he stayed at the Cambridge shop of the Antitois, withdrawing frequently to the jazz nights nearby of Ryle's restaurant. Balbalis drove the modified van of Dodge north into the increasingly heavy snowstorm. They bypassed the Pongo checkpoint at Methuen MA. They would place a large mirror in the deserted road and delude the tennis bus that it must leave the road to avoid impact; its own headlights would delude it. An old F.L.Q. trick. Two teams in the van's back assembled the mirror's components. Balbalis would not allow to stop for this assembly; the snowfall was worse in the Convexity because of the fans to the south. What used to be Montpelier in Vermont lay between E.W.D. grids but took bad fallout from the region of Champlain and was unoccupied and ghostly white with snow. Balbalis permitted at Montpelier a brief stop for final assembly and for those who were incontinent to change their bags. Balbalis pressed hard to the former place of St. Johnsbury, where the mirror was installed across the southbound lanes of the U.S. Interstate #91. Balbalis did not complain that there were no tracks in the snow of the road to be followed. He never complained. They arrived well early just south of the checkpoint at which Provincial Autoroute #55 became the Interstate #91. There was a brief period of the tension when it appeared that the night-vision attachment for the binoculars had been misplaced. Balbalis remained cool and it was located. The plan was to intercept the travelling team of players and allow A.F.R.s to arrive at the place in their stead. Marathe promised to conceive an excellent ruse to explain the wheelchairs and adult beards of the false players. There was no smoking in the van while they waited for the children tennis players of their country to appear at the checkpoint. The bus was forced to remain at the checkpoint for several minutes. The bus was large and chartered and appeared warm within. Above its windshield its lit rectangle of destination displayed the English word for charter. If the bus survived the swerve from the highway's mirror and was operational after the crash of swerving, Balbalis would drive this bus. There was one brief argument over who would be required to drive the van, for Balbalis refused to leave the van behind them even if the bus was operational. If the bus was not operational, no more than six junior children as survivors could be accommodated in the van. The rest would be allowed to die for *leur rai pays*. Balbalis, he showed no preference one or the other way.

Gately dreamed he was with Ennet House resident Joelle van Dyne in a Southern motel whose restaurant's authoritarian sign said simply EAT, in the U.S. South, in high summer, brutally hot, the foliage outside the room's broken windowscreen a parched khaki, the air glassy with heat, the ceiling fan rotating at a second-hand's rate, the room's bed a lavish four-poster, tall and squishy, the bedspread nubbly, Gately supine with his side on fire while newcomer Joelle v.D. raises her veil slightly to lick the sweat off his lids and temples, whispering so the veil flutters around and fans him, promising him a P.M. of near-terminal pleasures, undressing at the foot of the old tall bed, slowly, her loose light clothes moist with sweat and falling easily to the bare floor, and an incredible female body, an inhuman body, the sort of body Gately's only ever seen with a staple in its navel, a body like something you'd win in a raffle; and a fifth post forms on the four-poster, so to speak, which erect post's long-dormant height obscures the nude newcomer's figure; and then when she moves around out of the pulsing shadow to lean in close and press her inhuman body's face right up intimately close to his, she removes the veil, and on top of this body to die for is the unveiled historical likeness of fucking *Winston Churchill,* complete with cigar and jowls and bulldog scowl, and the ghastliness of the shock makes the rest of Gately's body go rigid, the pain of which wakes him with a jolted attempt to sit up that itself causes such a blast of pain that he half passes back out again and lies there with rolling eyes and a round mouth.

Gately's also powerless over memories of the older-type lady that had been their neighbor when he and his mother shared bed and board with the M.P. A Mrs. Waite. There was no Mr. Waite. The smeared window of the little empty garage the M.P. kept his weights in was right next to the spiny neglected garden Mrs. Waite kept in the narrow strip between the two houses. Mrs. Waite's house had been shall we say indifferently maintained. Mrs. Waite's house had made the Gately house look like the Taj. There was something wrong about Mrs. Waite. None of the parents said what it was, but none of the kids were allowed to play in her yard or ring her bell on Halloween. Gately never got clear on what was supposed to be wrong about her, but the little poor neighborhood's psyche throbbed with something dire about Mrs. Waite. Older kids drove across her lawn and shouted shit that Gately never quite made out, at night. The littler kids thought they had it: they were pretty sure Mrs. Waite was a witch. Yes, she did look a little witchy, but who over like fifty didn't? But the big thing was she kept jars of stuff she'd jarred herself in her little garage, brown-green viscous nameless vegetoid stuff in mayonnaise jars stacked on steel shelves and rusty-lidded and bearded with dust. The littler kids snuck in and broke some of the jars and stole one and ran away in mortal terror to break it elsewhere and then run again. They dared each other to ride their bikes in tiny diagonals across the edge of her lawn. They told each other stories of seeing Mrs. Waite in a pointy hat roasting missing kids whose pictures were on milk-cartons and pouring the juice into jars. Some of the bigger littler kids even tried that inevitable gag of putting a paper bag full of dog shit on her stoop and lighting it. It was somehow a further indictment of Mrs. Waite that she never complained. She rarely left her house. Mrs. Gately would never say what was wrong about Mrs. Waite but absolutely forbade Don to fuck with her in any way. Like Mrs. Gately was in any position to enforce any, like, for-biddings. Gately never fucked with Mrs. Waite's stored jars or rode across her lawn, and never much joined in on the witch-stories, which who needed witches to fear and despise when you had the good old M.P. right there at the kitchen table. But he was still scared of her. When he'd once seen her gnarly-eyed face up against the smeared garage window one P.M. when he had left the M.P. to beating Mrs. Gately and gone out to lift weights he screamed and almost dropped the bench-press bar on his Adam's apple. But over the long haul of a low-stimulation North Shore childhood, he'd gradu-ally developed a slight relationship with Mrs. Waite. He'd never all that much liked her; it wasn't like she was this lovable but misunderstood old lady; it's not like he ran to her dilapitated house to confide in her, or bond. But he went over once or twice, maybe, under circumstances he'd forgot, and had sat in her kitchen, interfaced a little. She was lucid, Mrs. Waite, and apparently continent, and there was no pointy hat anywhere in sight, but her house smelled bad, and Mrs. Waite herself had swollen veiny ankles and little white bits of that dried paste at the corners of her mouth and about a million newspapers stacked and mildewing all over the kitchen, and the old lady basically radiated whatever mixture of unpleasantness and vul-nerability it was that made you want to be cruel to people. Gately was never cruel to her, but it's not like he loved her or anything. When Gately went over there the couple times it was mostly when the M.P. was canning chow-der and his mother had passed out in vomit she expected somebody else to clean up, and he probably wanted to act out his kid's anger by doing some-thing Mrs. G.'d pathetically tried to forbid. He didn't eat much of whatever Mrs. Waite offered. She never offered him viscous material from a jar. His memories of whatever they discussed are unspecific. She hung herself, even-tually, Mrs. Waite — as in eliminated her own map — and because it was fall and cool she wasn't found for maybe weeks after. It wasn't Gately who found her. A meter-reader guy found her several weeks after Gately's eighth or ninth birthday. Gately's birthday was the same week as several other kids's in the neighborhood, by some chance. Usually Gately'd have his party over with some of the other kids that were having their birthdays with a party. Hats and Twister, X-Men videos, cake on Chinette plates, etc. Mrs. Gately was together enough to come a couple times. In retrospect, the other kids' parents let Gately have birthdays with them because they'd felt sorry for him, he's involuntarily realized. But at some sober neighbors' party, part of which was for his own eighth or ninth birthday, he remembers how Mrs. Waite had left her house and come rung the sober neighbor's bell and had brought a birthday cake. For the birthday. A neighborly gesture. Gately'd spilled the beans on the annual mass party at a kitchen-table interface with her. The cake was uneven and slightly tilted to one side, but it was dark chocolate and decorated with four cursive names and had clearly been made with care. Mrs. Waite had spared Gately the humiliation of putting just his name on the cake as if the cake was especially for him. But it was. Mrs. Waite had saved up for a long time to afford to make the cake, Gately knew. He knew she smoked like a chimney and had given up cigarettes for weeks to save up for something; she wouldn't tell him what; she'd tried to make her scary eyes twinkle when she wouldn't tell; but he'd seen the mayonnaise jar full of quarters on a pile of papers and had wrestled with himself over promoting it, and won. But there were only like nine candles on the cake when the party's Mom brought it in, and a couple of the kids having birthdays were like twelve, was the private tip-off on who the cake was really for. The party's Mom had taken the cake at the door and said Thank You but had neglected to invite Mrs. Waite in. Gately was in a position during Twister in the garage to see Mrs. Waite walking back home across the street, slowly but very straightly and dignified and upright. A lot of the kids went to the garage door to look: Mrs. Waite had rarely been seen outside her house before, and never off her property. The sober Mom brought the cake in the garage and said it was a Touching Gesture from Mrs. Waite across the street; but she wouldn't let anybody eat the cake or even come close enough to it to blow out the nine candles. The candles didn't all match. The candles burned down far enough so that there was a smell of burnt frosting before they went out. The cake sat tilted by itself in a corner of the clean garage. Gately didn't defy the sober Mom or any of the kids and eat a piece of the cake; he didn't even go near it. He didn't join in the delicious whispery arguments about what kind of medical waste or roasted-kid renderings were in the cake, but he didn't stand up and argue with the other kids about the fact of the poisoning, either. Before the party climaxed and the other kids that had got presents opened their presents, the sober Mom had taken the cake into the kitchen when she thought nobody was watching and threw it out in the wastebasket. Gately remembers the cake must have landed upside-down, because the unfrosted side was facing up in the wastebasket when he snuck in and had a look at the cake. Mrs. Waite had disappeared back inside her house way before the Mom threw the cake away. There's no way she could have seen the Mom take the uneaten cake back inside the house. A couple days later Gately had promoted a couple packs of Benson & Hedges 100s from a Store 24 and put them in Mrs. Waite's mailbox, where junk mail and utility bills were already piling up. He sometimes rang the bell but never saw her. Her bell had been a buzzer instead of a bell, he remembers. She got found by a frustrated meter-reader some indefinite number of weeks after that. The circumstances of her death and discovery became more dark myth for the littler kids. Gately wasn't so into self-torture as to think the cake getting not eaten and getting thrown out was in any way connected with Mrs. Waite hanging herself. Everybody had their own private troubles, Mrs. Gately had explained to him, and even at that age he could see her point. It's not like he'd like mourned Mrs. Waite, or missed her, or even thought about her even once for many years after that.

Which is what makes it somehow worse that his next, even more unpleasant Joelle van Dyne pain-and-fever dream takes place in what is, unmistakably and unavoidably, Mrs. Waite's kitchen, in great detail, right down to the ceiling's light-fixture full of dried bugs, the brimming ashtrays, the bar-graph of stacked *Globe*s, the maddening arrhythmic drip of the kitchen sink and the bad smell — a mixture of mildew and putrid fruit. Gately is in the ladder-back kitchen chair he used to sit in, the one with one rung broken, and Mrs. Waite is in her chair opposite, seated on the thing he thought then was a weird pink doughnut instead of a hemorrhoid pillow, except in the dream Gately's feet reach all the way to rest on the floor's dank tile, and Mrs. Waite is played by veiled U.H.I.D. House resident Joelle van D., except without her veil, and what's more without any clothes, as in starkers, gorgeous, with that same incredible body as in the other one except here this time with the face not of a jowly British P.M. but of a total female angel, not sexy so much as angelic, like all the world's light had gotten together and arranged itself into the shape of a face. Or something. It looks like somebody, Joelle's face, but Gately can't for the life of him place who, and it's not just the distraction of the inhumanly gorgeous naked bod below, because the dream is not like a sex-dream. Because in this dream, Mrs. Waite, who is Joelle, is Death. As in the figure of Death, Death incarnate. Nobody comes right out and says so; it's just understood: Gately's sitting here in this depressing kitchen interfacing with Death. Death is explaining that Death happens over and over, you have many lives, and at the end of each one (meaning life) is a woman who kills you and releases you into the next life. Gately can't quite make out if it's like a monologue or if he's asking questions and she's responding in a Q/A deal. Death says that this certain woman that kills you is always your next life's mother. This is how it works: didn't he know? In the dream everybody in the world seems to know this except Gately, like he'd missed that day in school when they covered it, and so Death's having to sit here naked and angelic and explain it to him, very patiently, more or less like Remedial Reading at Beverly H.S. Death says the woman who either knowingly or involuntarily kills you is always someone you love, and she's always your next life's mother. This is why Moms are so obsessively loving, why they try so hard no matter what private troubles or issues or addictions they have of their own, why they seem to value your welfare above their own, and why there's always a slight, like, twinge of selfishness about their obsessive mother-love: they're trying to make amends for a murder neither of you quite remember, except maybe in dreams. As Death's explanation of Death goes on Gately understands really important vague stuff more and more, but the more he understands the sadder he gets, and the sadder he gets the more unfocused and wobbly be-

850

comes his vision of the Death's Joelle sitting nude on the pink plastic ring, until near the end it's as if he's seeing her through a kind of cloud of light, a milky filter that's the same as the wobbly blur through which a baby sees a parental face bending over its crib, and he begins to cry in a way that hurts his chest, and asks Death to set him free and be his mother, and Joelle either shakes or nods her lovely unfocused head and says: Wait.

20 NOVEMBER
YEAR OF THE DEPEND ADULT UNDERGARMENT
GAUDEAMUS IGITUR

I was in a zoo. There were no animals or cages, but it was still a zoo. It was close to a nightmare and it woke me before 0500h. Mario was still asleep, gently lit by the window's view of tiny lights down the hill. He lay very still and soundless as always, his poor hands folded on his chest, as if awaiting a lily. I put in a plug of Kodiak. His four pillows brought Mario's chin to his chest when he slept. I was still producing excess saliva, and my one pillow was moist in a way I didn't want to turn on a light and investigate. I didn't feel good at all. A sort of nausea of the head. The feeling seemed worst first thing in the morning. I'd felt for almost a week as if I needed to cry for some reason but the tears were somehow stopping just millimeters behind my eyes and staying there. And so on.

I got up and went past the foot of Mario's bed to the window to stand on one foot. Sometime during the night heavy snow had begun to fall. I had been ordered by deLint and Barry Loach to stand on the left foot for fifteen minutes a day as therapy for the ankle. The countless little adjustments necessary to balance on one foot worked muscles and ligaments in the ankle that were therapeutically unreachable any other way. I always felt sort of dickish, standing on one foot in the dark with nothing to do.

The snow on the ground had a purple cast to it, but the falling and whirling snow was virgin white. Yachting-cap white. I stood on my left foot for maybe five minutes tops. The Boards and A.P.s[344] were three weeks from tomorrow at 0800 in the C.B.S.[345] auditorium at B.U. I could hear a night-custodial crew rolling a mop-bucket somewhere on another floor.

This was to be the first A.M. without dawn drills since Interdependence Day, and everybody was invited to sleep in until breakfast. There were to be no classes all weekend.

I'd awakened too early yesterday, too. I'd kept seeing Kevin Bain crawling my way in my sleep.

I straightened up my bed and put the pillow's wet side down and put on clean sweatpants and some socks that didn't smell foul.

The closest Mario comes to snoring is a thin sound he makes at the back of his throat. The sound is as if he's drawing out the word *key* over and over. It's not an unpleasant sound. I estimated a good 50 cm. of snow on the ground, and it was really coming down. In the purple half-light the West Courts' nets were half-buried. Their top halves shuddered in a terrible wind. All over the subdormitory I could hear doors rattling slightly in their frames, as they did only in a bad wind. The wind gave the snowfall a swirling diagonal aspect. Snow was hitting the exterior of the window with a sandy sound. The basic view outside the window was that of a briskly shaken paperweight — the kind with the Xmas diorama and shakeable snow. The grounds' trees, fences and buildings looked toylike and miniaturized somehow. In fact it was hard to distinguish new snow falling from extant snow simply whirling around in the wind. It only then occurred to me to wonder whether and where we would play today's exhibition meet. The Lung wasn't yet up, but the sixteen courts under the Lung wouldn't have accommodated more than an A-only meet anyway. A kind of cold hope flared in me because I realized this could be cancellation-weather. The backlash of this hope was an even worse feeling than before: I couldn't remember ever actively hoping not to have to play before. I couldn't remember feeling strongly one way or the other about playing for quite a long time, in fact.

Mario and I had begun to make a practice of keeping the phone console's power on at night but turning off the ringer. The console's digital recorder had a light that pulsed once for each incoming message. The double flash of the recorder's light set up an interesting interference pattern with the red battery-light on the ceiling's smoke detector, the two lights flashing in synch on every seventh phone-flash and then moving slowly apart in a visual Doppler. A formula for the temporal relation between two unsyncopated flashes would translate spatially into the algebraic formula for an ellipse, I could see. Pemulis had poured a terrific volume of practical pre-Boards math into my head for two weeks, taking his own time and not asking for anything in return, being almost suspiciously generous about it. Then, since the Wayne debacle, the little tutorials had ceased and Pemulis himself had been very scarce, twice missing meals and several times taking the truck for long periods without checking with any of the rest of us about our truck-needs. I didn't even try to factor in the rapid single flash of the phone's power-unit display on the side of the TP; this would make it some sort calculus thing, and even Pemulis had conceded that I was not hardwired for anything past algebra and conic sections.

Every November, between I. Day and the WhataBurger Invitational in Tucson AZ, the Academy holds a semipublic exhibition meet for the 'benefit' of E.T.A.'s patrons and alumni and friends in the Boston area. The exhibition is followed by a semiformal cocktail party and dance in the dining hall, where players are required to appear showered and semiformal and available for social intercourse with patrons. Some of them all but check our teeth. Last year Heath Pearson had appeared for the gala in a red vest and bellboy's cap and furry tail, carrying a little organ and inviting patrons to grind the organ while he capered around chattering. C.T. was unamused. The whole Fundraiser is a Charles Tavis innovation. C.T. is far better at public relations and pump-priming than was Himself. The exhibition and gala are possibly the climax of C.T.'s whole administrative year. He'd determined that mid-November was the best time for a fundraiser, with the weather not yet bad and the tax-year drawing to a close but the U.S. holiday season, with its own draining system of demands on goodwill, not yet under way. For the past three fiscal years, the Fundraiser's proceeds have all but paid for the spring's Southeast tour and the European *terre-batu*-fest of June–July.

The exhibition meet involved both genders' A and B teams and was always against some foreign junior squad, to give the whole Fundraising affair a patriotic kicker. The gentle fiction was that the meet was just one stop for the foreign squad on a whole vague general U.S. tour, but in truth C.T. usually flew the foreigners in special, and at some expense. We had in the past done battle with teams from Wales, Belize, the Sudan, and Mozambique. Cynics might point to an absence of tennis juggernauts among the opponents. Last year's Mozambique thing was a particular turkey-shoot, 70–2, and there'd been an ugly xeno-racist mood among some of the spectators and patrons, a couple of whom cheerily compared the meet to Mussolini's tanks rolling over Ethiopian spearchuckers. Y.D.A.U.'s opponents were to be the Québec Jr. Davis and Jr. Wightman Cup teams, and their arrival from M.I.A.-D'Orval[346] was keenly anticipated by Struck and Freer, who claimed that the Québecois Jr. Wightman girls were normally sequestered and saw very few coed venues and would be available for broadening intercultural relations of all kinds.

It was improbable that anything was going to be landing on time at Logan in this kind of snow, though.

The wind also produced a desolate moaning in all the ventilation ducts. Mario said 'key' and sometimes 'ski,' drawing them out. It occurred to me that without some one-hitters to be able to look forward to smoking alone in the tunnel I was waking up every day feeling as though there was nothing in the day to anticipate or lend anything any meaning. I stood on one foot for a couple more minutes, spitting into a coffee can I'd left on the floor near the phone from the night before. The implied question, then, would be whether the Bob Hope had somehow become not just the high-point of the day but its actual meaning. That would be pretty appalling. The Penn 4 that was my hand-strengthening ball for November was on the sill against the window. I'd neither carried nor squeezed my ball for several days. No one seemed to have noticed.

Mario cedes me full control over the phone's ringer and answering machine, since he has trouble holding the receiver and the only messages he ever gets are In-House ones from the Moms. I enjoyed leaving different outgoing messages on the machine. But I refused ever to back the messages with music or digitally altered bits of entertainment. None of the E.T.A. phones was video-capable — another C.T. decision. Under C.T. the Academy's manual of honor codes, rules, and procedures had almost tripled in length. Probably our room's best message ever was Ortho Stice doing his deadly C.T.-impression, taking 80 seconds to list possible reasons why Mario and I couldn't answer the phone and outlining our probable reactions to all possible caller-emotions provoked my our unavailability. But at 80 seconds the thing wore thin after a while. Our outgoing this week was something like 'This is the disembodied voice of Hal Incandenza, whose body is not now able . . . ,' and so on, and then the standard invitation to leave a message. It was honesty and abstinence week, after all, and this seemed a more truthful message to leave than the pedestrian 'This is Hal Incandenza . . . ,' since the caller would pretty obviously be hearing a digital recording of me rather than me. This observation owed a debt to Pemulis, who for years and with several different roommates has retained the same recursive message — 'This is Mike Pemulis's answering machine's answering machine; Mike Pemulis's answering machine regrets being unavailable to take a first-order message for Mike Pemulis, but if you'll leave a second-order message at the sound of the clapping hand, Mike Pemulis's answering machine will . . . ,' and so on, which has worn so thin that very few of Pemulis's friends or customers can abide waiting through the tired thing to leave a message, which Pemulis finds congenial, since no really relevant caller would be fool enough to leave his name on any machine of Pemulis's anyway.

Plus it was also creepy that, when the face's effulgence becomes the boiled white of the Trauma Wing ceiling as he comes up with a start up for air, the apparently real nondream Joelle van D. is leaning over the bed's crib-railing, wetting Gately's big forehead and horror-rounded lips with a cool cloth, wearing sweatpants and a sort of loose brocaded hulpil whose lavender almost matches the selvage on her clean veil. The hulpil's neckline is too high for there to be much cleavage-action as she leans over him, which Gately regards as probably kind of a mercy. The two brownies Joelle's got in her other hand (and her nails are bitten down to the ragged quick, just like Gately's) she says she liberated from the nurses' station and brought down for him, since Morris H. meant them for him and they're by all just rights his. But she can see he's in no shape to swallow, she says. She smells like peaches and cotton, and there's a sweet evil whiff of the discount Canadian gaspers so many of the residents smoke, and underneath those smells Gately can detect that she's got on a bit of perfume.[347]

To amuse him she says '*And Lo*' several times. Gately makes his chest go up and down rapidly to signify amusement. He declines either to moo or mew at her, out of embarrassment. Her veil this morning has a springy light-purple around the border, and the hair framing the veil seems a darker red, duskier, than when she'd first come into the House and refused meat. Gately hadn't been much into WYYY or Madame Psychosis, but he'd sometimes run into people who were — Organics men, mostly, opium and brown heroin, terrible mulled wine — and he feels on top of the febrile pain and the creepiness of the amphetaminic-wraith- and Winston-Churchill-face-Joelle- and angelic-maternal-Death-Joelle-dreams an odd vividness in himself at being swabbed and maybe even generally admired by someone who's an underground local intellectual-dash-art-type celebrity. He doesn't know how to explain it, like as if the fact that she's a public personage makes him feel somehow physically actuated, like more *there*-feeling, conscious of the way he's holding his face, hesitant to make his barnyard sounds, even breathing through his nose so she won't smell his unbrushed teeth. He feels self-conscious with her, Joelle can tell, but what's admirable is he has no idea how heroic or even romantic he looks, unshaven and intubated, huge and helpless, wounded in service to somebody who did not deserve service, half out of his tree from pain and refusing narcotics. The last and pretty much only man Joelle ever let herself admire in a romantic way had left and wouldn't even face up to why, instead erecting for himself a pathetic jealous fantasy about Joelle and his own poor father, whose only interest in Joelle had been first aesthetic and then anti-aesthetic.

Joelle doesn't know that newly sober people are awfully vulnerable to the delusion that people with more sober time than them are romantic and heroic, instead of clueless and terrified and just muddling through day-by-day like everybody else in AA is (except maybe the fucking Crocodiles).

Joelle says she can't stay long this time: all nonworking residents have to report for the House's A.M. daily-meditation meeting, as Gately knows only too well. He isn't sure what she means by 'this time.' She describes the newest male resident's weird limbo-injury posture, and the way Johnette Foltz has to cut up this Dave guy's supper and drop it into his open mouth bit by bit like a bird with a chick. Lifting her face to the ceiling makes the linen veil conform to the features of the face below, mouth open wide in imitation of a chick. The crewneckish hulpil makes her hair's loose curls look dark and her wrists and hands look pale. Her hands's skin is taut and freckled and treed with veins. His bed's metal bars keep Gately's rolling eyes from seeing anything much south of her thorax until Joelle finishes with the washcloth and retreats to the edge of the other bed, which at some point has become empty and the crying guy's chart removed, and its crib-railings folded down, and she sits on the edge of the bed and crosses her legs, supporting one huarache's heel on the railing's joint, revealing she's got on white socks under flesh-colored huaraches and ancient baggy old birch-colored sweatpants with B.U.M. down one leg, which Gately's pretty sure he's seen at the Sunday A.M. Big Book meeting on Ken Erdedy, and belong to Erdedy, and he feels a flash of something unpleasant that she'd be wearing the upscale kid's pants. The A.M. light outside has gone from sunny yellow-white to now a kind of old-dime gray, with what looks like serious wind.

Joelle eats the cream-cheese brownies Gately can't eat and works at pulling a kind of big notebookish thing out of her broad cloth purse. She talks about last night's St. Columbkill's[348] Meeting, where they'd all gone unsupervised because Johnette F. had to stay and keep an eye on Glynn who was sick and on Henderson and Willis, who were under legal quarantine upstairs. Gately racks his RAM for which fucking night St. Columbkill's is. Joelle says how last night's was St. Collie's once-a-month format where instead of a Commitment they had that round-robin discussion where somebody in the hall spoke for five minutes and then picked the next speaker out of the hall's crowd. There'd been a Kentuckian there, which Gately might recall she was from Kentucky? A Kentucky newcomer there, Wayne something, a real damaged-looking boy who hailed from the good old Blue Grass State but of late resided in a disconnected drainage pipe off a watershed facility down in the Allston Spur, he'd said. This guy, she said, said he was nineteen or thereabout, looked 40-some+, had clothes that looked to be decomposing on him even as he stood at the podium, had a ripe odor of drainage about him that produced hankies as far back as the fourth row, which he explained the odor by admitting his residential drainage pipe was in fact 'mostly' disconnected, like as in little-used. Joelle's voice is nothing like the hollow resonant radio-voice and she uses her hands a lot to talk, trying to recreate the whole thing for Gately. Trying to give him a little bit of a meeting, Gately realizes, with a slight tight smile of disbelief that he can't dredge up a mental meeting schedule so he'll know what day this is.

Some of the St. Columbkillers were saying it was the longest single black-out they'd ever heard of. This Wayne fellow'd said he had no idea when, why or how he'd ended up so far up north as metro Boston ten years after his last memory. Most compelling, visually, Wayne had had a deep diagonal furrow in his face, extending from right eyebrow to left lip-corner — Joelle traces the length and angle with a ragged-nailed finger across her veil — splaying his nose and upper lip and rendering him so violently cross-eyed he seemed to address both corners of the front row at the same time. This old Wayne boy'd sketched how the facial dent — what Wayne had called 'the

Flaw,' pointing at it like people might need help seeing what he was talking about — derived from his very own personal hard-drinking alcoholic & chicken-farmer Daddy, in the grip of the post-binge Horrors and seeing subjective pests in a big way, one day, up and hitting Wayne at age nine smack in the face with a hatchet one time when Wayne couldn't tell him where a certain Ball jar of distilled spirits had been hidden the day before, against the possibility of the Horrors. It had been just him and his Daddy and his Maw — ' "that was feeble" ' — and 7.7 acres of chicken farm, Wayne had said. Wayne said the Flaw had just about healed up fine with fresh air and plenty of exercise when his Daddy, trying one Monday P.M. to get outside a late lunch of mush and syrup, up and clutched his skull, turned red and then blue and then purple, and died. Little Wayne had reportedly wiped the face clean of mush, dragged the dead body under the farmhouse porch, wrapped it in Purina Chicken-Chow sacks, and told his feeble Maw his Daddy had gone off to lay up drunk. The diagonal-dented kid had apparently then gone off to school as usual, done some discreet w.o.m. advertising, and had brought home with him a different set of boys each day for almost a week, charging them a fiveski a head to crawl under the porch and eyeball a bona fried dead man. Late Friday P.M., he recollected, he'd set off with hard currency to the billiard establishment where the niggers[349] that sold distilled Ball jars to his late Daddy was at, getting set to ' "lay up drunk as a cock on jimson." ' The next thing this Wayne boy says he knows, he wakes up in the partially disconnected NNE pipe, one millennial decade older and with some ' "right nasty" ' medical issues the timer's bell prevents him from sharing in detail.

And this old Wayne boy had up and pointed to Joelle to come speak next. 'Almost as if he knew. As if he gut-intuited some sort of kinship, affinity of origin.'

Gately grunted softly to himself. He figured guys with ten-year blackouts who live in pipes probably didn't have to much to go on besides your gut-type intuitions. He knew he needed to be reminded that this strange girl was only about three weeks clean and still leaching Substances out of her tissues and still utterly clueless, but he felt like he resented it whenever he got reminded. Joelle had the big flat book in her lap and was looking down at her thumb and flexing it, watching it flex. What was disconcerting was that when her head was down the veil hung loose at the same vertical angle as when her head was up, only now it was perfectly smooth and untextured, a smooth white screen with nothing behind it. A loudspeaker down the hall gave those xylophone dings that meant God knows what all the time.

When Joelle's head came back up, the reassuring little hills and valleys of veiled features reappeared behind the screen. 'I'm going to have to take off here in a second,' she said. 'I could come on back after, if you want. I can bring anything you think you'd like.'

Gately hiked an eyebrow at her, to get her to smile.

'Hopefully since your fever went down they said they'll decide you're out of the woods and take that out, finally,' Joelle said, looking at Gately's mouth. 'It's got to hurt, and Pat said you'll feel better when you can start quote sharing what you're feeling.'

Gately hiked both eyebrows.

'And you can tell me what you'd like brought. Who you'd want to have come. Whom.'

Moving his left arm north along his chest and throat to get the left hand up to feel at his mouth made the whole right side sing with pain. A skin-warmed plastic tube led in from the right side and was taped to his right cheek and went into his mouth and went down his throat past where his fingers could feel at the back of his mouth. He hadn't been able to feel it in his mouth or going down the back of his throat to he didn't want to know where, or even the tape on his cheek. He'd had like this like tube in his throat the whole time and hadn't even known it. It had been in there so long by the time he came up for air he'd gotten like unconsciously used to it and hadn't even known it was there. Maybe it was a feeding tube. The tube was probably why he could only mew and grunt. He probably didn't have permanent voice damage. Thank God. He made his thoughts capitalized and Thanked God several times. He pictured himself at a lavish Commitment podium, like at an AA convention, off-handedly saying something that got an enormous laugh.

Either Joelle had some sort of problem with her thumb or she'd just got really interested in watching the thumb flex and twiddle. She was saying 'It's strange, not knowing it's coming, then standing up there to speak. Folks you don't know. Things I don't realize I think til I say them. On the show I was used to knowing quite well what I thought before I spoke. This isn't like that.' She seemed to be addressing herself to the thumb. 'I took a page from your manual and shared my complaint about the "But For the Grace of God," and you were right, they just laughed. But I also . . . I hadn't realized til I found myself telling them that I'd stopped seeing the "One Day at a Time" and "Keep It in the Day" as trite clichés. Patronizing.' Gately noticed she still talks about Recovery-issues in a stiff proper intellectualish way she doesn't talk about other stuff with. Her way of still keeping it all at arm's length a little. A mental thumb to pretend to look at while she talks. It was all right; Gately's own way of keeping it at arm's length at the start had involved an actual arm. He pictured her laughing as he tells her that, the veil billowing mightily in and out. He smiled around the tube, which Joelle saw as encouragement. She said 'And why Pat in counselling keeps telling me just to build a wall around each individual 24-hour period and not look over or back. And not to count days. Even when you get a chip for 14 days or 30 days, not to add them up. In counselling I'd just smile and nod. Being polite. But standing up there last night, I didn't even share it aloud, but I realized suddenly that this was why I'd never been able to stay off the stuff for more than a couple weeks. I'd always break down, go back. Freebase.' She looks up at him. 'I 'based, you know. You knew that. You all see the Intake forms.'

Gately smiles.

She said 'This was why I couldn't get off and stay off. Just as the cliché warns. I literally wasn't keeping it in the day. I was adding the clean days up in my head.' She cocked her head at him. 'Did you ever hear of this fellow Evel Knievel? This motorcycle-jumper?'

Gately nods slightly, being careful of a tube he now feels. This is why his throat had had that raped feeling in it. The tube. He actually has an old cutout action picture of the historical Evel Knievel, from an old *Life* magazine, in a white leather Elvisish suit, in the air, aloft, haloed in spotlights, upright on a bike, a row of well-waxed trucks below.

'At St. Collie only the Crocodiles'd heard of him. My own Daddy'd followed him, cut out pictures, as a boy.' Gately can tell she's smiling under there. 'But what I used to do, I'd throw away the pipe and shake my fist at the sky and say *As God is my fucking witness NEVER AGAIN, as of this minute right here I QUIT FOR ALL TIME.*' She also has this habit of absently patting the top of her head when she talks, where little barrettes and spongy clamps hold the veil in place. 'And I'd bunker up all white-knuckled and stay straight. And count the days. I was proud of each day I stayed off. Each day seemed evidence of something, and I counted them. I'd add them up. Line them up end to end. You know?' Gately knows very well but doesn't nod, lets her do this on just her own steam. She says 'And soon it would get . . . improbable. As if each day was a car Knievel had to clear. One car, two cars. By the time I'd get up to say like maybe about 14 cars, it would begin to seem like this staggering number. Jumping over 14 cars. And the rest of the year, looking ahead, hundreds and hundreds of cars, me in the air trying to clear them.' She left her head alone and cocked it. 'Who could do it? How did I ever think anyone could do it that way?'

Gately remembered some evil fucking personal detoxes. Broke in Malden. Bent with pleurisy in Salem. MCI/Billerica during a four-day lockdown that caught him short. He remembered Kicking the Bird for weeks on the floor of a Revere Holding cell, courtesy of the good old Revere A.D.A. Locked down tight, a bucket for a toilet, the Holding cell hot but a terrible icy draft down near the floor. Cold Turkey. Abrupt Withdrawal. The Bird. Being incapable of doing it and yet having to do it, locked in. A Revere Holding cage for 92 days. Feeling the edge of every second that went by. Taking it a second at a time. Drawing the time in around him real tight. Withdrawing. Any one second: he remembered: the thought of feeling like he'd be feeling this second for 60 more of these seconds — he couldn't deal. He could not fucking deal. He had to build a wall around each second just to take it. The whole first two weeks of it are telescoped in his memory down into like one second — less: the space between two heartbeats. A breath and a second, the pause and gather between each cramp. An endless Now stretching its gull-wings out on either side of his heartbeat. And he'd never before or since felt so excruciatingly alive. Living in the Present between pulses. What the White Flaggers talk about: living completely In The Moment. A whole day at a crack seemed like tit, when he Came In. For he had Abided With The Bird.

But this inter-beat Present, this sense of endless Now — it had vanished in Revere Holding along with the heaves and chills. He'd returned to himself, moved to sit on the bunk's edge, and ceased to Abide because he no longer had to.

His right side is past standing, but the hurt is nothing like the Bird's hurt was. He wonders, sometimes, if that's what Ferocious Francis and the rest want him to walk toward: Abiding again between heartbeats; tries to imagine what kind of impossible leap it would take to live that way all the time, by choice, straight: in the second, the Now, walled and contained between slow heartbeats. Ferocious Francis's own sponsor, the nearly dead guy they wheel to White Flag and call Sarge, says it all the time: It's a gift, the Now: it's AA's real gift: it's no accident they call it *The Present*.

'And yet it wasn't til that poor new pipe-fellow from home pointed at me and hauled me up there and I said it that I realized,' Joelle said. 'I don't *have* to do it that way. I get to choose how to do it, and they'll help me stick to the choice. I don't think I'd realized before that I could — I can really *do* this. I can do this for one endless day. I can. Don.'

The look he was giving her was meant to like validate her breakthrough and say yes yes she could, she could as long as she continued to choose to. She was looking right at him, Gately could tell. But he'd also gotten a personal prickly chill all over from his own thinking. He could do the dextral pain the same way: Abiding. No one single instant of it was unendurable. Here was a second right here: he endured it. What was undealable-with was the thought of all the instants all lined up and stretching ahead, glittering. And the projected future fear of the A.D.A., whoever was out there in a hat eating Third World fast food; the fear of getting convicted of Nuckslaughter, of V.I.P.-suffocation; of a lifetime on the edge of his bunk in M.C.I. Walpole, remembering. It's too much to think about. To Abide there. But none of it's as of now real. What's real is the tube and Noxzema and pain. And this could be done just like the Old Cold Bird. He could just hunker down in the space between each heartbeat and make each heartbeat a wall and live in there. Not let his head look over. What's unendurable is what his own head could make of it all. What his head could report to him, looking over and ahead and reporting. But he could choose not to listen; he could treat his head like G. Day or R. Lenz: clueless noise. He hadn't quite gotten this before now, how it wasn't just the matter of riding out the cravings for a Substance: everything unendurable was in the head, was the head not Abiding in the Present but hopping the wall and doing a recon and then returning with unendurable news you then somehow believed. If Gately got out of this, he decided, he was going to take the Knievel picture off his wall and mount it and give it to Joelle, and they'd laugh, and she'd call him Don or The Bimster, etc.

Gately rolls his eyes way over to the right to see Joelle again, who she's using both pale hands to get the big book open on her sweatpants' lap. Gray windowlight shines on clear plastic sheets like little laminates inside the thing.

'. . . idea to haul this out last night and was looking at it. I wanted to show you my own personal Daddy,' she says. She's holding the photo album out at him, wide open, like a kindergarten teacher at storytime. Gately makes a production of squinting. Joelle comes over and rests the big album on the top of Gately's crib-railing, peering down over the top and pointing at a snapshot in its little square sleeve.

'Right there's my Daddy.' In front of a low white porch-railing, a generic lean old guy with lines around his nose from squinting into sunlight and the composed smile of somebody that's been told to smile. A skinny dog at his side, half in profile. Gately's more interested in how the shadow of whoever took the photo is canted into the shot's foreground, darkening half the dog.

'And that's one of the dogs, a pointer that got hit right after that by a UPS truck out to 104,' she says. 'Where no animal with a lick of sense would think it had business being. My Daddy never names dogs. That one's just called the one that got hit by the UPS truck.' Her voice is different again.

Gately tries to Abide in seeing what she's pointing at. Most of the rest of the page's pictures are of farm-type animals behind wooden fences, looking the way things look that can't smile, that don't know a camera's looking. Joelle said her personal Daddy was a low-pH chemist, but her late mother's own Daddy had left them a farm, and Joelle's Daddy moved them out there and jick-jacked around with farming, mostly as an excuse to keep lots of pets and stick experimental low-pH stuff in the soil.

At some point in here an all-business nurse comes in and fucks with the I.V. bottles, then hunkers down and changes the catheter-receptacle under the bed, and for a second Gately likes to die of embarrassment. Joelle seems not even to be pretending not to notice.

'And this right here's a bull we used to call Mr. Man.' Her slim thumb moves from shot to shot. The sunlight in Kentucky looks bright-yellower than NNE's. The trees are a meaner green and have got weird mossy shit hanging from them. 'And this right here's a mule called Chet that could jump the fence and used to get at everybody's flowers out along Route 45 til

Daddy had to put him down. This is a cow. This right here's Chet's mama. It's a mare. I don't recollect any kind of name except "Chet's Mama." Daddy'd let her out to neighbors that really did farm, to sort of make up for folks' flowers.'

Gately nods studiously at each photo, trying to Abide. He hasn't thought about the wraith or the wraith-dream once since he woke up from the dream where Joelle was Mrs. Waite as a maternal Death-figure. Next life's Chet's Mama. He opens his eyes wide to clear his head. Joelle's head is down, looking down at the open album from overhead. Her veil hangs loose and blank again, so close he could reach his left hand up and lift it if he wanted. The open book she's moving her hand around in gives Gately an idea he can't believe he's only having now. Except he worries because he isn't left-handed. Which is to say *SINISTRAL*. Joelle's got her thumb by a weird old sepia shot of the ass and hunched back of some guy scrabbling up the slope of a roof. 'Uncle Lum,' she says, 'Mr. Riney, Lum Riney, my Daddy's partner over to the shop, that breathed some kind of fume at the shop when I was little, and got strange, and now he'll always try and climb up on top of shit, if you let him.'

He winces at the pain of moving his left arm to put a hand on her wrist to get her attention. Her wrist is thin across the top but oddly deep, thick-seeming. Gately gets her to look at him and takes the hand off her wrist and uses it to mime writing awkwardly in the air, his eyes rolling a bit from the pain of it. This is his idea. He points at her and then out the window and circles his hand back to her. He refuses to grunt or moo to emphasize anything. His forefinger is twice the size of her thumb as he again mimes holding an implement and writing on the air. He makes such a big slow obvious show of it because he can't see her eyes to be sure she gets what he's after.

If a halfway-attractive female so much as smiles at Don Gately as they pass on the crowded street, Don Gately, like pretty much all heterosexual drug addicts, has within a couple blocks mentally wooed, shacked up with, married and had kids by that female, all in the future, all in his head, mentally dandling a young Gately on his mutton-joint knee while this mental Mrs. G. bustles in an apron she sometimes at night provocatively wears with nothing underneath. By the time he gets where he's going, the drug addict has either mentally divorced the female and is in a bitter custody battle for the kids or is mentally happily still hooked up with her in his sunset years, sitting together amid big-headed grandkids on a special porch swing modified for Gately's mass, her legs in support-hose and orthopedic shoes still damn fine, barely having to speak to converse, calling each other 'Mother' and 'Papa,' knowing they'll kick within weeks of each other because neither could possibly live without the other, is how bonded they've got through the years.

The projective mental union of Gately and Joelle ('M.P.') van Dyne keeps foundering on the vision of Gately knee-dandling a kid in a huge blue- or pink-bordered veil, however. Or tenderly removing the spongy clamps of Joelle's veil in moonlight on their honeymoon in Atlantic City and discovering just like one eye in the middle of her forehead or a horrific Churchill-face or something.[350] So the addictive mental long-range fantasy gets shaky, but he still can't help envisioning the old X, with Joelle well-veiled and crying out *And Lo!* in that empty compelling way at the moment of orchasm — the closest Gately'd ever come to Xing a celebrity was the ragingly addicted nursing-student with the head-banging loft, who'd borne an incredible resemblance to the young Dean Martin. Having Joelle share personal historical snapshots with Gately leads his mind right over the second's wall to envision Joelle, hopelessly smitten with the heroic Don G., volunteering to bonk the guy in the hat outside the room over the head and sneak Gately and his tube and catheter out of St. E.'s in a laundry cart or whatever, saving him from the BPD Finest or Federal crew cuts or whatever direr legal retribution the guy in the hat might represent, or else selflessly offering to give him her veil and a big dress and let him hold the catheter under the muumuu and sashay right out while she huddles under the covers in impersonation of Gately, romantically endangering her recovery and radio career and legal freedom, all out of a *Liebestod*-type consuming love for Gately.

This last fantasy makes him ashamed, it's so cowardly. And even contemplating a romantic thing with a clueless newcomer is shameful. In Boston AA, newcomer-seducing is called 13th-Stepping[351] and is regarded as the province of true bottom-feeders. It's predation. Newcomers come in so whacked out, clueless and scared, their nervous systems still on the outside of their bodies and throbbing from detox, and so desperate to escape their own interior, to lay responsibility for themselves at the feet of something as seductive and consuming as their former friend the Substance. To avoid the mirror AA hauls out in front of them. To avoid acknowledging their old dear friend the Substance's betrayal, and grieving it. Plus let's not even mention the mirror-and-vulnerability issues of a newcomer that has to wear a U.H.I.D veil. One of Boston AA's stronger suggestions is that newcomers avoid all romantic relationships for at least a year. So somebody with some sober time predating and trying to seduce a newcomer is almost tantamount to rape, is the Boston consensus. Not that it isn't done. But the ones that do it never have the kind of sobriety anybody else respects or wants for themselves. A 13th-Stepper is still running from the mirror himself.

Not to mention that a Staffer seducing a new resident he's supposed to be there to help would be dicking over Pat Montesian and Ennet House on a grand scale.

Gately sees it's probably no accident that his vividest Joelle-fantasies are coincident with flight-from-Finest-and-legal-responsibility fantasies. That his head's real fantasy is this newcomer helping him avoid, escape, and run, joining him later in like Kentucky on a modified porch swing. He's still pretty new himself: wanting somebody else to take care of his mess, somebody else to keep him out of his various cages. It's the same delusion as the basic addictive-Substance-delusion, basically. His eyes roll up in his head at disgust with himself, and stay there.

I went down the hall to take out the tobacco and brush my teeth and rinse out the Spiru-Tein can, which had gotten an unpleasant crust along the sides. The subdorm halls were curved and had no corners as such, but you can see at most three doors and the jamb of the fourth from any point in the hall before the curve extrudes into your line of sight. I wondered briefly whether it was true that small children believed their parents could see them even around corners and curves.

The high wind's moan and doors' rattle were worse in the uncarpeted hall. I could hear faint sounds of early-morning weeping in certain rooms beyond my line of sight. Lots of the top players start the A.M. with a quick fit of crying, then are basically hale and well-wrapped for the rest of the day.

The walls of the subdorms' hallways are dinner-mint blue. The walls of the rooms themselves are cream. All the woodwork is dark and varnished, as is the guilloche that runs below all E.T.A. ceilings; and the dominant odor in the hallways is always a mixture of varnish and tincture of benzoin.

Someone had left a window open by the sinks in the boys' room, and a hump of snow lay on the sill, and on the floor beneath the window by the sink on the end, whose hot-water pipe shrieks, was a parabolic dusting of snow, already melting at the apex. I turned on the lights and the exhaust fan kicked on with them; for some reason I could barely stand its sound. When I put my head out the window the wind came from nowhere and everywhere, the snow swirling in funnels and eddies, and there were little grains of ice in the snow. It was brutally cold. Across the East Courts, the paths were obscured, and the pine's branches were near horizontal under their snow's weight. Schtitt's transom and observation tower looked menacing; it was still dark and snow-free on the lee side facing Comm.-Ad. The sight of distant ATHSCME fans displacing great volumes of snowy air northward is one of the better winter views from our hilltop, but visibility was now too poor to make out the fans, and the liquid hiss of the snow was too total to make out whether the fans were even on. The Headmaster's House wasn't much more than a humped shape off by the north tree-line, but I could picture poor C.T. at the living room window in leather slippers and Scotch-plaid robe, seeming to pace even when standing still, raising and lowering the antenna of the phone in his hand, with several calls out already to

Logan, M.I.A.-Dorval, WeatherNet-9000's recorded update, heavy-browed figures in Québec's O.N.A.N.T.A. office, C.T.'s forehead a washboard and lips moving soundless as he brainstormed his way toward a state of Total Worry.

I brought my head back in when I could no longer feel my face. I made my little ablutions. I hadn't had to go to the bathroom in a serious way in three days.

The digital display up next to the ceiling's intercom read **11–18-EST0456.**

When the whap-whap of the bathroom door subsided I heard a quiet voice with an odd tone farther up around the curve of the hallway. It turned out that good old Ortho Stice was sitting in a bedroom-chair in front of a hall window. He was facing the window. The window was closed, and he had his forehead up against the glass, either talking or chanting to himself very quietly. The whole lower part of the window was fogged with his breath. I came up behind him, listening. The back of his head was that shark-belly gray-white of crew cuts so short the scalp shows through. I was more or less right behind his chair. I couldn't tell whether he was talking to himself or chanting something. He didn't turn around even when I rattled my toothbrush in the NASA glass. He had on his classic Darknesswear: black sweatshirt, black sweatpants on which he'd had a red and gray *E.T.A.* silkscreened down both legs. His feet were bare on the cold floor. I was standing right beside the chair, and he still didn't look up.

'Who's that now?' he said, staring straight ahead through the window.

'Hi Orth.'

'Hal. You're up kind of early.'

I rattled my toothbrush a little to indicate a shrug. 'You know. Up and about.'

'What's the matter?'

'What do you mean?' I asked.

'Your voice. Shoot, are you crying? What's the matter?'

My voice had been neutral and a bit puzzled. 'I'm not crying, Orth.'

'Well then.' Stice breathed onto the window. He reached up without moving his head and scratched the back of his crew cut. 'Up and around. We going to play some furriners out there today or what?'

For the past ten days I'd always felt worst in the early A.M., before dawn. There's something elementally horrific about waking before dawn. The window was unobscured above The Darkness's breath-line. The snow wasn't swirling or pummelling the window as much on the building's east side, but the lee side's absence of wind showed just how hard new snow was coming down. It was like a white curtain endlessly descending. The sky was lightening here on the east side, a paler gray-white, not unlike Stice's crew-cut. I realized that from his position he could see only condensed breath on the window, no reflections. I made a few grotesque, distended, pop-eyed faces at him behind his back. They made me feel worse.

I rattled the brush. 'Well, if we do, it's not going to be out there. It's drifting about up to the tape on the west nets. They'll have to try to get us indoors somewhere.'

Stice breathed. 'There's no indoor place's got thirty-six courts, Inc. Winchester Club's got twelve is maybe the most. Fucking Mount Auburn's only got eight.'

'They'll have to move us around to different sites. It's a pain in the ass, but Schtitt's done it before. I think the real variable'll be whether the Québec kids got into Logan last night before whenever it was this hit.'

'Logan'll be shut down you're saying.'

'But I think we'd have heard if they got in last night. Freer and Struck were keeping tabs on an F.A.A. link ever since supper, Mario said.'

'Boys are looking to get X'd by some slow-witted hairy-legged foreign girls or *what*?'

'My guess is they're stuck up at Dorval. I'll bet C.T. is on the case even now. Get some sort of announcement at breakfast, probably.'

This was a clear opening for The Darkness to do a quick C.T. impression, wondering aloud over the phone to the Québecois coach whether he, C.T., should press for them to charter ground transport from Montreal or else rather urge them not to risk travel through the Concavity in a storm in such a generous but disappointed gesture the Québecois would think busing the 400 clicks to Boston in a blizzard was his own generous idea, C.T. wholly open, opening all different psych-strategies to the coach's inspection, with the frantic ruffling sound of the coach's French-English dictionary loud in the phone's background. But Stice just sat there with his forehead against the glass. His bare feet were tapping some sort of rhythm on the floor. The hallway was freezing, and his toes had a faint blue tinge. He blew air out of his lips in a tight sigh, making his fat cheeks flap a little; we called this his horse-sound.

'Were you talking to yourself out here, or chanting, or what?'

A silence ensued.

'Heard this one joke,' Stice said finally.

'Let's hear it.'

'You want to hear it?'

'I could use a quality laugh right now, Dark,' I said.

'You too?'

Another silence ensued. Two different people were weeping at different pitches behind closed doors. A toilet flushed on the second floor. One of the weepers was nearly skirling, an inhuman keening sound. There was no way to tell which E.T.A. male it was, which door back down past the walls' curve.

The Darkness scratched the back of his head again without moving his head. His hands looked almost luminous against the black sleeves.

'There's these three statisticians gone duck hunting,' he said. He paused. 'They're like statisticians by trade.'

'I'm with you so far.'

'And they gone off hunting duck, and they're hunkered down in the muck of a duck blind, for hunting, in waders and hats and all, your top-of-the-line Winchester double-aughts, so on. And they're quacking into one of them kazoos duck hunters always quack into.'

'Duck-calls,' I said.

'There you go.' Stice tried to nod against the window. 'Well and here comes this one duck come flying on by overhead.'

'Their quarry. The object of their being out there.'

'Damn straight, their *raisin-debt* and what have you, and they're getting set to blast the son of a whore into feathers and goo,' Stice said. 'And the first statistician, he brings up his Winnie and lets go, and the recoil goes and knocks him back on his ass kersplat in the muck, and but he's missed the duck, just low, they saw. And so the second statistician he up and fires then, and back he goes too on his ass too, these Winnies got a fucker of a recoil on them, and back on his ass the second one goes, from firing, and they see his shot goes just high.'

'Misses the duck as well.'

'Misses her just high. At which and then the third statistician commences to whooping and jumping up and down to beat the band, hollering "We got him, boys, we done got him!" '

Someone was crying out in a bad dream and someone else was yelling for quiet. I wasn't even pretending to laugh. Stice didn't seem to expect me to. He shrugged without moving his head. His forehead had not once left the cold glass.

I stood next to him in silence and held my NASA glass with the toothbrush and looked out over the top of Stice's head through the window's upper half. The snowfall was intense and looked silky. The East Courts' pavilion's green canvas roof bowed ominously down, its white GATORADE logo obscured. A figure was out there, not under the shelter of the pavilion but sitting in the bleachers behind the east Show Courts, leaning back with his elbows on one level and bottom on the next and feet stretched out below, not moving, wearing what seemed to be puffy and bright enough to be a coat, but getting buried by snow, just sitting there. It was impossible to tell the person's age or sex. Church spires off in Brookline were darkening as the sky lightened behind them. The beginning of dawn looked like moonlight through the snow. Several people were at their vehicles' windshields with scrapers down along Commonwealth Avenue. Their images were tiny and dark and fluttered; the Avenue's line of buried parked cars looked like igloo after igloo, some sort of Eskimo tract-housing thing. It had never before snowed like this in mid-November. A snow-covered B train labored uphill like a white slug. It seemed clear that the T would be suspending routes before long. The snow and cold sunrise gave everything a confected quality. The portcullis between the driveway and the parking lot was half up, probably to keep it from being frozen closed. I couldn't see who was in the portcullis's security booth. The attendants always came and went, most of them from the Ennet House place, trying to 'recover.' The flagpole's two flags were frozen and stuck right out straight, turning stiffly from side to side in the wind, like someone in a neck-brace, instead of flapping. The E.T.A. physical-post mailbox just inside the portcullis had a mohawk of snow. The whole scene had an indescribable pathos to it. Stice's fogged breath kept me from seeing anything closer than the mailbox and East Courts. The light was starting to diffract into colors at the perimeter of Stice's breath-fog on the window.

'Schacht heard that joke down at the Cranial place from some B.U. fellow with just terrible facial pain, he said,' Stice said.

'I'm going to go ahead and ask the question, D-man.'

'It's a statistics joke. You got to know your medials means and modes.'

'I get the joke, Orth. The question is how come you've got your forehead all up against the window like that when your breath's keeping you from seeing anything. What are you trying to look at? And isn't your forehead getting kind of cold?'

Stice didn't nod. He made his horse-sound again. He had always had the face of a fat man on a fit man's lean body. I hadn't noticed before that he had an odd little teardrop of extra flesh low down on his right jowl, like a bit of skin with mole-aspirations. He said 'The forehead stopped feeling cold a couple hours back, when I lost all my feeling in it.'

'You've been sitting here with bare feet and your forehead against the glass for a couple *hours?*'

'More like four, I think.'

I could hear a night-custodial crew laughing and clanking a bucket right below us. Only one was laughing. It was Kenkle and Brandt.

'My next question's pretty obvious, then, Orth.'

He gave another awkward shrug that didn't involve his head. 'Well. It's sort of embarrassing, here, Inc,' he said. He paused. 'It's stuck is what it is.'

'Your forehead's stuck to the window?'

'Best as I can recollect I wake up, it's just after 0100, fuckin Coyle's having them discharges again and there's no sleeping through that, boy.'

'I shudder to think, Orth.'

'And Coyle 'course just doesn't even hit the light just hauls out a fresh sheet from the stack under his bunk and goes right back to sawing logs. And I'm wide awake by this point in time, though, and then I couldn't get back under.'

'Couldn't get back to sleep.'

'Something's real wrong, I can tell,' The Darkness said.

'Pre-Fundraiser nerves? The WhataBurger coming up? You feel yourself starting to climb plateaux, starting to play the way you came here hoping one day to play, and part of you doesn't believe it, it feels wrong. I went through this. Believe me, I can und—'

Stice automatically tried to shake his head and then gave a small cry of pain. 'Not that. None of that. Long fucking story. I'm not even sure I'd want anybody to believe it. Forget that part. The point's I'm up there — I'm lying there real sweaty and hot and jittered. I jump on down and got a chair and brang it out here to set where it's cool.'

'And where you don't have to lie there and contemplate Coyle's sheet slowly ripening under his bunk,' I said, shuddering a little.

'And it's just starting to snow, then, out. It's about maybe like 0100. I thought how I'd just set and watch the snow a little and settle on down and then go grab some sack down in the V.R.' He scratched at the reddening back of his scalp again.

'And as you watched, you rested your head pensively against the glass for just a second.'

'And that was all she wrote. Forgot the forehead was sweated up. Whammo. Kertwanged my own self. Just like remember when Rader and them got Ingersoll to touch his tongue on that net-post last New Year's? Stuck here fucking tight as that tongue, Hal. Hell of a lot more total stuck area, too, than Ingersoll. He only did lose that smidgeon off the tip. Inc, I tried to pull her off her about 0230, and there was this fucking . . . *sound*. This sound and a feeling like the skin'll give before the bind will, sure. Frozen stuck. And this here's more skin than I care to say goodbye to, buddyruff.' He was speaking just above a whisper.

'Jesus, and you've just been sitting here all this time.'

'Well shit I was embarrassed. And it never got quite bad enough to yell out. I kept thinking if it gets a little worse I'll go on and yell out. And then along about 03 I quit feeling the forehead altogether.'

'You've just been sitting here waiting for someone to happen along. Chanting quietly to keep up your courage.'

'I was just praying like hell it wouldn't be Pemulis. God only knows what that son of a whore'd've thunk of to do to me here all helpless and immobilated. And Troeltsch is sawing logs just inside that door there, with his fucking mike and cable and ambitions. I've been praying he don't wake up. And let's don't even *mention* that son of a bitch Freer.'

I looked at the door. 'But that's Axhandle's single. What would Troeltsch be doing sleeping in Axhandle's room?'

Ortho shrugged. 'Trust that I've had plenty of time to listen and identify different folks' snores, Inc.'

I looked from Stice to Axford's door and back. 'So you've just been sitting here listening to sleep-noises and watching your breath expand and freeze on the window?' I said. Imagining it seemed somehow unendurable: me just sitting there, stuck, well before sunrise, alone, too embarrassed to call out, my own exhalations fouling the window and denying me even a view to divert attention from the horror. I stood there horrified, admiring The Darkness's ballsy calm.

'There was a kind of real bad half-hour when my upper lip up and got stuck too, in the breath, when the breath froze. But I breathed the sucker loose. I breathed real hot and fast. Goddamn near hyper-v'd. I was scared if I passed out I'd slump on forward and the whole face'd get stuck. Goddamn forehead's bad enough.'

I put my toothbrush and NASA glass down on the cantilevered vent-module. Rooms' vents were recessed, hallway-vents protrusive. E.T.A.'s annular heating system produced a lubricated hum I had stopped really hearing years ago. The Headmaster's House still had oil heat; it always sounded like a maniac was hammering at the pipes far below.

'Dark, prepare yourself mentally,' I said. 'I'm going to help pull you loose.'

Stice didn't seem to hear this. He seemed oddly preoccupied for a man occlusively sealed to a frozen window. He was feeling at the back of his head with real vigor, which is what he did when he was preoccupied. 'You believe in shit, Hal?'

'Shit?'

'I don't know. Little-kid shit. Telekiniption. Ghosts. Parabnormal shit.'

'Just going to get around behind you and yank and we'll pop you right off,' I said.

'Somebody did come by before,' he said. 'There was somebody standing back there about maybe an hour back. But he just stood there. Then he went away. Or . . . it.' A full-body shiver.

'It'll be like that last little bit of ankle-tape. We'll pull you back so hard and fast you won't feel a thing.'

'I'm getting these real unpleasant memories of that piece of Ingersoll's tongue on Nine's net-post that stayed there til spring.'

'This is no saliva-and-subzero-metal situation, Dark. This is some freakish occlusive seal. Glass doesn't conduct heat like metal conducts heat.'

'There ain't too fucking much heat involved in this window right here, buddy-ruff.'

'And I'm not sure what you mean, *paranormal*. I believed in vampires when I was small. Himself allegedly used to see his father's ghost on stairways sometimes, but then again toward the end he used to see black-widow spiders in his hair, too, and claimed I wasn't speaking sometimes when I was sitting right there speaking to him. So we kind of wrote it all off. Orth, I guess I don't know what to think about paranormal shit.'

'Then plus I think something bit me. On the back of the head here, some bug that knew I was helpless and couldn't see.' Stice dug again at the red area behind his ear. There was a kind of weltish bump there. It wasn't in a vampire-related area of the neck.

'And good old Mario says he's seen paranormal figures, and he's not kidding, and Mario doesn't lie,' I said. 'So belief-wise I don't know what to think. Subhadronic particles behave ghostishly. I think I withhold all prejudgment on the whole thing.'

'Well all right then. It was good it was you come by then.'

'The big thing's going to be to stiffen the old neck, Dark, to avoid whiplash. We'll pull you off there like a cork from a bottle of Moët.'

'Pull my sorry ass off here, Inc, and I'll take and show you some parabnormal shit that'll shake your personal tree but good,' Stice said, bracing. ''n't said nothing to nobody but Lyle about it, and I'm sick of the secretness of it. You won't pre-formulize any judgments, Inc, I know.'

'You're going to be fine,' I said. I got right behind Stice and bent slightly and got an arm around his chest. His wooden chair creaked as I braced my knee against it. Stice began breathing fast and hard. His parotitic jowls flapped a little as he breathed. Our cheeks were almost pressed together. I told him I was going to pull on the count of Three. I actually pulled on Two, so he couldn't brace himself. I pulled back as hard as I could, and after a stutter of resistance Stice pulled back with me.

There was a horrible sound. The skin of his forehead distended as we yanked his head back. It stretched and distended until a sort of shelf of stretched forehead-flesh half a meter long extended from his head to the window. The sound was like some sort of elastic from hell. The dermis of Stice's forehead was still stuck fast, but the abundant loose flesh of Stice's bulldog face had risen and gathered to stretch and connect his head to the window. And for a second I saw what might be considered Stice's real face, his features as they would be if not encased in loose jowly prairie flesh: as every mm. of spare flesh was pulled up to his forehead and stretched, I got a glimpse of Stice as he would appear after a radical face-lift: a narrow, fine-featured, and slightly rodential face, aflame with some sort of revelation, looked out at the window from beneath the pink visor of stretched spare skin.

All this took place in less than second. For just an instant we both stayed there, straining backward, listening to the little Rice-Krispie sound of his skin's collagen-bundles stretching and popping. His chair was leaning way back on its two rear legs. Then Stice shrieked in pain: 'Jesus God put it *back!*' The little second face's blue eyes protruded like cartoon eyes. The fine little thin-lipped second mouth was a round coin of pain and fear.

'Put it back put it back put it back!' Stice yelled.

I couldn't just let go, though, for fear that the elastic stretch would snap Stice forward into the window and send his face through the glass. I eased him forward, watching the chair's front legs descend slowly to the floor; and the tension of the forehead's skin decreased, and Stice's full fleshy round face reappeared over the small second face, and covered it, and we eased him forward until nothing but a few centimeters of decollagenated forehead-skin hanging and sagging at about eyelash-level remained as evidence of the horrific stretch.

'Jesus God,' Stice panted.

'You are really and truly stuck, Orth.'

'Fuck me *skating* did that ever hurt.'

I tried to rotate a kink out of my shoulder. 'We're going to have to thaw it off, Dark.'

'You're not getting close to this forehead with a saw, bud. I'll set right-cheer till spring first, see if I don't.'

Then Jim Troeltsch's towering A.M.-cowlick and then face and fist emerged through Axford's doorway just over Stice's hunched shoulder. Stice had been right. Being in somebody else's room even after Lights Out was an infraction; staying there overnight was too far out even to mention in the regulations. 'Reports of screaming have reached us here in the Eyewitness News-Center,' Troeltsch said into his fist.

'The fuck out of here, Troeltsch,' Stice said.

'*Thaw*, Ortho. Warm water. Heat the window. Hot water. Dissolve the adhesion. Heating pad. Hot pack from Loach's office or something.'

'Loach's door can't be dickied,' Stice said. 'Don't wake him up on Fundraiser day yet.'

Troeltsch extended the fist. 'Reports of high-pitched screams have led this reporter to an unfolding scene of dramatic crisis, and we're going to attempt to get a word with the youngster at the center of all the commotion.'

'Tell him to pipe down and get back with that hand or so help me Jesus, Hal.'

'The Darkness accidentally put his forehead against the window here when it was wet and it froze and he's been out here stuck all night,' I told Troeltsch, ignoring the big fist he held to my face. I squeezed Stice's shoulder. 'I'll go get Brandt to rig something warm.'

It was as if some tacit agreement had been reached not even to bring up Troeltsch's being in Axford's room or where Axford was. It was hard to know which would be more disturbing, Axford's not being in his room all night or Axford being in there behind the ajar door, meaning Troeltsch and Axford had both spent the night in one small single with exactly one bed. The universe seemed to have aligned itself so that even acknowledging it would violate some tacit law. Troeltsch seemed oblivious to any appearance of impropriety or unthinkable possibilities. It was hard to imagine he'd be this obnoxious if he felt he had something to be discreet about. He was standing on tiptoe to see over the window's breath-line, one hand cupped over his ear as if to hold a headset. He whistled softly. 'Plus in addition now reports of mind-boggling snowfall are coming in to the News-Center.'

I grabbed my toothbrush and NASA glass from the vent's protrusion; since the Betel Caper,[352] only the worst kind of naïf leaves his toothbrush unattended around E.T.A. 'Keep an eye on Stice and my NASA glass right there, Jim, if you would.'

'Any comment on the mixture of pain, cold, embarrassment, and weather-related feelings you must be feeling, Mr. Stice is it?'

'Don't leave me immobilated with Troeltsch, man, Hal. He's going to make me talk to his hand.'

'A weather-related drama unfolding around the original plight of an embarrassed man trapped by his own forehead,' Troeltsch was saying into his fist, facing his own reflection in the window, trying with the other big hand to quash the cowlick, as I trotted and slid to a stop in my socks just past the door to the stairwell.

Kenkle and Brandt were ageless in the special desiccated way janitors are ageless, somewhere between thirty-five and sixty. They were inseparable and essentially unemployable. Boredom had years ago led us to Lateral Alice Moore's minimally crypto-protected employee files, and Brandt's file had listed his S.-B. I.Q. as Submoronic-to-Moronic. He was bald and somehow at once overweight and wiry. Both right and left temples carried red jagged surgical scars of unknown origin. His affective range consisted of different intensities of grin. He lived with Kenkle in an attic apartment in Roxbury Crossing overlooking Madison Park High School's locked and cordoned playground, famed site of unsolved ritual mutilations in the Year of the Perdue Wonderchicken. His major attraction for Kenkle seemed to consist in the fact that he neither walked away nor interrupted when Kenkle was speaking. Even in the stairwell I could hear Kenkle discoursing on their Thanksgiving plans and directing Brandt's mop-work. Kenkle was technically black, as in Negroid, though he was more the burnt-sienna color of a spoiled pumpkin. But his hair was a black person's hair, and he wore it in thick dreadlocks that looked like a crown of wet cigars. An academic diamond in the very rough Roxbury Crossing, he'd received his doctorate in low-temperature physics from U.Mass. at twenty-one and taken a prestigious sinecure at the U.S. Office of Naval Research, then at twenty-three had been court-martialed out of the O.N.R. for offenses that changed each time you asked him. Some event between twenty-one and twenty-three seemed to have broken him at several strategic points, and he'd retreated from Bethesda back to the front stoop of his old Roxbury Crossing apartment building, where he read Ba'hai texts whose jackets he covered with intricately folded newspaper, and spat spectacular parabolas of quivering phlegm into New Dudley Street. He was dark-freckled and carbuncular and afflicted with excess phlegm. He was an incredible spitter, and alleged his missing incisors had been removed 'for facilitating the expec-toratory process.' We all suspected he was either hypomanic or 'drine-addicted or both. His expression was very serious at all times. He discoursed nonstop to poor Brandt, using spit as a sort of conjunction between clauses. He spoke loudly because they both wore earplugs of expanding foam — people's nightmare-cries gave them the fantods. Their custodial technique consisted of Kenkle spitting with pinpoint accuracy onto whatever surface Brandt was to clean next and Brandt trotting like a fine hunting dog from glob to glob, listening and grinning, laughing when appropriate. They were moving away from me down the hall toward the second floor's east window, Brandt making great shining arcs with his doll's-head mop, Kenkle pulling the gunmetal bucket and lobbing signifying phlegm over Brandt's bent back.

'And then the Yuletide season, Brandt my friend Brandt — Christmas — Christmas morning — What is the essence of Christmas morning but the childish co-eval of venereal interface, for a child? — A present, Brandt — Something you have not earned and which formerly was out of your po-ssession is now in your po-ssession — Can you sit there and try to say there is no symbolic rela-tion between unwrapping a Christmas present and undressing a young lady?'

Brandt bobbed and mopped, uncertain whether to laugh.

Himself had met Kenkle and Brandt on the T (Kenkle and Brandt apparently rode the T at night, recreationally), trying somehow to make it up to Enfield from the Back Bay via the Orange Line,[353] and somewhat the worse for wear. Kenkle and Brandt not only got Himself onto the right color train and kept him propped up between them all the way up the eternity of Comm. Ave., they'd seen him safely down the T-stop's steep iron stairs and across traffic and up the hill's serpentine driveway to the portcullis, and had been invited in at 0200 by Himself to continue whatever low-temperature discussion he and Kenkle had been having as Brandt carried Himself up the hill in a fireman's carry (Kenkle recalls that night's discussion being about the human nose as an erectile organ, but the only really sure bet is that it was one-sided); and the duo had ended up being cast as black-veiled Noh-style attendants in Himself's *Zero-Gravity Tea Ceremony,* and had been menially employed at E.T.A. ever since, though always on the graveyard shift, since Mr. Harde loathed Kenkle with a passion.

Kenkle hawked and hit a small strip of dust at the crease of baseboard and floor that the mop's arc had missed. 'For I am a missionary man, Brandt, is what I am — Brandt — as in give me the straight-forward vene-real in-terface of missionary congress or give me nihil and zilch — You know what I am saying? — Give me your best thoughts on alter-native po-sitions, Brandt — Brandt — For me, for my part at least, I say nix and nihil on the rear-entry or you might hear it termed Dog- or Canine-Style interface so favored in huts, blue car-tridges, Tan-tric etchings — Brandt, it's animal-istic — Why? — Why you say? — Brandt, it is an ess-entially *hunched* way to have interface — She hunches, you hunch over her — Inordi*nate*ly too much hunching, to my own way of —'

It was Brandt who heard me as I came up behind them in socks, trying to keep to the drier patches. I almost slipped twice. It was still coming down hard outside the east window.

'Otto Brandt here!' Brandt called to me, extending a hand, though I was still several meters away.

Kenkle's dreadlocks protruded from under a plaid hat. He turned with Brandt and raised his hand Indianishly in greeting. 'Good prince Hal. Up and dressed in dawn's ear-a-ly.'

'Let me introduce myself,' Brandt said. I shook his hand.

'In his socks and toothbrush. E.T.A.'s athe-ling, Brandt, whom I will wager rar-e-ly hunches.'

'The Darkness needs you guys upstairs ASAP,' I said, trying to dry a sock against a pant-leg. 'Dark's face is stuck to the window and he's in terrible pain and we couldn't pull it off and it's going to take hot water, but not too hot.' I indicated the bucket at Kenkle's feet. I noticed Kenkle's shoes didn't match.

'What may we ask is so amusing, then?' Kenkle asked.

'Name's Brandt and pleased to meet you,' Brandt said, out with the hand again. He dropped the mop where Kenkle pointed.

'Troeltsch is with him now, but he's in a bad way,' I said, shaking Brandt's hand.

'We are in route,' Kenkle said, 'but why the hilarity?'

'What hilarity?'

Kenkle looked from me to Brandt to me. 'What hilarity he says. Your face is a hilarity-face. It's working hilariously. At first it merely looked *a*-mused. Now it is open-ly *cach*-inated. You are almost doubled over. You can barely get your words out. You're all but slapping your knee. *That* hilarity, good Prince atheling Hal. I thought all you players were compadremundos in civilian life.'

Brandt beamed as he backed down the hall. Kenkle pushed his plaid cap back to scratch at some sort of eruption at the hairline. I drew myself up to full height and consciously composed my face into something deadly-somber. 'How about now?'

Brandt had the custodial closet unlocked. There was the sound of a metal bucket being filled at the closet's industrial tap.

Kenkle brought his cap back forward and narrowed his eyes at me. He came up close. His eyelashes were clotted with small crisp yellow flakes. There were Struck-like facial cysts in various stages of development. Kenkle's breath always smelled vaguely of egg salad. He felt at his mouth speculatively for a moment and said 'Somewheres now between amused and cach-inated. Mirth-ful, perhaps. The crinkled eyes. The dimples of mirth. The exposed gums. We can bounce this off Brandt's best thinking as well, if —'

From directly overhead came a ceiling-rattling 'GYAAAAAAA' from Stice. I was feeling at my face. Some doors opened along the hall, heads protruding. Brandt had a full metal bucket and was trying to run to the stairwell, the weight of the bucket canting his shoulder and steaming water sloshing onto the clean floor. He stopped with his hand on the stairwell door and looked back over his shoulder at us, reluctant to proceed without Kenkle.

'I elect to go with *mirthful*,' Kenkle said, giving my shoulder a little squeeze as he stepped past. I heard him saying different things to the heads in the doorways all the way down the hall.

'Jesus,' I said. Socks or no, I went forward into the really wet mopped area and tried to make out my face's expression in the east window. It was now too light, though, outside, off all the snow. I looked sketchy and faint to myself, tentative and ghostly against all that blazing white.

PARTIAL TRANSCRIPT OF WEATHER-DELAYED MEETING
BETWEEN:
(1) MR. RODNEY TINE SR., CHIEF OF
UNSPECIFIED SERVICES & WHITE HOUSE ADVISER
ON INTERDEPENDENT RELATIONS; (2) MS.
MAUREEN HOOLEY, VICE-PRESIDENT FOR CHILDREN'S
ENTERTAINMENT, INTERLACE TELENTERTAINMENT,
INC.; (3) MR. CARL E. ('BUSTER') YEE,
DIRECTOR OF MARKETING AND PRODUCT-
PERCEPTION, GLAD FLACCID RECEPTACLE
CORPORATION; (4) MR. R. TINE JR.,
DEPUTY REGIONAL COORDINATOR, U.S. OFFICE OF
UNSPECIFIED SERVICES; AND (5) MR. P. TOM VEALS,
VINEY AND VEALS ADVERTISING, UNLTD.
8TH FLOOR STATE HOUSE ANNEX BOSTON MA, U.S.A
20 NOVEMBER — YEAR OF THE DEPEND ADULT
UNDERGARMENT

MR. TINE SR.: Tom. Buster. Mo.
MR. VEALS: R. the G.
MR. YEE: Rod.
MR. TINE SR.: Guys.
MR. TINE JR.: Afternoon, Chief!

MR. TINE SR.: Mmmph.

MS. HOOLEY: Glad you could finally get in, Rod. May I say we're all extremely excited, on our end.

MR. TINE SR.: Never seen snow like this. Any of you ever seen snow remotely approaching anything like this?

MR. VEALS: [Sneezes.] Fucking town.

MR. YEE: Like an extra dimension out there. Less an element than its own dimension.

SOMEONE: [Shoe makes a squelching noise under the table.]

MR. YEE: With its own rules, laws. Awe-inspiring. Fearsome.

MR. VEALS: Cold. Wet. Deep. Slippery. More like.

MR. TINE JR.: [Tapping the edge of a ruler against the tabletop.] Their limo in from Logan did a 180 on Storrow. Mr. Yee was just telling —

MR. TINE SR.: [Tapping a telescoping weatherman's pointer against the edge of the tabletop.] So what's the poop. The skinny. What are we talking.

MS. HOOLEY: Spot ready for previewing. We need your go. I'm in from Phoenix via New New York.

MR. YEE: I'm in from Ohio. Choppered up from NNY with Mo here.

MS. HOOLEY: Spot's master's in the post-production lab down at V&V. All ready except for some final bugs with the matteing.

MR. VEALS: Maureen says we need you and Buster's green light to disseminate.

MS. HOOLEY: You and the titular sponsor here green-light it, we can have disseminatable product by the end of the weekend.

MR. VEALS: [Sneezes.] Assuming this fucking snow doesn't shut down our power.

MR. TINE SR.: [Motioning with weatherman's pointer to U.S.O. stenographer to transcribe verbatim.] Seen it yet, Buster?

MR. YEE: Negative, Rod. Just in with these folks here. Kennedy completely socked in. Mo had to charter a chopper. I'm sitting here cherry.

MR. TINE JR.: [Tapping edge of ruler on tabletop.] How'd you fare getting up here, Sir, if I may?

MR. TINE SR.: Mountain comes to Mohammed, eh Tom?

MR. VEALS: How come I only came two clicks down here and I'm the one with a fucking cold?

MR. TINE JR.: I've been here in Boston as well.

MR. VEALS: [Checking connections on Infernatron 210-Y Digital Player and Viewer System.] So shall we?

MR. TINE SR.: OK, for the record. Mo. Demographic target?

MS. HOOLEY: Ages six to ten, with marginally reduced efficacy four to six and ten to thirteen. Let's say target's four to twelve, white, native English-speaking, median income and above, capacity on Kruger

Abstraction Scale three or above. [Refers to notes.] Advertable attention-span of sixteen seconds with a geometric fall-off commencing at thirteen seconds.

MR. TINE SR.: Spot-length?

MS. HOOLEY: Thirty seconds with a traumatic graphic at fourteen seconds.

MR. VEALS: [Hawks phlegm.]

MR. YEE: Proposed insertion-vehicle, Mo?

MS. HOOLEY: The 'Mr. Bouncety-Bounce Show,' spontaneous dissemination at 1600 M to F. 1500 Central and Mountain. Cream of the crop. 82 Share on spontaneous receptions for the slot.

MR. YEE: Any data on what percentage of total viewing in the slot is Spontaneous versus Recorded cartridge?

MS. HOOLEY: We had 47% plus or minus two as of Year of the Yushityu 2007. That's the last year the data's firmed up for.

MR. TINE SR.: So say 40% of total viewing for the spot.

MR. YEE: Give or take. Impressive.

MR. TINE SR.: So check, check, check. We got rough costs?

MR. YEE: Production just over half a meg. Post-production —

MR. VEALS: Bupkus. 150K before matteing.

MR. YEE: I might add that Tom's pro-bonoing his part of the production.

MR. VEALS: So you all ready to eyeball this or what?

MS. HOOLEY: Since 'Mr. B-B' 's contracted as a no-public-service-spot vehicle, dissemination charge'll come out around 180K per slot.

MR. YEE: Which we're still of the position this seems a bit steep.

MR. TINE JR.: The upcoming year's Glad's year, Buster. You wanted the year. You want the Year of Glad to be the year half the nation stopped doing anything but staring bug-eyed at some sinister cartridge while little whorls went around in their eyes until they died of starvation in the middle of their own exc—?

MR. TINE SR.: Shut up, Rodney. And quit with the ruler-tapping. Buster I'm sure knows the incredible good will that's even now accruing from their proud sponsorship of probably the most important public-service spots ever conceived, given the potential threat here.

MR. VEALS: [Sneezes twice in abrupt succession.] [Comment unintelligible.]

MR. TINE SR.: [Taps telescoping weatherman's pointer on edge of tabletop.] Righto then. The spot itself, then. The spokesfigure icon thing. Still the singing Kleenex?

MR. YEE: The what-was-it, Frankie the No-Thankee Hankie, warning kids to say No Thankee to unlabelled or suspicious cartridges?

MS. HOOLEY: [Clears throat.] Tom?

MR. TINE JR.: [Taps ruler on edge of tabletop.]

MR. VEALS: [Hawks.] No. Had to shit-can the dancing Kleenex after the response groups' test data were analyzed. Various problems. The phrase 'No Thankee' itself perceived as archaic. Uncool. Crotchety-adult. Too New England or something. Summoned images of a leathery-faced old guy in overalls. Took attention away from what they're supposed to say No Thanks to. Plus phrase-recognition data was way under minimum slogan-parameters.

Ms. HOOLEY: Problems with the icon itself.

MR. VEALS: [Blowing nose one nostril at a time.] Kids hated Frankie the Hankie. We're talking levels past ambivalence. Associated the hankie with snot, basically. The word *booger* kept coming up. The singing didn't help.

Ms. HOOLEY: Which is why in this case thank God for response-group testing.

MR. YEE: This business'll make you old.

MR. VEALS: Had to go back and completely reboot at square one.

MR. YEE: Does anyone else smell a peculiar citrusy floral odor?

Ms. HOOLEY: Tom's boys've been at it twenty-four/seven. We're extremely excited at the result.

MR. VEALS: It's previewable but rough. Not really quite there yet. The first Phil's digitals had a bug.

MR. TINE JR.: Phil?

MR. VEALS: A small bug, but nasty. Dregs of a turbovirus in the graphic encoder. Phil's head kept detaching and floating off to the upper right. Not a good effect at all, given the message we want to send.

MR. YEE: Like orange blossoms, but with a kind of sick sweetness.

Ms. HOOLEY: Oh dear.

MR. VEALS: [Sneezes.] And debugging put us behind on some of the fonts, so you're going to have to use some imagination here. Has this 210 unit been downloaded for schematic matteing?

MR. TINE JR.: Excuse me. Phil?

MR. VEALS: Introducing Fully Functional Phil, the prancing ass.

Ms. HOOLEY: More like a mule, a burro. A burro.

MR. TINE JR.: [Tapping like mad.] An ass?

Ms. HOOLEY: Horse-characters were copyrighted by ChildSearch. Their 'Patch the Pony Who Says Nay to Strangers' spots.

MR. TINE JR.: A prancing ass?

Ms. HOOLEY: The perception of naïveté and clumsiness about a mule-icon provoked a kind of empathy in the response groups. Phil's not coming off as an authority-figure-joy-killer type. More like a peer. So the cartridge he warns against gets none of the forbidden-fruit-type boost of being warned against by an authority figure.

MR. VEALS: Plus the kid market's a frigging horror show. Near every species was copyrighted. Garfield. McGruff the freaking crime dog. Toucan Sam. The O.N.A.N. bird of prey. Let's not even get into the bears or bunnies. It was basically either an ass or a cockroach. Never again the kid's market as God is my witness. [Sneezes.]

Ms. HOOLEY: Once we went with the burro, Tom opted to accentuate the clumsy-incompetence factor. To almost ironize the icon. Buck teeth, crossed eyes —

MR. VEALS: Extravagantly crossed. Like he's just been whacked with a sock full of nickels. Eye-response was through the roof.

Ms. HOOLEY: Ears that won't stay upright. Legs keep getting all rubbery and tangled when he tries to prance.

MR. VEALS: But prance he does.

MR. YEE: But surely it doesn't present itself as an ass. Surely it doesn't prance out and say, 'Take it from me, an ass.'

MR. VEALS: A *fully functional* ass.

Ms. HOOLEY: Tom's rather ingeniously played up the functionality angle. The energy and verve versus passivity angle. He's never just Phil. He's Fully Functional Phil. He's a blur of kid-type activity — school, playing, teleputer-interfacing, prancing. Tom's got him storyboarded for a number of thirty-second activity-packed little adventures. He's a goof, an iconic child, but he's *active*. He stands for the attraction of capacity, agency, choice. As versus the spot's animated adult who we see in a recliner ostensibly watching the Canadian cartridge, little spirals going around and around in his eyes as his body sort of melts and his head starts growing and distending until the passive watching adult's image is just a huge five-o'clock-shadowed head in the recliner, his eyeballs huge and whirling.

MR. TINE JR.: [Taps his ruler against the edge of the tabletop.]

MR. VEALS: Let's just roll the thing for them, Mo.

MR. TINE SR.: I've got to say I foresee trouble selling a certain Commander in Chief on a prancing ass as an improvement over a singing Kleenex.

Ms. HOOLEY: Phil's message is that not every entertainment cartridge out there is necessarily a good old safe pre-approved InterLace TelEntertainment product. He says word's reached him during his fun-filled fully functional daily activities of a certain very wicked and sneaky cartridge that even has a little smiling face on the case and when you first start watching it looks like it promises to be more fun to watch than anything you've ever wished on a star or blown out a birthday-cake candle for. In a thought-bubble that becomes visible when Phil's ears flop down again —

MR. VEALS: [Sneezes.] Not yet matted in all the way —

MR. TINE SR.: You know how he is about Kleenex.

Ms. HOOLEY: — will be an image of an iconic cartridge case with a friendly smile and pudgy little harmless Pillsbury Doughboy arms and legs.

MR. YEE: [Loosening his collar.] Not the actual copyrighted Pillsbury iconic-limb animation-codes, though.

MR. VEALS: Relax. More like a reference. An allusion to plumpness, cuteness. Pudgy and harmless-looking limbs, is the thing.

MR. TINE JR.: [Tapping edge of tabletop with ruler.]

MR. TINE SR.: [Pointing at tapping ruler with weatherman's pointer.] You're close to losing that hand, bucko.

MS. HOOLEY: [Referring to notes.] Then Phil looks up and pops the thought-bubble with a needle and says But it's a liar, this smiling cartridge is, a wicked thing, lying, like the stranger who leans out of his car and offers you a ride home to your Mommy and Daddy but really wants to grab you and put his sweaty hand over your mouth and lock you in the car and take you far away with him to where you'll never see your Mommy, Daddy, or Mr. Bouncety-Bounce ever again.

MR. VEALS: Which and here's the traumatic graphic at fourteen, a dark-bordered new thought-bubble over Phil in which now the cartridge's limbs are like a dockworker's, it's a swart leering cartridge with yellow fangs and long nails in a plaid cap and overalls driving off with an animated kid splayed all screaming and horrified against the car's rear window, spirals starting to roll in the kid's eyes. Wait'll you see it.

MS. HOOLEY: It's so scary it's positively riveting.

MR. VEALS: [Sneezes twice.] Stuff of fucking nightmares.

MR. YEE: Urgle. Urgle urgle. Splarg. *Kaa*. [Falls from chair.]

MR. TINE JR.: Holy mackerel.

MR. TINE SR.: Buster? Buster?

MS. HOOLEY: Mr. Yee's epileptic. Severe. Untreatable. Happened twice on the chopper in. Stress or embarrassment brings it on. He'll be back up in a minute. Just act natural when he comes back up.

MR. YEE: [Heels drumming on terrazzo State House Annex floor tile.] Ack. Kaa.

MR. TINE SR.: Jesus.

MR. TINE JR.: [Tapping ruler on tabletop's edge.] Jesus W. Christ.

MR. TINE SR.: [Rising, indicating tapping ruler with extended weatherman's pointer.] All right, God damn it. Give me that thing. Give it here.

MR. TINE JR.: But Chief —

MR. TINE SR.: You heard me God damn it. You know it drives me bats. You'll get it back when we're done. Drives me up the wall. Always has. What is it with you and that ruler.

MS. HOOLEY: Be up and back in the game in a jiff. He won't remember the fit. Just don't mention it. The embarrassment of mentioning it'll set it off again. That's why twice on the chopper. I learned the hard way.

MR. YEE: Splar. Kak.

MR. VEALS: [Hawking.] For Christ's sake.

MS. HOOLEY: [Referring to notes.] As the cartridge in the car in the thought-bubble drives the splayed kid away, Phil prances a bit and warns that we don't even know for sure what the cartridge to watch out for is even about. He warns that the police only know that it's something that looks like you'd *really* want to watch it. He says all we know is it *looks* really entertaining. But that it *really* just wants to take away your functionality. He says we know it's . . . *Canadian*.

MR. VEALS: That's why the plaid cap in the traumatic graphic. Response data indicates a plaid cap with earflaps signifies the Big C to over 70% of the spot's target. The overalls drive the association home.

MS. HOOLEY: At nineteen seconds, Fully Functional Phil then dances his Warning Dance, a Native-American-cum-Breakdance-type dance we're hoping will catch on among younger dancers. His rhetorical thrust is to play it functional and safe and make sure and check with Mommy and/or Daddy before watching *any* entertainment you haven't seen before. I.e. to accept no Spontaneous Dissemination and play no post-delivered entertainment without checking with an authority figure.

MR. TINE JR.: But as a peer. More like, 'I'm thinking this is what *I* better do, if I want to stay fully functional.'

MR. YEE: [Back upright in chair.] Somebody's mentioned the floppy-ear and plastic-buck-teeth product tie-ins.

MR. TINE JR.: Jesus Mr. Yee, are you sure you're OK?

MS. HOOLEY: Ixnay on the entionmay.

MR. YEE: [Sweat-soaked, looking around.] What did he mean? He didn't mean . . . ?

MR. TINE SR.: God damn it, Rodney.

MR. YEE: Urg. Splarg. [Falls from chair.]

MS. HOOLEY: [Clears throat.] And finally, direly — can I say direly?

MR. VEALS: This is at 25.35 seconds.

MS. HOOLEY: Emphatically warns that if Mommy and/or Daddy have been observed sitting in one position in front of the home's viewer for an unusually long period of time —

MR. VEALS: — Without speaking. Without responding to stimuli.

MS. HOOLEY: — or acting in any way unusual or distracted or creepy or spooky with respect to an entertainment on the viewer —

MR. VEALS: We cut *spooky* on the last pass.

MR. YEE: Sklah. Nnngg.

MS. HOOLEY: — that the fully functional kid'll *never* attempt to rouse them himself, and Fully Functional Phil leans way in in a kind of fish-eye-lens close-up and says 'No-ho-ho-ho *way*' would he ever be so dumb as to even for a second plunk himself passively down and have a look at what it is his parents are so silently, creepily engrossed by, but to vacate the premises and prance as fast as he can to get a policeman, who'll know just how to cut the premises' power and help Mum and Dad.

MR. VEALS: His trademark expression is 'No-ho-ho-ho *way*.' He works it in whenever possible.

MR. TINE JR.: His equivalent to the Kleenex's 'No-Thankee.'

MR. TINE SR.: We're ready to view, I think.

MR. YEE: [Back in seat, necktie now wrapped all the way around neck like aviator's scarf.] Still hashing out the tie-ins with Hasbro et al.

MR. VEALS: We're all cued and ready.

MR. TINE SR.: Let's have a look at the sucker.

MS. HOOLEY: Since Tom's too modest to say so, I should say that Tom's already storyboarded an extremely exciting adolescent-targeted version of Fully Functional Phil, for music-video and soft-core disseminations, where Phil engages in a great deal more ironic self-parody, and in this version his trademark expression becomes 'It's *your* ass, ace.'

MR. TINE JR.: So let's have a look at the bastard.

MR. TINE SR.: Kid, your job here from here on out is to pipe down, now do you —?

MR. YEE: I've been asked to say for transcription how pleased the Glad Flaccid Receptacle Corporation is, during this potentially grave interval, to be a proud —

MR. VEALS: [At the Infernatron 210 Viewer.] Hit those lights over behind you, kid.

MR. TINE JR.: This'll make it difficult for the transcriber to transcribe, can I say.

MR. YEE: This spot doesn't happen to in any way optically pulse or strobe, does it?

MR. VEALS: Are we all set?

MR. TINE SR.: So lights already.

Gately's memories of 'Cheers!' 's Nom now are clearer and vivider than any memory of the wraith-dream or the whirling wraith who said death was just everything outside you getting really slow. The implication that there might at any given time in any room be whole swarms of wraiths flitting around the hospital on errands that couldn't affect anybody living, all way too fast to see and dropping by to watch Gately's chest rise and fall at the rate of the sun, none of this has sunk in enough to give him the howlers, not in the wake of Joelle's visit and the fantasies of romance and rescue, and the consequent shame. There's now a sandy sound of gritty sleetish stuff wind-driven against the room's window, the hiss of the heater, sounds of gunfire and brass bands from cartridge viewers on in other rooms. The room's other bed's still empty and tightly made. The intercom gives that triple ding every few minutes; he wonders if they just do it to bug people. The fact that he couldn't even finish *Ethan From* in 10th-grade English and hasn't got clue one about where ghostwords like *SINISTRAL* or *LIEBESTOD* mean or come from, much less *OMMATOPHORIC,* is just starting to percolate up to awareness when there's a cold hand on his good shoulder and he opens his eyes. Not to mention *ghostwords,* which is a real and esoteric word. He's been floating just under sleep's lid again. Joelle van D.'s gone. The hand is the nurse that had changed the catheter-bag. She looks hassled and unserene, and one cheekbone sticks out farther than the other, and her little slot of a mouth's got little vertical wrinkles all around it from being held tight all the time, not unlike the basically-late Mrs. G.'s tight little mouth.

'The visitor said you'd requested this, because of the tube.' It's a little stenographic notebook and Bic. 'Are you left-handed?' The nurse means *sinistral.* She's penguin-shaped and smells of cheap soap. The notebook is *STENOGRAPHIC* because its pages turn over at the top instead of to the side. Gately shakes his head gingerly and opens his left hand for the stuff. It makes him feel good all over again that Joelle had understood what he'd meant. She hadn't just come to tell her troubles to somebody that couldn't make human judgment-noises. Shaking his head slowly lets him see past the nurse's white hip. Ferocious Francis is sitting in the chair that the wraith and Ewell and Calvin Thrust had all sat in, his skinny legs uncrossed, gnarled and crew-cutted and clear-eyed behind his glasses and totally relaxed, holding his portable O_2-tank, his chest rising and falling at about the rate a phone rings, watching the nurse waddle tensely out. Gately can see a clean white T- under the open buttons of Ferocious Francis's flannel shirt. Coughing is F.F.'s way of saying hello.

'Still sucking air I see,' Ferocious Francis says when the fit's passed, making sure the little blue tubes are still taped under his nose.

Gately struggles with one hand to flip the notebook open and write 'YO!' in block caps. Except there's nothing to really hold the notebook up against and write; he has to sort of balance it flat on one thigh, so he can't see what he's writing, and writing with his left hand makes him feel like a stroke-victim must feel, and what he holds up at his sponsor looks more like ϫ ſ.

'Figured God needed a little help the other night did you?' Francis says, leaning way out to the side to get a red bandanna hankie out of a back pocket. 'What I heard.'

Gately tries to shrug, can't, smiles weakly. His right shoulder is so thickly bandaged it looks like a turbanned head. The old man probes a nostril and then examines the hankie with interest, just like the dream-wraith did. His fingers are swollen and misshapen and his nails are long and square and the color of old turtleshell.

'Poor sick bastard going around cutting up people's pets, cut up the wrong people's pets. This is the way I heard it.'

Gately wants to tell Ferocious Francis how he's discovered how no one second of even unnarcotized post-trauma-infection-pain is unendurable. That he can Abide if he must. He wants to share his experience with his Crocodile sponsor. And plus, now that somebody he trusts himself to need is here, Gately wants to weep about the pain and tell how bad the pain of it is, how he doesn't think he can stand it one more second.

'You saw yourself as in charge. Thought you'd step in. Protect your fellowman from his consequences. Which poor sick green Ennet House fuck was it?'

Gately struggles to try and get his knee up so he can see to write 'LENZ. WHITE WIG. ALWAYS NORTH. ALWAYS ON PHONE.' Again it looks cuneiform though, illegible. Ferocious Francis blows out a nostril and replaces the little tube. The tank in his lap makes no sound. It has a little valve but no dial or needles.

'You stepped in against six armed Hawaiians, I hear. Marshall Plan. Captain Courageous. God's personal Shane.' F.F. likes to send air through his nose's tubes in a mirthless burst, a kind of anti-laugh. His nose is large and cucumber-shaped and wide-pored, and pretty much its whole circulatory system is visible. 'Glenny Kubitz calls me and describes the thing blow by blowjob. Says I should see the other guys. Says about breaking a Hawaiian's nose, shoving the bits up into the brain. The old chop-and-stiff-arm he says. Big Don G.'s a Satanically tough motherfuck: this was his assessment. Said the way he heard it you could fight like you was born in a barfight. I tell Glenny I say I'm sure you'll be proud to hear him say it.'

Gately was trying with maddening sinistral care to write out 'HURT? DEAD ANY? FINIST? WHO HAT IN HALL?,' more like drawing than writing, when without warning one of the day-shift Trauma M.D.s sweeps in, radiating brisk health and painless cheer. Gately remembers dealing with this one M.D. some days ago in a kind of gray post-surgical fog. This M.D. is Indian or Pakistani and is glossily dark but with a sort of weirdly classically white-type face you could easily imagine profiling on a coin, plus teeth you could read by the gleam of. Gately hates him.

'So I am here with you again in this room!' The M.D. sings, kind of, when he talks. The name in gold piping on his white coat has a *D* and a *K* and a shitload of vowels. Gately almost had to reach up and swat this M.D. after surgery to keep him from hooking up a Demerol drip. That was between let's say four and eight days ago. It's probably But for the Grace that his Crocodilian sponsor Ferocious Francis G.'s sitting here watching blandly when the Pakistani M.D. sweeps in this time.

Plus they all have this flourishy M.D. way of sweeping Gately's chart up off their hip and holding it up to read it. The Pakistani purses his lips and puffs them out absently and sucks off his pen a little.

'Grade-two toxemia. Synovial inflammation. The pain of the trauma is very much worse today, yes?' the M.D. says to the chart. He looks up, the teeth emerge. 'Synovial inflammation: nasty nasty. The pain of synovial inflammation is compared in the medical literature to renal calculus and ectopic labor.' Partly it's the darkness of the classic face around them that makes the teeth seem so high-watt. The smile widens steadily without seeming to run out of new teeth to expose. 'And so you are now ready to let us provide the level of analgesia the trauma warrants instead of Toradol, simple headache ibuprofen, which these medications are boys doing a large man's duty here, yes? There has been reconsidering in light of the level? Yes?'

Gately is inscribing an enormous vowel in the notebook with incredible care.

'I make you aware of synthetic anipyretic analgesics which are no higher than Category C-III[354] for dependence.' Gately imagines the M.D. smiling incandescently as he wields a shepherd's crook. The guy has that odd clipped singsong way of talking of skinny guys in loincloths on mountains in films. Gately superimposes a big skull and crossbones over the glossy face, mentally. He holds up a palsied page-high A and brandishes it at the M.D. and then brings the notebook back down and swiftly up again, spells it out, figuring Ferocious Francis will step in and set this ad-man for the Disease straight once and for all, so Gately'll never have to face this kind of Pakistani temptation again with maybe nobody supportive here next time. C-III his ass. Fucking *Talwin*'s C-III, too.

'Oramorph SR for an instance. Very safe, very much relief. Fast relief.'

This is just morphine sulfate with a fancy corporate name, Gately knows. This raghead doesn't know who he's dealing with, or what he's.

'Now I must tell tell, I would make the personal first choice of titrated hydromorphone hydrochloride, in this case —'

Christ, this is Dilaudid. Blues. Fackelmann's Mount Doom. Kite's steep-angled decline, as well. Death on a Ritz. The Blue Bayou. Gene Fackelmann's killer, by and large. And also Gately pictures good old Nooch, tall skinny Vinnie Nucci, from the beach at Salem, who favored Dilaudid and spent over a year without ever taking the belt off his wing, dropping through Osco skylights at night on a rope with the belt all tight and ready just over his elbow already, Nucci never eating and getting skinnier and skinnier until he seemed to be just two cheekbones raised to a great silent height, even the whites of his eyes finally turning the blue of the bayou; and Fackelmann's eliminated map after the insane scam on Sorkin and a disastrous two nights of Dilaudid, when Sorkin'd —

'— though I say yes, this in truth is a C-II medication, and I wish to respect all wishes and concerns,' the M.D. half-sings, inclined at the waist now by Gately's railings, looking closely at the shoulder's dressing but not seeming at all disposed to even touch it, his hands behind his back. His ass is

886

more or less right in Ferocious Francis's face, who's just sitting there. The M.D. doesn't even seem to be aware 34-year-sober Ferocious Francis is there. And Francis isn't making a peep.

It also occurs to Gately that *esoteric* is another ghostword he's got no rights to throw around, mentally.

'For I am Moslem, and abstain also, by religious law, from all abusive compounds as well,' the M.D. says. 'Yet if I have suffered trauma, or the dentist of my teeth proposes to perform a painful process, I submit as a Moslem to the imperative of my pain and will accept relief, knowing no established religion's God wills needless suffering for His children.'

Gately has made two shaky smaller A's together on the next sheet and is stabbing emphatically at the sheet with his Bic. He wishes if the M.D. wouldn't shut up he'd at least move, so Gately could shoot a desperate Please-Jump-In-Here look at Ferocious Francis. The drug-question has nothing to do with established Gods.

The M.D.'s bobbing a little as he leans, his face coming in and then receding. 'This is a Grade-II trauma we are looking at in this room. Allow me to explain that the discomfort of right now will only intensify as the synovial nerves begin to reanimate. The laws of trauma dictate that the pain will intensify as healing begins to commence. I am a professional at my job, sir, as well as a Moslem. Hydrocodone bitartrate[355] — C-III. Levorphanol tartrate[356] — C-III. Oxymorphone hydrochloride[357] — admittedly, yes, C-II, but more than indicated in this degree of needless suffering.'

Gately can hear Ferocious Francis blowing his nose again behind the M.D. Gately's mouth floods with spittle at the memory of the sick-sweet antiseptic taste of hydrochloride that rises to the tongue with an injection of Demerol, the taste Kite and the lesbian burglars and even Equus ('I'll Stick Anything in Any Part of My Body') Reese all gagged at but that poor old Nooch and Gene Fackelmann and Gately himself had loved, came to love like a mother's warm hand. Gately's eyes wobble and his tongue protrudes from a shiny mouth-corner as he draws a crude syringe and arm and belt and then tries to draw a skull-and-bones over the whole shaky ensemble, but the skull looks more like a plain old smiley-face. He holds it out to the foreigner anyway. The dextral pain's so bad he wants to throw up, throat-tube or no.

The M.D. studies the palsied drawing, nodding the exact way Gately used to nod at Alfonso Parias-Carbo the totally ununderstandable Cuban. 'Oxycodone-nalaxone compound,[358] with a short half-life but only a C-III grading of abuse.' There's no way the guy could be like intentionally making his voice this wheedly-sounding; it's got to be Gately's own Disease. The Spider. Gately envisions his brain struggling in a silk cocoon. He keeps summoning to mind the little detox-story Ferocious Francis tells from the Commitment podium, how they gave him Librium[359] to help with the discomfort of Withdrawal, and how Francis says he just threw the Librium hard over his left shoulder, for luck, and has had very good luck ever since.

'Likewise as well the time-tested pentazocine lactate, which I can offer with assurances as a Moslem trauma-professional standing here in this room in person with you at your bed's side.'

Pentazocine lactate is Talwin, Gately's #2 trusted standard when he was Out There, which 120 mg. on an empty gut was like floating in oil the exact same temperature as your body, just like Percocet[360] except without the maddening back-of-the-eyeball itch that always wrecked a Percocet high for him.

'Surrender your courageous fear of dependence and let us do our profession, young sir,' the Pakistani sums up, standing right up next to the bed, the left side, his professional lab-coat hiding F.F., hands behind his back, the dull glint of the metal corner of Gately's chart just visible between his legs, immaculate of posture, smiling cheerily down, the whites of his eyes as ungodly white as his teeth. The memory of Talwin makes parts of his body Gately didn't know could drool drool. He knows what's coming next, Gately does. And if the Pakistani goes ahead and offers Demerol again Gately won't resist. And who the fuck'll be able to blame him, after all. Why should he have to resist? He'd received a bona fide Grade-Whatever dextral synovial trauma. Shot with a professionally modified .44 Item. He's post-trauma, in terrible pain, and everyone heard the guy say it: it was going to get worse, the pain. This was a trauma-pro in a white coat here making reassurances of legitimate fucking use. Gehaney heard him; what the fuck did the Flaggers want from him? This wasn't hardly like slipping over to Unit #7 with a syringe and a bottle of Visine. This was a stop-term measure, a short-gap-type measure, the probable intervention of a compassionate unjudging God. A quick Rx-squirt of Demerol — probably at the outside two, three days of a Demerol drip, maybe even one where they'd hook the drip to a rubber bulb he could hold and self-administer the Demerol only As Needed. Maybe it was the Disease itself telling him to be scared a medically necessary squirt would pull all his old triggers again, put him back in the cage. Gately pictures himself trying to shunt through a magnetic-contact burglar alarm with a hand and a hook. But surely if Ferocious Francis thought a medically advised short-term squirt suspect, at all, the old reptilian bastard would *say* something, do his fucking job as a Crocodile and sponsor, instead of just sitting there playing with his nostril's little noninvasive tube.

'Look kid, I'm gonna screw and let you settle this bullshit and come back up later,' comes Francis's voice, subdued and neutral, signifying nothing, and then the rasp of the chair's legs and the system of grunts that always accompanies F.F.'s getting up from a chair. His white crew cut rises like a slow moon over the Pakistani's shoulder, which the M.D.'s only sign of acknowledgment of Francis is to sort of tuck his chin down into his shoulder like a violinist, addressing Gately's sponsor for the first time:

'Then perhaps you would please, Mr. Gately Senior, if you please help us help your concerned and brave boy here but a boy I believe whose cavalier attitude underestimates the level of coming discomfort which is sadly unnecessary altogether if he will let us help him, sir,' the Pakistani sings over his shoulder to Ferocious Francis, as if they were the room's only adults. He's assuming Ferocious Francis is Gately's organic Dad.

Gately knows a Crocodile never bothers to correct anybody's misimpression. He's halfway to the door, moving with maddening slow care like always, as if walking on ice, twisted and seeming to limp off both legs and heartbreakingly assless in the baggy seat-shiny wide-waled old man's corduroys he always wears, the back of his red neck complexly creased as he moves off away, lifting one hand in a gesture of acknowledgment and dismissal of the M.D.'s request:

'Not my business to say one way or the other. Kid's gonna do what he decides he needs to do for himself. He's the one that's feeling it. He's the only one can decide.' He either pauses or slows down even further at the open door, looking back at Gately but not meeting his wide eyes. 'You keep your pecker up, kid, and I'll bring some of the son of a bitches by to look in again later.' He slips in 'Might want to Ask For Some Help, deciding.' The last of this comes from the white hall as the Pakistani's glossy head comes back in close with now a tight strained-patience smile, and Gately can hear him inhaling to get ready to say that of course in Grade-II traumas of this severe type the treatment of preferred indication is the admittedly C-II and highly abusable but unsurpassed for effectiveness and tightly controlled administration of one 50-mg. tab in a diluting saline drip q. 3–4 hours of mep—

Gately's good left hand skins a knuckle shooting out between the bars of the bedside crib-railing and plunging under the M.D.'s lab-coat and fastening onto the guy's balls and bearing down. The Pakistani pharmacologist screams like a woman. It isn't rage or the will to harm so much as just no other ideas for keeping the bastard from offering something Gately knows that he's powerless at this moment to refuse. The sudden exertion sends a blue-green sheet of pain over Gately that makes his eyes roll up as he bears down on the balls, but not enough to crush. The Pakistani curtsies deeply and bends forward, crumpling around Gately's hand, showing all 112 teeth as he screams higher and higher until he hits a jagged high note like a big opera lady in a Viking helmet so shattering it makes the crib-railings and windowglass shiver and woke Don Gately up with a start, his left arm through the railing and twisted with the force of his attempt to sit up so that the pain now made him hit almost the same high note as the dream's foreign

M.D. The sky outside the window was gorgeous, Dilaudid-colored; the room was full of serious A.M. light; no sleet on the window. The ceiling throbbed a little but did not breathe. The one visitor-chair was back over by the wall. He looked down. Either the stenographer's notebook and pen had got knocked off his bed or the dream had made up that part, too. The next bed was still empty and made up tight. It came to him all of a sudden why they called them hospital corners. But the railing Joelle van D. had folded down to sit on the bunk in the fucking Erdedy kid's sweats was still folded down, and the other railing was still up. So there was some like evidence of the one part, that she'd been really there, showing him the pictures. Gately brought his skinned hand gingerly back inside the railing and felt to make sure there really was a big invasive tube going into his mouth, and there was. He could roll his eyes way up and see his heart monitor going silently nuts. Sweat was coming off every part of him, and for the first time in the Trauma Wing he felt like he needed to take a shit, and he had no idea what arrangements there were for taking a shit but suspected they weren't going to be appetizing at all. Second. Second. He tried to Abide. No single second was past enduring. The intercom was giving triple dings. There really were sounds of other rooms' TPs, and of a meal cart being rolled down the hall, and the metally smell of food for the edible patients. He couldn't see anything like a hat-shadow in the hall, but it could have been all the sunlight.

The dream's vividness had been either fever or Disease, but either way it had fucking seriously rattled his cage. He heard the singsong voice promising about increasing discomfort. His shoulder beat like a big heart, and the pain was sickeninger than ever. No single second was past standing. Memories of good old Demerol rose up, clamoring to be Entertained. The thing in Boston AA is they try to teach you to accept occasional cravings, the sudden thoughts of the Substance; they tell you that sudden Substance-cravings will rise unbidden in a true addict's mind like bubbles in a toddler's bath. It's a lifelong Disease: you can't keep the thoughts from popping in there. The thing they try to teach you is just to Let Them Go, the thoughts. Let them come as they will, but do not *Entertain* them. No need to invite a Substance-thought or -memory in, offer it a tonic and your favorite chair, and chat with it about old times. The thing about Demerol wasn't just the womb-warm buzz of a serious narcotic. It was more like the, what, the aesthetics of the buzz. Gately'd always found Demerol with a slight Talwin kicker such a smooth and orderly buzz. A somehow deliciously *symmetrical* buzz: the mind floats easy in the exact center of a brain that floats cushioned in a warm skull that itself sits perfectly centered on a cushion of soft air some neckless distance above the shoulders, and inside all is a somnolent hum. Chest rises and falls on its own, far away. The easy squeak of your head's blood is like bedsprings in the friendly distance. The sun itself seems to be smiling. And when you nod off, you sleep like a man of wax, and awaken in the same last position you remember falling asleep in.

And pain of all sorts becomes a theory, a news-item in the distant colder climes way below the warm air you hum on, and what you feel is mostly gratitude at your abstract distance from anything that doesn't sit inside concentric circles and love what's happening.

Gately takes advantage of the fact that he's already facing ceilingward to seriously Ask For Help with the obsession. He thinks hard about anything else at all. Heading out w/ old Gary Carty in the pre-dawn reek of low tide off Beverly to bring up lobster traps. The M.P. and the flies. His mother sleeping slack-mouthed on a chintz divan. Cleaning the very grossest corner of the Shattuck Shelter. The billow of the veiled girl's veil. The traps' little cages of cross-hatched bars, the lobsters' eyes' stalks always poking through the squares so the eyes looked out at open sea. Or the bumper stickers on the M.P.'s old Ford — SEEEEE YAAAAAAA!! and DON'T TAILGATE ME OR I'LL FLICK A BOOGER ON YOUR WINDSHIELD! and MIA: ~~FORGOTTEN~~ and I HAVEN'T HAD SEX IN SO LONG I FORGET WHO GETS TIED UP! The fish asking about what's water. The sharp-nosed round-cheeked dead-eyed nurse with a weird Germanish accent that would sell Gately little sampler bottles of Sanofi-Winthrop Demerol syrup, 80 mg./bottle, vilely banana-flavored, then would lie back slack and dead-eyed while Gately X'd her, barely breathing, in an airless Ipswich apartment whose weird brown windowshades filled the place with light the color of weak tea. Named Egede or Egette, she eventually started telling Gately she couldn't come close to coming unless he burned her with a cigarette, which marked the first time Gately seriously tried to quit smoking.

Now a black outside-linebacker of a St. E.'s nurse rumbles in and checks his drips and writes on his chart and points the artillery of her tits down at him to ask how he's doing, and calls him 'Baby,' which nobody minds from enormous black nurses. Gately points at his lower abdomen in the area of his colon and tries to make a broad explosive gesture with just one arm, slightly less mortified than if it had been a human-size white nurse, at least.

Gately happened onto Demerol at age twenty-three when intra-ocular itching finally forced him to abandon Percocets and explore new vistas. Demerol was more expensive mg. for mg. than most synthetic narcs, but it was also easier to get, being the treatment of medical choice for mind-bending post-operative pain. Gately can't for the life of him remember who or just where in Salem he was first introduced to what the boys on the North Shore called Pebbles and Bams-Bams, 50 and 100 mg. Demerol tablets, respectively very tiny and tiny, chalky white scored discs with $\boxed{\text{D/35}}$ on one side and Sanofi-Winthrop Co.'s very-soon-beloved trademark, a kind of $\boxed{\text{W}}$, on the other, that rakish $\textit{W}$ just puncturing the square envelope of itchy-eyed North-Shore life. And remembering even the $\boxed{\text{D/35}}$ feels like Entertaining the

891

obsession. He knows it was not long after Nooch's funeral, because he'd been alone and crewless at whatever moment whoever handed him two 50 mg. tablets way too tiny for his big-fingered hands, in lieu of whatever else it was he'd wanted, laughing when Gately said What the fuck and They look like Bufferin for ants or some shit, saying: Trust Me.

It must have been his twenty-third summer Out There, because he remembers being shirtless and driving down 93 when he ran out of everything else and pulled off into the JFK Library lot to take them, so small and tasteless he had to check his open mouth in the rearview to make sure he'd gotten them down. And he remembers not wearing a shirt because he'd gotten to study his big bare hairless chest for a long time. And from that somnolent P.M. in the JFK lot on he'd been a faithful attendant at the goddess Demerol's temple, right to the very finish.

Gately remembers crewing — for good bits of both the Percocet and Demerol eras — with two other North Shore narcotics addicts, who Gately'd grown up with one and had broke digits for Whitey Sorkin the migrainous bookie with the other. They weren't burglars, either of them, these guys: Fackelmann and Kite. Fackelmann had a background in creative-type checks, plus access to equipment for manufacturing I.D., and Kite's background was he'd been a computer-wienie at Salem State before he got the Shoe for hacking the phone bills of certain guys deep in trouble over 900 sex-lines into the S.S. Administration's WATS account, and they became naturals at crewing together, F. and K., and had their own unambitious but elegant scam going that Gately was ever only marginally in on. What Fackelmann and Kite'd do, they'd rig up an identity and credit record sufficient to rent them a luxury furnished apt., then they'd rent a lot of upscale-type appliances from like Rent-A-Center or Rent 2 Own down in Boston, then they'd sell the luxury appliances and furnishings off to one of a couple dependable fences, then they'd bring in their own air mattresses and sleeping bags and canvas chairs and little legit-bought TP and viewer and speakers and camp out in the empty luxury apartment, getting very high on the rented goods' net proceeds, until they got their second Overdue Notice on the rent; then they'd rig up another identity and move on and do it all over. Gately took his turn being the one to bathe and shave and answer a luxury-apt.-rental ad in borrowed Yuppiewear and meet the property management people and sweep them off their Banfis with his I.D. and credit rating, and forge some name on the lease; and he usually crashed and got high in the apts. with Fackelmann and Kite, though he, Gately, had had his own digit-breaking and then later burglary career, and his own fences, and tended more and more to cop his own scrips and his own Percocets and then later Demerol.

Lying there, working on Abiding and not-Entertaining, Gately remembers how good old doomed Gene Fackelmann — that for a narcotics addict had had a truly raging libido — used to like to bring different girls home to whatever apt. they were scamming at the time, and how Fax'd open the door and look around in pretend-astonishment at the empty and carpetless luxury apt. and shout 'We been fuckin robbed!'

For Fackelmann and Kite, the rap on Gately was that he was a great and (for a narcotics addict, which places limits on rational trusting) stand-up guy, and a ferociously good friend and crewmate, but they just didn't for their lives see why Gately chose to be a narcotics man, why these were his Substances of his choice, because he was a great and cheerful stand-up jolly-type guy off the nod, but when he was Pebbled or narculated in any way he'd become this totally taciturn withdrawn dead-like person, they always said, like a totally different Gately, sitting for hours real low in his canvas chair, practically lying in this chair whose canvas bulged and legs bowed out, speaking barely at all, and then only the necessariest word or two, and then without ever seeming to open his mouth. He made whoever he got high with feel lonely. He got real, like, interior. Pamela Hoffman-Jeep's term was 'Other-Directed.' And it was worse when he shot anything up. You'd have to almost *pry* his chin off his chest. Kite used to say it was like Gately shot cement instead of narcotics.

McDade and Diehl come in around 1100h. from visiting Doony Glynn down somewheres in the Gastroenterology Dept. and try to give Gately's left hand archaic old unhip high fives as a goof and say the Bowel guys've got Glynn on a megadrip of a Levsin[361]-codeine diverticulitis compound, and the Doon seemed to have undergone a kind of spiritual experience vis-à-vis this compound, and was giving them ebubblient high fives and saying the Bowel M.D.s were saying that there was a chance the condition might be inoperable and chronic and that D.G.'d have to be on the compound for life, with a rubber bulb for Self-Administration, and the formerly fetal Doon was sitting up in a lotus position and seemed to be a very happy camper indeed. Gately makes pathetic sounds around his oral tube as McDade and Diehl start to interrupt each other apologizing for how it's looking like they might not be able to stand up and legally depose for Gately like they'd be ready to do in a fucking *hatbeat* if it weren't for various legal issues they're still under the clouds of that their P.D. and P.O. respectively say that walking voluntarily into Norfolk District Court in Enfield would be tittymount to like judicio-penal suicide, they're told.

Diehl looks at McDade and then says there's also disparaging news about the .44 Item, that by everybody's reconstruction of events it's more than likely Lenz might have promoted the Item up off the lawn when he legged it off the E.M.P.H.H. complex just ahead of the Finest. Because it's fucking vanished, and nobody'd have rat-holed it and not given it up knowing what's at stake for the good old G-Man in the deal. Gately makes a whole new kind of noise.

McDade says the more upbeat news is that Lenz has been possibly spotted, that Ken E. and Burt F. Smith had seen what looked like either R. Lenz or C. Romero after a wasting illness on their way back from wheeling Burt F.S. to a meeting in Kenmore Square, mostly from the side of the back they'd seen him, wearing a back-split tux and sombrero w/ balls, and apparently officially relapsed, back Out There, drunk as a maroon, so totally legless when they saw him he was doing a drunk's old hurricane-walk, fighting his way from parking meter to parking meter and clinging to each parking meter. Wade McDade here thinks to insert that the confirmed scuttlebutt is that E.M.P.H.H. is getting ready to rent out Unit #3 to a long-term mental-health agency caring for people with incapacitating agoraphobia, and that everybody at the House is speculating on what a constantly crowded and cabin-feverish place *that's* going to be, what with the terribleness of the predicted winter coming up. Diehl says his nasal sinus can always tell when it's going to snow, and his sinus is starting to predict at least flurries for maybe as early as tonight. They never think to tell Gately what day it is. That Gately can't communicate even this most basic of requests makes him want to scream. McDade, in what's either an intimate aside or a knife-twist at a Staffer who's in no position to enforce anything, confides that he and Emil Minty are arranging with Parias-Carbo — who works for an Ennet House alum at All-Bright Printing down near the Jackson-Mann School — for engraved-looking formal invitations for the agoraphobic folks in Unit #3 to all just come on out and over to Ennet House for a crowded noisy outdoor Welcome-to-the-E.M.P.H.H.-Neighborhood bash. And now Gately knows for sure it was McDade and Minty that put the HELP WANTED sign up under the window of the lady in Unit #4 that shouts for Help. The general level of tension in the room increases. Gavin Diehl clears his throat and says everybody says to say Gately's like wicked missed back at the House and everybody said to say ' 's up?' and that they hope the G-Man's up and back kicking residential ass very soon; and McDade produces an unsigned Get Well card from his pocket and puts it carefully through the railing's bars, where it lies next to Gately's arm and begins to open up from being folded and shoved in a pocket. It's clear the thing was shoplifted.

It's probably the pathetic unsigned folded hot card, but Gately's suddenly stricken by the heat of the waves of self-pity and resentment he feels about not only the card but about the prospect of these booger-chewing clowns not standing up to eyewitness for his *se offendendo* after he just tried to do his sober job on one of their behalf and is now lying here in a level of increasing dextral discomfort these limp punks couldn't imagine if they tried, getting ready to have to say no to grinning Pakistanis about his Disease's drug of choice with an invasive tube down his mouth and no notebook after he asked for one, and needing to shit and to know the day and no big black

894

nurse in view, and unable to move — it suddenly seems awful starry-eyed to be willing to look on the course of events as evidence of the protection and care of a Higher Power — it's a bit hard to see why a quote *Loving God* would have him go through the sausage-grinder of getting straight just to lie here in total discomfort and have to say no to medically advised Substances and get ready to go to jail just because Pat M. doesn't have the brass to make these selfish bottom-feeding dipshits stand up and do the right thing for once. The resentment and fear make cords stand out on Gately's purple neck, and he looks ferocious but not at all jolly. — Because what if God is really the cruel and vengeful figurant Boston AA swears up and down He isn't, and He gets you straight just so you can feel all the more keenly every bevel and edge of the special punishments He's got lined up for you? — Because why the fuck say no to a whole rubber bulbful of Demerol's somnolent hum, if these are the quote *rewards* of sobriety and rabidly-active work in AA? The resentment, fear and self-pity are almost narcotizing. Way beyond anything he'd felt when hapless Canadians punched or shot him. This was a sudden total bitter impotent Job-type rage that always sends any sober addict falling back and up inside himself, like vapor up a chimney. Diehl and McDade were backing away from him. As well they fucking might. Gately's big head felt hot and cold, and his pulse-line on the overhead monitor started to look like the Rockies.

The residents, between Gately and the door, wide-eyed, now suddenly parted to let someone pass. At first all Gately could see between them was the kidney-shaped plastic bedpan and a cylindrical syringe-snouted ketchup-bottlish thing with *FLEET* down the side in cheery green. It took this equipment a second to signify. Then he saw the nurse that came forward bearing the stuff, and his raging heart fell out of him with a thud. Diehl and McDade made hearty-farewell noises and melted out the door with the vague alacrity of seasoned drug-addicts. The nurse was no slot-mouthed penguin or booming mammy. This nurse looked like something out of a racy-nursewear catalogue, like somebody that had to detour blocks out of her way to avoid construction sites at lunchtime. Gately's projected image of his and this gorgeous nurse's union unfolded and became instantly grotesque: him prone and ass-up on the porch swing, she white-haired and angelic and bearing something away in a kidney-shaped pan to the towering pile behind the retirement-cottage. Everything angry in him evaporated as he got ready to just fucking die of mortification. The nurse stood there and twirled the bedpan on one finger and flexed the long Fleet cylinder a couple times and made an arc of clear fluid come out the tip and hang in the windowlight, like a gunslinger twirling his six-shooter around to casually show off, smiling in a way that simply snapped Gately's spine. He began to mentally recite the Serenity Prayer. When he moved he could smell his own sour smell. Not to mention the time and pain involved in rolling onto his left side and exposing his ass and pulling his knees to his chest with one arm — 'Hug those knees like they were your Sweetie, is what we say,' she said, putting a terribly soft cool hand on Gately's ass — without jostling the catheter or I.V.s, or the thick taped tube that went down his mouth to God knows where:

I was going to go back up to see about Stice's defenestration, to check on Mario and change my socks and examine my expression in the mirror for unintentional hilarity, to listen to Orin's phone-messages and then the protracted-death aria from *Tosca* once or twice. There is no music for free-floating misery like *Tosca*.

I was moving down the damp hall when it hit. I don't know where it came from. It was some variant of the telescopically self-conscious panic that can be so devastating during a match. I'd never felt quite this way off-court before. It wasn't wholly unpleasant. Unexplained panic sharpens the senses almost past enduring. Lyle had taught us this. You perceive things very intensely. Lyle's counsel had been to turn the perception and attention on the fear itself, but he'd shown us how to do this only on-court, in play. Everything came at too many frames per second. Everything had too many aspects. But it wasn't disorienting. The intensity wasn't unmanageable. It was just intense and vivid. It wasn't like being high, but it was still very: *lucid*. The world seemed suddenly almost edible, there for the ingesting. The thin skin of light over the baseboards' varnish. The cream of the ceiling's acoustic tile. The deerskin-brown longitudinal grain in the rooms' doors' darker wood. The dull brass gleam of the knobs. It was without the abstract, cognitive quality of Bob or Star. The turn-signal red of the stairwell's lit EXIT sign. Sleepy T. P. Peterson came out of the bathroom in a dazzling plaid robe, his face and feet salmon-colored from the showers' heat, and vanished across the hall into his room without seeing me wobbling, leaning against the cool mint wall of the hallway.

But the panic was there too, endocrinal, paralyzing, and with an overcognitive, bad-trip-like element that I didn't recognize from the very visceral on-court attacks of fear. Something like a shadow flanked the vividness and lucidity of the world. The concentration of attention did something to it. What didn't seem fresh and unfamiliar seemed suddenly old as stone. It all happened in the space of a few seconds. The familiarity of Academy routine took on a crushing cumulative aspect. The total number of times I'd schlepped up the rough cement steps of the stairwell, seen my faint red reflection in the paint of the fire door, walked the 56 steps down the hall to our room, opened the door and eased it gently back flush in the jamb to keep from waking Mario. I reexperienced the years' total number of steps, movements, the breaths and pulses involved. Then the number of times I would have to repeat the same processes, day after day, in all kinds of light, until I graduated and moved away and then began the same exhausting process of exit and return in some dormitory at some tennis-power university somewhere. Maybe the worst part of the cognitions involved the incredible volume of food I was going to have to consume over the rest of my life. Meal after meal, plus snacks. Day after day after day. Experiencing this food in toto. Just the thought of the meat alone. One megagram? Two megagrams? I experienced, vividly, the image of a broad cool well-lit room piled floor to ceiling with nothing but the lightly breaded chicken fillets I was going to consume over the next sixty years. The number of fowl vivisected for a lifetime's meat. The amount of hydrochloric acid and bilirubin and glucose and glycogen and gloconol produced and absorbed and produced in my body. And another, dimmer room, filled with the rising mass of the excrement I'd produce, the room's double-locked steel door gradually bowing outward with the mounting pressure. . . . I had to put my hand out against the wall and stand there hunched until the worst of it passed. I watched the floor dry. Its dull shine brightened behind me in the snowlight from the east window. The wall's baby blue was complexly filigreed with bumps and clots of paint. An unmopped glob of Kenkle's spit sat by the corner of V.R.5's door's jamb, quivering slightly as the door rattled in its frame. There were scuffles and thumps from upstairs. It was still snowing like hell.

I lay on my back on the carpet of Viewing Room 5, still on the second floor, fighting the sense that I'd either never been here before or had spent lifetimes just here. The entire room was panelled in a cool yellow shimmering material called Kevlon. The viewer took up half the south wall and was dead and gray-green. The carpet's green was close to this color, too. The instructional and motivational cartridges were in a large glass bookcase whose central shelves were long and whose top and bottom shelving tapered down to almost nothing. *Ovoid* would convey the case's shape. I had the NASA glass with my toothbrush in it balanced on my chest. It rose whenever I inhaled. I'd had the NASA glass since I was a little boy, and its decal of white-helmeted figures waving authoritatively through the windows of a prototype shuttle was faded and incomplete.

After a time, Sleepy T.P. Peterson put his wet-combed head in the door and said LaMont Chu wanted to know whether what was happening outside qualified as a blizzard. It took over a minute of my not saying anything for him to go away. The ceiling panels were grotesquely detailed. They seemed to come after you like some invasive E.T.A. patron backing you up against the wall at a party. The ankle throbbed dully in the snowstorm's low pressure. I relaxed my throat and simply let the excess saliva run postnasally back and down. The Moms's mother had been ethnic Québecois, her father Anglo-Canadian. The term used in the *Yale Journal of Alcohol Studies* for this man was *binge-drinker*. All my grandparents were deceased. Himself's middle name had been Orin, his father's own father's name. The V.R.'s entertainment cartridges were arrayed on wall-length shelves of translucent polyethylene. Their individual cases were all either clear plastic or glossy black plastic. My full name is Harold James Incandenza, and I am 183.6 cm. tall in stocking feet. Himself designed the Academy's indirect lighting, which is ingenious and close to full-spectrum. V.R.5 contained a large couch, four reclining chairs, a midsized recumbency, six green corduroy spectation-pillows stacked in a corner, three end tables, and a coffee table of mylar with inlaid coasters. The overhead lighting in every E.T.A. room came from a small carbon-graphite spotlight directed upward at a complexly alloyed reflecting plate above it. No rheostat was required; a small joystick controlled the brightness by altering the little spot's angle of incidence to the plate. Himself's films were arranged on the third shelf of the entertainment-case. The Moms's full name is Avril Mondragon Tavis Incandenza, Ed.D., Ph.D. She is 197 cm. tall in flats and still came up only to Himself's ear when he straightened and stood erect. For almost a month in the weight room, Lyle had been saying that the most advanced level of Vaipassana or 'Insight' meditation consisted in sitting in fully awakened contemplation of one's own death. I had held Big Buddy sessions in V.R.5 throughout the month of September. The Moms had grown up without a middle name. The etymology of the term *blizzard* is essentially unknown. The full-spectrum lighting system had been a labor of love from Himself to the Moms, who'd agreed to leave Brandeis and head up the Academy's academics and had an ethnic Canadian's horror of fluorescent light; but by the time the system had been installed and de-bugged, the gestalt of the Moms's lumiphobia had extended to all overhead lighting, and she never used her office's spot-and-plate system.

Petropolis Kahn put his large shaggy head in and asked what was all this brooha upstairs, the thumps and cryings-out. He asked whether I was going to breakfast. The scuttlebutt on breakfast was sausage-analog and OJ with palpable pulp, he said. I closed my eyes and recalled that I'd known Petropolis Kahn for three years and three months. Kahn went away. I could feel his head's withdrawal from the doorway: a very slight suction in the room's air. I needed to fart but had not so far farted. The atomic weight of carbon is 12.01 and change. A small and carefully monitored game of Eschaton slated for the mid-A.M., with (according to rumor) Pemulis himself as game-master, was certain to be snowed out. It had begun to occur to me, driving back from Natick on Tuesday, that if it came down to a choice between continuing to play competitive tennis and continuing to be able to get high, it would be a nearly impossible choice to make. The distant way in which this fact appalled me itself appalled me. The founder of the sub-14's'

Tunnel Club had been Heath Pearson as a very little boy. The rumor that Pemulis himself would don the beanie for the next Eschaton came from Kent Blott; Pemulis had been avoiding me ever since I returned from Natick on Tuesday — as if he sensed something. The woman behind the register at the Shell station last night had recoiled as I approached to present my card before pumping, as if she too had seen something in my expression I hadn't known was there. The *North American Collegiate Dictionary* claimed that any 'very heavy' snowstorm with 'high winds' qualified as a blizzard. Himself, for two years before his death, had had this delusion of silence when I spoke: I believed I was speaking and he believed I was not speaking. Mario averred that Himself had never accused him of not speaking. I tried to recall whether I had ever brought the subject up with the Moms. The Moms was at pains to be completely approachable on all subjects except Himself and what had been going on between her and Himself as Himself withdrew more and more. She never forbade questions about it; she just got so pained and blurry-faced that you felt cruel asking her anything. I considered whether Pemulis's cessation of the math-tutorials was perhaps an oblique affirmation, a kind of You Are Ready. Pemulis often communicated in a kind of esoteric code. It was true that I had kept mostly to myself in the room since Tuesday. The condensed *O.E.D.*, in a rare bit of florid imprecision, defined *blizzard* as 'A furious blast of frost-wind and blinding snow in which man and beast frequently perish,' claiming the word was either a neologism or a corruption of the French *blesser*, coined in English by a reporter for Iowa's *Northern Vindicator* in B.S. 1864. Orin alleged in Y.T.M.P. that when he took the Moms's car in the morning he sometimes observed the smeared prints of nude human feet on the inside of the windshield. V.R.5's heating duct's grille gave off a sterile hiss. All up and down the hall were sounds of the Academy coming to life, making competitive ablutions, venting anxiety and complaints at the possible blizzard outside — wanting to play. There was heavy foot-traffic in the third-floor hall above me. Orin was going through a period where he was attracted only to young mothers of small children. A hunched way: she hunches; you hunch. John Wayne had had a violent allergic reaction to a decongestant and had commandeered the WETA microphone and publicly embarrassed himself on Troeltsch's Tuesday broadcast, apparently, and had been taken to St. Elizabeth's overnight for observation, but had recovered quickly enough to come home and then finish ahead even of Stice in Wednesday's conditioning run. I missed the entire thing and was filled in by Mario on my return from Natick — Wayne had apparently said unkind things about various E.T.A. staff and administration, none of which anyone who knew Wayne and all he stood for had taken seriously. Relief that he was OK had dominated everyone's accounts of the whole incident; the Moms herself had apparently stayed by Wayne's side late into the night at St. E.'s, which Booboo felt was estimable and just like the Moms. Simply imagining the total number of times my chest will rise and fall and rise. If you want prescriptive specificity you go to a hard-ass: Sitney and Schneewind's *Dictionary of Environmental Sciences* required 12 cm./hour of continuous snowfall, minimum winds of 60 kph., and visibility of less than 500 meters; and only if these conditions obtained for more than three hours was it a blizzard; less than three hours was 'C-IV Squall.' The dedication and sustained energy that go into true perspicacity and expertise were exhausting even to think about.

It now lately sometimes seemed like a kind of black miracle to me that people could actually care deeply about a subject or pursuit, and could go on caring this way for years on end. Could dedicate their entire lives to it. It seemed admirable and at the same time pathetic. We are all dying to give our lives away to something, maybe. God or Satan, politics or grammar, topology or philately — the object seemed incidental to this will to give oneself away, utterly. To games or needles, to some other person. Something pathetic about it. A flight-from in the form of a plunging-into. Flight from exactly what? These rooms blandly filled with excrement and meat? To what purpose? This was why they started us here so young: to give ourselves away before the age when the questions *why* and *to what* grow real beaks and claws. It was kind, in a way. Modern German is better equipped for combining gerundives and prepositions than is its mongrel cousin. The original sense of *addiction* involved being bound over, dedicated, either legally or spiritually. To devote one's life, plunge in. I had researched this. Stice had asked whether I believed in ghosts. It's always seemed a little preposterous that Hamlet, for all his paralyzing doubt about everything, never once doubts the reality of the ghost. Never questions whether his own madness might not in fact be unfeigned. Stice had promised something boggling to look at. That is, whether Hamlet might be only *feigning* feigning. I kept thinking of the Film and Cartridge Studies professor's final soliloquy in Himself's unfinished *Good-Looking Men in Small Clever Rooms that Utilize Every Centimeter of Available Space with Mind-Boggling Efficiency*, the sour parody of academia that the Moms had taken as an odd personal slap. I kept thinking I really should go up and check on The Darkness. There seemed to be so many implications even to thinking about sitting up and standing up and exiting V.R.5 and taking a certain variable-according-to-stride-length number of steps to the stairwell door, on and on, that just the thought of getting up made me glad I was lying on the floor.

I was on the floor. I felt the Nile-green carpet with the back of each hand. I was completely horizontal. I was comfortable lying perfectly still and staring at the ceiling. I was enjoying being one horizontal object in a room filled with horizontality. Charles Tavis is probably not related to the Moms by actual blood. Her extremely tall French-Canadian mother died when the Moms was eight. Her father left their potato farm on 'business' a few months later and was gone for several weeks. He did this sort of thing with some frequency. A binge-drinker. Eventually there would be a telephone call from some distant province or U.S. state, and one of the hired men would go off to bail him out. From this disappearance, though, he returned with a new bride the Moms had known nothing about, an American widow named Elizabeth Tavis, who in the stilted Vermont wedding photo seems almost certainly to have been a dwarf — the huge square head, the relative length of the trunk compared to the legs, the sunken nasal bridge and protruding eyes, the stunted phocomelic arms around squire Mondragon's right thigh, one khaki-colored cheek pressed affectionately against his belt-buckle. C.T. was the infant son she'd brought to the new union, his father a ne'er-do-well killed in a freak accident playing competitive darts in a Brattleboro tavern just as they were trying to adjust the obstetric stirrups for the achondroplastic Mrs. Tavis's labor and delivery. Her smile in the wedding photo is homodontic. According to Orin, though, C.T. and the Moms claim Mrs. T. was not a true homodont the way — for instance — Mario is a true homodont. Every single one of Mario's teeth is a second bicuspid. So it was all rather up in the air. The account of the disappearance, darts-accident, and dental incongruity comes from Orin, who claimed to have decocted it all out of an extended one-sided conversation he had with a distraught C.T. in the waiting room of Brigham and Women's OB/GYN while the Moms was prematurely delivering Mario. Orin had been seven years old; Himself had been in the delivery room, where apparently Mario's birth was quite a touch-and-go thing. The fact that Orin was our one and only source for data shrouded the whole thing in further ambiguity, as far as I was concerned. Pinpoint accuracy had never been Orin's forte. The wedding photo was available for inspection, of course, and confirmed Mrs. Tavis as huge-headed and wildly short. Neither Mario nor I had ever approached the Moms on the issue, possibly out of fear of reopening psychic wounds from a childhood that had always sounded unhappy. All I knew for sure was that I had never approached her about it.

For their part, the Moms and C.T. have never represented themselves as anything other than unrelated but extremely close.

The attack of panic and prophylactic focus's last spasm now suddenly almost overwhelmed me with the intense horizontality that was all around me in the Viewing Room — the ceiling, floor, carpet, table-tops, the chairs' seats and the shelves at their backs' tops. And much more — the shimmering horizontal lines in the Kevlon wall-fabric, the very long top of the viewer, the top and bottom borders of the door, the spectation pillows, the viewer's bottom, the squat black cartridge-drive's top and bottom and the little push-down controls that protruded like stunted tongues. The seemingly endless horizontality of the couch's and chairs' and recumbency's seats, the wall of shelves' every line, the varied horizontal shelving of the ovoid case, two of every cartridge-case's four sides, on and on. I lay in my tight little sarcophagus of space. The horizontality piled up all around me. I was the meat in the room's sandwich. I felt awakened to a basic dimension I'd neglected during years of upright movement, of standing and running and stopping and jumping, of walking endlessly upright from one side of the court to the other. I had understood myself for years as basically vertical, an odd forked stalk of stuff and blood. I felt denser now; I felt more solidly composed, now that I was horizontal. I was impossible to knock down.

Gately's cognomen growing up and moving through public grades had been Bim or Bimmy, or The Bimulator, etc., from the acronymic B.I.M., 'Big Indestructible Moron.' This was on Boston's North Shore, mostly Beverly and Salem. His head had been huge, even as a kid. By the time he hit puberty at twelve the head seemed a yard wide. A regulation football helmet was like a beanie on him. His coaches had to order special helmets. Gately was worth the cost. Every coach past 6th grade told him he was a lock for a Division 1 college team if he bore down and kept his eye on the prize. Memories of half a dozen different neckless, buzz-cut, and pre-infarcted coaches all condense around a raspy emphasis on bearing down and predictions of a limitless future for Don G., Bimmy G., right up until he dropped out in high school's junior year.

Gately went both ways — fullback on offense, outside linebacker on D. He was big enough for the line, but his speed would have been wasted there. Already carrying 230 pounds and bench-pressing well over that, Gately clocked a 4.4 40 in 7th grade, and the legend is that the Beverly Middle School coach ran even faster than that into the locker room to jack off over the stopwatch. And his biggest asset was his outsized head. Gately's. The head was indestructible. When they needed yards, they'd shift to isolate Gately on one defender and get him the ball and he'd lower his head and charge, eyes on the turf. The top of his special helmet was like a train's cowcatcher coming at you. Defenders, pads, helmets, and cleats bounced off the head, often in different directions. And the head was fearless. It was like it had no nerve endings or pain receptors or whatever. Gately amused teammates by letting them open and close elevator doors on the head. He let people break things over the head — lunchboxes, cafeteria trays, bespectacled wienies' violin cases, lacrosse sticks. By age thirteen he never had to buy beers: he'd bet some kid a six he could take a shot with this or that object to the head. His left ear is permanently kind of gnarled from elevator-door impacts, and Gately favors a kind of long-sided Prince Valiantish bowl-cut to help cover the misshapen ear. One cheekbone still has a dented violet cast from 10th grade when a North Reading kid at a party bet him a twelve-pack on a shot with a sock full of nickels and then clocked him under the eye with it instead of the skull. It took Beverly's whole offensive line to pull Gately off what was left of the kid. The juvenile line on Gately was that he was totally jolly and laid-back and easygoing up to a certain point but that if you crossed that point with him you better be able to beat a 4.4 40.

He was always kind of a boys' boy. He had a jolly ferocity about him that scared girls. And he had no idea how to deal with girls except to try and impress them by letting them watch somebody do something to his head. He was never what you'd call a ladies' man. At parties he was always at the center of the crowd that drank instead of dancing.

It was surprising, maybe, given Gately's size and domestic situation, that he wasn't a bully. He wasn't kindly or heroic or a defender of the weak; it's not like he stepped kindly in to protect wienies and misfits from the predations of those kids that were bullies. He just had no interest in brutalizing the weak. It's still not clear to him if this was to his credit or not. Things might have been different if the M.P. had ever knocked Gately around instead of focusing all his attention on the progressively weaker Mrs. G.

He smoked his first duBois at age nine, a hard little needle-thin joint bought off jr.-high niggers and smoked with three other grade-school football players in a vacant summer cottage one had the key to, watching broadcast-televised niggers run amok in a flaming L.A. CA after some Finest got home-movied crewing on a nigger in the worst way. Then his first real drunk a few months later, after he and the players'd hooked up with an Orkin man that liked to get kids all blunt on screwdrivers and that wore brownshirts and jackboots in his off-hours and lectured them about Zog and *The Turner Diaries* while they'd drink the OJ and vodka he'd bought them and look at him blandly and roll their eyes at each other. Soon none of the football players Gately hung with were interested in much of anything except trying to get high and holding air-guitar and pissing contests and talking theoretically about Xing big-haired North Shore girls, and trying to think up things to break over Gately's head. They all had like domestic situations too. Gately was the only one of them truly dedicated to football, and that was probably just because he'd been told over and over that he had real talent and limitless futures. He was classified Attention-Deficit and Special-Ed. from grade school on, with particular Deficits in 'Language Arts,' but that was at least partly because Mrs. G. could barely read and Gately wasn't interested in making her feel worse. And but there was no Deficit in his attention to ball, or to cold foamers or screwdrivers or high-resin desBois, or especially to applied pharmacology, not once he'd done his first Quaalude[362] at age thirteen.

Just as Gately's whole recall of his screwdriver-and-sinsemilla beginnings tends to telescope into one memory of pissing orange juice into the Atlantic (he and the blunt cruel Beverly players and bullies he partied with drinking whole quarts of throat-warming OJ at a shot and standing ankle-deep in grit on a North Shore shore, facing east and sending long arcs of legal-pad-yellow piss into onrushing breakers that came in and creamed around their feet, the foam warm and yellow-shot with their piss — like spitting into the wind — Gately at the podium had started saying it turns out he was pissing on himself right from the start, with alcohol), in just the same way, the whole couple years before he discovered oral narcotics, the whole period 13–15 when he was a devotee of Quaaludes and Hefenreffer-brand beer collapses and gathers itself under what he still recalls as 'The Attack of the Killer Sidewalks.' Quaaludes and Hefenreffer also marked Gately's entree into a whole new rather more sinister and less athletic social set at B.M.S., one member of which was Trent Kite,[363] a dyed-in-wool laptop-carrying wienie, chinless and with a nose like a tapir, and pretty much the last fanatical Grateful Dead fan under age forty on the U.S. East Coast, whose place of honor in the sinister Beverly Middle School drug-set was due entirely to his gift for transforming the kitchen of any vacationing parents' house into a rudimentary pharmaceutical laboratory, using like BBQ-sauce bottles as Erlenmeyer Flasks and microwave ovens to cyclize OH and carbon into three-ring compounds, synthesizing methylenedioxy psychedelics[364] from nutmeg and sassafras oil, ether from charcoal-starter, designer meth from Tryptophan and L-Histidine, sometimes using only a gas-top range and parental Farberware, able even to decoct usable concentrations of tetra-hydrofruan from PVC Pipe Cleaner — which at that time best of British luck ordering tetrahydrofruan from any chemical company in the 48 contigs/6 provinces without getting paid an immediate visit by D.E.A. guys in three-piece suits and reflecting shades — and then using the tetrahydrofruan and ethanol and any protein-binding catalyst to turn plain old Sominex into something just one H_3C molecule away from good old biphasic metha-qualone, a.k.a. the intrepid Quaalude. Kite had called his Quaalude-isotopes 'QuoVadis,' and they were a great favorite for 13–15-year-old Bimmy G. and the slouched sharp-haired sinister set he dropped Ludes and QuoVadises with, washing them down with Hefenreffers, resulting in a kind of mnemonic brown-out where the entire two-year interval — the same interval during which the ex-M.P. found somebody else, a Newburyport divorcée who apparently put up a more sporting fight than Mrs. G., and decamped in his sticker-covered Ford with his seaman's bag and pea-coat — the whole period's become in Gately's sober memory just the vague era of The Attack of the Killer Sidewalks. Quaaludes and 16-oz. Hefenreffers awakened Gately and his new droogs to the usually-dormant-but-apparently-ever-lurking ill will of innocent-seeming public sidewalks everywhere. You didn't have to be brainy Trent Kite to figure out the equation (Quaaludes) + (not even that many beers) = getting whapped by the nearest sidewalk — as in you're walking innocently along down a sidewalk and out of nowhere the sidewalk comes rushing up to meet you: WHAP. Happened time after fucking time. It made the whole crew resent having to walk anywhere on QuoVadises because of not having driver's licenses yet, which gives you some idea of the sum-total I.Q. brought to bear on the problem of the Attacks. A tiny permanent cast in his left eye and what looks like a chin-dimple are Gately's legacy from the period before moving up to Percocets, which one advantage of the move deeper into oral narcs was that Percocets + Hefenreffers didn't allow you even enough upright mobility to make you vulnerable to sidewalks' ever-lurking ill will.

It was amazing that none of this stuff seemed much to hurt Gately's performance playing ball, but then he was as devoted to football as he was to oral CNS-depressants. At least for a while. He had disciplined personal rules back then. He absorbed Substances only at night, after practice. Not so much as a fractional foamer between 0900h. and 1800h. during the seasons of practice and play, and he settled for just a single duBois on Thursday evenings before actual games. During football season he ruled himself with an iron hand until the sun set, then threw himself on the mercy of sidewalks and the somnolent hum. He used class to catch up on REM-sleep. By freshman year he was starting on the Beverly-Salem H.S. Minutemen Varsity and was on academic probation. Most of the sinister set he'd hung with were expelled for truancy or trafficking or worse by sophomore year. Gately kept hanging in and on til seventeen.

But Quaaludes and QuoVadis and Percocets are lethal in terms of homework, especially washed down with Hefenreffer, and extra-especially if you're academically ambivalent and A.D.D.-classified and already using every particle of your self-discipline protecting football from the Substances. And — unhappily — high school is totally unlike higher education in terms of major-sport coaches' influence over instructors, athletes-and-grades-wise. Kite got Gately through math and Special Ed. science, and the French teacher was getting her strabysmic eyeballs fucked out by the Minutemen's tanned lounge-lizard of an Offensive Coordinator on the behalf of Gately and a semi-retarded tight end. But English just fucking killed him, Gately. All four of the English teachers the Athletic Dept. tried Gately on had this *sieg-heil* idea that it was somehow cruel to pass a kid that couldn't do the work. And the Athletic Dept. pointing out to them that Gately had an especially challenging domestic situation and that flunking Gately and rendering him ineligible for ball would eliminate his one reason even to stay on in school — these were to no, like, aveil. English was his sink-or-swim situation, what he then termed his 'Water Lou.' Term papers he could more or less swing; the football coach had wienies on retainer. But the in-class themes and tests killed Gately, who simply didn't have enough will left over after sunset to choose like the crushingly dull *Ethan From* over QuoVadis and Hefenreffer. Plus by this time three different schools' authorities had him convinced he was basically dumb, anyway. But mostly it was the Substances. This one particular B.-S.H.S.-Athletic-Dept.-hired wienie of an English tutor spent a sophomore-year March's worth of evenings in Gately's company, and by Easter the kid weighed 95 pounds and had a nose-ring and hand-tremors and was placed by his frantic, functional parents in a juvenile-intervention rehab, where the wienie's whole first week of Withdrawal was spent in a corner reciting *Howl* in high-volume Chaucerian English. Gately flunked Sophomore Comp. in May and lost the fall's eligibility and withdrew from school for a year to preserve his junior season. And but then, without the only other thing he'd been devoted to, the psychic emergency-brake was off, and Gately's sixteenth year is still mostly a gray blank, except for his mother's new red chintz TV-watching couch, and also the acquaintance of an accommodating Rite-Aid pharmacist's assistant with disfiguring eczema and serious gambling debts. Plus memories of terrible rear-ocular itching and of a basic diet of convenience-store crud, plus the vegetables from his mother's vodka glass, while she slept. When he finally returned for his sophomore year of class and junior year of ball at seventeen and 284 lbs., Gately was enervated, flabby, apparently narcoleptic, and on a need-schedule so inflexible that he needed 15 mg. of good old oxycodone hydrochloride out of his pocket's Tylenol bottle every three hours to keep the shakes off. He was like a huge confused kitten out on the field — the coach made him go in for P.E.T. Scans, fearing M.S. or Lou Gehrig's — and even the Classic Comics version of *Ethan From* was now beyond his abilities; and good old Kite was gone by that last September of Unsubsidized Time, admitted early on a full ride in Comp. Science by Salem State U., meaning Gately was now on his own in remedial math and chem. On offense, Gately lost his starting spot in the third game to a big clear-eyed freshman the coach said showed nearly limitless potential. Then Mrs. Gately suffered her cirrhotic hemorrhage and cerebral-blood thing in late October, just before the midterms Gately was getting ready to fail. Bored-eyed guys in white cotton blew blue bubbles and loaded her in the back of a leisurely sirenless ambulance and took her first to the hospital and then to a Medicaid L.T.I.[365] out across the Yirrell Beach span in Pt. Shirley. The backs of Gately's eyes were too itchy for him to even be able to stand out on the red pocked stoop's steps and see to wave adios. The first gasper he ever smoked was that day, a 100 out of a half-finished pack of his mother's generics, that she left. He didn't even ever go back to B.-S.H.S. to clean out his lockers. He never played organized ball again.

I may have been dozing. Some more heads came and awaited response and left. I may have dozed. It occurred to me that I didn't have to eat if I was not hungry. This presented itself as almost a revelation. I hadn't been hungry in over a week. I could remember when I was always hungry, constantly hungry.

Then at some point Pemulis's head appeared in the doorway, his strange twin-towered A.M. cowlick bobbing as he looked back over each shoulder out into the hall. His right eye was either twitchy or swollen from sleep; something was wrong with it.

'Mmyellow,' he said.

I pretended to shade my eyes. 'Howdy there stranger.'

It is not Pemulis's way to apologize or explain or worry that you might think ill of him. In this he reminded me of Mario. This almost regal lack of insecurity is hard to put together with his crippling neurasthenia on-court.

''s up?' he said, not moving from the doorway.

I could see my asking him where he'd been all week leading to so many different possible responses and further questions that the prospect was almost overwhelming, so enervating I could barely get out that I'd just been lying here on the floor.

'Lying here is all,' I told him.

'So I just got told,' he said. 'The Petropulator mentioned hysterics.'

It was almost impossible to shrug lying supine on thick shag. 'See for yourself,' I said.

Pemulis came all the way in. He became the only thing in the room that understood itself as basically vertical. He didn't look very good; his color wasn't good. He had not shaved, and a dozen little black bristles jutted from the ball of his chin. He gave the impression of chewing gum even though he was not chewing gum.

He said 'Thinking?'

'The opposite. Thought-prophylaxis.'

'Feeling a little punk?'

'Can't complain.' I rolled my eyes up at him.

He made a sharp glottal stop. He moved toward the periphery of my vision and fit himself into the seam of two walls behind me; I heard him sliding down to assume the back-supported squat he sometimes liked.

The Petropulator was Petropolis Kahn. I was thinking of the final film-lecture in *Good-Looking Men in Small Clever Rooms* . . . and then of C.T.'s misadventure at Himself's funeral. The Moms had had Himself interred in her family's traditional plot in L'Islet Province. I heard a whoop and two crashes directly overhead. My rib cage contracted and expanded.

'Incster?' Pemulis said after a time.

A noteworthy thing turned out to be that the mound of earth on a freshly-filled grave seems airy and risen and plump, like dough.

'Hal?' Pemulis said.

'Javol.'

'We've got some really important interfacing to do, brother.'

I didn't say anything. There were too many potential responses, both witty ones and earnest ones. I could hear Pemulis's cowlicks brush each wall as he looked to either side, and the slight sound of a small zipper being played with.

'I'm thinking we could go someplace discreet and really interface.'

'I'm a highly tuned horizontal antenna tuned in to you lying right here.'

'I was meaning could we go somewheres.'

'So this urgency all of a sudden?' I was trying to make my intonation Jewish-motherish, that melodic dip-rise-dip. 'All week: not a call, not a card. Now I should hear this about urgency?'

'Seen your Mums around lately?'

'Haven't seen her all week. Doubtless she's over helping C.T. arrange a weather-venue.' I paused. 'I haven't seen him all week either, come to think,' I said.

'The Eschaton's a no-go,' Pemulis said. 'The map's a mess out there.'

'We're going to get an announcement about the Québec kids very soon, I can feel it,' I said. 'I'm that highly tuned in this position.'

'What say let's skip the sausage-analog and whip down to Steak 'N Sundae and eat.'

There was an extended pause as I ran a response-tree. Pemulis was zipping and unzipping something with a short zipper. I couldn't decide. I finally had to choose almost at random. 'I'm trying to cut down on patronizing places with "'N" in their name.'

'Listen.' I heard his knees creak as he leaned in toward the top of my head. 'About the *tu-savez-quoi* —'

'The Eeday Emmay Eezay. The synthetic bacchanal. That's definitely off, Mike. Talk about the map being a mess.'

'That's part of what we need to interface about, if you'd get off your literally your ass here.'

I spent a minute watching the NASA glass fall and rise. 'Don't even start, M.M.'

'What start?'

'We're on hiatus, remember? We're living like Shi'ite Moslems for the thirty days you miraculously blarneyed the guy into giving us.'

'Blarney wasn't why we got it, Inc, is the thing.'

'And now, what, twenty days to go. We're going to produce urine like a mullah's babe, we agreed.'

'This isn't —' Pemulis started.

I farted, but it didn't produce a noise. I was bored. I couldn't remember a time when Pemulis had bored me. 'And I do not need you launching temptation-rhetoric my way,' I said.

Keith Freer appeared in the doorway, leaning against the jamb with his bare arms crossed. He was still wearing the weird unitard he slept in, which made him look like someone who tore phone books in half at a sideshow.

'Does somebody have an explanation why there's human flesh on the hall window upstairs?' he said.

'We're con*vers*ing here,' Pemulis told him.

I half sat up. 'Flesh?'

Freer looked down at me. 'This is nothing to laugh at I don't think Hal. There's I swear to fucking God a human strip of forehead-flesh upstairs on the hall window, and what looks like two eyebrows, and bits of nose. And now Tall Paul says down in the lobby Stice was seen coming out of the infirmary wearing something out of Zorro.'

Pemulis was completely vertical, standing again; I could hear his knees as he rose. 'It's like a tête-à-tête in here, brother. We're in here bunkered, mano a —'

'Stice got stuck to the window,' I explained, lying all the way back down. 'Kenkle and Brandt were going to detach him with warm water from a janitorial bucket.'

Pemulis said 'How do you get stuck to a window?'

'Well from the looks it looks like they detached half his face from his head,' Freer said, feeling at his own forehead and shuddering a little.

Kieran McKenna's little porcine snout appeared in a gap under Freer's arm. He still wore his stupid full-head gauze wrap for his supposed bruised skull. 'Did you guys get to see The Darkness? Gopnik said he looks like a piece of cheese pizza where somebody tore the cheese off. Gopnik said Troeltsch is charging two bucks a look.' He ran off toward the stairwell without waiting for a reply, his pocket jingling madly. Freer looked at Pemulis and opened his mouth, then apparently reconsidered and followed off down the hall. We could hear a couple of sarcastic whistles at Freer's unitard.

Pemulis reappeared at the top of my vision; his right eye was definitely twitching. 'This is what I meant about going someplace discreet. When have I ever urgently asked you to dialogue before, Inc?'

'Certainly not within the last few days, Mike, that's for sure.'

There was an extended pause. I raised my hands over my face and looked at their shapes against the indirect lights.

Pemulis finally said 'Well, I'm going to go make sure I eat before I have to see Stice without a fucking forehead.'

'Have an analog for me,' I said. 'Let me know if there's word on the meet. I'll eat if I'm going to have to play.'

Pemulis licked his palm and tried to get his cowlicks to behave. From my vantage he was high overhead and upside-down. 'So are you going to get up and go up and get dressed and stand on one foot with that opera thing on at some point? Because I could eat and then come up. We can tell Mario we need to mano-à-tête.'

Now I was making a cage of my hands and watching the light through its shape as I rotated it. 'Will you do me a favor? Get *Good-Looking Men in*

Small Clever Rooms That Utilize Every Centimeter of Available Space with Mind-Boggling Efficiency out for me. It's about a dozen cartridges in from the right on the third shelf down in the entertainment-case. Cue it up to about 2300, 2350 maybe? The last five minutes or so.'

'The third shelf down,' I said as he scanned, tapping a foot. 'They've got all Himself's stuff together on the third shelf.'

He scanned. '*Baby Pictures of Famous Dictators? Fun with Teeth? Annular Fusion Is Our Fiend?* I haven't even heard of half your Dad's shit that's here.'

'It's *Friend*, not *Fiend*. Either it's mislabeled or the label's peeling. And they're supposed to be alphabetized. It ought to be right next to *Flux in a Box.*'

'And me using the poor guy's lab,' Pemulis said. He loaded the player and turned on the viewer, his knees popping again as he squatted to set the cue to 2350. The huge screen hummed in a low pitch that ascended as it began to warm up, the screen taking on a milky blue aspect like the eye of a dead bird. Pemulis's feet were bare and I looked at the calluses on his heels. He tossed the cartridge's case carelessly on a couch or chair behind me and looked down. 'What the fuck's *Fun with Teeth* supposed to be about?'

I tried to shrug against the friction of the carpet. 'Pretty much what it says it's about.' The funeral had been held on 5 or 6 April in St. Adalbert, a small town built around spud-storage facilities fewer than five clicks west of the Great Concavity. We'd all had to fly up by way of Newfoundland because of the volume of waste-displacement launches that spring. And commercial airlines hadn't yet had data on high-altitude Dioxin levels over the Concavity. Cloud-cover prevented our seeing much of the New Brunswick coast, which I'm told was a mercy. What happened at the funeral service itself was simply that a circling gull scored a direct white hit on the shoulder of C.T.'s blue blazer, and that when he opened his mouth in shock at the direct hit, a large blue-bodied fly flew right into his mouth and was hard to extract. Several persons laughed. It was no huge or dramatic thing. The Moms probably laughed hardest of anyone.

The TP's tracker chugged and clicked, and the viewer bloomed. Pemulis had been wearing parachute pants and a tam-o'-shanter and lensless spectacles, but no shoes. The cartridge started close to what I'd wanted to review, the protagonist's climactic lecture. Paul Anthony Heaven, all 50 kilos of him, gripping the lectern with both hands so you could see that he was missing his thumbs, the sad dyed strands combed over his bald spot visible because he had his head down, reading the lecture in the deadening academic monotone that Himself so loved. The monotone was the reason why Himself used Paul Anthony Heaven, a nonprofessional, by trade a data-entry drone for Ocean Spray, in anything that required a deadening institutional presence — Paul Anthony Heaven had also played the threatening supervisor in *Wave Bye-Bye to the Bureaucrat*, the Massachusetts State Commissioner for Beach and Water Safety in *Safe Boating Is No Accident*, and a Parkinsonian corporate auditor in *Low-Temperature Civics*.

'Thus the Flood's real consequence is revealed to be desiccation, generations of hydrophobia on a pandemic scale,' the protagonist was reading aloud. Peterson's *The Cage* was running on a large screen behind the lectern. A number of shots of undergraduates with their heads on their desks, reading their mail, making origami animals, picking at their faces with blank intensity, established that the climactic lecture wasn't coming off as all that climactic to the audience within the film. 'We thus become, in the absence of death as teleologic end, ourselves desiccated, deprived of some essential fluid, aridly cerebral, abstract, conceptual, little more than hallucinations of God,' the academic read in a deadly drone, his eyes never leaving his lectern's text. The art-cartridge critics and scholars who point to the frequent presence of audiences inside Himself's films, and argue that the fact that the audiences are always either dumb and unappreciative or the victims of some grisly entertainment-mishap betrays more than a little hostility on the part of an *'auteur'* pegged as technically gifted but narratively dull and plotless and static and not entertaining enough — these academics' arguments seem sound as far as they go, but they do not explain the incredible pathos of Paul Anthony Heaven reading his lecture to a crowd of dead-eyed kids picking at themselves and drawing vacant airplane- and genitalia-doodles on their college-rule note-pads, reading stupefyingly turgid-sounding shit[366] — 'For while *clinamen* and *tessera* strive to revive or revise the dead ancestor, and while *kenosis* and *daemonization* act to repress consciousness and memory of the dead ancestor, it is, finally, artistic *askesis* which represents the contest proper, the battle-to-the-death with the loved dead' — in a monotone as narcotizing as a voice from the grave — and yet all the time weeping, Paul Anthony Heaven, as an upward hall full of kids all scan their mail, the film-teacher not sobbing or wiping his nose on his tweed sleeve but silently weeping, very steadily, so that tears run down Heaven's gaunt face and gather on his underslung chin and fall from view, glistening slightly, below the lectern's frame of sight. Then this too began to seem familiar.

He hadn't in the beginning burgled, Gately, as a full-time drug addict, though he did sometimes promote small valuables from the apartments of the strung-out nurses he X'd and copped samples from. After the bailout from school, Gately worked full-time for a time for a North Shore bookmaker, a guy that also owned several titty clubs down Rte. 1 in Saugus, Whitey Sorkin, that had sort of casually befriended him when Gately was still playing high-profile ball. His professional association with Whitey Sorkin continued part-time even after Gately discovered his real B&E vocation, though he tended more and more toward less taxing nonviolent crime.

But from age like eighteen to twenty-three, Gately and the prenominate Gene Fackelmann — a towering, slope-shouldered, wide-hipped, prematurely potbellied, oddly priapistic, and congenitally high-strung Dilaudid addict with a walrusy mustache that seemed to have a nervous life of its own — these two served as like Whitey Sorkin's operatives in the field, taking bets and phoning them in to Saugus, delivering winnings, and collecting debts. It was never clear to Gately why Whitey Sorkin was called Whitey, because he spent a huge amount of time under ultraviolet lamps as part of an esoteric cluster-headache-treatment regimen and so was the constant shiny color of a sort of like dark soap, with almost the same color and coin-of-the-realm classic profile as the cheery young Pakistani M.D. who'd told Gately at Our Lady of Solace Hospital in Beverly how Teddibly Soddy he was that Mrs. G.'s cirrhosis and cirrhotic stroke had left her at roughly the neurologic level of a Brussels sprout and then given him public-transportation directions to the Point Shirley L.T.I.

Eugene ('Fax') Fackelmann, who'd dropped out of the Lynn MA educational system at like ten, had met Whitey Sorkin through the same eczematic, gamble-happy pharmacist's assistant Gately had first met Sorkin through. Gately was now no longer called Bimmy or Doshka. He was Don now, nicknameless. Sometimes Donny. Sorkin referred to Gately and Fackelmann as his Twin Towers. They were more or less Sorkin's paid muscle. Except not in any sort of way important crime figures' paid muscle is portrayed in popular entertainment. They didn't stand impassively flanking Sorkin at crime-figure meetings or light his cigar or call him 'Boss' or anything. They weren't his bodyguards. In fact they weren't physically around him that much; they usually dealt with Sorkin and his Saugus office and secretary via beepers and cellular phones.[367]

And while they did collect debts for Sorkin, including bad debts (especially Gately), it's not like Gately went around breaking debtors' kneecaps. Even the threat of coercive violence was pretty rare. Partly, Gately and Fackelmann's sheer size was enough to keep delinquencies from getting out of hand. And partly it was that everybody involved usually knew each other — Sorkin, his bettors and debtors, Gately and Fackelmann, other drug addicts (who sometimes bet, or more often dealt with Gately and Fackelmann for guys that did), even the North Shore Finest's Vice guys, many of whom also sometimes bet with Sorkin because he gave the Finest special civil-servant reductions on vigorish. It was all like this community. Usually Gately's job on bad debts or delinquent vig was to go around to the debtor at whatever bar the guy watched satellite sports at and just inform him that the debt was threatening to get out of hand — making the debt itself seem like the delinquent party — and that Whitey was concerned about it, and work out some arrangement or payment-plan with the guy. Then the young Gately'd go into the bar's head and cell-phone Sorkin and get his OK on whatever arrangement they'd worked out. Gately was laid-back and affable and never had a hard word for anybody, hardly. Nor did Whitey Sorkin: a lot of his bettors were old and steady customers, and lines of credit went with the territory. Most of the rare debt-trouble that called for size and coercion involved guys with a gambling problem, kind of pathetic furtive guys addicted to the rush of the bet, who got themselves in a hole and then tried suicidally to bet their way out of the hole, and who'd bet with several bookies at once, and who'd lie and agree to payment-arrangements they had no intention of sticking to, suicidally betting they could keep all their debts in the air until they could square themselves with the major long-shot score they were always sure was around the corner. These types were painful, because usually Gately knew the debtors and they'd exploit his knowing them and beg and weep and tug at both Gately's and Whitey Sorkin's heart-strings with tales of loved ones and wasting illnesses. They'd sit there and look into Gately's eyes and lie and believe their own lies, and Gately would have to call in the debtors' lies and sob-stories and get Sorkin's explicit decision on if to believe them and what to do. These types were Gately's first exposure to the concept of real addiction and what it can turn someone into; he hadn't yet connected the concept to drugs really, except coke-heads and hardcore needle-jockeys, who at that point all seemed to him just as furtive and pathetic as the gambling-addicts, in their own way. These sob-story-, one-more-chance-types were also the types that put Whitey Sorkin through hell in terms of emotionally, causing Whitey cluster headaches and terrible cranio-facial neuralgia, and at a certain point Sorkin used to start adding (to the delinquent skeet, the vig, and the interest) extra charges for his own required intake of Cafergot[368] spansules and UV light and visits to Enfield MA's National Cranio-Facial Pain Foundation. The use of Gately and Fack-elmann's rump-roast-sized fists in actual hands-on coercion got called for only when a compulsive debtor's lies and hole got serious enough that Sor-kin became willing to forgo the guy's patronage in the future. At this sort of point, Whitey Sorkin's business-objective became to somehow induce the addicted debtor to cover his debts to Sorkin before the debtor covered his debts to any of the other books he was into, which meant for Sorkin that he had to vividly demonstrate to the debtor that Sorkin's was the least pleasant hole to be in and the most important one to get out of. Enter the Twin Towers. The violence was to be tightly controlled and gradually progressive in like stages. The first round of incentivizing hose-work — a light beating, maybe a broken digit or two — usually fell to Gene Fackelmann, not only because he was the naturally crueler of the Twin Towers and rather liked putting a digit in a car door, but also because he had a controlled restraint

Gately lacked: Sorkin found that once Gately got started in physically on somebody it was like something ferocious and uncontrolled on a slope inside the big kid got dislodged and started to roll on its own, and sometimes Gately wouldn't be able to stop himself before the debtor was reduced to a condition where he wasn't even going to be able to raise his head, much less funds, at which point not only did Sorkin have to write off the debt but the big kid Donny'd get so guilty and remorseful he'd triple his drug-intake and be no use to fucking nobody for a week. Sorkin learned how to use his Towers to maximize their strengths. Fackelmann got the first-round light work for coercive collections, but Gately was better than Fax at negotiating arrangements with guys so it never had to come to violence. And there were certain harder cases, cases that laid Sorkin out in bed with cranio-facial stress for days at a time because they were hard-case addicts that were either so far gone or so deep in so many holes that Fackelmann's light cruelty didn't resolve the situation. At an extreme point with some of these cases Sorkin got to a point where he was willing to forgo not only the debtor's future patronage but also the remittance due; at a certain point the goal was to minimize future *other* hard cases by making it clear that W. Sorkin was one book you couldn't just flagrantly stay in the hole with and lie to for month after month without having your map seriously fucking reconfigured. Here again, in this-type case Gately's internal out-of-control slope of ferocity was superior to Fackelmann's easy but ultimately shallow sadism.[369]

W. Sorkin, like most psychosomatic-level neurotics, was spiteful to his enemies and overgenerous to his friends. Gately and Fackelmann each received 5% vig on the 10% vigorish Sorkin took on every bet, and Sorkin made over $200,000 worth of book all over the North Shore on a week's pro ball alone, which for most diplomaless young Americans 1,000+ per pre-millennial week would have been a very handsome living, but for the Twin Towers' rigid physical scheduling of narcotics needs was not even 60% enough, weekly. Gately and Fackelmann moonlighted, and for a while separately — Fackelmann's sideline with I.D.s and creative personal checking, Gately working freelance Security for large card games and small drug-deliveries — but even before they were a real crew they copped as a unit, as in together, plus once in a moon with poor old V. Nucci, for whom Gately also occasionally held the rope on late-night Osco-and-Rite-Aid-skylight missions, his entree to formal burglary proper. The fact that Gately was devoted to Percocets and Bam-Bams and Fackelmann to Dilaudid allowed them a high level of trust with each other's stashes. Gately would do Blues, which had to be injected, only when no oral narcs were to be got and he was face to face with early Withdrawal. Gately feared and despised needles and was terrified of the Virus, which in those days was laying out needle-jockeys left and right. Fackelmann would cook up for Gately and tie him off and let

Gately watch closely as he took the plastic wrap off a mint-new syringe and needle-cartridge Fackelmann could get with a fake Medicaid Iletin[370] I.D. for diabetes mellitus. The worst thing about Dilaudid for Gately was that the hydromorphone's transit across the blood-brain barrier created a terrible five-second mnemonic hallucination where he was a gargantuan toddler in an XXL Fisher-Price crib in a sandy field under a storm-cloudy sky that bulged and receded like a big gray lung. Fackelmann would loosen the belt and stand back and watch Gately's eyes roll up as he broke a malarial sweat and stared up at the delusion's respiritic sky while his huge hands throttled the air in front him just like a toddler shakes at the bars of his crib. Then after five or so seconds the Dilaudid would cross over and kick, and the sky stopped breathing and turned blue. A Dilaudid nod made Gately mute and sodden for three hours.

Besides the maddening itch behind the eyes, Fackelmann didn't like oral narcotics because he said they gave him terrible sugar-cravings that his huge soft slumped weight wouldn't tolerate indulging. Not exactly the swiftest ship in Her Majesty's fleet in terms of like upstairs, Fackelmann was resistant to Gately's pointing out that Dilaudid also gave the Faxman terrible sugar-cravings, as did actually just about everything. The plain truth was that Fackelmann just really liked Dilaudid.

Then good old Trent Kite got the administrative Shoe from Salem State, who informed him he'd never study in the industry again, and Gately brought Kite into the crew, and Kite threw together some old-time Quo-Vadis for a small crew-warming party, and Fackelmann introduced Kite to pharmaceutical-grade Dilaudid, and Kite found a new friend for life, he said; and Kite and Fackelmann swiftly fell into the I.D.-, credit-history-and-furnished-luxury-apartment-scam, in which by this time Gately involved himself pretty much only as a hobby, preferring bold nighttime merchandise-promotion to fraud, which fraud tended to involve meeting the people you stole from, which Gately found slimy and kind of awkward.

Gately lay in the Trauma Ward in terrific infected pain, trying to Abide between cravings for relief by remembering a blinding white afternoon just after Xmas, when Fackelmann and Kite were off disposing of some of a furnished apartment's furnishings and Gately was killing time in the apartment laminating some false MA drivers licenses rush-ordered by rich Philips Andover Academy[371] kids for what turned out to be the last New Year's Eve of Unsubsidized Time. He'd been standing at an ironing board in the by now pretty much unfurnished apartment, ironing laminates onto the fake licenses, watching good old Boston U. play Clemson in the Ken-L-Ration-Magnavox-Kemper-Insurance Forsythia Bowl on a cumbersome first-generation Inter-Lace HDV hanging on the bare wall, the high-def viewer always now the last luxury furnishing to be fenced. The winter daylight through the penthouse windows was dazzling and fell across the viewer's big flat screen and made the players look bleached and ghostly. Through the windows off in the distance was the Atlantic O., gray and dull with salt. The B.U. punter was a hometown Boston kid the announcers kept inserting was a walk-on and an inspirational story that had never played a major sport until college and now was already one of the finest punt-specialists in N.C.A.A. history, and had the potential to be a lock for a pretty much limitless pro ball career if he bore down and kept his eye on the carrot. The B.U. punter was two years younger than Don Gately. Gately's big digits could barely fit around the iron's EZ-grip handle, and stooping over the ironing board made the small of his back ache, and he hadn't eaten anything except deep-fried stuff out of shiny plastic packaging for like a week, and the stink of the plastic laminates under the iron stunk wicked bad, and his big square face sagged lower and lower as he stared at the punter's ghostly digital image until he found himself starting to cry like a babe. It came out of emotional nowheres all of a sudden, and he found himself blubbering at the loss of organized ball, his one gift and other love, his own stupidity and lack of discipline, that blasted cocksucking *Ethan From,* his Mom's Sir Osis and vegetabilization and his failure after four years ever yet to visit, feeling suddenly lower than bottom-feeder-shit, standing over hot laminates and Polaroid squares and little stick-on D.M.V. letters for rich blond male boys, in the blazing winter light, blubbering amid fraudulent stink and tear-steam. It was two days later he got pinched for assaulting one bouncer with the unconscious body of another bouncer, in Danvers MA, and three months after that that he went to Billerica Minimum.

Entrepôt-bound, twitchy-eyed and checking both sides behind him as he comes, rounding the curve of Subdormitory B's hall with his stick and little solid frustum-shaped stool, Michael Pemulis sees at least eight panels of the drop-ceiling have somehow fallen out of their aluminum struts and are on the floor — some broken in that incomplete, hingey way stuff with fabric-content gets broken — including the relevant panel. No old sneaker is in evidence on the floor as he clears the panels to plant the stool, his incredibly potent Bentley-Phelps penlight in his teeth, looking up into the darkness of the struts' lattice.

Given the Faxter's historical proclavity for fraudulent scams, it was amazing to Gately that he didn't ever know how Fackelmann had been fraudulently getting over on Whitey Sorkin in all kinds of little ways almost from the start, and didn't even find it out until the not at all small scam with

Eighties Bill and Sixties Bob, which took place during the three months Gately was out on bail Sorkin had generously put up. By this time Gately had fallen in with two lesbian pharmaceutical-cocaine addicts he'd met at the gym doing upside-down sit-ups from the chin-up bar (the lesbians, not Gately, who was strictly from bench, curl, and squat). These vigorous girls ran a rather intriguing house-cleaning-and-key-copying-and-burglary operation in Peabody and Wakefield, and Gately had begun working heavy-merchandise-lifting and 4×4-vehicle-promotion for them, serious full-time burglary, as his taste for even the threat of violence diminished on account of remorse at the bouncer-damage he'd inflicted in that Danvers bar after just seven Hefenreffers and an innocent comment about the B.-S.H.S.'s Min-utemen's inferiority to the Danvers H.S. Roughriders; and Gately left more and more of Sorkin's transfer-and-collection work to Fackelmann, who by this time had gotten back into oral narcotics out of Virus-fears and stopped resisting the sugar-cravings he associated with oral narcs and gotten so fat and soft his shirtfront looked like an accordion when he sat down to eat Peanut M&M's and nod, and now also to a bad-news new guy Sorkin had lately befriended and put to work, a fuchsia-haired Harvard Square punk-type kid with a build like a stump and round black unblinking eyes, an old-fashioned street-junk needle-jockey that went by the moniker Bobby C or just 'C,' and liked to hurt people, the only I.V.-heroin addict Gately'd come across that actually preferred violence, with no lips at all and purple hair in three great towering spikes and little bare patches in the hair on his forearms — from constantly testing the edge on his boot-knife — and a leather jacket with way more zippers than anybody could ever need, and a pre-electric earring that hung way down and was a roaring skull in gold-plate flames.

Gene Fackelmann had, it turns out, for years been getting fraudulently over on Whitey Sorkin's bookmaking operation in all sorts of little ways that Gately and Kite (according to Kite) hadn't known about. Usually it was something like Fax taking long-shot action from marginal bettors not well known to Sorkin and not phoning the action in to Sorkin's secretary, and then, when the long-shot lost, collecting the skeet plus vig[372] from the bettor and rat-holing it all for himself. It had seemed to Gately after he found out about it a suicidal-type risk, since if any of these long-shots ever actually *won* Fack-elmann would be responsible for giving the bettor his winnings from 'Whitey' — meaning it would be Sorkin that would hear the complaint if Fackelmann didn't come up with the $ on his own and get it to the bettor — and the whole crew's pharmacological expenses meant they always existed on the absolutest margins of liquidity, at least that's what Gately and Kite (according to Kite) had always thought. It wasn't until Fackelmann's map had been presumably eliminated for keeps and Kite had returned from his long highatus and Gately and Kite were getting the late Fackelmann's stuff together to divvy up valuables and dump the rest and Gately found, taped to the underside of Fackelmann's porn-cartridge storage case, over $22,000 in mint-crisp O.N.A.N. currency, not until then that Gately realized that Fackelmann had through iron will kept unspent an emergency reserve skeet-payment stake for just such a worst-case possibility. Gately split this found Fackelmann-$ with Trent Kite, then but went and turned his half of it in to Sorkin, claiming it was all they'd found. It wasn't that he forked his half over to Sorkin out of any kind of fear — Sorkin would have regretfully had the C kid and his Nuck/fag crew demap him, Gately, too, along with Fackelmann, if he'd thought Gately had been part of Fax's scam — but out of guilt over having been clueless about his own fellow Twin Tower screwing Sorkin after Sorkin had been so neurasthenically over-generous to them both, and because Fackelmann's betrayal had ended up so hurting Sorkin and causing him so much psychosomatic grief that he'd spent a whole week in bed in Saugus in the dark with Lone Ranger–type sleep shades on, drinking VO and Cafergot and clutching his traumatized cranium and face, feeling betrayed and abandoned, he'd said, his whole faith in the human creature shaken, he'd wept to Gately over the cellular phone, after it all came out. Ultimately, Gately gave Sorkin his half of Fackelmann's secret $ mostly to try and cheer Sorkin up. Let him know somebody cared. He also did it for Fackelmann's memory, which he was mourning Fax's gruesome death even at the same time he cursed him for a liar and rat-punk. It was a time of moral confusion for Don G., and his half of the post-mortem $ seemed like the best he could do in terms of like a gesture. He didn't rat out that Kite had a whole other half, which Kite spent his half of the $ on Grateful Dead bootlegs and a portable semiconductor-refrigeration unit for his D.E.C. 2100's motherboard that upped his processing capacity to 32 mb^2 of RAM, roughly the same as an InterLace Disseminator-substation or an NNE Bell cellular SWITCHnet; though it wasn't two months before he'd pawned the D.E.C. and put it in his arm, and had become such a steeply-downhill-type Dilaudid-addict that when he signed on as Gately's new trusted associate for B&Es after Gately got out of Billerica the once-mighty Kite wasn't even able to dicky an alarm or shunt a meter, and Gately found himself the brains of the team, which it was a mark of his own high-angle decline that this fact didn't make him more nervous.

The R.N. that'd flushed his colon while Gately wept with shame is now back in the room with an M.D. Gately hasn't seen before. He lies there pinwheel-eyed from pain and efforts to Abide via memory. One eye has some sort of blurry sleep-goop film in it that won't blink or rub away. The room is filled with mournful gunmetal winter-P.M. light. The M.D. and gorgeous R.N. are doing something to the room's other bed, attaching something metally complex from out of a big case not unlike a good-table-silverware case, with molded purple velvet insides for metal rods and two half-circles of steel. The intercom dings. The M.D.'s got a beeper at his belt, an object with still more unhealthy associations. Gately hasn't exactly been asleep. The heat of his post-op fever makes his face feel tight, like standing too close to a fire. His right side's settled down to a sick ache like a kicked groin. Fackelmann's favorite phrase had been *'That's a goddamned lie!'* He'd used it in response to just about everything. His mustache always looked like it was getting ready to crawl off his lip. Gately's always despised facial hair. The former naval M.P. had had a great big yellow-gray mustache he waxed into two sharp protruding steer-horns. The M.P. was vain about his mustache and spent giant amounts of time clipping and grooming and waxing it. When the M.P. passed out, Gately used to come quietly up and gently push the stiff waxed sides of the mustache into crazy canted angles. Sorkin's new third field-operative C'd claimed to collect ears and to have a collection of ears. Bobby C with his lightless eyes and flat lipless head, like a reptile. The M.D. was one of those apprentice Residential M.D.s that looked about twelve, scrubbed and groomed to a dull pink shine. He radiated the bustling cheer they teach M.D.s how to radiate at you. He had a child's haircut, complete with spit-curl, and his thin neck swam in the collar of his white M.D.-coat, and his coat's pens' pocket-protector and the owlish glasses he kept pushing up, together with the little neck, gave Gately the sudden insight that most M.D.s and A.D.A.s and P.D./P.O.s and shrinks, the fearsomest authority figures in a drug addict's life, that these guys came from the pencil-necked ranks of the same weak-chinned wienie kids that drug addicts used to despise and revile and bully, as kids. The R.N. was so attractive in the gray light and goop-blur it was almost grotesque. Her tits were such that she had a little cleft of cleavage showing even over her R.N.'s uniform, which was not like a low-neckline thing. The milky cleavage that suggests tits like two smooth scoops of vanilla ice cream that your healthy-type girls all have probably got. Gately's forced to confront the fact that he's never once been with a really healthy girl, and not with even so much as a girl of any kind in sobriety. And then when she reaches way up to unscrew a bolt in some kind of steelish plate on the wall over the empty bed the like hemline of her uniform retreats up north so that the white stockings' rich violinish curves at the top of the insides of her legs in the white *LISLE* are visible in backlit silhouette, and an *EMBRASURE* of sad windowlight shines through her legs. The raw healthy sexuality of the whole thing just about makes Gately sick with longing and self-pity, and he wants to avert his head. The young M.D. is also staring at the lissome stretch and retreating hem, not even pretending to help with the bolt, missing as he goes to push up the glasses so that he stabs himself in the forehead. The M.D. and R.N. exchange several pieces of real technical medical language. The M.D. drops his clipboard twice. The R.N. either doesn't notice any of the sexual tension in the room because she's spent her whole life as the eye of a storm of sexual tension, or else she just pretends not to notice. Gately's almost positive the M.D.'s jacked off before to the thought of this R.N., and he feels sick that he totally empathizes with the M.D. It'd be *CIRCUMAMBIENT* sexual tension, would be the ghostword. Gately'd never even let an unhealthy strung-out-type female go into the head for at least an hour after he'd taken a dump in there, out of embarrassment, and now this sickening circumambient creature had with her own Fleet syringe and soft hands summoned a loose pathetic dump from the anus of Bimmy Gately, which anus she had thus seen close up, producing a dump.

It doesn't even register on Gately that it's spitting a little goopy sleet outside until he's made himself avert his head from the window and R.N. The ceiling's throbbing a little, like a dog when it's hot. The R.N. had told him, from behind, her name was Cathy or Kathy, but Gately wants to think of her as just the R.N. He can smell himself, a smell like sandwich-meat left in the sun, and feel greasy sweat purling all over his scalp, and his unshaved chin against his throat, and the tube taped into his mouth is tacky with the scum of sleep. The thin pillow is hot and he has no way to flip it over to the cool side of the pillow. It's like his shoulder's grown its own testicles and every time his heart beats some very small guy kicked him in them, the testicles. The M.D. sees Gately's open eyes and tells the nurse the gunshot patient is semiconscious again and is he Q'd for any kind of P.M. med. The sleetfall is slight; it sounds like somebody's throwing little fistfuls of sand at the window from real far away. The deadly R.N., helping the M.D. clamp some kind of weird steel back-braceish thing with what looks like a metal halo they'd put together from parts out of the big case, clamping the thing to the head of the bed and to little steel plates under the bed's heart monitor — it looks sort of like the upper part of an electric chair, he thinks — the R.N. looks down in mid-stretch and says Hi Mr. Gately and says Mr. Gately is allergic and doesn't get any meds except antipyretics and Toradol in a drip Dr. Pressburger do you Mr. Gately you poor brave allergic thing. Her voice is like you can just imagine what she'd sound like getting X'd and really liking it. Gately's repelled at himself for having taken a dump in front of this kind of R.N. The M.D.'s name had sounded just like 'Pressburger' or 'Prissburger,' and Gately's now sure the poor yutz'd taken daily ass-kickings from sinister future drug addicts, as a kid. The M.D.'s perspiring in the ambient sexuality of the R.N. He says (the M.D. does) So what's he intubated for if he's conscious and self-ventilating and on a drip. This is while the M.D.'s trying to screw the metal halo itself to the top of the back-braceish thing with bolt-head screws, one knee up on the bed and stretching so part of the red soft upper part of his ass is showing over his belt, not being able to get the thing screwed on, shaking the metal halo like it's its stubborn fault, and even lying there Gately can tell the guy's turning the bolt-head screws the wrong way. The R.N. comes over and puts a cool soft hand on Gately's forehead in a way that makes the forehead want to die with shame. What Gately can get from what she says to Dr. Pressburger is that there'd been concern that Gately might have got a fragment of whatever projectile he got invaded with in, through, or near his lower-something Trachea, since there'd been trauma to his Something-with-six-syllables-that-started-with-*Sterno,* she said the radiology results were indefinite but suspicious, and somebody called Pendleton had wanted a 16 mm. siphuncular nebulizer dispensing 4 ml. of 20% Mucomyst[373] q. 2 h. on the off-chance of hemorrhage or mucoidal flux, like just in case. The parts of this Gately can follow he doesn't care for one bit. He doesn't want to know his body even fucking *has* something with six syllables in it. The horrifying R.N. wipes Gately's face off as best she can with her hand and says she'll try to fit him in for a sponge bath before she goes off-shift at 1600h., at which Gately goes rigid with dread. The R.N.'s hand smells of Kiss My Face–brand Organic Hand and Body Lotion, which Pat Montesian also uses. She tells the poor M.D. to let her have a try at the cranial brace, those things are always a bear to screw in. Her shoes are those subaudible nurses' shoes that make no sound, so it seems like she glides away from Gately's bed instead of walks away. Her legs aren't visible until she gets a certain ways away. The M.D.'s own shoes have a wet squeak to the left one. The M.D. looks like he hasn't slept well in about a year. There's a faint vibe of prescription 'drines about the guy, on Gately's view. He paces squeakily at the foot of the bed watching the R.N. turn the screws the right way and pushes his owlish glasses up and says that Clifford Pendleton, scratch golfer or no, is a post-traumatic maroon, that nebulized Mucomyst is for (and here his voice makes it clear he's reciting from memory, like to show off) abnormal, viscid, or inspissated post-traumatic mucus, not potential hemorrhaging or edema, and that 16 mm. siphuncular intubation itself had been specifically discreditated as an intratracheal-edema prophylaxis in the second-to-latest issue of *Morbid Trauma Quarterly* as so diametrically invasive that it was more apt to exacerbate than to alleviate hemoptysis, according to somebody he calls 'Laird' or 'Layered.' Gately's listening in with the uncomprehending close attention of like a child whose parents are discussing something adultly complex about child-care in its presence. The condescension with which Prissburger inserts that *hemoptysis* means something called 'pertussive hemorrhage,' like Kathy the R.N. wasn't enough of a pro not to have to insert little technical explanations for, makes Gately sad for the guy — it's obvious the guy pathetically thinks this kind of limp condescending shit will impress her. Gately's got to admit he would have tried to impress her, too, though, if she hadn't met him by holding a kidney-shaped pan under his working anus. The R.N.'s finishing packing up the parts of the brace thing the M.D. couldn't seem to attach, meanwhile. She was saying the M.D. seemed awful well-up on methodology for something called a 2R, as they left, and Gately could tell the M.D. couldn't tell she was being a little sarcastic. The M.D. was struggling to try to carry the thing's case, which Gately judges weighs at most 30 kg. It occurs to him head-on for the first time that the real reason Stavros L. hired shelter-cleaning guys out of halfway houses was that he could get away with paying them like bupkis, and that he (Don G.) must surely on some level have known this all along but been in some kind of Denial about confronting it head-on that he was getting fucked over by Stavros the shoe-freak, and that the word *embrasure* had been surely another invasive-wraith ghostword, and then now also that nobody seems to exactly be falling all over themself to bring the paper and pen it had sure seemed like Joelle van D. had understood Gately's mimed request for, and that thus maybe Joelle's visit and show-and-tell with the snapshots had been just as much a febrile hallucination as the figuranted wraith, and that it has stopped spitting sleet but the clouds out there still look like they mean serious business out there over Brighton-Allston, and that if Joelle v.D.'s intimate visit with the photo album was a hallucination that at least meant it was also a hallucination she was wearing fucking college-kid Ken Erdedy's sweatpants, and that the low-angled sadness of the cloudy P.M. light meant it had to be pretty near 1600h. EST so that maybe There By The Grace he could avoid maybe getting an uncontrolled woodie getting sponged naked by the horrifyingly attractive K/Cathy and but still could get sponged by her linebacker of a replacement, because the sour meaty smell of himself was grim, only maybe miss the woodie-hazard and get sponged by the big hairy-moled 1600–2400h. nurse in support-hose to who Gately's anus was a stranger. Plus that 1600h. EST was Spontaneous-Dissemination time for Mr. Bouncety-Bounce, the mentally ill kiddy-show host Gately's always loved and used to try his best with Kite and poor old Fackelmann to be home and largely alert for, and that nobody's once offered to click on the HD viewer that hangs next to a myopic fake-Turner fog-and-boat print on the wall opposite Gately's and the former kid's beds, and that he had no remote with which to either activate the TP at 1600 or ask somebody else to activate it. That without some kind of notebook and pencil he couldn't communicate even the basicest question or like concept to anybody — it was like he was a vegetated hemorrhagic-stroke-victim. Without a pencil and notebook he couldn't even seem to get across a request for a notebook and pencil; it was like he was trapped inside his huge chattering head. Unless, his head then points out, Joelle van Dyne's visit had been real and her understanding of the pen-and-notebook gesture had been real, and but somebody out there in the hallway with a hat or at the Hospital President's office or at the nurses' station with his innerdicted M.-Hanley-brownies had also innerdicted the request for writing supplies, at the Finest's request, so he couldn't get his story straight with anybody before they came for him, that it was like a pre-interrogation softening-up thing, they were leaving him trapped in himself, a figurant, mute and unmoving and blank like the House's catatonic lady slumped moist and pale in her chair or the Advanced Basics Group's adopted girl's vegetable-kingdom sister, or the whole catatonic gang over at E.M.P.H.H.'s #5 Shed, silent and dead-faced even when touching a tree or propped up amid exploding front-lawn firecrackers. Or the wraith's nonexistent kid. It's got to be past 1600h., light-wise, unless it's the lowering clouds. There's roughly 0% or less visibility now outside the sleet-crusted window. The room's windowlight is darkening to that Kaopectate shade that has always marked the just-pre-sunset time of day that Gately (like most drug addicts) has always most dreaded, and had always either lowered his helmet and charged extra-murderous at somebody to block it out (the late-day dread) or else dropped QuoVadis or oral narcotics or turned on Mr. Bouncety-Bounce extra loud or busied himself in his silly chef's hat in the Ennet House kitchen or made sure he was at a Meeting sitting way up close in nose-pore range, to block it out (the late-day dread), the gray-light late-afternoon dread, always worse in winter, the dread, in winter's watered-down light — just like the secret dread he's always felt whenever everybody happened to ever leave the room and left him alone in a room, a terrible stomach-sinking dread that probably dates all the way back to being alone in his XXL Dentons and crib below Herman the Ceiling That Breathed.

It occurs to Gately that right now's just like when he was a toddler and his Mom and her companion were both passed out or worse: no matter how frightened or scared he might become he now again cannot get anybody to come or to hear or even *know* about it; the discredited tube to prevent vicious or inspired bleeding in his suspicious Trachea has left him completely Alone, worse off than a toddler that could at least bellow and yowl, rattling the bars of its playpen in terror that nobody tall was in any shape to hear him. Plus this dreadful time of weak gray late-day light is the time, was the time when the sad and nerdily dressed wraith appeared yesterday. Assuming that was yesterday. Assuming it was a real wraith. But the wraith, with its chinky Coke and theories of post-mortem speed, had been able to interface with Gately without aid of speech or gesture or Bic, was why even out of his mind Gately had had to admit to himself it must have been a delusion, a fever-dream. But he has to admit he'd kind of liked it. The dialogue. The give-and-take. The way the wraith could seem to get inside him. The way he said Gately's best thoughts were really communiqués from the patient and Abiding dead. Gately wonders if his organic father the ironworker is not now maybe dead and dropping in and standing very still from time to time for a communiqué. He felt slightly better. The room's ceiling was not breathing. It lay flat as a stucco sheet, rippling only slightly with the petroleum-fumes of fever and Gately's own smell. Then bubbling up out of nowhere again he suddenly confronts deep-focus memories of

Gene Fackelmann's final demise and Gately and Pamela Hoffman-Jeep's involvement in Fackelmann's demise.

Gately, for several months before he did his State assault-bit, was disastrously involved with one Pamela Hoffman-Jeep, his first girl ever with a hyphen, a sort of upscale but directionless and not very healthy and pale and incredibly passive Danvers girl that worked in Purchasing for a hospital-supply co. in Swampscott and was pretty definitely an alcoholic and drank bright drinks with umbrellas in Rte. 1 clubs in the late P.M. until she swooned and passed out with a loud clunk. That's what she called it — 'swooned.' The swooning and passing out with a loud clunk as her head hit the table was more or less a nightly thing, and Pamela Hoffman-Jeep fell automatically in love with any man she termed 'chivalrous'[374] enough to carry her out to the parking lot and drive her home without raping her, which rape of an unconscious head-lolling girl she termed 'Taking Advantage.' Gately got introduced to her by Fackelmann, who one time as he came up through a sports bar called the Pourhouse's parking lot to dialogue with a Sorkin-debtor Gately saw Fackelmann staggering along carrying this unconscious girl to his ride, one big hand quite a bit farther up her prom-looking taffeta gown than it really needed to be to carry her, and Fackelmann told Gately if Don'd give this gash a ride home he'd stay and do the collection, which Gately's heart wasn't in collections anymore and he jumped at the trade, as long as Fackelmann could promise him she could hold her various fluids in the 4×4 he was driving. So it was Fackelmann who told him, as he put the tiny and limp but still continent body in his arms in the parking lot of the Pourhouse, to watch his personal six, Gately, and be sure and violate her a little, because this gash here was like one of those South Sea–culture gashes in that if Gately took her home and she woke up nonviolated she'd be Gately's for life. But Gately obviously had no intention of raping an unconscious person, much less even putting his hand up the gown of a girl that might lose her fluids any second, and this locked him into the involvement. Pamela Hoffman-Jeep called Gately her 'Night-Errand' and fell passively in love with his refusal to Take Advantage. Gene Fackelmann, she confided, was not the gentleman Gately was.

What helped make the involvement disastrous was that Pamela Hoffman-Jeep was always either so leglessly drunk or so passively hungover all the time that any sort of sex any time at all with her would have classified as Taking Advantage.

This girl was the single passivest person Gately ever met. He never once saw P.H.-J. actually get from one spot to another under her own power. She needed somebody chivalrous to pick her up and carry her and lay her back down 24/7/365, it seemed like. She was a sort of sexual papoose. She spent most of her life passed out and sleeping. She was a beautiful sleeper, kittenish and serene, never drooling. She made passivity and unconsciousness look kind of beautiful. Fackelmann called her Death's Poster-Child. Even at work, at the hospital supply co., Gately imagined her horizontal, curled fetal on something soft, with all the hot slack facial intensity of a sleeping baby. He imagined her bosses and coworkers all tiptoeing around Purchasing whispering to each other to not wake her up. She never once rode in the actual front seat of any vehicle he drove her home in. But she also never threw up or pissed herself or even complained, just smiled and yawned an infant's little milky yawn and snuggled deeper into whatever Gately had swaddled her in. Gately started doing that thing about yelling they'd been robbed when he carried her into whatever stripped luxury apt. they were crewing in. P.H.-J. wasn't what you'd call great-looking, but she was incredibly sexy, Gately felt, because she always managed to look like you'd just X'd her into a state of total unmuscled swoon, lying there unconscious. Trent Kite told Fackelmann he thought Gately was out of his fucking mind. Fax observed that Kite himself was not exactly a W. T. Sherman with the ladies, even with coke-whores and strung-out nursing students and dipsoid lounge-hags whose painted faces swung loose from their heads. Fackelmann claimed to have started a Log just to keep track of Kite's attempted pickup lines — surefire lines like e.g. 'You're the second most beautiful woman I've ever seen, the first most beautiful woman I've ever seen being former British Prime Minister Margaret Thatcher,' and 'If you came home with me I'm unusually confident that I could achieve an erection,' and said that if Kite wasn't still cherry at twenty-three and a half it was proof of some kind of divine-type grace.

Sometimes Gately would come out of a Demerol-nod and look at pale passive Pamela lying there sleeping beautifully and undergo a time-lapse clairvoyant thing where he could almost visibly watch her losing her looks through her twenties and her face starting to slide over off her skull onto the pillow she held like a stuffed toy, becoming a lounge-hag right before his eyes. The vision aroused more compassion than horror, which Gately never even considered might qualify him as a decent person.

Gately's two favorite things about Pamela Hoffman-Jeep were: the way she would come out of her stupor and hold her cheek and laugh hysterically each time Gately carried her across the threshold of some stripped apartment and bellow that they'd been ripped off; and the way she always wore the long white linen gloves and bare-shoulder taffeta that made her seem like some upscale North Shore debutante who's had like one too many dippers of country-club punch and is just begging to be Taken Advantage of by some low-rent guy with a tattoo — she'd make a sort of languid very-slow-motion bullwhip-gesture with her hand in the long white glove as she lay wherever Gately had deposited her and simper out with an upscale inflection 'Don Honey, bring Mommy a highball' (she called a drink a highball), which it turned out was a deadly impression of her own Mom, who it turned out this lady made Gately's own Mom look like Carry Nation by comparison, lush-wise: the only four times Gately ever met Mrs. H.-J. were all at E.R.s and sanitaria.

Gately lies there pop-eyed with guilt and anxiety in the hiss and click of resumed sleet, in the twilit St. E.'s room, next to the glittering back-brace-and-skull-halo thing clamped exoskeletally to the empty next bed and gleaming dully at selected welds, Gately trying to Abide, remembering. It had been Pamela Hoffman-Jeep that finally clued Gately in on the little ways Gene Fackelmann had been historically getting over on Whitey Sorkin, and alerted him to the suicidal creek Fackelmann had got himself into with a certain mistaken-bet scam that had blown up right in his map. Even Gately had been able to tell something was the matter: for the last two weeks Fackelmann had been squatting sweatily in a corner of the stripped living room, right outside the little luxury bedroom Gately and Pamela were lying in, out there squatting over his Sterno cooker and incredible twin hills of sky-blue Dilaudid and many-hued M&M's, not much speaking or responding or moving or even seeming to cop a nod, just sitting there hunched and plump and glistening like some sort of cornered toad, his mustache flailing around on his lip. Things would have had to be bad indeed for Gately ever to try to get coherent data out of P.H.-J. Apparently the deal was that one of the bettors that bet with Sorkin through Fackelmann was a guy Gately and Fackelmann know only as Eighties Bill, an impeccably groomed guy that wore red suspenders under snazzy Zegna-brand menswear and tortoiseshell specs and Docksiders, an old-fashioned corporate take-overer and asset-plunderer, maybe fifty, with an Exchange Place office and a souvenir FREE MILKEN bumper sticker on his Beamer — it was a night of many highballs and much papoosing, and Gately had to keep flicking the top of P.H.-J.'s skull to keep her conscious long enough to free-associate her way through the details — who was on his fourth marriage to his third aerobics instructor, and who liked to bet only on Ivy League college hoops, but who when he did so — bet — bet amounts so huge that Fackelmann always had to get Sorkin's pre-approval on the bet and then call Eighties Bill back, and so on.

But so — according to Pamela Hoffman-Jeep — this Eighties Bill, who's a Yale alum and usually unabashedly sentimental about what Pamela H.-J. laughingly says Fackelmann called his 'al*mo*meter' — well, on this particular time it seems like a little impeccably groomed birdie has whispered in Eighties Bill's hairy ear, because this one time Eighties Bill wants to put $125K down on Brown U. against Yale U., i.e. betting against his almometer, only he wants (−2) points instead of the even spread Sorkin and the rest of the Boston books are taking off the Atlantic City line for a spread. And Fackelmann has to cell-phone down to Saugus to bounce this off Sorkin, except Sorkin's down in the city in Enfield at the National Cranio-Facial Pain Foundation office getting his weekly UV-bombardment and Cafergot refill from Dr. Robert ('Sixties Bob') Monroe — the septuagenarian pink-sunglasses-and-Nehru-jacket-wearing N.C.-F.P.F. ergotic-vascular-headache-treatment specialized, a guy who in yore-days interned at Sandoz and was one of T. Leary's original circle of mayonnaise-jar acid-droppers at T. Leary's now-legendary house in West Newton MA, and is now (60s B.) an intimate acquaintance of Kite, because Sixties Bob is an even bigger Grateful Dead fanatic maybe even than Kite, and sometimes got together with Kite and several other Dead devotees (most of who now had canes and O_2 tanks) and traded historical-souvenir-type tiger's eyes and paisley dou-blets and tie-dyes and lava lamps and bandannas and plasma spheres and variegated black-light posters of involuted geometric designs, and argued about which Dead shows and bootlegs of Dead shows were the greatest of all time in different regards, and just basically had a hell of a time. 60s B., an inveterate collector and haggling trader of shit, sometimes took Kite along on little expeditions of eclectic and seedy shops for Dead-related parapher-nalia, sometimes even informally fencing stuff for Kite (and so indirectly Gately), covering Kite with $ when Kite's rigid need-schedule didn't permit a more formal and time-consuming fence, Sixties Bob then trading the mer-chandise around various seedy locales for 60s-related shit nobody else'd even usually want. A couple times Gately had to actually finger an ice cube out of a highball and slip it under the shoulderless neckline of P.H.-J.'s prom gown to try and keep her on some kind of track. Like most incredibly pas-sive people, the girl had a terrible time ever separating details from what was really important to a story, is why she rarely ever got asked anything. But so the point is that the person that took Fackelmann's call about Eighties Bill's mammoth Yale-Brown bet wasn't in fact Sorkin but rather Sorkin's secretary, one Gwendine O'Shay, the howitzer-breasted old Green-Cardless former I.R.A.-moll who'd gotten hit on the head with a truncheon by a godless Belfast Bobbie once too often back on the Old Sod, and whose skull now was (in Fackelmann's own terminology) soft as puppy-shit in the rain, but who had just the seedy sort of distracted-grandmotherly air that makes her perfect for clapping her red-knuckled old hands to her cheeks and squealing as she claimed Mass Lottery lottery winnings whenever Whitey Sorkin and his MA-Statehouse bagmen-cronies arrange to have a Sorkinite buy a mysteriously winning Mass Lottery ticket from one of the countless convenience stores Sorkin & cronies own through dummy corporations all up and down the North Shore, and who, because she could not only give what Sorkin claimed was the only adequate cervical massage west of the Berne Hot Alp Springs Center but also could both word-process a shocking 110 wpm and wield a shillelagh like nobody's business — plus had been W. Sorkin's dear late I.R.A.-moll Mum's Scrabble-pal back in Belfast, on the Old Sod — served as Whitey's chief administrative aide, manning the cellular phones when Sorkin was out or indisposed.

And so but P.H.-J.'s point, which Gately has to just about crack her scalp open flicking out of her: Gwendine O'Shay, familiar with Eighties Bill and his Y.U. Bulldog sentimentality, plus cranially soft as a fucking grape, O'Shay took Fackelmann's call *wrong*, thought Fackelmann said Eighties Bill wanted 125K with (–2) points on *Yale* instead of (–2) on *Brown*, put Fackelmann on Hold and made him listen to Irish Muzak while she put in a call to a Yale Athletic Dept. mole out of Sorkin's Read-Protected database's MOLE file and learned that the Yale U. Bulldogs' star power forward had been diagnosed with an extremely rare neurologic disorder called Post-Coital Vestibulitis[375] in which for several hours after intercourse the power forward tended to suffer such a terrible vertiginous loss of proprioception that he literally couldn't tell his ass from his elbow, much less make an authoritative move to the bucket. Plus then O'Shay's second call, to Sorkin's Brown U. athletic mole (a locker-room attendant everybody thinks is deaf), reveals that several of Brown U.'s most sirenish and school-spirited hetero coeds had been recruited, auditioned, briefed, rehearsed (i.e. '*debriefed*,' giggles Pamela Hoffman-Jeep, whose giggles involve the sort of ticklish shoulder-writhing undulations of a much younger girl getting tickled by an authority figure and pretending not to like it), and stationed at strategic points — I–95 rest-stops, in the spare-tire compartment at the rear of the Bulldogs' chartered bus, in the evergreen shrubbery outside the teams' special entrance to the Pizzitola Athl. Center in Providence, in concave recesses along the Pizzitola tunnels between special entrance and Visitors' locker room, even in a specially enlarged and sensually-appointed locker next to the power forward's locker in the VLR, all prepared — like the Brown cheerleaders and Pep Squad, who've been induced to do the game pantyless, electrolysized and splits-prone to help lend a pyrotechnic glandular atmosphere to the power forward's whole playing-environment — prepared to make the penultimate sacrifice for squad, school, and influential members of the Brown Alumni Bruins Boosters Assoc. So that Gwendine O'Shay then switches back to Fackelmann and OKs the mammoth bet and point-spread, as like who wouldn't, with that kind of mole-reported fix in the works. Except of course she's taken the wager backwards, i.e. O'Shay thinks Eighties Bill's now got 125K on Yale coming within two points, while Eighties Bill — who it turns out's cast himself as White Knight in bidding for majority control of Providence's Federated Funnel and Cone Corp., O.N.A.N.'s leading manufacturer of conoid receptacles, with F.F.&C. CEO'd by a prominent Brown alumnus so rabid a Bruins-booster he actually wears a snarling hollow bear-head to conference games, whose ass Eighties Bill is going about kissing like nobody's beeswax, P.H.-J. inserts, hinting it was Eighties Bill who'd tipped the Bruins staff off about the power forward's Achilles' vas deferens — E.B. quite reasonably believes he's now got Brown within a deuce for 125 el grande's.

The wrench in the ointment that nobody in Providence has counted on is the picket-and-knuckleduster-wielding appearance of Brown University's entire Dworkinite Female Objectification Prevention And Protest Phalanx outside the Pizzitola Athl. Center's main gates right at game-time, two FOPPPs per motorcycle, who blow through the filigreed gates like they were so much wet Kleenex and storm the arena, plus a division of Brown's pluckier undergraduate N.O.W.s who execute a pincer-movement down from the cheap seats up top during the first time-out, at the precise moment the Brown cheerleaders' first pyramid-maneuver ends in a mid-air split that causes the Pizzitola's scoreboard's scorekeeper to reel backward against his controls and blow out both HOME's and VISITORS' zeroes, on the board, just as the FOPPPs' unmuffled Hawgs come blatting malevolently down through the ground-level tunnels and out onto the playing floor; and in the ensuing melee not only are cheerleaders, Pep Squad, and comely Brown U. sirens all either laid out with picket-signs wielded like shillelaghs or thrown kicking and shrieking over the burly shoulders of militant FOPPPs and carried off on roaring Hawgs, leaving the Yale power forward's delicate nervous system intact if overheated; but two Brown U. Bruin starters, a center and a shooting guard — both too wrung-out and dazed by a grueling week of comely-siren-auditioning and -rehearsing to have sense enough to run like hell once the melee spills out onto the Pizzitola hardwood — are felled, by a FOPPP knuckleduster and a disoriented referee with a martial-arts background, respectively; and so when the floor is finally cleared and stretchers borne off and the game resumes, Yale U. cleans Brown U.'s clock by upwards of 20.

Then so Fackelmann calls up Eighties Bill and arranges to pick up the skeet, which is $137,500 with the vig, which E.B. gives him in large-denomination pre-O.N.A.N. scrip in a *GO BROWN BRUINS* gym-bag he'd brought to the game to sit next to the ursine-headed CEO with and now has less than no use for, but so Fackelmann receives the skeet downtown and blasts up cheesy Route 1 to Saugus to deliver the skeet and pick up his vig on the vig ($625 U.S.) right away, needing to cop Blues in what's starting to be the worst way, etc. Plus Fackelmann's figuring on maybe a small bonus or at least some emotional validation from Sorkin for bringing in such a mammoth and promptly-remitted wager. But, when he gets to the Rte. 1 titty bar at the rear of which Sorkin has his administrative offices behind an unmarked fire door and all wallpapered in stuff that looks like ersatz wood panelling, Gwendine O'Shay wordlessly points behind her station at Sorkin's personal office door with a terse gesture Fackelmann doesn't think fits with the up-beatness of the occasion at all. The door's got a big poster of R. Limbaugh on it, from before the assassination. Sorkin's in there working spreadsheets with his special monitor-screen-light-filtering goggles on. The goggles' lenses on their long protruding barrels look like lobsters' eyes on stalks. Gately and Fackelmann and Bobby C never spoke to Sorkin until spoken to, not out of henchmanish obsequity but because they could never tell what Sorkin's cranio-facial vascular condition was or if he could tolerate sound until they verifiably heard him tolerating his own. (Sound.)

So G. Fackelmann waits wordlessly to hand over Eighties Bill's skeet, standing there tall and soft and palely sweating, the overall shape and color of a peeled boiled egg. When Sorkin hikes an eyebrow at the *GO BRUINS* bag and says the knee-slapping hilarity of the joke escapes him, Fackelmann's mustache positively takes off all over his upper lip, and he prepares to say what he always says when he's flummoxed, that whatever's being said is with all due respect a goddamn lie. Sorkin saves his data and pushes his desk chair back so he can reach all the way down to the fireproof drawer. The goggles are often used in data-processing sweatshops and list for a deuce. Sorkin grunts as he hauls out a huge old Mass Lottery box for Quik-Pick cards and heaves it onto the desk, where it bulges obscenely, filled with 112.5K U.S. — there's 112.5 fucking K in there, all in ones, 125K minus vig, what Sorkin via O'Shay believes to be Eighties Bill's winnings, all in small bills, because Sorkin's pissed off and can't resist making a little like gesture. Fackelmann doesn't say anything. His mustache goes limp as his mental machinery starts revving. Sorkin, massaging his temples, staring up at Fackelmann with his goggles like a crab in a tank, says he supposes he can't blame Fax or O'Shay, that he'd have OK'd the bet himself, what with the neurologic tip on the Yale forward they had. Who could have foreseen thuggish Feminazis screwing up the ointment. He utters a bit of Gaelic that Fackelmann doesn't know but assumes to be fatalistical. He peels six C-notes and an O.N.A.N.ite 25-spot off a wad the size of an artillery shell and pushes them across the metal desk at Fackelmann, his vig on the vig. He says What the fuck (Sorkin does), this Eighties Bill kid's irrational sentimentalism for Yale will sooner or later catch up with him. Veteran books tend to be statistically philosophical and patient. Fackelmann doesn't even bother to wonder why Sorkin refers to Eighties Bill as 'kid' when they're both about the same age. But a high-watt bulb is slowly beginning to incandesce over Fackelmann's moist head. As in the Faxter starts to conceptualize the overall concept of what must of happened. He still hasn't said anything, Pamela Hoffman-Jeep emphasizes. Sorkin looks Fackelmann over and asks if he's gained some asymmetrical-type weight, there. Fackelmann's left tit does look noticeably bigger than his right, under his sportcoat, because of the legal envelope with 137 1000s and one 500 in it, the skeet from an Eighties Bill who thought he'd lost. Just like Sorkin thought E.B.'d *won*. The slight high whine in the room that Sorkin thinks is his Infernatron disk-drive is really the whine of Fackelmann's high-speed mentation. His mustache roils like a cracked whip as he works his own internal mental spreadsheet. 250K in one lumpy sum represented like 375 sky-blue grams of hydromorphone hydrochloride[376] or like 37,500 10-mg. soluble tablets of the shit, available from a certain rapacious but discreet Chinatown opiate-dealer who'd only deal synthetic narcs in 100-gram weights — which all translated, assuming Kite could be persuaded to pack up his D.E.C. 2100 and move far far away with Fackelmann to help him set up a street-distribution matrix in some urban market far far away, into close to like let's see carry the one like 1.9 million in street-value, which sum meant that Fackelmann and to a lesser jr.-partner extent Kite could have their chins on their chests for the rest of their days without ever having to strip another apt., forge another passport, break another thumb. All if Fackelmann just kept his map shut about O'Shay's confabulation of Yale/ Brown//Brown/Yale, mumbled something about an I.V.-adulterant causing a sudden and temporary gigantism in one tit, and blasted out of there straight down Rte. 1 to this one Dr. Wo and Associates, Hung Toy's Cold Tea Emporium, Chinatown.

By this time Pamela Hoffman-Jeep had succumbed to the highballs and her own swaddled warmth and was irreversibly swooned, ice or fillip or no, twitching synaptically and murmuring to somebody named Monty that he was certainly no kind of gentleman in *her* book. But Gately could chart the rest of Fackelmann's shit-creek's course for himself. When approached by Fackelmann with a GO BROWN gym-bag of Dr. Wo's finest wholesale Dilaudid and invited to decamp with him and set up a distrib-matrix for their own drug-empire far far away, Kite would have staggered back in horror at Fackelmann's obviously not knowing that the bettor Eighties Bill was in fact none other than the *son of Sixties Bob*, viz. Whitey Sorkin's personal migrainologist, who Sorkin trusted and confided in as only a massive I.V.-dose of Cafergot can make you trust and confide, and whom Sorkin would undoubtedly tell all about the guy's own son's huge win on Yale, and who wasn't like Ward-and-Wally close with his son, Sixties Bob wasn't, but naturally kept distant paternal tabs on him, and would certainly have known that E.B.'d in fact bet Brown in an attempt to cozy up to the conic CEO, and so would know that there'd been some kind of mix-up; and also that (Kite'd still be staggering back in horror as all this added up) plus, even if Sorkin somehow didn't get told of Eighties Bill's loss and Fackelmann's scam from Sixties Bill, the fact was that Sorkin's newest savagest U.S. muscle, Bobby ('C') C, old-fashioned smack-addict, copped regular old organic Burmese heroin from this Dr. Wo on a regular basis, and was sure to hear about 300+ grams of wholesale Dilaudid bought by a Fackelmann known to be C's co-employee off Sorkin . . . and thus that Fackelmann, who when he came to Kite with the proposition was already in possession of a Brown-Booster bag full of 37,500 10-mg. Dilaudids and minus Sorkin's 250K — plus with as Gately later knew only 22K in suicidal-scam-backfire-insurance capital — was already dead: Fackelmann was a Dead Man, Kite

931

would have said, staggering back with horror at Fax's idiocy; Kite'd have said he could smell Fackelmann already biodegrading from here. Dead as a fucking post, he'd have told Fackelmann, already worrying about being seen sitting there with him in whatever titty bar they were in when Fax hit Kite with the proposal. And Gately, watching P.H.-J. sleep, could not only imagine but Identify fully with how Fackelmann, on hearing Kite say he could smell him dead and why, with how Fackelmann, instead of taking his bagful of Blues and gluing on a goatee and immediately fleeing to climes that'd never even fucking *heard* of metro Boston's North Shore — that the Faxter'd done what any drug addict in possession of his Substance would do when faced with fatal news and attendant terror: Facklemann'd made a fucking beeline for their luxury-stripped home and familiar safe-feeling hearth and had plopped down and immediately fired up the Sterno cooker and cooked up and tied off and shot up and nailed his chin to his chest and kept it there with staggering quantities of Dilaudid, trying to mentally blot out the reality of the fact that he was going to get demapped if he didn't take some kind of decisive remedial action at once. Because, Gately realized even then, this was your drug addict's basic way of dealing with problems, was using the good old Substance to blot out the problem. Also probably medicating his terror by stuffing himself with Peanut M&M's, which would explain all the wrappers littering the floor of the corner he hadn't moved from. That thus this is why Fackelmann has been squatting moist and silent in a corner of the living room right outside this very bedroom here for days; this was why the apparent contradiction of the staggering amount of Substance Fackelmann had in the gym-bag next to him together with the cornered-toad look of a man in the great fear one associates with Withdrawal. Charting and thinking, drumming his fingers absently on P.H.-J.'s unconscious skull, Gately realized he could more than empathize with Fackelmann's flight into Dilaudid and M&M's, but he now realizes that that was the first time it really ever dawned on him in force that a drug addict was at root a craven and pathetic creature: a thing that basically hides.

The most sexual thing Gately ever did with Pamela Hoffman-Jeep was he liked to unwrap her cocoon of blankets and climb in with her and spoon in real tight, fitting his bulk up close against all her soft concave places, and then go to sleep with his face in her nape. It bothered Gately that he could empathize with Fackelmann's desire to hide and blot out, but in the retrospect of memory now it bothers him more that he didn't lie there up next to the comatose girl being bothered for more than a few minutes before he felt the familiar desire that blots out all bother, and that that night he had unwrapped the cocoon of bedding and arisen so automatically in service of this desire. And feels the worst of all that he'd lumbered out of the bedroom in just jeans and belt out to the gloaming living room where Fackelmann was hunched moist and smeary-mouthed in the corner next to a mountain of

10 mg. Dilaudids and his mixing bowl of distilled water and works-kit and Sterno unit, that Gately had lumbered so automatically out to Fackelmann under the pretense — to himself, too, the pretense, was the worst thing — the pretense that he was just going to check on poor old Fackelmann, to maybe try and convince him to take some kind of action, go penitent to Sorkin or flee the clime instead of just hiding there in the corner with his mind in neutral and his chin on his chest and a stalactite of chocolated drool from his lower lip lengthening. Because he knew that the first thing Fackelmann would do when Gately left P.H.-J. and lumbered out to the defurnished living room would be to fumble in his GoreTex works-kit for a new factory-wrapped syringe and invite Gately to hunker on down and get right with the planet. I.e. ingest some of this mountain of Dilaudid, to keep Fackelmann company. Which to Gately's shame he did, had done, and no part of the reality of Fackelmann's creek and the need for action had even been brought up, so intent were they on the Blues' somnolent hum, blotting everything out, while Pamela Hoffman-Jeep lay wrapped tight in the other room dreaming of damsels and towers — Gately did, he remembers vividly, he let Fackelmann fix them both up but good, and told himself he was doing it to keep Fackelmann company, like sitting up with a sick friend, and (maybe worst) believed it was true.

Little entr'actes of feverish dreams punctuate memories and being conscious, like. He dreams he's riding due north on a bus the same color as its own exhaust, passing again and again the same gutted cottages and expanse of heaving sea, weeping. The dream goes on and on, without any kind of resolution or arrival, and he weeps and sweats as he lies there, stuck in it. Gately comes sharply around when he feels the little rough tongue on his forehead — not unlike Nimitz the M.P.'s little pet kitten's hesitant tongue, when the M.P. had still had the kitten, before the mysterious period when the kitten disappeared and the garbage disposal wouldn't run right for days and the M.P. sat hungover with his notebook at the kitchen table with his blond head in his hands, just sat there for several days, and Gately's Mom went around pale as hell and wouldn't go near the kitchen sink for days, and rushed to the bathroom when Gately finally asked what was the deal with the garbage disposal and where was Nimitz. When Gately gets his eyelids unstuck, though, the tongue is not even close to being Nimitz's. The wraith is back, right by the bed, dressed like before and blurred at the edges in the hat-shadowed spill of hallway-light, and except now with him is another, younger, way more physically fit wraith in kind of faggy biking shorts and a U.S. tank top who's leaning way over Gately's railing and . . . fucking *licking Gately's forehead* with a rough little tongue, and as Gately reflexively strikes out at the guy's map — no man put his tongue on D. W. Gately and lived — he has just enough time to realize the wraith's breath has no warmth to it, or smell, before both wraiths vanish and a blue forked bolt of pain from his sudden striking-out sends him back against his hot pillow with an arched spine and a tube-impeded scream, his eyes rolling back into the dove-colored light of whatever isn't quite sleep.

His fever is way worse, and his little snatches of dreams have a dismantled cubist aspect he associates in memory with childhood flu. He dreams he looks in a mirror and sees nothing and keeps trying to clean the mirror with his sleeve. One dream consists only of the color blue, too vivid, like the blue of a pool. An unpleasant smell keeps coming up his throat. He's both in a bag and holding a bag. Visitors flit in and out, but never Ferocious Francis or Joelle van D. He dreams there's people in his room but he's not one of them. He dreams he's with a very sad kid and they're in a graveyard digging some dead guy's head up and it's really important, like Continental-Emergency important, and Gately's the best digger but he's wicked hungry, like irresistibly hungry, and he's eating with both hands out of huge economy-size bags of corporate snacks so he can't really dig, while it gets later and later and the sad kid is trying to scream at Gately that the important thing was buried in the guy's head and to divert the Continental Emergency to start digging the guy's head up before it's too late, but the kid moves his mouth but nothing comes out, and Joelle van D. appears with wings and no underwear and asks if they knew him, the dead guy with the head, and Gately starts talking about knowing him even though deep down he feels panic because he's got no idea who they're talking about, while the sad kid holds something terrible up by the hair and makes the face of somebody shouting in panic: *Too Late.*

She'd come out of the St. E.'s doors and turned right for the quick walk back up to Ennet and a grotesquely huge woman whose hose bulged with stubble and whose face and head were four times larger than the largest woman Joelle had ever seen had grabbed her arm at the elbow and said she was sorry to be the one to tell her but that unbeknownst to her she was in almost mind-boggling danger.

It took rather a while for Joelle to look her up and down. 'This is supposed to be news?'

So and but that night's next A.M.'d found Gately and Fackelmann still there in Fackelmann's little corner, belts around their arms, arms and noses red from scratching, still at it, the ingestion, on a hell of a tear, cooking up and getting off and eating M&M's when they could find their mouths with their hands, moving like men deep under water, heads wobbling on strengthless necks, the empty room's ceiling sky-blue and bulging and under it hanging on the wall overhead to their right the apartment's upscale TP's viewer on a recursive slo-mo loop of some creepy thing Fackelmann liked that was just serial shots of flames from brass lighters, kitchen-matches, pilot lights, birthday candles, votive candles, pillar candles, birch shavings, Bunsen burners, etc., that Fackelmann had got from Kite, who just before dawn had come out dressed and declined to get high with them and coughed nervously and announced he had to leave for a few days or more for a 'totally key' and unmissable software trade-show in a different area code, not knowing Gately now knew he knew Fackelmann already to be dead, w/ Kite then trying to leave discreetly with every piece of hardware he owned in his arms, including the nonportable D.E.C., trailing cables. Then a bit later, as the A.M. light intensified yellowly and made both Gately and Fackelmann curse the fact that the curtains had been stripped and pawned, as they continued to hunch and cook and shoot, at maybe 0830h. Pamela Hoffman-Jeep was up and vomiting briskly and applying mousse against the worka-day day, calling Gately Honey and her Night Errand and asking if she'd done anything last night she'd have to explain to anybody today — kind of an A.M. routine in their relationship — applying blush and drinking her standard anti-hangover breakfast[377] and watching Gately and Fackel-mann's chins fall and rise at slightly different underwater rates. The smell of her perfume and high-retsin mints hung in the bare room long after she'd bid them both Ciao Bello. As the A.M. sun got higher and intolerable, in-stead of taking action and nailing a blanket or something over the window they opted instead to obliterate the reality of the eye-scalding light and be-gan truly bingeing on Blues, flirting with an O. D. They scaled Fackelmann's Mt. Dilaudid at a terrible clip. Fackelmann was by nature a binger. Gately was typically more like a maintenance user. He rarely went on a classic-type binge, which meant plunking down in one place with an enormous stash and getting loaded over and over again for long periods without moving. But when he did start a binge he might as well have been strapped to the snout of a missile for all the control he had over length or momentum. Fackelmann was having at the mountain of 10-mg. Blues like there was no tomorrow. Every time Gately even started to bring up the issue of how Faxter had come by such a huge blue haul of the Substance — trying maybe to invite Fackelmann to confront the reality of his trouble by describing it, like — Fackelmann would cut him off with a soft 'That's a goddamn lie.' This was pretty much all Fackelmann would ever say, when loaded, even in response to things like questions. You have to picture all the binge's verbal exchanges as occurring like very slowly, oddly distended, as if the time were honey:

'Serious fucking stash you managed to come by somehow right here, Fa—'

'That's a goddamn lie.'

'Man. Man. I just hope Gwendine or C's got the phone today out there, man. Instead of Whitey. No business getting done out of here today I don't thi—'

''s a goddamn lie.'

'That's for sure, Fax.'

''s a goddamn lie.'

'Fax. The Faxter. Count Faxula.'

'Goddamn *lie*.'

After a while in all the distension it got to be like a joke. Gately would haul his big head upright and try to allege the roundness of the planet, the three-dimensionality of the phenomenal world, the blackness of all black dogs —

''s a goddamn lie.'

They found it increasingly funny. After every exchange like this they laughed and laughed. Each exhalation of laughter seemed to take several minutes. The ceiling and the window's light receded. Fackelmann wet his pants; this was even funnier. They watched the pool of urine spread out against the hardwood floor, changing shape, growing curved arms, exploring the fine oak floor. The rises and valleys and little seams. It might of gotten later and then early A.M. again. The entertainment cartridge's myriad small flames were reflected in the spreading puddle, so that soon Gately could watch without taking his chin off his chest.

When the phone rang it was just a fact. The ringing was like an environment, not a signal. The fact of its ringing got more and more abstract. Whatever a ringing phone might signify was like totally overwhelmed by the overwhelming fact of its ringing. Gately pointed this out to Fackelmann. Fackelmann vehemently denied it.

At some point Gately tried to stand and was rudely assaulted by the floor, and wet his own pants.

The phone rang and rang.

At another point they got interested in rolling different colors of Peanut M&M's into the puddles of urine and watching the colored dye corrode and leave a vampire-white football of M&M in a nimbus of bright dye.

The intercom's buzzer to the luxury apartment complex's glass doors downstairs sounded, overwhelming both of them with the fact of its sound. It buzzed and buzzed. They discussed wishing it would stop the way you discuss wishing it would stop raining.

It became the ICBM of binges. The Substance seemed inexhaustible; Mt. Dilaudid changed shapes but never really much shrank that they could see. It was the first and only time ever that Gately I.V.'d narcotics so many times in one arm that he ran out of arm-vein and had to switch to the other arm. Fackelmann was no longer coordinated enough to help him tie off and boot. Fackelmann kept making a string of chocolaty drool appear and distend almost down to the floor. The acidity of their urine was corroding the apt.'s hardwood floor's finish in an observable way. The puddle had grown many arms like a Hindu god. Gately couldn't quite tell if the urine had explored its way almost back to their feet or if they were already sitting in urine. Fackelmann would see how close to the surface of the pond of their mixed piss he could get the tip of the string of spit before he sucked it back up and in. The little game had an intoxicating aura of danger to it. The insight that most people like play-danger but don't like real-life danger hit Gately like an epiphany. It took him gallons of viscous time to try and articulate the insight to Fackelmann so that Fackelmann could give it the imprimatur of a denial.

Eventually the buzzer stopped.

The phrase 'More tattoos than teeth' also kept going through Gately's head as it bobbed (the head), even though he had no idea where the phrase came from or who it was supposed to refer to. He hadn't been to Billerica Minimum yet; he was on bail that Whitey Sorkin had bonded.

The taste of the M&M's couldn't cut the weirdly sweet medical taste of hydromorphone in Gately's mouth. He watched an old stovetop-burner's crown of blue flame shimmer in the shine of the urine.

During a ruddled sunset-light period Fackelmann had had a small convulsion and a bowel movement in his pants and Gately hadn't had the coordination to go to Fackelmann's side during the seizure, to help and just be there. He had the nightmarish feeling that there was something crucial he had to do but had forgot what it was. 10-mg. injections of the Blue Bayou kept the feeling at bay for shorter and shorter periods. He'd never heard of somebody having a convulsion from an O.D., and Fackelmann had indeed seemed to bounce to his version of back.

The sun outside the big windows seemed to go up and down like a yo-yo.

They ran out of the distilled water Fackelmann had in the mixing bowl, and Fackelmann took a cotton and sopped up candy-dyed urine off the floor and cooked up with urine. Gately appeared to himself to be repulsed by this. But there was no question of trying to get to the stripped kitchen for the distilled-water bottle. Gately was tying off his right arm with his teeth, now, his left was so useless.

Fackelmann smelled very bad.

Gately nodded out into a dream where he was on a Beverly-Needham bus whose sides said PARAGON BUS LINES: THE GRAY LINE. In his stuporous recall over four years later in St. E.'s he realizes that this bus is the bus from the dream that wouldn't end and wouldn't go anywhere, but has the sickening realization that the connection between the two buses is itself a dream, or is in a dream, and it's now that his fever returns to new heights and his line on the heart monitor gets a funny little hitch like a serration at the 1st and 3rd nodes, which makes an amber light flash at the nurse's station down the hall.

When the buzzer sounded again they were watching the flames-film late at night. Now poor old Pamela Hoffman-Jeep's voice came to them through the intercom. The intercom and apt.-complex-front-doors-unlocker button were all the way across the living room by the apartment door. The ceiling bulged and receded. Fackelmann had made his hand into the shape of a claw and was studying the claw in the light of the TP's flames. Mt. Dilaudid was badly caved in on one side; a disastrous avalanche into Lake Urine was a possibility. P.H.-J. sounded drunk as a Nuck. She said to let her in. She said she knew they were in there. She used *party* as a verb several times. Fackelmann was whispering that it was a lie. Gately remembers he actually had to prod himself in the bladder to feel if he had to go to the bathroom. His Unit felt small and icy cold against his leg in the wet jeans. The ammoniac smell of urine and the breathing ceiling and drunk distant female voice . . . Gately reached in the dark for the bars of his playpen, grasped them with pudgy fists, hauled himself to his feet. His rising was more like the floor lowering. He wobbled like a toddler. The apt. floor below him feinted right, left, circling for an opening to attack. The luxury windows hung with starlight. Fackelmann had made his claw come alive into a spider and was letting the spider climb slowly down his chest-area. The starlight was smeary; there were no distinct stars. Everything out of the line of fire of the cartridge-viewer was dark as a pocket. The buzzer sounded angry and the voice pathetic. Gately put his foot out in the direction of the buzzer. He heard Fackelmann telling his hand's claw's spider it was witnessing the birth of an empire. Then when Gately put his foot down there was nothing there. The floor dodged his foot and rushed up at him. He caught a glimpse of bulged ceiling and then the floor caught him in the temple. His ears belled. The impact of the floor against him shook the whole room. A box of laminates teetered and fell and fanned clear laminates all over the wet floor. The viewer fell off the wall and cast ruddled flames on the ceiling. The floor jammed itself against Gately, pressing in tight, and he grayed out with his scrunched face toward Fackelmann and the windows beyond, with Fackelmann holding the spider out in mid-air at him for his inspection.

'Oh for Christ's sake then.

'I was in two scenes. What else is in there I do not know. In the first scene I'm going through a revolving door. You know, around in this glass revolving door, and going around out as I go in is somebody I know but apparently haven't seen for a long time, because the recognition calls for a shocked look, and the person sees me and gives an equally shocked look — we're supposedly formerly very close and now haven't seen each other in the longest time, and the meeting is random chance. And instead of going in

I keep going around in the door to follow the person out, which person is also still revolving in the door to follow me in, and we whirl in the door like that for several whirls.'

'Q.'

'The actor was male. He wasn't one of Jim's regulars. But the character I recognize in the door is epicene.'

'Q.'

'Hermaphroditic. Androgynous. It wasn't obvious that the character was supposed to be a male character. I assume you can Identify.

'The other had the camera bolted down inside a stroller or bassinet. I wore an incredible white floor-length gown of some sort of flowing material and leaned in over the camera in the crib and simply apologized.'

'Q.'

'Apologized. As in my lines were various apologies. "I'm so sorry. I'm so terribly sorry. I am so, so sorry. Please know how very, very, very sorry I am." For a real long time. I doubt he used it all, I strongly doubt he used it all, but there were at least twenty minutes of permutations of "I'm sorry." '

'Q.'

'Not exactly. Not exactly veiled.'

'Q.'

'The point of view was from the crib, yes. A crib's-eye view. But that's not what I mean by driving the scene. The camera was fitted with a lens with something Jim called I think an auto-wobble. Ocular wobble, something like that. A ball-and-socket joint behind the mount that made the lens wobble a little bit. It made a weird little tiny whirring noise, I recollect.'

'Q.'

'The mount's the barrel. The mount's what the elements of the lens are arranged in. This crib-lens's mount projected out way farther than a conventional lens, but it wasn't near as big around as a catadioptric lens. It looked more like an eye-stalk or a night-vision scope than a lens. Long and skinny and projecting, with this slight wobble. I don't know much about lenses beyond basic concepts like length and speed. Lenses were Jim's forte. This can't be much of a surprise. He always had a whole case full. He paid more attention to the lenses and lights than to the camera. His other son carried them in a special case. Leith was cameras, the son was lenses. Lenses Jim said were what he had to bring to the whole enterprise. Of filmmaking. Of himself. He made all his own.'

'Q.'

'Well I've never been around them. But I know there's something wobbled and weird about their vision, supposedly. I think the newer-born they are, the more the wobble. Plus I think a milky blur. Neonatal nystagmus. I don't know where I heard that term. I don't remember. It could have been Jim. It could have been the son. What I know about infants personally you could — it may have been an astigmatic lens. I don't think there's much doubt the lens was supposed to reproduce an infantile visual field. That's what you could feel was driving the scene. My face wasn't important. You never got the sense it was meant to be captured realistically by this lens.'

'Q.'

'I never saw it. I've got no idea.'

'Q.'

'They were buried with him. The Masters of everything unreleased. At least that was in his will.'

'Q.'

'It had nothing to do with killing himself. Less than nothing to do with it.'

'Q.'

'No I never saw his fucking will. He told me. He told me things.

'He'd stopped being drunk all the time. That killed him. He couldn't take it but he'd made a promise.'

'Q.'

'I don't know that he ever even got a finished Master. That's *your* story. There wasn't anything unendurable or enslaving in either of my scenes. Nothing like these actual-perfection rumors. These are academic rumors. He talked about making something quote too perfect. But as a *joke*. He had a thing about entertainment, being criticized about entertainment v. nonentertainment and stasis. He used to refer to the Work itself as "entertainments." He always meant it ironically. Even in jokes he never talked about an anti-version or antidote for God's sake. He'd never carry it that far. A joke.'

'. . .'

'When he talked about this thing as a quote perfect entertainment, terminally compelling — it was always ironic — he was having a sly little jab at me. I used to go around saying the veil was to disguise lethal perfection, that I was too lethally beautiful for people to stand. It was a kind of joke I'd gotten from one of his entertainments, the Medusa-Odalisk thing. That even in U.H.I.D. I hid by hiddenness, in denial about the deformity itself. So Jim took a failed piece and told me it was too perfect to release — it'd paralyze people. It was entirely clear that it was an ironic joke. To me.'

'Q.'

'Jim's humor was a *dry* humor.'

'Q.'

'If it got made and nobody's seen it, the Master, it's in there with him. Buried. That's just a guess. But I bet you.'

'. . .'

'Call it an *educated* bet.'

'Q.'

'. . .'

'Q, Q, Q.'

'That's the part of the joke he didn't know. Where he's buried is *itself* buried, now. It's in your annulation-zone. It's not even your *territory*. And now if you want the thing — he'd enjoy the joke very much, I think. Oh shit yes very much.'

By a rather creepy coincidence, it turned out that, up in our room, Kyle Dempsy Coyle and Mario were also watching one of Himself's old efforts. Mario had gotten his pants on and was using his special tool to zip and button. Coyle looked oddly traumatized. He was sitting on the edge of my bed, his eyes wide and his whole body with the slight tremble of something hanging from the tip of a pipette. Mario greeted me by name. Snow continued to whirl and eddy outside the window. The position of the sun was impossible to gauge. The net-posts were now buried almost up to their scorecard attachments. The wind was piling snow up in drifts against all Academy right angles and then pummelling the drifts into unusual shapes. The window's whole view had the gray grainy quality of a poor photo. The sky looked diseased. Mario worked his tool with great patience. It often took him several tries to catch and engage the tool's jaws on the tongue of his zipper. Coyle, still wearing his apnea-mouthguard, stared at our room's little viewer. The cartridge was Himself's *Accomplice!,* a short melodrama with Cosgrove Watt and a boy no one had ever seen before or since.

'You woke up early,' Mario said, smiling up from his fly. His bed was made up drum-tight.

I smiled. 'Turns out I wasn't the only one.'

'You look sad.'

I raised my hand with the NASA glass at Coyle. 'An unexpected pleasure, K.D.C.'

'Thtithe fickn meth,' Coyle said.

I put the glass and toothbrush on my dresser and straightened its doily. I picked some clothing up and began separating it by smell into wearable and unwearable.

'Kyle says Jim Troeltsch tore some of Ortho's face off trying to pull him off a window his face got glued to,' Mario said. 'And then Jim Troeltsch and Mr. Kenkle tried to put toilet tissue on the ripped parts, the way Tall Paul sometimes puts little bits of Kleenex on a shaving cut, but Ortho's face was a lot worse than a shaving cut, and they used a whole roll, and now Ortho's face is covered with toilet tissue, and the tissue's stuck now, and Ortho can't get it off, and at breakfast Mr. deLint was yelling at Ortho for letting them put toilet tissue on it, and Ortho ran to his and Kyle's room and locked the door, and Kyle doesn't have his key since the accident with the whirlpool.'

I helped Mario on with his police lock's vest and affixed the Velcro nice and tight. Mario's chest is so fragile-feeling that I could feel his heartbeat's tremble through the vest and sweatshirt.

Coyle removed the apnea-guard. Strings of white nighttime oral material appeared between his mouth and the guard as he extracted it. He looked to Mario. 'Tell him the worst part.'

I was watching Coyle very closely to see what he planned to do with the sickening mouthpiece he held.

'Hey Hal, your phone has messages, and Mike Pemulis came by and asked if you were up and about.'

'You haven't told him the worst part of it,' Coyle said.

'Don't even think about putting that thing down anywhere my bed, Kyle, please.'

'I'm holding it away from everything, don't worry.'

Mario used his tool to zip up the long curved zipper of his backpack. 'Kyle said there was a problem with a discharge again —'

'So I heard,' I said.

'— and Kyle says he woke up and Ortho was missing, and Ortho's bed was missing as well, so he turned on the light —'

Coyle gestured with the appliance: 'And lo and fucking-capital-B behold.'

'— yes *and lo*,' Mario said, 'Ortho's bed is up near the ceiling of their room. The frame has some way got lifted up and bolted to the ceiling sometime during the night without Kyle hearing it or waking up.'

'Until the discharge, that is,' I said.

'This is it,' said Coyle. 'The tin cans and accusations I'm moving his stuff around are one thing. I'm going to Lateral Alice for a switch like Troeltsch did. This is the *straw*.'

Mario said 'And his bed's up on the ceiling now, still, and if it falls it's going to go right through the floor and fall in Graham and Petropolis's room.'

'He's in there right now all mummified in toilet paper, sulking, with his bed hanging overhead, with the door locked, so I can't even get my apnea-guard-cleaning supplies,' Coyle said.

I'd heard nothing about Troeltsch apparently switching room-assignments with Trevor Axford. A gigantic wedge of snow slid down a steep part of the roof over our window and fell past the window and hit the ground below with a huge whump. For some reason the fact that something as major as a midterm room-switch could have taken place without my knowing anything about it filled me with dread. There were a few glitters of a possible incipient panic-attack again.

Mario's bedside table had a tube of salve for his pelvis's burn, unevenly squeezed. Mario was looking at my face. 'Is it you're sad about not getting to play if the Québec players are canceled?'

'And then to crown off the whole night he ends up with his face glued to a window,' Coyle said disgustedly.

'Frozen,' I corrected him.

'Except but now listen to Stice's explanation.'

'Let me guess,' I said.

'For the bed hovering.'

Mario looked at Coyle. 'You said bolted.'

'I said *presumably* bolted is what I said. I said the only rationale that's possible is bolts.'

'Let me guess,' I said.

'Let him guess,' Mario told Coyle.

'The Darkness thinks ghosts.' Coyle stood and came toward us. His two eyes were not set quite level in his face. 'Stice's explanation that he swore me to discretion but that was before the bed on the ceiling was he thinks he's been somehow selected or chosen to get haunted or possessed by some kind of beneficiary or guardian ghost that resides in and/or manifests in ordinary physical objects, that wants to teach The Darkness how to not underestimate ordinary objects and raise his game to like a supernatural level, to help his game.' One eye was subtly lower than the other, and set at a different angle.

'Or hurt somebody else's,' I said.

'Stice is mentally buckling,' Coyle said, still moving in. I was careful to stay just out of morning-breath range. 'He keeps staring at things with his temple-veins flexing, trying to exert will on them. He bet me 20 beans he could stand on his desk chair and lift it up at the same time, and then he wouldn't let me cancel the bet when I got embarrassed for him after half an hour, standing up there flexing his temples.'

I was also keeping a careful eye on the oral appliance. 'Did you guys hear sausage-analog and fresh-squeezed for breakfast?'

Mario asked again if I were sad.

Coyle said 'I was *down* there. Stice's map was taking the edge off appetites all over the room. Then deLint started in yelling at him.' He was looking at me oddly. 'I don't see what's so funny about it, man.'

Mario fell backward onto his bed and wriggled into his backpack's straps with practiced ease.

Coyle said 'I don't know if I should go to Schtitt, or Rusk, or what. Or Lateral Alice. What if they haul him off somewhere, and it's my fault?'

'There's no denying The Dark's raised his game this fall though.'

'There are machine messages on the machine, Hal, too,' Mario said as I held his hands carefully and pulled him upright.

'What if it's the mental buckling that's raised his game?' Coyle said. 'Does it still count as buckling?'

Cosgrove Watt had been one of the very few professional actors Himself ever used. Himself often liked to use rank amateurs; he wanted them simply to read their lines with an amateur's wooden self-consciousness off cue cards Mario or Disney Leith would hold up well to the side of wherever the character was supposed to be looking. Up until the last phase of his career, Himself had apparently thought the stilted, wooden quality of nonprofessionals helped to strip away the pernicious illusion of realism and to remind the audience that they were in reality watching actors acting and not people behaving. Like the Parisian-French Bresson he so admired, Himself had no interest in suckering the audience with illusory realism, he said. The apparent irony of the fact that it required *non*actors to achieve this stilted artificial I'm-only-acting-here quality was one of very few things about Himself's early projects that truly interested academic critics. But the real truth was that the early Himself hadn't wanted skilled or believable acting to get in the way of the abstract ideas and technical innovations in the cartridges, and this had always seemed to me more like Brecht than like Bresson. Conceptual and technical ingenuity didn't much interest entertainment-film audiences, though, and one way of looking at Himself's abandonment of anticonfluentialism is that in his last several projects he'd been so desperate to make something that ordinary U.S. audiences might find entertaining and diverting and conducive to self-forgetting[378] that he had had professionals and amateurs alike emoting wildly all over the place. Getting emotion out of either actors or audiences had never struck me as one of Himself's strengths, though I could remember arguments during which Mario had claimed I didn't see a lot of what was right there.

Cosgrove Watt was a pro, but he wasn't very good, and before Himself discovered him, Watt's career consisted mostly of regional-market commercials on broadcast television. His widest commercial exposure was as the Dancing Gland in a series of spots for a chain of East Coast endocrinology clinics. He'd worn a bulbous white costume, white toupee, and either a ball-and-chain or white tap-shoes, depending on whether he was portraying the Before-Gland or the After-Gland. Himself during one of these commercials had shouted Eureka at our HD Sony and travelled personally all the way to Glen Riddle, Pennsylvania, where Watt lived with his mother and her cats, to recruit him. He used Cosgrove Watt in almost every project for eighteen months. Watt for a time was to Himself as DeNiro was to Scorsese, McLachlin to Lynch, Allen to Allen. And up until Watt's temporal-lobe problem made his social presence unbearable, Himself had actually put Watt, mother, and cats up in a contiguous suite of what later became prorectors' rooms off the main E.T.A. tunnel, the Moms acquiescing in this but instructing Orin, Mario, and me never ever to remain in a room alone with Watt.

Accomplice! was one of Watt's later roles. It is a sad and simple cartridge, and so short that the TP retracked to the film's beginning in almost no time. Himself's film opens as a beautifully sad young bus-station male prostitute, fragile and epicene and so blond even his eyebrows and lashes are blond, is approached in the Greyhound coffee shop by a flabby, dissipated-looking old specimen with gray teeth and circumflex eyebrows and obvious temporal-lobe difficulties. Cosgrove Watt plays the depraved older man, who takes the boy home to his lush but somehow scuzzy co-op apartment, in fact the place Himself had rented for O. and the P.G.O.A.T. and had decorated in various gradations of scuz for the interiors of almost all his late projects.

The sad and beautiful Aryan-looking boy agrees to seduction by the dissipated old specimen, but only on the condition that the man wear protection. The boy, who is inarticulate, nevertheless makes this stipulation extremely clear. Safe Sex or No Sex, he stipulates, holding up a familiar foil packet. The hideous old specimen — now in a smoking jacket and ascot of apricot-colored silk, and smoking through a long white FDR-style filter — is offended, thinks the young male prostitute has sized him up as such a depraved and dissipated old specimen that he might well have It, the Human Immuno Virus, he thinks. His thoughts are rendered via animated thought-bubbles, which Himself at that late-middle stage hoped the audience would find at once self-consciously nonillusory and wildly entertaining. Watt's old specimen is grinning grayly in what he thinks is a pleasant way as he obligingly takes the foil packet and removes his ascot with what he believes to be a sensual flourish . . . but inside his thought-bubble he's having temporal-lobe spasms of sadistic rage at the sad blond boy for appearing to size him up as a health risk. The obvious health risk here is referred to, both orally and in the thought-bubble, merely as *It*. For example: 'Little bastard thinks I'm so dissipated-looking that I've been at this sort of thing so long that I'm likely to have *It*, does he,' the old specimen thinks, his thought-bubble going all jagged with rage.

So the flabby old specimen's now, at only six minutes into the cartridge, Track 510, he's now taking the sad beautiful boy, in the standard (extravagantly hunched) homosexual way, on the canopied bed of his tacky boudoir: the young male prostitute's dutifully assumed the hunched, homo-submissive position because the old ponce has showed him he's wearing the condom. The young prostitute, who's shown (hunched) only from the left side during the act itself, seems beautiful in a fragile, skinny-flanked, visible-ribs way, while the old specimen has the slack ass and pointy little breasts of a man made grotesque by years of dissipation. The intercourse scene is done under bright lamps, without any sort of soft focus or light-jazz background score to lighten the atmosphere of clinical detachment.

What the sad blond submissive boy doesn't know is that the dissipated old specimen had secretly palmed an old-fashioned one-sharp-sided razor blade when he'd gone into his burgundy-tiled bathroom to gargle with cinnamon mouthwash and dab Calvin Klein–brand Pheromonic Musk on his flabby pulse-points, and as he hunches animalistically over the boy, he's holding the business end of the blade right up next to the sad boy's anus as he takes his pleasure, so that the blade's sharp side slices into both condom and erect phallus on each outthrust, the hideous old specimen unmindful of the blood and whatever pain's involved in the phallic slicing as, still hunched and thrusting, he peels the slit condom off like the skin of a sausage. The young male prostitute, hunched submissively, feels the condom-peel and then the blood and starts struggling like a condemned man, trying to get the condomless bleeding flabby old specimen out and off of him. But the boy's thin and delicate, and the old man has no trouble holding him down with his soft slack flabby weight until he's grimaced and grunted and taken his pleasure to its end. It's apparently an explicit-homosexual-sex-scene convention that whoever takes the submissive hunched position keeps his face turned away from the camera while the dominant partner's phallus is inside him, and Himself honors this convention, though a self-conscious footnote subtitled along the bottom of the screen rather irritatingly points out that the scene is honoring a convention. The prostitute turns his agonized face around to the camera only after the depraved older homosexual has removed his bloody and deflating post-pleasure phallus, brings his blond-browed face around to his left to face the audience in a mute howl as he collapses onto his delicate chest with his arms out on the satin sheets and his violated bum hiked high in the air, revealing now at the crease of his bum and upper hamstring a vivid purple splotch, more vivid than any bruise and with eight spidery tentacles radiating from it that are, the older man's horrified thought-bubble reveals, the unmistakable eight-legged-vivid-contusion-blotch sign of Kaposi's Sarcoma, that most universal symptom of *It,* and the boy is sobbing that the depraved old homosexual has made him — the prostitute — a murderer, the boy's racking sobs making the hiked bum waggle in front of the old specimen's horrified face as the boy sobs into the chartreuse satin and shrieks '*Murderer! Murderer!*' over and over, so that almost a third of *Accomplice!*'s total length is devoted to the racked repetition of this word — way, way longer than is needed for the audience to absorb the twist and all its possible implications and meanings. This was just the sort of issue Mario and I argued about. As I see it, even though the cartridge's end has both characters emoting out of every pore, *Accomplice!*'s essential project remains abstract and self-reflexive; we end up feeling and thinking not about the characters but about the cartridge itself. By the time the final repetitive image darkens to a silhouette and the credits roll against it and the old man's face stops spasming in horror and the boy shuts up, the cartridge's real tension becomes the question: Did Himself subject us to 500 seconds of the repeated cry 'Murderer!'

946

for some reason, i.e. is the puzzlement and then boredom and then impatience and then excruciation and then near-rage aroused in the film's audience by the static repetitive final ⅓ of the film aroused for some theoretical-aesthetic end, or is Himself simply an amazingly shitty editor of his own stuff?

It was only after Himself's death that critics and theorists started to treat this question as potentially important. A woman at U. Cal–Irvine had earned tenure with an essay arguing that the reason-versus-no-reason debate about what was unentertaining in Himself's work illuminated the central conundra of millennial après-garde film, most of which, in the teleputer age of home-only entertainment, involved the question why so much aesthetically ambitious film was so boring and why so much shitty reductive commercial entertainment was so much fun. The essay was turgid to the point of being unreadable, besides using *reference* as a verb and pluralizing *conundrum* as *conundra*.[379]

From my horizontal position on the bedroom floor I could use the TP's remote to do everything but actually remove and insert cartridges into the drive's dock. The room's window was now a translucent clot of snow and steam. InterLace's Spontaneous Disseminations for New New England were all about weather. With our subscription system, E.T.A. got numerous large-market Spontaneous tracks. Each track took a slightly different angle on the weather. Each track had a slightly different focus. Remote reports from Boston's North and South shores, Providence, New Haven, and Hartford-Springfield served to establish a consensus that a terrific amount of snow had fallen and was continuing to fall and blow around and pile up. Cars were shown abandoned at hasty angles, and we got to see the universal white VW-Bug-shape of snow-buried cars. Black-helmeted gangs of adolescents on snowmobiles were shown prowling New Haven's streets, clearly up to no good. Pedestrians were shown bent over and floundering; remote-report journalists were shown trying to flounder over to them to get their thoughts and reflections. One floundering reporter in Quincy on the South Shore abruptly disappeared from view except for a hand with a microphone protruding bravely from some sort of sinkhole of snow; the bent backs of technicians were then shown floundering away from the remote camera to his aid. People with snow blowers stood in their own little blizzards. A pedestrian was filmed doing a spectacular pratfall. Cars at all angles in streets were shown with their tires spinning, shuddering in stasis. One track kept cutting back to a man endlessly trying to brush off a windshield that immediately whitened again behind each brushstroke. A bus sat with its snout in a monster-sized drift. ATHSCME fans atop the wall north of Ticonderoga NNY were shown making horizontal cyclones of snow in the air. Rouged somber women in InterLace studios concurred that this was the worst blizzard to hit the region since B.S. 1998 and the second-worst since

B.S. 1993. A man in a wheelchair was shown staring stonily at a two-meter drift across the ramp outside the State House. Satellite maps of east-central O.N.A.N. showed a white formation that was spiralled and shaggy and seemed to have what looked like claws. It was not a Nor'easter. A hot moist ridge from the Gulf of Mexico and an Arctic cold front had collided over the Concavity. The storm's satellite photo was superimposed on schemata of the '98 ass-kicker and shown to be just about identical. An unwelcome old acquaintance was back, a striking woman with black bangs and vivid lipstick said, smiling somberly. Another track iterated: this was not a Nor'easter. It might have been better to say 'smiling mirthlessly.' The flat glazed eyes of the man brushing impotently at his windshield seemed to represent an important visual image; different tracks kept returning to his face. He refused to acknowledge journalists or requests for thoughts. His was the creepy businesslike face of someone carefully picking up glass in the road after an accident in which his decapitated wife's been impaled on the steering wheel. Another track's anchor was a beautiful black woman with purple lipstick and what looked like a very tall crew cut. Reports of snow came in from all directions. After a while I stopped keeping track of the number of times the word *snow* was repeated. All synonyms for *snowstorm* were rapidly exhausted. Helmetless thrill-seekers on snowmobiles were doing doughnuts in Copley Square downtown. Homeless men hunched nearly drift-covered in doorways, readying snorkels of rolled-up newspaper. Jim Troeltsch, now apparently a resident of B-204, had liked to do a pretty funny impression of an InterLace anchorwoman having an orgasm. One of the thrill-seekers' snowmobiles spun out of control and plunged into a drift, and the remote camera stayed on the drift for several moments, but nothing emerged. Connecticut's National Guard Reserve had been ordered to assemble but had not assembled because travel in Connecticut was impossible. Three men in uniforms and gray helmets chased two men in white helmets, all on snowmobiles, for reasons an on-site journalist described as not yet emergent. Remote-site journalists used such words as *emergent, individual, alleged, utilize,* and *developing.* But all this impersonal diction was preceded by the anchorperson's first name, as if the report were part of an intimate conversation. An InterLace delivery-boy was shown delivering recorded cartridges on a snowmobile and was described as plucky. Otis P. Lord had undergone a procedure for the removal of the Hitachi monitor on Thursday, LaMont Chu had said. I had never once ridden a snowmobile, skied, or skated: E.T.A. discouraged them. DeLint described winter sports as practically getting down on one knee and begging for an injury. The snowmobiles on the viewer all made sounds like little chain-saws that were extra pugnacious to compensate for being so little. There was a poignant shot of a stuck plow in Northampton. 'Individuals who are not with emergency reasons to travel' (*sic*) were being officially discouraged from travelling by a state trooper in a hat with a chinstrap. A Brockton man in a Lands' End parka took a fall too burlesque to have been unstaged.

I could barely recall the '98 blizzard. The Academy had been open for only a few months. I remember the edges of the shaved hilltop were still square and steep and striped in sedimentary layers, final construction delayed by some nasty piece of litigation from the VA hospital below. The storm came barrelling in southeast from Canada in March. Dwight Flechette and Orin and the other players had had to be led to the Lung roped together, single file, Schtitt in the lead carrying a highway flare. A couple photos hung in C.T.'s waiting room. The last boy along the rope disappeared into a forlorn gray whirl. The Lung's new bubble had had to be taken down and fixed when snow-weight stove it in on one side. The T stopped running. I remember some of the younger players had cried and sworn up and down that the blizzard wasn't their fault. For days snow churned steadily out of a graphite sky. Himself had sat in a spindle-backed chair, at the same living-room window C.T. now uses for advanced worry, and aimed a series of nondigital cameras at the mounting snow. After years in which his consuming obsession was the establishment of E.T.A., Orin said, Himself had started in with the film-obsession almost immediately after the Academy was up and running. Orin has said the Moms had assumed the film thing was a passing obsession. Himself had seemed interested mostly in the lenses and rasters[380] at first, and in the consequences of their modification. He sat in that chair throughout the whole storm, sipping brandy from a one-handed snifter, his long legs not quite covered by a plaid blanket. His legs had seemed to me almost endlessly long back then. He always seemed to be right on the edge of coming down with something. His record up until then indicated that he remained obsessed with something until he became successful at it, then transferred his obsession to something else. From military optics to annular optics to entrepreneurial optics to tennis-pedagogy to film. In the chair during the blizzard he'd had beside him several different types of camera and a large leather case. The inside of the case was striated with lenses down both sides. He used to let Mario and me put different lenses in our eyes and squint to hold them, imitating Schtitt.

One way of looking at the film-obsession's endurance is that Himself was never really successful or accomplished at filmmaking. This was something else on which Mario and I had agreed to disagree.

It took almost a year to complete the move from Weston to E.T.A. The Moms had attachments in Weston and she drew things out. I was pretty small. I lay flat on my back on our room's carpet and tried to recall details of our home in Weston, twidgeling the TP's remote with my thumb. I do not have Mario's head for remembered detail. One dissemination-track simply panned the metro-Boston sky and horizons from atop the Hancock tower. On the FM band, WYYY was apparently doing its weather-report via mimesis, broadcasting raw static while the student staff doubtless did bongs in celebration of the storm and then went up sliding around the Union's cerebral rooftop. The Hancock camera's pan included the sinciput of the M.I.T. Union, its roof's convolutions filling with snow ahead of the rest of it, creepy filigrees of white against the roof's deep gray.

Our subdorm room's only carpet was an oversized corruption of the carpet page from the Lindisfarne Gospels in which you had to look very closely to make out the tiny pornographic scenes in the Byzantine weave surrounding the cross. I'd acquired the carpet years ago during a period of intense interest in Byzantine pornography inspired by what I'd seen as a titillating reference in the O.E.D. I too had moved serially between obsessions, as a child. I adjusted my angle on the carpet. I was trying to align myself along some sort of grain in the world I could barely feel, since Pemulis and I stopped. Meaning the grain, not the world. I realized I could not distinguish my own visual memories of the Weston house from my memories of hearing Mario's detailed reports of his memories. I remember a late-Victorian three-level on a low quiet street of elms, hyperfertilized lawns, tall homes with oval windows and screen porches. One of the street's homes had a pineapple finial. Only the street itself was low; the lots were humped up high and the houses so tall the broad street seemed nevertheless constricted, a sort of affluence-flanked defile. It seemed always to be summer or spring. I could remember the Moms's voice high overhead at a screen-porch door, calling us in as dusk drifted down and leaded fanlights began to light up at homes' doors in some sort of linear sync. Either our driveway or another driveway flanked with whitewashed stones the shapes of beads or drops. The Moms's intricate garden in a backyard enclosed by a fencework of trees. Himself on the screen porch, stirring a gin and tonic with his finger. The Moms's dog S. Johnson, not yet neutered, confined by psychosis in a sort of large fenced pen abutting the garage, running around and around the pen when thunder sounded. The smell of Noxzema: Himself behind Orin in the upstairs bathroom, towering over and down, teaching Orin to shave against the grain, upward. I remember S. Johnson leaping up on his hind legs and sort of playing the fence with his paws as Mario approached the pen: the rattling chain-link's pitch. The circle of earth worn bare by S.J.'s orbit in the pen when thunder sounded or planes crossed overhead. Himself sat low in chairs and could cross his legs and still have both feet flat on the floor. He'd hold his chin in his hand while he looked at you. My memories of Weston seemed like tableaux. They seemed more like snapshots than films. A weird isolated memory of summertime gnats knitting the air above the shaggy animal-head of a neighbor's topiary hedge. Our own round shrubs trimmed flat as tabletops by the Moms. More horizontals. The chatter of hedge-clippers, their power-cords bright orange. I had to swallow spit with almost every breath. I remembered climbing with a dawdler's heavy tread the cement steps up from the street to a gambrel-roofed late-Victorian whose narrow height from the steps gave it the distended look of thick liquid hanging: gingerbread eaves, undulate shingles of weathered red, zinc gutters the Moms's graduate students came and kept clean. A blue star in the front window and the words *BLOCK MOTHER,* which had always suggested either a rectangular woman or some type of football-crowd cheer. The inside cool and dim and a smell of Lemon Pledge. I had no visual memories of my mother without white hair; all that varied was the length. A touch-tone phone, with a cord running into the wall, on a horizontal surface in a recessed alcove near the front door. Cork floors and pre-mounted shelving of woody-smelling wood. The chilling framed print of Lang directing *Metropolis* in 1924.[381] A hulking black chest with strap-hinges of brass. A few of Himself's old heavy tennis trophies as bookends on the mounted shelving. An étagère filled with old-fashioned magnetic videos in bright adverting boxes, a cluster of blue-and-white delfts on the étagère's top shelf that had dwindled as one figurine after another got knocked off by Mario, stumbling or shoved. The blue-white chairs with the protective plastic that made your legs sweat. A divan done in some sort of burlapesque Iranian wool dyed to the color of sand mixed with ash — this may have been a neighbor's divan. Some cigarette burns in the fabric of the divan's arms. Books, videotapes, kitchen's cans — all alphabetized. Everything painfully clean. Several spindle-backed captain's chairs in contrasting fruit-woods. A surreal memory of a steamed lavatory mirror with a knife sticking out of the pane. A massive stereo television console of whose gray-green eye I was afraid when the television was off. Some of the memories have to be confabulated or dreamed — the Moms would never have had a divan with burns in it.

A picture window east, the direction of Boston, with claret-colored figures and a blue sun all suspended in a web of lead. The candy-colored summer sunrise through that window as I watched television in the A.M.

The tall thin quiet man, Himself, with his razor-burn and bent glasses and chinos too short, whose neck was slender and shoulders sloped, who slumped in candied east-window sunlight with his tailbone supported by windowsills, meekly stirring a glass of something with his finger while the Moms stood there telling him she'd long-since abandoned any reasonable hope that he could hear what she was telling him — this silent figure, of whom I still remember mostly endless legs and the smell of Noxzema shave-cream, seems, still, impossible to reconcile with the sensibility of something like *Accomplice!* It was impossible to imagine Himself conceiving of sodomy and razors, no matter how theoretically. I lay there and could almost remember Orin telling me something almost moving that Himself had once told him. Something to do with *Accomplice!* The memory hung somewhere just out of conscious reach, and its tip-of-the-tongue inaccessibility felt too much like the preface to another attack. I accepted it: I could not remember.

Off down the Weston street a church with an announcement-board in the grass out front — white plastic letters on a slotted black surface — and at least once Mario and I stood watching a goatish man change the letters and thus the announcement. One of the first occasions where I remember reading something involved the announcement-board announcing:

LIFE IS LIKE TENNIS
THOSE WHO SERVE
BEST USUALLY WIN

with the letters all spaced far out like that. A big fresh-cement-colored church, liberal with glass, denomination not recalled, but built in what was, in the B.S. 80's probably, modern — a parabolic poured-concrete shape billowed and peaked like a cresting wave. A suggestion in it of some paranormal wind somewhere that could make concrete billow and pop like a tucking sail.

Our own subdorm room now has three of those old Weston captain's chairs whose backs dent your spine if you don't fit it carefully between two spindles. We have an unused wicker basket for laundry on which are stacked some corduroy spectation-pillows. Floor plans for Hagia Sophia and S. Simeon at Qal'at Si'man on the wall over my bed, the really prurient part of *Consummation of the Levirates* over the chairs, also from the old interest in Byzantinalia. Something about the stiff and dismantled quality of *maniera greca* porn: people broken into pieces and trying to join, etc. At the foot of Mario's bed a surplus-store trunk for his own film equipment and a canvas director's chair where he's always laid out his police lock, lead weights, and vest for the night. A fiberboard stand for the compact TP and viewer, and a stenographer's chair for using the TP to type. Five total chairs in a room where no one ever sits in a chair. As in all the subdorm rooms and hallways, a guilloche ran around our walls half a meter from the ceiling. New E.T.A.s always drove themselves bats counting their room's guilloche's interwoven circles. Our room had 811 and truncated bits of -12 and -13, two left halves stuck like open parentheses up in the southwest corner. Between the ages of eleven and thirteen I'd had a plaster knock-off of a lewd Constantine frieze, the emperor with a hyperemic organ and an impure expression, hung by two hooks from the guilloche's lower border. Now I couldn't for the life of me recall what I'd done with the frieze, or which Byzantine seraglio the original had decorated. There had been a time when data like these were instantly available.

The Weston living room had had an early version of Himself's full-spectrum cove lighting and at one end an elevated fieldstone fireplace with a big copper hood that made a wonderful ear-splitting drum-head for wooden spoons, with memories of some foreign adult I didn't recognize grinding at her temples and pleading *Do* Stop. The Moms's jungle of Green Babies had spread out into the room from another corner, the plants' pots on stands of various heights, hanging in nests of twine suspended from clamps, arrayed at eye-height from projecting trellises of white-painted iron, all in the other-worldly glow of a white-hooded tube of ultraviolet light hung with thin chains from the ceiling. Mario can recall violet-lit laces of ferns and the wet meaty gloss of rubber-tree leaves.

And a coffee table of green-shot black marble, too heavy to move, on whose corner Mario knocked out a tooth after what Orin swore up and down was an accidental shove.

Mrs. Clarke's varicotic calves at the stove. The way her mouth overhead would disappear when the Moms reorganized something in the kitchen. My eating mold and the Moms's being very upset that I'd eaten it — this memory was of Orin's telling the story; I had no childhood memory of eating fungus.

My trusty NASA glass still rested on my chest, rising when my rib cage rose. When I looked down my own length, the glass's round mouth was a narrow slot. This was because of my optical perspective. There was a concise term for *optical perspective* that I again could not quite make resolve.

What made it hard really to recall our old house's living room was that so many of its appointments were now in the living room of the Headmaster's House, the same and yet altered, and by more than rearrangement. The onyx coffee table Mario had fallen against (*specular* is what refers to optical perspective; it came to me after I stopped trying to recall it) now supported compact disks and tennis magazines and a cello-shaped vase of dried eucalyptus, and the red-steel stand for the family Xmas tree, when in season. The table had been a wedding gift from Himself's mother, who died of emphysema shortly before Mario's surprise birth. Orin reports she'd looked like an embalmed poodle, all neck-tendons and tight white curls and eyes that were all pupil. The Moms's birth-mother had died in Québec of an infarction when she — the Moms — was eight, her father during her sophomore year at McGill under circumstances none of us knew. The hydrant-sized Mrs. Tavis was still alive and somewhere in Alberta, the original L'Islet potato farm now part of the Great Concavity and forever lost.

Orin and Bain et al. at Family Trivia during that terrible first year's blizzard, Orin imitating the Moms's high breathy 'My son ate this! God, please!,' never tiring of it.

Orin had liked also to recreate for us the spooky kyphotic hunch of Himself's mother, in her wheelchair, beckoning him closer with a claw, the way she seemed always caved in over and around her chest as if she'd been speared there. An air of deep dehydration had hung about her, he said, as if she osmosized moisture from whoever came near. She spent her last few years living in the Marlboro St. brownstone they'd had before Mario and I were born, tended by a gerontologic nurse Orin said always wore the expression of every post-office mug shot you've ever seen. When the nurse was off, a small silver bell was apparently hung from an arm of the old lady's wheelchair, to be rung when she could not breathe. A cheery silver tinkle announcing asphyxiation upstairs. Mrs. Clarke would still pale whenever Mario asked about her.

It's become easier to see the climacteric changes in the Moms's own body since she began confining herself more and more to the Headmaster's House. This occurred after Himself's funeral, but in stages — the gradual withdrawal and reluctance to leave the grounds, and the signs of aging. It is hard to notice what you see every day. None of the physical changes has been dramatic — her nerved-up dancer's legs becoming hard, stringy, a shrinking of the hips and a girdly thickening at the waist. Her face settles a little lower on her skull than it did four years ago, with a slight bunching under the chin and an emerging potential for something pruny happening around her mouth, in time, I thought I could see.

The word that best connoted why the glass's mouth looked slotty was probably *foreshortened.*

The Q.R.S. Infantilist would no doubt join the old grief-therapist in asking how watching one's Moms begin to age makes you feel inside. Questions like these become almost koans: you have to lie when the truth is Nothing At All, since this appears as a textbook lie under the therapeutic model. The brutal questions are the ones that *force* you to lie.

Either our old kitchen or a neighbor's kitchen panelled with walnut and hung with copper pâté-molds and herbal sprigs. An unidentified woman — not Avril or Mrs. Clarke — standing in that kitchen in snug cherry slacks, loafers over bare feet, waggling a mixing spoon, laughing at something, a long-tailed comet of flour on her cheek.

It occurred to me then with some force that I didn't want to play this afternoon, even if some sort of indoor exhibition-meet came off. Not even neutral, I realized. I would on the whole have preferred not to play. What Schtitt might have to say to that, v. what Lyle would say. I was unable to stay with the thought long enough to imagine Himself's response to my refusal to play, if any.

But this was the man who made *Accomplice!,* whose sensibility informed the hetero-hardcore *Möbius Strips* and the sado-periodontal *Fun with Teeth* and several other projects that were just thoroughgoingly nasty and sick.

Then it occurred to me that I could walk outside and contrive to take a spill, or squeeze out the window on the rear staircase of HmH and fall several meters to the steep embankment below, being sure to land on the bad ankle and hurt it, so I'd not have to play. That I could carefully plan out a fall from the courts' observation transom or the spectators' gallery of whatever club C.T. and the Moms sent us to to help raise funds, and fall so carefully badly I'd take out all the ankle's ligaments and never play again. Never have to, never get to. I could be the faultless victim of a freak accident and be knocked from the game while still on the ascendant. Becoming the object of compassionate sorrow rather than disappointed sorrow.

I couldn't stay with this fantastic line of thought long enough to parse out whose disappointment I was willing to cripple myself to avoid (or forgo).

And then out of nowhere it returned to me, the moving thing Himself had said to Orin. This was concerning 'adult' films, which from what I've seen are too downright sad to be truly nasty, or even really entertainment, though the adjective *adult* is kind of a misnomer.

Orin had told me that once he and Smothergill, Flechette, and I think Penn's older brother had gotten hold of a magnetic video of some old hardcore X-film — *The Green Door* or *Deep Throat,* one of those old chestnuts of cellulite and jism. There were excited plans to convene in V.R.3 and watch the thing in secret after Lights Out. The Viewing Rooms at that point had broadcast televisions and magnetic VCR-devices, instructional mag-vids from Galloway and Braden, etc. Orin and co. were all around fifteen at the time, bombed by their own glands — they were pop-eyed at the prospect of genuine porn. There were rules about videos' suitability for viewing in the Honor Code, but Himself was not noted for his discipline, and Schtitt didn't yet have deLint — the first generation of E.T.A.s did pretty much as they pleased off-court, as long as they were discreet.

Nevertheless, word about this 'adult' film got around, and somebody — probably Mary Esther Thode's sister Ruth, then a senior and insufferable — ratted the boys' viewing-plans out to Schtitt, who took the matter to Himself. Orin said he was the only one Himself called into the Headmaster's office, which in that era had only one door, which Himself asked Orin to close. Orin recalled seeing none of the unease that always accompanied Himself's attempts at stern discipline. Instead Himself invited Orin to sit and gave him a lemon soda and stood facing him, leaning back slightly so that the front edge of his desk supported him at the tailbone. Himself took his glasses off and massaged his closed eyes delicately — almost trea-suringly, his old eyeballs — in the way Orin knew signified that Himself was ruminative and sad. One or two soft interrogatives brought the whole affair out in the open. You could never lie to Himself; somehow you just never had the heart. Whereas Orin made almost an Olympic sport of lying to the Moms. Anyway, Orin quickly confessed to everything.

What Himself said then moved him, Orin told me. Himself told Orin he wasn't going to forbid them to watch the thing if they really wanted to. But just please to keep it discreet, just Bain and Smothergill and Orin's immediate circle, nobody younger, and nobody whose parents might hear about it, and for God's sake don't let your mother get wind. But that Orin was old enough to make his own entertainment-decisions, and if he decided he wanted to watch the thing. . . . And so on.

But Himself said that if Orin wanted his personal, fatherly as opposed to headmasterly, take on it, then he, Orin's father — though he wouldn't forbid it — would rather Orin didn't watch a hard-porn film yet. He said this with such reticent earnestness there was no way Orin couldn't ask him how come. Himself felt his jaw and pushed his glasses up several times and shrugged and finally said he supposed he was afraid of the film giving Orin the wrong idea about having sex. He said he'd personally prefer that Orin wait until he'd found someone he loved enough to want to have sex with and had had sex with this person, that he'd wait until he'd experienced for himself what a profound and really quite moving thing sex could be, before he watched a film where sex was presented as nothing more than organs going in and out of other organs, emotionless, terribly lonely. He said he supposed he was afraid that something like *The Green Door* would give Orin an impoverished, lonely idea of sexuality.

What poor old O. claimed to have found so moving was Himself's assumption that O. was still cherry. What moved *me* to feel sorry for Orin was that it seemed pretty obvious that that had nothing to do with what Himself was trying to talk about. It was the most open I'd ever heard of Himself being with anybody, and it seemed terribly sad to me, somehow, that he'd wasted it on Orin. I'd never once had a conversation nearly that open or intimate with Himself. My most intimate memory of Himself was the scratchiness of his jaw and the smell of his neck when I fell asleep at supper and he carried me upstairs to bed. His neck was thin but had a good meaty warm smell; I now for some reason associate it with the odor of Coach Schtitt's pipe.

I tried briefly to picture Ortho Stice hoisting his bunk up and bolting it to the ceiling without waking Coyle. Our room's door remained ajar from Mario's exit with Coyle to find someone with a master key. Yardguard and Wagenknecht's heads popped in briefly and urged me to come have a look at The Darkness's ruined map and withdrew when they got no response. The second floor was pretty quiet; most of them were still dawdling at breakfast, awaiting some announcement on the weather and Québecois squads. Snow hit the windows with a gritty sound. The angle of the wind had made a kind of whistle out of one corner of the subdorm building, and the whistling came and went.

Then I heard John Wayne's stride in the hall outside, light and even and easy on floors, the stride of a guy with stellar calf-development. I heard his low sigh. Then, though the door was too far behind me to see, for a moment or two I could somehow tell for sure that John Wayne's head was inside the open door. I could feel it clearly, almost painfully. He was looking down at me lying there on the Lindisfarne carpet. There was none of the gathering tension of a person deciding whether or not to speak. I could feel my throat's equipment move when I swallowed. John Wayne and I never had much to say to one another. There wasn't even hostility between us. He ate dinner with us at HmH every so often because he and the Moms were tight. The Moms made little attempt to disguise her attachment to Wayne. Now his breathing behind me was light and very even. No waste, complete utilization of each breath.[382]

Of us three, it was Mario who had spent the most time with Himself, sometimes travelling with him for location-work. I had no idea what they spoke about together, or how openly. None of us had ever pressed Mario to say much about it. It occurred to me to wonder why this was so.

I decided to get up but then did not in fact get up. Orin was convinced that Himself was a virgin when he met the Moms in his late thirties. I find this pretty hard to believe. Orin will also grant that there's no doubt Himself was faithful to the Moms right up to the end, that his attachment to Orin's fiancée was not sexual. I had a sudden and lucid vision of the Moms and John Wayne locked in a sexual embrace of some kind. John Wayne had been involved with the Moms sexually since roughly the second month after his arrival. They were both expatriates. I hadn't yet been able to identify a strong feeling one way or the other about the liaison, nor about Wayne himself, except for admiring his talent and total focus. I did not know whether Mario knew of the liaison, to say nothing of poor C.T.

It was impossible for me to imagine Himself and the Moms being explicitly sexual together. I bet most children have this difficulty where their parents are concerned. Sex between the Moms and C.T. I imagined as both frenetic and weary, with a kind of doomed timeless Faulknerian feel to it. I imagined the Moms's eyes open and staring blankly at the ceiling the whole time. I imagined C.T. never once shutting up, talking around and around whatever was taking place between them. My coccyx had gone numb from the pressure of the floor through the thin carpet. Bain, graduate students, grammatical colleagues, Japanese fight-choreographers, the hairy-shouldered Ken N. Johnson, the Islamic M.D. Himself had found so especially torturing — these encounters were imaginable but somehow generic, mostly a matter of athleticism and flexibility, different configurations of limbs, the mood one more of cooperation than complicity or passion. I tended to imagine the Moms staring expressionlessly at ceilings throughout. The complicit passion would have come after, probably, with her need to be sure the encounter was hidden. Peterson-allusions notwithstanding, I wondered about some hazy connection between this passion for hiddenness and the fact that Himself had made so many films titled *Cage*, and that the amateur player he became so attached to was the veiled girl, Orin's love. I wondered whether it was possible to lie supine and throw up without aspirating vomit or choking. The plumed spout of a whale. The tableau of John Wayne and my mother in my imagination was not very erotic. The image was complete and sharply focused but seemed stilted, as if composed. She reclines against four pillows, at an angle between seated and supine, staring upward, motionless and pale. Wayne, slim and brown-limbed, smoothly muscled, also completely motionless, lies over her, his untanned bottom in the air, his blank narrow face between her breasts, his eyes unblinking and his thin tongue outthrust like a stunned lizard's. They stay just like that.

She wasn't dumb — she figured it was likely that they'd let her loose just to see where she'd go.

She went home. She went to the House. She got one of the last trains before they closed the T, probably. It took forever to get from Comm. Ave. down to Enfield Marine in her clogs and skirt in the snow, and melt soaked the veil and made it adhere to the features below. She'd been close to removing the veil to get away from the outside-linebacker of a federal lady anyway. She looked now just like a linen-pale version of what she really looked like. But there was no one about in the snow. She figured if she could speak with Pat M. Pat M. might be prevailed upon to put her in quarantine with Clenette and Yolanda, not let in no law. She could tell Pat about the wheelchairs, try to convince her to dismantle the ramp. The visibility was so bad she didn't see it til she cleared the Shed, the Middlesex County Sheriff's car, fiercely snow-tired, lights going bluely, parked idling in the roadlet outside the ramp, wipers on Occasional, a uniform at the wheel absently feeling his face.

He says 'I'm Mikey, alcoholic and addict and a sick fuck, you know what I'm saying?'

And they laugh and shout out 'You definitely are' as he stands there rocking the podium slightly, blurred a bit through the linen, smearing one side of his face with a laborer's hand as he tries to think what to say. It's another of these round-robin-speaker deals, each speaker picking the next from the smoky lunchtime crowd, jogging up to the fiberboard podium trying to think what to say, and how, for the five minutes each is allotted. The chairperson at the table up by the podium has a clock and a novelty-shop gong.

'Well,' he says, "well so I seen some of the old Mikey come back out yesterday, you know what I'm saying? Fucking scared me to see it. What it was, I was going to take my kid down to the lanes and bowl a couple. With my kid. Who he just got the cast off. So I'm all happy and whatnot, got the day off, see the kid. Quality sober time with the kid. So on and so forth. So I'm all on the happy wagon and like that, about seeing the kid, you know what I'm saying? So, what, so I call up my cunt of a sister. He's living back with them, with Ma and my sister, so I'm calling up my sister to see can I come get the kid at such-and-such time and whatnot. Because you know how the judge said I got to get one of them's fucking consent to even see my kid. You know what I'm saying? Because of the restraining order on the old Mikey, from before. I got to get their permission. And I, what, accept that, I say OK, so I'm calling up all accepting and on the happy wagon for my sister to consent, and she out of the goodness of her heart she makes me wait while she says she's got to check it with Ma. And they consent, finally. And I, what, accept that, you know what I'm saying? And I say I was going to be there at such-and-such time and whatnot, and my sister says ain't I even going to say thank you? Like with the attitude, you know what I'm saying? And I say 't the fuck, what, you want a fucking medal for letting me see my own kid? And the cunt hangs *up* on me. Oh. Fucking *oh*. Ever since the judge with the order, it's with the attitude over there, the cunt and Ma both. So after she just hangs up on me a little of the old Mikey I think starts to come out and I go over there and yes all right I got to be honest I do I park on the grass of their fucking lawn, and I go up and go up and I see her and I'm like Fuck you you cunt, and Ma's in the hall behind her in the door, I go Fucking hang up on me why don't you, you should go for some fucking counselling you know what I'm saying? And they don't neither one of them like that verbal comment too much, right? The cunt almost starts laughing and goes, like, *I'm* telling *her* to go for counseling?'

Crowd-laughter.

'I mean I ain't exactly coming over there with long-term sobriety, right? And I accept that. But the cunt's got the hook on the door and she's going Who the fuck are *you* to be telling *me* to go for fucking counselling after the sick fucking little like stunt you and that *bimbo* pulled on that kid who only just now even got the cast off? Oh, and no sign of the fucking kid anywhere. Just her and Ma through the screen door, all over the place with the attitude. And now they tell me to get the fuck off their porch, No they tell me, as in like Permission Denied, consent to see my own kid fucking *refused*. And the cunt still in her fucking bathrobe after noon, and Ma behind her half in the bag already and hanging on to the fucking wall. You know what I'm saying? My serenity's like: *See* yaa! And I say up *boat-ayouse's* asses, I'm here for my goddamn kid. And now my sister says she's going for the phone, and Ma's saying The fuck, get the fuck out, Mikey. And plus did I mention no sign of the kid, and I ain't to even like *touch* the screen door, not without consent. And I'm wanting to fucking kill somebody here, you know what I'm saying? And my sister's getting the antenna out on the phone, and so I go OK I'm fucking leaving, but I like grab my balls at the both of them and go Eat me the boatayouse, you know what I'm saying? Cause now it's the old Mikey back, and now *I* got with the attitude now, also. I'm wanting to light my cunt of a sister up so bad I can't hardly see to get the truck off the lawn and leave. But and so and but so I'm driving back home, and I'm so mad I all of a sudden try and pray. And I try and pray, driving along and whatnot, and it comes to me I see irregarding of their fucked-up attitude I still need to go back and apologize irregardless, for grabbing my balls at them, cause that's old fucking behavior. I see for my own sobriety's sake I need to go back and try and say I'm sorry. The thought of it just about makes me puke, you know what I'm — but I go back and pull the truck up out front on the street and pray and go back up on the porch, and I fucking apologize, and I go to my sister Please can I at least see the kid to see the cast off, and the cunt goes Fuck you, get the fuck out, we don't accept your fucking apology. And no sign of Ma, and the fucking kid there's no sign of him, so I got to accept her word and don't even know for sure if the cast is even off. But why I needed to share I think is it scared me. *I* scared me, you know what I'm saying? I was at the counsellor's after and I told him I go I got to get some kind of hold on this fucking temper or I'm going to end up right back in front of the fucking judge for lighting somebody up again, you know what I'm saying? And God fucking forbid it should be somebody that's in my family, because I been that route once too many times already. And I go like Am I nuts, Dr., or what? Do I got a like death-wish or what? You know what I'm saying? The cast just only now finally comes off and I'm wanting to light up the fucking cunt that's got to *consent* I should get closer than a hundred m.'s to the kid? Is it like I'm *trying* to set myself up for a drink or what exactly is it with this spring-loaded temper, if I'm sober? The temper and judge is why I fucking got sober in the first place. So what the fuck is this? Well fuck me. I'm just grateful I got some of that out. It's been up in my head, renting space, you know what I'm saying? I see Vinnie's getting ready to fucking gong me. I want to hear from Tommy E. back there against the wall. Yo Tom*my!* What are you, spanking the hog back there or what? But I'm just glad to be here. I just wanted to get some of that shit out.'

The man's pants' crease was gone at the knee and his Cardin topcoat looked slept in.

'It was good of you to grant me an easement.'

Pat M. tried to recross her legs and shrugged. 'You said you weren't here professionally.'

'Good of you to believe me.' The Assistant District Attorney for Suffolk County's 4th Circuit up on the near North Shore's hat was a good dress Stetson with a feather in the band. He held it up in his lap by the brim and slowly rotated it by moving his fingers along the brim. He'd re-crossed his legs twice. 'We met you and Mars at the Marblehead Regatta for the McDonald's House thing for children, not this summer but either the sum—'

'I know who you are.' Pat's husband wasn't a celebrity but knew a lot of local celebrities, from the mint-reconditioned-sports-car upscale network around Boston.

'Well it's good of you. I'm here about one of your residents.'

'But not professionally,' Pat said. It wasn't a question or verification. She was cool steel when it came to protecting the residents and House. Then back home in her own home she was a shattered husk of a wreck.

'Frankly I'm not sure why I am here. You're just down the hill from the hospital. I've been up at Saint Elizabeth's off and on for three days. Perhaps I need to simply air this. The 5th District boys — the P.D.s — speak well of the place. Your House here. Perhaps I need simply to share this, to work up the nerve. My sponsor's no help. He's simply said do it if you want to have any hope of things getting better.'

Anything less than a combination thoroughgoing professional and AA-longtimer would have at least hiked an eyebrow at one of the most powerful and remorseless constables in three counties saying *sponsor*.

'It's Phob-Comp-Anon,' the A.D.A. said. 'I went through Choices[383] last winter and have been working a program of recovery in Phob-Comp-Anon a day at a time to the best of my ability ever since then.'

'I see.'

'It's Tooty,' the A.D.A. said. He did a pause with his eyes closed and then smiled, still with his eyes closed. 'It is, rather, me, and my enmeshment-issues with Tooty's . . . condition.'

Phob-Comp-Anon was a decade-old 12-Step splinter from Al-Anon, for codependency-issues surrounding loved ones who were cripplingly phobic or compulsive, or both.

'It's a long story and not a particularly interesting one, I'm sure,' the A.D.A. said. 'Suffice to say that Tooty's been in torment over some oral-dental-hygienic-violation issues that have their roots we're discovering in some issues from a childhood whose dysfunctionality we — well, which she'd been in denial about for quite some time. It doesn't matter what. My program's my own. The hiding the car keys, the cutting off her credit with different dentists, the checking the wastebaskets for new brush-wrappers five times an hour — my unmanageability's my own, and I'm doing what I can, day by day, to let go and detach with love.'

'I think I understand.'

'I'm working Nine, now.'

Pat said 'The Ninth Step.'

The A.D.A. reversed the hat's rotation by moving his fingers in the opposite direction along the brim.

'I'm trying to make direct amends to whosoever my Fourth- and Eighth-Step work's revealed I've harmed, except in cases where to do so would injure them or others.'

A tiny spiritual slip from Pat in the form of a patronizing smile. 'I have a nodding acquaintance with Nine myself.'

The A.D.A. was barely there, his eyes fixed and dilated. The remorselessly ingathered eyebrow-angle Pat had always seen in his photos was completely reversed. The brows now formed a little peaked roof of pathos.

'One of your residents,' he said. 'A Mr. Gately, Court-Remanded out of the 5th Circuit, Peabody I believe. Or Staff counselor, alumni, some status.'

Pat made a kind of exaggerated innocent trying-to-place-the-name-type face.

The A.D.A. said 'It doesn't matter. I'm aware of your constraints. I want nothing from you on him. It's him I've been up at Saint Elizabeth's to see.'

Pat allowed herself one slightly flared nostril at this news.

The A.D.A. leaned forward, hat rotating between his calves, elbows on knees in the odd defecatory posture men used to try to communicate earnestness in their sharing. 'I'm told — I owe the — Mr. Gately — an amend. I need to make an amend to Mr. Gately.' He looked up. 'You too — this remains within these walls, as if it were my anonymity. All right?'

'Yes.'

'It doesn't matter what for. I blamed the — I've harbored a resentment, against this Gately, concerning an incident I'd considered responsible for making Tooty's phobia reflare. It doesn't matter. The specifics, or his culpability or exposure to prosecution in the incident — I've come to believe these don't matter. I've harbored this resentment. The kid's picture's been up on my Priority-board with the pictures of far more objectively important threats to the public weal. I've been biding my time, waiting to get him. This latest incident — no, don't say it, you needn't say a thing — seemed like just the opening. My last chance went federal and then fizzled.'

Pat allowed herself a very slightly puzzled forehead.

The man waved the hat. 'It doesn't matter. I've hated, *hated* this man. You know that Enfield's Suffolk County. This incident with the Canadian assault, the alleged firearm, the witnesses who can't depose because of their own exposure. . . . My sponsor, my entire Group — they say if I act on the resentment I'm doomed. I'll get no relief. It won't help Tooty. Tooty's lips will still be white pulp from the peroxide, her enamel in tatters from the constant irrational brushing and brushing and *brushing and* —' he clamped his fine clean hand over his mouth and produced a high-pitched noise that frankly gave Pat the howlers, his right eyelid twitching.

He took several breaths. 'I need to let it go. I've come to believe that. Not just the prosecution — that's the easy part. I've already tossed the file, though whatever civil liability the — Mr. Gately might face is another matter, not my concern. It's so damnably *ironic*. The man's going to two-step out of at the very least a probation-violation and prosecution on all his old *highly* convictable charges because I have to pitch the case, for the sake of my own recovery, I, who wanted nothing so much as to see this man locked down in a cell with some psychopathic cellmate for the rest of his natural life, who shook my fist at the ceiling and *vowed* —' and again the noise, this time muffled by the fine hat and so less well-muffled, his shoes pounding a little on the carpet in rage so that Pat's dogs raised their heads and looked quizzically at him, and the epileptic one had a very small loud-noise seizure.

'I hear you saying this is very hard but you've decided what you need to do.'

'Worse,' the A.D.A. said, blotting his brow with an unfolded handkerchief. 'I have to make an amend, my sponsor's said. If I want the growth that promises real relief. I have to make direct amends, put out my hand and say that I'm sorry and ask the man's forgiveness for my own failure to forgive. This is the only way I'll be able to forgive him. And I can't detach with love from Tooty's phobic compulsion until I've forgiven the b— the man I've blamed in my heart.'

Pat looked him in the eye.

'Of course I can't say I've tossed the Canadian case's file, I needn't go that far they say. That would expose me to conflict of interest — the *irony* — and could hurt Tooty, if my position's threatened. I've been told I can simply let him simmer on that until time passes and nothing moves forward.' He raised his own eyes. 'Which means you cannot tell anyone either. Declining to prosecute for personal spiritual reasons — the office — it would be hard for others to understand. This is why I've come to you in explicit confidence.'

'I hear your request and I'll honor it.'

'But listen. I can't do it. Cannot. I've sat outside that hospital room saying the Serenity Prayer over and over and praying for willingness and thinking of my own spiritual interests and believing this amend is my Higher Power's will for my own growth and I haven't been able to go in. I go and sit paralyzed outside the room for several hours and drive home and pry Tooty away from the sink. It can't go on. I have to look that rotten — no, *evil*, I'm convinced in my heart, that son of a bitch is *evil* and *deserves* to be removed from the community. I have to walk in there and extend my hand and tell him I've wished him ill and blamed him and ask for forgiveness — *him* — if you *knew* what sick, *twisted*, sadistically *evil* and *sick* thing he did to us, to her — and ask him for forgiveness. Whether he forgives or not is not the issue. It's my own side of the street I need to clean.'

'It sounds very, very hard,' Pat said.

The fine hat was almost spinning between the man's calves, the pantcuffs of which had been pulled up in the defecatory forward lean to reveal socks that weren't, it seemed, both quite the same texture of wool. The mismatched socks spoke to Pat's heart more than anything else.

'I don't even know why I came here,' he said. 'I couldn't simply leave again and drive home. Yesterday she'd been at her tongue with one of those old NoCoat LinguaScraper appliances until it bled. I can't go home and look on that again without having cleaned house.'

'I hear you.'

'And you were just down the hill.'

'I understand.'

'I don't expect help or counsel. I already believe I have to do it. I've accepted the injunction to do it. I believe I have no choice. But I can't do it. I haven't been able to do it.'

'Willing, maybe.'

'Haven't yet been willing. Yet. I wish to emphasize *yet*.'

20 NOVEMBER
YEAR OF THE DEPEND ADULT UNDERGARMENT
IMMEDIATELY PRE-FUNDRAISER-EXHIBITION-FÊTE
GAUDEAMUS IGITUR

Usually, part of the experience of having the place you live in throw a gala is watching different people arrive for the festivities — the Warshavers, the Gartons and Peltasons and Prines, the Chins, the Middlebrooks and Gelbs, an incidental Lowell, the Buckmans in their claret-colored Volvo driven by their silent grown son who you never see except when he's driving Kirk and Binnie Buckman someplace. Dr. Hickle and his creepy niece. The Chawafs and Heavens. The Reehagens. The palsied and megawealthy Mrs. Warshaver with her pair of designer canes. The Donagan brothers from Svelte Nail. But usually we never get to see them arriving, the friends and patrons of E.T.A., for the Fundraising exhibition and gala. Usually while they're arriving and getting greeted by Tavis we're all down in the lockers, dressing and stretching, getting ready to exhibit. Getting shaved and taped by Loach, etc.

It must usually be an unusual occasion for the guests, too, because for the first few hours they're there to watch us play — they're all audience — then at some point with the last couple matches winding down the guys in white jackets with trays start appearing in Comm.-Ad., and the gala starts, and then it's the guests who become the participants and performers.

Dressing and stretching, wrapping grips with Gauze-Tex or filling a pouch with fuller's earth (Coyle, Freer, Stice, Traub) or sawdust (Wagenknecht, Chu), getting taped, those in puberty getting shaved and taped. A ritual. Even the conversation, usually, such as it is, has a timeless ceremonial aspect. John Wayne hunched as always on the bench before his locker with his towel like a hood over his head, running a coin back and forth over the backs of his fingers. Shaw pinching the flesh between his thumb and first finger, acupressure for a headache. Everyone had gone into their like auto-pilot ritual. Possalthwaite's sneakers were pigeon-toed under a stall door. Kahn was trying to spin a tennis ball on his finger like a basketball. At the sink, Eliot Kornspan was blowing out his sinuses with hot water; no one else was anywhere near the sink. A certain number of hysterical pre-competition rumors about the Québec Jr. Team and the severity of the weather circulated and were refuted and shifted antigens and returned. You could hear the high-register end of the wind even down here. The Csikszentmihalyi kid was doing a kind of piaffer in place, his knees hitting his chest, stretching his hip-flexors out. Troeltsch sat up against his locker near Wayne, wearing a disconnected headset and broadcasting his own match in advance. There were fart-accusations and -denials. Rader snapped a towel at Wagenknecht, who liked to stand for long periods of time bent at the waist with his head against his knees. Arslanian sat very still in a corner, blindfolded in what was either an ascot or a very fey necktie, his head cocked in the attitude of the blind. It was unclear whether B squads would even get to play; no one was sure how many courts the M.I.T. Union had inside. Rumors flew this way and that. Michael Pemulis was nowhere to be seen since early this A.M., at which time Anton Doucette said he'd seen Pemulis quote 'lurking' out by the West House dumpsters looking quote 'anxiously depressed.'

Then a small but univocal cheer went up from some of the players when Otis P. Lord appeared at the door, his cadaverous dad escorting him, O.P.L. out of post-op and pale but looking his old self, with just a thin little choker-width bandage of gauze around his neck from the monitor's removal and an odd ellipse of dry red skin around his mouth and nostrils. He came in and shook a few hands and used the stall next to Postal Weight and left; he wasn't playing today.

J. L. Struck was applying an astringent to areas of his jaw.

An hysterical rumor that the Québec players had been spotted coming down a ramp out of a charter-bus in the main lot and were by all appearances not the Québec J.D.C. and -W.C. squads but some sort of Special-Olympicish Québec adult *wheelchair*-tennis contingent — this rumor flew wildly around the locker room and then died out when a couple of the sub-14's who burned nervous energy by scampering around checking rumors scampered out and up the stairs to check the rumor and failed to return.

Across the wall on the Female side we could easily hear Thode and Donni Stott invoking Camilla, goddess of speed and light step. Thode had had an hysterical tantrum after breakfast because Poutrincourt hadn't showed for the Females' pre-match Staff thing and looked to be AWOL. Loach et al. had outfitted Ted Schacht with a complex knee-brace with jointed aluminum struts down both sides and a coin-sized hole in the elastic over the kneecap for dermal ventilation, and Schacht was lumbering around between the stalls and the locker with his arms straight out and his weight on his heels pretending to walk like Frankenstein. Several people talked to themselves at their lockers. Barry Loach was down on one knee shaving Hal's left ankle for tape. A couple of us remarked how Hal wasn't eating the usual customary Snickers bar or AminoPal. Hal had his hands on Loach's shoulders as the tape went on. A match-wrap is two horizontal layers just above the malleolus knob-thing, then straight down and four times around the tarsus just in front of the joint, so there's a big gap for flexion of the joint, but a compacting and supportive wrap. Then Loach puts a liner-sock and a wick-sock over the tape, then slides on the little inflatable AirCast deal and pumps it to the right pressure, checking with a little gauge, and Velcros it just tight enough for support plus max-flexion. Hal was on the bench with his hands on Loach's shoulders through the whole little routine. Everybody's had his hands on Loach's shoulders at one time or another. Hal's shave and wrap take four minutes. Schacht's knee and Fran Unwin's hamstring thing each take over ten. Wayne's quarter looked like it was dancing on his knuckles. Because of the towel over his head all you could see was a very thin oval section of his face, like an almond on its end. Wayne got to have a small disk-player in his locker, and Joni Mitchell was playing, which nobody ever minded because he kept it very low. Stice was blowing a purple bubble. Freer was trying to touch his toes. Traub and Whale, also on the wrap-bench, later said Hal was being weird. Like they said asking Loach if the pre-match locker room ever gave him a weird feeling, occluded, electric, as if all this had been done and said so many times before it made you feel it was recorded, they all in here existed basically as Fourier Transforms of postures and little routines, locked down and stored and call-uppable for rebroadcast at specified times. What Traub heard as *Fourier Transforms* Whale heard as *Furrier Transforms*. But also, as a consequence, erasable, Hal had said. By whom? Hal before a match usually had a wide-eyed ingenuish anxiety of someone who'd never been in a situation even remotely like this before. His face today had assumed various expressions ranging from distended hilarity to scrunched grimace, expressions that seemed unconnected to anything that was going on. The word was that Tavis and Schtitt had chartered three buses to take the squads to an indoor venue Mrs. Inc had had alumnus Corbett Th-Thorp call in mammoth favors to arrange — several mostly unused courts somewhere in the deep-brain tissue of the M.I.T. Student Union — and that the whole gala would be moved over to the Student Union, and that the Québec team and most of the guests were being contacted by cellular about the cancellation of the previous cancellation and the change in venue, and that those guests who didn't hear about the change would ride in the buses with the players and staff, some of them in formal- and evening-wear, probably, the guests. Traub also says he also heard Hal use the word *moribund,* but Whale couldn't confirm. Schacht entered a stall and drove the latch home with a certain purposeful sound that produced that momentary gunslinger-enters-saloon-type hush through-out the locker room. Nobody in the vicinity could say they heard Barry Loach respond one way or another to any of the strange moody things Hal was saying as Loach locked down the ankle for high-level play. Wagenknecht apparently really did fart.

The consensus among E.T.A.s is that Head Trainer Barry Loach resembles a wingless fly—blunt and scuttly, etc. One E.T.A. tradition consists of Big Buddies recounting to new or very young Little Buddies the saga of Loach and how he ended up as an elite Head Trainer even though he doesn't have an official degree in Training or whatever from Boston College, which is where he'd gone to school. In outline form, the saga goes that Loach grew up as the youngest child of an enormous Catholic family, the parents of which were staunch Catholics of the old school of extremely staunch Catholicism, and that Mrs. Loach (as in the mom)'s life's most fervent wish was that one of her countless children would enter the R.C. clergy, but that the eldest Loach boy had done a two-year U.S.N. bit and had gotten de-mapped early on in the Brazilian O.N.A.N./U.N. joint action of Y.T.M.P.; and that within weeks of the wake the next oldest Loach boy had died of ciquatoxic food-poisoning eating tainted blackfin grouper; and the next oldest Loach, Therese, through a series of adolescent misadventures had ended up in Atlantic City NJ as one of the women in sequined leotards and high heels who carries a large posterboard card with the Round # on it around the ring between rounds of professional fights, so that hopes for Therese becoming a Carmelite dimmed considerably; and on down the line, one Loach falling helplessly in love and marrying right out of high school, another burning only to play the cymbals with a first-rate philharmonic (now crashing away with the Houston P.O.). And so on, until there was just one other Loach child and then Barry Loach, who was the youngest and also totally under Mrs. L.'s thumb, emotionally; and that young Barry had breathed a huge sigh of relief when his older brother — always a pious and contemplative and big-hearted kid, brimming over with abstract love and an innate faith in the indwelling goodness of all men's souls — began to show evidence of a true spiritual calling to a life of service in the R.C. clergy, and ultimately entered Jesuit seminary, removing an enormous weight from his younger brother's psyche because young Barry — ever since he first slapped a Band-Aid on an X-Men figure — felt his true calling was not to the priesthood but to the liniment-and-adhesive ministry of professional athletic training. Who, finally, can say the whys and whences of each man's true vocation? And then so Barry was a Training major or whatever at B.C., and by all accounts proceeding satisfactorily toward a degree, when his older brother, quite far along toward getting ordained or frocked or whatever as a licensed Jesuit, suffered at age twenty-five a sudden and dire spiritual decline in which his basic faith in the innate indwelling goodness of men like spontaneously combusted and disappeared — and for no apparent or dramatic reason; it just seemed as if the brother had suddenly contracted a black misanthropic spiritual outlook the way some twenty-five-year-old men contract Sanger-Brown's ataxia or M.S., a kind of degenerative Lou Gehrig's Disease of the spirit — and his interest in serving man and God-in-man and nurturing the indwelling Christ in people through Jesuitical pursuits underwent an understandable nosedive, and he began to do nothing but sit in his dormitory room at St. John's Seminary — right near Enfield Tennis Academy, coincidentally, on Foster Street in Brighton off Comm. Ave., right by the Archdiocese H.Q. or whatever — sitting there trying to pitch playing-cards into a wastebasket in the middle of the floor, not going to classes or vespers or reading his Hours, and talking frankly about giving up the vocation altogether, which all had Mrs. Loach just about prostrate with disappointment, and had young Barry suddenly re-weighted with dread and anxiety, because if his brother bailed out of the clergy it would be nearly irresistibly incumbent on Barry, the very last Loach, to give up his true vocation of splints and flexion and enter seminary himself, to keep his staunch and beloved Mom from dying of disappointment. And so a series of personal interviews with the spiritually necrotic brother took place, Barry having to station himself on the other side of the playing-cards' wastebasket so as even to get the older brother's attention, trying to talk the brother down from the misanthropic spiritual ledge he was on. The spiritually ill brother was fairly cynical about Barry Loach's reasons for trying to talk him down, seeing as how both men knew that Barry's own career-dreams were on the line here as well; though the brother smiled sardonically and said he'd come to expect little better than self-interested #1-looking-out from human beings anyway, since his practicum work out among the human flocks in some of Boston's nastier downtown venues — the impossibility of conditions-changing, the ingratitude of the low-life homeless addicted and mentally ill flocks he served, and the utter lack of compassion and basic help from the citizenry at large in all Jesuitical endeavors — had killed whatever spark of inspired faith he'd had in the higher possibilities and perfectibility of man; so he opined what should he expect but that his own little brother, no less than the coldest commuter passing the outstretched hands of the homeless and needy at Park Street Station, should be all-too-humanly concerned with nothing but the care and feeding of Numero Uno. Since a basic absence of empathy and compassion and taking-the-risk-to-reach-out seemed to him now an ineluctable part of the human character. Barry Loach was understandably way out his depth on the theological turf of like Apologia and the redeemability of man — though he was able to relieve a slight hitch in the brother's toss that was stressing his card-throwing arm's flexor carpi ulnaris muscle and so to up the brother's card-in-wastebasket percentage significantly — but he was not only desperate to preserve his mother's dream and his own indirectly athletic ambitions at the same time, he was actually rather a spiritually upbeat guy who just didn't buy the brother's sudden despair at the apparent absence of compassion and warmth in God's supposed self-mimetic and divine creation, and he managed to engage the brother in some rather heated and high-level debates on spirituality and the soul's potential, not that much unlike Alyosha and Ivan's conversations in the good old *Brothers K.,* though probably not nearly as erudite and literary, and nothing from the older brother even approaching the carcinogenic acerbity of Ivan's Grand Inquisitor scenario.

In outline, it eventually boiled down to this: a desperate Barry Loach — with Mrs. L. now on 25 mg. of daily Ativan[384] and just about camped out in front of the candle-lighting apse of the Loach's parish church — Loach challenges his brother to let him prove somehow — risking his own time, Barry's, and maybe safety somehow — that the basic human character wasn't as unempathetic and necrotic as the brother's present depressed condition was leading him to think. After a few suggestions and rejections of bets too way-out even for Barry Loach's desperation, the brothers finally settle on a, like, experimental challenge. The spiritually despondent brother basically challenges Barry Loach to not shower or change clothes for a while and make himself look homeless and disreputable and louse-ridden and clearly in need of basic human charity, and to stand out in front of the Park Street T-station on the edge of the Boston Common, right alongside the rest of the downtown community's lumpen dregs, who all usually stood there outside the T-station stemming change, and for Barry Loach to hold out his unclean hand and instead of stemming change simply ask passersby to touch him. Just to touch him. Viz. extend some basic human warmth and contact. And this Barry does. And does. Days go by. His own spiritually upbeat constitution starts taking blows to the solar plexus. It's not clear whether the verminousness of his appearance had that much to do with it; it just turned out that standing there outside the station doors and holding out his hand and asking people to touch him ensured that just about the last thing any passerby in his right mind would want to do was touch him. It's possible that the respectable citizenry with their bookbags and cellulars and dogs with little red sweater-vests thought that sticking one's hand way out and crying 'Touch me, just touch me, *please*' was some kind of new stem-type argot for 'Lay some change on me,' because Barry Loach found himself hauling in a rather impressive daily total of $ — significantly more than he was earning at his work-study job wrapping ankles and sterilizing dental prostheses for Boston College lacrosse players. Citizens found his pitch apparently just touching enough to give him $; but B. Loach's brother — who often stood there in collarless mufti up against the plastic jamb of the T-station's exit, slouched and smirking and idly shuffling a deck of cards in his hands — was always quick to point out the spastic delicacy with which the patrons dropped change or $ into Barry Loach's hand, these kind of bullwhip-motions or jagged in-and-outs like they were trying to get something hot off a burner, never touching him, and they rarely broke stride or even made eye-contact as they tossed alms B.L.'s way, much less ever getting their hand anywhere close to contact with B.L.'s disreputable hand. The brother not unreasonably nixed the accidental contact of one commuter who'd stumbled as he tried to toss a quarter and then let Barry break his fall, not to mention the bipolarly ill bag-lady who got Barry Loach in a headlock and tried to bite his ear off near the end of the third week of the Challenge. Barry L. refused to concede defeat and misanthropy, and the Challenge dragged on week after week, and the older brother got bored eventually and stopped coming and went back to his room and waited for the St. John's Seminary administration to give him his walking papers, and Barry Loach had to take Incompletes in the semester's Training courses, and got canned from his work-study job for not showing up, and he went through weeks and then months of personal spiritual crisis as passerby after passerby interpreted his appeal for contact as a request for cash and substituted abstract loose change for genuine fleshly contact; and some of the T-station's other disreputable stem-artists became intrigued by Barry's pitch — to say nothing of his net receipts — and started themselves to take up the cry of 'Touch me, please, please, *someone!*,' which of course further compromised Barry Loach's chances of getting some citizen to interpret his request literally and lay hands on him in a compassionate and human way; and Loach's own soul began to sprout little fungal patches of necrotic rot, and his upbeat view of the so-called normal and respectable human race began to undergo dark revision; and when the other scuzzy and shunned stem-artists of the downtown district treated him as a compadre and spoke to him in a collegial way and offered him warming drinks from brown-bagged bottles he felt too disillusioned and coldly alone to be able to refuse, and thus started to fall in with the absolute silt at the very bottom of the metro Boston socio-economic duck-pond. And then what happened with the spiritually infirm older brother and whither he fared and what happened with his vocation never gets resolved in the E.T.A. Loach-story, because now the focus becomes all Loach and how he was close to forgetting — after all these months of revulsion from citizens and his getting any kind of nurturing or empathic treatment only from homeless and addicted stem-artists — what a shower or washing machine or a ligamental manipulation even were, much less career-ambitions or a basically upbeat view of indwelling human goodness, and in fact Barry Loach was dangerously close to disappearing forever into the fringes and dregs of metro Boston street life and spending his whole adult life homeless and louse-ridden and stemming in the Boston Common and drinking out of brown paper bags, when along toward the end of the ninth month of the Challenge, his appeal — and actually also the appeals of the other dozen or so cynical stem-artists right alongside Loach, all begging for one touch of a human hand and holding their hands out — when all these appeals were taken literally and responded to with a warm handshake — which only the more severely intoxicated stemmers didn't recoil from the profferer of, plus Loach — by E.T.A.'s own Mario Incandenza, who'd been sent dashing out from the Back Bay co-op where his father was filming something that involved actors dressed up as God and the Devil playing poker with Tarot cards for the soul of Cosgrove Watt, using subway tokens as the ante, and Mario'd been sent dashing out to get another roll of tokens from the nearest station, which because of a dumpster-fire near the entrance to the Arlington St. station turned out to be Park Street, and Mario, being alone and only fourteen and largely clueless about anti-stem defensive strategies outside T-stations, had had no one worldly or adult along with him there to explain to him why the request of men with outstretched hands for a simple handshake or High Five shouldn't automatically be honored and granted, and Mario had extended his clawlike hand and touched and heartily shaken Loach's own fuliginous hand, which led through a convoluted but kind of heartwarming and faith-reaffirming series of circumstances to B. Loach, even w/o an official B.A., being given an Asst. Trainer's job at E.T.A., a job he was promoted from just months later when the then-Head Trainer suffered the terrible accident that resulted in all locks being taken off E.T.A. saunas' doors and the saunas' maximum temperature being hard-wired down to no more than 50°C.

The inverted glass was the size of a cage or small jail cell, but it was still recognizably a bathroom-type tumbler, as if for gargling or post-brushing swishing, only huge and upside-down, on the floor, with him inside. The tumbler was like a prop or display; it was the sort of thing that would have to be made special. Its glass was green and its bottom over his head was pebbled and the light inside was the watery dancing green of extreme ocean depths.

There was a kind of louvered screen or vent high on one side of the glass, but no air was coming out. In. The air inside the huge glass was pretty clearly limited, as well, because there was already CO_2 steam on the sides. The glass was too thick to break or to kick his way out, and it felt like he might have possibly broken the leg's foot already trying.

There were some green and distorted faces through the glass's side's steam. The face at eye-level belonged to the latest Subject, the dexterous and adoring Swiss hand-model. She stood looking at him, her arms crossed, smoking, exhaling greenly through her nose, then looked down to confer with another face, seeming to float at about waist-level, that belonged to the shy and handicapped fan who O.'d realized had shared the Subject's Swiss accent.

The Subject behind the glass would meet Orin's eye steadily but did not acknowledge him or anything he shouted. When Orin had tried to kick his way out was when he'd recognized that the Subject was looking *at* his eyes rather than *into* them as previously. There were now smeared footprints on the glass.

Every few seconds Orin wiped the steam of his breath away from the thick glass to see what the faces were doing.

His foot really was hurt, and the remains of whatever had made him fall asleep so hard really were making him sick to his stomach, and in sum this experience was pretty clearly not one of his bad dreams, but Orin, #71, was in deep denial about its not being a dream. It was like the minute he'd come to and found himself inside a huge inverted tumbler he'd opted to figure: dream. The stilted amplified voice that came periodically through the small screen or vent above him, demanding to know Where Is The Master Buried, was surreal and bizarre and inexplicable enough to Orin to make him grateful: it was the sort of surreal disorienting nightmarish incomprehensible but vehement demand that often gets made in really bad dreams. Plus the bizarre anxiety of not being able to get the adoring Subject to acknowledge anything he said through the glass. When the speaker's screen slid back, Orin looked away from the glass's faces and up, figuring that they were going to do something even more surreal and vehement that would really nail down the undeniable dream-status of the whole experience.

Mlle. Luria P——, who disdained the subtler aspects of technical interviews and had lobbied simply to be given a pair of rubber gloves and two or three minutes alone with the Subject's testicles (and who was not really Swiss), had predicted accurately what the Subject's response would be when the speaker's screen was withdrawn and the sewer roaches began pouring blackly and shinily through, and as the Subject splayed itself against the tumbler's glass and pressed its face so flat against the absurd glass's side that the face changed from green to stark white, and, much muffled, shrieked at them 'Do it to her! *Do it to her!*,' Luria P—— inclined her head and rolled her eyes at the A.F.R. leader, whom she had long regarded as something of a ham.

Human beings came and went. An R.N. felt his forehead and yanked her hand back with a yelp. Somebody down the hall was jabbering and weeping. At one point Chandler F., the recently graduated nonstick-cookware salesman, seemed to be there in the classic resident-confiteor position, his chin on his hands on the bedside crib-railing. The room's light was a glowing gray. The Ennet House House Manager was there, fingering the place her missing eyebrow'd been, trying to explain something about how Pat M. hadn't come because she and Mr. M.'d had to kick Pat's little girl out of the house for using something synthetic again, and was in a too shaky place spiritually to even leave home. Gately felt physically hotter than he'd ever felt. It felt like a sun in his head. The crib-type railings got tapered on top and writhed a little, like flames. He imagined himself on the House's aluminum platter with an apple in his mouth, his skin glazed and crispy. The M.D. that looked age twelve appeared with others wreathed in mist and said Up it to 30 q 2 and Let's Try Doris,[385] that the poor son of a bitch was burning down. He wasn't talking to Gately. The M.D. was not addressing Don Gately. Gately's only conscious concern was Asking For Help to refuse Demerol. He kept trying to say *addict*. He remembered being young on the playground and telling Maura Duffy to look down her shirt and spell *attic*. Somebody else said Ice Bath. Gately felt something rough and cool on his face. A voice that sounded like his own brain-voice with an echo said to never try and pull a weight that exceeds you. Gately figured he might die. It wasn't calm and peaceful like alleged. It was more like trying to pull something heavier than you. He heard the late Gene Fackelmann saying to get a load of this. He was the object of much bedside industry. A brisk clink of I.V. bottles overhead. Slosh of bags. None of the overhead voices talking to him. His input unrequired. Part of him hoped they were putting Demerol in his I.V without him knowing. He gurgled and mooed, saying *addict*. Which was the truth, that he was, he knew. The Crocodile that liked to wear Hanes, Lenny, that at the podium liked to say 'The truth will you set you free, but not until it's done with you.' The voice down the hall was weeping like its heart would break. He imagined the A.D.A. with his hat off earnestly praying Gately would live so he could send him to M.D.C.-Walpole. The harsh sound he heard up close was the tape around his unshaved mouth getting ripped off him so quick he hardly felt it. He tried to avoid projecting how his shoulder would feel if they started pounding on his chest like they pound on dying people's chests. The intercom calmly dinged. He heard conversing people in the hall passing the open door and stopping for a second to look in, but still conversing. It occurred to him if he died everybody would still exist and go home and eat and X their wife and go to sleep. A conversing voice at the door laughed and told somebody else it was getting harder these days to tell the homosexuals from the people who beat up homosexuals. It was impossible to imagine a world without himself in it. He remembered two of his Beverly High teammates beating up a so-called homosexual kid while Gately walked away, wanting no part of either side. Disgusted by both sides of the conflict. He imagined having to become a homosexual in Walpole. He imagined going to one meeting a week and having a shepherd's crook and parrot and playing cribbage for a cigarette a point and lying on his side in his bunk in his cell facing the wall, jacking off to the memory of tits. He saw the A.D.A. with his head bowed and his hat against his chest.

Somebody overhead asked somebody else if they were ready, and somebody commented on the size of Gately's head and gripped Gately's head, and then he felt an upward movement deep inside that was so personal and horrible he woke up. Only one of his eyes would open because the floor's impact had shut the other one up plump and tight as a sausage. His whole front side of him was cold from lying on the wet floor. Fackelmann around somewhere behind him was mumbling something that consisted totally of *g*'s.

His open eye could see the luxury apt. window. It was dawn outside, a glowing gray, and birds had plenty to say out in the bare trees; and at the big window was a face and a windmill of arms. Gately tried to adjust the vertical hold on his vision. Pamela Hoffman-Jeep was at the window. Their apt. was on the second floor of the luxury complex. She was up in a tree right outside the window, standing on a branch, looking in, either gesturing wildly or trying to keep her balance. Gately felt a rush of concern about her falling out of the tree and was preparing to ask the floor to maybe please relax its hold a second and let him go when P.H.-J.'s face suddenly fell and exited the bottom of the window and was replaced by the face of Bobby ('C') C. Bobby C raised a slow two-finger salute to his temple in an impassively mocking Hello as he scanned the evidence of serious bingeing in the room, through the window. Eyeballing Mt. Dilaudid with special attention, nodding down to somebody down under the tree. He edged forward on the branch until he was right up flush with the window and pushed up on its frame with one hand, trying to open the locked window. The rising sun behind him cast a shadow of his head against the wet floor. Gately called out to Fackelmann and tried to roll and sit up. His bones felt full of busted glass. Bobby C held up a six-pack of Hefenreffer and waggled it suggestively, like wanting in. Gately had just managed to sit partly up when C's fist in its fingerless glove came through the window, spraying double-pane glass. The fallen TP screen continued to show shots of small flames, Gately could see. C's arm came through and groped for the latch and raised the window. Fackelmann was bleating like a sheep but not moving; a syringe he hadn't bothered with removing hung from the inside of his elbow. Gately saw Bobby C had glass in his purple hair and a vintage Taurus-PT 9 mm. jammed into his spike-studded belt. Gately sat there dumbly as C clambered on in and kind of tip-toed through the various puddles and rolled Fackelmann's head back to check his pupils. C clucked his tongue and let Fackelmann's head fall back against the wall, Fax still softly bleating. He turned smartly on his boot's heel and started across toward the apartment door, and Gately sat there looking at him. When he got to where Gately was sitting on the floor with his wet legs curved parenthesized out in front of him like some sort of huge pre-verbal rug-rat C stopped as if to say something he'd just remembered, looking down at Gately, his smile wide and warm, and Gately noticed he had a black front tooth just as C caught him over the ear with the Taurus-PT and put him back down. The floor got the back of Gately's head worse than the gun-butt did. His ears belled. It wasn't stars he saw. Then Bobby C kicked Gately in the balls, S.O.P. to keep your man down, and Gately drew his knees up and turned his head and was sick out onto the floor. He heard the apartment door opening and the leisurely sound of C's boots going down the stairs to the complex's door. Between spasms, Gately urged Fackelmann to go for the window as rickety-tick as he could. Fackelmann was slumped back against the wall; he was looking at his legs and saying he couldn't feel his legs, that he was numb from the scalp on down and climbing.

C returned shortly, and at the head of a whole entourage-type group of people Gately didn't like the looks of at all. There were DesMonts and Pointgravè, Canadian Harvard Square small-time thug-types Gately knew slightly, small-time freelancers, too Canadianly dumb for anything but the brutalest work. Gately was unglad to see them. They wore overalls and nonmatching flannel shirts. The poor eczematic pharmacist's-assistant guy was behind them, carrying a black Dr.-bag. Gately was on his back pedalling his legs in the air, which is what anybody that's played organized ball knows is what you do for a brody to the groin. The pharmacist's assistant stopped behind C and stood there looking at his own Weejuns. Three big unfamiliar girls entered in red leather coats and badly laddered hose. Then poor old Pamela Hoffman-Jeep, her taffeta torn and stained and her face gray with shock, got borne in through the door by two Oriental punks in shiny leather jackets. They had their hands under her ass and carried her as if seated, one leg out and a white stick of bone protruding from her shin, which her shin was a serious mess. Gately saw all this upside-down, pedalling his legs until he could get up. One of the big girls carried an old-type Graphix bong and a Glad Cinch-Sak kitchen-can bag. Either Pointgravè or DesMonts — Gately could never remember which of them was who — carried a case of bonded liquor. C asked generally if it was Party Time. The room brightened as the sun climbed. The room was filling up. Another of the girls made negative comments about the urine on the floor. Fackelmann in the corner began saying it was all a goddamned lie. C pretended to answer himself in a falsetto and said Yes indeedyweedy it was Party Time. Now a very bland groomed collegeish guy in a Wembley tie entered with a TaTung Corp. box and put it down by where the pharmacist's assistant was still standing, and the bland guy rehung the teleplayer on the wall and ejected the TP's small-flame cartridge, dropping it on the wet floor. The two Oriental toughs carried Pamela Hoffman-Jeep over to a far corner of the living room, and she screamed when they dropped her onto a box of counterfeit little Commonwealth of MA peel-off seals. They were small, the Orientals, and they were looking down at him, but neither had bad skin. A small grim woman with a tight gray bun and sensible shoes entered last and shut the apt. door behind her. Gately rolled slowly to his knees and stood up, still bent a bit at the waist, not moving, one eye still swollen shut. He could hear Fackelmann trying to stand. P.H.-J. stopped shrieking and blacked out and slumped down until her chin was on her chest and her ass half off the box. The room smelled like Dilaudid and urine and Gately's vomit and Fackelmann's bowel movement and the red leather girls's fine leather coats. C came on over and reached up and put his arm around Gately's shoulders and stood with him like that while two of the tough girls in their coats passed around bottles of bourbon from the case. Gately could focus best when he squinted. The A.M. sun hung in the window, up and past the tree, yellowing. The bottles were the black-labelled boxy bottles that signified Jack Daniels. A churchbell off in the Square struck seven or eight. Gately had had a bad experience with Jack Daniels at age fourteen. The bland groomed corporate guy had inserted a different TP cartridge and now was getting a portable CD player out of the TaTung box while the pharmacist's assistant watched him. Fackelmann said whatever it was was a total goddamn lie. Pointgravè or DesMonts took the bottle C had taken from the tough girls and handed to Gately. The sunlight on the floor through the window was spidered with shadows of branches. Everybody in the room's shadows were moving around on the west wall. C also held a bottle. Soon just about everybody had their own individual bottle of Jack. Gately heard Fackelmann asking somebody to open his for him he was numb to the ceiling and climbing and he couldn't feel his hands. The small grim librarianish woman went to Fackelmann, removing her purse from her shoulder. Gately was figuring out what he was going to say on the Faxter's behalf when Whitey Sorkin arrived. Until then he figured it was C's party and just not to unnecessarily rile C. It seemed to take a long time to formulate mental thoughts. Pamela Hoffman-Jeep's shin looked like ground chuck. C lifted his square bottle and asked for general permission to like propose a toast. P.H.-J.'s lips were blue with shock. Gately felt bad that he felt so little romantic concern now that she'd fallen out of the tree. He spent no time wondering if she'd ratted them out, if she'd brought Bobby C to them or vice-versy. At least one of the girls in the red leather coats had an awful big Adam's apple for a girl. C roughly turned Gately's shoulders toward Fackelmann in the corner and toasted to old friends and new friends and what looked like a serious fucking-A score for Gene Gene the Fax Machine, given the size of this Dilaudid-pile and all the evidence of some serious fucking partying they could see, and smell. Everyone drank from their bottle. The grim-faced little woman had to help Fackelmann find his mouth with the mouth of his bottle. All three of the big women displayed Adam's apples when they tilted way back to chug. The polite swallow of Jack almost made Gately heave. C's Item in his belt pressed against Gately's thigh and so did some of the belt's spikes. DesMonts and Pointgravè both had S&W Items in shoulder-holsters. The Oriental punks didn't display any arms but had a look about them like they didn't ever even shower unarmed; safe bet they at least had little weird sharp chinky things you threw at people, Gately figured. Several of C's group chugged their whole bottle. One of the big girls hurled her bottle at the west wall, but it didn't break. Why is it you feel it in your gut and not your nuts per se, when you get brodied? Gately was turning and looking wherever C's arm was turning him. The contorted face on the rehung viewer from the corporate guy's cartridge was Whitey Sorkin's, a portrait Sorkin had let some neuralgic painter do of him having a cluster-headache out at the National Cranio-Facial Pain Foundation in the city, for a series for an ad for aspirin. The cartridge seemed like just a continuous still of the painting, so that it looked like Sorkin on the wall was sort of presiding over the gathering in a mute pained way. The librarianish little woman was threading a sewing needle with thread, her mouth real tight. The pharmacist's assistant was getting little skin-flakes all over the black bag as he hunkered down over the bag removing several syringes from the bag and filling them out of a 2500-IU ampule and handing them up to be passed around. The N.C.-F.P.F. painting had a red fist pulling a handful of brain out of the top of Sorkin's skull while Sorkin's face looked out of the viewer with the classic migraine-sufferer's look of super-intense thought, almost more meditative than hurt-looking. One Oriental kid was squatting chinkishly in the corner drinking Jack and the other was sweeping up spilled laminates off the floor, using a flap from the TaTung box for a dustpan. Chinks could do some serious sweeping, Gately reflected. Another of the girls threw her bottle at the wall. It was when C didn't even have Gately facing them that it dawned on Gately the girls in coats and slatternly hose were fags dressed up as girls, like as in transvestals. Bobby C was beaming. The first bit of real personal-ass fear Gately felt was when he realized these people looked like mostly members of Bobby C's personal set, that they weren't the people Sorkin would dispatch if he was sending his own people and coming himself, soon, that Sorkin's painting on the wall was symbolic of Sorkin wasn't coming, that Sorkin had given Bobby C free rain on this piece of painful business. The pharmacist's assistant removed two pre-filled syringes from the bag, unwrapping their crinkly plastic. C told Gately quietly how Whitey said to say he knew Donnie wasn't part of Fackelmann's score to fuck Sorkin and Eighties Bill. That he didn't need to do anything except kick back and enjoy the party and let Fackelmann face his own music and to not let any like 19th-century notions of defending the weak and pathetic drag Gately into this. C said he was sorry about the bit of the beating, he had to make sure Gately didn't try and get Fackelmann out the window while he was down unlocking the door. That he hoped Gately wouldn't hold it against him 'cause he wished him no particular ill and wanted no beef, later. This was all said very quietly and intensively while the two fags in wigs that had tried to break bottles were sitting on a box filling the Graphix's huge party-bowl with grass from the Glad bag, which contained grass. DesMontes sat in a director's chair. Everybody else was drinking out of their square bottle, standing around the sunny room in the awkward postures of way more people than seats. Their arms were pale and hairless. The two Oriental toughs were tying each other off. The draft through the fist-hole in the window made Gately shiver. The other fag was making like comments about Gately's physique. Gately asked C quietly if he and Fackelmann couldn't get cleaned up real quick and they could all go see Sorkin together and Whitey and Gene could reason together and work out an accord. Fackelmann found his voice and asked loudly if anybody wanted to hike on over here to Mt. Dilaudid and get fucking fucked *up*. Gately winced. Bobby C smiled at Fackelmann and said it looked like Fax had had about enough. But at the same time the psoriatic assistant came to Fackelmann and checked his pupils with a penlight and then shot him up with a pre-filled, using an artery in his neck. The back of Fackelmann's head hit the wall several times, his face flushing violently in the standard clinical reaction to Narcan.[386] The pharmacist then came C and Gately's way. The portable CD player started in with poor old Linda McCartney as C held Gately and the asst. pharmacist tied him off with an M.D.'s rubber strap. Gately stood there slightly hunched. Fackelmann was making sounds like a long-submerged man coming up for air. C told Gately to fasten his seatbelt. Urine had turned part of the apt.'s luxury-hardwood floor's finish soft and white, like soap-scum. The CD playing was one C'd played all the fucking time in the car when Gately had been with him in a car: somebody had taken an old disk of McCartney and the Wings — as in the historical Beatles's McCartney — taken and run it through a Kurtzweil remixer and removed every track on the songs except the tracks of poor old Mrs. Linda McCartney singing backup and playing tambourine. When the fags called the grass 'Bob' it was confusing because they also called C 'Bob.' Poor old Mrs. Linda McCartney just fucking could not sing, and having her shaky off-key little voice flushed from the cover of the whole slick multitrack corporate sound and pumped up to solo was to Gately unspeakably depressing — her voice sounding so lost, trying to hide and bury itself inside the pro backups' voices; Gately imagined Mrs. Linda McCartney — in his Staff room's wall's picture a kind of craggy-faced blonde — imagined her standing there lost in the sea of her husband's pro noise, feeling low esteem and whispering off-key, not knowing quite when to shake her tambourine: C's depressing CD was past cruel, it was somehow sadistic-seeming, like drilling a peephole in the wall of a handicapped bathroom. Two of the transvestals were doing the Swim to the awful tape in the swept center of the floor; the other had one of Fackelmann's arms while the bland guy in the Wembley tie gripped Fackelmann's other arm and was slapping Fackelmann lightly as the Dilaudid fought the Narcan. They'd seated Fackelmann in his corner in Gately's special Demerol-chair. Gately's balls throbbed with his pulse. The pharmacist's assistant's face was right up in Gately's. His cheeks and chin were a mess of silvery scaly flakes, and an oily sweat on his forehead caught the window's sunlight as he gave Gately a tight smile.

'I'm pretty much straight already, C-man, after that nut-shot,' Gately said, 'if you don't want to waste the Narcan.'

'Oh this isn't no Narcan,' C said softly, holding Gately's arm.

'Hadly,' said the assistant, uncapping the syringe.

C said 'Hold on to your hat.' He poked the assistant's shoulder. 'Tell him.'

'It's pharm-grade Sunshine,'[387] the assistant said, tapping for a good vein.

'Hold on to your heart,' C said, watching the needle go in. The pharmacist slid it in expertly, horizontal and flush to the skin. Gately had never done Sunshine. Next to ungettable outside a Canadian hospital. He watched his own blood ruddle the serum as the pharmacist extended his thumb to ease the plunger back. The pharmacist's assistant could really boot. C's tongue was in the corner of his mouth as he watched. The corporate guy had Fackelmann's arms held tight and a transvestal who'd gotten in behind the chair held his head by the chin and hair as the gray lady knelt before him with her threaded needle. Gately couldn't keep himself from watching the stuff go in him. There was no pain. He wondered for a second if it was a hot shot: it seemed like a whole lot of trouble to go to just to get him off. The pharmacist's thumbnail was ingrown. There were a couple eczema-flakes on Gately's arm where the guy was inclined over it. You get to like the sight of your own blood after a while. The pharmacist had him half booted when Fackelmann started screaming. The scream's pitch got higher as it drew out. When Gately could look away from the stuff going in, he saw the librarian-type lady was sewing Fackelmann's eyelids open to the skin above his eyebrows. As in they were sewing poor old Count Faxula's eyes open. A kid on the playground had used to turn his lids inside out at girls like they were doing now to the poor old Faxter. Gately gave a reflexive jerk toward him, and C hugged him tight with one arm.

'Easy,' C said very softly.

The taste of the hydrochloride in the Sunshine was the same, delicious, the taste of the smell of every Dr.'s office everywhere. He'd never done Talwin-PX. Impossible to get scrips for, the PX, a Canadian blend; U.S. Talwin's[388] got .5 mg. of naloxone mixed in, to cut the buzz, is why Gately only did NX on top of Bam-Bams. He understood they'd given Fackelmann the anti-narc so he'd feel the needle as they sewed his eyes open. *Cruel* is spelled with a *u*, he remembered. The two Orientals left the room at C's direction. Linda McC. sounded borderline-psychotic. The little gray lady worked fast. The eye that was already sewed open bulged obscenely. Everybody in the room except C and the corporate guy and grim lady started shooting dope. Two of the fags had their eyes shut and their faces at the ceiling as if they couldn't take watching what they were doing to their arm. The pharmacist was tying off the passed-out Pamela Hoffman-Jeep, which seemed like insult + injury. There was every different kind of style and skill-level of injection and boot going on. Fackelmann's face was still a scream-face. The corporate-tool type was dropping fluid from a pipette into Fackelmann's sewed-open eye while the lady rethreaded the needle. It was just seeming to Gately he'd seen the fluid-in-eye thing in a cartridge or movie the M.P.'d liked when he was a Bim playing ball on the chintz in the sea when the Sunshine crossed the barrier and came on.

You could see why the U.S. made them cut the buzz. The air in the room got overclear, a glycerine shine, colors brightening terribly. If colors themselves could catch fire. The word on the C-II Talwin-PX was it was intense but short-acting, and pricey. No word on its interaction with massive residual amounts of I.V.-Dilaudid. Gately tried to figure while he still could. If they were going to eliminate his map with an O.D. they'd have used something cheap. And if the librarian was going to sew his eyes open. Gately was trying to think. Too they wouldn't have got him. Him. Got him off.

The very air of the room bulged. It ballooned. Fackelmann's screams about lies rose and fell, hard to hear against the arterial roar of the Sun. McC. was trying to muffle a cough. Gately couldn't feel his legs. He could feel C's arm around him taking more and more of his weight. C's arms's muscles rising and hardening: he could feel this. His legs were, like: opting out. Attack of floors and sidewalks. Kite used to sing a ditty called '32 Uses For Sterno Me Lad.' C was starting to let him down easy. Strong squat hard kid. Most heroin-men you can knock down with a Boo. C: there was a gentleness about C, for a kid with the eyes of a lizard. He was letting him down real easy. C was going to protect Bimmy Don from the bad floor's assault. The supported swoon spun Gately around, C moving around him like a dancer to slow the fall. Gately got a rotary view of the whole room in almost untakable focus. Pointgravè was vomiting chunkily. Two of the fags were sliding down the wall they had their backs to. Their red coats were aflame. The passing window exploded with light. Or else it was DesMontes that was vomiting and Pointgravè was taking the TP's viewer off the wall and stretching its fibroid wire over toward Fackelmann against the wall. One of Fax's eyes was as open as his mouth, disclosing way more eye than you ever want to see on somebody. He was no longer struggling. He stared piratically straight ahead. The librarian was starting on his other eye. The bland man had a rose in his lapel and he'd put on glasses with metal lenses and was blind-high and missing Fax's eye with the dropper half the time, saying something to Pointgravè. A transvestal had P.H.-J.'s torn hem hiked up and a spiderish hand on her flesh-colored thigh. P.H.-J.'s face was gray and blue. The floor came up slowly. Bobby C's squat face looked almost pretty, tragic, half lit by the window, tucked up under Gately's spinning shoulder. Gately felt less high than disembodied. It was obscenely pleasant. His head left his shoulders. Gene and Linda were both screaming. The cartridge with the held-open eyes and dropper had been the one about ultra-violence and sadism. A favorite of Kite. Gately thinks *sadism* is pronounced 'saddism.' The last rotating sight was the chinks coming back through the door, holding big shiny squares of the room. As the floor wafted up and C's grip finally gave, the last thing Gately saw was an Oriental bearing down with the held square and he looked into the square and saw clearly a reflection of his own big square pale head with its eyes closing as the floor finally pounced. And when he came back to, he was flat on his back on the beach in the freezing sand, and it was raining out of a low sky, and the tide was way out.

O

NOTES AND ERRATA

1. Methamphetamine hydrochloride, a.k.a. crystal meth.

2. Orin's never once darkened the door of any sort of therapy-professional, by the way, so his takes on his dreams are always generally pretty surface-level.

3. E.T.A. is laid out as a cardioid, with the four main inward-facing bldgs. convexly rounded at the back and sides to yield a cardioid's curve, with the tennis courts and pavilions at the center and the staff and students' parking lots in back of Comm.-Ad. forming the little bashed-in dent that from the air gives the whole facility the Valentine-heart aspect that still wouldn't have been truly cardioid if the buildings themselves didn't have their convex bulges all derived from arcs of the same r, a staggering feat given the uneven ground and wildly different electrical-and-plumbing-conduit wallspace required by dormitories, administrative offices, and polyresinous Lung, pull-offable probably by on the whole East Coast one guy, E.T.A.'s original architect, Avril's old and very dear friend, the topology world's closed-curve-mapping-Übermensch A.Y. ('Vector-Field') Rickey of Brandeis U., now deceased, who used to wow Hal and Mario in Weston by taking off his vest without removing his suit jacket, which M. Pemulis years later exposed as a cheap parlor-trick-exploitation of certain basic features of continuous functions, which revelation Hal mourned in a Santa's-not-real type of secret way, and which Mario simply ignored, preferring to see the vest thing as plain magic.

4. Those younger staffers who double as academic and athletic instructors are, by convention at North American tennis academies, known as 'prorectors.'

5. Known usually as 'drines — i.e. lightweight speed: Cylert, Tenuate,[a] Fastin, Preludin, even sometimes Ritalin. It's worth an N.B. that, unlike Jim Troeltsch or the Preludin-happy Bridget Boone, Michael Pemulis (out of maybe some queer sort of blue-collar street-type honor) rarely ingests any 'drines before a match, reserving them for recreation — some people are wired to find heart-pounding eye-wobbling 'drine-stimulation recreational.

    a. Tenuate's the trade name of diethylpropion hydrochloride, Marion Merrell Dow Pharmaceuticals, technically a prescription antiobesity agent, favored by some athletes for its mildly euphoric and resources-rallying properties w/o the tooth-grinding and hideous post-blood-spike crash that the hairier-chested 'drines like Fastin and Cylert inflict, though with a discomfitting tendency to cause post-spike ocular nystagmus. Nystagmus or no nystagmus, Tenuate's a particular favorite of Michael Pemulis, who hoards for personal ingestion every 75-mg. white Tenuate capsule he can lay hands on, and does not sell or trade them, except sometimes to roommate Jim Troeltsch, who nags Pemulis for them and also goes into Pemulis's special entrepôt-yachting-cap and promotes still more of them on the sly, a couple at a time, feeling that they help his sports-color-commentary loquacity, which secret promotions Pemulis knows about all too well, and is biding his time to retaliate, never you fear.

6. Lightweight tranqs: Valium-III and Valrelease, good old dependable Xanax, Dalmane, Buspar, Serax, even Halcion (legally available in Canada, unbelievably, still); with those kids inclined toward a heavier slide — reds, Meprospan, 'Happy Patch' transdermals, Miltown, Stelazine, the odd injury-'scrip Darvon) never lasting for more than a couple seasons for the obvious reason that serious tranqs can make even breathing seem

like too much trouble to go to, the cause of a meaty percentage of tranq-related deaths being attributed off the record by Emergency Room personnel to 'P.S.' or 'Pulmonary Sloth.'

7. Top jr. players are for the most part pretty cautious with alcohol, mostly because the physical consequences of heavy intake — like nausea and dehydration and poor hand-eye interface — make high-level performance almost impossible. Very few other standard substances have prohibitive short-term hangovers, actually, though an evening of even synthetic cocaine will make the next day's Dawn Drills very unpleasant indeed, which is why so few of E.T.A.'s hard core do cocaine, though there's also the issue of expense: though many E.T.A.s are the children of upscale parents, the children themselves are rarely flush with $ from home, since the gratification of pretty much every physical need is either taken care of or prohibited by E.T.A. itself. It's maybe worth noting that the same people hardwired to enjoy recreational 'drines also tend to gravitate toward cocaine and methedrine and other engine-revvers, while another broad class of more naturally higher-strung types tend more toward the edge-bevelling substances: tranqs, cannabis, barbiturates, and — yes — alcohol.

8. I.e.: psylocibin; Happy Patches[a]; MDMA/Xstasy (bad news, though, X); various low-tech manipulations of the benzene-ring in methoxy-class psychedelics, usually home-makable; synthetic dickies like MMDA, DMA, DMMM, 2CB, para-DOT I–VI, etc. — though note this class doesn't and shouldn't include CNS-rattlers like STP, DOM, the long-infamous West-U.S.-Coast 'Grievous Bodily Harm' (gamma hydroxybutyric acid), LSD-25 or -32, or DMZ/M.P. Enthusiasm for this stuff seems independent of neurologic type.

    a. Homemade transdermals, usually MDMA or Muscimole, with DDMS or the over-counter-available DMSO as the transdermal carrier.

9. A.k.a. LSD-25, often with a slight 'drine kicker added, called 'Black Star' because in metro Boston the available acid usually comes on chip-sized squares of thin cardboard with a black stencilled star on them, all from a certain shadowy node of supply down in New Bedford. All acid and Grievous Bodily Harm, like cocaine and heroin, come into Boston mostly from New Bedford MA, which in turn gets most of its supply from Bridgeport CT, which is the true lower intestine of North America, Bridgeport, be advised, if you've never been through there.

10. Like most sports academies, E.T.A. maintains the gentle fiction that 100% of its students are enrolled at their own ambitious volition and not that of, say for instance, their parents, some of whom (tennis-parents, like the stage-mothers of Hollywood legend) are bad news indeed.

11. An involved Arab women's game involving little shells and a quilted gameboard — rather like mah jongg without rules, by the diplomatic and medical husbands' estimate.

12. Meperedine hydrochloride and pentazocine hydrochloride, Schedule C-II and C-IV[a] narcotic analgesics, respectively, both from the good folks over at Sanofi Winthrop Pharm-Labs, Inc.

    a. Following the Continental Controlled Substance Act of Y.T.M.P., O.N.A.N.D.E.A.'s hierarchy of analgesics/antipyretics/anxiolytics establishes drug-classes of Category-II through Category-VI, with C-II's (e.g. Dilaudid, Demerol) being judged the heaviest w/r/t dependence and possible abuse, down to C-VI's that are about as potent as a kiss on the forehead from Mom.

13. Though masked in the evidentiary photo and never once given up or named by Gately to anyone, this can be presumed to have been one Trent ('Quo Vadis') Kite, Gately's old and once-gifted friend from his Beverly MA childhood.

14. This A.D.A.'s little personal trademark was that he always wore an anachronistic but

quality Stetson-brand businessman's hat with a decorative feather in the band, and frequently touched or played with the hat in tense situations.

15. The Bureau of Alcohol/Tobacco/Firearms, at that time under the temporary aegis of the United States Office of Unspecified Services.

16. Extremely unpleasant Québecois-insurgents-and-cartridge-related subsequent developments make it clear that this was (again) Trent ('Quo Vadis') Kite.

17. The codeineless kind, though — almost the first physical datum Gately took in in the nasty flashbulb-flash shock of the occupied bedroom's light coming on, to give you an idea of an oral-narcotics man's depth of psychic investment.

18. On top of the seascape safe's more negotiable contents, themselves on top of an unplugged and head-parked and absolutely top-hole genuine InterLace state-of-the-art TP/viewer ensemble in a multishelved hardwood rollable like entertainment-system-console thing, with a cartridge-dock and double-head drive in a compartment underneath with doors with classy little brass maple-leaf knob things and several shelves crammed tight with upscale arty-looking film cartridges, which latter Don Gately's colleague just about drooled all over the parquet flooring at the potential discriminating-type-fence-value of, potentially, if they were rare or celluloid-transferred or not available on the InterLace Dissemination Grid.

19. 'Une Personne de l'Importance Terrible,' presumably.

20. Fluorescence has been banned in Québec, as have computerized telephone solicitations, the little ad-cards that fall out of magazines and have to be looked at to be picked up and thrown in the trash, and the mention of any religious holiday whatsoever to sell any sort of product or service, is just one reason why his volunteering to come live down here was selfless.

21. Q.v. Note 211 sub.

22. Trade name of terfenadine, Marion Merrell Dow Pharmaceuticals, the tactical nuclear weapon of nondrowsy antihistamines and mucoidal desiccators.

23. Office of Naval Research, U.S.D.D.

24.

JAMES O. INCANDENZA: A FILMOGRAPHY[a]

The following listing is as complete as we are able to make it. Because the twelve years of Incandenza's directorial activity also coincided with large shifts in film venue — from public art cinemas, to VCR-capable magnetic recordings, to InterLace TelEntertainment laser dissemination and reviewable storage disk laser cartridges — and because Incandenza's output itself comprises industrial, documentary, conceptual, advertorial, technical, parodic, dramatic noncommercial, nondramatic ('anti-confluential') noncommercial, nondramatic commercial, and dramatic commercial works, this filmmaker's career presents substantive archival challenges. These challenges are also compounded by the facts that, first, for conceptual reasons, Incandenza eschewed both L. of C. registration and formal dating until the advent of Subsidized Time, secondly, that his output increased steadily until during the last years of his life Incandenza often had several works in production at the same time, thirdly, that his production company was privately owned and underwent at least four different changes of corporate name, and lastly that certain of his high-conceptual projects' agendas required that they be titled and subjected to critique but never filmed, making their status as film subject to controversy.

Accordingly, though the works are here listed in what is considered by archivists to be their

a. From Comstock, Posner, and Duquette, 'The Laughing Pathologists: Exemplary Works of the Anticonfluential Après Garde: Some Analyses of the Movement Toward Stasis in North American Conceptual Film (w/ Beth B., Vivienne Dick, James O. Incandenza, Vigdis Simpson, E. and K. Snow).' ONANite Film and Cartridge Studies Annual, vol. 8, nos. 1–3 (Year of D.P. from the A.H.), pp. 44–117.

probable order of completion, we wish to say that the list's order and completeness are, at this point in time, not definitive.

Each work's title is followed: by either its year of completion, or by 'B.S.,' designating undated completion before Subsidization; by the production company; by the major players, if credited; by the storage medium's ('film' 's) gauge or gauges; by the length of the work to the nearest minute; by an indication of whether the work is in black and white or color or both; by an indication of whether the film is silent or in sound or both; by (if possible) a brief synopsis or critical overview; and by an indication of whether the work is mediated by celluloid film, magnetic video, InterLace Spontaneous Dissemination, TP-compatible InterLace cartridge, or privately distributed by Incandenza's own company(ies). The designation UNRELEASED is used for those works which never saw distribution and are now publicly unavailable or lost.

Cage.[b] Dated only 'Before Subsidization.' Meniscus Films, Ltd. Uncredited cast; 16 mm.; .5 minutes; black and white; sound. Soliloquized parody of a broadcast-television advertisement for shampoo, utilizing four convex mirrors, two planar mirrors, and one actress. UNRELEASED

Kinds of Light. B.S. Meniscus Films, Ltd. No cast; 16 mm.; 3 minutes; color; silent. 4,444 individual frames, each of which photo depicts lights of different source, wavelength, and candle power, each reflected off the same unpolished tin plate and rendered disorienting at normal projection speeds by the hyperretinal speed at which they pass. CELLULOID, LIMITED METROPOLITAN BOSTON RELEASE, REQUIRES PROJECTION AT .25 NORMAL SPROCKET DRIVE

Dark Logics. B.S. Meniscus Films, Ltd. Players uncredited; 35 mm.; 21 minutes; color; silent w/ deafening Wagner/Sousa soundtrack. Griffith tribute, Iimura parody. Child-sized but severely palsied hand turns pages of incunabular manuscripts in mathematics, alchemy, religion, and bogus political autobiography, each page comprising some articulation or defense of intolerance and hatred. Film's dedication to D. W. Griffith and Taka Iimura. UNRELEASED

Tennis, Everyone? B.S. Heliotrope Films, Ltd./U.S.T.A. Films. Documentary cast w/ narrator Judith Fukuoka-Hearn; 35 mm.; 26 minutes; color; sound. Public relations/advertorial production for United States Tennis Association in conjunction with Wilson Sporting Goods, Inc. MAGNETIC VIDEO

'There Are No Losers Here.' B.S. Heliotrope Films, Ltd./ U.S.T.A. Films. Documentary cast w/ narrator P. A. Heaven; 35 mm.; color; sound. Documentary on B.S. 1997 U.S.T.A. National Junior Tennis Championships, Kalamazoo MI and Miami FL, in conjunction with United States Tennis Association and Wilson Sporting Goods. MAGNETIC VIDEO

Flux in a Box. B.S. Heliotrope Films, Ltd./Wilson Inc. Documentary cast w/ narrator Judith Fukuoka-Hearn; 35 mm.; 52 minutes; black and white/color; sound. Documentary history of box, platform, lawn, and court tennis from the 17th-century Court of the Dauphin to the present. MAGNETIC VIDEO

Infinite Jest (I). B.S. Meniscus Films, Ltd. Judith Fukuoka-Hearn; 16/35 mm.; 90(?) minutes; black and white; silent. Incandenza's unfinished and unseen first attempt at commercial entertainment. UNRELEASED

Annular Fusion Is Our Friend. B.S. Heliotrope Films, Ltd./Sunstrand Power & Light Co. Documentary cast w/ narrator C. N. Reilly; Sign-Interpreted for the Deaf; 78 mm.; 45 minutes; color; sound. Public relations/advertorial production for New England's Sunstrand Power and Light utility, a nontechnical explanation of the processes of DT-cycle lithiumized annular fusion and its applications in domestic energy production. CELLULOID, MAGNETIC VIDEO

Annular Amplified Light: Some Reflections. B.S. Heliotrope Films/Sunstrand Power & Light

---

b. With the possible exception of *Cage III — Free Show*, Incandenza's *Cage* series bears no discernible relation to Sidney Peterson's 1947 classic, *The Cage*.

Co. Documentary cast w/ narrator C. N. Reilly; Sign-Interpreted for the Deaf; 78 mm.; 45 minutes; color; sound. Second infomercial for Sunstrand Co., a nontechnical explanation of the applications of cooled-photon lasers in DT-cycle lithiumized annular fusion. CELLULOID, MAGNETIC VIDEO

Union of Nurses in Berkeley. B.S. Meniscus Films, Ltd. Documentary cast; 35 mm.; 26 minutes; color; silent. Documentary and closed-caption interviews with hearing-impaired RNs and LPNs during Bay Area health care reform riots of 1996. MAGNETIC VIDEO, PRIVATELY RELEASED BY MENISCUS FILMS, LTD.

Union of Theoretical Grammarians in Cambridge. B.S. Meniscus Films, Ltd. Documentary cast; 35 mm.; 26 minutes; color; silent w/ heavy use of computerized distortion in facial close-ups. Documentary and closed-caption interviews with participants in the public Steven Pinker–Avril M. Incandenza debate on the political implications of prescriptive grammar during the infamous Militant Grammarians of Massachusetts convention credited with helping incite the M.I.T. language riots of B.S. 1997. UNRELEASED DUE TO LITIGATION

Widower. B.S. Latrodectus Mactans Productions. Cosgrove Watt, Ross Reat; 35 mm.; 34 minutes; black and white; sound. Shot on location in Tucson AZ, parody of broadcast television domestic comedies, a cocaine-addicted father (Watt) leads his son (Reat) around their desert property immolating poisonous spiders. CELLULOID; INTERLACE TELENT CARTRIDGE RERELEASE #357–75–00 (Y.P.W.)

Cage II. B.S. Latrodectus Mactans Productions. Cosgrove Watt, Disney Leith; 35 mm.; 120 minutes; black and white; sound. Sadistic penal authorities place a blind convict (Watt) and a deaf-mute convict (Leith) together in 'solitary confinement,' and the two men attempt to devise ways of communicating with each other. LIMITED CELLULOID RUN; RERELEASED ON MAGNETIC VIDEO

Death in Scarsdale. B.S. Latrodectus Mactans Productions. Cosgrove Watt, Marlon R. Bain; 78 mm.; 39 minutes; color; silent w/ closed-caption subtitles. Mann/Allen parody, a world-famous dermatological endocrinologist (Watt) becomes platonically obsessed with a boy (Bain) he is treating for excessive perspiration, and begins himself to suffer from excessive perspiration. UNRELEASED

Fun with Teeth. B.S. Latrodectus Mactans Productions. Herbert G. Birch, Billy Tolan, Pam Heath; 35 mm.; 73 minutes; black and white; silent w/ non-human screams and howls. Kosinski/Updike/Peckinpah parody, a dentist (Birch) performs sixteen unanesthetized root-canal procedures on an academic (Tolan) he suspects of involvement with his wife (Heath). MAGNETIC VIDEO, PRIVATELY RELEASED BY LATRODECTUS MACTANS PROD.

Infinite Jest (II). B.S. Latrodectus Mactans Productions. Pam Heath; 35/78 mm.; 90(?) minutes; black and white; silent. Unfinished, unseen attempt at remake of *Infinite Jest (I).* UNRELEASED

Immanent Domain. B.S. Latrodectus Mactans Productions. Cosgrove Watt, Judith Fukuoka-Hearn, Pam Heath, Pamela-Sue Voorheis, Herbert G. Birch; 35 mm.; 88 minutes; black and white w/ microphotography; sound. Three memory-neurons (Fukuoka-Hearn, Heath, Voorheis (w/ polyurethane costumes)) in the Inferior frontal gyrus of a man's (Watt's) brain fight heroically to prevent their displacement by new memory-neurons as the man undergoes intensive psychoanalysis. CELLULOID; INTERLACE TELENT CARTRIDGE RERELEASE #340–03–70 (Y.P.W.)

Kinds of Pain. B.S. Latrodectus Mactans Productions. Anonymous cast; 35/78 mm.; 6 minutes; color; silent. 2,222 still-frame close-ups of middle-aged white males suffering from almost every conceivable type of pain, from an ingrown toenail to cranio-facial neuralgia to inoperable colo-rectal neoplastis. CELLULOID, LIMITED METRO BOSTON RELEASE, REQUIRES PROJECTION AT .25 NORMAL SPROCKET-DRIVE

Various Small Flames. B.S. Latrodectus Mactans Productions. Cosgrove Watt, Pam Heath, Ken N. Johnson; 16 mm.; 25 minutes w/ recursive loop for automatic replay; color; silent w/ sounds of human coitus appropriated from and credited to Caballero Control Corp. adult videos. Parody of neoconceptual structuralist films of Godbout and Vodriard, n-frame images of myriad varieties of small household flames, from lighters and birthday candles to stovetop gas rings and grass clippings ignited by sunlight through a magnifying glass, alternated with antinarrative sequences of a man (Watt) sitting in a dark bedroom drinking bourbon while his wife (Heath) and an Amway representative (Johnson) have acrobatic coitus in the background's lit hallway. UNRELEASED DUE TO LITIGATION BY 1960s US CONCEPTUAL DIRECTOR OF *VARIOUS SMALL FIRES* ED RUSCHA — INTERLACE TELENT CARTRIDGE RERELEASE #330-54-94 (Y.T.-S.D.B.)

Cage III — Free Show. B.S. Latrodectus Mactans Productions/Infernatron Animation Concepts, Canada. Cosgrove Watt, P. A. Heaven, Everard Maynell, Pam Heath; partial animation; 35 mm.; 65 minutes; black and white; sound. The figure of Death (Heath) presides over the front entrance of a carnival sideshow whose spectators watch performers undergo unspeakable degradations so grotesquely compelling that the spectators' eyes become larger and larger until the spectators themselves are transformed into gigantic eyeballs in chairs, while on the other side of the sideshow tent the figure of Life (Heaven) uses a megaphone to invite fairgoers to an exhibition in which, if the fairgoers consent to undergo unspeakable degradations, they can witness ordinary persons gradually turn into gigantic eyeballs. INTERLACE TELENT FEATURE CARTRIDGE #357-65-65

'*The Medusa v. the Odalisque.*' B.S. Latrodectus Mactans Productions. Uncredited cast; zoneplating laser holography by James O. Incandenza and Urquhart Ogilvie, Jr.; holographic fight-choreography by Kenjiru Hirota courtesy of Sony Entertainment–Asia; 78 mm.; 29 minutes; black and white; silent w/ audience-noises appropriated from network broadcast television. Mobile holograms of two visually lethal mythologic females duel with reflective surfaces onstage while a live crowd of spectators turns to stone. LIMITED CELLULOID RUN; PRIVATELY RERELEASED ON MAGNETIC VIDEO BY LATRODECTUS MACTANS PRODUCTIONS

The Machine in the Ghost: Annular Holography for Fun and Prophet. B.S. Heliotrope Films, Ltd./National Film Board of Canada. Narrator P. A. Heaven; 78 mm.; 35 minutes; color; sound. Nontechnical introduction to theories of annular enhancement and zone-plating and their applications in high-resolution laser holography. UNRELEASED DUE TO US/CANADIAN DIPLOMATIC TENSIONS

Homo Duplex. B.S. Latrodectus Mactans Productions. Narrator P. A. Heaven; Super-8 mm.; 70 minutes; black and white; sound. Parody of Woititz and Shulgin's 'poststructural antidocumentaries,' interviews with fourteen Americans who are named John Wayne but are not the legendary 20th-century film actor John Wayne. MAGNETIC VIDEO (LIMITED RELEASE)

Zero-Gravity Tea Ceremony. B.S. Latrodectus Mactans Productions. Ken N. Johnson, Judith Fukuoka-Hearn, Otto Brandt, E. J. Kenkle; 35 mm.; 82 minutes; black and white/color; silent. The intricate *Ocha-Kai* is conducted 2.5 m. off the ground in the Johnson Space Center's zero-gravity-simulation chamber. CELLULOID; INTERLACE TELENT RERELEASE #357-40-01 (Y.P.W.)

Pre-Nuptial Agreement of Heaven and Hell. B.S. Latrodectus Mactans Productions/ Infernatron Animation Concepts, Canada. Animated w/ uncredited voices; 35 mm.; 59 minutes; color; sound. God and Satan play poker with Tarot cards for the soul of an alcoholic sandwich-bag salesman obsessed with Bernini's 'The Ecstasy of St. Teresa.' PRIVATELY RELEASED ON CELLULOID AND MAGNETIC VIDEO BY LATRODECTUS MACTANS PRODUCTIONS

The Joke. B.S. Latrodectus Mactans Productions. Audience as reflexive cast; 35 mm. × 2 cameras; variable length; black and white; silent. Parody of Hollis Frampton's 'audience-specific events,' two Ikegami EC-35 video cameras in theater record the 'film' 's audience and project the resultant raster onto screen — the theater audience watching itself watch itself get the obvious 'joke' and become increasingly self-conscious and uncomfortable and hostile supposedly comprises the film's involuted 'antinarrative' flow. Incandenza's first truly controversial project, *Film & Kartridge Kultcher's* Sperber credited it with 'unwittingly sounding the deathknell of post-poststructural film in terms of sheer annoyance.' NONRECORDED MAGNETIC VIDEO SCREENABLE IN THEATER VENUE ONLY, NOW UNRELEASED

Various Lachrymose U.S. Corporate Middle-Management Figures. Unfinished. UNRELEASED

Every Inch of Disney Leith. B.S. Latrodectus Mactans Productions/Medical Imagery of Alberta, Ltd. Disney Leith; computer-enlarged 35 mm./× 2 m.; 253 minutes; color; silent. Miniaturized, endoscopic, and microinvasive cameras traverse entire exterior and interior of one of Incandenza's technical crew as he sits on a folded serape in the Boston Common listening to a public forum on uniform North American metricization. PRIVATE RELEASE ON MAGNETIC VIDEO BY LATRODECTUS MACTANS PRODUCTIONS; INTERLACE TELENT RERELEASE #357–56–34 (Y.P.W.)

Infinite Jest (III). B.S. Latrodectus Mactans Productions. Uncredited cast; 16/35 mm.; color; sound. Unfinished, unseen remake of *Infinite Jest (I), (II).* UNRELEASED

Found Drama I.
Found Drama II.
Found Drama III. . . . conceptual, conceptually unfilmable. UNRELEASED

The Man Who Began to Suspect He Was Made of Glass. Year of the Whopper. Latrodectus Mactans Productions. Cosgrove Watt, Gerhardt Schtitt; 35 mm.; 21 minutes; black and white; sound. A man undergoing intensive psychotherapy discovers that he is brittle, hollow, and transparent to others, and becomes either transcendentally enlightened or schizophrenic. INTERLACE TELENT FEATURE CARTRIDGE #357–59–00

Found Drama V.
Found Drama VI. . . . conceptual, conceptually unfilmable. UNRELEASED

The American Century as Seen Through a Brick. Year of the Whopper. Latrodectus Mactans Productions. Documentary cast w/ narration by P. A. Heaven; 35 mm.; 52 minutes; color w/ red filter and oscillophotography; silent w/ narration. As U.S. Boston's historical Back Bay streets are stripped of brick and repaved with polymerized cement, the resultant career of one stripped brick is followed, from found-art temporary installation to displacement by E.W.D. catapult to a waste-quarry in southern Québec to its use in the F.L.Q.-incited anti-O.N.A.N. riots of January/Whopper, all intercut with ambiguous shots of a human thumb's alterations in the interference pattern of a plucked string. PRIVATELY RELEASED ON MAGNETIC VIDEO BY LATRODECTUS MACTANS PRODUCTIONS

The ONANtiad. Year of the Whopper. Latrodectus Mactans Productions/Claymation action sequences © Infernatron Animation Concepts, Canada. Cosgrove Watt, P. A. Heaven, Pam Heath, Ken N. Johnson, Ibn-Said Chawaf, Squyre Frydell, Marla-Dean Chumm, Herbert G. Birch, Everard Meynell; 35 mm.; 76 minutes; black and white/color; sound/silent. Oblique, obsessive, and not very funny claymation love triangle played out against live-acted backdrop of the inception of North American Interdependence and Continental Reconfiguration. PRIVATELY RELEASED ON MAGNETIC VIDEO BY LATRODECTUS MACTANS PRODUCTIONS

The Universe Lashes Out. Year of the Whopper. Latrodectus Mactans Productions. Documentary cast w/ narrator Herbert G. Birch; 16 mm.; 28 minutes; color; silent w/ narration. Documentary on the evacuation of Atkinson NH/New Québec at the inception of Continental Reconfiguration. MAGNETIC VIDEO (LIMITED RELEASE)

*Poultry[1] in[1] Motion.*Year of the Whopper. Latrodectus Mactans Productions. Documentary cast w/ narrator P. A. Heaven; 16 mm.; 56 minutes; color; silent w/ narration. Documentary on renegade North Syracuse NNY turkey farmers' bid to prevent toxification of Thanksgiving crop by commandeering long, shiny O.N.A.N. trucks to transplant over 200,000 pertussive fowl south to Ithaca. MAGNETIC VIDEO (LIMITED RELEASE)

Found[1] Drama[1] IX.
Found[1] Drama[1] X.
Found[1] Drama[1] XI. . . conceptual, conceptually unfilmable. UNRELEASED

*Möbius[1] Strips.*Year of the Whopper. Lactrodectus Mactans Productions. 'Hugh G. Rection,' Pam Heath, 'Bunny Day,' 'Taffy Appel'; 35 mm.; 109 minutes; black and white; sound. Pornography-parody, possible parodic homage to Fosse's *All[1] That[1] Jazz,* in which a theoretical physicist ('Rection'), who can only achieve creative mathematical insight during coitus, conceives of Death as a lethally beautiful woman (Heath). INTERLACE TELENT FEATURE CARTRIDGE #357–65–32 (Y.W.)

*Wave[1] Bye-Bye[1] to[1] the[1] Bureaucracy.*Year of the Whopper. Latrodectus Mactans Productions. Everard Maynell, Phillip T. Smothergill, Paul Anthony Heaven, Pamela-Sue Voorheis; 16 mm.; 19 minutes; black and white; sound. Possible parody/homage to B.S. public-service-announcement cycle of Church of Jesus Christ of Latter-Day Saints,[c] a harried commuter is mistaken for Christ by a child he knocks over.

*Blood[1] Sister:[1] One[1] Tough[1] Nun.*Year of the Tucks Medicated Pad. Latrodectus Mactans Productions. Telma Hurley, Pam Heath, Marla-Dean Chumm, Diane Saltoone, Soma Richardson-Levy, Cosgrove Watt; 35 mm.; 90 minutes; color; sound. Parody of revenge/recidivism action genre, a formerly delinquent nun's (Hurley's) failure to reform a juvenile delinquent (Chumm) leads to a rampage of recidivist revenge. INTERLACE TELENT PULSE-DISSEMINATION 21 JULY Y.T.M.P., CARTRIDGE #357–87–04

*Infinite[1] Jest[1] (IV)*Year of the Tucks Medicated Pad. Latrodectus Mactans Productions. Pam Heath (?), 'Madame Psychosis'(?); 78 mm.; 90 minutes(?); color; sound. Unfinished, unseen attempt at completion of *Infinite[1] Jest[1] (III)*UNRELEASED

*Let[1] There[1] Be[1] Lite.*Year of the Tucks Medicated Pad. Poor Yorick Entertainment Unlimited. Documentary cast w/ narrator Ken N. Johnson; 16mm.; 50 minutes(?); black and white; silent w/ narration. Unfinished documentary on genesis of reduced-calorie bourbon industry. UNRELEASED

Untitled. Unfinished. UNRELEASED

*No[1] Troy.*Year of the Whopper. Latrodectus Mactans Productions. No cast; liquid-surface holography by Urquhart Ogilvie, Jr.; 35 mm.; 7 minutes; enhanced color; silent. Scale-model holographic recreation of Troy NY's bombardment by miscalibrated Waste Displacement Vehicles, and its subsequent elimination by O.N.A.N. cartographers. MAGNETIC VIDEO (PRIVATE RELEASE LIMITED TO NEW BRUNSWICK, ALBERTA, QUÉBEC) Note: Archivists in Canada and the U.S. West Coast do not list *No[1] Troy*but do list titles *The[1] Violet[1] City*and *The[1] Violet[1] Ex-City*respectively, leading scholars to conclude that the same film was released under several different appellations.

Untitled. Unfinished. UNRELEASED

*Valuable[1] Coupon[1] Has[1] Been[1] Removed.*Year of the Tucks Medicated Pad. Poor Yorick Enter-

---

c. See Romney and Sperber, 'Has James O. Incandenza Ever Even Once Produced One Genuinely Original or Unappropriated or Nonderivative Thing?' *Post-Millennium[1] Film[1] Cartridge[1] Journal,*vols. 7–9 (Fall/Winter, Y.P.W.), pp. 4–26.

tainment Unlimited. Cosgrove Watt, Phillip T. Smothergill, Diane Saltoone; 16 mm.; 52 minutes; color; silent. Possible Scandinavian-psychodrama parody, a boy helps his alcoholic-delusional father and disassociated mother dismantle their bed to search for rodents, and later he intuits the future feasibility of D.T.-cycle lithiumized annular fusion. CELLULOID (UNRELEASED)

Baby Pictures of Famous Dictators. Year of the Tucks Medicated Pad. Poor Yorick Entertainment Unlimited. Documentary or uncredited cast w/ narrator P. A. Heaven; 16 mm.; 45 minutes; black and white; sound. Children and adolescents play a nearly incomprehensible nuclear strategy game with tennis equipment against the real or holographic(?) backdrop of sabotaged ATHSCME 1900 atmospheric displacement towers exploding and toppling during the New New England Chemical Emergency of Y.W. CELLULOID (UNRELEASED)

Stand Behind the Men Behind the Wire. Year of the Tucks Medicated Pad. Poor Yorick Entertainment Unlimited. Documentary cast w/ narrator Soma Richardson-Levy; Super-8 mm.; 52 minutes; black and white/color; sound. Shot on location north of Lowell MA, documentary on Essex County Sheriff's Dept. and Massachusetts Department of Social Services' expedition to track, verify, capture, or propitiate the outsized feral infant alleged to have crushed, gummed, or picked up and dropped over a dozen residents of Lowell in January, Y.T.M.P. INTERLACE TELENT CARTRIDGE #357-12-56

As of Yore. Year of the Tucks Medicated Pad. Poor Yorick Entertainment Unlimited. Cosgrove Watt, Marlon Bain; 16/78 mm.; 181 minutes; black and white/color; sound. A middle-aged tennis instructor, preparing to instruct his son in tennis, becomes intoxicated in the family's garage and subjects his son to a rambling monologue while the son weeps and perspires. INTERLACE TELENT CARTRIDGE # 357-16-09

The Clever Little Bastard. Unfinished, unseen. UNRELEASED

The Cold Majesty of the Numb. Unfinished, unseen. UNRELEASED

Good-Looking Men in Small Clever Rooms That Utilize Every Centimeter of Available Space With Mind-Boggling Efficiency. Unfinished due to hospitalization. UNRELEASED

Low-Temperature Civics. Year of the Tucks Medicated Pad. Poor Yorick Entertainment Unlimited. Cosgrove Watt, Herbert G. Birch, Ken N. Johnson, Soma Richardson-Levy, Everard Maynell, 'Madame Psychosis,' Phillip T. Smothergill, Paul Anthony Heaven; 35 mm.; 80 minutes; black and white; sound. Wyler parody in which four sons (Birch, Johnson, Maynell, Smothergill) intrigue for control of a sandwich-bag conglomerate after their CEO father (Watt) has an ecstatic encounter with Death ('Psychosis') and becomes irreversibly catatonic. NATIONAL DISSEMINATION IN INTERLACE TELENT'S 'CAVALCADE OF EVIL' SERIES — JANUARY/YEAR OF TRIAL-SIZE DOVE BAR — AND INTERLACE TELENT CARTRIDGE #357-89-05

(At Least) Three Cheers for Cause and Effect. Year of the Tucks Medicated Pad. Poor Yorick Entertainment Unlimited. Cosgrove Watt, Pam Heath, 'Hugh G. Rection'; 78 mm.; 26 minutes; black and white; sound. The headmaster of a newly constructed high-altitude sports academy (Watt) becomes neurotically obsessed with litigation over the construction's ancillary damage to a V.A. hospital far below, as a way of diverting himself from his wife's (Heath's) poorly hidden affair with the academically renowned mathematical topologist who is acting as the project's architect ('Rection'). CELLULOID (UNRELEASED)

(The) Desire to Desire. Year of the Tucks Medicated Pad. Poor Yorick Entertainment Unlimited. Robert Lingley, 'Madame Psychosis,' Marla-Dean Chumm; 35 mm.; 99 minutes(?); black and white; silent. A pathology resident (Lingley) falls in love with a beautiful cadaver ('Psychosis') and the paralyzed sister (Chumm) she died rescuing from the attack of an oversized feral infant. Listed by some archivists as unfinished. UNRELEASED

Safe Boating Is No Accident. Year of the Tucks Medicated Pad(?). Poor Yorick Entertainment

Unlimited/X-Ray and Infrared Photography by Shuco-Mist Medical Pressure Systems, Enfield MA. Ken N. Johnson, 'Madame Psychosis,' P. A. Heaven. Kierkegaard/Lynch (?) parody, a claustrophobic water-ski instructor (Johnson), struggling with his romantic conscience after his fiancée's ('Psychosis''s) face is grotesquely mangled by an outboard propeller, becomes trapped in an overcrowded hospital elevator with a defrocked Trappist monk, two overcombed missionaries for the Church of Jesus Christ of Latter-Day Saints, an enigmatic fitness guru, the Massachusetts State Commissioner for Beach and Water Safety, and seven severely intoxicated opticians with silly hats and exploding cigars. Listed by some archivists as completed the following year, Y.T.-S.D.B. UNRELEASED

Very Low Impact. Year of the Tucks Medicated Pad. Poor Yorick Entertainment Unlimited. Marla-Dean Chumm, Pam Heath, Soma Richardson-Levy-O'Byrne; 35 mm.; 30 minutes; color; sound. A narcoleptic aerobics instructor (Chumm) struggles to hide her condition from students and employers. POSTHUMOUS RELEASE Y.W.-Q.M.D.; INTERLACE TELENT CARTRIDGE # 357–97–29

The Night Wears a Sombrero. Year of the Tucks Medicated Pad (?). Ken N. Johnson, Phillip T. Smothergill, Dianne Saltoone, 'Madame Psychosis'; 78 mm.; 105 minutes; color; silent/sound. Parody/homage to Lang's *Rancho Notorious*, a nearsighted apprentice cowpoke (Smothergill), swearing vengeance for a gunslinger's (Johnson's) rape of what he (the cowpoke) mistakenly believes is the motherly brothel-owner (Saltoone) he (the cowpoke) is secretly in love with, loses the trail of the gunslinger after misreading a road sign and is drawn to a sinister Mexican ranch where Oedipally aggrieved gunslingers are ritually blinded by a mysterious veiled nun ('Psychosis'). Listed by some archivists as completed the preceding year, Y.W. INTERLACE TELENT CARTRIDGE #357–56–51

Accomplice! Year of the Tucks Medicated Pad. Poor Yorick Entertainment Unlimited. Cosgrove Watt, Stokely 'Dark Star' McNair; 16 mm.; 26 minutes; color; sound. An aging pederast mutilates himself out of love for a strangely tattooed street hustler. INTERLACE TELENT CARTRIDGE # 357–10–10 withdrawn from dissemination after *Cartridge Scene* reviewers called *Accomplice!* '. . . the stupidest, nastiest, least subtle and worst-edited product of a pretentious and wretchedly uneven career.' NOW UNRELEASED

Untitled. Unfinished. UNRELEASED

Untitled. Unfinished. UNRELEASED

Untitled. Unfinished. UNRELEASED

Dial C for Concupiscence. Year of the Trial-Size Dove Bar. Poor Yorick Entertainment Unlimited. Soma Richardson-Levy-O'Byrne, Marla-Dean Chumm, Ibn-Said Chawaf, Yves Francoeur; 35 mm.; 122 minutes; black and white; silent w/ subtitles. Parodic *noir*-style tribute to Bresson's *Les Anges du Peché,* a cellular phone operator (Richardson-Levy-O'Byrne), mistaken by a Québecois terrorist (Francoeur) for another cellular phone operator (Chumm) the FLQ had mistakenly tried to assassinate, mistakes his mistaken attempts to apologize as attempts to assassinate her (Richardson-Levy-O'Byrne) and flees to a bizarre Islamic religious community whose members communicate with each other by means of semaphore flags, where she falls in love with an armless Near Eastern medical attaché (Chawaf). RELEASED IN INTERLACE TELENT'S 'HOWLS FROM THE MARGIN' UNDERGROUND FILM SERIES — MARCH/ Y.T.-S.D.B. — AND INTERLACE TELENT CARTRIDGE #357–75–43

Insubstantial Country. Year of the Trial-Size Dove Bar. Poor Yorick Entertainment Unlimited. Cosgrove Watt; 16 mm.; 30 minutes; black and white; silent/sound. An unpopular après-garde filmmaker (Watt) either suffers a temporal lobe seizure and becomes mute or else is the victim of everyone else's delusion that his (Watt's) temporal lobe seizure has left him mute. PRIVATE CARTRIDGE RELEASE BY POOR YORICK ENTERTAINMENT UNLIMITED

It Was a Great Marvel That He Was in the Father Without Knowing Him. Year of the Trial-Size Dove Bar. Poor Yorick Entertainment Unlimited. Cosgrove Watt, Phillip T. Smothergill;

16 mm.; 5 minutes; black and white; silent/ sound. A father (Watt), suffering from the delusion that his etymologically precocious son (Smothergill) is pretending to be mute, poses as a 'professional conversationalist' in order to draw the boy out. RELEASED IN INTERLACE TELENT'S 'HOWLS FROM THE MARGIN' UNDERGROUND FILM SERIES — MARCH/ Y.T.-S.D.B — AND INTERLACE TELENT CARTRIDGE #357–75–50

Cage IV — Web. Unfinished. UNRELEASED

Cage V — Infinite Jim. Unfinished. UNRELEASED

Death and the Single Girl. Unfinished. UNRELEASED.

The Film Adaptation of Peter Weiss's 'The Persecution and Assassination of Marat as Performed by the Inmates of the Asylum at Charenton Under the Direction of the Marquis de Sade.' Year of the Trial-Size Dove Bar. Poor Yorick Entertainment Unlimited. James O. Incandenza, Disney Leith, Urquhart Ogilvie, Jr., Jane Ann Prickett, Herbert G. Birch, 'Madame Psychosis,' Marla-Dean Chumm, Marlon Bain, Pam Heath, Soma Richardson-Levy-O'Byrne-Chawaf, Ken N. Johnson, Dianne Saltoone; Super-8 mm.; 88 minutes; black and white; silent/ sound. Fictional 'interactive documentary' on Boston stage production of Weiss's 20th-century play within play, in which the documentary's chemically impaired director (Incandenza) repeatedly interrupts the inmates' dumbshow-capering and Marat and Sade's dialogues to discourse incoherently on the implications of Brando's Method Acting and Artaud's Theatre of Cruelty for North American filmed entertainment, irritating the actor who plays Marat (Leith) to such an extent that he has a cerebral hemorrhage and collapses onstage well before Marat's scripted death, whereupon the play's nearsighted director (Ogilvie), mistaking the actor who plays Sade (Johnson) for Incandenza, throws Sade into Marat's medicinal bath and throttles him to death, whereupon the extra-dramatic figure of Death ('Psychosis') descends *deus ex machina* to bear Marat (Leith) and Sade (Johnson) away, while Incandenza becomes ill all over the theater audience's first row. 8 MM. SYNC-PROJECTION CELLULOID. UNRELEASED DUE TO LITIGATION, HOSPITALIZATION

Too Much Fun. Unfinished. UNRELEASED

The Unfortunate Case of Me. Unfinished. UNRELEASED

Sorry All Over the Place. Unfinished. UNRELEASED

Infinite Jest (V?). Year of the Trial-Size Dove Bar. Poor Yorick Entertainment Unlimited. 'Madame Psychosis'; no other definitive data. Thorny problem for archivists. Incandenza's last film, Incandenza's death occurring during its post-production. Most archival authorities list as unfinished, unseen. Some list as completion of *Infinite Jest (IV)*, for which Incandenza also used 'Psychosis,' thus list the film under Incandenza's output for Y.T.M.P. Though no scholarly synopsis or report of viewing exists, two short essays in different issues of *Cartridge Quarterly East* refer to the film as 'extraordinary'[d] and 'far and away [James O. Incandenza's] most entertaining and compelling work.'[e] West Coast archivists list the film's gauge as '16 . . . 78 . . . *n* mm.,' basing the gauge on critical allusions[f] to 'radical experiments in viewers' optical perspective and context' as *IJ(V?)*'s distinctive feature. Though Canadian archivist Tête-Bêche lists the film as completed and privately distributed by P.Y.E.U. through posthumous provisions in the filmmaker's will, all other comprehensive filmographies have the film either unfinished or UNRELEASED, its Master cartridge either destroyed or vaulted *sui testator*.

---

d. E. Duquette, 'Beholden to Vision: Optics and Desire in Four Après Garde Films,' *Cartridge Quarterly East,* vol. 4 no. 2, Y.W.-Q.M.D., pp. 35–39.

e. Anonymous, 'Seeing v. Believing,' *Cartridge Quarterly East,* vol. 4 no. 4, Y.W.-Q.M.D., pp. 93–95.

f. Ibid.

25. More like July–October, actually.

26. Synthetically enhanced enkephalin, an opiate-like pentapeptide or so-called endorphin manufactured in the human spine, one of the compounds prominently involved in the infamous 'CadaverGate' scandal that brought down so many funeral directors in the Year of the Perdue Wonderchicken.

27. Metro Boston subdialectical argot — origin unknown — for cannabis, pot, grass, duBois, dope, ganja, bhang, herb, hash, m. jane, kif, etc.; with 'Bing Crosby' designating cocaine and organic methoxies ('drines), and — inexplicably — 'Doris' standing for synthetic dickies, psychs, and phenyls.

28. Monoamine-oxidase inhibitors, a venerable class of antidepressants/anxiolytics, of which Parnate — SmithKline Beecham's product-name for tranylcypromine sulfate — is a member. Zoloft is sertraline hydrochloride, a serotonin-reuptake-inhibitor (SRI) not all that dissimilar to Prozac, manufactured by Pfizer-Roerig.

29. Electro-Convulsive Therapy.

30. A neutral boric acid eyewash, a kind of turbo-charged Visine, available over-counter from Wyeth Labs, with its own eye-cup of apothecary-blue plastic that's downright gorgeous when held up to a window's light.

31. Schtitt's term for Mr. A. deLint, which means technically 'soulmate' or 'spouse' but isn't meant at all sexually w/r/t deLint, we can rest assured.

32. Roughly, 'They Can Kill You, But the Legalities of Eating You Are Quite a Bit Dicier.'

33. I.e., 'Before Subsidization' or the beginning of the subsidized O.N.A.N.ite lunar calendar under President Gentle; see *sub*.

34. A.k.a. 'E.L.D.,' that still-green shoot off the pure branch of math that deals with systems and phenomena whose chaos is beyond even Mandelbrotian math's Strange Equations and Random Attractants, a delimiting reaction against the Chaos Theories of fractal-happy meteorologists and systems analysts, E.L.D., whose post-Gödelian theorems and nonexistence proofs amount to extremely lucid and elegant admissions of defeat in certain cases, hands thrown up w/ complete deductive justification. Incandenza, whose frustrated interest in grand-scale failure was unflagging through four different careers, would have been all over Extra-Linear Dynamics like white on rice, had he survived.

35. I.e., presumably, 'of-Georg-Cantor,' Cantor being a 1900s-era set-theorist (German also) and more or less founder of transfinite mathematics, the man who proved some infinities were bigger than other infinities, and whose 1905-ish Diagonal Proof demonstrated that there can be an infinity of things between any two things no matter how close together the two things are, which D. Proof deeply informed Dr. J. Incandenza's sense of the transstatistical aesthetics of serious tennis.

36. Low-Bavarian for something like 'wandering alone in blasted disorienting territory beyond all charted limits and orienting markers,' supposedly.

37. Wheelchair.

38. Ghostly light- and monster-shadow phenomenon particular to certain mountains; e.g. q.v. Part I of Goethe's *Faust*, the Walpurgisnacht six-toed danceathon on the Harz-Bröcken, in which there's described a classic '*Bröckengespenstphänom.*' (*Gespenst* means specter or wraith.)

39. Marathe's superior in the A.F.R.,[a] the leader of the Wheelchair Assassins' U.S.A. cell, and the former boyhood friend of Rémy Marathe's late older brothers, both struck and killed by trains.[b]

    a. *Les Assassins des Fauteuils Rollents*, a.k.a. Wheelchair Assassins, pretty much Québec's most dreaded and rapacious anti-O.N.A.N. terrorist cell.

    b. See Note 304 *sub*.

40. In other words, M. Fortier and the A.F.R. (as far as Marathe knew) believed that Marathe was functioning as a kind of 'triple agent' or duplicitous 'double agent' — at Fortier's direction, Marathe had pretended to approach B.S.S. seeking to trade knowledge of the A.F.R.'s anti-O.N.A.N. activities for protection and medical care for his hideously ill wife (Marathe's) — only (as far as Marathe can know) Marathe and very few B.S.S. operatives know that Marathe is now only *pretending* to pretend to betray, that M. Steeply is fully aware that Marathe responds to B.S.S.'s summonses with what M. Fortier believes is his (Fortier's) full knowledge, that M. Fortier is not (as far as Marathe and Steeply can reasonably posit) aware that Steeply and B.S.S. are aware that Fortier is aware of Marathe's meetings with Steeply, and that Marathe's own violent death will be the smallest of his (Marathe's) problems should his Mont-Tremblant countrymen come to suspect the even-numbered total of his final loyalties.

41. Intra-O.N.A.N. sobriquet for 'acting as a double agent'; similarly w/ 'tripling,' and so on.

42. The 'thing of important' seems to be that Marathe's A.F.R. superiors believe he only is pretending to betray them in order to secure advanced U.S. cardiac-prosthetic technology for his wife; but that in fact he really *is* betraying them (the superiors, his country) — probably actually for that medical tech — and is thus only pretending only to pretend.

43. Chronic inflammation of the terminal ileum and adjacent tissues, named in dubious honor of a Dr. Crohn in B.S. 1932.

44. Professional euphemism for involuntary interrogation, either w/ or w/o physical inducements.

45. See Note 304 *sub*.

46. Over-the-counter topical stuff for the corticatization of skin, tincture of benzoin facilitates the development of the kinds of callus that don't get blood-blisters underneath. Way more common and universal among serious players than Lemon Pledge. Finding the smell of t. of b. nauseous, some junior players prefer an applied layer of corn starch or baby powder, which makes the t. of b. easier to wash off later but also leaves weird little white fingerprints over everything you touch.

47. *Le Front de la Libération de la Québec,* rather a younger and rowdier and less implacably businesslike cell than the A.F.R., and symbolically adopting certain cultural customs, musics and motifs associated with Hawaii, supposedly an ironic nod to the idea that Québec is now, too, a kind of annex or territory of the U.S., a Canadian province only on paper, and separated from its real captor-nation by distances of space and culture that are unbridgeable.

48. The progressive asymmetrical narrowing of one or more cardiac sinuses; can be either atherosclerotic or neoplastic; rare before continental Interdependence; now the third-leading cause of death among adults of Québec and New Brunswick and the seventh among adults of the Northeastern U.S.A.; associated with chronic low-level exposure to 2,3,7,8 Tetrachlorodibenzo-P-Di- and -Trioxin compounds.

49. Redundancy *sic.*

50. Said galoots also known, in the old founder's AA circle, Enfield MA's White Flag Group, as 'The Crocodiles.'

51. Syntax *sic,* which had helped drive Mrs. Avril Incandenza — her Op-Ed letters and formal complaints apparently ignored at every political level — to help found the Militant Grammarians of Massachusetts, ever since a bramble in the flank of advertisers, corporations, and all fast-and-loose-players with the integrity of public discourse — see *sub*.

52. The Gas Chromatography/Mass Spectrometry scan uses particle-bombardment and a

positive-ion read by a spectrometer. It's the mid-range test of choice for corporations and athletic bodies, way less expensive than chromosomatic breakdowns of hair samples, but — as long as environmental controls on the hardware're strictly observed — more comprehensive and reliable than the older E.M.I.T. and AbuScreen/RIA urine tests.

53. Eschaton is a real-participant and tennis-court-modified version of the EndStat® ROM-run nuclear-conflagration game.

54. Viz. Prescriptive Grammar (Grade 10), Descriptive Grammar (11), Grammar and Meaning (12).

55. Hal, who personally thinks the term that'd apply here would be *suborned,* not *entrapped* — unless the caller were himself a police officer — keeps his own counsel on this point and basically goes along to get along.

56. ... or PMA, Grievous Bod., nutmeg's myristicin, or Hawaiian baby-woodrose seeds' ergine, or the African iboga's ibogaine, the yagé's harmaline ... or the fly agaric fungus's well-known muscimole, which fitviavi's derived DMZ resembles chemically sort of the way an F-18 resembles a Piper Cub. ...

57. Ingesters' accounts of the temporal-perception consequences of DMZ in the literature are, as far as Pemulis is concerned, vague and inelegant and more like mystical in the *Tibetan-Dead-Book* vein than rigorous or referentially clear; one account Pemulis doesn't completely get but can at least get the neuro-titillating gist of is one monograph's toss-off quote from an Italian lithographer who'd ingested DMZ once and made a lithograph comparing himself on DMZ to a piece of like Futurist sculpture, plowing at high knottage through time itself, kinetic even in stasis, plowing temporally ahead, with time coming off him like water in sprays and wakes.

58. Certified (by the Commonwealth of Massachusetts) Substance Abuse Counselor.

59. Oxycodone hydrochloride w/ acetaminophen, C-II Class, Du Pont Pharmaceuticals.

60. Replacing the old neo-Georgian J. A. Stratton Student Center, right off Mass. Ave. and gutted with C4 during the so-called M.I.T. Language Riots of twelve₁ years past.

61. An après-garde digital movement, a.k.a. 'Digital Parallelism' and 'Cinema of Chaotic Stasis,' characterized by a stubborn and possibly intentionally irritating refusal of different narrative lines to merge into any kind of meaningful confluence, the school derived somewhat from both the narrative bradykineticism of Antonioni and the disassociative formalism of Stan Brakhage and Hollis Frampton, comprising periods in the careers of the late Beth B., the Snow brothers, Vigdis Simpson, and the late J. O. Incandenza (middle period).

62. At the zenith of the self-help-group movement in the B.S. mid-1990s, there were estimated to be over 600 wholly distinct Step-based fellowships in the U.S.A., all modelled, however heretically or flakily, on the '12 Steps' of Alcoholics Anonymous. By Y.D.A.U., the number has dropped to about one-third of that.

63. (the student engineer's analogy)

64. Not 100% clear on this, but the thrust is that the T and Q are the two basic courses of study leading historically to the like 18th-century equivalent of a H.S. diploma and a B.A., or maybe M.A., respectively, at nodes of hoary classicality like Oxford and Cambridge U. during the time of Samuel Johnson — more or less the original grammato-lexical-and-pedagogical hard-ass — and that the trivium makes you take grammar, logic, and rhetoric, and then if you're still standing you get the quadrivium of math, geometry, astronomy, and music, and that none of the classes — including the potentially lightweight astronomy and music — were in fact lightweight, which is one possible reason why the

portraits of all these classical and neo-classical B.A.s and D.Phil.s at Oxford and Cambridge look so pale and wasted and haunted and grim. Not to mention that the only day E.T.A.s get off classes is Sunday, partly to make up for how much they're away from the classroom on trips; and back at E.T.A. classless Sunday is a three-session day on the courts, all of which strikes people outside academies as almost fanatically brutal. For more general pedagogy here see P. Beesley's somewhat frumpy and dated B.S.-era *Revival of the Humanities in American Education,* or better yet Dr. A. M. Incandenza's updated version of same, with its prose updated and typos eradicated and argument rather more keenly honed, available on CD-ROM through InterLace @cornup3.COM or in trade paperback from Cornell University Press, 3rd edition © Year of the Tucks Medicated Pad.

65. E.T.A.s' moniker for the Headmaster's House.

66. Some M.I.T.s are compulsive about taping the shows and then listening to the musics again and trying to track them down in stores and college archives, not unlike the way some of their parents had killed whole evenings trying to parse out the lyrics on R.E.M. and Pearl Jam tapes, etc.

67. A couple of the Enfield Marine Public Health Hospital Security officers know E.T.A.'s Hal Incandenza from having met his brother Mario when James O. Incandenza had hired the officers as lineless figurant background-extra cops for both *Dial C for Concupiscence* and *Three Cheers for Cause and Effect.* The E.M. officers are sometimes down in The Unexamined Life tavern on Blind Bouncer nights when Hal is in there with like Axford, Hal hitting The Life quite a bit less frequently than Axford and Struck and Troeltsch, who rarely miss a Bring-Your-Braille-I.D. theme-night at The Unexamined Life, and seem able to function during A.M. drills even after several parasolled Mudslides or the House-Specialty Blue Flame cognac-based things you have to blow out before sipping from their huge blue-rimmed snifters. The E.M. cops are both young dim big good regular blue(literally)-collar Boston guys, high-school tackles now going soft, their jowls razor-burned and purpling with gin, and they'll sometimes regale the E.T.A.s w/r/t some of the more colorful E.M. specimens they're paid to keep secure. There's something a little compulsive about the cops' particular interest in #5 chronic catatonics, especially. The E.M. cops call Unit #5 'The Shed,' they say, because its residents don't seem housed there so much as more like *stored* there. The E.M. cops pronounce *stored* 'stew-wad.' The chronic catatonics themselves they refer to as 'objay darts,' which is something else Don G. over in #6 has never understood. Over Mudslides, they'll often give little thumbnail anecdotes about various of The Shed's objay darts, and one of the reasons why they regale the E.T.A.s only when Hal's down there at The Unexamined Life is that Hal is the only E.T.A. who seems truly interested, which is the sort of thing your veteran off-duty cop can always sense. E.g. one of the objay darts they're into is the lady who sits very still with her eyes closed. The cops explain that the lady is not catatonic in the strict sense of *catatonic* but rather a 'D.P.,' which is mental-health-facility slang for *Debilitatingly Phobic.* Her deal is apparently that she's almost psychotically terrified of the possibility that she might be either blind or paralyzed or both. So e.g. she keeps her eyes shut tight 24/7/365 out of the reasoning that as long as she keeps her eyes shut tight she can find hope in the possibility that if she was to open them she'd be able to see, they say; but that if she were ever to actually open her eyes and actually not be able to see, she reasons, she's lost that precious like margin of hope that she's maybe not blind. Then they run through her similar reasoning behind sitting absolutely motionless out of a phobia of being paralyzed. After each anecdote-tale like (they've got like an anecdote-routine, the E.M. cops), the shorter E.M. Security officer always uses his tongue to manipulate the little green parasol from one side of his mouth to the other as he holds his snifter tight in both hands and makes his jowls accordionize as he nods and posits that the terrifying thing is that the common unifying symptom of most of The Shed's objay darts is a terror so terrifying it makes the object of the terror come true, somehow, which observation

always makes both of the big dim workingmen shiver an identical and kind of almost delicious-looking shiver, pushing their hats back and shaking their heads at their glasses, as Hal blows out the fire of the second Blue Flame they've bought him, making a wish before he blows.

68. Freer's 'The Viking' moniker is his own invention, and nobody else uses it, instead referring to him as just 'Freer,' and regarding it as a classic pathetic Freer-type move that he goes around trying to get people to refer to him as 'The Viking.'

69. NA = Narcotics Anonymous; CA = Cocaine Anonymous. In some cities there are also Psychedelics Anonymous, Nicotine Anonymous (also, confusingly, called NA), Designer Drugs Anonymous, Steroids Anonymous, even (especially in and around Manhattan) something called Prozac Anonymous. In none of these Anonymous fellowships anywhere is it possible to avoid confronting the God stuff, eventually.

70. Not to mention, according to some hard-line schools of 12-Step thought, yoga, reading, politics, gum-chewing, crossword puzzles, solitaire, romantic intrigue, charity work, political activism, N.R.A. membership, music, art, cleaning, plastic surgery, cartridge-viewing even at normal distances, the loyalty of a fine dog, religious zeal, relentless helpfulness, relentless other-folks'-moral-inventory-taking, the development of hard-line schools of 12-Step thought, ad darn near infinitum, including 12-Step fellowships themselves, such that quiet tales sometimes go around the Boston AA community of certain incredibly advanced and hard-line recovering persons who have pared away potential escape after potential escape until finally, as the stories go, they end up sitting in a bare chair, nude, in an unfurnished room, not moving but also not sleeping or meditating or abstracting, too advanced to stomach the thought of the potential emotional escape of doing anything whatsoever, and just end up sitting there completely motion- and escape-less until a long time later all that's found in the empty chair is a very fine dusting of off-white ashy stuff that you can wipe away completely with like one damp paper towel.

71. The Boston AA slogan w/r/t this phenomenon is 'You Can't Unring a Bell.'

72. About which Pakistani manager and his ancestry and ratty little mustache and officious management style McDade has a colorful thing or two to say, boy.

73. One of the graduate prorectors' little tasks is supposedly to go around to different Subdorm floors and check the rooms for things like are the beds made up drum-tight, with unpleasant little extra drills added to the regimens of bed-making and toothpaste-cap-replacing slackers, though few of the prorectors have the combination anality and drive actually to go around to their assigned rooms with a checklist, the exceptions being Aubrey deLint, Mary Esther Thode, and the hatchet-faced Kenyan Tony Nwangi, who's got the Pemulis/Troeltsch/Schacht suite under extremely beady scrutiny at all times.

74. Davis Cup is male, Wightman female.

75. Hal's private dread is that Tavis will want him to offer up his personal competitive map and dignity to John ('N.R.') Wayne — who's never in several matches lost more than three games in a set to Hal — for the titillation of the alumni and patrons at the November Fundraiser-gala's exhibitions, though this is pretty unlikely right before the What-aBurger, when Hal'll be apt to face Wayne in the semis anyway, and Schtitt isn't apt to want an utter demapping that fresh in Hal's mind right before a major event.

76. Hal Incandenza had been thought for a while as a toddler to have some sort of Attention Deficit Disorder — partly because he read so fast and spent so little time on each level of various pre-CD-ROM video games, partly because just about any upscale kid even slightly to port or starboard of the bell curve's acme was thought at that time to have A.D.D. — and for a while there'd been a certain amount of specialist-shuttling, and many of the specialists were veterans of Mario and were preconditioned to see Hal as also

damaged, but thanks to the diagnostic savvy of Brandeis's Child Development Center the damage assessments were not only retracted but reversed way out to the other side of the Damaged-to-Gifted continuum, and for much of the glabrous part of his childhood Hal'd been classified as somewhere between 'Borderline Gifted' and 'Gifted' — though part of this high cerebral rank was because B.C.D.C.'s diagnostic tests weren't quite so keen when it came to distinguishing between raw neural gifts and the young Hal's mono-maniacally obsessive interest and effort, as if Hal were trying as if his very life were in the balance to please some person or persons, even though no one had ever even hinted that his life depended on seeming gifted or precocious or even exceptionally pleasing — and when he'd committed to memory entire dictionaries and vocab-check software and syntax manuals and then had gotten some chance to recite some small part of what he'd pounded into his RAM for a proudly nonchalant mother or even a by-this-time-as-far-as-he-was-concerned-pretty-much-out-there father, at these times of public performance and pleasure — the Weston MA School District in the early B.S. 1990s had had interschool range-of-reading-and-recall spelling-beeish competitions called 'Battle of the Books,' which these were for Hal pretty much of a public turkey-shoot and approval-fest — when he'd extracted what was desired from memory and faultlessly pronounced it before cer-tain persons, he'd felt almost that same pale sweet aura that an LSD afterglow conferred, some milky corona, like almost a halo of approved grace, made all the milkier by the faultless nonchalance of a Moms who made it clear that his value was not contingent on winning first or even second prize, ever.

77. Granted, Pemulis, over the summer (he boards at E.T.A. during the summer but hasn't qualified for the European trip since Y.P.W.), had made and distributed (at cost) a few copies of a highly amusing low-memory TP game whose graphics featured a picture of deLint and a mock-up of the hell-panel from H. Bosch's tryptich *The Garden of Earthly Delights,* which TP game continues to enjoy a select late-night vogue among the sub-16's.

78. (Subject to O.N.A.N. Dept. of Weights and Measures Oversight Committee ratifica-tion of final contract between G.F.R. Co., Zanesville OH, and the Bureau of Endorsement Revenue, United States Office of Unspecified Services, Vienna VA, 15 December Y.D.A.U.)

79. And, it goes w/o saying, w/o one of those video-recorded suicide notes or fond fare-wells from the terminally ill, which digital halloos from beyond the grave were, after a brief and videophony-like vogue, by the Year of the Trial-Size Dove Bar used only by the tasteless and trailer-park tacky, w/ the very tackiest using Tableaux w/ famous dead Elvis-/Carson-grade celebrities to convey their farewells.

80. Orin Incandenza knew that Joelle van Dyne and Dr. James O. Incandenza weren't lovers; Mrs. Avril Incandenza did not know that they weren't lovers, although by the time of Joelle's acquaintance with him Jim wasn't in a position to be lovers with anybody, neurologically speaking, though it's not clear to Joelle whether Avril even knew this, since Jim and Avril hadn't been intimate with each other, i.e. conjugally, for quite some time, though Jim hadn't known the precise reason why Avril was so sanguine about their not being intimate until the incident with the Volvo, where apparently Avril had been with someone (Orin would not say who or whether he knew who) in the Volvo and had idly — and disastrously, whether w/ unconscious intent or not — and presumably post-coitally idly written the person's first name in the steam of the steamed-up car window, which name had disappeared with the steam but had reappeared the next time the window had steamed up, which had been when James had been driving to this very brownstone, to shoot Joelle in the weird wobble-lensed maternal 'I'm-so-terribly-sorry' monologue-scene of the last thing he'd done, and then never shown her, and had ordered the cartridge's burial in the brass casket w/ him in the same testament in which he'd willed Joelle an absurd (and addiction-enabling) annuity, which Avril'd never have

lowered herself to the level of contesting, but which could hardly be expected not to have solidified the appearance that they'd been lovers, Joelle and Jim.

81. 'Theory and Praxis in Peckinpah's Use of Red,' *Classic Cartridge Studies* vol. IX, nos. 2 & 3, YY2007MRCVMETIUFI/ITPSFH,O,OM(s).

82. Maybe in like psychic opposition to their Moms's compulsive cleaning thing, both Orin when he was at E.T.A. and now Hal are horrific slobs. In Hal's case this is facilitated by the fact that the third floor of Subdorm C's prorector is the incredibly lax and laid-back Corbett Thorp, who may stutter and go in for half-baked motivational experiments on the younger players but never comes around with a white glove and clipboard. Mario makes his bed without fail, but you have to keep in mind that it's not like he's got all that much else to do. Hal's fitted sheet and sheet are Bean-James River flannels in matching green and black Night Watch plaid, and for a comforter he uses a green fiberfill winter-camp sleeping bag that's of unknown origin and price because he got it for Xmas and it had all the tags removed.

83. Boston Police Department.

84. Available on ROM via InterLace @deltad3.COM or in (remaindered) paperback from Delta/Delacorte division of Bantam-Doubleday-Dell-Little,-Brown, itself a division of Bell Atlantic/TCI.

85. = no academy affiliation.

86. The O.N.A.N.T.A. junior tour allows court-side oxygen ever since an unfortunate embolism in Raleigh NC, Y.W.Q.M.D.

87. Q.v. Note 24 *supra*.

88. Since claiming rampant and mysterious breakage and then one time having the Dunlop rep passing through Allston on his way out of Boston from E.T.A. see not one but three kids on three separate corners hawking shiny new Dunlop sticks in what amounted, Dunlop charged, almost to Conspiracy to Defraud, in YY2007MRCVMETIUFI/ITPSFH,O,OM(s).

89. The fact that it's not at all clear day-to-day what this *it* and *caring* mean, or how you can be expected both to care passionately and not care at all, that huge amounts of internal psychic energy get expended on trying to come to some acceptable understanding of all this stuff, particularly from 16 to like 18, is not accidental or a weakness in E.T.A. pedagogy, in Schacht's opinion, though a sizable contingent of E.T.A.s view Schtitt as bats and essentially a figurehead and choose to steer more by head prorector deLint's clipboard and reductive statistics, which at least afford you a firm idea of where you stand, comparatively, at all times.

90.
   E.g.:

SELECTED SNIPPET FROM THE INDIVIDUAL-RESIDENT-INFORMAL-INTERFACE HOURS OF D. W. GATELY, LIVE-IN STAFF, ENNET HOUSE DRUG AND ALCOHOL RECOVERY HOUSE, ENFIELD MA, ON AND OFF FROM JUST AFTER THE BROOKLINE YOUNG PEOPLE'S AA MTNG UP TO ABOUT 2329H., WEDNESDAY 11 NOVEMBER Y.D.A.U.

'I fear I simply have to deny the insinuation that it's disloyal or ungrateful to find oneself troubled by certain quite *glaring* inconsistencies in this master quote unquote Program you all seem to expect us simply to open up and blindly swallow whole and then walk around glazed with our arms right out straight in front of us parroting, reciting.'

'Geoff — Geoffrey, man, I don't think anybody's trying to insinuate anything over on you, brother. I know I ain't trying to.'

1000

'No, you simply sit there with your arms crossed nodding with that timeless patience that communicates condescension and judgment without exposing you to responsibility for insinuating anything aloud.'

'Maybe when I look patient I'm really trying to be patient with myself, for not finishing school and etcetera and having a hard time keeping up with you.'

'This AA tactic of masking condescension behind humility. . . .'

'I guess I'm just sorry for you you're feeling frustrated with the Program today. I know there's lots of days I'm frustrated with it. So I don't know what to say helpful to you except what they said to me, to just hang in there.'

'One Day at a One Day at a One Day.'

'Brother, that's just all I know to tell you that's worked for me. I know for me it don't matter if there's days I fucking *hate* it. I just have to do it. And it don't help me or anybody else if I go around negativing on newcomers and trying to take out my issues on trying to fuck them up with God-puzzles.'

'Mr. Gately Sir, I found myself sitting tonight in yet another Alcoholics Anonymous Meeting the central Message of which was the importance of going to still more Alcoholics Anonymous Meetings. This infuriating carrot-and-donkey aspect of trudging to Meetings only to be told to trudge to still more Meetings.'

'I hear you.'

'As if, I mean, what's supposedly going to be communicated at these *future* meetings I'm exhorted to trudge to that cannot simply be communicated *now,* at *this* meeting, instead of the glazed recitation of exhortations to attend these vague future revelatory meetings?'

'I'm doing my best to stay with you here Day man.'

'And tonight I'm just settling in in yet another uneven-legged chair, cultivating that glazed passive spectatorial state of mind that is *clearly* what they're trying to inspire in the ephebe, settling in next to a positively *redolent* Emil M. and trying to hold my poor addled Denial-ridden mind open with all available main, listening to this ravaged-looking Yalie in yellow slacks detail episodes of tremens whose gruesomeness interdicted any possible Identification —'

'I'm remembering I heard Pat tell you that thinking people who are walking ahead of you are following you is a pretty bad kind of D.T.s, brother.'

'And I in*formed* her that there's a well-known surveillance tactic known as the *Box*-surveillance, which involves certain members of the surveillance team establishing themselves in *front* of the subject.'

'Except I don't ever remember you explaining why a sociology teacher weaving his way from his fourth bar to his fifth bar is important enough for four guys from some you-never-mentioned-what kind of conspiracy to be pulling this real complex surveillance thing.'

'. . .'

'Except I was interrupting your point you were sharing, I know, and I'm sorry.'

'Your basic decency is why you're whom I bring my thoughts to, Don. You know that.'

'That makes me feel good Day man.'

'I mean to whom else might I speak? The girl who takes her eye out and fondles it? Poor Ewell with his obsessive tattoo charts? *Lenz?*'

'It makes me feel good you think I'm decent to talk to. That's supposed to be why I'm here. I sure needed to talk, at the start. Can you remember where you were headed before I broke i— interrupted?'

'Something this broken Ivy Leaguer said, some AA sally. He said that only one newcomer in a million actually trudges into an Alcoholics Anonymous Closed Meeting and in fact doesn't belong there.'

'Meaning doesn't turn out to have the Disease you mean.'

'Yes. And that he said that quote if *You* — looking *right* at yours truly, seemingly,

with that wearily amused patient expression you all must practice in front of the mirror —
he said that only one newcomer in a million doesn't belong here, and if quote *You* think
You're that one-in-a-million, *You definitely* belong here. And everyone howled with
mirth, stomped their feet and blew coffee through their noses and wiped their eyes with
the backs of their hands and elbowed each other. Howled with mirth.'

'But you were, like, unsmiling at it.'

'And everyone labels as Denial or ingratitude what's actually *horror,* Don. The *horror*
of acknowledging that you do apparently have some sort of problem with mild sedatives
and fine Chianti, and wanting with all sincerity to give every fair chance to a treatment-
modality which millions swear up and down has helped them with their own problem.'

'You're talking about AA.'

'To want very much to believe in it, and to try, and then to your *horror* find the
Program riddled with these obvious and idiotic fallacies and reductia ad absurdum
which —'

'I'm going to need to ask you to try and say that again in words I can follow, Geoffrey,
if you want me to be right there alongside with you. And I'm sorry if that seems descending.'

'Don, I am sincere when I say I'm *frightened* when I find that there are things about
this allegedly miraculous Program's doctrine that simply do not follow. That do not co-
here. That do not make anything resembling rational sense.'

'I'm with you on that one now, brother.'

'Tonight's example of the one-in-a-million, say. Don, let me ask you, Don. In all earnest. Why shouldn't every human being in the world be in AA?'

'Now I'm not with you anymore again, Geoffrey.'

'Don, why doesn't every featherless biped on earth qualify for AA? By AA's reasoning,
why isn't everyone everywhere an alcoholic?'

'Well Geoffrey man it's a totally private decision to admit the Disease, nobody can go
tell another man he's —'

'But indulge me for a moment. By AA's own professed logic, everyone ought to be in
AA. If you have some sort of Substance-problem, then you belong in AA. But if you say
you do *not* have a Substance-problem, in other words if you *deny* that you have a
Substance-problem, why then you're by definition in *Denial,* and thus you apparently
need the Denial-busting Fellowship of AA even more than someone who can admit his
problem.'

'. . .'

'Don't look at me like that. Show me the flaw in my reasoning. I beg you. Show me
why not everyone should be in AA, given the way AA regards those who don't believe
they belong there.'

'. . .'

'And now you don't know what to say. There's no cockle-warming cliché that applies.'

'The slogan I've heard that might work here is the slogan *Analysis-Paralysis.*'

'Oh lovely. Oh very nice. By all means don't *think* about the validity of what they're
claiming your life hinges on. Oh do not ask what *is* it. Do not ask not whether it's not
insane. Simply open wide for the spoon.'

'For me, the slogan means there's no set way to argue intellectual-type stuff about the
Program. Surrender To Win, Give It Away To Keep It. God As You Understand Him. You
can't think about it like an intellectual thing. Trust me because I been there, man. You can
analyze it til you're breaking tables with your forehead and find a cause to walk away,
back Out There, where the Disease is. Or you can stay and hang in and do the best you
can.'

'AA's response to a question about its axioms, then, is to invoke an axiom about the
inadvisability of all such questions.'

'I ain't AA Day man. No one like individual can respond for AA.'

'Am I out of line in seeing something totalitarian about it? Something dare I say un-American? To interdict a fundamental doctrinal question by invoking a doctrine against questioning? Wasn't this the very horror the Madisonians were horrified of in 1791? Amendments I and IX? My Grievance is disallowed because my Petition for Redress is a priori interdicted by the inadvisability of all Petitioning?'

'I'm about to get fucking lapped here I'm so not-following. You honestly don't see what's a little whacked-out about what you're saying about Denial?'

'I'm thinking your failure to engage me on the question itself means either I'm right, and AA's whole Belonging-versus-Denial matrix is constructed on logical sand, in which case *horror,* or else it means you're stupefied with condescending pity for me for some reason I fail to grasp, doubtless because of Denial, in which case the look on your face right now is the same weary patience that makes me want to *scream* in meetings.'

'So scream. They can't kick you out.'

'How comforting.'

'This is a thing I do know. They can't kick you out.'

91. *Pillow-biter*'s a North Shore term, one Gately grew up with, and it and the *f*-term are the only terms for male homosexuals he knows, still.

92. Diane Prins, Perth Amboy NJ.

93. An anxiety-fest captured nicely by the banner-shaped posters deLint used to have D. Harde put up each fall over the senior-locker sections of both locker rooms that had *WINNERS NEVER HAVE TO QUIT* until some of the other prorectors went to Schtitt and got him to make deLint take them down.

94. It's surely been spelled out already that prorectors teach one marginal class per term and serve as on-court assistants to Schtitt's *Lebensgefährtin* Aubrey deLint, and that their existence at E.T.A. is marginal and low-prestige and their spiritual state on the low continuum between embittered and accepting, and for many of the more neurasthenic E.T.A. students the prorectors are kind of repellent the way hideously old people are repellent, reminding the students of the kind of low-prestige purgatorial fate that awaits the marginal and low-ranked jr. player; and while a couple of the prorectors are feared, none of them is all that much respected, and they're avoided, and stick together with one another and keep to themselves and seem on the whole sad, with that grad-schoolish sense of arrested adolescence and reality-avoidance about them.

95. *Pink* being Microsoft Inc.'s first post-Windows DOS, quickly upgraded to Pink$_2$ when InterLace took everything 100% interactive and digital; by Y.D.A.U. it's kind of a dinosaur, but it's still the only DOS that'll run a Mathpak\EndStat tree without having to stop and recompile every few seconds.

96. A kind of prorectorishly sad post in Amateur Sports Administration at tiny Throppinghamshire Provincial College in Fredericton N.B., C.T.'s undergrad alma mater.

97. It's both perverse and kind of understandable that getting some sort of college scholarship (or 'Ride'), while very few E.T.A.s (and certainly not Orin Incandenza) have any real kind of financial need, that nevertheless a scholarship is enormously important self-esteem-wise, since opting for the college-tennis route in the first place is kind of an admission of defeat and a surrender of dearly held dreams of the professional Show.

98. And to keep a distant but weirdly beady and obsessive eye on Mario, from whose lordotic presence in a room Tavis'd flee just as Avril was fleeing from the temptation of overlobbying Orin on B.U., such that for a few days when both Orin and Mario entered a room there'd be the sound of a tremendous collision in the hall outside as C.T. and Avril's flights' vectors met.

99. MA Dept. of Revenue.

100. The way a White Flagger formulates this, e.g., is that 99.9% of what goes on in one's life is actually none of one's business, with the .1% under one's control consisting mostly of the option to accept or deny one's inevitable powerlessness over the other 99.9%, which just trying to parse this out makes Don Gately's forehead turn purple.

101. Some of their earliest dates were watching big-budget commercial films, and Orin had one time completely unpremeditatedly told her it was a strange feeling watching commercial films with a girl who was prettier than the women in the films, and she'd punched him hard in the arm in a way that just about drove him wild.

102. International Brotherhood of Pier, Wharf, and Dock Workers.

103. A quote 'episode of excessive neuronal discharge manifested by motor, sensory and/or [psychic] dysfunction, with or without unconsciousness and/or convulsive [movements],' plus eye-rolling and tongue-swallowing.

104. In order for O.N.A.N.T.A. academies to qualify as actual schools and not just like extended-term sports camps, all instructors and prorectors except the Head have to be listed as more like academic instructors who prorect on the side.

105. A Dworkinite heavy-leather organization whose membership on the U.S. East Coast was in the five figures up until the ugly Pizzitola Riots of Providence RI in Y.W.-Q.M.D. discredited the F.O.P.P.P.s, and fragmented them.

106. There's a Viewing Room on each subdorm floor, and room-size TP's w/ phone consoles and (if a kid wants) modems are standard issue, but only E.T.A. juniors and seniors get to have actual cartridge-viewers in their subdorm rooms — a two-year-old administrative concession the credit for which goes largely to Troeltsch, who made such a pest of himself with Charles Tavis over the issue that Tavis finally relented just to keep the kid from lurking in his office's waiting room, speaking into his fist, pretending to report on 'the flames of controversy surrounding individual rights raging here in quaint and peaceful Enfield' — and none of these viewers (likewise the Viewing Room's units) can have motherboard-cards for Spontaneous InterLace Disseminations or for ROM-caliber games, which broadcasts and videoish games encourage a stuporous passivity that E.T.A.'s philosophy now regards as venomous to the whole set of reasons the kids are enrolled there in the first place.

107. E.g. the WhataBurger Invitational will allegedly be recorded for fringe-market, order-only viewing, later this month.

108. Sometimes, especially in early fall and late spring, this can involve a lapse of several weeks; WETA doesn't broadcast when most of the kids are away at some competitive thing, and Saturday classes are likewise often canceled — this is one reason why so many prorectors' classes are relegated by Mrs. A.M.I. to Saturdays.

109. Apparently the Parti Q. is provincial, intra-Québecois; the Bloc's its federal counterpart, w/ members in Parliament, and so on and so forth.

110.
Q.v. here later in the same day, 11/7, as Hal Incandenza sits on the edge of his unmade bed, undressed, with the good right leg curled under him and the bad ankle soaking in a janitor-pail of dissolved Epsom salts, looking through one of Mario's old Hush Puppy shoeboxes of letters and snapshots. Saturdays involve classes and drills and P.M. matches but no conditioning run or weight circuits. Afternoon's odd mismatched challenge matches held on staff-squeegeed Center Courts under a steady metal sunless sky. The air still damp after lunchtime's rain. Hal's own odd match was truncated when C-squadder Hugh Pemberton took a ball in the eye up at net and began wandering the service box in wobbled circles. Hal skipped a quick trip down to the Pump Room and got to shower nearly solo in the main locker room. Tomorrow's Interdependence Day communal

supper at E.T.A. is a big deal and includes each person's own specially selected hat, plus real dessert, and a post-prandial Mario-made film, and sometimes a sing-along. Hal and Pemulis, Struck and Axford and Troeltsch and Schacht and sometimes Stice have their own special private day-before-I.-Day-ritualistic-supper-out-and-trip-to-The-Unexamined-Life blowout-gala, since Sunday is a day of total mandatory R&R. The untruncated matches are winding down out there, Hal can hear. The sun is coming out just in time to go down. The Comm.-Ad. pipes start to moan and sing with crowded showering kids. Pale net-shadows are starting to elongate acutely across the sidelines of the courts' north sides. Mario is more or less the Incandenza family archivist ex officio. Mario has been closeted with Disney Leith all day preparing things for Sunday's post-prandial gala and filmfest. The phone sits mute atop the answering-machine attachment on the telephone's power unit's console. Its antenna is retracted and it simply sits there, exuding the vague contained menace of mute phones. The phone's ringer sort of twitters instead of ringing. The audio-only comm.-system's power console is bolted to a receptacle on the side of Hal and Mario's TP, and its red power light blinks at the slow liquid rate of a radio tower. The phone and answering machine are hand-me-downs from Orin's days at E.T.A., old models of transparent plastic, so you can see everything's quad-colored pasta of wires and chips and tin disks. The only message when Hal got in was from Orin at 1412h. Orin had said he'd just called to ask whether by any chance Hal'd ever realized that all of Emily Dickinson — as in the Belle of Amherst Emily Dickinson, the canonical agoraphobic poet — that every single one of Ms. Dickinson's canonical poems could by sung without loss or syllabic distortion to the tune of 'The Yellow Rose (of Texas).' 'Be*cause* I *could* not *stop* for *Death* He *kin*dly *stopped* for *Me*,' Orin had sung illus-tratively onto the recording. 'I *hope* the *Father in* the *skies* Will *lift* his *little Girl*.' Actually more like sort of sung. There'd been professional-locker-room sounds in the background — locker doors banging, bass voices on tile and steel, personal stereos, hisses of antiperspirant and styling-spritz. The odd enclosed echo of locker rooms everywhere, junior or pro. 'On *my* vol*ca*no *grows* the *Grass* A *meditative spot*,' and so on. The fleshy pop of a professionally snapped towel on adult skin. A black man's falsetto laughter. Orin's recorded voice said he'd just grabbed an odd free second to inquire what Hal's machine might make of this fact.

Hal spits Kodiak tobacco juice into an old rocket-emblazoned NASA glass on the bedside table, idly and for no special reason riffling through densely packed letters tri-folded and packed upright, a kind of Rolodex of different mementos and postal corre-spondence Mario's rescued from wastebaskets and recycling bins and dumpsters and quietly saved in shoeboxes. Mario has no problem with Hal perusing his closet's stuff. Mario's closet has a canvas strap instead of a knob. Ideally there would also be a bucket of very cold water, and Hal would move the bad ankle from one bucket to the other and back again. A whistle sounds from down near the girls' West Courts. Someone little in the hall outside the closed door shouts 'Guess again!' to someone else farther down the hall. None of the Hush Puppy box's snail-mail letters are to or from Mario. Mario's bed is loosely, unanally made. Hal's bed is unmade. Hal and Mario's mother had done her undergraduate Honors work at McGill on the use of hyphens, dashes, and colons in E. Dickinson. The Epsom-water whitens his calluses. Unlaundered bedding swims around him. The phone twitters. *Ample make this bed,* or *Ample make* this *bed*. The phone twitters again.

20 June Y.W.-Q.M.D.

Dear Filbert,[a]

It's been a quiet week here on Mount Gawdforsaken[b] — today is perishing hot, windless, quiet as a tomb, lush and pretty. Every floral unit on the grounds has its pistil aprick and petals atremble in a truly shameless fashion, for the bees are about. The whole hill hums drowsily. Yesterday, your Uncle Charles was accosted on the north path by a bumblebee that he alleges was so enormous it sounded like a tuba, and he dispatched Mr. Harde and the grounds crew with skeet rifles and orders to ' . . .bring the Sikorski-sized bugger down.' I shall spare you details of the subsequent misadventures of the grounds crew, two of whom are now recovering satisfactorily.

The paucity of decibels here is due in part to all six A-teams' departure yesterday for Milan, with Gerhardt, Aubrey, Carolyn, and Urquhart at the pedagogical tiller. It seems not so many moons ago that we were seeing you, Marlon, Ross, and the rest off on the European clay junket. I recall pressing the maternal beak to the terminal window's glass, trying to make my Filbert out somewhere behind the airplane's impossible little bullet-hole windows. I cried like a fool every time, as of course I did all over again yesterday, embarrassing everyone but Mario, who also cried.

As for me, I've swotted and wakked all morning, cranking up your Uncle Charles's videophone and trying to cajole the editors of various supermarket trade publications to run M.G.M.'s[c] latest plea for amending *Less* to *Fewer* in those !*#!*# Express Check-Out lanes. One old editorial codger said that he'd dearly love to help me out but that his newsletter was devoted exclusively to issues of promotional display. When I suggested that a little comic relief in the form of the L——$>F$ bulletin might not be amiss, he chortled. Chortling is good. We like chortling. However, I did manage to twist the arms (harder to do telephonically than one might think) of *Produce Weekly*, Star Market's *Quarterly Register*, and PriceChopper's *Shelf and Cart*, so the wheels of adjectival justice continue, albeit creakily, to turn.

The very last gobbet of Academy news is that your Uncle Charles had his blood cholesterol tested late last week. Though the verdict rendered was no worse than a rather unperspicuous "Normal to Upper-normal" (*sic*), the penultimate modifier has caused, as you might anticipate, much pacing and high-decibel whingeing, as well as vows of eternal xerophagy from here on out. Your Uncle Charles has already, for some months now, made a practice of swallowing three teaspoons of fish-liver oil just before he hurls the administrative skeleton bedward for the night. Your brothers have taken to trekking over on slow nights to watch him swallow his oil, purely out of enthusiasm for the faces Charles makes as the stuff goes gulletward. I e-ordered the poor man a low-lipid, artery-friendly cookbook as a sort of Whatthehell present the day the results came in, and your Uncle Charles has already pored over the thing and marked several yummers. We're to have a swot at cabbage patties tonight, fast-laners that we are. I do suppose the poor man will find a way to ladle rice bran[d] into his toothpaste before this spasm of angst subsides. Bless his heart — as it were!

My, this machine does let one maunder on. I'd best get back to harrying grocers. One of this fall's matriculates[e] is the son of a man who's apparently become an immensely wealthy Telegrocer[f] in the Upper Midwest, so perhaps the Express Lane-Solecism issue will simply disappear in these here parts as well.

It goes without saying that you are of course wearing your halo and mouth-guard at all appropriate times and eating at least one green, leafy vegetable per day.

Oh — 'twas *won*derful to hear about the arbitration and contract. Mr. deLint read a detailed account and told us all about it. Proud, as ever, to know you.

Miss You and Love You Lots,

and c.

Dear _____Ms. Incandenza_____,

Due to the large number of mail the New Orleans Saints® are so fortunate enough to receive from all across the 2nd InterLace Gridᵇ, we regrettably say _____ORIN INCANDENZA #71_____ can not answer your letter in person, however, on behalf of the New Orleans Saints® _____"ORIN"_____ has asked me to say Thank-You for your message of support, and best wishes.

Inclosed, please accept a special, color 20 × 25 centimeter personally autographed action photo of _____ORIN INCANDENZA   #71_____, as our way of saying Thank-You and how important you're letter has been to us.

Cordjally,

Jethro Bodine

Assistant Mailroom Technician

And c.

'Mmyellow.'

'Presenting Speedy Seduction Strategy Number 7.'

'Orin. Happy Inter-Day Eve. E Unibus Pluram and so on. Still dodging the disabled?'

'A proviso up-front, Hallie: Number 7 never misses.'

'And not every Dickinson poem is singable to 'Yellow Rose,' O. Sorry to disappoint you. For instance like "*Ample make this bed — Make this bed with awe*" isn't even iambic, much less quatrameter/trimeter.'

'Just a theory. Just tossing it out for the machine's consideration.'

'A practice to be encouraged. This particular theory's unfortunately a dink. Plus I don't think you quite meant *proviso*.'

'Number 7 remains a no-miss proposal, though. Picture this. Obtain a ring. As in a wedding band. So you present yourself to the Subject as visibly married.'

'You know I hate these Strategy calls.'

'Also of course works if you really *do* happen to be married. In which case you've got a ring already.'

'I'm sitting here soaking my ankle, O.'

'The object being to present yourself to the Subject as married, as in happily married, and you engage her in a conversation in which you make a big deal of how head-over-heels in love you are with your wife, how wonderful she is, the wife, how blue and clean the pilot-light of passion still burns in the central heating system of your love for her, your wife, even after all these several years you've been hitched.'

'I'm sitting here looking through an old box of letters to kill just a very few minutes before a bunch of us climb in the tow truck for Pemulis's annual I.-Day-Eve town-painting.'

'But as you're saying all this to the Subject, your manner is nevertheless indicating that you're attracted to her.'

'It's poignant somehow that you always use the word *Subject* when you mean the exact obverse.'

'But it's not like flirtatious or salivious, your manner. More like just strongly involuntarily attracted. Almost as if hypnotized against your will. Your manner can indicate this just by following the Subject's conversational movements and changes of posture or facial expression in that sort of vacant intense way a hungry person watches somebody eating. Following the movements of the fork as if memerized. With, of course now, the occasional flicker of pain and conflict in your eyes, at the fact that here you are involuntarily memerized by somebody other than your serapic wife, which the point —'

'Time. Yo. I think you mean *seraphic*. I also think you meant *lascivious* and *mesmerized*.'

'You know what your problem is, Hallie?'

'I have just one problem?'

'But hang on until you see that 7's worth not making me digress away from, though. Because the point being to get across how it's an incredible tribute to the Subject's overwhelming female charms that you can even really even *see* her, the Subject, since you're so in love with your wife you barely even see most women as even female anymore, much less be involuntarily attracted to the Subject, much less have maybe the thought of infidelity skitter no matter how involuntarily across your devoted mind. And it's not like you'll have to volunteer any of this directly. The Subject'll draw the observations on her own. That's the point of the conflicted flickers in your memerized eyes, or at the most an involuntary tortured groan, a quick bite of the knuckle of the forefinger.'

'A heel of the hand to the forehead or something like that.'

'Get your manner down just conflicted-looking enough and the Subject herself'll actually start drawing you out on this fact, the involuntary attraction that's so painful to you and so flattering and tributary to her.'

'So wait. This is like a conversation where you're affecting all this flickering and groaning? Like you mean a cocktail-party-small-talk conversation? Or do you just brandish your fake ring at some girl at a bus stop and start a tortured tribute to your seraphic wife?'

'It takes place anywhere. Venue-adjustable. 7's portable and never-miss. The point is to maneuver the issue of your devoted attracted conflicted pain to the point where you can appear to almost sort of break down and can ask the Subject in all tortured sincerity if she thinks your involuntarily finding her so visibly female and attractive makes you a bad husband. Display vulnerability and ask her to evaluate the like integrity of your heart. Seem desperate. Your whole married self-concept shaken. Practically beg the Subject to reassure you you're not a bad-hearted man. Plead with the Subject to say what she thinks it might be about her charms that could drive your serapic wife even momentarily from your heart. You present the attraction you feel for the Subject as this involuntary identity-threatening soul-searing-type crisis you just desperately need her help with, the Subject's, person to person.'

'Sounds very moving.'

'And if it so happens you really are married, the additional advantage to 7's pitch is that you and the Subject both, however briefly, get to believe it. The pitch. The involuntary passionate doomed knight-errant-type pitch.'

'And of course, O., the Subject just happens to be married herself, often with small children, putting her directly in your crosshairs.'

'A matter of what's the word personal preference and taste that doesn't impact 7's surefire no-miss quality one way or the other. It's the doomed involuntary conflicted good-man's-downfall-type quality that no Subject can seemingly resist.'

'. . .'

'Ainsi, then.'

'Well O. the thing's sick. It's even sicker than 4. Was it 4? The one you said that Loach inspired, where you'd supposedly just that very day dropped out of Jesuit seminary after umpteen years of disciplined celibacy because of carno-spiritual yearnings you hadn't even been quite in touch with as carno-spiritual in nature until you just now this very moment laid eyes on the Subject? With the breviary and rented collar?'

'That was 4, yes. 4's pretty much of a gynecopia also, but within a kind of narrower demographic psychological range of potential Subjects. Notice I never said 4 was no-miss.'

'Well you must be a very proud young man. This is even sicker. The fake ring and fictional spouse. It's like you're inventing somebody you love just to seduce somebody else into helping you betray her. What's it like. It's like suborning somebody into helping you desecrate a tomb they don't know is empty.'

'This is what I get for passing down priceless fruits of hard experience to somebody who still thinks it's exciting to shave.'

'I ought to go. I have a blackhead I have to see to.'

'You haven't asked why I called right back. Why I'm calling during high-toll hours.'

'Plus I feel some kind of toothache starting, and it's the weekend, and I want to see Schacht before Mrs. Clarke's confectionery day in the sun tomorrow. Plus I'm naked.'

'I'm surprised you were even there. In person. I was expecting the Disembodied Voice and asking you to call back ASAP on this. What is it out there, 1600? Why aren't you outside hard at play? Don't tell me Schtitt started cancelling P.M.'s for I.-Day Eve.'

'I tagged this kid Pemberton in the eye up at net. It was inadvertent. We were only four games in. He hit a big soft fluffy goose of an approach and I was trying to handcuff him. I hit it at him only to handcuff him. He never even got his stick up. Right in the left socket. It made a sound like a champagne cork. A prorector named Corbett Thorp said he thought Pemberton might have detached a retina. Something sure seemed detached. He was walking around in diminishing circles like he'd been hit with a mallet.'

'You sound really, like, remorse-riddled.'

'Kitchens and heat, O. I've taken my share of balls in various spots. And whence bizarre metric theories about Emily Dickinson all of a sudden, by the way? And what's up with the lurking figures with wheelchairs?'

'You're a Top-Ten junior stickman suddenly now this year, Hallie, what's Schtitt doing giving you a cloth mouse like Hugh Pemberton to bat around anyway?'

'You remember him?'

'Who could forget a kid that looks like he's curtsying when he serves? With the white visor and the little amber glasses? That kid's been hanging from the bottom of the ladder by his nails since he was nine.'

'It's been carnage all week. Schtitt's playing the C teams against the A's. It's for the C's' development, Donni said. Also because today word's down from the tower some of the staff thought some of the A's looked tentative against Port Wash.'

'They despise tentativity.'

'I think they want us just short of cocky for the Fundraiser and then the WhataBurger, where Wayne's got a chance to knock this Veach kid off the pole.'

'Let's not forget you though either, H. I can get down for at least the WhataBurger semis if you get there, if you want incentive.'

'As in in person, O.?'

'Word is you're worth watching now.'

'Word?'

'I keep my ear to the cement, Hallie.'

'At least for very short Subjects, I'd imagine.'

'We take off for the Patriots that Friday, what is that like the 27th or -8th, but it's a

Saturday afternoon game. I can be down there by midday Sunday if you're still in the thick.'

'You'll probably need to wear some sort of sign around your neck so I know it's you.'

'. . .'

'So then you'll be up here just as we're down there, oddly, playing.'

'It goes without saying you'd give me the advance skinny if anybody I didn't want to see was by any chance flying down there with you guys.'

'The C versus A thing's been more like grotesque than confidence-building. Guys are taking out stress in kind of twisted ways. Struck beat Gloeckner in 40 minutes and then made a show of revealing he'd had 3-kilo ankle-weights on under his socks. Wayne made van Slack cry right there in front of everybody.'

'Word is Wayne has exactly one gear.'

'Then Thursday Coyle had his left wrist tied to his right ankle and was still beating this new kid Stockhausen until Schtitt sent Tex Watson down to tell him to knock it off.'

'So but the reason I'm really calling, Hallie.'

'And you're being evasive about the dread about the disabled. The like rolling stalkers.'

'I haven't seen wheel one in days. I'm thinking possibly this was a kind of very shy sort of fan club of people without legs that look up to me —'

'Grotesque entendre, O.'

'— as, like, the ultimate leg. They use different ruses to follow me around and never come close or say anything because they're really shy because they don't have legs. So now my mind's resting easier.'

'Now if the roach- and spiders-at-heights fears'd subside you could really hold the head high.'

'So the reason I'm calling.'

'I already said I'd let you know when and if. No sightings of any journalists. Your *Moment* profiler.'

'I'm actually glad I got you in person. I was going to ask you to call me ASAP.'

'I'm pleased to call you a sap whenever you like, O.'

'That's below you. And I can hear you still chewing that grisly shit. That shit's going to make your lower jaw fall right off. I've seen it happen down here, believe me. And you're wondering why the tooth problems all the time suddenly.'

'Snuff's saliva-stimulating. It's actually oral-hygiene-enhancing, when you factor in all the extra brushing. The caries are Himself's legacy. You know that. The Himself whose root canals put Dr. Zegarelli's kids through Andover.'

'This basically nonsocial call, H., is because I need your feedback on some issues from these half-dozen or so very complex and far-ranging and in-depth conversations I had with a certain Subject.'

'Not the mobile-home person, surely.'

'Whole different ballpark of Subject. The Dickinson theory I have to admit came from these conversations.'

'Sounds like one deep lady.'

'Whole levels and dimensions to this one. We've had a whole series of very intense verbal interchanges. Transcendentalist poetics was just one of the in-depth issues ranged over. This subject keeps me on the cerebral toes.'

'Dickinson's about as Transcendentalist as Poe. Your Subject's 0 for 2.'

'This is all off to the side of the call. I told this Subject I'd consider certain issues very carefully before I really responded.'

'Which meant you'd consider what she wanted to hear and how to ladle it on until she begs you to have intercourse with her.'

'I hence need considered-sounding responses to two basic questions.'

'Why this sick thing of making me complicit in these Strategic pursuits when you know I think they're troubled and sick? It's like asking somebody to help you culture anthrax or something.'

'Just two questions is all.'

'Now I'm beginning almost to be able to feel my pulse in the tooth, it feels like the infection's gathering force so fast.'

'Firstly, what does the following word I can't find in the dictionary mean: s-a-m-i-z-d-a-t.'

'*Samizdat.* Russian compound noun. Soviet twentieth-century idiom. *Sam* — stem: "self"; *izdat* — undeclined verb: "to publish." I think the literal denotation's technically archaic: the sub-rosa dissemination of politically charged materials that were banned when the Eschaton-era Kremlin was going around banning things. Connotatively, the generic meaning now is any sort of politically underground or beyond-the-pale press or the stuff published thereby. There's no real samizdat in the U.S. per se, First Amendment–wise, I don't think. I suppose ultra-radical Québecois and Albertan stuff could be considered O.N.A.N.ite samizdat.'

'Pow.'

'Not just Séparatisteur pamphlets, now. It'd have to be more incendiary. Materials advocating violence, destruction of property, disruption of Grids, anti-O.N.A.N. terrorism and so on. I don't think O.N.A.N.'s got technical bans per se, I don't think, but Poutrincourt said the R.C.M.P.s are empowered to impound literature and even desktop-publishing and InterLink hardware et cetera without any sort of warrant.'

'R.C.M.P.'

'Mounties, O.'

'The Nelson Eddy guys in silly hats and equestrian jaspers.'

'Close enough. Next question.'

'So you'd have no idea why The Mad Stork's name would come up in connection with somebody saying *samizdat.*'

'This is the second question?'

'Call it 1(a).'

'Not in any strict sense of the term. I guess I could see some Séparatisteurs trying to read *The ONANtiad* or *Brick* as anti-Reconfiguration films. Maybe stuff like *Poultry in Motion.* A lot of Himself's stuff was self-distributed, too. And *Immanent Domain*'s allegedly on one level an allegory about the Concavity, though that overlooks that Gentle wasn't even President when the thing came out. But you can tell your Subject that Himself's work was all very self-consciously American. His interest in politics was subordinate to form. Always. And none of it's banned. Whatever's still on the InterLace back-menus is inter-Grid: you can order *The ONANtiad* in Manitoba, Vera Cruz, anywhere.'

'Speaking of Québec Separatism, interestingly.'

'Why do I get a sinking feeling this is going to be 1(a)-point-one or something. Maybe I could call you back tomorrow and we could chat on and on. I'm going to be here reading for Boards till the Eschaton at 1400. Holiday tolls are low.'

'It's my nickel, here.'

'Or maybe you could simply call the person who's really the person to chat with about all issues Canadian, O.'

'Droll.'

'Moving right along to question 2, then — my Epsom salts are getting cold.'

'The big one is what you'd have to say if some tough-minded and spectacular Subject asked you what you have to say about the way every Nuck Séparatisteur up there, from the Bloc Québecois and Fils de Montcalm all the way out to the really bug-eyed radical fringe-type sects and terroristic cells —'

'I'm going to have to object to the word *Nuck,* O.'

'Beg pardon. The issue being why the whole Québec-Séparatisteur collection up there dropped the original Québec-independence objective like a rock and switched seemingly overnight to putting everything into agitating against O.N.A.N. and the Reconfiguration and forcing the return of the Concavity to our map.'

'O., this is O.N.A.N.ite politics. I'd look my Subject right in the big blue eye and tell her straight-out that the field of nanomicroscopy is not yet advanced enough to measure my interest in the intricacies of O.N.A.N.ite politics. Poutrincourt's class is disquieting enough. The whole thing's unpleasant and dry and repetitive and mostly dull. Thevet has a kind of compelling romanto-historical yarn to spin, though, about —'

'I'm serious. You've had some background, at least. The only Nuck prorector we ever got taught ceramics.'

'But you're the one with the Pléiades and the 5 on the French Achievement boards and the ability to trill your R's.'

'That's Parisian. And now I don't even watch the sports summaries, much less the political stuff. Just try for just one second. This Subject raised issues that were way out of my depth.'

'That's not even coherent enough to be a mixed metaphor, O. Are you honestly telling me you want your depth increased? Or are you just looking for some Cliff-Note summary so you can incorporate the impression of depth into some new panty-removal campaign? Are you going to tell her you studied O.N.A.N.ite politics under the Jesuits?'

'The whole thing was dicey. I had to tell the Subject that I had to think about it and ponder, that I always took time to ponder at depth before I just dashed off an opinion.'

'And don't tell me: this is your *Moment* profiler? Your Boswell in an E cup? Is this why she's en route? Was the whole familio-historical profile story last week a dodge? Am I really just supposed to sit down with her and paint you now as a political-minded exseminarian who's married to someone only some sort of heroically proportioned goddess could tempt you to betray? Because I'll tell you right now that Schtitt's not going to let any of us here talk to anybody from some glossy rag like *Moment* without him or deLint sitting right there with us. Gone are the days of Himself not caring how many who's-thenext-Venus-Williams-hype journalists haunt the grounds, man. Schtitt's now calling the shots on who talks to whom. DeLint has a whole scathing appendix to the Admissions Manual about junior development and toxic hype.'

'Helen'll be able to get in.'

'Schtitt's not going to let me hype your political acuity or pseudo-wife or anything else. He's got C.T. seeing this place as a sort of prophylactic against commercial attention. He thinks junior commercial attention's deforming. The Manual now invites us to see ourselves as in utero and hype as thalidomide. Schtitt'll let her in and stick her in with C.T. and let C.T. filibuster her till she throws herself out the window like that journalist from Condé Nast last fall.'

'Forget the profile. Speak to her or don't. This is personal.'

'Meaning you've discovered she has small children and maybe a marriage you can deform.'

'I'm ignoring all this. Helen's a different sort of Subject. I've discovered levels and dimensions to Helen that have nothing to do with profiles.'

'Meaning she's a tough nut. Meaning you've set your crosshairs and she hasn't succumbed. And she knows you're not married and not a tormented Jesuit. She's Strategyresistant because she knows too much to fall for a persona.'

'Co-ponder with me a second, if you're through. Stop me at any time. Jump right in at any time. On both the ultra-left and -right, the brass ring up there has always been independent secession for Québec, historically, no? Am I off? The Fronte Libération and so on? The Fils de Montcalm. Or is it maybe *du*? Are they the ones in Spandex and pancake makeup? The giant pies dropped on Ottawa after the third Meech Lake Accord?'

'. . .'

'Parizeau et all and so on. Feel free to stop me or jump in. It all'd been about getting Québec out of Canada, right? The Meech Lake and Charlottetown revolts. The Crétien assassination. "Notre Rai Pays." Terrorists in plaid flannel. French Canada for the Francophonic. Acadian Zionism. "La Québecois Toujours." "On ne parle d'Anglais ici." '

'With all the terrorism especially directed at Ottawa, pressure on Ottawa and Canada. "Permettez Nous Partir, Permettez Nous Être." Or we blow up the Frontenac. Or we irradiate Winnipeg. Or we put a railroad-spike through Crétien's eye. This is not exactly deep-depth, O.'

'Yes and then but suddenly everything changes when Ottawa, under duress or no, puts itself under the surgically sterile like thumb of O.N.A.N., with the advent of O.N.A.N., Gentle, quote unquote Experialism.'

'You don't sound like you need any input from me on all this, O.'

'But so but then in *immediate unison* all the various different Separatist groups drop secession and independence like rocks and all transfer their insurgent resentment to O.N.A.N. and the U.S., and now insurge against O.N.A.N. on behalf of the same Canada they'd spent decades treating like the enemy. Does this seem a little bit odd?'

'. . .'

'Doesn't this seem a little odd, Hallie?'

'I'm really the wrong blood-relative to ask about the intricacies of the Canadian radical mind, O. We have a blood-relative who's got dual citizenship, if you recall. Who I'm sure'd be overjoyed to ponder Separatist ideological flux with you all you want and then some. I'm sure. Once her jaw recovered from being unhinged by joy that you actually called.'

'I'm slapping not one but both knees at the dro—'

' 'd you know she's never once asked me whether Booboo and I hear from you? Not once. A sort of appalled pride. She's ashamed of even hurting over it, some —'

'Kidding all off to the side, I'm serious about this. The oddness of it. You know I respect your frontal lobes, Hallie. I'm asking for depth, not any kind of expertise.'

'You just ignored the meat of everything I just said. You're like an old person about this. With an old person's weird selective hearing.'

'I'm going to let this whole pot-insulting-the-kettle on selective awareness of things just slide right on by. As a gesture that this is a serious call. Why they all seemingly with one mind switched objectives.'

'And acting on behalf of the whole of Canada, Québec, suddenly, is what you want explained. Or do you simply want it confirmed as odd?'

'The Subject cited polls from when they were still bothering to take polls up there that said like upwards of four-fifths of all Canadians wanted out of O.N.A.N. and hoped President Gentle had a ghastly accident in his UV-booth, et cetera.'

'So the second and final question concerns this shift from anti-Canadian Québecer nationalism to anti-O.N.A.N. Canadian nationalism.'

'What I was thinking is is this maybe a textbook case of Johnny-Gentle-type-find-an-enemy-for-a-divided-nation-to-come-together-by-blaming-and-hating theory in action? Is this somehow Québec like circling its wagons with Alberta and all the other provinces in the face of a common enemy?'

'. . .'

'Hal?'

'You could always point out to the profiler that there's a nice little irony to Gentle's strategy ending up bringing Canada together at our expense, when it was pretty obviously meant to bring us together at Canada's expense.'

'But you sound like you think the more deeply pondered response would be something else.'

'All I know is some very basic schoolboy history from Poutrincourt's class. And from the advantage of occasional contact with the Moms.'

'Hit me.'

'The historical record indicates pretty clearly that the one and only nationalism in the Québecois soul is Québecois nationalism. It's been "Nous v. La Plupart Toujours," and the more so the farther out on the fringes you get. I can't see the Séparatisteurs considering Québec a true part of Canada any more than Lesotho saw itself as part of SOUTHAF. Poutrincourt keeps thumping the fact that there's no valid comparison between Québec and our own antebellum South. Why do you think Meech Lake III[h] failed? It's because at root they've never seen themselves as anything other than hostages of Ottawa and the Anglophone provinces. Even moderate Séparatisteurs like Parizeau spoke of the final surrender on the Plains of Abraham as a kind of forced property-transfer, the whole original war[i] as one in which French-Canadians weren't the losers so much as the spoils. Booty.'

'This all checks with the Subject's take.'

'The impression I get is that Québec's hatred of anglophone Canada transcends anything they could work up against O.N.A.N. Just mention 1759 and the Moms's lips disappear. Pemulis and Axford keep coming early and putting a big gothic 1759 on the blackboard before G&M[j] just to watch the Moms's lips disappear when she comes in and sees it.'

'My sense is the Subject concurs on the hatred-assessment. They want plain out, always have. Health-care and NAFTA be damned. That's why they sabotaged all three Meech Lake Accords, she says. She seems to imply the anti-O.N.A.N. thing is some sort of anomalous dodge or something.'

'I've got to confess a sort of curiosity now about this profiler you just last week were preparing to fend off about Himself. Not to mention comparing her to defensive linemen. Rubensian was never your type, I didn't think.'

'. . .'

'Plus any Subject you're bothering about even giving the impression of depth to. This is more work than your type of Subject tends to demand, usually, isn't it?'

'. . .'

'This is something else that isn't you. You've never exactly been shy about discussing Subjects with me.'

'It's complex. She's grown on me.'

'It's this certain *way* she takes notes on your explanation of Coffin-Corner punts.'

'It's complicated. There's a lot I'm not saying. She's got levels. I've discovered levels and dimensions to her I didn't know were originally there.'

'Oh O., *please* don't let it just be you've just discovered she's married with little kids. That's not it by any chance is it? Please let it be something other than little kids.'

'. . .'

'Let it be something other than the hordes of other Subjects I've sat and listened to excruciatingly detailed sadistic blow-by-blow Strategic accounts of. Orin "Homewrecker" Incandenza, this is what the team calls you, in like jest? You sick pup.'

'*I'm* a sick pup? *I'm* the sick one?'

'. . . Wants to blame her, won't admit it, needs to, won't admit it, sweepingly blames the whole affair of Himself on her, won't interface with her or worse even acknowledge her, resents even the fact she forgives things like you and Marlon Bain killing her dog —'

'— a hit-and-run-and-back-up-and-hit-again driver, I *told* you rep—'

'— pretends he gets the most retardate PR staffer he can make hold the crayon to send grotesque solecistic pseudo-impersonal replies to her pathetic letters. Jethro Bodine, O.? Jethro *Bodine?*'

'A private chuckle. She'd never get it.'

'Disowns her — worse, sicker, tells himself he's convinced himself she doesn't even exist, as if she never existed, but by some coincidence has this rapacious fetish for young married mothers he can strategize into betraying their spouses and maybe damaging their kids for all time, and has this apparently even more rapacious compulsive need to call the blood-relative he hasn't even seen in four years and tell him all about every Subject and Strategy, blow-by-blow, long distance, in nanomicroscopic detail. Let's stop and ponder *this* all for a moment, O., what say?'

'I'm letting all this be just water off a duck's back. I can tell it's the tooth talking. I can remember the stress of the place. All I can say is that trust me here: this *Moment* Subject is like strickenly dissimilar from what you're indicting. The levels and circumstances aren't the ones you're so anxious to call rapacious. Is all I can say at this juncture.'

'Why do I suspect it's simply that you tried to make the big X with her and she demurred and this simply piqued your interest? During my can't-miss nail-interval you were saying how enormous interior linemen were making comments about her bottom being so huge and soft you could whack it over and over with a car antenna and not hurt it.'

'Hallie I never said any such fucking thing. You pulled that out of the air. And *I'm* sick?'

'You said she was obese.'

'I said she was a girl and a half in all directions. Which all of a sudden there was something that seemed cross-cultural about it: I had this sudden flash of understanding how cultures can regard largeness as erotic. More of someone to love. Not to mention queerly and oddly intense and alive and vibrant.'

'And she declined a casual advance, and showed you pictures of her like enormous offspring, and you came to attention.'

'With a heartbreakingly lovely face, too, Hal, all peachy and lissome, like big pretty girls get.'

'I'm going to have to keep her away from this kid Ortho Stice up here, because he really is a Rubensophile. After P.M.s when we sit around he'll go on and on about enormous breasts and melon bellies and quivering laps until we're all grimacing and pinching our nose-bridges. And whatever you meant was not *lissome*.'

'The reserve QB who's next to me in these godawful pre-game costumed swoop-and-glides said something I liked. Helen passed him in the locker room and he — do you want to hear this?'

'She was in the locker room?'

'It's the law. The pros aren't a PR-gulag. He said she had a face that'd break your heart and then also break the heart of whoever like rushed over to your aid as you pitched over sideways grabbing your chest.'

'That is a pretty good one, O.'

'But so far we concur on the basic oddness, it sounds like. If the radicals want Québec loose from Canada still, and that's always been the priceless pearl, why like dissipate themselves trying to wreak mayhem down here almost the precise moment Interdependence is declared? 'ce pas?'

'I'd rather just agree it's a stumper and then go dry my ankle and find a clean shirt and grab Schacht and hit him up for some Anbesol before we hit the truck.'

'Right? And do these different groups get along, amongst themselves, the different Separatist flanges?'

'Not according to Poutrincourt they don't.'

'So why then the united concerted switch from like Let Québec Go or we stick knives in the eyes of Canadian VIPs and drop huge confections on Rue Sherbrooke during St. Jean-Baptiste Day to all of a sudden Let Canada Go or we blow up ATHSCME towers and stretch mirrors across U.S. highways and hang fleur-de-lis banners from U.S. monuments and disrupt InterLace pulses and skywrite Nuck obscenities over Buffalo and dicky with waste-vehicle launchers so it rains moose-guano on New Haven and shoot O.N.A.N.ite V.I.P.s on U.S. soil and only barely get foiled from injecting anaerobic toxins into jars of Planters peanuts?'

'The New Haven Brown Rain thing was sort of a chortle, though, you have to admit.'

'Chortles are good. We like chortles. But what's the political motivation for the about-face? Account for this for me. All it has to do is sound soberly considered.'

'Orin, I'm trying to reconcile your doubtless sincere seriousness about this with your choice\of me as co-ponderer.'

'All —'

'I'm a privileged white seventeen-year-old U.S. male. I'm a student at a tennis academy that sees itself as a prophylactic. I eat, sleep, evacuate, highlight things with yellow markers, and hit balls. I lift things and swing things and run in huge outdoor circles. I am just about as apolitical as someone can be. I am out of all loops but one, by design. I'm sitting here naked with my foot in a bucket. What exactly is it you hope to get from me on this? I keep losing focus on whether you want a deep-sounding line of patter to facilitate Xing this fleshy Subject or have somehow been seduced into believing it's really worth pondering the weedy thought-processes of fringe Canadians. Of fringe *anybody*. How consistent do the Brazilian *Nuevo Contras*' objectives look? The *Noie Störkraft*'s? Shining Path's? The Belgian CCC's'? Pro-Life assault squads? The *Ez-ed-Dean-el-Qassan*? P.E.T.A. fur-farm arsonists' objectives? Jesus, Gentle and the poor C.U.S.P.s?'k

'*Poor C.U.S.P.s?*'

'Why not just soberly shrug and invoke the term *wacko* and leave it at that? Why not tell her you're a radically simple and somewhat sick young man who kicks balls really high in the air for a living?'

'All I —'

'Why not just say *who cares?* This stuff isn't about you and me. The person this stuff is about is the person you say you've erased from all RAM. Why not tell the damn truth for once?'

'*Me* tell the truth? *Me* lie?'

'What, this ascapartic bathroom-mag journalist is going to give you like an SAT entrance-test on Francophone extremism? Like a gyno-entrance exam? You have to place above a certain percentile to get her to let you X her on the floor of the nursery right next to the bassinet? Whom are you trying to kid? Whom do you think this is really about? Can you be that sick that you can't even admit it over the fucking *phone?*'

'. . .'

'Or what?'

'. . .'

'I'm sorry, O. I apologize.'

'Think nothing of it. I know you didn't mean it.'

'I hate losing the temper.'

'You don't sound good, Hallie. You sound ground down.'

Hal grinds at his eye with a finger. 'These tooth-episodes make me feel like that wobbled shrieking figure in that Munch lithograph.'

'That chew's going to eat right through your membranes. It's a vicious vice. I'm urging in all earnest. Ask that Schacht kid.'

Michael Pemulis cracks Hal's door slowly and slowly pokes his head and one shoulder in, saying nothing. He has showered but is still flushed, and his right eye gets wobbly in this certain way when two or three Tenuates are wearing off. He has his yachting cap, gold epaulets of fake naval braid, and in one ear a piratical gold hoop that lights up in sync with his pulse. With the door just cracked and his head poked in he brings his other arm in over from behind like it's not his arm, his hand in the shape of a claw just over his head, and makes as if the claw from behind is pulling him back out into the hall. W/ an eye-rolling look of fake terror.

Hal is hunched, examining his finger for eye-material. 'In all the excitement we've neglected the most obvious response, then, O. Your answer for the exam, and then I can go dry the ankle.' He can hear Pemulis asking Petropolis Kahn and Stephan Wagenknecht something off down the hall through the cracked door.

'I think I already tried the obvious response on her, but hit me.'

'Pemulis just made his first pass and left the door ajar. I'm sitting here nude in a draft through an open door neglecting the maybe deceptively obvious fact that something like, what, three-quarters of the Concavity's northern border runs contiguous to Québec.'

'Exactamundo.'

'So that so what if Ottawa didn't formally subjoin the Concavity to any particular province. Really big favor, I'm sure. Because the map speaks for itself. Bits of western New Brunswick and a smidgeon of Ontario aside, the Concavity — the physical fact and fallout of the Concavity — it's Québec's problem. Something like 750 clicks of border along the Concavity, with attendant seepage, for Notre Rai Pays.'

'Yes plus the brunt of the airborne wastes from the high-altitude ATHSCMEs, plus being the province that gets splatted when the E.W.D. vehicles overshoot the Concavity. This is what I tried right off the bat on her.'

'So what's the puzzle. Put yourself in Québec's shoes. Once again they get the gooey end of the Canadian dipstick. It's mostly now western Québecer kids the size of Volkswagens shlumpfing around with no skulls. It's Québecers with cloracne and tremors and olfactory hallucinations and infants born with just one eye in the middle of their forehead. It's eastern Québec that gets green sunsets and indigo rivers and grotesquely asymmetrical snow-crystals and front lawns they have to beat back with a machete to get to their driveways. They get the feral-hamster incursions and the Infant-depredations and the corrosive fogs.'

'Although people aren't exactly flocking to New Brunswick or Lake Ontario either. And the coastal ATHSCMEs send the coastal phenols out over Fundy, and supposedly the lobsters out there are like monsters in old Japanese films, and supposedly Nova Scotia glows, at night, in satellite photos.'

'Still and all, O., tell her proportionally speaking it's Québec that's borne the brunt of what Canada had to take. The brunt *again*, to their way of thinking, remember. Small wonder the fringe mentalities are violently anti-O.N.A.N. up there. There's got to be a real straw-and-camel feel to the whole thing.'

The door swings all the way open and clunks against the wall behind it. Michael Pemulis has pretended to kick it in. 'Good Lard preserve us he's nekkid,' he says, coming in and closing the door to check behind it. Hal holds up a hand for him to wait a second.

'Except here's the thing,' Orin says. Pemulis stands expectantly in an uncluttered patch of Hal's half of the floor and makes a show of looking at his wrist as if there were a watch there. Hal nods at him and holds up one finger.

'Except here's the thing,' Orin is saying. 'The issue she raises is is there really any sort of realistic hope of Québec getting Gentle to get O.N.A.N. to reverse the Reconfiguration. Take back the Concavity, shut down the fans, make us acknowledge the waste as fundamentally American waste.'

'Well probably of course not.' Hal looks up at Pemulis and makes his own hand into a claw and makes clawing motions at the phone. Pemulis is compulsively going around zipping and unzipping everything in the room with a zipper, a habit of his Hal loathes. 'But now she's got you falling back into demanding realistic and consistent logic from fringe mentalities again.'

'But Hallie just hang on. Canada as a whole couldn't oppose O.N.A.N. Wouldn't. Ottawa's so far in now they wouldn't say shit if they had three times the mouthful they already have. Of shit I mean.'

Pemulis is pointing vehemently out the west window at the parking lot where the tow truck is parked and making exaggerated Henry VIII–like rending and chewing motions. His eyes, under the waning influence of P.M. stimulants, do not get mirthful or glazed.

They just get tiny and lightless and even closer together in his narrow face, like a second set of nostrils. The right eye's little wobble is out of sync with the pulse of his earring.

There's the sound of Orin switching phone-hands. 'So then I'll ask you what she seemed like she rhetorically asked: are the Separatists' and fringe cells' pathetic little anti-O.N.A.N. campaigns and gestures down here basically just hopeless and pathetic?'

'Does fish-shit drift slowly bottomward, O.? How could she see it as anything but, if she's as savvy as you say?' Hal removes his pruned white foot from the janitor-bucket and dries it on a woppsed-up sheet. He points at a pair of underwear near Pemulis's Docksider. Pemulis picks the briefs up off the floor with two fingers and tosses them to Hal with a pretend-shudder.

'So simply largely symbolic at best, then?'

Hal's lying back trying to get his legs into the briefs with one hand. 'Tell her after much chin-stroking simply *yes*, O. O., Pemulis is standing here already in his hat pretending to clang a dinner bell. He's got big glittery ropes of drool swinging from his lower lip.' Pemulis is actually making a complex system of motions indicating both the procedures for rolling a duBois and the lateness of the hour. For the past two years, Hal and Pemulis and Struck and Troeltsch and sometimes B. Boone have made a little ritual of nipping out to the little hidden clearing behind West House's parking lot's dumpsters and sharing an obscene cigar-sized duBois before the I.-Day-Eve expedition and supper out, while Schacht and sometimes Ortho Stice sit inside the tow truck, faces green in the green glow of the truck's instruments, warming it up. Hal sits up and makes a waggling go-on-ahead-on-down motion to Pemulis.

'But you have the . . . Mr. *Hope*,' Pemulis stage-whispers.

'One moment please.' Hal clamps a hand hard over the phone and covers phone and hand with two pillows and some bedding, and stage-whispers 'Where's your part of the Mr. H. all of a sudden? Why do we have to roll a zeppelin out of *my* part of the Hope I bought retail from *you* not three days ago?'

The nystagmus makes the eye-rolling lurider. 'Extenuations. We can get it all sorted out right later. Nobody's going to like *exploit* you.'

And then it's hard to extract the hand and phone. 'O., I'm going to have to book out of here in just about one second.'

'Just how about this. Ponder this in advance for me and try and stay upright til you can call me back. This was the Subject's crux-type proposal. You can call collect if you want.'

'I don't have to respond,' Hal says.

'Correct.'

'I just listen and then break the connection.'

'Calling me like tonight or tomorrow before lunch, collect if I.-Day's full-toll.'

'I just sit here very briefly and then the conversation's over and we can go.' Hal's directing all this more at Pemulis, who's pacing and holding the Constantine bust in his hands and examining it at close range, shaking his head.

'All set? This is it. Are you set?'

'So go already.'

'Her poser goes roughly like this. If the Separatists' big object has always been to independently secede, and if they've got about a snowball's chance of ever really getting O.N.A.N. de-Reconfigured, and if pretty much all Canadians despise Gentle and the transfer of the Concavity and the whole Experialist merde sandwich, but especially the Concavity, the cartographic fact of a Concavity in our map and a new Convexity in theirs, that the maps now say it's Canadian soil, this toxified like area: grant that all this is obviously right; then why don't the Separatists in Québec use the fact of the odiousness of the Concavity to go put their parliamentary wigs on and go to Ottawa to parliament and say to the rest of Canada like: Look, let us secede, and we'll take the Concavity *with* us when we secede, it'll be our problem not yours, it'll go on the maps as Québecois and not Canadian, it'll be *our* blot and *our* bone of dissension with O.N.A.N., and Canadian honor will be desmirched, and Canada's pathetic standing in O.N.A.N. and the like world community of standings will be rehabilitated because of the ingenious way Ottawa's parliament will have re-gerrymandered O.N.A.N.'s map without taking on the U.S. directly? Why not this? Why don't they go to Ottawa and say Cuibono all around and say This way everybody wins? We get our own Notre Rai Pays, and you get the slap in the face of the Concavity off your map. The Subject posited why the Nucks don't see the odiousness of the Concavity as maybe the best thing that ever happened to them in terms of Canada's persuadability into letting Québec go. She hit me with Why wouldn't your thinking militant Nucks use the Concavity as a bargaining chip for independence, why would they want O.N.A.N. to take back the one thing odious enough to be a chip?'

'Who's this you're talking to you can't call back?' Pemulis says loudly, pacing back and forth with little toy-soldier about-faces, his hoop flickering like mad.

Hal lowers the phone but doesn't cover it. 'It's Orin, wanting to know why Québec and the F.L.Q. and so on haven't tried bargaining with the Canadian administration, offering Québec's cartographic adoption of the Concavity in exchange for Separation.' Hal cocks his head slightly. 'This could be Poutrincourt's so-called Separation and return's real meaning, it occurs to me.'

'Orin as in your brother, with the leg?'

'He's all in a swivet about inter-O.N.A.N.ite politics.'

Pemulis makes a megaphone of his hands. 'Tell him who gives a bright flaming fart! Tell him to go read a book! Tell him to access any one of a dozen D-bases off of the Net! Tell him you're pretty sure he can afford it!' Pemulis's hands are slender and red-knuckled and his fingers long and sort of falcate. 'Tell him you can hear the truck getting impatiently revved as on one of the very few totally free nights we ever get our friends get ready to leave without you. Remind him how we have to eat on schedule up here or we get the wobbles. Tell him we read books and tirelessly access D-bases and run our asses off all day here and need to eat instead of we don't just stand there and swing one leg up and down over and over for seven-plus figures.'

'Tell Penisless to go sit on something sharp,' Orin says.

'O., he's right, I can feel that feeling of my body starting to feed on itself. You said I could think and call you back. I'll use your pager if you like.'

Pemulis has used one foot to clear a path through laundry and diskettes and books and gear to the west window, where he's making broad involved gestures with a person or persons outside down on the grounds whom the window's big sill keeps Hal from being able to see. Hal's underwear is at a diagonal across his pelvis. Orin on the phone is saying:

'Picture this and see what you think. Imagine this. The F.L.Q. and other various Separatist cells all suddenly divert their terror's energies away from Canada and suddenly start mounting an insurgent campaign of U.S. and Mexican harassment. But the thing is they make a big deal of terroristically insurging against O.N.A.N. on the behalf of *all* of Canada. They even find a way to bring the Albertan ultra-rightists in on it, plus other provincial fringes, so it looks to O.N.A.N. like maybe all of Canada as a whole is in on the insurging.'

'I don't have to picture it. It's what's going on. The C.P.C.P.[1] makes incursions against Montana like clockwork. There was that horrific jamming of InterLace pulses and substitution of porn-films for children's programming around Duluth in June traced to that psycho quintet in southwest Ontario. The Interstates north of Saratoga are still supposed to be undrivable after sunset.'

'Exactly.'

'So some point for me to ponder needs to emerge really fast, here, Orin.'

'The point is I was rhetorically invited by the Subject to entertain the picture of it all really being the Nucks. The pan-Canadian thing being a dodge. The Separatists all somehow united and orchestrating the anti-O.N.A.N.ism. The rhetorical question becomes to imagine this and ask: Why would they do this?'

'We're wearing a groove in the same track again, O. It's because the Concavity impacts mainly Québec.'

'No, I mean she meant why would they make such a noise about insurging on behalf of all of *Canada* and go to such lengths to orchestrate the appearance of pan-*Canadian* anti-O.N.A.N.ism.'

'And then judging by precedent the Subject gave a hypothetical answer to her own question. Have you gotten to get a word in edgewise throughout this series of interviews, O.?'

'What if it's that the Nuck Separatists know totally well that if the O.N.A.N. administration sees Canada as a big enough roach in the ointment, Gentle and Unspecified Services' boys in white can get together with Mexico's Vichified puppet-state and make things like really unpleasant *indeed* for Ottawa. They could make Canada the sort of black scapegoat of all of O.N.A.N. There's little you can picture that might be worse than being the one country in a three-country continental Anschluss that the other two countries are ganging up on and making things unpleasant for.'

'*Vichified? Anschluss?* This doesn't sound like any Orin I know. These are rabidly political catchwords. What kind of heartbreaking Rubensian *Moment*-type fluff-journalist is this you're so determined to —?'

'The unpleasantness is pretty easy to imagine a picture of. The E.W.D. vectors could easily be recalibrated further north, Gentle could tell them. Our waste-resources are extensive. At the mildest, he could say, good-sized chunks of Canada could be Concavitized.'

'I have to go. Pemulis is slumped back against the wall with his hands over his stomach and is slumping all the way down the wall looking wobbly and pale.'

'Ponder the picture of the parliament's nails bitten all the way down to the ragged pink pulpy stuff as the Nucks orchestrate the terrorism so it looks more and more like Canada versus O.N.A.N.'

Hal's in slacks and one street-sock and one athletic sock and picking different shirts up off the floor, trying to smell a clean one. 'But this is all —'

'Kyaaaa!' Pemulis vaults a corner of Hal's bed and tries to claw at the transparent phone's antenna like he's going to break it off. Hal turns to protect the phone with a shoulder, whipping at Pemulis with a sweatshirt.

Orin is saying 'What I'm asking is for you to ponder could it maybe end up that Québec, after wreaking various mayhi down here and making it look like it's all of Canada, the P.Q.s or somebody respectable gets wigged up and go to Ottawa and offers this deal: Parliament gets the P.M. and the government to get the other provinces to let Québec go, Separate, *aller, partir* — and in return Québec'll step up the anti-O.N.A.N. harassment and insurgency while *dropping* the pretense of other provinces being involved and all of Canada insurging and make it publicly clear that it's Québec and Québec alone that's O.N.A.N.'s real nemesis. They tell Ottawa they'll offer the contiguousness of the Concavity as their reason and send absolutely everything they've got in terms of terrorism at O.N.A.N. and Gentle, taking full credit each time. Offering themselves as the culprit and de-Reconfiguration as the objective.'

'So your multilevelled journalist's hypothesizing a kind of meta-extortion.' Hal can hear Pemulis's whistle-lipped breathing. 'Separation is still the Québecer insurgents' real goal, and their anti-O.N.A.N. insurgency is not what it appears.' Hal's in the dark under the desk that the fold-out TP and drives and phone console and modem are stacked on one corner of, surrounded by nests of wires, trying to find his other street-shoe. 'It's supposedly just been a ruse to arouse O.N.A.N.'s ire at Canada so the Québecers can use the U.S. and Mexico as levers on Ottawa.'

'Trying to engineer it so that Canada'll be more than happy to disassociate from them,'

Orin says. 'And I'm saying I don't have the background or lobes to even know whether she might be putting me on, testing my depth.'

'You've always had a special dread of depth-testing.'

'How about why don't you just toss me the Bob and Axhandle and me'll go down and get things ready and wait for you,' Pemulis stage-whispers to Hal's slacks' bottom, which is pretty much all that's visible from under the desk. Hal's hand comes up out of the leg-space under the desk and raises one finger and shakes it a little for emphasis. Pemulis is standing next to the small TP viewer — which is propped up like a large photo with a buttressy thing that folds out of its back — and the TP's disk- and cartridge-drive, which takes up less than a quarter of the desktop and has the phone's console and power unit bolted into a receptacle on the drive's side.

Hal's voice is muffled and has the strained pitch of someone trying to clear nests of dust-bunnied wire to find something. 'Except Orin I don't see a great deal of pondering required here. The total anti-U.S. insurgency so far's been too hapless and small-potato for her theory to work. The odd pie- and guano-bombardment, stretching mirrors across lonely roads, even demapping officials and botulizing the occasional peanut jar. None of this is exactly bringing anyone to his knees. None of this is making Canada or Québec look like any kind of serious threat.'

Michael Pemulis, his jaunty cap pushed back and his lips pursed as if whistling, but not whistling, is very casually brushing his hand over the drive and console's power unit, as if killing time by casually dusting. His other hand's jingling pocket-change. There's the sound of Hal clunking his head on something under the desk. His bottom is bony and his belt has missed two loops. The power unit's toggle's next to a little red jewel of a power-light that blinks at the same rate as a smoke alarm when the toggle's on ON.

Hal sneezes twice. Pemulis taps his fingers in a little anapestic gallop over the unit's top. Orin sounds like he's sitting up straight. 'Hallie kid now you're right with me, this is where your pondering lobes come in, because that was just my response, that there was nothing sufficiently more than just an annoying gnat-like annoyance about the insurgencies, which is where she moved beyond my depth back into 1(a), if you remember, when she raised this *samizdat*-word in connec—'.

a. Don't ask.

b. Ibid.

c. I.e., the Militant Grammarians of Massachusetts, a syntactic-integrity PAC Avril had put together with two or three very dear friends and colleagues around metro Boston.

d. The Year of the Whisper-Quiet Maytag Dishmaster's anti-sclerotic miracle-food craze.

e. The then-skinny Eliot Kornspan, before Loach and Freer got hold of him.

f. At once high-tech and somehow atavistic, Telegrocery services let you order off your TP and then have the stuff brought right to your door by college-studenty types, often within hours, saving one the stress and fluorescent hassle of public food-shopping. As of Y.D.A.U. it's still very big in some areas and not all that big in others. The first Tele-grocery service didn't even launch in metro Boston until YY2007MRCVMETIUFI/ITPSFH,O,OM(*s*), and it's still mostly in Boston a downscale and blue-collar thing, oddly.

g. InterLace serves just about all of habitable O.N.A.N.; each nation comprises (roughly speaking) an entertainment-dissemination 'Grid.'

h. After Meech Lake I, Charlottetown I and II, and Meech Lake II, this was Ottawa's fifth and final attempt to placate Québec with a constitutional amendment formalizing the Gallic province's right to 'preserve and promote' a 'distinct society and culture.'

i. The French and Indian War, known to Québecers as 'La Guerre des Britanniques et des Sauvages,' BS c. 1754–60, at the final battles of which, at the Plains of Abraham in '59 and Montreal in '60, the English and Americans kicked ass and took names in a large way that's never quite been forgotten by the Québecois, whose memory for insult is the stuff of legend. The wily Amherst was there, too, at Ticonderoga and Montreal, with his trusty smallpox-blankets.

j. Grammar and Meaning.

k. The Clean U.S. Party of Johnny Gentle, Famous Crooner.

l. The Calgarian pro-Canadian Phalanx.

111. Hal's term, actually an Incandenza-family term, actually not inappropriate here because like most Incandenza-family terms put into family usage by Avril, who's an expatriate Québecer, *whinge* is some east-Canadian idiom for vigorous high-pitched complaining, almost like whining except with a semantic tinge of legitimacy to the complaint.

112. The soon to be all-too-well-known and dread-inspiring *Assassins des Fauteuils Rollents* of the E.W.D.-receptacle-festooned Papineau region of southwestern Québec.

113. Which sinewy stuff is described by the OB-GYN specialist in his DictaChart as 'neural-gray.'

114. © B.S. MCMLXII, The Glad Flaccid Receptacle Corporation, Zanesville OH, sponsor of the very last year of O.N.A.N.ite Subsidized Time (q.v. Note 78). All Rights Reserved.

115. Volkmann's contracture's some kind of severe serpentine deformation of the arms following a fracture that hadn't been set right or splinted or where the arm's been allowed to stay all woundedly bent in as it heals; *bradyauxesis* refers to some part(s) of the body not growing as fast as the other parts of the body — Himself and the Moms got plenty familiar with these sorts of congenital-challenge terms and many more, re Mario, particularly the variations on the medical root *brady,* from the Greek *bradys* meaning slow, such as bradylexia (w/r/t reading), bradyphenia (practical-problem-solving-type thinking), nocturnal bradypnea (dangerously slow breathing during sleep sometimes, which is why Mario uses four pillows minimum), bradypedestrianism (obvious), and especially bradykinesia, an almost gerontologic lentissimo about most of Mario's movements, an exaggerated slowness that both resembles and permits extremely close slow attention to whatever's being done.

116. Pretty much the BMW of 16mm. digital-cartridge recorders, brought out in limited numbers by Paillard Cinématique of Sherbrooke, Québec, CAN, just weeks before its manufacturing facilities were annularly hyperfloriated and the company went belly-up.

117. . . . overshot the place to mention that Mario's head — in perverse contradistinction to the arm-trouble — is *hyper*auxetic, and two to three times the size of your more average elf-to-jockey-sized head and facies.

118. You'd somehow think that Mario would be thick as thieves with the blue-collar custodial and kitchen and physical plant/grounds staff, but it's odd, he and they never have much to say to each other, and with rare exceptions none of the E.T.A.s including Mario has anything interpersonal to do with the nine-month part-time halfway-house rehabilitating workers, who mostly mow and mop and empty trash and load dishes into the dining hall's steamer, and who radiate a kind of slitty-eyed reserve that seems far more sullen and ungrateful than shy.

119. . . . also overshot the spot to include that Mario's a homodont: all his teeth are bicuspids and identical, front and back, not unlike a porpoise; it's a source of unending struggle for Ted Schacht, who tends to avoid Mario because whenever he's around him he has to fight the urge to have him open up and submit to scrutiny, which Schacht can well imagine would hurt his feelings: nobody wants to be an object of clinical interest like that.

120. This basic phenomenon being what more abstraction-capable post-Hegelian adults call 'Historical Consciousness.'

121. Eschaton's pre- and post-procedures are convolved enough so that an actual game gets gotten up every like month or so at most, almost always on Sunday, but even then not all twelve of a year's kids can get the hours off to play, which is why the latitude and surplus in game-personnel.

122. O.N.A.N.ite Classroom Cartographic Series W–520–500–268–6^W–9^W–9^W–14^{W4}, © B.S. 1994, Rand McNally & Company.

123. Pemulis here, dictating to Inc, who can just sit there making a steeple out of his fingers and pressing it to his lip and not take notes and wait and like inscribe [*sic*] it anytime in the next week and get it verbatim, the smug turd. Using the Mean-Value formula for dividing available megatonnage among Combatants whose GNP/Military // Military/Nuke ratios vary from Eschaton to Eschaton keeps you from needing to crunch out a new ratio for each Combatant each time, plus lets you multi-regress the results so Combatants get rewarded for past thermonuclear largesse [occasional verbal flourishes Hal's — HJI]. The formula's also provable by the Extreme Value Theorem, which the EV Theorem itself has a proof that's just about the biggest Unit-twisting bitch in the whole of applied differentiation, but I see Hal grimacing, so we'll keep it compact, even though this whole thing is real interesting if you're interested and whatnot.

· Say you've got a Combatant and a record of his past GNP/Military // Military/Nuke ratios. We want to give the Combatant the like exact average of all the past megatonnages he's gotten in the past. The exact average is called the 'Mean Value,' which ought to give us a bit of a giggle, given the hostility of the context here.

So then but let A stand for the Mean Value of a Combatant's constantly fluctuating ratio and so constantly fluctuating initial megatonnage. We want to find A and give the Combatant exactly A megatons. How to do it's pretty elegant, and all you need for it is two pieces of data: the most his ratio's ever been and the least it's ever been. These two datums [*sic*] are called the Extreme Values of the cn-n function for which A's the Mean Value, by the way.

So then but so let f be a continuous non-negative function (meaning the ratio) on the interval [a, b] (meaning the difference between the least the ratio's ever been and the most it's ever been and whatnot). Are these little explanations aggravating [*sic*]? Inc's looking at me like butter would freeze. It's hard to know what to assume v. what to explain. I'm trying to be as clear as I can be [*sic*]. And now he's looking at me like I'm digressing. Why don't you just pass that certain item back on over here, Inculator. But so we've got f and we've got [a, b]. And let r and R be the smallest and biggest values of the function $f(x)$ on the interval [a, b]. So now check out the rectangles of height r and height R over the interval [a, b] in the diagram marked let's go ahead and mark it say PEEMSTER:

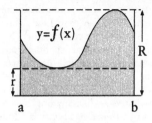

PEEMSTER

The Mean Value we're after, A, can now be expressed integrally as the Area of some intermediate-type rectangle whose height is taller [*sic*] than r but shorter [*sic*] than R. From here on it's just tit. We need a constant. You always need a constant. Inc's nodding his head sarcastically like I think I'm saying something sage. Let d be any constant, for computational reasons the closer to 1 the better, so like let d be the size of Hal's Unit.

Hal Incandenza's Addendum: In meters.

Michael Pemulis's Resumption: Very funny. So now, just looking at the wicked-illuminating PEEMSTER diagram above, you can see that this Area we want:

$$A = \int_a^b f(x)dx$$

is going to be bigger than the area of the rectangle with height r and but also smaller than the area of the rectangle with height R. Pure mental reason [sic] *compels,* then, that [*sic*] somewhere in there between r and R there's an exact height, $f(x')$, such that (I have to say that every demonstration of a stats theorem has *Let* and *such that* in them, mostly I think because they're so wicked much fun to say) such that the rectangle of this height $f(x')$ over the whole interval [a, b] has *exactly* the Area we want, the Mean Value of all the historic [*sic*] expenditure-ratios; in other words in abstracted form:

$$\int_a^b f(x)dx = f(x')(b - a)$$

where (b − a) is just the size of the interval. And so have a look at the revealing diagram labeled HALSADICK:

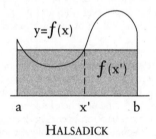

$$y = f(x)$$

$$f(x')$$

a   x'   b

HALSADICK

This fucking *works.* You don't have to crunch out a whole new ratio each time for each Combatant to dole out the ordnance. You just skim the highest and lowest ratios off the Eschaton records the Beanie-man keeps on each time. This is *wicked.* This is fucking *elegant.* Note that (*Note that*'s another like compulsitory [*sic*] term) note that the Combatant's Mean-Value megatonnage will change, slightly, from Eschaton to Eschaton, exactly the way a like hitter's season average will alter just a bit from at-bat to at-bat, depending integrally on what he delivered on his last trip to the plate and whatnot. Note also that you can use this Mean-Value time-saver with anything that varies within a (*definable*) set of boundaries and whatnot — like any line, or a tennis court's boundaries, or like maybe say a certain drug's urine-level range between Clean and Royally Pinched. As a like exercise, if you're interested, play three hours of high-level competitive jr. top-level [*sic*] tennis and then calculate the Mean Value of the ratios of first serves to appearances at net and appearances at net to points won; for a serve-and-volleyer, this is how to tell how serve-dependent his match-performance is. DeLint does this kind of exercise every morning sitting on the can. It's going to be interesting to see if [*sic*] Hal, who thinks he's just too sly trying to outline Eschaton in the 3rd-person tense [*sic*] like some jowly old

Eschatologist with leather patches on his elbows [*sic*], if Inc can transpose [*sic?*] the math here without help from his Mumster. Later.

P.S. Allston Rules.

124. Both EndStat and Mathpak are registered trademarks of Aapps Inc., itself now a division of InterLace TelEntertainment.

125. Plastic-mesh laundry baskets take two hands to carry and keep you from being able to dribble up more balls with your stick's face; the cast-off janitorial buckets are the size of like a middle-size wastebasket, but they have a sturdy steel pail-type handle, and their hard-polymer composition makes for lasting wear. It was into just such a bucket that Pemulis threw up before his kind of suspicious V.D. down at Port Washington.

(Various gear-companies sell various specially designed ball receptacles with names like 'Ball-Hopper' and 'Ball-Bank' — the general Academy consensus is these are for dilettantes and pussies.)

126. It being well-nigh impossible to keep the present from infecting even a playful and childlike Historical Consciousness, Canadians often end up playing picayune but villainous roles in Eschatonic TRIGSITs.

127. A lot of these little toss-ins and embellishments are Inc amusing himself, not Otis's TRIGSIT, which is 100% all biz.

P.S. Wolf-Spiders Ruleth the Land.

128. Most Valuable Lobber.

129. M. Pemulis is, in the best Allston MA tradition, a good friend and a bad-news enemy, and even E.T.A.s who don't like him are careful not to do or even say anything that might call for score-settling, because Pemulis is a thoroughgoing chilled-revenge gourmet, and is not one bit above dosing someone's water-jug or voltaging their door-knob or encoding something horrid in your E.T.A. med-files or dickying with the mirror over the bureau in the little recessed part of your subdorm room so that when you look in the mirror in the A.M. to comb or tend to a blackhead or something you see something staring back at you that you'll never entirely get over, which is what took over two years to finally happen to M. H. Penn, who afterward wouldn't say what he'd seen but stopped shaving altogether and, it's agreed, has never been quite himself since.

130. Pemulis doesn't actually literally say 'breath and bread.'

131. Before Boston Groups' regular speaker meetings there are often closed, half-hour Beginners' Discussion Meetings, where newcomers can share their cluelessness, weakness, and despair in a warm supportive private atmosphere.

132. The word *Group* in *AA Group* is always capitalized because Boston AA places enormous emphasis on joining a Group and identifying yourself as a member of this larger thing, the Group. Likewise caps in like *Commitment, Giving It Away,* and c.

133. Gately's little bedroom in the damp Ennet House basement is plastered all over every part of every wall that's dry enough to take tape with cutout Scotch-taped photos of all sorts of variegated and esoteric celebrities past and present, which are varied as residents throw magazines into the E.M.P.H.H. dumpsters and are frequently selected because the celebrities are somehow grotesque; it's a kind of compulsive habit held over from Gately's fairly dysfunctional North Shore childhood, when he'd been a clipping and taping fiend.

134. And if you're brand-new, as in like your first three days, and so on mandatory nonpunitive House Restriction — like veiled Joelle van Dyne, who entered the House just today, 11/8, Interdependence Day, after the E.R. physician at Brigham and Women's Hospital who last night had pumped her full of Inderal[a] and nitro had looked upon her unveiled face and been deeply affected, and had taken a special interest, a consequence of which after Joelle regained consciousness and speech had involved placing a call to Pat

Montesian, whose paralyzing alcoholic stroke the physician had treated in this very same E.R. almost seven years before, and in whose case he'd also taken a special interest and had followed, such that he was now a personal friend of the sober Pat M.'s and sat honorarily on Ennet House's Board of Directors, so that his call to Pat's home on Saturday night had gotten Joelle into the House on the spot, as of Interdependence Day A.M.'s discharge from B&W, leap-frogging literally dozens of waiting-list people and putting Joelle into Ennet House's intensive program of residential treatment literally before she even knew what was happening, which in retrospect might have been lucky — if you're this new you're actually not supposed ever to leave the Staffer's sight, though in practice this rule gets suspended when you have to go to the ladies' room and the Staffer's male, or vice versa.

    a. Propranolol hydrochloride, Wyeth-Ayerst, a beta-blocking antihypertensive.

135. A conviction common to all who Hang In with AA, after a while, and abstracted in the slogan 'My Best Thinking Got Me Here.'

136. Trade-name Fastin, ®SmithKline Beecham Inc., a low-level 'drine not unlike Tenuate, though w/ more associated tooth-grinding.

137. None of these are Don Gately's terms.

138. In e.g. Boston: join Group, get Active, get phone #s, get sponsor, audio-call sponsor daily, hit meetings daily, pray like fiend for release from Disease, don't kid self that you can still buy rodneys in liquor stores or date your dealer's niece or think for a second you can still hang out in bars playing darts and just drinking Millennial Fizzies or vanilla Yoo-Hoos, etc.

139. Volunteer Counselor Eugenio ('Gene') M. favors entomologic tropes and analogies, which is especially effective with brand-new residents fresh from subjective safaris through the Kingdom of Bugs.

140. Don G.'s North Shore's vulgate signifier for trite/banal is: *limp*.

141. Likewise that his private term for blacks is *niggers*, which is unfortunately still all he knows.

142. The speaker doesn't actually use the terms *thereon, most assuredly,* or *operant limbic system,* though she really had, before, said *chordate phylum.*

143. *Sic.*

144. E.g. see Ursula Emrich-Levine (University of California-Irvine), 'Watching Grass Grow While Being Hit Repeatedly Over the Head With a Blunt Object: Fragmentation and Stasis in James O. Incandenza's *Widower, Fun with Teeth, Zero-Gravity Tea Ceremony,* and *Pre-Nuptial Agreement of Heaven and Hell,' Art Cartridge Quarterly,* vol. III, nos. 1–3, Year of the Perdue Wonderchicken.

145.
TRANSCRIPT-FRAGMENT FROM INTERVIEW SERIES FOR PUTATIVE
MOMENT MAGAZINE SOFT PROFILE ON PHOENIX CARDINAL
PROFESSIONAL PUNTER O. J. INCANDENZA, BY PUTATIVE *MOMENT*
MAGAZINE SOFT-PROFILE-WRITER HELEN STEEPLY,
3 NOVEMBER Y.D.A.U.

    'Q.'
    'Well, there are odd sorts of consolations in having somebody go progressively bats in front of your eyes, such as for example sometimes The Mad Stork would go off on things in sort of a funny way. We always thought he was funny a good bit of the time.
    'You've got to remember he came at entertainment more from an interest in lenses and light. Most arty directors I think get more abstract as they go on. With him it was the opposite. A lot of his funniest stuff was very abstract. Are those earrings real copper? Can you wear real copper?'

'Q.'

'You've got to remember that he came out of all these old artish directors that were really "ne pas à la mode" anymore by the time he broke in, not just Lang and Bresson and Deren but the anti–New Wave abstracters like Frampton, wacko Nucks like Godbout, anticonfluential directors like Dick and the Snows who not only really belonged in a quiet pink room somewhere but were also self-consciously behind the times, making all sorts of heavy art-gesture films about film and consciousness and isness and diffraction and stasis et cetera. Most extremely beautiful women I've ever met complain of getting a sort of itchy green crust when they wear real copper. So the tenure-jockeys and critics who were hailing this millennial new Orthochromatic Neorealism thing as the real new avant-garde thing were getting tenure by blasting Dick and Godbout and the flying Snow Brothers and The Stork for trying to be avant-garde, when really they were self-consciously trying to be more like *après*-garde. I never did get straight on what *Orthochromatic* means, but it was very trendy. But The Mad Stork talked a lot about intentional atavism and retrogradism and stasis. Plus the academics who hated him hated the artificial sets and the chiaroscuro lighting, which the Stork had a total fetish for weird lenses and chiaroscuro.

'After the thing about the Medusa and the Odalisque came out, and *The Joke,* and the film-establishment theory-queers were holding their noses and saying Incandenza's still mired in this late-century self-referencing unentertaining formalism and unrealistic abstraction, after a while Himself, The Stork, in his own progressively bats way, decided to get revenge. He planned a lot of it out at McLean Hospital, which's out in Belmont, which is where Himself had almost his own private reserved room, by then. He made up a genre that he considered the ultimate Neorealism and got some film-journals to run some proclamatory edictish things he wrote about it, and he got Duquette at M.I.T. and a couple other younger tenure-jockeys who were in on it to start referring and writing little articles in journals and quarterlies about it and talking at art openings and avant-garde theater and film openings, feeding it into the grapevine, hailing some new movement they called Found Drama, this supposedly ultimate Neorealism thing that they all declared was like the future of drama and cinematic art, etc.

'Because I'm thinking if you like copper stuff and little Aztec suns there's a small place down in Tempe where I know the owner and he has some incredible little copper pieces we could parp down and have you look at. My own theory is it takes an incredible natural complexion to be able to wear the baser metals, though it might just be an allergy-thing, the way some women react and some don't.'

'Q.'

'What Found Drama was — and you've got to keep in mind that Duquette and a Brandeis critic named like Posener who was in on the revenge each got a mammoth grant for this, and The Mad Stork got two smaller ones somewhere, grants, to go cross-country to graduate film programs giving turgid theoretical deadly-serious lectures on this Found Drama, and then they'd come back up home to Boston and The Stork and the couple critics would lay up drunk and invent new Found-Drama theoretical lectures and chortle and laugh till there was evidence it was time for Himself to go back to detox again.'

'Q.'

'Like a family nickname. Hal and I either called him Himself or The Sad Stork. The Moms was the first to say *Himself,* which I think is a Canadian thing. Hal mostly said Himself. God knows what Mario used to call him. Who knows. I said *Mad,* The Mad Stork.'

'Q.'

'No see there *weren't* any real cartridges or pieces of Found Drama. This was the joke. All it was was you and a couple cronies like Leith or Duquette got out a metro Boston phone book and tore a White Pages page out at random and thumbtacked it to the wall and then The Stork would throw a dart at it from across the room. At the page. And the name it hit becomes the subject of the Found Drama. And whatever happens to the protagonist with the name you hit with the dart for like the next hour and a half is the

Drama. And when the hour and a half is up, you go out and have drinks with critics who like chortlingly congratulate you on the ultimate in Neorealism.'

'Q.'

'You do whatever you want during the Drama. You're not there. Nobody knows what the name in the phone book's doing.'

'Q.'

'The joke's theory was there's no audience and no director and no stage or set because, The Mad Stork and his cronies argued, in Reality there are none of these things. And the protagonist doesn't know he's the protagonist in a Found Drama because in Reality nobody thinks they're in any sort of Drama.'

'Q.'

'Almost nobody. That's a very good point. Almost nobody. I'm going to take a chance and just tell you I'm a little bit intimidated here.'

'Q.'

'I'm worried this might sound sexist or offensive. I've been around very, very beautiful women before, but I'm not accustomed to them being really acute and sharp and politically savvy and penetrating and multilevelled and intimidatingly intelligent. I'm sorry if that sounds sexist. It's simply been my experience. I'll go ahead and simply tell you the truth and take the chance that you might think I'm some kind of stereotypical Neanderthal athlete or sexist clown.'

'Q.'

'Absolutely no, no, nothing got recorded or filmed. Reality being camera-free, being the joke I'll again underline. Nobody even knew what the guy in the phone book had been doing, nobody knew what the Drama had been. Although they liked to speculate when they'd go out after the time was up to have drinks and pretend to review how the Drama went. Himself usually imagined the guy was sitting there watching cartridges, or counting some pattern in his wallpaper, or looking out the window. It wasn't impossible maybe even the name you hit with the dart was somebody dead in the last year and the phone book hadn't caught up, and here was this guy who was dead and just a random name in a phone book and the subject of what people for a few months — until Himself couldn't keep a straight face anymore or had had enough revenge on the critics, because the critics were hailing — not just the critics in on the joke, but actual tenure-jockeys who were getting tenure to assess and dismiss and hail — they were hailing this as the ultimate in avant-garde Neorealism, and saying maybe The Stork deserved reappraisal, for a Drama with no audience and oblivious actors who might have moved away or died. A certain Mad Stork got two grants out of it and later made a lot of enemies because he refused to give them back after the hoax was like unveiled. The whole thing was kind of bats. He spread the grant money for Found Drama around a couple of local improvisation companies. It's not like he kept the money. It's not like he needed it. I think he especially liked the idea that the star of the show might have already moved away or recently died and there was no way to know.'

146. See for example Incandenza's first narrative collaboration w/ Infernatron-Canada, the animated *Pre-Nuptial Agreement of Heaven and Hell,* made at the acknowledged height of his anticonfluential period — B.S. Private Release, L.M.P.

147. The festivity here being due largely to the fact that both he and Gerhardt Schtitt returned from putting on little E.T.A. presentations at various tennis clubs too late to have been informed about the degenerative Eschaton free-for-all and serious Lord-, Ingersoll-, and Penn-injuries, both trainer Barry Loach and prorector Rik Dunkel having told Avril, and Schtitt to be told by whichever of Nwangi and deLint first works up the pluck, and the issue of telling Tavis being as would be S.O.P. left up to Avril, who will — because Tavis has already lost a certain amount of sleep preparing emotionally and rhetorically for the impending arrival of putative *Moment* journalist 'Helen' Steeply, whom he's been

convinced to let onto the grounds by Avril's argument that the *Moment* office promises the profile's subject and inevitable hype involve only an E.T.A. alumnus (Avril neglected to tell Tavis she was pretty sure it was Orin) and that a certain amount of soft-news-publicity for E.T.A.-qua-institution couldn't hurt in either the fundraising- or the recruiting-goodwill department — who will almost certainly wait and tell Tavis (who's in far too festive a mood to notice three or four younger kids ominously absent from the supper and gala) in the morning, if the poor man's to have a chance at any real sleep at all (also giving Avril time to figure out how upperclass heads can roll, as of course they must, given chaos and season-ending injuries under the direct gaze of designated Big Buddies, without those heads including that of Hal, who — unlike, thank God, John — was identified at the scene with that Pemulis person). Hal can tell just by the dining hall's emotional gestalt that neither Schtitt nor Tavis knows about the Eschaton, but the Moms is next to impossible to read, and Hal won't know whether she's been told of the debacle until he is able to pry Mario away from Anton ('The Boogerman') Doucette and get the Moms-skinny right from Booboo direct, after the film.

148. Troeltsch wears an InterLace Sports baseball cap, and Keith Freer a two-horned operatic Viking helmet along with his leather vest, and Fran Unwin a fez, and fierce little Josh Gopnik the white beanie with the dirty cart-wheel-track across it from this afternoon's debacle. Tex Watson wears a tan Stetson with a really high crown, and little Tina Echt an outlandishly large plaid beret that covers half her little head, the Vaught twins a freakish bowler with two domes and one brim, Stephan Wagenknecht a plastic sallet — this is just scanning at random; the headwear goes on and on, a whole topography of hats — and Carol Spodek a painter's cap with the name of a paint company, and Bernadette Longley a calpac that obstructs the view of people behind her. Duncan van Slack in a harquebus w/ buckle. Should probably also mention Avril's wearing a Fukoama microfiltration mask, it being way too early in the day for supper for her anyway. Ortho Stice wears a calotte and the U.S.S. Millicent Kent a slanted noir-style fedora and Tall Paul Shaw, way in back, a conquistadorial helmet and escudo, and Mary Esther Thode a plain piece of cardboard propped on her head that says HAT. Idris Arslanian's spectacular bearskin shako is held in place with a chinstrap.

149. (I.e. silk-suited Vocalists snapping their fingers and telling their casino audiences they were beautiful human beings and but when it comes time to actually start crooning the Vocalists' lips move but nothing Velvety emerges, all sound withheld, a Job Action, rendered even more chilling by the skill with which the Frankies and Tonies lip-synch to utter silence — and the way the beautiful casino audiences, hit someplace they lived, somehow, clearly, responded with near-psychotic feelings of deprivation and abandonment, became a mob, almost tore lounges down, upended little round tables, threw free ice-intensive drinks, audiences in their well-heeled majority behaving like dysfunctional or inadequately nurtured children.)

150. The years right around the millennium being a terrible U.S. time for waste, then, ozone-wise and landfill-wise and shoddily-disposed-of-dioxins-wise, w/ DT-cycle annular fusion at the stage where they had the generating-massive-amounts-of-high-R-waste part down a lot more pat than the consuming-the-waste-in-a-nuclear-process-whose-own-waste-was-the-fuel-for-the-first-waste-intensive-phase-of-the-circle-of-reactions part.

151. Actual term employed is *downer-type*.

152. A lightless and eye-averted late-night weight room being not exactly a last-name type of place.

153. Sometimes it's as straightforward as directing someone to give her fiancé the roundhouse forehand slap she's been secretly aching to give him ever since he'd once teased her about putting some Band-Aids on those insect bites on her chest.

154. = the anticonfluental *Cage III — Free Show;* q.v. Note 24 *supra.*

155. The Medusa wears a kind of chain-mail backless evening gown and Hellenic sandals, the Odalisque a Merry Widow.

156. Mario's speculative puppet-show comes down maybe a little hard on the implication that former O.C.D.-support-group-sponsor and later Clean U.S. Party campaign manager and now O.U.S. Chief Rodney P. Tine is the real dark force behind Reconfiguration and New England's de-mapping and the transfer of the Great Concavity, that Johnny Gentle, Famous Crooner was and remains a slightly unbent but basically genial and befuddled figurehead, content mostly to twirl his mike and immolate his epidermis so long as his office is clean and his food's pre-tasted, and that it's actually been Tine behind C.U.S.P.'s geopolitical anality and Experialism, and that Tine was essentially pulling Gentle's strings all through the Concavity Cabinet and subsequent Reconfiguration and mass relocation. This is, in point of fact, simply one theory and direction for finger-pointing, and tends to founder on the unexplained issue of just what would motivate Tine to undertake all this anyway, since his own O.C.D. has been documented to be ruminative rather than hygienic, not to mention the fact that he's hopelessly smitten with the Québecer Luria P——. J. O. Incandenza's own *ONANtiad,* being an adult production, was considerably more restrained and ambiguous on the whole Tine-as-dark-force issue.

157. An oblique little in-tribute from Mario to the Moms, at which line every year Avril at the Headmaster's Table takes off the witch's hat and holds it by the brim and whips it around in an enthused circle three times over her head.

158. The umpires on the U.S. junior tour tend to be retired high-school principals whose only renumeration is the chance to exercise again some slight authority over the young.

159. Clipperton eventually perfecting the toss-with-the-same-hand-you-serve-with maneuver pioneered by South African doubles specialist Colin van der Hingle after a hideous turbo-prop-charter-aircraft-propeller accident took off his right arm, ear, and sideburn in only the second year of his Show career, in Durban.

160. Certain other and doubtless really disturbing footage of Clipperton's suicide still exists, having — with perhaps half a dozen other emotionally or professionally sensitive cartridge-Masters — been designated Unviewable by testatory codicil and, as far as either Hal or Orin knows, enclosed in some sort of vault-apparatus that only Himself's attorneys and maybe Avril have access to. As far as can be determined, only those lawyers, Avril, Disney Leith, and perhaps Mario know that the cartridges were, in fact, along with his case of special lenses, interred right there with J. O. Incandenza's dead body[a] — yickily enough — there having been room in the bronze casket only because Incandenza's extreme height dictated a casket-size that his thin physique didn't nearly fill the width and depth of.

> a. (in the Mondragon-family-plot area of Le Cimetière du St. Adalbert in the now overlush potato-growing country off Provincial Autoroute 204 in L'Islet Province, Québec, just over the border from what is now the eastern Concavity, such that the funeral had to be delayed and then rushed to be fit in between annulation-cycles)

161. The other having been that predictive call for the catatonic hero, also for Ogilvie's Entertainment 2-termer.

162. Every Nielsen respondent seemed to respond with especial neural repulsion to one or another particular portrait. There was one of a woman with every carpenter's tool known to God exiting her face. One of a young male with a spear of scarlet light through the right temple and coming clear out the other side. A woman with her crown between the incisors of some sort of shark so huge it passes from view past the frame. A grandmotherly type with roses, human hands, a pencil, and other lush-type flora all coming

serpentine out of her open skull's top. A head coming out in a long string from a throttled tube of paste; a Talmudic scholar bearded in needles; a Baconian pope with his hat on fire. Three or four dental ones that sent people scrambling to the bathroom to floss themselves bloody. The painting that had particularly nailed nine-year-old Hal and had had him popping Nunhagen compulsively until his ears started ringing and didn't stop for almost a week had been of a deeply parlor-tanned and vaguely familiar upscale male, a disembodied fist yanking a handful of brains out of the guy's left ear while the guy's overhealthy face, like most of the ad's faces, wears a queer look of intense unhappy concentration, one more of like brooding than conventionally expressive of pain.

163. NoCoat Inc. ended up occupying the #346 spot vacated by Hoechst's CBS, Hal noted with surprisingly little irony.

164. Granted that this stuff is all grossly simplified in Hal's ephebic account; Lace-Forché and Veals are in fact transcendent geniuses of a particularly complex right-time-and-place sort, and their appeals to an American ideology committed to the *appearance of freedom* almost unanalyzably compelling.

165. Granted, *pace* critics, this was partly to forestall A.C.D.C.'s apellate-court claims that InterLace was basically hopping up and down on the B.S. 1890 Sherman Act with spike heels.

166. 'Reduced Instruct-Set Computers,' descendents of the IBM/Apple 'Power PCs,' with mainframe-caliber response-time and .25 terabytes of DRAM and numerous expansion-slots for various killer apps.

167. A couple of Incandenza's more accessible early documentaries were bought by Inter-Lace on a distribution-factored contingency basis, but except for a flat PBS-ish one on the lay priciples of DT-annulation they never brought Meniscus/Latrodectus more than a fraction of the interest on the interest from Himself's rearview-mirror fortune. InterLace ended up optioning rights to only a couple of his higherbrow productions for its 'Howls from the Margin' low-volume-expectation product-line during Himself's lifetime; the bulk of his stuff didn't make any ILT menus until after his untimely death.

168. It didn't do J. Gentle F.C.'s original grass-roots-intensive campaign a whole lot of good around ultra-liberal Enfield that one of his earliest sign-carrying faithful had been E.T.A.'s own Gerhardt Schtitt, who politically listed so far to starboard that even people without watches looked at their watches and referred vaguely to just-recalled appointments whenever Schtitt's eyes got a certain particular navy-blue cast and he uttered any one of such terms as *America, decadence, State,* or *Law*; but Mario I. was pretty much the only one clued in to the fact that Schtitt's attraction to Gentle had more to do with Schtitt's take on tennis than anything else: the Coach was swept away with the athleto-Wagnerian implications of Gentle's proposals for waste, this business of sending from yourself what you hope will not return.

169. Triaminotetralin, a synthesized hallucinogen whose high transdermal bioavailability makes it a popular ingredient in the 'Happy Patches' so prevalent in the American West and Southwest of Subsidized Time — *Pharmochemical Quarterly* 17, 18 (Spring, Year of the Trial-Size Dove Bar) provides a detailed account of the synthesis and transdermal physiochemistry of aminotetralins in general.

170. Québecois French: 'working up steam.'

171. 'Homestyle. Ready to Serve.'

172. 'Pursuit of happiness.'

173. Q.v. Note 304 *sub*.

174. 'Absolutely no bonking,' presumably.

175. The both-hands-full logistics of which are hard to envision, but realism wasn't really the point of the image for the bitter Brigade boys.

176. It's also where Mario's most derivative of Himself, whose own *ONANtiad* was more centrally concerned with doomed high-office claymation romance than with political comment, though the love thing in Incandenza Sr.'s film had concerned not Tine and a Québecois fatale but an alleged doomed and unconsummated affair between President J. Gentle and the equally hygiene-and-germ-obsessed wife of Canada's 'Minister of Environment and Resource-Development Enterprises,' the affair presented as doomed and unconsummated because the Minister hires a malevolent young Canadian *Candida albicans* specialist to induce in his wife a severe and more or less permanent yeast infection, driving both wife and Gentle to ardent-desire-v.-hygienic-neurosis breakdowns during which the wife throws herself across the tracks in front of a Québecois bullet-train and Gentle decides to exact his revenge on a macrocartographic scale. The *ONANtiad* was not Himself's strongest effort by a long shot, and pretty much everybody around E.T.A. agrees that Mario's own Reconfiguration-explanation-parody is funnier and more accessible than Himself's, if also a bit heavier-handed.

177. The officially spun term for making Canada take U.S. terrain and letting us dump pretty much everything we don't want onto it is *Territorial Reconfiguration*. *Great Concavity* and *Grand Convexité* are more like U.S./Canadian street argot that got adopted and genericized by the media.

178. A more abstract but truer epigram that White Flaggers with a lot of sober time sometimes change this to goes something like: 'Don't worry about getting in touch with your feelings, they'll get in touch with you.'

179. Presumably North Shore AA meetings, but Gately never recollects hearing the word *AA;* all he remembers from the time is just 'Meetings' and a Diagnosis he'd construed as chivalric.

180. But Avril had gotten former M.I.T. #1 Men's Singles Corbett Thorp to drive Mario down to V.F. Rickey's cerebral Student Union thing, where Thorp used his old student I.D. (thumb over expiration date) to get them past the Security lady at the Rectus Bulbi and down to the YYY studio's freezing pink basement, where the only person who didn't talk like an angry cartoon character, a severely carbuncular man at the engineer's board, would by way of comment point only at a tripartite onionskin screen that stood folded beneath a handless wall-clock, possibly signifying that no hiatus could be all that long if the absent party hadn't taken her trusty screen. Mario hadn't had any idea M.P.'d used a screen, on-air. That's when he'd gotten agitated.

181. Corbett Thorp's sobriquet among the less kind kids is 'Th-th-th-th.'

182. Known also sometimes as 'Pukers.'

183. The dull-metal Kenkle & Brandt kind, not the white plastic industrial-solvent buckets associated with Eschaton and yesterday's debacle.

184. Moving fast in one direction and having the ball hit someplace behind you and having to try to stop and reverse direction very quickly is known also as a 'wrong-foot' or '*contre-pied,*' and it results in a fair number of injuries to junior knees and ankles; ironically enough it's Hal, since the explosion, who's known as the real E.T.A. master of placement and opponent-yanking-around and the old *contre-pied*. Also a quick insertion that Dennis van der Meer, father of Side-to-Sides, was a Dutch immigrant low-level pro who became a major pro coach and tennis-education-theory guru, on the same level with like a Harry Hopman or Vic Braden.

185. Stice's legendarily dysfunctional parents are in Kansas, but he's got two vaguely lesbianic maiden aunts or great-aunts or something up in Chelsea who keep bringing him foods the staff won't let him eat.

186. Serious juniors never pick up tennis balls with their hands. Males tend to bend down and dribble the balls up with the face of their stick; there are various little substyles of this. Females and some younger males less into bending stand and trap the ball between their shoe and racquet and bring their foot up in a quick little twitch, the stick bringing the ball up with it. Males who do this trap the ball against the inside of the shoe, while females trap the ball against the outside of the shoe, which looks a bit more feminine. Reverse-snobbism at E.T.A. has never reached the point of people bending way down and picking balls up manually, which, like wearing a visor, is regarded as the true sign of the novice or hack.

187. N.b.: Europeans and Australians refer to overheads as 'overhands,' while South Africans sometimes also call them 'pointers.'

188. The budget doesn't allow for communal suppers on weekends, and the weekly menu has below SATR and SUND the word *forage,* which with a certain percentage of this fall's residents ends up being literal.

189. Expanding where appropriate on Note 12: Demerol is meperidine hydrochloride, a Schedule C-II synthetic narcotic, available from Sanofi Winthrop Laboratories in banana-flavored syrup; 25, 50, 75, and 100 mg./ml. cartridge-needle units; and (most popular w/ D.W.G.) the 50 and 100 mg. tablets known up on the Shore as Pebbles and Bam-Bam, respectively. (D&D of course means Drunk and Disorderly, and P.D. and P.O. respectively mean Public Defender and Probation Officer or 'Probie,' by the way.)

190. If somebody dies during the commission of a felony, even from so much as a defective pacemaker or a lightning bolt, the felon's facing Murder-2 and unbargainable time, at least in MA, a ghastly statutory provision as far as most active drug addicts are concerned, since even though they're not violence-oriented, efficiency and safety-consciousness are not exactly hallmarks of addiction-motivated crimes, which tend to be impulsive and fuzzily thought out at best.

191. Also known as a case being 'Blue-Filed,' meaning put in a kind of judicial limbo for a specified period, and reopenable ('Red-Filed') at any time P.O.s and Boards decide the defendant isn't making 'satisfactory progress.'

192. She didn't literally say *shitstorm.*

193. Gately didn't get any of this from Pat Montesian; it's mostly like Ennet House mythology, with some hard facts from Gene M. and Calvin Thrust, both of whom think Pat M. just about hung the moon.

194. A totally different thing than Volkmann's contracture (cf. Note 115).

195. Which he had to make a fucking Financial Amend to have fixed, which luckily semi-Crocodile Sven R. was a refinisher and voluntarily fixed the crack with some weird fake-wood-resin, so Gately only had to pay for the tube of fake-wood-resin instead of a whole new institutional table.

196. E.g. 'Kid, sobriety's like a hard-on: the minute you get it, you want to fuck with it'; they'd rattle this kind of stuff off; they had a million of them.

197. (Never yet having checked the side of a box of pasta for possible directions.)

198. Project MK-Ultra, U.S.-C.I.A. inception 4/3/B.S.53: 'The central activity of the MK-Ultra program was conducting and funding brainwashing experimentation with dangerous drugs and other techniques [*sic*] performed on persons who were not volunteers by

C.I.A. Technical Service Division employees, agents, and contractors.' — Civil Action #80-3163, *Orlikow et al. v. United States of America*, B.S. 1980.

199. Alprazolam, Upjohn Inc.'s big hat-throw into the benzodiazepine ring, only Schedule C-IV but wickedly dependence-producing, w/ severe unpleasant abrupt-withdrawal penalties.

200. Ennet House near-alumnus Chandler Foss's analysis, which you can bet was developed outside Gately's earshot.

201. Another vestige: Gately still always automatically notices bars and mesh, the foil and little magnetic contacts of residential alarms, plunger-buttons on the inside of hinges, etc.

202. Local argot for Storrow Drive, which runs along the Charles from the Back Bay out to Alewife, with multiple lanes and Escherian signs and On- and Off-ramps within car-lengths of each other and no speed limit and sudden forks and the overall driving experience so forehead-drenching it's in the metro Police Union's contract they don't have to go anywhere near it.

203. Whether English misspelling or Québecois solecism, *sic*.

204. Jolly-Jolt® hand-buzzers, Whoopi-Daisy® (celebrity-endorsed) cushions, Blammo® cigars, Oh, Waiter® plastic-ice-cubes-w/-fly, I See London!® X-ray specs, etc. usually just trucked over, along w/ the Saprogenic Greetings® treacly greeting and postcards, from the Waltham facilities of Acmé Inc., a.k.a. 'The Acmé Family of Gags 'N Notions, Pre-Packaged Emotions, Jokes and Surprises and Wacky Disguises,' at a substantial and politically motivated discount, seeing that the company's owned by the Québec-sympathetic shadowy Albertan mogul who'd been such a force in the anti-broadcast A.C.D.C., and who over a decade back had exploited the then-U.S.-owned then-Acme's severe PR and cash-flow problems right after the serial Blammo Cigar tragedies to move in and hostile t/o the firm for about 30% of its real worth.

205. Unknown to the hapless Antitois, this doesn't mean they're necessarily blank. Copy-Capable cartridges, a.k.a. Masters, require a 585-r.p.m.-drive viewer or TP to run, and on a conventional 450-drive decline to give off so much as static, appearing rather empty and blank. Q.v. here Note 301 *sub*.

206. Being out of the sociolinguistic loop, L.A. has no way of knowing that 'To hear the squeak' is itself the very darkest of contemporary Canada's euphemisms for sudden and violent de-mapping.

207. L.A. having a pretty good intuition that the lone communicable '*va chier, putain!*' wouldn't be a good idea in this context.

208. From Ch. 16, 'The Awakening of My Interest in Annular Systems,' in *The Chill of Inspiration: Spontaneous Reminiscences by Seventeen Pioneers of DT-Cycle Lithiumized Annular Fusion,* ed. Prof. Dr. Günther Sperber, Institut für Neutronenphysik und Reaktortechnik, Kernforschungszentrum Karlsruhe, U.R.G., available in English in ferociously expensive hardcover only, © Y.T.M.P. from Springer-Verlag Wien NNY.

209. E.g.: Ted Schacht adjusting his wristbands and sash. Carol Spodek stretching for a volley at net, her whole body distended, face grim and full of cords. An old one of Marlon Bain at the follow-through of a big forehand, a corona of sweat shimmering around him, his bigger arm crossed across his throat. Ortho Stice doing a handstand. Yardguard gliding down through a low backhand. Wayne this summer sliding on Rome's fine clay, a red cloud hiding everything below the knees. Pemulis and Stice standing cross-armed against desert light and a fence. Shaw without his silly wispy pseudo-Newcombe mustache. The photos have been looked at so often they're pale. Hal at the height of his toss, knees more

bent than he'd like. Wayne holding up a silver plate. The European-contingent males three summers past all lined up outside a square van with its steering wheel on the wrong side, somebody with either two or three fingers held up over Axford's head. Schtitt addressing kids you can only see the backs of. Todd Possalthwaite shaking a small black kid's hand at net. Troeltsch pretending to interview Felicity Zweig. The Vaught twins sharing a foot-long frank at a stand at the Bronx's U.S. Jr. Open. Todd Possalthwaite at the net with a P.W.T.A. kid. Every muscle in Amy Wingo's front leg ridged as she gets a little ahead of herself on a backhand. On and on. They're not in a straight line; they're more like chaotically placed. Heath Pearson, former tow-truck shareholder, now at Pepperdine, facing away from the camera, under Lung-light, running. The Palmer Academy courts looking cheesy in the heat. A lot of the photos are stills from Mario. Peter Beak falling nastily after a stretch-volley, both feet off what looks like Longwood's synthetic grass. The photos surrounded by locationless clouds and sky. Freer in the bleachers at Brisbane in thongs and a tank-top, giving the camera a peace-sign. The Lung in mid-assembly with Pearson and Penn and Vandervoort and Mackey and the rest of that year's seniors out in the pavilion's webbed chairs, feet up in the cold, kibbitzing Hal and Schacht and the other kids lugging parts. One of Mrs. Clarke's cooks in a hairnet mixing something with an arm-sized pestle in a bowl she has to tilt to hold. None of Mario or Orin. A battalion of kids in sweats doing sprints up the hill in deep snow, two or three well behind and ominously bent over. Some lighter-blue rectangles where pictures have been taken down and not yet replaced. A shirtless Freer playing microtennis with Lori Clow. A close-up of bespectacled Gretchen Holt staring in disbelief at a linesman's call. Wayne and a Manitoban in T-shirts with leaves on them, hands over their hearts, facing north. Kent Blott with a horrified boomerang mouth and his nose a protrusion in the supporter fit over his ears and nose and Traub and Lord collapsing around him in either hilarity or horror. Hal and Wayne at the net in doubles, both leaning way over left like the whole court's tilted.

210. Hal and Mario have long since had to accept[a] the fact that Avril, at 50+, is still endocrinologically compelling to males.

    a. 'Accept' isn't the same as 'be crazy about,' of course.

211. As with the neuro-gastric thing, only Ted Schacht and Hal know that Pemulis's deepest dread is of academic or disciplinary expulsion and ejection, of having to schlepp back down Comm. Ave. into blue-collar Allston diploma- and ticket-outless, and now in his final E.T.A. year the dread's increased many-fold, and is one reason Pemulis takes such elaborate precautions in all extracurriculars — making a Substance-customer explicitly suborn him, etc. — and is why Hal and Schacht presented him on his last birthday with the poster over Pemulis's room's console that has a careworn large-crowned King sitting on his throne stroking his chin and brooding, with the caption: YES, I'M PARANOID — BUT AM I PARANOID *ENOUGH*?

212. Though it's unmentioned, everyone in the waiting room except Ann Kittenplan is keenly aware that Lord and Postal Weight are Pemulis's charges, Penn and Ingersoll Axhandle's; plus that neither Struck nor Troeltsch seems to have been summoned for potential discipline.

213. Since tennis courts are laid side to side and played on by hard-hitting but fallible humans, errant shots are always going off sticks' frames and net-posts and even fences and bouncing and rolling into other people's territory. In starting at usually the quarter-final rounds of serious tournaments there are ballboys to retrieve them. In early rounds and practice, though, the delicate etiquette is that you suspend play and get other people's balls for them, if they come rolling across, and shoot them back over to the court of origin. The way to signal for this sort of help is to yell 'Sorry!' or 'A little help on Three?' or something. But both Hal and Axford seem constitutionally incapable of doing this, asking for help with errant balls. They both have to hold everything and go and run all the

way over to some other court, halting at each intervening court to wait for a point to be finished, to get their own balls. It's a curious inability to request aid that no amount of negative reinforcement from Tex Watson or Aubrey deLint can seem to correct.

214. Where it's a non-overhead run-back-to-the-baseline-after-an-offensive-lob-then-run-all-the-way-back-up-and-tap-the-netcord-with-your-stick-just-as-Nwangi-or-Thode-hits-another-offensive-lob-over-your-head-you-have-to-run-back-and-get-successfully-back-or-they-pile-extra-lobs-onto-your-regular-allotment pure pain-fest.

215. A Clipperton-level legend involves the now long-gone little E.T.A. who in Y.W.-Q.M.D. had called MA's Department of Social Services and characterized disciplinary Pukers as child abuse, resulting in the appearance at the portcullis of two stitchy-mouthed and humorless D.S.S.-ladies who hung creepily around all day and required Schtitt's actually confining Aubrey deLint to his room, so purply furious was deLint with the kid who'd dropped the dime.

216. No clue.

217. Hal had missed out on the soft grass, clay, and Har-Tru surfaces of the Jr. Slams, because a singular disadvantage of attending a North American academy is that O.N.A.N.T.A. rules for Jr. Slams permit just one entrant per academy in each age-division, and John Wayne got the nods.

218. The late J. O. Incandenza's Meniscus Optical Products Ltd.'s development of those weird wide-angle rear-view mirrors on the sides of automobiles that so diminish the cars behind you that federal statute requires them to have printed right on the glass that Objects In Mirror Are Closer Than They Appear, which little imprints Incandenza found so disconcerting that he was kind of shocked when U.S. automakers and importers bought rights on the mirrors, way back, for Incandenza's first unsettling entrepreneurial payday — E.T.A.s like to postulate that the mirrors had been inspired by the always-foreshortened Charles Tavis.

219. Extremely annoying host of InterLace Spontaneous-Dissemm. children's program.

220. ® CardioMed Fitness Products, a fourth-generation StairMasterish thing except set more to resemble a down-escalator somehow dickied to a sadistically high number of r.p.m.s, so that the exerciser has to sort of run climbing for his life to avoid getting hurled backwards all the way across the office by the machine, which is what accounts for the big square weight-room floor-mat attached to the cleared expanse of office wall opposite the rear of the machine, which Tavis had moved up to from his StairMaster after a frightening cholesterol-count report, and had had kind of a tricky time with at first, once requiring a back-brace.

221. The Satellite pro Hal'd gotten a set from, a barrel-chested Latvian who thought Hal's name was *All*.

222. N.b. again that Marathe's native tongue is not good old contemporary idiomatic Parisio/European French but cont. id. Québecois French, which is about on a par with Basque in terms of difficulty, being full of weird idioms and having both inflected and uninflected grammatical features, an inbred and obstreperous dialect, and which in fact Steeply barely got an 'Acceptable' in, in U.S.O. technical-interview training in Vienna / Falls Church VA, and which does not admit of easy coeval expression in English.

223. Viz. at the allusion to the supposed *samizdateur*'s anticonfluential and meta-entertainmentish and hologram-intensive Medusa-v.-Odalisque thing, which in fact the play-within-film fight-scene part can be broken down into a series of what are called 'Fast Fourier Transforms,' though what the hell 'ALGOL' is is anybody's guess, unless it's not

an acronym but some actual Québecois term, '*l'algol,*' which if so it isn't in any dictionaries or on-line lexical sources anywhere in the 2nd or 3rd IL/IN Grid.

224. Q.v. William James on '. . . that latent process of unconscious preparation often preceding a sudden awakening to the fact that the mischief is irretrievably done,' the line that actually snapped Lenz to what he was up to when he chanced to read it in a huge large-print edition he'd found behind a bookshelf along the north wall of the Ennet living room of something he'd called *The Principles of Psychology with The Gifford Lectures on Natural Religion,* by William James (obviously), available in EZC large-font print from Microsoft/NAL–Random House–Ticknor, Fields, Little, Brown and Co., © Y.T.M.P., a volume that's come to mean a great deal to Lenz.

225. ® The Mobil Chemical Co.'s Consumer Products Branch's Plastics Division, Pittsford NNY.

226. ® Ibid.

227. A.k.a. Haloperidol, McNeil Pharmaceutical, 5 mg./ml. pre-filled syringes: picture several cups of Celestial Seasonings' Cinnamon Soother tea followed by a lead-filled sap across the back of the skull.

228. National Security Agency, absorbed w/ A.T.F. and D.E.A., C.I.A. and O.N.R. and Secret Service into the ambit of the Office of Unspecified Services.

229. The A.A.O.A.A., Unspecified Services' most elite and least specific division, which on Hugh Steeply's latest field-assignment is paying his salary, though his checks and alimony's garnishment are routed through something called the 'Foundation for Continental Freedom,' which one fervently hopes is a shell/dummy.

230. Charlestown/Southie street term for meters.

231. Powdered vitamin B_{12}, convincingly bitter and talc-textured, which Lenz has always preferred B_{12} to Manitol as a cut because Manitol gives him this allergic thing where he got very tiny red bumps with weird pale caps on his fingertips.

232. Hydrolysis is the metabolic process by which organic cocaine's broken down into benzoylecgonine, methanol, ecgonine, and benzoic acid, and one reason not everybody is wired to enjoy Crosbulation is that the process is essentially toxic and can yield unpleasant neurosomatic fallout in certain systems: e.g. in Don Gately's neurosystem, spider angiomas and a tendency to pluck at the skin on the backs of his hands, due to which tendency he's always loathed and hated coke and most cokeheads; in Bruce Green's system, binocular nystagmus and a walloping depression even while the coke-high's still on that accounts for the tendency toward fits of weeping with his nystagmic face hidden in the crook of his big right arm; in Ken Erdedy an unstoppable rhinorrhagia that sent him to the Emergency Room both times he ever did cocaine; in Kate Gompert blepharospecticity and now instant cerebral hemorrhage because she's on Parnate, an M.A.O.-inhibiting antidepressant; in Emil Minty a ballism so out-of-control he snorted Bing only once. Hemispasms of the oral labia are a common effect of coke-hydrolysis, one mild enough so that people can get them and still enjoy Bing very much; the spasming can range from a mild gnawing/writhing affect in Lenz, Thrale, Cortilyu, and Foss to an alternating series of Edvard Munch–Jimmy Carter–Paliacci–Mick Jagger–like expressive contortions so severe that everyone in a room except for them is embarrassed. In former cokehead Calvin Thrust, hydrolysis had caused a priapism that led directly to his early choice of career. Randy Lenz also gets nystagmus, but of the right eye only, as well as vascular constriction, diuresis extremus, phosphenism, compulsive tooth-grinding, megalomania, phobophobia, euphoric recall, delusions of persecution and/or homicidal envy, sociosis, postnasal drip, a mild priapism that makes the diuresis a dicey and gymnastic affair, occasional acne rosea and/or rhinophyma, and — especially if there's synergism from almost a whole pack of

filterless Winstons and four cups of nipple-hardeningly strong and alkaline B.Y.P. coffee — confabulation concurrent with a manic garrulousness sufficient to cause lingual tendinitis, pulmonary phasece, and a complete inability to send from his presence anyone who seems at all willing to listen to him.

233. A.k.a. lignocaine, xylocaine-L, a diethylamino-oxylidide compound used as a dental and maxillofacial anesthetic, the world's best Bing-cut because it numbs and produces a bitter drip just like the Bingster, and also even temporarily heightens the rush of I.V. coke, though if it's 'based it tastes nothing like oxidized coke, and it's also more expensive than Manitol or B_{12} and harder to get because it's prescription, meaning the orthodontist was a very popular fellow with dealers indeed.

234.

TRANSCRIPT-FRAGMENTS FROM INTERVIEW SERIES FOR
PUTATIVE *MOMENT* MAGAZINE SOFT PROFILE ON PHOENIX
CARDINAL PROFESSIONAL PUNTER O. J. INCANDENZA,
BY PUTATIVE *MOMENT* MAGAZINE SOFT-PROFILE WRITER
HELEN STEEPLY — NOVEMBER Y.D.A.U.

'I'm not going to talk about why I don't talk to the Moms anymore.'
'Q.'
'Or The Mad Stork's adventures in the mental-health community, either.'
'Q.'
'We're not off to a good start here, ma'am, no matter how lovely you're looking in that pantsuit.'
'Q.'
'Because the question doesn't mean anything is why. *Insane* is just like a catch-term, it doesn't describe anything, it isn't a reason for anything. The Stork was a full-blown demented alcoholic for the last three years of his life, and he put his head in the microwave, and I think just in terms of unpleasantness you'd have to be sort of insane to kill yourself in such a painful way. So but was he insane. In the last five years of his life he put together a tennis academy and got together a national-caliber coaching staff and U.S.T.A. accreditation and sanction and multi-Grid funding and set up the start of an endowment for E.T.A., and also came up with that new kind of window glass that doesn't fog or smudge from people touching it or breathing on it and drawing little finger-oil faces on it, then sold it to Mitsubishi, and also managed the revenues from all his previous patents, plus of course drank himself blind on a daily basis and then needed at least two hours to sit there naked under a scratchy blanket and shake, and went around impersonating various kinds of health-care professionals during the periods he believed he was a health-care professional, from when he had the delirium-tremen-type career delusions, and *in his spare time* made in-depth documentaries and a dozen art-films that people are still writing doctoral theses on. So was he insane? It's true, the *New Yorker* guy, the film guy who replaced the guy who replaced Rafferty, what was his name, it's true he kept saying the films were like the planet's most psychotic psyche working out its shit right there on the screen and asking you to pay to watch him. But you have to remember that that guy got third-degree burned by the whole Found Drama scam. That guy was one of the high-caliber critics who said in print that here Incandenza had put drama ahead three or four leaps in one visionary leap, and after The Stork finally couldn't keep a straight face anymore and spilled the beans on NPR radio during a 'Fresh Air' dramaturgy-panel the *New Yorker* guy dropped from critical sight for like a year and then when he came back he had it in for Himself in a very big way, which is understandable.'
'Q.'
'What I started to say is if quote unquote sources you cannot name say the reason I'm not in contact is I claim the Moms is insane, well, what is *insane* supposed to mean. Do I

trust her I do not. Do I want to be in association with her in any way — that is a neg. Do I think she's irretrievably bats? One of her best friends is the E.T.A. counselor, Rusk, with doctorates in both Gender and Deviance. Does she think the Moms is bats?'

'Q.'

'The criteria I was analogizing to The Stork is does the Moms function. And the Moms functions and then some. The Moms careers through the day turboed and in fifth gear. You've got the assorted Deaning at E.T.A. You've got the full teaching load there. You've got accreditation reports and structuring both quadrivium and trivium three years ahead of time at the start of every year. You've got writing prescriptive linguistics books that come out every thirty-six months so you could set your watch by them. You've got grammatical conferences and conventions, which she doesn't leave the grounds ever anymore but she's there videophonically rain or shine for them all. You've got the Militant Grammarians of Massachusetts, which she co-founded with a couple quote cherished academic friends, also bats, where the M.G.M.s for instance go around to Mass. supermarkets and dun the manager if the Express Checkout sign says 10 ITEMS OR LESS instead of OR FEWER and so on. The year before The Mad Stork's death the Orange Crush people had an ad on billboards and little magazine-fall-out cards that said CRUSH: WITH A TASTE THAT'S ALL IT'S OWN, with like a possessive IT'S, and I swear the M.G.M. squad lost their minds; the Moms spent five weeks going back and forth to NNY City, organized two different rallies on Madison Avenue that got very ugly, acted as her own attorney in the suit the Crush people brought, never slept, never once slept, lived on cigarettes and salad, huge salads always consumed very late at night, the Moms has a thing about never eating until it's late.'

'Q.'

'Apparently it's the noise, she can't take urban noise, she says, is why Hallie says she hasn't set glass-slipper-one off the Grounds in — you'd have to ask Hallie. The Volvo was already up on blocks when I was at college downtown. But I know she went to The Stork's funeral, which was off the grounds. Now she's got a tri-modem and videophony out the bazoo, though she'd never use a Tableau, I know.'

'Q.'

'Well it's been pretty obvious since early on out in Weston the Moms has O.C.D. Obsessive-Compulsive Disorder. The only reason she's never been diagnosed or treated for it is that in her the Disorder doesn't prevent her from functioning. It all seems to come back to functioning. Traversion is character, according to Schtitt. One guy I was close to at E.T.A. for years developed the kind of impairing O.C.D. where you need treatment — Bain wasted huge amounts of time on all these countless rituals of washing, cleaning, checking things, walking, had to have a T-square on the court to make sure all the strings on his stick were intersecting at 90°, could only go through a doorway if he'd felt all around the frame of the doorway by hand, checking the frame for God knows what, and then was totally unable to trust his senses and always had to recheck the doorway he'd just checked. We had to physically carry Bain out of the locker room, before tournaments. Actually we've been close all our lives, notwithstanding that Marlon Bain is the single sweatiest human being you'd ever want to get within a click of. I think the O.C.D. might have started as a result of the compulsive sweat, which the sweat itself started after his parents were killed in a grotesque freak accident, Bain's. Unless the strain of the constant rituals and fussing itself exaculates the perspiring. The Stork used Marlon in Death in Scarsdale, if you want to see way more than you want to know about perspiration. But the E.T.A. staff indulged Bain's pathology about doorways because Schtitt's own mentor had been pathologically devoted to this idea that you are what you walk between. It's so nice to be able to end a sentence with a preposition when it's easier. Jesus I'm thinking usage again. This is why I avoid the topic of the Moms. The whole topic starts to infect me. It takes me days to clean myself out of it. Traversion being character according to Schtitt. It takes a certain type of woman to look that good in a pantsuit, I think. I've always —'

'Q.'

'I think the point being that with actual clinical Obsessive-Compulsive Disorder I had to watch much of my ex-doubles partner's life grind to a halt because it'd take him three hours to shower and then another two to get out through the shower door. He was in this sort of paralysis of compulsive motions that didn't serve any kind of function. The Moms, on the other hand, can function with the compulsions because she's also compulsively efficient and practical about her compulsions. Whether this makes her more insane than Marlon Bain or less insane than Marlon Bain, who can like say. As an instance the Moms solved a lot of her threshold-problems by having no real doors or doorways built on the first floor of HmH so the rooms are all split off by angles and partitions and plants. The Moms kept to a Prussian bathroom-schedule so she couldn't spend hours in there washing her hands until the skin fell off the way Bain's did, he had to wear cotton gloves the whole summer right before he left E.T.A. The Moms for a while had video cameras installed so she could obsessively check whether Mrs. Clarke'd left the oven on or check her plants' arrangement or whether all the bathroom towels are lined up with their fringes flush without physically checking; she had a little wall of monitors in her study at HmH; The Stork put up with the cameras but the sense I get is that Tavis isn't going to be keen on being photorecorded in the bathroom or anyplace else, so maybe she's had to have other recourse.[a] You can check that yourself out there. What I'm trying to say is she's compulsively efficient even about her obsessions and compulsions. Of course there are doors upstairs, lockable doors, but that's in service of other compulsions. The Moms's. You can go ahead and ask her what I mean. She's so compulsive she's got the compulsions themselves arranged so efficiently that she can get everything done and still have plenty of time left over for her children. These are a constant drain on her batteries. She's got to keep Hal's skull lashed tight to hers without being so overt about it that Hallie has any idea what's going on, to keep him from trying to pull his skull away. The kid's still obsessed with her approval. He lives for applause from exactly two hands. He's still performing for her, syntax- and vocabulary-wise, at seventeen, the same way he did when he was ten. The kid is so shut down talking to him is like throwing a stone in a pond. The kid has no idea he even knows something's wrong. Plus the Moms has to obsess over Mario and Mario's various challenges and tribulations and little patheticnesses and worship Mario and think Mario's some kind of secular martyr to the mess she'd made of her adult life, all the while having to keep up a front of laissez-faire laid-back management where she pretends to let Mario go his own way and do his own thing.'

'Q.'

'I'm not going to talk about it.'

'Q.'

'No and don't insult my intelligence, I'm not going to talk about why I don't want to talk about it. If this is going to be a *Moment* article, Hallie's going to read it, and then he'll read it to Booboo, and I'm not talking about The Stork's death or the Moms's stability in a thing where they'll read about it and have to read some authoritative report on my take on it instead of coming to their own terms about it. With it, rather. Terms with, terms about. No, terms with it.'

'. . .'

'They both might have to wait until they get away from there before they can even realize what's going on, that the Moms is unredeemably fucking bats. All these terms that became clichés — *denial, schizogenic, pathogenic family like systems* and so on and so forth. A former acquaintance said The Mad Stork always used to say clichés earned their status as clichés because they were so obviously true.'

'. . .'

'I never once saw the two of them fight, not once in eighteen domestic and Academy years, is all I'll say.'

'Q.'

'The late Stork was the victim of the most monstrous practical joke ever played, in my opinion, is all I'll say.'

'. . .'

'All right, I'll relate one antidote[b] that might be more revealing of the Moms's emotional weather than any adjective. Jesus, see, I start explicitly referring to parts of speech just thinking about the whole thing. The thing about people who are truly and malignantly crazy: their real genius is for making the people around them think they *themselves* are crazy. In military science this is called Psy-Ops, for your info.'

'Q.'

'I'm sorry? Right then, one illustrative thing. Which thing to pick. Embarrassment of riches. I'll pick one at random. I think I was maybe twelve. I was in 12's, I know, on that summer's tour. Though I was playing 12's when I was still ten. It was ten to thirteen that I was regarded as gifted, with a tennis future. I began to decline around what should have been puberty. Call me let's say twelve. People were talking about NAFTA and something called the quote Information Turnpike and there was still broadcast TV, though we had a satellite dish. The Academy wasn't even a twinkle in anybody's eye. The Stork would disappear periodically when money came in. I think he kept going back up to Lyle in Ontario. Call me age ten. We still lived in Weston, known also as Volvoland. The Moms gardened like a fiend out there. This was something else she *had* to do. Had a thing about. Hadn't gone to indoor plants yet. Called the garden's crops her Green Babies. Wouldn't let us eat the zucchini. Never picked it, it got monstrous and dry and fell off and rotted. Big fun. But her real thing was preparing the garden every spring. She started making lists and pricing supplies and drafting outlines in January. Did I mention her own father had been a potato farmer, at one time a millionaire potato-baron-type farmer, in Québec?

'But so it's early March. Are those earrings electric, or is it you? How come I've never seen those earrings up to now? I thought women who could bring off copper earrings never wore anything but copper. You should see yourself in this light. Fluorescence isn't kind to most women. It must take an exceptional kind —'

'Q.'

'In the Moms's family plot. St.-Quelquechose Quebec or something. Never been there. His will said only not anywhere near his own dad's plot. Right near Maine. Heart of the Concavity. The Moms's home town's wiped off the map. Bad ecocycles, real machete-country. I'd have to try to recall the town. But so but then so the Moms is out in the cold garden. It's March and it's co-*wold*. I've got this story down. I've related this incident to several family-type professionals, and not one eyebrow stayed steady among them. This is the sort of antidote that makes pathogenic-systems-pros' eyebrows go all the way up and over their skull and disappear down the back of their neck.'

'. . .'

'So then I'm let's say thirteen, which means Hallie's four. The Moms is in the backyard garden, tilling the infamously flinty New England soil with a rented Rototiller. The situation is ambiguous between whether it's the Moms steering the Rototiller or vice versa. The old machine, full of gas I'd slopped through a funnel — the Moms secretly believes petroleum products give you leukemia, her solution is to pretend to herself she doesn't know what's wrong when the thing won't work and to stand there wringing her hands and let some eager-to-please thirteen-year-old puff out his chest at being able to diagnose the problem, and then I pour the gas. The Rototiller is loud and hard to control. It roars and snorts and bucks and my mother's stride behind it is like the stride of someone walking an untrained St. Bernard, she's leaving drunken staggery footprints behind her in the tilled dirt, behind the thing. There's something about a very very tall woman trying to operate a Rototiller. The Moms is incredibly tall, way taller than everybody except The Stork, who towered even over the Moms. Of course she'd be horrified if she ever brought herself to recognize what she was doing, orchestrating a little kid into handling the gas that she thinks might be cancerous; she doesn't even *know* she's phobic about gas. She's wearing two pairs of work-gloves and plastic surgery-type bags over her espadrilles, which were the only footwear she could garden in. And a Fukoama microfiltration pollution mask, which you might remember those from that period. Her toes are blue in the dirty plastic bags. I'm a few meters ahead of the Moms, in charge of preemptive rock- and clod-removal. That's her term. Preemptive rock- and clod-removal.

'Now work with me, see this with me. In the middle of this tilling here comes my little brother Hallie, maybe like four at the time and wearing some kind of fuzzy red pajamas and a tiny little down coat, and slippers that had those awful Nice-Day yellow smile-faces on both toes. We've been at it maybe an hour and half, and the garden's dirt is just about tilled when Hal comes out and down off the pressure-treated redwood deck and comes walking very steadily and seriously toward the border of the garden the Moms had surveyed out with little sticks and string. He has his little hand out, he's holding out something small and dark and he's coming toward the garden as the Rototiller snorts and rattles behind me, dragging the Moms. As he gets closer the thing in his hand resolves into something that just doesn't look pleasant at all. Hal and I look at each other. His expression is very serious even despite that his lower lip is having a sort of little epileptic fit, which means he's getting ready to bawl. That's with a *w*. I remember the air was gray with dust and the Moms had her glasses on. He holds the thing out toward the Moms's figure. I squint. The thing covering his palm and hanging over the sides of the palm is a rhombusoid patch of fungus. Big old patch of house-mold. Underline *big* and *old*. It must have come from some hot furnace-hidden corner of the basement, some corner she must have missed with the flamethrower, after the flooding we had every January thaw. I heft a clod or rock, I'm staring, every follicle I've got is bunched and straining. You could feel the tension, it was like standing down at Sunstrand Plaza when they fired the transformers, every follicle bunches and strains. It was a sort of nasal green, black-speckled, hairy like a peach is hairy. Also some orange speckles. A patch of very bad-news-type mold. Hal looks at me in the noise, his lower lip all over the place. He looks to the Moms, the Moms is intent on a plumb-straight Rototilled line, weaving. The pièce is that the mold looks, like, strangely incomplete. As in it dawns on me right then *chewed on,* Helen. And yes as I squint some sickening hairy stuff is still there like impacted in the kid's front teeth and hairily smeared around the mouth.

'Be there with me, Helen. Feel the sort of Wagnerish clouds gather. Hallie always said there was always this sense as a kid with the Moms that the whole cosmos was just this side of fulminating into boiling clouds of elemental gas and was being held materially together only through heroic exercise of will and ingenuity on the part of the Moms.

'Everything slows waaay down. She's coming around with the machine at the end of a row and sees Hallie wearing his happy-slippers outside in the cold, which just in itself is enough to gut-shot the cosmos as far as she's concerned, usually. Now we're seeing the Rototiller get shut down as she bends way down to where I'd showed her the choke. The machine diesels a little and farts some blue smoke. The machine sucks the nub of its starter-rope into itself. I can feel the voltage like I'm still there. Post-racket tingling quiet descends. There's the tentative chirp of a bird. The Moms comes toward Hal standing there in his little red coat. She's tucking a wisp of hair back under the special plastic cap's elastic. Her hair at that time was dark brown, she's addressing him, she has an unbelievably humiliating little family pet name for the kid that I'll show him the mercy of never telling anybody.

'But so she's coming over. Hal is standing there. Holds the horrific patch of fungus out. The Moms sees at first only her child holding something out, and like all moms hardwired for motherhood she reaches to take whatever her baby holds out. The one sort of case where she wouldn't check before reaching out toward something held out.'

'Q.'

'The Moms though now stops just inside the border of string and she squints, her glasses have dust, she starts to see and process just what it is the kid's holding out to her. Her hand's outstretched in the air over the garden's string and she stops.

'Hallie takes one step forward, arm up and out in a kind of like Nazi salute. He goes "I ate this."'

'The Moms says she begs his pardon.

'Helen, you decide. But consider the fragility of the obsesso-compulsive's control. The terrible life-ruling phobias. Her four horsemen: enclosure, communicational imprecision, and untidiness, which you can't get much untidier than basement-mold.'

'Q.'

'The fourth horseman stays hidden, of course, like in all quality eschatologies, the unturned card, under wraps till actual game-time.

' "I ate this" Hal goes, he's still holding the thing out, not crying, a kind of clinical grimness to him about it, like the mold's some audit it's his job to show her. And do you want to know if she touched it?'

'Q.'

'It suddenly occurs to me that if you want stuff on the Moms and The Mad Stork you could contact Bain. He practically lived with us in Weston. As like a secondary source. I'm sure he'd discuss the Moms's foibles all you want. The man still practically holds up a crucifix at any mention. His little greeting-card company has just been bought up by a huge novelty concern, so I'm sure he's in his big room lying there having palm-fronds waved and his forehead wiped, feeling flush and voluble. I guess I'd rather you didn't ask him about my foibles, but he's inexhaustible on the subject of the Moms and O.C.D. He never leaves home, which home is one room, the converted Children's Reading Room of what used to be the Waltham Public Library, which is the whole third floor. He learned from the Moms how to minimize doorways to traverse. I'm afraid he's not InterNetted and has an O.C.D.-phobic thing about e-mail. His snail-mail address is Marlon K. Bain, Saprogenic Greetings Inc., BPL-Waltham Bldg., 1214 Totten Pond Road, Waltham MA 021549872/4. It'd also be good if you could avoid mentioning the number 2 to him. He has problems with the number 2. I don't know if his not leaving home is similar to the Moms's not leaving home. This is the most I've thought about the Moms in a dog's age, to be honest with you. You have this way of getting stuff out of me. It's like you do nothing but sit there with that cigarette and you're all I can see and all I want is to please you. It's like I can't help it. Is this just good journalism, Helen?'

'. . .'

'Or is there something more going on here, some kind of strange bond I feel between us that sort of like tears down all my normal personal-life boundaries and makes me open totally to you? I guess I have to hope you won't take advantage. Does this all sound like some kind of line? Maybe if it was a line it'd sound less lame. I guess I do wish I could come off more suave. I don't know what else to do except just tell what's going on inside me, even if it sounds lame. I never have any clue what you're thinking about it.'

'. . .'

' "Help! My son ate this!" She screamed the same thing over and over, holding the mold-rhombus up like a torch, running around just inside the string border while I and Hallie staggered back, literally like staggered back, gaping at our first taste of apocalypse, a corner of the universe suddenly peeled back to reveal what seethed out there just beyond tidiness. What lay just north of order.

' "Help! My son ate this! My son has eaten this! Help!" she kept screaming, running in tight little right-faces just inside this perfect box of string, and I'm seeing The Mad Stork's face at the glass door over the deck, palms out and thumbs together to make a frame, and Mario my other brother next to him as usual down around his knee, with Mario's face all squished against the glass from supporting his weight, their breath on the window spreading, Hal inside the string finally and trying to follow her, crying, and not impossibly I also crying a little, just from the infectious stress, and those two through the back door's glass just watching, and fucking Booboo also trying to make that frame with his hands, so finally it was Mr. Reehagen next door, who was so-called "friends" with her, who had to come out and over and finally had to hook up the hose.'

    a. This may be a lie — no one else at E.T.A. knows anything else about there having been any cameras in HmH's kitchen, bathroom, etc.
    b. *sic.*

235. She'd arrayed the photos herself, from her purse, on the dresser; he hadn't had to ask her to; it added to the sense of synchronous mercy, a cosmic kindness balancing out the jacuzzi's dead bird and the frigidly invasive reporter.

236. E.T.A. shorthand: Vector/Angle/Pace/Spin.

237. The NW-to-NE angle at the former Monteplier VT isn't quite 90°, but it is very close. By the way, the Syracuse-Ticonderoga-Salem triangle is one of those endless-based 25-130-25 triangles that looks so hideous when projected onto one of Corbett Thorp's distorting globes in the Trivium's Cubular Trigonometry.

238. Quod vide here Ch. 7, 'It All Started with a Colorectal Neoplastis, an Openness to Communicative Manifestations of Divine Grace, and a Seedy-Looking Fellow That Publicly Lifted a Chair He Was Standing On, That Was Clearly Just Such a Manifestation,' in *The Chill of Inspiration: Spontaneous Reminiscences by Seventeen Pioneers of DT-Cycle Lithiumized Annular Fusion*, ed. Prof. Dr. Günther Sperber, Institut für Neutronenphysik und Reaktortechnik, Kernforschungszentrum Karlsruhe, U.R.G., available in English in ferociously expensive hardcover only, © Y.T.M.P. from Springer-Verlag Wien NNY. (N.b. that while the annular meta-disease treatment is highly effective on metastatic cancers, it proved a disappointment on the HIV-spectrum viri, since AIDS is itself a meta-disease.)

239. Because he'd been sworn to secrecy, Green doesn't tell Lenz that Charlotte Treat had shared with Green that her adoptive father had been one-time Chair of the Northeast Regional Board of Dental Anesthesiologists, and had been pretty liberal with the use of the old N_2O and thiopental sodium around the Treats' Revere MA household, for personal and extremely unsavory reasons.

240. ® The Mauna Loa Macadamia Nut Corp., Hilo HI — 'A LOW SODIUM FOOD.'

241. Popular corporate-hard-rock bands, though it shows where Bruce Green's psychic decline really started that, except for TBA_5, these bands were all truly big two or three years past, and are now slightly passé, with Choosy Mothers having split up entirely by now to explore individual creative directions.

242. This is one reason why he consents to be hung way out into space from Schtitt's transom for filming all-court play, held only by some prorector with a firm grip on the back of his lock's vest, which the players looking up at Mario's forward ski-jump posture off the crow's nest find incredibly terrifying and audacious and ballsy, and Avril won't even leave HmH during all-court filmings.

243. This though Avril's never come right out and articulated her worry about his P.M. safety to Mario, not wanting to seem as though she's making a special issue of his deficits and vulnerability or to seem inconsistent when she lets Hal go off nightly wherever he likes or just basically in any way to inhibit Mario's sense of autonomy and freedom by causing him to worry about her worrying — which he does, rather a lot, worry about Avril's worrying about him. If that makes sense.

244. Mario, like his maternal uncle Charles Tavis, has a dislike of fluorescent lighting.

245. Viz.: 'You feeling better?'
    'Will be soon.'
    'Is that supposed to mean something? What's that supposed to mean?'

'Nothing. Literally nothing.'

246. A depressing new Sober Club in Somerville's Davis Square where AAs and NAs — mostly new and young — get heartbreakingly dolled up and dance stiffly and tremble with sober sexual anxiety and they stand around with Cokes and M.F.s telling each other how great it is to be in an intensely social venue with all your self-conscious inhibitions unmedicated and screaming in your head. The smiles alone in these places are excruciating to see.

247. A Restriction means just no Overnight that week and an extra Chore; a House Restriction means you have to be back an hour after work and nightly meetings; Full House is no leaving the House except for work and meetings, and 15 minutes to get back, and no even leaving to buy smokes or a paper, or even to go out in the lawn for oxygen, and one violation means a Discharge: F.H.R. is Ennet's version of the Hole, and it's dreaded.

248. Ennet House takes its urines over to the methadone clinic, which has all manner of clients who have to submit weekly urines to courts and programs, and the clinic lets Ennet put its urines gratis in the weekly batch the clinic sends out to an E.M.I.T.-mill clinic all the way out in Natick, and in return every once in a while Pat gets a call from the trollish little social worker who runs #2 about some client down there who's decided he wants off the methadone, as well, and Pat will shoot the client way up on the Interview list and give him an interview and usually let the client in — Calvin T. and Danielle S. had both originally gotten into Ennet House this way, i.e. via #2.

249. It's maybe significant that Don Gately never once failed to clean up any vomit or incontinence his mother'd just drunkenly left there or passed out in, no matter how pissed off or disgusted he was or how sick he himself was: not once.

250. (who owns a Lincoln, Henderson does, origins unknown and suspicious)

251. This is all for Insurance Reasons, the Staff sheet on which Gately doesn't understand all the language of, and fears.

252. It's against House rules to smoke upstairs in the bedrooms — more Insurance Reasons — and a week's Restriction is supposed to be mandatory, and Pat's personally a fanatic about the rule, but Gately, much as he fears the grim boilerplate on the Insurance Sheet, always pretends he doesn't see anything when he sees somebody smoking up here, since when he was a resident he actually used to sometimes smoke *in his sleep* he was so tense, and every once in a while will wake up and find that he has again, i.e. lit a gasper and apparently smoked it and put it out all in his sleep, down in bed in his Staff oubliette in the basement.

253. (the items from the House's donated-clothes baskets that fit Gately being few and far)

254. Gately's made it an iron point never again ever to run, once he got straight.

255. NNE street argot for any kind of handgun.

256. (Erdedy's hands still up, w/ keys)

257. (NNE Region, trying hard not to irritate Tine Sr. by fidgeting)

258. (Desert-SW Region, understated in a massive peasant skirt and sensible flats)

259. These, ® a number of fine companies, are like enormous versions of the little windshield-washer implements at service stations — an industrial mop-handle w/ a canted rubber blade at the end, used for spreading puddle-water out so it dries faster, at some academies replaced with the EZ-DRI hinged-roller-of-dense-sponge-at-the-end court-

dryer, which E.T.A. eschews because of how fast the rolling sponge at the end mildews and smells bad.

260. Mrs. Incandenza always grades everything in blue ink.

261. A phenomenon not unknown, viz. menial employees and shift-workers mining E.T.A.'s collected waste for cast-off value, and permitted by the administration and Mr. Harde, or rather just not actively discouraged, since 'One man's trash . . .' and so on, with the only requirement being a certain visual discretion when carrying off E.T.A.'s offal, simply because the whole thing's kind of embarrassing for everybody.

262. I.e. the Women's Tennis Association, the distaff equivalent of the A.T.P.

263. *Sic,* presumably for Betamax (®Sony).

264. *Sic,* but it's pretty obvious what Marathe means here.

265. Reinforced Aluminum Spectation Unit.

266. The occasional upscale parent could be seen exiting Comm.-Ad. and crossing behind the West Courts' south fence to the asphalt lot and what were unmistakably parental autos, all remarkable for their textbook tire-pressure and bristles of cellular antennae and the absence of any little dust-smiles on their rear or side windows. Charles Tavis had spent the morning interfacing with parents of those E.T.A. kids injured in I.-Day's Eschaton free-for-all. Lateral Alice Moore, for a treat, had been listening to Tavis and parents on her headphones, while typing, instead of her collection of aerobic favorites. Struck and Pemulis had cruised by before lunch and blarneyed her into putting the exchanges on her intercom's speaker for a couple minutes. You should hear C.T. enclosed with parents sometime. It was only some of the parents — Todd Possalthwaite's dad was on honeymoon in the Azores, and Otis P. Lord's mother had some inner-ear thing and the Lords couldn't fly. But Pemulis and Struck concurred that everyone with any kind of administration in his blood should hear E.T.A.'s Headmaster with parents and a placative mission, a master charmer past all social gauge, a Houdini with the manacles of fact, the interfaces like fluidless seductions — Pemulis said the man's missed a genuine calling in sales — everyone practically wanting to smoke a cigarette afterward, the parents leave weeping, pumping Tavis's hands — one parent per hand — practically begging him to accept both their thanks and their apologies for daring to even possibly *think,* even for a *moment.* Then, supporting each other, making their way over Lateral Alice's third rail and past the beaming extremely *polite* lads by her desk and out through the pressurized glass lobby doors and down off the white-pillared neo-Georgian porch and past courts and bleachers and into their well-maintained autos and out the portcullis and very slowly down the hill's brick drive before they even recall they'd forgotten to pop in on their injured kid, sign his cast, feel his forehead, say Hey.

267. I.e. ace/double fault, rather like the ratio of strikeouts to walks for a pitcher.

268. It was like Steeply'd never seen so many left-handed people: both Hal Incandenza and the boy in black were left-handed, one of the two little girls four courts down was left-handed, deLint was marking the chart with his left hand. Both A.F.R. turncoat Rémy Marathe and Québecer triple-operative Luria P——— were southpaws, though Steeply realized that this could hardly be called significant.

269.

Saprogenic Greetings*

WHEN YOU CARE ENOUGH TO LET A PROFESSIONAL SAY IT FOR YOU

*a proud member of the ACMÉ Family of Gags 'N Notions,
Pre-Packaged Emotions, Jokes and Surprises and Wacky Disguises

Ms. Helen Steepley
And So On
November Y.D.A.U.

. . . (1) Orin Incandenza and I played, practiced, and generally hung out through
most of what seemed at the time to be our formative years. We met because I kept
encountering him across the net in the local tennis tournaments we played around metro
Boston, Boys' 10's. We were the two best 10-year-old males in Boston. We soon became
practice partners, our mothers driving us every weekday afternoon to a junior development program at the Auburndale Tennis Club in West Newton. After my own parents
were horribly killed on the Jamaica Way commuter road one morning in the freak crash
of a radio traffic-report helicopter, I became a sort of hanger-on at the Incandenza house
out in Weston. When J.O.I. founded the Academy, I was one of the first matriculants.
Orin and I were inseparable until around age 15, when I reached my own zenith in terms
of early puberty and athletic promise and began to be able to beat him. He took it hard.
We were never inseparable again. We spent quantity time together again briefly for a
few months the next year, during a period when we both experimented heavily with
recreational substances. We both ended up losing enthusiasm for substances after only a
couple years, Orin because he had finally entered puberty and had discovered the
weaker sex and found he needed all his faculties and guile, myself because a couple of
really negative methoxy-psychedelic experiences left me with certain Disabilities that to
this day make normal life an exceptional challenge, and which I tend to blame on having
done deadly-serious hallucinogens at a sort of larval psychological stage during which
no N. American adolescent should be allowed to do hallucinogens. These Disabilities
led to my departure from the Enfield Tennis Academy at 17, prior to graduation, and
my withdrawal from competitive junior tennis and contemporary life as we know it.
Orin was largely burned out on tennis too by 17, though no one in his right mind could
have foreseen a defection to organized U.S. football in his future.

A grunting, crunching ballet of repressed homoeroticism, football, Ms. Steepley, on
my view. The exaggerated breadth of the shoulders, the masked eradication of facial
personality, the emphasis on contact-vs.-avoidance-of-contact. The gains in terms of
penetration and resistance. The tight pants that accentuate the gluteals and hamstrings
and what look for all the world like codpieces. The gradual slow shift of venue to
"artificial surface," "artificial turf." Don't the pants' fronts look fitted with codpieces?
And have a look at these men whacking each other's asses after a play. It is like Swin-
burne sat down on his soul's darkest night and designed an organized sport. And pay no
attention to Orin's defense of football as a ritualized substitute for armed conflict.
Armed conflict is plenty ritualized on its own, and since we have real armed conflict
(take a spin through Boston's Roxbury and Mattapan districts some evening) there is no
need or purpose for a substitute. Football is pure homophobically repressed nancy-ism,
and do not let O. tell you different.

. . . (3c) I cannot help you too much with the facts surrounding Dr. Incandenza's
suicide. I know that he erased his own cartography in a grisly way. I was told that in the
year leading up to his death Dr. Incandenza was abusing ethyl alcohol on a daily basis
and was working on a whole new genre of film-cartridge that Orin at the time claimed
was driving Dr. Inc insane.

. . . (3e) The supposed cause of their separation is that Dr. Incandenza began using
her in his work more and more extensively and eventually asked her to perform in the
prenominate completely radical new type of filmed entertainment that supposedly was
driving him to a breakdown. They supposedly became close, James and Jo-Ellen, though
Orin in my judgment is not a reliable source of information about their relationship.
The only other apposite fact I have — and I have this not from Orin but from an

1047

innocent female relative of mine who was (briefly) in a position to interface with our punter in an intimate and unguarded way impossible between hetero males — is that some incident occurred in the Incandenzas' Volvo involving one of the windows and a word — all I am given is that O. reports that in the days prior to Dr. Incandenza's felo de se, a so-called "word" appeared on a "fogged" "window" of Mrs. Inc's pale yellow Volvo, and the word cast a conjugal pall in all sorts of directions. This is it.

. . . (5) The "vailed warning" (typo?) you refer to in my postal response to you is simply that you have to take what Orin says in a fairly high-sodium way. I am not sure I would stand and point at Orin as an example of a classic pathological liar, but you have only to watch him in certain kinds of action to see that there can be such a thing as *sincerity with a motive*. I have no idea what your relationship with Orin is or what your feelings are — and if Orin wishes it I am afraid I can predict your feelings for him will be strong — so I shall just tell you that for instance at E.T.A. I saw Orin in bars or at post-tournament dances go up to a young lady he would like to pick up and use this fail-safe cross-sectional pick-up Strategy that involved an opening like "Tell me what sort of man you prefer, and then I'll affect the demeanor of that man." Which in a way of course is being almost pathologically open and sincere about the whole picking-up enter-prise, but also has this quality of Look-At-Me-Being-So-Totally-Open-And-Sincere-I-Rise-Above-The-Whole-Disingenuous-Posing-Process-Of-Attracting-Someone-,-And-I-Transcend-The-Common-Disingenuity-In-A-Bar-Herd-In-A-Particularly-Hip-And-Witty-Self-Aware-Way-,-And-If-You-Will-Let-Me-Pick-You-Up-I-Will-Not-Only-Keep-Being-This-Wittily,-Transcendently-Open-,-But-Will-Bring-You-Into-This-World-Of-Social-Falsehood-Transcendence, which of course he cannot do because the whole openness-demeanor thing is *itself* a purposive social falsehood; it is a pose of poselessness; Orin Incandenza is the *least open man* I know. Spend a little time with Orin's Uncle Charles a.k.a. "Gretel the Cross-Sectioned Dairy Cow" Tavis if you want to see real openness in motion, and you will see that genuine pathological openness is about as seductive as Tourette's syndrome.

It is not that Orin Incandenza is a liar, but that I think he has come to regard the truth as *constructed* instead of *reported*. He came by this idea educationally, is all I will add. He studied for almost eighteen years at the feet of the most consummate mind-fucker I have ever met, and even now he remains so flummoxed he thinks the way to escape that person's influence is through renunciation and hatred of that person. Defining yourself in opposi-tion to something is still being anaclitic on that thing, isn't it? I certainly think so. And men who believe they hate what they really *fear* they *need* are of limited interest, I find.

. . . Again I will remind you that Orin and I are on the outs a bit at the moment, so some of my judgments may be temporarily short on charity.

One reason Orin is not a straight-out liar is that Orin is not a particularly skillful liar. The few times I saw him try consciously to lie were pathetic. This is one reason why his juvenile recreational-chemical phase passed so quickly compared to some of our colleagues at E.T.A. If you are going to do serious drugs while you are still a minor and under your parents' roof, you are going to have to lie often and lie well. Orin was a strangely stupid liar. I am recalling there was one afternoon on Mrs. Clarke's day off when Mrs. Inc had to go off and overfunction somewhere and Orin was supposed to baby-sit Mario and Hal, who were at the kind of crazed-toddler age where they would hurt themselves if they were not closely supervised, and I was over, and Orin and I decided to dart up to the loft over the Weston house's garage to smoke a bit of Bob Hope, which is to say high-resin marijuana, and in the loft, high, wandered disastrously into the sort of pseudophilosophical mental labyrinth that Bob Hope–smokers are al-ways wandering into and getting trapped in and wasting huge amounts of time[a] inside

a. This tendency to involuted abstraction is sometimes called "Marijuana Thinking"; and by the way, the so-called "Amotivational Syndrome" consequent to massive Bob Hope–consumption is a mis-nomer, for it is not that Bob Hope-smokers lose interest in practical functioning, but rather Marijuana-Think themselves into labyrinths of reflexive abstraction that seem to cast doubt on the very possibility of practical functioning, and the mental labor of finding one's way out consumes all available attention and makes the Bob Hope–smoker look physically torpid and apathetic and amoti-vated sitting there, when really he is trying to claw his way out of a labyrinth. Note that the over-whelming hunger (the so-called "munchies") that accompanies cannabis intoxication may be a natural defense mechanism against this kind of loss of practical function, since there is no more practical function anywhere than foraging for food.

an intellectual room they cannot negotiate their way out of, and by the time we hadn't resolved the abstract problem that had put us into the labyrinth but just as always had gotten so hungry we abandoned it and stumbled out and down the loft's wooden ladder, the sun was all the way on the other side of the sky over Wayland and Sudbury, and the whole afternoon had passed without Hal and Mario having received any protective supervision; and Hal and Mario somehow survived the afternoon, but when Mrs. Incandenza returned that night she asked Orin what we and the supervised toddlers had done all afternoon and Orin lied that we had all been right here, respectively playing and supervising, and Mrs. Incandenza expressed puzzlement to Orin because she said she had tried to call the house several times that afternoon but was unable to get through, and Orin replied that while supervising he had herded the toddlers carefully into rooms with phone-jacks and made calls and had been on the phone several times for long periods of time for this that or the other thing, was why she had been unable to get through, at which Mrs. Incandenza (who is extremely tall) had blinked several times and looked very confused and said that but the phone had not been busy, it had just rung and rung and rung. At a juncture like this, men and boys get separated in terms of prevarication, I submit. And all Orin could come up with was a steady gaze as he said, as if from the Rose Garden: "I have no response to that." Which incredibly stupid response he and I found very funny for weeks afterward, especially since Mrs. Incandenza *never punished* and refused to act as if she believed lying was even a possibility as far as her children were concerned, and treated an exploded lie as an insoluble cosmic mystery instead of an exploded lie.

The worst instance of both Orin's mendacious idiocy and Mrs. Incandenza's unwillingness to countenance an idiotic lie came one grisly day soon after Orin had finally gotten his vehicle operator's license. O. and I found ourselves with an idle weekday afternoon off in August after losing early at a synthetic-grass tournament down at Longwood, and Hal was still alive in what was then Boys' 10's and thus a good bit of the E.T.A. summer community was still down at Longwood, including Mario and Mrs. Incandenza, who'd been driven down I remember by a sort of swarthily foreign-looking monilial-internist medical resident Mrs. Inc had introduced as a so-called "dear and cherished friend" but hadn't explained how they'd met, and Dr. Incandenza was indisposed and not in a position to bother anyone that day, I remember, and Orin and I had most of E.T.A. to ourselves, even the gate's portcullis unmanned and up, and this being at the acme of our interest in such things we wasted little time in ingesting some sort of recreational substance, I cannot recall what kind but I remember them as particularly impairing, and we decided however that we weren't yet impaired enough, and decided to drive down the hill to one of the disreputable liquor stores along Commonwealth Avenue that accepted your word of honor as proof of age, and we hopped into the Volvo and blasted down the hill and down Commonwealth Avenue, severely impaired, and wondered in a speculative way why people on the sidewalks all along Commonwealth seemed to be waving at us and holding their heads and pointing and jumping wildly up and down, and Orin waving cheerfully back and holding his own head in a sort of friendly imitation, but it was not until we got all the way down to the Commonwealth–Brighton Ave. split that the horrible realization hit us: Mrs. Incandenza often during summer days kept the Incandenzas' beloved dog S. Johnson leashed to the back of her Volvo within reach of his water and Science Diet bowls, and Orin and I had peeled out in the car without even thinking to check for whether S. Johnson was attached to it. I will not try to describe what we found when we pulled into a parking lot and slunk to the rear of the car. Let's call it a nubbin. Let's say what we found was a leash and collar, and a nubbin. According to the couple of witnesses who were able to speak, S. Johnson had made a valiant go of trying to keep up back there for at least a couple blocks down Commonwealth, but at some point he either lost his footing or got his canine affairs in order and figured it was his day to shuffle off, and gave up, and hit the pavement, after which the scene the witnesses described was unspeakable. There was fur and let's call it material down the middle of the inside east-bound lane for five or six blocks. What we had left to take slowly back up the Academy's hill was a leash, a collar with tags describing medication-allergies and food-sensitivities, and a nubbin of let's call it attached material.

The point is that I defy you to imagine how it felt later that day to stand there with Orin in the HmH living room before the prone and piteously weeping Mrs. Incandenza and listen to Orin try to construct a version of events in which he and I had sensed somehow that S. Johnson was dying for a good brisk August walk and were walking him down Commonwealth,[b] saying there we were walking good old S. Johnson demurely down the sidewalk when a hit-and-run driver not only swerved up onto the sidewalk to run the dog down but then backed up and ran him over again and backed up and ran him over again, and on and on, so more like a *pulverize*-and-run driver, while Orin and I had stood there too paralyzed with horror and grief even to think of noticing the make and color of the car, much less the fiend's license plate. Mrs. Incandenza on her knees (there's something surreal about a very tall woman on her knees), weeping and pressing her hand to her collarbone but nodding in confirmation at every syllable of Orin spinning this pathetic lie, O. holding up the leash and collar (and nubbin) like Exhibit A, with me next to him wiping my forehead and wishing the immaculately polished and sterilized hardwood floor would swallow up the whole scene in toto.

. . . (7) Ms. Steeples, to my way of thinking, the word "abuse" is vacuous. Who can define "abuse"? The difficulty with really interesting cases of abuse is that the ambiguity of the abuse becomes part of the abuse. Thanks over the decades to the energetic exercise of your own profession, Ms. Steeley, we have all heard ACOAs and AlaTeens and ACONAs and ACOGs and WHINERS relate clear cases of different kinds of abuse: beatings, diddlings, rapes, deprivations, domineerment, humiliation, captivity, torture, excessive criticism or even just utter disinterest. But at least the victims of this sort of abuse can, when they have dredged it back up after childhood, confidently call it "abuse." There are, however, more ambiguous cases. Harder to profile, one might say. What would you call a parent who is so neurasthenic and depressive that any opposition to his parental will plunges him into the sort of psychotic depression where he does not leave his bed for days and just sits there in bed cleaning his revolver, so that the child would be terrified of opposing his will and plunging him into a depression and maybe causing him to suicide? Would that child qualify as "abused"? Or a father who is so engrossed by mathematics that he gets engrossed helping his child with his algebra homework and ends up forgetting the child and doing it all himself so that the child gets an A in Fractions but never in fact learns fractions? Or even say a father who is extremely handy around the house and can fix anything, and has the son help him, but gets so engrossed in his projects (the father) that he never thinks to explain to the son how the projects actually get done, so that the son's "help" never advances past simply handing the father a specified wrench or getting him lemonade or Phillips-head screws until the day the father is crushed into aspic in a freak accident on the Jamaica Way and all opportunities for transgenerational instruction are forever lost, and the son never learns how to be a handy homeowner himself, and when things malfunction around his own one-room home he has to hire contemptuous filthy-nailed men to come fix them, and feels terribly inadequate (the son), not only because he is not handy but because this handiness seemed to him to have represented to his father everything that was independent and manly and non-Disabled in an American male. Would you cry "Abuse!" if you were the unhandy son, looking back? Worse, *could* you call it abuse without feeling that you were a pathetic self-indulgent piss-puddle, what with all the genuine cases of hair-raising physical and emotional abuse diligently reported and analyzed daily by conscientious journalists (and profiled?))?

I am not sure whether you could call this abuse, but when I was (long ago) abroad in the world of dry men, I saw parents, usually upscale and educated and talented and functional and white, patient and loving and supportive and concerned and involved in their children's lives, profligate with compliments and diplomatic with constructive criticism, loquacious in their pronouncements of unconditional love for and approval of their children, conforming to every last jot/tittle in any conceivable definition of a good parent, I saw parent after unimpeachable parent who raised kids who were (a) emotionally retarded or (b) lethally self-indulgent or (c) chronically depressed or (d) bor-

---

b. Now, Orin had never once walked S. Johnson. Orin was not even all that keen on S. Johnson, because the dog was always trying to mate with his left leg. And anyway, S. Johnson was very much Mrs. Incandenza's dog, and was normally exercised only by Mrs. Incandenza, and at rigidly specific times of day.

derline psychotic or (e) consumed with narcissistic self-loathing or (f) neurotically driven/addicted or (g) variously psychosomatically Disabled or (h) some conjunctive permutation of (a) . . . (g).

Why is this. Why do so many parents who seem relentlessly bent on producing children who feel they are good persons deserving of love produce children who grow to feel they are hideous persons not deserving of love who just happen to have lucked into having parents so marvelous that the parents love them even though they are hideous?

Is it a sign of abuse if a mother produces a child who believes not that he is innately beautiful and lovable and deserving of magnificent maternal treatment but somehow that he is a hideous unlovable child who has somehow lucked in to having a really magnificent mother? Probably not.

But could such a mother then *really* be all that magnificent, if that's the child's view of himself?

I am not speaking about my own mother, who was decapitated by a plummeting rotorblade long before she could have much effect one way or the other on my older brother and innocent younger sister and me.

I think, Mrs. Starkly, that I am speaking of Mrs. Avril M.-T. Incandenza, although the woman is so multileveled and indictment-proof that it is difficult to feel comfortable with any sort of univocal accusation of anything. Something just was not *right*, is the only way to put it. Something *creepy*, even on the culturally stellar surface. For instance, after Orin had pretty clearly killed her beloved dog S. Johnson in a truly awful if accidental way, and then had tried to evade responsibility for it with a lie that a parent far less intelligent than Avril could have seen right through, Mrs. Inc's response was not only not conventionally abusive, but seemed almost too unconditionally loving and compassionate and selfless to possibly be true. Her response to Orin's pathetic pulverize-and-run-driver lie was not to act credulous so much as to act as if the entire grotesque fiction had never reached her ears. And her response to the dog's death itself was bizarrely furcated. On the one hand, she mourned S. Johnson's death very deeply, took the leash and collar and canine nubbin tenderly and arranged lavish memorial and funeral arrangements, including a heartbreakingly small cherrywood coffin, cried in audible private for weeks, etc. But the other half of her emotional energies went into being overly solicitous and polite toward Orin, upping the daily compliment-and-reinforcement-dose, arranging for favorite foods at E.T.A. meals, having his favorite little tennis appurtenances appear magically in his bed and locker with loving notes attached, basically making the thousands of little gestures by which the technically stellar parent can make her child feel particularly valued[c] — all out of concern that Orin *in no way* think she resented him for S. Johnson's death or blamed him or loved him less in any way because of the whole incident. Not only was there no punishment or even visible pique, but the love-and-support-bombardment *increased*. And all this was coupled with elaborate machinations to keep the mourning and funeral arrangements and moments of wistful dog-remembrance hidden from Orin, for fear that he might see that the Moms was hurt and so feel bad or guilty, so that in his presence Mrs. Inc became even more cheerful and loquacious and witty and intimate and benign, even suggesting in oblique ways that life was now somehow suddenly *better* without the dog, that some kind of unrecognized albatross had been somehow removed from her neck, and so on and so forth.

What does a trained analyst of our cultural profile's soft contours like yourself make of this, Mrs. Starksaddle? Is it mind-bogglingly considerate and loving and supportive, or is there something . . . *creepy* about it? Maybe a more perspicuous question: Was the almost pathological generosity with which Mrs. Inc responded to her son taking her car in an intoxicated condition and dragging her beloved dog to its grotesque death and then trying to lie his way out of it, was this generosity for Orin's sake, or for Avril's own? Was it Orin's "self-esteem" she was safeguarding, or her own vision of herself as a more stellar Moms than any human son could ever hope to feel she merits?

When Orin does his impression of Avril — which I doubt you or anyone else can get him to do anymore, though it was a party-stopper back in our days at the Academy — what he will do is assume an enormous warm and loving smile and move steadily toward you until he is in so close that his face is spread up flat against your own face and

---

c. Yes — all right — this may start to touch on it: not "valu*able*" but "val*ued*."

your breaths mingle. If you can get to experience it — the impression — which will seem worse to you: the smothering proximity, or the unimpeachable warmth and love with which it's effected?

For some reason now I am thinking of the sort of philanthropist who seems humanly repellent not in spite of his charity but *because* of it: on some level you can tell that he views the recipients of his charity not as persons so much as pieces of exercise equipment on which he can develop and demonstrate his own virtue. What's creepy and repellent is that this sort of philanthropist clearly *needs* privation and suffering to continue, since it is his own virtue he prizes, instead of the ends to which the virtue is ostensibly directed.

Everything Orin's mother is about is always terribly well-ordered and multivalent. I suspect she was badly abused as a child. I have nothing concrete to back this up.

But if, Ms. Bainbridge, you have yielded your own charms to Orin, and if Orin strikes you as a wonderfully gifted and giving lover — which by various accounts he is — not just skilled and sensuous but magnificently generous, empathic, attentive, loving — if it seems to you that he does, truly, derive his own best pleasure from giving you pleasure, you might wish to reflect soberly on this vision of Orin imitating his dear Moms as philanthropist: a person closing in, arms open wide, smiling.

270. ® The Glad Flaccid Receptacle Corporation, Zanesville OH.

271. (including K. McKenna, who claims to have a bruised skull but does not in fact have a bruised skull)

272. This is why Ann Kittenplan, way more culpable for Eschaton-damage than any of the other kids, isn't down here on the punitive cleanup crew, is that it's become a defacto Tunnel Club operation. LaMont Chu was nominated to tell her she could blow it off and they'd mark her down as present, which was just fine with Ann Kittenplan, since even the butchest little girls don't seem to have this proto-masculine fetish for enclosure underneath things.

273. = Stars, shooting stars, falling stars.

274. Poutrincourt uses the Nuck idiom *réflechis* instead of the more textbook *réflexes*, and does indeed sound like the real Canadian McCoy, though her accent is without the long moany suffixes of Marathe, and but anyway it is for certain that a certain 'journalist' will be e-mailing Falls Church VA on the U.S.O.'s Clipper-proof line for the unexpurgated files on one 'Poutrincourt, Thierry T.'

275. Using *s'annuler* instead of the more Québecois *se détruire*.

276. Using the vulgate Québecois *transperçant,* whose idiomatic connotation of doom Poutrincourt shouldn't have had any reason to think the Parisian-speaking Steeply would know, which is the slip that indicates that Poutrincourt's figured out that Steeply is neither a civilian soft-profiler nor even a female, which Poutrincourt's probably known ever since Steeply'd lit his Flanderfume with the elbow of his lighter-arm *out* instead of *in*, which only males and radically butch lesbians ever do, and which together with the electrolysis-rash comprises the only real chink in the operative's distaff persona, and would require an almost professionally hypervigilant and suspicious person to notice the significance of.

277. Trois-Rivières-region idiom, meaning basically 'reason to get out of bed in the morning.'

278. Where was *Mrs.* Pemulis all this time, late at night, with dear old Da P. shaking Matty 'awake' until his teeth rattled and little Micky curled up against the far wall, shell-breathing, silent as death, is what I'd want to know.

279. The kid's the former E.T.A. whose name keeps eluding and torturing Hal, who hasn't gone over twenty-four hours without getting high in secret for well over a year, and doesn't feel very good at all, and finds the kid's name's elusiveness infuriating.

280. *Anhedonia* was apparently coined by Ribot, a Continental Frenchman, who in his 19th-century *Psychologie des Sentiments* says he means it to denote the psychoequivalent of *analgesia,* which is the neurologic suppression of pain.

281. This had been one of Hal's deepest and most pregnant abstractions, one he'd come up with once while getting secretly high in the Pump Room. That we're all lonely for something we don't know we're lonely for. How else to explain the curious feeling that he goes around feeling like he misses somebody he's never even met? Without the universalizing abstraction, the feeling would make no sense.

282. (the big reason why people in pain are so self-absorbed and unpleasant to be around)

283. S.S.R.I.s, of which Zoloft and the ill-fated Prozac were the ancestors.

284. A crude and cheap form of combustible methedrine, favored by the same sort of addictive class that sniffs gasoline fumes or coats the inside of a paper bag with airplane glue and puts the bag over their face and breathes until they fall down and start to convulse.

285. This has got to be a mispronunciation or catachresis on R.v.C.'s part, since Clonidine — 2-(2,6-Dichloroanilino)-2-imidazoline — is a decidedly adult-strength antihypertensive; the infant'd have to be N.F.L.-sized to tolerate it.

286. Kate G.'s never done Ice, or crack/'base/crank, nor even cocaine or low-impact 'drines. Drug addicts tend to fall into different classes: those who like downs and Mr. Hope rarely enjoy stimulants, while coke- and 'drine-fiends as a rule abhor marijuana. This is an area of potentially fruitful study in addictionology. Note that pretty much every class of addicts drinks, though.

287. Since last winter, when a stale smell, litter of dental stimulators, and single slender spit-wet butt signified that a certain upperclassman had been smoking panatelas late at night in V.R.3.

288. The Continent's Best Yogurt®.

289. In point of a fact wholly unknown to Hal, *BS:OTN* was in fact a very sad self-hate-festival on Himself's part, a veiled allegory of sponsorship and Himself's own miserable distaste for the vacant grins and reductive platitudes of the Boston AA that M.D.s and counselors kept referring him to.

290. Whether the girl's hideous facial burn-scars are the result of a freebase accident is never made explicit in the film. Bernadette Longley says she kind of hopes that's the case, because otherwise the scars would function as symbols of some deeper and more spiritual wound/hideousness, and the symbolic equation of facial with moral deformity strikes everybody over thirteen in the room as terribly gooey and heavy and stock.

291. After a heyday during the pre-millennial self-help craze, CA's receded back to being a splinter of the still-enormous Narcotics Anonymous; and Pat Montesian and the Ennet House Staff, while they have nothing against a resident with cocaine-issues hitting the occasional CA venue, strongly suggest that residents stick with AA or NA and not make splinters like CA or Designer Drug Addicts Anonymous or Prescription Tranquilizers Anonymous their primary fellowship for recovery, mostly because the splinters tend to have way fewer Groups and meetings — and some none at all in certain parts of the U.S. — and because their extremely specific Substance-focus tends to narrow the aperture of recovery and focus too much on abstinence from just one Substance instead of complete sobriety and a new spiritual way of life in toto.

292. Fearful partly because the Ennet House Staff strongly discourages residents forming

any kind of sentimental attachment to members of the opposite sex during their nine-month stay,[a] to say nothing of attachments to Staffers.

a. This is a corollary of Boston AA's suggestion that single newcomers not get romantically involved for the first year of sobriety. The big reason for this, Boston AAs with time will explain if pinned down, is that the sudden removal of Substances leaves an enormous ragged hole in the psyche of the newcomer, the pain of which the newcomer's supposed to feel and be driven kneeward by and pray to have filled by Boston AA and the old Higher Power, and intense romantic involvements offer a delusive analgesic for the pain of the hole, and tend to make the involvees clamp onto one another like covalence-hungry isotopes, and substitute each other for meetings and Activity in a Group and Surrender, and then if the involvement doesn't pan out (which like how many between newcomers do you suppose do) both involvees are devastated and in even more hole-pain than before and now don't have the intensive-work-in-AA-dependent strength to make it through the devastation without going back to the Substance. Relevant gnomes here might include 'Addicts Don't Have Relationships, They Take Hostages' (sic) and 'An Alcoholic Is a Relief-Seeking Missile.' And so on. The no-involvement thing tends to be the Waterloo of all suggestions, for newcomers, and celibacy's often the issue that separates those who Hang from those who Go Back Out There.

293. Apparently the current colored word for other coloreds. Joelle van Dyne, by the way, was aculturated in a part of the U.S.A. where verbal attitudes toward black people are dated and unconsciously derisive, and is doing pretty much the best she can — *colored* and so on — and anyway is a paragon of racial sensitivity compared to the sort of culture Don Gately was conditioned in.

294. It's a Boston-colored thing on Commitments to make all speech a protracted apostrophe to some absent 'Jim,' Joelle's observed in a neutral sociologic way.

295. Boston Housing Authority.

296. Mixes 5/1 with ferric chloride to produce 'A + B Blood,' an F/X staple of low-budget splatter-films.

297. The cartridge's repetitive emphasis on the Mother Superior's desire to *silence* the novitiate leads B. Boone — a lazy student but very bright girl — to opine that the silent brown-cowled Trappists who've been hanging superfluously around the film's edges like some mute Greek chorus have been serving a symbolic rather than a narrative function, which strikes Hal as perceptive.

298. It's also a sly Schtitt-directed à-clef, of course, amounting to something like We Are What We Revile or We Are What We Scurry Around As Fast As Possible With Our Eyes Averted, though when Schtitt mentions the motto he never attaches any moral connotation to it, or for that matter ever translates it, allowing prorectors and Big Buddies to adjust their translations to suit the needs of the pedagogical moment.

299. © the Commonwealth of MA's Lottery Authority.

300. Easily found when pawning a cordless M. Café® Café-au-Lait Maker at a Brookline shop of pawning, for Fortier and Marathe and the A.F.R. knew well M. DuPlessis's passion of breakfast café au lait.

301. Having in her M.B.A. program absorbed the litigatory lessons of music producers v. cassette-tape manufacturers and film-production companies v. videotape-rental chains, Noreen Lace-Forché protected InterLace's golden goose's copyrights by specifying that all consumer-TP-compatible laser cartridges be engineered as Read-Only — copyable Master cartridges require special OS-codes and special hardware to run,[a] and you need licenses for both the codes and the hardware, which keeps most consumers out of the bootleg-

cartridge business but is not a hard hurdle to clear if you've got financial resources and political incentive (i.e., to dupe off a Master).

a. N.L.-F. had even rigged it so that Masters have to be run at 585 r.p.m. instead of a consumer-TP's cartridge-drive's 450 r.p.m.

302. Thanks to the betrayal of Marathe, this pure-malice agenda is known to the Office of Unspecified Services, though it is not impossible that Fortier deliberately allowed Marathe to pass along this datum, Marathe knows, for the hope of instilling even deeper chills of fear in *Sans-Christe* Gentle and his O.N.A.N. *chiens-courants*. Suspected but unknown by Marathe, Fortier plans to have Marathe view the Entertainment by force before plans for the dissemination of copies from a Master are firm in execution. This not because Fortier for a moment suspects Marathe's love of his wife's health of prompting his betrayal of *Leur Rai Pays* — Fortier had overseen both *jeux du prochain train*[a] at which Marathe's elder brothers had been struck and killed, and Fortier has long nursed a suspicion that Marathe nurses dreams of redress for this.

a. Q.v. Note 304 *sub*.

303. Though hope springs eternal in the breasts, this news had been expected by Broullîme and Fortier the moment they witnessed the shop's brothers active and alert. For they believed no Master cartridge would have lain unshelved in a bag or damp box: even the dim brothers Antitoi, seeing the unique case and slightly larger size of a Master, would have put this to the special side, and arranged for the special 585-r.p.m. hardware to view it to check for special value, and been already lost.

304.

Q.v. @ 2030h. on 11 November Year of the D.A.U., 308 Subdorm B, Enfield Tennis Academy, where James Albrecht Lockley Struck Jr. sits slumped, chin in hands, forehead slathered in $(C_2H_5CO)_2O_2$[a], elbows on tiny cleared spots on desktop, TP compactly humming, word-processing converter plugged into its green-lit dock, HD screen set atop the cartridge-viewer chassis on its fold-out support like a loved one's photo, keyboard hauled out of McGee-like chaos of closet and set on Heavy Touch, cursor throbbing softly at screen's upper left before Struck, hunched blearily over what's starting to emerge as like unabsorbable amounts of research material for his post-Midterm termpaper for Ms. Poutrincourt's History of Canadian Unpleasantness course thing. Struck always refers mentally to his classes as 'things.' Original hopes for at least originality of topic have long since gone over the side of the boat, emotionally. It turns out the more luridly absorbing the angle of topic you choose, the more people have already been there before you with their footprints to fill and their obscurely academic-type-journal articles to try and absorb and, like, synthesize. Struck's been at this over an hour, and his original sights have lowered considerably. He's been feeling a bit punk all day, sinuses with that infallible storm's-on-the-way feeling of weight and clot and a goalie-mask headache that throbs with his heart, and he's now trying to find some new resource in the piles that's obscure and amateurish enough for him to transpose and semi-plagiarize without worrying about Poutrincourt having read it or smelling a rat in the woodpile.

'Almost as little of irreproachable scholarly definitiveness is known about the infamous Separatist "Wheelchair Assassins" (*Les Assassins des Fauteuils Rollents* or A.F.R.s) of southwestern Quebec as is accepted as axiomatic about the herds of oversized "Feral Infants" allegedly reputed to inhabit the periodically overinhabitable forested sections of the eastern Reconfiguration.'

A B.P.L. ArchFax database search off the conjunctive key terms *A.F.R., wheelchair, fauteuil rollent, Quebec, Québec, Separatism, terrorist, Experialism, history,* and *cult,* which you'd think would narrow things down nicely, yielded over 400 items, articles, essays, and papers, in everything from *The Continent* to *Us,* from *Foreign Affairs* to something called *Wild Conceits,* a woebegone little marginal archaic desktop-pub.-

looking thing put out by someplace called Bayside Community College up I-93 in Medford, nowhere near any bays, and edited by the same-named guy whose *Wild Conceits* wheelchair-killers essay Struck, after having to read the first sentence a bunch of times to even make sense of it, gauges he's pretty safe in ripping off, since no way Poutrincourt'd have spent the time to E.S.L. her way through U.S. Academese this insufferable:

'. . . that the prenominate oversized infants reputedly do exist, are anomalous and huge, grow but do not develop, feed on the abundance of annularly available edibles the overgrowth periods in the region represent, do deposit titanically outsized scat, and presumably do crawl thunderously about, occasionally sallying south of murated retention lines and into populated areas of New New England.' In a twist on the usual plagiarism-situation, the hardest work for Struck here is going to be sanitizing the prose in this *Wild Conceits* guy's thing, or at least bringing the verbs and modifiers down out of the like total ozone, which the Academese here on the whole sounds to Struck like the kind of foam-flecked megalograndiosity he associates with Quaaludes and red wine and then the odd Preludin to pull out of the grandiose nosedive of the Quaaludes and red wine. Plus let's not even mention repair-work on the freewheeling transitions; Poutrincourt has a fetishy thing about transitions.

'The massive, feral infants, formed by toxicity and sustained by annulation, however, are, from the vulgate perspective of this Year of the Whisper-Quiet Maytag Dishmaster, essentially passive icons of the Experialist gestalt. Would that the infamous *Assassins des Fauteuils Rollents* were, as well.' Struck can almost see Poutrincourt putting a big red triple-underlined QUOI? under a transition this tortured and freewheeling. Struck pictures the *Wild Conceits* guy totally strafed as he goes, weaving over his foam-flecked desktop, almost. 'For the infamous Quebecker Separatist *A.F.R.* cell's claims to irreduceably active status include the following. The legless Quebecker Wheelchair Assassins, although legless and confined to wheelchairs, nevertheless contrive to have situated large reflective devices across odd-numbered United States highways for the purpose of disorienting and endangering northbound Americans, to have disrupted pipelines between processing points in the eastern Reconfiguration's annular fusion grid, have been linked to attempts at systemic damage of the federally contracted Empire Waste Displacement's launch and reception facilities on both sides of the Reconfigured intracontinental border, and, perhaps most infamously, derive their cell's own sobriquet in the vox populi —— "Wheelchair Assassins" —— from the active practice of assassinating prominent Canadian officials who support or even tolerate what they —— the *A.F.R.*s, in infrequent public communiqués —— regard as both Quebec and Canada *in toto*'s "Sudetenlandization" by the —— as the *A.F.R.* characterize it —— same American-dominated Organization of North American Nations which forced ecologically distorted and possibly mutagenic territory into their —— the nation of Canada, and most specifically and intensively the province of Quebec —— aegis in the newly subsidized Year of the Whopper . . .' — Struck, canted slightly in his desk-chair from the overdevelopment of his body's right side, is also trying to carve up each of this diarrheatic G. T. Day, M.S. guy's clauses into less-long self-contained sentences that sound more earnest and pubescent, like somebody earnestly struggling toward truth instead of flecking your forehead with spittle as he ranted grandiosely — '. . . the Wheelchair Assassins at these all too publicly familiar assassinations materializing, quote "as if from nowhere" unquote, masters of stealth, striking terror into prominent, Canadian hearts, affording no warning excepting the ominous squeak of slow wheels, striking swiftly and without warning, assassinating prominent Canadians and then dissolving back into the dark night' — as opposed to a light night? Struck forces sudden air through his full nose, producing a low and horn-like derisive sound — 'striking always at night, a type of performative signature, to strike at night only, leaving behind only sinuous networks of thin, double tracks in snow, dew, leaves, or earth, as performative signatures, such that a double sinuous *S* shaped line across the traditional *fleur-de-lis* motif of Quebecois Separatism is the *A.F.R.* cell's standard, its escutcheon or "symbol," if you will, in their infrequent and always hostile communiqués to the administrations of Canada and O.N.A.N. Such that, quote, "To hear the squeak," unquote, is now an understood euphemistic locution among officials highly placed in Quebecois, Canadian, and O.N.A.N.ite power structures for instant, terrifying, and violent death. And for the media, as well. As in, quote, "Before many thousands of shocked subscribers, newly elected Bloc Quebecois leader Gilles Duceppe and an aide, guarded by no fewer than a dozen units of the Domestic Detail's elite mounted Cuirassiers, nevertheless heard the squeak last night during a spontaneously disseminated address at the lakeside resort of Pointe Claré."[4]

Struck, clutching his head with one hand, is trying to find *euphemismic* in the TP's Lex-Base.

'. . . Affiliations, sometimes purported, between the Root Cult core of *Les Assassins* on one hand and the more extreme and violently subversive of Quebec's *Séparatisteur* organizations —— the *Fronte de la Libération de la Quebec,* the *Fils de Montcalm,* the ultra right anti-Reconfigurative vishnu of the *Bloc Quebecois* —— tend, however, to be contradicted by both stated agendas —— the conventional Separatist phalances demanding only the independent secession of provincial Quebec and the elimination of Anglo-American cognates from public discourse, while the A.F.R.s' stated aims being nothing less total than the total return of all Reconfigured territories to American administration, the cessation of all E.W.D. airborne waste displacement and ATHSCME rotary air mass displacement activity within 175 kilometers of Canadian soil, the removal of all fission/waste/fusion annulars north of the 42°-N. Parallel, and the secession of Canada *in toto* from the Organization of North American Nations —— and by the fact that all too many prominent figures in the recent sociohistory of the Separatist movement —— for e.g., Schnede, Charest, Remillard, both Sr. and Jr. Bouchards —— have, in the last 24 months —— particularly, in the violent and bloody autumn of the Year of the Trial-Size Dove Bar —— "heard the squeak." '

Struck's little TP's internal Lex files confirm *vishnu,* at least. Plus there's a kind of almost savage edge to the article's incoherence that Struck's getting almost to like, a little: he keeps imagining the little hyphen of wrinkle Poutrincourt gets between her eyebrows when she doesn't follow something and can't quite tell if it's your English's fault or her English's fault. 'Prior to Y.P.W.c.'s Freedom of Speculation Act, credible sociohistorical data on the origins and evolution of *Les Assassins des Fauteuils Rollents* from obscure, adolescent, nihilistic Root Cult to one of the most feared cells in the annals of Canadian extremism was regrettably patchy and dependent on the hearsay of sources whose scholarly veracity was of an integrity somewhat less than unimpeachable.' Struck here pictures Thierry Poutrincourt, who tends to get that little annoyed-confusion wrinkle sometimes even with the lucidest of term papers, lowering her tall head and charging into a wall. One sinus feels noticeably bigger than the other sinus, and there's something not quite right with his neck from sitting hunched all this time, and he'd kill relatives for a quick DuBois.

'*Les Assassins des Fauteuils Rollents* of Quebec are essentially cultists, locating both their political *raison d'etre* and their philosophical *dasein* within the North American sociohistorical interval of intensive special interest diffraction that preceded —— nay, one might daresay stood in integral causal relation with respect to —— the nearly simultaneous inaugurations of O.N.A.N.ite governance, continental Interdependence, and the commercial subsidization of a lunar O.N.A.N. calendar. Like most Canadian cult extensions, however, the Wheelchair Assassins and their cultic derivations have proven substantially more fanatical, less benign, less reasonable, and substantially more malignant —— in sum, more difficult for responsible authorities to anticipate, control,

---

[4] CBC/PATHÉ 1200h.–0000h. Summary Cartridge # 911–24–04, 4 May Y.P.Wc., © Y.P. Wc., PATHÉ Nouvelle Toujours, Ltd.

interdict, or reason with than even the most passionate U.S. kabals. This scholarly essay concurs in many essential respects with the thesis that Canadian and other non American Root Cults, in contrast to all but what Phelps and Phelps argue are isolated pockets of antihistorical American stelliformism, persist so queerly in directing their reverent fealty toward principles, quote, "often not only isomorphic with but activally *opposed* to the cultists' own individual pleasure, comfort, *cui bono*, or entertainment as to be all but outside the ken of both the sophisticated predictive models of psychosocial science and the rudimentary comprehension of human reason."[5]

This all takes serious labor for Struck to decoct the gist out of and then recast in rather less uptown and more basic studential prose. Twice in the hall outside his and Shaw's and Pemberton's room, Rader and Wagenknecht and some other 16's-sounding males go down the hall, all of them together going 'Er, ah, ee, oo, ah, er, ah, ee . . . ,' and so on. 'It is an accepted fact that Les Assassins' Root Cult, in a fashion typical of those whose objects are divorced from the rational advancement of individual interest, takes, for its rites and personality, rituals intimately bound up with "*Les jeux pour-memes*," formal competitive games whose end is less any sort of "prize" than it is a manner of basic identity: i.e., that is, "game" as metaphysical environment and psychohistorical locus and geatalt.' Struck's own historical dad, during Jim's own childhood in Rancho Mirage, was an inveterate red-wine-with-heavy-tranqs-on-the-side drinker, who used to make late-night phone calls to people he didn't know very well and make statements he later had to retract at great length, until finally one autumn night the Dad had staggered out and attempted a one-and-a-half tuck into the Struck family's backyard pool that he hadn't recalled had been drained, resulting in a neck brace for life that ended his career as a low-80s golfer, resulting in incredible bitterness and family trauma, before little J.A.L.S. Jr. was shipped off to the Rolling Hills Academy.

'It is, for example, largely conceded that Les Assassins' confinement to their epithetic wheelchairs can be traced to rural southwestern pre-Experialist Quebec's infamous "*Le Jeu du Prochain Train*," and that the A.F.R.'s Root Cult itself was comprised largely or perhaps even entirely of veteran devotees and practitioners of this savage, nihilistic, and mettle testing *jeu pour-meme*.

' "*La Culte du Prochain Train*," often translated as "The Cult of the Next Train," is known to have originated at least a decade prior to Reconfiguration among the male offspring of asbestos, nickel and zinc miners in the desolate Papineau region of what was then extreme southwest Quebec. The chilling game's competition and its upspringing cult soon spread throughout the network of non-ionized and pre-Interdependent railroad lines which carried raw minerals south to Ottawa and the United States' Great Lake Ports.' Over Struck's little desk hangs a model airplane made entirely from different parts of beer cans. While Inc was keen on the whole lurid mirror-across-highway terrorism thing of early O.N.A.N., and Schacht's paper's focus was the violent French-Catholic protests against municipal fluoridation under Mulroney, Struck had picked the A.F.R.-and-Russian-Roulettish-train-jumping-cult-thing connection, and was sticking to it with the same tenacity that kept him on the 18's A-squad despite a serve that deLint described as resembling a debutante's curtsy. The plane's got flattened cans for wings, smunched-flat cans for wheels, part of a tallboy for fuselage and snout.

'As with many games, *Le Jeu du Prochain Train* was itself substantially simpler than

---

5 in Phelps and Phelps, *The Cults of the Unwavering I: A Field Guide to Cults of Currency Specula-tion, Melanin, Fitness, Bioflavinoids, Spectation, Assassination, Stasis, Property, Agoraphobia, Re-pute, Celebrity, Acraphobia, Performance, Amway, Fame, Infamy, Deformity, Scopophobia, Syntax, Consumer Technology, Scopophilia, Presleyism, Hunterism, Inner Children, Eros, Xenophobia, Sur-gical Enhancement, Motivational Rhetoric, Chronic Pain, Solipsism, Survivalism, Preterition, Anti-Abortionism, Kevorkianism, Allergy, Albinism, Sport, Chiliasm, and Telentertainment in pre-O.N.A.N. North America*, © Y.P.W.

the organization of the competition.' A cool smile from Struck. 'It was played after sunset at specified sites, specifically *les passages à niveau de voie ferrée* that marked every rural Quebecker road's intersection with a railroad track. In the Year of the Whopper, there were over two thousand (2,000) such intersections in the Papineau region alone, though not all saw heavy enough flow to accommodate the complexities of true competition.

'Six boys, miners' sons, ages ten to roughly sixteen, Quebecois French speaking boys, line up on six railroad ties' juts just outside the track. Two hundred sixteen (216) boys —— never either more nor less —— are involved in a night's opening rounds, organized into sixes, each group of six taking its turn with a different train, standing on consecutive juts just outside one track, waiting, doubtless tense, awaiting the procession of a fearsome bride, indeed. The night's heavily travelled crossing's schedule of trains is known to *Le Jeu du Prochain Train*'s episcopate of *les directeurs de jeu* —— older, post-adolescent boys, veterans of previous *les jeux,* many of them legless and in wheelchairs or —— for the sons of asbestos miners, many orphaned and desperately poor —— on crude rolling boards. No timepieces are permitted the players, who are under the absolute discretion of the game's *directeurs,* whose decisions are final and often brutally enforced. They all are silent, listening for the sound of the engine's whistle, a sound which is sad and cruel at the same time, as the sound approaches and begins to subtly undergo Doppler Effects. They tense palely muscled legs beneath hand me down corduroys as the next train's one white eye rounds the track's curve and bears down on the game's waiting boys.'

Struck keeps bogging down in these parts where it seems like the guy just totally abandons a scholarly tone, and even probably starts making up or hallucinating details which there's no way Jim Struck could represent himself as having been there to see, and he's blue-delete-looping all over the place, plus grinding his eye and picking at his forehead, his two more or less constant responses to creative stress.

'*Le Jeu du Prochain Train* itself is simplicity in motion. The object: Be the last of your round's six to jump from one side of the tracks to the other —— that is, across the tracks —— before the train passes. Your only real opponents are your six's other five. Never is the train itself regarded as an opponent. The speeding, screaming train is regarded rather as *le jeu*'s boundary, arena, and reason. Its size, its speed down the extremely gradual north-to-south grade of what was then southwestern Quebec, and the precise mechanical specifications of each scheduled train —— these are known to the *directeurs,* they comprise the constants in a game the variables of which are the respective wills of the six ranged along the track, and their estimates of one another's will to risk all to win.'

Struck transposes clearly nonadolescent uptown material like this into: 'The variable of the game isn't so much a matter of the train, but the player's courage and will.'

'The last few instants, vanishingly small, when the player may hurl himself athwart the expanse of track, across timber ties, creosote stench, gravel and scarred iron, amid the ear splitting scream of the whistle almost overhead, able to feel the huge push of terrible air from the transport's cow catcher or express train's rounded nose, to go sprawling in the gravel past the tracks' other side and roll to see wheels and flanges, couplings and driving rods, the furious back and forth of transverse axles, feeling the whistle's steam condense to drizzle all around —— these few seconds are known, familiar as their own pulse, to the boys who assemble and play.' Struck's now progressed to grinding the whole heel of his hand into his eyesocket, producing a kind of ectoplasmic pinwheel of red in there. Did like even pre-bullet railroad engines have flanges and cowcatchers and whistles that steamed?

In a disastrous lapse, Struck copies *hurl himself athwart,* a decidedly un-Struckish-sounding verb phrase, verbatim into his text.

'. . . that the true variable which renders *le Jeu du Prochain Train* a contest and not merely a game involves the nerve and heart and willingness to risk all of any or all of the five waiting beside you at the track. How long can they wait? When will they choose? Their lives and limb worth how much Queen-headed coin this night? More radical by far than the American youth automobile game of "Chicken" to which its principle is frequently compared (five, not one, different wills to comparatively gauge, in addition to your own will's resolve, and no motion or action to distract you from the tension of waiting motionlessly to move, waiting as one by one the other five quail and save themselves, leap to beat the train . . . ,' and then the sentence just ends, without even a close to the parenthesis, though Struck, with a canny sense for this sort of thing, knows the analogy to Chicken'll ring just the right bell, term-paper-wise.

'Le Jeu's historic best, reportedly, however, ignore their five competitors completely, concentrating their entire attention on determining the last viable instant in which to leap, regarding the last, final, and only true opponent in the game to be their own will, mettle, and intuition about the last viable instant in which to leap. These nerveless few, le Jeu's finest —— many of whom will go on to directeur future jeux (if not, often, to membership in Les Assassins or its stelliform offshoots) —— these nerveless and self-contained virtuosi never see their opponents' flinches or tics or the darkenings at corduroys' crotches, none of the normal signs of will faltering which lesser players scan for —— for the game's finest players frequently close their eyes entirely as they wait, trusting the railroad ties' vibration and the whistle's pitch, as well as intuition, and fate, and whatever numinous influences lie just beyond fate.' Struck at certain points imagines himself gathering this Wild Conceits guy's lapels together with one hand and savagely and repeatedly slapping him with the other — forehand, backhand, forehand.

'The cult's game's principle is simple. The last of the six to jump before the train and land intact wins the round. The fifth through the second to leap have lost, but acquitted themselves.

'The first in a round to quail and jump walks home from there, alone under the moon, disgraced and ashamed.

'But even the first to quail and jump has jumped. Far beyond prohibited, not to jump at all is regarded as impossible. To "perdre son coeur" and not jump at all is outside le Jeu's limit. The possibility simply does not exist. It is unthinkable. Only once, in le Jeu du Prochain Train's extensive oral history, has a miner's son not jumped, lost his heart and frozen, remaining on his jut as the round's train passed. This player later drowned. "Perdre son coeur," when it is mentioned at all, is known also as "Faire un Bernard Wayne," in dubious honor of this lone unjumping asbestos miner's son, about whom little beyond his subsequent drowning in the Baskatong Reservoir is known, his name denoting a figure of ridicule and disgust among speakers of the Papineau Region vulgate.' Disastrously, Struck blithely transposes this stuff too, with not even a miniature appliance-size bulb flickering anywhere over his head.

'The game's object is to jump last and land still fully limbed upon the opposite embankment.

'Expresses are 30 k.p.h. faster than conventional transports, but a transport's cow catcher mangles. A boy struck head on by a moving train is shot as from a cannon, knocked out of his shoes, describes a towering, flailing arc, and is transported home in a burlap sack. A player caught beneath a wheel and run over is frequently spread out along a hundred red meters or more of reddened track, and is transported home in a number of ceremonial asbestos and nickel mining shovels provided by the Jeu's older and frequently dismembered directeurs.

'As happens more often, purportedly, a boy who has dived more than half way across the tracks when he is struck and hit, loses one or more legs —— either there on the spot, if lucky, or later, under surgical gas and orthopedic saws applied to what are customarily violently angled masses of unrecognizably contuded meat.' The paradox here for Struck as plagiarist, who needs something with sufficient detail to be able to basically just rehash, is that this thing here has almost too much detail, much of it purple; it doesn't even seem all that scholarly; it seems more like the Wild Conceits Bayside C.C. guy seemed to get more and more tipsy as the thing went on until he felt free to make a lot of it up, like e.g. the contuded-meat bits, etc.

What's interesting to Hal Incandenza about his take on Struck, sometimes Pemulis, Evan Ingersoll, et al. is that congenital plagiarists put so much more work into camouflaging their plagiarism than it would take just to write up an assignment from conceptual scratch. It usually seems like plagiarists aren't lazy so much as kind of navigationally insecure. They have trouble navigating without a detailed map's assurance that somebody has been this way before them. About this incredible painstaking care to hide and camouflage the plagiarism — whether it's dishonesty or a kind of kleptomaniacal thrill-seeking or what — Hal hasn't developed much of any sort of take.

'It is frightfully simple and straightforward. Sometimes the last of the six to jump is struck; then the second to last leaper becomes the last and victor, and advances, each winner literally "surviving" into the game's next round, a sort of sextupled semi final, six rounds of six Canadian boys each: the, quote, "*Les Trente-Six*" for the evening. The initial rounds' boys —— those who have been neither the last nor the disgraceful first to leap —— are permitted to stay at the *le passage à niveau de voie ferree,* assembled to become the semi finals' silent audience. The entire *Le Jeu du Prochain Train* is customarily conducted in silence.' In a disastrous and maybe unconsciously self-destructive set of lapses, Struck rehabilitates the prose but keeps a lot of the hallucinatory specific descriptive stuff in, unfootnoted, though there's obviously no way he could pretend to have been there.

'The surviving losers from among the *Les Trente-Six* then swell the ranks of the silent gallery as the six nerveless winners —— the finalists, this night's "*attendants longtemps ses tours*" —— some bleeding or gray with shock, survivors already of two separate long delayed leaps and hairbreadth escapes, eyes blank or closed, mouths working in savored distaste, await the nightly 2359 Express, the ultra ionized "*Le Train de la Foudre*" from Mont Tremblant to Ottawa. They will jump athwart the tracks in front of its high speed nose at the final moment, each trying to be the last to leap and live. It is not rare for several of the *le Jeu's* finalists to be struck.' Struck tries to decide whether it'd be unrealistic or unself-consciously realistic to keep using his own name as a verb — would a man with anything to camouflage use his own name as a verb?

'. . . that several among the *La Culte du Prochain Train's* survivors and organizational directorate went on to found and comprise *Les Assassins des Fauteuils Rollents* is beyond sociohistorical dispute, though the precise ideological relation between the B.S. era's simultaneously chivalric and nihilistic Cult of the Train's savage tournaments and the present's limbless cell of anti-O.N.A.N. extremists remains the subject of the same scholarly debate that surrounds the evolution of northern Quebec's *La Culte de Baiser Sans Fin* into the not particularly dreaded but media savvy *Fils de Montcalm* cell credited with the helicoptered dropping of the 12 meter, human waste filled, pie shell onto the rostrum of U.S. President Gentle's second Inaugural.

'As with the *La Culte du Prochain Train,* the Cult of the Endless Kiss of the iron mining regions surrounding the Gulf of St. Lawrence, coalesced around a periodic, tournament style competition, this one comprised of 64 adolescent Canadian participants, of whom one half were female.[6] Thus, the first round pitted 32 couples, each of which consisted of one male and one female Quebecker.' Struck is trying to phone Hal, but gets only his room's wearisome phone-machine-message; can you ever say *pitted* without some kind of *against* in there someplace later in the sentence? Struck envisions the *Wild Conceit* scholar utterly strafed by this time, the guy's eyes crossed and his head lolling and having to cover one eye with a hand just to see a single screen, and typing with his nose. But with the apparent self-destructive credulity that characterizes many plagiarists, no matter how gifted, Struck goes ahead and puts in the complementless *pitted,* imagining forehand and backhand slaps all the while. 'Of each pair, one half, designated by lot, filled his or her lungs to capacity with inhaled air, while the other exhaled maximally to empty his or hers. Their mouths were then fitted together and quickly sealed by an

---

6 Except in certain very esoteric variations on the game.

organizing cultist with occlusive tape, who then expertly employed the thumb and forefinger of both hands to seal the combatants' nostrils. Thus, the battle of the Endless Kiss had been joined. The entire lung contents of the designatedly inhaled player was then exhaled orally into the emptied lungs of his or her opponent, who in turn exhaled the inhalation back to its original owner, and so forth, back and forth, the same air being traded back and forth, with oxygen and carbon dioxide ratios becoming progressively more Spartan, until the organizer holding their nostrils closed officially declared one combatant or the other to be "*evanoui*," or, "swooned," either fallen to the ground or out on his or her feet. The theoretics of the contest lends itself to an appreciation of the patient, attritive, grinding down tactics of traditional Quebecois *Séparatisteurs* such as *Les Fils de Montcalm* and the *Fronte de la Libération du Québec,* as opposed to the viciousness and brinksmanship of "*Le Prochain Train*"'s Root Cult's disabled heirs. The figurative object of the "*Baisser*" competition appears —— according to Phelps and Phelps —— to involve using what one is given with maximally exhaustive levels of efficiency and endurance before excreting it back whence it came, a stoic stance toward waste utilization that the Phelps somewhat cavalierly employ to illuminate the *Montcalmistes'* relative indifference to a continental Reconfiguration that constitutes *Les Assassins des Fauteuils Rollents'* whole "*raison de la guerre outrance.*" 'b

    a. Pimple cream.

    b. 'Reason for all-out war,' which Struck inserts without bothering even to check for the definition Day'd been too befogged to give, which is in and of itself almost suicidal, given that Poutrincourt knows exactly how much French facility Struck's got, or rather hasn't.

305. (she thought then)

306. Some of her and Jim's best arguments had been over the connotations of 'Everybody's a critic,' which Jim had liked to repeat with all different shades and pitches of ironic double-edge.

307. Joelle van Dyne and Orin Incandenza each remember themselves as the original approachee. It's unclear which if either's memory is accurate, though it's noteworthy that this is one of only two total times Orin has perceived himself as the approachee, the other being the 'Swiss hand-model' on whose nude flank he's been furiously tracing infinity signs all during the *Moment* Subject's absence.

308. = point of view.

309. In the Chestnut Hills Shopping Center on Boylston/Rte. 9, which the E.T.A. A-squad staggers past several times a week, on runs — a chain, but a very top-shelf and fine one, and the Brookline Legal puts on a particularly fine marine spread, and the boniface seemed to know Dr. Incandenza and called him by name, and brought him a double bonded without being asked.

310. Jargon: Film/Cartridge Studies.

311. Trilateral North American immigration bureaucracy.

312. Boston AA jargon. *Y.E.T.* is 'You're Eligible Too,' a denial-buster for those who compare others' ghastly consequences to their own so far, the point being to get you to see the street-guy with socks for gloves drinking Listerine at 0700h. as just slightly farther down the same road you're on, when you Come In. Or something close to that.

313. The bureaucracy of Québecois pensions, which had ruled against buying anything more than a used Kenbeck pacemaker for Marathe's father, now deceased.

314. See Note 304 *supra.*

315. Marathe's malentendu of *live-in.*

316. Like e.g. the times C.T. and the Moms would come out to Logan to pick Mario and Himself up from a filming trip, Mario lugging gear, Himself damp and pasty from the cabin pressure and not enough leg-room and his sportcoat pockets always clicking with little plastic bottles with unopenable caps, and in the car up to Enfield Mario's uncle

would keep up an Opheliac mad monologue of chatter that would get Himself's poor teeth grinding so bad that when they pulled over to the breakdown lane and Mario came around to open the door and let Himself lean out and be ill there'd be grit in the throw-up that came out, white dental visible grit, from all the grinding.

317. © B.S. 1981, Routledge & Kegan Paul Plc, London UK, wildly expensive hdcover; not on disk.

318. Maine having been lost altogether, recall.

319. Incandenza family idiom for leftovers.

320. Main library, M.I.T., East Cambridge.

321.
Q.v. for a confirming example 1930h. Thurs., 12 November Y.D.A.U., Rm. 204 Subdorm B:
'No, look, it's still Rise Over Run. The derivative's the slope of the tangent at some point along the function. It doesn't matter what point until they give you the point on the test.'
'Will this even be on the Boards? Do they go past trig?'
'This *is* fucking trig. They'll give you word problems that may involve changing quantities — something accelerating, a voltage, inflation of O.N.A.N. currency over U.S. currency. Differentiation'll save you half the time, all those triangles inside triangles to figure change with trig. Trig's a Unit-bender on rate-changes. Derivatives're just trig with some imagination. You imagine the points moving inexorably toward each other until for all practical purposes they're the same point. The slope of a defined line becomes the slope of a tangent to one point.'
'One point that's in fact actually two points?'
'You use your goddamn *imagination,* Inc, plus a couple prescribed limits. Which they won't fuck with you on limits on the general test, trust me. This is a big pink titty compared to an Eschaton calculation. You move the two points you're doing Rise-over-Run on infitesimally close together, you end up with a plug-in formula.'
'Can I tell you about my dream now and then we'll use the momentum from that to plow through this?'
'Just write this on your wrist or something. Function x, exponent n, the derivative's going to be $nx + x^{n-1}$ for any kind of first-order rate-of-increase thing they're going to ask you. This assumes a definable limit, of course, which no way they're going to fuck with you on limits on the fucking Boards.'
'It was a DMZ-dream.'
'Do you see how you're going to apply this to a rate-of-increase-type little story they'll pose?'
'It involved your experimental soldier, the massive dose.'
'Let me just close this door, here.'
'It was the Leavenworth convict. The one you said had left the planet. The one belting out Ethel Merman. It was horrific, Mikey. In the dream I was the soldier.'
'So you're now going to assume a real you-know-what experience will be similar to the experience of a nightmare.'
'Aha. Why nightmare? Why do you assume it was a nightmare? Did I use the word *nightmare?*'
'You used the word *horrific.* I assume it wasn't a romp through the heather.'
'In the dream the horror was that I wasn't really singing "There's No Business Like Show Business." I was really screaming for help. I was screaming like "Help! I'm screaming for help and everybody's acting as if I'm singing Ethel Merman covers! It's me! It's me, screaming for help!"'
'A Rusk-level dream, Inc. A standard nobody-understands-me dream. The DMZ and Mermanization were incidental.'
'There was a quality of *loneliness* to it, though. Unlike anything. To be screaming that

I'm screaming for help instead of singing a show-tune and to have the wardens and doctors gathered around snapping their fingers and tapping their feet.'

'Have I mentioned DMZ doesn't show up on a G.C./M.S.? Struck tracked this down off an obscure Digestive-Flora footnote. It's the fitviavi-mold base. If the stuff shows up at all it shows as a slight case of imbalanced yeast.'

'I thought only girls got yeast.'

'Inc, don't be so fucking naïve. Data number two is Struck is halfway toward nailing down that this stuff's original intent was to induce what they called quote transcendent experiences in get this chronic alcoholics in the like 1960s at Verdun Protestant Hospital in Montreal.'

'How come everywhere I turn this fall now everybody's suddenly mentioning Québec in all kinds of radically different contexts? Orin's calling with some protracted obsession about anti-O.N.A.N. Québecers.'

'. . . Tavis up and announces Québec are the lambs in this year's fundraiser. Your Mum's from Québec.'

'And then this term of all terms I take Poutrincourt's insurgency class, which is basically a Québecathon.'

'Oh I *definitely* I'd suspect some kind of conspiracy or trap. It's obvious everything's pointing toward getting you in a cell belting out Mermanalia. Inc, I think your hinges are starting to squeak. I think this is what plateaux-hopping up to the top does to somebody. I think a meaningful transcendent DMZ-type non-uremic-fallout interlude before Tucson is just what the carpenter ordered, for the old hinges. Keep you from going back to just smoking that Bob Hope day in day out when the test's up. Shit'll kill your lungs. Shit'll make you fat, soft, moist and pale, Inc. Seen it happen. You need something more than a 30-day cleanout. The *tu-sais-qué* could be just the reconfiguration you need to start branching out, leave the Bob Hope alone, find something you can take to college or the Show and not get paralyzed. Shit'll paralyze you over time, Incblob. Saw it happen time and over, back in the neighborhood. Once-promising stand-up guys spending their lives in front of the TP, eating Nutter Butters and whacking off into an old sock. The shit-fairy moves in with luggage for an extended stay, Inc. Plus indecisive? You haven't seen indecisive til you've seen a guy with little fat-titties slumped in a chair in his tenth year of nonstop Bob Hope. It's not pretty. Incster my friend it's not pretty at all. A transcendent experience with me and the Axhandle could be just what the hinges are squeaking for. Be around some other people for a change. Don't make me sit there with just Axhandle babbling about Yale. Leave the Visine at home.'

'Was it *transcendent*? The term in Struck's literature? Or was it *transcendental?*'

' 's the difference for Christ's sake?'

'Mike, what if I said I've been moving toward more than just a month off.'

'Abandon All Hope.[a] This what I was talking.'

'I mean maybe make a decision. Forever. What if it was that I was doing it more and more and it was getting less fun but I was still doing it more and more, and the only way to moderate would be to like wave a hankie at it altogether.'

'I applaud. Some low-risk transcendentalism with me and the Human Hatchet could be just the impotence for this kind of like major re—'

'But it'd be everything. Blue Flames, the odd 'drine. If I do anything I know I'd go back to the Bob. I'd drop Madame Psychosis with you guys and all my firmest resolve would melt and I'd have the one-hitter out and be sniveling at you to spring some eternal Hope on me.'

'You're so naïve, Inc. You're so sharp in one way and such a little bald little fat-legged baby in the woods in others. You think you're just going to go Here I go, deciding, and reverse total thrust and quit everything?'

'What I said was what if.'

'Hal, you are my friend, and I've been friends to you in ways you don't even have a clue. So brace yourself for a growth-spurt. You want to quit because you're starting to see you need it, and —'

'That's exactly it. Peems, think how horrible that'd be, if somebody *needed* it. Not just *liked* it a great great great deal. Needing it becomes a whole separate order of. . . . It seems horrific. It seems like the difference between really loving something and being —'

'Say the word, Inc.'

'. . .'

'Because you know why? What if it's true? The word. What if you are? So the answer's just walk away? If you're addicted you *need* it, Hallie, and if you *need* it what do you imagine happens if you just hoist the white flag and try to go on without it, without anything?'

'. . .'

'You lose your mind, Inc. You die inside. What happens if you try and go without something the machine *needs*? Food, moisture, sleep, O_2? What happens to the machine? Think about it.'

'You were just now applauding the idea of Abandoning All Hope. You were just invoking an image of me with breasts, masturbating into laundry, with cobwebs between my ass and a chair.'

'That's the *Bob*. I didn't hear me say *everything*. If you need the Bob, Inc, you can only quit the Bob if you move onward and up to something else.'

'Harder drugs. Just like those old filmstrips about pot opening the door to larger drugs, where Jiminy Cricket —'

'Oh fuck you. It doesn't have to be harder. It just has to be something. I know guys quit heroin, coke. How? They make the strategic move to a case a day of Coors. Or to methadone, whatever. I know hard-drinking guys Inc that got off the booze by switching to the Bob Hope. Me myself, you've seen, I switch all the time. The trick is the right switch for a man's wiring. I'm saying a real cobweb-blaster with me and Axford after the Fundraiser could help you get some serious perspective, cut the babytalk and sweeping bullshit decisions there's no way you can do and start getting a real handle on how you're going to branch out away from this Bob thing, which I applaud the getting away from the Bob for you, Inc, it's not your thing, you were starting to get that look of a guy that'll end up with tits.'

'So you're in a very subtle way lobbying for a DMZ-drop by saying you don't believe I could simply quit everything. Since you sure don't plan to quit. With your left eye wobbling all over the place. You haven't even quit the Tenuate. "Winners don't ever have to quit" and all deLint's little —'

'I didn't hear me say none of that. And I think you probably could quit it all. For a while. You're not a pussy. You've got balls, I know. I bet you could gut it out.'

'For a while, you're saying.'

'And but what do you think would happen after a while, though? Without something you *need*?'

'What, you're saying I'd grab my chest and keel over? Clutch my head in the middle of a Tap & Whack and die of an aneurism like that girl last year at Atwood?'

'No. But you'd die inside. Maybe outside too. But what I've seen, if you're the real thing and *need* it and just cut yourself off of it altogether, you die inside. You lose your mind. I've seen it happen. Cold Turkey they call it, the Bird. White-knuckling. Guys that'd just quit everything because they were in too deep and quit it all and just died.'

'A Clipperton, you mean? You're saying Himself killed himself because he got sober? Because he didn't get sober. There was a thing of Wild Turkey right there on the counter by the oven he blew his fucking head up with. So don't try to kertwang me with *him*, Mike.'

'Inc, what I know about your Da could be inscribed with a blunt crayon along the rim of a shot glass. I'm talking guys I *know*. Wolf Spiders. Allston guys, that quit. Some did a Clipperton, yes. Some ended up in the Mental Marriott. Some got through by they joined NA or a cult or some bug-eyed church and went around with ties talking about Jesus or

Surrendering, but that shit's not going to work for you because you're too sharp to ever buy the God-Squad shit. Most nothing big happened, that needed it and quit. They got up and went to work and came home and ate and went to sleep and got up, day after day. But dead. Like machines; you could almost see the keys in their backs. You looked into their maps and something was gone. The walking dead. They loved it so much they needed it and gave it up and now they were waiting to die. Something was all over, inside.'

'Their *joie de vivre.* The fire in the belly.'

'Hal, it's been what, now, for you, two-and-a-half days without? three days? How you feeling in there already, brother?'

'I'm all right.'

'Uh-*huh.* Incpuddle, all I know's I'm your friend. I am. You don't want to communate with the Madame, you can hold me and Ax's purses for us. You do what you want and point me toward whoever tells you different. I'm just giving you the advice to look a little further past that second of deciding something I know you won't let yourself take back.'

'Some vital part of my like personhood would die without something to ingest. This is your view.'

'Sometimes you don't listen real well, Hallie. That's all right. Spend some time figuring out this *needing.* Like what part of you's come to *need* it, do you think.'

'You're alleging that's the part that'll die.'

'Just whatever part you feel has come to *need* what you're planning to take away from it.'

'The part that's dependent or incomplete, you mean. The *addict.*'

'That's just a word.'

a. q.v. Note 334 *sub.*

322. Johnette F., whose very first stepmother had been a Chelsea MA police officer, was conditioned in early childhood to refer to police as 'police' or 'the Law,' since most B.P.D. personnel find the street term *the Finest* sardonic.

323. People outside the Boston AA community always use *The* and say *The Ennet House;* this is one way to always tell somebody new or from outside the community.

324.
17 NOVEMBER — YEAR OF THE DEPEND ADULT UNDERGARMENT
Sometimes at odd little times of day the E.T.A. males' locker room downstairs in Comm.-Ad. is empty, and you can go in there and sort of moon around and listen to the showers drip and the drains gurgle. You can feel the odd stunned quality customarily crowded places have at empty times. You can take your time dressing, flex in front of the big plate mirror over the sink; the mirror has projecting side-mirrors so you can check out the old biceps from either side, see the jawline in profile, practice expressions, try to look all natural and uncomposed so you can try to see what you really might normally look like to other people. The air in the locker room hangs heavy with the smells of underarms, deodorant, benzoin, camphonated powder, serious feet, old steam. Also Lemon Pledge and a slight smell of electrical burn from overused blow-dryers. Traces of powder and fuller's earth[a] on the blue carpeting, down in too deep to get out without a steamer. You can take a comb out of the big jar of Barbicide on the shelf by the sink, and like a .38-caliber blow-dryer, and experiment boldly. It's the best mirror in the Academy, intricately lit from all perspectives. Dr. J. O. Incandenza knew his adolescents. At slack times, sometimes head custodian Dave ('F.D.V.') Harde can be found in here, taking a tiny nap on one of the benches that run in front of the lockers, which he claims the benches do something palliative for his spinal funiculi. More often there's one of Dave's incredibly old and interchangeable menial-task janitors in here running a carpet sweeper or spraying industrial disinfectant in the urinals. You can go into the shower area and not turn the water on and sing, really let go. Michael Pemulis's own vocals sound pro-quality good to him, but only when he's surrounded by shower-tile. Sometimes when it's empty in here you can

catch snatches of voices and intriguing feminine-hygienic noises from the females' locker room on the other side of the lockers' wall.

At most other times of day, your certain type of more delicately constituted E.T.A. jr. uses the primitive subdorm hall showers and sinks and avoids the packed locker room at almost all costs. No way Western man ever should have conceived of commodes and hot showers in the same crowded air-space. T. Schacht can clear out most of a steamy locker room just by lumbering into a commode-stall and driving the latch home with a certain purposeful force.

The prorectors have their own showers in a kind of lounge near their rooms in the secondary tunnel, with a Viewer and recliners and a little fridgelet and a dicky-proof door.

When M. M. Pemulis came down to dress for P.M.s at about 1420h.,[b] the only people in the locker room were 14-A lobber nonpareil Todd Possalthwaite, hunched and weeping, and Keith Freer, whom Pemulis was to play and who looked in no hurry to get dressed and out there to play, and could very possibly have been the thing that was making Postal Weight weep. The so-called 'Viking' was shirtless and had a towel around his neck and was at the mirror ministering to his skin. He had high hard white-blond hair and an extremely muscular neck and lower jaw, with a certain type of protrusive gonions that made his upper face look tapered and sly. His hair always reminded Hal Incandenza of frozen surf, Hal said. Todd Possalthwaite was near-nude and hunched on the bench under his locker, his face in his hands, with its nose's white bandages visible through spread fingers, weeping softly, shoulders trembling.

Pemulis, who's Postal Weight's Big Buddy and sort of lob-and-Eschaton-mentor and genuinely likes the kid, dropped his gear and gave him a sort of male-affectionate fake one-two punch like Think Fast. ' 's the nose, Todder?' Like all of them, Pemulis could do his locker's combination by feel, from months and years of constant combination-doing. He was looking all around himself and the room. Freer made a slight noise when Pemulis asked the Postman if there was anything he could do.

'Nothing's true,' Postal Weight sobbed, his voice palm-muffled, rocking slightly on the bench. His locker was open and little-boy cluttered. He was wearing only an an unbuttoned little flannel shirt and a Johnson & Johnson jr. jock strap, and had tiny white feet[c] and delicate little shell-like toes. He was supposed to be in Donni Stott's Valley-Map laugher right now, Pemulis knew.

'What, metaphysical angst at thirteen?' Pemulis directs the question to the quote-Viking's reflection's eye in the mirror. Freer's back is tapered and uncolloped and for a tennis player's back has superb latissimal definition but is mottled slightly from repeated applications and defoliations of Pledge, Freer being a profligate Pledge-user because he is complexion-obsessed and has the sort of Nordicular skin that peels instead of tanning. He still has his jeans and loafers on, Pemulis sees. Pemulis keeps waiting for the distinctive attitudinal upswing of two pre-match Tenuate spansules.[d] Pemulis's locker is both full and very precisely ordered, practically alphabetized, like the trunk of an experienced seaman. Disassemblable scale and armamentarium and mood-altering substances used to be concealed in several factory-concealed niches in the special system of niche-riddled portable shelving Pemulis had installed at age 15. Plus small cloth packets of ground cayenne pepper, to foil the always-remotely-possible sniffer-dog, when he was a callow youth. This was before the discovery of the ultimate entrepôt above the false ceiling in Subdorm B's male hallway.

'Just a disappointed dinkle.' Freer's chuckle tends to be mirthless. 'What I could get out of him before the waterworks, Postal Weight's old man promised him so-and-so if the kid accomplishes thus-and-such.' His speech was distorted because he was ballooning his cheek with his tongue and applying flesh-tinted cream to a possible pimple there. 'And the Postmaster here feels like he's held up his side of the accomplishment, and now I get the drift Daddy's backing out.'

Possalthwaite's shoulders continued to tremble as he cried into his hands.

'In other words welching you're saying the Dad is,' Pemulis said to Freer.

'I gather now the Dad's trying to restructure the original deal all of a sudden.'

Pemulis undid his belt. 'The dangled carrot's snatched away, the brass ring plays hard to get, to coin a maxim.'

'Something about Disney World, before the wa-wa started.'

Pemulis removed his nonplay sneakers by scraping downward at one heel with the other sneaker's toe, looking down into the tender little whorl in the center of Possalthwaite's hair. He'd never be so ephebic as to verbally ask Freer if he had plans to suit up so they could get out there; he'd never let Freer think he was renting Freer space in his head before the match started. 'Postman, is this because of the Eschaton incident? Is it because of the nose? Because I can get on the horn and tell old Postal Weight Sr. they're blaming nobody under 17, it turns out, you should tell him, Todder. There's whole land-barges of shit, but none of it's spraying in you guys's direction, you should take comfort.'

'*Nothing's true,*' Possalthwaite keened, not looking up, muffled, flat-nippled, fatless in the young gut, feet spectral below his legs' brown, rocking, shaking his head, looking terribly young and innocently vulnerable, sort of pre-moral. Little white strips of bandage protuded from his palms' outer edges, from I.-Day's apocalypse.

'Well, not much is *fair,* anyway,' Pemulis conceded. The Viking made a noise at himself.

Pemulis calls Postal Weight's father up on-screen. Minneapolis-area developer. Malls, corporate parks, bustling places at the edges of roaring beltways. Late forties, slim, an overmanaged tan, a little oversharp in the dress dept., with a motivational-seminar-type hard-sell charm. A dagger of a Dad, with a pencil mustache and blinding shoe-leather. He tried to conjure an image of this paternal figure hitting Keith Freer on the noggin with a rolling pin and a bald cartoon lump rising from Freer's skull. (Pemulis calculates a win or even three-setter w/ Freer would mean a place on the WhataBurger plane, is why he's willing to violate a kind of personal honor-code and take pre-match Tenuate, which even with the 36-hour-elimination curve is kind of cavalier, given that he and Inc'd escaped on-spot urinalysis only because Pemulis implied to Mrs. Incandenza that he'd tell the Incster about Avril having some sort of major-sport interlude with John Wayne, and Avril is kind of a coldly-biding-her-time-not-to-be-fucked-with administrative figure, and along with C. ['Gretel the Cross-Sectioned Cow'] Tavis isn't exactly a fan of Pemulis anyway, certainly since the electrified-Rusk-doorknob-and-litigation incident. The 'drines didn't seem to be kicking in. Instead of the surge of stomachless competitive verve, all Pemulis felt was a slight unpleasant spaciness and a kind of enforced-feeling dryness in his eyes and mouth, like he's facing into a warm wind.) Pemulis had never once seen his own Da in anything other than a white Hanes T-shirt gone permanent yellow under the arms.

'Nothing's fair because nothing's *true,*' Possalthwaite wept into his palms. His little flannel shoulders shook.

Something old in one of the shower drains sighed and gurgled, a nauseous sound.

'Buck up.' Pemulis was removing all necessary match-articles and refolding them and placing them in his noncomplimentary Dunlop gear-bag with military precision. He put a foot on the bench and looked briefly to either side. 'Because if that's your burr then rest in my assurance, Postalcode: certain things are rock-solid, high-grade true.'

Freer had made a pincer of his fingers and was at the other cheek. 'Let him cry. Let baby have his dinkle. Piss and moan. Thirteen for Christ's sake. A kid thirteen hasn't even been in the same room with real disappointment yet. Hasn't even locked eyes across a room with real disillusion and and frustration and pain. Thirteen: pain's a rumor. What's the word. Angst. Baby wouldn't know genuine-article angst if it walked up and got him in a headlock.'

'Not like real true real possible-little-cheek-pimple angst, Vike, hey?'

'Flip it over and squat, Pemulis,' without bothering to look. Both Pemulis and Freer had pronounced a hard *g* in *angst,* Hal would have observed. The Viking contorted his mouth and raised his big chin to check the flesh of his jaw, turning slightly to use the side-mirrors as well.

Pemulis smiled broadly, trying to envision Keith Freer sitting in a canvas restraint-wrap in full lotus, staring blankly, hitting all the high notes in 'No Business Like Show Business' as orderlies in boiled whites and prim nurses in bent hats stand around snapping their fingers, clean white cheap institutional-care sneakers tapping noiselessly through all eternity. He was down to chinos and bare light-brown feet. He considered a blue T-shirt with a black wolf-spider on it v. a coincidentally red-on-gray T-shirt that had 'Vodka is the Enemy of Production' in presumably Russian. His good four Dunlop sticks were stacked on the bench to Possalthwaite's left. He picked up two and tested the strings' tension by hitting the side of one stick's head against the the strung face of the other and listening to the strings and then switching sticks and repeating the process. The exact right tension has a certain pitch. Midsized Dunlop Enqvist TL Composites. $304.95 U.S. retail. Real catgut strings have a kind of a dentalish sweet stink. The dot-and-circumflex logo. He didn't much look at Possalthwaite. He chose the Cyrillic shirt with the bottle-glyph. He rolled it up and put his head through the head-hole first, his late great Da's old-fashioned way. The upscaler kids here all did the arm-holes first. Then they did the head. You can also tell the scholarship kids because for some reason they put on a sock and a shoe and then a sock and a shoe. See for instance Wayne, who'd been in their room right after lunch when Pemulis had made the decision to come up for some pre-match Tenuate. Wayne's room was right nearby and he was standing there over Troeltsch's pharmacopic bedside table with no shirt and wet hair, rheumy-eyed and shiny-nostriled from mois-turizer on his Kleenex-chafed nostrils. The Viking was squeezing a damp tennis ball with his left hand while he scanned his forehead by mostly feel. Pemulis's psychic counter-strategy was not to appear in any hurry to dress and stretch and get out there either. Pemulis — who feared and hated unauthorized people being in his room, and who was constantly on Schacht's back about forgetting to lock up when he left, and who wasn't intimidated by Wayne's talent and success and affectless reserve, but was cautious around him, John Wayne, sort of the way a formidable predator will be unintimidated but cau-tious around another formidable predator, particularly since the virtuosic but tense per-formance in a certain administrative office a week ago, which had been mentioned by neither man — had coolly asked Wayne if he could help him, and Wayne had just as coolly not looked up from rattling through sickly Jim Troeltsch's bedside table's stuff and said he'd come in for some of Troeltsch's Seldane^e, which Pemulis had indeed heard Troeltsch at breakfast describing to a nose-blowing Wayne as the battlefield-nuke of anti-histamines that didn't make you too drowsy to function at an incredibly high level of function. Pemulis adjusted his jock's rear straps, trying to remember this Wayne-memory's point. Wayne had wanted a clear head and high pulmonary function because he was down to play the Syrian Satelliter in an informal exhibition at 1515h. Wayne hadn't offered this explanation; Pemulis got it off the e-board. One reason Pemulis was cau-tiously unassertive about Wayne's unauthorized presence in the room was the leaflet, which given a certain office-incident it wasn't impossible Wayne might choose to suspect seeing Pemulis's hand in the Olde-English-fonted leaflet up at various boards and inserted on the E.T.A. TPs' communal e-board for 11/14 announcing a joint John Wayne/Dr. Avril Incandenza arithmetic presentation to the pre-quadrivial 14-and-Unders on how 17 can actually go into 56 way more than 3.294 times. The point was that the half-dressed Wayne had been standing there with one foot bare and one in a sock and shoe. Pemulis shook his head slightly and looked down at Possalthwaite and tried to gather spit.

The speaker out up by the clock in the cement hall by the sauna crackled to life for the start of weekly WETA, with its glass-shattering Joan Sutherland theme. Pemulis put his street-sneakers on his street-shoe shelf. 'Buck up, T.P. It's just an angst-spasm. You're just reeling from a temporary paternal kertwang. Philosophical truth's jutting out all over the place. Disney World or no. Nose or no. Eschaton lives on, believe me. Underground or no. You have a calling, a talent. A missileman of your caliber. Reach down and rally, me little button.'

Possalthwaite had taken his face from his hands and was staring stonily up somewhere past Pemulis, lips moving in the habitual sucking reflex for which he took so much guff. His face had the pink scrubbed look of a crying child all right. His hands had left brown spiders of tincture of benzoin on his cheeks. He had two little smudges of bruise under the eyes. He sniffed meatily through a nose still covered in horizontal strips of surgical tape. 'I ab dot a little button.'

'That's what all the little buttons say, kid,' the Viking said levelly, removing something from a nostril with tweezers. Pemulis's sinuses felt like four-laners and his sense of smell was a lot keener than a man in a locker room might wish. Freer's locker next to Gloeckner's next to good old Inc's was agape, the bolted colposcope gleaming in the overhead lights and his Fox large-head sticks a nauseous West-Coast fluorescent orange with the trademark fox-glyph painted on the strings.

Possalthwaite scratched at one foot with the nails of the other foot. 'If you can't trust your folks. . .'

'Let me both validate and remind you that the kertwang you're reeling under is emotion-based and not fact-based.'

Possalthwaite opened his mouth.

'You're getting ready to say if you can't trust the ostensively loving patriarchal bosom you can't trust anyone at all, and if you can't trust people what can you trust, in terms of unvarying dependability, Postal Weight, am I right?'

'Oh Jesus H. Christmastree here it comes,' the Viking said to his forehead's reflection.

Pemulis was putting on a sock and a shoe, his mouth right down by Postal Weight's ear. 'This is not a bullshit problem. This is a like serious emotiono-philosophical deal you're confronting. I think it's a good sign you're coming to me instead of holding it all impactedly inside.'

'Who's coming to you?' Freer turned the big face this way and that. 'He was already in here having his little wa-wa-dinkle.'

Pemulis tried envisioning Keith Freer being bent over the net by Bedouins in purple turbans and roundly buggered, making the sort of sounds Leith's historical b/w J. Gleason made when in pain. To Possalthwaite he was saying 'Cause I can remember staring down the exact same-type thing, though from a more like philosophicalized kertwang than emotions.'

Freer said 'Do not ask him what he means, kid.'

Then a couple of 16s came in, G. ('Yardguard') Rader and a marginal Slavic kid whose first name was Zoltan and whose last name nobody could pronounce, and ignored Freer's advice to run for their lives because the good Dr. Pemulis had been prescribing for himself again and was going to begin to rant, and threw down their gear and proceeded immediately to get fresh towels from the dispenser over by the showers and to snap them at each other.

'What do you mean?' said Possalthwaite.

'The snare closes, the trap closes, here it comes.'

Rader rolled his wrists and spiraled the towel for what he called maximum painage. The Viking turned and said if he felt so much as a terrycloth breeze on this personal ass right here they were toast, the two. Pemulis was taking racquets out. E.T.A.'s male 16s were as a group inbent, conspiratorial, glandular, cliqueish. They excluded anyone not in their set. They had techniques and strategems of exclusion way more advanced than the 18s or 14s. (They tended to exclude Stice, mostly because he roomed with Coyle and drilled a lot of the time up with the 18s, and mixed with them, and more recently Kornspan, excluded, basically because he was cretinous and cruel and now consensually suspected of having tortured and killed the two collarless cats whose burnt corpses had been found on the hillside during pre-drill sprints a couple weeks back.) They had their own dialect

1070

and codes, in-jokes inside in-jokes.ᶠ And at E.T.A. only 16s snapped towels, and only for a year or two, but they went at it with a vengeance, towel-snapping, a brief flared genuflection to jock-stereotype, a stage where there's this primate-like passion for red-assed bonding in steamy rooms. They were the age staring down the barrel not of Is anything true but of Am I true, of What am I, of What is this thing, and it made them strange.

Then 18's-B/C fence-sitter Duncan van Slack, the kid who carried a guitar around with himself everyplace but never played it, and refused all late-night-sitting-around-someone's-room requests to play, and who was suspected of not being able to play the thing at all, and whose own Da was supposedly a redoubted gene-sequencer in Savannah, poked his head and guitar's neck in the door and said to *come quick* and then withdrew his head before anybody could ask what was up.

'If you didn't have such a way with a launch-vector I wouldn't be sure you're ready to hear this, Postalscale.'

'It occurs to me this is your boring man's true talent: the talent for ensnaring,' says the Viking. 'Flee while you can, kid.'

Possalthwaite blew his nose in the crook of his elbow and left it there.

Pemulis, who still used genuine catgut strings, zipped the two sticks he'd chosen into their Dunlop covers. He put an arch-support shoe up on the bench by Postalweight's bottom, looking quickly right and left:

'Todder, you can trust math.'

Freer said 'You heard it here first.'

Pemulis compulsively zipped and unzipped one of the covers. 'Take a breather, Keith. Todd, trust math. As in Matics, Math E. First-order predicate logic. Never fail you. Quantities and their relation. Rates of change. The vital statistics of God or equivalent. When all else fails. When the boulder's slid all the way back to the bottom. When the headless are blaming. When you do not know your way about. You can fall back and regroup around math. Whose truth is deductive truth. Independent of sense or emotionality. The syllogism. The identity. Modus Tollens. Transitivity. Heaven's theme song. The nightlight on life's dark wall, late at night. Heaven's recipe book. The hydrogen spiral. The methane, ammonia, H_2O. Nucleic acids. A and G, T and C. The creeping inevibatility. Caius is mortal. Math is not mortal. What it is is: listen: it's true.'

'This from a man on academic probation for who knows the length.'

Something involving Freer and a saline-moistened cattle-prod refused to quite mentally gel. There was still none of Tenuate's stomachless verve or well-being, just a glittered hum in his head and sinuses that felt like wind-tunnels. Pemulis tended to be a mouth-breather. The Viking raised one leg to fart toward Pemulis in a vaudevillian way, getting a laugh from Csikszentmihalyi and Rader, who'd mostly undressed and taken seats on the bench opposite Pemulis and Postal Weight, towels hung unwinding in their hands, watching, and were only every once in a while and in a halfhearted way pretending to look like they were getting ready to snap each other.

'I'm not a math person, Dad says,' said Postal Weight. Again the nose made the words come out *dot* and *bath* and *persod*. Csikszentmihalyi feinted a lunge and then really lunged and there was brief flurry of terrycloth.

Pemulis unzipped the cover. 'The axiom. The lemma. Listen: "If two different sets of parametric equations represent the same curve J, but the curve is traced in opposite directions in the two cases, then the two sets of equations produce values for a line integral over J that are negatives of each other." Not "*If* thus-and-such." Not "*unless* a gladhanding commercial réaltor from Boardman MN in $400 Banfi loafers changes his mind." Always and ever. As in puts the *a* in *a priori*. An honest lamp in the inkiest black, Toddleposter.'

There were voices and running feet like some sort of ruckus. McKenna stuck his head in and looked wildly around and withdrew without saying anything. Csikszentmihalyi went out after him. Freer and Rader both said What the fuck. Pemulis had only one button of his fly buttoned and was pointing at the ceiling with a finger:

'. . . Only that at times like this, when you're directionless in a dark wood, trust to the abstract deductive. When driven to your knees, kneel and revere the double S. Leap like a knight of faith into the arms of Peano, Leibniz, Hilbert, L'Hôpital. You will be lifted up. Fourier, Gauss, LaPlace, Rickey. Borne up. Never let fall. Wiener, Reimann, Frege, Green.'

Csikszentmihalyi came back in with Ortho Stice, their color high.

Pemulis compulsively zips and unzips zippers, is the reason why he wears only button-fly pants and tennis shorts.

Cs/yi said 'There is expression. You must immediately come.'

Freer turned from the mirror, both hands on a comb. 'What the fuck's going on?'

'John Wayne is insanely holding forth innermost thoughts for public ears.'

'Never trust the father you can see,' Pemulis told Possalthwaite.

Stice was already on his way back out and said over his shoulder, 'Troeltsch's got Wayne on the air and Wayne's lost his mind.'

a. Like dry loamy clay, highly absorbent, used by some for traction on their grips, eschewed by others because it has a lot of aluminum silicates and the Y.T.M.P.'s 'aluminum-causes-impotence' panic still weighs hard on some pubescent players' minds.

b. A good many seniors' schedules have no last-period classes, or have Independent-Study stuff slated for last period, and when two of these seniors — e.g. Pemulis & Freer — are scheduled for a P.M. challenge-match, they get to start at 1430h. instead of 1515h., and usually then finish up early, which is a great perk, given that they'll get to hit both the weight room and the locker room at slack and empty times.

c. An advantage of competitive mediocrity is you get to sit in the stands and get lots of sun on your feet and chest, because you're knocked out of competition by like the second round. Hence grotesquely pale feet are sort of a perverse mark of competitive status, maybe like toothlessness in hockey or something.

d. Specially engineered to react very fast with the hydrolytic enzyme esterase and thus to be completely out of the tissues within 36 hrs.

e. Q.v. Note 22 *supra*.

f. For example, during the first month of last summer's Euroclay junket, at some prear-ranged signal the male 16s would all hunch and hop around brachiatishly with their knuckles just off the ground in a circle, hitting their chests and going 'Er ah ee oo ah,' over and over, until prorector N. Hartigan finally lost his patience as they did it again in the line for Customs at L'Aéroport Orly and had hysterics so gruesome in someone that tall that the practice stopped as mysteriously as it'd started.

325. (whose theories of detection and interview are strongly informed by the b/w noir films Tine so enjoyed as a boy late at night on local broadcast television, and misses)

326. (and then some)

327. Bolex H64, -32 and -16 models come with a turret that accepts three C-mount lenses, which gives the models a kind of multi-eyed, alien-facial look.

328. (though never unveiled)

329. (which is actually complete horseshit, but goes unchallenged by the O.U.S. opera-tives, who are pretty savvy at choosing their heuristic battles)

330. (given the guy's track record with ingestion)

331. *Picaresque* pretty obviously referring to the comic-Surrealist tradition of Bay Area avant-gardeists like Peterson & Broughton, since Peterson's *Potted Psalm*'s mother-and-Death stuff and *The Cage*'s cranial-imprisonment and disconnected-eyeball stuff are pretty obvious touchstones in a lot of Himself's more parodic-slapstick productions.

332.

17 NOV. Y.D.A.U.

'Gracious me and mine,' Pemulis said, clutching the ankle of the leg he'd crossed to keep the foot from joggling.

'Rusk and Charles and Mrs. Incandenza are with him now. Schtitt's been up to see him. Loach has done a thorough reflex-check. John Wayne's going to be OK.'

'Well thank heavens for that load off everyone's mind,' Pemulis said.

It was Pemulis, deLint, Nwangi, and Watson in the Dean of Academic Affairs' Office. Mrs. Inc's ventilator hissed and something up in there whirred a little. DeLint was behind the high desk, looking like a mean little boy. Nobody'd said if anybody higher up than deLint was going to show. Pemulis didn't know if this was good or bad.

'Let's make perfectly sure we got this in order and in your words.' Nwangi and Watson were window-dressing. This was A. deLint's show. His face kind of came apart when he smiled. 'With no prior knowledge of anything untoward, you're pulled from the locker room and stand out in the hall with several other students, which is your first knowledge anything's untoward with Wayne.'

Pemulis figured none of the administrators had heard the thing; they always shut their soundproof doors at 1435h.; Pemulis had no idea what Wayne's said about anything, or Jim Troeltsch, who very prudently hasn't shown facial-feature one in their room since the apocalyptic broadcast. It'd taken Pemulis about half the salivaless sprint up to B-204 to figure out what had happened and to find his pilfered Tenuates in the little pecker's Seldane bottle. Pemulis sort of shuddered to imagine the impact of the 'drine on Wayne's cherry-red and virgin bloodstream. The slight whir of his cortex working at full speed was masked by the hiss of the ventilator and the sound of whistles and play and Schtitt's megaphone outside.

'I'm in there suiting up waiting for Freer and doing a little B.B.-intervention on Possalthwaite who was in crisis and Zoltan and The Darkness come like spasming in saying Troeltsch'd jury-rigged the Duke into candid sharing for the WETA broadcast.'

'They said what, that Troeltsch had tricked Wayne into speaking candidly without awareness it's going out over WETA into all the rooms?'

Pemulis realized the limpness of this, in like that anybody'd see that Wayne'd have to have been sitting right there with Troeltsch by the little old-time gunmetal handheld mike at Lateral Alice Moore's curved desk. He'd already heard from Lateral Alice that it was more like Wayne had come rattling in and shoved Troeltsch aside and grabbed the mike and started ranting while Troeltsch and Lateral Alice Moore had looked on aghastly; and that Dave Harde, down doing some maintainance to L.A.M.'s deactivated third rail, had been so aghasted he'd pitched forward narcoleptically and stayed like that with his face in the blue carpet and ass in the air for nearly an hour, and that Lateral Alice's own stress had brought on an aggravation of her chronic cyanosis to the point where her whole face was still blue-tinged and between her knees when Pemulis had got to her.

'This was more like a general sort of impression which I feel like I might have misbegotten from the agitation of the guys. Plus how completely un-Wayneish Wayne sounded, like how could anybody ever have said that shit if they thought it wasn't just them and Troeltsch alone, much less Wayne, who as we all know is pretty much reserve in motion.'

DeLint's nostrils got that pale flare they got, Pemulis knew, when he smelled horseshit and knew you knew it. Pemulis knows deLint's been laying for him ever since the incident with the P.W.T.A. guy who started to wobble and then rant down at P.W.T.A., which was a totally different type of deal. The irony was that the Wayne-dosing had been a total accident and in no way Pemulis's deal, if anybody's Troeltsch's, but the cortex couldn't nail down any way to get this across without admitting to possession of a 'drine, which given the shaky pharmaceutical ground since the Eschaton and O.N.A.N.T.A. urologist would be tantamount to Clippertonizing himself. Nwangi showed almost blinding 3rd-World teeth but was saying nothing. Watson's eyes had almost this nictitater of stupidity-film on them, less a dullness than a deadness, the dead porch light of nobody home at chez Tex Watson. Pemulis saw the leaflet about Wayne and Mrs. I. and deviant division in the papers deLint held.

'Which is in your words your first knowledge of untowardness with Wayne.'

'My first is I get out there still trying to counsel the Postheimer and here on the speaker's Wayne doing what Keith observed may have been a sort of imitation of Dr. Tavis.'

It had been uncanny. It had made Stice look like a rank amateur. Wayne had told Troeltsch to pretend he was some adolescent girl: this was adolescent Tavis asking her for a date; Pemulis shuddered; he couldn't exactly remember all the little mannerisms, which Wayne'd clearly gotten locked down from Tavis always sitting next to him on the bus back from victories going at him nonstop, but in outline it was Chuckie Tavis coming up to some Canadian cheerleader or something and telling her he was going to be completely open with her: he had a terrible fear of rejection; he was telling her up-front now that tomorrow he was going to ask her out for a date and was *begging* her not openly to reject him if she didn't want to go, to think up some plausible excuse — though of course he said he realized that what he was saying would make that excuse hard to believe, now that he's openly asked her to make up an excuse.

'Whereupon the whole Academy hears Mr. Troeltsch prompt Wayne into making public castigations of his various peers and instructors.'

'I've got to say it did seem like Troeltsch had kind of orchestrated things somehow, sir, was my impression.'

'Referring to Corbett Thorp as a —' pretending to riffle through the papers so Pemulis'd have to see the 17-into-56 leaflet several times as it came up in the riffle.

'I believe the expression was "a palsied twit," ' Nwangi said to deLint.

'Yes "palsied twit." And Francis Unwin quote "has the on-court look of a cornered rodent." And Disney R. Leith: the quote "sort of man you always end up sitting next to at civic functions." Ms. Richardson-Levy-o'Byrne-Chawaf as chair of some sort of commit-tee dealing with the topic of the quote "Itty Bitty Titty." On Coach Schtitt, quote, seeming as if he'd been "denied some kind of vitally important moisture from birth hencefor-ward." Our own Mr. Nwangi here being in rough quote if I've got it quote "the sort of fellow who'll be in a Chinese restaurant with you and won't even share food or trade food." '

'Meaning mean-spirited.' Nwangi threw his head back and beamed like he was blind. What was chilling was that in Wayne's scenario Tavis does succeed, Wayne projects, in seducing the Canadian cheerleader or whatever, even when he's totally open on the date about the fact that he'd deliberately told her he was afraid of rejection in the first place only as a strategy to make him seem to her different from other boys, more honest and open, so that the scenario was that the honesty was so exhausting she'd basically just laid back exhausted and let him X her just to shut him up. Except — chillingly — he hadn't shut up.

'— including some sort of imitation of Dr. Tavis carrying on a monologue during the act of sexual intercourse,' deLint said, trying to find it in the sheaf. 'On Bernadette Long-ley: "Bernadette Longley looks like her hair grew her head instead of the other way around." On Mary Esther Thode: "a face like a pancake." On the Academy's own late Founder and husband of the Dean of Ac.-Aff.: "so full of himself he could have shit limbs." Unquote. On his own doubles partner Hal Incandenza: "by all appearances addicted to everything that is not tied down, cannot outrun him, and is fittable in the mouth." '

'I'm remembering the word as *insertable*.' Pemulis kicked himself, mentally. The pancake thing had been expanded to like fifteen seconds as Wayne had sketched M. E. Thode's face as circular, burned, freckled, cratered, doughy, shiny, soggy, on and on. Plus somehow even more chilling was that Pemulis knew from Inc that Wayne's pseudo-Tavis 'I-live-in-fear-of-rejection' ploy was actually in the top five or ten of the troubling

'Strategies' that Inc's brother Orin the punter called up to Hal about employing to young married women.

'Donni Stott has we're informed "skin like an attaché case and is a compelling advt tisement for sunscreen." I myself am, here I quote, quote "a man who would not lend h own mother a quarter for a rubber tip for her crutch." '

'Is the emerging point that this is going to impact my getting to go on the WhataBurge1 trip?'

Nwangi crumpled and slapped his knee. His face literally looked like a very dark hatchet. Tex Watson reached down behind the console he was slumped in his chair by and brought out Pemulis's special yachting cap and dangled it like something you want a dog to jump for. From someplace under Nwangi's chair were brought out two pharmaceutical scales, several jeweller's loupes, the tow truck's supply of empty sterile Visine bottles, and plus every bottle from Troeltsch's bedside table, which clearly Troeltsch had eaten some enormous wedge of putrid deal-cutting cheese.

Pemulis tasted the metallic taste of a seriously anxious stomach. 'I request to see the Dean of Ac.-Aff. before any of this goes further.'

'We have again Ms. Heath, apparently on someone's mind very much today, now said to be the sort of person who quote "cries at card tricks." We have a Rik Dunkel who "could not find his own bottom with both hands and a nautical compass of exacting precision." We have a return engagement with Ms. Heath, described as "dwelling always at the edge of some vast continent of menstrual hysteria." We have our own beloved Tex, sitting right here, described as having "a tiny liquid-filled nubbin at the top of the spine" in lieu of higher cortex function.'

'Aubs, no kidding: something pressing I have to interface about with Mrs. Inc. Tell her it concerns U.S.-Canadian relations.'

Nwangi's laugh was high and had the slight teakettle-wheeze to it of the laughs of large black men the world over. 'She sends you her *regards,* the Dean said to tell you.' He slapped his knee three times.

DeLint looked a little less happy because he clearly didn't know what any of it was about and didn't like playing coded messenger, but he still looked pretty happy: 'Michael Mathew Pemulis, the Academy's Dean of Academic Affairs said to tell you the adminis-tration's too naturally concerned about the state of one of our two very finest current talents, who it's clear he's been unwittily dosed with an artificial stimulant prohibited by federal statute, O.N.A.N.T.A. regulations, and the Enfield Tennis Academy Honor-Code Specs on Artificial Substances, to permit itself the satisfaction of giving you the Dean's very best regards and her wish that quote "may the road rise up to meet you whitherever your future travels lie." ' DeLint probed his ear. 'I think that was it in a nutshell.'

Pemulis got very cool and brass-mask-faced. He was breathing very clearly through his nose, and the office air seemed mentholated. Everything got very cool and formal inside and glycerine-clear. 'Aubs, before anything gets nailed in stone that we'll all I promise you and Mrs. Inc we'll all of us regret —'

DeLint said 'I was given to understand you can either finish out the term for credit or you can hit the trail with your little sailing cap full of pockets on a stick like a bandanna to some other O.N.A.N.T.A. institution and see if they'll take a senior without any kind of positive reference, which the sense I get is the administration says fat chance on any kind of reference.'

Tex Watson said something about urine.

Pemulis recrossed his leg. DeLint looked at Nwangi:

'I believe the kid is speechless.'

'I believe he has nothing to say.'

'I don't believe it.'

'And something about you're invited to shout whatever you threatened the administra-tion to shout about from the highest hill you can find, which pretty soon won't be this one.'

ιrough laughter: 'And that the administrative office doorknobs have
grounded, the administrative files all recryptographilated, everyone's
.nodized and sealed with Plastic Wood, Mrs. Inc said to tell you.'
.-of-cards riffle of the wings of the Shit Fairy, which he privately envi-
f violet incubus with the Da's saggy frown. Pemulis scratched very coolly
'And this affects the WhataBurger, my chances?'
.1 Pemulis he just fucking slayed him while Watson looked from face to face
rocked and wheezed and slapped at his knee, and Pemulis, close-mouthed
.ng with terrible ease, found their good humor almost infectious.

.t out by the Mass Division of S.A.S., listing meetings of all but the very most
.-fringe-type 12-Step Programs in city, sub-, and exurbs, all up and down both
.s, the Cape, and Nantucket.

ι. Hal's Pemulis-inspired trope for putting down the secret daily Bob H., which started
a wry dark mental joke and now within a week has become the way Hal characterizes
.bstinence to himself, which any Boston AA would tell him isn't a very promising way to
think about it at all, in terms of self-pity.

335. Except of course for a certain hardwired type of pornography- and onanistic sex-
addict, which has given rise to a couple exceptionally icky Step-based fellowships.

336. (according to his sudoriferous and and agora-compulsive younger brother, M. Bain)

337. Latin blunder for self-defense's *se defendendo* is *sic,* either a befogged muddling of a
professional legal term, or a post-Freudian slip, or (least likely) a very oblique and
subtle jab at Gately from a Ewell intimate with the graveyard scene from *Hamlet* —
namely V.i. 9.

338. Ketorolac tromethamine, a non-narcotic analgesic, little more than Motrin with
ambition — ®Syntex Labs.

339. International Brotherhood of Electrical Workers.

340. Doxycycline hyclate, an I.V.-antibiotic — ®Parke-Davis Pharmaceuticals.

341. Oxycodone hydrochloride + acetaminophen, a Schedule C-III narcotic oral
analgesic — ®Du Pont Pharmaceuticals.

342. Or possibly *Babel.*

343. Boston AA slogan meaning trying to quit addictive Substance-use without working
any kind of Recovery Program.

344. E.T.S.'s[a] Advanced Placement Standardized Subject Tests, which Hal Incandenza's
signed up to take in English and (Parisian) French.

   a. Educational Testing Service Inc., Princeton NJ.

345. The College of Basic Studies Bldg. on Commonwealth and Granby, approx. 3 clicks
east-southeast of E.T.A.

346. Montréal International Airport-D'Orval, Cartierville Airport being now restricted
to intra-Québec flights only.

347. (Which in fact she doesn't, but she had had perfume on the last time she wore the
hulpil.)

348. An R. Catholic church just off Brighton Center.

349. *Sic.*

350. Or a face writhing in involuntary disgust at Don G.'s own armlessness and hook, maybe.

351. As in a combination of the First and Twelfth Steps, goes the AA joke: 'My Life Is Unmanageable and I'd Like to Share It With You.'

352. Reference to January-February Y.D.A.U., when person or persons unknown went around coating selected toothbrushes of the Boys and Girls 16's with what was finally pinpointed as betel-nut extract, causing panic and internecine finger-pointing and resulting in serial oxidation-treatment visits to Dr. E. Zegarelli, D.D.S., by half a dozen E.T.A.s until the brush-tamperings ceased as suddenly as they'd begun; and now nine months later no one still has the slightest idea re perpetrator or point.

353. Which runs not to Enfield-Brighton but to Roxbury and Mattapan, places where it is very bad nighttime joss indeed to be both white and incapacitated.

354. Q.v. note a to Note 12.

355. Anexsia — ®SmithKline Beecham Laboratories.

356. Levo-Dromoran — ®Roche Laboratories.

357. Numorphan, kind of a watered-down Dilaudid — ®Du Pont Pharmaceuticals.

358. Perwin NX — ®Boswell Medications Ltd., Canada — which accounts for the C-III, because the Canadians are notoriously insane when it comes to forecasting abuse-potential.

359. A.k.a. Chlordiazepoxide hydrochloride — ®Roche, Inc. — a low-grade Valiumish tranq.

360. A C-III and sort of entry-level oral narcotic, the side-effects and inconsistent buzz of which often send abusers up the ladder to C-II compounds.

361. A.k.a. hyoscyamine sulfate — ®Schwarz Pharma Kremers Urban, Inc. — an anti-spasmodic for anything from colitis to Irritable Bowel Syndrome.

362. A.k.a. methaqualone, now manufactured outside O.N.A.N. jurisdiction under the trade name Parestol.

363. Later one-third of the rent-and-strip-luxury-apts. crew, and even later Gately's trusted colleague on some of his most disastrous and bottom-hastening home-invasions, including that of one G. DuPlessis, which Kite ended up regretting exponentially more than Gately did, once the A.F.R. got through with him.

364. MDA, MDMA ('X'), MMDA-2 ('Love Boat'), MMDA-3a ('Eve'), DMMDA-2 ('Starry Night'), etc.

365. Long-Term Institution.

366. Sounding rather suspiciously like Professor H. Bloom's turgid studies of artistic *influenza* — though it's unclear how either Flood- or dead-ancestor discussions have any connection to S. Peterson's low-budget classic *The Cage*, which is mostly about a peripatetic eyeball rolling around, other than the fact that J. O. Incandenza loved this film and stuck little snippets of it or references to it just about anywhere he could; maybe the 'disjunction' or 'disconnection' between the screen's film and Ph.D.'s scholastic discussion of art is part of the point.[a]

    a. (Which of course assumes there's a point.)

367. Though they did, just as in depictions of organized crime in popular entertainment, often change the cell-phones they used, to avoid potential taps or Pen Registers — Sorkin

buying new units and #s, Gately more often borrowing student R.N.s' cellulars and then returning them after a few days. One of Gately's biggest challenges in this career was remembering all the different fucking phone numbers and addresses of luxury-apts.-of-the-week when he was strafed on Bam-Bams just about all the time.

368. Cimetidine — ®SmithKline Beecham Pharmaceuticals — 800-mg. spansules for generalized cranio-vascular woe (derived, kind of interestingly, from the same ergot rye-mold as LSD).

369. For the two maps Sorkin had to have eliminated altogether during this period, it's maybe worth observing that he eschewed both Towers and instead used the thuggish ex-Québecer muscleboys DesMontes and Pointgravè, who had no real loyalties or membership in any community and hired themselves out as enforcers for books and high-interest lenders all up and down both Shores. Gately did, as a coercive collector, demap one person, but it was essentially an accident — the debtor had been blond, and drinking Heinekens, and then when things got physical he'd squirted Gately in the face with Mace, and a red curtain of rage had descended over Gately's sight, and when he'd come back to himself the debtor's head was turned 180° around on his neck and had the little Mace can all the way up one nostril, and it was the most professionally horrified Gately had ever been up until the thing with the suffocated Canadian *P.I.T.*, which anyway occurred much later and when Gately was way more nonviolence-prone.

370. Purified pork insulin in a zinc suspension — ®Lilly Pharmaceuticals.

371. An elite private high school up near the Methuen salient.

372. Surely *skeet* and *vig*, meaning debt and bookmaker's automatic percentage (usually 10% subtracted from winnings or added to skeet) are not just metro Boston terms.

373. A.k.a. Acetylcysteine-20 — ®Bristol Laboratories — a nebulizable prophylaxis against the post-traumatic buildup of abnormal, viscid, or inspissated mucus.

374. With the hard-*ch* sound distinctive of North Shore pronun. of words like *Chicago* and *champagne*.

375. Known less sensitively among neuro-urology residents as 'Dizzy Dick Disorder' or sometimes just '3-D.'

376. Knoll Laboratories' good old Dilaudid — $666.00/g. wholesale and $5/mg. street at Y.W.-Q.M.D. valuations.

377. A 'Phillips Screwdriver,' vodka and Milk of Magnesia, which Gately finds nauseous and privately refers to as a 'lowball.'

378. (As opposed to self-confronting, presumably.)

379. See Note 144 *supra*.

380. The 1.3:1-aspect-ratio rectangle scanned by electron beams in video imaging, now replaced by multi-interlace[a] solid-field HD digital imaging.

a. Why Noreen Lace-Forché's seminal corporation's name was a kind of wry pun: 2:1 *interlace* was pre-HD television's term for breaking the picture frame into two 262.5-line fields for standard 525-line raster-scanning.... A very in-type joke designed to appeal to the same Big Four that Noreen L.-F. was then wooing.

381. More like B.S. 1926, according to the Still Photo Archive at NNY City's Museum of Modern Art. Plus n.b. the print — which Hal correctly remembers Avril always loathing [a] — long pre-dated J.O.I.'s ever picking up a camera.

a. Hence the relative queerness of its still being up on the HmH living room wall four years after Incandenza's felo de se — it's not like anybody asked her to keep the thing up.

382. Whether in singles against him or doubles alongside, when Hal is on-court with Wayne he always gets the creepy feeling that Wayne has control out there not just of his voluntary CNS but also of his heartrate and blood pressure, the diameter of his pupils, etc., which feeling is not only creepy but distracting, adding to the tension of playing with Wayne.

383. Winter Park FL facility for enmeshment-, codependency-, and compulsivity-related Issues.

384. A.k.a. Lorazepam — ®Wyeth-Aherst Labs — a venerable anti-anxiety tranq, of which 25 mg./day is enough to anxiolytize a good-sized Clydesdale.

385. Probably meaning Doryx, Parke-Davis's doxycycline hyclate, the Cruise missile of gram-negative antibiotics.

386. Nalaxone hydrochloride, the Exocet missile of narcotic antagonists — ®DuPont Pharm. — 2 ml./20ml.-saline pre-filled syringes.

387. Metro Boston's third-hardest thing to street-cop after raw Vietnamese opium and the incredibly potent DMZ, Sunshine is pentazocine hydrochloride and mefenamic acid[a] — ®Sanofi Winthrop, Canada, Inc. — w/ trade-name Talwin-PX — Day-Glo-yellow serum, 7ml./20ml.-saline pre-filled syringes.

   a. A non-narc analgesic marketed in the U.S. as Ponstel — ®Parke-Davis — mostly (oddly enough) for dysmenorrhea, sort of like nuclear-grade Mydol.

388. Talwin-NX — ®Sanofi Winthrop U.S.

ABOUT THE AUTHOR

David Foster Wallace is the recipient of a MacArthur Fellowship and numerous other awards. He is the author of several books, including the novels *The Broom of the System* and *Infinite Jest,* the story collections *Girl with Curious Hair, Brief Interviews with Hideous Men,* and *Oblivion;* and the nonfiction collections *A Supposedly Fun Thing I'll Never Do Again* and *Consider the Lobster.* He lives in California.

Also by David Foster Wallace

A Supposedly Fun Thing I'll Never Do Again

Essays and Arguments

"Animated by wonderfully exuberant prose.... This volume not only reconfirms Mr. Wallace's stature as one of his generation's preeminent talents, but it also attests to his virtuosity.... His novelist's radar for the incongruous detail and the revealing remark — along with his hyperkinetic language and natural storytelling gifts — make him a remarkably able reporter."　　　　　— Michiko Kakutani, *New York Times*

"Further cements Wallace's reputation as probably the most ambitious and prodigious literary talent of his generation, an erupting Vesuvius of prose and ideas and intellect."　　— John Marshall, *Seattle Post-Intelligencer*

"The title essay is worth the price of the book . . . irrefutable proof of comic genius. . . . Yes, he's a great writer, get used to it."　　　　　— Adam Begley, *New York Observer*

"Wallace puts enough energy, attitude, thought, 'fun' (in and out of quotes), and sheer information into any single page to wear me out. But they don't. . . . As long as he's willing to get down and rassle with this stuff, I'm glad to sit here and read all about it."　　— David Gates, *Newsweek*

"A heady, often hilarious tour of American diversions. . . . A remarkably talented, fluid, and arresting young voice."　　　　　— Alex Abramovich, *Entertainment Weekly*

"Mr. Wallace's distinctive and infectious style, an acrobatic cartwheeling between high intellectual discourse and vernacular insouciance, makes him tremendously entertaining to read, whatever his subject."　　　　　— Laura Miller, *New York Times Book Review*

"He's the real thing. . . . Beneath the fun and the verbal high jinks, there is a passionate and deeply serious writer at work."　　　　　— Brigitte Frase, *San Francisco Chronicle*

Back Bay Books

Available in paperback wherever books are sold

Also by David Foster Wallace

Brief Interviews with Hideous Men

"A supersonic delight, a full-scale harassment of the short story form. . . . David Foster Wallace is one badass fiction writer."
— Benjamin Weissman, *LA Weekly*

"At just about the time this reviewer was putting on a black suit to attend the funeral of American fiction, David Foster Wallace showed up. . . . Wallace, like Nabokov, the writer whom he most resembles, has a seemingly inexhaustible bag of literary tricks." — Andrei Codrescu, *Chicago Tribune*

"Wallace can make you laugh out loud with his devilish wit."
— George Gurley, *Kansas City Star*

"In his eccentric obsession and his sinister experiments, Wallace is beginning to resemble another mad scientist of American literature: Edgar Allan Poe. And his hideous men, like Poe's, are vexed by demons that haunt us all." — Adam Goodheart, *New York Times Book Review*

"A strikingly original collection. . . . *Brief Interviews with Hideous Men* is meant to interrogate the reader, to elicit fresh responses to horrors that have lost their edge in the age of information overload. . . . It displays a range of intellect and talent that is unseemly for any one writer to have, let alone show off." — R. Z. Sheppard, *Time*

"A brilliant book. . . . One of the most ambitious and talented writers of his generation. Wallace's work is bitingly funny and remarkably, even wildly, imaginative; at the same time he aims for very large psychological, emotional, and social issues, issues of how we live or fail to live, love and fail to love, survive or destroy ourselves. . . . Wallace has planted himself firmly as the American writer of his generation to watch, to match, and, most urgently, to read." — Vince Passaro, *Salon*

Also by David Foster Wallace

Consider the Lobster

And Other Essays

"There is no writer alive more incisive and hilarious, more ruthlessly tender, when it comes to documenting the perversities of modern American life. . . . What makes Wallace an exceptional writer isn't his big old brain, but the fact that his brain does the bidding of an even larger heart."
— Steve Almond, *Los Angeles Times Book Review*

"Wallace can do sad, funny, silly, heartbreaking, and absurd with equal ease; he can even do them all at once."
— Michiko Kakutani, *New York Times*

"Rabidly intelligent. . . . Wallace is a master of flipping a world inside out through its own lingo, of swallowing it whole and then destroying it from the inside on its own terms."   — John Freedman, *Boston Globe*

"Wallace is bracingly insightful . . . so vast is his intellectual energy and ambition."   — Pankaj Mishra, *New York Times Book Review*

"Wallace does not like irony. He does like serious issues, seriously discussed. These appear gradually, however, and reaching them is great fun, as the reader swoops and swirls and doubles back and races down the final reaches of Wallace's prose. It's as if Wallace had been, not a tennis star, but a snowboarder. A snowboarder with a PhD."
— Peter Grier, *Christian Science Monitor*

"What is remarkable is Wallace's freewheeling mind and that mind's ability to weave through the most far-reaching source material to get at the core questions that drive us but are also so easily forgotten or obscured: What is true? What does it mean to be 'good'? Why are we here, anyway? . . . For anyone who cares about such questions, *Consider the Lobster* is essential reading."   — Traver Kauffman, *Rocky Mountain News*

Back Bay Books
Available in paperback wherever books are sold

Also by David Foster Wallace

Oblivion

Stories

"Stunning. . . . Wallace is an astonishing storyteller whose fiction reminds us why we learned to read in the first place."
— Andrew Ervin, *San Francisco Chronicle*

"Reading David Foster Wallace is like listening to the best kind of rock band."
— David Amsden, *BlackBook*

"Wallace masters every area he writes about. . . . He has the vocabulary. He has the energy. He has the big ideas. He has the attitude."
— Walter Kirn, *New York Times Book Review*

"A wordsmith of the first water. . . . Wallace is fearless and insanely imaginative, and the adventuresome reader who follows his labyrinthine plot strands — Russian dolls within Russian dolls — will be rewarded with, simply put, some of the best writing, sentence for sentence, in fiction today."
— Corey Mesler, *Memphis Flyer*

"David Foster Wallace has earned a place as one of America's most daring and talented young writers. . . . His eye for cultural detail is ever sharp, his humor ever dry. . . . Wallace transcends mere dazzling displays and explores human emotions with sensitivity."
— Scott Morris, *Los Angeles Times Book Review*

"Wallace is a writer who still believes in asking readers to participate actively in the experience of literature, even when he's being aneurysm-inducingly funny."
— Ken Babstock, *Globe and Mail*

"At once cool and intimate, *Oblivion* reads, to creepy effect, like an X-ray of one of John Updike's classics of marital strain."
— Troy Patterson, *Entertainment Weekly*

"Pay attention to this writer. . . . He's telling us a lot about the hypocrisy and the sordidness of modern life, and he doesn't spare anyone."
— Debra Bruno, *Chicago Sun-Times*

Back Bay Books
Available in paperback wherever books are sold